On the Way to the Wedding

In which:

Firstly, Gregory Bridgerton falls in love with the wrong woman, and

Secondly, she falls in love with someone else, but

Thirdly, Lucy Abernathy decides to meddle; however,

Fourthly, she falls in love with Gregory, which is highly inconvenient because

Fifthly, she is practically engaged to Lord Haselby, but

Sixthly, Gregory falls in love with Lucy.

Which leaves everyone in a bit of a pickle.

Watch them all find their happy endings in:

The stunning conclusion
to the Bridgerton series
by the incomparable Julia Quinn

JULIA QUINN

ON THE WAY TO THE WEDDING

AVON BOOKS
An Imprint of HarperCollins*Publishers*

This is a work of fiction. Names, characters, places, and incidents are products of the author's imagination or are used fictitiously and are not to be construed as real. Any resemblance to actual events, locales, organizations, or persons, living or dead, is entirely coincidental.

AVON BOOKS
An Imprint of HarperCollins*Publishers*
10 East 53rd Street
New York, New York 10022-5299

Copyright © 2006 by Julie Cotler Pottinger
ISBN-13: 978-0-06-053125-6
ISBN-10: 0-06-053125-8
www.avonromance.com

First Avon Books paperback printing: July 2006

Avon Trademark Reg. U.S. Pat. Off. and in Other Countries, Marca Registrada, Hecho en U.S.A.
HarperCollins® is a registered trademark of HarperCollins Publishers Inc.

Printed in the U.S.A.

10 9 8 7 6 5 4 3 2 1

For Lyssa Keusch.
Because you're my editor.
Because you're my friend.

And also for Paul.
Just because.

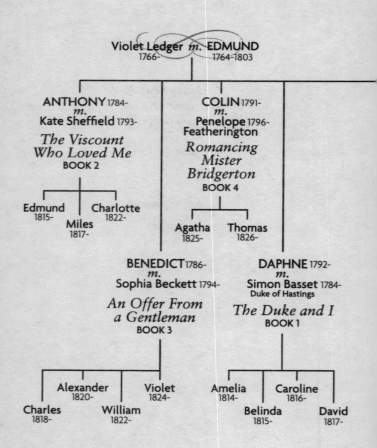

Violet Ledger *m.* EDMUND
1766-   1764-1803

ANTHONY 1784-
m.
Kate Sheffield 1793-

*The Viscount
Who Loved Me*
BOOK 2

Edmund   Charlotte
1815-   1822-
      Miles
      1817-

COLIN 1791-
m.
Penelope 1796-
Featherington

*Romancing
Mister
Bridgerton*
BOOK 4

Agatha   Thomas
1825-   1826-

BENEDICT 1786-
m.
Sophia Beckett 1794-

*An Offer From
a Gentleman*
BOOK 3

DAPHNE 1792-
m.
Simon Basset 1784-
Duke of Hastings

The Duke and I
BOOK 1

Alexander   Violet
1820-   1824-
Charles   William
1818-   1822-

Amelia   Caroline
1814-   1816-
Belinda   David
1815-   1817-

𝓑ridgerton
FAMILY
TREE

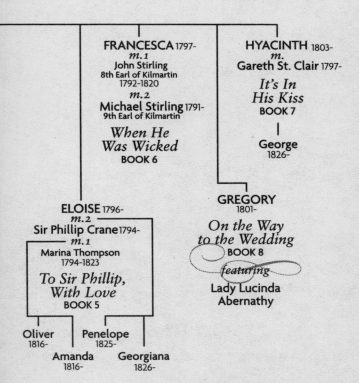

FRANCESCA 1797-
m.1
John Stirling
8th Earl of Kilmartin
1792-1820
m.2
Michael Stirling 1791-
9th Earl of Kilmartin

*When He
Was Wicked*
BOOK 6

HYACINTH 1803-
m.
Gareth St. Clair 1797-

*It's In
His Kiss*
BOOK 7

George
1826-

GREGORY
1801-

*On the Way
to the Wedding*
BOOK 8

featuring

Lady Lucinda
Abernathy

ELOISE 1796-
m.2
Sir Phillip Crane 1794-
m.1
Marina Thompson
1794-1823

*To Sir Phillip,
With Love*
BOOK 5

Oliver
1816-

Amanda
1816-

Penelope
1825-

Georgiana
1826-

Prologue

London, not far from St. George's, Hanover Square
Summer, 1827

*H*is lungs were on fire.

Gregory Bridgerton was running. Through the streets of London, oblivious to the curious stares of onlookers, he was running.

There was a strange, powerful rhythm to his movements— *one two three four, one two three four*—that pushed him along, propelling him forward even as his mind remained focused on one thing and one thing only.

The church.

He had to get to the church.

He had to stop the wedding.

How long had he been running? One minute? Five? He

couldn't know, couldn't concentrate on anything but his destination.

The church. He had to get to the church.

It had started at eleven. This thing. This ceremony. This thing that should never have happened. But she'd done it anyway. And he had to stop it. He had to stop *her*. He didn't know how, and he certainly didn't know why, but she was doing it, and it was wrong.

She had to know that it was wrong.

She was *his*. They belonged together. She knew that. God damn it all, she knew that.

How long did a wedding ceremony take? Five minutes? Ten? Twenty? He'd never paid attention before, certainly never thought to check his watch at the beginning and end.

Never thought he'd need the information. Never thought it would matter this much.

How long had he been running? Two minutes? Ten?

He skidded around a corner and onto Regent Street, grunting something that was meant to take the place of "Excuse me," as he bumped into a respectably dressed gentleman, knocking his case to the ground.

Normally Gregory would have stopped to aid the gentleman, bent to retrieve the case, but not today, not this morning.

Not now.

The church. He had to get to the church. He could not think of anything else. He must not. He must—

Damn! He skidded to a halt as a carriage cut in front of him. Resting his hands on his thighs—not because he wanted to, but rather because his desperate body demanded it—he sucked in huge gulps of air, trying to relieve the screaming pressure in his chest, that horrible burning, tearing feeling as—

The carriage moved past and he was off again. He was close now. He could do it. It couldn't have been more than five minutes since he'd left the house. Maybe six. It felt like thirty, but it couldn't have been more than seven.

He had to stop this. It was wrong. He had to stop it. He *would* stop it.

He could see the church. Off in the distance, its gray steeple rising into the bright blue sky. Someone had hung flowers from the lanterns. He couldn't tell what kind they were—yellow and white, yellow mostly. They spilled forth with reckless abandon, bursting from the baskets. They looked celebratory, cheerful even, and it was all so wrong. This was not a cheerful day. It was not an event to be celebrated.

And he *would* stop it.

He slowed down just enough so that he could run up the steps without falling on his face, and then he wrenched the door open, wide, wider, barely hearing the slam as it crashed into the outer wall. Maybe he should have paused for breath. Maybe he should have entered quietly, giving himself a moment to assess the situation, to gauge how far along they were.

The church went silent. The priest stopped his drone, and every spine in every pew twisted until every face was turned to the back.

To him.

"Don't," Gregory gasped, but he was so short of breath, he could barely hear the word.

"Don't," he said, louder this time, clutching the edge of the pews as he staggered forward. "Don't do it."

She said nothing, but he saw her. He saw her, her mouth open with shock. He saw her bouquet slip from her hands, and he knew—by God he knew that she'd stopped breathing.

She looked so beautiful. Her golden hair seemed to catch the light, and it shone with a radiance that filled him with strength. He straightened, still breathing hard, but he could walk unassisted now, and he let go of the pew.

"Don't do it," he said again, moving toward her with the stealthy grace of a man who knows what he wants.

Who knows what should be.

Still she didn't speak. No one did. It was strange, that. Three hundred of London's biggest busybodies, gathered into one building, and no one could utter a word. No one could take his eyes off him as he walked down the aisle.

"I love you," he said, right there, right in front of everyone. Who cared? He would not keep this a secret. He would not let her marry someone else without making sure all the world knew that she owned his heart.

"I love you," he said again, and out of the corner of his eye he could see his mother and sister, seated primly in a pew, their mouths open with shock.

He kept walking. Down the aisle, each step more confident, more sure.

"Don't do it," he said, stepping out of the aisle and into the apse. "Don't marry him."

"Gregory," she whispered. "Why are you doing this?"

"I love you," he said, because it was the only thing to say. It was the only thing that mattered.

Her eyes glistened, and he could see her breath catch in her throat. She looked up at the man she was trying to marry. His brows rose as he gave her a tiny, one-shouldered shrug, as if to say, *It is your choice.*

Gregory sank to one knee. "Marry me," he said, his very soul in his words. "Marry *me*."

He stopped breathing. The entire church stopped breathing.

She brought her eyes to his. They were huge and clear and everything he'd ever thought was good and kind and true.

"Marry me," he whispered, one last time.

Her lips were trembling, but her voice was clear when she said—

One

In which Our Hero falls in love.

Two months earlier

Unlike most men of his acquaintance, Gregory Bridgerton believed in true love.

He'd have to have been a fool not to.

Consider the following:

His eldest brother, Anthony.

His eldest sister, Daphne.

His other brothers, Benedict and Colin, not to mention his sisters, Eloise, Francesca, and (galling but true) Hyacinth, all of whom—*all* of whom—were quite happily besotted with their spouses.

For most men, such a state of affairs would produce nothing quite so much as bile, but for Gregory, who had been born with an uncommonly cheerful, if occasionally (according to his younger sister) annoying, spirit, it simply meant that he had no choice but to believe the obvious:

Love existed.

It was not a wispy figment of the imagination, designed to keep the poets from complete starvation. It might not be something that one could see or smell or touch, but it was out there, and it was only a matter of time before he, too, found the woman of his dreams and settled down to be fruitful, multiply, and take on such baffling hobbies as papier-mâché and the collection of nutmeg graters.

Although, if one wanted to put a fine point on it, which did seem rather precise for such an abstract sort of concept, his dreams didn't exactly include a woman. Well, not one with any specific and identifiable attributes. He didn't know anything about this woman of his, the one who was supposed to transform his life completely, turning him into a happy pillar of boredom and respectability. He didn't know if she would be short or tall, dark or fair. He'd like to think she would be intelligent and in possession of a fine sense of humor, but beyond that, how was he to know? She could be shy or outspoken. She might like to sing. Or maybe not. Maybe she was a horsewoman, with a ruddy complexion born of too much time out of doors.

He didn't know. When it came to this woman, this impossible, wonderful, and currently nonexistent woman, all he really knew was that when he found her . . .

He'd know.

He didn't know how he'd know; he just knew that he would. Something this momentous, this earth-shattering and life-altering . . . well, really, it wasn't going to whisper its way into existence. It would come full and forceful, like the proverbial ton of bricks. The only question was when.

And in the meantime, he saw no reason not to have a fine time while he anticipated her arrival. One didn't need to behave like a monk while waiting for one's true love, after all.

Gregory was, by all accounts, a fairly typical man about London, with a comfortable—although by no means extravagant—allowance, plenty of friends, and a level enough head to know when to quit a gaming table. He was considered a decent enough catch on the Marriage Mart, if not precisely the top selection (fourth sons never did command a great deal of attention), and he was always in demand when the society matrons needed an eligible man to even up the numbers at dinner parties.

Which did make his aforementioned allowance stretch a bit further—always a benefit.

Perhaps he ought to have had a bit more purpose in his life. Some sort of direction, or even just a meaningful task to complete. But that could wait, couldn't it? Soon, he was sure, everything would come clear. He would know just what it was he wished to do, and whom he wished to do it with, and in the meantime, he'd—

Not have a fine time. Not just at *this* moment, at least.

To explain:

Gregory was presently sitting in a leather chair, a rather accommodating one, not that that really had any bearing on the matter other than the fact that the lack of discomfort was conducive to daydreaming, which in turn was conducive to not listening to his brother, who, it should be noted, was standing approximately four feet away, droning on about something or other, almost certainly involving some variation of the words *duty* and *responsibility*.

Gregory wasn't really paying attention. He rarely did.

Well, no, occasionally he did, but—

"Gregory? Gregory!"

He looked up, blinking. Anthony's arms were crossed, never a good sign. Anthony was the Viscount Bridgerton, and had been for more than twenty years. And while he was, Gregory would be the first to insist, the very best of brothers, he would have made a rather fine feudal lord.

"Begging your pardon for intruding upon your thoughts, such as they are," Anthony said in a dry voice, "but have you, perhaps—just perhaps—heard anything I've said?"

"Diligence," Gregory parroted, nodding with what he deemed sufficient gravity. "Direction."

"Indeed," Anthony replied, and Gregory congratulated himself on what had clearly been an inspired performance. "It was well past time that you finally sought some direction in your life."

"Of course," Gregory murmured, mostly because he'd missed supper, and he was hungry, and he'd heard that his sister-in-law was serving light refreshments in the garden. Besides, it never made sense to argue with Anthony. Never.

"You must make a change. Choose a new course."

"Indeed." Maybe there would be sandwiches. He could eat about forty of those ridiculous little ones with the crusts cut off right then.

"Gregory."

Anthony's voice held that tone. The one that, while impossible to describe, was easy enough to recognize. And Gregory knew it was time to pay attention.

"Right," he said, because truly, it was remarkable how well a single syllable could delay a proper sentence. "I expect I'll join the clergy."

That stopped Anthony cold. Dead, frozen, cold. Gregory paused to savor the moment. Too bad he had to become a bloody vicar to achieve it.

"I beg your pardon," Anthony finally murmured.

"It's not as if I've many choices," Gregory said. And as the words emerged, he realized it was the first time he'd spoken them. It somehow made them more real, more permanent. "It's the military or the clergy," he continued, "and, well, it's got to be said—I'm a beastly bad shot."

Anthony didn't say anything. They all knew it was true.

After a moment of awkward silence, Anthony murmured, "There are swords."

"Yes, but with my luck I'll be posted to the Sudan." Gregory shuddered. "Not to be overly fastidious, but really, the heat. Would *you* want to go?"

Anthony demurred immediately. "No, of course not."

"And," Gregory added, beginning to enjoy himself, "there is Mother."

There was a pause. Then: "She pertains to the Sudan . . . how?"

"She wouldn't very well like my going, and then you, you must know, will be the one who must hold her hand every time she worries, or has some ghastly nightmare about—"

"Say no more," Anthony interrupted.

Gregory allowed himself an inner smile. It really wasn't fair to his mother, who, it was only sporting to point out, had never once claimed to portend the future with anything so wispy as a dream. But she *would* hate his going to the Sudan, and Anthony *would* have to listen to her worry over it.

And as Gregory didn't particularly wish to depart England's misty shores, the point was moot, anyway.

"Right," Anthony said. "Right. I am glad, then, that we have finally been able to have this conversation."

Gregory eyed the clock.

Anthony cleared his throat, and when he spoke, there was an edge of impatience to his voice. "And that you are finally thinking toward your future."

Gregory felt something tighten at the back of his jaw. "I am but six-and-twenty," he reminded him. "Surely too young for such repeated use of the word *finally*."

Anthony just arched a brow. "Shall I contact the archbishop? See about finding you a parish?"

Gregory's chest twisted into an unexpected coughing spasm. "Er, no," he said, when he was able. "Not yet, at least."

One corner of Anthony's mouth moved. But not by much, and not, by any stretch of the definition, into a smile. "You could marry," he said softly.

"I could," Gregory agreed. "And I shall. In fact, I plan to."

"Really?"

"When I find the right woman." And then, at Anthony's dubious expression, Gregory added, "Surely you, of all people, would recommend a match of love over convenience."

Anthony was rather famously besotted with his wife, who was in turn rather inexplicably besotted with him. Anthony was also rather famously devoted to his seven younger siblings, so Gregory should not have felt such an unexpected wellspring of emotion when he softly said, "I wish you every happiness that I myself enjoy."

Gregory was saved from having to make a reply by the very loud rumbling of his stomach. He gave his brother a sheepish expression. "Sorry. I missed supper."

"I know. We expected you earlier."

Gregory avoided wincing. Just.

"Kate was somewhat put out."

That was the worst. When Anthony was disappointed that was one thing. But when he claimed that his wife had been somehow pained . . .

Well, that was when Gregory *knew* he was in trouble. "Got a late start from London," he mumbled. It was the truth, but still, no excuse for bad behavior. He had been expected at the house party in time for supper, and he had not come through. He almost said, "I shall make it up to her," but at the last moment bit his tongue. Somehow that would make it worse, he knew, almost as if he was making light of his tardiness, assuming that he could smooth over any transgression with a smile and a glib comment. Which he often could, but for some reason this time—

He didn't want to.

So instead he just said, "I'm sorry." And he meant it, too.

"She's in the garden," Anthony said gruffly. "I think she means to have dancing—on the patio, if you can believe it."

Gregory could. It sounded exactly like his sister-in-law. She wasn't the sort to let any serendipitous moment pass her by, and with the weather so uncommonly fine, why not organize an impromptu dance al fresco?

"See that you dance with whomever she wishes," Anthony said. "Kate won't like any of the young ladies to feel left out."

"Of course not," Gregory murmured.

"I will join you in a quarter of an hour," Anthony said, moving back to his desk, where several piles of paper awaited him. "I have a few items here yet to complete."

Gregory stood. "I shall pass that along to Kate." And then, the interview quite clearly at an end, he left the room and headed out to the garden.

It had been some time since he'd been to Aubrey Hall, the ancestral home of the Bridgertons. The family gathered here in Kent for Christmas, of course, but in truth, it wasn't home for Gregory, and never really had been. After his father had died, his mother had done the unconventional and uprooted her family, electing to spend most of the year in London. She had never said so, but Gregory had always suspected that the graceful old house held too many memories.

As a result, Gregory had always felt more at home in town than in the country. Bridgerton House, in London, was the home of his childhood, not Aubrey Hall. Still, he enjoyed his visits, and he was always game for bucolic pursuits, such as riding and swimming (when the lake was warm enough to permit it), and strangely enough, he liked the change of pace. He liked the way the air felt quiet and clean after months in the city.

And he liked the way he could leave it all behind when it grew *too* quiet and clean.

The night's festivities were being held on the south lawn, or so he'd been told by the butler when he'd arrived earlier that evening. It seemed a good spot for an outdoor fête—level ground, a view to the lake, and a large patio with plenty of seating for the less energetic.

As he approached the long salon that opened to the outside, he could hear the low murmur of voices buzzing in through the French doors. He wasn't certain how many people his sister-in-law had invited for her house party—probably something between twenty and thirty. Small enough to be intimate, but still large enough so that one could escape for some peace and quiet without leaving a gaping hole in the gathering.

As Gregory passed through the salon, he took a deep breath, trying in part to determine what sort of food Kate had decided to serve. There wouldn't be much, of course; she would have already overstuffed her guests at supper.

Sweets, Gregory decided, smelling a hint of cinnamon as he reached the light gray stone of the patio. He let out a disappointed breath. He was starving, and a huge slab of meat sounded like heaven right then.

But he was late, and it was nobody's fault but his own, and Anthony would have his head if he did not join the party immediately, so cakes and biscuits it would have to be.

A warm breeze sifted across his skin as he stepped outside. It had been remarkably hot for May; everyone was talking about it. It was the sort of weather that seemed to lift the mood—so surprisingly pleasant that one couldn't help but smile. And indeed, the guests milling about seemed to be in happy spirits; the low buzz of conversation was peppered with frequent rumbles and trills of laughter.

Gregory looked around, both for the refreshments and for someone he knew, most preferably his sister-in-law Kate, whom propriety dictated he greet first. But as his eyes swept across the scene, instead he saw . . .

Her.

Her.

And he knew it. He knew that she was the one. He stood frozen, transfixed. The air didn't rush from his body; rather, it seemed to slowly escape until there was nothing left, and he just stood there, hollow, and aching for more.

He couldn't see her face, not even her profile. There was just her back, just the breathtakingly perfect curve of her neck, one lock of blond hair swirling against her shoulder.

And all he could think was—*I am wrecked.*

For all other women, he was wrecked. This intensity, this fire, this overwhelming sense of rightness—he had never felt anything like it.

Maybe it was silly. Maybe it was mad. It was probably both those things. But he'd been waiting. For this moment, for so long, he'd been waiting. And it suddenly became clear—why he hadn't joined the military or the clergy, or taken his brother up on one of his frequent offers to manage a smaller Bridgerton estate.

He'd been waiting. That's all it was. Hell, he hadn't even realized how much he'd been doing nothing but waiting for this moment.

And here it was.

There *she* was.

And he knew.

He knew.

He moved slowly across the lawn, food and Kate forgotten. He managed to murmur his greetings to the one or two people he passed on his way, still keeping his pace. He had to reach her. He had to see her face, breathe her scent, know the sound of her voice.

And then he was there, standing mere feet away. He was breathless, awed, somehow fulfilled merely to stand in her presence.

She was speaking with another young lady, with enough animation to mark them as good friends. He stood there for a moment, just watching them until they slowly turned and realized he was there.

He smiled. Softly, just a little bit. And he said . . .

"How do you do?"

Lucinda Abernathy, better known to, well, everyone who knew her, as Lucy, stifled a groan as she turned to the gentleman who had crept up on her, presumably to make calf eyes at Hermione, as did, well, everyone who met Hermione.

It was an occupational hazard of being friends with Hermione Watson. She collected broken hearts the way the old vicar down by the Abbey collected butterflies.

The only difference, being, of course, that Hermione didn't jab her collection with nasty little pins. In all fairness, Hermione didn't wish to win the hearts of gentlemen, and she certainly never set out to break any of them. It just . . . happened. Lucy was used to it by now. Hermione was Hermione, with pale blond hair the color of butter, a heart-shaped face, and huge, wide-set eyes of the most startling shade of green.

Lucy, on the other hand, was . . . Well, she wasn't Hermione, that much was clear. She was simply herself, and most of the time, that was enough.

Lucy was, in almost every visible way, just a little bit *less* than Hermione. A little less blond. A little less slender. A little less tall. Her eyes were a little less vivid in color—bluish-gray, actually, quite attractive when compared with anyone other than Hermione, but that did her little good, as she never *went* anywhere without Hermione.

She had come to this stunning conclusion one day while not paying attention to her lessons on English Composition and Literature at Miss Moss's School for Exceptional Young Ladies, where she and Hermione had been students for three years.

Lucy was a little bit less. Or perhaps, if one wanted to put a nicer sheen on it, she was simply *not quite*.

She was, she supposed, reasonably attractive, in that healthy, traditional, English rose sort of manner, but men were rarely (oh, very well, never) struck dumb in her presence.

Hermione, however . . . well, it was a good thing she was such a nice person. She would have been impossible to be friends with, otherwise.

Well, that and the fact that she simply could not dance. Waltz, quadrille, minuet—it really didn't matter. If it involved music and movement, Hermione couldn't do it.

And it was *lovely*.

Lucy didn't think herself a particularly shallow person, and she would have insisted, had anyone asked, that she would freely throw herself in front of a carriage for her dearest friend, but there was a sort of satisfying fairness in the fact that the most beautiful girl in England had two left feet, at least one of them club.

Metaphorically speaking.

And now here was another one. Man, of course, not foot. Handsome, too. Tall, although not overly so, with warm brown hair and a rather pleasing smile. And a twinkle in his eyes as well, the color of which she couldn't quite determine in the dim night air.

Not to mention that she couldn't actually *see* his eyes, as he wasn't looking at her. He was looking at Hermione, as men always did.

Lucy smiled politely, even though she couldn't imagine that he'd notice, and waited for him to bow and introduce himself.

And then he did the most astonishing thing. After disclosing his name—she should have known he was a Bridgerton from the looks of him—he leaned down and kissed *her* hand first.

Lucy's breath caught.

Then, of course, she realized what he was doing.

Oh, he was *good*. He was really good. Nothing, *nothing* would endear a man to Hermione faster than a compliment to Lucy.

Too bad for him that Hermione's heart was otherwise engaged.

Oh well. It would be amusing to watch it all play out, at least.

"I am Miss Hermione Watson," Hermione was saying, and Lucy realized that Mr. Bridgerton's tactics were doubly clever. By kissing Hermione's hand second, he could linger over it, and her, really, and then she would be the one required to make the introductions.

Lucy was almost impressed. If nothing else, it marked him as slightly more intelligent than the average gentleman.

"And this is my dearest friend," Hermione continued, "Lady Lucinda Abernathy."

She said it the way she always said it, with love and devotion, and perhaps just the barest touch of desperation, as if to say—*For heaven's sake, spare Lucy a glance, too.*

But of course they never did. Except when they wanted advice concerning Hermione, her heart, and the winning thereof. When that happened, Lucy was always in high demand.

Mr. Bridgerton—Mr. Gregory Bridgerton, Lucy mentally corrected, for there were, as far as she knew, three Mr. Bridgertons in total, not counting the viscount, of course—turned and surprised her with a winning smile and warm eyes. "How do you do, Lady Lucinda," he murmured.

"Very well, thank you," and then she could have kicked herself for she actually stammered before the V in *very*, but for heaven's sake, they never looked at her after gazing upon Hermione, never.

Could he possibly be interested in *her*?

No, impossible. They never were.

And really, did it matter? Of course it would be rather charming if a man fell madly and passionately in love with her for a change. Really, she wouldn't *mind* the attention. But the truth was, Lucy was practically engaged to Lord Haselby and had been for years and years and years, so there was no use in having a besotted admirer of her own. It wasn't as if it could lead to anything useful.

And that besides, it certainly wasn't Hermione's fault that she'd been born with the face of an angel.

So Hermione was the siren, and Lucy was the trusty friend, and all was right with the world. Or if not right, then at least quite predictable.

"May we count you among our hosts?" Lucy finally asked, since no one had said anything once they'd all finished with the requisite "Pleased to meet yous."

"I'm afraid not," Mr. Bridgerton replied. "Much as I would like to take credit for the festivities, I reside in London."

"You are very fortunate to have Aubrey Hall in your family," Hermione said politely, "even if it is your brother's."

And that was when Lucy knew. Mr. Bridgerton fancied Hermione. Forget that he'd kissed her hand first, or that he'd actually looked at her when she said something, which most men never bothered to do. One had only to see the way he regarded Hermione when she spoke to know that he, too, had joined the throngs.

His eyes had that slightly glazed look. His lips were parted. And there was an intensity there, as if he'd like to gather Hermione up and stride down the hill with her, crowds and propriety be damned.

As opposed to the way he looked at her, which could be quite easily catalogued as polite disinterest. Or perhaps it was—*Why are you blocking my way, thus preventing me from sweeping Hermione up in my arms and striding down the hill with her, crowds and propriety be damned?*

It wasn't disappointing, exactly. Just . . . not . . . undisappointing.

There ought to be a word for that. Really, there ought.

"Lucy? Lucy?"

Lucy realized with a touch of embarrassment that she had not been paying attention to the conversation. Hermione was regarding her curiously, her head tilted in that manner of hers that men always seemed to find so fetching. Lucy had tried it once. It had made her dizzy.

"Yes?" she murmured, since some sort of verbal expression seemed to be in order.

"Mr. Bridgerton has asked me to dance," Hermione said, "but I have told him that I *cannot*."

Hermione was forever feigning twisted ankles and head colds to keep herself off the dance floor. Which was also all good and fine, except that she fobbed off all her admirers on Lucy. Which was all good and fine *at first*, but it had got so common that Lucy suspected that the gentlemen now thought they were being shoved in her direction out of pity, which couldn't have been further from the truth.

Lucy was, if she did say so herself, a rather fine dancer. And an excellent conversationalist as well.

"It would be my pleasure to lead Lady Lucinda in a dance," Mr. Bridgerton said, because, really, what else could he say?

And so Lucy smiled, not entirely heartfelt, but a smile nonetheless, and allowed him to lead her to the patio.

Two

**In which Our Heroine displays a decided
lack of respect for all things romantic.**

𝒢regory was nothing if not a gentleman, and he hid his disappointment well as he offered his arm to Lady Lucinda and escorted her to the makeshift dance floor. She was, he was sure, a perfectly charming and lovely young lady, but she wasn't Miss Hermione Watson.

And he had been waiting his entire life to meet Miss Hermione Watson.

Still, this *could* be considered beneficial to his cause. Lady Lucinda was clearly Miss Watson's closest friend—Miss Watson had positively gushed about her during their brief conversation, during which time Lady Lucinda gazed off at something beyond his shoulder, apparently not listening to a word. And with four sisters, Gregory knew a thing or two about women, the most important of which was that it was always a good idea to befriend the friend, provided they really *were* friends, and not just that odd thing women did where they pretended to be friends and were actually just waiting for the perfect moment to knife each other in the ribs.

Mysterious creatures, women. If they could just learn to say what they meant, the world would be a far simpler place.

But Miss Watson and Lady Lucinda gave every appearance of friendship and devotion, Lady Lucinda's woolgathering aside. And if Gregory wished to learn more about Miss Watson, Lady Lucinda Abernathy was the obvious place to start.

"Have you been a guest at Aubrey Hall very long?" Gregory asked politely as they waited for the music to begin.

"Just since yesterday," she replied. "And you? We did not see you at any of the gatherings thus far."

"I only arrived this evening," he said. "After supper." He grimaced. Now that he was no longer gazing upon Miss Watson, he remembered that he was rather hungry.

"You must be famished," Lady Lucinda exclaimed. "Would you prefer to take a turn around the patio instead of dancing? I promise that we may stroll past the refreshment table."

Gregory could have hugged her. "You, Lady Lucinda, are a capital young lady."

She smiled, but it was an odd sort of smile, and he couldn't quite tell what it meant. She'd liked his compliment, of that he was fairly certain, but there was something else there as well, something a little bit rueful, maybe something a little bit resigned.

"You must have a brother," he said.

"I do," she confirmed, smiling at his deduction. "He is four years my elder and always hungry. I will be forever amazed we had any food in the larder when he was home from school."

Gregory fit her hand in the crook of his elbow, and together they moved to the perimeter of the patio.

"This way," Lady Lucinda said, giving his arm a little tug

when he tried to steer them in a counterclockwise direction. "Unless you would prefer sweets."

Gregory felt his face light up. "Are there savories?"

"Sandwiches. They are small, but they are quite delicious, especially the egg."

He nodded, somewhat absently. He'd caught sight of Miss Watson out of the corner of his eye, and it was a bit difficult to concentrate on anything else. Especially as she had been surrounded by men. Gregory was sure they had been just waiting for someone to remove Lady Lucinda from her side before moving in for the attack.

"Er, have you known Miss Watson very long?" he asked, trying not to be too obvious.

There was a very slight pause, and then she said, "Three years. We are students together at Miss Moss's. Or rather we were students together. We completed our studies earlier this year."

"May I assume you plan to make your debuts in London later this spring?"

"Yes," she replied, nodding toward a table laden with small snacks. "We have spent the last few months preparing, as Hermione's mother likes to call it, attending house parties and small gatherings."

"Polishing yourselves?" he asked with a smile.

Her lips curved in answer. "Exactly that. I should make an excellent candlestick by now."

He found himself amused. "A mere candlestick, Lady Lucinda? Pray, do not understate your value. At the very least you are one of those extravagant silver urns everyone seems to need in their sitting rooms lately."

"I am an urn, then," she said, almost appearing to consider the idea. "What would that make Hermione, I wonder?"

A jewel. A diamond. A diamond set in gold. A diamond set in gold surrounded by . . .

He forcibly halted the direction of his thoughts. He could

perform his poetic gymnastics later, when he wasn't expected to keep up one end of a conversation. A conversation with a different young lady. "I'm sure I do not know," he said lightly, offering her a plate. "I have only barely made Miss Watson's acquaintance, after all."

She said nothing, but her eyebrows rose ever so slightly. And that, of course, was when Gregory realized he was glancing over her shoulder to get a better look at Miss Watson.

Lady Lucinda let out a small sigh. "You should probably know that she is in love with someone else."

Gregory dragged his gaze back to the woman he was meant to be paying attention to. "I beg your pardon?"

She shrugged delicately as she placed a few small sandwiches on her plate. "Hermione. She is in love with someone else. I thought you would like to know."

Gregory gaped at her, and then, against every last drop of his good judgment, looked back at Miss Watson. It was the most obvious, pathetic gesture, but he couldn't help himself. He just . . . Dear God, he just wanted to look at her and look at her and never stop. If this wasn't love, he could not imagine what was.

"Ham?"

"What?"

"Ham." Lady Lucinda was holding out a little strip of sandwich with a pair of serving tongs. Her face was annoyingly serene. "Would you care for one?" she asked.

He grunted and held out his plate. And then, because he couldn't leave the matter as it was, he said stiffly, "I'm sure it is none of my business."

"About the sandwich?"

"About Miss Watson," he ground out.

Even though, of course, he meant no such thing. As far as he was concerned, Hermione Watson was very much his business, or at least she would be, very soon.

It was somewhat disconcerting that *she* had apparently not been hit by the same thunderbolt that had struck him. It had never occurred to him that when he did fall in love, his intended might not feel the same, and with equal immediacy, too. But at least this explanation—her thinking she was in love with someone else—assuaged his pride. It was much more palatable to think her infatuated with someone else than completely indifferent to him.

All that was left to do was make her realize that whoever the other man was, he was not the one for her.

Gregory was not so filled with conceit that he thought he could win any woman upon whom he set his sights, but he certainly had never had *difficulties* with the fairer sex, and given the nature of his reaction to Miss Watson, it was simply inconceivable that his feelings could go unrequited for very long. He might have to work to win her heart and hand, but that would simply make victory all the sweeter.

Or so he told himself. Truth was, a mutual thunderbolt would have been far less trouble.

"Don't feel badly," Lady Lucinda said, craning her neck slightly as she surveyed the sandwiches, looking, presumably, for something more exotic than British pig.

"I don't," he bit off, then waited for her to actually return her attention to him. When she didn't, he said again, "I don't."

She turned, gazed at him frankly, and blinked. "Well, that's refreshing, I must say. Most men are crushed."

He scowled. "What do you mean, most men are crushed?"

"Exactly what I said," she replied, giving him an impatient glance. "Or if they're not crushed, they become rather unaccountably angry." She let out a ladylike snort. "As if any of it could be considered her fault."

"Fault?" Gregory echoed, because in truth, he was having a devil of a time following her.

"You are not the first gentleman to imagine himself in love with Hermione," she said, her expression quite jaded. "It happens all the time."

"I don't *imagine* myself in love—" He cut himself off, hoping she didn't notice the stress on the word *imagine*. Good God, what was happening to him? He used to have a sense of humor. Even about himself. Especially about himself.

"You don't?" She sounded pleasantly surprised. "Well, that's refreshing."

"Why," he asked with narrowed eyes, "is that refreshing?

She returned with: "Why are you asking so many questions?"

"I'm not," he protested, even though he was.

She sighed, then utterly surprised him by saying, "I am sorry."

"I beg your pardon?"

She glanced at the egg salad sandwich on her plate, then back up at him, the order of which he did not find complimentary. He usually rated above egg salad. "I thought you would wish to speak of Hermione," she said. "I apologize if I was mistaken."

Which put Gregory in a fine quandary. He could admit that he'd fallen headlong in love with Miss Watson, which was rather embarrassing, even to a hopeless romantic such as himself. Or he could deny it all, which she clearly wouldn't believe. Or he could compromise, and admit to a mild infatuation, which he might normally regard as the best solution, except that it could only be insulting to Lady Lucinda.

He'd met the two girls at the same time, after all. And he wasn't headlong in love with *her*.

But then, as if she could read his thoughts (which frankly scared him), she waved a hand and said, "Pray do not worry yourself over my feelings. I'm quite used to this. As I said, it happens *all* the time."

Open heart, insert blunt dagger. Twist.

"Not to mention," she continued blithely, "that I am practically engaged myself." And then she took a bite of the egg salad.

Gregory found himself wondering what sort of man had found himself attached to this odd creature. He didn't pity the fellow, exactly, just . . . wondered.

And then Lady Lucinda let out a little "Oh!"

His eyes followed hers, to the spot where Miss Watson had once stood.

"I wonder where she went," Lady Lucinda said.

Gregory immediately turned toward the door, hoping to catch one last glimpse of her before she disappeared, but she was already gone. It was damned frustrating, that. What was the point of a mad, bad, immediate attraction if one couldn't do anything about it?

And forget *all* about it being one-sided. Good Lord.

He wasn't sure what one called sighing through gritted teeth, but that's exactly what he did.

"Ah, Lady Lucinda, there you are."

Gregory looked up to see his sister-in-law approaching.

And remembered that he'd forgotten all about her. Kate wouldn't take offense; she was a phenomenally good sport. But still, Gregory did usually try to have better manners with women to whom he was not blood related.

Lady Lucinda gave a pretty little curtsy. "Lady Bridgerton."

Kate smiled warmly in return. "Miss Watson has asked me to inform you that she was not feeling well and has retired for the evening."

"She has? Did she say—Oh, never mind." Lady Lucinda gave a little wave with her hand—the sort meant to convey nonchalance, but Gregory saw the barest hint of frustration pinching at the corners of her mouth.

"A head cold, I believe," Kate added.

Lady Lucinda gave a brief nod. "Yes," she said, looking a bit less sympathetic than Gregory would have imagined, given the circumstances, "it would be."

"And you," Kate continued, turning to Gregory, "have not even seen fit to greet me. How are you?"

He took her hands, kissed them as one in apology. "Tardy."

"That I knew." Her face assumed an expression that was not irritated, just a little bit exasperated. "How are you otherwise?"

"Otherwise lovely." He grinned. "As always."

"As always," she repeated, giving him a look that was a clear promise of future interrogation. "Lady Lucinda," Kate continued, her tone considerably less dry, "I trust you have made the acquaintance of my husband's brother, Mr. Gregory Bridgerton?"

"Indeed," Lady Lucinda replied. "We have been admiring the food. The sandwiches are delicious."

"Thank you," Kate said, then added, "and has Gregory promised you a dance? I cannot promise music of a professional quality, but we managed to round together a string quartet amongst our guests."

"He did," Lady Lucinda replied, "but I released him from his obligation so that he might assuage his hunger."

"You must have brothers," Kate said with a smile.

Lady Lucinda looked to Gregory with a slightly startled expression before replying, "Just one."

He turned to Kate. "I made the same observation earlier," he explained.

Kate let out a short laugh. "Great minds, to be sure." She turned to the younger woman and said, "It is well worth understanding the behavior of men, Lady Lucinda. One should never underestimate the power of food."

Lady Lucinda regarded her with wide eyes. "For the benefit of a pleasing mood?"

"Well, *that*," Kate said, almost offhandedly, "but one really shouldn't discount its uses for the purpose of winning an argument. Or simply getting what you want."

"She's barely out of the schoolroom, Kate," Gregory chided.

Kate ignored him and instead smiled widely at Lady Lucinda. "One is never too young to acquire important skills."

Lady Lucinda looked at Gregory, then at Kate, and then her eyes began to sparkle with humor. "I understand why so many look up to you, Lady Bridgerton."

Kate laughed. "You are too kind, Lady Lucinda."

"Oh, please, Kate," Gregory cut in. He turned to Lady Lucinda and added, "She will stand here all night if you keep offering compliments."

"Pay him no attention," Kate said with a grin. "He is young and foolish and knows not of what he speaks."

Gregory was about to make another comment—he couldn't very well allow Kate to get away with that—but then Lady Lucinda cut in.

"I would happily sing your praises for the rest of the evening, Lady Bridgerton, but I believe that it is time for me to retire. I should like to check on Hermione. She has been under the weather all day, and I wish to assure myself that she is well."

"Of course," Kate replied. "Please do give her my regards, and be certain to ring if you need anything. Our housekeeper fancies herself something of an herbalist, and she is always mixing potions. Some of them even work." She grinned, and the expression was so friendly that Gregory instantly realized that she approved of Lady Lucinda. Which meant something. Kate had never suffered fools, gladly or otherwise.

"I shall walk you to the door," he said quickly. It was the least he could do to offer her this courtesy, and besides, it would not do to insult Miss Watson's closest friend.

They said their farewells, and Gregory fit her arm into the

crook of his elbow. They walked in silence to the door to the drawing room, and Gregory said, "I trust you can make your way from here?"

"Of course," she replied. And then she looked up—her eyes were bluish, he noticed almost absently—and asked, "Would you like me to convey a message to Hermione?"

His lips parted with surprise. "Why would you do that?" he asked, before he could think to temper his response.

She just shrugged and said, "You are the lesser of two evils, Mr. Bridgerton."

He wanted desperately to ask her to clarify that comment, but he could not ask, not on such a flimsy acquaintance, so he instead worked to maintain an even mien as he said, "Give her my regards, that is all."

"Really?"

Damn, but that look in her eye was annoying. "Really."

She bobbed the tiniest of curtsies and was off.

Gregory stared at the doorway through which she had disappeared for a moment, then turned back to the party. The guests had begun dancing in greater numbers, and laughter was most certainly filling the air, but somehow the night felt dull and lifeless.

Food, he decided. He'd eat twenty more of those tiny little sandwiches and then he'd retire for the night as well.

All would come clear in the morning.

Lucy *knew* that Hermione didn't have a headache, or any sort of ache for that matter, and she was not at all surprised to find her sitting on her bed, poring over what appeared to be a four-page letter.

Written in an extremely compact hand.

"A footman brought it to me," Hermione said, not even looking up. "He said it arrived in today's post, but they forgot to bring it earlier."

Lucy sighed. "From Mr. Edmonds, I presume?"

Hermione nodded.

Lucy crossed the room she and Hermione were currently sharing and sat down in the chair at the vanity table. This wasn't the first piece of correspondence Hermione had received from Mr. Edmonds, and Lucy knew from experience that Hermione would need to read it twice, then once again for deeper analysis, and then finally one last time, if only to pick apart any hidden meanings in the salutation and closing.

Which meant that Lucy would have nothing to do but examine her fingernails for at least five minutes.

Which she did, not because she was terribly interested in her fingernails, nor because she was a particularly patient person, but rather because she knew a useless situation when she saw one, and she saw little reason in expending the energy to engage Hermione in conversation when Hermione was so patently uninterested in anything she had to say.

Fingernails could only occupy a girl for so long, however, especially when they were already meticulously neat and groomed, so Lucy stood and walked to the wardrobe, peering absently at her belongings.

"Oh, dash," she muttered, "I hate when she does that." Her maid had left a pair of shoes the wrong way, with the left on the right and the right on the left, and while Lucy knew there was nothing earth-shatteringly wrong with that, it did offend some strange (and extremely tidy) little corner of her sensibilities, so she righted the slippers, then stood back to inspect her handiwork, then planted her hands on her hips and turned around. "Are you finished yet?" she demanded.

"Almost," Hermione said, and it sounded as if the word had been resting on the edge of her lips the whole time, as if she'd had it ready so that she could fob off Lucy when she asked.

Lucy sat back down with a huff. It was a scene they had

played out countless times before. Or at least four.

Yes, Lucy knew exactly how many letters Hermione had received from the romantic Mr. Edmonds. She would have liked *not* to have known; in fact, she was more than a little irritated that the item was taking up valuable space in her brain that might have been devoted to something useful, like botany or music, or good heavens, even another page in *De-Brett's,* but the unfortunate fact was, Mr. Edmonds's letters were nothing if not an *event,* and when Hermione had an event, well, Lucy was forced to have it, too.

They had shared a room for three years at Miss Moss's, and since Lucy had no close female relative who might help her make her bow into society, Hermione's mother had agreed to sponsor her, and so here they were, still together.

Which was lovely, really, except for the always-present (in spirit, at least) Mr. Edmonds. Lucy had made his acquaintance only once, but it certainly *felt* as if he were always there, hovering over them, causing Hermione to sigh at strange moments and gaze wistfully off into the distance as if she were committing a love sonnet to memory so that she might include it in her next reply.

"You are aware," Lucy said, even though Hermione had not indicated that she was finished reading her missive, "that your parents will never permit you to marry him."

That was enough to get Hermione to set the letter down, albeit briefly. "Yes," she said with an irritated expression, "you've said as much."

"He is a secretary," Lucy said.

"I realize that."

"A secretary," Lucy repeated, even though they'd had this conversation countless times before. "Your *father's* secretary."

Hermione had picked the letter back up in an attempt to ignore Lucy, but finally she gave up and set it back down, confirming Lucy's suspicions that she had long since finished it and was now in the first, or possibly even second, rereading.

"Mr. Edmonds is a good and honorable man," Hermione said, lips pinched.

"I'm sure he is," Lucy said, "but you can't *marry* him. Your father is a viscount. Do you really think he will allow his only daughter to marry a penniless secretary?"

"My father loves me," Hermione muttered, but her voice wasn't exactly replete with conviction.

"I am not trying to dissuade you from making a love match," Lucy began, "but—"

"That is exactly what you are trying to do," Hermione cut in.

"Not at all. I just don't see why you can't try to fall in love with someone of whom your parents might actually approve."

Hermione's lovely mouth twisted into a frustrated line. "You don't understand."

"What is there to understand? Don't you think your life might be just a touch easier if you fell in love with someone suitable?"

"Lucy, we don't get to choose who we fall in love with."

Lucy crossed her arms. "I don't see why not."

Hermione's mouth actually fell open. "Lucy Abernathy," she said, "you understand nothing."

"Yes," Lucy said dryly, "you've mentioned."

"How can you possibly think a person can choose who she falls in love with?" Hermione said passionately, although not so passionately that she was forced to rouse herself from her semireclined position on the bed. "One doesn't *choose*. It just happens. In an instant."

"Now *that* I don't believe," Lucy replied, and then added, because she could not resist, "not for an instant."

"Well, it does," Hermione insisted. "I know, because it

happened to me. I wasn't *looking* to fall in love."

"Weren't you?"

"No." Hermione glared at her. "I wasn't. I fully intended to find a husband in London. Really, who would have expected to meet anyone in *Fenchley*?"

Said with the sort of disdain found only in a native Fenchleyan.

Lucy rolled her eyes and tilted her head to the side, waiting for Hermione to get on with it.

Which Hermione did not appreciate. "Don't look at me like that," she snipped.

"Like what?"

"Like *that*."

"I repeat, like what?"

Hermione's entire face pinched. "You know exactly what I'm talking about."

Lucy clapped a hand to her face. "Oh my," she gasped. "You looked *exactly* like your mother just then."

Hermione drew back with affront. "That was unkind."

"Your mother is lovely!"

"Not when her face is all pinchy."

"Your mother is lovely even with a pinchy face," Lucy said, trying to put an end to the subject. "Now, do you intend to tell me about Mr. Edmonds or not?"

"Do you plan to mock me?"

"Of course not."

Hermione lifted her brows.

"Hermione, I promise I will not mock you."

Hermione still looked dubious, but she said, "Very well. But if you do—"

"*Hermione.*"

"As I told you," she said, giving Lucy a warning glance, "I wasn't expecting to find love. I didn't even know my father had hired a new secretary. I was just walking in the garden, deciding which of the roses I wished to have cut for the table, and then . . . *I saw him.*"

Said with enough drama to warrant a role on the stage.

"Oh, Hermione," Lucy sighed.

"You said you wouldn't mock me," Hermione said, and she actually jabbed a finger in Lucy's direction, which struck Lucy as sufficiently out of character that she quieted down.

"I didn't even see his face at first," Hermione continued. "Just the back of his head, the way his hair curled against the collar of his coat." She sighed then. She actually sighed as she turned to Lucy with the most pathetic expression. "And the color. Truly, Lucy, have you ever seen hair such a spectacular shade of blond?"

Considering the number of times Lucy had been forced to listen to gentlemen make the same statement about Hermione's hair, she thought it spoke rather well of her that she refrained from comment.

But Hermione was not done. Not nearly. "Then he turned," she said, "and I saw his profile, and I swear to you I heard music."

Lucy would have liked to point out that the Watsons' conservatory was located right next to the rose garden, but she held her tongue.

"And then he turned," Hermione said, her voice growing soft and her eyes taking on that *I'm-memorizing-a-love-sonnet* expression, "and all I could think was—*I am ruined.*"

Lucy gasped. "Don't *say* that. Don't even hint at it."

Ruin was not the sort of thing any young lady mentioned lightly.

"Not *ruined* ruined," Hermione said impatiently. "Good heavens, Lucy, I was in the rose garden, or haven't you been listening? But I knew—I *knew* that I was ruined for all other men. There could never be another to compare."

"And you knew all this from the back of his neck?" Lucy asked.

Hermione shot her an exceedingly irritated expression. "And his profile, but that's not the point."

Lucy waited patiently for the point, even though she was quite certain it wouldn't be one with which she would agree. Or probably even understand.

"The point is," Hermione said, her voice growing so soft that Lucy had to lean forward to hear her, "that I cannot possibly be happy without him. Not possibly."

"Well," Lucy said slowly, because she wasn't precisely certain how she was meant to add to *that,* "you seem happy now."

"That is only because I know he is waiting for me. And"— Hermione held up the letter—"he writes that he loves me."

"Oh dear," Lucy said to herself.

Hermione must have heard her, because her mouth tightened, but she didn't say anything. The two of them just sat there, in their respective places, for a full minute, and then Lucy cleared her throat and said, "That nice Mr. Bridgerton seemed taken with you."

Hermione shrugged.

"He's a younger son, but I believe he has a nice portion. And he is certainly from a good family."

"Lucy, I told you I am not interested."

"Well, he's very handsome," Lucy said, perhaps a bit more emphatically than she'd meant to.

"You pursue him, then," Hermione retorted.

Lucy stared at her in shock. "You know I cannot. I'm practically engaged to Lord Haselby."

"Practically," Hermione reminded her.

"It might as well be official," Lucy said. And it was true. Her uncle had discussed the matter with the Earl of Davenport, Viscount Haselby's father, years ago. Haselby was about ten years older than Lucy, and they were all simply waiting for her to grow up.

Which she supposed she'd done. Surely the wedding wouldn't be too far off now.

And it was a good match. Haselby was a perfectly pleasant fellow. He didn't speak to her as if she were an idiot, he seemed to be kind to animals, and his looks were pleasing enough, even if his hair was beginning to thin. Of course, Lucy had only actually met her intended husband three times, but everyone knew that first impressions were extremely important and usually spot-on accurate.

Besides, her uncle had been her guardian since her father had died ten years earlier, and if he hadn't exactly showered her and her brother Richard with love and affection, he had done his duty by them and raised them well, and Lucy knew it was her duty to obey his wishes and honor the betrothal he had arranged.

Or practically arranged.

Really, it didn't make much difference. She was going to marry Haselby. Everyone knew it.

"I think you use him as an excuse," Hermione said.

Lucy's spine stiffened. "I beg your pardon."

"You use Haselby as an excuse," Hermione repeated, and her face took on a lofty expression Lucy did not enjoy one bit. "So that you do not allow your heart to become engaged elsewhere."

"And just where else, precisely, might I have engaged my heart?" Lucy demanded. "The season has not even begun!"

"Perhaps," Hermione said, "but we have been out and about, getting 'polished' as you and my mother like to put it. You have not been living under a rock, Lucy. You have met any number of men."

There was really no way to point out that none of those men ever even *saw* her when Hermione was near. Hermione would try to deny it, but they would both know that she was lying in an attempt to spare Lucy's feelings. So Lucy instead grumbled something under her breath that was meant to be a reply without actually *being* a reply.

And then Hermione did not say anything; she just looked at her in that arch manner that she never used with anyone else, and finally Lucy had to defend herself.

"It's not an excuse," she said, crossing her arms, then planting her hands on her hips when that didn't feel right. "Truly, what would be the point of it? You know that I'm to marry Haselby. It's been planned for ages."

She crossed her arms again. Then dropped them. Then finally sat down.

"It's not a bad match," Lucy said. "Truthfully, after what happened to Georgiana Whiton, I should be getting down on my hands and knees and kissing my uncle's feet for making such an acceptable alliance."

There was a moment of horrified, almost reverent silence. If they had been Catholic, they would have surely crossed themselves. "There but for the grace of God," Hermione finally said.

Lucy nodded slowly. Georgiana had been married off to a wheezy seventy-year-old with gout. And not even a titled seventy-year-old with gout. Good heavens, she ought to have at least earned a "Lady" before her name for her sacrifice.

"So you see," Lucy finished, "Haselby really isn't such a bad sort. Better than most, actually."

Hermione looked at her. Closely. "Well, if it is what you wish, Lucy, you know that I shall support you unreservedly. But as for me . . ." She sighed, and her green eyes took on that faraway look that made grown men swoon. "I want something else."

"I know you do," Lucy said, trying to smile. But she couldn't even begin to imagine how Hermione would achieve her dreams. In the world they lived in, viscounts' daughters did not marry viscounts' secretaries. And it seemed to Lucy that it would make far more sense to adjust Hermione's dreams than to reshape the social order. Easier, too.

But right now she was tired. And she wanted to go to bed. She would work on Hermione in the morning. Starting with that handsome Mr. Bridgerton. He would be perfect for her friend, and heaven knew he was interested.

Hermione would come around. Lucy would make sure of it.

Three

In which Our Hero tries very, very hard.

$\mathcal{T}$he following morning was bright and clear, and as Gregory helped himself to breakfast, his sister-in-law appeared at his side, smiling faintly, clearly up to something.

"Good morning," she said, far too breezy and cheerful.

Gregory nodded his greeting as he heaped eggs on his plate. "Kate."

"I thought, with the weather so fine, that we might organize an excursion to the village."

"To buy ribbons and bows?"

"Exactly," she replied. "I do think it is important to support the local shopkeepers, don't you?"

"Of course," he murmured, "although I have not recently found myself in great need of ribbons and bows."

Kate appeared not to notice his sarcasm. "All of the young ladies have a bit of pin money and nowhere to spend it. If I do not send them to town they are liable to start a gaming establishment in the rose salon."

Now *that* was something he'd like to see.

"And," Kate continued quite determinedly, "if I send them to town, I will need to send them with escorts."

When Gregory did not respond quickly enough, she repeated, *"With escorts."*

Gregory cleared his throat. "Might I assume you are asking me to walk to the village this afternoon?"

"This morning," she clarified, *"and,* since I thought to match everyone up, *and,* since you are a Bridgerton and thus my favorite gentleman of the bunch, I thought I might inquire if there happened to be anyone with whom you might prefer to be paired."

Kate was nothing if not a matchmaker, but in this case Gregory decided he ought to be grateful for her meddling tendencies. "As a matter of fact," he began, "there is—"

"Excellent!" Kate interrupted, clapping her hands together. "Lucy Abernathy it is."

Lucy Aber— "Lucy Abernathy?" he repeated, dumbfounded. "The Lady Lucinda?"

"Yes, the two of you seemed so well-matched last evening, and I must say, Gregory, I like her tremendously. She says she is practically engaged, but it is my opinion that—"

"I'm not interested in Lady Lucinda," he cut in, deciding it would be too dangerous to wait for Kate to draw breath.

"You're not?"

"No. I'm not. I—" He leaned in, even though they were the only two people in the breakfast room. Somehow it seemed odd, and yes, a little bit embarrassing to shout it out. "Hermione Watson," he said quietly. "I would like to be paired with Miss Watson."

"Really?" Kate didn't look disappointed exactly, but she did look slightly resigned. As if she'd heard this before. Repeatedly.

Damn.

"Yes," Gregory responded, and he felt a rather sizable

surge of irritation washing over him. First at Kate, because, well, she was right there, and he'd fallen desperately in love and all she could do was say, "Really?" But then he realized he'd been rather irked all morning. He hadn't slept well the night before; he hadn't been able to stop thinking about Hermione and the slope of her neck, the green of her eyes, the soft lilt of her voice. He had never—never—reacted to a woman like this, and while he was in some way relieved to have finally found the woman he planned to make his wife, it was a bit disconcerting that she had not had the same re- action to *him*.

Heaven knew he'd dreamed of this moment before. When- ever he'd thought about finding his true love, she had always been fuzzy in his thoughts—nameless, faceless. But she had always felt the same grand passion. She hadn't sent him off dancing with her best friend, for God's sake.

"Hermione Watson it is, then," Kate said, exhaling in that way females did when they meant to tell you something you couldn't possibly begin to understand even if they had cho- sen to convey it in English, which, of course they did not.

Hermione Watson it was. Hermione Watson it would be.

Soon.

Maybe even that morning.

"Do you suppose there is anything to purchase in the village aside from bows and ribbons?" Hermione asked Lucy as they pulled on their gloves.

"I certainly hope so," Lucy responded. "They do this at every house party, don't they? Send us off with our pin money to purchase ribbons and bows. I could decorate an entire house by now. Or at the very least, a small thatched cottage."

Hermione smiled gamely. "I shall donate mine to the cause, and together we shall remake a . . ." She paused, thinking, then smiled. "A large thatched cottage!"

Lucy grinned. There was something so *loyal* about Hermione. Nobody ever saw it, of course. No one ever bothered to look past her face. Although, to be fair, Hermione rarely shared enough of herself with any of her admirers for them to realize what lay behind her pretty exterior. It wasn't that she was shy, precisely, although she certainly wasn't as outgoing as Lucy. Rather, Hermione was private. She simply did not care to share her thoughts and opinions with people she did not know.

And it drove the gentlemen mad.

Lucy peered out the window as they entered one of Aubrey Hall's many drawing rooms. Lady Bridgerton had instructed them to arrive promptly at eleven. "At least it doesn't look as if it might rain," she said. The last time they'd been sent out for fripperies it had drizzled the entire way home. The tree canopy had kept them moderately dry, but their boots had been nearly ruined. And Lucy had been sneezing for a week.

"Good morning, Lady Lucinda, Miss Watson."

It was Lady Bridgerton, their hostess, striding into the room in that confident way of hers. Her dark hair was neatly pulled back, and her eyes gleamed with brisk intelligence. "How lovely to see you both," she said. "You are the last of the ladies to arrive."

"We are?" Lucy asked, horrified. She *hated* being late. "I'm so terribly sorry. Didn't you say eleven o'clock?"

"Oh dear, I did not mean to upset you," Lady Bridgerton said. "I did indeed say eleven o'clock. But that is because I thought to send everyone out in shifts."

"In shifts?" Hermione echoed.

"Yes, it's far more entertaining that way, wouldn't you agree? I have eight ladies and eight gentlemen. If I sent the lot of you out at once, it would be impossible to have a proper conversation. Not to mention the width of the road. I would hate for you to be tripping over one another."

There was also something to be said for safety in numbers,

but Lucy kept her thoughts to herself. Lady Bridgerton clearly had some sort of agenda, and as Lucy had already decided that she greatly admired the viscountess, she was rather curious as to the outcome.

"Miss Watson, you will be paired with my husband's brother. I believe you made his acquaintance last night?"

Hermione nodded politely.

Lucy smiled to herself. Mr. Bridgerton had been a busy man that morning. Well done.

"And you, Lady Lucinda," Lady Bridgerton continued, "will be escorted by Mr. Berbrooke." She smiled weakly, almost in apology. "He is a relation of sorts," she added, "and, ah, truly a good-natured fellow."

"A relation?" Lucy echoed, since she wasn't exactly certain how she was meant to respond to Lady Bridgerton's uncharacteristically hesitant tone. "Of sorts?"

"Yes. My husband's brother's wife's sister is married to his brother."

"Oh." Lucy kept her expression bland. "Then you are close?"

Lady Bridgerton laughed. "I like you, Lady Lucinda. And as for Neville . . . well, I am certain you will find him entertaining. Ah, here he is now. Neville! Neville!"

Lucy watched as Lady Bridgerton moved to greet Mr. Neville Berbrooke at the door. They had already been introduced, of course; introductions had been made for everyone at the house party. But Lucy had not yet conversed with Mr. Berbrooke, nor truly even seen him except from afar. He seemed an affable enough fellow, rather jolly-looking with a ruddy complexion and a shock of blond hair.

"Hallo, Lady Bridgerton," he said, somehow crashing into a table leg as he entered the room. "Excellent breakfast this morning. Especially the kippers."

"Thank you," Lady Bridgerton replied, glancing nervously at the Chinese vase now teetering on the tabletop. "I'm sure you remember Lady Lucinda."

The pair murmured their greetings, then Mr. Berbrooke said, "D'you like kippers?"

Lucy looked first to Hermione, then to Lady Bridgerton for guidance, but neither seemed any less baffled than she, so she just said, "Er . . . yes?"

"Excellent!" he said. "I say, is that a tufted tern out the window?"

Lucy blinked. She looked to Lady Bridgerton, only to discover that the viscountess would not make eye contact. "A tufted tern you say," Lucy finally murmured, since she could not think of any other suitable reply. Mr. Berbrooke had ambled over to the window, so she went to join him. She peered out. She could see no birds.

Meanwhile, out of the corner of her eye she could see that Mr. Bridgerton had entered the room and was doing his best to charm Hermione. Good heavens, the man had a nice smile! Even white teeth, and the expression extended to his eyes, unlike most of the bored young aristocrats Lucy had met. Mr. Bridgerton smiled as if he meant it.

Which made sense, of course, as he was smiling at Hermione, with whom he was quite obviously infatuated.

Lucy could not hear what they were saying, but she easily recognized the expression on Hermione's face. Polite, of course, since Hermione would never be impolite. And maybe no one could see it but Lucy, who knew her friend so well, but Hermione was doing no more than tolerating Mr. Bridgerton's attentions, accepting his flattery with a nod and a pretty smile while her mind was far, far elsewhere.

With that cursed Mr. Edmonds.

Lucy clenched her jaw as she pretended to look for terns, tufted or otherwise, with Mr. Berbrooke. She had no reason to think Mr. Edmonds anything but a nice young man, but the simple truth was, Hermione's parents would never countenance the match, and while Hermione might think she would be able to live happily on a secretary's salary, Lucy was quite certain that once the first bloom of marriage faded, Hermione would be miserable.

And she could do *so* much better. It was obvious that Hermione could marry anyone. Anyone. She wouldn't need to settle. She could be a queen of the *ton* if she so desired.

Lucy eyed Mr. Bridgerton, nodding and keeping one ear on Mr. Berbrooke, who was back on the subject of kippers. Mr. Bridgerton was perfect. He didn't possess a title, but Lucy was not so ruthless that she felt Hermione had to marry into the highest available rank. She just could not align herself with a secretary, for heaven's sake.

Plus, Mr. Bridgerton was extremely handsome, with dark, chestnut hair and lovely hazel eyes. And his family seemed perfectly nice and reasonable, which Lucy had to think was a point in his favor. When you married a man, you married his family, really.

Lucy couldn't imagine a better husband for Hermione. Well, she supposed she would not complain if Mr. Bridgerton were next in line for a marquisate, but really, one could not have everything. And most importantly, she was quite certain that he would make Hermione happy, even if Hermione did not yet realize this.

"I will make this happen," she said to herself.

"Eh?" from Mr. Berbrooke. "Did you find the bird?"

"Over there," Lucy said, pointing toward a tree.

He leaned forward. "Really?"

"Oh, Lucy!" came Hermione's voice.

Lucy turned around.

"Shall we be off? Mr. Bridgerton is eager to be on his way."

"I am at your service, Miss Watson," the man in question said. "We depart at your discretion."

Hermione gave Lucy a look that clearly said that *she* was eager to be on her way, so Lucy said, "Let us depart, then," and she took Mr. Berbrooke's proffered arm and allowed him to lead her to the front drive, managing to yelp only once, even though she thrice stubbed her toe on heaven knew what, but somehow, even with a nice, lovely expanse of grass, Mr. Berbrooke managed to find every tree root, rock, and bump, and lead her directly to them.

Gad.

Lucy mentally prepared herself for further injury. It was going to be a painful outing. But a productive one. By the time they returned home, Hermione would be at least a little intrigued by Mr. Bridgerton.

Lucy would make sure of it.

If Gregory had had any doubts about Miss Hermione Watson, they were banished the moment he placed her hand in the crook of his elbow. There was a rightness to it, a strange, mystical sense of two halves coming together. She fit perfectly next to him. *They* fit.

And he wanted her.

It wasn't even desire. It was strange, actually. He wasn't feeling anything so plebian as bodily desire. It was something else. Something within. He simply wanted her to be his. He wanted to look at her, and to know. To *know* that she would carry his name and bear his children and gaze lovingly at him every morning over a cup of chocolate.

He wanted to tell her all this, to share his dreams, to paint a picture of their life together, but he was no fool, and so he simply said, as he guided her down the front path, "You look exceptionally lovely this morning, Miss Watson."

"Thank you," she said.

And then said nothing else.

He cleared his throat. "Did you sleep well?"

"Yes, thank you," she said.

"Are you enjoying your stay?"

"Yes, thank you," she said.

Funny, but he'd always thought conversation with the woman he'd marry would come just a *little* bit easier.

He reminded himself that she still fancied herself in love with another man. Someone unsuitable, if Lady Lucinda's comment of the night before was any indication. What was that she had called him—the lesser of two evils?

He glanced forward. Lady Lucinda was stumbling along ahead of him on the arm of Neville Berbrooke, who had never learned to adjust his gait for a lady. She seemed to be managing well enough, although he did think he might have heard a small cry of pain at one point.

He gave his head a mental shake. It was probably just a bird. Hadn't Neville said he'd seen a flock of them through the window?

"Have you been friends with Lady Lucinda for very long?" he asked Miss Watson. He knew the answer, of course; Lady Lucinda had told him the night before. But he couldn't think of anything else to ask. And he needed a question that could not be answered with *yes, thank you* or *no, thank you.*

"Three years," Miss Watson replied. "She is my dearest friend." And then her face finally took on a bit of animation as she said, "We ought to catch up."

"To Mr. Berbrooke and Lady Lucinda?"

"Yes," she said with a firm nod. "Yes, we ought."

The last thing Gregory wanted to do was squander his precious time alone with Miss Watson, but he dutifully called out to Berbrooke to hold up. He did, stopping so suddenly that Lady Lucinda quite literally crashed into him.

She let out a startled cry, but other than that was clearly unhurt.

Miss Watson took advantage of the moment, however, by disengaging her hand from his elbow and rushing forward. "Lucy!" she cried out. "Oh, my dearest Lucy, are you injured?"

"Not at all," Lady Lucinda replied, looking slightly confused by the extreme level of her friend's concern.

"I must take your arm," Miss Watson declared, hooking her elbow through Lady Lucinda's.

"You must?" Lady Lucinda echoed, twisting away. Or rather, attempting to. "No, truly, that is not necessary."

"I insist."

"It is not necessary," Lady Lucinda repeated, and Gregory wished he could see her face, because it *sounded* as if she were gritting her teeth.

"Heh heh," came Berbrooke's voice. "P'rhaps I'll take your arm, Bridgerton."

Gregory gave him a level look. "*No.*"

Berbrooke blinked. "It was a joke, you know."

Gregory fought the urge to sigh and somehow managed to say, "I was aware." He'd known Neville Berbrooke since they'd both been in leading strings, and he usually had more patience with him, but right now he wanted nothing so much as to fit him with a muzzle.

Meanwhile, the two girls were bickering about something, in tones hushed enough that Gregory couldn't hope to make out what they were saying. Not that he'd likely have understood their language even if they'd been shouting it; it was clearly something bafflingly female. Lady Lucinda was still tugging her arm, and Miss Watson quite simply refused to let go.

"She is injured," Hermione said, turning and batting her eyelashes.

Batting her eyelashes? She chose *this* moment to flirt?

"I am not," Lucy returned. She turned to the two gentlemen. "I am not," she repeated. "Not in the slightest. We should continue."

Gregory couldn't quite decide if he was amused or insulted by the entire spectacle. Miss Watson quite clearly did not wish for his escort, and while some men loved to pine for the unattainable, he'd always preferred his women smiling, friendly, and willing.

Miss Watson turned then, however, and he caught sight of the back of her neck (what *was* it about the back of her neck?). He felt himself sinking again, that madly in love feeling that had captured him the night before, and he told himself not to lose heart. He hadn't even known her a full day; she merely needed time to get to know him. Love did not strike everyone with the same speed. His brother Colin, for example, had known his wife for years and years before he'd realized they were meant to be together.

Not that Gregory planned to wait years and years, but still, it did put the current situation in a better perspective.

After a few moments it became apparent that Miss Watson would not acquiesce, and the two women would be walking arm in arm. Gregory fell in step beside Miss Watson, while Berbrooke ambled on, somewhere in the vicinity of Lady Lucinda.

"You must tell us what it is like to be from such a large family," Lady Lucinda said to him, leaning forward and speaking past Miss Watson. "Hermione and I each have but one sibling."

"Have three m'self," said Berbrooke. "All boys, all of us. 'Cept for my sister, of course."

"It is . . ." Gregory was about to give his usual answer, about it being mad and crazy and usually more trouble than it was worth, but then somehow the deeper truth slipped across his lips, and he found himself saying, "Actually, it's comforting."

"Comforting?" Lady Lucinda echoed. "What an intriguing choice of word."

He looked past Miss Watson to see her regarding him with curious blue eyes.

"Yes," he said slowly, allowing his thoughts to coalesce before replying. "There is comfort in having a family, I think. It's a sense of . . . just *knowing,* I suppose."

"What do you mean?" Lucy asked, and she appeared quite sincerely interested.

"I know that they are there," Gregory said, "that should I ever be in trouble, or even simply in need of a good conversation, I can always turn to them."

And it was true. He had never really thought about it in so many words, but it was true. He was not as close to his brothers as they were to one another, but that was only natural, given the age difference. When they had been men about town, he had been a student at Eton. And now they were all three married, with families of their own.

But still, he knew that should he need them, or his sisters for that matter, he had only to ask.

He never had, of course. Not for anything important. Or even most things unimportant. But he knew that he could. It was more than most men had in this world, more than most men would ever have.

"Mr. Bridgerton?"

He blinked. Lady Lucinda was regarding him quizzically.

"My apologies," he murmured. "Woolgathering, I suppose." He offered her a smile and a nod, then glanced over at Miss Watson, who, he was surprised to see, had also turned to look at him. Her eyes seemed huge in her face, clear and dazzlingly green, and for a moment he felt an almost electric connection. She smiled, just a little, and with a touch of embarrassment at having been caught, then looked away.

Gregory's heart leaped.

And then Lady Lucinda spoke again. "That is *exactly*

how I feel about Hermione," she said. "She is the sister of my heart."

"Miss Watson is truly an exceptional lady," Gregory murmured, then added, "As, of course, are you."

"She is a superb watercolorist," Lady Lucinda said.

Hermione blushed prettily. *"Lucy."*

"But you are," her friend insisted.

"Like to paint myself," came Neville Berbrooke's jovial voice. "Ruin my shirts every time, though."

Gregory glanced at him in surprise. Between his oddly revealing conversation with Lady Lucinda and his shared glance with Miss Watson, he'd almost forgotten Berbrooke was there.

"M'valet is up in arms about it," Neville continued, ambling along. "Don't know why they can't make paint that washes out of linen." He paused, apparently in deep thought. "Or wool."

"Do you like to paint?" Lady Lucinda asked Gregory.

"No talent for it," he admitted. "But my brother is an artist of some renown. Two of his paintings hang in the National Gallery."

"Oh, that is marvelous!" she exclaimed. She turned to Miss Watson. "Did you hear that, Hermione? You must ask Mr. Bridgerton to introduce you to his brother."

"I would not wish to inconvenience either Mr. Bridgerton," she said demurely.

"It would be no inconvenience at all," Gregory said, smiling down at her. "I would be delighted to make the introduction, and Benedict always loves to natter on about art. I rarely am able to follow the conversation, but he seems quite animated."

"You see," Lucy put in, patting Hermione's arm. "You and Mr. Bridgerton have a great deal in common."

Even Gregory thought that was a bit of a stretch, but he did not comment.

"Velvet," Neville suddenly declared.

Three heads swung in his direction. "I beg your pardon?" Lady Lucinda murmured.

"S'the worst," he said, nodding with great vigor. "T'get the paint out of, I mean."

Gregory could only see the back of her head, but he could well imagine her blinking as she said, "You wear velvet while you paint?"

"If it's cold."

"How . . . unique."

Neville's face lit up. "Do you think so? I've always wanted to be unique."

"You are," she said, and Gregory did not hear anything other than reassurance in her voice. "You most certainly are, Mr. Berbrooke."

Neville beamed. "Unique. I like that. Unique." He smiled anew, testing the word on his lips. "Unique. *Unique.* You-oo-oooooo-neek."

The foursome continued toward the village in amiable silence, punctuated by Gregory's occasional attempts to draw Miss Watson into a conversation. Sometimes he succeeded, but more often than not, it was Lady Lucinda who ended up chatting with him. When she wasn't trying to prod Miss Watson into conversation, that was.

And the whole time Neville chattered on, mostly carrying on a conversation with himself, mostly about his newfound uniqueness.

At last the familiar buildings of the village came into view. Neville declared himself uniquely famished, whatever that meant, so Gregory steered the group to the White Hart, a local inn that served simple but always delicious fare.

"We should have a picnic," Lady Lucinda suggested. "Wouldn't that be marvelous?"

"Capital idea," Neville exclaimed, gazing at her as if she

were a goddess. Gregory was a little startled by the fervor of his expression, but Lady Lucinda seemed not to notice.

"What is your opinion, Miss Watson?" Gregory asked. But the lady in question was lost in thought, her eyes unfocused even as they remained fixed on a painting on the wall.

"Miss Watson?" he repeated, and then when he finally had her attention, he said, "Would you care to take a picnic?"

"Oh. Yes, that would be lovely." And then she went back to staring off into space, her perfect lips curved into a wistful, almost longing expression.

Gregory nodded, tamping down his disappointment, and set out making arrangements. The innkeeper, who knew his family well, gave him two clean bedsheets to lay upon the grass and promised to bring out a hamper of food when it was ready.

"Excellent work, Mr. Bridgerton," Lady Lucinda said. "Don't you agree, Hermione?"

"Yes, of course."

"Hope he brings pie," Neville said as he held the door open for the ladies. "I can always eat pie."

Gregory tucked Miss Watson's hand in the crook of his arm before she could escape. "I asked for a selection of foods," he said quietly to her. "I hope there is something that meets your cravings."

She looked up at him and he felt it again, the air swooshing from his body as he lost himself in her eyes. And he knew she felt it, too. She had to. How could she not, when he felt as if his own legs might give out beneath him?

"I am sure that it will be delightful," she said.

"Are you in possession of a sweet tooth?"

"I am," she admitted.

"Then you are in luck," Gregory told her. "Mr. Gladdish has promised to include some of his wife's gooseberry pie, which is quite famous in this district."

"Pie?" Neville visibly perked up. He turned to Lady Lucinda. "Did he say we were getting pie?"

"I believe he did," she replied.

Neville sighed with pleasure. "Do you like pie, Lady Lucinda?"

The barest hint of exasperation washed over her features as she asked, "What sort of pie, Mr. Berbrooke?"

"Oh, any pie. Sweet, savory, fruit, meat."

"Well . . ." She cleared her throat, glancing about as if the buildings and trees might offer some guidance. "I . . . ah . . . I suppose I like most pies."

And it was in that minute that Gregory was quite certain Neville had fallen in love.

Poor Lady Lucinda.

They walked across the main thoroughfare to a grassy field, and Gregory swept open the sheets, laying them flat upon the ground. Lady Lucinda, clever girl that she was, sat first, then patted a spot for Neville that would guarantee that Gregory and Miss Watson would be forced to share the other patch of cloth.

And then Gregory set about winning her heart.

Four

**In which Our Heroine offers advice,
Our Hero takes it, and everyone eats too much pie.**

He was going about it all wrong.

Lucy glanced over Mr. Berbrooke's shoulder, trying not to frown. Mr. Bridgerton was making a valiant attempt to win Hermione's favor, and Lucy had to admit that under normal circumstances, with a different female, he would have succeeded handily. Lucy thought of the many girls she knew from school—any one of them would be head over heels in love with him by now. *Every* one of them, as a matter of fact.

But not Hermione.

He was trying too hard. Being too attentive, too focused, too . . . too . . . Well, too in love, quite frankly, or at least too infatuated.

Mr. Bridgerton was charming, and he was handsome, and obviously quite intelligent as well, but Hermione had *seen* all this before. Lucy could not even begin to count the number of gentlemen who had pursued her friend in much the same manner. Some were witty, some were earnest. They gave flowers, poetry, candy—one even brought Hermione a puppy (instantly refused by Hermione's mother, who had informed the poor gentleman that the natural habitat of dogs did not include Aubusson carpets, porcelain from the Orient, or herself).

But underneath they were all the same. They hung on her every word, they gazed at her as if she were a Greek goddess come down to earth, and they fell over each other in an attempt to offer the cleverest, most romantic compliments ever to rain down upon her pretty ears. And they never seemed to understand how completely unoriginal they all were.

If Mr. Bridgerton truly wished to pique Hermione's interest, he was going to need to do something different.

"More gooseberry pie, Lady Lucinda?" Mr. Berbrooke asked.

"Yes, please," Lucy murmured, if only to keep him busy with the slicing as she pondered what to do next. She really didn't want Hermione to throw her life away on Mr. Edmonds, and truly, Mr. Bridgerton was perfect. He just needed a little help.

"Oh, look!" Lucy exclaimed. "Hermione doesn't have any pie."

"No pie?" Mr. Berbrooke gasped.

Lucy batted her eyelashes at him, not a mannerism with which she had much practice or skill. "Would you be so kind as to serve her?"

As Mr. Berbrooke nodded, Lucy stood up. "I believe I will stretch my legs," she announced. "There are lovely flowers on the far side of the field. Mr. Bridgerton, do you know anything about the local flora?"

He looked up, surprised by her question. "A bit." But he didn't move.

Hermione was busy assuring Mr. Berbrooke that she adored gooseberry pie, so Lucy took advantage of the moment and jerked her head toward the flowers, giving Mr. Bridgerton the sort of urgent look that generally meant "*Come with me now.*"

For a moment he appeared to be puzzled, but he quickly recovered and rose to his feet. "Will you allow me to tell you a bit about the scenery, Lady Lucinda?"

"That would be marvelous," she said, perhaps a touch too enthusiastically. Hermione was staring at her with patent suspicion. But Lucy knew that she would not offer to join them; to do so would encourage Mr. Bridgerton to believe she desired his company.

So Hermione would be left with Mr. Berbrooke and the pie. Lucy shrugged. It was only fair.

"That one, I believe, is a daisy," Mr. Bridgerton said, once they had crossed the field. "And that stalky blue one— Actually, I don't know what it's called."

"Delphinium," Lucy said briskly, "and you must know that I did not summon you to speak of flowers."

"I had an inkling."

She decided to ignore his tone. "I wished to give you some advice."

"Really," he drawled. Except it wasn't a question.

"Really."

"And what might your advice be?"

There was really no way to make it sound any better than it was, so she looked him in the eye and said, "You're going about this all wrong."

"I beg your pardon," he said stiffly.

Lucy stifled a groan. Now she'd pricked his pride, and he would surely be insufferable. "If you want to win Hermione," she said, "you have to do something different."

Mr. Bridgerton stared down at her with an expression that almost bordered on contempt. "I am well able to conduct my own courtships."

"I am sure you are . . . with other ladies. But Hermione is different."

He remained silent, and Lucy knew that she had made her point. He also thought Hermione different, else he wouldn't be making such an effort.

"Everyone does what you do," Lucy said, glancing over at the picnic to make sure that neither Hermione nor Mr. Berbrooke had got up to join them. "Everyone."

"A gentleman does love to be compared to the flock," Mr. Bridgerton murmured.

Lucy had any number of rejoinders for *that,* but she kept her mind on the task at hand and said, "You cannot act like the rest of them. You need to set yourself apart."

"And how do you propose I do that?"

She took a breath. He wasn't going to like her answer. "You must stop being so . . . devoted. Don't treat her like a princess. In fact, you should probably leave her alone for a few days."

His expression turned to distrust. "And allow all the other gentleman to rush in?"

"They will rush in anyway," she said in a matter-of-fact voice. "There is nothing you can do about that."

"Lovely."

Lucy plodded on. "If *you* withdraw, Hermione will be curious as to the reason why."

Mr. Bridgerton looked dubious, so she continued with, "Do not worry, she will know that you're interested. Heavens, after today she'd have to be an idiot not to."

He scowled at that, and Lucy herself couldn't quite believe she was speaking so frankly to a man she barely knew, but desperate times surely called for desperate measures . . . or desperate speech. "She will know, I promise you. Hermione is very intelligent. Not that anyone seems to notice. Most men can't see beyond her face."

"I would like to know her mind," he said softly.

Something in his tone hit Lucy squarely in the chest. She looked up, right into his eyes, and she had the strangest sense that she was somewhere else, and he was somewhere else, and the world was dropping away around them.

He was different from the other gentlemen she'd met. She wasn't sure how, exactly, except that there was something more to him. Something different. Something that made her ache, deep in her chest.

And for a moment she thought she might cry.

But she didn't. Because, really, she couldn't. And she wasn't that sort of female, anyway. She didn't wish to be. And she certainly did not cry when she did not know the reason for it.

"Lady Lucinda?"

She'd stayed silent too long. It was unlike her, and— "She will not wish to allow you to," she blurted out. "Know her mind, I mean. But you can . . ." She cleared her throat, blinked, regained her focus, and then planted her eyes firmly on the small patch of daisies sparkling in the sun. "You can convince her otherwise," she continued. "I am sure that you can. If you are patient. And you are true."

He didn't say anything right away. There was nothing but the faint whistle of the breeze. And then, quietly, he asked, "Why are you helping me?"

Lucy turned back to him and was relieved that this time the earth remained firmly fixed beneath her feet. She was herself again, brisk, no-nonsense, and practical to a fault. And he was just another gentleman vying for Hermione's hand.

All was normal.

"It's you or Mr. Edmonds," she said.

"Is that his name," he murmured.

"He is her father's secretary," she explained. "He is not a bad man, and I don't think he is only after her money, but any fool could see that you are the better match."

Mr. Bridgerton cocked his head to the side. "Why, I wonder, does it sound as if you have just called Miss Watson a fool?"

Lucy turned to him with steel in her eyes. "Do not *ever* question my devotion to Hermione. I could not—" She shot a quick glance at Hermione to make sure she wasn't looking before she lowered her voice and continued. "I could not love her better if she were my blood sister."

To his credit, Mr. Bridgerton gave her a respectful nod and said, "I did you a disservice. My apologies."

Lucy swallowed uncomfortably as she acknowledged his words. He looked as if he meant them, which went a long way toward mollifying her. "Hermione means the world to me," she said. She thought about the school holidays she had spent with the Watson family, and she thought about the lonely visits home. Her returns had never seemed to coincide with those of her brother, and Fennsworth Abbey was a cold and forbidding place with only her uncle for company.

Robert Abernathy had always done his duty by his two charges, but he was rather cold and forbidding as well. Home meant long walks alone, endless reading alone, even meals alone, as Uncle Robert had never shown any interest in dining with her. When he had informed Lucy that she would be attending Miss Moss's, her initial impulse had been to throw her arms around him and gush, "Thank you thank you *thank you*!"

Except that she had never hugged him before, not in the seven years he'd been her guardian. And besides that, he had been seated behind his desk and had already returned his attention to the papers in front of him. Lucy had been dismissed.

When she arrived at school, she had thrown herself into her new life as a student. And she had adored every moment. It was so marvelous just to have people to talk to. Her brother Richard had left for Eton at the age of ten, even before their father had died, and she'd been wandering the halls of the Abbey for nearly a decade with no one but her officious governess for company.

At school people liked her. That had been the best part of all. At home she was nothing more than an afterthought, but at Miss Moss's School for Exceptional Young Ladies the other students sought her company. They asked her questions and actually waited to hear her answer. Lucy might not have been the queen bee of the school, but she had felt that she belonged, and that she had mattered.

She and Hermione had been assigned to share a room that first year at Miss Moss's, and their friendship had been almost instant. By nightfall of that first day, the two were laughing and chattering as if they had known each other all of their lives.

Hermione made her feel . . . better somehow. Not just their friendship, but the knowledge of their friendship. Lucy *liked* being someone's best friend. She liked having one, too, of course, but she really liked knowing that in all the world, there was someone who liked her best. It made her feel confident.

Comfortable.

It was rather like Mr. Bridgerton and what he'd said about his family, actually.

She knew she could count on Hermione. And Hermione knew the same was true of her. And Lucy wasn't sure that there was anyone else in the world she could say that of. Her brother, she supposed. Richard would always come to her aid if she needed him, but they saw each other so rarely these days. It was a pity, really. They had been quite close when they were small. Shut away at Fennsworth Abbey, there was rarely anyone else with whom to play, and so they'd had no choice but to turn to each other. Luckily, they'd got along, more often than not.

She forced her mind back to the present and turned to Mr. Bridgerton. He was standing quite still, regarding her with an expression of polite curiosity, and Lucy had the strangest sense that if she told him everything—about Hermione and Richard and Fennsworth Abbey and how lovely it had been to leave for school . . .

He would have understood. It seemed impossible that he could, coming from such a large and famously close family. He couldn't possibly know what it was to be lonely, to have something to say but no one to say it to. But somehow—it was his eyes, really, suddenly greener than she'd realized, and so focused on her face—

She swallowed. Good heavens, what was happening to her that she could not even finish her own thoughts?

"I only wish for Hermione's happiness," she managed to get out. "I hope you realize that."

He nodded, then flicked his eyes toward the picnic. "Shall we rejoin the others?" he asked. He smiled ruefully. "I do believe Mr. Berbrooke has fed Miss Watson three pieces of pie."

Lucy felt a laugh bubbling within her. "Oh dear."

His tone was charmingly bland as he said, "For the sake of her health, if nothing else, we ought to return."

"Will you think about what I said?" Lucy asked, allowing him to place her hand on his arm.

He nodded. "I will."

She felt herself grip him a little more tightly. "I am right about this. I promise you that I am. No one knows Hermione better than I. And no one else has watched all those gentlemen try—and fail—to win her favor."

He turned, and his eyes caught hers. For a moment they stood perfectly still, and Lucy realized that he was assessing her, taking her measure in a manner that should have been uncomfortable.

But it wasn't. And that was the oddest thing. He was staring at her as if he could see down to her very soul, and it didn't feel the least bit awkward. In fact, it felt oddly . . . nice.

"I would be honored to accept your advice regarding Miss Watson," he said, turning so that they might return to the picnic spot. "And I thank you for offering to help me win her."

"Th-thank you," Lucy stammered, because really, hadn't that been her intention?

But then she realized that she no longer felt quite so nice.

Gregory followed Lady Lucinda's directives to the letter. That evening, he did not approach Miss Watson in the drawing room, where the guests had assembled before supper. When they removed themselves to the dining room, he made no attempt to interfere with the social order and have his seat switched so that he might sit next to her. And once the gentlemen had returned from their port and joined the ladies in the conservatory for a piano recital, he took a seat at the rear, even though she and Lady Lucinda were standing quite alone, and it would have been easy—expected, even—for him to pause and murmur his greetings as he passed by.

But no, he had committed to this possibly ill-advised scheme, and so the back of the room it was. He watched as Miss Watson found a seat three rows ahead, and then settled into his chair, finally allowing himself the indulgence of gazing upon the back of her neck.

Which would have been a perfectly fulfilling pastime were he not *completely* unable to think of anything other than her absolute lack of interest. In him.

Truly, he could have grown two heads and a tail and he would have received nothing more than the polite half-smile she seemed to give everyone. If that.

It was not the sort of reaction Gregory was used to receiving from women. He did not expect universal adulation, but really, when he did make an effort, he usually saw better results than this.

It was damned irritating, actually.

And so he watched the two women, willing them to turn,

to squirm, to do something to indicate that they were cognizant of his presence. Finally, after three concertos and a fugue, Lady Lucinda slowly twisted in her seat.

He could easily imagine her thoughts.

Slowly, slowly, act as if you're glancing at the door to see if someone came in. Flick your eyes ever so slightly at Mr. Bridgerton—

He lifted his glass in salute.

She gasped, or at least he hoped she did, and turned quickly around.

He smiled. He probably shouldn't take such joy in her distress, but truly, it was the only bright spot in the evening thus far.

As for Miss Watson—if she could feel the heat of his stare, she gave no indication. Gregory would have liked to have thought that she was studiously ignoring him—that at least might have indicated some sort of awareness. But as he watched her glance idly around the room, dipping her head every so often to whisper something in Lady Lucinda's ear, it became painfully clear that she wasn't ignoring him at all. That would imply that she noticed him.

Which she quite obviously did not.

Gregory felt his jaw clench. While he did not doubt the good intentions behind Lady Lucinda's advice, the advice itself had been quite patently dreadful. And with only five days remaining to the house party, he had wasted valuable time.

"You look bored."

He turned. His sister-in-law had slipped into the seat next to him and was speaking in a low undertone so as not to interfere with the performance.

"Quite a blow to my reputation as a hostess," she added dryly.

"Not at all," he murmured. "You are splendid as always."

Kate turned forward and was silent for a few moments before saying, "She's quite pretty."

Gregory did not bother to pretend that he didn't know what she was talking about. Kate was far too clever for that. But that didn't mean he had to encourage the conversation. "She is," he said simply, keeping his eyes facing front.

"My suspicion," said Kate, "is that her heart is otherwise engaged. She has not encouraged any of the gentlemen's attentions, and they have certainly all tried."

Gregory felt his jaw tense.

"I have heard," Kate continued, surely aware that she was being a bother, not that that would stop her, "that the same has been true all of this spring. The girl gives no indication that she wishes to make a match."

"She fancies her father's secretary," Gregory said. Because, really, what was the point of keeping it a secret? Kate had a way of finding everything out. And perhaps she could be of help.

"Really?" Her voice came out a bit too loud, and she was forced to murmur apologies to her guests. "Really?" she said again, more quietly. "How do you know?"

Gregory opened his mouth to reply, but Kate answered her own question. "Oh, of course," she said, "the Lady Lucinda. She would know everything."

"Everything," Gregory confirmed dryly.

Kate pondered this for a few moments, then stated the obvious. "Her parents cannot be pleased."

"I don't know that they are aware."

"Oh my." Kate sounded sufficiently impressed by this gossipy tidbit that Gregory turned to look at her. Sure enough, her eyes were wide and sparkling.

"Do try to contain yourself," he said.

"But it's the most excitement I've had all spring."

He looked her squarely in the face. "You need to find a hobby."

"Oh, Gregory," she said, giving him a little nudge with her elbow. "Don't allow love to turn you into such a stuff.

You're far too much fun for that. Her parents will never allow her to marry the secretary, and she's not one to elope. You need only to wait her out."

He let out an irritated exhale.

Kate patted him comfortingly. "I know, I know, you wish to have things done. Your sort is never one for patience."

"My sort?"

She flicked her hand, which she clearly considered enough of an answer. "Truly, Gregory," she said, "this is for the best."

"That she is in love with someone else?"

"Stop being so dramatic. I meant that it will give you time to be certain of your feelings for her."

Gregory thought of the gut-punched feeling he got every time he looked at her. Good God, especially the back of her neck, strange as that seemed. He couldn't imagine he needed time. This was everything he'd ever imagined love to be. Huge, sudden, and utterly exhilarating.

And somehow crushing at the same time.

"I was surprised you didn't ask to be seated with her at supper," Kate murmured.

Gregory glared at the back of Lady Lucinda's head.

"I can arrange it for tomorrow, if you wish," Kate offered.

"Do."

Kate nodded. "Yes, I— Oh, here we are. The music is ending. Pay attention now and look like we're polite."

He stood to applaud, as did she. "Have you ever *not* chattered all the way through a music recital?" he asked, keeping his eyes front.

"I have a curious aversion to them," she said. But then her lips curved into a wicked little smile. "And a nostalgic sort of a fondness, as well."

"Really?" *Now* he was interested.

"I don't tell tales, of course," she murmured, quite purposefully not looking at him, "but really, have you ever seen me attend the opera?"

Gregory felt his brows lift. Clearly there was an opera singer somewhere in his brother's past. Where *was* his brother, anyway? Anthony seemed to have developed a remarkable talent for avoiding most of the social functions of the house party. Gregory had seen him only twice aside from their interview the night he arrived.

"Where *is* the scintillating Lord Bridgerton?" he asked.

"Oh, somewhere. I don't know. We'll find each other at the end of the day, that is all that matters." Kate turned to him with a remarkably serene smile. Annoyingly serene. "I must mingle," she said, smiling at him as if she hadn't a care in the world. "Do enjoy yourself." And she was off.

Gregory hung back, making polite conversation with a few of the other guests as he surreptitiously watched Miss Watson. She was chatting with two young gentlemen—annoying sops, the both of them—while Lady Lucinda stood politely to the side. And while Miss Watson did not appear to be flirting with either, she certainly was paying them more attention than *he'd* received that evening.

And there was Lady Lucinda, smiling prettily, taking it all in.

Gregory's eyes narrowed. Had she double-crossed him? She didn't seem the sort. But then again, their acquaintance was barely twenty-four hours old. How well did he know her, really? She *could* have an ulterior motive. And she *might* be a very fine actress, with dark, mysterious secrets lying below the surface of her—

Oh, blast it all. He was going mad. He would bet his last penny that Lady Lucinda could not lie to save her life. She was sunny and open and most definitely *not* mysterious. She had meant well, of that much he was certain.

But her advice had been excremental.

He caught her eye. A faint expression of apology seemed to flit across her face, and he thought she might have shrugged.

Shrugged? What the hell did *that* mean?

He took a step forward.

Then he stopped.

Then he thought about taking another step.

No.

Yes.

No.

Maybe?

Damn it. He didn't know what to do. It was a singularly unpleasant sensation.

He looked back at Lady Lucinda, quite certain that his expression was not one of sweetness and light. Really, this was all her fault.

But of course now she wasn't looking at him.

He did not shift his gaze.

She turned back. Her eyes widened, hopefully with alarm.

Good. Now they were getting somewhere. If he couldn't feel the bliss of Miss Watson's regard, then at least he could make Lady Lucinda feel the misery of his.

Truly, there were times that just didn't call for maturity and tact.

He remained at the edge of the room, finally beginning to enjoy himself. There was something perversely entertaining about imagining Lady Lucinda as a small defenseless hare, not quite sure if or when she might meet her untimely end.

Not, of course, that Gregory could ever assign himself the role of hunter. His piss-poor marksmanship guaranteed that he couldn't hit anything that moved, and it was a damned good thing he wasn't responsible for acquiring his own food.

But he *could* imagine himself the fox.

He smiled, his first real one of the evening.

And then he knew that the fates were on his side, because he saw Lady Lucinda make her excuses and slip out the conservatory door, presumably to attend to her needs.

As Gregory was standing on his own in the back corner, no one noticed when he exited the room through a different door.

And when Lady Lucinda passed by the doorway to the library, he was able to yank her in without making a sound.

Five

In which Our Hero and Heroine
have a most intriguing conversation.

One moment Lucy was walking down the corridor, her
nose scrunched in thought as she tried to recall the location
of the nearest washroom, and the next she was hurtling
through air, or at the very least tripping over her feet, only to
find herself bumping up against a decidedly large, decidedly
warm, and decidedly human form.

"Don't scream," came a voice. One she knew.

"Mr. Bridgerton?" Good heavens, this seemed out of character. Lucy wasn't quite certain if she ought to be scared.

"We need to talk," he said, letting go of her arm. But he
locked the door and pocketed the key.

"Now?" Lucy asked. Her eyes adjusted to the dim light
and she realized they were in the library. "Here?" And then
a more pertinent question sprang to mind. "Alone?"

He scowled. "I'm not going to ravish you, if that's what
worries you."

She felt her jaw clench. She hadn't thought he *would,* but

he didn't need to make his honorable behavior sound so much like an insult.

"Well, then, what is this about?" she demanded. "If I am caught here in your company, there will be the devil to pay. I'm practically engaged, you know."

"I know," he said. In *that* sort of tone. As if she'd informed him of it ad nauseam, when she knew for a fact she had not mentioned it more than once. Or possibly twice.

"Well, I am," she grumbled, just knowing that she would think of the perfect retort two hours later.

"What," he demanded, "is going on?"

"What do you mean?" she asked, even though she knew quite well what he was talking about.

"Miss Watson," he ground out.

"Hermione?" As if there was another Miss Watson. But it did buy her a bit of time.

"Your advice," he said, his gaze boring into hers, "was abysmal."

He was correct, of course, but she'd been hoping he might not have noticed.

"Right," she said, eyeing him warily as he crossed his arms. It wasn't the most welcoming of gestures, but she had to admit that he carried it off well. She'd heard that his reputation was one of joviality and fun, neither of which was presently in evidence, but, well, hell hath no fury and all that. She supposed one didn't need to be a woman to feel a tad bit underwhelmed at the prospect of unrequited love.

And as she glanced hesitantly at his handsome face, it occurred to her that he probably didn't have much experience with unrequited love. Really, who *would* say no to this gentleman?

Besides Hermione. But she said no to everyone. He shouldn't take it personally.

"Lady Lucinda?" he drawled, waiting for a response.

"Of course," she stalled, wishing he didn't seem so very *large* in the closed room. "Right. Right."

He lifted a brow. "Right."

She swallowed. His tone was one of vaguely paternal indulgence, as if she were mildly amusing but not quite worthy of notice. She knew that tone well. It was a favorite of older brothers, for use with younger sisters. And any friends they might bring home for school holidays.

She hated that tone.

But she plowed on nonetheless and said, "I agree that my plan did not turn out to be the best course of action, but truthfully, I am not certain that anything else would have been an improvement."

This did not appear to be what he wished to hear. She cleared her throat. Twice. And then again. "I'm terribly sorry," she added, because she did feel badly, and it was her experience that apologies always worked when one wasn't quite certain what to say. "But I really did think—"

"You told me," he interrupted, "that if I ignored Miss Watson—"

"I didn't tell you to *ignore* her!"

"You most certainly did."

"No. No, I did not. I told you to back away a bit. To try to be not quite so obvious in your besottedment."

It wasn't a word, but really, Lucy couldn't be bothered.

"Very well," he replied, and his tone shifted from slightly-superior-older-brother to outright condescension. "If I wasn't meant to ignore her, just what precisely do you think I should have done?"

"Well . . ." She scratched the back of her neck, which suddenly felt as if it were sprouting the most horrid of hives. Or maybe it was just nerves. She'd almost rather the hives. She didn't much like this queasy feeling growing in her stomach as she tried to think of something reasonable to say.

"Other than what I did, that is," he added.

"I'm not sure," she ground out. "I haven't *oceans* of experience with this sort of thing."

"Oh, *now* you tell me."

"Well, it was worth a try," she shot back. "Heaven knows, you certainly weren't succeeding on your own."

His mouth clamped into a line, and she allowed herself a small, satisfied smile for hitting a nerve. She wasn't *normally* a mean-spirited person, but the occasion did seem to call for just a little bit of self-congratulation.

"Very well," he said tightly, and while she would have preferred that he apologized and then said—explicitly—that she was right and he was wrong, she supposed that in *some* circles, "Very well" *might* pass for an acknowledgment of error.

And judging by his face, it was the most she was likely to receive.

She nodded regally. It seemed the best course of action. Act like a queen and maybe she would be treated like one.

"Have you any other brilliant ideas?"

Or not.

"Well," she said, pretending that he'd actually sounded as if he cared about the answer, "I don't think it's so much a question of what to do as why what you did didn't work."

He blinked.

"No one has ever given up on Hermione," Lucy said with a touch of impatience. She hated when people did not understand her meaning immediately. "Her disinterest only makes them redouble their efforts. It's embarrassing, really."

He looked vaguely affronted. "I beg your pardon."

"Not *you*," Lucy said quickly.

"My relief is palpable."

Lucy should have taken offense at his sarcasm, but his sense of humor was so like her own she couldn't help but enjoy it. "As I was saying," she continued, because she always did like to remain on the topic at hand, "no one ever seems to admit defeat and move on to a more attainable lady. Once everyone realizes that everyone *else* wants her, they seem to go mad. It's as if she's nothing but a prize to be won."

"Not to me," he said quietly.

Her eyes snapped to his face, and she realized instantly that he meant that Hermione was *more* than a prize. He cared for her. He truly cared for her. Lucy wasn't sure why, or even how, as he had barely made her friend's acquaintance. And Hermione hadn't been terribly forthcoming in her conversations, not that she ever was with the gentlemen who pursued her. But Mr. Bridgerton cared for the woman inside, not just the perfect face. Or at least he thought he did.

She nodded slowly, letting all this sink in. "I thought that perhaps if someone actually *stopped* dancing attendance on her, she might find it intriguing. Not," she hastened to assure him, "that Hermione sees all of this gentlemanly attention as her due. Quite to the contrary. To be honest, for the most part it's a nuisance."

"Your flattery knows no bounds." But he was smiling—just a little bit—as he said it.

"I've never been very skilled at flattery," she admitted.

"Apparently not."

She smiled wryly. He hadn't meant his words as an insult, and she wasn't going to take them as such. "She will come around."

"Do you think so?"

"I do. She will have to. Hermione is a romantic, but she understands how the world works. Deep down she knows she cannot marry Mr. Edmonds. It simply cannot be done. Her parents will disown her, or at the very least they will threaten to, and she is not the sort to risk that."

"If she really loved someone," he said softly, "she would risk anything."

Lucy froze. There was something in his voice. Something

rough, something powerful. It shivered across her skin, raising goosebumps, leaving her strangely unable to move.

And she had to ask. She had to. She had to *know*. "Would you?" she whispered. "Would you risk anything?"

He didn't move, but his eyes burned. And he didn't hesitate. "Anything."

Her lips parted. With surprise? Awe? Something else?

"Would *you*?" he countered.

"I . . . I'm not sure." She shook her head, and she had the queerest feeling that she didn't quite know herself any longer. Because it ought to have been an easy question. It would have been, just a few days ago. She would have said of course not, and she would have said she was far too practical for that sort of nonsense.

And most of all, she would have said that that sort of love did not exist, anyway.

But something had changed, and she didn't know what. Something had shifted within her, leaving her off-balance.

Unsure.

"I don't know," she said again. "I suppose it would depend."

"On what?" And his voice grew even softer. Impossibly soft, and yet she could make out every word.

"On . . ." She didn't know. How could she not know what it would depend upon? She felt lost, and rootless, and . . . and . . . and then the words just came. Slipped softly from her lips. "On love, I suppose."

"On love."

"Yes." Good heavens, had she ever had such a conversation? Did people actually talk about such things? And were there even any answers?

Or was she the only person in the world who didn't understand?

Something caught in her throat, and Lucy suddenly felt far too alone in her ignorance. He knew, and Hermione knew, and the poets claimed they did as well. It seemed *she* was the only lost soul, the only person who didn't understand what love was, who wasn't even sure it existed, or if it did, whether it existed for her.

"On how it felt," she finally said, because she didn't know what else to say. "On how love felt. How it feels."

His eyes met hers. "Do you think there is a variation?"

She hadn't expected another question. She was still reeling from the last one.

"How love feels," he clarified. "Do you think it could possibly be different for different people? If you loved someone, truly and deeply, wouldn't it feel like . . . like *everything*?"

She didn't know what to say.

He turned and took a few steps toward the window. "It would consume you," he said. "How could it not?"

Lucy just stared at his back, mesmerized by the way his finely cut coat stretched across his shoulders. It was the strangest thing, but she couldn't seem to pull her gaze from the little spot where his hair touched his collar.

She almost jumped when he turned around. "There would be no doubting it," he said, his voice low with the intensity of a true believer. "You would simply know. It would feel like everything you'd ever dreamed, and then it would feel like more."

He stepped toward her. Once. Then again. And then he said, "That, I think, is how love must feel."

And in that moment Lucy knew that she was not destined to feel that way. If it existed—if love existed the way Gregory Bridgerton imagined it—it did not wait for her. She couldn't imagine such a maelstrom of emotion. And she would not enjoy it. That much she knew. She didn't want to feel lost to the whirlwind, at the mercy of something beyond her control.

She didn't want misery. She didn't want despair. And if that meant she also had to forsake bliss and rapture, so be it.

She lifted her eyes to his, made breathless by the gravity of her own revelations. "It's too much," she heard herself say. "It would be too much. I wouldn't . . . I wouldn't . . ."

Slowly, he shook his head. "You would have no choice. It would be beyond your control. It just . . . happens."

Her mouth parted with surprise. "That's what she said."

"Who?"

And when she answered, her voice was strangely detached, as if the words were being drawn straight from her memory. "Hermione," she said. "That's what Hermione said about Mr. Edmonds."

Gregory's lips tightened at the corners. "Did she?"

Lucy slowly nodded. "Almost precisely. She said it just happens. In an instant."

"She said that?" The words sounded like an echo, and indeed, that was all he could do—whisper inane questions, looking for verification, hoping that maybe he had misheard, and she would reply with something entirely different.

But of course she did not. In fact, it was worse than he'd feared. She said, "She was in the garden, that's what she said, just looking at the roses, and then she saw him. And she knew."

Gregory just stared at her. His chest felt hollow, his throat tight. This wasn't what he wanted to hear. *Damn* it, this was the one thing he didn't want to hear.

She looked up at him then, and her eyes, gray in the dim light of the night, found his in an oddly intimate manner. It was as if he knew her, knew what she would say, and how her face would look when she said it. It was strange, and terrifying, and most of all, discomforting, because this wasn't the Honorable Miss Hermione Watson.

This was Lady Lucinda Abernathy, and she was not the woman with whom he intended to spend the rest of his life.

She was perfectly nice, perfectly intelligent, and certainly more than attractive. But Lucy Abernathy was not for him.

And he almost laughed, because it all would have been so much easier if his heart had flipped the first time he saw *her*. She might be practically engaged, but she wasn't in love. Of that he was certain.

But Hermione Watson . . .

"What did she say?" he whispered, dreading the answer.

Lady Lucinda tilted her head to the side, and she looked nothing so much as puzzled. "She said that she didn't even see his face. Just the back of his head—"

Just the back of her neck.

"—and then he turned, and she thought she heard music, and all she could think was—"

I am wrecked.

"—'I am ruined.' That is what she said to me." She looked up at him, her head still tilting curiously to the side. "Can you imagine? Ruined? Of all things. I couldn't quite grasp it."

But *he* could. He could.

Exactly.

He looked at Lady Lucinda, and he saw that she was watching his face. She looked puzzled still. And concerned. And just a little bit bewildered when she asked, "Don't you find it odd?"

"Yes." Just one word, but with his entire heart wrapped around it. Because it *was* strange. It cut like a knife. She wasn't supposed to feel that way about someone else.

This wasn't the way it was supposed to happen.

And then, as if a spell had been broken, Lady Lucinda turned and took a few steps to the right. She peered at the bookshelves—not that she could possibly make out any of the titles in this light—then ran her fingers along the spines.

Gregory watched her hand; he didn't know why. He just watched it as it moved. She was quite elegant, he realized. It wasn't noticeable at first, because her looks were so wholesome and traditional. One expected elegance to shimmer like silk, to glow, to transfix. Elegance was an orchid, not a simple daisy.

But when Lady Lucinda moved, she looked different. She seemed to . . . flow.

She would be a good dancer. He was sure of it.

Although he wasn't quite sure why that mattered.

"I'm sorry," she said, turning quite suddenly around. "About Miss Watson?"

"Yes. I did not mean to hurt your feelings."

"You didn't," he said, perhaps a little too sharply.

"Oh." She blinked, perhaps with surprise. "I'm glad for that. I didn't mean to."

She wouldn't mean to, he realized. She wasn't the sort.

Her lips parted, but she didn't speak right away. Her eyes seemed to focus beyond his shoulder, as if she were searching behind him for the correct words. "It was just that . . . Well, when you said what you said about love," she began, "it just sounded so familiar. I couldn't quite fathom it."

"Nor could I," he said softly.

She held silent, not quite looking at him. Her lips were pursed—just a touch—and every now and then she would blink. Not a fluttery sort of movement but rather something quite deliberate.

She was thinking, he realized. She was the sort who *thought* about things, probably to the neverending frustration of anyone charged with the task of guiding her through life.

"What will you do now?" she asked.

"About Miss Watson?"

She nodded.

"What do you suggest I do?"

"I'm not sure," she said. "I can speak to her on your behalf, if you would like."

"No." Something about that seemed far too juvenile. And Gregory was only just now beginning to feel that he was truly a man, well and grown, ready to make his mark.

"You can wait, then," she said with a tiny shrug. "Or you can proceed and try again to woo her. She won't have the opportunity to see Mr. Edmonds for at least a month, and I would think . . . eventually . . . she would come to see . . ."

But she didn't finish. And he wanted to know. "Come to see what?" he pressed.

She looked up, as if pulled from a dream. "Why, that you . . . that you . . . just that you are so much *better* than the rest. I don't know why she cannot see it. It's quite obvious to me."

From anyone else it would have been a strange statement. Overly forward, perhaps. Maybe even a coy hint of availability.

But not from her. She was without artifice, the sort of girl a man could trust. Rather like his sisters, he supposed, with a keen wit and a sharp sense of humor. Lucy Abernathy would never inspire poetry, but she would make a very fine friend.

"It will happen," she said, her voice soft but certain. "She will realize. You . . . and Hermione . . . You will be together. I am sure of it."

He watched her lips as she spoke. He didn't know why, but the shape of them was suddenly intriguing . . . the way they moved, formed their consonants and vowels. They were ordinary lips. Nothing about them had attracted his attention before. But now, in the darkened library, with nothing in the air but the soft whisper of their voices . . .

He wondered what it would mean to kiss her.

He stepped back, feeling suddenly and overwhelmingly *wrong*.

"We should return," he said abruptly.

A flicker of hurt passed over her eyes. Damn. He hadn't meant to sound like he was so eager to be rid of her. None of this was her fault. He was just tired. And frustrated. And she was there. And the night was dark. And they were alone.

And it hadn't been desire. It couldn't be desire. He'd been waiting his entire life to react to a woman the way he had to Hermione Watson. He couldn't possibly feel desire for another woman after that. Not Lady Lucinda, not anyone.

It was nothing. *She* was nothing.

No, that was not fair. She was something. Quite a bit, actually. But not for him.

Six

In which Our Hero makes progress.

Dear God, what had she said?

That single thought pounded through Lucy's mind as she lay in bed that night, too horrified even to toss and turn. She lay on her back, staring at the ceiling, utterly still, utterly mortified.

And the next morning, as she peered in the mirror, sighing at the weary lavender color beneath her eyes, there it was again—

Oh, Mr. Bridgerton, you are so much better than the rest.

And every time she relived it, the voice in her memory grew higher, more simpering, until she turned into one of those awful creatures—the girls who fluttered and swooned every time someone's older brother came to visit at school.

"Lucy Abernathy," she muttered under her breath, "you silly cow."

"Did you say something?" Hermione looked up at her

from her position near the bed. Lucy already had her hand on the doorknob, ready to leave for breakfast.

"Just doing sums in my head," Lucy lied.

Hermione went back to putting on her shoes. "For heaven's sake, *why*?" she said, mostly to herself.

Lucy shrugged, even though Hermione was not looking at her. She always said that she was doing sums in her head when Hermione caught her talking to herself. She had no idea why Hermione believed her; Lucy detested sums, almost as much as she hated fractions and tables. But it seemed like the sort of thing she might do, practical as she was, and Hermione had never questioned it.

Every now and then Lucy mumbled a number, just to make it more authentic.

"Are you ready to go down?" Lucy asked, twisting the knob. Not that *she* was. The last thing she wished was to see, well, anyone. Mr. Bridgerton in particular, of course, but the thought of facing the world at large was just ghastly.

But she was hungry, and she was going to have to show herself eventually, and she didn't see why her misery ought to wallow on an empty stomach.

As they walked to breakfast, Hermione peered at her curiously. "Are you well, Lucy?" she asked. "You look a little strange."

Lucy fought the urge to laugh. She *was* strange. She was an idiot, and probably shouldn't be let loose in public.

Good God, had she actually told Gregory Bridgerton that he was better than the rest?

She wanted to die. Or at the very least hide under a bed.

But no, she couldn't even manage to feign illness and have a good lying-in. It hadn't even occurred to her to try. She was so ridiculously normal and routineish that she was up and ready to depart for breakfast before she'd even managed a single coherent thought.

Aside from the pondering of her apparent madness, of course. *That* she had no trouble focusing upon.

"Well, you look very fine, anyway," Hermione said as they reached the top of the staircase. "I do like your choice of the green ribbon with the blue dress. I wouldn't have thought of it, but it's very smart. And so lovely with your eyes."

Lucy looked down at her clothing. She had no recollection of dressing herself. It was a miracle she did not look as if she had escaped from a Gypsy circus.

Although . . .

She let out a little sigh. Running off with the Gypsies sounded rather appealing just then, practical even, since she was quite certain she ought never to show her face in polite society again. Clearly she was missing an extremely important connecting vessel between her brain and her mouth, and heaven only knew what might emerge from her lips next.

Good gracious, she might as well have told Gregory Bridgerton that she thought him a god.

Which she did not. Not at all. She merely thought him a rather fine catch for Hermione. And she'd told him so. Hadn't she?

What *had* she said? Precisely, what had she said?

"Lucy?"

What she said was . . . What she said *was*—

She stopped cold.

Dear *God.* He was going to think *she* wanted him.

Hermione walked another few paces before she realized Lucy was no longer in step beside her. "Lucy?"

"Do you know," Lucy said, her voice coming out just a little bit squeaky, "I don't believe I'm hungry after all."

Hermione looked incredulous. "For breakfast?"

It *was* a bit farfetched. Lucy always ate like a sailor at breakfast.

"I . . . ah . . . I think something did not quite agree with me last night. Perhaps the salmon." She put her hand on her belly for added effect. "I think I should lie down."

And never get up.

"You do look a bit green," Hermione said.

Lucy smiled wanly, making a conscious decision to be thankful for small favors.

"Would you like me to bring you something?" Hermione asked.

"Yes," Lucy said fervently, hoping Hermione hadn't heard the rumble of her stomach.

"Oh, but I shouldn't," Hermione said, placing one thoughtful finger to her lips. "You probably shouldn't eat if you are feeling queasy. The last thing you want is to bring it all up again."

"It's not queasiness, exactly," Lucy improvised.

"It's not?"

"It's . . . ah . . . rather difficult to explain, actually. I . . ." Lucy sagged against the wall. Who knew she had it in her to be such a fine actress?

Hermione rushed to her side, concern knitting her brow. "Oh dear," she said, supporting Lucy with an arm around her back. "You look ghastly."

Lucy blinked. Maybe she *was* taking ill. Even better. That would keep her sequestered for days.

"I am returning you to bed," Hermione said, her tone brooking no argument. "And then I will summon Mother. She will know what to do."

Lucy nodded with relief. Lady Watson's remedy for any sort of ailment was chocolate and biscuits. Unorthodox, to be sure, but as it was what Hermione's mother chose whenever she claimed to be ill, she couldn't very well deny it to anyone else.

Hermione guided her back to their bedchamber, even going so far as to remove Lucy's slippers for her before she lay atop the bed. "If I didn't know you so well," Hermione said, tossing the slippers carelessly into the armoire, "I would think you were faking."

"I would never."

"Oh, you would," Hermione said. "You absolutely would. But you could never carry it off. You're far too traditional."

Traditional? What had *that* to do with anything?

Hermione let out a little huff of air. "I'm probably going to have to sit with that wearisome Mr. Bridgerton at breakfast now."

"He's not so dreadful," Lucy said, with perhaps a bit more verve than one might expect from someone with a belly full of bad salmon.

"I suppose not," Hermione acceded. "He's better than most, I daresay."

Lucy winced at the echo of her own words. *So much better than the rest. So much better than the rest.*

It was quite possibly the most appalling thing ever to cross her lips.

"But he is not for me," Hermione continued, oblivious to Lucy's distress. "He will realize it soon enough. And then he will move on to someone else."

Lucy doubted that, but she didn't say anything. What a coil. Hermione was in love with Mr. Edmonds, Mr. Bridgerton was in love with Hermione, and Lucy was *not* in love with Mr. Bridgerton.

But he thought she was.

Which was nonsense, of course. She would never allow that to happen, practically engaged as she was to Lord Haselby.

Haselby. She nearly groaned. This would all be so much easier if she could remember his face.

"Perhaps I'll ring for breakfast," Hermione said, her face lighting up as if she had just discovered a new continent. "Do you think they will send up a tray?"

Oh, blast. There went all her plans. Now Hermione had

an excuse to remain in their chamber all day. And the next, too, if Lucy continued to feign illness.

"I don't know why I didn't think of it sooner," Hermione said, heading to the bellpull. "I would much rather remain here with you."

"Don't," Lucy called out, her brain spinning madly.

"Why not?"

Indeed. Lucy thought quickly. "If you have them bring a tray, you might not get what you want."

"But I know what I want. Coddled eggs and toast. Surely they can manage that."

"But *I* don't want coddled eggs and toast." Lucy tried to keep her expression as pitiful and pathetic as she could manage. "You know my taste so well. If you go to the breakfast room, I'm sure you would find something exactly right."

"But I thought you weren't going to eat."

Lucy put her hand back on her belly. "Well, I might want to eat a little."

"Oh, very well," Hermione said, by now sounding more impatient than anything else. "What do you want?"

"Er, perhaps some bacon?"

"With a fishy stomach?"

"I'm not sure it was the fish."

For the longest moment, Hermione just stood there and stared at her. "Just bacon, then?" she finally asked.

"Ehm, and anything else you think I might enjoy," Lucy said, since it would have been easy enough to ring for bacon.

Hermione let out a pent-up breath. "I shall return soon." She regarded Lucy with a slightly suspicious expression. "Don't overexert yourself."

"I won't," Lucy promised. She smiled at the door as it closed behind Hermione. She counted to ten, then hopped out of bed and ran to the wardrobe to straighten her slippers. Once that was done to her satisfaction, she snatched up a book and crawled back in to settle down and read.

All in all, it was turning out to be a lovely morning.

By the time Gregory entered the breakfast room, he was feeling much better. What had happened the night before— it was nothing. Practically forgotten.

It wasn't as if he'd *wanted* to kiss Lady Lucinda. He'd merely wondered about it, which was worlds apart.

He was just a man, after all. He'd wondered about hundreds of women, most of the time without *any* intention of even speaking to them. Everybody wondered. It was whether one acted upon it that made the difference.

What was that his brothers—his happily married brothers, he might add—had once said? Marriage didn't render them *blind*. They might not be looking for other women, but that didn't mean they didn't notice what was standing right in front of them. Whether it was a barmaid with extremely large bosoms or a proper young lady with a—well, with a pair of lips—one couldn't very well not *see* the body part in question.

And if one saw, then of course one would wonder, and—

And nothing. It all added up to nothing.

Which meant Gregory could eat his breakfast with a clear head.

Eggs were good for the soul, he decided. Bacon, too.

The only other occupant of the breakfast room was the fiftyish and perpetually starchy Mr. Snowe, who was thankfully more interested in his newspaper than in conversation. After the obligatory grunts of greeting, Gregory sat down at the opposite end of the table and began to eat.

Excellent sausage this morning. And the toast was exceptional as well. Just the right amount of butter. A bit of salt needed for the eggs, but other than that they were rather tasty.

He tried the salted cod. Not bad. Not bad at all.

He took another bite. Chewed. Enjoyed himself. Thought very deep thoughts about politics and agriculture.

Moved on determinedly to Newtonian physics. He really should have paid more attention at Eton, because he couldn't quite recall the difference between force and work.

Let's see, work was that bit with the foot-pounds, and force was . . .

It wasn't even really *wondering*. Honestly, it could all be blamed on a trick of the light. And his mood. He'd been feeling a bit off. He'd been looking at her mouth because she'd been talking, for heaven's sake. Where else was he meant to look?

He picked up his fork with renewed vigor. Back to the cod. And his tea. Nothing washed everything away like tea.

He took a long sip, peering over the edge of his cup as he heard someone coming down the hall.

And then *she* filled the doorway.

He blinked with surprise, then glanced over her shoulder. She'd come without her extra appendage.

Now that he thought about it, he didn't think he'd ever seen Miss Watson without Lady Lucinda.

"Good morning," he called out, in precisely the right tone. Friendly enough so as not to sound bored, but not *too* friendly. A man never wanted to sound desperate.

Miss Watson looked over at him as he stood, and her face registered absolutely no emotion whatsoever. Not happiness, not ire, nothing but the barest flicker of acknowledgment. It was quite remarkable, really.

"Good morning," she murmured.

Then, hell, why not. "Will you join me?" he asked.

Her lips parted and she paused, as if not quite sure what she wished to do. And then, as if to offer perverse proof that they did in fact share some sort of higher connection, he read her mind.

Truly. He knew exactly what she was thinking.

Oh, very well, I suppose I have to eat breakfast, anyway.
It positively warmed the soul.

"I cannot stay very long," Miss Watson said. "Lucy is unwell, and I promised to bring her a tray."

It was difficult to imagine the indomitable Lady Lucinda taking ill, although Gregory didn't know why. It wasn't as if he *knew* her. Really, it had been nothing but a few conversations. If that. "I trust it is nothing serious," he murmured.

"I don't think so," she replied, taking a plate. She looked up at him, blinking those astounding green eyes. "Did you eat the fish?"

He looked down at his cod. "Now?"

"No, last night."

"I imagine so. I usually eat everything."

Her lips pursed for a moment, then she murmured, "I ate it as well."

Gregory waited for further explanation, but she didn't seem inclined to offer any. So instead he remained on his feet as she placed delicate portions of eggs and ham on her plate. Then, after a moment's deliberation—

Am I really hungry? Because the more food I put on my plate, the longer it will take to consume it. Here. In the breakfast room. With him.

—she took a piece of toast.

Hmmm. Yes, I'm hungry.

Gregory waited until she took a seat across from him, and he sat down. Miss Watson offered him a small smile—the sort that was really nothing more than a shrug of the lips—and proceeded to eat her eggs.

"Did you sleep well?" Gregory asked.

She dabbed at her mouth with her serviette. "Very well, thank you."

"I did not," he announced. Hell, if polite conversation failed to draw her out, perhaps he ought to opt for surprise.

She looked up. "I'm so sorry." And then she looked back down. And ate.

"Terrible dream," he said. "Nightmare, really. Ghastly."

She picked up her knife and cut her bacon. "I'm so sorry," she said, seemingly unaware that she'd uttered those very same words mere moments earlier.

"I can't quite recall what it was," Gregory mused. He was making it all up, of course. He hadn't slept well, but not because of a nightmare. But he was going to get her to talk to him or die trying. "Do you remember your dreams?" he asked.

Her fork stopped midway to her mouth—and there was that delightful connection of the minds again.

In God's name, why is he asking me this?

Well, maybe not in God's name. That would require a bit more emotion than she seemed to possess. At least with him.

"Er, no," she said. "Not usually."

"Really? How intriguing. I recall mine about half of the time, I would estimate."

She nodded.

If I nod, I won't have to come up with something to say.

He plowed on. "My dream from last night was quite vivid. There was a rainstorm. Thunder and lightning. Very dramatic."

She turned her neck, ever so slowly, and looked over her shoulder.

"Miss Watson?"

She turned back. "I thought I heard someone."

I hoped I heard someone.

Really, this mind-reading talent was beginning to grow tedious.

"Right," he said. "Well, where was I?"

Miss Watson began to eat very quickly.

Gregory leaned forward. She wasn't going to escape so easily. "Oh, yes, the rain," he said. "It was pouring. Absolute deluge. And the ground began to melt beneath my feet. Dragged me down."

He paused, purposefully, and then kept his eyes on her face until she was forced to say something.

After a few moments of exceedingly awkward silence, she finally moved her gaze from her food to his face. A small piece of egg trembled on the edge of her fork.

"The ground was melting," he said. And almost laughed.

"How . . . unpleasant."

"It *was*," he said, with great animation. "I thought it would swallow me whole. Have you ever felt like that, Miss Watson?"

Silence. And then— "No. No, I can't say that I have."

He idly fingered his earlobe, and then said, quite offhandedly, "I didn't much like it."

He thought she might spit her tea.

"Well, really," he continued. "Who would?"

And for the first time since he'd met her, he thought he saw the disinterested mask slip from her eyes as she said, with quite a bit of feeling, "I have no idea."

She even shook her head. Three things at once! A complete sentence, a spot of emotion, *and* a shake of the head. By George, he might be getting through to her.

"What happened next, Mr. Bridgerton?"

Good *God,* she had asked him a question. He might tumble from his chair. "Actually," he said, "I woke up."

"That's fortunate."

"I thought so as well. They say if you die in your dreams, you die in your sleep."

Her eyes widened. "They do?"

"*They* being my brothers," he admitted. "You may feel free to assess the information based upon its source."

"I have a brother," she said. "He delights in tormenting me."

Gregory offered her a grave nod. "That is what brothers are meant to do."

"Do you torment your sisters?"

"Mostly just the younger one."

"Because she's smaller."

"No, because she deserves it."

She laughed. "Mr. Bridgerton, you are terrible."

He smiled slowly. "You haven't met Hyacinth."

"If she bothers you enough to make you wish to torment her, I am sure I would adore her."

He sat back, enjoying this feeling of ease. It was nice not to have to work so hard. "Your brother is your elder, then?"

She nodded. "He *does* torment me because I'm smaller."

"You mean you don't deserve it?"

"Of course not."

He couldn't quite tell if she was being facetious. "Where is your brother now?"

"Trinity Hall." She took the last bite of her eggs. "Cambridge. Lucy's brother was there as well. He has been graduated for a year."

Gregory wasn't quite certain why she was telling him this. He wasn't interested in Lucinda Abernathy's brother.

Miss Watson cut another small piece of bacon and lifted her fork to her mouth. Gregory ate as well, stealing glances at her as he chewed. Lord, but she was lovely. He didn't think he'd ever seen another woman with her coloring. It was the skin, really. He imagined that most men thought her beauty came from her hair and eyes, and it was true that those were the features that initially stopped a man cold. But her skin was like alabaster laid over a rose petal.

He paused mid-chew. He had no idea he could be so poetic.

Miss Watson set down her fork. "Well," she said, with the tiniest of sighs, "I suppose I should prepare that plate for Lucy."

He stood immediately to assist her. Good heavens, but she actually sounded as if she didn't wish to leave. Gregory congratulated himself on an extremely productive breakfast.

"I shall find someone to carry it back for you," he said, signaling to a footman.

"Oh, that would be lovely." She smiled gratefully at him, and his heart quite literally skipped a beat. He'd thought it merely a figure of speech, but now he knew it was true. Love really could affect one's internal organs.

"Please do offer Lady Lucinda my well wishes," he said, watching curiously as Miss Watson heaped five slices of meat on the plate.

"Lucy likes bacon," she said.

"I see that."

And then she proceeded to spoon eggs, cod, potatoes, tomatoes, and then on a separate plate muffins and toast.

"Breakfast has always been her favorite meal," Miss Watson said.

"Mine as well."

"I shall tell her that."

"I can't imagine that she will be interested."

A maid had entered the room with a tray, and Miss Watson placed the heaping plates upon it. "Oh, she will," she said breezily. "Lucy is interested in everything. She does sums in her head, even. For entertainment."

"You're joking." Gregory couldn't imagine a less pleasant way to keep oneself occupied.

She placed her hand on her heart. "I swear it to you. I think she must be trying to improve her mind, because she was never very good at maths." She walked to the door, then turned to face him. "Breakfast was lovely, Mr. Bridgerton. Thank you for the company and the conversation."

He inclined his head. "The pleasure was all mine."

Except that it wasn't. She had enjoyed their time together, too. He could see it in her smile. And her eyes.

And he felt like a king.

"Did you know that if you die in your dreams, you die in your sleep?"

Lucy didn't even pause in her cutting of her bacon. "Nonsense," she said. "Who told you that?"

Hermione perched on the edge of the bed. "Mr. Bridgerton."

Now *that* rated above bacon. Lucy looked up immediately. "Then you saw him at breakfast?"

Hermione nodded. "We sat across from each other. He helped me arrange for the tray."

Lucy regarded her massive breakfast with dismay. Usually she managed to hide her ferocious appetite by dallying at the breakfast table, then getting another serving once the first wave of guests had departed.

Oh well, nothing to do about it. Gregory Bridgerton already thought her a widgeon—he might as well think her a widgeon who would weigh twelve stone by the year's end.

"He's rather amusing, actually," Hermione said, absently twirling her hair.

"I've heard he's quite charming."

"Mmmm."

Lucy watched her friend closely. Hermione was gazing out the window, and if she didn't quite have that ridiculous memorizing-a-love-sonnet look to her, she had at least worked her way up to a couplet or two.

"He is extremely handsome," Lucy said. There seemed no harm in confessing it. It wasn't as if she was planning to set her cap for him, and his looks were fine enough that it could be interpreted as a statement of fact rather than opinion.

"Do you think so?" Hermione asked. She turned back to Lucy, her head tilting thoughtfully to the side.

"Oh yes," Lucy replied. "His eyes, particularly. I'm quite partial to hazel eyes. I always have been."

Actually, she'd never considered it one way or the other, but now that she thought about it, hazel eyes *were* rather fine. Bit of brown, bit of green. Best of both worlds.

Hermione looked at her curiously. "I didn't know that."

Lucy shrugged. "I don't tell you everything."

Another lie. Hermione was privy to every boring detail of Lucy's life and had been for three years. Except, of course, for her plans to match Hermione with Mr. Bridgerton.

Mr. Bridgerton. Right. Must return the conversation to the subject of *him*.

"But you must agree," Lucy said in her most pondering of voices, "he's not *too* handsome. It's a good thing, really."

"Mr. Bridgerton?"

"Yes. His nose has a great deal of character, wouldn't you say? And his eyebrows aren't quite even." Lucy frowned. She hadn't realized she was quite so familiar with Gregory Bridgerton's face.

Hermione did nothing but nod, so Lucy continued with "I don't think I should want to be married to someone who was *too* handsome. It must be terribly intimidating. I would feel like a duck every time I opened my mouth."

Hermione giggled at that. "A duck?"

Lucy nodded and decided not to quack. She wondered if the men who courted Hermione worried about the same thing.

"He's quite dark," Hermione said.

"Not so dark." Lucy thought his hair a medium-brown.

"Yes, but Mr. Edmonds is so fair."

Mr. Edmonds did have lovely blond hair, so Lucy decided not to comment. And she knew she had to be very careful at this point. If she pushed Hermione too hard in Mr. Bridgerton's direction, Hermione would surely balk and go right back to being in love with Mr. Edmonds, which, of course, was utter disaster.

No, Lucy was going to need to be subtle. If Hermione was going to switch her devotion to Mr. Bridgerton, she was going to have to figure it out for herself. Or think she did.

"And his family is very smart," Hermione murmured.

"Mr. Edmonds's?" Lucy asked, deliberately misinterpreting.

"No, Mr. Bridgerton's, of course. I have heard such interesting things about them."

"Oh, yes," Lucy said. "I have as well. I rather admire Lady Bridgerton. She's been a marvelous hostess."

Hermione nodded her agreement. "I think she prefers you to me."

"Don't be silly."

"I don't mind," Hermione said with a shrug. "It's not as if she *doesn't* like me. She just likes you better. Women always like you better."

Lucy opened her mouth to contradict but then stopped, realizing that it was true. How odd that she had never noticed it. "Well, it's not as if you'd be marrying *her,*" she said.

Hermione looked at her sharply. "I didn't say I wished to marry Mr. Bridgerton."

"No, of course not," Lucy said, mentally kicking herself. She'd known the words were a mistake the minute they'd escaped her mouth.

"But . . ." Hermione sighed and proceeded to stare off into space.

Lucy leaned forward. So this was what it meant to hang on a word.

And she hung, and she hung . . . until she could bear it no longer. "Hermione?" she finally queried.

Hermione flopped back onto the bed. "Oh, Lucy," she moaned, in tones worthy of Covent Garden, "I'm so confused."

"Confused?" Lucy smiled. This had to be a good thing.

"Yes," Hermione replied, from her decidedly inelegant position atop the bed. "When I was sitting at the table with Mr. Bridgerton—well, actually at first I thought him quite mad—but then I realized I was enjoying myself. He was funny, actually, and made me laugh."

Lucy did not speak, waiting for Hermione to gather the rest of her thoughts.

Hermione made a little noise, half-sigh, half-moan. Wholly distressed. "And then once I realized that, I looked up at him, and I—" She rolled onto her side, leaning on her elbow and propping her head up with one hand. "I *fluttered*."

Lucy was still trying to digest the *mad* comment. "Fluttered?" she echoed. "What is *fluttered*?"

"My stomach. My heart. My—my something. I don't know what."

"Similar to when you saw Mr. Edmonds for the first time?"

"No. *No.* No." Each no was said with a different emphasis, and Lucy had the distinct sense that Hermione was trying to convince herself of it.

"It wasn't the same at all," Hermione said. "But it was . . . a little bit the same. On a much smaller scale."

"I see," Lucy said, with an admirable amount of gravity, considering that she didn't understand at all. But then again, she never understood this sort of thing. And after her strange conversation with Mr. Bridgerton the night before, she was quite convinced she never would.

"But wouldn't you think—if I am so desperately in love with Mr. Edmonds—wouldn't you think I would never flutter with anyone else?"

Lucy thought about that. And then she said, "I don't see why love has to be desperate."

Hermione pushed herself up on her elbows and looked at her curiously. "That wasn't my question."

It wasn't? Oughtn't it have been?

"Well," Lucy said, choosing her words carefully, "perhaps it means—"

"I know what you are going to say," Hermione cut in. "You're going to say that it probably means I am not as in love with Mr. Edmonds as I thought. And then you will say that I need to give Mr. Bridgerton a chance. And then you will tell me that I ought to give all of the other gentlemen a chance."

"Well, not *all* of them," Lucy said. But the rest of it was rather close.

"Don't you think this has all occurred to me? Don't you realize how terribly distressing all of this is? To doubt myself so? And good heavens, Lucy, what if this is not the end of it? What if this happens again? With someone else?"

Lucy rather suspected she was not meant to answer, but still she spoke. "There is nothing wrong with doubting yourself, Hermione. Marriage is an enormous undertaking. The biggest choice you will ever make in your life. Once it's done, you can't change your mind."

Lucy took a bite of her bacon, reminding herself how grateful she was that Lord Haselby was so suitable. Her situation could have been ever so much worse. She chewed, swallowed, and said, "You need only to give yourself a bit of time, Hermione. And you should. There is never any good reason to rush into marriage."

There was a long paused before Hermione answered. "I reckon you're right."

"If you are truly meant to be with Mr. Edmonds, he will wait for you." Oh, heavens. Lucy couldn't *believe* she'd just said that.

Hermione jumped from the bed, just so that she could rush to Lucy's side and envelop her in a hug. "Oh, Lucy, that was the sweetest thing you have ever said to me. I know you don't approve of him."

"Well . . ." Lucy cleared her throat, trying to think of an

acceptable reply. Something that would make her feel not *quite* so guilty for not having meant it. "It's not that—"

A knock sounded at the door.

Oh, thank goodness.

"Enter," the two girls called out in unison.

A maid came in and bobbed a quick curtsy. "M'lady," she said, looking at Lucy, "Lord Fennsworth has arrived to see you."

Lucy gaped at her. "My *brother*?"

"He is waiting in the rose salon, m'lady. Shall I tell him you will be right down?"

"Yes. Yes, of course."

"Will there be anything else?"

Lucy slowly shook her head. "No, thank you. That will be all."

The maid departed, leaving Lucy and Hermione staring at each other in shock.

"Why do you think Richard is here?" Hermione asked, her eyes wide with interest. She had met Lucy's brother on a number of occasions, and they had always got on well.

"I don't know." Lucy quickly climbed out of bed, all thoughts of feigning an upset stomach forgotten. "I hope nothing is amiss."

Hermione nodded and followed her to the wardrobe. "Has your uncle been unwell?"

"Not that I have been made aware." Lucy fished out her slippers and sat on the edge of the bed to put them back on her feet. "I had best get down to see him. If he is here, it is something important."

Hermione regarded her for a moment, then asked, "Would you like for me to accompany you? I shan't intrude upon your conversation, of course. But I will walk down with you, if you like."

Lucy nodded, and together they departed for the rose salon.

Seven

**In which Our Unexpected
Guest delivers distressing news.**

$\mathscr{G}$regory had been chatting with his sister-in-law in the breakfast room when the butler informed her of their unexpected guest, and so naturally he decided to accompany her to the rose salon to greet Lord Fennsworth, elder brother to Lady Lucinda. He had nothing better to do, and it somehow seemed he ought to go meet the young earl, given that Miss Watson had been chattering on about him a quarter of an hour earlier. Gregory knew him only by reputation; the four years' difference in their ages had ensured that they had not crossed paths at university, and Fennsworth had not yet chosen to take his place in London society.

Gregory had been expecting a studious, bookish sort; he'd heard that Fennsworth had elected to remain at Cambridge even when school was not in session. Indeed, the gentleman waiting by the window in the rose salon did possess a certain gravitas that made him seem slightly older than his years. But Lord Fennsworth was also tall, fit, and although perhaps a touch shy, he carried himself with an air of self-possession that came from something more primal than a title of nobility.

Lady Lucinda's brother knew who he was, not just what he was born to be called. Gregory liked him immediately.

Until it became obvious that he, like the rest of male humanity, was in love with Hermione Watson.

The only mystery, really, was why Gregory was surprised.

Gregory had to commend him—Fennsworth managed a full minute of inquiries about his sister's welfare before he added, "And Miss Watson? Will she be joining us as well?"

It wasn't so much the words as the tone, and even that not so much as the flicker in his eyes—that spark of eagerness, anticipation.

Oh, call a spade a spade. It was desperate longing, pure and simple. Gregory ought to know—he was quite certain it had flashed through his own eyes more than once in the past few days.

Good God.

Gregory supposed he still found Fennsworth a good enough fellow, even with his annoying infatuation, but really, the entire situation was beginning to grow tiresome.

"We are so pleased to welcome you to Aubrey Hall, Lord Fennsworth," Kate said, once she had informed him that she did not know if Miss Watson would be accompanying his sister down to the rose salon. "I do hope that your presence does not indicate an emergency at home."

"Not at all," Fennsworth replied. "But my uncle has requested that I fetch Lucy and bring her home. He wishes to speak with her on a matter of some importance."

Gregory felt one corner of his lips quirk in an upward direction. "You must be quite devoted to your sister," he said, "to come all this way yourself. Surely you could have simply sent a carriage."

To his credit, Lucy's brother did not appear flustered by

the question, but at the same time, he did not have an immediate answer. "Oh no," he said, the words coming out rather quickly after the long pause. "I was more than happy to make the trip. Lucy is good company, and we have not visited for quite some time."

"Must you leave right away?" Kate asked. "I have been so enjoying your sister's company. And we would be honored to count you among our guests as well."

Gregory wondered just what she was about. Kate was going to have to locate another female to even up the numbers if Lord Fennsworth was to join the party. Although he supposed that if Lady Lucinda left, she would have to do the exact same thing.

The young earl hesitated, and Kate took advantage of the moment with a beautifully executed "Oh, do say that you will remain. Even if it cannot be for the duration of the party."

"Well," Fennsworth said, blinking as he considered the invitation. It was clear that he wanted to stay (and Gregory was quite certain he knew the reason why). But title or no, he was still young, and Gregory imagined that he answered to his uncle on all matters pertaining to the family.

And said uncle clearly desired Lady Lucinda's swift return.

"I suppose there would be no harm in taking an extra day," Fennsworth said.

Oh, dandy. He was willing to defy his uncle to gain extra time with Miss Watson. And as Lady Lucinda's brother, he was the one man who Hermione would never brush away with her usual polite boredom. Gregory readied himself for another day of tedious competition.

"Please say you will stay until Friday," Kate said. "We are planning a masked ball for Thursday evening, and I would hate for you to miss it."

Gregory made a mental note to give Kate an extremely ordinary gift for her next birthday. Rocks, maybe.

"It's only one more day," Kate said with a winning smile.

It was at that moment that Lady Lucinda and Miss Watson entered the room, the former in a morning dress of lightish blue and the latter in the same green frock she'd worn to breakfast. Lord Fennsworth took one look at the duo (more at one than the other, and suffice it to say that blood was not thicker than unrequited love), and he murmured, "Friday it is."

"Delightful," Kate said, clasping her hands together. "I shall have a room readied for you straightaway."

"Richard?" Lady Lucinda queried. "Why are you here?" She paused in the doorway and looked from person to person, apparently confused by Kate's and Gregory's presence.

"Lucy," her brother said. "It has been an age."

"Four months," she said, almost unthinkingly, as if some little part of her brain required absolute accuracy, even when it hardly mattered.

"Heavens, that is a long time," Kate said. "We will leave you now, Lord Fennsworth. I am sure you and your sister wish to have a few moments of privacy."

"There is no rush," Fennsworth said, his eyes flicking briefly to Miss Watson. "I would not wish to be rude, and I haven't yet had the opportunity to thank you for your hospitality."

"It wouldn't be rude at all," Gregory put in, anticipating a swift departure from the salon with Miss Watson on his arm.

Lord Fennsworth turned and blinked, as if he'd forgotten Gregory's presence. Not terribly surprising, as Gregory had remained uncharacteristically silent through the exchange.

"Pray do not trouble yourself," the earl said. "Lucy and I will have our conversation later."

"Richard," Lucy said, looking somewhat concerned, "are you certain? I was not expecting you, and if there is anything amiss . . ."

But her brother shook his head. "Nothing that cannot

wait. Uncle Robert wishes to speak with you. He asked me to bring you home."

"Now?"

"He did not specify," Fennsworth replied, "but Lady Bridgerton has very graciously asked us to remain until Friday, and I agreed. That is"—he cleared his throat—"assuming you wish to remain."

"Of course," Lucy replied, looking confused and adrift. "But I—well . . . Uncle Robert . . ."

"We should leave," Miss Watson said firmly. "Lucy, you should have a moment with your brother."

Lucy looked at her brother, but he had taken advantage of Miss Watson's entry into the conversation by looking at *her,* and he said, "And how are you, Hermione? It has been far too long."

"Four months," Lucy said.

Miss Watson laughed and smiled warmly at the earl. "I am well, thank you. And Lucy is correct, as always. We last spoke in January, when you visited us at school."

Fennsworth dipped his chin in acknowledgment. "How could I have forgotten? It was such a pleasant few days."

Gregory would have bet his right arm that Fennsworth had known down to the minute how long it had been since he had last laid eyes on Miss Watson. But the lady in question was clearly oblivious to the infatuation, because she just smiled and said, "It was, wasn't it? It was so sweet of you to take us ice skating. You are always such good company."

Good God, how could she be so oblivious? There was no way she would have been so encouraging had she realized the nature of the earl's feelings for her. Gregory was certain of it.

But while it was obvious that Miss Watson was extremely fond of Lord Fennsworth, there was no indication that she held him in any sort of romantic esteem. Gregory consoled himself with the knowledge that the two had certainly known each other for years, and naturally she would be friendly with Fennsworth, given how close she was to Lady Lucinda.

Practically brother and sister, really.

And speaking of Lady Lucinda—Gregory turned in her direction and was not surprised to find that she was frowning. Her brother, who had traveled at least a day to reach her side, now seemed in no hurry whatsoever to speak with her.

And indeed, everyone else had fallen silent, as well. Gregory watched the awkward tableau with interest. Everyone seemed to be glancing about, waiting to see who might speak next. Even Lady Lucinda, whom no one would call shy, seemed not to know what to say.

"Lord Fennsworth," Kate said, thankfully breaking the silence, "you must be famished. Will you have some breakfast?"

"I would appreciate that greatly, Lady Bridgerton."

Kate turned to Lady Lucinda. "I did not see you at breakfast, either. Will you have something now?"

Gregory thought of the massive tray Miss Watson had had brought up for her and wondered how much of it she'd managed to wolf down before having to come meet her brother.

"Of course," Lady Lucinda murmured. "I should like to keep Richard company, in any case."

"Miss Watson," Gregory cut in smoothly, "would you care to take a turn about the gardens? I believe the peonies are in bloom. And those stalky blue things—I always forget what they are called."

"Delphinium." It was Lady Lucinda, of course. He'd known she would not be able to resist. Then she turned and looked at him, her eyes narrowing ever so slightly. "I told you that the other day."

"So you did," he murmured. "I've never had much of a head for details."

"Oh, Lucy remembers everything," Miss Watson said breezily. "And I would be delighted to view the gardens with you. That is, if Lucy and Richard do not mind."

Both assured her that they did not, although Gregory was quite certain he saw a flash of disappointment and—dare he say it—irritation in Lord Fennsworth's eyes.

Gregory smiled.

"I shall find you back in our room?" Miss Watson said to Lucy.

The other girl nodded, and with a feeling of triumph—there was nothing quite like besting one's competition—Gregory placed Miss Watson's hand in the crook of his elbow and led her out of the room.

It was going to be an excellent morning, after all.

Lucy followed her brother and Lady Bridgerton to the breakfast room, which she did not mind one bit, as she had not had a chance to eat very much of what Hermione had brought her earlier. But it did mean that she had to endure a full thirty minutes of meaningless conversation while her brain raced about, imagining all sorts of disasters that could be responsible for her unexpected summons home.

Richard couldn't very well speak to her about anything important with Lady Bridgerton and half of the house party blithering on about coddled eggs and the recent rainfall, so Lucy waited uncomplainingly while he finished (he'd always been an annoyingly slow eater), and then she tried her best not to lose her patience as they strolled out to the side lawn, Richard first asking her about school, then Hermione, and then Hermione's mother, and then her upcoming debut, and then Hermione again, with a side tangent to Hermione's brother, whom he'd apparently run across in Cambridge, and then it was back to the debut, and to what extent she was to share it with Hermione . . .

Until finally Lucy halted in her tracks, planted her hands

on her hips, and demanded that he tell her why he was there.

"I told you," he said, not quite meeting her eyes. "Uncle Robert wishes to speak with you."

"But *why*?" It was not a question with an obvious answer. Uncle Robert hadn't cared to speak with her more than a handful of times in the past ten years. If he was planning to start now, there was a reason for it.

Richard cleared his throat a number of times before finally saying, "Well, Luce, I think he plans to marry you off."

"Straightaway?" Lucy whispered, and she didn't know why she was so surprised. She'd known this was coming; she'd been practically engaged for years. And she had told Hermione, on more than one occasion, that a season for her was really quite foolish—why bother with the expense when she was just going to marry Haselby in the end?

But now . . . suddenly . . . she didn't want to do it. At least not so soon. She didn't want to go from schoolgirl to wife, with nothing in between. She wasn't asking for adventure— she didn't even *want* adventure—truly, she wasn't the sort.

She wasn't asking for very much—just a few months of freedom, of laughter.

Of dancing breathlessly, spinning so fast that the candle flames streaked into long snakes of light.

Maybe she was practical. Maybe she was "that old Lucy," as so many had called her at Miss Moss's. But she liked to dance. And she wanted to do it. Now. Before she was old. Before she became Haselby's wife.

"I don't know when," Richard said, looking down at her with . . . was it regret?

Why would it be regret?

"Soon, I think," he said. "Uncle Robert seems somewhat eager to have it done."

Lucy just stared at him, wondering why she couldn't stop thinking about dancing, couldn't stop picturing herself, in a gown of silvery blue, magical and radiant, in the arms of—

"Oh!" She clapped a hand to her mouth, as if that could somehow silence her thoughts.

"What is it?"

"Nothing," she said, shaking her head. Her daydreams did not have a face. They could not. And so she said it again, more firmly, "It was nothing. Nothing at all."

Her brother stooped to examine a wildflower that had somehow missed the discerning eyes of Aubrey Hall's gardeners. It was small, blue, and just beginning to open.

"It's lovely, isn't it?" Richard murmured.

Lucy nodded. Richard had always loved flowers. Wildflowers in particular. They were different that way, she realized. She had always preferred the order of a neatly arranged bed, each bloom in its place, each pattern carefully and lovingly maintained.

But now . . .

She looked down at that little flower, small and delicate, defiantly sprouting where it didn't belong.

And she decided that she liked the wild ones, too.

"I know you were meant to have a season," Richard said apologetically. "But truly, is it so very dreadful? You never really wanted one, did you?"

Lucy swallowed. "No," she said, because she knew it was what he wanted to hear, and she didn't want him to feel any worse than he already did. And she hadn't really cared one way or the other about a season in London. At least not until recently.

Richard pulled the little blue wildflower out by the roots, looked at it quizzically, and stood. "Cheer up, Luce," he said, chucking her lightly on the chin. "Haselby's not a bad sort. You won't mind being married to him."

"I know," she said softly.

"He won't hurt you," he added, and he smiled, that slightly

false sort of smile. The kind that was meant to be reassuring and somehow never was.

"I didn't think he would," Lucy said, an edge of . . . of *something* creeping into her voice. "Why would you bring such a thing up?"

"No reason at all," Richard said quickly. "But I know that it is a concern for many women. Not all men give their wives the respect with which Haselby will treat you."

Lucy nodded. Of course. It was true. She'd heard stories. They'd all heard stories.

"It won't be so bad," Richard said. "You'll probably even like him. He's quite agreeable."

Agreeable. It was a good thing. Better than disagreeable.

"He will be the Earl of Davenport someday," Richard added, even though of course she already knew that. "You will be a countess. Quite a prominent one."

There was that. Her schoolfriends had always said she was so lucky to have her prospects already settled, and with such a lofty result. She was the daughter of an earl and the sister of an earl. And she was destined to be the wife of one as well. She had nothing to complain about. Nothing.

But she felt so empty.

It wasn't a bad feeling precisely. But it was disconcerting. And unfamiliar. She felt rootless. She felt adrift.

She felt not like herself. And that was the worst of it.

"You're not surprised, are you, Luce?" Richard asked. "You knew this was coming. We all did."

She nodded. "It is nothing," she said, trying to sound her usual matter-of-fact self. "It is only that it never felt quite so immediate."

"Of course," Richard said. "It is a surprise, that is all. Once you grow used to the idea, it will all seem so much better. Normal, even. After all, you have always known you were to be Haselby's wife. And think of how much you will enjoy planning the wedding. Uncle Robert says it is to be a grand affair. In London, I believe. Davenport insists upon it."

Lucy felt herself nod. She did rather like to plan things. There was such a pleasant feeling of being in charge that came along with it.

"Hermione can be your attendant, as well," Richard added.

"Of course," Lucy murmured. Because, really, who else would she choose?

"Is there a color that doesn't favor her?" Richard asked with a frown. "Because you will be the bride. You don't want to be overshadowed."

Lucy rolled her eyes. That was a brother for you.

He seemed not to realize that he had insulted her, though, and Lucy supposed she shouldn't have been surprised. Hermione's beauty was so legendary that no one took insult with an unfavorable comparison. One would have to be delusional to think otherwise.

"I can't very well put her in black," Lucy said. It was the only hue she could think of that turned Hermione a bit sallow.

"No, no you couldn't, could you?" Richard paused, clearly pondering this, and Lucy stared at him in disbelief. Her brother, who had to be regularly informed of what was fashionable and what was not, was actually *interested* in the shade of Hermione's attendant dress.

"Hermione can wear whatever color she desires," Lucy decided. And why not? Of all the people who would be in attendance, there was no one who meant more to her than her closest friend.

"That's very kind of you," Richard said. He looked at her thoughtfully. "You're a good friend, Lucy."

Lucy knew she should have felt complimented, but instead she just wondered why it had taken him so long to realize it.

Richard gave her a smile, then looked down at the flower, still in his hands. He held it up, twirled it a few times, the stem rolling back and forth between his thumb and index finger. He blinked, his brow furrowing a touch, then he placed the flower in front of her dress. They were the same blue—slightly purple, maybe just a little bit gray.

"You should wear this color," he said. "You look quite lovely just now."

He sounded a little surprised, so Lucy knew that he was not just saying it. "Thank you," she said. She'd always thought the hue made her eyes a bit brighter. Richard was the first person besides Hermione ever to comment on it. "Perhaps I will."

"Shall we walk back to the house?" he asked. "I am sure you will wish to tell Hermione everything."

She paused, then shook her head. "No, thank you. I think I shall remain outside for a short while." She motioned to a spot near the path that led down to the lake. "There is a bench not too far away. And the sun feels rather pleasant on my face."

"Are you certain?" Richard squinted up at the sky. "You're always saying you don't want to get freckles."

"I already have freckles, Richard. And I won't be very long." She hadn't planned to come outside when she'd gone to greet him, so she had not brought her bonnet. But it was early yet in the day. A few minutes of sunshine would not destroy her complexion.

And besides that, she wanted to. Wouldn't it be nice to do something just because she wanted to, and not because it was expected?

Richard nodded. "I will see you at dinner?"

"I believe it is laid at half one."

He grinned. "You would know."

"There is nothing like a brother," she grumbled.

"And there is nothing like a sister." He leaned over and kissed her brow, catching her completely off-guard.

"Oh, Richard," she muttered, aghast at her soppy reaction. She never cried. In fact, she was known for her complete lack of flowerpot tendencies.

"Go on," he said, with enough affection to send one tear rolling down her cheek. Lucy brushed it away, embarrassed that he'd seen it, embarrassed that she'd done it.

Richard squeezed her hand and motioned with his head toward the south lawn. "Go stare at the trees and do whatever you need to do. You'll feel better after you have a few moments to yourself."

"I don't feel poorly," Lucy said quickly. "There is no need for me to feel *better*."

"Of course not. You are merely surprised."

"Exactly."

Exactly. Exactly. Really, she was delighted, really. She'd been waiting for this moment for years. Wouldn't it be nice to have everything settled? She liked order. She liked being settled.

It was just the surprise. That was all. Rather like when one saw a friend in an unexpected location and almost didn't recognize her. She hadn't expected the announcement now. Here, at the Bridgerton house party. And that was the only reason she felt so odd.

Really.

Eight

*In which Our Heroine learns a truth about her brother
(but does not believe it), Our Hero learns a secret
about Miss Watson (but is not concerned by it),
and both learn a truth about themselves
(but are not aware of it).*

An hour later, Gregory was still congratulating himself
on the masterful combination of strategy and timing that
had led to his outing with Miss Watson. They had had a
perfectly lovely time, and Lord Fennsworth had—well,
Fennsworth may have also had a perfectly lovely time, but if
so, it had been in the company of his sister and not the lovely
Hermione Watson.

Victory was indeed sweet.

As promised, Gregory had taken her on a stroll through
the Aubrey Hall gardens, impressing them both with his
stupendous recall of six different horticultural names. Delphinium, even, though in truth that was all Lady Lucinda's
doing.

The others were, just to give credit where it was due: rose,
daisy, peony, hyacinth, and grass. All in all, he thought he'd
acquitted himself well. Details never had been his forte.
And truly, it was all just a game by that point.

Miss Watson appeared to be warming to his company, as well. She might not have been sighing and fluttering her lashes, but the veil of polite disinterest was gone, and twice he had even made her laugh.

She hadn't made *him* laugh, but he wasn't so certain she'd been trying to, and besides, he had certainly smiled. On more than one occasion.

Which was a good thing. Really. It was rather pleasant to once again have his wits about him. He was no longer struck by that punched-in-the-chest feeling, which one would think had to be good for his respiratory health. He was discovering he rather enjoyed breathing, an undertaking he seemed to find difficult while gazing upon the back of Miss Watson's neck.

Gregory frowned, pausing in his solitary jaunt down to the lake. It *was* a rather odd reaction. And surely he'd seen the back of her neck that morning. Hadn't she run ahead to smell one of the flowers?

Hmmm. Perhaps not. He couldn't quite recall.

"Good day, Mr. Bridgerton."

He turned, surprised to see Lady Lucinda sitting by herself on a nearby stone bench. It was an odd location for a bench, he'd always thought, facing nothing but a bunch of trees. But maybe that was the point. Turning one's back on the house—and its many inhabitants. His sister Francesca had often said that after a day or two with the entire Bridgerton family, trees could be quite good company.

Lady Lucinda smiled faintly in greeting, and it struck him that she didn't look quite herself. Her eyes seemed tired, and her posture was not quite straight.

She looks vulnerable, he thought, rather unexpectedly. Her brother must have brought unhappy tidings.

"You're wearing a somber expression," he said, walking politely to her side. "May I join you?"

She nodded, offering him a bit of a smile. But it wasn't a smile. Not quite.

He took a seat beside her. "Did you have an opportunity to visit with your brother?"

She nodded. "He passed along some family news. It was . . . not important."

Gregory tilted his head as he regarded her. She was lying, clearly. But he did not press further. If she'd wanted to share, she would have done. And besides, it wasn't his business in any case.

He was curious, though.

She stared off in the distance, presumably at some tree. "It's quite pleasant here."

It was an oddly bland statement, coming from her.

"Yes," he said. "The lake is just a short walk beyond these trees. I often come in this direction when I wish to think."

She turned suddenly. "You do?"

"Why are you so surprised?"

"I—I don't know." She shrugged. "I suppose you don't seem the sort."

"To think?" Well, really.

"Of course not," she said, giving him a peevish look. "I meant the sort who needed to get away to do so."

"Pardon my presumptuousness, but you don't seem the sort, either."

She thought about that for a moment. "I'm not."

He chuckled at that. "You must have had quite a conversation with your brother."

She blinked in surprise. But she didn't elaborate. Which again didn't seem like her. "What are you here to think about?" she asked.

He opened his mouth to reply, but before he could utter a word, she said, "Hermione, I suppose."

There seemed little point in denying it. "Your brother is in love with her."

That seemed to snap her out of her fog. "*Richard?* Don't be daft."

Gregory looked at her in disbelief. "I can't believe you haven't seen it."

"I can't believe you *have*. For heaven's sake, she thinks of him as a brother."

"That may well be true, but he does not return the sentiment."

"Mr. Br—"

But he halted her with a lifted hand. "Now, now, Lady Lucinda, I daresay I have been witness to more fools in love than you have—"

The laughter quite literally exploded from her mouth. "Mr. Bridgerton," she said, once she was able, "I have been constant companion these last three years to Hermione Watson. *Hermione Watson*," she added, just in case he hadn't understood her meaning. "Trust me when I tell you there is no one who has been witness to more lovesick fools than I."

For a moment Gregory did not know how to respond. She did have a point.

"Richard is not in love with Hermione," she said with a dismissive shake of her head. And a snort. A ladylike one, but still. She *snorted* at him.

"I beg to differ," he said, because he had seven siblings, and he certainly did not know how to gracefully bow out of an argument.

"He can't be in love with her," she said, sounding quite certain of her statement. "There is someone else."

"Oh, really?" Gregory didn't even bother to get his hopes up.

"Really. He's always nattering on about a girl he met through one of his friends," she said. "I think it was someone's sister. I can't recall her name. Mary, perhaps."

Mary. Hmmph. He *knew* that Fennsworth had no imagination.

"Ergo," Lady Lucinda continued, "he is not in love with Hermione."

At least she seemed rather more like herself. The world seemed a bit steadier with Lucy Abernathy yipping along like a terrier. He'd felt almost off-balance when she'd been staring morosely at the trees.

"Believe what you will," Gregory said with a lofty sigh. "But know this: your brother will be nursing a broken heart ere long."

"Oh, really?" she scoffed. "Because you are so convinced of your own success?"

"Because I'm convinced of his lack of it."

"You don't even know him."

"And now you are defending him? Just moments ago you said he wasn't interested."

"He's not." She bit her lip. "But he is my brother. And if he *were* interested, I would have to support him, wouldn't you think?"

Gregory lifted a brow. "My, how quickly your loyalties shift."

She looked almost apologetic. "He *is* an earl. And you . . . are not."

"You shall make a fine society mama."

Her back stiffened. "I beg your pardon."

"Auctioning your friend off to the highest bidder. You'll be well-practiced by the time you have a daughter."

She jumped to her feet, her eyes flashing with anger and indignation. "That is a terrible thing to say. My most important consideration has always been Hermione's happiness. And if she can be made happy by an earl . . . who happens to be my *brother* . . ."

Oh, brilliant. Now she was going to *try* to match Hermione with Fennsworth. Well done, Gregory. Well done, indeed.

"She can be made happy by me," he said, rising to his feet. And it was true. He'd made her laugh twice this morning, even if she had not done the same for him.

"Of course she can," Lady Lucinda said. "And heavens, she probably will if you don't muck it up. Richard is too young to marry, anyway. He's only two-and-twenty."

Gregory eyed her curiously. Now she sounded as if she were back to him as the best candidate. What was she about, anyway?

"And," she added, impatiently tucking a lock of her dark blond hair behind her ear when the wind whipped it into her face, "he is *not* in love with her. I'm quite certain of it."

Neither one of them seemed to have anything to add to *that*, so, since they were both already on their feet, Gregory motioned toward the house. "Shall we return?"

She nodded, and they departed at a leisurely pace.

"This still does not solve the problem of Mr. Edmonds," Gregory remarked.

She gave him a funny look.

"What was that for?" he demanded.

And she actually giggled. Well, perhaps not a giggle, but she did do that breathy thing with her nose people did when they were rather amused. "It was nothing," she said, still smiling. "I'm rather impressed, actually, that you didn't pretend to not remember his name."

"What, should I have called him Mr. Edwards, and then Mr. Ellington, and then Mr. Edifice, and—"

Lucy gave him an arch look. "You would have lost all of my respect, I assure you."

"The horror. Oh, the horror," he said, laying one hand over his heart.

She glanced at him over her shoulder with a mischievous smile. "It was a near miss."

He looked unconcerned. "I'm a terrible shot, but I do know how to dodge a bullet."

Now *that* made her curious. "I've never known a man who would admit to being a bad shot."

He shrugged. "There are some things one simply can't

avoid. I shall always be the Bridgerton who can be bested at close range by his sister."

"The one you told me about?"

"All of them," he admitted.

"Oh." She frowned. There ought to be some sort of prescribed statement for such a situation. What *did* one say when a gentleman confessed to a shortcoming? She couldn't recall ever hearing one do so before, but surely, sometime in the course of history, some gentleman had. And someone would have had to make a reply.

She blinked, waiting for something meaningful to come to mind. Nothing did.

And then—

"Hermione can't dance." It just popped out of her mouth, with no direction whatsoever from her head.

Good gracious, *that* was meant to be meaningful?

He stopped, turning to her with a curious expression. Or maybe it was more that he was startled. Probably both. And he said the only thing she imagined one *could* say under the circumstances:

"I beg your pardon?"

Lucy repeated it, since she couldn't take it back. "She can't dance. That's why she won't dance. Because she can't."

And then she waited for a hole to open up in the ground so that she could jump into it. It didn't help that he was presently staring at her as if she were slightly deranged.

She managed a feeble smile, which was all that filled the impossibly long moment until he finally said, "There must be a reason you are telling this to me."

Lucy let out a nervous exhale. He didn't sound angry— more curious than anything else. And she hadn't *meant* to insult Hermione. But when he said he couldn't shoot, it just seemed to make an odd sort of sense to tell him that Hermione couldn't dance. It fit, really. Men were supposed to shoot, and women were supposed to dance, and trusty best friends were supposed to keep their foolish mouths shut.

Clearly, all three of them needed a bit of instruction.

"I thought to make you feel better," Lucy finally said. "Because you can't shoot."

"Oh, I can *shoot*," he said. "That's the easy part. I just can't aim."

Lucy grinned. She couldn't help herself. "I could show you."

His head swung around. "Oh, *gad*. Don't tell me *you* know how to shoot."

She perked up. "Quite well, actually."

He shook his head. "The day only needed this."

"It's an admirable skill," she protested.

"I'm sure it is, but I've already four females in my life who can best me. The last thing I need is—oh, gad *again*, please don't say Miss Watson is a crack shot as well."

Lucy blinked. "Do you know, I'm not sure."

"Well, there is still hope there, then."

"Isn't that peculiar?" she murmured.

He gave her a deadpan look. "That I have hope?"

"No, that—" She couldn't say it. Good heavens, it sounded silly even to her.

"Ah, then you must think it peculiar that you don't know whether Miss Watson can shoot."

And there it was. He guessed it, anyway. "Yes," she admitted. "But then again, why would I? Marksmanship wasn't a part of the curriculum at Miss Moss's."

"To the great relief of gentlemen everywhere, I assure you." He gave her a lopsided smile. "Who did teach you?"

"My father," she said, and it was strange, because her lips parted before she answered. For a moment she thought she'd been surprised by the question, but it hadn't been that.

She'd been surprised by her answer.

"Good heavens," he responded, "were you even out of leading strings?"

"Just barely," Lucy said, still puzzling over her odd reaction. It was probably just because she didn't often think of her father. He had been gone so long that there weren't many questions to which the late Earl of Fennsworth constituted the reply.

"He thought it an important skill," she continued. "Even for girls. Our home is near the Dover coast, and there were always smugglers. Most of them were friendly—everyone knew who they were, even the magistrate."

"He must have enjoyed French brandy," Mr. Bridgerton murmured.

Lucy smiled in recollection. "As did my father. But not all of the smugglers were known to us. Some, I'm sure, were quite dangerous. And . . ." She leaned toward him. One really couldn't say something like this without leaning in. Where would the fun be in that?

"And . . . ?" he prompted.

She lowered her voice. "I think there were spies."

"In Dover? Ten years ago? Absolutely there were spies. Although I do wonder at the advisability of arming the infant population."

Lucy laughed. "I was a bit older than *that*. I believe we began when I was seven. Richard continued the lessons once my father had passed on."

"I suppose he's a brilliant marksman as well."

She nodded ruefully. "Sorry."

They resumed their stroll toward the house. "I won't challenge him to a duel, then," he said, somewhat offhandedly.

"I'd rather you didn't."

He turned to her with an expression that could only be called sly. "Why, Lady Lucinda, I do believe you have just declared your affection for me."

Her mouth flapped open like an inarticulate fish. "I have n— what could possibly lead you to that conclusion?" And *why* did her cheeks feel so suddenly hot?

"It could never be a fair match," he said, sounding remarkably at ease with his shortcomings. "Although in all truth, I don't know that there is a man in Britain with whom I could have a fair match."

She still felt somewhat light-headed after her previous surprise, but she managed to say, "I'm sure you overstate."

"No," he said, almost casually. "Your brother would surely leave a bullet in my shoulder." He paused, considering this. "Assuming he wasn't of a mind to put one in my heart."

"Oh, don't be silly."

He shrugged. "Regardless, you must be more concerned for my welfare than you were aware."

"I'm concerned for everybody's welfare," she muttered.

"Yes," he murmured, "you would be."

Lucy drew back. "Why does that sound like an insult?"

"Did it? I can assure you it wasn't meant to."

She stared at him suspiciously for so long that he finally lifted his hands in surrender. "It was a compliment, I swear to you," he said.

"Grudgingly given."

"Not at all!" He glanced over at her, quite obviously unable to suppress a smile.

"You're laughing at me."

"No," he insisted, and then of course he laughed. "Sorry. Now I am."

"You could at least *attempt* to be kind and say that you are laughing *with* me."

"I could." He grinned, and his eyes turned positively devilish. "But it would be a lie."

She almost smacked him on the shoulder. "Oh, you are terrible."

"Bane of my brothers' existence, I assure you."

"Really?" Lucy had never been the bane of anyone's existence, and right then it sounded rather appealing. "How so?"

"Oh, the same as always. I need to settle down, find purpose, apply myself."

"Get married?"

"That, too."

"Is that why you are so enamored of Hermione?"

He paused—just for a moment. But it was there. Lucy felt it.

"No," he said. "It was something else entirely."

"Of course," she said quickly, feeling foolish for having asked. He'd told her all about it the night before—about love just happening, having no choice in the matter. He didn't want Hermione to please his brother; he wanted Hermione because he couldn't *not* want her.

And it made her feel just a little bit more alone.

"We are returned," he said, motioning to the door to the drawing room, which she had not even realized they had reached.

"Yes, of course." She looked at the door, then looked at him, then wondered why it felt so awkward now that they had to say goodbye. "Thank you for the company."

"The pleasure was all mine."

Lucy took a step toward the door, then turned back to face him with a little "Oh!"

His brows rose. "Is something wrong?"

"No. But I must apologize—I turned you quite around. You said you like to go that way—down toward the lake—when you need to think. And you never got to."

He looked at her curiously, his head tilting ever so slightly to the side. And his eyes—oh, she wished she could describe what she saw there. Because she didn't understand it, didn't quite comprehend how it made her tilt her head in concert with his, how it made her feel as if the moment were stretching . . . longer . . . longer . . . until it could last a lifetime.

"Didn't you wish for time for yourself?" she asked, softly . . . so softly it was almost a whisper.

Slowly, he shook his head. "I did," he said, sounding as if the words were coming to him at that very moment, as if the thought itself was new and not quite what he had expected.

"I did," he said again, "but now I don't."

She looked at him, and he looked at her. And the thought quite suddenly popped into her head—

He doesn't know why.

He didn't know why he no longer wanted to be by himself.

And she didn't know why that was meaningful.

Nine

In which Our Story takes a turn.

The following night was the masked ball. It was to be a grand affair, not *too* grand, of course—Gregory's brother Anthony wouldn't stand for that much disruption of his comfortable life in the country. But nevertheless, it was to be the pinnacle of the house party events. All the guests would be there, along with another hundred or so extra attendees—some down from London, others straight from their homes in the country. Every last bedchamber had been aired out and prepared for occupants, and even with that, a good number of partygoers were staying at the homes of neighbors, or, for an unlucky few, at nearby inns.

Kate's original intention had been to throw a fancy dress party—she'd been longing to fashion herself as Medusa (to the surprise of no one)—but she had finally abandoned the idea after Anthony informed her that if she had her way with this, *he* would choose his own costume.

The look he gave her was apparently enough for her to declare an immediate retreat.

She later told Gregory that he had still not forgiven her for costuming him as Cupid at the Billington fancy dress ball the previous year.

"Costume too cherubic?" Gregory murmured.

"But on the bright side," she had replied, "I now know exactly how he must have looked as a baby. Quite darling, actually."

"Until this moment," Gregory said with a wince, "I'm not sure I understood exactly how much my brother loves you."

"Quite a bit." She smiled and nodded. "Quite a bit indeed."

And so a compromise was reached. No costumes, just masks. Anthony didn't mind that one bit, as it would enable him to abandon his duties as host entirely if he so chose (who would notice his absence, after all?), and Kate set to work designing a mask with Medusish snakes jumping out in every direction. (She was unsuccessful.)

At Kate's insistence, Gregory arrived in the ballroom at precisely half eight, the ball's announced start. It meant, of course, that the only guests in attendance were he, his brother, and Kate, but there were enough servants milling about to make it seem not quite so empty, and Anthony declared himself delighted with the gathering.

"It's a much better party without everyone else jostling about," he said happily.

"When did you grow so opposed to social discourse?" Gregory asked, plucking a champagne flute off a proffered tray.

"It's not that at all," Anthony answered with a shrug. "I've simply lost patience for stupidity of any kind."

"He is not aging well," his wife confirmed.

If Anthony took any exception to her comment, he made no show of it. "I simply refuse to deal with idiots," he told

Gregory. His face brightened. "It has cut my social obligations in half."

"What's the point of possessing a title if one cannot refuse one's invitations?" Gregory murmured wryly.

"Indeed," was Anthony's reply. "Indeed."

Gregory turned to Kate. "You have no arguments with this?"

"Oh, I have many arguments," she answered, craning her neck as she examined the ballroom for any last-minute disasters. "I always have arguments."

"It's true," Anthony said. "But she knows when she cannot win."

Kate turned to Gregory even though her words were quite clearly directed at her husband. "What I *know* is how to choose my battles."

"Pay her no mind," Anthony said. "That is just her way of admitting defeat."

"And yet he continues," Kate said to no one in particular, "even though he knows that I always win in the end."

Anthony shrugged and gave his brother an uncharacteristically sheepish grin. "She's right, of course." He finished his drink. "But there is no point in surrendering without a fight."

Gregory could only smile. Two bigger fools in love had yet to be born. It was endearing to watch, even if it did leave him with a slight pang of jealousy.

"How fares your courtship?" Kate asked him.

Anthony's ears perked up. "Your courtship?" he echoed, his face assuming its usual *obey-me-I-am-the-viscount* expression. "Who is she?"

Gregory shot Kate an aggravated look. He had not shared his feelings with his brother. He wasn't sure why; surely in part because he hadn't actually *seen* much of Anthony in the past few days. But there was more. It just didn't seem like the sort of thing one wished to share with one's brother.

Especially one who was considerably more father than brother.

Not to mention . . . If he didn't succeed . . .

Well, he didn't particularly wish for his family to know.

But he *would* succeed. Why was he doubting himself? Even earlier, when Miss Watson was still treating him like a minor nuisance, he had been sure of the outcome. It made no sense that now—with their friendship growing—he should suddenly doubt himself.

Kate, predictably, ignored Gregory's irritation. "I just adore it when you don't know something," she said to her husband. "Especially when I do."

Anthony turned to Gregory. "You're sure you want to marry one of these?"

"Not that one precisely," Gregory answered. "Something rather like it, though."

Kate's expression turned somewhat pinched at having been called an "it," but she recovered quickly, turning to Anthony and saying, "He has declared his love for—" She let one of her hands flutter in the air as if waving away a foolish idea. "Oh, never mind, I think I won't tell you."

Her phrasing was a bit suspect. She probably had meant to keep it from him all along. Gregory wasn't sure which he found more satisfying—that Kate had honored his secret or that Anthony had been flummoxed.

"See if you can guess," Kate said to Anthony with an arch smile. "That should lend your evening a sense of purpose."

Anthony turned to Gregory with a level stare. "Who is it?"

Gregory shrugged. He always sided with Kate when it came to thwarting his brother. "Far be it from me to deny you a sense of purpose."

Anthony muttered, "Arrogant pup," and Gregory knew that the evening was off to a fine start.

The guests began to trickle in, and within an hour, the ballroom sang with the low buzz of conversation and laughter. Everyone seemed a bit more adventurous with a mask on the face, and soon the banter grew more risqué, the jokes more ribald.

And the laughter . . . It was difficult to put the right word on it, but it was different. There was more than merriment in the air. There was an edge to the excitement, as if the party-goers somehow knew that this was the night to be daring.

To break free.

Because in the morning, no one would know.

All in all, Gregory liked nights like these.

By half nine, however, he was growing frustrated. He could not be positive, but he was almost certain that Miss Watson had not made an appearance. Even with a mask, she would find it nearly impossible to keep her identity a secret. Her hair was too startling, too ethereal in the candlelight for her to pass as anyone else.

But Lady Lucinda, on the other hand . . . She would have no trouble blending in. Her hair was certainly a lovely shade of honeyish blond, but it was nothing unexpected or unique. Half the ladies of the *ton* probably had hair that color.

He glanced around the ballroom. Very well, not half. And maybe not even a quarter. But it wasn't the spun moonlight of her friend's.

He frowned. Miss Watson really ought to have been present by then. As a member of the house party, she need not deal with muddy roads or lame horses or even the long line of carriages waiting out front to deliver the guests. And while he doubted she would have wished to arrive as early as he had done, surely she would not come over an hour late.

If nothing else, Lady Lucinda would not have tolerated it. She was clearly a punctual sort.

In a good way.

As opposed to an insufferable, nagging way.

He smiled to himself. She wasn't like that.

Lady Lucinda was more like Kate, or at least she would be, once she was a bit older. Intelligent, no-nonsense, just a little bit sly.

Rather good fun, actually. She was a good sport, Lady Lucinda was.

But he didn't see her among the guests, either. Or at least he didn't think he did. He couldn't be quite sure. He did see several ladies with hair the approximate shade of hers, but none of them seemed quite right. One of them moved the wrong way—too clunky, maybe even a little bit lumbering. And another was the wrong height. Not very wrong, probably just a few inches. But he could tell.

It wasn't she.

She was probably wherever Miss Watson was. Which he did find somewhat reassuring. Miss Watson could not possibly get into trouble with Lady Lucinda about.

His stomach growled, and he decided to abandon his search for the time being and instead seek sustenance. Kate had, as always, provided a hearty selection of food for her guests to nibble upon during the course of the evening. He went directly to the plate of sandwiches—they looked rather like the ones she'd served the night he'd arrived, and he'd liked those quite well. Ten of them ought to do the trick.

Hmmm. He saw cucumber—a waste of bread if ever he saw one. Cheese—no, not what he was looking for. Perhaps—

"Mr. Bridgerton?"

Lady Lucinda. He'd know that voice anywhere.

He turned. There she was. He congratulated himself. He'd been right about those other masked honey blonds. He definitely hadn't come across her yet this evening.

Her eyes widened, and he realized that her mask, covered with slate blue felt, was the exact color of her eyes. He wondered if Miss Watson had obtained a similar one in green.

"It *is* you, isn't it?"

"How did you know?" he returned.

She blinked. "I don't know. I just did." Then her lips parted—just enough to reveal a tiny little gleam of white teeth, and she said, "It's Lucy. Lady Lucinda."

"I know," he murmured, still looking at her mouth. What was it about masks? It was as if by covering up the top, the bottom was made more intriguing.

Almost mesmerizing.

How was it he hadn't noticed the way her lips tilted ever so slightly up at the corners? Or the freckles on her nose. There were seven of them. Precisely seven, all shaped like ovals, except for that last one, which looked rather like Ireland, actually.

"Were you hungry?" she asked.

He blinked, forced his eyes back to hers.

She motioned to the sandwiches. "The ham is very nice. As is the cucumber. I'm not normally partial to cucumber sandwiches—they never seem to satisfy although I do like the crunch—but these have a bit of soft cheese on them instead of just butter. It was a rather nice surprise."

She paused and looked at him, tilting her head to the side as she awaited his reply.

And he smiled. He couldn't help it. There was something so uncommonly entertaining about her when she was prattling on about food.

He reached out and placed a cucumber sandwich on his plate. "With such a recommendation," he said, "how could I refuse?"

"Well, the ham is nice, too, if you don't like it."

Again, so like her. Wanting everyone to be happy. *Try this. And if you don't like it, try this or this or this. And if that doesn't work, have mine.*

She'd never said it, of course, but somehow he knew she would.

She looked down at the serving platter. "I do wish they weren't all mixed up."

He looked at her quizzically. "I beg your pardon?"

"Well," she said—that singular sort of *well* that foretold a long and heartfelt explanation. "Don't you think it would have made far more sense to separate the different types of sandwiches? To put each on its own smaller plate? That way, if you found one you liked, you would know exactly where to go to get another. *Or*"—at this she grew even more animated, as if she were attacking a problem of great societal importance—"*if* there was another. Consider it." She waved at the platter. "There might not be a single ham sandwich left in the stack. And you couldn't very well sift through them all, looking. It would be most impolite."

He regarded her thoughtfully, then said, "You like things to be orderly, don't you?"

"Oh, I do," she said with feeling. "I really do."

Gregory considered his own disorganized ways. He tossed shoes in the wardrobe, left invitations strewn about . . . The year before, he had released his valet-secretary from service for a week to visit his ailing father, and when the poor man had come back, the chaos on Gregory's desk alone had nearly done him in.

Gregory looked at Lady Lucinda's earnest expression and chuckled. He'd probably drive her mad in under a week as well.

"Do you like the sandwich?" she asked, once he'd taken a bite. "The cucumber?"

"Very intriguing," he murmured.

"I wonder, is food meant to be intriguing?"

He finished the sandwich. "I'm not certain."

She nodded absently, then said, "The ham is nice."

They lapsed into a companionable silence as they glanced out across the room. The musicians were playing a lively waltz, and the ladies' skirts were billowing like silken bells as they spun and twirled. It was impossible to watch the scene and not feel as if the night itself were alive . . . restless with energy . . . waiting to make its move.

Something would happen that night. Gregory was sure of it. Someone's life would change.

If he was lucky, it would be his.

His hands began to tingle. His feet, too. It was taking everything he had just to stand still. He wanted to move, he wanted to *do* something. He wanted to set his life in motion, reach out and capture his dreams.

He wanted to move. He couldn't stand still. He—

"Would you like to dance?"

He hadn't meant to ask. But he'd turned, and Lucy was right there beside him, and the words just tumbled out.

Her eyes lit up. Even with the mask, he could see that she was delighted. "Yes," she said, almost sighing as she added, "I love to dance."

He took her hand and led her to the floor. The waltz was in full swing, and they quickly found their place in the music. It seemed to lift them, render them as one. Gregory needed only to press his hand at her waist, and she moved, exactly as he anticipated. They spun, they twirled, the air rushing past their faces so quickly that they had to laugh.

It was perfect. It was breathless. It was as if the music had crept under their skin and was guiding their every movement.

And then it was over.

So quickly. *Too* quickly. The music ended, and for a moment they stood, still in each other's arms, still wrapped in the memory of the music.

"Oh, that was lovely," Lady Lucinda said, and her eyes shone.

Gregory released her and bowed. "You are a superb dancer, Lady Lucinda. I knew you would be."

"Thank you, I—" Her eyes snapped to his. "You did?"

"I—" Why had he said that? He hadn't meant to say that. "You're quite graceful," he finally said, leading her back to the ballroom's perimeter. Far more graceful than Miss Watson, actually, although that did make sense given what Lucy had said about her friend's dancing ability.

"It is in the way you walk," he added, since she seemed to be expecting a more detailed explanation.

And that would have to do, since he wasn't about to examine the notion any further.

"Oh." And her lips moved. Just a little. But it was enough. And it struck him—she looked happy. And he realized that most people didn't. They looked amused, or entertained, or satisfied.

Lady Lucinda looked happy.

He rather liked that.

"I wonder where Hermione is," she said, looking this way and that.

"She didn't arrive with you?" Gregory asked, surprised.

"She did. But then we saw Richard. And he asked her to dance. *Not*," she added with great emphasis, "because he is in love with her. He was merely being polite. That is what one does for one's sister's friends."

"I have four sisters," he reminded her. "I know." But then he remembered. "I thought Miss Watson does not dance."

"She doesn't. But Richard does not know that. No one does. Except me. And you." She looked at him with some urgency. "Please do *not* tell anyone. I beg of you. Hermione would be mortified."

"My lips are sealed," he promised.

"I imagine they went off to find something to drink," Lucy said, leaning slightly to one side as she tried to catch a glimpse of the lemonade table. "Hermione made a comment about being overheated. It is her favorite excuse. It almost always works when someone asks her to dance."

"I don't see them," Gregory said, following her gaze.

"No, you wouldn't." She turned back to face him, giving her head a little shake. "I don't know why I was looking. It was some time ago."

"Longer than one can sip at a drink?"

She chuckled. "No, Hermione can make a glass of lemonade last an entire evening when she needs to. But I think Richard would have lost patience."

It was Gregory's opinion that her brother would gladly cut off his right arm just for the chance to gaze upon Miss Watson while she pretended to drink lemonade, but there was little point in trying to convince Lucy of that.

"I imagine they decided to take a stroll," Lucy said, quite obviously unconcerned.

But Gregory immediately felt an unease. "Outside?"

She shrugged. "I suppose. They are certainly not here in the ballroom. Hermione cannot hide in a crowd. Her hair, you know."

"But do you think it is wise for them to be off alone?" Gregory pressed.

Lady Lucinda looked at him as if she couldn't quite understand the urgency in his voice. "They're hardly off alone," she said. "There are at least two dozen people outside. I looked out through the French doors."

Gregory forced himself to stand perfectly still while he considered what to do. Clearly he needed to find Miss Watson, and quickly, before she was subjected to anything that might be considered irrevocable.

Irrevocable.

Jesus.

Lives could turn on a single moment. If Miss Watson really was off with Lucy's brother . . . If someone caught them . . .

A strange heat began to rise within him, something angry and jealous and entirely unpleasant. Miss Watson might be in danger . . . or she might not. Maybe she welcomed Fennsworth's advances . . .

No. No, she did not. He practically forced the thought down his throat. Miss Watson thought she was in love with that ridiculous Mr. Edmonds, whoever he was. She wouldn't welcome advances from Gregory *or* Lord Fennsworth.

But had Lucy's brother seized an opportunity that *he* had missed? It rankled, lodged itself in his chest like a hot cannonball—this *feeling,* this emotion, this bloody . . . awful . . . pissish . . .

"Mr. Bridgerton?"

Foul. Definitely foul.

"Mr. Bridgerton, is something wrong?"

He moved his head the inch required to face Lady Lucinda, but even so, it took several seconds for him to focus on her features. Her eyes were concerned, her mouth pressed into a worried line.

"You don't look well," she said.

"I'm fine," he ground out.

"But—"

"Fine," he positively snapped.

She drew back. "Of course you are."

How had Fennsworth done it? How had he got Miss Watson off alone? He was still wet behind the ears, for God's sake, barely out of university and never come down to London. And Gregory was . . . Well, more experienced than that.

He should have been paying more attention.

He should never have allowed this.

"Perhaps I'll look for Hermione," Lucy said, inching away. "I can see that you would prefer to be alone."

"No," he blurted out, with a bit more force than was strictly polite. "I will join you. We shall search together."

"Do you think that's wise?"

"Why wouldn't it be wise?"

"I . . . don't know." She stopped, stared at him with wide, unblinking eyes, finally saying, "I just don't think it is. You yourself just questioned the wisdom of Richard and Hermione going off together."

"You certainly cannot search the house by yourself."

"Of course not," she said, as if he were foolish for even having suggested it. "I was going to find Lady Bridgerton."

Kate? Good God. "Don't do *that*," he said quickly. And perhaps a bit disdainfully as well, although that hadn't been his intention.

But she clearly took umbrage because her voice was clipped as she asked, "And why not?"

He leaned in, his tone low and urgent. "If Kate finds them, and they are not as they should be, they will be married in less than a fortnight. Mark my words."

"Don't be absurd. Of course they will be as they should," she hissed, and it took him aback, actually, because it never occurred to him that she might stand up for herself with quite so much vigor.

"Hermione would never behave in an untoward manner," she continued furiously, "and neither would Richard, for that matter. He is my brother. My *brother*."

"He loves her," Gregory said simply.

"No. He. *Doesn't*." Good God, she looked ready to explode. "And even if he did," she railed on, "which he does not, he would *never* dishonor her. Never. He wouldn't. He wouldn't—"

"He wouldn't what?"

She swallowed. "He wouldn't do that to *me*."

Gregory could not believe her naiveté. "He's not thinking of *you*, Lady Lucinda. In fact, I believe it would be safe to say that you have not crossed his mind even once."

"That is a terrible thing to say."

Gregory shrugged. "He's a man in love. Hence, he is a man insensible."

"Oh, is *that* how it works?" she retorted. "Does that render *you* insensible as well?"

"No," he said tersely, and he realized it was actually true. He had already grown accustomed to this strange fervor. He'd regained his equilibrium. And as a gentleman of considerably more experience, he was, even when Miss Watson was not an issue, more easily in possession of his wits than Fennsworth.

Lady Lucinda gave him a look of disdainful impatience. "Richard is not in love with her. I don't know how many ways I can explain that to you."

"You're wrong," he said flatly. He'd been watching Fennsworth for two days. He'd been watching him watching Miss Watson. Laughing at her jokes. Fetching her a cool drink.

Picking a wildflower, tucking it behind her ear.

If that wasn't love, then Richard Abernathy was the most attentive, caring, and unselfish older brother in the history of man.

And as an older brother himself—one who had frequently been pressed into service dancing attendance upon his sisters' friends—Gregory could categorically say that there did not exist an older brother with such levels of thoughtfulness and devotion.

One loved one's sister, of course, but one did not sacrifice one's every waking minute for the sake of her best friend without some sort of compensation.

Unless a pathetic and unrequited love factored into the equation.

"I am not wrong," Lady Lucinda said, looking very much as if she would like to cross her arms. "And I'm getting Lady Bridgerton."

Gregory closed his hand around her wrist. "That would be a mistake of magnificent proportions."

She yanked, but he did not let go. "Don't patronize me," she hissed.

"I'm not. I'm instructing you."

Her mouth fell open. Really, truly, flappingly open.

Gregory would have enjoyed the sight, were he not so furious with everything else in the world just then.

"You are insufferable," she said, once she'd recovered.

He shrugged. "Occasionally."

"*And* delusional."

"Well done, Lady Lucinda." As one of eight, Gregory could not help but admire any well-placed quip or retort. "But I would be far more likely to admire your verbal skills if I were not trying to stop you from doing something monumentally stupid."

She looked at him through narrowed eyes, and then she said, "I don't care to speak to you any longer."

"Ever?"

"I'm getting Lady Bridgerton," she announced.

"You're getting me? What is the occasion?"

It was the last voice Gregory wanted to hear.

He turned. Kate was standing in front of them both, regarding the tableau with a single lifted brow.

No one spoke.

Kate glanced pointedly at Gregory's hand, still on Lady Lucinda's wrist. He dropped it, quickly stepping back.

"Is there something I should know about?" Kate asked, and her voice was that perfectly awful mix of cultured inquiry and moral authority. Gregory was reminded that his sister-in-law could be a formidable presence when she so chose.

Lady Lucinda—*of course*—spoke immediately. "Mr. Bridgerton seems to feel that Hermione might be in danger."

Kate's demeanor changed instantly. "Danger? Here?"

"No," Gregory ground out, although what he really meant was—*I am going to* kill *you*. Lady Lucinda, to be precise.

"I haven't seen her for some time," the annoying twit continued. "We arrived together, but that was nearly an hour ago."

Kate glanced about, her gaze finally settling on the doors leading outside. "Couldn't she be in the garden? Much of the party has moved abroad."

Lady Lucinda shook her head. "I didn't see her. I looked."

Gregory said nothing. It was as if he were watching the world destructing before his very eyes. And really, what could he possibly say to stop it?

"Not outside?" Kate said.

"I didn't think anything was amiss," Lady Lucinda said, rather officiously. "But Mr. Bridgerton was instantly concerned."

"He was?" Kate's head snapped to face him. "You were? Why?"

"May we speak of this at another time?" Gregory ground out.

Kate immediately dismissed him and looked squarely at Lucy. "Why was he concerned?"

Lucy swallowed. And then she whispered, "I think she might be with my brother."

Kate blanched. "That is not good."

"Richard would never do anything improper," Lucy insisted. "I promise you."

"He is in love with her," Kate said.

Gregory said nothing. Vindication had never felt less sweet.

Lucy looked from Kate to Gregory, her expression almost bordering on panic. "No," she whispered. "No, you're wrong."

"I'm not wrong," Kate said in a serious voice. "And we need to find them. Quickly."

She turned and immediately strode toward the door. Gregory followed, his long legs keeping pace with ease. Lady Lucinda seemed momentarily frozen, and then, jumping into action, she scurried after them both. "He would never do anything against Hermione's will," she said urgently. "I promise you."

Kate stopped. Turned around. Looked at Lucy, her expression frank and perhaps a little sad as well, as if she recognized that the younger woman was, in that moment, losing a bit of her innocence and that she, Kate, regretted having to be the one to deliver the blow.

"He might not have to," Kate said quietly.

Force her. Kate didn't say it, but the words hung in the air all the same.

"He might not have— What do you—"

Gregory saw the moment she realized it. Her eyes, always so changeable, had never looked more gray.

Stricken.

"We have to find them," Lucy whispered.

Kate nodded, and the three of them silently left the room.

Ten

In which love is triumphant—
but not for Our Hero and Heroine.

Lucy followed Lady Bridgerton and Gregory into the hallway, trying to stem the anxiety she felt building within her. Her belly felt queer, her breath not quite right.

And her mind wouldn't quite clear. She needed to focus on the matter at hand. She knew she needed to give her full attention to the search, but it felt as if a portion of her mind kept pulling away—dizzy, panicked, and unable to escape a horrible sense of foreboding.

Which she did not understand. Didn't she *want* Hermione to marry her brother? Hadn't she just told Mr. Bridgerton that the match, while improbable, would be superb? Hermione would be her sister in name, not just in feeling, and Lucy could not imagine anything more fitting. But still, she felt . . .

Uneasy.

And a little bit angry as well.

And guilty. Of course. Because what right did she have to feel angry?

"We should search separately," Mr. Bridgerton directed, once they had turned several corners, and the sounds of the masked ball had receded into the distance. He yanked off his mask, and the two ladies followed suit, leaving all three on a small lamp table that was tucked into a recessed nook in the hallway.

Lady Bridgerton shook her head. "We can't. *You* certainly can't find them by yourself," she said to him. "I don't wish to even ponder the consequences of Miss Watson being alone with two unmarried gentlemen."

Not to mention his reaction, Lucy thought. Mr. Bridgerton struck her as an even-tempered man; she wasn't sure that he could come across the pair alone without thinking he had to spout off about honor and the defense of virtue, which always led to disaster. Always. Although given the depth of his feelings for Hermione, his reaction might be a little less honor and virtue and a little more jealous rage.

Even worse, while Mr. Bridgerton might lack the ability to shoot a straight bullet, Lucy had no doubt that he could blacken an eye with lethal speed.

"And *she* can't be alone," Lady Bridgerton continued, motioning in Lucy's direction. "It's dark. And empty. The gentlemen are wearing masks, for heaven's sake. It does loosen the conscience."

"I wouldn't know where to look, either," Lucy added. It was a large house. She'd been there nearly a week, but she doubted she'd seen even half of it.

"We shall remain together," Lady Bridgerton said firmly.

Mr. Bridgerton looked as if he wanted to argue, but he held his temper in check and instead bit off, "Fine. Let's not waste time, then." He strode off, his long legs establishing a pace that neither of the two women was going to find easy to keep up with.

He wrenched open doors and then left them hanging ajar, too driven to reach the next room to leave things as he'd found them. Lucy scrambled behind him, trying rooms on the other side of the hall. Lady Bridgerton was just up ahead, doing the same.

"Oh!" Lucy jumped back, slamming a door shut.

"Did you find them?" Mr. Bridgerton demanded. Both he and Lady Bridgerton immediately moved to her side.

"No," Lucy said, blushing madly. She swallowed. "Someone else."

Lady Bridgerton groaned. "Good God. Please say it wasn't an unmarried lady."

Lucy opened her mouth, but several seconds passed before she said, "I don't know. The masks, you realize."

"They were wearing masks?" Lady Bridgerton asked. "They're married, then. And not to each other."

Lucy desperately wanted to ask how she had reached that conclusion, but she couldn't bring herself to do so, and besides, Mr. Bridgerton quite diverted her thoughts by cutting in front of her and yanking the door open. A feminine shriek split the air, followed by an angry male voice, uttering words Lucy dare not repeat.

"Sorry," Mr. Bridgerton grunted. "Carry on." He shut the door. "Morley," he announced, "and Winstead's wife."

"Oh," Lady Bridgerton said, her lips parting with surprise. "I had no idea."

"Should we do something?" Lucy asked. Good heavens, there were people committing *adultery* not ten feet away from her.

"It's Winstead's problem," Mr. Bridgerton said grimly. "We have our own matters to attend to."

Lucy's feet remained rooted to the spot as he took off again, striding down the hallway. Lady Bridgerton glanced at the door, looking very much as if she wanted to open it and peek inside, but in the end she sighed and followed her brother-in-law.

Lucy just stared at the door, trying to figure out just what it was that was niggling at her mind. The couple on the table —on the *table,* for God's sake—had been a shock, but something else was bothering her. Something about the scene wasn't quite right. Out of place. Out of context.

Or maybe something was sparking a memory.

What *was* it?

"Are you coming?" Lady Bridgerton called.

"Yes," Lucy replied. And then she took advantage of her innocence and youth, and added, "The shock, you know. I just need a moment."

Lady Bridgerton gave her a sympathetic look and nodded, but she carried on her work, inspecting the rooms on the left side of the hall.

What had she seen? There was the man and the woman, of course, and the aforementioned table. Two chairs, pink. One sofa, striped. And one end table, with a vase of cut flowers . . .

Flowers.

That was it.

She knew where they were.

If she was wrong and everybody else was right, and her brother really was in love with Hermione, there was only one place he would have taken her to try to convince her to return the emotion.

The orangery. It was on the other side of the house, far from the ballroom. And it was filled, not just with orange trees, but with flowers. Gorgeous tropical plants that must have cost Lord Bridgerton a fortune to import. Elegant orchids. Rare roses. Even humble wildflowers, brought in and replanted with care and devotion.

There was no place more romantic in the moonlight, and no place her brother would feel more at ease. He loved flowers. He always had, and he possessed an astounding memory for their names, scientific and common. He was always picking something up, rattling off some sort of informational tidbit—this one only opened in the moonlight, that one was related to some such plant brought in from Asia. Lucy had always found it somewhat tedious, but she could see how it might seem romantic, if it weren't one's brother doing the talking.

She looked up the hall. The Bridgertons had stopped to speak to each other, and Lucy could see by their postures that the conversation was intensely felt.

Wouldn't it be best if she were the one to find them? Without *any* of the Bridgertons?

If Lucy found them, she could warn them and avert disaster. If Hermione wanted to marry her brother . . . well, it could be her choice, not something she had to do because she'd been caught unawares.

Lucy knew how to get to the orangery. She could be there in minutes.

She took a cautious step back toward the ballroom. Neither Gregory nor Lady Bridgerton seemed to notice her.

She made her decision.

Six quiet steps, backing up carefully to the corner. And then—one last quick glance thrown down the hall—she stepped out of sight.

And ran.

She picked up her skirts and ran like the wind, or at the very least, as fast as she possibly could in her heavy velvet ball gown. She had no idea how long she would have before the Bridgertons noticed her absence, and while they would not know her destination, she had no doubt that they would find her. All Lucy had to do was find Hermione and Richard first. If she could get to them, warn them, she could push Hermione out the door and claim she'd come across Richard alone.

She would not have much time, but she could do it. She knew she could.

Lucy made it to the main hall, slowing her pace as much

as she dared as she passed through. There were servants about, and probably a few late-arriving guests as well, and she couldn't afford to arouse suspicion by running.

She slipped out and into the west hallway, skidding around a corner as she took off again at a run. Her lungs began to burn, and her skin grew damp with perspiration beneath her gown. But she did not slow down. It wasn't far now. She could do it.

She knew she could.

She had to.

And then, amazingly, she was there, at the heavy double doors that led out to the orangery. Her hand landed heavily on one of the doorknobs, and she meant to turn it, but instead she found herself bent over, struggling to catch her breath.

Her eyes stung, and she tried to stand, but when she did she was hit with what felt like a wall of panic. It was physical, palpable, and it rushed at her so quickly that she had to grab on to the wall for support.

Dear God, she didn't want to open that door. She didn't want to see them. She didn't want to know what they had been doing, didn't want to know how or why. She didn't want this, any of this. She wanted it all back as it was, just three days earlier.

Couldn't she have that back? It was just *three days*. Three days, and Hermione would still be in love with Mr. Edmonds, which really wasn't such a problem since nothing would come of it, and Lucy would still be—

She would still be herself, happy and confident, and only practically engaged.

Why did everything have to *change*? Lucy's life had been perfectly acceptable the way it was. Everyone had his place, and all was in perfect order, and she hadn't had to *think* so hard about everything. She hadn't cared about what love meant or how it felt, and her brother wasn't secretly pining for her best friend, and her wedding was a hazy plan for the future, and she had been happy. She had been happy.

And she wanted it all back.

She grasped the knob more tightly, tried to turn it, but her hand wouldn't move. The panic was still there, freezing her muscles, pressing at her chest. She couldn't focus. She couldn't think.

And her legs began to tremble.

Oh, dear God, she was going to fall. Right there in the hallway, inches from her goal, she was going to crumple to the floor. And then—

"Lucy!"

It was Mr. Bridgerton, and he was running to her, and it occurred to her that she'd failed.

She'd failed.

She'd made it to the orangery. She'd made it in time, but then she'd just stood at the door. Like an idiot, she'd stood there, with her fingers on the bloody knob and—

"My God, Lucy, what were you thinking?"

He grabbed her by the shoulders, and Lucy leaned into his strength. She wanted to fall into him and forget. "I'm sorry," she whispered. "I'm sorry."

She did not know what she was sorry for, but she said it all the same.

"This is no place for a woman alone," he said, and his voice sounded different. Hoarse. "Men have been drinking. They use the masks as a license to—"

He fell silent. And then— "People are not themselves."

She nodded, and she finally looked up, pulling her eyes from the floor to his face. And then she saw him. Just saw him. His face, which had become so familiar to her. She seemed to know every feature, from the slight curl of his hair to the tiny scar near his left ear.

She swallowed. Breathed. Not quite the way she was meant to, but she breathed. More slowly, closer to normal.

"I'm sorry," she said again, because she didn't know what else to say.

"My God," he swore, searching her face with urgent eyes, "what happened to you? Are you all right? Did someone—"

His grip loosened slightly as he looked frantically around. "Who did this?" he demanded. "Who made you—"

"No," Lucy said, shaking her head. "It was no one. It was just me. I—I wanted to find them. I thought if I— Well, I didn't want you to— And then I— And then I got here, and I—"

Gregory's eyes moved quickly to the doors to the orangery. "Are they in there?"

"I don't know," Lucy admitted. "I think so. I couldn't—" The panic was finally receding, almost gone, really, and it all seemed so silly now. She felt so stupid. She'd stood there at the door, and she'd done nothing. Nothing.

"I couldn't open the door," she finally whispered. Because she had to tell him. She couldn't explain it—she didn't even understand it—but she had to tell him what had happened.

Because he'd found her.

And that had made the difference.

"Gregory!" Lady Bridgerton burst on the scene, practically hurtling against them, quite clearly out of breath from having tried to keep up. "Lady Lucinda! Why did you— Are you all right?"

She sounded so concerned that Lucy wondered what she looked like. She felt pale. She felt small, actually, but what could possibly be in her face that would cause Lady Bridgerton to look upon her with such obvious worry.

"I'm fine," Lucy said, relieved that she had not seen her as Mr. Bridgerton had. "Just a bit overset. I think I ran too quickly. It was foolish of me. I'm sorry."

"When we turned around and you were gone—" Lady Bridgerton looked as if she were trying to be stern, but worry was creasing her brow, and her eyes were so very kind.

Lucy wanted to cry. No one had ever looked at her like that. Hermione loved her, and Lucy took great comfort in that, but this was different. Lady Bridgerton couldn't have been that much older than she was—ten years, maybe fifteen—but the way she was looking at her . . .

It was almost as if she had a mother.

It was just for a moment. Just a few seconds, really, but she could pretend. And maybe wish, just a little.

Lady Bridgerton hurried closer and put an arm around Lucy's shoulders, drawing her away from Gregory, who allowed his arms to return to his sides. "Are you certain you are all right?" she asked.

Lucy nodded. "I am. Now."

Lady Bridgerton looked over to Gregory. He nodded. Once.

Lucy didn't know what that meant.

"I think they might be in the orangery," she said, and she wasn't quite certain what had caught at her voice—resignation or regret.

"Very well," Lady Bridgerton said, her shoulders pushing back as she went to the door. "There's nothing for it, is there?"

Lucy shook her head. Gregory did nothing.

Lady Bridgerton took a deep breath and pulled open the door. Lucy and Gregory immediately moved forward to peer inside, but the orangery was dark, the only light the moon, shining through the expansive windows.

"Damn."

Lucy's chin drew back in surprise. She'd never heard a woman curse before.

For a moment the trio stood still, and then Lady Bridgerton stepped forward and called out, "Lord Fennsworth! Lord Fennsworth, please reply. Are you here?"

Lucy started to call out for Hermione, but Gregory clamped a hand over her mouth.

"Don't," he whispered in her ear. "If someone else is here, we don't want them to realize we're looking for them both."

Lucy nodded, feeling painfully green. She'd thought she'd known something of the world, but as each day passed, it seemed she understood less and less. Mr. Bridgerton stepped away, moving farther into the room. He stood with his hands on his hips, his stance wide as he scanned the orangery for occupants.

"Lord Fennsworth!" Lady Bridgerton called out again.

This time they heard a rustling. But soft. And slow. As if someone were trying to conceal his presence.

Lucy turned toward the sound, but no one came forward. She bit her lip. Maybe it was just an animal. There were several cats at Aubrey Hall. They slept in a little hutch near the door to the kitchen, but maybe one of them had lost its way and got locked in the orangery.

It had to be a cat. If it were Richard, he'd have come forward when he heard his name.

She looked at Lady Bridgerton, waiting to see what she would do next. The viscountess was looking intently at her brother-in-law, mouthing something and motioning with her hands and pointing in the direction of the noise.

Gregory gave her a nod, then moved forward on silent feet, his long legs crossing the room with impressive speed, until—

Lucy gasped. Before she had time to blink, Gregory had charged forward, a strange, primal sound ripping from his throat. Then he positively leaped through the air, coming down with a thud and a grunt of "I have you!"

"Oh no." Lucy's hand rose to cover her mouth. Mr. Bridgerton had someone pinned to the floor, and his hands looked to be very close to his captive's throat.

Lady Bridgerton rushed toward them, and Lucy, seeing her, finally remembered her own feet and ran to the scene. If it was Richard—*oh, please don't let it be Richard*—she needed to reach him before Mr. Bridgerton killed him.

"Let . . . me . . . *go!*"

"Richard!" Lucy called out shrilly. It was his voice. There could be no mistaking it.

The figure on the floor of the orangery twisted, and then she could see his face.

"Lucy?" He looked stunned.

"Oh, Richard." There was a world of disappointment in those two words.

"Where is she?" Gregory demanded.

"Where is who?"

Lucy felt sick. Richard was feigning ignorance. She knew him too well. He was lying.

"Miss Watson," Gregory ground out.

"I don't know what y—"

A horrible gurgling noise came from Richard's throat.

"Gregory!" Lady Bridgerton grabbed his arm. "Stop!"

He loosened his hold. Barely.

"Maybe she's not here," Lucy said. She knew it wasn't true, but somehow it seemed the best way to salvage the situation. "Richard loves flowers. He always has. And he doesn't like parties."

"It's true," Richard gasped.

"Gregory," Lady Bridgerton said, "you must let him up."

Lucy turned to face her as she spoke, and that was when she saw it. Behind Lady Bridgerton.

Pink. Just a flash. More of a strip, actually, just barely visible through the plants.

Hermione was wearing pink. That very shade.

Lucy's eyes widened. Maybe it was just a flower. There were heaps of pink flowers. She turned back to Richard. Quickly.

Too quickly. Mr. Bridgerton saw her head snapping around.

"What did you see?" he demanded.

"Nothing."

But he didn't believe her. He let go of Richard and began to move in the direction Lucy was looking, but Richard rolled to the side and grabbed one of his ankles. Gregory went down with a yell, and he quickly retaliated, catching hold of Richard's shirt and yanking with enough force to scrape his head along the floor.

"Don't!" Lucy cried, rushing forward. Good God, they were going to kill each other. First Mr. Bridgerton was on top, then Richard, then Mr. Bridgerton, then she couldn't tell *who* was winning, and the whole time they were just *pummeling* each other.

Lucy wanted desperately to separate them, but she didn't see how without risking injury to herself. The two of them were beyond noticing anything so mundane as a human being.

Maybe Lady Bridgerton could stop them. It was her home, and the guests her responsibility. She could attack the situation with more authority than Lucy could hope to muster.

Lucy turned. "Lady Br—"

The words evaporated in her throat. Lady Bridgerton was not where she had been just moments earlier.

Oh *no.*

Lucy twisted frantically about. "Lady Bridgerton? Lady Bridgerton?"

And then there she was, moving back toward Lucy, making her way through the plants, her hand wrapped tightly around Hermione's wrist. Hermione's hair was mussed, and her dress was wrinkled and dirty, and—dear God above—she looked as if she might cry.

"Hermione?" Lucy whispered. What had happened? What had Richard done?

For a moment Hermione did nothing. She just stood there like a guilty puppy, her arm stretched limply in front of her, almost as if she'd forgotten that Lady Bridgerton still had her by the wrist.

"Hermione, what happened?"

Lady Bridgerton let go, and it was almost as if Hermione were water, let loose from a dam. "Oh, Lucy," she cried, her voice catching as she rushed forward. "I'm so sorry."

Lucy stood in shock, embracing her . . . but not quite. Hermione was clutching her like a child, but Lucy didn't quite know what to do with herself. Her arms felt foreign, not quite attached. She looked past Hermione's shoulder, down to the floor. The men had finally stopped thrashing about, but she wasn't sure she cared any longer.

"Hermione?" Lucy stepped back, far enough so that she could see her face. "What happened?"

"Oh, Lucy," Hermione said. *"I fluttered."*

An hour later, Hermione and Richard were engaged to be married. Lady Lucinda had been returned to the party, not that she would be able to concentrate on anything anyone was saying, but Kate had insisted.

Gregory was drunk. Or at the very least, doing his best to get there.

He supposed the night had brought a few small favors. He hadn't actually come across Lord Fennsworth and Miss Watson in flagrante delicto. Whatever they'd been doing— and Gregory was expending a great deal of energy to *not* imagine it—they had stopped when Kate had bellowed Fennsworth's name.

Even now, it all felt like a farce. Hermione had apologized, then Lucy had apologized, then *Kate* had apologized, which had seemed remarkably out of character until she finished her sentence with, "but you are, as of this moment, engaged to be married."

Fennsworth had looked delighted, the annoying little sod, and then he'd had the gall to give Gregory a triumphant little smirk.

Gregory had kneed him in the balls.

Not *too* hard.

It could have been an accident. Really. They were still on the floor, locked into a stalemate position. It was entirely plausible that his knee could have slipped.

Up.

Whatever the case, Fennsworth had grunted and collapsed. Gregory rolled to the side the second the earl's grip loosened, and he moved fluidly to his feet.

"So sorry," he'd said to the ladies. "I'm not certain what's come over him."

And that, apparently, was that. Miss Watson had apologized to him—after apologizing to first Lucy, then Kate, then Fennsworth, although heaven knew why, as he'd clearly won the evening.

"No apology is needed," Gregory had said tightly.

"No, but I—" She looked distressed, but Gregory didn't much care just then.

"I did have a lovely time at breakfast," she said to him. "I just wanted you to know that."

Why? Why would she *say* that? Did she think it would make him feel better?

Gregory hadn't said a word. He gave her a single nod, and then walked away. The rest of them could sort the details out themselves. He had no ties to the newly affianced couple, no responsibilities to them or to propriety. He didn't care when or how the families were informed.

It was not his concern. None of it was.

So he left. He had a bottle of brandy to locate.

And now here he was. In his brother's office, drinking his brother's liquor, wondering what the hell this all meant. Miss Watson was lost to him now, that much was clear. Unless of course he wanted to kidnap the girl.

Which he did not. Most assuredly. She'd probably squeal like an idiot the whole way. Not to mention the little matter of her possibly having given herself to Fennsworth. Oh, and

Gregory destroying his good reputation. There was that. One did not kidnap a gently bred female—especially one affianced to an earl—and expect to emerge with one's good name intact.

He wondered what Fennsworth had said to get her off alone.

He wondered what Hermione had meant when she'd said she fluttered.

He wondered if they would invite him to the wedding.

Hmmm. Probably. Lucy would insist upon it, wouldn't she? Stickler for propriety, that one. Good manners all around.

So what now? After so many years of feeling slightly aimless, of waiting waiting waiting for the pieces of his life to fall into place, he'd thought he finally had it all figured out. He'd found Miss Watson and he was ready to move forward and conquer.

The world had been bright and good and shining with promise.

Oh, very well, the world had been perfectly bright and good and shining with promise before. He hadn't been unhappy in the least. In fact, he hadn't really minded the waiting. He wasn't even sure he'd wanted to find his bride so soon. Just because he knew his true love existed didn't mean he wanted her right away.

He'd had a very pleasant existence before. Hell, most men would give their eyeteeth to trade places.

Not Fennsworth, of course.

Bloody little bugger was probably plotting every last detail of his wedding night that very minute.

Sodding little b—

He tossed back his drink and poured another.

So what did it mean? What did it mean when you met the woman who made you forget how to breathe and she up and married someone else? What was he supposed to do now?

Sit and wait until the back of someone else's neck sent him into raptures?

He took another sip. He'd had it with necks. They were highly overrated.

He sat back, plunking his feet on his brother's desk. Anthony would hate it, of course, but was he in the room? No. Had he just discovered the woman he'd hoped to marry in the arms of another man? No. More to the immediate point, had his face recently served as a punching bag for a surprisingly fit young earl?

Definitely not.

Gregory gingerly touched his left cheekbone. And his right eye.

He was not going to look attractive tomorrow, that was for sure.

But neither would Fennsworth, he thought happily.

Happily? He was happy? Who'd have thought?

He let out a long sigh, attempting to assess his sobriety. It had to be the brandy. Happiness was not on the agenda for the evening.

Although . . .

Gregory stood. Just as a test. Bit of scientific inquiry. Could he stand?

He could.

Could he walk?

Yes!

Ah, but could he walk straight?

Almost.

Hmmm. He wasn't nearly as foxed as he'd thought.

He might as well go out. No sense in wasting an unexpectedly fine mood.

He made his way to the door and put his hand on the knob. He stopped, cocking his head in thought.

It had to be the brandy. Really, there was no other explanation for it.

Eleven

*In which Our Hero does the one thing
he would never have anticipated.*

The irony of the evening was not lost on Lucy as she made her way back to her room.

Alone.

After Mr. Bridgerton's panic over Hermione's disappearance . . . after Lucy had been thoroughly scolded for running off by herself in the middle of what was turning out to be a somewhat raucous evening . . . after one couple had been forced to become engaged, for heaven's sake—no one had noticed when Lucy left the masked ball by herself.

She still couldn't believe that Lady Bridgerton had insisted upon returning her to the party. She had practically led Lucy back by the collar, depositing her in the care of someone or other's maiden aunt before retrieving Hermione's mother, who, it must be presumed, had no idea of the excitement that lay in wait for her.

And so Lucy had stood at the edge of the ballroom like a fool, staring at the rest of the guests, wondering how they could possibly not be aware of the events of the evening. It seemed inconceivable that three lives could be upended so completely, and the rest of the world was carrying on as usual.

No, she thought, rather sadly, actually—it was four; there was Mr. Bridgerton to be considered. His plans for the future had been decidedly different at the outset of the evening.

But no, everyone else appeared perfectly normal. They danced, they laughed, they ate sandwiches that were still distressingly mixed up on a single serving platter.

It was the strangest sight. Shouldn't something seem different? Shouldn't someone come up to Lucy and say, eyes quizzical—*You look somewhat altered. Ah, I know. Your brother must have seduced your closest friend.*

No one did, of course, and when Lucy caught sight of herself in a mirror, she was startled to see that she appeared entirely unchanged. A little tired, perhaps, maybe a little pale, but other than that, the same old Lucy.

Blond hair, not *too* blond. Blue eyes—again, not too blue. Awkwardly shaped mouth that never quite held still the way she wanted it to, and the same nondescript nose with the same seven freckles, including the one close to her eye that no one ever noticed but her.

It looked like Ireland. She didn't know why that interested her, but it always had.

She sighed. She'd never been to Ireland, and she probably never would. It seemed silly that this would suddenly bother her, as she didn't even want to go to Ireland.

But if she did wish to, she'd have to ask Lord Haselby, wouldn't she? It wasn't much different from having to ask Uncle Robert for permission to do, well, anything, but somehow . . .

She shook her head. Enough. It had been a strange night, and now she was in a strange mood, stuck in all her strangeness in the middle of a masked ball.

Clearly what she needed to do was go to bed.

And so, after thirty minutes of trying to look as if she were enjoying herself, it finally became apparent that the maiden aunt entrusted with her care did not quite understand the scope of the assignment. It wasn't difficult to deduce; when Lucy had attempted to speak to her, she had squinted through her mask and screeched, "Lift your chin, gel! Do I know you?"

Lucy decided that this was not an opportunity to be wasted, and so she had replied, "I'm sorry. I thought you were someone else," and walked right out of the ballroom.

Alone.

Really, it was almost funny.

Almost.

She wasn't foolish, however, and she'd traversed enough of the house that evening to know that while the guests had spilled to the west and south of the ballroom, they had not ventured to the north wing, where the family kept their private rooms. Strictly speaking, Lucy ought not to go that way, either, but after what she'd been through in the past few hours, she rather thought she deserved a bit of latitude.

But when she reached the long hall that led to the north, she saw a closed door. Lucy blinked with surprise; she'd never noticed a door there before. She supposed the Bridgertons normally left it open. Then her heart sank. Surely it would be locked—what was the purpose of a closed door if not to keep people out?

But the doorknob turned with ease. Lucy carefully shut the door behind her, practically melting with relief. She couldn't face going back to the party. She just wanted to crawl into bed, curl up under the covers, close her eyes, and sleep sleep sleep.

It sounded like heaven. And with any luck, Hermione would not yet have returned. Or better yet, her mother would insist upon her remaining overnight in her room.

Yes, privacy sounded extremely appealing just then.

It was dark as she walked, and quiet, too. After a minute or so, Lucy's eyes adjusted to the dim light. There were no lanterns or candles to illuminate the way, but a few doors had been left open, allowing pale shafts of moonlight to make parallelograms on the carpet. She walked slowly, and with an odd sort of deliberation, each step carefully measured and aimed, as if she were balancing on a thin line, stretching right down the center of the hall.

One, two . . .

Nothing out of the ordinary. She frequently counted her steps. And *always* on the stairs. She'd been surprised when she got to school and realized that other people did not.

. . . three, four . . .

The runner carpet looked monochromatic in the moonlight, but Lucy knew that the big diamonds were red, and the smaller ones were gold. She wondered if it were possible to step only on gold.

. . . five, six . . .

Or maybe red. Red would be easier. This wasn't a night to challenge herself.

. . . seven, eight, n—

"Oomph!"

She crashed into something. Or dear heaven, some*one.* She'd been looking down, following the red diamonds, and she hadn't seen . . . but shouldn't the other person have seen *her*?

Strong hands caught her by the arms and steadied her. And then—"Lady Lucinda?"

She froze. "Mr. Bridgerton?"

His voice was low and smooth in the darkness. "Now *this* is a coincidence."

She carefully disentangled herself—he had grabbed her by the arms to keep her from falling—and stepped back. He seemed very large in the close confines of the hall. "What are you doing here?" she asked.

He offered her a suspiciously easy grin. "What're *you* doing here?"

"Going to bed. This hallway seemed the best route," she explained, then added with a wry expression, "given my state of unaccompaniment."

He cocked his head. Scrunched his brow. Blinked. And finally: "Is that a word?"

For some reason that made her smile. Not her lips, exactly, but on the inside, where it counted. "I don't think so," she replied, "but really, I can't be bothered."

He smiled faintly, then motioned with his head to the room he must have just exited. "I was in my brother's office. Pondering."

"Pondering?"

"Quite a bit to ponder this evening, wouldn't you say?"

"Yes." She looked around the hall. Just in case there was someone else about, even though she was quite certain there was not. "I really shouldn't be here alone with you."

He nodded gravely. "I wouldn't want to disrupt your practical engagement."

Lucy hadn't even been thinking of *that*. "I meant after what happened with Hermione and—" And then it seemed somehow insensitive to spell it out. "Well, I'm sure you're aware."

"Indeed."

She swallowed, then tried to make it appear as if she weren't looking at his face to see if he was upset.

He just blinked, then he shrugged, and his expression was . . .

Nonchalant?

She chewed on her lip. No, that couldn't be. She must have misread him. He had been a man in love. He had told her so.

But this was none of her business. This required a certain measure of self-remindering (to add another word to her rapidly growing collection), but there it was. It was none of her business. Not one bit.

Well, except for the part about her brother and her best friend. No one could say that *that* didn't concern her. If it had just been Hermione, or just been Richard, there *might* have been an argument that she should keep her nose out of it, but with the both of them—well, clearly she was involved.

As regarded Mr. Bridgerton, however . . . *none* of her business.

She looked at him. His shirt collar was loosened, and she could see a tiny scrap of skin where she knew she ought not look.

None. None! Business. Of hers. None of it.

"Right," she said, ruining her determined tone with a decidedly involuntary cough. Spasm. Coughing spasm. Vaguely punctuated by: "Should be going."

But it came out more like . . . Well, it came out like something that she was quite certain could not be spelled with the twenty-six letters of the English language. Cyrillic might do it. Or possibly Hebrew.

"Are you all right?" he queried.

"Perfectly well," she gasped, then realized she was back to looking at that spot that wasn't even his neck. It was more his chest, which meant that it was more someplace decidedly unsuitable.

She yanked her eyes away, then coughed again, this time on purpose. Because she had to do *some*thing. Otherwise her eyes would be right back where they ought not be.

He watched her, almost a bit owlish in his regard, as she recovered. "Better?"

She nodded.

"I'm glad."

Glad? *Glad?* What did *that* mean?

He shrugged. "I hate it when that happens."

Just that he is a human being, Lucy you dolt. One who knows what a scratchy throat feels like.

She was going mad. She was quite certain of it.

"I should go," she blurted out.

"You should."

"I really should."

But she just stood there.

He was looking at her the *strangest* way. His eyes were narrowed—not in that angry way people usually associated with squinty eyes, but rather as if he were thinking exceptionally hard about something.

Pondering. That was it. He was pondering, just as he'd said.

Except that he was pondering *her*.

"Mr. Bridgerton?" she asked hesitantly. Not that she knew what she might inquire of him when he acknowledged her.

"Do you drink, Lady Lucinda?"

Drink? "I beg your pardon?"

He gave her a sheepish half-smile. "Brandy. I know where my brother keeps the good stuff."

"Oh." *Goodness.* "No, of course not."

"Pity," he murmured.

"I really couldn't," she added, because, well, she felt as if she had to explain.

Even though *of course* she did not drink spirits.

And *of course* he would know that.

He shrugged. "Don't know why I asked."

"I should go," she said.

But he didn't move.

And neither did she.

She wondered what brandy tasted like.

And she wondered if she would ever know.

"How did you enjoy the party?" he asked.

"The party?"

"Weren't you forced to go back?"

She nodded, rolling her eyes. "It was strongly suggested."

"Ah, so then she dragged you."

To Lucy's great surprise, she chuckled. "Rather close to it. And I didn't have my mask, which made me stick out a bit."

"Like a mushroom?"

"Like a—?"

He looked at her dress and nodded at the color. "A blue mushroom."

She glanced at herself and then at him. "Mr. Bridgerton, are you intoxicated?"

He leaned forward with a sly and slightly silly smile. He held up his hand, his thumb and index finger measuring an inch between them. "Just a little bit."

She eyed him dubiously. "Really?"

He looked down at his fingers with a furrowed brow, then added another inch or so to the space between them. "Well, perhaps this much."

Lucy didn't know much about men or much about spirits, but she knew enough about the two of them together to ask, "Isn't that always the case?"

"No." He lifted his brows and stared down his nose at her. "I usually know exactly how drunk I am."

Lucy had no idea what to say to that.

"But do you know, tonight I'm not sure." And he sounded surprised at that.

"Oh." Because she was at her articulate best this evening.

He smiled.

Her stomach felt strange.

She tried to smile back. She really should be going.

So naturally, she did not move.

His head tilted to the side and he let out a thoughtful exhale, and it occurred to her that he was doing exactly what he'd said he'd been doing—pondering. "I was thinking," he said slowly, "that given the events of the evening . . ."

She leaned forward expectantly. Why did people always let their voices trail off just when they were about to say something meaningful? "Mr. Bridgerton?" she nudged, because now he was just staring at some painting on the wall.

His lips twisted thoughtfully. "Wouldn't you think I ought to be a bit more upset?"

Her lips parted with surprise. "You're not upset?" How was that possible?

He shrugged. "Not as much as I should be, given that my heart practically stopped beating the first time I saw Miss Watson."

Lucy smiled tightly.

His head went back to vertical, and he looked at her and blinked—perfectly clear-eyed, as if he had just reached an obvious conclusion. "Which is why I suspect the brandy."

"I see." She didn't, of course, but what else could she say? "You . . . ah . . . you certainly seemed upset."

"I was cross," he explained.

"You're not any longer?"

He thought about that. "Oh, I'm still cross."

And Lucy felt the need to apologize. Which she *knew* was ridiculous, because none of this was her fault. But it was so ingrained in her, this need to apologize for everything. She couldn't help it. She wanted everyone to be happy. She always had. It was neater that way. More orderly.

"I'm sorry I didn't believe you about my brother," she said. "I didn't know. Truly, I didn't know."

He looked down at her, and his eyes were kind. She wasn't sure when it had happened, because a moment ago, he'd been flip and nonchalant. But now . . . he was different.

"I know you didn't," he said. "And there is no need to apologize."

"I was just as startled when we found them as you were."

"I wasn't very startled," he said. Gently, as if he were

trying to spare her feelings. Make her feel not such a dunce for not seeing the obvious.

She nodded. "No, I suppose you wouldn't have been. You realized what was happening, and I did not." And truly, she did feel like a half-wit. How could she have been so completely unaware? It was Hermione and her brother, for heaven's sake. If anyone were to detect a budding romance, it ought to have been she.

There was a pause—an awkward one—and then he said, "I will be well."

"Oh, of course you will," Lucy said reassuringly. And then *she* felt reassured, because it felt so lovely and *normal* to be the one trying to make everything right. That's what she did. She scurried about. She made sure everyone was happy and comfortable.

That was who she was.

But then he asked —oh *why* did he ask—"Will you?"

She said nothing.

"Be well," he clarified. "Will you be well"—he paused, then shrugged— "as well?"

"Of course," she said, a little too quickly.

She thought that was the end of it, but then he said, "Are you certain? Because you seemed a little . . ."

She swallowed, waiting uncomfortably for his assessment.

". . . overset," he finished.

"Well, I was surprised," she said, glad to have an answer. "And so naturally I was somewhat disconcerted." But she heard a slight stammer in her voice, and she was wondering which one of them she was trying convince.

He didn't say anything.

She swallowed. It was uncomfortable. *She* was uncomfortable, and yet she kept talking, kept explaining it all. And she said, "I'm not entirely certain what happened."

Still, he did not speak.

"I felt a little . . . Right here . . ." Her hand went to her chest, to the spot where she had felt so paralyzed. She looked up at him, practically begging him with her eyes to say something, to change the subject and end the conversation.

But he didn't. And the silence made her explain.

If he'd asked a question, said even one comforting word, she wouldn't have told him. But the silence was too much. It had to be filled.

"I couldn't move," she said, testing out the words as they left her lips. It was as if by speaking, she was finally confirming what had happened. "I reached the door, and I couldn't open it."

She looked up at him, searching for answers. But of course he did not have any.

"I—I don't know why I was so overcome." Her voice sounded breathy, nervous even. "I mean—it was Hermione. And my brother. I—I'm sorry for your pain, but this is all rather tidy, really. It's nice. Or at least it should be. Hermione will be my sister. I have always wanted a sister."

"They are occasionally entertaining." He said it with a half-smile, and it did make Lucy feel better. It was remarkable how much it did. And it was just enough to cause her words to spill out, this time without hesitation, without even a stammer.

"I could not believe they had gone off together. They should have said something. They should have told me that they cared for one another. I shouldn't have had to discover it that way. It's not right." She grabbed his arm and looked up at him, her eyes earnest and urgent. "It's not right, Mr. Bridgerton. It's not right."

He shook his head, but only slightly. His chin barely moved, and neither did his lips as he said, "No."

"Everything is changing," she whispered, and she wasn't talking about Hermione any longer. But it didn't matter, except that she didn't want to think anymore. Not about that.

Not about the future. "It's all changing," she whispered, "and I can't stop it."

Somehow his face was closer as he said, again, "No."

"It's too much." She couldn't stop looking at him, couldn't move her eyes from his, and she was still whispering it— "It's all too much"—when there was no more distance between them.

And his lips . . . they touched hers.

It was a kiss.

She had been kissed.

Her. Lucy. For once it was about her. She was at the center of her world. It was life. And it was happening to *her.*

It was remarkable, because it all felt so *big,* so transforming. And yet it was just a little kiss—soft, just a brush, so light it almost tickled. She felt a rush, a shiver, a tingly lightness in her chest. Her body seemed to come alive, and at the same time freeze into place, as if afraid that the wrong movement might make it all go away.

But she didn't want it to go away. God help her, she wanted this. She wanted this moment, and she wanted this memory, and she wanted . . .

She just *wanted.*

Everything. Anything she could get.

Anything she could feel.

His arms came around her, and she leaned in, sighing against his mouth as her body came into contact with his. This was it, she thought dimly. This was the music. This was a symphony.

This was a flutter. More than a flutter.

His mouth grew more urgent, and she opened to him, reveling in the warmth of his kiss. It spoke to her, called to her soul. His hands were holding her tighter, tighter, and her own snaked around him, finally resting where his hair met his collar.

She hadn't meant to touch him, hadn't even thought about

it. Her hands seemed to know where to go, how to find him, bring him closer. Her back arched, and the heat between them grew.

And the kiss went on . . . and on.

She felt it in her belly, she felt it in her toes. This kiss seemed to be everywhere, all across her skin, straight down to her soul.

"Lucy," he whispered, his lips finally leaving hers to blaze a hot trail along her jaw to her ear. "My God, Lucy."

She didn't want to speak, didn't want to do anything to break the moment. She didn't know what to call him, couldn't quite say *Gregory,* but *Mr. Bridgerton* was no longer right.

He was more than that now. More to her.

She'd been right earlier. Everything *was* changing. She didn't feel the same. She felt . . .

Awakened.

Her neck arched as he nipped at her earlobe, and she moaned—soft, incoherent sounds that slid from her lips like a song. She wanted to sink into him. She wanted to slide to the carpet and take him with her. She wanted the weight of him, the heat of him, and she wanted to *touch* him—she wanted to *do* something. She wanted to act. She wanted to be daring.

She moved her hands to his hair, sinking her fingers into the silky strands. He let out a little groan, and just the sound of his voice was enough to make her heart beat faster. He was doing remarkable things to her neck—his lips, his tongue, his teeth—she didn't know which, but one of them was setting her on fire.

His lips moved down the column of her throat, raining fire along her skin. And his hands—they had moved. They were cupping her, pressing her against him, and everything felt so *urgent.*

This was no longer about what she wanted. It was about what she needed.

Was this what had happened to Hermione? Had she innocently gone for a stroll with Richard and then . . . *this*?

Lucy understood it now. She understood what it meant to want something you knew was wrong, to allow it to happen even though it could lead to scandal and—

And then she said it. She tried it. "Gregory," she whispered, testing the name on her lips. It felt like an endearment, an intimacy, almost as if she could change the world and everything around her with one single word.

If she said his name, then he could be hers, and she could forget everything else, she could forget—

Haselby.

Dear God, she was engaged. It was not just an understanding any longer. The papers had been signed. And she was—

"No," she said, pressing her hands on his chest. "No, I can't."

He allowed her to push him away. She turned her head, afraid to look at him. She knew . . . if she saw his face . . .

She was weak. She wouldn't be able to resist.

"Lucy," he said, and she realized that the sound of him was just as hard to bear as his face would have been.

"I can't do this." She shook her head, still not looking at him. "It's wrong."

"Lucy." And this time she felt his fingers on her chin, gently urging her to face him.

"Please allow me to escort you upstairs," he said.

"No!" It came out too loud, and she stopped, swallowing uncomfortably. "I can't risk it," she said, finally allowing her eyes to meet his.

It was a mistake. The way he was looking at her— His eyes were stern, but there was more. A hint of softness, a touch of warmth. And curiosity. As if . . . As if he wasn't quite sure what he was seeing. As if he were looking at her for the very first time.

Dear heaven, that was the part she couldn't bear. She

wasn't even sure why. Maybe it was because he was looking at *her*. Maybe it was because the expression was so . . . *him*. Maybe it was both.

Maybe it didn't matter.

But it terrified her all the same.

"I will not be deterred," he said. "Your safety is my responsibility."

Lucy wondered what had happened to the slightly intoxicated, rather jolly man with whom she'd been conversing just moments earlier. In his place was someone else entirely. Someone quite in charge.

"Lucy," he said, and it wasn't exactly a question, more of a reminder. He would have his way in this, and she would have to acknowledge it.

"My room isn't far," she said, trying one last time, anyway. "Truly, I don't need your assistance. It's just up those stairs."

And down the hall and around a corner, but he didn't need to know that.

"I will walk you to the stairs, then."

Lucy knew better than to argue. He would not relent. His voice was quiet, but it had an edge she wasn't quite certain she'd heard there before.

"And I will remain there until you reach your room."

"That's not necessary."

He ignored her. "Knock three times when you do so."

"I'm not going to—"

"If I don't hear your knock, I will come upstairs and personally assure myself of your welfare."

He crossed his arms, and as she looked at him she wondered if he'd have been the same man had he been the firstborn son. There was an unexpected imperiousness to him. He would have made a fine viscount, she decided, although she wasn't certain she would have liked him so well. Lord Bridgerton quite frankly terrified her, although he must have had a softer side, adoring his wife and children as he so obviously did.

Still . . .

"Lucy."

She swallowed and grit her teeth, hating to have to admit that she'd lied. "Very well," she said grudgingly. "If you wish to hear my knock, you had better come to the top of the stairs."

He nodded and followed her, all the way to the top of the seventeen steps.

"I will see you tomorrow," he said.

Lucy said nothing. She had a feeling that would be unwise.

"I will see you tomorrow," he repeated.

She nodded, since it seemed to be required, and she didn't see how she was meant to avoid him, anyway.

And she wanted to see him. She shouldn't want to, and she *knew* she shouldn't do it, but she couldn't help herself.

"I suspect we will be leaving," she said. "I'm meant to return to my uncle, and Richard . . . Well, he will have matters to attend to."

But her explanations did not change his expression. His face was still resolute, his eyes so firmly fixed on hers that she shivered.

"I will see you in the morning," was all he said.

She nodded again, and then left, as quickly as she could without breaking into a run. She rounded the corner and finally saw her room, just three doors down.

But she stopped. Right there at the corner, just out of his sight.

And she knocked three times.

Just because she could.

Twelve

In which nothing is resolved.

When Gregory sat down to breakfast the next day, Kate was already there, grim-faced and weary.

"I'm so sorry," was the first thing she said when she took the seat next to him.

What *was* it with apologies? he wondered. They were positively rampant these past few days.

"I know you had hoped—"

"It is nothing," he interrupted, flicking a glance at the plate of food she'd left on the other side of the table. Two seats down.

"But—"

"Kate," he said, and even he didn't quite recognize his own voice. He sounded older, if that was possible. Harder.

She fell silent, her lips still parted, as if her words had been frozen on her tongue.

"It's nothing," he said again, and turned back to his eggs. He didn't want to talk about it, he didn't want listen to explanations. What was done was done, and there was nothing he could do about it.

Gregory was not certain what Kate was doing while he concentrated on his food—presumably looking around the room, gauging whether any of the guests could hear their conversation. Every now and then he heard her shifting in her seat, unconsciously changing her position in anticipation of saying something.

He moved on to his bacon.

And then—he knew she would not be able to keep her mouth shut for long—"But are you—"

He turned. Looked at her hard. And said one word.

"Don't."

For a moment her expression remained blank. Then her eyes widened, and one corner of her mouth tilted up. Just a little. "How old were you when we met?" she asked.

What the devil was she about? "I don't know," he said impatiently, trying to recall her wedding to his brother. There had been a bloody lot of flowers. He'd been sneezing for weeks, it seemed. "Thirteen, perhaps. Twelve?"

She regarded him curiously. "It must be difficult, I think, to be so very much younger than your brothers."

He set his fork down.

"Anthony and Benedict and Colin—they are all right in a row. Like ducks, I've always thought, although I'm not so foolish to say so. And then—hmmm. How many years between you and Colin?"

"Ten."

"Is that all?" Kate looked surprised, which he wasn't sure he found particularly complimentary.

"It's a full six years from Colin to Anthony," she continued, pressing one finger against her chin as if that were to indicate deep thought. "A bit more than that, actually. But I suppose they are more commonly lumped together, what with Benedict in the middle."

He waited.

"Well, no matter," she said briskly. "Everyone finds his place in life, after all. Now then——"

He stared at her in amazement. How could she change the subject like that? Before he had any idea what she was talking about.

"——I suppose I should inform you of the remainder of the events of last night. After you left." Kate sighed—groaned really—shaking her head. "Lady Watson was a bit put out that her daughter had not been closely supervised, although really, whose fault is that? And *then* she was put out that Miss Watson's London season was over before she had a chance to spend money on a new wardrobe. Because, after all, it is not as if she will make a debut now."

Kate paused, waiting for Gregory to say something. He lifted his brows in the tiniest of shrugs, just enough to say that he had nothing to add to the conversation.

Kate gave him one more second, then continued with: "Lady Watson did come about rather quickly when it was pointed out that Fennsworth is an earl, however young."

She paused, twisting her lips. "He *is* rather young, isn't he?"

"Not so much younger than I am," Gregory said, even though he'd thought Fennsworth the veriest infant the night before.

Kate appeared to give that some thought. "No," she said slowly, "there's a difference. He's not . . . Well, I don't know. Anyway——"

Why did she keep changing the subject just when she started to say something he actually wanted to hear?

"——the betrothal is done," she continued, picking up speed with that, "and I believe that all parties involved are content."

Gregory supposed he did not count as an involved party.

But then again, he felt more irritation than anything else. He did not like being beaten. At anything.

Well, except for shooting. He'd long since given up on that.

How was it that it never occurred to him, not even once, that he might not win Miss Watson in the end? He had accepted that it would not be easy, but to him, it was a fait accompli. Predestined.

He'd actually been making progress with her. She had laughed with him, by gad. Laughed. Surely that had to have meant something.

"They are leaving today," Kate said. "All of them. Separately, of course. Lady and Miss Watson are off to prepare for the wedding, and Lord Fennsworth is taking his sister home. It's why he came, after all."

Lucy. He had to see Lucy.

He'd been trying not to think about her.

With mixed results.

But she was there, all the time, hovering at the back of his mind, even while he was stewing over the loss of Miss Watson.

Lucy. It was impossible now to think of her as Lady Lucinda. Even if he hadn't kissed her, she would be Lucy. It was who she was. It fit her perfectly.

But he *had* kissed her. And it had been magnificent.

But most of all, unexpected.

Everything about it had surprised him, even the very fact that he'd done it. It was Lucy. He wasn't supposed to kiss *Lucy.*

But she'd been holding his arm. And her eyes—what was it about her eyes? She'd been looking up at him, searching for something.

Searching *him* for something.

He hadn't meant to do it. It just happened. He'd felt pulled, inexorably tugged toward her, and the space between them had grown smaller and smaller . . .

And then there she was. In his arms.

He'd wanted to melt to the floor, lose himself in her and never let go.

He'd wanted to kiss her until they both fell apart from the passion of it.

He'd wanted to—

Well. He'd wanted to do quite a bit, to tell the truth. But he'd also been a little bit drunk.

Not very. But enough to doubt the veracity of his response.

And he'd been angry. And off-balance.

Not with Lucy, of course, but he was quite certain it had impaired his judgment.

Still, he should see her. She was a gently bred young lady. One didn't kiss one of *those* without making explanations. And he ought to apologize as well, although that didn't really feel like what he wanted to do.

But it was what he *should* do.

He looked up at Kate. "When are they leaving?"

"Lady and Miss Watson? This afternoon, I believe."

No, he almost blurted out, *I meant Lady Lucinda.* But he caught himself and kept his voice unconcerned as he said instead, "And Fennsworth?"

"Soon, I think. Lady Lucinda has already been down for breakfast." Kate thought for a moment. "I believe Fennsworth said he wished to be home by supper. But they can make the journey in one day. They don't live too very far away."

"Near Dover," Gregory murmured absently.

Kate's brow furrowed. "I think you're right."

Gregory frowned at his food. He'd thought to wait here for Lucy; she would not be able to miss breakfast. But if she'd already eaten, then the time of her departure would be growing near.

And he needed to find her.

He stood. A bit abruptly—he knocked his thigh against the edge of the table, causing Kate to look up at him with a startled expression.

"You're not going to finish your breakfast?" she asked.

He shook his head. "I'm not hungry."

She looked at him with patent disbelief. She'd been a member of the family for over ten years, after all. "How is that possible?"

He ignored the question. "I bid you a lovely morning."

"Gregory?"

He turned. He didn't want to, but there was a slight edge to her voice, just enough for him to know he needed to pay attention.

Kate's eyes filled with compassion—and apprehension. "You're not going to seek out Miss Watson, are you?"

"No," he said, and it was almost funny, because that was the last thing on his mind.

Lucy stared at her packed trunks, feeling tired. And sad. And confused.

And heaven knew what else.

Wrung out. That was how she felt. She'd watched the maids with the bath towels, how they twisted and twisted to wring out every last drop of water.

So it had come to this.

She was a bath towel.

"Lucy?"

It was Hermione, quietly entering their room. Lucy had already been asleep when Hermione had returned the night before, and Hermione had been asleep when Lucy had left for breakfast.

When Lucy had returned, Hermione had been gone. In many ways, Lucy had been grateful for that.

"I was with my mother," Hermione explained. "We depart this afternoon."

Lucy nodded. Lady Bridgerton had found her at breakfast and informed her of everyone's plans. By the time she had returned to her bedchamber, her belongings were all packed and ready to be loaded onto a carriage.

That was it, then.

"I wanted to talk with you," Hermione said, perching on the edge of the bed but keeping a respectful distance from Lucy. "I wanted to explain."

Lucy's gaze remained fixed on her trunks. "There is nothing to explain. I'm very happy that you will be marrying Richard." She managed a weary smile. "You shall be my sister now."

"You don't sound happy."

"I'm tired."

Hermione was quiet for a moment, and then, when it was apparent that Lucy was done speaking, she said, "I wanted to make sure that you knew that I was not keeping secrets from you. I would never do that. I hope you know I would never do that."

Lucy nodded, because she did know, even if she had felt abandoned, and perhaps even a little betrayed the night before.

Hermione swallowed, and then her jaw tightened, and then she took a breath. And Lucy knew in that moment that she had been rehearsing her words for hours, tossing them back and forth in her mind, looking for the exact right combination to say what she felt.

It was exactly what Lucy would have done, and yet somehow it made her want to cry.

But for all Hermione's practice, when she spoke she was still changing her mind, choosing new words and phrases. "I really did love— No. No," she said, talking more to herself than to Lucy. "What I mean is, I really did *think* I loved Mr. Edmonds. But I reckon I didn't. Because first there was Mr. Bridgerton, and then . . . Richard."

Lucy looked sharply up. "What do you mean, first there was Mr. Bridgerton?"

"I . . . I'm not sure, actually," Hermione answered, flustered by the question. "When I shared breakfast with him it was as if I was awakened from a long, strange dream. Do you remember, I spoke to you about it? Oh, I didn't hear music or any some such, and I did not even feel . . . Well, I don't know how to explain it, but even though I was not in any way *overcome*—as I was with Mr. Edmonds—I . . . I wondered. About him. And whether maybe I *could* feel something. If I tried. And I did not see how I could possibly be in love with Mr. Edmonds if Mr. Bridgerton made me wonder."

Lucy nodded. Gregory Bridgerton made her wonder, too. But not about whether she could. That she knew. She just wanted to know how to make herself *not.*

But Hermione did not see her distress. Or perhaps Lucy hid it well. Either way, Hermione just continued with her explanation. "And then . . ." she said, "with Richard . . . I'm not certain how it happened, but we were walking, and we were talking, and it all felt so pleasant. But more than pleasant," she hastily added. "Pleasant sounds dull, and it wasn't that. I felt . . . right. Like I'd come home."

Hermione smiled, almost helplessly, as if she couldn't quite believe her good fortune. And Lucy was glad for her. She really was. But she wondered how it was possible to feel so happy and so sad at the same time. Because she was never going to feel that way. And even if she hadn't believed in it before, she did now. And that made it so much worse.

"I am sorry if I did not appear happy for you last night," Lucy said softly. "I am. Very much so. It was the shock, that is all. So many changes all at one time."

"But *good* changes, Lucy," Hermione said, her eyes shining. "Good changes."

Lucy wished she could share her confidence. She wanted to embrace Hermione's optimism, but instead she felt overwhelmed. But she could not say that to her friend. Not now, when she was glowing with happiness.

So Lucy smiled and said, "You will have a good life with Richard." And she meant it, too.

Hermione grasped her hand with both of her own, squeezing tightly with all the friendship and excitement inside of her. "Oh, Lucy, I know it. I have known him for so long, and he's *your* brother, so he has always made me feel safe. Comfortable, really. I don't have to worry about what he thinks of me. You've surely already told him everything, good and bad, and he still believes I'm rather fine."

"He doesn't know you can't dance," Lucy admitted.

"He doesn't?" Hermione shrugged. "I will tell him, then. Perhaps he can teach me. Does he have any talent for it?"

Lucy shook her head.

"Do you see?" Hermione said, her smile wistful and hopeful and joyful all at once. "We are perfectly matched. It has all become so clear. It is so easy to talk with him, and last night . . . I was laughing, and he was laughing, and it just felt so . . . *lovely*. I can't really explain."

But she didn't have to explain. Lucy was terrified that she knew exactly what Hermione meant.

"And then we were in the orangery, and it was so beautiful with the moonlight shining through the glass. It was all dappled and blurry and . . . and then I looked at him." Hermione's eyes grew misty and unfocused, and Lucy knew that she was lost in the memory.

Lost and happy.

"I looked at him," Hermione said again, "and he was looking down at me. I could not look away. I simply could not. And then we kissed. It was . . . I didn't even think about it. It just happened. It was just the most natural, wonderful thing in the world."

Lucy nodded sadly.

"I realized that I didn't understand before. With Mr. Edmonds—oh, I thought myself so violently in love with him, but I did not know what love was. He was so handsome, and he made me feel shy and excited, but I never longed to kiss him. I never looked at him and leaned in, not because I wanted to, but just because . . . because . . ."

Because what? Lucy wanted to scream. But even if she'd had the inclination, she lacked the energy.

"Because it was where I belonged," Hermione finished softly, and she looked amazed, as if she hadn't herself realized it until that very moment.

Lucy suddenly began to feel very queer. Her muscles felt twitchy, and she had the most insane desire to wrap her hands into fists. What did she *mean*? Why was she saying this? Everyone had spent so much time telling her that love was a thing of magic, something wild and uncontrollable that came like a thunderstorm.

And now it was something else? It was just *comfort*? Something peaceful? Something that actually sounded *nice*? "What happened to hearing music?" she heard herself demand. "To seeing the back of his head and *knowing*?"

Hermione gave her a helpless shrug. "I don't know. But I shouldn't trust it, if I were you."

Lucy closed her eyes in agony. She didn't need Hermione's warning. She would never have trusted that sort of feeling. She wasn't the sort who memorized love sonnets, and she never would be. But the other kind—the one with the laughing, the comfort, the feeling *nice*—that she would trust in a heartbeat.

And dear God, that was what she'd felt with Mr. Bridgerton.

All that and music, too.

Lucy felt the blood drain from her face. She'd heard *music* when she kissed him. It had been a veritable symphony, with soaring crescendos and pounding percussion and even that pulsing little underbeat one never noticed until it crept up and took over the rhythm of one's heart.

Lucy had floated. She'd tingled. She'd felt all those things Hermione had said she'd felt with Mr. Edmonds—and everything she'd said she felt with Richard, as well.

All with one person.

She was in love with him. She was in love with Gregory Bridgerton. The realization couldn't have been more clear . . . or more cruel.

"Lucy?" Hermione asked hesitantly. And then again— "Luce?"

"When is the wedding?" Lucy asked abruptly. Because changing the subject was the only thing she could do. She turned, looked directly at Hermione and held her gaze for the first time in the conversation. "Have you begun making plans? Will it be in Fenchley?"

Details. Details were her salvation. They always had been.

Hermione's expression grew confused, then concerned, and then she said, "I . . . no, I believe it is to be at the Abbey. It's a bit more grand. And . . . are you certain you're all right?"

"Quite well," Lucy said briskly, and she *sounded* like herself, so maybe that would mean she would begin to feel that way, too. "But you did not mention when."

"Oh. Soon. I'm told there were people near the orangery last night. I am not certain what was heard—or repeated—but the whispering has begun, so we will need to have it all settled posthaste." Hermione gave her a sweet smile. "I don't mind. And I don't think Richard does, either."

Lucy wondered which of them would reach the altar first. She hoped it was Hermione.

A knock sounded on the door. It was a maid, followed by two footmen, there to remove Lucy's trunks.

"Richard desires an early start," Lucy explained, even though she had not seen her brother since the events of the previous night. Hermione probably knew more about their plans than she did.

"Think of it, Lucy," Hermione said, walking her to the door. "We shall both be countesses. I of Fennsworth, and you of Davenport. We shall cut quite a dash, we two."

Lucy knew that she was trying to cheer her up, so she used every ounce of her energy to force her smile to reach her eyes as she said, "It will be great fun, won't it?"

Hermione took her hand and squeezed it. "Oh, it will, Lucy. You shall see. We are at the dawn of a new day, and it will be bright, indeed."

Lucy gave her friend a hug. It was the only way she could think to hide her face from view.

Because there was no way she could feign a smile this time.

Gregory found her just in time. She was in the front drive, surprisingly alone, save for the handful of servants scurrying about. He could see her profile, chin tipped slightly up as she watched her trunks being loaded onto the carriage. She looked . . . composed. Carefully held.

"Lady Lucinda," he called out.

She went quite still before she turned. And when she did, her eyes looked pained.

"I am glad I caught you," he said, although he was no longer sure that he was. She was not happy to see him. He had not been expecting that.

"Mr. Bridgerton," she said. Her lips were pinched at the corners, as if she thought she was smiling.

There were a hundred different things he could have said,

so of course he chose the least meaningful and most obvious. "You're leaving."

"Yes," she said, after the barest of pauses. "Richard desires an early start."

Gregory looked around. "Is he here?"

"Not yet. I imagine he is saying goodbye to Hermione."

"Ah. Yes." He cleared his throat. "Of course."

He looked at her, and she looked at him, and they were quiet.

Awkward.

"I wanted to say that I am sorry," he said.

She . . . she didn't smile. He wasn't sure what her expression was, but it wasn't a smile. "Of course," she said.

Of course? *Of course?*

"I accept." She looked slightly over his shoulder. "Please, do not think of it again."

It was what she had to say, to be sure, but it still niggled at Gregory. He had kissed her, and it had been stupendous, and if he wished to remember it, he damned well would.

"Will I see you in London?" he asked.

She looked up at him then, her eyes finally meeting his. She was searching for something. She was searching for something in him, and he did not think she found it.

She looked too somber, too tired.

Too not like *her*.

"I expect you shall," she replied. "But it won't be the same. I am engaged, you see."

"*Practically* engaged," he reminded her, smiling.

"No." She shook her head, slow and resigned. "I truly am now. That is why Richard came to fetch me home. My uncle has finalized the agreements. I believe the banns will be read soon. It is done."

His lips parted with surprise. "I see," he said, and his mind raced. And raced and raced, and got absolutely nowhere. "I wish you the best," he said, because what else could he say?

She nodded, then tilted her head toward the wide green lawn in front of the house. "I believe I shall take a turn around the garden. I have a long ride ahead of me."

"Of course," he said, giving her a polite bow. She did not wish for his company. She could not have made herself more clear if she had spoken the words.

"It has been lovely knowing you," she said. Her eyes caught his, and for the first time in the conversation, he *saw* her, saw right down to everything inside of her, weary and bruised.

And he saw that she was saying goodbye.

"I am sorry . . ." She stopped, looked to the side. At a stone wall. "I am sorry that everything did not work out as you had hoped."

I'm not, he thought, and he realized that it was true. He had a sudden flash of his life married to Hermione Watson, and he was . . .

Bored.

Good God, how was it he was only just now realizing it? He and Miss Watson were not suited at all, and in truth, he had made a narrow escape.

He wasn't likely to trust his judgment next time when it came to matters of the heart, but that seemed far more preferable to a dull marriage. He supposed he had Lady Lucinda to thank for that, although he wasn't sure why. She had not prevented his marriage to Miss Watson; in fact, she had encouraged it at every turn.

But somehow she was responsible for his coming to his senses. If there was any one true thing to be known that morning, that was it.

Lucy motioned to the lawn again. "I shall take that stroll," she said.

He nodded his greeting and watched her as she walked off. Her hair was smoothed neatly into a bun, the blond strands catching the sunlight like honey and butter.

He waited for quite some time, not because he expected her to turn around, or even because he hoped she would.

It was just in case.

Because she might. She might turn around, and she might have something to say to him, and then he might reply, and she might—

But she didn't. She kept on walking. She did not turn, did not look back, and so he spent his final minutes watching the back of her neck. And all he could think was—

Something is not right.

But for the life of him, he did not know what.

Thirteen

In which Our Heroine sees a glimpse of her future.

One month later

The food was exquisite, the table settings magnificent, the surroundings beyond opulent.

Lucy, however, was miserable.

Lord Haselby and his father, the Earl of Davenport, had come to Fennsworth House in London for supper. It had been Lucy's idea, a fact which she now found painfully ironic. Her wedding was a mere week away, and yet until this night she hadn't even seen her future husband. Not since the wedding had shifted from probable to imminent, anyway.

She and her uncle had arrived in London a fortnight earlier, and after eleven days had passed without a glimpse of her intended, she had approached her uncle and asked if they might arrange some sort of gathering. He had looked rather irritated, although not, Lucy was fairly certain, because he thought the request foolish. No, her mere presence was all it required to bring on such an expression. She was standing in front of him, and he had been forced to look up.

Uncle Robert did not like to be interrupted.

But he apparently saw the wisdom in allowing an affianced couple to share a word or two before they met at a church, so he had curtly told her that he would make the arrangements.

Buoyed by her small victory, Lucy had also asked if she might attend one of the many social events that were taking place practically right outside her door. The London social season had begun, and each night Lucy stood at her window, watching the elegant carriages roll by. Once there had been a party directly across St. James's Square from Fennsworth House. The line of carriages had snaked around the square, and Lucy had snuffed the candles in her room so that she would not be silhouetted in the window as she watched the proceedings. A number of partygoers had grown impatient with the wait, and since the weather was so fine, they had disembarked on her side of the square and walked the rest of the way.

Lucy had told herself that she just wanted to see the gowns, but in her heart she knew the truth.

She was looking for Mr. Bridgerton.

She didn't know what she would do if she actually *saw* him. Duck out of sight, she supposed. He had to know that this was her home, and surely he would be curious enough to glance at the façade, even if her presence in London was not a widely known fact.

But he didn't attend that party, or if he did, his carriage had deposited him right at the front doorstep.

Or maybe he wasn't in London at all. Lucy had no way of knowing. She was trapped in the house with her uncle and her aging, slightly deaf aunt Harriet, who had been brought in for the sake of propriety. Lucy left the house for trips to the dressmaker and walks in the park, but other than that, she was completely on her own, with an uncle who did not speak, and an aunt who could not hear.

So she was not generally privy to gossip. About Gregory Bridgerton or anyone, for that matter.

And even on the odd occasion when she did see someone she knew, she couldn't very well *ask* after him. People would think she was interested, which of course she was, but no one, absolutely no one, could ever know of it.

She was marrying someone else. In a week. And even if she weren't, Gregory Bridgerton had shown no sign that he might be interested in taking Haselby's place.

He had kissed her, that was true, and he had seemed concerned for her welfare, but if he was of the belief that a kiss demanded a proposal of marriage, he had made no indication. He had not known that her engagement to Haselby had been finalized—not when he'd kissed her, and not the following morning when they had stood awkwardly in the drive. He could only have believed that he was kissing a girl who was entirely unattached. One simply did not *do* such a thing unless one was ready and willing to step up to the altar.

But not Gregory. When she *had* finally told him, he hadn't looked stricken. He hadn't even looked mildly upset. There had been no pleas to reconsider, or to try to find a way out of it. All she'd seen in his face—and she had *looked,* oh, how she'd looked—was . . . nothing.

His face, his eyes—they had been almost blank. Maybe a touch of surprise, but no sorrow or relief. Nothing to indicate that her engagement meant anything to him, one way or another.

Oh, she did not think him a cad, and she was quite sure he would have married her, had it been necessary. But no one had seen them, and thus, as far as the rest of the world was concerned, it had never happened.

There were no consequences. For either of them.

But wouldn't it have been nice if he'd seemed just a little bit upset? He'd kissed her, and the earth had *shook*—surely he'd felt it. Shouldn't he have wanted more? Shouldn't he have wanted, if not to marry her, then at least the possibility of doing so?

Instead he'd said, "I wish you the best," and it had sounded so final. As she'd stood there, watching her trunks being loaded into the carriage, she had *felt* her heart breaking. Felt it, right there in her chest. It had *hurt*. And as she walked away, it had just got worse, pressing and squeezing until she thought it would steal her very breath. She'd begun to move faster—as fast as she could while maintaining a normal gait, and then finally she rounded a corner and collapsed onto a bench, letting her face fall helplessly into her hands.

And prayed that no one saw her.

She'd wanted to look back. She'd wanted to steal one last glance at him and memorize his stance—that singular way he held himself when he stood, hands behind his back, legs slightly apart. Lucy knew that hundreds of men stood the same way, but on him it was different. He could be facing the other direction, yards and yards away, and she would know it was he.

He walked differently, too, a little bit loose and easygoing, as if a small part of his heart was still seven years old. It was in the shoulders, the hips maybe—the sort of thing almost no one would notice, but Lucy had always paid attention to details.

But she hadn't looked back. It would have only made it worse. He probably wasn't watching her, but if he were . . . and he saw her turn around . . .

It would have been devastating. She wasn't sure why, but it would. She didn't want him to see her face. She had managed to remain composed through their conversation, but once she turned away, she had felt herself change. Her lips had parted, and she'd sucked in a huge breath, and it was as if she had hollowed herself out.

It was awful. And she didn't want him to see it.

Besides, he wasn't interested. He had all but fallen over himself to apologize for the kiss. She knew it was what he had to do; society dictated it (or if not that, then a quick trip to the altar). But it hurt all the same. She'd wanted to think he'd felt at least a tiny fraction of what she had. Not that anything could come of it, but it would have made her feel better.

Or maybe worse.

And in the end, it didn't matter. It didn't matter what her heart did or didn't know, because she couldn't do anything with it. What was the point of feelings if one couldn't use them toward a tangible end? She had to be practical. It was what she was. It was her only constant in a world that was spinning far too quickly for her comfort.

But still—here in London—she wanted to see him. It was silly and it was foolish and it was most certainly unadvisable, but she wanted it all the same. She didn't even have to speak with him. In fact she probably *shouldn't* speak with him. But a glimpse . . .

A glimpse wouldn't hurt anyone.

But when she had asked Uncle Robert if she might attend a party, he had refused, stating that there was little point in wasting time or money on the season when she was already in possession of the desired outcome—a proposal of marriage.

Furthermore, he informed her, Lord Davenport wished for Lucy to be introduced to society as Lady Haselby, not as Lady Lucinda Abernathy. Lucy wasn't sure why this was important, especially as quite a few members of society already knew her as Lady Lucinda Abernathy, both from school and the "polishing" she and Hermione had undergone that spring. But Uncle Robert had indicated (in his inimitable manner, that is to say, without a word) that the interview was over, and he had already returned his attention to the papers on his desk.

For a brief moment, Lucy had remained in place. If she said his name, he might look up. Or he might not. But if he did, his patience would be thin, and she would feel like an annoyance, and she wouldn't receive any answers to her questions, anyway.

So she just nodded and left the room. Although heaven only knew why she had bothered to nod. Uncle Robert never looked back up once he dismissed her.

And now here she was, at the supper she herself had requested, and she was wishing—fervently—that she had never opened her mouth. Haselby was fine, perfectly pleasant even. But his father . . .

Lucy prayed that she would not be living at the Davenport residence. Please *please* let Haselby have his own home.

In Wales. Or maybe France.

Lord Davenport had, after complaining about the weather, the House of Commons, and the opera (which he found, respectively, rainy, full of ill-bred idiots, and *by God not even in English!*) then turned his critical eye on her.

It had taken all of Lucy's fortitude not to back up as he descended upon her. He looked rather like an overweight fish, with bulbous eyes and thick, fleshy lips. Truly, Lucy would not have been surprised if he had torn off his shirt to reveal gills and scales.

And then . . . *eeeeuhh* . . . she shuddered just to remember it. He stepped close, so close that his hot, stale breath puffed around her face.

She stood rigidly, with the perfect posture that had been drilled into her since birth.

He told her to show her teeth.

It had been humiliating.

Lord Davenport had inspected her like a broodmare, even going so far as to place his hands on her hips to measure them for potential childbirth! Lucy had gasped and glanced frantically at her uncle for help, but he was stone-faced and staring resolutely at a spot that was not her face.

And now that they had sat to eat . . . good heavens! Lord Davenport was *interrogating* her. He had asked every conceivable question about her health, covering areas she was quite certain were not suitable for mixed company, and then, just when she thought the worst of it was over—

"Can you do your tables?"

Lucy blinked. "I beg your pardon?"

"Your tables," he said impatiently. "Sixes, sevens."

For a moment Lucy could not speak. He wanted her to do *maths*?

"Well?" he demanded.

"Of course," she stammered. She looked again to her uncle, but he was maintaining his expression of determined disinterest.

"Show me." Davenport's mouth settled into a firm line in his jowly cheeks. "Sevens will do."

"I . . . ah . . ." Utterly desperate, she even tried to catch Aunt Harriet's eye, but she was completely oblivious to the proceedings and in fact had not uttered a word since the evening had begun.

"Father," Haselby interrupted, "surely you—"

"It's all about breeding," Lord Davenport said curtly. "The future of the family lies in her womb. We have a right to know what we're getting."

Lucy's lips parted in shock. Then she realized she'd moved a hand to her abdomen. Hastily she allowed it to drop. Her eyes shot back and forth between father and son, not sure whether she was supposed to speak.

"The last thing you want is a woman who thinks too much," Lord Davenport was saying, "but she ought to be able to do something as basic as multiplication. Good God, son, think of the ramifications."

Lucy looked to Haselby. He looked back. Apologetically. She swallowed and shut her eyes for a fortifying moment.

When she opened them, Lord Davenport was staring straight at her, and his lips were parting, and she realized he was going to speak again, which she positively could not bear, and—

"Seven, fourteen, twenty-one," she blurted out, cutting him off as best she could. "Twenty-eight, thirty-five, forty-two . . ."

She wondered what he would do if she botched it. Would he call off the marriage?

". . . forty-nine, fifty-six . . ."

It was tempting. So tempting.

". . . sixty-three, seventy, seventy-seven . . ."

She looked at her uncle. He was eating. He wasn't even looking at her.

". . . eighty-two, eighty-nine . . ."

"Eh, that's enough," Lord Davenport announced, coming in right atop the *eighty-two*.

The giddy feeling in her chest quickly drained away. She'd rebelled—possibly for the first time in her entire life—and no one had noticed. She'd waited too long.

She wondered what else she should have done already.

"Well done," Haselby said, with an encouraging smile.

Lucy managed a little smile in return. He really wasn't bad. In fact, if not for Gregory, she would have thought him a rather fine choice. Haselby's hair was perhaps a little thin, and actually *he* was a little thin as well, but that wasn't really anything to complain about. Especially as his personality—surely the most important aspect of any man—was perfectly agreeable. They had managed a short conversation before supper while his father and her uncle were discussing politics, and he had been quite charming. He'd even made a dry, sideways sort of joke about his father, accompanied by a roll of the eyes that had made Lucy chuckle.

Truly, she shouldn't complain.

And she didn't. She wouldn't. She just wished for something else.

"I trust you acquitted yourself acceptably at Miss Moss's?" Lord Davenport asked, his eyes narrowed just enough to make his query not precisely friendly.

"Yes, of course," Lucy replied, blinking with surprise. She'd thought the conversation had veered away from her.

"Excellent institution," Davenport said, chewing on a piece of roasted lamb. "They know what a girl should and should not know. Winslow's daughter went there. Fordham's, too."

"Yes," Lucy murmured, since a reply seemed to be expected. "They are both very sweet girls," she lied. Sybilla Winslow was a nasty little tyrant who thought it good fun to pinch the upper arms of the younger students.

But for the first time that evening, Lord Davenport appeared to be pleased with her. "You know them well, then?" he asked.

"Er, somewhat," Lucy hedged. "Lady Joanna was a bit older, but it's not a large school. One can't really *not* know the other students."

"Good." Lord Davenport nodded approvingly, his jowls quivering with the movement.

Lucy tried not to look.

"These are the people you will need to know," he went on. "Connections that you must cultivate."

Lucy nodded dutifully, all the while making a mental list of all the places she would rather be. Paris, Venice, Greece, although weren't they at war? No matter. She would still rather be in Greece.

". . . responsibility to the name . . . certain standards of behavior . . ."

Was it very hot in the Orient? She'd always admired Chinese vases.

". . . will not tolerate any deviation from . . ."

What was the name of that dreadful section of town? St. Giles? Yes, she'd rather be there as well.

". . . obligations. Obligations!"

This last was accompanied by a fist on the table, causing the silver to rattle and Lucy to jerk in her seat. Even Aunt Harriet looked up from her food.

Lucy snapped to attention, and because all eyes were on her, she said, "Yes?"

Lord Davenport leaned in, almost menacingly. "Someday you will be Lady Davenport. You will have obligations. Many obligations."

Lucy managed to stretch her lips just enough to count as a response. Dear God, when would this evening end?

Lord Davenport leaned in, and even though the table was wide and laden with food, Lucy instinctively backed away. "You cannot take lightly your responsibilities," he continued, his voice rising scarily in volume. "Do you understand me, gel?"

Lucy wondered what would happen if she clasped her hands to her head and shouted it out.

God in heaven, put an end to this torture!!!

Yes, she thought, almost analytically, that might very well put him off. Maybe he would judge her unsound of mind and—

"Of course, Lord Davenport," she heard herself say.

She was a coward. A miserable coward.

And then, as if he were some sort of wind-up toy that someone had twisted off, Lord Davenport sat back in his seat, perfectly composed. "I am glad to hear of it," he said dabbing at the corner of his mouth with his serviette. "I am reassured to see that they still teach deference and respect at Miss Moss's. I do not regret my choice in having sent you there."

Lucy's fork halted halfway to her mouth. "I did not realize you had made the arrangements."

"I had to do something," he grunted, looking at her as if

she were of feeble mind. "You haven't a mother to make sure you are properly schooled for your role in life. There are things you will need to know to be a countess. Skills you must possess."

"Of course," she said deferentially, having decided that a show of absolute meekness and obedience would be the quickest way to put an end to the torture. "Er, and thank you."

"For what?" Haselby asked.

Lucy turned to her fiancé. He appeared to be genuinely curious.

"Why, for having me sent to Miss Moss's," she explained, carefully directing her answer at Haselby. Maybe if she didn't *look* at Lord Davenport, he would forget she was there.

"Did you enjoy it, then?" Haselby asked.

"Yes, very much," she replied, somewhat surprised at how very *nice* it felt to be asked a polite question. "It was lovely. I was extremely happy there."

Haselby opened his mouth to reply, but to Lucy's horror, the voice that emerged was that of his father.

"It's not about what makes one happy!" came Lord Davenport's blustery roar.

Lucy could not take her eyes off the sight of Haselby's still-open mouth. *Really,* she thought, in a strange moment of absolute calm, *that had been almost frightening.*

Haselby shut his mouth and turned to his father with a tight smile. "What is about, then?" he inquired, and Lucy could not help but be impressed at the absolute lack of displeasure in his voice.

"It is about what one learns," his father answered, letting one of his fists bang down on the table in a most unseemly manner. "And who one befriends."

"Well, I did master the multiplication tables," Lucy put in mildly, not that anyone was listening to her.

"She will be a countess," Davenport boomed. "A countess!"

Haselby regarded his father equably. "She will only be a countess when you die," he murmured.

Lucy's mouth fell open.

"So really," Haselby continued, casually popping a minuscule bite of fish into his mouth, "it won't matter much to you, will it?"

Lucy turned to Lord Davenport, her eyes very very wide.

The earl's skin flushed. It was a horrible color—angry, dusky, and deep, made worse by the vein that was positively jumping in his left temple. He was staring at Haselby, his eyes narrowed with rage. There was no malice there, no wish to do ill or harm, but although it made absolutely no sense, Lucy would have sworn in that moment that Davenport hated his son.

And Haselby just said, "Fine weather we're having." And he smiled.

Smiled!

Lucy gaped at him. It was pouring and had been for days. But more to the point, didn't he realize that his father was one cheeky comment away from an apoplectic fit? Lord Davenport looked ready to spit, and Lucy was quite certain she could hear his teeth grinding from across the table.

And then, as the room practically pulsed with fury, Uncle Robert stepped into the breach. "I am pleased we have decided to hold the wedding here in London," he said, his voice even and smooth and tinged with finality, as if to say—*We are done with that, then.* "As you know," he continued, while everyone else regained his composure, "Fennsworth was married at the Abbey just two weeks ago, and while it does put one in the mind of ancestral history—I believe the last seven earls held their weddings in residence—really, hardly anyone was able to attend."

Lucy suspected that had as much to do with the hurried nature of the event as with its location, but this didn't seem the time to weigh in on the topic. And she had loved the wedding for its smallness. Richard and Hermione had been so very happy, and everyone in attendance had come out of love and friendship. It had truly been a joyous occasion.

Until they had left the next day for their honeymoon trip to Brighton. Lucy had never felt so miserable and alone as when she'd stood in the drive and waved them away.

They would be back soon, she reminded herself. Before her own wedding. Hermione would be her only attendant, and Richard was to give her away.

And in the meantime she had Aunt Harriet to keep her company. And Lord Davenport. And Haselby, who was either utterly brilliant or completely insane.

A bubble of laughter—ironic, absurd, and highly inappropriate—pressed in her throat, escaping through her nose with an inelegant snort.

"Enh?" Lord Davenport grunted.

"It is nothing," she hastily said, coughing as best she could. "A bit of food. Fishbone, probably."

It was almost funny. It would have been funny, even, if she'd been reading it in a book. It would have had to have been a satire, she decided, because it certainly wasn't a romance.

And she couldn't bear to think it might turn out a tragedy.

She looked around the table at the three men who presently made up her life. She was going to have to make the best of it. There was nothing else to do. There was no sense in remaining miserable, no matter how difficult it was to look on the bright side. And truly, it could have been worse.

So she did what she did best and tried to look at it all from a practical standpoint, mentally cataloguing all the ways it could have been worse.

But instead, Gregory Bridgerton's face kept coming to mind—and all the ways it could have been better.

Fourteen

**In which Our Hero and Heroine are reunited,
and the birds of London are ecstatic.**

When Gregory saw her, right there in Hyde Park his first day back in London, his first thought was—

Well, of course.

It seemed only natural that he would come across Lucy Abernathy in what was literally his first hour out and about in London. He didn't know *why*; there was no logical reason for them to cross paths. But she had been much in his thoughts since they had parted ways in Kent. And even though he'd thought her still off at Fennsworth, he was strangely unsurprised that hers would be the first familiar face he'd see upon his return after a month in the country.

He'd arrived in town the night before, uncommonly weary after a long trip on flooded roads, and he'd gone straight to bed. When he woke—rather earlier than usual, actually—the world was still wet from the rains, but the sun had popped out and was shining brightly.

Gregory had immediately dressed to go out. He loved the

way the air smelled clean after a good, stormy rain—even in London. No, *especially* in London. It was the only time the city smelled like that—thick and fresh, almost like leaves.

Gregory kept a small suite of rooms in a tidy little building in Marylebone, and though his furnishings were spare and simple, he rather liked the place. It felt like home.

His brother and his mother had, on multiple occasions, invited him to live with them. His friends thought him mad to refuse; both residences were considerably more opulent and more to the point, better staffed than his humble abode. But he preferred his independence. It wasn't that he minded them telling him what to do—they knew he wasn't going to listen, and he knew he wasn't going to listen, but for the most part, everyone remained rather good-natured about it.

It was the scrutiny he couldn't quite tolerate. Even if his mother was pretending not to interfere in his life, he knew that she was always watching him, taking note of his social schedule.

And *commenting* on it. Violet Bridgerton could, when the inclination struck, converse on the topic of young ladies, dance cards, and the intersection thereof (as pertained to her unmarried son) with a speed and facility that could make a grown man's head spin.

And frequently did.

There was this young lady and that young lady and would he please be sure to dance with both of them—twice—at the next soiree, and above all, he must never, ever forget the *other* young lady. The one off by the wall, didn't he see her, standing by herself. Her aunt, he must recall, was a close personal friend.

Gregory's mother had a lot of close personal friends.

Violet Bridgerton had successfully ushered seven of her eight children into happy marriages, and now Gregory was bearing the sole brunt of her matchmaking fervor. He adored her, of course, and he adored that she cared so much for his well-being and happiness, but at times she made him want to pull his hair out.

And Anthony was worse. He didn't even have to *say* anything. His mere presence was usually enough to make Gregory feel that he was somehow not living up to the family name. It was difficult to make one's way in the world with the mighty Lord Bridgerton constantly looking over one's shoulder. As far as Gregory could determine, his eldest brother had never made a mistake in his life.

Which made his own all the more egregious.

But, as luck would have it, this was a problem more easily solved than not. Gregory had simply moved out. It required a fair portion of his allowance to maintain his own residence, small though it was, but it was worth it, every last penny.

Even something as simple as this—just leaving the house without anyone wondering why or where (or in his mother's case, to *whom*)—it was lovely. Fortifying. It was strange how a mere stroll could make one feel like one's own man, but it did.

And then there she was. Lucy Abernathy. In Hyde Park when by all rights she ought to still be in Kent.

She was sitting on a bench, tossing bits of bread at a scruffy lot of birds, and Gregory was reminded of that day he'd stumbled upon her at the back of Aubrey Hall. She had been sitting on a bench then as well, and she had seemed so subdued. In retrospect, Gregory realized that her brother had probably just told her that her engagement had been finalized.

He wondered why she hadn't said anything to him.

He wished she'd said something to him.

If he had known that she was spoken for, he would never have kissed her. It went against every code of conduct to which he held himself. A gentleman did not poach upon another man's bride. It was simply not done. If he had known the truth, he would have stepped away from her that night, and he would have—

He froze. He didn't know what he would have done. How was it that he had rewritten the scene in his mind countless times, and he only now realized that he had never quite got to the point where he pushed her away?

If he had known, would he have set her on her way right at that first moment? He'd had to take hold of her arms to steady her, but he could have shifted her toward her destination when he let go. It would not have been difficult—just a little shuffle of the feet. He could have ended it then, before anything had had a chance to begin.

But instead, he had smiled, and he had asked her what she was doing there, and then—good *God,* what had he been thinking—he'd asked her if she drank brandy.

After that—well, he wasn't sure how it had happened, but he remembered it all. Every last detail. The way she was looking at him, her hand on his arm. She'd been clutching him, and for a moment it had almost felt like she needed him. He could be her rock, her center.

He had never been anyone's center.

But it wasn't that. He hadn't kissed her for that. He'd kissed her because . . .

Because . . .

Hell, he didn't know *why* he'd kissed her. There had just been that moment—that strange, inscrutable moment—and it had all been so quiet—a fabulous, magical, mesmerizing silence that seemed to seep into him and steal his breath.

The house had been full, teeming with guests, even, but the hallway had been theirs alone. Lucy had been gazing up at him, her eyes searching, and then . . . somehow . . . she was closer. He didn't recall moving, or lowering his head, but her face was just a few inches away. And the next he knew . . .

He was kissing her.

From that moment on, he had been quite simply gone. It was as if he'd lost all knowledge of words, of rationality and thought. His mind had become a strange, preverbal thing. The world was color and sound, heat and sensation. It was as if his mind had been subsumed by his body.

And now he wondered—when he let himself wonder—if he could have stopped it. If she hadn't said no, if she hadn't pressed her hands to his chest and told him to stop—

Would he have done so on his own?

Could he have done so?

He straightened his shoulders. Squared his jaw. Of course he could have. She was Lucy, for heaven's sake. She was quite wonderful, in quite a number of ways, but she wasn't the sort men lost their heads over. It had been a temporary aberration. Momentary insanity brought on by a strange and unsettling evening.

Even now, sitting on a bench in Hyde Park with a small fleet of pigeons at her feet, she was clearly the same old Lucy. She hadn't seen him yet, and it felt almost luxurious just to observe. She was on her own, save for her maid, who was twiddling her thumbs two benches over.

And her mouth was moving.

Gregory smiled. Lucy was talking to the birds. Telling them something. Most likely she was giving them directions, perhaps setting a date for future bread-tossing engagements.

Or telling them to chew with their beaks closed.

He chuckled. He couldn't help himself.

She turned. She turned, and she saw him. Her eyes widened, and her lips parted, and it hit him squarely in the chest—

It was *good* to see her.

Which struck him as a rather odd sort of reaction, given how they'd parted.

"Lady Lucinda," he said, walking forward. "This is a surprise. I had not thought you were in London."

For a moment it seemed she could not decide how to act,

and then she smiled—perhaps a bit more hesitantly than he was accustomed to—and held forward a slice of bread.

"For the pigeons?" he murmured. "Or me?"

Her smile changed, grew more familiar. "Whichever you prefer. Although I should warn you—it's a bit stale."

His lips twitched. "You've tried it, then?"

And then it was as if none of it had happened. The kiss, the awkward conversation the morning after . . . it was gone. They were back to their odd little friendship, and all was right with the world.

Her mouth was pursed, as if she thought she ought to be scolding him, and he was chuckling, because it was such good fun to bait her.

"It's my second breakfast," she said, utterly deadpan.

He sat on the opposite end of the bench and began to tear his bread into bits. When he had a good-sized handful, he tossed them all at once, then sat back to watch the ensuing frenzy of beaks and feathers.

Lucy, he noticed, was tossing her crumbs methodically, one after another, precisely three seconds apart.

He counted. How could he not?

"The flock has abandoned me," she said with a frown.

Gregory grinned as the last pigeon hopped to the feast of Bridgerton. He threw down another handful. "I always host the best parties."

She turned, her chin dipping as she gave him a dry glance over her shoulder. "You are insufferable."

He gave her a wicked look. "It is one of my finest qualities."

"According to whom?"

"Well, my mother seems to like me quite well," he said modestly.

She sputtered with laughter.

It felt like a victory.

"My sister . . . not as much."

One of her brows lifted. "The one you are fond of torturing?"

"I don't torture her because I *like* to," he said, in a rather instructing sort of tone. "I do it because it is *necessary*."

"To whom?"

"To all Britain," he said. "Trust me."

She looked at him dubiously. "She can't be that bad."

"I suppose not," he said. "My mother seems to like her quite well, much as that baffles me."

She laughed again, and the sound was . . . *good.* A nondescript word, to be sure, but somehow it got right to the heart of it. Her laughter came from within—warm, rich, and true.

Then she turned, and her eyes grew quite serious. "You like to tease, but I would bet all that I have that you would lay down your life for her."

He pretended to consider this. "How much do you have?"

"For shame, Mr. Bridgerton. You're avoiding the question."

"Of course I would," he said quietly. "She's my little sister. Mine to torture and mine to protect."

"Isn't she married now?"

He shrugged, gazing out across the park. "Yes, I suppose St. Clair can take care of her now, God help him." He turned, flashing her a lopsided smile. "Sorry."

But she wasn't so high in the instep to take offense. And in fact, she surprised him utterly by saying—with considerable feeling, "There is no need to apologize. There are times when only the Lord's name will properly convey one's desperation."

"Why do I feel you are speaking from recent experience?"

"Last night," she confirmed.

"Really?" He leaned in, terribly interested. "What happened?"

But she just shook her head. "It was nothing."

"Not if *you* were blaspheming."

She sighed. "I did tell you you were insufferable, didn't I?"

"Once today, and almost certainly several times before."

She gave him a dry look, the blue of her eyes sharpening as they fixed upon him. "You've been counting?"

He paused. It was an odd question, not because she'd asked it—for heaven's sake, he would have asked the very thing, had he been given the same bait. Rather, it was odd because he had the eerie feeling that if he thought about it long enough, he might actually know the answer.

He liked talking with Lucy Abernathy. And when she said something to him . . .

He remembered it.

Peculiar, that.

"I wonder," he said, since it seemed a good time to change the topic. "Is *sufferable* a word?"

She considered that. "I think it must be, don't you?"

"No one has ever uttered it in my presence."

"This surprises you?"

He smiled slowly. With appreciation. "You, Lady Lucinda, have a smart mouth."

Her brows arched, and in that moment she was positively devilish. "It is one of my best-kept secrets."

He started to laugh.

"I'm more than just a busybody, you know."

The laughter grew. Deep in his belly it rumbled, until he was shaking with it.

She was watching him with an indulgent smile, and for some reason he found that calming. She looked warm . . . peaceful, even.

And he was happy to be with her. Here on this bench. It was rather pleasant simply to be in her company. So he turned. Smiled. "Do you have another piece of bread?"

She handed him three. "I brought the entire loaf."

He started tearing them up. "Are you trying to fatten the flock?"

"I have a taste for pigeon pie," she returned, resuming her slow, miserly feeding schedule.

Gregory was quite sure it was his imagination, but he would have sworn the birds were looking longingly in his direction. "Do you come here often?" he asked.

She didn't answer right away, and her head tilted, almost as if she had to think about her answer.

Which was odd, as it was a rather simple question.

"I like to feed the birds," she said. "It's relaxing."

He hurled another handful of bread chunks and quirked a smile. "Do you think so?"

Her eyes narrowed and she tossed her next piece with a precise, almost military little flick of her wrist. The following piece went out the same way. And the one after that, as well. She turned to him with pursed lips. "It is if you're not trying to incite a riot."

"Me?" he returned, all innocence. "You are the one forcing them to battle to the death, all for one pathetic crumb of stale bread."

"It's a very fine loaf of bread, well-baked and extremely tasty, I'll have you know."

"On matters of nourishment," he said with overdone graciousness, "I shall always defer to you."

Lucy regarded him dryly. "Most women would not find that complimentary."

"Ah, but you are not most women. And," he added, "I have seen you eat breakfast."

Her lips parted, but before she could gasp her indignation, he cut in with: "That was a compliment, by the way."

Lucy shook her head. He really was insufferable. And she was *so* thankful for that. When she'd first seen him, just standing there watching her as she fed the birds, her stomach had dropped, and she'd felt queasy, and she didn't know what to say or how to act, or really, anything.

But then he'd ambled forward, and he'd been so . . . *him-*

self. He'd put her immediately at ease, which, under the circumstances, was really quite astonishing.

She was, after all, in love with him.

But then he'd smiled, that lazy, familiar smile of his, and he'd made some sort of joke about the pigeons, and before she knew it, she was smiling in return. And she felt like herself, which was so reassuring.

She hadn't felt like herself for weeks.

And so, in the spirit of making the best of things, she had decided not to dwell upon her inappropriate affection for him and instead be thankful that she could be in his presence without turning into an awkward, stammering fool.

There *were* small favors left in the world, apparently.

"Have you been in London all this time?" she asked him, quite determined to maintain a pleasant and perfectly normal conversation.

He drew back in surprise. Clearly, he had not expected that question. "No. I only just returned last night."

"I see." Lucy paused to digest that. It was strange, but she hadn't even considered that he might not be in town. But it would explain— Well, she wasn't sure what it would explain. That she hadn't caught a glimpse of him? It wasn't as if she'd been anywhere besides her home, the park, and the dressmaker. "Were you at Aubrey Hall, then?"

"No, I left shortly after you departed and went to visit my brother. He lives with his wife and children off in Wiltshire, quite blissfully away from all that is civilized."

"Wiltshire isn't so very far away."

He shrugged. "Half the time they don't even receive the *Times.* They claim they are not interested."

"How odd." Lucy didn't know anyone who did not receive the newspaper, even in the most remote of counties.

He nodded. "I found it rather refreshing this time, however. I have no idea what anyone is doing, and I don't mind it a bit."

"Are you normally such a gossip?"

He gave her a sideways look. "Men don't gossip. We talk."

"I see," she said. "That explains so much."

He chuckled. "Have *you* been in town long? I had assumed you were also rusticating."

"Two weeks," she replied. "We arrived just after the wedding."

"We? Are your brother and Miss Watson here, then?"

She hated that she was listening for eagerness in his voice, but she supposed it couldn't be helped. "She is Lady Fennsworth now, and no, they are on their honeymoon trip. I am here with my uncle."

"For the season?"

"For my wedding."

That stopped the easy flow of conversation.

She reached into her bag and pulled out another slice of bread. "It is to take place in a week."

He stared at her in shock. "That soon?"

"Uncle Robert says there is no point in dragging it out."

"I see."

And maybe he did. Maybe there was some sort of etiquette to all this that she, sheltered girl from the country that she was, had not been taught. Maybe there *was* no point in postponing the inevitable. Maybe it was all a part of that making the best of things philosophy she was working so diligently to espouse.

"Well," he said. He blinked a few times, and she realized that he did not know what to say. It was a most uncharacteristic response and one she found gratifying. It was a bit like Hermione not knowing how to dance. If Gregory Bridgerton could be at a loss for words, then there was hope for the rest of humanity.

Finally he settled upon: "My felicitations."

"Thank you." She wondered if he had received an invitation. Uncle Robert and Lord Davenport were determined to hold the ceremony in front of absolutely everyone. It was, they said, to be her grand debut, and they wanted all the world to know that she was Haselby's wife.

"It is to be at St. George's," she said, for no reason whatsoever.

"Here in London?" He sounded surprised. "I would have thought you would marry from Fennsworth Abbey."

It was most peculiar, Lucy thought, how *not* painful this was—discussing her upcoming wedding with him. She felt more numb, actually. "It was what my uncle wanted," she explained, reaching into her basket for another slice of bread.

"Your uncle remains the head of the household?" Gregory asked, regarding her with mild curiosity. "Your brother is the earl. Hasn't he reached his majority?"

Lucy tossed the entire slice to the ground, then watched with morbid interest as the pigeons went a bit mad. "He has," she replied. "Last year. But he was content to allow my uncle to handle the family's affairs while he was conducting his postgraduate studies at Cambridge. I expect that he will assume his place soon now that he is"—she offered him an apologetic smile—"married."

"Do not worry over my sensibilities," he assured her. "I am quite recovered."

"Truly?"

He gave her a small, one-shouldered shrug. "Truth be told, I count myself lucky."

She pulled out another slice of bread, but her fingers froze before pinching off a piece. "You do?" she asked, turning to him with interest. "How is that possible?"

He blinked with surprise. "You *are* direct, aren't you?"

And she blushed. She felt it, pink and warm and just *horrible* on her cheeks. "I'm sorry," she said. "That was terribly rude of me. It is only that you were so very much—"

"Say no more," he cut her off, and then she felt even worse, because she had been about to describe—probably in meticulous detail—how lovesick he'd been over Hermione. Which, had she been in his position, she'd not wish recounted.

"I'm sorry," she said.

He turned. Regarded her with a contemplative sort of curiosity. "You say that quite frequently."

"I'm sorry?"

"Yes."

"I . . . I don't know." Her teeth ground together, and she felt quite tense. Uncomfortable. Why would he point out such a thing? "It's what I do," she said, and she said it firmly, because . . . Well, because. That ought to be enough of a reason.

He nodded. And that made her feel even worse. "It's who I am," she added defensively, even though he'd been agreeing with her, for heaven's sake. "I smooth things over and I make things right."

And at that, she hurled the last piece of bread to the ground.

His brows rose, and they both turned in unison to watch the ensuing chaos. "Well done," he murmured.

"I make the best of things," she said. "Always."

"It's a commendable trait," he said softly.

And at that, somehow, she was angry. Really, truly, beastly angry. She didn't want to be commended for knowing how to settle for second-best. That was like winning a prize for the prettiest shoes in a footrace. Irrelevant and *not* the point.

"And what of you?" she asked, her voice growing strident. "Do you make the best of things? Is that why you claim yourself recovered? Weren't you the one who waxed rhapsodic over the mere thought of love? You said it was *everything,* that it gave you no choice. You said—"

She cut herself off, horrified by her tone. He was staring at her as if she'd gone mad, and maybe she had.

"You said many things," she mumbled, hoping that might end the conversation.

She ought to go. She had been sitting on the bench for at least fifteen minutes before he'd arrived, and it was damp and breezy, and her maid wasn't dressed warmly enough, and if she thought long and hard enough about it, she probably had a hundred things she needed to do at home.

Or at least a book she could read.

"I am sorry if I upset you," Gregory said quietly.

She couldn't quite bring herself to look at him.

"But I did not lie to you," he said. "Truthfully, I no longer think of Miss—excuse me, Lady Fennsworth—with any great frequency, except, perhaps, to realize that we should not have been well-suited after all."

She turned to him, and she realized she wanted to believe him. She really did.

Because if he could forget Hermione, maybe she could forget him.

"I don't know how to explain it," he said, and he shook his head, as if he were every bit as perplexed as she. "But if ever you fall madly and inexplicably in love . . ."

Lucy froze. *He wasn't going to say it. Surely, he couldn't say it.*

He shrugged. "Well, I shouldn't trust it."

Dear God. Hermione's words. Exactly.

She tried to remember how she had replied to Hermione. Because she had to say something. Otherwise, he would notice the silence, and then he'd turn, and he'd see her looking so unnerved. And then he would ask questions, and she wouldn't know the answers, and—

"It's not likely to happen to me," she said, the words practically pouring from her mouth.

He turned, but she kept her face scrupulously forward. And she wished desperately that she had not tossed out all the bread. It would be far easier to avoid looking at him if she could pretend to be involved with something else.

"You don't believe that you will fall in love?" he asked.

"Well, perhaps," she said, trying to sound blithe and sophisticated. "But not *that*."

"That?"

She took a breath, hating that he was forcing her to explain. "That desperate sort of thing you and Hermione now disavow," she said. "I'm not the sort, don't you think?"

She bit her lip, then finally allowed herself to turn in his direction. Because what if he could tell that she was lying? What if he sensed that she was already in love—with him? She would be embarrassed beyond comprehension, but wouldn't it be better to *know* that he knew? At least then, she wouldn't have to wonder.

Ignorance wasn't bliss. Not for someone like her.

"It is all beside the point, anyway," she continued, because she couldn't bear the silence. "I am marrying Lord Haselby in one week, and I would *never* stray from my vows. I—"

"Haselby?" Gregory's entire body twisted as he swung around to face her. "You're marrying *Haselby*?"

"Yes," she said, blinking furiously. What sort of reaction was *that*? "I thought you knew."

"No. I didn't—" He looked shocked. Stupefied.

Good heavens.

He shook his head. "I can't imagine why I didn't know."

"It wasn't a secret."

"No," he said, a bit forcefully. "I mean, no. No, of course not. I did not mean to imply."

"Do you hold Lord Haselby in low esteem?" she asked, choosing her words with extreme care.

"No," Gregory replied, shaking his head—but just a little, as if he were not quite aware that he was doing it. "No. I've known him for a number of years. We were at college together. And university."

"Are you of an age, then?" Lucy asked, and it occurred to her that something was a bit wrong if she did not know the age of her fiancé. But then again, she wasn't certain of Gregory's age, either.

He nodded. "He's quite . . . affable. He will treat you well." He cleared his throat. "Gently."

"Gently?" she echoed. It seemed an odd choice of words.

His eyes met hers, and it was only then that she realized he had not precisely looked at her since she'd told him the name of her fiancé. But he didn't speak. Instead he just stared at her, his eyes so intense that they seemed to change color. They were brown with green, then green with brown, and then it all seemed almost to blur.

"What is it?" she whispered.

"It is of no account," he said, but he did not sound like himself. "I . . ." And then he turned away, broke the spell. "My sister," he said, clearing his throat. "She is hosting a soiree tomorrow evening. Would you like to attend?"

"Oh yes, that would be lovely," Lucy said, even though she knew she should not. But it had been so long since she'd had any sort of social interaction, and she wasn't going to be able to spend time in his company once she was married. She ought not torture herself now, longing for something she could not have, but she couldn't help it.

Gather ye rosebuds.

Now. Because really, when else—

"Oh, but I *can't*," she said, disappointment turning her voice to nearly a whine.

"Why not?"

"It is my uncle," she replied, sighing. "And Lord Davenport—Haselby's father."

"I know who he is."

"Of course. I'm sor—" She cut herself off. She wasn't going to say it. "They don't wish for me to make my bow yet."

"I beg your pardon. Why?"

Lucy shrugged. "There is no point in my being introduced to society as Lady Lucinda Abernathy when I'm to be Lady Haselby in a week."

"That's ridiculous."

"It is what they say." She frowned. "And I don't think they wish to suffer the expense, either."

"You will attend tomorrow evening," Gregory said firmly. "I shall see to it."

"You?" Lucy asked dubiously.

"Not *me*," he answered, as if she'd gone mad. "My mother. Trust me, when it comes to matters of social discourse and niceties, she can accomplish anything. Have you a chaperone?"

Lucy nodded. "My aunt Harriet. She is a bit frail, but I am certain she could attend a party if my uncle allowed it."

"He will allow it," Gregory said confidently. "The sister in question is my eldest. Daphne." He then clarified: "Her grace the Duchess of Hastings. Your uncle would not say no to a duchess, would he?"

"I don't think so," she said slowly. Lucy could not think of anyone who would say no to a duchess.

"It's settled, then," Gregory said. "You shall be hearing from Daphne by afternoon." He stood, offering his hand to help her up.

She swallowed. It would be bittersweet to touch him, but she placed her hand in his. It felt warm, and comfortable. And safe.

"Thank you," she murmured, taking her hand back so that she might wrap both around the handle of her basket. She nodded at her maid, who immediately began walking to her side.

"Until tomorrow," he said, bowing almost formally as he bade her farewell.

"Until tomorrow," Lucy echoed, wondering if it were

true. She had never known her uncle to change his mind before. But maybe . . .

Possibly.

Hopefully.

Fifteen

**In which Our Hero learns that he is not,
and probably never will be, as wise as his mother.**

$\mathscr{O}$ne hour later, Gregory was waiting in the drawing room
at Number Five, Bruton Street, his mother's London home
since she had insisted upon vacating Bridgerton House upon
Anthony's marriage. It had been his home, too, until he had
found his own lodgings several years earlier. His mother
lived there alone now, ever since his younger sister had married. Gregory made a point of calling upon her at least twice
a week when he was in London, but it never ceased to surprise him how quiet the house seemed now.

"Darling!" his mother exclaimed, sailing into the room
with a wide smile. "I had not thought to see you until this
evening. How was your journey? And tell me everything
about Benedict and Sophie and the children. It is a crime
how infrequently I see my grandchildren."

Gregory smiled indulgently. His mother had visited Wiltshire just one month earlier, and did so several times per
year. He dutifully passed along news of Benedict's four chil-

dren, with added emphasis on little Violet, her namesake. Then, once she had exhausted her supply of questions, he said, "Actually, Mother, I have a favor to ask of you."

Violet's posture was always superb, but still, she seemed to straighten a bit. "You do? What is it you need?"

He told her about Lucy, keeping the tale as brief as possible, lest she reach any inappropriate conclusions about his interest in her.

His mother tended to view any unmarried female as a potential bride. Even those with a wedding scheduled for the week's end.

"Of course I will assist you," she said. "This will be easy."

"Her uncle is determined to keep her sequestered," Gregory reminded her.

She waved away his warning. "Child's play, my dear son. Leave this to me. I shall make short work of it."

Gregory decided not to pursue the subject further. If his mother said she knew how to ensure someone's attendance at a ball, then he believed her. Continued questioning would only lead her to believe he had an ulterior motive.

Which he did not.

He simply liked Lucy. Considered her a friend. And he wished for her to have a bit of fun.

It was admirable, really.

"I shall have your sister send an invitation with a personal note," Violet mused. "And perhaps I shall call upon her uncle directly. I shall lie and tell him I met her in the park."

"Lie?" Gregory's lips twitched. "You?"

His mother's smile was positively diabolical. "It won't matter if he does not believe me. It is one of the advantages of advanced years. No one dares to countermand an old dragon like me."

Gregory lifted his brows, refusing to fall for her bait. Violet Bridgerton might have been the mother of eight adult children, but with her milky, unlined complexion and wide smile, she did not look like anyone who could be termed old. In fact, Gregory had often wondered why she did not remarry. There was no shortage of dashing widowers clamoring to take her in to supper or stand up for a dance. Gregory suspected any one of them would have leaped at the chance to marry his mother, if only she would indicate interest.

But she did not, and Gregory had to admit that he was rather selfishly glad of it. Despite her meddling, there was something quite comforting in her single-minded devotion to her children and grandchildren.

His father had been dead for over two dozen years. Gregory hadn't even the slightest memory of the man. But his mother had spoken of him often, and whenever she did, her voice changed. Her eyes softened, and the corners of her lips moved—just a little, just enough for Gregory to see the memories on her face.

It was in those moments that he understood why she was so adamant that her children choose their spouses for love.

He'd always planned to comply. It was ironic, really, given the farce with Miss Watson.

Just then a maid arrived with a tea tray, which she set on the low table between them.

"Cook made your favorite biscuits," his mother said, handing him a cup prepared exactly as he liked it—no sugar, one tiny splash of milk.

"You anticipated my visit?" he asked.

"Not this afternoon, no," Violet said, taking a sip of her own tea. "But I knew you could not stay away for long. Eventually you would need sustenance."

Gregory offered her a lopsided smile. It was true. Like many men of his age and status, he did not have room in his apartments for a proper kitchen. He ate at parties, and at his club, and, of course, at the homes of his mother and siblings.

"Thank you," he murmured, accepting the plate onto which she'd piled six biscuits.

Violet regarded the tea tray for a moment, her head cocked slightly to the side, then placed two on her own plate. "I am quite touched," she said, looking up at him, "that you seek my assistance with Lady Lucinda."

"Are you?" he asked curiously. "Who else would I turn to with such a matter?"

She took a delicate bite of her biscuit. "No, I am the obvious choice, of course, but you must realize that you rarely turn to your family when you need something."

Gregory went still, then turned slowly in her direction. His mother's eyes—so blue and so unsettlingly perceptive—were fixed on his face. What could she possibly have meant by that? No one could love his family better than he did.

"That cannot be true," he finally said.

But his mother just smiled. "Do you think not?"

His jaw clenched. "I *do* think not."

"Oh, do not take offense," she said, reaching across the table to pat him on the arm. "I do not mean to say that you do not love us. But you do prefer to do things for yourself."

"Such as?"

"Oh, finding yourself a wife—"

He cut her off right then and there. "Are you trying to tell me that Anthony, Benedict, and Colin welcomed your interference when they were looking for wives?"

"No, of course not. No man does. But—" She flitted one of her hands through the air, as if she could erase the sentence. "Forgive me. It was a poor example."

She let out a small sigh as she gazed out the window, and Gregory realized that she was prepared to let the subject drop. To his surprise, however, he was not.

"What is wrong with preferring to do things for oneself?" he asked.

She turned to him, looking for all the world as if she had not just introduced a potentially discomforting topic. "Why, nothing. I am quite proud that I raised such self-sufficient sons. After all, three of you must make your own way in the world." She paused, considering this, then added, "With some help from Anthony, of course. I should be quite disappointed if he did not watch out for the rest of you."

"Anthony is exceedingly generous," Gregory said quietly.

"Yes, he is, isn't he?" Violet said, smiling. "With his money *and* his time. He is quite like your father in this way." She looked at him with wistful eyes. "I am so sorry you never knew him."

"Anthony was a good father to me." Gregory said it because he knew it would bring her joy, but he also said it because it was true.

His mother's lips pursed and tightened, and for a moment Gregory thought she might cry. He immediately retrieved his handkerchief and held it out to her.

"No, no, that's not necessary," she said, even as she took it and dabbed her eyes. "I am quite all right. Merely a little—" She swallowed, then smiled. But her eyes still glistened. "Someday you will understand—when you have children of your own—how lovely it was to hear that."

She set the handkerchief down and picked up her tea. Sipping it thoughtfully, she let out a little sigh of contentment.

Gregory smiled to himself. His mother adored tea. It went quite beyond the usual British devotion. She claimed it helped her to think, which he would normally have lauded as a good thing, except that all too often *he* was the subject of her thoughts, and after her third cup she had usually devised a frighteningly thorough plan to marry him off to the daughter of whichever friend she had most recently paid a morning call to.

But this time, apparently, her mind was not on marriage. She set her cup down, and, just when he thought she was ready to change the subject, she said, "But he is not your father."

He paused, his own teacup halfway to his mouth. "I beg your pardon."

"Anthony. He is not your father."

"Yes?" he said slowly, because really, what could possibly be her point?

"He is your brother," she continued. "As are Benedict and Colin, and when you were small—oh, how you wished to be a part of their affairs."

Gregory held himself very still.

"But of course they were not interested in bringing you along, and really, who can blame them?"

"Who indeed?" he murmured tightly.

"Oh, do not take offense, Gregory," his mother said, turning to him with an expression that was a little bit contrite and little bit impatient. "They were wonderful brothers, and truly, very patient most of the time."

"Most of the time?"

"Some of the time," she amended. "But you were so much smaller than they were. There simply wasn't much in common for you to do. And then when you grew older, well . . ."

Her words trailed off, and she sighed. Gregory leaned forward. "Well?" he prompted.

"Oh, it's nothing."

"Mother."

"Very well," she said, and he knew right then and there that she knew *exactly* what she was saying, and that any sighs and lingering words were entirely for effect.

"I think that you think you must prove yourself to them," Violet said.

He regarded her with surprise. "Don't I?"

His mother's lips parted, but she made no sound for several seconds. "No," she finally said. "Why would you think you would?"

What a silly question. It was because— It was because—

"It's not the sort of thing one can easily put into words," he muttered.

"Really?" She sipped at her tea. "I must say, that was not the sort of reaction I had anticipated."

Gregory felt his jaw clench. "What, precisely, did you anticipate?"

"Precisely?" She looked up at him with just enough humor in her eyes to completely irritate him. "I'm not certain that I can be precise, but I suppose I had expected you to deny it."

"Just because I do not wish it to be the case does not render it untrue," he said with a deliberately casual shrug.

"Your brothers respect you," Violet said.

"I did not say they do not."

"They recognize that you are your own man."

That, Gregory thought, was not precisely true.

"It is not a sign of weakness to ask for help," Violet continued.

"I have never believed that it was," he replied. "Didn't I just seek your assistance?"

"With a matter that could only be handled by a female," she said, somewhat dismissively. "You had no choice but to call on me."

It was true, so Gregory made no comment.

"You are used to having things done for you," she said.

"Mother."

"Hyacinth is the same way," she said quickly. "I think it must be a symptom of being the youngest. And truly, I did not mean to imply that either of you is lazy or spoiled or mean-spirited in any way."

"What did you mean, then?" he asked.

She looked up with a slightly mischievous smile. "Precisely?"

He felt a bit of his tension slipping away. "Precisely," he said, with a nod to acknowledge her wordplay.

"I merely meant that you have never had to work particularly hard for anything. You're quite lucky that way. Good things seem to happen to you."

"And as my mother, you are bothered by this . . . how?"

"Oh, Gregory," she said with a sigh. "I am not bothered at all. I wish you nothing but good things. You know that."

He wasn't quite sure what the proper response might be to this, so he held silent, merely lifting his brows in question.

"I've made a muddle of this, haven't I?" Violet said with a frown. "All I am trying to say is that you have never had to expend much of an effort to achieve your goals. Whether that is a result of your abilities or your goals, I am not certain."

He did not speak. His eyes found a particularly intricate spot in the patterned fabric covering the walls, and he was riveted, unable to focus on anything else as his mind churned.

And yearned.

And then, before he even realized what he was thinking, he asked, "What has this to do with my brothers?"

She blinked uncomprehendingly, and then finally murmured, "Oh, you mean about your feeling the need to prove yourself?"

He nodded.

She pursed her lips. Thought. And then said, "I'm not sure."

He opened his mouth. That was not the answer he had been expecting.

"I don't know everything," she said, and he suspected it was the first time that particular collection of words had ever crossed her lips.

"I suppose," she said, slowly and thoughtfully, "that you . . . Well, it's an odd combination, I should think. Or perhaps not so odd, when one has so many older brothers and sisters."

Gregory waited as she collected her thoughts. The room was quiet, the air utterly still, and yet it felt as if something were bearing down on him, pressing at him from all sides.

He did not know what she was going to say, but somehow . . .

He knew . . .

It mattered.

Maybe more than anything else he'd ever heard.

"You don't wish to ask for help," his mother said, "because it is so important to you that your brothers see you as a man grown. And yet at the same time . . . Well, life has come easily to you, and so I think sometimes you don't try."

His lips parted.

"It is not that you refuse to try," she hastened to add. "Just that most of the time you don't have to. And when something is going to require too much effort . . . If it is something you cannot manage yourself, you decide that it is not worth the bother."

Gregory found his eyes pulling back toward that spot on the wall, the one where the vine twisted so curiously. "I know what it means to work for something," he said in a quiet voice. He turned to her then, looking her full in the face. "To want it desperately and to know that it might not be yours."

"Do you? I'm glad." She reached for her tea, then apparently changed her mind and looked up. "Did you get it?"

"No."

Her eyes turned a little bit sad. "I'm sorry."

"I'm not," he said stiffly. "Not any longer."

"Oh. Well." She shifted in her seat. "Then I am not sorry. I imagine you are a better man for it now."

Gregory's initial impulse leaned toward offense, but to his great surprise, he found himself saying, "I believe you are correct."

To his even greater surprise, he meant it.

His mother smiled wisely. "I am so glad you are able to see it in that light. Most men cannot." She glanced up at the clock and let out a chirp of surprise. "Oh dear, the time. I promised Portia Featherington that I would call upon her this afternoon."

Gregory stood as his mother rose to her feet.

"Do not worry about Lady Lucinda," she said, hurrying to the door. "I shall take care of everything. And please, finish your tea. I do worry about you, living all by yourself with no woman to care for you. Another year of this, and you will waste away to skin and bones."

He walked her to the door. "As nudges toward matrimony go, that was particularly unsubtle."

"Was it?" She gave him an arch look. "How nice for me that I no longer even try for subtlety. I have found that most men do not notice anything that is not clearly spelled out, anyway."

"Even your sons."

"*Especially* my sons."

He smiled wryly. "I asked for that, didn't I?"

"You practically wrote me an invitation."

He tried to accompany her to the main hall, but she shooed him away. "No, no, that's not necessary. Go and finish your tea. I asked the kitchen to bring up sandwiches when you were announced. They should arrive at any moment and will surely go to waste if you don't eat them."

Gregory's stomach grumbled at that exact moment, so he bowed and said, "You are a superb mother, did you know that?"

"Because I feed you?"

"Well, yes, but perhaps for a few other things as well."

She stood on her toes and kissed him on the cheek. "You are no longer my darling boy, are you?"

Gregory smiled. It had been her endearment for him for as long as he remembered. "I am for as long as you wish it, Mother. As long as you wish it."

Sixteen

In which Our Hero falls in love. Again.

*W*hen it came to social machinations, Violet Bridgerton was every bit as accomplished as she claimed, and indeed, when Gregory arrived at Hastings House the following evening, his sister Daphne, the current Duchess of Hastings, informed him that Lady Lucinda Abernathy would indeed be attending the ball.

He found himself rather unaccountably pleased at the outcome. Lucy had looked so disappointed when she'd told him that she would not be able to go, and really, shouldn't the girl enjoy one last night of revelry before she married Haselby?

Haselby.

Gregory still couldn't quite believe it. How could he have not known that she was marrying Haselby? There was nothing he could do to stop it, and really, it wasn't his place, but dear God, it was *Haselby*.

Shouldn't Lucy be told?

Haselby was a perfectly amiable fellow, and, Gregory had

to allow, in possession of a more than acceptable wit. He wouldn't beat her, and he wouldn't be unkind, but he didn't . . . he couldn't . . .

He would not be a husband to her.

Just the thought of it left him grim. Lucy wasn't going to have a regular marriage, because Haselby didn't *like* women. Not the way a man was meant to.

Haselby would be kind to her, and he'd probably provide her with an exceedingly generous allowance, which was more than many women had in their marriages, regardless of their husbands' proclivities.

But it did not seem fair that, of all people, Lucy was destined for such a life. She deserved so much more. A house full of children. And dogs. Perhaps a cat or two. She seemed the sort who'd want a menagerie.

And flowers. In Lucy's home there would be flowers everywhere, he was certain of it. Pink peonies, yellow roses, and that stalky blue thing she liked so well.

Delphinium. That was it.

He paused. Remembered. Delphinium.

Lucy might claim that her brother was the horticulturalist of the family, but Gregory could not imagine her living in a home without color.

There would be laughter and noise and splendid disarray—despite her attempts to keep every corner of her life neat and tidy. He could see her easily in his mind's eye, fussing and organizing, trying to keep everyone on a proper schedule.

It almost made him laugh aloud, just to think of it. It wouldn't matter if there was a fleet of servants dusting and straightening and shining and sweeping. With children nothing was ever quite where one put it.

Lucy was a manager. It was what made her happy, and she ought to have a household to manage.

Children. Lots of them.

Maybe eight.

He glanced around the ballroom, which was slowly beginning to fill. He didn't see Lucy, and it wasn't so crowded yet that he might miss her. He did, however, see his mother.

She was heading his way.

"Gregory," she said, reaching out to him with both hands when she reached him, "you look especially handsome this evening."

He took her hands and raised them to his lips. "Said with all the honesty and impartiality of a mother," he murmured.

"Nonsense," she said with a smile. "It is a fact that all of my children are exceedingly intelligent and good-looking. If it were merely my opinion, don't you think someone would have corrected me by now?"

"As if any would dare."

"Well, yes, I suppose," she replied, maintaining an impressively impassive face. "But I shall be stubborn and insist that the point is moot."

"As you wish, Mother," he said with perfect solemnity. "As you wish."

"Has Lady Lucinda arrived?"

Gregory shook his head. "Not yet."

"Isn't it odd that I haven't met her," she mused. "One would think, if she has been in town a fortnight already . . . Ah well, it matters not. I am certain I will find her delightful if you made such an effort to secure her attendance this evening."

Gregory gave her a look. He knew this tone. It was a perfect blend of nonchalance and utter precision, usually utilized whilst digging for information. His mother was a master at it.

And sure enough, she was discreetly patting her hair and not quite looking at him as she said, "You said you were introduced while you were visiting Anthony, did you not?"

He saw no reason to pretend he did not know what she was about.

"She is engaged to be married, Mother," he said with great emphasis. And then for good measure he added, "In one week."

"Yes, yes, I know. To Lord Davenport's son. It is a long-standing match, I understand."

Gregory nodded. He couldn't imagine that his mother knew the truth about Haselby. It was not a well-known fact. There were whispers, of course. There were always whispers. But none would dare repeat them in the presence of ladies.

"I received an invitation to the wedding," Violet said.

"Did you?"

"It's to be a very large affair, I understand."

Gregory clenched his teeth a bit. "She is to be a countess."

"Yes, I suppose. It's not the sort of thing one can do up small."

"No."

Violet sighed. "I adore weddings."

"Do you?"

"Yes." She sighed again, with even more drama, not that Gregory would have imagined it possible. "It is all so romantic," she added. "The bride, the groom . . ."

"Both are considered standard in the ceremony, I understand."

His mother shot him a peevish look. "How could I have raised a son who is so unromantic?"

Gregory decided there could not possibly be an answer to that.

"Fie on you, then," Violet said, "I plan to attend. I almost never refuse an invitation to a wedding."

And then came *the voice*. "Who is getting married?"

Gregory turned. It was his younger sister, Hyacinth. Dressed in blue and poking her nose into everyone else's business as usual.

"Lord Haselby and Lady Lucinda Abernathy," Violet answered.

"Oh yes." Hyacinth frowned. "I received an invitation. At St. George's, is it not?"

Violet nodded. "Followed by a reception at Fennsworth House."

Hyacinth glanced around the room. She did that quite frequently, even when she was not searching for anyone in particular. "Isn't it odd that I haven't met her? She is sister to the Earl of Fennsworth, is she not?" She shrugged. "Odd that I have not met him, either."

"I don't believe Lady Lucinda is 'out,' " Gregory said. "Not formally, at least."

"Then tonight will be her debut," his mother said. "How exciting for us all."

Hyacinth turned to her brother with razor-sharp eyes. "And how is it that you are acquainted with Lady Lucinda, Gregory?"

He opened his mouth, but she was already saying, "And do not say that you are not, because Daphne has already told me everything."

"Then why are you asking?"

Hyacinth scowled. "She did not tell me how you *met*."

"You might wish to revisit your understanding of the word *everything*." Gregory turned to his mother. "Vocabulary and comprehension were never her strong suits."

Violet rolled her eyes. "Every day I marvel that the two of you managed to reach adulthood."

"Afraid we'd kill each other?" Gregory quipped.

"No, that I'd do the job myself."

"Well," Hyacinth stated, as if the previous minute of conversation had never taken place, "Daphne said that you were most anxious that Lady Lucinda receive an invitation, and Mother, I understand, even penned a note saying how much she enjoys her company, which as we all know is a bald-faced lie, as none of us has ever met the—"

"Do you ever cease talking?" Gregory interrupted.

"Not for you," Hyacinth replied. "How *do* you know her? And more to the point, how well? *And* why are you so eager to extend an invitation to a woman who will be married in a week?"

And then, amazingly, Hyacinth *did* stop talking.

"I was wondering that myself," Violet murmured.

Gregory looked from his sister to his mother and decided he hadn't meant any of that rot he'd said to Lucy about large families being a comfort. They were a nuisance and an intrusion and a whole host of other things, the words for which he could not quite retrieve at that moment.

Which may have been for the best, as none of them were likely to have been polite.

Nonetheless, he turned to the two women with extreme patience and said, "I was introduced to Lady Lucinda in Kent. At Kate and Anthony's house party last month. And I asked Daphne to invite her this evening because she is an amiable young lady, and I happened upon her yesterday in the park. Her uncle has denied her a season, and I thought it would be a kind deed to provide her with an opportunity to escape for one evening."

He lifted his brows, silently daring them to respond.

They did, of course. Not with words—words would never have been as effective as the dubious stares they were hurling in his direction.

"Oh, for heaven's sake," he nearly burst out. "She is *engaged*. To be married."

This had little visible effect.

Gregory scowled. "Do I appear to be attempting to put a halt to the nuptials?"

Hyacinth blinked. Several times, the way she always did when she was thinking far too hard about something not her affair. But to his great surprise, she let out a little *hmm* of acquiescence and said, "I suppose not." She glanced about the room. "I should like to meet her, though."

"I'm sure you will," Gregory replied, and he congratulated himself, as he did at least once a month, on not strangling his sister.

"Kate wrote that she is lovely," Violet said.

Gregory turned to her with a sinking feeling. "*Kate* wrote to you?" Good God, what had she revealed? It was bad enough that Anthony knew about the fiasco with Miss Watson—he had figured it out, of course—but if his mother found out, his life would be utter hell.

She would kill him with kindness. He was sure of it.

"Kate writes twice a month," Violet replied with a delicate, one-shouldered shrug. "She tells me everything."

"Is Anthony aware?" Gregory muttered.

"I have no idea," Violet said, giving him a superior look. "It's really none of his business."

Good God.

Gregory just managed to not say it aloud.

"I gather," his mother continued, "that her brother was caught in a compromising position with Lord Watson's daughter."

"Really?" Hyacinth had been perusing the crowd, but she swung back for that.

Violet nodded thoughtfully. "I had wondered why that wedding was so rushed."

"Well, that's why," Gregory said, a little bit like a grunt.

"Hmmmm." This, from Hyacinth.

It was the sort of sound one never wished to hear from Hyacinth.

Violet turned to her daughter and said, "It was quite the to-do."

"Actually," Gregory said, growing more irritated by the second, "it was all handled discreetly."

"There are always whispers," Hyacinth said.

"Don't you add to them," Violet warned her.

"I won't say a word," Hyacinth promised, waving her

hand as if she had never spoken out of turn in her life.

Gregory let out a snort. "Oh, *please.*"

"I won't," she protested. "I am superb with a secret as long as I *know* it is a secret."

"Ah, so what you mean, then, is that you possess no sense of discretion?"

Hyacinth narrowed her eyes.

Gregory lifted his brows.

"How *old* are you?" Violet interjected. "Goodness, the two of you haven't changed a bit since you were in leading strings. I half expect you to start pulling each other's hair right on the spot."

Gregory clamped his jaw into a line and stared resolutely ahead. There was nothing quite like a rebuke from one's mother to make one feel three feet tall.

"Oh, don't be a stuff, Mother," Hyacinth said, taking the scolding with a smile. "He knows I only tease him so because I love him best." She smiled up at him, sunny and warm.

Gregory sighed, because it was true, and because he felt the same way, and because it was, nonetheless, exhausting to be her brother. But the two of them were quite a bit younger than the rest of their siblings, and as a result, had always been a bit of a pair.

"He returns the sentiment, by the way," Hyacinth said to Violet, "but as a man, he would never say as much."

Violet nodded. "It's true."

Hyacinth turned to Gregory. "And just to be perfectly clear, I never pulled your hair."

Surely his signal to leave. Or lose his sanity. Really, it was up to him.

"Hyacinth," Gregory said, "I adore you. You know it. Mother, I adore you as well. And now I am leaving."

"Wait!" Violet called out.

He turned around. He should have known it wouldn't be that easy.

"Would you be my escort?"

"To what?"

"Why, to the wedding, of course."

Gad, *what* was that awful taste in his mouth? "Whose wedding? Lady Lucinda's?"

His mother gazed at him with the most innocent blue eyes. "I shouldn't like to go alone."

He jerked his head in his sister's direction. "Take Hyacinth."

"She'll wish to go with Gareth," Violet replied.

Gareth St. Clair was Hyacinth's husband of nearly four years. Gregory liked him immensely, and the two had developed a rather fine friendship, which was how he knew that Gareth would rather peel his eyelids back (and leave them that way for an indefinite amount of time) than sit through a long, drawn-out, all-day society affair.

Whereas Hyacinth was, as she did not mind putting it, *always* interested in gossip, which meant that she surely would not wish to miss such an important wedding. Someone would drink too much, and someone else would dance too close, and Hyacinth would *hate* to be the last to hear of it.

"Gregory?" his mother prompted.

"I'm not going."

"But—"

"I wasn't invited."

"Surely an oversight. One that will be corrected, I am certain, after your efforts this evening."

"Mother, as much as I would like to wish Lady Lucinda well, I have no desire to attend her or anyone's wedding. They are such sentimental affairs."

Silence.

Never a good sign.

He looked at Hyacinth. She was regarding him with large owlish eyes. "You like weddings," she said.

He grunted. It seemed the best response.

"You do," she said. "At my wedding, you—"

"Hyacinth, you are my sister. It is different."

"Yes, but you also attended Felicity Albansdale's wedding, and I distinctly recall—"

Gregory turned his back on her before she could recount his merriness. "Mother," he said, "thank you for the invitation, but I do not wish to attend Lady Lucinda's wedding."

Violet opened her mouth as if to ask a question, but then she closed it. "Very well," she said.

Gregory was instantly suspicious. It was not like his mother to capitulate so quickly. Further prying into her motives, however, would eliminate any chance of a quick escape.

It was an easy decision.

"I bid you both *adieu*," he said.

"Where you going?" Hyacinth demanded. "And why are you speaking French?"

He turned to his mother. "She is all yours."

"Yes," Violet sighed. "I know."

Hyacinth immediately turned on her. "What does *that* mean?"

"Oh, for heaven's sake, Hyacinth, you—"

Gregory took advantage of the moment and slipped away while their attention was fixed on each other.

The party was growing more crowded, and it occurred to him that Lucy might very well have arrived while he was speaking with his mother and sister. If so, she wouldn't have made it very far into the ballroom, however, and so he began to make his way toward the receiving line. It was a slow process; he had been out of town for over a month, and everyone seemed to have something to say to him, none of it remotely of interest.

"Best of luck with it," he murmured to Lord Trevelstam, who was trying to interest him in a horse he could not afford. "I am sure you will have no difficulty—"

His voice left him.

He could not speak.

He could not *think*.

Good God, not again.

"Bridgerton?"

Across the room, just by the door. Three gentlemen, an elderly lady, two matrons, and—

Her.

It was her. And he was being pulled, as sure as if there were a rope between them. He needed to reach her side.

"Bridgerton, is something—"

"I beg your pardon," Gregory managed to say, brushing past Trevelstam.

It was her. Except . . .

It was a different her. It wasn't Hermione Watson. It was— He wasn't sure who she was; he could see her only from the back. But there it was—that same splendid and terrible feeling. It made him dizzy. It made him ecstatic. His lungs were hollow. *He* was hollow.

And he wanted her.

It was just as he'd always imagined it—that magical, almost incandescent sense of knowing that his life was complete, that *she* was the one.

Except that he'd done this before. And Hermione Watson *hadn't* been the one.

Dear God, could a man fall insanely, stupidly in love twice?

Hadn't he just told Lucy to be wary and scared, that if she was ever overcome with such a feeling, she should not trust it?

And yet . . .

And yet there she was.

And there *he* was.

And it was happening all over again.

It was just as it had been with Hermione. No, it was worse. His body tingled; he couldn't keep his toes still in his boots. He wanted to jump out of his skin, rush across the room and . . . just . . . just . . .

Just *see* her.

He wanted her to turn. He wanted to see her face. He wanted to know who she was.

He wanted to know *her*.

No.

No, he told himself, trying to force his feet in the other direction. This was madness. He should leave. He should leave right now.

But he couldn't. Even with every rational corner of his soul screaming at him to turn around and walk away, he was rooted to the spot, waiting for her to turn.

Praying for her to turn.

And then she did.

And she was—

Lucy.

He stumbled as if struck.

Lucy?

No. It couldn't be possible. He knew Lucy.

She did not do this to him.

He had seen her dozens of times, kissed her even, and never once felt like this, as if the world might swallow him whole if he did not reach her side and take her hand in his.

There had to be an explanation. He had felt this way before. With Hermione.

But this time—it wasn't quite the same. With Hermione it had been dizzying, new. There had been the thrill of discovery, of conquest. But this was Lucy.

It was Lucy, and—

It all came flooding back. The tilt of her head as she explained why sandwiches ought to be properly sorted. The delightfully peeved look on her face when she had tried to explain to him why he was doing everything wrong in his courtship of Miss Watson.

The way it had felt so right simply to sit on a bench with her in Hyde Park and throw bread at the pigeons.

And the kiss. Dear God, *the kiss.*

He still dreamed about that kiss.

And he wanted her to dream about it, too.

He took a step. Just one—slightly forward and to the side so that he could better see her profile. It was all so familiar now—the tilt of her head, the way her lips moved when she spoke. How could he not have recognized her instantly, even from the back? The memories had been there, tucked away in the recesses of his mind, but he hadn't wanted—no he hadn't allowed himself—to acknowledge his presence.

And then she saw him. Lucy saw him. He saw it first in her eyes, which widened and sparkled, and then in the curve of her lips.

She smiled. For him.

It filled him. To near bursting, it filled him. It was just one smile, but it was all he needed.

He began to walk. He could barely feel his feet, had almost no conscious control over his body. He simply moved, knowing from deep within that he had to reach her.

"Lucy," he said, once he was next to her, forgetting that they were surrounded by strangers, and worse, friends, and he should not presume to use her given name.

But nothing else felt right on his lips.

"Mr. Bridgerton," she said, but her eyes said, *Gregory.*

And he knew.

He loved her.

It was the strangest, most wonderful sensation. It was exhilarating. It was as if the world had suddenly become open to him. Clear. He understood. He understood everything he needed to know, and it was all right there in her eyes.

"Lady Lucinda," he said, bowing deeply over her hand. "May I have this dance?"

Seventeen

In which Our Hero's sister moves things along.

$\mathcal{I}$t was heaven.

Forget angels, forget St. Peter and glittering harpsichords. Heaven was a dance in the arms of one's true love. And when the one in question had a mere week before marrying someone else entirely, aforementioned one had to grab heaven tightly, with both hands.

Metaphorically speaking.

Lucy grinned as she bobbed and twirled. Now there was an image. What would people say if she charged forward and grabbed him with both hands?

And never let go.

Most would say she was mad. A few that she was in love. The shrewd would say both.

"What are you thinking about?" Gregory asked. He was looking at her . . . differently.

She turned away, turned back. She felt daring, almost magical. "Wouldn't you care to know?"

He stepped around the lady to his left and returned to his place. "I would," he answered, smiling wolfishly at her.

But she just smiled and shook her head. Right now she wanted to pretend she was someone else. Someone a little less conventional. Someone a great deal more impulsive.

She did not want to be the same old Lucy. Not tonight. She was sick of planning, sick of placating, sick of never doing anything without first thinking through every possibility and consequence.

If I do this, then that will happen, but if I do that, then this, this, and the other thing will happen, which will yield an entirely different result, which could mean that—

It was enough to make a girl dizzy. It was enough to make her feel paralyzed, unable to take the reins of her own life.

But not tonight. Tonight, somehow, through some amazing miracle named the Duchess of Hastings—or perhaps the dowager Lady Bridgerton, Lucy was not quite certain—she was wearing a gown of the most exquisite green silk, attending the most glittering ball she could ever have imagined.

And she was dancing with the man she was quite certain she would love until the end of time.

"You look different," he said.

"I feel different." She touched his hand as they stepped past each other. His fingers gripped hers when they should have just brushed by. She looked up and saw that he was gazing at her. His eyes were warm and intense and he was watching her the same way—

Dear God, he was watching her the way he'd watched Hermione.

Her body began to tingle. She felt it in the tips of her toes, in places she did not dare to contemplate.

They stepped past each other again, but this time he leaned in, perhaps a bit more than he ought, and said, "I feel different as well."

Her head snapped around, but he had already turned so

that his back was to her. How was he different? Why? What did he *mean*?

She circled around the gentleman to her left, then moved past Gregory.

"Are you glad you attended this evening?" he murmured.

She nodded, since she had moved too far away to answer without speaking too loudly.

But then they were together again, and he whispered, "So am I."

They moved back to their original places and held still as a different couple began to process. Lucy looked up. At him. At his eyes.

They never moved from her face.

And even in the flickering light of the night—the hundreds of candles and torches that lit the glittering ballroom—she could see the gleam there. The way he was looking at her—it was hot and possessive and proud.

It made her shiver.

It made her doubt her ability to stand.

And then the music was done, and Lucy realized that some things must truly be ingrained because she was curtsying and smiling and nodding at the woman next to her as if her entire life had not been altered in the course of the previous dance.

Gregory took her hand and led her to the side of the ballroom, back to where the chaperones milled about, watching their charges over the rims of their glasses of lemonade. But before they reached their destination, he leaned down and whispered in her ear.

"I need to speak with you."

Her eyes flew to his.

"Privately," he added.

She felt him slow their pace, presumably to allow them more time to speak before she was returned to Aunt Harriet. "What is it?" she asked. "Is something amiss?"

He shook his head. "Not any longer."

And she let herself hope. Just a little, because she could not bear to ponder the heartbreak if she was wrong, but maybe . . . Maybe he loved her. Maybe he wished to marry her. Her wedding was less than a week away, but she had not said her vows.

Maybe there was a chance. Maybe there was a way.

She searched Gregory's face for clues, for answers. But when she pressed him for more information, he just shook his head and whispered, "The library. It is two doors down from the ladies' retiring room. Meet me there in thirty minutes."

"Are you mad?"

He smiled. "Just a little."

"Gregory, I—"

He gazed into her eyes, and it silenced her. The way he was looking at her—

It took her breath away.

"I cannot," she whispered, because no matter what they might feel for each other, she was still engaged to another man. And even if she were not, such behavior could only lead to scandal. "I can't be alone with you. You know that."

"You must."

She tried to shake her head, but she could not make herself move.

"Lucy," he said, "you must."

She nodded. It was probably the biggest mistake she would ever make, but she could not say no.

"Mrs. Abernathy," Gregory said, his voice sounding overly loud as he greeted her aunt Harriet. "I return Lady Lucinda to your care."

Aunt Harriet nodded, even though Lucy suspected she had no idea what Gregory had said to her, and then she turned to Lucy and yelled, "I'm sitting down!"

Gregory chuckled, then said, "I must dance with others."

"Of course," Lucy replied, even though she rather suspected she was not wholly cognizant of the various intricacies involved in scheduling an illicit meeting. "I see someone I know," she lied, and then, to her great relief, she actually did see someone she knew—an acquaintance from school. Not a good friend, but still, a familiar enough face to offer greetings.

But before Lucy could even flex her foot, she heard a female voice call out Gregory's name.

Lucy could not see who it was, but she could see Gregory. He had shut his eyes and looked quite pained.

"Gregory!"

The voice had drawn close, and so Lucy turned to her left to see a young woman who could only be one of Gregory's sisters. The younger one, most probably, else she was remarkably well-preserved.

"This must be Lady Lucinda," the woman said. Her hair, Lucy noted, was the precise shade of Gregory's—a rich, warm chestnut. But her eyes were blue, sharp and acute.

"Lady Lucinda," Gregory said, sounding a bit like a man with a chore, "may I present my sister, Lady St. Clair."

"Hyacinth," she said firmly. "We must dispense with the formalities. I am certain we shall be great friends. Now then, you must tell me all about yourself. And then I wish to hear about Anthony and Kate's party last month. I had wished to go, but we had a previous engagement. I heard it was vastly entertaining."

Startled by the human whirlwind in front of her, Lucy looked to Gregory for advice, but he just shrugged and said, "This would be the one I am fond of torturing."

Hyacinth turned to him. "I beg your pardon."

Gregory bowed. "I must go."

And then Hyacinth Bridgerton St. Clair did the oddest thing. Her eyes narrowed, and she looked from her brother to Lucy and back again. And then again. And then one more time. And then she said, "You'll need my help."

"Hy—" Gregory began.

"You will," she cut in. "You have plans. Do not try to deny it."

Lucy could not believe that Hyacinth had deduced all that from one bow and an *I must go*. She opened her mouth to ask a question, but all she got out was, "How—" before Gregory cut her off with a warning look.

"I know that you have something up your sleeve," Hyacinth said to Gregory. "Else you would not have gone to such lengths to secure her attendance this evening."

"He was just being kind," Lucy tried to say.

"Don't be silly," Hyacinth said, giving her a reassuring pat on the arm. "He would never do that."

"That's not true," Lucy protested. Gregory might be a bit of a devil, but his heart was good and true, and she would not countenance anyone—even his sister—saying otherwise.

Hyacinth regarded her with a delighted smile. "I like you," she said slowly, as if she were deciding upon it right then and there. "You are wrong, of course, but I like you, anyway." She turned to her brother. "I like her."

"Yes, you've said as much."

"And you need my help."

Lucy watched as brother and sister exchanged a glance that she couldn't begin to understand.

"You will need my help," Hyacinth said softly. "Tonight, and later, too."

Gregory stared at his sister intently, and then he said, in a voice so quiet that Lucy had to lean forward to hear it, "I need to speak with Lady Lucinda. Alone."

Hyacinth smiled. Just a touch. "I can arrange that."

Lucy had a feeling she could do anything.

"When?" Hyacinth asked.

"Whenever is easiest," Gregory replied.

Hyacinth glanced around the room, although for the life

of her, Lucy could not imagine what sort of information she was gleaning that could possibly be pertinent to the decision at hand.

"One hour," she announced, with all the precision of a military general. "Gregory, you go off and do whatever it is you do at these affairs. Dance. Fetch lemonade. Be seen with that Whitford girl whose parents have been dangling after you for months.

"You," Hyacinth continued, turning to Lucy with an authoritarian gleam in her eye, "shall remain with me. I shall introduce you to everyone you need to know."

"Who do I need to know?" Lucy asked.

"I'm not sure yet. It really doesn't matter."

Lucy could only stare at her in awe.

"In precisely fifty-five minutes," Hyacinth said, "Lady Lucinda will tear her dress."

"I will?"

"*I* will," Hyacinth replied. "I'm good at that sort of thing."

"You're going to tear her dress?" Gregory asked doubtfully. "Right here in the ballroom?"

"Don't worry over the details," Hyacinth said, waving him off dismissively. "Just go and do your part, and meet her in Daphne's dressing room in one hour."

"In the duchess's bedchamber?" Lucy croaked. She couldn't possibly.

"She's Daphne to us," Hyacinth said. "Now then, everyone, off with you."

Lucy just stared at her and blinked. Wasn't she meant to stay at Hyacinth's side?

"That means him," Hyacinth said.

And then Gregory did the most startling thing. He took Lucy's hand. Right there, in the middle of the ballroom where anyone might see, he took her hand and kissed it. "I leave you in good hands," he told her, stepping back with a polite nod. He gave his sister a look of warning before adding, "As difficult as that might be to believe."

Then he went off, presumably to dote on some poor unsuspecting female who had no idea she was nothing but an innocent pawn in his sister's master plan.

Lucy looked back at Hyacinth, somewhat exhausted by the entire encounter. Hyacinth was beaming at her.

"Well done," she said, although to Lucy it sounded more like she was congratulating herself. "Now then," she continued, "why does my brother need to speak with you? And don't say that you have no idea, because I will not believe you."

Lucy pondered the wisdom of various replies and finally decided upon "I have no idea." It wasn't precisely the truth, but she wasn't about to divulge her most secret hopes and dreams to a woman she'd met only minutes earlier, no matter whose sister she might be.

And it made her feel as if she might have won the point.

"Really?" Hyacinth looked suspicious.

"Really."

Hyacinth was clearly unconvinced. "Well, you're clever, at least. I shall grant you that."

Lucy decided she would not be cowed. "Do you know," she said, "I thought I was the most organized and managing person I knew, but I think you're worse."

Hyacinth laughed. "Oh, I am not at all organized. But I *am* managing. And we shall get on famously." She looped her arm through Lucy's. "Like sisters."

One hour later, Lucy had realized three things about Hyacinth, Lady St. Clair.

First, she knew everyone. And everything about everyone.

Second, she was a wealth of information about her brother. Lucy had not needed to ask a single question, but by the time they left the ballroom, she knew Gregory's favorite color (blue) and food (cheese, any sort), and that as a child he had spoken with a lisp.

Lucy had also learned that one should never make the mistake of underestimating Gregory's younger sister. Not only had Hyacinth torn Lucy's dress, she had carried it out with enough flair and cunning so that four people were aware of the mishap (and the need for repair). And she had done all her damage to the hem, so as to conveniently preserve Lucy's modesty.

It was really quite impressive.

"I've done this before," Hyacinth confided as she guided her out of the ballroom.

Lucy was unsurprised.

"It's a useful talent," Hyacinth added, sounding utterly serious. "Here, this way."

Lucy followed her up a back staircase.

"There are very few excuses available to women who wish to leave a social function," Hyacinth continued, displaying a remarkable talent for sticking to her chosen topic like glue. "It behooves us to master every weapon in our arsenal."

Lucy was beginning to believe that she'd led a very sheltered life.

"Ah, here we are." Hyacinth pushed open a door. She peered in. "He's not here yet. Good. That gives me time."

"For what?"

"To mend your dress. I confess I forgot that detail when I formulated my plan. But I know where Daphne keeps needles."

Lucy watched as Hyacinth strode to a dressing table and opened a drawer.

"Right where I thought they were," Hyacinth said with a triumphant smile. "I do love it when I am right. It makes life so much more convenient, wouldn't you agree?"

Lucy nodded, but her mind was on her own question. And then she asked it—"Why are you helping me?"

Hyacinth looked at her as if she were daft. "You can't go back in with a torn dress. Not after we told everyone we'd gone off to mend it."

"No, not that."

"Oh." Hyacinth held up a needle and regarded it thoughtfully. "This will do. What color thread, do you think?"

"White, and you did not answer my question."

Hyacinth ripped a piece of thread off a spool and slid it through the eye of the needle. "I like you," she said. "And I love my brother."

"You know that I am engaged to be married," Lucy said quietly.

"I know." Hyacinth knelt at Lucy's feet, and with quick, sloppy stitches began to sew.

"In a *week*. Less than a week."

"I know. I was invited."

"Oh." Lucy supposed she ought to have known that. "Erm, do you plan to attend?"

Hyacinth looked up. "Do you?"

Lucy's lips parted. Until that moment, the idea of not marrying Haselby was a wispy, far-fetched thing, more of a *oh-how-I-wish-I-did-not-have-to-marry-him* sort of feeling. But now, with Hyacinth watching her so carefully, it began to feel a bit more firm. Still impossible, of course, or at least . . .

Well, maybe . . .

Maybe not quite impossible. Maybe only mostly impossible.

"The papers are signed," Lucy said.

Hyacinth turned back to her sewing. "Are they?"

"My uncle *chose* him," Lucy said, wondering just who she was trying to convince. "It has been arranged for ages."

"Mmmm."

Mmmm? What the devil did *that* mean?

"And he hasn't . . . Your brother hasn't . . ." Lucy fought for words, mortified that she was unburdening herself to a near stranger, to Gregory's own sister, for heaven's sake. But Hyacinth wasn't *saying* anything; she was just sitting there with her eyes focused on the needle looping in and out of Lucy's hem. And if Hyacinth didn't say anything, then Lucy had to. Because— Because—

Well, because she did.

"He has made me no promises," Lucy said, her voice nearly shaking with it. "He stated no intentions."

At that, Hyacinth did look up. She glanced around the room, as if to say, *Look at us, mending your gown in the bedchamber of the Duchess of Hastings.* And she murmured, "Hasn't he?"

Lucy closed her eyes in agony. She was not like Hyacinth St. Clair. One needed only a quarter of an hour in her company to know that she would dare anything, take any chance to secure her own happiness. She would defy convention, stand up to the harshest of critics, and emerge entirely intact, in body and spirit.

Lucy was not so hardy. She wasn't ruled by passions. Her muse had always been good sense. Pragmatism.

Hadn't she been the one to tell Hermione that she needed to marry a man of whom her parents would approve?

Hadn't she told Gregory that she didn't want a violent, overwhelming love? That she just wasn't the sort?

She wasn't that kind of person. She wasn't. When her governess had made line drawings for her to fill, she had always colored between the lines.

"I don't think I can do it," Lucy whispered.

Hyacinth held her gaze for an agonizingly long moment before turning back to her sewing. "I misjudged you," she said softly.

It hit Lucy like a slap in the face.

"Wh . . . wh . . ."

What did you say?

But Lucy's lips would not form the words. She did not wish to hear the answer. And Hyacinth was back to her brisk self, looking up with an irritated expression as she said, "Don't fidget so much."

"Sorry," Lucy mumbled. And she thought—*I've said it again. I am so predictable, so utterly conventional and unimaginative.*

"You're still moving."

"Oh." Good God, could she do nothing right this evening? "Sorry."

Hyacinth jabbed her with the needle. "You're *still* moving."

"I am not!" Lucy almost yelled.

Hyacinth smiled to herself. "That's better."

Lucy looked down and scowled. "Am I bleeding?"

"If you are," Hyacinth said, rising to her feet, "it's nobody's fault but your own."

"I beg your pardon."

But Hyacinth was already standing, a satisfied smile on her face. "There," she announced, motioning to her handiwork. "Certainly not as good as new, but it will pass any inspection this evening."

Lucy knelt to inspect her hem. Hyacinth had been generous in her self-praise. The stitching was a mess.

"I've never been gifted with a needle," Hyacinth said with an unconcerned shrug.

Lucy stood, fighting the impulse to rip the stitches out and fix them herself. "You might have told me," she muttered.

Hyacinth's lips curved into a slow, sly smile. "My, my," she said, "you've turned prickly all of a sudden."

And then Lucy shocked herself by saying, "*You've* been hurtful."

"Possibly," Hyacinth replied, sounding as if she didn't much care one way or the other. She glanced toward the door with a quizzical expression. "He ought to have been here by now."

Lucy's heart thumped strangely in her chest. "You still plan to help me?" she whispered.

Hyacinth turned back. "I am hoping," she replied, her eyes meeting Lucy's with cool assessment, "that you have misjudged yourself."

Gregory was ten minutes late to the assignation. It couldn't be helped; once he had danced with one young lady, it had become apparent that he was required to repeat the favor for a half-dozen others. And although it was difficult to keep his attention on the conversations he was meant to be conducting, he did not mind the delay. It meant that Lucy and Hyacinth were well gone before he slipped out the door. He intended to find some way to make Lucy his wife, but there was no need to go looking for scandal.

He made his way to his sister's bedchamber; he had spent countless hours at Hastings House and knew his way around. When he reached his destination, he entered without knocking, the well-oiled hinges of the door giving way without a sound.

"Gregory."

Hyacinth's voice came first. She was standing next to Lucy, who looked . . .

Stricken.

What had Hyacinth done to her?

"Lucy?" he asked, rushing forward. "Is something wrong?"

Lucy shook her head. "It is of no account."

He turned to his sister with accusing eyes.

Hyacinth shrugged. "I will be in the next room."

"Listening at the door?"

"I shall wait at Daphne's escritoire," she said. "It is halfway across the room, and before you make an objection, I cannot go farther. If someone comes you will need me to rush in to make everything respectable."

Her point was a valid one, loath as Gregory was to admit it, so he gave her a curt nod and watched her leave the room, waiting for the click of the door latch before speaking.

"Did she say something unkind?" he asked Lucy. "She can be disgracefully tactless, but her heart is usually in the right place."

Lucy shook her head. "No," she said softly. "I think she might have said exactly the right thing."

"Lucy?" He stared at her in question.

Her eyes, which had seemed so cloudy, appeared to focus. "What was it you needed to tell me?" she asked.

"Lucy," he said, wondering how best to approach this. He'd been rehearsing speeches in his mind the entire time he'd been dancing downstairs, but now that he was here, he didn't know what to say.

Or rather, he did. But he didn't know the order, and he didn't know the tone. Did he tell her he loved her? Bare his heart to a woman who intended to marry another? Or did he opt for the safer route and explain why she could not marry Haselby?

A month ago, the choice would have been obvious. He was a romantic, fond of grand gestures. He would have declared his love, certain of a happy reception. He would have taken her hand. Dropped to his knees.

He would have kissed her.

But now . . .

He was no longer quite so certain. He trusted Lucy, but he did not trust fate.

"You can't marry Haselby," he said.

Her eyes widened. "What do you mean?"

"You can't marry him," he replied, avoiding the question. "It will be a disaster. It will . . . You must trust me. You must not marry him."

She shook her head. "Why are you telling me this?"

Because I want you for myself.

"Because . . . because . . ." He fought for words. "Because you have become my friend. And I wish for your happiness. He will not be a good husband to you, Lucy."

"Why not?" Her voice was low, hollow, and heartbreakingly unlike her.

"He . . ." Dear God, how did he say it? Would she even understand what he meant?

"He doesn't . . ." He swallowed. There had to be a gentle way to say it. "He doesn't . . . Some people . . ."

He looked at her. Her lower lip was quivering.

"He prefers men," he said, getting the words out as quickly as he was able. "To women. Some men are like that."

And then he waited. For the longest moment she made no reaction, just stood there like a tragic statue. Every now and then she would blink, but beyond that, nothing. And then finally—

"Why?"

Why? He didn't understand. "Why is he—"

"No," she said forcefully. "Why did you tell me? Why would you say it?"

"I told you—"

"No, you didn't do it to be kind. Why did you tell me? Was it just to be cruel? To make me feel the way you feel, because Hermione married my brother and not you?"

"No!" The word burst out of him, and he was holding her, his hands wrapped around her upper arms. "No, Lucy," he said again. "I would never. I want you to be happy. I want . . ."

Her. He wanted her, and he didn't know how to say it. Not then, not when she was looking at him as if he'd broken her heart.

"I could have been happy with him," she whispered.

"No. No, you couldn't. You don't understand, he—"

"Yes, I could," she cried out. "Maybe I wouldn't have loved him, but I could have been happy. It was what I expected. Do you understand, it was what I was prepared for. And you . . . you . . ." She wrenched herself away, turning until he could no longer see her face. "You ruined it."

"How?"

She raised her eyes to his, and the look in them was so stark, so deep, he could not breathe. And she said, "Because you made me want you instead."

His heart slammed in his chest. "Lucy," he said, because he could not say anything else. "Lucy."

"I don't know what to do," she confessed.

"Kiss me." He took her face in his hands. "Just kiss me."

This time, when he kissed her, it was different. She was the same woman in his arms, but *he* was not the same man. His need for her was deeper, more elemental.

He loved her.

He kissed her with everything he had, every breath, every last beat of his heart. His lips found her cheek, her brow, her ears, and all the while, he whispered her name like a prayer—

Lucy Lucy Lucy.

He wanted her. He needed her.

She was like air.

Food.

Water.

His mouth moved to her neck, then down to the lacy edge of her bodice. Her skin burned hot beneath him, and as his fingers slid the gown from one of her shoulders, she gasped—

But she did not stop him.

"Gregory," she whispered, her fingers digging into his hair as his lips moved along her collarbone. "Gregory, oh my G— Gregory."

His hand moved reverently over the curve of her shoulder. Her skin glowed pale and milky smooth in the candlelight, and he was struck by an intense sense of possession. Of pride.

No other man had seen her thus, and he prayed that no other man ever would.

"You can't marry him, Lucy," he whispered urgently, his words hot against her skin.

"Gregory, don't," she moaned.

"You can't." And then, because he knew he could not allow this to go any further, he straightened, pressing one last kiss against her lips before setting her back, forcing her to look him in the eye.

"You cannot marry him," he said again.

"Gregory, what can I—"

He gripped her arms. Hard. And he said it.

"I love you."

Her lips parted. She could not speak.

"I love you," he said again.

Lucy had suspected—she'd hoped—but she hadn't really allowed herself to believe. And so, when she finally found words of her own, they were: "You do?"

He smiled, and then he laughed, and then he rested his forehead on hers. "With all of my heart," he vowed. "I only just realized it. I'm a fool. A blind man. A—"

"No," she cut in, shaking her head. "Do not berate yourself. No one ever notices me straightaway when Hermione is about."

His fingers gripped her all the tighter. "She does not hold a candle to you."

A warm feeling began to spread through her bones. Not

desire, not passion, just pure, unadulterated happiness. "You really mean it," she whispered.

"Enough to move heaven and earth to make sure you do not go through with your wedding to Haselby."

She blanched.

"Lucy?"

No. She could do it. She would do it. It was almost funny, really. She had spent three years telling Hermione that she had to be practical, follow the rules. She'd scoffed when Hermione had gone on about love and passion and hearing music. And now . . .

She took a deep, fortifying breath. And now she was going to break her engagement.

That had been arranged for years.

To the son of an earl.

Five days before the wedding.

Dear God, the scandal.

She stepped back, lifting her chin so that she could see Gregory's face. His eyes were watching her with all the love she herself felt.

"I love you," she whispered, because she had not yet said it. "I love you, too."

For once she was going to stop thinking about everyone else. She wasn't going to take what she was given and make the best of it. She was going to reach for her own happiness, make her own destiny.

She was not going to do what was expected.

She was going to do what *she* wanted.

It was time.

She squeezed Gregory's hands. And she smiled. It was no tentative thing, but wide and confident, full of her hopes, full of her dreams—and the knowledge that she would achieve them all.

It would be difficult. It would be frightening.

But it would be worth it.

"I will speak with my uncle," she said, the words firm and sure. "Tomorrow."

Gregory pulled her against him for one last kiss, quick and passionate with promise. "Shall I accompany you?" he asked. "Call upon him so that I might reassure him of my intentions?"

The new Lucy, the daring and bold Lucy, asked, "And what *are* your intentions?"

Gregory's eyes widened with surprise, then approval, and then his hands took hers.

She felt what he was doing before she realized it by sight. His hands seemed to slide along hers as he descended . . .

Until he was on one knee, looking up at her as if there could be no more beautiful woman in all creation.

Her hand flew to her mouth, and she realized she was shaking.

"Lady Lucinda Abernathy," he said, his voice fervent and sure, "will you do me the very great honor of becoming my wife?"

She tried to speak. She tried to nod.

"Marry me, Lucy," he said. "Marry me."

And this time she did. "Yes." And then, "Yes! Oh, yes!"

"I will make you happy," he said, standing to embrace her. "I promise you."

"There is no need to promise." She shook her head, blinking back the tears. "There is no way you could not."

He opened his mouth, presumably to say more, but he was cut off by a knock at the door, soft but quick.

Hyacinth.

"Go," Gregory said. "Let Hyacinth take you back to the ballroom. I will follow later."

Lucy nodded, tugging at her gown until everything was back in its proper place. "My hair," she whispered, her eyes flying to his.

"It's lovely," he assured her. "You look perfect."

She hurried to the door. "Are you certain?"

I love you, he mouthed. And his eyes said the same.

Lucy pulled open the door, and Hyacinth rushed in. "Good heavens, the two of you are slow," she said. "We need to be getting back. Now."

She strode to the door to the corridor, then stopped, looking first at Lucy, then at her brother. Her gaze settled on Lucy, and she lifted one brow in question.

Lucy held herself tall. "You did not misjudge me," she said quietly.

Hyacinth's eyes widened, and then her lips curved. "Good."

And it was, Lucy realized. It was very good, indeed.

Eighteen

In which Our Heroine makes a terrible discovery.

She could do this.

She could.

She needed only to knock.

And yet there she stood, outside her uncle's study door, her fingers curled into a fist, as if *ready* to knock on the door.

But not quite.

How long had she stood like this? Five minutes? Ten? Either way, it was enough to brand her a ridiculous ninny. A coward.

How did this happen? *Why* did it happen? At school she had been known as capable and pragmatic. She was the girl who knew how to get things done. She was not shy. She was not fearful.

But when it came to Uncle Robert . . .

She sighed. She had always been like this with her uncle. He was so stern, so taciturn.

So unlike her own laughing father had been.

She'd felt like a butterfly when she left for school, but whenever she returned, it was as if she had been stuffed right back in her tight little cocoon. She became drab, quiet.

Lonely.

But not this time. She took a breath, squared her shoulders. This time she would say what she needed to say. She would make herself heard.

She lifted her hand. She knocked.

She waited.

"Enter."

"Uncle Robert," she said, letting herself into his study. It felt dark, even with the late afternoon sunlight slanting in through the window.

"Lucinda," he said, glancing briefly up before returning to his papers. "What is it?"

"I need to speak with you."

He made a notation, scowled at his handiwork, then blotted his ink. "Speak."

Lucy cleared her throat. This would be a great deal easier if he would just *look up* at her. She hated speaking to the top of his head, hated it.

"Uncle Robert," she said again.

He grunted a response but kept on writing.

"Uncle Robert."

She saw his movements slow, and then, finally, he looked up. "What is it, Lucinda?" he asked, clearly annoyed.

"We need to have a conversation about Lord Haselby." There. She had said it.

"Is there a problem?" he asked slowly.

"No," she heard herself say, even though that wasn't at all the truth. But it was what she always said if someone asked if there was a problem. It was one of those things that just came out, like *Excuse me,* or *I beg your pardon.*

It was what she'd been trained to say.

Is there a problem?

No, of course not. No, don't mind my wishes. No, please don't worry yourself on my account.

"Lucinda?" Her uncle's voice was sharp, almost jarring.

"No," she said again, louder this time, as if the volume would give her courage. "I mean yes, there is a problem. And I need to speak with you about it."

Her uncle gave her a bored look.

"Uncle Robert," she began, feeling as if she were tiptoeing through a field of hedgehogs, "did you know . . ." She bit her lip, glancing everywhere but at his face. "That is to say, were you aware . . ."

"Out with it," he snapped.

"Lord Haselby," Lucy said quickly, desperate just to get it over with. "He doesn't like women."

For a moment Uncle Robert did nothing but stare. And then he . . .

Laughed.

He *laughed*.

"Uncle Robert?" Lucy's heart began to beat far too quickly. "Did you know this?"

"Of course I knew it," he snapped. "Why do you think his father is so eager to have you? He knows you won't talk."

Why wouldn't she talk?

"You should be thanking me," Uncle Robert said harshly, cutting into her thoughts. "Half the men of the *ton* are brutes. I'm giving you to the only one who won't bother you."

"But—"

"Do you have any idea how many women would love to take your place?"

"That is not the point, Uncle Robert."

His eyes turned to ice. "I beg your pardon."

Lucy stood perfectly still, suddenly realizing that this was it. This was her moment. She had never countermanded him before, and she probably never would again.

She swallowed. And then she said it. "I do not wish to marry Lord Haselby."

Silence. But his eyes . . .

His eyes were thunderous.

Lucy met his stare with cool detachment. She could feel a strange new strength growing inside of her. She would not back down. Not now, not when the rest of her life was at stake.

Her uncle's lips pursed and twisted, even as the rest of his face seemed to be made of stone. Finally, just when Lucy was certain that the silence would break her, he asked, his voice clipped, "May I ask why?"

"I—I want children," Lucy said, latching on to the first excuse she could think of.

"Oh, you'll have them," he said.

He smiled then, and her blood turned to ice.

"Uncle Robert?" she whispered.

"He may not like women, but he will be able to do the job often enough to sire a brat off you. And if he can't . . ." He shrugged.

"What?" Lucy felt panic rising in her chest. "What do you mean?"

"Davenport will take care of it."

"His father?" Lucy gasped.

"Either way, it is a direct male heir, and that is all that is important."

Lucy's hand flew to her mouth. "Oh, I can't. I can't." She thought of Lord Davenport, with his horrible breath and jiggly jowls. And his cruel, cruel eyes. He would not be kind. She didn't know how she knew, but he wouldn't be kind.

Her uncle leaned forward in his seat, his eyes narrowing menacingly. "We all have our positions in life, Lucinda, and yours is to be a nobleman's wife. Your duty is to provide an heir. And you will do it, in whatever fashion Davenport deems necessary."

Lucy swallowed. She had always done as she was told. She had always accepted that the world worked in certain ways. Dreams could be adjusted; the social order could not.

Take what you are given, and make the best of things.

It was what she had always said. It was what she had always done.

But not this time.

She looked up, directly into her uncle's eyes. "I won't do it," she said, and her voice did not waver. "I won't marry him."

"What . . . did . . . you . . . say?" Each word came out like its own little sentence, pointy and cold.

Lucy swallowed. "I said—"

"I know what you said!" he roared, slamming his hands on his desk as he rose to his feet. "How dare you question me? I have raised you, fed you, given you every bloody thing you need. I have looked after and protected this family for ten years, when none of it—*none of it*—will come to me."

"Uncle Robert," she tried to say. But she could barely hear her own voice. Every word he had said was true. He did not own this house. He did not own the Abbey or any of the other Fennsworth holdings. He had nothing other than what Richard might choose to give him once he fully assumed his position as earl.

"I am your guardian," her uncle said, his voice so low it shook. "Do you understand? You will marry Haselby, and we will never speak of this again."

Lucy stared at her uncle in horror. He had been her guardian for ten years, and in all that time, she had never seen him lose his temper. His displeasure was always served cold.

"It's that Bridgerton idiot, isn't it?" he bit off, angrily swiping at some books on his desk. They tumbled to the floor with a loud thud.

Lucy jumped back.

"Tell me!"

She said nothing, watching her uncle warily as he advanced upon her.

"Tell me!" he roared.

"Yes," she said quickly, taking another step back. "How did you— How did you know?"

"Do you think I'm an idiot? His mother and his sister *both* beg the favor of your company on the same day?" He swore under his breath. "They were obviously plotting to steal you away."

"But you let me go to the ball."

"Because his sister is a duchess, you little fool! Even Davenport agreed that you had to attend."

"But—"

"Christ above," Uncle Robert swore, shocking Lucy into silence. "I cannot believe your stupidity. Has he even promised marriage? Are you really prepared to toss over the heir to an earldom for the *possibility* of a viscount's fourth son?"

"Yes," Lucy whispered.

Her uncle must have seen the determination on her face, because he paled. "What have you done?" he demanded. "Have you let him touch you?"

Lucy thought of their kiss, and she blushed.

"You stupid cow," he hissed. "Well, lucky for you Haselby won't know how to tell a virgin from a whore."

"Uncle Robert!" Lucy shook with horror. She had not grown so bold that she could brazenly allow him to think her impure. "I would never— I didn't— How could you think it of me?"

"Because you are acting like a bloody idiot," he snapped. "As of this minute, you will not leave this house until you leave for your wedding. If I have to post guards at your bedchamber door, I will."

"No!" Lucy cried out. "How could you do this to me? What does it matter? We don't need their money. We don't need their connections. Why can't I marry for love?"

At first her uncle did not react. He stood as if frozen, the only movement a vein pounding in his temple. And then, just when Lucy thought she might begin to breathe again, he cursed violently and lunged toward her, pinning her against the wall.

"Uncle Robert!" she gasped. His hand was on her chin, forcing her head into an unnatural position. She tried to swallow, but it was almost impossible with her neck arched so tightly. "Don't," she managed to get out, but it was barely a whimper. "Please . . . Stop."

But his grip only tightened, and his forearm pressed against her collarbone, the bones of his wrist digging painfully into her skin.

"You will marry Lord Haselby," he hissed. "You'll marry him, and I will tell you why."

Lucy said nothing, just stared at him with frantic eyes.

"You, my dear Lucinda, are the final payment of a long-standing debt to Lord Davenport."

"What do you mean?" she whispered.

"Blackmail," Uncle Robert said in a grim voice. "We have been paying Davenport for years."

"But why?" Lucy asked. What could they have possibly done to warrant blackmail?

Her uncle's lip curled mockingly. "Your father, the beloved eighth Earl of Fennsworth, was a traitor."

Lucy gasped, and it felt as if her throat were tightening, tying itself into a knot. It couldn't be true. She'd thought perhaps an extramarital affair. Maybe an earl who wasn't really an Abernathy. But treason? Dear God . . . *no*.

"Uncle Robert," she said, trying to reason with him. "There must be a mistake. A misunderstanding. My father . . . He was not a traitor."

"Oh, I assure you he was, and Davenport knows it."

Lucy thought of her father. She could still see him in her mind—tall, handsome, with laughing blue eyes. He had spent money far too freely; even as a small child she had known that. But he was not a traitor. He could not have been. He had a gentleman's honor. She remembered that. It was in the way he'd stood, the things he'd taught her.

"You are lying," she said, the words burning in her throat. "Or misinformed."

"There is proof," her uncle said, abruptly releasing her and striding across the room to his decanter of brandy. He poured a glass and took a long gulp. "And Davenport has it."

"How?"

"I don't know how," he snapped. "I only know that he does. I have seen it."

Lucy swallowed and hugged her arms to her chest, still trying to absorb what he was telling her. "What sort of proof?"

"Letters," he said grimly. "Written in your father's hand."

"They could be forged."

"They have his seal!" he thundered, slamming his glass down.

Lucy's eyes widened as she watched the brandy slosh over the side of the glass and off the edge of the desk.

"Do you think I would accept something like this without verifying it myself?" her uncle demanded. "There was information—details—things only your father could have known. Do you think I would have paid Davenport's blackmail all these years if there was a chance it was false?"

Lucy shook her head. Her uncle was many things, but he was not a fool.

"He came to me six months after your father died. I have been paying him ever since."

"But why me?" she asked.

Her uncle chuckled bitterly. "Because you will be the perfect upstanding, obedient bride. You will make up for Haselby's deficiencies. Davenport had to get the boy married to someone, and he needed a family that would not talk." He gave her a level stare. "Which we will not. We cannot. And he knows it."

She shook her head in agreement. She would never speak of such things, whether she was Haselby's wife or not. She *liked* Haselby. She did not wish to make life difficult for him. But neither did she wish to be his wife.

"If you do not marry him," her uncle said slowly, "the entire Abernathy family will be ruined. Do you understand?"

Lucy stood frozen.

"We are not speaking of a childhood transgression, a Gypsy in the family tree. Your father committed high treason. He sold state secrets to the French, passed them off to agents posing as smugglers on the coast."

"But why?" Lucy whispered. "We didn't need the money."

"How do you think we *got* the money?" her uncle returned caustically. "And your father—" He swore under his breath. "He always had a taste for danger. He probably did it for the thrill of it. Isn't that a joke upon us all? The very earldom is in danger, and all because your father wanted a spot of adventure."

"Father wasn't like that," Lucy said, but inside she wasn't so sure. She had been just eight when he had been killed by a footpad in London. She had been told that he had come to the defense of a lady, but what if that, too, was a lie? Had he been killed because of his traitorous actions? He was her father, but how much did she truly know of him?

But Uncle Robert didn't appear to have heard her comment. "If you do not marry Haselby," he said, his words low and precise, "Lord Davenport will reveal the truth about your father, and you will bring shame upon the entire house of Fennsworth."

Lucy shook her head. Surely there was another way. This couldn't rest all upon her shoulders.

"You think not?" Uncle Robert laughed scornfully. "Who

do you think will suffer, Lucinda? You? Well, yes, I suppose you will suffer, but we can always pack you off to some school and let you moulder away as an instructor. You'd probably enjoy it."

He took a few steps in her direction, his eyes never leaving her face. "But do think of your brother," he said. "How will he fare as the son of a known traitor? The king will almost certainly strip him of his title. And most of his fortune as well."

"No," Lucy said. *No.* She didn't want to believe it. Richard had done nothing wrong. Surely he couldn't be blamed for his father's sins.

She sank into a chair, desperately trying to sort through her thoughts and emotions.

Treason. How could her father have done such a thing? It went against everything she'd been brought up to believe in. Hadn't her father loved England? Hadn't he told her that the Abernathys had a sacred duty to all Britain?

Or had that been Uncle Robert? Lucy shut her eyes tightly, trying to remember. Someone had said that to her. She was sure of it. She could remember where she'd stood, in front of the portrait of the first earl. She remembered the smell of the air, and the exact words, and—blast it all, she remembered everything save the person who'd spoken them.

She opened her eyes and looked at her uncle. It had probably been he. It sounded like something he would say. He did not choose to speak with her very often, but when he did, duty was always a popular topic.

"Oh, Father," she whispered. How could he have done this? To sell secrets to Napoleon—he'd jeopardized the lives of thousands of British soldiers. Or even—

Her stomach churned. Dear God, he may have been responsible for their deaths. Who knew what he had revealed to the enemy, how many lives had been lost because of his actions?

"It is up to you, Lucinda," her uncle said. "It is the only way to end it."

She shook her head, uncomprehending. "What do you mean?"

"Once you are a Davenport, there can be no more blackmail. Any shame they bring upon us would fall on their shoulders as well." He walked to the window, leaning heavily on the sill as he looked out. "After ten years, I will finally— *We* will finally be free."

Lucy said nothing. There was nothing to say. Uncle Robert peered at her over his shoulder, then turned and walked toward her, watching her closely the entire way. "I see you finally grasp the gravity of the situation," he said.

She looked at him with haunted eyes. There was no compassion in his face, no sympathy or affection. Just a cold mask of duty. He had done what was expected of him, and she would have to do the same.

She thought of Gregory, of his face when he had asked her to marry him. He loved her. She did not know what manner of miracle had brought it about, but he loved her.

And she loved him.

God above, it was almost funny. She, who had always mocked romantic love, had fallen. Completely and hopelessly, she'd fallen in love—enough to throw aside everything she'd thought she believed in. For Gregory she was willing to step into scandal and chaos. For Gregory she would brave the gossip and the whispers and the innuendo.

She, who went mad when her shoes were out of order in her wardrobe, was prepared to jilt the son of an earl four days before the wedding! If that wasn't love, she did not know what was.

Except now it was over. Her hopes, her dreams, the risks she longed to take—they were all over.

She had no choice. If she defied Lord Davenport, her family would be ruined. She thought of Richard and

Hermione—so happy, so in love. How could she consign them to a life of shame and poverty?

If she married Haselby her life would not be what she wanted for herself, but she would not suffer. Haselby was reasonable. He was kind. If she appealed to him, surely he would protect her from his father. And her life would be . . .

Comfortable.

Routine.

Far better than Richard and Hermione would fare if her father's shame was made public. Her sacrifice was nothing compared to what her family would be forced to endure if she refused.

Hadn't she once wanted nothing more than comfort and routine? Couldn't she learn to want this again?

"I will marry him," she said, sightlessly gazing at the window. It was raining. When had it begun to rain?

"Good."

Lucy sat in her chair, utterly still. She could feel the energy draining from her body, sliding through her limbs, seeping out her fingers and toes. Lord, she was tired. Weary. And she kept thinking that she wanted to cry.

But she had no tears. Even after she'd risen and walked slowly back to her room—she had no tears.

The next day, when the butler asked her if she was at home for Mr. Bridgerton, and she shook her head—she had no tears.

And the day after that, when she was forced to repeat the same gesture—she had no tears.

But the day after that, after spending twenty-hours holding his calling card, gently sliding her finger over his name, of tracing each letter—*The Hon. Gregory Bridgerton*—she began to feel them, pricking behind her eyes.

Then she caught sight of him standing on the pavement, looking up at the façade of Fennsworth House.

And he saw her. She knew he did; his eyes widened and

his body tensed, and she could feel it, every ounce of his bewilderment and anger.

She let the curtain drop. Quickly. And she stood there, trembling, shaking, and yet still unable to move. Her feet were frozen to the floor, and she began to feel it again—that awful rushing panic in her belly.

It was wrong. It was all so wrong, and yet she knew she was doing what had to be done.

She stood there. At the window, staring at the ripples in the curtain. She stood there as her limbs grew tense and tight, and she stood there as she forced herself to breathe. She stood there as her heart began to squeeze, harder and harder, and she stood there as it all slowly began to subside.

Then, somehow, she made her way to the bed and lay down.

And then, finally, she found her tears.

Nineteen

**In which Our Hero takes matters—
and Our Heroine—into his own hands.**

By Friday Gregory was desperate.

Thrice he'd called upon Lucy at Fennsworth House. Thrice he'd been turned away.

He was running out of time.

They were running out of time.

What the *hell* was going on? Even if Lucy's uncle had denied her request to stop the wedding—and he could not have been pleased; she was, after all, attempting to jilt a future earl—surely Lucy would have attempted to contact him.

She loved him.

He knew it the way he knew his own voice, his own heart. He knew it the way he knew the earth was round and her eyes were blue and that two plus two would always *always* be four.

Lucy loved him. She did not lie. She could not lie.

She *would* not lie. Not about something like this.

Which meant that something was wrong. There could be no other explanation.

He had looked for her in the park, waiting for hours at the bench where she liked to feed pigeons, but she had not appeared. He had watched her door, hoping he might intercept her on her way to carry out errands, but she had not ventured outside.

And then, after the third time he had been refused entry, he saw her. Just a glimpse through the window; she'd let the curtains fall quickly. But it had been enough. He'd not been able to see her face—not well enough to gauge her expression. But there had been something in the way she moved, in the hurried, almost frantic release of the curtains.

Something was wrong.

Was she being held against her will? Had she been drugged? Gregory's mind raced with the possibilities, each more dire than the last.

And now it was Friday night. Her wedding was in less than twelve hours. And there was not a whisper—not a peep—of gossip. If there were even a hint that the Haselby-Abernathy wedding might not take place as planned, Gregory would have heard about it. If nothing else, Hyacinth would have said something. Hyacinth knew everything, usually before the subjects of the rumors themselves.

Gregory stood in the shadows across the street from Fennsworth House and leaned against the trunk of a tree, staring, just staring. Was that her window? The one through which he'd seen her earlier that day? There was no candle-light peeking through, but the draperies were probably heavy and thick. Or perhaps she'd gone to bed. It was late.

And she had a wedding in the morning.

Good God.

He could not let her marry Lord Haselby. He could not. If there was one thing he knew in his heart, it was that he and Lucinda Abernathy were meant to be husband and wife. Hers was the face he was supposed to gaze upon over eggs and bacon and kippers and cod and toast every morning.

A snort of laughter pressed through his nose, but it was that nervous, desperate kind of laughter, the sound one made when the only alternative was to cry. Lucy had to marry him, if only so that they could eat masses and masses of food together every morning.

He looked at her window.

What he *hoped* was her window. With his luck he was mooning over the servants' washroom.

How long he stood there he did not know. For the first time in his memory, he felt powerless, and at least this—watching a bloody window—was something he could control.

He thought about his life. Charmed, for sure. Plenty of money, lovely family, scads of friends. He had his health, he had his sanity, and until the fiasco with Hermione Watson, an unshakable belief in his own sense of judgment. He might not be the most disciplined of men, and perhaps he should have paid more attention to all those things Anthony liked to pester him about, but he knew what was right, and he knew what was wrong, and he'd known—he had absolutely *known*—that his life would play out on a happy and contented canvas.

He was simply that sort of person.

He wasn't melancholy. He wasn't given to fits of temper.

And he'd never had to work very hard.

He looked up at the window, thoughtfully.

He'd grown complacent. So sure of his own happy ending that he hadn't believed—he *still* couldn't quite believe—that he might not get what he wanted.

He had proposed. She had accepted. True, she had been promised to Haselby, and still was, for that matter.

But wasn't true love supposed to triumph? Hadn't it done

so for all his brothers and sisters? Why the hell was he so unlucky?

He thought about his mother, remembered the look on her face when she had so skillfully dissected his character. She had got most everything right, he realized.

But only most.

It was true that he had never had to work very hard at anything. But that was only part of the story. He was not indolent. He would work his fingers to the very bone if only . . .

If only he had a reason.

He stared at the window.

He had a reason now.

He'd been waiting, he realized. Waiting for Lucy to convince her uncle to release her from her engagement. Waiting for the puzzle pieces that made up his life to fall into position so that he could fit the last one in its place with a triumphant "Aha!"

Waiting.

Waiting for love. Waiting for a calling.

Waiting for clarity, for that moment when he would know exactly how to proceed.

It was time to stop waiting, time to forget about fate and destiny.

It was time to act. To work.

Hard.

No one was going to hand him that second-to-last piece of the puzzle; he had to find it for himself.

He needed to see Lucy. And it had to be now, since it appeared he was forbidden to call upon her in a more conventional manner.

He crossed the street, then slipped around the corner to the back of the house. The ground floor windows were tightly shut, and all was dark. Higher on the façade, a few curtains fluttered in the breeze, but there was no way Gregory could scale the building without killing himself.

He took stock of his surroundings. To the left, the street. To the right, the alley and mews. And in front of him . . .

The servants' entrance.

He regarded it thoughtfully. Well, why not?

He stepped forward and placed his hand on the knob.

It turned.

Gregory almost laughed with delight. At the very least, he went back to believing—well, perhaps just a little—about fate and destiny and all that rot. Surely this was not a usual occurrence. A servant must have sneaked out, perhaps to make his own assignation. If the door was unlocked, then clearly Gregory was meant to go inside.

Or he was mad in the head.

He decided to believe in fate.

Gregory shut the door quietly behind him, then gave his eyes a minute to become accustomed to the dark. He appeared to be in a large pantry, with the kitchen off to the right. There was a decent chance that some of the lower servants slept nearby, so he removed his boots, carrying them in one hand as he ventured deeper into the house.

His stockinged feet were silent as he crept up the back stairs, making his way to the second floor—the one he thought housed Lucy's bedchamber. He paused on the landing, stopping for a brief moment of sanity before stepping out into the hall.

What was he thinking? He hadn't the slightest clue what might happen if he were caught here. Was he breaking a law? Probably. He couldn't imagine how he might not be. And while his position as brother to a viscount would keep him from the gallows, it would not wipe his slate clean when the home he'd chosen to invade belonged to an earl.

But he had to see Lucy. He was done with waiting.

He took a moment on the landing to orient himself, then walked toward the front of the house. There were two doors at the end. He paused, painting a picture of the house's façade in his mind, then reached for the one on the left. If Lucy had indeed been in her own room when he'd seen her, then this was the correct door. If not . . .

Well, then, he hadn't a clue. Not a clue. And here he was, prowling in the Earl of Fennsworth's house after midnight.

Good God.

He turned the knob slowly, letting out a relieved breath when it made no clicks or squeaks. He opened the door just far enough to fit his body through the opening, then carefully shut it behind him, only then taking the time to examine the room.

It was dark, with scarcely any moonlight filtering in around the window coverings. His eyes had already adjusted to the dimness, however, and he could make out various pieces of furniture—a dressing table, a wardrobe . . .

A bed.

It was a heavy, substantial thing, with a canopy and full drapes that closed around it. If there was indeed someone inside, she slept quietly—no snoring, no rustling, nothing.

That's how Lucy would sleep, he suddenly thought. Like the dead. She was no delicate flower, his Lucy, and she would not tolerate anything less than a perfectly restful night. It seemed odd that he would be so certain of this, but he was.

He *knew* her, he realized. He truly knew her. Not just the usual things. In fact, he *didn't* know the usual things. He did not know her favorite color. Nor could he guess her favorite animal or food.

But somehow it didn't matter if he didn't know if she preferred pink or blue or purple or black. He knew her heart. He *wanted* her heart.

And he could not allow her to marry someone else.

Carefully, he drew back the curtains.

There was no one there.

Gregory swore under his breath, until he realized that the

sheets were mussed, the pillow with a fresh indent of someone's head.

He whirled around just in time to see a candlestick swinging wildly through the air at him.

Letting out a surprised grunt, he ducked, but not fast enough to avoid a glancing blow to his temple. He swore again, this time in full voice, and then he heard—

"Gregory?"

He blinked. "Lucy?"

She rushed forward. "What are you doing here?"

He motioned impatiently toward the bed. "Why aren't you asleep?"

"Because I'm getting married tomorrow."

"Well, that's why I'm here."

She stared at him dumbly, as if his presence was so unexpected that she could not muster the correct reaction. "I thought you were an intruder," she finally said, motioning to the candlestick.

He allowed himself the tiniest of smiles. "Not to put too fine a point on it," he murmured, "but I am."

For a moment it looked as if she might return the smile. But instead she hugged her arms to her chest and said, "You must go. Right now."

"Not until you speak with me."

Her eyes slid to a point over his shoulder. "There is nothing to say."

"What about 'I love you'?"

"Don't say that," she whispered.

He stepped forward. "I love you."

"Gregory, please."

Even closer. "I love you."

She took a breath. Squared her shoulders. "I am marrying Lord Haselby tomorrow."

"No," he said, "you're not."

Her lips parted.

He reached out and captured her hand in his. She did not pull away.

"Lucy," he whispered.

She closed her eyes.

"Be with me," he said.

Slowly, she shook her head. "Please don't."

He tugged her closer and pulled the candlestick from her slackening fingers. "Be with me, Lucy Abernathy. Be my love, be my wife."

She opened her eyes, but she held his gaze for only a moment before twisting away. "You're making it so much worse," she whispered.

The pain in her voice was unbearable. "Lucy," he said, touching her cheek, "let me help you."

She shook her head, but she paused as her cheek settled into his palm. Not for long. Barely a second. But he felt it.

"You can't marry him," he said, tilting her face toward his. "You won't be happy."

Her eyes glistened as they met his. In the dim light of the night, they looked a dark, dark gray, and achingly sad. He could imagine the entire world there, in the depths of her gaze. Everything he needed to know, everything he might *ever* need to know—it was there, within her.

"You won't be happy, Lucy," he whispered. "You know that you won't."

Still, she didn't speak. The only sound was her breath, moving quietly across her lips. And then, finally—

"I will be content."

"*Content?*" he echoed. His hand dropped from her face, falling to his side as he stepped back. "You will be content?"

She nodded.

"And that's *enough?*"

She nodded again, but smaller this time.

Anger began to spark within him. She was willing to toss him away for that? Why wasn't she willing to fight?

She loved him, but did she love him enough?

"Is it his position?" he demanded. "Does it mean so much to you to be a countess?"

She waited too long before replying, and he knew she was lying when she said, "Yes."

"I don't believe you," he said, and his voice sounded terrible. Wounded. Angry. He looked at his hand, blinking with surprise as he realized he was still holding the candlestick. He wanted to hurl it at the wall. Instead he set it down. His hands were not quite steady, he saw.

He looked at her. She said nothing.

"Lucy," he begged, "just tell me. Let me help you."

She swallowed, and he realized she was no longer looking at his face.

He took her hands in his. She tensed, but she did not pull away. Their bodies were facing each other, and he could see the ragged rise and fall of her chest.

It matched what he felt in his own.

"I love you," he said. Because if he kept saying it, maybe it would be enough. Maybe the words would fill the room, surround her and sneak beneath her skin. Maybe she would finally realize that there were certain things that could not be denied.

"We belong together," he said. "For eternity."

Her eyes closed. One single, heavy blink. But when she opened them again, she looked shattered.

"Lucy," he said, trying to put his very soul into one single word. "Lucy, tell me—"

"Please don't say that," she said, turning her head so that she was not quite looking at him. Her voice caught and shook. "Say anything else, but not that."

"Why not?"

And then she whispered, "Because it's true."

His breath caught, and in one swift movement he pulled her to him. It was not an embrace; not quite. Their fingers were entwined, their arms bent so that their hands met between their shoulders.

He whispered her name.

Lucy's lips parted.

He whispered it again, so soft that the words were more of a motion than a sound.

Lucy Lucy.

She held still, barely breathing. His body was so close to hers, yet not quite touching. There was heat, though, filling the space between them, swirling through her nightgown, trembling along her skin.

She tingled.

"Let me kiss you," he whispered. "One more time. Let me kiss you one more time, and if you tell me to go, I swear that I will."

Lucy could feel herself slipping, sliding into need, falling into a hazy place of love and desire where right was not quite so identifiable from wrong.

She loved him. She loved him so much, and he could not be hers. Her heart was racing, her breath was shaking, and all she could think was that she would never feel this way again. No one would ever look at her the way Gregory was, right at that very moment. In less than a day she was to marry a man who wouldn't even wish to kiss her.

She would never feel this strange curling in the core of her womanhood, the fluttering in her belly. This was the last time she'd stare at someone's lips and *ache* for them to touch hers.

Dear God, she wanted him. She wanted *this*. Before it was too late.

And he loved her. He loved her. He'd said it, and even though she couldn't quite believe it, she believed *him*.

She licked her lips.

"Lucy," he whispered, her name a question, a statement, and a plea—all in one.

She nodded. And then, because she knew she could not lie to herself or to him, she said the words.

"*Kiss me.*"

There would be no pretending later, no claiming she had been swept away by passion, stripped of her ability to think. The decision was hers. And she'd made it.

For a moment Gregory did not move, but she knew that he heard her. His breath sucked raggedly into him, and his eyes turned positively liquid as he gazed at her. "Lucy," he said, his voice husky and deep and rough and a hundred other things that turned her bones to milk.

His lips found the hollow where her jaw met her neck. "Lucy," he murmured.

She wanted to say something in return, but she could not. It had taken all she had just to ask for his kiss.

"I love you," he whispered, trailing the words along her neck to her collarbone. "I love you. I love you."

They were the most painful, wonderful, horrible, magnificent words he could have said. She wanted to cry—with happiness *and* sorrow.

Pleasure and pain.

And she understood—for the first time in her life—she understood the prickly joy of complete selfishness. She shouldn't be doing this. She knew she shouldn't, and she knew he probably thought that this meant that she would find a way out of her commitment to Haselby.

She was lying to him. As surely as if she'd said the words.

But she could not help herself.

This was her moment. Her one moment to hold bliss in her hands. And it would have to last a lifetime.

Emboldened by the fire within her, she pressed her hands roughly to his cheeks, pulling his mouth against hers for a torrid kiss. She had no idea what she was doing—she was sure there must be rules to all this, but she did not care. She just wanted to kiss him. She couldn't stop herself.

One of his hands moved to her hips, burning through the thin fabric of her nightgown. Then it stole around to her bottom, squeezing and cupping, and there was no more space between them. She felt herself sliding down, and then they were on the bed, and she was on her back, his body pressed against hers, the heat and the weight of it exquisitely male.

She felt like a woman.

She felt like a goddess.

She felt like she could wrap herself around him and never let go.

"Gregory," she whispered, finding her voice as she twined her fingers in his hair.

He stilled, and she knew he was waiting for her to say more.

"I love you," she said, because it was true, and because she needed *some*thing to be true. Tomorrow he would hate her. Tomorrow she would betray him, but in this, at least, she would not lie.

"I want you," she said, when he lifted his head to gaze into her eyes. He stared at her long and hard, and she knew that he was giving her one last chance to back out.

"I want you," she said again, because she wanted him beyond words. She wanted him to kiss her, to take her, and to forget that she was not whispering words of love.

"Lu—"

She placed a finger to his mouth. And she whispered, "I want to be yours." And then she added, "Tonight."

His body shuddered, his breath moving audibly over his lips. He groaned something, maybe her name, and then his mouth met hers in a kiss that gave and took and burned and consumed until Lucy could not help but move underneath him. Her hands slid to his neck, then inside his coat, her fingers desperately seeking heat and skin. With a roughly mumbled curse, he rose up, still straddling her, and yanked off the coat and cravat.

She stared at him with wide eyes. He was removing his shirt, not slowly or with finesse, but with a frantic speed that underscored his desire.

He was not in control. She might not be in control, but neither was he. He was as much a slave to this fire as she was.

He tossed his shirt aside, and she gasped at the sight of him, the light sprinkling of hair across his chest, the muscles that sculpted and stretched under his skin.

He was beautiful. She hadn't realized a man could be beautiful, but it was the only word that could possibly describe him. She lifted one hand and gingerly placed it against his skin. His blood leaped and pulsed beneath, and she nearly pulled away.

"No," he said, covering her hand with his own. He wrapped his fingers around hers and then took her to his heart.

He looked into her eyes.

She could not look away.

And then he was back, his body hard and hot against hers, his hands everywhere and his lips everywhere else. And her nightgown— It no longer seemed to be covering quite so much of her. It was up against her thighs, then pooled around her waist. He was touching her—not *there,* but close. Skimming along her belly, scorching her skin.

"Gregory," she gasped, because somehow his fingers had found her breast.

"Oh, Lucy," he groaned, cupping her, squeezing, tickling the tip, and—

Oh, dear God. How was it possible that she felt it *there?*

Her hips arched and bucked, and she needed to be closer. She needed something she couldn't quite identify, something that would fill her, complete her.

He was tugging at her nightgown now, and it slipped over

her head, leaving her scandalously bare. One of her hands instinctively rose to cover her, but he grabbed her wrist and held it against his own chest. He was straddling her, sitting upright, staring down at her as if . . . as if . . .

As if she were beautiful.

He was looking at her the way men always looked at Hermione, except somehow there was *more*. More passion, more desire.

She felt worshipped.

"Lucy," he murmured, lightly caressing the side of her breast. "I feel . . . I think . . ."

His lips parted, and he shook his head. Slowly, as if he did not quite understand what was happening to him. "I have been waiting for this," he whispered. "For my entire life. I didn't even know. I didn't know."

She took his hand and brought it to her mouth, kissing the palm. She understood.

His breath quickened, and then he slid off of her, his hands moving to the fastenings of his breeches.

Her eyes widened, and she watched.

"I will be gentle," he vowed. "I promise you."

"I'm not worried," she said, managing a wobbly smile.

His lips curved in return. "You look worried."

"I'm not." But still, her eyes wandered.

Gregory chuckled, lying down beside her. "It might hurt. I'm told it does at the beginning."

She shook her head. "I don't care."

He let his hand wander down her arm. "Just remember, if there is pain, it will get better."

She felt it beginning again, that slow burning in her belly. "How much better?" she asked, her voice breathy and unfamiliar.

He smiled as his fingers found her hip. "Quite a bit, I'm told."

"Quite a bit," she asked, now barely able to speak, "or . . . rather a lot?"

He moved over her, his skin finding every inch of hers. It was wicked.

It was bliss.

"Rather a lot," he answered, nipping lightly at her neck. "More than rather a lot, actually."

She felt her legs slide open, and his body nestled in the space between them. She could feel him, hard and hot and pressing against her. She stiffened, and he must have felt it, because his lips crooned a soft, "Shhhh," at her ear.

From there he moved down.

And down.

And down.

His mouth trailed fire along her neck to the hollow of her shoulder, and then—

Oh, dear God.

His hand was cupping her breast, making it round and plump, and his mouth found the tip.

She jerked beneath him.

He chuckled, and his other hand found her shoulder, holding her immobile while he continued his torture, pausing only to move to the other side.

"Gregory," Lucy whimpered, because she did not know what else to say. She was lost to the sensation, completely helpless against his sensual onslaught. She couldn't explain, she couldn't fix or rationalize. She could only feel, and it was the most terrifying, thrilling thing imaginable.

With one last nip, he released her breast and brought his face back up to hers. His breathing was ragged, his muscles tense.

"Touch me," he said hoarsely.

Her lips parted, and her eyes found his.

"Anywhere," he begged.

It was only then that Lucy realized that her hands were at her sides, gripping the sheets as if they could keep her sane. "I'm sorry," she said, and then, amazingly, she began to laugh.

One side of his mouth curved up. "We're going to have to break you of that habit," he murmured.

She brought her hands to his back, lightly exploring his skin. "You don't want me to apologize?" she asked. When he joked, when he teased—it made her comfortable. It made her bold.

"Not for this," he groaned.

She rubbed her feet against his calves. "Ever?"

And then his hands started doing unspeakable things. "Do you want me to apologize?"

"No," she gasped. He was touching her intimately, in ways she didn't know she could be touched. It should have been the most awful thing in the world, but it wasn't. It made her stretch, arch, squirm. She had no idea what it was she was feeling—she couldn't have described it with Shakespeare himself at her disposal.

But she wanted more. It was her only thought, the only thing she knew.

Gregory was leading her somewhere. She felt pulled, taken, transported.

And she wanted it all.

"Please," she begged, the word slipping unbidden from her lips. "Please . . ."

But Gregory, too, was beyond words. He said her name. Over and over he said it, as if his lips had lost the memory of anything else.

"Lucy," he whispered, his mouth moving to the hollow between her breasts.

"Lucy," he moaned, slipping one finger inside of her.

And then he gasped it. *"Lucy!"*

She had touched him. Softly, tentatively.

But it was she. It was her hand, her caress, and it felt as if he'd been set on fire.

"I'm sorry," she said, yanking her hand away.

"*Don't* apologize," he ground out, not because he was angry but because he could barely speak. He found her hand and dragged it back. "This is how much I want you," he said, wrapping her around him. "With everything I have, everything I am."

His nose was barely an inch from hers. Their breath mingled, and their eyes . . .

It was like they were one.

"I love you," he murmured, moving into position. Her hand slid away, then moved to his back.

"I love you, too," she whispered, and then her eyes widened, as if she were stunned that she'd said it.

But he didn't care. It didn't matter if she'd meant to tell him or not. She'd said it, and she could never take it back. She was his.

And he was hers. As he held himself still, pressing ever so softly at her entrance, he realized that he was at the edge of a precipice. His life was now one of two parts: before and after.

He would never love another woman again.

He *could* never love another woman again.

Not after this. Not as long as Lucy walked the same earth. There could be no one else.

It was terrifying, this precipice. Terrifying, and thrilling, and—

He jumped.

She let out a little gasp as he pushed forward, but when he looked down at her, she did not seem to be in pain. Her head was thrown back, and each breath was accompanied by a little moan, as if she could not quite keep her desire inside.

Her legs wrapped around his, feet running down the

length of his calves. And her hips were arching, pressing, begging him to continue.

"I don't want to hurt you," he said, every muscle in his body straining to move forward. He had never wanted anything the way he wanted her in that moment. And yet he had never felt less greedy. This had to be for her. He could not hurt her.

"You're not," she groaned, and then he couldn't help himself. He captured her breast in his mouth as he pushed through her final barrier, embedding himself fully within her.

If she'd felt pain, she didn't care. She let out a quiet shriek of pleasure, and her hands grabbed wildly at his head. She writhed beneath him, and when he attempted to move to her other breast, her fingers grew merciless, holding him in place with a ferocious intensity.

And all the while, his body claiming her, moving in a rhythm that was beyond thought or control.

"Lucy Lucy Lucy," he moaned, finally tearing himself away from her breast. It was too hard. It was too much. He needed room to breathe, to gasp, to suck in the air that never quite seemed to make it to his lungs.

"Lucy!"

He should wait. He was trying to wait. But she was grabbing at him, digging her nails into his shoulders, and her body was arching off the bed with enough strength to lift him as well.

And then he felt her. Tensing, squeezing, shuddering around him, and he let go.

He let go, and the world quite simply exploded.

"I love you," he gasped as he collapsed atop her. He'd thought himself beyond words, but there they were.

They were his companion now. Three little words.

I love you.

He would never be without them.

And that was a splendid thing.

Twenty

In which Our Hero has a very bad morning.

$\mathcal{S}$ometime later, after sleep, and then more passion, and then not quite sleep, but a peaceful quiet and stillness, and then more passion—because they just could not help themselves—it was time for Gregory to go.

It was the most difficult thing he had ever done, and yet he was still able to do it with joy in his heart because he knew that this was not the end. It was not even goodbye; it was nothing so permanent as that. But the hour was growing dangerous. Dawn would arrive shortly, and while he had every intention of marrying Lucy as soon as he could manage it, he would not put her through the shame of being caught in bed with him on the morning of her wedding to another man.

There was also Haselby to consider. Gregory did not know him well, but he had always seemed an affable fellow and did not deserve the public humiliation that would follow.

"Lucy," Gregory whispered, nudging her cheek with his nose, "it is near to morning."

She made a sleepy sound, then turned her head. "Yes," she said. Just *Yes,* not *It's all so unfair* or *It shouldn't have to be this way.* But that was Lucy. She was pragmatic and prudent and charmingly reasonable, and he loved her for all that and more. She didn't want to change the world. She just wanted to make it lovely and wonderful for the people she loved.

The fact that she had done this—that she had let him make love to her and was planning to call off her wedding *now,* the very morning of the ceremony—it only showed him how deeply she cared for him. Lucy didn't look for attention and drama. She craved stability and routine, and for her to make the leap she was preparing for—

It humbled him.

"You should come with me," he said. "Now. We should leave together before the household wakes."

Her bottom lip stretched a bit from side to side in an *oh dear*–ish expression that was so fetching he simply had to kiss her. Lightly, since he had no time to get carried away, and just a little peck on the corner of her mouth. Nothing that interfered with her answer, which was a disappointing "I cannot."

He drew back. "You cannot remain."

But she was shaking her head. "I . . . I must do the right thing."

He looked at her quizzically.

"I must behave with honor," she explained. She sat then, her fingers clutching the bedclothes so tightly that her knuckles turned white. She looked nervous, which he supposed made sense. He felt on the edge of a brand-new dawn, whereas she—

She still had a rather large mountain to scale before she reached her happy ending.

He reached out, trying to take one of her hands, but she was not receptive. It wasn't that she was tugging away from him; rather, it almost felt as if she was not even aware of his touch.

"I cannot sneak away and allow Lord Haselby to wait in vain at the church," she said, the words rushing out, tumbling from her lips as her eyes turned to his, wide and imploring.

But just for a moment.

Then she turned away.

She swallowed. He could not see her face, but he could see it in the way she moved.

She said, softly, "Surely you understand that."

And he did. It was one of the things he loved best about her. She had such a strong sense of right and wrong, sometimes to the point of intractability. But she was never moralistic, never condescending.

"I will watch for you," he said.

Her head turned sharply, and her eyes widened in question.

"You may need my assistance," he said softly.

"No, it won't be necessary. I'm sure I can—"

"I insist," he said, with enough force to silence her. "This shall be our signal." He held up his hand, fingers together, palm out. He twisted at the wrist then, once, to bring his palm around to face him, and then again, to return it to its original position. "I shall watch for you. If you need my help, come to the window and make the signal."

She opened her mouth, as if she might protest one more time, but in the end she merely nodded.

He stood then, opening the heavy draperies that ringed her bed as he searched for his clothing. His garments were strewn about—his breeches here, his shirt remarkably over there, but he quickly gathered what he needed and dressed.

Lucy remained in bed, sitting up with the sheets tucked

under her arm. He found her modesty charming, and he almost teased her for it. But instead he decided just to offer an amused smile. It had been a momentous night for her; she should not be made to feel embarrassed for her innocence.

He walked to the window to peer out. Dawn had not yet broken, but the sky hung with anticipation, the horizon painted with that faint shimmer of light one saw only before the sunrise. It glowed gently, a serene purplish-blue, and was so beautiful he beckoned to her to join him. He turned his back while she donned her nightgown and then, once she had padded across the room in her bare feet, he pulled her gently against him, her back to his chest. He rested his chin on top of her head.

"Look," he whispered.

The night seemed to dance, sparkling and tingling, as if the air itself understood that nothing would ever be the same. Dawn was waiting on the other side of the horizon, and already the stars were beginning to look less bright in the sky.

If he could have frozen time, he would have done so. Never had he experienced a single moment that was so magical, so . . . full. Everything was there, everything that was good and honest and true. And he finally understood the difference between happiness and contentment, and how lucky and blessed he was to feel both, in such breathtaking quantities.

It was Lucy. She completed him. She made his life everything he had known it could someday be.

This was his dream. It was coming true, all around him, right there in his arms.

And then, right as they were standing at the window, one of the stars shot through the sky. It made a wide, shallow arc, and it almost seemed to Gregory that he heard it as it traveled, sparking and crackling until it disappeared from sight.

It made him kiss her. He supposed a rainbow would do the same, or a four-leafed clover, or even a simple snowflake, landing on his sleeve without melting. It was simply impossible to enjoy one of nature's small miracles and *not* kiss her. He kissed her neck, and then he turned her around in his arms so that he could kiss her mouth, and her brow, and even her nose.

All seven freckles, too. God, he loved her freckles.

"I love you," he whispered.

She laid her cheek against his chest, and her voice was hoarse, almost choked as she said, "I love you, too."

"Are you certain you will not come with me now?" He knew her answer, but he asked, anyway.

As expected, she nodded. "I must do this myself."

"How will your uncle react?"

"I'm . . . not sure."

He stepped back, taking her by the shoulders and even bending at the knees so that his eyes would not lose contact with hers. "Will he hurt you?"

"No," she said, quickly enough so that he believed her. "No. I promise you."

"Will he try to force you to marry Haselby? Lock you in your room? Because I could stay. If you think you will need me, I could remain right here." It would create an even worse scandal than what currently lay ahead for them, but if it was a question of her safety . . .

There was nothing he would not do.

"Gregory—"

He silenced her with a shake of his head. "Do you understand," he began, "how completely and utterly this goes against my every instinct, leaving you here to face this by yourself?"

Her lips parted and her eyes—

They filled with tears.

"I have sworn in my heart to protect you," he said, his

voice passionate and fierce and maybe even a little bit reve-
latory. Because today, he realized, was the day he truly became a man. After twenty-six years of an amiable and, yes,
aimless existence, he had finally found his purpose.

He finally knew why he had been born.

"I have sworn it in my heart," he said, "and I will swear it
before God just as soon as we are able. And it is like acid in
my chest to leave you alone."

His hand found hers, and their fingers twined.

"It is not right," he said, his words low but fierce.

Slowly, she nodded her agreement. "But it is what must be
done."

"If there is a problem," he said, "if you sense danger, you
must promise to signal. I will come for you. You can take
refuge with my mother. Or any one of my sisters. They
won't mind the scandal. They would care only for your happiness."

She swallowed, and then she smiled, and her eyes grew
wistful. "Your family must be lovely."

He took her hands and squeezed them. "They are *your*
family now." He waited for her to say something, but she did
not. He brought her hands to his lips and kissed them each
in turn. "Soon," he whispered, "this will all be behind us."

She nodded, then glanced over her shoulder at the door.
"The servants will be waking shortly."

And he left. He slipped out the door, boots in hand, and
crept out the way he'd come in.

It was still dark when he reached the small park that filled
the square across from her home. There were hours yet before the wedding, and surely he had enough time to return
home to change his clothing.

But he was not prepared to chance it. He had told her he
would protect her, and he would never break that promise.

But then it occurred to him—he did not need to do this
alone. In fact, he should not do it alone. If Lucy needed him,

she would need him well and full. If Gregory had to resort to force, he could certainly use an extra set of hands.

He had never gone to his brothers for help, never begged them to extricate him from a tight spot. He was a relatively young man. He had drunk spirits, gambled, dallied with women.

But he had never drunk too much, or gambled more than he had, or, until the previous night, dallied with a woman who risked her reputation to be with him.

He had not sought responsibility, but neither had he chased trouble.

His brothers had always seen him as a boy. Even now, in his twenty-sixth year, he suspected they did not view him as quite fully grown. And so he did not ask for help. He did not place himself in any position where he might need it.

Until now.

One of his older brothers lived not very far away. Less than a quarter of a mile, certainly, maybe even closer to an eighth. Gregory could be there and back in twenty minutes, including the time it took to yank Colin from his bed.

Gregory had just rolled his shoulders back and forth, loosening up in preparation for a sprint, when he spied a chimney sweep, walking across the street. He was young—twelve, maybe thirteen—and certainly eager for a guinea.

And the promise of another, should he deliver Gregory's message to his brother.

Gregory watched him tear around the corner, then he crossed back to the public garden. There was no place to sit, no place even to stand where he might not be immediately visible from Fennsworth House.

And so he climbed a tree. He sat on a low, thick branch, leaned against the trunk, and waited.

Someday, he told himself, he would laugh about this. Someday they would tell this tale to their grandchildren, and it would all sound very romantic and exciting.

As for now . . .

Romantic, yes. Exciting, not so much.

He rubbed his hands together.

Most of all, it was cold.

He shrugged, waiting for himself to stop noticing it. He never did, but he didn't care. What were a few blue fingertips against the rest of his life?

He smiled, lifting his gaze to her window. There she was, he thought. Right there, behind that curtain. And he loved her.

He loved her.

He thought of his friends, most of them cynics, always casting a bored eye over the latest selection of debutantes, sighing that marriage was such a chore, that ladies were interchangeable, and that love was best left to the poets.

Fools, the lot of them.

Love existed.

It was right there, in the air, in the wind, in the water. One only had to wait for it.

To watch for it.

And fight for it.

And he would. As God was his witness, he would. Lucy had only to signal, and he would retrieve her.

He was a man in love.

Nothing could stop him.

"This is not, you realize, how I had intended to spend my Saturday morning."

Gregory answered only with a nod. His brother had arrived four hours earlier, greeting him with a characteristically understated "This is interesting."

Gregory had told Colin everything, even down to the events of the night before. He did not like telling tales of Lucy, but one really could not ask one's brother to sit in a tree for hours without explaining why. And Gregory had found a certain comfort in unburdening himself to Colin. He had not lectured. He had not judged.

In fact, he had understood.

When Gregory had finished his tale, tersely explaining why he was waiting outside Fennsworth House, Colin had simply nodded and said, "I don't suppose you have something to eat."

Gregory shook his head and grinned.

It was good to have a brother.

"Rather poor planning on your part," Colin muttered. But he was smiling, too.

They turned back to the house, which had long since begun to show signs of life. Curtains had been pulled back, candles lit and then snuffed as dawn had given way to morning.

"Shouldn't she have come out by now?" Colin asked, squinting at the door.

Gregory frowned. He had been wondering the same thing. He had been telling himself that her absence boded well. If her uncle were going to force her to marry Haselby, wouldn't she have left for the church by now? By his pocket watch, which admittedly wasn't the most accurate of timepieces, the ceremony was due to begin in less than an hour.

But she had not signaled for his help, either.

And that did not sit well with him.

Suddenly Colin perked up.

"What is it?"

Colin motioned to the right with his head. "A carriage," he said, "being brought 'round from the mews."

Gregory's eyes widened with horror as the front door to Fennsworth House opened. Servants spilled out, laughing and cheering as the vehicle came to a stop in front of Fennsworth House.

It was white, open, and festooned with perfectly pink flowers and wide rosy ribbons, trailing behind, fluttering in the light breeze.

It was a wedding carriage.

And no one seemed to find that odd.

Gregory's skin began to tingle. His muscles burned.

"Not yet," Colin said, placing a restraining hand on Gregory's arm.

Gregory shook his head. His peripheral vision was beginning to fade from view, and all he could see was that damned carriage.

"I have to get her," he said. "I have to go."

"Wait," Colin instructed. "Wait to see what happens. She might not come out. She might—"

But she did come out.

Not first. That was her brother, his new wife on his arm.

Then came an older man—her uncle, most probably—and that ancient woman Gregory had met at his sister's ball.

And then . . .

Lucy.

In a wedding dress.

"Dear God," he whispered.

She was walking freely. No one was forcing her.

Hermione said something to her, whispered in her ear.

And Lucy smiled.

She smiled.

Gregory began to gasp.

The pain was palpable. Real. It shot through his gut, squeezed at his organs until he could no longer move.

He could only stare.

And think.

"Did she tell you she wasn't going to go through with it?" Colin whispered.

Gregory tried to say yes, but the word strangled him. He tried to recall their last conversation, every last word of it. She had said she must behave with honor. She had said she must do what was right. She had said that she loved him.

But she had never said that she would not marry Haselby.

"Oh my God," he whispered.

His brother laid his hand over his own. "I'm sorry," he said.

Gregory watched as Lucy stepped up into the open carriage. The servants were still cheering. Hermione was fussing with her hair, adjusting the veil, then laughing when the wind lifted the gauzy fabric in the air.

This could not be happening.

There had to be an explanation.

"No," Gregory said, because it was the only word he could think to say. "No."

Then he remembered. The hand signal. The wave. She would do it. She would signal to him. Whatever had transpired in the house, she had not been able to halt the proceedings. But now, out in the open, where he could see, she would signal.

She had to. She knew he could see her.

She knew he was out there.

Watching her.

He swallowed convulsively, never taking his eyes off her right hand.

"Is everyone here?" he heard Lucy's brother call out.

He did not hear Lucy's voice in the chorus of replies, but no one was questioning her presence.

She was the bride.

And he was a fool, watching her ride away.

"I'm sorry," Colin said quietly, as they watched the carriage disappear around the corner.

"It doesn't make sense," Gregory whispered.

Colin jumped down out of the tree and silently held out his hand to Gregory.

"It doesn't make sense," Gregory said again, too bewildered to do anything but let his brother help him down. "She wouldn't do this. She loves me."

He looked at Colin. His eyes were kind, but pitying.

"No," Gregory said. "No. You don't know her. She would not— No. You don't know her."

And Colin, whose only experience with Lady Lucinda Abernathy was the moment in which she had broken his brother's heart, asked, "Do *you* know her?"

Gregory stepped back as if struck. "Yes," he said. "Yes, I do."

Colin didn't say anything, but his brows rose, as if to ask, *Well, then?*

Gregory turned, his eyes moving to the corner around which Lucy had so recently disappeared. For a moment he stood absolutely still, his only movement a deliberate, thoughtful blink of his eyes.

He turned back around, looked his brother in the face. "I know her," he said. "I do."

Colin's lips drew together, as if trying to form a question, but Gregory had already turned away.

He was looking at that corner again.

And then he began to run.

Twenty-one

In which Our Hero risks everything.

"*A*re you ready?"

Lucy regarded the splendid interior of St. George's—the bright stained glass, the elegant arches, the piles and piles of flowers brought in to celebrate her marriage.

She thought about Lord Haselby, standing with the priest at the altar.

She thought about the guests, all more-than-three-hundred of them, all waiting for her to enter on her brother's arm.

And she thought about Gregory, who had surely seen her climb up into the bridal carriage, dressed in her wedding finery.

"Lucy," Hermione repeated, "are you ready?"

Lucy wondered what Hermione might do if she said no.

Hermione was a romantic.

Impractical.

She would probably tell Lucy that she did not have to go through with it, that it did not matter that they were standing just outside the doors to the church sanctuary, or that the prime minister himself was seated inside.

Hermione would tell her that it did not matter that papers had been signed and banns had been read, in three different parishes. It did not matter that by fleeing the church Lucy would create the scandal of the decade. She would tell Lucy that she did not have to do it, that she should not settle for a marriage of convenience when she could have one of passion and love. She would say—

"Lucy?"

(Is what she actually said.)

Lucy turned, blinking in confusion, because the Hermione of her imagination had been giving quite an impassioned speech.

Hermione smiled gently. "Are you ready?"

And Lucy, because she was Lucy, because she would always be Lucy, nodded.

She could do nothing else.

Richard joined them. "I cannot believe you are getting married," he said to Lucy, but not before gazing warmly at his wife.

"I am not so very much younger than you are, Richard," Lucy reminded him. She tilted her head toward the new Lady Fennsworth. "And I am two months older than Hermione."

Richard grinned boyishly. "Yes, but she is not my sister."

Lucy smiled at that, and she was grateful for it. She needed smiles. Every last one she could manage.

It was her wedding day. She had been bathed and perfumed and dressed in what had to be the most luxurious gown she had ever laid eyes upon, and she felt . . .

Empty.

She could not imagine what Gregory thought of her. She had deliberately allowed him to think that she planned to call off the wedding. It was terrible of her, cruel and dishonest, but she did not know what else to do. She was a coward, and she could not bear to see his face when she told him she still intended to marry Haselby.

Good God, how could she have explained it? He would have insisted that there was another way, but he was an idealist, and he had never faced true adversity. There *wasn't* another way. Not this time. Not without sacrificing her family.

She let out a long breath. She could do this. Truly. She could. She could.

She closed her eyes, her head bobbing a half inch or so as the words echoed in her mind.

I can do this. I can. I can.

"Lucy?" came Hermione's concerned voice. "Are you unwell?"

Lucy opened her eyes, and said the only thing Hermione would possibly believe. "Just doing sums in my head."

Hermione shook her head. "I hope Lord Haselby likes maths, because I vow, Lucy, you are mad."

"Perhaps."

Hermione looked at her quizzically.

"What is it?" Lucy asked.

Hermione blinked several times before finally replying. "It is nothing, really," she said. "Just that that sounded quite unlike you."

"I don't know what you mean."

"To agree with me when I call you mad? That's not at all what you would say."

"Well, it's obviously what I did say," Lucy grumbled, "so I don't know what—"

"Oh, pish. The Lucy I know would say something like, 'Mathematics is a very extremely important endeavor, and really, Hermione, you ought to consider practicing sums yourself.'"

Lucy winced. "Am I truly so officious?"

"Yes," Hermione replied, as if she were mad even to question it. "But it's what I love best about you."

And Lucy managed another smile.

Maybe everything would be all right. Maybe she would be happy. If she could manage two smiles in one morning, then surely it couldn't be that bad. She needed only to keep moving forward, in her mind and her body. She needed to have this thing done, to make it permanent, so she could place Gregory in her past and at least pretend to embrace her new life as Lord Haselby's wife.

But Hermione was asking Richard if she might have a moment alone with Lucy, and then she was taking her hands, leaning in and whispering, "Lucy, are you certain you wish to do this?"

Lucy looked up at her in surprise. Why was Hermione asking her this? Right at the moment when she most wanted to run.

Hadn't she been smiling? Hadn't Hermione seen her smiling?

Lucy swallowed. She tried to straighten her shoulders. "Yes," she said. "Yes, of course. Why would you ask such a thing?"

Hermione did not answer right away. But her eyes—those huge, green eyes that rendered grown men senseless—they answered for her.

Lucy swallowed and turned away, unable to bear what she saw there.

And Hermione whispered, *"Lucy."*

That was all. Just Lucy.

Lucy turned back. She wanted to ask Hermione what she meant. She wanted to ask why she said her name as if it were a tragedy. But she didn't. She couldn't. And so she hoped Hermione saw her questions in her eyes.

She did. Hermione touched her cheek, smiling sadly. "You look like the saddest bride I've ever seen."

Lucy closed her eyes. "I'm not sad. I just feel . . ."

But she didn't know what she felt. What was she supposed

to feel? No one had trained her for this. In all her education, with her nurse, and governess, and three years at Miss Moss's, no one had given her lessons in *this.*

Why hadn't anyone realized that this was far more important than needlework or country dances?

"I feel . . ." And then she understood. "I feel like I'm saying goodbye."

Hermione blinked with surprise. "To whom?"

To myself.

And she was. She was saying goodbye to herself, and everything she might have become.

She felt her brother's hand on her arm. "It's time to begin," he said.

She nodded.

"Where is your bouquet?" Hermione asked, then answered herself with, "Oh. Right there." She retrieved the flowers, along with her own, from a nearby table and handed them to Lucy. "You shall be happy," she whispered, as she kissed Lucy's cheek. "You must. I simply will not tolerate a world in which you are not."

Lucy's lips wobbled.

"Oh dear," Hermione said. "I sound like you now. Do you see what a good influence you are?" And then, with one last blown kiss, she entered the chapel.

"Your turn," Richard said.

"Almost," Lucy answered.

And then it was.

She was in the church, walking down the aisle. She was at the front, nodding at the priest, looking at Haselby and reminding herself that despite . . . well, despite certain habits she did not quite understand, he would make a perfectly acceptable husband.

This was what she had to do.

If she said no . . .

She could not say no.

She could see Hermione out of the corner of her eye, standing beside her with a serene smile. She and Richard had arrived in London two nights earlier, and they had been so *happy*. They laughed and they teased and they spoke of the improvements they planned to make at Fennsworth Abbey. An orangery, they had laughed. They wanted an orangery. And a nursery.

How could Lucy take that from them? How could she cast them into a life of shame and poverty?

She heard Haselby's voice, answering, "I will," and then it was her turn.

Wilt thou have this Man to thy Wedded Husband, to live together after God's ordinance in the holy estate of Matrimony? Wilt thou obey him, and serve him, love, honor, and keep him in sickness and in health; and, forsaking all other, keep thee only unto him, so long as ye both shall live?

She swallowed and tried not to think of Gregory. "I will."

She had given her consent. Was it done, then? She didn't feel different. She was still the same old Lucy, except she was standing in front of more people than she ever cared to stand in front of again, and her brother was giving her away.

The priest placed her right hand in Haselby's, and he pledged his troth, his voice loud, firm, and clear.

They separated, and then Lucy took his hand.

I, Lucinda Margaret Catherine . . .

"I, Lucinda Margaret Catherine . . ."

. . . take thee, Arthur Fitzwilliam George . . .

". . . take thee, Arthur Fitzwilliam George . . ."

She said it. She repeated after the priest, word for word. She said her part, right up until she meant to give Haselby her troth, right up until—

The doors to the chapel slammed open.

She turned around. Everyone turned around.

Gregory.

Dear God.

He looked like a madman, breathing so hard he was barely able to speak.

He staggered forward, clutching the edges of the pew for support, and she heard him say—

"*Don't.*"

Lucy's heart stopped.

"Don't do it."

Her bouquet slipped from her hands. She couldn't move, couldn't speak, couldn't do anything but stand there like a statue as he walked toward her, seemingly oblivious to the hundreds of people staring at him.

"Don't do it," he said again.

And no one was talking. Why was no one talking? Surely someone would rush forward, grab Gregory by the arms, haul him away—

But no one did. It was a spectacle. It was theater, and it seemed no one wanted to miss the ending.

And then—

Right there.

Right there in front of everyone, he stopped.

He stopped. And he said, "I love you."

Beside her Hermione murmured, "Oh my goodness."

Lucy wanted to cry.

"I love you," he said again, and he just kept walking, his eyes never leaving her face.

"Don't do it," he said, finally reaching the front of the church. "Don't marry him."

"Gregory," she whispered, "why are you doing this?"

"I love you," he said, as if there could be no other explanation.

A little moan choked in her throat. Tears burned her eyes, and her entire body felt stiff. Stiff and frozen. One little wind, one little *breath* would knock her over. And she couldn't manage to think anything but *Why?*

And *No.*

And *Please.*

And—oh heavens, *Lord Haselby!*

She looked up at him, at the groom who had found himself demoted to a supporting role. He had been standing silently this entire time, watching the unfolding drama with as much interest as the audience. With her eyes she pleaded with him for guidance, but he just shook his head. It was a tiny movement, far too subtle for anyone else to discern, but she saw it, and she knew what it meant.

It is up to you.

She turned back to Gregory. His eyes burned, and he sank to one knee.

Don't, she tried to say. But she could not move her lips. She could not find her voice.

"Marry me," Gregory said, and she *felt* him in his voice. It wrapped around her body, kissed her, embraced her. "Marry *me.*"

And oh dear Lord, she wanted to. More than anything, she wanted to sink to her knees and take his face in her hands. She wanted to kiss him, she wanted to shout out her love for him—here, in front of everyone she knew, possibly everyone she ever would know.

But she had wanted all of that the day before, and the day before that. Nothing had changed. Her world had become more public, but it had not changed.

Her father was still a traitor.

Her family was still being blackmailed.

The fate of her brother and Hermione was still in her hands.

She looked at Gregory, aching for him, aching for them both.

"Marry me," he whispered.

Her lips parted, and she said—

"No."

Twenty-two

In which all hell breaks loose.

*A*ll hell broke loose.

Lord Davenport charged forward, as did Lucy's uncle and Gregory's brother, who had just tripped up the steps to the church after chasing Gregory across Mayfair.

Lucy's brother dashed forward to move both Lucy and Hermione from the melee, but Lord Haselby, who had been watching the events with the air of an intrigued spectator, calmly took the arm of his intended and said, "I will see to her."

As for Lucy, she stumbled backward, her mouth open with shock as Lord Davenport leaped atop Gregory, landing belly down like a—well, like nothing Lucy had ever seen.

"I have him!" Davenport yelled triumphantly, only to be smacked soundly with a reticule belonging to Hyacinth St. Clair.

Lucy closed her eyes.

"Not the wedding of your dreams, I imagine," Haselby murmured in her ear.

Lucy shook her head, too numb to do anything else. She should help Gregory. Really, she should. But she felt positively drained of energy, and besides, she was too cowardly to face him again.

What if he rejected her?

What if she could not resist him?

"I do hope he will be able to get out from under my father," Haselby continued, his tone as mild as if he were watching a not-terribly-exciting horse race. "The man weighs twenty stone, not that he would admit it."

Lucy turned to him, unable to believe how calm he was given the near riot that had broken out in the church. Even the prime minister appeared to be fending off a largish, plumpish lady in an elaborately fruited bonnet who was swatting at anyone who moved.

"I don't think she can see," Haselby said, following Lucy's gaze. "Her grapes are drooping."

Who *was* this man she had—dear heavens, had she married him yet? They had agreed to something, of that she was certain, but no one had declared them man and wife. But either way, Haselby was bizarrely calm, given the events of the morning.

"Why didn't you say anything?" Lucy asked.

He turned, regarding her curiously. "You mean while your Mr. Bridgerton was professing his love?"

No, while the priest was droning on about the sacrament of marriage, she wanted to snap.

Instead, she nodded.

Haselby cocked his head to the side. "I suppose I wanted to see what you'd do."

She stared at him in disbelief. What would he have done if she'd said yes?

"I am honored, by the way," Haselby said. "And I shall be

a kind husband to you. You needn't worry on that score."

But Lucy could not speak. Lord Davenport had been removed from Gregory, and even though some other gentleman she did not recognize was pulling him back, he was struggling to reach her.

"Please," she whispered, even though no one could possibly hear her, not even Haselby, who had stepped down to aid the prime minister. "Please don't."

But Gregory was unrelenting, and even with two men pulling at him, one friendly and one not, he managed to reach the bottom of the steps. He lifted his face, and his eyes burned into hers. They were raw, stark with anguish and incomprehension, and Lucy nearly stumbled from the unleashed pain she saw there.

"Why?" he demanded.

Her entire body began to shake. Could she lie to him? Could she do it? Here, in a church, after she had hurt him in the most personal and the most public way imaginable.

"Why?"

"Because I had to," she whispered.

His eyes flared with something—disappointment? No. Hope? No, not that, either. It was something else. Something she could not quite identify.

He opened his mouth to speak, to ask her something, but it was at that moment that the two men holding him were joined by a third, and together they managed to haul him from the church.

Lucy hugged her arms to her body, barely able to stand as she watched him being dragged away.

"How could you?"

She turned. Hyacinth St. Clair had crept up behind her and was glaring at her as if she were the very devil.

"You don't understand," Lucy said.

But Hyacinth's eyes blazed with fury. "You are weak," she hissed. "You do not deserve him."

Lucy shook her head, not quite sure if she was agreeing with her or not.

"I hope you—"

"Hyacinth!"

Lucy's eyes darted to the side. Another woman had approached. It was Gregory's mother. They had been introduced at the ball at Hastings House.

"That will be enough," she said sternly.

Lucy swallowed, blinking back tears.

Lady Bridgerton turned to her. "Forgive us," she said, pulling her daughter away.

Lucy watched them depart, and she had the strangest sense that all this was happening to someone else, that maybe it was just a dream, just a nightmare, or perhaps she was caught up in a scene from a lurid novel. Maybe her entire life was a figment of someone else's imagination. Maybe if she just closed her eyes—

"Shall we get on with it?"

She swallowed. It was Lord Haselby. His father was next to him, uttering the same sentiment, but in far less gracious words.

Lucy nodded.

"Good," Davenport grunted. "Sensible girl."

Lucy wondered what it meant to be complimented by Lord Davenport. Surely nothing good.

But still, she allowed him to lead her back to the altar. And she stood there in front of half of the congregation who had not elected to follow the spectacle outside.

And she married Haselby.

"What were you thinking?"

It took Gregory a moment to realize that his mother was demanding this of Colin, and not of him. They were seated in her carriage, to which he had been dragged once they had left the church. Gregory did not know where they were going. In random circles, most probably. Anywhere that wasn't St. George's.

"I tried to stop him," Colin protested.

Violet Bridgerton looked as angry as any of them had ever seen her. "You obviously did not try hard enough."

"Do you have any idea how fast he can run?"

"Very fast," Hyacinth confirmed without looking at them. She was seated diagonally to Gregory, staring out the window through narrowed eyes.

Gregory said nothing.

"Oh, Gregory," Violet sighed. "Oh, my poor son."

"You shall have to leave town," Hyacinth said.

"She is right," their mother put in. "It can't be helped."

Gregory said nothing. What had Lucy meant—*Because I had to?*

What did that *mean*?

"I shall never receive her," Hyacinth growled.

"She will be a countess," Colin reminded her.

"I don't care if she is the bloody queen of—"

"Hyacinth!" This, from their mother.

"Well, I don't," Hyacinth snapped. "No one has the right to treat my brother like that. No one!"

Violet and Colin stared at her. Colin looked amused. Violet, alarmed.

"I shall ruin her," Hyacinth continued.

"No," Gregory said in a low voice, "you won't."

The rest of his family fell silent, and Gregory suspected that they had not, until the moment he'd spoken, realized that he had not been taking part in the conversation.

"You will leave her alone," he said.

Hyacinth ground her teeth together.

He brought his eyes to hers, hard and steely with purpose. "And if your paths should ever cross," he continued, "you shall be all that is amiable and kind. Do you understand me?"

Hyacinth said nothing.

"Do you understand me?" he roared.

His family stared at him in shock. He never lost his temper. Never.

And then Hyacinth, who'd never possessed a highly developed sense of tact, said, "No, as a matter of fact."

"I beg your pardon?" Gregory, said, his voice dripping ice at the very moment Colin turned to her and hissed, "Shut *up.*"

"I don't understand you," Hyacinth continued, jamming her elbow into Colin's ribs. "How can you possibly possess sympathy for her? If this had happened to me, wouldn't you—"

"This didn't happen to you," Gregory bit off. "And you do not know her. You do not know the reasons for her actions."

"Do *you*?" Hyacinth demanded.

He didn't. And it was killing him.

"Turn the other cheek, Hyacinth," her mother said softly.

Hyacinth sat back, her bearing tense with anger, but she held her tongue.

"Perhaps you could stay with Benedict and Sophie in Wiltshire," Violet suggested. "I believe Anthony and Kate are expected in town soon, so you cannot go to Aubrey Hall, although I am sure they would not mind if you resided there in their absence."

Gregory just stared out the window. He did not wish to go to the country.

"You could travel," Colin said. "Italy is particularly pleasant this time of year. And you haven't been, have you?"

Gregory shook his head, only half listening. He did not wish to go to Italy.

Because I had to, she'd said.

Not because she wished it. Not because it was sensible.

Because she had to.

What did that mean?

Had she been forced? Was she being blackmailed?

What could she have possibly done to warrant blackmail?

"It would have been very difficult for her not to go through with it," Violet suddenly said, placing a sympathetic hand on his arm. "Lord Davenport is not a man anyone would wish as an enemy. And really, right there in the church, with everyone looking on . . . Well," she said with a resigned sigh, "one would have to be extremely brave. And resilient." She paused, shaking her head. "And prepared."

"Prepared?" Colin queried.

"For what came next," Violet clarified. "It would have been a huge scandal."

"It already is a huge scandal," Gregory muttered.

"Yes, but not as much as if she'd said yes," his mother said. "Not that I am glad for the outcome. You know I wish you nothing but your heart's happiness. But she will be looked upon approvingly for her choice. She will be viewed as a sensible girl."

Gregory felt one corner of his mouth lift into a wry smile. "And I, a lovesick fool."

No one contradicted him.

After a moment his mother said, "You are taking this rather well, I must say."

Indeed.

"I would have thought—" She broke off. "Well, it matters not what I would have thought, merely what actually is."

"No," Gregory said, turning sharply to look at her. "What would you have thought? How should I be acting?"

"It is not a question of *should*," his mother said, clearly flustered by the sudden questions. "Merely that I would have thought you would seem . . . angrier."

He stared at her for a long moment, then turned back to the window. They were traveling along Piccadilly, heading west toward Hyde Park. Why *wasn't* he angrier? Why wasn't he putting his fist through the wall? He'd had to be dragged from the church and forcibly stuffed into the carriage, but once that had been done, he had been overcome by a bizarre, almost preternatural calm.

And then something his mother had said echoed in his mind.

You know I wish you nothing but your heart's happiness.

His heart's happiness.

Lucy loved him. He was certain of it. He had seen it in her eyes, even in the moment she'd refused him. He knew it because she had told him so, and she did not lie about such things. He had felt it in the way she had kissed him, and in the warmth of her embrace.

She loved him. And whatever had made her go ahead with her marriage to Haselby, it was bigger than she was. Stronger.

She needed his help.

"Gregory?" his mother said softly.

He turned. Blinked.

"You started in your seat," she said.

Had he? He hadn't even noticed. But his senses had sharpened, and when he looked down, he saw that he was flexing his fingers.

"Stop the carriage."

Everyone turned to face him. Even Hyacinth, who had been determinedly glaring out the window.

"Stop the carriage," he said again.

"Why?" his mother asked, clearly suspicious.

"I need air," he replied, and it wasn't even a lie.

Colin knocked on the wall. "I'll walk with you."

"No. I prefer to be alone."

His mother's eyes widened. "Gregory . . . You don't plan to . . ."

"Storm the church?" he finished for her. He leaned back, giving her a casually lopsided smile. "I believe I've embarrassed myself enough for one day, wouldn't you think?"

"They'll have said their vows by now, anyway," Hyacinth put in.

Gregory fought the urge to glare at his sister, who never seemed to miss an opportunity to poke, prod, or twist. "Precisely," he replied.

"I would feel better if you weren't alone," Violet said, her blue eyes still filled with concern.

"Let him go," Colin said softly.

Gregory turned to his older brother in surprise. He had not expected to be championed by him.

"He is a man," Colin added. "He can make his own decisions."

Even Hyacinth did not attempt to contradict.

The carriage had already come to a halt, and the driver was waiting outside the door. At Colin's nod, he opened it.

"I wish you wouldn't go," Violet said.

Gregory kissed her cheek. "I need air," he said. "That is all."

He hopped down, but before he could shut the door, Colin leaned out.

"Don't do anything foolish," Colin said quietly.

"Nothing foolish," Gregory promised him, "only what is necessary."

He took stock of his location, and then, as his mother's carriage had not moved, deliberately set off to the south.

Away from St. George's.

But once he reached the next street he doubled around.

Running.

Twenty-three

In which Our Hero risks everything. Again.

$\mathcal{I}$n the ten years since her uncle had become her guardian, Lucy had never known him to host a party. He was not one to smile upon any sort of unnecessary expense—in truth, he was not one to smile at all. So it was with some suspicion that she approached the lavish fête being thrown in her honor at Fennsworth House following the wedding ceremony.

Lord Davenport had surely insisted upon it. Uncle Robert would have been content to serve tea cakes at the church and be done with it.

But no, the wedding must be an event, in the most extravagant sense of the word, and so as soon as the ceremony was over, Lucy was whisked to her soon-to-be-former home and given just enough time in her soon-to-be-former bedchamber to splash some cool water on her face before she was summoned to greet her guests below.

It was remarkable, she thought as she nodded and received

the well wishes of the attendees, just how good the *ton* was at pretending nothing had happened.

Oh, they would be speaking of nothing else tomorrow, and she could probably look forward to being the main topic of conversation for the next few months, even. And certainly for the next year no one would say her name without appending, "You know the one. With the *wedding*."

Which would surely be followed by, "Ohhhhhhhh. *She's* the one."

But for now, to her face, there was nothing but "Such a happy occasion," and "You make a beautiful bride." And of course, for the sly and daring—"Lovely ceremony, Lady Haselby."

Lady Haselby.

She tested it out in her mind. She was Lady Haselby now.

She could have been Mrs. Bridgerton.

Lady Lucinda Bridgerton, she supposed, as she was not required to surrender her honorific upon marriage to a commoner. It was a nice name—not as lofty as Lady Haselby, perhaps, and certainly nothing compared to the Countess of Davenport, but—

She swallowed, somehow managing not to dislodge the smile she'd affixed to her face five minutes earlier.

She would have liked to have been Lady Lucinda Bridgerton.

She *liked* Lady Lucinda Bridgerton. She was a happy sort, with a ready smile and a life that was full and complete. She had a dog, maybe two, and several children. Her house was warm and cozy, she drank tea with her friends, and she laughed.

Lady Lucinda Bridgerton laughed.

But she would never be that woman. She had married Lord Haselby, and now she was his wife, and try as she might, she could not picture where her life might lead. She did not know what it meant to be Lady Haselby.

The party hummed along, and Lucy danced her obligatory dance with her new husband, who was, she was relieved to note, quite accomplished. Then she danced with her brother, which nearly made her cry, and then her uncle, because it was expected.

"You did the right thing, Lucy," he said.

She said nothing. She didn't trust herself to do so.

"I am proud of you."

She almost laughed. "You have never been proud of me before."

"I am now."

It did not escape her notice that this was not a contradiction.

Her uncle returned her to the side of the ballroom floor, and then—dear *God*—she had to dance with Lord Davenport.

Which she did, because she knew her duty. On this day, especially, she knew her duty.

At least she did not have to speak. Lord Davenport was at his most effusive, and more than carried the conversation for the both of them. He was delighted with Lucy. She was a magnificent asset to the family.

And so on and so forth until Lucy realized that she had managed to endear herself to him in the most indelible manner possible. She had not simply agreed to marry his dubiously reputationed son; she had affirmed the decision in front of the entire *ton* in a scene worthy of Drury Lane.

Lucy moved her head discreetly to the side. When Lord Davenport was excited, spittle tended to fly from his mouth with alarming speed and accuracy. Truly, she wasn't sure which was worse—Lord Davenport's disdain or his everlasting gratitude.

But Lucy managed to avoid her new father-in-law for most of the festivities, thank heavens. She managed to avoid most everyone, which was surprisingly undifficult, given that she was the bride. She didn't want to see Lord Davenport, because she detested him, and she didn't want to see her uncle, because she rather suspected she detested him, as well. She didn't want to see Lord Haselby, because that would only lead to thoughts of her upcoming wedding night, and she didn't want to see Hermione, because she would ask questions, and then Lucy would cry.

And she didn't want to see her brother, because he was sure to be with Hermione, and besides that, she was feeling rather bitter, alternating with feeling rather guilty for feeling bitter. It wasn't Richard's fault that he was deliriously happy and she was not.

But all the same, she'd rather not have to see him.

Which left the guests, most of whom she did not know. And none of whom she wished to meet.

So she found a spot in the corner, and after a couple of hours, everyone had drunk so much that no one seemed to notice that the bride was sitting by herself.

And certainly no one took note when she escaped to her bedchamber to take a short rest. It was probably very bad manners for a bride to avoid her own party, but at that moment, Lucy simply did not care. People would think she'd gone off to relieve herself, if anyone noticed her absence. And somehow it seemed appropriate for her to be alone on this day.

She slipped up the back stairs, lest she come across any wandering guests, and with a sigh of relief, she stepped into her room and shut the door behind her.

She leaned her back against the door, slowly deflating until it felt like there was nothing left within her.

And she thought—*Now I shall cry.*

She wanted to. Truly, she did. She felt as if she'd been holding it inside for hours, just waiting for a private moment. But the tears would not come. She was too numb, too dazed by the events of the last twenty-four hours. And so she stood there, staring at her bed.

Remembering.

Dear heaven, had it been only twelve hours earlier that she had lain there, wrapped in his arms? It seemed like years. It was as if her life were now neatly divided in two, and she was most firmly in *after*.

She closed her eyes. Maybe if she didn't see it, it would go away. Maybe if she—

"Lucy."

She froze. Dear God, *no*.

"Lucy."

Slowly, she opened her eyes. And whispered, "Gregory?"

He looked a mess, windblown and dirty as only a mad ride on horseback could do to a man. He must have sneaked in the same way he'd done the night before. He must have been waiting for her.

She opened her mouth, tried to speak.

"Lucy," he said again, and his voice flowed through her, melted around her.

She swallowed. "Why are you here?"

He stepped toward her, and her heart just *ached* from it. His face was so handsome, and so dear, and so perfectly wonderfully familiar. She knew the slope of his cheeks, and the exact shade of his eyes, brownish near the iris, melting into green at the edge.

And his mouth—she knew that mouth, the look of it, the feel of it. She knew his smile, and she knew his frown, and she knew—

She knew far too much.

"You shouldn't be here," she said, the catch in her voice belying the stillness of her posture.

He took another step in her direction. There was no anger in his eyes, which she did not understand. But the way he was looking at her—it was hot, and it was possessive, and it was nothing a married woman should ever allow from a man who was not her husband.

"I had to know why," he said. "I couldn't let you go. Not until I knew why."

"Don't," she whispered. "Please don't do this."

Please don't make me regret. Please don't make me long and wish and wonder.

She hugged her arms to her chest, as if maybe . . . maybe she could squeeze so tight that she could pull herself inside out. And then she wouldn't have to see, she wouldn't have to hear. She could just be alone, and—

"Lucy—"

"Don't," she said again, sharply this time.

Don't.

Don't make me believe in love.

But he moved ever closer. Slowly, but without hesitation. "Lucy," he said, his voice warm and full of purpose. "Just tell me why. That is all I ask. I will walk away and promise never to approach you again, but I must know why."

She shook her head. "I can't tell you."

"You won't tell me," he corrected.

"No," she cried out, choking on the word. "I can't! Please, Gregory. You must go."

For a long moment he said nothing. He just watched her face, and she could practically *see* him thinking.

She shouldn't allow this, she thought, a bubble of panic beginning to rise within her. She should scream. Have him ejected. She should run from the room before he could ruin her careful plans for the future. But instead she just stood there, and he said—

"You're being blackmailed."

It wasn't a question.

She did not answer, but she knew that her face gave her away.

"Lucy," he said, his voice soft and careful, "I can help you. Whatever it is, I can make it right."

"No," she said, "you can't, and you're a fool to—" She cut

herself off, too furious to speak. What made him think he could rush in and fix things when he knew nothing of her travails? Did he think she had given in for something small? Something that could be easily overcome?

She was not that weak.

"You don't know," she said. "You have no idea."

"Then tell me."

Her muscles were shaking, and she felt hot . . . cold . . . everything in between.

"Lucy," he said, and his voice was so calm, so even—it was like a fork, poking her right where she could least tolerate it.

"You can't fix this," she ground out.

"That is not true. There is nothing anyone could hold over you that could not be overcome."

"By what?" she demanded. "Rainbows and sprites and the everlasting good wishes of your family? It won't work, Gregory. It won't. The Bridgertons may be powerful, but you cannot change the past, and you cannot bend the future to suit your whims."

"Lucy," he said, reaching out for her.

"No. No!" She pushed him away, rejected his offer of comfort. "You don't understand. You can't possibly. You are all so happy, so perfect."

"We are not."

"You *are*. You don't even know that you are, and you can't conceive that the rest of us are not, that we might struggle and try and be good and still not receive what we wish for."

Through it all, he watched her. Just watched her and let her stand by herself, hugging her arms to her body, looking small and pale and heartbreakingly alone.

And then he asked it.

"Do you love me?"

She closed her eyes. "Don't ask me that."

"Do you?"

He saw her jaw tighten, saw the way her shoulders tensed and rose, and he knew she was trying to shake her head.

Gregory walked toward her—slowly, respectfully.

She was hurting. She was hurting so much that it spread through the air, wrapped around him, around his heart. He ached for her. It was a physical thing, terrible and sharp, and for the first time he was beginning to doubt his own ability to make it go away.

"Do you love me?" he asked.

"Gregory—"

"Do you love me?"

"I can't—"

He placed his hands on her shoulders. She flinched, but she did not move away.

He touched her chin, nudged her face until he could lose himself in the blue of her eyes. "Do you love me?"

"Yes," she sobbed, collapsing into his arms. "But I can't. Don't you understand? I shouldn't. I have to make it stop."

For a moment Gregory could not move. Her admission should have come as a relief, and in a way it did, but more than that, he felt his blood begin to race.

He believed in love.

Wasn't that the one thing that had been a constant in his life?

He believed in love.

He believed in its power, in its fundamental goodness, its rightness.

He revered it for its strength, respected it for its rarity.

And he knew, right then, right there, as she cried in his arms, that he would dare anything for it.

For love.

"Lucy," he whispered, an idea beginning to form in his mind. It was mad, bad, and thoroughly inadvisable, but he could not escape the one thought that was rushing through his brain.

She had not consummated her marriage.

They still had a chance.

"*Lucy.*"

She pulled away. "I must return. They will be missing me."

But he captured her hand. "Don't go back."

Her eyes grew huge. "What do you mean?"

"Come with me. Come with me now." He felt giddy, dangerous, and just a little bit mad. "You are not his wife yet. You can have it annulled."

"Oh no." She shook her head, tugging her arm away from him. "No, Gregory."

"Yes. Yes." And the more he thought about it, the more it made sense. They hadn't much time; after this evening it would be impossible for her to say that she was untouched. Gregory's own actions had made sure of that. If they had any chance of being together, it had to be now.

He couldn't kidnap her; there was no way he could remove her from the house without raising an alarm. But he could buy them a bit of time. Enough so that he could sort out what to do.

He pulled her closer.

"No," she said, her voice growing louder. She started really yanking on her arm now, and he could see the panic growing in her eyes.

"Lucy, yes," he said.

"I will scream," she said.

"No one will hear you."

She stared at him in shock, and even he could not believe what he was saying.

"Are you threatening me?" she asked.

He shook his head. "No. I'm saving you." And then, before he had the opportunity to reconsider his actions, he grabbed her around her middle, threw her over his shoulder, and ran from the room.

Twenty-four

*In which Our Hero leaves
Our Heroine in an awkward position.*

"Y ou are tying me to a *water closet*?"

"Sorry," he said, tying two scarves into such expert knots that she almost worried that he had done this before. "I couldn't very well leave you in your room. That's the first place anyone would look." He tightened the knots, then tested them for strength. "It was the first place *I* looked."

"But a water closet!"

"On the third floor," he added helpfully. "It will take hours before anyone finds you here."

Lucy clenched her jaw, desperately trying to contain the fury that was rising within her.

He had lashed her hands together. *Behind her back.*

Good Lord, she had not known it was possible to be so angry with another person.

It wasn't just an emotional reaction—her entire body had erupted with it. She felt hot and prickly, and even though she knew it would do no good, she jerked her arms against the piping of the water closet, grinding her teeth and letting out a frustrated grunt when it did nothing but produce a dull clang.

"Please don't struggle," he said, dropping a kiss on the top of her head. "It is only going to leave you tired and sore." He looked up, examining the structure of the water closet. "Or you'll break the pipe, and surely that cannot be a hygienic prospect."

"Gregory, you have to let me go."

He crouched so that his face was on a level with hers. "I cannot," he said. "Not while there is still a chance for us to be together."

"Please," she pleaded, "this is madness. You must return me. I will be ruined."

"I will marry you," he said.

"I'm already married!"

"Not quite," he said with a wolfish smile.

"I said my vows!"

"But you did not consummate them. You can still get an annulment."

"That is not the point!" she cried out, struggling fruitlessly as he stood and walked to the door. "You don't understand the situation, and you are selfishly putting your own needs and happiness above those of others."

At that, he stopped. His hand was on the doorknob, but he stopped, and when he turned around, the look in his eyes nearly broke her heart.

"You're happy?" he asked. Softly, and with such love that she wanted to cry.

"No," she whispered, "but—"

"I've never seen a bride who looked so sad."

She closed her eyes, deflated. It was an echo of what Hermione had said, and she knew it was true. And even then, as she looked up at him, her shoulders aching, she could not escape the beatings of her own heart.

She loved him.

She would always love him.

And she hated him, too, for making her want what she could not have. She hated him for loving her so much that he would risk everything to be together. And most of all, she hated him for turning her into the instrument that would destroy her family.

Until she'd met Gregory, Hermione and Richard were the only two people in the world for whom she truly cared. And now they would be ruined, brought far lower and into greater unhappiness than Lucy could ever imagine with Haselby.

Gregory thought that it would take hours for someone to find her here, but she knew better. No one would locate her for days. She could not remember the last time anyone had wandered up here. She was in the nanny's washroom—but Fennsworth House had not had a nanny in residence for years.

When her disappearance was noticed, first they would check her room. Then they'd try a few sensible alternatives—the library, the sitting room, a washroom that had not been in disuse for half a decade . . .

And then, when she was not found, it would be assumed that she'd run off. And after what had happened at the church, no one would think she'd left on her own.

She would be ruined. And so would everyone else.

"It is not a question of my own happiness," she finally said, her voice quiet, almost broken. "Gregory, I beg of you, please don't do this. This is not just about me. My family— We will be ruined, all of us."

He walked to her side and sat. And then he said, simply, "Tell me."

She did. He would not give in otherwise, of that she was certain.

She told him everything. About her father, and the written proof of his treason. She told him about the blackmail. She told him how she was the final payment and the only thing that would keep her brother from being stripped of his title.

Lucy stared straight ahead throughout the telling, and for that, Gregory was grateful. Because what she said—it shook him to his very core.

All day Gregory had been trying to imagine what terrible secret could possibly induce her to marry Haselby. He'd run twice through London, first to the church and then here, to Fennsworth House. He had had plenty of time to think, to wonder. But never—not once—had his imagination led him to this.

"So you see," she said, "it is nothing so common as an illegitimate child, nothing so racy as an extramarital affair. My father—an earl of the realm—committed treason. *Treason*." And then she laughed. *Laughed*.

The way people did when what they really wanted was to cry.

"It's an ugly thing," she finished, her voice low and resigned. "There is no escaping it."

She turned to him for a response, but he had none.

Treason. Good God, he could not think of anything worse. There were many ways—many *many* ways—one could get oneself thrown out of society, but nothing was as unforgivable as treason. There wasn't a man, woman, or child in Britain who had not lost someone to Napoleon. The wounds were still too fresh, and even if they weren't . . .

It was *treason*.

A gentleman did not forsake his country.

It was ingrained in the soul of every man of Britain.

If the truth about Lucy's father were known, the earldom of Fennsworth would be dissolved. Lucy's brother would be left destitute. He and Hermione would almost certainly have to emigrate.

And Lucy would . . .

Well, Lucy would probably survive the scandal, especially

if her surname was changed to Bridgerton, but she would never forgive herself. Of that, Gregory was certain.

And finally, he understood.

He looked at her. She was pale and drawn, and her hands were clenched tightly in her lap. "My family has been good and true," she said, her voice shaking with emotion. "The Abernathys have been loyal to the crown since the first earl was invested in the fifteenth century. And my father has shamed us all. I cannot allow it to be revealed. I cannot." She swallowed awkwardly and then sadly said, "You should see your face. Even you don't want me now."

"No," he said, almost blurting out the word. "No. That is not true. That could never be true." He took her hands, held them in his own, savoring the shape of them, the arch of her fingers and the delicate heat of her skin.

"I am sorry," he said. "It should not have taken me so long to collect myself. I had not imagined treason."

She shook her head. "How could you?"

"But it does not change how I feel." He took her face in his hands, aching to kiss her but knowing he could not.

Not yet.

"What your father did— It is reprehensible. It is—" He swore under his breath. "I will be honest with you. It leaves me sick. But you—*you*, Lucy—you are innocent. You did nothing wrong, and you should not have to pay for his sins."

"Neither should my brother," she said quietly, "but if I do not complete my marriage to Haselby, Richard will—"

"Shhh." Gregory pressed a finger to her lips. "Listen to me. I love you."

Her eyes filled with tears.

"I love you," he said again. "There is nothing in this world or the next that could ever make me stop loving you."

"You felt that way about Hermione," she whispered.

"No," he said, almost smiling at how silly it all seemed

now. "I had been waiting so long to fall in love that I wanted the love more than the woman. I never loved Hermione, just the idea of her. But with you . . . It's different, Lucy. It's deeper. It's . . . it's . . ."

He struggled for words, but there were none. Words simply did not exist to explain what he felt for her. "It's *me*," he finally said, appalled at the inelegance of it. "Without you, I . . . I am . . ."

"Gregory," she whispered, "you don't have to—"

"I am nothing," he cut in, because he wasn't going to allow her to tell him that he didn't have to explain. "Without you, I am nothing."

She smiled. It was a sad smile, but it was true, and it felt as if he'd been waiting years for that smile. "That's not true," she said. "You know that it's not."

He shook his head. "An exaggeration, perhaps, but that is all. You make me better, Lucy. You make me wish, and hope, and aspire. You make me want to *do* things."

Tears began to trickle down her cheeks.

With the pads of his thumbs he brushed them away. "You are the finest person I know," he said, "the most honorable human being I have ever met. You make me laugh. And you make me *think*. And I . . ." He took a deep breath. "I love you."

And again. "I love you."

And again. "I love you." He shook his head helplessly. "I don't know how else to say it."

She turned away then, twisting her head so that his hands slid from her face to her shoulders, and finally, away from her body completely. Gregory could not see her face, but he could hear her—the quiet, broken sound of her breathing, the soft whimper in her voice.

"I love you," she finally answered, still not looking at him. "You know that I do. I will not demean us both by lying about it. And if it were only me, I would do anything—anything for that love. I would risk poverty, ruin. I would move to America, I would move to darkest Africa if that were the only way to be with you."

She let out a long, shaky breath. "I cannot be so selfish as to bring down the two people who have loved me so well and for so long."

"Lucy . . ." He had no idea what he wanted to tell her, just that he didn't want her to finish. He knew he did not want to hear what she had to say.

But she cut him off with—"Don't, Gregory. Please. I'm sorry. I cannot do it, and if you love me as you say you do, you will bring me back now, before Lord Davenport realizes I've gone missing."

Gregory squeezed his fingers into fists, then flexed them wide and straight. He knew what he should do. He should release her, let her run downstairs to the party. He should sneak back out the servants' door and vow never to approach her again.

She had promised to love, honor, and obey another man. She was supposed to forsake all others.

Surely, he fell under that aegis.

And yet he couldn't give up.

Not yet.

"One hour," he said, moving into a crouching position beside her. "Just give me one hour."

She turned, her eyes doubtful and astonished and maybe—*maybe*—just a little bit hopeful as well. "One hour?" she echoed. "What do you think you can—"

"I don't know," he said honestly. "But I will promise you this. If I cannot find a way to free you from this blackmail in one hour, I will return for you. And I will release you."

"To return to Haselby?" she whispered, and she sounded—

Did she sound disappointed? Even a little?

"Yes," he said. Because in truth it was the only thing he

could say. Much as he wished to throw caution to the wind, he knew that he could not steal her away. She would be respectable, as he would marry her as soon as Haselby agreed to the annulment, but she would never be happy.

And he knew that he could not live with himself.

"You will not be ruined if you go missing for one hour," he said to her. "You can simply tell people you were overset. You wished to take a nap. I am sure that Hermione will corroborate your story if you ask her to."

Lucy nodded. "Will you release my bindings?"

He gave his head a tiny shake and stood. "I would trust you with my life, Lucy, but not with your own. You're far too honorable for your own good."

"Gregory!"

He shrugged as he walked to the door. "Your conscience will get the better of you. You know that it will."

"What if I promise—"

"Sorry." One corner of his mouth stretched into a not quite apologetic expression. "I won't believe you."

He took one last look at her before he left. And he had to smile, which seemed ludicrous, given that he had one hour to neutralize the blackmail threat against Lucy's family and extract her from her marriage. During her wedding reception.

By comparison, moving heaven and earth seemed a far better prospect.

But when he turned to Lucy, and saw her sitting there, on the floor, she looked . . .

Like herself again.

"Gregory," she said, "you cannot leave me here. What if someone finds you and removes you from the house? Who will know I am here? And what if . . . and what if . . . and then what if . . ."

He smiled, enjoying her officiousness too much to actually listen to her words. She was definitely herself again.

"When this is all over," he said, "I shall bring you a sandwich."

That stopped her short. "A sandwich? A *sandwich*?"

He twisted the doorknob but didn't yet pull. "You want a sandwich, don't you? You always want a sandwich."

"You've gone mad," she said.

He couldn't believe she'd only just come to the conclusion. "Don't yell," he warned.

"You know I can't," she muttered.

It was true. The last thing she wanted was to be found. If Gregory was not successful, she would need to be able to slip back into the party with as little fuss as possible.

"Goodbye, Lucy," he said. "I love you."

She looked up. And she whispered, "One hour. Do you really think you can do it?"

He nodded. It was what she needed to see, and it was what he needed to pretend.

And as he closed the door behind him, he could have sworn he heard her murmur, "Good luck."

He paused for one deep breath before heading for the stairs. He was going to need more than luck; he was going to need a bloody miracle.

The odds were against him. The odds were *extremely* against him. But Gregory had always been one to cheer for the underdog. And if there was any sense of justice in the world, any existential fairness floating through the air . . . If *Do unto others* offered any sort of payback, surely he was due.

Love existed.

He knew that it did. And he would be damned if it did not exist for him.

Gregory's first stop was Lucy's bedchamber, on the second floor. He couldn't very well stroll into the ballroom and request an audience with one of the guests, but he thought there was a chance that someone had noticed Lucy's absence and gone off looking for her. God willing it would be someone sympathetic to their cause, someone who actually cared about Lucy's happiness.

But when Gregory slipped inside the room, all was exactly as he'd left it. "Damn," he muttered, striding back to the door. Now he was going to have to figure out how to speak to her brother—or Haselby, he supposed—without attracting attention.

He placed his hand on the knob and yanked, but the weight of the door was all wrong, and Gregory wasn't certain which happened first—the feminine shriek of surprise or the soft, warm body tumbling into his.

"You!"

"You!" he said in return. "Thank God."

It was Hermione. The one person he *knew* cared for Lucy's happiness above all else.

"What are you doing here?" she hissed. But she closed the door to the corridor, surely a good sign.

"I had to talk to Lucy."

"She married Lord Haselby."

He shook his head. "It has not been consummated."

Her mouth quite literally fell open. "Good God, you don't mean to—"

"I will be honest with you," he cut in. "I don't know what I mean to do, other than find a way to free her."

Hermione stared at him for several seconds. And then, seemingly out of nowhere, she said, "She loves you."

"She told you that?"

She shook her head. "No, but it's obvious. Or at least with hindsight it is." She paced the room, then turned suddenly around. "Then why did she marry Lord Haselby? I know she feels strongly about honoring commitments, but surely she could have ended it before today."

"She is being blackmailed," Gregory said grimly.

Hermione's eyes grew very large. "With what?"

"I can't tell you."

To her credit, she did not waste time protesting. Instead, she looked up at him, her eyes sharp and steady. "What can I do to help?"

Five minutes later, Gregory found himself in the company of both Lord Haselby and Lucy's brother. He would have preferred to have done without the latter, who looked as if he might cheerfully decapitate Gregory were it not for the presence of his wife.

Who had his arm in a viselike grip.

"Where is Lucy?" Richard demanded.

"She is safe," Gregory replied.

"Pardon me if I am not reassured," Richard retorted.

"Richard, stop," Hermione cut in, forcibly pulling him back. "Mr. Bridgerton is not going to hurt her. He has her best interests at heart."

"Oh, really?" Richard drawled.

Hermione glared at him with more animation than Gregory had ever seen on her pretty face. "He loves her," she declared.

"Indeed."

All eyes turned to Lord Haselby, who had been standing by the door, watching the scene with a strange expression of amusement.

No one seemed to know what to say.

"Well, he certainly made it clear this morning," Haselby continued, settling into a chair with remarkably easy grace. "Wouldn't you agree?"

"Er, yes?" Richard answered, and Gregory couldn't really blame him for his uncertain tone. Haselby did seem to be taking this in a most uncommon manner. Calm. So calm that Gregory's pulse seemed to feel the need to race twice as fast, if only to make up for Haselby's shortcomings.

"She loves me," Gregory told him, balling his hand into a fist behind his back—not in preparation for violence, but rather because if he didn't move *some* part of his body, he was liable to jump out of his skin. "I'm sorry to say it, but—"

"No, no, not at all," Haselby said with a wave. "I'm quite aware she doesn't love *me*. Which is really for the best, as I'm sure we can all agree."

Gregory wasn't sure whether he was meant to answer that. Richard was flushing madly, and Hermione looked completely confused.

"Will you release her?" Gregory asked. He did not have time to dance around the subject.

"If I weren't willing to do that, do you really think I'd be standing here speaking with you in the same tones I use to discuss the weather?"

"Er . . . no?"

Haselby smiled. Slightly. "My father will not be pleased. A state of affairs which normally brings me great joy, to be sure, but it does present a host of difficulties. We shall have to proceed with caution."

"Shouldn't Lucy be here?" Hermione asked.

Richard resumed his glaring. "Where *is* my sister?"

"Upstairs," Gregory said curtly. That narrowed it down to only thirty-odd rooms.

"Upstairs *where*?" Richard ground out.

Gregory ignored the question. It really wasn't the best time to reveal that she was presently tied to a water closet.

He turned back to Haselby, who was still seated, one leg crossed casually over the other. He was examining his fingernails.

Gregory felt ready to climb the walls. How could the bloody man sit there so calmly? This was the single most critical conversation either of them would ever have, and all he could do was inspect his *manicure*?

"Will you release her?" Gregory ground out.

Haselby looked up at him and blinked. "I said I would."

"But will you reveal her secrets?"

At that, Haselby's entire demeanor changed. His body seemed to tighten, and his eyes grew deadly sharp. "I have no idea what you're talking about," he said, each word crisp and precise.

"Nor do I," Richard added, stepping close.

Gregory turned briefly in his direction. "She is being blackmailed."

"Not," Haselby said sharply, "by me."

"My apologies," Gregory said quietly. Blackmail was an ugly thing. "I did not mean to imply."

"I always wondered why she agreed to marry me," Haselby said softly.

"It *was* arranged by her uncle," Hermione put in. Then, when everyone turned to her in mild surprise, she added, "Well, you know Lucy. She's not the sort to rebel. She *likes* order."

"All the same," Haselby said, "she did have a rather dramatic opportunity to get out of it." He paused, cocking his head to the side. "It's my father, isn't it?"

Gregory's chin jerked in a single, grim nod.

"That is not surprising. He is rather eager to have me married. Well, then—" Haselby brought his hands together, twining his fingers and squeezing them down. "What shall we do? Call his bluff, I imagine."

Gregory shook his head. "We can't."

"Oh, come now. It can't be that bad. What on earth could Lady Lucinda have done?"

"We really should get her," Hermione said again. And then, when the three men turned to her again, she added, "How would you like your fate to be discussed in your absence?"

Richard stepped in front of Gregory. "Tell me," he said.

Gregory did not pretend to misunderstand. "It is bad."

"Tell me."

"It is your father," Gregory said in a quiet voice. And he proceeded to relate what Lucy had told to him.

"She did it for us," Hermione whispered once Gregory was done. She turned to her husband, clutching his hand. "She did it to save us. Oh, *Lucy.*"

But Richard just shook his head. "It's not true," he said.

Gregory tried to keep the pity out of his eyes as he said, "There is proof."

"Oh, really? What sort of proof?"

"Lucy says there is written proof."

"Has she seen it?" Richard demanded. "Would she even know how to tell if something were faked?"

Gregory took a long breath. He could not blame Lucy's brother for his reaction. He supposed he would be the same, were such a thing to come to light about his own father.

"Lucy doesn't know," Richard continued, still shaking his head. "She was too young. Father wouldn't have done such a thing. It is inconceivable."

"You were young as well," Gregory said gently.

"I was old enough to know my own father," Richard snapped, "and he was not a traitor. Someone has deceived Lucy."

Gregory turned to Haselby. "Your father?"

"Is not that clever," Haselby finished. "He would cheerfully commit blackmail, but he would do it with the truth, not a lie. He is intelligent, but he is not creative."

Richard stepped forward. "But my uncle is."

Gregory turned to him with urgency. "Do you think he has lied to Lucy?"

"He certainly said the one thing to her that would guarantee that she would not back out of the marriage," Richard said bitterly.

"But why does *he* need her to marry Lord Haselby?" Hermione asked.

They all looked to the man in question.

"I have no idea," he said.

"He must have secrets of his own," Gregory said.

Richard shook his head. "Not debts."

"He's not getting any money in the settlement," Haselby remarked.

Everyone turned to look at him.

"I may have let my father choose my bride," he said with a shrug, "but I wasn't about to marry without reading the contracts."

"Secrets, then," Gregory said.

"Perhaps in concert with Lord Davenport," Hermione added. She turned to Haselby. "So sorry."

He waved off her apology. "Think nothing of it."

"What should we do now?" Richard asked.

"Get Lucy," Hermione immediately answered.

Gregory nodded briskly. "She is right."

"No," said Haselby, rising to his feet. "We need my father."

"Your father?" Richard bit off. "He's hardly sympathetic to our cause."

"Perhaps, and I'm the first to say he's intolerable for more than three minutes at a time, but he will have answers. And for all of his venom, he is mostly harmless."

"Mostly?" Hermione echoed.

Haselby appeared to consider that. "Mostly."

"We need to act," Gregory said. "Now. Haselby, you and Fennsworth will locate your father and interrogate him. Find out the truth. Lady Fennsworth and I will retrieve Lucy and bring her back here, where Lady Fennsworth will remain with her." He turned to Richard. "I apologize for the arrangements, but I must have your wife with me to safeguard Lucy's reputation should someone discover us.

She's been gone nearly an hour now. Someone is bound to notice."

Richard gave him a curt nod, but it was clear he was not happy with the situation. Still, he had no choice. His honor demanded that he be the one to question Lord Davenport.

"Good," Gregory said. "Then we are agreed. I will meet the two of you back in . . ."

He paused. Aside from Lucy's room and the upstairs washroom, he had no knowledge of the layout of the house.

"Meet us in the library," Richard instructed. "It is on the ground floor, facing east." He took a step toward the door, then turned back and said to Gregory, "Wait here. I will return in a moment."

Gregory was eager to be off, but Richard's grave expression had been enough to convince him to remain in place. Sure enough, when Lucy's brother returned, barely a minute later, he carried with him two guns.

He held one out to Gregory.

Good God.

"You may need this," Richard said.

"Heaven help us if I do," Gregory said under his breath.

"Beg pardon?"

Gregory shook his head.

"Godspeed, then." Richard nodded at Haselby, and the two of them departed, moving swiftly down the hall.

Gregory beckoned to Hermione. "Let us go," he said, leading her in the opposite direction. "And do try not to judge me when you see where I am leading you."

He heard her chuckle as they ascended the stairs. "Why," she said, "do I suspect that, if anything, I shall judge you very clever indeed?"

"I did not trust her to remain in place," Gregory confessed, taking the steps two at a time. When they reached the top, he turned to face her. "It was heavy-handed, but there was nothing else I could do. All I needed was a bit of time."

Hermione nodded. "Where are we going?"

"To the nanny's washroom," he confessed. "I tied her to the water closet."

"You tied her to the— Oh my, I cannot wait to see this."

But when they opened the door to the small washroom, Lucy was gone.

And every indication was that she had not left willingly.

Twenty-five

**In which we learn what happened,
a mere ten minutes earlier.**

Had it been an hour? Surely it had been an hour.

Lucy took a deep breath and tried to calm her racing nerves. Why hadn't anyone thought to install a clock in the washroom? Shouldn't someone have realized that *eventually* someone would find herself tied to the water closet and *might* wish to know the hour?

Really, it was just a matter of time.

Lucy drummed the fingers of her right hand against the floor. Quickly, quickly, index to pinky, index to pinky. Her left hand was tied so that the pads of her fingers faced up, so she flexed, then bent, then flexed, then bent, then—

"Eeeeeuuuuuhhh!"

Lucy groaned with frustration.

Groaned? Grunted.

Groaned.

It should have been a word.

Surely it had been an hour. It must have been an hour.

And then . . .

Footsteps.

Lucy jerked to attention, glaring at the door. She was furious. And hopeful. And terrified. And nervous. And—

Good God, she wasn't meant to possess this many simultaneous emotions. One at a time was all she could manage. Maybe two.

The knob turned and the door jerked backward, and—

Jerked? Lucy had about one second to sense the wrongness of this. Gregory wouldn't jerk the door open. He would have—

"Uncle Robert?"

"You," he said, his voice low and furious.

"I—"

"You little whore," he bit off.

Lucy flinched. She knew he held no great affection for her, but still, it hurt.

"You don't understand," she blurted out, because she had no idea what she should say, and she refused—she absolutely *refused* to say, "I'm sorry."

She was done with apologizing. Done.

"Oh, really?" he spat out, crouching down to her level. "Just what don't I understand? The part about your fleeing your wedding?"

"I didn't flee," she shot back. "I was abducted! Or didn't you notice that I am *tied to the water closet*?"

His eyes narrowed menacingly. And Lucy began to feel scared.

She shrank back, her breath growing shallow. She had long feared her uncle—the ice of his temper, the cold, flat stare of his disdain.

But she had never felt frightened.

"Where is he?" her uncle demanded.

Lucy did not pretend to misunderstand. "I don't know."

"Tell me!"

"I don't know!" she protested. "Do you think he would have tied me up if he trusted me?"

Her uncle stood and cursed. "It doesn't make sense."

"What do you mean?" Lucy asked carefully. She wasn't sure what was going on, and she wasn't sure just whose wife she would be, at the end of the proverbial day, but she was fairly certain that she ought to stall for time.

And reveal nothing. Nothing of import.

"This! You!" her uncle spat out. "Why would he abduct you and leave you here, in Fennsworth House?"

"Well," Lucy said slowly. "I don't think he could have got me out without someone seeing."

"He couldn't have got into the party without someone seeing, either."

"I'm not sure what you mean."

"How," her uncle demanded, leaning down and putting his face far too close to hers, "did he grab you without your consent?"

Lucy let out a short puff of a breath. The truth was easy. And innocuous. "I went to my room to lie down," she said. "He was waiting for me there."

"He knew which room was yours?"

She swallowed. "Apparently."

Her uncle stared at her for an uncomfortably long moment. "People have begun to notice your absence," he muttered.

Lucy said nothing.

"It can't be helped, though."

She blinked. What was he talking about?

He shook his head. "It's the only way."

"I—I beg your pardon?" And then she realized—he wasn't talking to her. He was talking to himself.

"Uncle Robert?" she whispered.

But he was already slicing through her bindings.

Slicing? *Slicing?* Why did he have a knife?

"Let's go," he grunted.

"Back to the party?"

He let out a grim chuckle. "You'd like that, wouldn't you?"

Panic began to rise in her chest. "Where are you taking me?"

He yanked her to her feet, one of his arms wrapped vise-like around her. "To your husband."

She managed to twist just far enough to look at his face. "My—Lord Haselby?"

"Have you another husband?"

"But isn't he at the party?"

"Stop asking so many questions."

She looked frantically about. "But where are you taking me?"

"You are not going to ruin this for me," he hissed. "Do you understand?"

"No," she pleaded. Because she didn't. She no longer understood anything.

He yanked her hard against him. "I want you to listen to me, because I will say this only once."

She nodded. She wasn't facing him, but she knew he could feel her head move against his chest.

"This marriage will go forward," he said, his voice deadly and low. "And I will personally see to it that it is consummated tonight."

"What?"

"Don't argue with me."

"But—" She dug her heels in as he started to drag her to the door.

"For God's sake, don't fight me," he muttered. "It's nothing that you wouldn't have had to do, anyway. The only difference is that you will have an audience."

"An audience?"

"Indelicate, but I will have my proof."

She began to struggle in earnest, managing to free one

arm long enough to swing wildly through the air. He quickly restrained her, but his momentary shift in posture allowed her to kick him hard in the shins.

"God *damn* it," he muttered, wrenching her close. "Cease!"

She kicked out again, knocking over an empty chamber pot.

"Stop it!" He jammed something against her ribs. "Now!"

Lucy stilled instantly. "Is that a knife?" she whispered.

"Remember this," he said, his words hot and ugly against her ear. "I cannot kill you, but I can cause you great pain."

She swallowed a sob. "I am your niece."

"I don't care."

She swallowed and asked, her voice quiet, "Did you ever?"

He nudged her toward the door. "Care?"

She nodded.

For a moment there was silence, and Lucy was left with no means to interpret it. She could not see her uncle's face, could sense no change in his stance. She could do nothing but stare at the door, at his hand as he reached for the knob.

And then he said, "No."

She had her answer, then.

"You were a duty," he clarified. "One I fulfilled, and one I am pleased to discharge. Now come with me, and don't say a word."

Lucy nodded. His knife was pressing ever harder against her ribs and already she had heard a soft crunching sound as it poked through the stiff fabric of her bodice.

She let him move her along the corridor and down the stairs. Gregory was here, she kept telling herself. He was here, and he would find her. Fennsworth House was large, but it was not massive. There were only so many places her uncle could stash her.

And there were hundreds of guests on the ground floor.

And Lord Haselby—surely he would not consent to such a scheme.

There were at least a dozen reasons her uncle would not succeed in this.

A dozen. Twelve. Maybe more. And she needed only one—just one to foil his plot.

But this was of little comfort when he stopped and yanked a blindfold over her eyes.

And even less when he threw her into a room and tied her up.

"I will be back," he bit off, leaving her on her bottom in a corner, bound hand and foot.

She heard his footsteps move across the room, and then it burst from her lips—a single word, the only word that mattered—

"Why?"

His footsteps stopped.

"Why, Uncle Robert?"

This couldn't be just about the family honor. Hadn't she already proved herself on that score? Shouldn't he trust her for that?

"Why?" she asked again, praying he had a conscience. Surely he couldn't have looked after her and Richard for so many years without some sense of right and wrong.

"You know why," he finally said, but she knew that he was lying. He had waited far too long before answering.

"Go, then," she said bitterly. There was no point in stalling him. It would be far better if Gregory found her alone.

But he didn't move. And even through her blindfold she could feel his suspicion.

"What are you waiting for?" she cried out.

"I'm not sure," he said slowly. And then she heard him turn.

His footsteps drew closer.

Slowly.

Slowly . . .

And then—

"Where is she?" Hermione gasped.

Gregory strode into the small room, his eyes taking in everything—the cut bindings, the overturned chamber pot. "Someone took her," he said grimly.

"Her uncle?"

"Or Davenport. They are the only two with reason to—" He shook his head. "No, they cannot do her harm. They need the marriage to be legal and binding. And long-standing. Davenport wants an heir off Lucy."

Hermione nodded.

Gregory turned to her. "You know the house. Where could she be?"

Hermione was shaking her head. "I don't know. I don't know. If it's her uncle—"

"Assume it's her uncle," Gregory ordered. He wasn't sure that Davenport was agile enough to abduct Lucy, and besides that, if what Haselby had said about his father was true, then Robert Abernathy was the man with secrets.

He was the man with something to lose.

"His study," Hermione whispered. "He is always in his study."

"Where is it?"

"On the ground floor. It looks out the back."

"He wouldn't risk it," Gregory said. "Too close to the ballroom."

"Then his bedchamber. If he means to avoid the public rooms, then that is where he would take her. That or her own chamber."

Gregory took her arm and preceded her out the door. They made their way down one flight of stairs, pausing before opening the door that led from the servants' stairs to the second floor landing.

"Point out his door to me," he said, "and then go."

"I'm not—"

"Find your husband," he ordered. "Bring him back."

Hermione looked conflicted, but she nodded and did as he asked.

"Go," he said, once he knew where to go. "Quickly."

She ran down the stairs as Gregory crept along the hall. He reached the door Hermione had indicated and carefully pressed his ear to it.

"What are you waiting for?"

It was Lucy. Muffled through the heavy wood door, but it was she.

"I don't know," came a male voice, and Gregory realized that he could not identify it. He'd had few conversations with Lord Davenport and none with her uncle. He had no idea who was holding her hostage.

He held his breath and slowly turned the knob.

With his left hand.

With his right hand he pulled out his gun.

God help them all if he had to use it.

He managed to get the door open a crack—just enough to peer in without being noticed.

His heart stopped.

Lucy was bound and blindfolded, huddled in the far corner of the room. Her uncle was standing in front of her, a gun pointed between her eyes.

"What are you up to?" he asked her, his voice chilling in its softness.

Lucy did not say anything, but her chin shook, as if she was trying too hard to hold her head steady.

"Why do you wish for me to leave?" her uncle demanded.

"I don't know."

"Tell me." He lunged forward, jamming his gun between her ribs. And then, when she did not answer quickly enough, he yanked up her blindfold, leaving them nose to nose. "Tell me!"

"Because I can't bear the waiting," she whispered, her voice quivering. "Because—"

Gregory stepped quietly into the room and pointed his gun at the center of Robert Abernathy's back. *"Release her."*

Lucy's uncle froze.

Gregory's hand tightened around the trigger. "Release Lucy and step slowly away."

"I don't think so," Abernathy said, and he turned just enough so that Gregory could see that his gun was now resting against Lucy's temple.

Somehow, Gregory held steady. He would never know how, but his arm held firm. His hand did not quiver.

"Drop your gun," her uncle ordered.

Gregory did not move. His eyes flicked to Lucy, then back to her uncle. Would he hurt her? Could he? Gregory still wasn't certain just why, precisely, Robert Abernathy needed Lucy to marry Haselby, but it was clear that he did.

Which meant that he could not kill her.

Gregory gritted his teeth and tightened his finger on the trigger. "Release Lucy," he said, his voice low, strong, and steady.

"Drop your gun!" Abernathy roared, and a horrible, choking sound flew from Lucy's mouth as one of his arms jammed up and under her ribs.

Good God, he was mad. His eyes were wild, darting around the room, and his hand—the one with the gun—was shaking.

He would shoot her. Gregory realized that in one sickening flash. Whatever Robert Abernathy had done—he thought he had nothing left to lose. And he would not care whom he brought down with him.

Gregory began to bend at his knees, never taking his eyes off Lucy's uncle.

"Don't do it," Lucy cried out. "He won't hurt me. He can't."

"Oh, I can," her uncle replied, and he smiled.

Gregory's blood ran cold. He would try—dear God, he would try with everything he had to make sure that they both came through this alive and unhurt, but if there was a choice—if only one of them was to walk out the door . . .

It would be Lucy.

This, he realized, was love. It was that sense of rightness, yes. And it was the passion, too, and the lovely knowledge that he could happily wake up next to her for the rest of his life.

But it was more than all that. It was this feeling, this knowledge, this *certainty* that he would give his life for her. There was no question. No hesitation. If he dropped his gun, Robert Abernathy would surely shoot him.

But Lucy would live.

Gregory lowered himself into a crouch. "Don't hurt her," he said softly.

"Don't let go!" Lucy cried out. "He won't—"

"Shut up!" her uncle snapped, and the barrel of his gun pressed even harder against her.

"Not another word, Lucy," Gregory warned. He still wasn't sure how the hell he was going to get out of this, but he knew that the key was to keep Robert Abernathy as calm and as sane as possible.

Lucy's lips parted, but then their eyes met . . .

And she closed them.

She trusted him. Dear God, she trusted him to keep her safe, to keep them both safe, and he felt like a fraud, because all he was doing was stalling for time, keeping all the bullets in all the guns until someone else arrived.

"I won't hurt you, Abernathy," Gregory said.

"Then drop the gun."

He kept his arm outstretched, the gun now positioned sideways so he could lay it down.

But he did not let go.

And he did not take his eyes off Robert Abernathy's face as he asked, "Why do you need her to marry Lord Haselby?"

"She didn't tell you?" he sneered.

"She told me what you told her."

Lucy's uncle began to shake.

"I spoke with Lord Fennsworth," Gregory said quietly. "He was somewhat surprised by your characterization of his father."

Lucy's uncle did not respond, but his throat moved, his Adam's apple shifting up and down in a convulsive swallow.

"In fact," Gregory continued, "he was quite convinced that you must be in error." He kept his voice smooth, even. Unmocking. He spoke as if at a dinner party. He did not wish to provoke; he only wished to converse.

"Richard knows nothing," Lucy's uncle replied.

"I spoke with Lord Haselby as well," Gregory said. "He was also surprised. He did not realize that his father had been blackmailing you."

Lucy's uncle glared at him.

"He is speaking with him now," Gregory said softly.

No one spoke. No one moved. Gregory's muscles were screaming. He had been in his crouch for several minutes, balancing on the balls of his feet. His arm, still outstretched, still holding the gun sideways but steady, felt like it was on fire.

He looked at the gun.

He looked at Lucy.

She was shaking her head. Slowly, and with small motions. Her lips made no sound, but he could easily make out her words.

Go.

And *please.*

Amazingly, Gregory felt himself smile. He shook his head, and he whispered, "Never."

"What did you say?" Abernathy demanded.

Gregory said the only thing that came to mind. "I love your niece."

Abernathy looked at him as if he'd gone mad. "I don't care."

Gregory took a gamble. "I love her enough to keep your secrets."

Robert Abernathy blanched. He went absolutely bloodless, and utterly still.

"It was you," Gregory said softly.

Lucy twisted. "Uncle Robert?"

"Shut up," he snapped.

"Did you lie to me?" she asked, and her voice sounded almost wounded. "Did you?"

"Lucy, *don't*," Gregory said.

But she was already shaking her head. "It wasn't my father, was it? It was *you*. Lord Davenport was blackmailing you for your *own* misdeeds."

Her uncle said nothing, but they all saw the truth in his eyes.

"Oh, Uncle Robert," she whispered sadly, "how could you?"

"I had nothing," he hissed. "Nothing. Just your father's droppings and leftovers."

Lucy turned ashen. "Did you kill him?"

"No," her uncle replied. Nothing else. Just no.

"Please," she said, her voice small and pained. "Do not lie to me. Not about this."

Her uncle let out an aggravated breath and said, "I know only what the authorities told me. He was found near a gambling hell, shot in the chest and robbed of all of his valuables."

Lucy watched him for a moment, and then, her eyes brimming with tears, gave a little nod.

Gregory rose slowly to his feet. "It is over, Abernathy," he said. "Haselby knows, as does Fennsworth. You cannot force Lucy to do your bidding."

Lucy's uncle gripped her more tightly. "I can use her to get away."

"Indeed you can. By letting her go."

Abernathy laughed at that. It was a bitter, caustic sound.

"We have nothing to gain by exposing you," Gregory said carefully. "Better to allow you to quietly leave the country."

"It will never be quiet," Lucy's uncle mocked. "If she does not marry that freakish fop, Davenport will shout it from here to Scotland. And the family will be ruined."

"No." Gregory shook his head. "They won't. You were never the earl. You were never their father. There will be a scandal; that cannot be avoided. But Lucy's brother will not lose his title, and it will all blow over when people begin to recall that they'd never quite liked you."

In the blink of an eye, Lucy's uncle moved the gun from her belly to her neck. "You watch what you say," he snapped.

Gregory blanched and took a step back.

And then they all heard it.

A thunder of footsteps. Moving quickly down the hall.

"Put the gun down," Gregory said. "You have only a moment before—"

The doorway filled with people. Richard, Haselby, Davenport, Hermione—they all dashed in, unaware of the deadly confrontation taking place.

Lucy's uncle jumped back, wildly pointing his gun at the lot of them. "Stay away," he yelled. "Get out! All of you!" His eyes flashed like those of a cornered animal, and his arm waved back and forth, leaving no one untargeted.

But Richard stepped forward. "You bastard," he hissed. "I will see you in—"

A gun fired.

Gregory watched in horror as Lucy fell to the ground. A guttural cry ripped from his throat; his own gun rose.

He aimed.

He fired.

And for the first time in his life, he hit his mark.

Well, almost.

Lucy's uncle was not a large man, but nonetheless, when he landed on top of her, it hurt. The air was forced completely from her lungs, leaving her gasping and choking, her eyes squeezed shut from the pain.

"Lucy!"

It was Gregory, tearing her uncle from atop her.

"Where are you hurt?" he demanded, and his hands were everywhere, frantic in their motions as he searched for a wound.

"I didn't—" She fought for breath. "He didn't—" She managed to look at her chest. It was covered with blood. "Oh my heavens."

"I can't find it," Gregory said. He took her chin, positioning her face so that she was looking directly into his eyes.

And she almost didn't recognize him.

His eyes . . . his beautiful hazel eyes . . . they looked lost, nearly empty. And it almost seemed to take away whatever it was that made him . . . *him.*

"Lucy," he said, his voice hoarse with emotion, "*please.* Speak to me."

"I'm not hurt," she finally got out.

His hands froze. "The blood."

"It's not mine." She looked up at him and brought her hand to his cheek. He was shaking. Oh dear God, he was shaking. She had never seen him thus, never imagined he could be brought to this point.

The look in his eyes— She realized it now. It had been terror.

"I'm not hurt," she whispered. "Please . . . don't . . . it's all right, darling." She didn't know what she was saying; she only wanted to comfort him.

His breath was ragged, and when he spoke, his words were broken, unfinished. "I thought I'd— I don't know what I thought."

Something wet touched her finger, and she brushed it gently away. "It's over now," she said. "It's over now, and—"

And suddenly she became aware of the rest of the people in the room. "Well, I think it's over," she said hesitantly, pushing herself into a seated position. Was her uncle dead? She knew he'd been shot. By Gregory or Richard, she did not know which. Both had fired their weapons.

But Uncle Robert had not been mortally wounded. He had pulled himself to the side of the room and was propped up against the wall, clutching his shoulder and staring ahead with a defeated expression.

Lucy scowled at him. "You're lucky he's not a better shot."

Gregory made a rather strange, snorting sound.

Over in the corner, Richard and Hermione were clutching each other, but they both appeared unharmed. Lord Davenport was bellowing about something, she wasn't sure what, and Lord Haselby—good God, her *husband*—was leaning idly against the doorjamb, watching the scene.

He caught her eye and smiled. Just a bit. No teeth, of course; he never smiled quite so broadly.

"I'm sorry," she said.

"Don't be."

Gregory rose to his knees beside her, one arm draped protectively over her shoulder. Haselby viewed the tableau with patent amusement, and perhaps just a touch of pleasure as well.

"Do you still desire that annulment?" he asked.

Lucy nodded.

"I'll have the papers drawn up tomorrow."

"Are you certain?" Lucy asked, concerned. He was a lovely man, really. She didn't want his reputation to suffer.

"Lucy!"

She turned quickly to Gregory. "Sorry. I didn't mean— I just—"

Haselby gave her a wave. "Please, don't trouble yourself. It was the best thing that could possibly have happened. Shootings, blackmail, treason . . . No one will ever look to *me* as the cause of the annulment now."

"Oh. Well, that's good," Lucy said brightly. She rose to her feet because, well, it seemed only polite, given how generous he was being. "But do you still wish for a wife? Because I could help you find one, once I'm settled, that is."

Gregory's eyes practically rolled back in his head. "Good *God*, Lucy."

She watched as he stood. "I feel I must make this right. He thought he was getting a wife. In a way, it's not precisely fair."

Gregory closed his eyes for a long moment. "It is a good thing I love you so well," he said wearily, "because otherwise, I should have to fit you with a muzzle."

Lucy's mouth fell open. "Gregory!" And then, "Hermione!"

"Sorry!" Hermione said, one hand still clapped over her mouth to muffle her laughter. "But you *are* well-matched."

Haselby strolled into the room and handed her uncle a handkerchief. "You'll want to staunch that," he murmured. He turned back to Lucy. "I don't really want a wife, as I'm sure you're aware, but I suppose I must find some way to procreate or the title'll go to my odious cousin. Which would be a shame, really. The House of Lords would surely elect to disband if ever he decided to take up his seat."

Lucy just looked at him and blinked.

Haselby smiled. "So, yes, I should be grateful if you found someone suitable."

"Of course," she murmured.

"You'll need my approval, too," Lord Davenport blustered, marching forward.

Gregory turned to him with unveiled disgust. "You," he bit off, "may shut up. Immediately."

Davenport drew back in a huff. "Do you have any idea to whom you are speaking, you little whelp?"

Gregory's eyes narrowed and he rose to his feet. "To a man in a very precarious position."

"I beg your pardon."

"You will cease your blackmail immediately," Gregory said sharply.

Lord Davenport jerked his head toward Lucy's uncle. "He was a traitor!"

"And you chose not to turn him in," Gregory snapped, "which I would imagine the king would find equally reprehensible."

Lord Davenport staggered back as if struck.

Gregory rose to his feet, pulling Lucy up along with him. "You," he said to Lucy's uncle, "will leave the country. Tomorrow. Don't return."

"I shall pay his passage," Richard bit off. "No more."

"You are more generous than I would have been," Gregory muttered.

"I want him gone," Richard said in a tight voice. "If I can hasten his departure, I am happy to bear the expense."

Gregory turned to Lord Davenport. "You will never breathe a word of this. Do you understand?"

"And you," Gregory said, turning to Haselby. "Thank you."

Haselby acknowledged him with a gracious nod. "I can't help it. I'm a romantic." He shrugged. "It does get one in trouble from time to time, but we can't change our nature, can we?"

Gregory let his head shake slowly from side to side as a wide smile began to spread across his face.

"You have no idea," he murmured, taking Lucy's hand. He couldn't quite bear to be separated from her just then, even by a few inches.

Their fingers twined, and he looked down at her. Her eyes were shining with love, and Gregory had the most overwhelming, absurd desire to laugh. Just because he could.

Just because he loved her.

But then he noticed that her lips were tightening, too. Around the corners, stifling her own laughter.

And right there, in front of the oddest assortment of witnesses, he swept her into his arms and kissed her with every last drop of his hopelessly romantic soul.

Eventually—very eventually—Lord Haselby cleared his throat.

Hermione pretended to look away, and Richard said, "About that wedding . . ."

With great reluctance, Gregory pulled away. He looked to the left. He looked to the right. He looked back at Lucy.

And he kissed her again.

Because, really, it had been a long day.

And he deserved a little indulgence.

And God only knew how long it would be before he could actually marry her.

But mostly, he kissed her because . . .

Because . . .

He smiled, taking her head in his hands and letting his nose rest against hers. "I love you, you know."

She smiled back. "I know."

And he finally realized why he was going to kiss her again.

Just because.

Epilogue

**In which Our Hero and Heroine
exhibit the industriousness
of which we knew they were capable.**

*T*he first time, Gregory had been a wreck.

The second time was even worse. The memory of the first time had done little to calm his nerves. Just the opposite, in fact. Now that he had a better understanding of what was happening (Lucy had spared him no detail, a pox on her meticulous little soul) every little noise was subject to morbid scrutiny and speculation.

It was a damned good thing men couldn't have children. Gregory took no shame in admitting that the human race would have died out generations earlier.

Or at the very least, *he* would not have contributed to the current batch of mischievous little Bridgertons.

But Lucy seemed not to mind childbirth, as long as she could later describe the experience to him in relentless detail.

Whenever she wished.

And so by the third time, Gregory was a little more himself. He still sat outside the door, and he still held his breath when he heard a particularly unpleasant groan, but all in all, he wasn't wracked with anxiety.

The fourth time he brought a book.

The fifth, just a newspaper. (It did seem to be getting quicker with every child. Convenient, that.)

The sixth child caught him completely unawares. He'd popped out for a quick visit with a friend, and by the time he'd returned, Lucy was sitting up with the babe in her arms, a cheerful and not the least bit tired smile on her face.

Lucy frequently reminded him of his absence, however, so he took great care to be present for the arrival of number seven. Which he was, as long as one did not deduct points for his having abandoned his post outside her door in search of a middle-of-the-night snack.

At seven, Gregory thought they ought to be done. Seven was a perfectly fine number of children, and, as he told Lucy, he could barely recall what she looked like when she wasn't expecting.

"Well enough for you to make sure I'm expecting again," Lucy had replied pertly.

He couldn't very well argue with that, so he'd kissed her on the forehead and gone off to visit Hyacinth, to expound upon the many reasons seven was the ideal number of children. (Hyacinth was not amused.)

But then, sure enough, six months after the seventh, Lucy sheepishly told him that she was expecting another baby.

"No more," Gregory announced. "We can scarcely afford the ones we already possess." (This was not true; Lucy's dowry had been exceedingly generous, and Gregory had discovered that he possessed a shrewd eye for investments.)

But really, eight *had* to be enough.

Not that he was willing to curtail his nocturnal activities with Lucy, but there *were* things a man could do—things he probably already should have done, to tell the truth.

And so, since he was convinced that this would be his final child, he decided he might as well see what this was all about, and despite the horrified reaction of the midwife, he remained at Lucy's side through the birth (at her shoulder, of course.)

"She's an expert at this," the doctor said, lifting the sheet to take a peek. "Truly, I'm superfluous at this point."

Gregory looked at Lucy. She had brought her embroidery.

She shrugged. "It really does get easier every time."

And sure enough, when the time came, Lucy laid down her work, gave a little grunt, and—

Whoosh!

Gregory blinked as he looked at the squalling infant, all wrinkled and red. "Well, that was much less involved than I'd expected," he said.

Lucy gave him a peevish expression. "If you'd been present the first time, you would have—ohhhhhhh!"

Gregory snapped back to face her. "What is it?"

"I don't know," Lucy replied, her eyes filling with panic. "But this is not right."

"Now, now," the midwife said, "you're just—"

"I know what I am supposed to feel," Lucy snapped. "And this is not it."

The doctor handed the new baby—a girl, Gregory was pleased to learn—to the midwife and returned to Lucy's side. He laid his hands upon her belly. "Hmmmm."

"Hmmmm?" Lucy returned. And not with a great deal of patience.

The doctor lifted the sheet and peered below.

"Gah!" Gregory let out, returning to Lucy's shoulder. "Didn't mean to see that."

"What is going on?" Lucy demanded. "What do you— ohhhhhhh!"

Whoosh!

"Good heavens," the midwife exclaimed. "There are two."

No, Gregory thought, feeling decidedly queasy, there were nine.

Nine children.

Nine.

It was only one less than ten.

Which possessed two digits. If he did this again, he would be in the double-digits of fatherhood.

"Oh dear Lord," he whispered.

"Gregory?" Lucy said.

"I need to sit down."

Lucy smiled wanly. "Well, your mother will be pleased, at the very least."

He nodded, barely able to think. Nine children. What did one do with nine children?

Love them, he supposed.

He looked at his wife. Her hair was disheveled, her face was puffy, and the bags under her eyes had bypassed lavender and were well on their way to purplish-gray.

He thought she was beautiful.

Love existed, he thought to himself.

And it was grand.

He smiled.

Nine times grand.

Which was very grand, indeed.

Two men say
they're the Duke of Wyndham.
One of them must be wrong.

The Two Dukes
of Wyndham

The next great romance
from Julia Quinn
Coming Summer 2007

You'll ne~~ver get enough of these cowboys!~~

Talented Harlequin Blaze author Debbi Rawlins
makes all your cowboy dreams come true with her
popular miniseries

Made in Montana.

The little town of Blackfoot Falls isn't so sleepy
anymore...

In fact, it seems everyone's staying up late!

Get your hands on a hot cowboy with

#837 *Anywhere with You*

(March 2015)

#849 *Come On Over*

(June 2015)

#861 *This Kiss*

(September 2015)

*And remember, the sexiest cowboys are Made in
Montana!*

Dear Reader,

I think I'm starting to have a thing for rodeo cowboys. In *This Kiss* you'll meet Ethan Styles, a champion bull rider and the third rodeo hero I've written for the Made in Montana series.

During late spring and throughout the summer, there are a number of rodeos that take place close to my home. I like most of the events—not so much others, which I'll refrain from naming though you'll probably be able to guess from reading this book. But something occurred to me while doing some research, and by that I mean I begin "skimming" one of my rodeo books and forget to put it down. It seems my growing fondness for this true American sport has a lot to do with the cowboys, for whom rodeo is not just a sport or a job but a way of life. These men are a different breed. So much passion and dedication. What's not to love?

The heroine, Sophie, is a bit younger than most of my heroines, but she is so perfect for Ethan, I couldn't resist.

I hope everyone is enjoying their summer!

All my best,

Debbi Rawlins

Debbi Rawlins

This Kiss

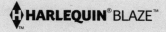
HARLEQUIN® BLAZE™

ISBN-13: 978-0-373-79865-0

This Kiss

Copyright © 2015 by Debbi Quattrone

The publisher acknowledges the copyright holder of the additional work:

Hard Knocks

Copyright © 2014 by Lori Foster

Recycling programs for this product may not exist in your area.

This edition published by arrangement with Harlequin Books S.A.

For questions and comments about the quality of this book, please contact us at CustomerService@Harlequin.com.

® and TM are trademarks of Harlequin Enterprises Limited or its corporate affiliates. Trademarks indicated with ® are registered in the United States Patent and Trademark Office, the Canadian Intellectual Property Office and in other countries.

Printed in U.S.A.

CONTENTS

Debbi Rawlins grew up in the country and loved Western movies and books. Her first crush was on a cowboy—okay, he was an actor in the role of a cowboy, but she was only eleven, so it counts. It was in Houston, Texas, where she first started writing for Harlequin, and now she has her own ranch...of sorts. Instead of horses, she has four dogs, four cats, a trio of goats and free-range cattle on a few acres in gorgeous rural Utah.

Books by Debbi Rawlins

HARLEQUIN BLAZE

Made in Montana

Barefoot Blue Jean Night
Own the Night
On a Snowy Christmas Night
You're Still the One
No One Needs to Know
From This Moment On
Alone with You
Need You Now
Behind Closed Doors
Anywhere with You
Come On Over

To get the inside scoop on Harlequin Blaze and its talented writers, be sure to check out BlazeAuthors.com.

All backlist available in ebook format.

Visit the Author Profile page at Harlequin.com for more titles.

THIS KISS

Debbi Rawlins

1

"GOTCHA!" SOPHIE MICHAELS grinned when she saw the motel's address on the computer screen. After a quick sip of morning coffee, she sent the file to her partner, Lola, who was sitting in the next office.

The rush from *getting her man* lasted barely a minute. Sophie sank back in her chair and sighed. Lately, the thrill of success was fleeting and not all that sweet.

Locating the deadbeat dad was rewarding because, well…he had three kids to support. But if he was going to jump bail anyway, couldn't he have done a better job of covering his tracks? For God's sake, a fourth grader could've found him.

After four years the job was finally getting to her. Too much sitting at the computer. Too much of the same old thing every day. Skip traces, lame excuses, shaken or re-signed parents putting up collateral for their wayward children or, almost as frequently, the roles being reversed. Here in Wattsville, Wyoming, nothing much exciting happened. Oh, they had bank robberies occasionally and liquor store holdups, but those types of criminals tended to be really stupid and that made her job boring.

Sophie sighed. Working in the bail bond business

wouldn't be forever. Mostly she'd signed on to help Lola get the company off the ground. Sophie looked on her cousin more like a sister. And Lola didn't mind that Sophie was sticking around only until she'd figured out what to do with her life.

Rolling her chair away from her dinged-up metal desk, Sophie dropped her chin to her chest and stretched her neck to the side. Feeling the strain of muscles that had been worked too hard earlier at the gym, she tried not to whimper. At least not loud enough for Lola to hear.

The front door to the reception area squeaked open and she glanced at the clock. "Oh, come on," she muttered. How could it be only eight-fifteen? It felt like noon.

They were expecting Mandy, the third member of their team, to return from Jackson Hole sometime this morning. But in case it was a potential client, Sophie got up. When she heard Hawk's voice, she promptly sat back down. And wished her door was closed. Hawk was Lola's sleazy boyfriend of three months. Sophie didn't like him, but so far she'd kept her mouth shut.

Lola hadn't had much luck with men in the past, but two people had never been less suited to each other. Hawk wasn't very bright, was sometimes crude and was under the delusion that riding a Harley and wearing black leather made him a badass.

He was a poser, no doubt in Sophie's mind. She knew something about desperately pretending to be someone you weren't just to fit in. A tiny bit of sympathy for him stopped her from telling Lola that his real name was Floyd and he was a high school dropout.

Sophie smiled. The idiot didn't get that she was really, really good with computers. And she knew a whole lot more about him than she'd let on.

Which she'd keep to herself. Unless Floyd kept pissing

her off. She wasn't the quiet, naive young girl she used to be in high school. Unlike Floyd aka Hawk, she had put a great deal of effort into transforming herself.

"Hey, Shorty," Hawk said, lounging against her office door frame. "Missed you at the gym this morning."

She hated the nickname, which he knew. Anyway, five-four wasn't that short. She gave his tall, lanky body a once-over. "Like you've ever seen the inside of a gym."

He laughed. "Gotta admit, you're looking pretty buff," he said, pushing back his straggly hair and eyeing her legs.

"Lola's in her office."

"I know. She's busy."

"So am I." Resisting the urge to tug down the hem of her bike shorts, Sophie swiveled in her chair so that her legs were under the desk, her gaze on the monitor.

"You guys working on something big?"

She noticed that line 2 was lit. Lola was on the phone. "Why are you still here?"

"Chillax, Shorty. Just making conversation while I wait for the old lady."

The front door opened again and Hawk glanced over his shoulder. His look of dread made Sophie smile. It had to be Mandy. She'd been working as a bounty hunter in Colorado before Lola hired her two years ago, and she could be intimidating at times. Plus, she didn't like Hawk any more than Sophie did. Only, Mandy wasn't as circumspect.

A whoop came from Lola's office. "Okay, ladies, we've got a live one. Mandy, are you here?"

Sophie leaped out of her chair and barreled past Hawk, who had enough smarts to get out of her way. "Somebody jumped bail?"

"Oh yeah." Lola walked out of her office waving a piece of paper. "You'll never guess who."

The waiting area was small, with two chairs, a ficus that

was alive only because Lola remembered to water it and a rack of magazines, where Mandy stood, tall, beefed-up and calm as could be. She wasn't the excitable type. "Ethan Styles," she said, and dropped her duffel bag.

Lola shoved back her long red hair and sighed. "How did you know?"

"Ethan Styles," Sophie murmured under her breath. She must've heard wrong. If his name was on the list of bonds they'd posted, she would've noticed. She knew him…sort of… "Who did you say?"

Lola's concerned gaze found Sophie. "I'm pretty sure you remember Ethan."

"The rodeo guy, right?" Hawk moved to the circle and sidled up to Lola when Sophie and Mandy gave him butt-out glares. "He's that hotshot bull rider."

Lola nodded and looked at Mandy. "You just get back from Jackson Hole?"

"An hour ago," Mandy said with a curious glance at Sophie. "I turned Jergens over to Deputy Martin."

Sophie couldn't seem to slow down her brain. Too many memories of Ethan revolved like a slide show on speed. She hadn't seen him up close since high school. She'd gone to a few rodeos just to see him, but only from the bleachers and it had been a while. Sometimes she watched him on TV, but not often. She wasn't a kid anymore and there was only so much daydreaming a woman could do without feeling like a dope.

"You get any sleep yet?" Lola asked Mandy, who just smiled.

"I hate to send you out again, but I got a tip that Styles might be headed for northwest Montana. A town called Blackfoot Falls."

"No shit. Pretty boy has an outstanding warrant?" Hawk

laughed. "What did he get locked up for? Screwing somebody's wife?"

The expression on Lola's face hinted that Hawk might not be far off the mark.

It wouldn't surprise Sophie if he was in trouble because of a woman. Half the girls in school had had the hots for him. Even now he left female fans across the country panting, but so what? Lola was mistaken if she thought Ethan's reputation with the ladies bothered Sophie. He didn't faze her. Not anymore.

"Why didn't he pay his own bail? Between his winnings and endorsement deals, he has to have money," Sophie said, mostly thinking out loud.

Lola shrugged. "He wouldn't be the first pro athlete to blow his cash on stupid things," she said. "We have the pink slip for his motor coach as collateral, so I had no problem with posting. I have to say, though, I'm surprised he skipped. He's not due in court until Monday, but he wasn't supposed to leave the state."

"I'll do it." Sophie squared her shoulders when they all stared at her. "I'll go after him."

Lola shook her head. "Not a good idea, Soph."

"You've never worked in the field." Mandy's quiet reminder somehow felt like a betrayal.

Even though Sophie had started kickboxing and tae kwon do back in college, it was Mandy who'd inspired her to go all out, work her body to its full potential. Sophie was in the best physical shape of her life and Mandy knew it. Anyway, Ethan might not come along willingly, but he wasn't the type to get rough.

"I told you guys I wanted to be more involved." She glared first at Lola, and then Mandy. "I know Ethan. I can bring him back with the least amount of fuss."

Hawk snorted. "No way. You don't know Styles."

"Shut up," Mandy said without looking at him. Her gaze stayed on Sophie. "You think you're ready?"

"I know I am." She glanced at Lola, who'd just given Hawk an impatient look. So maybe all wasn't peachy keen with the lovebirds. Good. Her cousin deserved better.

Lola met her gaze. "No, not Ethan. You can have the next one."

"I'm not asking for permission. I own half this company." Flexing her tense shoulders, Sophie ignored the looks of surprise. She and Lola never argued. Not over business, or their personal lives. "Text me the details. I'll go home, grab a few things and leave within the hour."

"Come on, Soph." Lola pinched the bridge of her nose. "Let's talk privately. Please."

"What she says makes sense." Hawk cut Lola short, earning him a warning look, which he obviously didn't like judging by his creepy scowl. "Why not let her go after him?"

"Excuse me—" Sophie stopped. Hawk was defending her? Okay, now, that was weird. She didn't need his help, but hey, bonus points for trying. "This isn't up for discussion," she said. "All we're doing is wasting time."

"Knowing him might not be an advantage," Mandy said. "Surprise is your best weapon. He sees you, he could run."

"Ethan won't remember me." Sophie avoided Lola's gaze. "Even if he does, he won't associate me with Lola's Bail Bonds."

Lola followed Sophie into her office. "We need to talk, kiddo," she said, closing the door behind her.

"You're not changing my mind." Sophie sifted through her cluttered drawer and found her wallet. Now, where were her keys?

She crouched to check under her desk and found them

next to a protein bar she'd misplaced yesterday. Grabbing them both, she pushed to her feet.

"Will you at least hear me out?" Her cousin's dark eyes weren't just worried but annoyed.

"Go ahead." Sophie unwrapped the bar and stuck half of it in her mouth, since she wouldn't have time to eat anything else. She had to get on the road fast. No telling how much of a head start Ethan had... "When did he leave for Montana, do you know?"

"Are you going to listen to me at all?"

"Probably not."

"Goddammit, Sophie." Lola paused and lowered her voice. "We can't afford for you to get all goo-goo-eyed over him. He'll sweet-talk you into letting him go and we'll be screwed."

Sophie chewed a bit, then said, "Wow, your faith in me is really touching."

"It's not that. The money's important, but I hate to think of you getting all twisted up over him again."

"Oh, for God's sake, I was never twisted up."

"Yes, you were." Lola smiled. "Don't forget, I was there. Anyway, that was high school, so you were allowed."

"Exactly. It was high school. I was fifteen. We had a fleeting encounter. Don't make a big deal out of it."

"He was your hero," Lola said, her voice softening.

Sophie turned away to pick up her gym bag. "You're only twenty-eight. I'm sure you still remember what it was like to be fifteen."

At the beginning of her freshman year, Sophie and her mom had moved to Wyoming. Lola had been a junior and the only person Sophie knew in her new school. They hadn't become friends quickly. Her cousin had had her own clique, and back then, Sophie had entered a nerdy phase, trying to balance her high IQ and an awkward social life.

That alone hadn't made her the target of bullies. Having had the audacity to wear the *wrong* dress was the line she'd crossed. She found out later that the most popular girl in school had worn the same sundress the week before Sophie even started at Wattsville High. The whole thing was ridiculous, considering that Ashley had huge boobs and Sophie had little more than two mosquito bites. So of course Ashley had looked so much better in the spaghetti-strap dress.

God, Sophie still remembered what it had felt like to have those girls come after her with scissors. They'd cut her dress to ribbons before Ethan had stopped them and put his jacket over her shoulders.

Turned out Ashley was Ethan's girlfriend. But he'd been furious when he stepped in and warned them off. After that, the girls still gave her evil looks, but they kept their distance.

Damn straight he'd been her hero.

"Are you still following his career?" Lola asked.

"No." Sophie set the gym bag on her chair and shut down her laptop, refusing to look up. "I know you saw me at my worst, sneaking around, following him, trying to stay on his radar. Frankly it embarrasses me to even think about it." All while he'd acted as if she hadn't existed. That part she left out, and met Lola's gaze. "Did you and Hawk have a fight?"

Lola's brows went up. "Why?"

"I saw the look you gave him."

"No, it's just…" Lola waved dismissively. "I'd already told him he shouldn't be hanging around here."

Sophie tucked her tablet under her arm. "Look, the thing with Ethan happened a long time ago. I was a kid." She smiled. "I can do this."

Lola studied her for a moment. "Okay," she said with a resigned sigh. "I just don't understand why you'd want to."

"I know," Sophie said softly. She didn't quite get it herself. It wasn't as if she needed closure, but in a weird way, that was exactly how it felt. She stopped halfway to the door. "Don't you think it's odd he jumped bail? Ethan has a reputation for being a stand-up guy."

"I don't know what he's thinking. He certainly doesn't have a low profile."

"Nope. The National Finals Rodeo in Las Vegas starts in about a week. He's going for his second championship title—" She saw the concern in Lola's eyes. "I read something about it online the other day," she murmured. "Try not to worry, okay? I've got this."

She hoped.

THE WATERING HOLE was noisy, crowded with cowboys drinking beer and gorgeous accommodating women dressed to kill. Ethan Styles had frequented hundreds of bars just like this one in the nine years since he turned pro. He knew what it was like the night before a rodeo, especially in a small town like Blackfoot Falls. So why in the hell had he suggested meeting his friend Matt here?

Somehow Ethan had gotten the dumb idea that this rodeo would be different. No prize money was involved or qualifying points. The event was a fund-raiser for Safe Haven, a large animal sanctuary, so all the ticket and concession money went directly to them. But he should've known better. Rodeo fans were a loyal bunch, and having to travel to this remote Montana town obviously hadn't bothered them.

Normally he was up for signing autographs and getting hit on by hot women. But with the finals a week away he'd been on edge since he hit Montana late this morning.

After that bogus arrest in Wyoming and then hearing how fellow bull rider Tommy Lunt had busted his knee, foreboding had prickled the back of his neck.

He'd missed the finals himself because of injuries. Twice. Last year broken ribs and a punctured lung had sidelined him. Two seasons before that, it had been an elbow injury. So he had cause to be jumpy.

"Hey, Styles, 'bout time you showed up." Kenny Horton stood at the bar with another bronc rider and three women, who all turned to eyeball Ethan.

He shook his head when Kenny motioned for him to join them. "Maybe later. I'm meeting someone."

"Right behind you."

At the sound of Matt Gunderson's voice, Ethan grinned and turned around to shake his hand. "Glad to see you, buddy."

"Same here. What's it been…a year?"

"About that." Ethan moved aside for a short, curvy blonde who'd just entered the bar. Their gazes met briefly, surprise flickering in her brown eyes. But then she brushed past him. "So, how's retirement?" he asked Matt and shifted so he could watch the blonde walk up to the bar.

The seats were all taken. A cowboy jumped to his feet and offered her his stool. Shaking her head, she dug into her pocket. Her tight jeans didn't leave room for much, but she managed to pull out a cell phone. She wasn't wearing a wedding ring. He always checked, though it hadn't done him any good last week.

Wendy hadn't been wearing one when he met her at the Ponderosa Saloon last Saturday, or when she invited him to her ranch that night. That hadn't made her any less married, and to a mean, rich son of a bitch on top of everything.

"Retirement? Shit, I work twice as hard for half the money," Matt said with a laugh. "But yeah, it was time."

That part Ethan didn't understand. Matt had been the one to beat. Yet out of the blue he'd just quit competing. Talk around the tour was that his new wife might've had something to do with it. "So, no regrets?"

"Not a one." Matt frowned. "You can't be thinking of getting out—"

"Hell no. Now that you're off the circuit, maybe I can finally win another title."

"Right." Matt laughed. "I seem to remember you leaving me in the dust more than a few times."

"Never when it counted."

"Man, you've had some bad luck right before the finals. I should've convinced you to drop out when we changed the date. You're the main draw this weekend. A lot of people are coming to see you ride Twister, but I should've thought this through."

"Come on, you probably figured I wouldn't make it to the finals."

Matt reared his head back, eyes narrowed. "What the hell's the matter with you, Styles?"

Ethan grinned. "Just joking." No way he'd admit that he had considered bailing because he couldn't risk injury. But then he'd only be superstitious about bad karma or some other bullshit. "It's a worthy cause. I'm glad to do it."

Just before Ethan turned to check on the blonde, he caught his friend's sympathetic look. Most rodeo cowboys started young and came from families of die-hard fans. Matt had been a casual fan who'd climbed onto his first bull at a late age, and yet he understood the pressure coming at Ethan from all sides. Winning another gold buckle wasn't just about ego or satisfying a lifelong dream. He came from rodeo royalty. Both his parents held multiple

world champion titles. Most of their fans were also his fans.
A lot of expectations drove him to succeed.

The woman was still standing at the bar, guys on either
side of her vying for her attention, but she didn't seem interested. She slowly sipped a drink, checked her phone
and then leaned over the bar to talk to the older woman
filling pitchers of beer.

Ethan smirked to himself. Bending over like that sure
wouldn't discourage guys from hitting on her. She knew how
to wear a pair of plain faded jeans. Her boots were brown,
low-heeled, scuffed. And the long-sleeve blue T-shirt was
nothing fancy. No, she sure wasn't dressed to be noticed like
the other women circling the room. Maybe she lived on a
nearby ranch and had just quit work.

Damn, she was hot.

And familiar. Yeah, women were plentiful for a bull
rider, and he was no saint. He also wasn't the type to forget a name or face. It sure felt as though he'd run into her
before. More than that, he felt this odd pull... The kind
of pull that could get him into trouble. Which he did not
need, especially not now.

Someone called out to Matt and he waved in acknowledgment. "We're not gonna find a table or a place at the
bar. Maybe we should head over to the diner. Unless you're
looking to hook up with that blonde."

"What blonde?" Ethan asked, and Matt smiled. "That
describes half the women in here."

"I'm talking about the one at the bar you've been eyeing."

"Nah, I'm not looking for company. I'm keeping my
nose clean until the finals."

"A whole week? You'll never make it."

"Probably not." Ethan laughed and glanced back at the
bar. "Is she local?"

Matt studied her for a moment. "I don't think so."

"Well, I'll be damned if it isn't the twins," a voice boomed from the back room.

Ethan and Matt exchanged glances. They both knew it was Tex, a bronc rider from Dallas. Though he wasn't the only one who called them *the twins*. They'd joined the pro tour within months of each other, and in the beginning they'd often been mistaken for brothers. Ethan figured it wasn't so much because they shared similar builds, or even because they both had light brown hair and blue eyes. It was their height. Six feet was tall for a bull rider.

"What are you boys doing standing there talking like two old women?" Tex yelled, a pool stick in one hand, an empty mug in the other. "Grab yourselves a pitcher and get on back here."

"Guess he's had a few," Ethan said. Tex was quiet by nature. But after a couple of beers…

"He'd better be able to ride tomorrow," Matt muttered, then turned when someone else shouted his name.

More people had poured into the bar. Ethan was willing to bet the place had reached capacity before the last ten customers had squeezed inside. And now that big-mouthed Tex had called attention to them, fans were approaching him and Matt for autographs.

They each accepted a pen and began scrawling their names. "You check in at The Boarding House yet?" Matt asked under his breath.

"An hour ago."

"It's not too late. You can stay out at the Lone Wolf. We've got a big house, trailer hookups. The inn's overbooked, so the owner won't have any trouble renting out your room. And my wife's dying to meet you."

"Hey, that's right. You're a married man now. Sorry I missed your wedding."

"No problem. I warned Rachel there'd be conflicts no matter which weekend she chose."

Ethan smiled as he passed the Safe Haven flyer he'd just signed to a middle-aged woman wearing a promotional Professional Bull Riders T-shirt from the 2010 finals, the year he wanted wiped from his memory forever. To be kept from the finals because of an injury was one thing, but to make it that far and then get hurt in the third round? Talk about fate landing a sucker punch.

This year nothing was going to keep him from the finals. Or from winning another gold buckle.

Nothing. Period.

2

SOPHIE SURE WISHED she'd known he was here in Blackfoot Falls for a rodeo before she'd left Wyoming. The event was a fund-raiser, so of course it wasn't listed on the PBR tour. The whole town, which wasn't saying much, since it was so small they had no traffic lights, was busting at the seams with rodeo fans. There was only one inn, a dude ranch twenty minutes away and a number of impromptu bed-and-breakfasts scattered around the area, all of which were booked. So was the large trailer park over thirty minutes away, not that a vacancy there would do her any good.

Somehow she had to get him alone. No clue how she was going to do it with so many fans clamoring for his attention. Those crazy people would string her up if they knew she planned to drag their favorite bull rider back to Wyoming.

The buckle bunnies worried her the most. Turning completely around so that her back was against the bar, she sipped her tonic water and watched the women practically line up, just waiting their turns to hit on Ethan.

She didn't care one bit. If he had enough stamina to screw every last one of them, then God bless him. She was twenty-six, not a silly teenager anymore, and he no

longer haunted her dreams. Though if he took one of those
eager young ladies back to his room for the night, Sophie
could have a problem.

It might mean she'd have to wait till morning to bag
him. That left her a very narrow window before the rodeo
started at noon.

Maybe she'd have to seduce him herself.

The thought sent a bolt of heat zinging through her
body. A hurried sip of tonic water barely made it down
her throat. He was still hot as hell. She'd be fooling herself if she couldn't admit that much. Tall and lean with
the perfect proportion of muscle, and those dreamy blue
eyes... Good Lord.

Bumping into him when she first entered the bar had
thrown her. She hadn't been prepared at all. But the wig
had done its job. Even up close he hadn't recognized her,
and now she was ready for him.

In the middle of signing an autograph, he swung a look
at her and she shifted her weight to her other foot. Okay,
maybe his gaze hadn't landed on her but vaguely in her
direction. Unfortunately her female parts couldn't tell the
difference.

Seducing him? That might have to take a few steps
back to plan Z.

"Now, why are you sittin' here drinkin' alone, darlin'?"
The same husky and very tipsy cowboy who'd offered her
a beer earlier wove too close, nearly unseating the guy on
her left.

She steadied Romeo with a brief hand on his shoulder. Boy, she sure didn't need either of the men making a
scene. "Are you here for the rodeo tomorrow?" she asked.

"You bet."

"Fan or rider?"

He frowned, clearly affronted.

Sophie smiled, despite the wave of beer breath that reached her. "Better go easy on the booze if you're competing."

The younger cowboy sitting on the stool twisted around and grinned. "Yeah, Brady, you don't wanna give those calves a leg up."

Ah, they knew each other. Made sense, since they were both probably here for the rodeo. Sophie relaxed a bit, and while the two men traded barbs, she slid a glance at Ethan, who was still surrounded by women.

Oddly he didn't seem all that interested in any of them. Not even the blondes. According to the articles and blogs she'd read earlier, his past three girlfriends had been blondes. Although it seemed he hadn't stayed with any of them for more than a few months. Probably thought he was too hot for any one woman to handle. Or decided it was his duty to spread the hotness around.

The cowboy, whose name was apparently Brady and who continued to stand too close, said something she didn't catch. Shifting her attention to him, she wondered if a well-placed knee could seem accidental. "Excuse me?"

He turned his head to look at Ethan. "Okay, now I see why you're being so uppity. You've already got your sights set on Styles. Figures." Lifting his beer, he mumbled, "Damn bull riders," before taking a gulp.

Oh, crap. Was she being that obvious? "Who's Styles?"

Brady frowned. "Are you kiddin'?"

She shook her head, the picture of innocence.

"See, Brady?" Grinning, the other cowboy elbowed him. "She's not snubbing you 'cause you're a calf roper. I bet she's got a whole lot more reasons than that."

Sophie ignored the troublemaker. "A calf roper?"

"That's right, darlin'. You're lookin' at a two-time champ."

"So you're one of those guys who chases the poor little calves and then ties them up?"

Brady's boastful grin slipped. "It's all for sport, darlin', don't you understand?"

"No, I don't. Not at all." She faked a shudder. "I always feel so sorry for the calves."

Even the guy sitting on the stool had shut up and swiveled around to face the other way. Brady just stared at her, then shook his head and walked off.

Sophie hid a smile behind a sip of tonic and turned back to Ethan. He was watching her. This time there was nothing vague about it. He gave her a slow smile and a small nod. She had no idea what that was supposed to mean. Other than she might need something stronger than tonic water.

Her nipples had tightened, and thank God the room was dim, because her entire body blushed. He couldn't have overheard her taunting Brady, not from over twenty feet away and with all the noisy laughter competing with the jukebox. And no way did Ethan recognize her.

He'd been a senior the year she started at Wattsville High, so he hadn't seen her in eleven years. She doubted he'd recognized her even once since the day he rescued her. How many times had she taken great pains to be in the perfect spot, like the cafeteria or near the boys' locker room so he couldn't miss her? Yet he did, and with unflattering consistency.

A fan stuck a piece of paper in his face and only then did he look away from her. Her heart hadn't stopped pounding.

"Sophie?"

She jumped so hard she nearly knocked over the waitress's loaded tray.

The woman moved back. "Sorry, didn't mean to startle you. Sophie, right?"

What the hell? No one here knew her. She nodded.

"Sadie asked me to give you this," she said, inclining

her head at the bartender and passing Sophie a piece of paper. "It's a name and phone number. She said you're looking for a place to stay tonight?"

Ah. Sophie smiled. "Yes," she said, accepting the paper. "Thank you."

"It's a long shot. The Meyers have probably rented out their spare rooms by now. But Kalispell is only a forty-five-minute drive from here." The waitress was already pushing through the crowd. "Good luck."

Sophie sighed. She thought she was so smart, but she stank at this covert stuff. Using her real name had been a stupid rookie move. No matter how doubtful it was that Ethan remembered her.

She studied the scribbled phone number, then glanced at Ethan. Fortunately he was too busy being mobbed to pay her any more attention. Both he and the man with him gave her the impression they'd bolt as soon as possible. She'd be a fool to let Ethan out of her sight, but it was too noisy to make a call in the bar. She'd have to step outside and just stay close to the door.

If she were to find a room, she'd be shocked. But she had to at least try in case she was forced to stay till morning. Or, God forbid, until after the rodeo was over in two days.

It would be so much easier to grab him tonight and leave Blackfoot Falls pronto. She didn't need his buddies interfering, because if they did, what could she do, really? And returning to Wyoming empty-handed wasn't an option.

She thought back to her earlier idea. Coaxing him to ask her to his room might be her best bet. But not if she couldn't get the damn jitters under control. Who was she kidding, anyway? There were several gorgeous women waiting for him to say the word. The only guy she'd attracted was one who roped and tied baby cows.

Hoping her half-full glass of tonic would hold her spot at the bar, she squeezed her way toward the door. The standing crowd was truly ridiculous, oblivious of anyone trying to pass, and forcing her in Ethan's direction.

"Boy howdy, was I shocked to hear you'd be riding this weekend, Ethan! Aren't you afraid of getting injured and missing the finals again?"

Sophie stopped. She turned and saw Ethan tighten his jaw. The people closest to him grew quiet and watchful.

The stout, ruddy-faced fan who'd asked the moronic question continued heedlessly. "I told the wife I figured you'd be too superstitious to take the chance, especially for no prize money."

"It's for a good cause," Ethan said quietly.

"Don't get me wrong, son. I'm glad you're here. I'm looking forward to seeing you ride tomorrow." The man rubbed his palms together, ignoring the blushing woman tugging at his arm. "I understand Matt Gunderson has raised some hard-bucking bulls."

"Yep. I heard the same thing." Ethan's jaw clenched again, then he smiled and moved back a little. "I sure hope all you folks are generous to Safe Haven. They take in a lot of animals who otherwise wouldn't have a chance of surviving. Any donation you'd like to add to the price of the ticket would be appreciated."

Unable to listen anymore, she shouldered her way to the door. No, she told herself. *Uh-uh.* She could not, and would not, feel sympathy for Ethan. As he'd said, Safe Haven was a good cause. He'd volunteered to ride. Great. Good for him. He wasn't letting superstition spook him. That didn't mean she wouldn't drag his ass back to Wyoming. He'd broken the condition of his bail by taking off. And clearly he didn't care at all about screwing her and Lola out of the money they'd posted for his bond. Sure, they had his motor coach as collateral. But until they could sell it, they were on the hook for a lot of cash.

Finally she made it outside. The biting cold November air nipped at her heated cheeks. She drew in a deep breath and immediately started coughing from all the cigarette smoke.

She turned to go the other way. Great. Smokers overran the sidewalk. She refused to stray too far from the door in case Ethan left, so she ducked behind a silver truck. No doubt he was anxious to get away from the stupid questions. And who could blame him?

The lighting was poor. She dug out her phone but could barely make out the number on the crumpled paper. Using the Bic app on her cell to see, she memorized the seven digits, then called. And promptly got the no she'd expected. Disconnecting, she sighed.

"No luck, huh?"

Sophie knew that voice. She slanted a look at Ethan, who stood on the sidewalk, his hands stuffed in his jeans pockets.

He wore a tan Western-style shirt, no jacket. His broad shoulders were hunched slightly, against the cold, she imagined.

"You must have me mixed up with someone else," she said, reminding herself to breathe. "I don't believe we've met."

"No?" He studied her a beat longer than she could manage to keep still. Thankfully he stepped back when she slipped between him and the truck to return to the sidewalk. "I thought maybe we had," he said, shrugging.

She shook her head, held her breath. "Nope."

Jeez. Of course he didn't recognize her. Or really think they'd met before. It was a pickup line guys used all the time.

"You're looking for a place to stay tonight," he said. "Aren't you?"

That stopped her again. "How do you know that?"

"The waitress." His intense stare wasn't helping her nerves, so she moved into the shadows. "I asked her."

Sophie huffed a laugh. "And of course she told you, because..." She closed her mouth. Because of that damn sexy smile of his, that was why, but this was what Sophie wanted, to get him alone, so she'd better lose the attitude.

"Because she's my buddy Matt's sister-in-law," he said, and glanced over his shoulder when the door opened and raucous laughter spilled out into the moonlit night. "Hey, how about we go someplace else? Get away from the bar."

"Sure." She tried not to seem too eager. Or irritated. Picking up a woman was this easy for a guy like Ethan. Just a look, a smile, and he was all set. She moved closer to him. The Boarding House Inn, where she knew he was staying, was within walking distance. "What did you have in mind?"

He looked both ways down Main Street. "How about the diner? Shouldn't be too crowded."

"The diner?"

"Is that all right? We can cross after this next truck."

"Um, sure. I guess."

Glancing at her, he asked, "You have somewhere else in mind?"

A diner? Okay, she was officially insulted. "I was thinking someplace more private," she whispered, linking arms with him.

Surprise flashed across his face. His eyes found hers, then he lowered his gaze to her lips. "I'm Ethan."

"I know who you are."

"And you're Sophie?"

So stupid. She nodded, promising herself that after this,

she'd stick to her desk job. At least her name hadn't triggered his memory. If he were to remember anything, it would probably be the pesky twerp who'd kept popping up in the weirdest places half his senior year.

The door to the bar opened again and they both turned. A tall brunette and her blonde sidekick walked out, scanning the groups of smokers.

The moment their gazes lit on Ethan, he tensed. "Let's go," he said, and draped his arm across the back of her shoulders. "Mind walking? It's not far."

"Fine." She huddled close, soaking in the warmth of his body and trying to decide if it would be too much to slide her arm around his waist.

He walked at a fast clip, and with her shorter legs she had some trouble keeping up. "Sorry," he said. "I'll slow down."

She saw her green Jeep parked at the curb just ahead, and two things flashed through her mind. She needed the handcuffs she'd left in her glove compartment, but she couldn't stop for them because of her Wyoming plates. If he knew the Jeep was hers, he could easily put two and two together.

"Cold?" he asked, pulling her closer.

"What?" She realized she'd tensed. "A little." Checking random plates, she saw a variety of out-of-state vehicles from Colorado, Utah, even an SUV from Wyoming. It was worth taking the chance. She really, really needed the cuffs. "Could we stop a minute?"

Ethan frowned and glanced back at the Watering Hole. "Am I still walking too fast?"

"No. We just passed my car and I wanted to grab my jacket."

He started to follow her, but she shook her head while inching backward and digging for the key in her pocket.

"It's kind of a mess," she said, relieved that he only smiled and stayed put.

She unlocked the driver's door. And kept an eye on him while she quickly transferred the handcuffs from the glove box to a deep pocket in the puffy down jacket she'd left on the passenger seat. Pausing, she considered scooping up her purse hidden on the floorboard.

Couldn't hurt. She probably could use some lip gloss about now. Jeez. *This is not a date.*

The door was closed and locked, her purse in hand before she considered the incriminating ID and *bail piece* authorizing her to arrest him inside her bag. It didn't matter, since she was going to do this thing quickly. Preferably the minute they were inside his room.

Instead of continuing to walk when she rejoined him, he studied her car. "I've always liked Jeeps. Looks new. Have you had it long?"

"I bought it last year." She drew in a breath. He was staring at her plates.

"You from Wyoming?"

"Not originally, but I've lived there for a few years now."

"What part?"

"Sheridan," she lied, purposely choosing the farthest town from Wattsville that she could think of.

"I'm from outside Casper myself." Either he was a very good actor or the Wyoming coincidence didn't bother him.

"Really? We're not exactly neighbors, but still…"

"Here, let me help you with your jacket."

Sophie thought she heard the handcuffs clink and clutched the jacket to her chest. Giving him a come-hither smile, she said, "I'd rather have your arm around me."

"Always happy to oblige a beautiful woman." Ethan took her free hand and drew her close. The jacket served as an unwanted buffer. "You aren't a rodeo fan, are you, Sophie?"

"Um, a little…"

He smiled. "It's okay. My ego isn't that fragile."

"I know who you are. That should count for something."

His puzzled frown sent up a warning flag. It lasted only a moment before the smile returned, and he started them walking again. "So you aren't here for the rodeo."

"No." Wrong answer. She wasn't sure why, but it felt wrong. She was missing something. "Well, yes, sort of. Does it matter?"

"I suppose not." He checked for traffic and guided her across the street, his arm tightening around her shoulders.

The Boarding House Inn was just up ahead. They had another half a block to go and she hoped the men standing on the porch steps deep in conversation would hurry up and leave. If she did her job well, by tomorrow morning it would appear that Ethan Styles had disappeared into thin air. And she preferred not to be identified as the last person seen with him.

That was where the wig came in handy. As a blonde, she barely recognized herself.

Luckily the porch cleared just as they approached. The silence that had fallen between her and Ethan was beginning to feel awkward. She slanted him a glance and caught him watching her. The porch light shone in both of their faces and he stopped, right there, several feet from the steps. Turning to face her, he nudged up her chin and studied her mouth.

She held her breath, certain he was about to kiss her.

"I have one question," he said. "Are you a reporter?"

"What? No."

Something in her expression must have made him doubt

her. His gaze narrowed, he seemed to be trying hard to remember...

"Why on earth would you think I'm a reporter?" It hit her then that everything would have been so much easier if she'd just pretended to be one of his buckle bunny fans. The wariness in his face convinced her to fix that situation right now.

"Okay, I lied," she blurted, the words rushing out of her mouth before she could think. "I'm a huge rodeo fan. The biggest. I go to rodeos all the time. I'm a buckle bunny. I didn't want to admit it and I—" She cleared her throat. "I wanted to stand out to get your attention, and that's why I lied. About not being a fan." She held in a sigh. "Does that make sense?"

Ethan looked as if he was going to laugh.

So she threw her arms around his neck and pulled him down into a blazing kiss.

3

ETHAN RECOVERED FROM her sudden burst of enthusiasm, thankful he hadn't landed on his ass. Sophie was small but strong, too. Strong enough that she'd forced him back a step. He put his arms around her and slowed down the kiss, taking the time to explore and sample the sweet taste of her mouth.

They were standing on the porch, under the light, in full view of Main Street where anyone passing the inn could see them. That didn't bother him. He just couldn't figure out what had caused her unexpected display of passion.

Way before he was finished with the kiss she stepped back, only to stare up at him with dazed eyes, and was that regret? Probably not. He wasn't seeing so clearly himself.

Damn, he should've moved them to his room before now. "How about we go inside where it's warm?" he asked.

She jerked a nod, clutched the jacket to her chest and inched farther away from him, as if she was afraid he was going to grab her.

Wondering if she'd ever picked up a guy before, Ethan was careful to give her some space. More practiced women who followed the circuit had a completely different air about them. He opened the door and motioned for her to go inside. The lobby was tiny, furnished with a desk and two wing chairs, a small oak table on which rolls and coffee would be set out in the morning, or so he'd been told.

"Turn right," he said, and she did so without a word or a backward glance. "I'm near the end."

He watched her as she led the way, admiring the view. Sophie claimed they'd never met, but he wasn't so sure that was true. Once he'd seen her up close, he was even more convinced they'd met before. The shape of her pouty lips had given him the first inkling that he knew her from somewhere. Even now, watching the slight sway of her hips tugged at his memory. It wasn't a particularly distinctive walk, so he didn't get it.

Hell, he could've seen her in the crowd at a rodeo. She'd admitted she was a fan. But that didn't feel right, either. If it turned out she'd lied and really was a reporter, man, he was going to be pissed. So far he'd been lucky. The public didn't know about his arrest. But one more media question about the black cloud that seemed to follow him to the finals every year and he'd shut them all out. No more interviews. No more sound bites. Screw 'em.

Sophie stopped to examine the baseboards and then looked up at the ceiling. "I think this place really was a boardinghouse at one time."

"Yep," Ethan said, glad she seemed more relaxed. "It was built around the 1920s. The new owner bought the place last year and kept the renovations as close to the original structure as possible. She even tried to replicate the detail in the moldings."

Sophie grinned at him. "I like that you know all that stuff."

With a laugh, he pulled the key out of his pocket. "It was on the website."

"The halls are awfully narrow. Men couldn't have had

very broad shoulders back in the twenties..." Her voice trailed off, her gaze flickering away from his chest.

"Two doors down," he said, staying right where he was, waiting for her to start walking again so he wouldn't crowd her.

He had to decide what to tell her. That kiss kind of ruined his plan. He hadn't actually been hitting on her. Blackfoot Falls was small, and with all the fans in town, he'd been rethinking Matt's offer to stay at his ranch. Ethan knew some of the guys had parked their motor coaches there instead of at the RV park outside of Kalispell.

Still, it would be quiet out there. He could help Sophie out by giving her his room. And staying at Matt's meant less chance for Ethan to get in any trouble.

He stuck the key in the lock and glanced at Sophie. With those soft brown eyes and that generous mouth, she looked like big trouble to him, tasted like it, too.

Who was he kidding? If he'd really wanted to just give her his room, he would have said something when they were outside. By her Jeep. Now, though, it would be awkward as hell to pack up and leave. He pushed the door open and she went right on inside.

After glancing around at the antique chair and the old armoire, she focused on the queen-size four-poster bed that took up most of the small room. She moved closer to it, stopping a moment to check out the patchwork quilt, and then ran her hand down the oak post close to the wall.

His cock pulsed.

When she wrapped her fingers around the smooth wood and stroked up, Ethan had to turn away. Yeah, he needed to erase that image real fast.

Between her obvious interest in the bed and his dick's growing interest in her, he decided it was time to offer the room as he'd intended, even if it would make him look like an ass.

"It's nice," she said, smiling, walking close enough he could inhale her sweet scent. "Quaint. Too bad the furniture is so small. I bet you can't even sit on the chair."

She laid her jacket over the back of it, sat on the edge and pulled off a boot.

And there went his last good intention. Ethan sighed. If even her red-striped sock turned him on, he wasn't going anywhere. She was already here. He was here. They were consenting adults. So he couldn't see a reason to deny himself a little recreation before heading to the Lone Wolf. Matt had left the invitation open.

"Need help with your boots?" she asked, mesmerizing him with those eyes the color of melted chocolate.

He pulled both his boots off before she'd finished removing her second one. "Tell me you're over twenty-one," he said, straightening and pausing at the first snap on his shirt.

Sophie laughed. "Are you serious? I don't look that young."

"I just like to be sure."

"Well, you can relax. I'm twenty-six. Anyway, I think the age of consent is sixteen in Montana."

The same as in Wyoming, not that he paid it any mind. Twenty-one was his personal cutoff.

Getting to her feet, she pulled her shirt from her jeans, then stopped and frowned. "Is something wrong?"

His snaps were still intact. "I have one last question."

"Okay," she said, taking a step closer, her sultry smile designed to scramble his brain.

"Are you married?"

Her eyebrows arched and her lips parted. She looked startled, and maybe confused. "No. Of course not." She shook her head, her eyebrows lowering into a delicate frown. "No, I'm not married, nor have I ever been married." She drew in a breath, seemed to calm herself and took over unsnapping his shirt. "Would it really matter?"

"If you have to ask, damn good thing you're still single." He could see he'd irritated her. Too bad. He wasn't about to get into another scrape like the mess he'd narrowly escaped in Wyoming. After discovering Wendy was married, he'd refused to sleep with her. To get back at him, she'd filed a false charge that he'd stolen some jewelry.

Sophie looked torn for a moment and then unfastened his next snap.

He caught her hand and inspected her ring finger. No mark, not even a faded one. "Sorry, but I'm touchy about the issue," he said, staring into her wary eyes and lifting her hand to his lips for a brief kiss before releasing her. "It's nothing personal."

Without another word, she finished unsnapping him, her eyes cast downward, until she parted the front of his shirt and pushed it off his shoulders. Her preoccupation with his bare chest was flattering but somewhat awkward. He finished shrugging out of the shirt, impatient to see what was under hers.

Uncertainty betrayed itself in the soft, hesitant palms she skimmed over his ribs and then his pecs. Her touch was almost reverent, her expression dreamlike. A few buckle bunnies he'd been with had tried to use their phones to sneak pictures of him shirtless, and even buck naked. But this was different. This seemed more…personal.

Jesus, he hoped it didn't turn out she was one of those crazy stalkers.

He captured her hands and gently lowered them from his chest. When he tried to draw up her T-shirt, she tensed, angling in a way that cut him off.

He took half a step back. "You change your mind?" he asked, keeping his tone low and even, letting her know it was all good. She was allowed.

"No," she said, shaking her head. "I haven't."

He tipped her chin up so he could see her face. "It's okay if you have. Tell me to stop and I will."

Sighing, she pulled off her own shirt and tossed it somewhere over her shoulder. He was too busy taking in the pink bra and creamy skin to see where it landed. Her breasts were the perfect size. They'd fit nicely in his hands. Her arms and shoulders were well toned, and her abs...a woman didn't get that kind of definition from casual exercise. Sophie took her workouts seriously. But she hadn't gone overboard, either, which he greatly appreciated.

He drew his thumb across the silky skin mounding above her bra. She had no freckles, just the faint remnant of a summer tan.

Damned if he wasn't the one staring now.

She shivered and shrank back.

"You're beautiful," he said, and looked up to meet eyes filled with disbelief. "I'm sure you get that line a lot, but I mean it."

She let out a short laugh and went for his belt buckle. He wished she wasn't so nervous. But if he brought it up, it would probably spook her into leaving.

Would that be the right thing to do?

Her frenzied movements confused him. It was as if she was racing the clock. Or...maybe she had someplace else she needed to be. Dammit, he couldn't figure her out. Although once they were in bed, he could slow things down. Make her feel real good.

"Hey."

When she looked up, he caught her chin and kissed her, taking his time, enjoying the velvety texture of her lips, trying to show her he was in no hurry. Although his dick wanted to argue.

She opened up for him and he slid his tongue inside, where it found its mate. The funny little tango that followed made them both smile. He'd always liked kissing best when tongues were involved, but simply moving his lips over hers felt more than satisfying. They found their rhythm and he deepened the kiss while pulling her tighter against him.

Sophie made a startled little sound in the back of her throat and stiffened. But she had to know she was making him hard. Thank God she didn't pull away. She pressed even closer, until her breasts pillowed his chest.

He reached behind to unfasten her bra, anxious to see her bare breasts, to watch her nipples harden and beg for his mouth. With his free hand he cupped her nape, slid his fingers into her hair. A sexy moan filled the inside of his mouth with her warm breath.

All of a sudden she froze.

She let out a squeak and wiggled out of his arms, her hand shooting to the top of her head.

"What happened?" Staying on the safe side, he kept his hands in plain sight. "Did I hurt you?"

They just stared at each other.

She didn't strike him as a woman who'd care if a man mussed up her hair. So what the hell?

"Sorry," she said, her cheeks pink. "Really sorry. I'm not freaking out or anything. About being here…you know…in the room with you. I promise I'm not."

Could've fooled him. "Look, we don't have to—"

"Let's get in bed, okay? I'll feel more relaxed then."

After a quick look at her parted lips, he watched the alarm fade from her eyes. "You don't like leaving the light on?" Ethan asked, worried he was missing something that would come back to bite him. "Is that it?"

"I don't care about the light." She smoothed back her hair and smiled as if nothing had happened.

Now that his body had cooled off some, he needed to think before she took another step toward him. This year he faced more pressure than ever to claim another championship title, partly because of his age, and also because of his kid sister. Mostly, though, it was about his left shoulder. It didn't hurt all the time, but he knew his rodeo days were numbered.

Sophie came up flush against him and looped her arms around his neck. Her pink lips parted slightly as she tilted her head back. She was still wearing the damn bra, not that it seemed to matter, since his mind went blank.

He put his hands on her waist, waiting, hoping he wasn't in for another surprise squeal. Her skin was soft and warm above the jeans waistband. The satiny texture made him itch to explore the rest of her. He settled for rubbing the small of her back, then moved his hands over the curve of her firm backside. Squeezing through denim was better than nothing, he supposed.

Screw that.

The jeans and bra both had to come off.

His request was preempted by an urgent tug. Sophie pulled his head down while she lifted herself up to meet his lips. When she leaned into him, moving her hips against his born-again erection, his whole body tightened. He slid his tongue inside her mouth and touched the tip of hers before circling and sampling the sweetness of her.

"Bed," she whispered.

He lifted her in his arms. With a soft gasp, she hung on tight even after he'd laid her down against the pillows. She resumed the kiss, refusing to let go of his neck, even as he followed her down. The fierce way she was cling-ing to him made things tricky. He stretched out alongside her, keeping his weight off her and on his braced elbow.

He dragged his mouth away from hers and trailed his lips along her jaw to her ear, wondering where she might be sensitive. After a few nips at her earlobe, he cupped a breast and murmured, "How about we get rid of this bra?"

She vaguely nodded, then stiffened. "Wait."

"For?"

She sat up and sighed. "I forgot something."

Ethan fell onto his back. She just wasn't going to make it easy, was she? "What did you forget?" he asked as she crawled over him and got off the bed.

"Just one sec," she said, raising one finger before she headed for the chair with her jacket draped over the back.

Ethan watched her rifle through the pockets and found it in his heart to forgive her for the interruption. Only be-cause she had one helluva nice ass. Which he hoped to see in the flesh, preferably before the next full moon.

Okay. He finally understood the problem. "I have a con-dom," he said, rolling to the side and reaching into his back pocket. "It's right here. You can stop looking."

She murmured something he couldn't make out, yet managed to give him the impression she hadn't heard him.

"Sophie?"

She turned to face him, holding the jacket against her front. Fortunately not so her breasts were hidden. Yeah, except the bra took care of that. Shit. Not being able to see and touch was driving him crazy.

He took the packet out of his wallet and tossed both on the nightstand. "Did you hear me?" Why the hell was she bringing the jacket with her? "I have a condom."

"What? Oh." She stopped by the side of the bed. "No, we don't need one."

"Uh, yeah, we do." He never broke that rule.

"I changed my mind about the light." She smiled and leaned down to give him a quick kiss and quite a view. "I think I want it off."

Ethan had never met a woman who ran so hot and cold, and at the speed of sound on top of that. He'd ridden a hundred ornery bulls that had given him less trouble. *Trouble* being the keyword here. Maybe this—Sophie—was an omen he needed to take more seriously.

She kissed him again, lingering this time, using her tongue, while trailing her fingers down his chest. She traced a circle around his navel and then rested her hand on his buckle. "I'll be right back."

Jesus. "What now?"

"The light."

Something else that was confusing. He knew she wasn't shy, and she had a killer body. "How about we leave the one in the bathroom on with the door closed partway?"

She straightened, thought for a moment and then nodded. "I think that might work better, actually."

Yep. She was a strange one, all right. But that nice round bottom of hers wasn't easily dismissed. He watched her walk to the bathroom, flip on the light and angle the door just so.

"I doubt you'll need the jacket," he said.

She only smiled and moved to the wall switch that controlled the two lamps.

"Why don't you get rid of those jeans while you're up?" He'd take care of the bra, no problem.

"Okay. Good idea." The room dimmed. "You take off yours, too."

Ethan watched her approach while he unbuckled and unzipped. It was a little too dark for his taste. Once he finally got her naked, he wanted to see her. Staying right where he was, he lifted his ass and pushed down his jeans.

"Here, let me help." She pulled them off his feet and flung the Wranglers at the chair.

He considered asking her to let a little more light into the room, but she dropped her jacket and climbed onto the bed. She got on her knees and steadied herself with a hand on his belly. And then threw a leg over his thighs and straddled him.

His cock seemed determined to test the resilience of his boxer briefs. "Your turn," he said, reaching for her zipper.

With a throaty laugh, she shoved his hand away. "Not when I have you exactly where I want you."

"I'll make it worth your while," he murmured, rubbing the back of his knuckles against her denim-covered crotch.

She gasped and squeezed her thighs together, only his hips were in the way. He already knew she was strong, but how she was gripping him…holy shit. Managing to move his trapped hand, he put more pressure on her crotch.

Sophie made a strangled sound. Shifting her body, she captured his hand. Intertwining her fingers with his, she pulled his arm up over his head as she leaned down to bite his lip. The aggressive move surprised him in a good way. With his free hand he unhooked her bra.

The left strap slid off her shoulder and bared her breast. He could see the rosy tip, though not as clearly as he wanted. The moment she realized what had happened, she released him. She leaned back, cursing, and trying to pull the bra up.

Like hell.

He slid his hand in before she could cover herself. And cupped her exposed breast, rubbing his thumb over the hard nipple while baring the other.

"You're beautiful," he whispered. "Don't hide yourself."

Closing her eyes, she arched slightly, filling his palm. He kneaded gently and she sighed, a soft breathy sound he wanted to hear again.

"No." She shrank back.

"Please, Sophie. I know you're nervous, but I promise I'll make you feel better."

"Stop," she said, eyes wide but impossible to read in the dimness.

He immediately lowered his hands. "Did I do something wrong?"

An awkward silence fell between them. She hadn't climbed off, so he figured that was a good sign. She also hadn't fixed her bra, but he was afraid to so much as glance anywhere below her neck until he understood what had just happened. He'd never had a woman tell him no or to stop before. This was brand-new territory and he was at a complete loss on how to respond. Ego played no part here. If anything, he felt like shit.

"Whatever I did to upset you, I'm very sorry," he said, resisting the urge to touch her, offer her comfort the only way he knew how. "I really am."

"Don't apologize," she said, shaking her head. "It's me, I shouldn't have let— Oh, shit. I hate this." She leaned over the side of the bed and reached for the jacket on the floor.

"Hate what?" He tried to do the honorable thing and not stare at her breasts. Apparently he had the willpower of a rutting bull, which he wasn't proud of.

She pulled something out of the pocket and hid it behind her back before he dragged his attention away from her breasts. Cosmic justice, he figured.

He barely had time to blink before she was all over him again. Kissing him, playing the aggressor once more, forcing his arm over his head, her warm soft body pressed close, her hard nipples grazing his chest...the feel of cold metal...

The hard band closing around his wrist jerked him from his haze. He heard a click. Confusion still messed with his brain. Sophie drew back, staring down at him, breathing hard.

He looked at his wrist handcuffed to the bedpost.

Sophie was into that kind of stuff? He wasn't, but he didn't mind accommodating her.

4

"You could've just told me." Ethan smiled. "This isn't my thing, but I'll play for a while," he said, and touched her breast.

"Oh, brother." She slapped his hand away, jerking back. For God's sake, she'd forgotten she had no top on. "This isn't a game, you idiot." She climbed off, glanced around the room for her shirt. Finding it near the chair, she pulled the tee over her head.

"What the hell is going on?"

The wig got caught and shifted. Boy, was she glad to get rid of that stupid thing. No one had warned her it would itch like crazy. She grabbed a handful of the fake blond locks and yanked it off her head.

"Jesus. What the—"

Pulling pins from her own hair, she shook it loose from the tight bun and glanced at Ethan, lying against the cream-colored sheets, his muscled chest smooth, bare and tanned. A light smattering of dark hair swirled just below his belly button and disappeared into the waistband of his boxer briefs.

Oh no. No looking there for her.

"I know you," he said, narrowing his gaze.

The light from the bathroom washed over his face, the tanned skin bringing out the blue of his eyes, as he studied her with an intensity that made her turn away. Did seeing her as a brunette trigger a memory? Doubtful. He'd barely noticed her after his grand gesture outside the cafeteria right in the middle of lunch period.

She walked into the bathroom and groaned at her image in the mirror. Well, of course her hair was plastered to her head and looking as unattractive as possible. He hadn't been staring because he remembered her. She could've just stepped off the set of some horror movie.

Rubbing her itchy scalp, she bent at the waist and fluffed out her hair. She straightened to look in the mirror again, not expecting much. And that was exactly what she got.

"Are you gonna get out here and explain what the hell is going on?" Ethan sounded angry.

"You jumped bail," she said, strolling back into the room and picking up her phone. Mostly so she didn't have to look at him. "Without giving a thought to the large bond that was posted on your behalf."

"No, I didn't. Jump bail, I mean. The charges were dropped."

"When?" If that was true, Lola would've told her by now. But he sounded so certain she had to look at him. "When?" she repeated.

"I'm not sure."

A lock of sun-streaked brown hair had fallen across his forehead. His face was lean and spare like the rest of him. Same square jaw she remembered, except for the dark stubble. And that perfect straight nose. He was even hotter now than he'd been back in high school.

Some friggin' nerve.

"So, you weren't sure if you had to show up in court or not and decided to take off anyway. Brilliant move."

"No, it's not like that." He jerked his wrist, clanging the handcuffs against the wooden post. "Is this necessary?"

Well, that had to be rhetorical. She checked for texts or voice mails. "If the charges were dropped, my partner would've notified me. So guess you're out of luck."

"Okay, look, my friend Arnie... Can we turn on more lights?"

"No." She sat on the chair and faced him. "Continue."

Ethan's normal, easygoing expression had vanished, replaced by a piercing frown that made her tense. "Who are you?"

"Sophie's my real name."

"You know what I'm asking."

"I'm a fugitive retrieval agent—"

"Fugitive?"

"You asked."

He cut loose a pithy four-letter word. "What's that, a fancy name for a bounty hunter?"

"Yep."

"And that gives you the right to slap handcuffs on me?"

"It sure does. Didn't you read the bail bond contract?" By signing the document, he'd given her and Lola more authority to arrest him than even the police.

She watched him scrub at his face with his free hand and waited out his mumbled curses. Leaving him with an unrestricted hand wasn't a smart move. The bedpost was made from solid wood and plenty sturdy...she'd checked first thing. But Ethan was agile and strong.

The memory of his hands on her body made her shudder.

Dammit, she should've brought two pairs of cuffs. Mandy preferred using zip ties and had given Sophie a few. But they were sitting in the Jeep.

"So that's why you're in such great shape," he murmured.

"Excuse me?"

"I thought maybe you were a personal trainer or something, but that didn't make sense, either," he said, letting his gaze wander over her.

"What are you talking about?"

"Look, if you just let me make a phone call, I can straighten this out in no time."

"I have a better idea. You can do it in person when I take you back to Wyoming."

"Bullshit."

Sophie smiled. "It's late. No sense driving tonight. We'll leave first thing in the morning."

He jerked hard on the cuffs. The whole bed seemed to shake. "You know I won't let you do that."

"Oh?" She rose. "What are you going to do? Scream?"

Wow, that sure pissed him off. His face reddened, and his eyes turned positively frosty. He looked as if he wanted to put his hands around her neck and strangle the life out of her.

It gave her a new respect for what Mandy had to do all the time. Face down criminals who might actually want to hurt her. Ethan was angry, and he'd try to get away if he could, but Sophie wasn't afraid of him. She knew he would never do her harm.

She walked to the window and parted the drapes, just enough so she could take a peek down the street. The Watering Hole wasn't visible from here. Neither was her Jeep. Lots of people were still milling around, though. Another reason she wouldn't try forcing Ethan into her car tonight.

Damn, she wished she'd grabbed her bag along with the jacket. She needed her toothbrush, face cream, a change of clothes, all that stuff... And she hated leaving Ethan alone while she ran to the Jeep. She turned and caught him staring at her butt.

He gave her a lazy smile.

Oh, so he was pulling out the charm again.

"Aren't you gonna ask if I did it?"

"What's the point?" Sophie said. "Unless you have proof, your answer means nothing. And if you had proof, I wouldn't be here."

His face darkened. "I didn't steal a goddamn thing. Wendy lied."

"Hmm, well, that's what you get for sleeping with a married woman."

"You mean, for *not* sleeping with her." Ethan shook his head, briefly closing his eyes. "Wendy lied about that, too. When I found out she was married, I left. She was pissed. I knew that... I just didn't know how bad."

Sophie thought back to earlier when he'd asked if she was married. He'd even inspected her ring finger. Maybe he was telling the truth, or maybe he'd learned an expensive lesson. The thing was, she didn't believe that he'd stolen anything. It made no sense. Even if he did need money, she'd seen the teenage Ethan's moral center, and age didn't change a person that much. But what she believed didn't matter.

"If I'm supposed to have a hundred grand in stolen jewelry, why would I need someone to post my bond?"

"You didn't have enough time to sell it?"

"Get real. I earned a lot more than that in endorsements alone this year. Plus my winnings."

"Okay, so..." What was she doing? Sophie knew better than to get involved. Her job was to take him back to Wyoming, period. "Why not use your own money to post bond?"

"I don't have that kind of cash lying around. My money's invested. I start withdrawing funds and I get questions. The media are already all over my ass about the finals in a week."

"Why?" She hadn't realized that she'd walked closer to him until she bumped her knee on a corner of the bed.

"Because of my track record. Every year I—" He plowed his fingers through his hair, the action drawing attention to the muscles in his arms and shoulders. "It doesn't matter."

"What?" She snapped her gaze back to his face. "I'm sorry, I missed that last bit."

He was staring at her again, with the same intensity as earlier. Trying to decide if she was the girl from school? Maybe. "My friend Arnie, he was supposed to take care of it. He knows the charge is bogus and said it would never make it to court."

"Is he an attorney?"

Ethan sighed. "He dropped out of law school."

She remembered an Arnie, a dopey junior who used to tag along behind Ethan. If this was the same guy, she sure wouldn't have trusted him with anything important. "Hope he didn't quit before he learned the part that would keep you from getting locked up."

Ethan blew out a breath. It seemed clear he'd had the same thought. "How about we call him? Can I at least do that?"

Sophie wandered toward the window while she tried to think. Talking to Arnie wouldn't help. Only Lola could tell her if Ethan was in the clear and the bond reimbursed. And for some reason Sophie wasn't anxious to admit she'd found him already. Why, she didn't know. She should be ecstatic and gloating.

"Tomorrow's the Safe Haven Benefit Rodeo," Ethan said. "They could really use the money. Since I'm the main attraction, it would be a shame if I missed—"

"Shut up." She glared at him. "I know about the rodeo. And guess what, genius...trying to make me feel bad isn't helping your cause. It's just pissing me off. I didn't create this problem. You did."

He glared back. "You're gonna deny me a goddamn lousy phone call?"

"Where's your cell?"

Frowning, he glanced at the nightstand. "My shirt... where is it?"

"What am I, your maid?" she grumbled, and spotted it on the floor by the chair. She picked up the shirt and then noticed his phone sitting on the armoire. Tempted to toss the cell to him, she moved close enough to drop it on the mattress barely within his reach.

With the most irritating grin, he strained toward the cell and grabbed it. "What are you afraid of? Huh? What did you think I was going to do to you? I've got one wrist cuffed to this post," he said in a taunting tone of voice. "What are you doing to my shirt?"

"What?" She looked down at the garment she was hugging to her chest. "Nothing."

"Were you sniffing it?"

"No. Ew." She flung the shirt toward the chair. *Oh God, oh God, oh God.* Heat stung her cheeks. She kept her face averted, knowing it must be red, and pulled out her own phone.

If he was laughing at her...

If?

Did she really have any doubt?

One word. Just one wrong word out of his mouth, and she'd drag him to her car in front of the whole damn town. Announce to everyone he was a fugitive from justice.

Her sigh ended in a shudder. She hadn't even been aware of smelling his shirt.

He was awfully quiet.

"Arnie?"

Sophie let out a breath and slowly turned to see Ethan holding the cell to his ear and glaring at the ceiling.

"Don't pull that you're-breaking-up bullshit on me," Ethan said, his voice furious. "What the hell, dude? I thought you were taking care of the charges."

Sophie perched on the edge of the chair to send a quick text to Lola.

"That's good, right?" Ethan stacked two pillows behind his back. "If she insists on lying, her husband will know she's been cruising bars and picking up men while he's out of town." He listened for a few seconds. "And I had to call you to find all this out?"

Before hitting Send, she glanced up again.

Ethan looked worried. His chest rose and fell on a sigh. "Jesus, Arnie, you've got to find out by tomorrow. The finals are in a week. You know this year could be it for me…"

The despair in his voice made her stomach clench. Thank God she had her phone to occupy her, because she couldn't stand to look at him right now. This year could be it for him? Why?

"Maybe I should call my agent," he said, his eyes meeting hers when she looked up. "Brian's going to find out anyway. They think I jumped bail. I've got a damn bounty hunter staring at me right now."

"Fugitive retrieval agent," she muttered.

"She's got me cuffed to the friggin' bed. Plans on dragging me back to Wyoming tomorrow." He paused. "Shut the fu—" He glanced at her. "Just make the damn call and get back to me first thing tomorrow. And, Arnie, this is your last chance." Ethan disconnected and threw the cell down. Hard.

No point in pretending she hadn't been listening. Anyway, the second he'd left her and Lola holding the bond, so to speak, he forfeited his right to privacy. And no, she absolutely would not feel sorry for him. He'd done this to himself.

She watched him inspect the handcuffs and flex his hand. Then he stared up at the ceiling, thumping his head back against the wooden bed rail, working the muscle at his jaw.

"I wouldn't trust Arnie if I were you," Sophie said. "At this point you really do need an attorney."

Ethan brought his chin down, a faint smile tugging at the corners of his mouth. "You know Arnie?"

Oh, crap. This was what she got for being nice. "No, but it sounded like you don't have confidence in him. So I'm saying, you should go with your instinct." She shrugged, carefully keeping her gaze level with his. "Didn't you mention something about calling your agent?"

His eyes continued to bore into hers. He hadn't so much as blinked. All she could think to do was stare back. She doubted that little slip about Arnie had been the thing that convinced Ethan of her identity. Just because she looked familiar didn't mean he remembered they'd gone to the same high school together for seven months, one week and two days.

Yeah, okay, so she'd counted. Down to the minute, actually, but when she'd been... Fifteen. *Jeez.*

"What did he say, anyway?"

"Arnie?"

"Yes, Arnie." Her phone signaled a new text. She glanced at the brief message. No surprise there. "I texted a friend who works in the sheriff's office to check on whether the charges were dropped. It seems you already know the answer."

He tightened his mouth. "Can you recommend an attorney?"

"Not really. I know a few, but I couldn't say if they're any good." Except for Craig, but she tried to stay clear of him. "What about your agent? Bet he knows one."

"Brian lives in Dallas. I can't call him this late. But yeah, he knows everybody. I trust he'll steer me right."

"You should've called him before you jumped bail."

Ethan sighed. "I didn't realize I'd jumped bail," he said with forced patience. "The charges were supposed to have been dropped."

"What about your parents? I would think they either have someone they use or know of someone."

"It's clear you're not a rodeo fan, yet you know who they are?"

She shrugged. "I think everyone in Beatrice County knows the name Styles. They own that big ranch and rodeo camp near Otter Lake. And didn't your dad win something like five championship titles for calf roping, and a few more for something else?"

Ethan nodded. "All-around cowboy three years in a row."

"Even your mom has four gold buckles for barrel racing, right?"

"You get all that from doing homework on me? Or did you already know this stuff?"

"Half and half."

"So you probably read about my kid sister." His tone stayed noncommittal and his expression blank.

Nevertheless, she'd bet there were a lot of emotions bubbling under the surface. She'd definitely seen pride in his eyes, but she wondered if there might be some jealousy in the mix.

"Last December Cara won her first championship title on her twenty-first birthday," he said. "She'll be competing for her second title next week. She'll be headed to Vegas with me. Assuming I get to go." He jerked on the cuffs so hard the post shook.

"Ah." Sophie nodded.

"Ah?"

"Sibling rivalry. I get it." She didn't have any siblings, but she could imagine the pressure Ethan was feeling. And a kid sister besting him? Ouch. "Well, I know barrel racing is a woman's event, so I'm guessing that's what she won?"

He nodded.

"Your dad won first place for tying up poor little calves—"

Ethan stared as though she'd just grown fangs.

"And your mom and sister got prizes for riding a horse around a few barrels without knocking them over."

Ethan started laughing.

"I'm not finished," she said. "And you're a bull rider. Correct me if I'm wrong, but don't you compete in the hardest, most dangerous event in rodeo?"

"Look," he said, his laughter ending with a sigh, "I don't know what your point is. I just need to make it to the finals." His mood had soured again. "So, what's it gonna take, Sophie? Tell me."

"You have to return to Wyoming and face the judge."

"I can't ride the next two days here, then go back to Wyoming and the unknown, and trust that I can still make it to Vegas for the finals."

She sucked in a deep breath. He wasn't thinking it through. "It's not as if you have a low profile," she reminded him. "If you fail to appear in court on Monday, the judge will issue a warrant and someone will be waiting in Vegas to arrest you."

"No. No, that can't happen. How can they come after me? I didn't do it. Dammit."

She bit down to keep from stating the obvious. Besides, Ethan had to know the legal system was far from perfect. Or maybe his charmed existence had spared him life's injustices. "Look, I know you don't want the publicity, but your folks live in the next county, along with lots of rodeo fans who adore them. You're probably the most popular bull rider in the country. Who do you think people are going to believe? You or what's her name?"

"Wendy." Ethan's mouth curved in a derisive smile. "Wendy Fullerton."

Fullerton? "Any relation to Broderick Fullerton?"

"His wife."

"Oh, shit."

"Exactly what I said." Ethan's sigh sounded a lot like defeat.

"How could you not know who she was?" Fullerton owned half the county. People generally feared him more than they liked him. But the fact remained, he provided over 60 percent of the jobs and his bank owned a ton of mortgages and notes. Including Sophie and Lola's business loan.

"Wendy is wife number four. They've been married for eight months." He shrugged. "How the hell would I know, anyway? I don't read the society pages and I'm rarely home. Jesus. Here I've been keeping my head down. Staying healthy. Staying out of trouble…"

"You picked up a strange woman in a bar," she muttered, really hating this whole mess. No room for sympathy now. Everything had to go by the book. "And instead of learning your lesson you came here and did it again."

"When?"

Sophie got to her feet so she could pace, hoping to

loosen up. Maybe she should be more concerned with toughening up. She'd started to soften toward Ethan, wondering how she could help him out. But anything she did would reflect on Lola, too. Their business loan wasn't in jeopardy. They'd been late with their payment only once in four years. It was silly to worry.

Ethan's response from a moment ago finally sank in and she faced him. "*When?* Is that a joke?"

"Do you see me laughing?" he said, his stare unflinching.

"Did you forget how I ended up here with you?"

"Nope. But you obviously did."

She pushed her fingers through her tangled hair. This was good, him being an ass. Made it easier to shove sympathy aside, be more objective. "Okay, I'll bite. Go ahead."

"Nothing. It's just that you hit on me."

She gaped at him. "Are you nuts?" It took a few more seconds to find her voice again. "You're crazy, you know that. You brought me to your room."

"Actually I was going to give it to you."

"What the hell are you talking about?"

"My friend Matt invited me to stay at his ranch. So when I heard you needed a room, I'd decided to give you this one and I would move over to the Lone Wolf," he said slowly, and with exaggerated patience. "Then you hit on me, and I...I went with the flow." He smiled. "I was only trying to be a gentleman."

"Oh, that's right. I forgot. You like to play hero and then move on." She held her breath. She couldn't believe she'd actually said *play hero*.

With a single lifted eyebrow, he held her gaze until she turned away. He didn't seem surprised or curious about what she'd meant, just faintly amused. So he'd probably remembered...

Swallowing, she stalked to the window, shoved the drapes aside and stared at nothing.

The stupid bastard had recognized her from school and hadn't said a word.

5

FINE. SO WHAT if he remembered? It didn't really matter. Sophie stayed at the window, though nothing happening outside was of particular interest. She simply knew better than to look at Ethan while she planned her next move. The inn sat directly on Main Street. And Blackfoot Falls was crawling with out-of-town fans. The only chance for an uneventful exit would be if they left in the middle of the night. Not her first choice, but...

The more she thought about it, the more she liked the idea. Once the Watering Hole closed, there wouldn't be anything for these people to do. They'd return to the trailer parks and dude ranches, or wherever they were staying. She could pull her Jeep up close to the porch and stuff him into the backseat. She'd gag him if she had to. But she doubted that would be necessary. He wouldn't want to call attention to himself.

Later, once they were on the open road, he'd try to make a move. Plenty of lonely stretches of highway between here and Wyoming for him to give it his all. But that was okay because she'd be ready for him. Sure, he could easily overpower her if he somehow broke free of his restraints. That was why she'd brought pepper spray.

Despite wanting to smack him, she hoped he was considering what she'd said about finding an attorney. With his high profile he'd be arrested sooner rather than later, and she really didn't want that to happen.

"I have a question," Ethan said.

Good for him. She had a million. Like whether he'd honestly intended to give her the room. And when exactly had he recognized her. He might've thought she seemed familiar and figured he'd met her in another bar, another town. Until she'd made the *hero* crack.

None of those things mattered, really. Her job was to take him back to Wyoming. And that was exactly what she was going to do. As long as she stayed focused, avoided looking at him whenever possible. Because she had enough wits about her to know he was dangerous to her self-control, to her ability to reason. If she wasn't careful, she'd revert to that same smitten fifteen-year-old girl who'd finished her freshman year with a bunch of newly awakened hormones and a broken heart.

Even now, ten feet away, she swore she could smell him. His rugged masculine scent drifted over to her, distracting her. Tempting her to forget she had a job to do.

"Why the blond wig?" he asked after she'd refused to so much as glance at him. "You're much prettier with dark hair."

"Oh, please." Sophie rubbed her eyes. This sucked. She was too tired to drive tonight. And she had to get him back as quickly as possible. For her own peace of mind, if nothing else.

"I'm not trying to butter you up. It's the truth. Were you worried I'd recognize you?"

She knew he was playing her. Or maybe he was still fuzzy about her identity and was looking for confirmation.

She wasn't about to fill in the blanks for him. "You like blondes, that's why."

"Who told you that?"

"Every one of your girlfriends has been blonde. Think that might've given me a hint?"

"It's been three years since I've had a steady girlfriend. And she was a brunette...who happened to dye her hair blond."

Sophie snorted a laugh. "Do you ever hear yourself?" Without thinking, she spun around...and let out a squeal. "What are you doing?"

The bastard was using something to pick the lock.

"No. Oh no, you don't."

She dove onto the mattress and crawled over to him. She leaned across his chest, trying to pry his free hand away from the handcuffs. Her right breast smooshed his face, startling him. Her, too. But it was probably the only thing that saved her, since she had barely reached his hand in time.

Unable to get a good grip of his wrist, she threw a leg over him. Straddling him hadn't been the objective, but there she was. She didn't know which was worse, sitting on his junk and squeezing his hips with her thighs or having her boob in his face. But she couldn't back down now.

Pulling on his arm was like trying to move a boulder. "Damn you, Styles. Don't you get it? You're going back to Wyoming one way or another. Why are you making this so hard?"

He grinned.

Okay, unfortunate word choice. He didn't have to be a child about it. She ignored him, other than to use all her might to pull his hand away...

He went completely still. Relaxed his arm. Dropped the small pocketknife.

"Would you stop that?" he growled. "I know you're a lunatic, but my dick doesn't, okay? So ease up. Damn."

"What did you say?"

"Stop wiggling."

"Oh." She stayed right where she was but tried not to move. *Holy shit.* There was a bulge under her left butt cheek. "Then stop trying to pick the lock."

"And how am I supposed to go to the bathroom, huh? Answer me that."

"Is that what this is about? You could've said—"

"No. I don't need to go now. But the point is, you can't keep me prisoner like this. You know damn well it isn't practical…" He trailed off and quietly exhaled, his eyes, wary and watchful, meeting hers dead-on.

Sophie couldn't tell if she was breathing or not. Heat coursed slowly through her body as she fought the urge to touch his muscled shoulders and chest.

They just stared at each other. His pupils were so big and dark she hardly saw any blue. She hated to think what she looked like with her wild tangled hair. Though the bulge under her fanny hadn't subsided, so she couldn't be the utter mess she imagined.

She finally shifted her gaze to his hand, still secured to the bedpost, and she picked up the pocketknife. She had no reason to be sitting on him. Or staring at his bare chest.

She gave the cuffs a reassuring tug, mostly for show, then lifted herself off him. Very carefully. No peeking, no unnecessary touching.

One thing was for certain. She didn't want to be tempted by his bare chest all night, so she'd have to figure a way for him to put his shirt on. As for his lower half, the sheet draped over his lap would have to do for now. It sure wasn't lying flat, though.

"So, how do you plan to deal with bathroom trips? Are you going in with me to be my...handler, so to speak?"

Luckily it took very little for him to annoy the hell out of her. "You're despicable."

Ethan laughed. "I'll make a deal with you."

Sophie rolled to the side of the bed and jumped off. "You have nothing I want."

"You sure about that?"

She glanced back at him. "When you get thrown off a bull, you must land on your head a lot."

"Ah, rodeo humor. Not very good, though. Hey, don't lose my pocketknife."

She shoved it deep into her jeans pocket. "Oh, so now I have everything you want, and you have nothing of interest to me." She swept a pointed gaze over his body. "So, as for making a deal..." She shrugged. "Too bad."

"I'm being serious."

"You should be. You're in a lot of trouble, Ethan." If he made her regret this, she'd save the court time and money and just shoot him. "What is it you want?"

He started to smirk, then gave up the smug act. "Let me ride for Safe Haven," he said, steadily meeting her eyes. "And you have my word I won't run."

"What about the finals?"

"I'll make it to Vegas."

Sophie was on the verge of a colossal headache. He hadn't been a stupid boy in school, and she assumed he hadn't lost any IQ points since then. "I doubt you can do both and still meet your legal obligation."

"Watch me."

"How am I supposed to believe you won't take off on me?"

"Because I gave you my word."

"Right." She rubbed her left temple.

"Just like I gave Matt Gunderson my word I'd ride for Safe Haven." He sure seemed intent on making a mess of his career. His life. "They haven't done one of these benefits before. If it goes well, it'll become an annual event. What do you think will happen if their headliner scratches at the last minute?"

She sighed. Her job would be a lot easier if he was only pretending to be noble. But this wasn't an act. Even back in high school Ethan had had a reputation for stepping in for the underdog, and not just her.

With a small shake of her head, she reached into her pocket for the key. "What time do you ride?"

"I think I'm last."

"Of course you are," she muttered. "So, after that we leave, right?"

"I'm on the lineup for Sunday, too."

"What if you get thrown on your ass before the eight seconds tomorrow?"

With a deadpan expression, he said, "This isn't about qualifying, so it doesn't matter."

Boy, did she hope she'd packed aspirin. "We'll split the difference. You ride tomorrow and then Sunday we drive straight to Wyoming. That way you can—"

He was already shaking his head. "People paid a lot of money for tickets."

"I bet they pay even more for the finals."

"Let me worry about that."

"Oh yeah? Hmm." She frowned at the key, and then at the lock. Anything to avoid those hypnotic eyes. "That should take care of everything."

"Sarcasm? Sure, that helps."

She glared at him then. "Your main problem is that you're not concerned enough."

He had the most annoying habit of looking like the boy

next door one minute, and sex wearing a Stetson the next. It had to stop. Being in the same room with him was nerve-racking enough. But this close?

Just as she was about to free him, someone knocked on the door.

"Oh, Ethan… Ethan Styles?" It was a woman's sing-song voice. "Are you in there, sugar?"

Sophie stepped back. "You expecting company?"

He shook his head, staring mutely at her.

"Obviously you gave out your room number."

"Nope," he said, keeping his voice low.

Was she being a total idiot? Once Sophie released him, that was it. She could barely stand this close to him without her skin feeling flushed.

There was another knock. At someone else's door.

Sophie strained to hear.

"Oh, Ethan…" Same woman, same question. Trying every door? That was sick.

Kind of like her back in school. Sophie cringed at the memory of hiding under the bleachers to watch him run track. Begging for a transfer to auto shop, of all the dumb things, just so she could be in the same class as Ethan.

Teenagers did lots of crazy stuff. She couldn't let it get to her. And anyway, she'd bet the woman in the hall was a lot older than fifteen.

She held the key poised at the lock. "Wait," she said, and started when he put a shushing finger to her lips.

It was unnecessary. No one in the hall could've heard her low pitch. And she'd bet he knew that. Yet she simply stood there, staring into the vivid blue of his eyes, while he lightly skimmed the pad of his thumb across her bottom lip before lowering his hand. The move was so subtle, she'd be a fool to make anything of it.

Her cousin was right. Lola had worried Sophie would

have trouble dealing with Ethan. But she'd honestly thought he no longer had any effect on her. She was wrong. She would just be more cautious, that was all. Ultimately she trusted he'd keep his word.

"We haven't come to terms on Sunday yet," she said, voice low and firm.

Their eyes dueled a moment.

"We'll renegotiate tomorrow," he said with a sexy smile that could get a ninety-year-old woman in trouble. "After the rodeo."

She laughed. "Oh, hell no." Sophie jabbed a finger at him. "You will stick to me like glue until I tell you otherwise. I want your word on *that*."

He grinned as if he was enjoying this. "You've got it."

"And shut up when I tell you to shut up."

"Yes, ma'am."

"Without the smirk," she murmured as she inserted the small key, narrowing her attention to the task as she gathered her courage. "You think you know me. From where?"

"Wattsville High."

Her heartbeat went bonkers, and heat flooded her face, but she refused to look at him. "Because I used my real name?"

"No. I didn't remember that."

Okay, at least that was settled. The second the lock sprang, she thought of something else. "Dammit."

"What?" He was quick to pull his wrist free.

It was too late but she should've considered leaving him cuffed until she brought the Jeep closer and got her bag. She glanced at the cuffs still clamped to the bedpost. Maybe she'd leave it there for now.

"Don't worry. I'm staying right here," Ethan said. "I'm not even going for that beer I'd wanted at the Watering Hole."

"You're right about that."

He put a hand on her hip, and a soft gasp slipped past her lips.

"Hands off," she warned, as much with a glare as with words.

"Mind moving so I can get up?"

She ignored the subtle undertone of amusement in his voice and headed back to the window. After she saw him grab his jeans, she looked out through the parted drapes, aware of him moving behind her. The bathroom door closed and she sighed with relief.

Her swirling thoughts would drive her insane if she didn't get a handle on what to tell Lola. Sophie had had no business making any kind of deal with him. Would Mandy ever negotiate with a bail jumper? Not in a million years.

The minute the rodeo started tomorrow, anyone who cared would know exactly where Ethan Styles was, so she had to tell Lola something.

The smartest story to tell was mostly true. Ethan had unknowingly violated the terms of his bail and he was willing to cooperate. Which saved Sophie from having to fight off hordes of fans. Yes, some gray area existed, since she had Ethan in her clutches at this very moment, but no one had to know...

It didn't feel good lying to Lola like that. In fact, Sophie couldn't recall having ever lied to her cousin, not about anything important, anyway. And here she was doing it now because of Ethan?

God, he was like a drug. And she felt like a junkie. A cocky junkie telling herself she'd clocked in enough sobriety. She could resist him. Easy. Might as well have had *denial* tattooed across her forehead. She'd tempted fate, and fate had kicked her right in the butt.

Her phone buzzed. It was Lola's ringtone. Sophie hesitated, briefly before deciding it was better to talk now, while she had privacy.

Just as she accepted the call, Ethan opened the door.

With his damp hair slicked back, it looked darker, more like the dusting of hair visible above the waistband of his jeans. Which she could swear now rode even lower on his hips than before.

"Sophie? You there?"

"Yeah. What's up?" She started to turn, then decided she'd rather keep an eye on him. He really needed to put his shirt on.

"I thought I'd hear from you by now," Lola said. "Where are you?"

"Blackfoot Falls. I texted you when I arrived."

"Yeah, two hours ago. Have you seen him yet?"

"Yes." She watched him open the closet and pull out a duffel bag. He appeared to be ignoring her, but she wasn't stupid. He was listening, hoping to hear something he could use to his advantage. Fine. As long as he stayed quiet.

"And?" Lola's impatience came through.

"I'll have to call you later."

"Got it. Just tell me this," Lola said. "Will you be able to pick him up tonight?"

She swallowed. "No."

Ethan turned in time to see her wince. Or maybe her voice had given away her guilt over the lie. He studied her a moment before swinging his bag onto the bed and sorting through his clothes.

Lola was still there—Sophie could hear the police scanner her cousin liked to keep on low volume in the background—but she hadn't said boo.

"Okay." Sophie swallowed. "Give me an hour."

"Hey, kiddo." Lola's voice had softened. "This turning out harder than you thought it would?"

Sophie sighed. Her head hurt, as did every lying bone in her body. "Yes," she admitted. "But I can do this." She realized what she'd said and spun to face the window. It was too late. Ethan had heard. "Gotta go."

She disconnected, then stared out at Main Street until she was satisfied no telltale blush stained her cheeks.

Ethan was watching her when she turned to him. He gave her a small crooked smile that didn't help at all.

"I have to move my car and get my bag," she said with deliberate gruffness. "You going to be here when I get back?"

"I gave you my word."

"Okay." She glanced around, pretending to search for the keys she knew were sitting under her jacket. "Guess I'll just have to hope that means something to you."

"I expect so," he said, his tone making it clear he didn't like his integrity questioned. "Mind picking up a six-pack? There's a market at the other end of Main." He dug deep in his pocket, pushing the jeans down another inch before producing a twenty.

It occurred to her that he was trying to buy time by sending her to the store. Not likely. She believed his word did matter to him. And even if she was wrong, he knew he'd be a sitting duck tomorrow, so why bother disappearing now?

She grabbed her jacket and keys. "What kind?"

"Your choice."

Sophie laughed. "You're not getting me drunk."

"Sharing a six-pack? I didn't think so."

Funny, she didn't remember him having such an intense stare. It made her jumpy. She spotted the room key and scooped it up as she passed him.

He caught her arm. "You forgot this," he said, trying to give her the money.

"My treat." She pulled away. His touch had given her goose bumps she didn't want him to see. "A condemned man always gets a last meal."

Ethan's slow smile wasn't altogether pleasant. "I was going to be a gentleman and sleep on the floor. Not anymore. We're sharing the bed."

"I wouldn't have it any other way," she said with a toss of her hair, and then fled the room before she hyperventilated.

6

FUZZY WITH SLEEP, Ethan opened his eyes to slits, just enough to see if the room was dark or if morning was trying to sneak in. He wasn't a big believer in alarm clocks and only used them if he had to.

Still black as night. Good.

Yawning, he changed positions and tried to get comfortable. The mattress wasn't bad, but not great, either. He lifted his lids again, trying to remember where he was...

Not Sioux City. That was last month.

Ah, Blackfoot Falls.

That's right...the Safe Haven Rodeo.

The shock of seeing the steel handcuffs dangling from the bedpost jerked him awake. Memories of a dark-haired beauty teased him. Not just any beauty, but the girl he remembered from Wattsville High.

He looked over his shoulder at Sophie. Her long brown hair was everywhere, and so was the rest of her. One arm was thrown out clear to his pillow while she slept partially on her side, her body slightly curled away from him. Her left leg was straight, but her right leg bent at the knee, bringing her foot up near his ass.

How could someone her size take up most of the bed?

No wonder he felt cramped and achy. He needed more room to stretch out.

He rolled over to give her a gentle nudge but stopped. His eyes had adjusted to the darkness, but he couldn't see much with her other arm plopped over her face. Her chin was visible, and so were those damn pouty lips that had distracted him as a teenager and were doing a number on him now.

Ethan had a feeling she underestimated how sexy she was. More so now that she was in her twenties and had filled out. He smiled at the oversize U of Wyoming T-shirt and men's plaid pajama pants that couldn't hide her curvy body. Sophie had insisted on sleeping on top of the covers while he stayed cozy under the sheet and blanket. As if that would've stopped them from doing anything if the mood had struck.

Hell, the mood had struck plenty. At least for him. He just refused to do anything about it.

Sophie was the sort of trouble he needed to avoid. Not because she wanted to drag him back to Wyoming, although the phony accusation bullshit was something he had to straighten out. Sophie herself was the problem. That nice toned body and gorgeous face would turn any man's head, so, yeah, the packaging didn't hurt, but half the women following the tour fit that description.

But he couldn't think of a single one who had Sophie's keen curious brown eyes. The kind a man could stare into and know he was in for a real interesting ride. Hell, he knew he'd get thrown before it was all over, maybe even stomped on. But for as long as he managed to stay in the saddle, he sure wouldn't be bored.

He liked that she wore her hair longer now, past her shoulders and kind of messy. What he liked most was that she didn't seem to give a shit how it looked. Which had been pretty bad when she pulled the wig off. Any other woman he knew, including his grandmother, would've fixed it until it was just so. But not Sophie, and when she tossed back all that long hair, it was with impatience. She sure wasn't flirting.

Another thing that struck him as sexy was the way she walked. Slow and easy. And with that almost-smile teasing her lips. That was why he'd noticed her in the bar. He hadn't recognized her then. But it was the same understated sexiness that had gotten her bullied in school.

Unfortunately Ethan might've had something to do with the bullying, too.

She shifted in her sleep, making a soft throaty sound that got his cock's attention.

God, he wanted to touch her.

The thought had barely flickered when she pulled her arm from his pillow, effectively removing his best excuse. And then she turned completely over on her side, her body curling away from him so that he couldn't see her face.

Well, shit.

No, he was better off staying away. This close to the finals he needed her cooperation more than he needed anything else she could offer. Because he still wasn't convinced that he shouldn't head straight to Vegas while his agent figured things out.

Statistically the odds were against him winning another championship title. At twenty-nine he was getting too old. He had to compete against younger riders. The guys who made it to the top ten were mostly in their mid-twenties. Very few guys close to his age had claimed the title in the past fifteen years. And lately, each time he strained his left shoulder, it took longer to heal.

Damn, he wanted that second title. He wished he could say winning was strictly about funding the rodeo camp he was eager to build. But his pride was equally invested in getting that buckle for the family trophy case. His sister had a good chance of claiming another title this year. The little shit wouldn't let him forget that she'd shown him up. He knew Cara didn't really mean anything with all the jabs. In their family, competitiveness was a sport unto itself.

He stared at the back of Sophie's head, then followed the line of her body, the dip at her waist, the narrow strip of exposed skin where her shirt had ridden up, the curve of her hip.

Her hair had spread to his pillow and he picked up a lock. Rubbed the silkiness between his thumb and forefinger. He hadn't expected it to be this soft. Or to smell faintly of roses. He figured she'd be into something more edgy, spicier. But the floral scent was nice, too.

This wasn't doing him any favors. His heart started pumping faster. He should be trying to go back to sleep, not letting himself get worked up. Had to be close to sunrise. Turning his head, he searched for the time. The small bedside clock reflected the old boardinghouse feel. It was useless in the dark.

He could flip on the lamp. Instead he rolled back to face Sophie. She hadn't moved. He didn't think she was faking sleep, either. She would've tugged down her shirt and covered herself.

Hell. She was just too tempting.

Ethan inched closer. He listened to her steady even breathing before sliding in to spoon her. She didn't move, not one tiny muscle. He'd half expected a startled jerk, or an elbow to his ribs. Was she used to sleeping with someone? Maybe she had a boyfriend. Yeah, probably. Why wouldn't she?

Now, why did that idea rub him the wrong way? He

hadn't seen her in over ten years. And he'd barely known her then. What did he care if she was involved with someone?

He waited a moment and then carefully put an arm around her waist. She'd stubbornly refused to take the blanket, and now her skin was cool. A lit candle would do a better job than the overtaxed heater.

Sophie moved suddenly. Just when he thought he was about to get busted, she wiggled back until they were touching from knees to chest. Her body was instinctively seeking warmth, and he was fine with that. But if she were to wake up right now, she'd blame him for where she'd stuck her sweet round bottom. And slap him into next year.

It would be worth it.

Tightening his arm, he buried his face in her hair and closed his eyes. She was soft and sweet. They fit together real well. It felt so nice having her in his arms that maybe he could get a couple more hours of sleep. He settled in and she pressed her backside closer. His damn boner would be the thing that woke her.

"What time is it?" she murmured, her voice husky.

Ethan braced himself. "Go back to sleep," he whispered, waiting for her to go all out ninja on him.

Slipping her small hand in his, she let out a soft contented sigh.

The moment passed. Her breathing returned to steady and even. Ethan closed his eyes again, hoping for sleep. So he'd quit wondering whom Sophie thought was snuggled against her.

SOPHIE SQUINTED INTO the sunlight that managed to creep in between the drapes and hit her in the face. Morning was always her favorite time of the day. She took pride in being one of those annoyingly energetic people who jumped out of bed ready to conquer the world.

Today she felt sluggish. No, that wasn't right. The feeling was more pleasant. Warm. Comfy. Safe. Was she coming out of a dream? Smiling, she closed her eyes again and snuggled down under the weight of a—

Her eyes popped open.

She pushed the arm off and shot up from the bed.

"What the—" Ethan lifted a hand to block the sun now shining in his face. He rolled onto his back, rubbing his shoulder and frowning at her. "Christ, you damn near took my arm off."

"Don't put it where it doesn't belong." Sophie tugged down her T-shirt, then remembered she wasn't wearing a bra.

"Huh?" His expression dazed, he seemed to be having trouble focusing on her. He was still under the blanket, his lower half, anyway. Okay, so he must've been sleeping and hadn't pressed against her on purpose.

She could see how that might happen. He was probably used to having a different woman in his bed every night. Arms folded across her chest, she headed for the bathroom.

It was too cool in the room. She vaguely remembered trying to adjust the thermostat last night, for all the good it had done. Since the inn had been recently renovated, she would've expected a better heater. Tonight she was using the blanket. Ethan could just—

No. Tonight they'd be long gone. Headed back to Wyoming. No more negotiating. Someday Ethan would realize she was doing him a favor. His best shot at making the finals was to show up in court Monday.

After taking care of more urgent business, she turned on the shower. The water didn't have to be hot, just warm. That was all she asked. And since she'd stupidly forgotten her bag, if it were to suddenly appear, that would be great, too. Fresh out of magic wishes, she sighed and opened the bathroom door, then made a dash for the leather carry-on she'd left by the closet.

Ethan didn't say a word and she risked a look at him. He was lying on his stomach, arms around his bunched pillow, his face buried. No shirt. She paused just inside the bathroom to admire his well-defined shoulders and back. He had to keep himself in good shape to ride bulls. But she was glad he didn't go overboard like so many guys she knew at the gym.

His elbow moved and she hurriedly closed the door. First, she tested the water. A bit warmer would've been more to her liking, but she wasn't complaining. She stripped off her clothes and got under the spray.

Damn, she shouldn't have been so hasty to leap out of bed. Of course she'd had no way of knowing he was asleep. But if she'd lain still a few seconds to find out, it would've been nice to feel his arm around her. To bask in his heat, maybe touch him and pretend...

Oh, brother. Did she want him to carry her books and save her a seat at lunch, too? She was almost twenty-seven, had pretty much taken care of her mom and herself after her father left on Sophie's fourteenth birthday, and she had a master's degree in computer science. So how was it that she could stay stuck at fifteen when it came to Ethan?

She finished showering, dried off and got dressed without once letting her mind stray from the day ahead. The rodeo started at two. Whether he liked it or not, she was waking his ass up right now. She wanted him packed, their bags stowed in her Jeep and both of them ready to go the minute his event was finished.

Breathing in deeply, she reminded herself she was a warrior, not a silly schoolgirl. She grabbed her bag and flung the door open. Ready for whatever he—

The bed was empty.

Sophie blinked. Panic rushed through her. "Son of a bitch."

"Looking for me?"

She turned toward the sound of his voice. He stood to her left pulling a shirt out of the closet with a look of amusement. "The bathroom's all yours," she muttered, and set her bag on the bed so she could rummage through it.

Somewhere in the mishmash of clothes and toiletries was a Ziploc bag with a tube of mascara, an eyeliner pencil and lip gloss. She found it and saw a couple of blush samples the saleswoman at the makeup counter had given her some months back, maybe a year. Sophie wondered if they were still good.

She felt him watching her and looked up. "Need something?"

He shook his head, his gaze narrowed. "You didn't have to rush. If you still need time in there," he said with a nod at the bathroom. "No problem."

"Nope. Go for it."

"Okay." He drawled out the word, but it was his faint smile that made her think she should be worried. He pulled out jeans and socks from his duffel. "I'll be quick so we'll have time to grab some breakfast."

"Fine. I'll run to the Food Mart now while you—"

"We're going to the diner," he said, walking over to her and forcing her chin up. "So you'll probably want to fix your face."

Sophie gasped. She reared back and shoved his hand away. "Forgive me for not meeting your standards."

He looked confused. "That's not what I meant," he said, and had the nerve to sound frustrated.

"Go. Take your shower." She turned back to her bag, trying to hide her disappointment and hurt.

The second he closed the bathroom door, she sank onto

the edge of the bed. Screw him. The stupid insensitive jerk. She pushed her fingers through her damp hair, working past the tangles and wincing at each tug on her scalp.

She eyed the bag beside her. She doubted she had a mirror, and even if she did she'd hate herself for caring enough to look. He thought she should fix her face? Asshole.

Gee, she wondered if she looked sufficiently presentable to pick up breakfast at the Food Mart. He could forget about the diner.

All of a sudden she felt totally drained. The kind of bone-deep exhaustion that followed an adrenaline high. Great. So much for getting a good start for Wyoming tonight.

How could Ethan have said something so hurtful?

She fell back on the mattress and rubbed her eyes. After a pot of coffee and some protein, she'd feel better. She wouldn't let the remark bother her.

She had to stay sharp, remember her objective. Pulling herself into a sitting position, she glanced at the clock.

No way. It couldn't be almost noon.

She yanked her phone from the charger and stared at the numbers. This wasn't possible. She'd never slept so late in her life. Never. Last night she drank one beer. Read for an hour while Ethan watched TV. The moment he'd fallen asleep, she got into bed and conked out herself around midnight.

Huh.

She noticed something black on her fingertips. She checked the phone, but it was fine, so she set it down. Her other hand was also smudged. Glancing down at her red shirt, she saw that it was clean. And her jeans, well, who could tell…they were brand-new and still dark blue.

The dye maybe?

A thought struck her.

She grabbed her bag and turned it upside down on the bed, not sure whether or not she wanted to be right about the cause of the mysterious smudges. After checking every inside pocket, she dumped the meager contents of the purse she hated carrying but kept on hand.

God bless Lola and her makeup addiction. And for giving Sophie some of her castoffs. The blush compact was small, the mirror tiny. But it did the job.

Sophie stared at her raccoon eyes and laughed. She wasn't used to wearing the epic amount of makeup she'd put on with the wig and obviously had done a poor job of removing all of it.

She found some tissue and went to work fixing her face, relieved she'd misunderstood Ethan. Though she had the feeling she would've been better off thinking he was a jerk.

7

"ARE YOU SURE this is a private ranch?" Sophie asked as they pulled into the Lone Wolf in Ethan's truck. They'd argued over who would drive and ended up flipping a coin.

"Yeah, I'm sure. It's been in the Gunderson family for several generations. Matt owns it now. Keep an eye out for a place to park."

Sophie recognized his friend from the bar last night. "Look, isn't that Matt motioning for you?"

"Yep. He must've saved us a spot."

Sophie glanced around at the rows of parked cars close to the gravel drive, the trailers and motor homes lined up to the right of the beautiful two-story ranch house with green shutters. The two barns were easy to identify, and so was the large stable, but she had no idea about all the other smaller buildings.

"That must be the new arena he built," Ethan said as he pulled up to Matt and lowered his window.

Sophie saw the large structure standing north of the corrals. Behind it were acres of sloping pastureland.

"Were you expecting this kind of turnout?" Ethan asked his friend.

Matt's sigh ended with a mild curse. "We've got some

kinks to work out, that's for sure." He looked at Sophie, nodded and then did a double take.

"Long story," Ethan muttered. "I'll explain later."

"Should be good. See that kid with the yellow flag?" Matt pointed. "He's holding a place for you. I'll catch up with you in a few minutes." He smacked the side of the truck and stepped back.

They were shown to a parking spot next to the arena. The huge building was definitely new with a green roof and rust-colored wooden siding. She couldn't imagine what it was used for besides hosting a rodeo, and she wouldn't find out anytime soon judging by the mob about to converge on them.

Or rather on Ethan.

The crowd barely let the poor guy climb out of the truck before they swarmed him. Two reporters pushed their way to the front. The thirtysomething man wore credentials around his neck, and the woman had a cameraman with her. A cowboy Sophie had seen at the bar last night stood to the side, grinning and watching fans shove pens and pictures in Ethan's face.

He accepted the attention better than she would have. He smiled politely, greeted a few people by name and pretty much ignored the pair of blondes wearing skintight jeans and showing off their boob jobs.

Sophie took a discreet glance at herself. Okay, so she had no room to talk. Her jeans could've been sprayed on. The boobs were all hers, though. She pulled her shoulders back. It helped some.

A heavyset man wearing a diamond pinkie ring the size of her Jeep, and who'd been talking with Ethan, turned and gave her a friendly smile. "Now, who do we have here?"

Sophie had purposely stayed back and hadn't expected

any interaction. She cleared her throat. "Sophie," she said, and stuck out her hand.

He seemed surprised but broadened his grin and shook hands with her. "You're here with Ethan?"

They should've discussed this in case someone asked. For God's sake, why hadn't they? She smiled, nodded, managed a quiet "Yes." And hoped the man would leave it at that.

"Sorry, Hal," Ethan said, appearing at her side. "I should've introduced you two right off." He slid an arm around her shoulders and smiled at her, his eyes asking her to go with it. "Sophie's my girlfriend."

"You don't say." The man seemed delighted. "Good for you, Styles. Though you best watch yourself. Your young lady has quite a grip," he said, chuckling and flexing his hand.

"Um, sorry." She'd been told that many times.

"No need to apologize," he said, winking at her. "This boy needs a firm hand." Hal was mostly bald, had no facial hair, but for some reason he reminded her of an overly friendly Santa Claus. "I'll leave you to finish signing autographs, son. I'm sure we'll meet again, Sophie." He gave her a nod and then wandered toward the arena entrance.

"Hal's a good guy," Ethan said, intently watching the older man stop and shake hands with a young cowboy. "I didn't expect to see him here."

She wondered if Ethan realized his arm was still around her shoulders. "Who is he?"

"Hal and his brother own Southern Saddles." He glanced at the sponsor patch he was wearing on his sleeve, then returned his watchful gaze to Hal and the young man. "Probably checking out the new talent. Danny just joined the pro tour this year, but he's kicking ass."

"What does he do?"

"Bull rider." Ethan finally lowered his arm from her shoulders but then resettled it around her waist.

"You're not worried about being replaced, are you? Companies sponsor more than one athlete all the time."

He shrugged. "If I miss the finals again, yeah, I'd expect they might replace me. That's what I'd do if I were in their shoes."

"That's not fair," she said, and noted his small tolerant smile. "I understand it's just business, of course I do. But if you miss the finals, for whatever reason, yeah, it'll totally suck, but the fact remains that out of hundreds you qualified to ride in the first place. That has to count for something."

He just kept staring at her and smiling. "How about a kiss?"

With a laugh, Sophie leaned away from him. "People are waiting for autographs."

"How long does a kiss take?"

She moved back in close, brushed her lips across his ear and whispered, "Depends how slow and deep you go."

Ethan promptly released her and started laughing. "Yeah, thanks, I need to ride a nineteen-hundred-pound bull while I'm distracted by a hard-on."

"Go sign autographs. That should cool you off."

He kissed her right on the mouth before she could stop him. "Remember, anybody asks, you're my girlfriend."

"I could've just as easily been your cousin," she grumbled, which she knew he'd heard as he walked back toward his waiting fans.

Ethan Styles's girlfriend for the day, she thought, and actually caught herself stupidly twirling her hair around her finger.

How pathetic.

ANOTHER THIRTY MINUTES and the rodeo would officially start. Sophie sure hoped Ethan wouldn't give her a hard time about getting on the road right after his event.

Damn, the man knew everyone. Rabid fans, casual fans, the volunteers from Safe Haven who'd helped organize the fund-raiser...

Sophie couldn't keep track of all the people she'd met. But she'd taken an instant liking to Matt and his wife, Rachel. She was friendly and outgoing and treated Ethan and Sophie as though she'd known them forever.

The four of them stood near the stable, the only open area where cars weren't parked bumper to bumper.

"If we do this again next year," Matt said, eyeing the swelling crowd with unease, "we're setting up a table for autographs. Off to the side, maybe near the east barn."

"Oh, trust me, we'll be doing this again." Rachel scanned the list on her clipboard. "Here you go, Ethan," she said, and passed him a number to wear.

Ethan removed the protective sheet to expose the sticky back and slapped it on the front of his shirt.

"This should've been a one-day event," Matt muttered, too preoccupied with what was going on around them to keep up with the conversation. Poor guy. He did seem tense.

"I wondered about that," Ethan said.

Matt strained to look beyond them and nodded to someone.

"My fault." Rachel sighed. "You warned me, and I was stubborn and wanted to help, but..."

"It's okay." Matt caught her hand and pulled her close. Looking into her eyes, he smiled before kissing her. Someone yelled for him, but he was completely focused on his wife. "Ethan and I have to go. Call me if you need anything." Matt gave her another quick kiss before pulling back and winking. "Everything will be just fine."

Rachel nodded. "Thank you," she whispered.

Busy being a voyeur, Sophie hadn't noticed Ethan moving closer. She felt his hand at her waist and with a start turned to him. "What?"

So much for a tender moment à la Matt and Rachel. Sophie had barked like an old harridan.

Ethan grinned. "I'm waiting for my kiss."

She knew Rachel was watching, so Sophie leaned in to plant a peck at the corner of his mouth.

He slid his hand behind her neck, preventing a retreat. "I know you can do better," he murmured near her ear. "Kiss me like you did last night."

She was about to warn him not to push it, but he slipped his tongue inside her mouth and didn't pull back until her heart almost thumped out of her chest.

"Come on, Styles," Matt yelled. "She's not going anywhere."

"He's right about that," Sophie whispered with a gentle shove to his chest.

Ethan stared at her a moment, his smile so faint it barely qualified. "You had to ruin it."

Her breath caught. She had no idea what he meant. Or how to respond. Somehow he seemed disappointed and it bothered her.

And dammit, that bothered her, too. Why should she care?

He glanced at Rachel, touched the brim of his hat, then turned and jogged toward Matt.

"Did you mess up his ritual?"

Sophie dragged her gaze from him and looked at Rachel. "Excuse me?"

"I know a lot of rodeo cowboys are superstitious, especially right before they ride. At least that's what Matt told me. I wasn't around when he was part of the tour."

"Did you meet him after he quit?"

"No. I've known Matt most of my life. We both grew up here in Blackfoot Falls. Although we had a ten-year interruption." Rachel waved an acknowledgment to someone motioning for her. "Mind walking with me?"

"Not at all. If you have something for me to do, put me to work."

"I probably will," Rachel said, grinning at first, and then she glanced back toward the guys and sighed. "Poor Matt. I don't know how he puts up with me. I had no idea this thing would be such a headache. He's right. One day would've been enough, but everyone in town got so excited about the business the rodeo was bringing and I just figured, why not add a day?"

"You want to help your community. That's nice." Sophie smiled, starting to feel better. She liked Rachel and really hoped there was a way to help. "I have a feeling Matt isn't too upset with you."

"Oh, I'm sure he'll think of some way for me to make it up to him," she said, her green eyes sparkling even as she blushed.

"How long have you guys been married?"

"Almost eight months."

"Wow. Not that long. You mentioned a ten-year interruption?"

"Matt's four years older and he left town at nineteen. I had a stupid crush on him and was completely convinced my life was over. Oh, but please don't tell anyone. God forbid the other half of the town should find out." Rachel rolled her eyes, making Sophie laugh. "A few years later I went off to college. After graduate school I came home—it was only supposed to be for the summer." She shrugged. "I stayed to help with my family's ranch and never left again."

They reached the frazzled woman who'd waved for

Rachel. How to handle the collected entry tickets was briefly discussed and then Rachel and Sophie headed for the concessions.

"What do you do here at the Lone Wolf?"

"Not much. Most of the hired men have been here forever, so they take care of the cattle. Matt's more interested in raising rodeo stock. The horses and bulls they're using today are his. In fact, that's why he built that monstrosity," she said, glancing at the building that housed the arena. "He wanted a year-round place for demonstrations and such."

"Is he riding today?"

"Oh, God no. I'd be a nervous wreck." Rachel pressed her lips together. "Sorry, I shouldn't have—"

"No, it's fine." Sophie shrugged. "Frankly I'm not a fan. But I try not to say much."

"Yes." They exchanged looks of mutual understanding, and then Rachel said, "Okay, I want to hear all about you and Ethan."

"It's not what you think." Sophie saw they were approaching the hot dog booth and hoped a mini crisis would distract Rachel. Nothing big or awful. Just a little something—

"Oh? How long have you two been together?"

"We're not, really. When he calls me his girlfriend, it's not like— We knew each other in high school." Sophie was a horrible liar. "And honestly we hadn't been in touch for years until…well, recently."

"Huh. How weird. Kind of like Matt and me."

Sophie sniffed the chilly air. "I think the hot dogs might be burning."

"Oh, great." Rachel glanced over her shoulder. "We'll talk later. At the barbecue." She was already backing toward the booth. "There won't be too many people staying."

"Barbecue?"

"Yes, at the house. Ethan said you two could make it. Didn't he tell you?"

A woman passing out programs intercepted Rachel. Sophie thought about reiterating her offer to help, but she figured she'd mostly be in the way. She also was anxious to go inside and find a seat, though not thrilled about having to sit through so many other events before it was Ethan's turn.

Dammit, she was nervous for him.

Bull riding was dangerous enough without Ethan's eerie penchant for having one thing or another go wrong just before the finals. So how could he not be distracted? Which only upped the chances of something bad happening.

Sophie felt her stomach knot. A stiff breeze coming off the mountains made her shiver. The Lone Wolf was a beautiful spread carved into the foothills. Thousands of pines made up for the barren trees. Up this far north and at this altitude, the leaves had fallen weeks ago.

She looked up at the overcast sky and wondered if snow was expected.

Her Jeep was okay in snow. Though she had yet to put it to a real test, since the county where she lived kept the roads plowed. Out here, driving could get tricky. They could take Ethan's truck and get to Wyoming in time, but not if he insisted on being pigheaded.

A barbecue?

Right.

Under different circumstances it might've been fun, Sophie thought as she finally entered the new arena. The place was huge and, according to some people in line, had only been completed last week. There were rows of bleachers on two sides, wooden picnic benches and folding chairs directly across. Metal pens and chutes for the animals finished the makeshift rectangular arena. The floor was a combination of concrete and dirt, and whiffs of sweat and manure had already taken Sophie by surprise. She tried not to inhale too deeply. No wonder the food concessions had been set up outside.

She studied the ticket Rachel had given her earlier. Her seat was supposed to be close to the action. She sure hoped it wasn't in the row of folding chairs. Yes, there was a steel barrier separating spectators from the bucking animals. And yes, she was confident Matt knew what he was doing. But no way in hell was Sophie going to sit that close.

Volunteers from Safe Haven, identified by orange vests, were running around, answering questions, directing people to seats and, in general, looking harried.

Wow, there were a lot of people. Families with kids dressed as little cowboys were just too adorable. Herds of teenage boys crowded the barricaded pens, dividing their attention between the horses and the lists of names printed on the white poster boards hanging on the wall. An older gentleman climbed a metal ladder and, with a fat felt-tipped marker, added another name. *Mayhem.*

Horse or bull? Sophie wondered. Then decided she didn't want to know.

Of course the buckle bunnies had turned out in considerable numbers. The women stood close to the chutes, mostly in pairs, and some of them were really gorgeous. Sophie wished she'd put a bit more effort into her makeup.

When her phone rang, she saw it was Lola and quickly picked up. "Sorry. I meant to call you earlier."

"Everything okay?"

"Yes." Sophie pressed a finger to her free ear to buffer the noise and walked as far away from the crowd as possible.

"Sounds like you're at the rodeo," Lola said.

"I am, but it hasn't started yet. And unfortunately Ethan rides last."

"A lot of people show up?"

"I'm guessing over four hundred."

"Whoa. He'll get mobbed when it's over."

"I know. He's already been overrun with kids wanting autographs." She saw Rachel walk in, and the first thing that popped into Sophie's mind was the barbecue. "Oh, did I mention it might snow?"

Lola responded with silence. And then, "Is that pertinent?"

"No. Not at all." Sophie gritted her teeth.

"So what's the plan?"

Luckily an announcement that the rodeo would begin in three minutes bounced off the walls at an ear-shattering volume. The crowd responded proportionately.

"Lola? It's crazy in here. I can't hear you very well. I'll have to call you later."

The noise level was settling down and Sophie could've finished their conversation. Instead she disconnected and turned off her phone.

8

AFTER SITTING THROUGH three hours of calf roping, team calf roping, steer wrestling, saddle bronc riding and having to listen to the pair next to her, Sophie figured her penance for blowing off Lola was paid in full.

The two middle-aged men had opinions about every damn thing in the whole universe. They certainly were entitled to express themselves. Sophie didn't have to listen. Now, the tobacco chewing? That was getting to her.

She was mentally rehearsing what she could politely say to get them to keep their tobacco juice to themselves when the announcer mentioned Ethan's name. She straightened and concentrated on what the commentator was saying. His slight twang wasn't always easy to understand.

"Think he'll wear a helmet?"

"Shh." Sophie scowled at the bearded man next to her. Then she processed what he'd said. "Who?"

The man gave her a long look, then nodded toward the area behind the chutes. "Ethan Styles."

Sophie panned the faces of three cowboys. "I don't see him."

"He's not riding yet. Danny Young is up next. Then Cody Clark. Weren't you listening?"

Sophie sucked it up and just smiled. Okay, now she remembered. There were supposed to be three bull riders today.

Danny Young was announced and she leaned forward, watching him secure a protective blue helmet, then lower himself onto the back of a bull already bucking to get out of the chute.

So far all the other cowboys had worn Stetsons or another brand of cowboy hat. But then their events weren't as dangerous as bull riding. She couldn't recall seeing a helmet in Ethan's truck. She knew not all bull riders liked wearing a helmet...

After wrapping a short bull rope around his left hand, the rider gave the nod. The chute gate swung open and the black bull charged out bucking and whirling and twisting. Dirt flew from the animal's hooves. With his free hand held up high, the rider clung to the rope with his other gloved hand. The crowd shouted and cheered.

A buzzer sounded and more cheering as the crowd leaped to their feet. The rider pulled the rope free and bailed to the right, landing on his feet while two cowboys distracted the bull. As the announcer sang his praises, Danny Young jogged to safety and then pulled off the helmet and grinned at the crowd.

"I bet the kid makes it to the finals next year," the bearded man said. "He finished the season ranked forty-ninth. Damn good for this being only his second tour."

"I'd sure like to see how he does on a fiercer bucker," said his friend with the weathered face.

Sophie turned and stared at him. "Are you saying that bull wasn't scary as hell?"

The other guy laughed and leaned back. "Hey, Lenny, she's talking to you."

"What?"

Sophie sighed. "That bull looked pretty intimidating to me."

"Is this your first rodeo, honey?" Lenny asked, his craggy features softened by a kind smile.

"No, but..." She breathed in deeply and glanced toward the chute. She wished she could see Ethan. Wearing a helmet. "Bull riding is nerve-racking."

"Then you might want to sit out the last ride."

"The last— You mean Ethan Styles," she said, a sickening wave of dread swelling inside her. "Why?"

"Matt Gunderson's new to the stock contracting business. But he's raising some good rodeo bulls. I heard Twister is one mean son of a—" Lenny gave her a sheepish grin, then shifted his gaze to the arena.

She realized the next rider—Cody something or other—was being announced, so she kept quiet and let the two men enjoy the event. Although how they could voluntarily watch a bloodthirsty bull try to pulverize someone, she'd never comprehend.

Yes, she understood some rodeo basics. For instance, the bulls were scored on their performance, just as the riders were. The scores were then combined for a potential of one hundred points. So clearly the more difficult the bull was to ride, the more points the rider received overall. But points didn't matter here. Ethan had told her so last night. Matt was supposed to be his friend. So why give Ethan a son of a bitch to ride?

No, it hadn't been Matt who'd made that call. It had been Ethan. She'd bet anything he'd insisted on riding the toughest bull. Stupid, reckless idiot.

She stared down at her aching hands. And only stopped wringing them to drag her damp palms down her jeans. The crowd's collective gasp made her look up.

The rider had been thrown over the bull's massive head.

He landed face-first in the dirt and then crawled until he could finally stand. When he staggered, it was Matt who jumped into the arena and helped the cowboy to the side. The bull continued to furiously buck, trampling the man's tan Stetson. Why wasn't he wearing a helmet?

He lifted a hand to let everyone know he was all right.

The crowd responded with deafening applause. Sophie squeezed her eyes shut. Ethan was next.

Please, please, please be wearing a helmet.

"All right, folks, you all know who's up next... Having finished the season at number two, Ethan Styles is arguably the hottest rider on tour," the announcer said, which inspired a few catcalls. "Whose agility and athleticism has won him the respect of his fans. And once again a trip to the finals in Las Vegas—"

Applause and cheering nearly drowned the man out. Handmade signs had popped up in the crowd. Some clever, some incredibly corny. One sign read Marry me, Ethan.

"Settle down, folks. It might be another minute or two. Looks like he might be having some trouble with Twister, who I've been told is a savage bucker. Like the other two bulls we've seen today, Twister belongs to Matt Gunderson. No stranger to you all, but new to the world of raising bulls. He assured me we won't be disappointed with Twister, says he's a real killer. I guess we'll all find out soon enough..."

The announcer continued talking, but Sophie had stopped listening. She rose from her seat, trying to catch a glimpse of Ethan. She could see his sun-streaked hair as the bull rocked him against the metal railing. No helmet. Damn him.

"Miss? You mind sitting down? We can't see from back here."

Sophie heard the voice behind her, but not until someone touched her arm did it register the man was speaking to her. With an apology she sank back onto her seat. Maybe it was a blessing that she couldn't see. Her nerves were already frayed. Why wouldn't he wear a helmet? It was just plain foolish.

"Styles is nuts," Lenny said. "I can't figure out why he's riding this weekend. With his track record you'd think he'd be holed up somewhere with the door double-locked."

The bearded man spat into a cup. "That's what I would do. He gets injured today, he won't never forgive himself. Sure would be a shame if he missed the finals again."

"You get a chance to see him ride Bad Company at the season opener?" Lenny asked his friend. "Reminds me of this bull. Thrashing and lunging against the gate like that, he ain't about to let Styles get comfortable. What was it that happened last year before the finals? Was it his elbow—"

"Please stop saying those things." Sophie turned to the two men. "Riders are superstitious enough. Ethan doesn't need to be reminded of what's happened in the past. So, please…"

Lenny frowned at her. "It ain't like we're saying it so he can hear."

"But you're still putting it out there in the universe."

The men glanced at each other and laughed. "Ma'am, you might wanna find another sport that's easier on your blood pressure," Lenny said.

Sophie hadn't been looking for a clear shot of Ethan. But that was what she got between a pair of Stetson-wearing cowboys sitting two rows in front of her. He was still tying his rope.

"What's he doing?" Lenny mumbled. "He can't be using a suicide wrap."

"He'd be a dang fool, since he's not looking to qualify."

"A what?" Sophie asked, but the men ignored her. A suicide wrap? Okay, maybe it was better she didn't know.

Gripping the edge of her seat, she leaned forward, her heart racing. "Damn you, Ethan," she muttered under her breath, her attention glued to him. "Put on the goddamn helmet."

"You know Styles personally?" Lenny asked, frowning at her.

"Yes," she said, swallowing when she saw him give the nod. "I'm his girlfriend."

AFTER WHAT FELT like an hour inside a blender, Ethan heard the buzzer. Another two seconds and he ripped free of the bull rope and jumped off Twister. He managed to land on his feet while a bullfighter lured the bull in the other direction. Pulling off his Stetson, Ethan waved it at the cheering crowd.

Good for Gunderson. He had a winner with Twister. That son of a bitch could buck and change direction with the best of them. When he'd burst out of the chute and cut to the left, Ethan almost let go.

Sophie wasn't in her seat.

What the hell?

He'd known exactly where she was sitting. He'd spotted her after watching Kenny get an ass-whooping by one of Matt's broncs.

People were on their feet, still applauding, so Ethan waved again before he exited the arena. Once he made it to the reserved area behind the pens, he stopped to dust off his hat and the front of his shirt. Matt was waiting for him with a mile-wide grin.

Ethan laughed. "You trying to kill me, Gunderson?"

"What did I tell you?"

"I didn't think the bastard was gonna let me outta the

chute." Ethan wiped his face with the back of his sleeve. "You ride him yet?"

"Nope." Matt handed him a clean rag. "If Twister didn't kill me, Rachel would."

"Smart woman."

Ethan recognized the irritated voice even before he turned around.

Sophie had slipped behind the fence, ignoring the man who tried to stop her.

"It's okay," Matt told the cowboy, and the man backed off.

It didn't appear Sophie was aware of anything going on around her. She was focused solely on Ethan, and she looked pissed.

She stopped a foot away and glared up at him. "Styles, there is something very wrong with you."

"Okay." He grinned and put on his hat. Her cheeks were pink, her dark eyes flashing. He couldn't imagine what this was about, but he didn't like that her lower lip had quivered. "Are you gonna tell me why?"

"We'll talk later," Matt said, nodding at Sophie as he passed her.

She gave him an apologetic smile. When she met Ethan's eyes again, she didn't look angry but afraid. "Why didn't you wear a helmet?" Her voice was so soft he barely heard her. "I know you don't owe me an answer," she said. "I do. But God, Ethan, you're a smart man. Bull riding is dangerous. And I'm just trying to understand—"

He touched her hand, and she threw her arms around his neck. She'd looked so sad and small standing there he wasn't sure what to do or say. Except to hold her close until she stopped trembling. He just rubbed her back and waited for her pounding heart to slow.

"I'm sorry if I'm embarrassing you," she murmured,

her face buried against his chest. "Just give me a minute, okay?"

"Hell, you're not embarrassing me." He almost made a joke, but the words seemed to stick in his throat. "A beautiful woman cares about whether I wear a helmet or not, and I should be embarrassed?"

Keeping her face down, she bumped him with her knee.

"Ethan?" The soft voice belonged to a Safe Haven volunteer. "Sorry to interrupt, but folks are waiting for autographs."

Sophie tried to pull away, but he held her tight.

"Tell them it'll be a few more minutes," he told the older woman standing at the fence. "Please."

"Will do." With a smile she turned and left.

"No, Ethan." Sophie pushed at his chest. "Go. I'm fine."

"Twister couldn't buck me off. You think I can't hold on to a little thing like you?"

"Oh, brother." She sniffed. "Watch it. I kickbox," she said, and slowly lifted her chin. Her eyes were bright, but no tears. "Don't make those people wait."

"Why not? They get bored and hit the concessions, that's more money for Safe Haven."

Sophie laughed. "And here I thought you were just a pretty face."

"See how wrong you can be?" He smiled at her mock glare and wondered what had set her off. He doubted it was just about him not wearing a helmet. But he couldn't get into it now. "How about you come with me?"

"Oh, for heaven's sake, I'm fine. Embarrassed as hell," she said. "Though not fatally. I'm sure I'll live to embarrass myself another day. So go." She tugged at his arm. "Good grief, I think your muscles have muscles."

Ethan caught her chin and tipped her face up so he could look into her eyes. "I usually do wear a helmet. But I left

Wyoming in a rush to get here and forgot it." He brushed a kiss across her mouth. "That's no excuse. It was dumb to forget something so important."

Her bottom lip quivered again. Not from fear this time. How was he supposed to go shake hands and sign autographs when all he could think about was tasting every inch of her? He trailed a finger down her throat, then traced the ridge of her collarbone. The satiny texture of her skin drove him nuts. So smooth and soft everywhere he touched. What must the skin of her inner thighs feel like?

"We can pick one up tomorrow," she whispered, pressing into him and making it damn near impossible for him to think straight.

"Pick what up?"

"A helmet." Her eyes started to drift closed, but then she widened them. "Oh no. We leave tonight."

"I'm not going to do that, Sophie."

"Ethan…"

He kissed her lips, silencing her. And tormenting himself. All he wanted was for them to be someplace far away, alone, without distractions. Someplace where he could explore her body with his hands and mouth. Listen to her soft breathless moans when their kissing got hot and heavy. He wondered what sound she would make when he sank deep inside her.

Her stubborn lips finally yielded, letting him slip his tongue between them.

He jerked a little when her fingers dug into his bum shoulder.

"Can people see us?" she asked, slightly breathless.

"Probably."

"An awful lot of kids are out there."

"Yeah." Ethan straightened and released her. "Let's get this over with," he said, taking her hand.

She pulled it back. "I'll wait in the truck."

"Come on…" Wasn't this just great? They were gonna end up arguing. So be it, but they weren't leaving tonight. "Matt and Rachel are barbecuing."

"I heard," she said, staying a step ahead of him.

"There won't be a lot of people, mostly the riders who are staying here in their trailers." He watched her squeeze between the fence post and the wall. No way he'd fit so he just moved the whole damn temporary fence. "Did you hear me?"

"Yes, I heard you, and you already know what I have to say to that."

"My agent called," he said, and that stopped her. "He's in the middle of something with a football client. We're talking later."

"Did you not tell him how important this is?"

"I will."

She shook her head. Then without so much as a glance, she walked in the direction of the truck, leaving him to face a dozen squealing kids and a pack of buckle bunnies.

9

SOPHIE WAS IN TROUBLE. She slumped down in the truck's passenger seat, grateful for the tinted windows, and checked her texts. Two from Lola, one from Mandy and a voice mail from her mom. Since she could set a clock by her mom's Saturday phone calls, she'd listen to the message later.

But Lola was getting impatient, and Sophie could hardly blame her.

She thumped her head back on the leather headrest. It was far too comfortable to knock any real sense into her thick skull.

God, she was being stupid. Not just stupid. She'd risen to the level of too-stupid-to-live. When had she become the kind of ridiculous airhead she and Mandy liked to make fun of in bars?

Well, payback was a bitch. She was allowing Ethan to make a complete fool out of her. He probably knew she'd gotten all giddy inside when he'd announced she was his girlfriend. He was only using her to buy time and to keep the buckle bunnies at bay.

And yet, a part of her refused to believe that he'd be so heartless. Something other than ego was driving him to go after that second championship. Maybe that something was more important than her ending up as collateral damage.

She really hadn't expected to like Ethan. He was nothing like the self-centered man she'd imagined. But he was being naive. Clearly he hadn't explained the gravity of his situation to his agent. If he had, Brian wouldn't be shelving the problem for later.

Sitting up straighter, she adjusted the rearview mirror, hoping she could see how the fan schmoozing was going. She recognized a young saddle bronc rider dividing his attention between a blonde and signing a kid's T-shirt. The crowd had thinned, but her view was still limited. She couldn't see Ethan and assumed he was around the corner of the building.

A volunteer picked up trash while two more were closing down the hot dog concession. Hopefully the fans would clear out soon. The sun had gone down, and so had the temperature. She should probably offer to help. But there was a call she should make first.

Ethan needed a lawyer. And Craig Langley was an excellent defense attorney. Every deputy and assistant DA she knew couldn't stand the man, which spoke to his success at getting his clients off. The reason she didn't care for him was more personal. For months he'd been asking her out with the same dogged persistence he used to wear down prosecutors. But he was too smooth in his thousand-dollar suits and not at all her type.

She stared at her phone, well aware that if she asked Craig for help, she'd owe him. Just the thought of having dinner with him gave her the creeps. And if any of the deputies found out, she'd be the laughingstock of the whole county.

"Damn you, Ethan." She sucked in a breath and checked old incoming calls. Yep, there was his number.

Craig answered on the second ring. "Sophie?"

"Hey." She forced a smile, hoping it helped make her sound less as though she'd rather be eating worms. "Got a minute?"

"Well, now, honey, for you I've got all night."

"I need a favor," she said on an exhale, and then summed up the problem, leaving out names for now.

"Hmm, you know I always have a full caseload..." he drawled.

She held back a sigh. Fine. She'd figured he would milk the situation. "I know you're busy, Craig," she said shamelessly using that husky tone men liked. "That's why I hated to even ask, but it's a time-sensitive matter. And frankly there's no one I could trust more with this little problem."

"You were absolutely right to call me. How about we meet for dinner to discuss the details?"

"I'd love that. I really would, except I'm out of town at the moment. In Montana, actually."

"Montana? When will you be back?"

"Monday, I hope."

"All right, that's the day after tomorrow. How about I make dinner reservations at La Maison? Would you like that?"

Cringing, Sophie shoved a hand through her hair. "See, this little problem my friend has, it really can't wait that long," she said, then tensed at his silence. "But dinner at La Maison sounds—"

She hadn't realized Ethan had opened the driver's door until she saw him standing there.

"That sounds great," she said in a rush, and saw Ethan frown. "But I need to go right now."

"We don't have to eat at La Maison," Craig said, sounding confused. "I know this little bistro—"

"I'll call you later, okay?"

"Sophie?"

She hung up on him. "All done?" she asked Ethan.

He frowned. "Am I interrupting?"

"Nope. Let's go."

He slid behind the wheel and closed the door. "Did you have to cancel a date?"

"No." She noticed he didn't have his keys out.

"The food's good at La Maison."

"You've been there?"

"A few times."

"Don't they require a jacket and tie?"

Ethan cocked an eyebrow. "I happen to have both."

"Huh. I can't picture you in a tie," she said, and failed to see why he seemed to find that objectionable. "Come on, why aren't we moving?"

"Because I'm not ready to move." He turned most of his body toward her. "Do you have a boyfriend?"

"No." He had some nerve. So why did she want so badly to help him stay out of jail? Might as well change her forehead tattoo from *denial* to *stupid*.

"Well, somebody sure wants to impress you."

She glared at him. "And if he does?"

"Nothing." Ethan took his hat off and tossed it into the backseat. "I'm sorry I screwed up your date. If you want to go to La Maison, I'll take you there myself."

Sophie snorted a laugh. Good to know it wasn't just her who was acting like a ridiculous child.

"What?"

"You like the food at La Maison? How about I bring you a takeout while you're sitting in jail?"

It was Ethan's turn to glare. "You're picking a fight so we don't go to the barbecue."

"You're unbelievable," she said. "You really are." She laid her head back and rubbed her eyes, careful not to streak her mascara. Out of her peripheral vision she saw him take out his phone.

"Arnie? Tell me something good." Ethan stared out the windshield while he listened. His mouth tightened. "Arnie." He drawled the name into a warning, then waited, listening, the muscle in his jaw working double time. "You dumb fuck, you slept with her, didn't you?"

Sophie lifted her head and stared outright.

He dropped the phone into his lap and hit the steering wheel with the heel of his hand.

Cursed.

Hit the wheel again.

"Tell me," she said, the tension in her chest beginning to hurt.

"Wendy isn't going to admit she lied. She can't change her story now."

"But her husband…"

"Fullerton already knows. His ranch foreman doesn't like Wendy, so he told the old man he saw me leaving around midnight. That's why she made up a story about turning me down at the bar and me following her home."

"But as far as Fullerton knows, you could've just been giving her a ride home or dropping something off…"

Ethan smiled.

"It's possible," Sophie said, annoyed that he thought she was the one being naive. "So, why did Arnie sleep with her? And anyway, doesn't that just prove she's a serial cheater?"

"She played him. Wendy found the perfect way to keep the dumb ass from telling her husband the truth. Claiming I'd ripped her off was overkill. She must've regretted it as soon as she realized she'd have to get rid of the jewelry and deal with an insurance investigation. So when Arnie showed up in front of a bunch of witnesses she jumped at the chance to tell everyone he'd brought the jewelry back to get her to drop the charges. He made it real easy for her to keep her jewelry and stick to the lie."

"That's crazy."

"Crazy or not, I don't need that kind of publicity dogging me at the finals."

"Yeah, but who'd believe you would do something like that?"

"Probably no one but her husband, if only to keep the marriage intact and save face."

"Men and their damn egos." She saw his eyebrows go up. "Yes, I'm talking about you, too." She huffed out a breath. Something had been bothering her... "What's a suicide wrap?"

His eyes narrowed. "Where did you hear that?"

"Some guys sitting next to me on the bleachers."

Shaking his head, he sighed. "We wrap the hand we use to hold on to the leather strap. Weaving the rope between the ring finger and pinkie makes it harder for the bull to pull it out of your hand," he said. "It also makes it harder for a rider to let go."

"And he can get hung up on a thrashing bull."

"Yes, sometimes that happens."

She tried to control a shudder. "Did you use one of those wraps today?"

"No."

"Do you ever?"

"Yes," he said, his gaze steady. "But I'm not reckless, Sophie."

"Uh, do you even know what the word *suicide* means?"

"Sorry we can't all be as smart as you," he said, his expression stony. "That doesn't mean I'm stupid."

Sophie briefly closed her eyes. "I'm sorry. I know I'm snide sometimes—of course I wasn't saying you're stupid." This was another reason kids had picked on her. She just didn't know when to keep her mouth shut. "If anyone's stupid, it's me. I'm supposed to be taking you back, not trying to find a way to— You don't even care what happens. Why should I?"

He caught her waving hands and held them both in one of his. "I care," he said, and looked directly into her eyes. "I thought Arnie would come through. Brian will, but probably not in time to avoid court, so we'll head to Wyoming tomorrow."

"In the morning?" she asked hopefully.

"No. After my ride."

"That's cutting it close."

He shrugged. "I got here in twelve hours with one stop. What about you?"

"The same."

"I'll talk to Matt about switching the schedule. We should be able to leave by midafternoon. Stop at a motel halfway and get a few hours' sleep." Ethan leaned over the console to brush a kiss across her lips. "How's that?"

She nodded, happy she could call Lola and not have to lie. Happy she was sitting here in Ethan's truck, feeling his warm breath on her face. "You might still need an attorney."

"I guess it'll depend on how far Wendy pushes her story."

"I bet she wants this to go away as much as you do."

"Sure hope so." He cupped the side of her face and studied her lips, his mouth curving in a slow smile.

"Wait. Let me say this before we get crazy and I forget."

A low chuckle rumbled in his throat. "Make it quick."

"Uh-huh." She touched his jaw, intrigued by the stubble that hadn't been there this morning. The rasp against her fingertips was oddly arousing. Imagining how amazing it would feel pressed to her breasts had her holding her breath.

"Last chance," he said, sliding his fingers into her hair.

Whatever she'd been about to say was already in the wind. She hoped it wasn't important. It didn't matter. She was more interested in what Ethan was doing to her scalp. His touch was sheer heaven. The soothing massage turned into a slight tug. She realized she'd closed her eyes.

Apparently he wanted them open. Watching her face, he held her still as he lowered his mouth. Their lips barely touched and lightning shot through her. His tongue didn't politely wait for an invitation. He demanded entrance, coaxing and teasing his way inside, stoking the fire that had ignited low in her belly.

She clutched his arm, digging her fingers into hard muscle, and met each stroke of his tongue. The console was in their way. She wished they could push it to the floor. Or what if they climbed into the backseat?

A light came on somewhere behind him, closer to the house. She didn't care. Her existence had narrowed to the urgency of Ethan's touch, his greedy mouth, the feel of his warm hard body and the longing about to burst out of her chest. Her young girlish fantasies hadn't prepared her for this, not for Ethan in the flesh.

He moved his shoulder to block the light from hitting her face. But he kept kissing her, touching her jaw, the side of her chin, testing how their mouths fit together from different angles. He traced her ear with his thumb, then followed the curve of her neck, and dipped his fingers under the neckline of her top. He thrust his tongue deeper into her mouth and still she couldn't get enough of him. Finally, gasping for air, they pulled apart.

Trying to catch her breath, she looked around. When

had it gotten so dark? Where was everyone? Low-voltage security lights from the stable and barns provided a soft glow. A couple of ranch hands stood outside the well-lit bunkhouse. Lots of activity happening where the fifth-wheelers and motor coaches were parked. But it was the porch light from the house that had shone in her face. No one was close enough to see them, though.

The fog had lifted from her brain and she looked at Ethan, who was staring at her.

She smiled at him.

He smiled back.

A wave of distant laughter came from the direction of the house.

"The barbecue," they said at the same time.

"Bet they won't miss us," Ethan said, reaching for her again.

Who cared if they did? she thought, and bumped his nose in her haste to get to his mouth. He murmured an "Ouch" and she started giggling.

"I barely touched you, Mr. Big-Tough-Bull-Rider."

"I never said I was tough. I get a paper cut and I cry like a baby." He ran a palm down her arm, then worked his thumb underneath the sleeve, stretching the fabric as far as it would go so he could probe her muscles. "You're the one who feels pretty tough. Work out much?"

She knew the question was rhetorical. "Every chance I get," she said anyway, and punctuated it with a quick teasing kiss.

"Remind me not to mess with you."

"I tried to warn—" She gasped at the feel of his hand sliding under her shirt.

"Nice abs." He smiled against her mouth, then brushed his tongue over hers. His hand skimmed her right breast, proving the bra an ineffective barrier.

Her nipples tightened immediately. He dipped his fingers inside the satin cup and grazed the puckered flesh. His touch sparked a surge of liquid heat that spread throughout her body, seeking release. Seeking more...

"We're making out in your truck," she whispered.

"I noticed," he murmured, his breath coming quick and short.

"People are inside..." She tried to swallow, but her mouth was parched. "The barbecue. We have to—"

"No, we don't."

"We can't stay here—"

"Right." He caught her earlobe between his teeth and tugged lightly. His fingers pushed deeper, plucking at her nipple, while his lips trailed the side of her neck. "I don't know where my keys are."

"They aren't in my bra." She felt his smile against her flushed skin.

"You sure? I should check."

"In high school you might've found tissue, no keys, though."

Pulling back to look at her, he laughed.

Sophie sighed. Not something she would've shared had she not been so fuzzy-headed. "That was a joke."

"I figured," he said, still laughing.

She cupped the bulge straining his jeans, and that shut him up. Holy cow, he was hard. Yeah, they definitely had to go someplace private. And the second she got her thoughts and mouth in working order, she'd tell him just that.

And after he stopped hissing.

And she supposed she'd also have to move her hand. Eventually. She shifted in her seat, causing the light to shine in her eyes again.

She lifted her hand to blot the brightness.

Ethan leaned way back against the seat, and it took

her a moment to realize he was having trouble sliding his hand into his pocket.

"We have to go inside," she said.

"No, we don't. Matt doesn't care."

"You have to talk to him about changing the schedule. So we can leave early tomorrow."

With a grunt, Ethan finally withdrew the keys. "I'll call him in the morning."

"It's better to give him a lot of notice. So you won't put him in a tight spot. Otherwise you'll give in and we'll be delayed." She watched his jaw clench and understood why he was resisting. She wanted to get back to the inn, herself. "Please. I really don't want to have to go out with Craig," she murmured.

"Who's Craig?"

"What?" Oh, crap. That thought wasn't supposed to have left her brain. "Craig who?"

"That was my question."

Dammit. If they were both naked already, they wouldn't be talking. "He's an attorney. From Casper. A very good attorney, and if you need him, then…" She waved a hand, wishing he'd just go inside already. "I can probably make that happen…" She trailed off as she turned her head to stare at the darkness outside her window.

Finally he opened the door, which triggered the interior light. Something she could've done without. "We won't need your friend Craig," Ethan said, and got out of the truck.

"He's not my friend. I don't even like him." She opened her door and slid off the seat. By the time she met him on the driver's side something had occurred to her. "There's really no reason for me to—"

Ethan cut her off by backing her against the truck. He had a good eight inches on her, and with his shoulders broad as they were she couldn't see the porch or even the house. But she heard a door open and close. Heard voices and laughter.

And then Ethan's big, rough hand touched her face. The fingers from his other hand were tangled in her hair. Aware that he had pinned her with a thigh partially nudged between hers, she stood in shock for a moment, feeling the truck's cold metal against her back.

"Ethan?"

"They can't see you," he whispered, and kissed her. "You don't know them."

"But—"

His openmouthed kiss silenced her. She heard the catcalls, so of course he did, too. And when a man with a heckling tone called Ethan's name, one hand briefly disappeared followed by rowdy laughter, so she was pretty sure Ethan had flipped him off. But even then Ethan didn't miss a beat. He slanted his mouth across hers, hungry and demanding, deepening the kiss until he'd left her breathless.

She gulped in air. "What are you doing?"

"Come on," he murmured, not breathing so easily, either. "Let's go."

She eyed the hand circling her arm and realized he meant they should leave the Lone Wolf. "But you were going to talk to Matt."

"I can't go in there. I'll call him."

A funny feeling slithered down her spine. Since she couldn't bodily force him inside the house, she rounded the hood and climbed back into the truck. He already had the keys in the ignition. "You've changed your mind about going back tomorrow, haven't you?"

He frowned at her, then reversed the truck. "No, I have not." Once he'd steered them toward the driveway, he said, "This has nothing to do with tomorrow. And everything to do with a certain physical condition that is completely your fault."

Sophie smiled when he stopped to kiss her hand. She just wished she believed him.

10

BAD VIBES WERE coming off Sophie in waves. They were halfway to town and Ethan still couldn't figure out what had caused the shift in her. It had started right after he told her he wouldn't be going inside to talk to Matt. Whether Ethan called him to change tomorrow's schedule or asked in person made no difference. And she was well aware of the damn hard-on that wouldn't quit. He couldn't have walked into the house like that.

"Did I embarrass you?" he asked after a long silence.

"When?"

"Just before we left. When I kissed you in front of Travis and those other folks."

"No. You said I didn't know them." She finally turned and looked at him. "But why *did* you kiss me like that in front of those people?"

"Travis Mills. I heard his voice and I did the first thing I could think of to avoid him." Saying it out loud made him sound like an ass. "That was rude. I'm sorry." He tugged at his snug jeans. "I got paid back, though. This hard-on is never gonna ease up."

"You could do a commercial for one of those pharmaceutical companies. I bet they'd give you a nice endorsement contract."

Ethan choked out a laugh. Nice to hear the smile back in her voice. "Yeah, I think I'll pass on that." He saw a turnout and pulled off the highway. He had a feeling he knew what could be bothering her. Might as well put her uncertainty to rest.

"What are you doing?" She twisted around to peer at the dark road behind them.

"Don't worry, I won't jump you. Not yet, anyway." He got out his phone. "I'm calling Matt."

"We'll be in town in ten minutes."

"Like you said, better to give him as much notice as possible." He listened to the rings, aware that the tension in the cab was easing. So she hadn't believed that he was serious about returning to Wyoming. It irritated him, since he'd given his word, but then he hung around with a dumb ass like Arnie, so what was she supposed to think?

Arnie didn't know it yet, but this time Ethan had had it with him. Back in school the jocks had picked on Arnie; so had the geeks, which was really pathetic. Ethan used to think he was one of those kids who just couldn't catch a break and he'd gone out of his way to befriend him. Once Ethan had turned pro he hired Arnie to do odd jobs and help him manage his schedule and social media. But the bastard hadn't only screwed Wendy; he'd screwed Ethan. And it hurt.

No surprise he was sent to voice mail, what with Matt having a houseful and all, but he hated leaving a message. For Sophie's sake, he left one anyway. It was short, to the point, and judging by her smile, it did the trick. He was glad she seemed relieved.

"I'm going to call Lola—she's my partner—oh, and my cousin. She was a year behind you in school."

He watched her pull out her phone. She was about to hit speed dial when her words sank in. "Your partner?"

She looked up, her expression wary. "We own Lola's Bail Bonds together. I'm good with computers. And Lola…" Sophie shrugged. "She's better with just about everything else."

"Why isn't your name in there?"

"I nixed it. The business is more Lola's gig. I wanted to help her get started. She knows I don't want to do this forever."

"Yeah, I'm thinking you're a little better than good with computers." He sat back and left the truck idling. "When I first thought I recognized you, I figured I had to be wrong. I mean, why would someone like you be working as a bounty hunter?"

"Fugitive retrieval agent," she muttered. "Scratch that. I like bounty hunter. Sounds pretty cool."

Was she acting flighty on purpose? Sophie was crazy smart. It wouldn't surprise him if she'd skipped her senior year and had gone on to college early. "Is this something you don't like to talk about?"

"I don't understand why you would think I'm such a computer whiz or why the bail bond business wouldn't be for me."

"Because you're too smart, that's why. Jesus. You were a freshman taking junior and senior classes and you were still bored."

She stared at him, her mouth open. "How would you know that?"

Shrugging, he put the truck in gear and eased them back on the highway. "You don't think I noticed you, but I did." He smiled at a memory of her hiding under the bleachers, nearly choking to death on her first and only cigarette. "You used to wear that ugly, oversize blue coat. Remember that? It could be a hundred degrees outside, the sun hotter than hell, and you'd be wearing that damn thing."

She was still staring at him. "After that day you saved me outside the locker room, you never said a word or even looked at me..."

Oh, he'd looked plenty, before and after. Only, he'd learned to be more sly about it after the friggin' incident over the dress. "I *saved* you? When did you get so dramatic?"

She turned away and fixed her gaze on the road ahead, arms crossed in front of her. "You did save me," she said softly. "You were my hero."

Grinding his teeth, he stepped on the accelerator. Kept his attention on the road, wishing like hell he hadn't brought up the coat or the past. He'd been such an asshole.

"You were popular. Everyone liked you. You don't understand what it's like to be different from everyone else and be thrown into a new environment with no friends or...or anybody who's willing to give you a chance." Sophie sighed. "Or pull you aside and explain why everyone thinks you're nothing but a dork."

The sadness in her voice made his gut clench. "I promise you those girls didn't think you were a dork," he said, reliving the anger and shame.

He should've broken up with Ashley that very day. She and her spiteful followers had been mean to Sophie, and who knew how many other girls. All because he'd looked one second too long and Ashley had felt threatened. But he'd put up with her random cruelty because she gave great head. Yeah, some hero.

Sophie surprised him with a laugh. "You don't have to say that, Ethan. It was a long time ago. I'm over it. If anyone calls me a dork now, I'd just put them in a body cast."

He looked over and saw her flexing her left biceps. He relaxed enough to smile. "I'll keep that in mind."

"Excellent idea." She slumped back and blew out a breath. "Okay, I have to say it… You can't claim to have noticed me now, not when you basically treated me as if I were invisible back then. Why didn't you ever talk to me after that day?"

"Well, for one thing, I had a girlfriend."

"Um, yeah. Ashley. I know. Anyway, I said *talk* to me, not ask me out on a date."

"That's the other thing. You were a lot younger than me."

"Guess what? The math hasn't changed."

Ethan shook his head. "Okay, I'll say this…being sarcastic doesn't do you any favors."

"Yes, I've heard that before," she murmured sheepishly. "I'll try to remember."

How was it that he could feel this comfortable with her? She said what she wanted without holding back. And he said whatever he said, and they just moved on, no sweat. Go figure. "You were fifteen. I was eighteen. At those ages it mattered."

"I see your point."

He opened and closed his mouth. Hell, he needed to think about what he was willing to admit. Or whether telling her anything would make her feel worse.

"Just so you know…" She pulled her legs up and hugged her knees. "I thought you deserved better than Ashley. She was a total bitch. But I respect your loyalty and that you didn't mess around with other girls."

"Look, Ashley was…" How should he put this?

"Hot. I get it. You were probably thinking with your dick," she said, and Ethan had to laugh. "How long after graduation were you guys together?"

"We broke up that night."

"No way." Sophie lowered her feet to the floorboard. "There was that big party at what's his name's house."

"Justin."

She'd turned in her seat so she was facing him. "What happened with Ashley?"

"She had one of her tantrums because I complimented her friend Shannon."

"Huh. I always thought they were BFFs."

"So did everyone else, including Shannon."

"Ashley didn't break it off, though. She was too crazy about you." It wasn't a question, but Sophie was obviously waiting for an answer.

He stretched his neck to the side to loosen a kink. "I couldn't take it anymore. She was a little drunk at the party and tried to use it as an excuse, but I knew that was bullshit. Like you said, I was thinking with the wrong body part."

"Wow. See? I was so far out of the loop I hadn't even heard about it. Had to be pretty big news."

"I don't know. I was so glad to be done with school I stayed out of the loop myself."

"Why? You must've had decent grades, since you weren't on the need-a-tutor list like most of the jocks."

"I never really considered myself a jock."

"Yeah, you kind of were. You and the quarterback were the two hottest guys in school."

"Says you."

"Said a whole locker room full of girls every friggin' day. It got pretty annoying."

"Glad I didn't know." He was straight-up serious. It would've been embarrassing. "Some of the guys I hung with thought you were hot."

She stayed quiet a long time, and then she turned back to face the windshield.

He swung his attention between her and the road. "What?"

"I don't understand why you feel the need to lie. I mean, yeah, if I think about those days too much, I can get cranky. But I'm good with my life."

"Do you know why Ashley and her posse destroyed your dress?"

"Because she'd worn the same one a week before I started at Wattsville. So?"

"That was enough to piss her off," he said. "But there was more to it. She overheard me telling the guys that you looked better in the dress. And two of them agreed."

"Why would you say something like that?"

"It was true." He saw lights up ahead and hoped it was Blackfoot Falls.

"You actually said that I looked better?"

"Swear to God."

Her laugh was nervous. "That's crazy. Ashley had the biggest boobs in school."

"Not all guys like big breasts, Sophie."

"You sure?"

Ethan smiled. "Yep, pretty sure I know what I'm talking about."

She stared at him in silence for almost a minute. Who knew what was going on in that head of hers? But it gave him time to recall last night, her standing there braless in a T-shirt while he'd been handcuffed to the bedpost. Sophie fell into the perfect category. He'd had a sample feel less than an hour ago and he was itching for more. His foot automatically pressed down on the gas.

They were getting closer to the lights.

Lord, please let this be Blackfoot Falls.

"I think I like you even more now," she said finally.

Considering that he hadn't gotten to know her in school, and it had been years since he'd laid eyes on her, it was odd how she already wasn't surprising him much. It was that comfort level and familiarity he'd been feeling with her. She wasn't flirty, and she didn't try to dress sexy, which was kind of sexy in itself.

"I had fantasies about you," she said. "When I was a kid."

"Uh, do I want to hear this?"

She adjusted the seat and leaned back. "After you rescued me, I felt really special. I mean, you even loaned me your jacket and told those girls to back off. And they did. Ashley and Shannon gave me the stink-eye, but that was it. Then I heard that you'd stepped in before. For other kids who'd been bullied. Like Arnie. So I knew I wasn't so special after all."

"I'd never gotten in between girls before."

"Really?"

"Nope. The rest of the guys thought I was nuts."

"You were brave. And noble."

More than the words themselves, the conviction in her voice made him feel like crap. "I hate bullies just about more than anything, but what I did had nothing to do with being noble." Guilt had played a big part. "Can we leave it alone?" he slipped in quickly when he saw by her body language she was ready to beat the issue to death.

"Okay." Sophie smiled. "Remember this moment. So you know I can be reasonable."

Ethan held in a laugh. "We're about two minutes from the inn. Have you eaten since breakfast?"

"No. You?"

He shook his head. "I guess we should get something in our bellies." Now that he thought about it, he was hungry. He just hadn't wanted to waste time eating. After they turned onto Main Street, he reached for her hand. "We can hit the diner, or pick up something to eat in the room."

"I vote for the second option," she said, lacing their fingers together.

"Sounds good. I want to shower first, though."

"I can pick up the food. And we should make it an early night, since we might have a lot of driving to do—"

He brought her hand up and kissed the back. "I think we can forget the early night."

"You're probably right," she said, her voice a husky whisper.

"I know I am." He resented having to release her because he needed both hands on the wheel. After he pulled up to the curb, he slid an arm behind her shoulders. He leaned in just as she turned her head.

"This is the diner," she said, and then turned back to him. "I thought—" She blinked, her confused expression fading as she realized he'd been about to kiss her.

He brushed his lips across hers. "What did you think?"

"That you would shower while I got takeout."

"Or…" He zeroed in on that sweet spot at the pulse in her neck. "We could shower together," he whispered.

Her throaty moan hit him low in the belly. "Who needs food?" she murmured, turning to meet his lips.

Ethan felt her tongue slip into his mouth. She practically climbed over the console, which he was seriously tempted to rip out. People strolled down the sidewalk past the truck. Half of them probably rodeo fans, trying to peer through the darkened windows. What the hell was wrong with him? He should've driven them straight to the inn.

He promised himself he'd do just that, in a minute, probably two. Sophie tasted like heaven with a scoop of sin. Her heat filled the cab and fogged the windows. He wanted her so damn bad it was messing with his head.

From her pouty lips to her untamed hair and curvy body, they all did it for him. Those soft brown eyes, though, they got to him the most.

It had taken him months to blot out the image of her the day he'd slipped his jacket over her shoulders. She'd looked so small, her dress in tatters, but she hadn't cried or uttered a single mean word. She'd just looked up at him with so much trust and gratitude that he hadn't deserved. Afterward he'd nearly busted a hand punching his metal locker. Fixing the big dent he'd left had come out of his own pocket.

After that he'd avoided her as much as possible. Arnie had retrieved the jacket from her the next day. Once Ethan left for college the memory had started to fade and eventually disappeared.

When he realized his hand had slipped down to her breast, he tried to cool down the X-rated kiss. Sophie wasn't interested in complying, so he forced himself to pull back.

"What's wrong?" she asked, then jerked a look at the center console under her left knee. She sank back into her seat, ducked her head and swept a gaze down the sidewalk.

"Yep. Too many people around."

"Oh, jeez. Well, they don't know me, but most of them probably recognize you. Sorry."

"I'm not." He drew the pad of his thumb across her lips. They were puffier than usual. From the kissing. He wanted more of that. Leaning forward got him a firm hand to the front of his shoulder.

"We should go," she said, laughing. "As in right now. Before we get carried away again."

"Honey, we haven't even gotten warmed up yet." He turned the key. The engine made a god-awful grinding noise.

Heads turned. They both cringed.

Fine way to learn the truck had been idling all along.

He shook his head, and Sophie laughed.

The drive to the inn would take three minutes tops. He doubted he could make it.

11

SOPHIE GRABBED THE room key from him and unlocked the door. She laughed when she felt his hand mold to her backside, then quickly sobered and huffed. "What did I tell you? No touching until we're…"

He gave her ass a light squeeze and smiled.

Oh Lord. He wasn't listening, so why had she bothered? She practically shoved him inside the room before their neighbors from down the hall caught up with them.

"Wait. Okay? Just wait."

"Why?"

She turned away from him because she couldn't think straight while staring into his darkened blue eyes. But Ethan put his arms around her and pulled her back against his chest. There was no missing his very insistent erection. So avoiding his gaze wasn't working at all. She was beginning to think nothing would.

He kissed the side of her neck and then trailed his lips to the slope of her shoulder. She closed her eyes, wondering if he knew what he could do to her with only a look, a smile, a brush of his lips.

It was humbling to accept that she was defenseless when it came to Ethan. In the past five years she'd made progress. She could honestly say she hadn't thought about him much. She'd stopped monitoring his standing with the tour. If a rodeo was televised, she'd sometimes watched him. But she hadn't gone out of her way.

But after only twenty-four hours in his company, she could no longer deny the cold, hard truth. Once an addict, always an addict. And when this was all over, and she and Ethan again went their separate ways... Well, God help her. The road to recovery was going to be infinitely harder this time.

With a sigh, she pushed aside the silly notion that she could save herself some pain by walking away now. No chance of that happening.

She turned around in his arms and pulled on the front of his Western-cut shirt. The snaps came apart easily. He yanked her top up and over her head. Her peach-colored bra distracted him while she pushed his shirt open, exposing well-developed pecs.

He slipped the bra strap off her shoulder, then bent his head to kiss the narrow strip of skin he'd uncovered. The light touch of his lips on flesh that had never been sensitive before almost sent her through the roof.

She went for his belt buckle and he reached behind to unclasp her bra, which he seemed determined to get rid of. Except she was equally interested in unzipping his jeans. Their arms momentarily tangled. Then it became a free-for-all with shirts, boots and socks flying everywhere.

Sophie couldn't contain her laughter, intensified by Ethan's impatient battle with her snug jeans. He was still wearing his Wranglers and wouldn't let her near the zipper while he struggled to get her jeans down, making it only as far as her hips.

"Peel, don't pull," she said, then yelped when he picked her up and dumped her on the bed.

His piercing gaze took her in, starting with her hair and eyes, before locking on her breasts. "You're perfect," he whispered, the gravel in his voice a turn-on all by itself.

"Take off your jeans," she said, her eyes feasting on his strong chest and muscled shoulders, on the flexing and release of his pecs. His skin was still tanned, no sleeve lines, nothing along his low-riding waistband, which made her wonder about a whole bunch of things. Like what she was going to find under those jeans. "Please."

He leaned over and touched his tongue to her left nipple. The light contact sent warm pleasure flowing through her body. His mouth was hot, and so was the hand he used to cup her other breast. So she didn't understand why she was shivering. Or why she couldn't seem to stop.

Ethan took the hard tip into his mouth and gently sucked while he eased the jeans down to her thighs. She put a hand on his shoulder, and with the other she strained to reach his zipper. He intercepted her, using less effort than it took to swat a fly.

But he got the message to hurry it up. In seconds he'd pulled off her jeans, leaving her in skimpy peach panties that seemed to fascinate him. She sat up, but he gently forced her back down and put his mouth on the tiny triangle of silk. His warm breath breached the material and sparked a fire inside her.

"Dammit, you're killing me," she murmured, afraid she was going to have the quickest orgasm in history.

He lifted his head. "I didn't want to rush you," he said, and slipped a finger under the material. With a sharp intake of breath, he pushed his finger intimately between her lips. "Jesus, you're wet."

His patience evaporated, replaced by a fevered haste. He stripped off her panties, dropped them right there on the floor and scooped her into his arms.

Startled, she hung on to his neck. "Where are—"

They reached the bathroom. The very small bathroom with its tiny shower. He set her on her feet and turned on the water.

"I don't know about this," she said. "It's going to be a tight squeeze."

"Luckily I'm very good at that."

Sophie looked at him and laughed. He held a hand under the spray, the other one rested on the curve of her butt and in his eyes, amusement and pure want warred for dominance.

He slipped his arm around her waist, pulled her against him and kissed her. "The water's warm," he murmured against her lips.

"Are you planning to shower with your jeans on?"

"Nope." His kiss was slow and thorough, and with her breasts pushing against his bare chest, she was never going to stop shivering. He broke the kiss. "You're going to get under this warm spray while I take off my jeans."

"Hurry, or I'll use up all the hot water." She stepped inside the narrow stall. It was almost too small for two people. They'd have to be careful—

Sophie found the soap and turned to see if Ethan was getting out of his jeans. He'd unzipped them but was just standing there watching her. It was startling. She'd never been watched like this before, and her first instinct was to yank the shower curtain closed all the way. But it was made of clear plastic, and this was Ethan. It was kind of hot knowing those hooded eyes were focused completely on her.

She rubbed the soap between her breasts and tipped her head back as she slid the bar up to her throat, taking her time and working up a lather. With her free hand she followed the suds sliding down her body, then cupped the white foam and brought it to her breast. She lingered on her nipples, plucking at the stiff peaks with her thumb and forefinger, before soaping around them.

It was easy to sneak a look at him. He sure wasn't staring at her eyes. Never in her life had she been happier that she took working out seriously. Her body was by no means perfect, but she was in good shape, especially considering her weakness for dark chocolate.

Ethan had pushed down the Wranglers, but he'd made it only to his hips. She knew the brand was one of his sponsors, and oh Lord, if they advertised with a picture of him right now, the company would sell out of jeans into the next millennium.

Their problem, not hers. She needed to give him a reason to speed things along. Slowly she turned around and used both hands to soap her butt and the back of her thighs before "dropping" the bar of soap.

Oops.

She bent all the way over until she could flatten her palms on the shower floor, knowing exactly what she was putting on display for him. Before she had a chance to straighten she heard the curtain being yanked across the rod.

Dammit. She'd wanted to get a good look at him before he—

His large hands settled on the curve of her hips. His erection slid up against her butt as he bent forward to kiss the middle of her back.

"You're driving me crazy," he practically growled the words, and removed his hand only to aim the intrusive shower spray toward the wall.

As she rose he banded an arm around her lower ribs, pulling her against him and kneading her left breast, tugging gently at her nipple. She felt his hot breath at the

side of her neck, and then the slightly rough texture of his
tongue, the scrape of his teeth on her skin.

She reached behind, trying in vain to touch him. But
he held her body so tight to his she doubted a breeze could
sneak in between them. Turned out the stall had room to
spare.

"Do you even know how much I want you, Sophie?"
he whispered hoarsely. "I've thought about this all day."

She hoped he'd pinch her soon. Just so she'd know this
was real. That she wasn't having one of her adolescent
fantasies.

No, she couldn't have come up with this scenario as a
teenager.

When she tried to turn around, he wouldn't cooperate. His mouth went from her neck to her shoulder and
his hand switched to kneading her other breast. But when
she forced the issue, he loosened his hold. She whirled
around to face him. And made herself dizzy. She laughed
and swayed against him.

Holy crap, he was hard.

She had to look.

He seemed to know what she wanted and even took a
step back for her. But he didn't release her arms. Good
thing. If he hadn't been holding her up, she would've gone
straight down to her knees.

God, he was beautiful. His tan ended about three inches
below his belly button. She put her hand out to touch him.

Ethan dropped to a crouch. Apparently he had something else in mind. She gasped at the first intimate brush
of his tongue. He parted her sensitive flesh and she slapped
a palm against the tile for support. His tongue was sure
and pointed, using just the right amount of pressure, circling the spot where she wanted it most. He dipped in for a

quick second, just long enough to convince her that dying of bliss wouldn't be so terrible.

His leisurely and confusing retreat turned her thoughts to *his* possible demise instead.

And then he was kissing and licking the soft skin of her inner thigh and he was somewhat forgiven.

He slipped two fingers deep inside her, and she clenched her inner muscles for all she was worth. Her stranglehold on his fingers had him moaning and cursing under his breath.

As soon as she released him he pushed to his feet. "Jesus, Sophie," he murmured, the rasp in his voice making her skin tingle.

He took her face in his hands and claimed her mouth. Thrusting his tongue between her lips, he probed deep inside, stroking her tongue, circling it and keeping her off balance with the heady dance.

He lowered his palms to her breasts. They'd been aching, waiting for his touch, though she hadn't known it until he closed his hands over them. Her head and body swam with so many shimmering sensations that she almost missed her chance.

Finally the path was clear. She curled trembling fingers around his hard, pulsing erection. The smooth taut skin was hot to the touch.

His breath caught in her mouth. His whole body tensed. She fully expected him to shove her hand aside, and damned if she would let that happen. She stroked upward, adjusting her grip in harmony with the urgency of his moans.

He didn't try to stop her. His hips moved in a slight thrust against her palm before he went still. She slid her hand to the base of his cock, hoping to break through the tight control he was struggling to maintain. Not very nice of her, considering that she was fighting the same battle herself. They were both dangerously close to the edge.

And she wanted to push him over first.

"We should switch to cold water," he said, partly laughing, mostly groaning.

"Don't you dare." She shivered just thinking about it.

"I'll keep you warm, honey," Ethan whispered close to her ear, and released her breasts. His hands slipped around and over her bottom and firmly pulled her against him.

She lost her grip, the damn sneak. "Hey, no fair cutting short my playtime."

"Tough," he murmured, his lips and teeth doing amazing things to the curve of her neck.

Somehow he'd managed to take the soap from her. Or maybe she'd dropped it. Things were starting to blur. With a wicked smile, he slid the soap between her breasts, then over her ribs, down to her belly. She snatched the small bar from him. His hand just kept heading south until it slipped between her thighs.

"You're a devil."

His gaze locked on her face, Ethan wiggled his fingers.

Sophie bit her lip, moved a little to the left and gasped. "If I have heart failure, it's your fault."

"I'll take full responsibility." He leaned back to look down at her breasts, the tips flushed to a deep rose. Lowering his chin, he tried to catch a nipple with his mouth, but there wasn't enough room to maneuver. He sighed. "I hate this shower."

"I know." She smiled at his grouchy expression, then got up on her toes and kissed him. It wasn't a long kiss or especially sexy, but his attitude quickly shifted to enthusiastic. She dragged her mouth from his and reached behind him to give his rock-hard backside a light smack. "Turn around so I can get your back."

Wrapping her in his arms, he lifted her off the shower floor.

"Hey," she said with a muffled giggle. "What are you doing?"

"Hang on." He redistributed her weight and lifted her higher. A little nudge from him and she locked her legs around his waist. Her arms circled his neck. "You should be able to reach my back from there," he murmured, his stubbled chin lightly scraping the tender skin above her breasts.

Even if she stretched she'd only be able to reach his shoulder blades. "Um, pretty sure there's an easier way." As good as his trailing lips felt, she was kind of anxious to trade the cramped shower for the queen-size bed…

She gasped at the unexpected brush against her clit.

Oh hell, the bed would still be there.

Another fleeting touch and her body jerked, then quickly settled, hoping…no, begging for more. Begging for Ethan. She tightened her thighs around him and the pressure increased.

It was his thumb. Right? Had to be his thumb, she thought, her speeding pulse in obvious disagreement.

With each tiny movement she felt more pressure build. Heat swept off his body in great waves. Calloused fingertips dug into her butt while his palms supported her, shifting her higher when she started to sag…

Oh God, it wasn't his thumb.

She dropped the soap and clutched his shoulders.

"Don't worry," he whispered. "I won't enter you without a condom."

She just nodded, barely managing to do that. The weak shower spray glanced off the tile and hit her hair and the side of her face. She'd put herself there by moving her hips, seeking his touch. And now her hair was completely wet, yet her mouth was so dry she had to moisten her lips.

He watched the swipe of her tongue, his eyes black with desire and torment, but he kept moving, rubbing the swollen head of his penis over her clit. He was doing this for her. And she loved the hot feel of him. But God, how she wished she could sink down, let him fill her to the brink. This was torture. Mostly for him, she imagined.

"Put me down, Ethan," she said, her hand sliding off his shoulder and pausing at his bulging biceps.

"Am I not hitting you right?" he asked, repositioning both of them and rocking her against his erection. The friction made her breath catch. "Is this better?"

"The only thing better would be you inside me." She kissed him. Hard and fast. Before they got distracted again.

His lids lowered to half-mast as he lifted a hand to her face. The arm still anchored around her waist kept her suspended while he exacted a more satisfying kiss.

She wasn't that light, either. She pulled back. "Jesus, you're going to hurt yourself."

He smiled. "I bet you aren't even a hundred pounds."

"That would be a horrible bet."

Somehow he'd found another way to rub her clit, the pressure lasting until her feet hit the floor. She raised her eyebrows at him. "One for the road," she said, and then blushed like crazy. She didn't even know why.

She tried to laugh it off and would've escaped him if she hadn't tangled with the stupid shower curtain. One thing she both loved and hated about Ethan was that penetrating gaze of his. He seemed to be constantly watching her, mostly in a good way. Like when they were making out, it was nice to know he was fully engaged. But if she was being sneaky or wanted to slide something by him, forget it.

Turned out she needn't have worried. Ethan finished

washing up while she dried herself and blotted some of the
moisture from her hair. She thought about turning down
the covers but she wanted that perfect view of him that
she'd been cheated out of earlier.

With her damp towel wrapped around her, she waited
for him to turn off the water and push back the shower curtain. He shook back his wet hair and smiled at the dry towel
she held up for him. The light hit him just right. Drops of
water glistened on his bronzed skin. His erection had gone
down some. Such a pity. Although there was still enough
heft there to make her happy.

"Where did you get the tan, cowboy?"

"Mending fences."

"You lie."

"What? You think all I do is ride bulls and pimp products? I have a ranch to take care of."

"Really?" Why didn't she know about that?

"Yes, ma'am, I do. You gonna bring me that towel?"

"Nope. Come and get it."

"All right," he said, stepping out of the stall. "But you
can bet that sweet little bottom of yours I'm coming for
more than that."

"Bring it."

A second later it was *her* towel wrapped around *his*
hips, a smug grin curving his mouth. He used the other
towel to dry his hair and chest while he gave her a leisurely once-over.

Well, duh. He had lightning reflexes. Terribly stupid
thing for her to forget.

She felt like an idiot standing there naked and trying to
hide the goods with her hands over her breasts, her bent leg
angled over the other thigh barely covering the short landing strip from her last waxing. Ridiculous, considering that

she'd given him a show through the shower curtain. She probably looked like a damn cartoon character.

Ethan wasn't laughing, though. The feral intensity of his eyes had her on the move.

"Watch it," she said, backing out of the bathroom. "The handcuffs are ready and waiting…"

Sophie froze.

Oh, shit.

She looked at him, her eyes wide.

He stopped in the doorway, staring back at her, realizing the same thing.

They both turned and looked at the gleaming metal cuffs dangling from the bedpost. The bed had been made. The whole room had been picked up.

"Oh God," Sophie groaned.

Ethan choked out a laugh.

"I'm glad my name isn't on the register," she muttered.

"Yeah, thanks." He caught her hand. "How about you make it up to me?" The towel fell from his hips before he pulled her close, chest to chest, thighs to thighs, skin to breathtaking skin.

12

ETHAN SKIMMED A HAND down Sophie's back and she pressed her body closer to his, as if they hadn't already melded together. She liked touching him. Not in just a sexual way. It was the smooth, firm texture of his skin that felt so good under her fingertips, the ridges of lean muscle absent of bulk that allowed him to move with grace. He truly was a gorgeous man.

"What's that smile for?" Without waiting for an answer he kissed her.

He didn't rush, even as his arousal grew harder and thicker. His lips moved over hers at a leisurely pace. How many times had they kissed already? And yet he was nibbling and tasting as though he were learning her mouth for the first time. Her breasts were tight and beginning to ache. He might've sensed her waning patience, or lost some of his own. Sliding his hands to her hips, he moved her back toward the bed.

She crawled in between the sheets first, and Ethan, his hand on her ass, slid in right behind her.

"We used the same soap," he said, cupping her breasts and squeezing gently. "Why do you smell so good?"

"You do, too."

"Not the same." He rolled his tongue over her nipple, pulled back to study it, then plucked at it with his lips. At the same time he rubbed his thumb across the other one, over and over, until she was ready to scream.

"What are you doing?"

He lifted his head and did a quick check. "Watching them darken," he said with a self-satisfied smile.

Before she could even blink he'd spread her legs and wedged himself between them. Propping himself on both elbows, he got into a position that put his mouth over her chest. He kissed each nipple, then cupped the sides of her breasts, pushing them together and sucking both nipples at the same time.

She wasn't quite busty enough to make the task easy. But he managed to send her back into an arch as she clawed at his arm.

"Your nipples are hypersensitive," he murmured, looking at her face and kissing one tip very gently. "Am I sucking too hard?"

"No. They usually aren't this sensitive. But what you were doing— It's perfect. All of it."

He used his tongue to swirl and soothe, and then reached over her, putting his chest just above her nose. She surged up and licked his flat brown nipple. He jerked, managed to grab the pillow he was after and tucked it next to her hip.

"For that," he said, dropping back down to his elbows and shifting so that his mouth was closer to her belly, "I will show no mercy."

With her legs still spread, she couldn't be in a more vulnerable position. Or be more excited about what was sure to come. Well, besides her.

Ethan moved down a few more inches and kissed inside each thigh before lifting his head. "What? No 'bring it'?"

Sophie frowned. She had no idea what he was talking—

Oh, right. "Yes," she murmured, already out of breath, her brain misfiring. "Do that."

He smiled, but courteously didn't laugh. He tapped her hip so she'd lift her butt, and he slid the pillow underneath her. Reaching behind her head, she centered and plumped the pillow supporting her neck. She wanted to watch.

Their gazes met.

Ethan dipped his chin. She felt the long, flat swipe of his moist tongue against the seam of her lips. Her insides clenched, and her lids drooped.

"Open your eyes, Sophie," he said softly, and took another long, slow lick.

She tried not to whimper. Even when he parted her and slid his tongue along her sex. But then he used his fingers, too, and the steamy blend of sensations elicited a moan from her that could've been made by an animal in the wild.

She clutched at his shoulder, at the sheets, and finally caught a handful of his hair. His answer was to slip his hands beneath her butt and pull her more firmly against his mouth. His fingers went right back to work, plunging in so deep she couldn't breathe. And he refused to stop.

"Ethan?" She tugged on his hair. "Condom. Now."

He lightly sucked her clit.

Sophie exploded.

Her orgasm rocked the bed, shook the entire room. Maybe the whole building. Closing her eyes, opening them, it didn't matter. She couldn't see. Cold one second, and hot the next. Trying to drag air into her lungs, she wiggled and squirmed and whimpered. She pulled Ethan's hair and shoved at his shoulder until he finally eased up.

"Shh," he whispered close to her ear. He was lying beside her, propped on one elbow and petting her hair.

"What?" she mumbled. When had he moved up? "Was I loud?"

He smiled and kissed her mouth.

Able to taste herself on his lips, she shuddered.

Coming from the hall outside the room she heard receding laughter.

Reality heralded its rude reentry. "Oh God." She was never loud. Or this breathless. Or still this warm and tingly. "On a scale of one to ten?" she asked, cringing. "Ten meaning I didn't need a mic."

Ethan didn't answer, but the grin he was trying to hold back told her a lot.

"Okay," she said, wrapping her hand around his erection. "Let's see you top that."

Two strokes and his head fell back.

She took the smooth, velvety head in her mouth, and his groan filled the room. She licked and sucked the crown and stroked the rest of him with her hand until his breathing grew ragged. His long fingers circled her wrist and he gently tugged her hand away. He already had a condom out. Wow, she really had missed a lot.

Ethan tore open the foil packet and sheathed himself. Slowly. Very slowly, his tortured expression hot as hell. He'd been ready for her a long time and close to climaxing himself. Yet he'd been patient and generous, making sure he'd taken care of her first. She hoped she didn't disappoint him. She wouldn't orgasm just with him inside her. Long ago she'd given up on the elusive G-spot. The damn thing was a myth, and no one could convince her otherwise.

She pressed her lips to his shoulder. He seemed surprised when she swung a leg over his hips to straddle him. Surprised, but not displeased. He stacked a second pillow behind his head and then held on to her hips as she sank onto him.

Every millimeter sent new waves of bliss shooting

straight to her pleasure centers. She slowed down, just until she could inhale once more before she died.

Before she knew it, he pulled her up, then flipped her over, sliding his knee between hers and settling in with a kiss that was so hot it left her breathless.

"What was that?" she asked. "Are you okay?"

He smiled as he nodded. "I didn't want to come too fast."

"Oh. Well, I was kind of hoping this part of the evening would include you. Inside me."

"Ah, so you didn't want to just chat, hmm?"

"I—" She closed her mouth, tilted her head and said, "No. In fact, if you don't do something right now, I'll—"

"You'll what?"

"Ethan. I swear to God…"

He raised his right eyebrow as he lifted both of her knees to his shoulders.

She waited, watched as he pressed a kiss on each nipple. Then, with the control of a man who rode bulls for a living, he entered her. In one swift, sure move.

"Holy mother of—" Sophie put her arms over her head and braced herself on the headboard.

"Okay?"

"Quit talking. And don't hold back."

With a feral growl he thrust again. Only this time he changed the angle just a bit. She moaned, and when he started to pull back, Sophie squeezed his cock.

"Sorry," she said, when it sounded as though she'd hurt him. "Are you all right?"

"On a tightrope here. Real tight."

"Wouldn't hurt you to fall," she said, touching his hair with one hand.

"Not yet." He shifted his angle once more. Higher than she was used to, and when he pushed in again, she cried out.

This was different. She had to rethink the whole G-spot issue. Damn, Ethan had found it.

He thrust again. And she let out a scream.

Again.

Another scream.

God, they were so going to get kicked out. But she didn't want him to stop. It was the sweetest torture she'd ever endured. She'd given up trying to keep her eyes open.

One more thrust and then...

Her whole back arched and she came so hard things turned a little gray, shifted upside down, started spinning. They both hit their final shudders within seconds of each other. She'd always known Ethan was a drug, and he'd just proven it.

It took a while to catch her breath, and Ethan, too, but he still managed to lower her legs. When her heart rate slowed to about a hundred beats per minute, she shifted and he tossed himself to the left side of the bed. Good thing he had a lot of practice on his dismounts.

Thinking how loud she'd been, she pressed a hand to her warm cheek. "I can never come back to this town, can I?"

"Nope," he said, and they both laughed.

ETHAN ROLLED ONTO his back and tucked her against his hard, languid body. They sure hadn't needed the heater tonight. His skin was warm from exertion and downright hot in some places. Places that happened to be some of Sophie's favorites. In fact, she was pretty toasty herself.

She barely had the energy to glance at the clock. It was two-thirty and they'd just finished making love for the second time. They'd managed to sleep for a couple of hours before that, but then Ethan had gotten frisky again and she'd been more than happy to oblige him.

And the thing with Ethan—a very admirable, wonderful thing—there was no rushing him when it came to sex. He liked taking his time, trying different angles, milking every last drop of pleasure out of her. Now that she knew she could orgasm without manual stimulation, she wanted to do it every time. She really had to give him props for being the most patient lover ever. Although she'd been with only three other guys and they'd been just okay.

Drowsy and sated, her cheek pressed to his chest, she traced a circle around his belly button, wondering if he'd been like this as a teenager. Probably not. But if he had, good thing she hadn't slept with him. A bar set that high first time around…she would've been destined for disappointment.

"Sleepy?" he asked, idly rubbing her back.

"Why?"

Ethan laughed. "Don't worry. I'm not going to ravish you again so soon."

"Ravish? Is that what you said?"

"Too many syllables for you?"

"Ha." She stifled a yawn. "Probably." Not just sleepy, but exhausted. Yet she was unwilling to give up a single minute with him. Tomorrow they'd have twelve hours together on the drive back to Wyoming, if one or the other wasn't snoozing. "Tell me about your ranch."

"Ah yes. The ranch," he said with a quiet chuckle. "I wondered when you'd bring it up."

"Meaning?"

"I'm busted."

"What?" She brought her head up. "You lied?"

"Technically, no. I own five hundred acres over in Carver County. Including a dilapidated barn and a two-room cabin that were on the property when I bought it."

"You live there?"

"Hell no. I'm a cowboy through and through, but I like

my modern comforts. And describing the place as rustic is putting it way too nicely." He shrugged. "Someday I'll build a house. I don't know—maybe next year."

She hated that he'd tensed, though she didn't know why. He'd been living on the road most of his adult life. Maybe the idea of putting down roots made him nervous. "So, would you raise cattle? Breed horses?"

"Don't ever cut your hair." He pushed his fingers through the thick wavy mass, stopping at a tangle and working some magic that quickly loosened it.

"I hate my hair. I always have." She'd made peace and given up on it. "At least with it long I can pull it back."

"How can you hate this?" he asked, fisting a handful and holding it up before slowly letting the locks fall over her shoulder and onto his chest.

"It's frizzy and wavy and yuck."

He shook his head. "Soft and sweet—" he tugged on a curl and smiling at it "—and very sexy."

"Too many concussions," she murmured, not knowing what else to say. Joking was her go-to when she was embarrassed. Or she'd escape through sarcasm, but she was working on that particular shortcoming.

"You know Matt's arena?"

Sophie nodded, curious and confused. He was still preoccupied with her hair, but his tone had changed.

"After I build the house, I'm going to put up something similar. Probably not quite as big, but I'll leave room to expand. And I'll have to do something about the barn. Hell, it may have to be torn down and built from scratch. Then there's the stable, and after that the corrals, more fencing. I've got a lot of work ahead of me."

"Are you going to do most of it yourself?"

"If I wanted to live in a lean-to, sure." He laughed. "I can handle the corrals and fences, but that's about it."

"Okay." She was still processing the information. "Building an arena means you're going to have rodeos?"

"Not the kind you're thinking of." He stretched his back and neck, but his jaw was clamped tight as he stared up at the ceiling. "I want to open a kids' rodeo camp."

"Oh, like your parents have."

"That's not what they do. For one thing, they cater to adults and it's strictly for profit." He glanced at her. "Nothing wrong with that. It's a business. And mine will be, too. I'll charge a fee. But I won't turn away a deserving kid just because his parents don't have the money or he's not athletic. The goal is to help the kids with self-esteem. Let them come into themselves at their own pace."

"Wow, Ethan." She pushed up to look at him full on. "That's terrific."

"Yeah?" Some of the tension seemed to melt from his jaw and shoulders. "You think so?"

"Are you kidding? That is so awesome." She meant it with all her heart. For a guy like Ethan, who had money, good looks and skills that most men could only dream about, it was amazing that he understood not everyone was handed a life wrapped with a pretty bow. "I'm so excited for you."

"I can tell." He was grinning when he leaned over to kiss her. "Somehow I knew you'd understand."

"Well, of course I do. I was the one who got picked on, remember?" She placed a palm on his chest, right over his big wonderful heart.

"You weren't bullied a lot, were you? You seemed like a pretty confident kid."

"If I kept to myself, then no, I wasn't bothered much. But basically, a smart kid thrown into a new school isn't generally well liked."

"I'm sorry, Sophie." He covered the hand she'd put on his chest and squeezed before he kissed her fingertips.

"Okay, what you just did?" She snuggled against him. "Made it all worth it."

"I'm serious," he said quietly.

"Me, too." She shrugged. "I spent a lot of time in my own head. Only-child syndrome, I guess. Plus, before my dad left my mom and me, he hadn't been around all that much."

"What do you mean by *left*? He just walked out on you?"

"He worked in construction and jumped around for different jobs while my mom and I stayed in Idaho. And then he met a woman—a waitress working at a diner, I think. Anyway, he came home to pick up his things and that was that."

"Jesus, what an ass."

"Oh, I had a much stronger word for him," she said with a wry grin. "Once Mom and I moved to Wattsville to be near my aunt and her family, things were better." Sophie sat up to look into his eyes. "If there's ever a single-parent kid who wants to go to your camp but doesn't have the money, you have to take him or her in, okay? Promise me."

He tucked a lock of her hair behind her ear and smiled. "I promise."

She nodded, satisfied that he'd keep his word. "Are you thinking of a day camp, or more like a summer thing where you board the kids?"

"I haven't decided for sure, but I imagine it'll end up being both. I'd prefer to have the kids for six weeks at a time, but that means we'd open only for the summer."

"That's kind of too bad." Sophie thought for a moment. "You know, lots of schools are open year-round now. I'd have to check, but I think that means they have three weeks off between sessions."

"I hadn't thought of that. Three weeks at a time isn't bad." His brow furrowed in thought, he stared off and absently rubbed her arm. "So maybe I could offer different programs for three weeks or six weeks and put something together in the afternoons for the local kids."

Her hand still rested on his chest and she liked feeling his heartbeat accelerate with his excitement. "Anyway, you have a lot of time to mull over all your options."

He looked at her, his mouth curving in a peculiar smile. "Between you and me, I've already hired a contractor. He's drawing up plans for me to look at after the finals."

"Ethan! That's so terrific."

"You can't say anything. No one else knows."

"Not even your parents?"

"Especially not them." He sighed, looking as if he regretted the remark. "It's nothing. Just another story in itself."

"Want to hear something I've never told anyone?" She lowered her hand to his belly. Not on purpose, but now it seemed he might be interested in something other than what she wanted to share.

"What's that?" he asked, moving her hand up a few inches.

"It's kind of weird, but I've thought about doing something with kids, too. Not on such a grand scale as what you have in mind. I don't have that kind of money, but just a small no-frills martial arts studio. I didn't take up kickboxing and tae kwon do until my first year of college but getting physical and learning discipline made a big difference in my life. I know a couple of qualified people who would volunteer to help teach the kids."

Ethan was silent for a few moments. "I can see how that changed things for you," he said, his slight frown confusing her. "And don't get me wrong, I think it's great you want to give back. But I still don't get why you're not doing something more challenging. I mean, now that I know you're not even from the area, I can't figure out why you'd stick around."

"You sound like my cousin." Sophie sighed. "I told you about my dad, who I don't see and don't care to see ever again. And my mom is a perfectly nice woman who also happens to be clueless. If I were to tell her I was leaving for the moon tomorrow, she would say what she always does, 'That's nice, dear.'" Sophie saw his left eyebrow shoot up. "Seriously. I like being around family. My aunt and uncle, my cousins...we all do stuff on holidays, and if somebody's car is in the shop, we help out.

"I know, it sounds corny. Whatever." She leaned into him while her hand reclaimed those few inches of warm belly. "Who knows? Now that I've gotten you out of my system, maybe I can move on to bigger things."

She felt him tense. Not just his chest and stomach but his whole body seemed to tighten. He should be relieved that she had no expectations beyond this weekend, but instead he looked annoyed.

"We have a long drive tomorrow. You should get some more sleep," she said, and pulled her hand away.

He caught it and peeled open her fingers. "Later," he said, and put her hand back on his lower belly.

13

SOPHIE CRANED HER NECK to see inside the arena. Now that she finally had some time alone, she'd phoned Lola. This was supposed to have been a quick call, but her cousin kept placing her on hold. "Is something wrong?"

"What do you mean?" Lola was rarely this curt. With others, yes, but usually not with Sophie. And here she'd called with good news. Lola sighed. "Sorry. It's that fight I had with Hawk. I think I told you about it—well, now he's being a goddamn baby and not taking my calls."

"Let him stew," Sophie suggested when she really wanted to say good riddance. "Stop calling him and he'll get worried and call you."

"Yeah, you're probably right. So, tell me again. You're at the rodeo now, but you think you'll be leaving in an hour?"

"Basically, yes. Ethan had hoped to be moved up on the schedule sooner, but there was a mix-up. We're still leaving earlier than we originally thought." Sophie waited. "You're quiet."

"Are you a hundred percent sure he isn't playing you?"

"Two hundred percent." A nasty remark about not mistaking Ethan for Hawk sat on the tip of Sophie's tongue. It was mean, so she pressed her lips together. "Do you want me to call you once we're on the road?"

"Are you driving straight through?"

"I don't know. It depends. We're both really tired." The last word had barely tripped off her tongue and she wanted to shoot herself. Eventually she'd tell Lola about Ethan, but not yet.

"Damn," Lola muttered, half to herself. "Hold on, would you?"

"I'll call you later," Sophie slipped in. Then she disconnected without knowing if Lola had heard. She wasn't about to wait around on hold for the umpteenth time and miss Ethan's ride.

She reentered the building, but instead of returning to her seat, she stood by the privacy fence close to the arena. A few buckle bunnies had made camp near the gate used by the riders and volunteers. In the looks department the women ranged from gorgeous to holy shit. And Sophie had overheard enough earlier to know that half the buckle bunnies here had come because of Ethan.

It made her smile to imagine their reaction over him choosing plain Jane her over any of them. There had been a time when she would've been beside herself with jealousy, crippled by self-doubt and mired in suspicion over his motives.

The suspicion part, that wasn't something to be ignored in her line of work. So yeah, she'd been wary at first, wondering if he was playing her. But the 200 percent she'd quoted Lola, that was real. Ethan was one of the good guys. Who just happened to be hot.

On the other hand, maybe she'd idealized him for so long she was being selective about what she wanted to see. He certainly was no monk, not that she expected him to be, but she wondered how difficult it was going to be for him to give up being a rodeo star. Being the guy all the women wanted. Having a slew of companies eager to give him money to endorse their products. Some of that would carry over into his post rodeo career. And it seemed as if his head was on straight enough he could separate his ego from all the nonsense.

But, again, was that what she wanted to see? And heaven help her, she couldn't discount last night. The most incredible, stupendous, holy-crap-I've-died-and-gone-to-heaven night of her entire life. Past and future. And screw anyone who said otherwise.

Ethan wanted to open a camp for kids to help with their self-esteem. Oh, for God's sake, he was just a little too perfect. Maybe she was being punked. Maybe a tiny camera had been hidden in the room. She'd see herself on some stupid reality show in two weeks. Lying next to him in bed, staring at him with big goo-goo eyes. And then she'd have to move to outer Mongolia. Sadly, last night would still have been worth it.

Sophie sighed so loudly the woman next to her turned to eye her. She hoped she wasn't going to be this same idiotic person for the rest of her twenties. So this was what happened after only three hours' sleep.

And in a few minutes Ethan, who'd had the same amount of sleep, would climb on top a two-thousand-pound bull that wanted to annihilate him.

Okay, now she was feeling nauseated.

She pressed a hand to her tummy and watched a young woman with long blond hair, tight jeans and killer boots walk up to the fence. The other buckle bunnies who'd staked their claim an hour ago turned to give her a sizing-up. She ignored them and called out to some of the bronc riders, who acknowledged her with waves. Popular girl.

The team roping event finally ended, and bull riding

was up next. Murmurs rose from the crowd. Fans were used to the bull riders being last. Sophie just wanted the whole thing to be over, period.

Her phone signaled an incoming text. It was from Peggy, Sophie's contact at the sheriff's office. Nothing had changed as far as the charges against Ethan went. And Sophie owed Peggy lunch at her favorite barbecue joint.

Sophie liked the older woman, so hanging out with her was always fun. Now, dinner with Craig, that she dreaded as much as a pap smear. She stared at her phone, trying to decide if it was time to suck it up and call him back.

Ethan's name being announced stole her attention. The signs held by fans shot up in the bleachers. She recognized a few from yesterday. The blonde newcomer let out an ear-piercing whistle, stomped one of her pricy boots and yelled, "Go get 'em, Styles."

His other female fans cast her looks of disdain. She either hadn't noticed or didn't care. Sophie ignored everyone and moved to a spot where she could see Ethan getting ready to be let out of the chute. Again without a helmet, since there hadn't been time to drive to Kalispell and back to buy one.

Today he was riding another bull and not Twister, so she was thankful for that. Although she'd missed the name of the brown bull that was giving him a fit. If Matt had found reason to call him something like the Devil's Spawn, she didn't want to know.

She saw Ethan give the nod for the gate, and then everything happened quickly. The instant the bull lunged from the chute and the clock started, Sophie began counting the seconds.

One thousand one, one thousand two...

The furious animal reared and bucked and did everything in its power to throw Ethan off its back.

One thousand five, one thousand six...

The bull whirled, then changed directions.

She closed her eyes. The crowd's roar had them popping back open.

Ethan was on the ground scrambling away from the monstrous animal. He made it clear of the dangerous hooves coming down like spiked sledgehammers and waved to the fans. The buzzer had gone off at seven and a half seconds. The announcer said something about the heartbreak score and lucky this wasn't the finals.

Sophie wasn't a violent person, but she really wanted to smack the man. He was safe from her. She couldn't move. Not until she was certain Ethan wasn't limping or holding his arm funny. He seemed fine as he left the arena, dusting off his hat and himself. Finally able to breathe again, she headed off to meet him in the back.

She recognized the husky Lone Wolf ranch hand who was acting as security guard and smiled at him when he opened the gate for her. She'd made it a few steps in when the blonde with the cute boots came barreling past her. The poor ranch hand tried to stop her, but the determined woman was too fast.

At the burst of commotion Ethan turned. With a shriek, the blonde jumped at him. He caught her, but unprepared, he staggered back.

"What the hell are you doing here?" Ethan set her down and gestured to the cowboy that it was okay.

Sophie wasn't quite sure what to do. Ethan's gaze had swept over her, so she knew he'd seen her. But his attention was directed at the other woman.

"I bet you're pissed. Damn. Half a second." The blonde shrugged. "At least it didn't count." She jerked a look toward the pen where another bull waited, cupped her hands around her mouth and yelled, "Hey, Matt, the place looks awesome."

Matt flashed her a smile, then went back to doing whatever he and another guy were doing to ready a scary-looking bull for the next rider.

Ethan scrubbed at his face and motioned for Sophie to join them. Nope, he wasn't a happy camper.

"So I was on my way to Vegas, and I thought what the hell…?" The woman paused when she noticed Sophie standing there. Her gaze swept from Sophie's hair to her boots. With a dismissive frown, the blonde turned back to Ethan. "I figured I'd zip up here and see how you were doing. Make sure you weren't laid up in the local hospital in traction or anything."

"Yeah, thanks." Ethan sighed.

Sophie wasn't feeling quite as charitable. The woman was much younger than Sophie initially thought, but that didn't excuse her stupidity.

Blondie grinned, then turned abruptly back to Sophie, staring at her as if she were an intruder. "Who are you?"

"If you'd shut up long enough," Ethan said, "I'd introduce you."

Something in his expression or tone spurred a sudden realization. "You must be Ethan's sister," Sophie said, noting a faint resemblance around the mouth and eyes. "Cara?"

She nodded and shook Sophie's outstretched hand.

"I'm Sophie," she said, and because Cara had the decency to look embarrassed, Sophie liked her better. "A friend of Ethan's."

"Sure, go ahead, introduce yourselves. You don't need me," he said, and Sophie gave him a private look that said otherwise.

She wanted more than anything to put her arms around

him, make sure nothing hurt and kiss him into tomorrow. But not with his sister watching.

Cara barely spared him a glance. "Sorry about before," she said, staring at Sophie with open curiosity. "Some of the buckle bunnies get too pushy and I try to run interference. The ladies seem to just looove my brother. I don't get it." She gave him a cheeky grin. "They don't know you like I do."

He was still grumpy. Probably overtired. And here they were supposed to hit the road right away.

Damn. It occurred to her that Cara showing up out of the blue could complicate things.

Sophie studied his face, the weariness around his eyes, the smudge at his left temple, the streak of grime on his chin. Everything else fell away. Nothing mattered as long as he was okay. She promised herself she would never let him stay up so late the night before a rodeo again.

That is, assuming she'd be in a position to carry out the promise.

He was staring back at her with those intense blue eyes, the corners of his mouth quirking up a bit.

"How are you?" she asked softly. "Everything in working order?"

His smile took over. "Come check for yourself."

Sophie hesitated. Silence doubled the awkwardness that fueled her uncertainty.

Cara must've felt it, too. She glanced around, then looked from Sophie to Ethan. "How do you guys know each other?"

"From high school," he said as he wiped the remaining dust from his face and moved to stand next to Sophie. "I want to have a few words with Matt…" He trailed off, leaving words unsaid, his gaze steady with hers. "Okay with you?"

"Of course." She knew he meant before they left, but he was reluctant to talk in front of Cara. That proved they had a problem.

When he moved in to kiss her, Sophie gave him her cheek. Clearly he didn't care for that one bit. He caught her chin and forced her to face him before he pressed his lips to hers.

"Okay, then," Cara muttered, glancing around again. "I'm gonna grab a hot dog. You guys want anything?"

Ethan might've responded in some way. Sophie hadn't said a word, but she saw that Cara was already headed for the gate.

Sophie raised her eyebrows at him.

"Look, before you rip me a new one, I kissed you because you looked as though you didn't know what to do in front of my sister." He shrugged and touched her arm. "And I figured it might get rid of Cara for a few minutes." He sighed. "Goddammit, I kissed you because I wanted to. Is that a problem?"

"No," she said. "Are you done?"

Ethan frowned. "Kissing you?"

A short laugh escaped her. "You know what? No more late nights." Sophie rolled her eyes at his instant grin. "I mean it. You could've gotten hurt today."

"Oh hell, I'm pumped so full of adrenaline before a ride I could go all night." His eyes lit and he ducked in to steal another kiss. "We should test that out."

Sophie laughed and pushed him away. "We kind of did last night."

"Let's go for two out of three."

"Come on, we have to get serious," she said, glancing over her shoulder and ignoring his murmured assurance that he was extremely serious. "I'm assuming Cara doesn't know about your little legal problem."

"No." That sobered him. "Definitely not and it's gonna stay that way."

"Okay, so—any idea why she's really here?"

"She has a friend who lives in Great Falls, maybe that's part of the reason." Ethan looked out toward the crowd, frowning. "It won't be easy getting out of here without kids wanting autographs."

Sophie groaned. "You couldn't have thought of that yesterday?"

"Did you?"

"Sorry. Guess I'm tired, too." She sniffed. "One of us didn't have that extra adrenaline boost."

He barked out a laugh. "You did okay without it."

Sophie tried to think of something clever, but settled for "Oh." And then of course she had to blush.

Ethan's gaze darkened. "Come on, baby," he murmured near her ear. "Don't make me hard. Not here."

Indignant, she drew back and stared. At his face. Nothing lower. "I didn't do anything."

His quiet groan sounded so damn sexy it vibrated all the way down her spine and pooled in the most inconvenient place. And then he had the nerve to look deep into her eyes and smile as if he knew exactly what he'd just done.

Wow, she'd have to figure out what had set him off. She'd definitely do it again. Later, though. She checked her watch. Right now they had to get out of Blackfoot Falls as soon as possible.

"Go sign a few autographs," she said. "You know you'll feel bad if you don't. And if you need to talk to Matt, just please be quick?"

Ethan shook his head. "I realized the timing is wrong. He's got too much on his plate until the rodeo is over. I'll call him tomorrow."

She saw him discreetly adjust the front of his jeans and she tried not to smile. "What about Cara?"

"I don't know. But she's headed back this way."

To make room for the other riders leaving the arena, Ethan and Sophie met Cara closer to the gate. Going beyond that would put them at the mercy of insistent fans. Sophie had really had no idea how much fan and media activity surrounded the riders. A minute ago she'd seen Cara get stopped for her autograph by two excited kids dressed like cowgirls.

"I just talked to Dad," Cara said after chewing a bite of hot dog. "I told him you're still in one piece. Nothing broken that I could see. He's still pissed at you, by the way."

Ethan shrugged. It seemed he couldn't care less about his father's disposition. Except Sophie saw his jaw clench long enough to tell a different tale.

"Mom and I just think you're crazy." She grinned, her eyes sparkling with mischief. "If I were you, bro, I'd be sitting in an isolation chamber until five minutes before the finals started."

"If you were me," Ethan said, "you'd have the good sense to keep your mouth shut." He turned to watch a rider lower himself onto a restless bull thrashing against the metal chute. "Matt has himself a good contender there with Tornado Alley. That sucker's gonna be a high scorer."

"I like Matt," Cara said, ignoring her brother's dismissal. "I always have, you know that. But I think it was shitty of him to ask you to ride this close to the finals."

"The benefit was planned for September. Something got screwed up. When he told me it got pushed back, I could've dropped out. So don't blame Matt."

"Well, that just makes you even more stupid." Cara tossed back her hair. "You get hurt between now and next weekend, and you'll regret it. I'm taking home my second buckle from Vegas this year. You know I will," she said with a nasty gleam in her eye. "And won't your little corner of the family trophy case look lonely?"

Sophie fumed. She pressed her lips together to keep from saying something sarcastic to the little twit. How could she treat her brother like that?

"Too bad you drove all this way to tell me something I already know, runt." Ethan ruffled her hair, which she obviously didn't like. "Why are you here?"

Cara smoothed back her hair. "I told you, to make sure you're in one piece and haven't done anything stupid. Well, stupider than this," she said, gesturing to nothing in particular. "Miss the finals again and you'll feel like a big loser."

"Wow." Sophie couldn't keep quiet a second longer. "I used to wonder what it would be like to have a brother or sister. If this is any example—" she shook her head "—I'm glad I don't have any siblings."

Cara glared at her, a deep red creeping up from her chest to her face.

Sophie tried not to glare back. She figured she'd said enough when Ethan put an arm around her and sighed.

"Cara didn't mean anything," he said. "Our family is competitive. And sometimes we egg each other on."

"Would you ever call Cara stupid and a loser? You can't tell me that doesn't hurt, Ethan." Sophie's voice cracked at the end. Ethan visibly swallowed, and she knew she'd struck a nerve. She lowered her lashes, thoroughly ashamed of her outburst. "I'm sorry. I shouldn't have said anything." She forced herself to look at Cara. "I really am sorry."

The woman's stricken expression made Sophie feel worse. "I wouldn't hurt my brother," Cara said, reverting to her bratty temperament with a contemptuous glare. The next second she deflated into a look of dismay. "Did I, Ethan? Did I hurt you?"

He left Sophie's side to ruffle Cara's hair again. "Hell, runt, you have to do a lot better than that to get under my skin."

He was lying, of course. And Sophie for one was glad he'd done so. For now, it was better that the tension eased.

"Quit messing up my hair," Cara said through gritted teeth. She made a show of smoothing back the long blond locks. Mostly, Sophie guessed, to hide the sheen of tears in her blue eyes. Sophie was right behind her in that department.

She glanced helplessly at Ethan.

He smiled and to Cara he said, "You still haven't told me why you're really here."

Cara dumped the rest of her hot dog in the trash can behind her. "I thought we could drive to Vegas together. But you already have company, so no problem."

"I'm going back to Wyoming first. I have some business to take care of in Casper tomorrow morning."

"Are you serious?" Her eyes widened. "You have to be in Vegas in four days."

"I know."

"Ethan..." She darted a look at Sophie, who wasn't about to say a word. "Can't your business wait? I mean, you don't want to cut it too close."

"No." Ethan inhaled deeply. "No, I don't. But I'll get to Vegas in time. No matter what it takes."

"I hope so," Cara said with a concerned frown.

Jitters flared in Sophie's tummy. She hoped so, too.

14

SOPHIE WASN'T THRILLED about leaving her Jeep behind, but it would be safe in Blackfoot Falls. The main thing worrying her as they drove toward Wyoming was Ethan's uncertain future. It was possible he'd have to fly to Vegas to get there in time. And it was also possible that he wouldn't make it to the finals at all. The thought made Sophie's stomach turn.

If that crazy Wendy Fullerton refused to drop the charges and Ethan ended up spending time in jail, not having a car would be the least of Sophie's worries.

Sophie adjusted the truck's air vents for the hundredth time. They were only five miles outside town. Maybe they should turn around and get the Jeep. The sensible thing was to follow Ethan to Wyoming. No, they were both too tired to drive separately.

"What's wrong?" Ethan took her hand. "You've been quiet and edgy. Are you still upset about Cara?"

"I'm mad at myself for butting in," Sophie admitted. "And I hope your sister doesn't hate me forever, but I'm okay. Just tired." She liked that he had twined their fingers together. "So are you. Don't forget I can take over driving anytime."

"Cara doesn't hate you. And she's really not a bad kid."

"I doubt she'd like being referred to as a kid," Sophie said. "She's only four years younger than me."

Ethan frowned. "Really? Only four years?"

"Technically, four and a half. But we women of a certain age have let that half thing go."

He smiled. "Cara can be a spoiled brat at times. That's for damn sure. And sometimes her teasing can get out of hand, but you have to understand, we were raised in a competitive environment."

"You mean, like riding in junior rodeos and stuff?"

"No. Well, yeah, we did some of that later on. But I'm talking about our parents and how they viewed childrearing. Always pushing us to succeed, to be the best. They can be fairly intense at times. I don't know that I agree with their method. I think using more praise would've been better, but I wanted to explain where Cara's coming from."

Sophie didn't dare say a word. She wouldn't dream of bad-mouthing his parents. But they sounded like bullies and they might've turned Cara into one. Lucky for Ethan, he'd taken the opposite path. No wonder as a teenager he'd championed the underdogs and misfits who'd been picked on. He'd understood what it was like to be bullied, though she doubted he saw it that way.

Her chest hurt suddenly. So much made sense now. His need to win that second title. Even the kids' camp he wanted to build. More than taking the opposite path, Ethan had turned out to be a really good man. Did his family value him for *that*? He did the right thing, and not the easy thing. Like riding for the Safe Haven Benefit even if it ended up costing him a trip to the finals.

"Did you fall asleep on me?" he asked, lightly squeezing her hand.

"No." She managed a small laugh. "I'm just thinking."

"Uh-oh. That doesn't always turn out so well."

"You got that right," she muttered, her brain beginning to speed ahead. "I have an idea." She forced herself to slow down. "First, may I totally butt into your life again?"

"So, now you're asking?"

"I'm being serious here," she said, looking at him.

He gave her a sober nod before turning back to the road and putting both hands on the wheel.

"I know you said your agent would find you an attorney, but it won't be quick enough." Sophie had done a brief search on the man. He was good, had an A-1 client list. Big sports names who made a lot of money. Like the football star he was currently tied up with. If push came to shove, Ethan wouldn't be the agent's priority. Not that she'd tell Ethan any of that. "I should call Craig."

"The La Maison guy?"

"Yes, but I promise that's not important. He's local and good. If there's a way to nip this thing, he'll figure it out. Next, Wendy Fullerton needs a wake-up call. She has to know, or at least believe, that you're willing to let the media have a field day with her accusation and the arrest, everything. Her husband may pull a lot of weight in Beatrice County, but you have fans across the country and a lot of other parts of the world."

"Jesus. I'm trying to keep it out of the media."

"She doesn't have to know that. And anyway, if the charge messes up your chance to go to the finals, you won't have any choice about what's reported." She saw his lips thin and she touched his arm. "I'm sorry, but that's the truth. And honestly I'm thinking it won't go that far. Even if it's a matter of getting a continuance."

Ethan gave a grudging nod.

Sophie took a deep breath. "Hell, if Wendy still refuses

to tell the truth, I can always tell the judge you were with me that night. I'll say you came over after you left the bar."

He slowly turned to her. "Forget it. I won't have you perjuring yourself for me."

"I know it's wrong, but so is what's happening to you. I'd just be canceling out Wendy's lie. Hey, what are you doing?"

He pulled the truck off the road, only there was no exit or turnout. And not all that much of a shoulder for anything other than an emergency.

Ethan left the engine idling and turned to her.

She twisted around to see if any cars were coming.

"We're fine," he said with a quick glance in the rear-view mirror. "I want you to know I understand how much it took for you to make that offer. And how much I appreciate your belief in me. But I would sit in jail for a year before I'd let you do that."

Sophie sighed.

He kissed her. "Thank you." He stroked her cheek and looked into her eyes for as long as he dared considering where they were parked. "I mean it, you're a special woman, Sophie."

She dropped her chin, embarrassed and a little sad. Feeling helpless wasn't one of her strengths. "Yeah, let's go before I end up a special pancake in the middle of the highway."

"I've been watching. You think I'd let anything happen to you?" he said as he got them back on the highway.

Oddly she truly believed that if it was within his power, he would do anything to keep her safe. Just as he'd done eleven years ago.

Somebody really needed to call Wendy and ask the lying cheat if she was prepared for a media circus. Not only would Wendy and Broderick Fullerton's names be dragged through the mud, but who knew how many guys might come out of the woodwork willing to tell the world Wendy had picked them up in bars, as well? Sounded like a good job for Ethan's agent.

Sophie was suddenly exhausted. All she wanted to do was stop thinking. About the past. About his sister's taunts. About how his parents had failed to appreciate what a terrific son they'd raised in spite of themselves. She needed to turn off her brain. Maybe take a nap. At least they were on their way back to Wyoming.

She'd laid her head back as soon as they were on the highway again, but the shutting-down-her-brain thing? It wasn't going to happen. She kept thinking over and over how this whole situation was so unfair on every level.

What if she was leading him back to the slaughter? He needed a top-notch lawyer, someone local who understood Fullerton's reach. With enough pull in the DA's office, Fullerton could be petty and have Ethan locked up long enough to miss the finals. Craig might be his best hope. "Ethan?" she said, and smiled at the hand he'd placed on hers. "We should get off at the next exit."

"Sure." He didn't ask why.

"We need to talk," she said, and stifled a yawn. Screw Wendy, screw his family, screw the unfairness of it all. "About turning around and going to Las Vegas. It's your call. Whatever you decide, I'm with you a hundred percent."

ETHAN LET HER SLEEP. It was already dark. They'd been driving for three hours and he knew she was exhausted. So was he, but not so much that he'd come up with the crazy idea to drive to Vegas.

Maybe he should've argued with her more. Or simply turned the truck around and headed back toward Wyoming after she'd fallen asleep. Hell, she'd made it clear that it was his career, his life, his decision.

It was weird because all along she'd been adamant about him showing up in court tomorrow, but now she seemed to think they could handle things— No, not they—he had to stop thinking of her as a partner in this nightmare. Not only was this his problem, but Sophie could get burned if things went sideways.

She had a lot of faith in this Craig guy, not him personally, but his legal skills. And she seemed confident that through him Ethan could take care of everything long-distance. Damn, he wished he knew what the favor would cost her. Beyond dinner at La Maison.

Ethan snorted. Like hell. He'd pay the hotshot attorney twice his fee before he'd let Sophie go on a date with Mr. Slick. What kind of man coerced a woman into going out with him by doing her a favor? For that reason alone, Ethan didn't like the guy. But Sophie had convinced him to get over himself, that his situation was too serious for him to be a dumb ass. Her exact words. They made him smile.

Sophie made him smile. A lot.

He saw their exit coming up. He hoped the motel he'd found on his iPhone was decent. In rural places like this part of Montana, you couldn't be too choosy. But if they continued on to Vegas as planned, they didn't have to rush. So no sense driving more than they had to tonight.

Once they arrived in Vegas, Sophie was going to be real happy with the suite he already had booked. He could almost hear her squeals when she saw the huge jetted tub. On second thought maybe he should find something off the strip. Damn, she could get loud when she came.

Almost on cue, she brought her head up and yawned just as he parked near the motel's ugly stucco office. He surveyed the row of mud-brown rooms. Damn place looked nothing like the website pictures.

"Where are we?" she asked after a second yawn.

"Some motel I found online. They exaggerated by a lot. We don't have to stay here."

She blinked at him. "Have you slept?"

Ethan laughed. "Not that I'm aware."

"Oh, right. You were driving." She gave him a sweet drowsy smile. "Neither of us should be driving, so this is fine. We're just going to sleep here."

"I hope not," he said, and opened his door.

She made a face at the overhead light.

"Stay here while I register." He quickly got out and closed the door so the light turned off.

The owner seemed keen on making small talk, but Ethan took care of business quickly and drove them to the room at the end. He found out their closest neighbor was two doors down. Just in case.

"It's not so bad," Sophie said, glancing around at the queen bed with a green-and-tan floral comforter that matched the curtains.

Ethan put their two bags in the closet. "Brace yourself, they even have a luggage rack."

"Oh my. Very fancy." She seemed to be waking up. "I want to see the bathroom. The size of the shower is the true test."

"Why?" He followed her inside and put his arms around her from behind. "What do you have in mind?"

"I don't even know what to call that color," she said, leaning back against him as they studied the ugly tile walls.

"Well," he said, deeply inhaling her sweet scent until he felt as if he'd had one beer too many. "The bathroom is bigger than the one at The Boarding House, and so is the shower."

"And everything is very clean."

"No bugs."

"Oh." Her gaze darted across the floor and she shifted her feet. "Why did you have to say that?"

He laughed. "Don't worry. I'll protect you."

"Yes, you will. I don't do bugs or mice."

He kept the straightest face he could. "Now, if the bed isn't lumpy or too soft—"

"And doesn't squeak."

He turned her to face him. "And since I have the most beautiful woman in all of Montana in my arms…"

"Right," she drawled with a mocking sigh, and glanced at the ceiling.

"Hey, you're talking about someone I happen to like very much. So knock it off."

Sophie blinked and blushed.

Ethan smiled and kissed her nose. Man, he liked it when she blushed. He didn't know why, but it got to him every time. "I'm thinking shower. Sex. Nap. More sex."

She was smiling up at him, her hands flat on his chest, her brown eyes sparkling. "Individual showers." He started to object and she pressed a silencing finger to his lips. "Only to save time."

He sucked her finger into his mouth.

She pressed closer. "This isn't working."

He released her finger. "Pardon me, ma'am. Please continue."

"Then sex."

"Now we're talking."

"Then sleep for as long as we can. If there's time when we wake up, then maybe…"

This wasn't what he'd expected at all. "You're serious?" He leaned back and searched her face. "This is, what…our third date and you're already cutting me off."

Sophie laughed. "Oh, sweetie, you think we've been dating?"

"Ah, that's right. You're just getting me out of your system." The remark had pissed him off and apparently he was still getting over it. Now wasn't the time to talk about it, though. He released her. "I'll take a shower first if you don't mind."

Staring at him, she nodded. She stepped around him to leave the bathroom, then looked back. "I was just teasing about the dating thing. I mean, I did handcuff you."

"I know." He smiled. "If you change your mind, you can shower with me."

"Actually I have to make a couple of calls."

He nodded, closed the door and turned the water on in the shower, but he didn't get in yet.

Looking in the mirror at the dark stubble shadowing his jaw, he thought about the past three days since he'd met up with Sophie again. Two days, three nights if he counted tonight. Jesus. Not long, but it felt like it. She was easy to be around, even when they disagreed. Or when things got prickly. His sister showing up, for instance.

He knew Sophie had gotten the wrong impression of his family. His parents weren't self-centered ogres. They did what they thought was best. But since when did he give a shit whether a woman he was involved with liked his family? That right there was the problem. He was feeling things that he probably shouldn't.

He pulled off his boots and unsnapped his shirt. Normally he'd wait and shave in the morning, but he wouldn't do that to Sophie. He opened the door and saw her sitting on the bed, talking on her cell.

She looked up in surprise but then smiled at him, her gaze slowly lowering to his open shirt. The way she moistened her lips was so damn sexy he had to force himself to keep moving to the closet. His shaving kit sat on top of his bag.

"I heard you," she said into the phone. "Call me tomorrow as soon as you find out, okay? The earlier the better. Yes, I do."

Just as he was about to close the bathroom door, he heard her say, "Thanks, Craig. I owe you."

15

"I HAVE A QUESTION," Sophie said after she'd had her shower and was crawling into bed with Ethan.

"Why do you have clothes on?"

"It's just a T-shirt."

Ethan was sitting up, pillow behind his back, the sheets at his waist, showing off a chest of the gods while looking at her with the frown of a ten-year-old. "It hides everything."

"Well, duh." She laughed until he pointed the remote at the TV and turned it off. "Okay," she said, and pulled the shirt over her head.

His hands were covering her breasts before she could even ditch the tee.

"Impatient, aren't we?" Already she was shivering from his touch. So much for them having a talk first.

"Damn right." He dragged his gaze away from the nipple he was circling with his thumb and looked at her mouth. "Kiss me now," he said in a dramatically low voice.

"Oh no, were you watching cartoons again?"

Before she knew it, he'd pulled her against his chest and claimed her mouth. She readily opened for him. He tasted minty and achingly familiar. Which was such a crazy thought she could hardly stand it. No, this wasn't a

young girl's fantasy, but it wasn't her real life, either. They
were two people attracted to each other and using sex to
deal with a stressful situation.

His hand moved to her face and he stroked her cheek
with the back of his fingers. She liked the smooth feel of his
jaw against her chin and cheeks. But she also liked it when
he had a day or two's worth of stubble. His tongue stroked
hers, gently, seductively, taking nothing for granted. She
might be a sure thing, but Ethan wanted her to be present,
eager to take this journey with him because she was helpless to do anything but.

If she slid the hand she had pressed to his chest lower,
she'd find him hard and ready. It would be easy to get lost
in the many ways he could make her feel so good, so content, put her in a state of temporary euphoria. She was an
addict, after all.

Oh yes, she had no doubt he could make her forget the
things she had to tell him. The difficult question she had
to ask, if only to ease her own mind. And hopefully his.

His mouth moved to her throat, leaving a trail of kisses
and light nips down to her collarbone. She quickly drew in
air and then leaned back, breaking contact with his mouth.

He looked up with a lazy smile. "Where do you think
you're going?" he murmured, and wrapped an arm around
her.

Constantly amazed at the gentleness of his large hands
and strong arms, she tried to remain firm and not give in
to his seeking mouth. "I'm not going anywhere," she said.
"Actually I wanted to talk." She saw his expression fall,
and with a laugh she cupped his jaw. "It's nothing horrible." She lowered her hand. "At least I hope not."

He sat back against the pillow and leveled his intense
gaze with her eyes. She took a moment to arrange her own

pillow, quickly compose herself and pull the sheet up to her breasts. He very obviously didn't care for that.

"When I said—" She cleared her throat. "The other night, when I made a crack about getting you out of my system…I swear I didn't mean anything by it."

Ethan snorted, shrugged a shoulder. "I know that."

She shook her head. "I hurt you. And I'm so sorry."

"You think you hurt me?" He lifted his eyebrows and gave her a look that bordered on patronizing.

Sophie didn't just think, she knew. She'd seen the same wounded expression in his eyes with Cara. Fleeting but unmistakable.

"All right, I mentioned it earlier, so I get why you think it upset me, but you're wrong. So don't worry about it."

"It was a thoughtless line directed more at myself than at you." She sighed at his stony reaction. "I had a huge crush on you after that day in school. It was so bad I couldn't even concentrate on studying."

His features softened. "Huh. For what it's worth, I couldn't tell. And I'd checked you out plenty."

"Liar."

"I did," he said with an odd laugh that told her he might be telling the truth. "But I was a lot more careful so Ashley wouldn't go nuts again."

"Wow, high school really sucked."

"Yes, in many ways it did." He reached for her hand. "Is that it? That's what you wanted to tell me?"

She held his gaze. "You haven't asked me about what the lawyer I hired on your behalf had to say."

"Craig?"

"Yes, Craig Langley."

"Okay." He released her hand. "I'm listening."

Oh, brother. It wasn't as if she'd done something behind his back. Ethan knew she was going to contact Craig. And yet the same brooding expression was on his face from a minute ago. "He's contacting the sheriff's office for a copy of the arrest report and Wendy's statement. Then he'll get back to us tomorrow first thing. He understands this is time-sensitive." She absolutely had no idea what Ethan was thinking. He'd closed her off. "I know you don't like talking about this, but—"

"I don't like that you feel you owe the guy. Certainly not on my behalf. Hell, it's not as if we're asking him to represent me for free."

Sophie relaxed a bit. "He's super busy, so yeah, I do owe him. And I don't care even a tiny bit. I've said it before, and I'll say it again. Craig is your best shot at making this all go away."

Ethan stared back a moment too long. "Why are you here, Sophie? Helping me like this. Do you feel you owe me?"

It was a fair question, she supposed. The answer, though, wasn't an easy one. Not if she wanted to be truthful. She swallowed around the lump forming in her throat. "No," she said. "I don't feel like I do, which is kind of odd, actually." She forced herself to keep her eyes even with his. "That stupid crush I told you about…I might still have a tiny itty-bitty piece of it left."

Ethan's mouth curved in a heart-stopping smile. "Good," he said, gathering her in his arms. "I might have a crush on you, too."

Before she could respond, he began kissing and biting her neck. She let out a shriek of laughter, then promptly covered her loud mouth.

"It's okay," he murmured, taking another nip. "The next two rooms are vacant."

She shoved him away to look at him. "And you know this because…?"

"Yes, honey," he said without apology, "I asked."

Sophie gasped, embarrassed, flustered… And then she just laughed.

Mostly because he was tickling behind her ear with his tongue. His hands were busy rubbing a nipple and cupping her butt. She loved having the freedom to skim her palm over his pecs while watching his shoulder muscles ripple. He was so damn beautiful it almost wasn't fair.

"Have you ever modeled for your sponsors?" she asked, and when he didn't answer, she rephrased it. "Like for a magazine ad?"

He kissed her collarbone, paused. "Once. When I was younger," he said, and continued blazing a path to her breast.

"Shirtless?"

When he didn't answer, she grinned. How had she not found the ad in one of her many searches back in her obsessive years?

He flicked his tongue over a very hard, sensitive nipple. Just as she thought she couldn't stand another second, he sucked it into his mouth and she arched slightly. The moment she relaxed he slid a hand between her thighs, then surprised her by going in the direction she hadn't expected.

He cradled the back of her calf in his palm, lightly caressing the muscle as he moved toward her ankle. His mouth moved to her other nipple, lightly biting the tight bud, then licking and sucking it until fire had spread through her veins.

Sophie reached under the sheets and found her prize. He hissed at her touch. Groaned when she wrapped her hand tighter and stroked him to the base of his erection. She took her time learning his shape, the smooth texture of his fever-hot flesh. She wanted to feel everything before she got lost in all the sexy things he did to her.

Ethan murmured some indistinct words—it might've been a mild curse—and then he pulled the sheet back and stared down at her hand wrapped around him, stroking upward. She paused at the rim of the crown and kissed him there.

"Sophie," he whispered, his breathless rasp so hot she felt it all the way to her swollen center.

He'd abandoned her leg, and she was sorry she interrupted him before seeing where he was going with that. But then he urged her thighs apart and slid a finger along the seam of her lips, and her mind went blank. Unconsciously she squeezed him tighter, and he dipped two fingertips inside her. Not far, just enough to tease her. To make her whimper.

He leaned forward at a slight angle so he could kiss her mouth. He kept his fingertips inside her and she hadn't given up her hold on his erection.

"I want to try something," he murmured against her mouth before leaning back to look at her.

"Okay," she said, and released him. It briefly occurred to her she should probably be wary. Or at least ask what he had in mind, but gazing into his blue eyes, she knew he wouldn't harm her.

He brought their faces close together and rested his forehead against hers. "It's nothing kinky or weird," he said. "I promise."

"I didn't think it would be."

Ethan smiled as he drew back. His fingers were still inside her. He pushed in a little deeper, his nostrils flaring, his expression strained, as if he might be rethinking his plan. Finally he pulled out.

He threw the covers to the foot of the bed. Grabbed a condom off the nightstand. Pushed the pillows out of the way so there was a clear spot in the middle of the mattress.

He shifted until he was sitting close to the center, his legs crossed loosely at the ankles.

She tried not to stare at his erection, but that was asking too much of herself. She figured out what he wanted to do, and her heart was already racing toward the finish line.

"I want you to sit on me," he said as he rolled on the condom. "As if you were going to wrap your legs around my waist. You'll be sort of sitting on my thighs at first. We'll find a fit to accommodate our height difference."

She nodded, and Ethan put his hands on her waist to help guide her as she climbed on board.

"Making the adjustments should be fun," she said.

Ethan's laugh turned into a groan as she sank down on him.

Maybe that was why he didn't notice that it was still an awkward arrangement. If her legs were a tad longer, it would be easier. She wiggled into a better position and ignored his tormented groans.

He reached behind and cupped her butt with both hands. He lifted her a tiny bit to the right and an inch closer against him. The angle of his erection covered a lot of territory...

Her breath caught at the base of her throat. No air was going in or out. He lifted his hips in the slightest thrust and he filled her utterly and completely to the max. A small cry escaped her lips when she felt her body stretch for him. How could he keep filling her?

She hoped this was good for him.

For her it was like hitting the jackpot.

One hand stayed on her butt, and the other slipped between them and found her clit. His thumb circled and rubbed with varying pressure.

Sensations bombarded her from both sides. They came down from the top and up from the bottom. Everywhere.

They shimmered around her, ruled over her. Awareness of her surroundings slipped in and out. She knew she was with Ethan, though. He was doing all of these miraculous things to her.

His body was warm and solid. Her hands rested on his shoulders, her fingers curling into his flesh and muscle.

"Open your eyes, Sophie," he whispered softly. "Come on, look at me."

She forced them open.

He was right there, his face inches from her face. His darkened eyes looking deeply into hers. And his smile... God, his smile melted anything that might've been left of her.

Holding his gaze, she rocked gently against him. He was still rubbing her, but she moved his hand away. It felt amazing, but she wanted to wait. She wanted to stay in this moment with him for as long as they could bear it.

Each of their movements was so tiny, so overwhelming. Neither of them had blinked. She was too afraid of missing something in his gorgeous blue eyes. He was trembling, his whole body straining to hold back. Sophie couldn't decide if that was what she really wanted.

Freezing this particular snapshot in time was amazing, but watching this incredible man shatter...for her... She had a feeling that would keep her heart warm forever.

She moved her face closer to his, wanting to kiss him without losing eye contact.

It didn't work.

Ethan's smile widened a little. He knew what she was doing. "Guess you have to make a choice," he said, his voice sounding weak from the strain of his tight control.

"Why?" She barely got the word out.

"Can't have both." He ran his fingers through her hair and it felt so great she almost closed her eyes.

"I think I might die," she said. "Right here. In whatever town this is. Cause of death…sensation overload."

"Then I'd better hurry up and come."

She laughed and the forward motion had him hissing through his teeth. It affected her, too. She could've sworn he'd rubbed her, but he didn't have a hand down there.

"I made a decision," she said.

"Good." His eyes were completely black. "I don't think I'm gonna last."

Sophie smiled. "Ready to rock and roll?"

In answer Ethan lifted his hips and her.

"Dammit. You made me blink."

Still watching her face, he smiled. And thrust again, only deeper.

She had to hang on to him.

He used both hands to anchor her hips, holding her steady to receive his thrusts. Semi-controlled at first, consistent, precise, but then that disappeared along with the eye contact.

She wound her arms tightly around his neck, her breasts cradled by his chest, the friction caused by his thrusts driving her crazy. Their whimpers and moans permeated the room.

Again, the pressure began building inside her, expanding and stretching, accelerating beyond her limit. And the heat. God, the heat rolled over them in shimmering waves of otherworldly pleasure, seducing them into the fire, fooling them into thinking they were warm and safe. Suspended here in the eye of the storm.

Ethan's strangled groan penetrated the sensual fog. His arms shook. Sweat beaded on his skin. His hands slipped from her hips. One landed on her thigh. She hadn't let go of his neck. Her own body hadn't stopped quaking. The spasms quivering inside her left her breathless and as weak as a newborn kitten.

She knew she should climb off. She couldn't move.

Ethan kissed the corner of her mouth. He lifted her up and laid her back on the mattress carefully, so her head landed on the pillow. Letting out a big whoosh of breath, he collapsed at her side.

"I think I know what it feels like to ride a bull," she murmured between gulps of air.

His laugh barely made it out. "You stayed on for more than eight seconds."

"I expect a buckle," she said, and then just breathed for a while. "That position really was ridiculously amazing. We have to do it again."

"Not right now."

"Wuss."

Chuckling, he rolled toward her. "We will. Do it again. And again."

"Many times."

He kissed the side of her neck. "Many times," he agreed, the warmth in his voice bringing a tightness to her chest.

She snuggled up against him.

He drew away for a moment, but just to pull the covers over them. And then he wrapped an arm around her, bringing her close.

Many times.

Repeating the words in her head made her smile. Though it was easy to say glib things now when she was here with Ethan, quite literally the man of her dreams.

But there was only one thing she knew for certain.

Ethan Styles was impossible. Impossible to understand. And impossible to resist...

16

SOPHIE WAS SITTING on a picnic bench near a snack bar about two hours from the motel where they'd stayed last night. No one else was sitting outside. The air was warm for November, but that wasn't saying much. The sun felt good, though, and she wanted to get the dreaded conversation with Lola over with—if she'd ever call back.

If Craig called soon, that would make her exceedingly happy, but she wasn't expecting to hear from him for another hour. He would've only received the paperwork this morning.

Lola was beginning to worry her. She hadn't been answering her texts or calls. Which wasn't like her at all. She couldn't be *that* busy just because Sophie was gone. Anyway, Lola had been anxious to keep in close touch, and since she was expecting Sophie and Ethan to be arriving in Wattsville this morning, it seemed very odd she wouldn't answer her phone.

Sophie sure hoped this weird behavior didn't have anything to do with Hawk. When Sophie checked him out early on, she hadn't found anything significant or violent in his past. She would've definitely alerted Lola.

Just to make herself feel better, she texted Mandy to

see if she knew what was happening at the office. Talking to her would be better, but Sophie wanted to be the one to tell Lola about the last-minute decision to go to Las Vegas. Yes, she could've left a heads-up on a voice mail, but she hadn't felt right doing that. She wanted to explain everything, even let Lola yell and scream at her if she wanted.

Best-case scenario, everything with Lola was fine— just the regular Monday madness keeping her busy. And Sophie would hear from Craig telling her the charges had been dropped, and Lola and Sophie wouldn't be on the hook for the full hundred-thousand-dollar bond.

If only she lived in a perfect world…

She looked up from her phone to take the cup of coffee Ethan had brought her. He bent to kiss her and even before their lips touched, she got that giddy feeling in her tummy that had been hanging around since they left Blackfoot Falls yesterday.

"They didn't have lattes or anything fancy. You should've seen the look I got when I asked for your part-skim, caramel-drizzled whatever."

"Well, if you didn't know what to ask for, how do you know if they have it or not?"

"Trust me, the second I mentioned the word *latte*, the old guy stopped listening. He was too busy mumbling something about yuppies ruining the world."

She eyed the Danish he'd brought for himself. "We just had breakfast."

"So?" He took a big bite, chewed, then sipped his coffee. "Do you know how many meals I've missed since I hooked up with you?"

"Is it my fault you think sex is a meal replacement?"

Ethan touched the brim of his hat and smiled at some phantom person behind her. "Mornin', ma'am."

"Yeah, like I'm going to fall for that," Sophie said,

and heard a tsking sound. She refused to turn all the way around, but managed to catch sight of the little white-haired woman walking toward the snack counter.

She looked at Ethan and they both laughed.

"You're the one who wanted to sit out here in the sun for a while," he said.

"Yes, and now I want a bite of that Danish."

"Then you'd better ask nicer." His next bite demolished half the pastry.

Her phone buzzed and she completely forgot about everything but the fact that she had a confession to make to Lola. And she sure didn't want to do it in front of Ethan.

As if he'd read her mind, he got to his feet. "I'll go pick up more Danish," he said.

"Hey, Lola, you were starting to worry me," Sophie said, watching Ethan stroll toward the snack bar.

"Where are you?" Lola asked. She sounded as if she'd been crying.

"Are you okay?"

"No. Not really."

"Are you at the office?"

"I was, but I'm at home now."

Sophie's chest hurt. Lola practically lived at the office. "Does this have anything to do with Hawk?"

Lola burst out crying. She tried to talk but couldn't seem to catch her breath.

"Can you tell me if Hawk is there with you now? Just say yes or no."

"No," Lola managed to choke out.

Sophie swallowed, feeling helpless and close to tears herself. "Did he hurt you?"

"No. Yes." Her voice broke, but the sobs were easing. "Not like you think."

"Okay, don't rush. I'll be right here when you can talk."

Sophie caught herself rocking back and forth, an arm wrapped across her stomach. She quickly glanced around. No sign of Ethan. She didn't want him to see her like this. He'd want an explanation she might not be comfortable giving. "Lola? I just wanted you to know I'm still here."

"I'm okay," she said. "Or getting there. Where are you? Are you close by?"

"No, I'm not." Sophie bit her lip. "I'm sorry. Is Mandy there?"

Lola sniffed. "No. I have to call her, though. She needs to help me find that goddamn, lying son of a bitch. I could kill that bastard."

Sighing with relief, Sophie listened to her cousin throw in a few more curses. Lola was sounding more like herself. Anger would serve her better than hurt right now.

Sophie's cell signaled an incoming call. She saw that it was Craig and winced. He'd have to leave a message. "Lola? Can you tell me what happened?"

A sob broke. "I'm sorry, Soph. Please don't hate me. I was such a fool. My God, I can't believe I'm that woman."

"I'm not going to hate you, Lola. Just tell me what happened."

Silence turned to quiet sobbing before Lola finally spoke. "He ripped us off," she said. "Hawk stole everything."

Sophie tried to quickly process the information. They really didn't have much for him to steal. "What exactly did Hawk take?"

"I really do mean everything, Soph," Lola said softly, then paused, trying to control her breathing. "He got into the safe."

Sophie felt the blood drain from her face. A violent shiver surged through her body. "How did—" She wouldn't ask. It didn't matter. Staying calm, keeping Lola calm, those were her priorities. Not dropping her phone would be good, too. Her hands were beginning to shake. "Since you guys had a fight maybe he's just trying to get your attention."

"No, I think he might've been planning this for a while. I'm gonna kill him. I am. God, I'm so stupid. This is all my fault."

"Don't go there, Lola. We need to stay focused. Okay?" Hell, Sophie was one to talk. She'd made her own mess. "How long ago could he have done this?"

"Last night, I think. Late. After we talked around midnight."

It was eleven-forty now. That gave the prick a head start. Sophie had to get to the research she'd done on him a few months ago. With any luck, there would be a clue as to where he'd gone. First, she'd get a hold of Mandy. And she had to talk to Craig. Jesus. Ethan was supposed to be in court in two hours. Hopefully Craig had worked his magic and it was a moot point by now. But she couldn't count on it.

"You're awfully calm," Lola said. "Do you understand what I'm telling you? He took *everything*." Her voice had risen and she sounded close to losing it again.

"I know. I'm just trying to think about our next step."

They'd always disagreed about how much cash to keep in the office. But after business had picked up, Lola had stubbornly insisted on having a minimum of twenty thousand dollars they could get their hands on quickly. "Okay... so, I'm going to call Mandy first, but she'll still want you to fill in the details, and then I'm going to see if I can track him electronically. We both know Hawk is too stupid to hide his trail."

"Yeah," Lola said with a small laugh. "There is that."

"So..." Sophie had to ask. "Just so I know what we're

dealing with, can you narrow down what you mean by *everything*?"

Lola let out a sob. "Thirty-five thousand cash," she said, and Sophie wanted to faint. "And two pieces of jewelry we were holding as collateral."

Sophie held her breath. How could she have forgotten about the collateral items? "Do you mean the antique brooch Mrs. Sellars gave us for her son's bond?"

"Yes," Lola choked out. "And the signed Mohammad Ali glove from Mr. Polinski."

Sophie held in a whimper. Mrs. Sellar's ruby-and-diamond brooch alone was worth about sixty thousand. So Lola's Bail Bonds was pretty much ruined financially. "Anything else?"

"I don't know how you can be this calm. I really don't."

Guilt, probably, because Sophie had created her own mess. She turned and saw Ethan approaching. He looked worried, so she tried to clean up her body language. "I don't know. Maybe I'm still in shock," Sophie said. "But let's use it to our advantage. Let's hang up and I'll contact Mandy, then get online."

"You have to call me soon, or you know I'll go nuts," Lola said. "I think I'll go to the bar and ask around. Hawk might've shot off his mouth."

"Mandy should probably do that."

"Everyone there knows me." Lola sighed. "They probably all think I'm a dumb ass, too, so what the hell?"

"For the record, I didn't say you were a dumb ass, nor do I think you are a dumb ass. We all have our blind spots," Sophie said, watching Ethan advance on her. "I'll call you soon."

"Wait. You have Styles, right? He'll make it to court?"

"Let's worry about Hawk for now."

"We really don't need to fork out money for Styles."

"I know that," she snapped, adding another layer of guilt to the growing pile. "Sorry."

"Nope. You have every right. Call me." Lola disconnected.

Sophie wanted to lay her head down and sob her heart out. She found a smile for Ethan when he set the paper bag on the table in front of her.

"Problem?" he asked, his eyes narrowed.

"Nothing I can't handle. Duty calls, though, and I have to get my tablet out of my bag." She glanced around, mostly because she was having trouble with that intense gaze of his. She couldn't explain anything now. She'd lose it and be tempted to hide in the comfort of his arms. He'd feel guilty they hadn't returned to Wyoming and she didn't want that. He had the finals to worry about.

THERE WAS ANOTHER ISSUE. She needed privacy and good Wi-Fi. "How about we find someplace where you can get some rest while I do a little work? Would that be okay?" she asked lightly. "I don't care if we go back to the same motel for a while."

Ethan's eyebrows went up. He looked as though he had a hundred questions. "Whatever you want."

"I have to make a quick call first, okay? To Mandy. She works in our office," Sophie said, trying like hell to sound normal. "Oh, and Craig called while I was talking to Lola. I had to let him go to voice mail, but I'll get back to him. Fingers crossed that he has good news."

Ethan stood there stone-faced, just watching her. She wasn't fooling him at all. He stepped back so she could get up, then offered her a hand. His skin was warm, his grip solid and sure. She felt safe with him. Alive. Happy. Whole. Which made her feel all the more a fool. This bubble in which they'd existed for the past three days was only a blip in time. A page torn from their normal lives and soon to be discarded. Yet she'd been willing to give up so much of herself, jeopardize the reputation of the business she'd built with Lola.

But Sophie couldn't afford self-pity or to let her shame interfere with finding Hawk. There would be plenty of time for all that later.

They were halfway to the truck when a sudden flash of memory stopped her cold. That day in the office when she'd announced she was going after Ethan... Hawk had sided with her. Lola had already been annoyed with him, yet he'd spoken out against her, taking Sophie's side. It made sense now. Lola was right. The bastard had been planning the theft for a while. Hawk knew Sophie didn't like him and he'd wanted her out of the way. But even worse, he'd used Lola.

Sophie was going to find that asshole. She would, because she was smarter than him and she knew so much more about him than he could imagine. And when she finally got her hands on him...

"Sophie? Please." Ethan put his arms around her. She'd never seen him look this worried, not even about his own problem. "Is it me? Am I causing you this grief?"

This wasn't fair to him. And anyway, she couldn't avoid his gaze forever. "We have a problem at the office. It's—" She cleared her throat. "My cousin Lola's boyfriend... We were robbed. The office safe was cleaned out."

"Jesus." Ethan touched her cheek. "I'm sorry. Did he get away with a lot?"

Despite trying to be stoic, she let out a whimper. "It's bad. He stole a lot of cash, some expensive jewelry we were holding as collateral, a piece of valuable sports memorabilia that might be irreplaceable."

When Ethan touched her cheek again, she realized he'd

been wiping tears. She jerked away, embarrassed and twice as furious with Hawk.

"Obviously we have to do something," Ethan said, easily staying abreast of her on the brisk walk to his truck. "I'm sure you have an idea."

"*You* will do nothing. Except whatever it is you do to get ready for the finals." She checked her cheeks for moisture. "I'm calling Mandy, a bounty hunter who works with us. She's the real deal. Totally badass. She'll help me find the stupid prick. Hawk really is stupid, probably left electronic footprints all over the country. I'll work on that while Mandy does her thing. Oh, we will find him, and when we do…"

They got to the truck and Ethan opened the passenger door for her.

"Look," she said, keeping her gaze lowered, "I feel horrible for Lola because she's blaming herself, and she shouldn't. This has nothing to do with you." As soon as Sophie was seated, she glanced at Ethan. He'd been so quiet.

His expression grim, he closed the door. She watched him round the hood. He looked angry.

She understood. She'd been incensed with Wendy Fullerton on his behalf, so she got it. Of course Ethan would be upset for her. And then she thought of something else. Damn. She couldn't afford to lose it now. Craig. She had to return his call. God, she really, really hoped the news was good. She wasn't about to leave Ethan twisting in the wind. Maybe he was angry because he thought she'd dropped the ball on him.

After he slid behind the wheel, she laid a hand on his arm. "I haven't forgotten you. I'm calling Craig now."

"You think I'm pissed about that?" His eyes were blazing mad when he turned to her. "You're a smart, capable woman, Sophie, I'll give you that. But obviously you're in trouble. Do you honestly think I could stand by and not help? Is that the kind of man you think I am?"

"No, of course not, but—"

"Frankly I don't give a shit what you have to say about it. I'm going to help you any way I'm able."

She'd never seen him this angry. Maybe that day back in high school. "Okay."

Looking straight ahead, he turned the key and started the truck. His lips were a thin line, his jaw clenched. Leaving the engine idling, he reached over the console, grabbed her upper arms and pulled her toward him.

"Damn independent little cuss," he muttered, and then kissed her hard on the mouth. He released her, took a deep breath and asked, "Now where the hell are we going?"

17

AFTER CONTACTING MANDY and receiving the bad news from Craig, Sophie worked from her tablet at the small table in the dinky motel they'd found three miles down from the snack bar. The room sucked, but the Wi-Fi was good.

Ethan had stepped outside so he wouldn't disturb her while he called his agent. Brian would probably come in person to strangle Sophie. If they'd gone straight to Wyoming last night as they'd planned, Ethan wouldn't be missing his court date in—she looked at the time and felt a little sick—five minutes.

There was still a possibility that everything would work out for him. Mandy was on the case, and Sophie had a great deal more faith in the bounty hunter than she had in herself at the moment. Sophie was pretty damn close to blowing everything.

Craig was furious that she hadn't warned him about Wendy being Broderick Fullerton's wife. Apparently Craig was on retainer with two of Fullerton's subsidiaries. They'd exchanged a few choice words, and Sophie might've called Craig a yellow-bellied chickenshit. It was actually one of the nicer names that had come to mind after discovering he'd called Lola and told her everything. So now her poor cousin was a complete basket case, worrying that Fullerton would have his bank call in their loan and kill their line of credit.

Sophie had only herself to blame.

Sighing, she rubbed her eyes. The screen blurred. She was tired from stress and lack of sleep, and staring at Hawk's—no, Floyd's—background file was frustrating. She was missing something, but she couldn't seem to pinpoint it. For the third time, she searched through his late teenage years, the job-hopping, being nailed for shoplifting cigarettes, petty stuff. Mostly his past was uneventful.

Her cell buzzed. She picked it up and read the text from Lola. A warrant had just been issued for Ethan's arrest. Sophie briefly closed her eyes. She wanted to call Mandy, but there was no point. If she had news, she would've called.

Sophie stared at the text, wanting so very much to curl up into a ball. Oh God, what had she done? He could've made it to court. They had been on their way to Wyoming. Did she have to pick then to rail against life's injustices? Did she need any more proof that she was hopeless when it came to Ethan? She had no judgment, no ability to reason, and now two people she deeply cared about had been caught in her well-intentioned but destructive wake.

She wondered if she should call Lola. And say what? Sorry I wasn't there for you? Sorry I was too busy chasing a childish dream? Sorry I didn't warn you about Hawk? Sophie could go on forever about the ways in which she'd failed. And she hadn't even gotten to Ethan yet.

Speaking of which… She heard the door being unlocked. She looked up as Ethan walked into the room. He looked grim but gave her a smile. She tried to return it. Had he been keeping track of the time? Was he expecting to hear about the warrant? She had to say something.

She moistened her lips. "A warrant has—"

"I know."

"I'm sorry, Ethan."

"Why? You tried to warn me." He slipped behind her chair and massaged her cramped shoulders.

His strong, gentle hands felt so good, but she didn't deserve his kindness. Or his forgiveness. She didn't deserve him. "I'm also the person who encouraged you to drive to Vegas instead. I was so sure Craig would come through, or that Wendy would finally—"

"Shh, it doesn't matter."

"Of course it does." She stopped when her voice shook.

"Aren't you going to check that?" he asked.

"What?" She realized she'd gotten an alert and looked at the corner of the screen. Floyd had used his credit card to buy gas—he was in Reno, Nevada.

Ethan took the other chair. "This is good. You've located him, right?"

"For now." Something clicked in the back of her mind that made sense about him being in Reno. "I have to check something before I call Mandy," she said, knowing Mandy would head for the airport as soon as she heard the news. So if she hadn't made progress solving Ethan's problem... Well, that was that.

"You should be happy," he said, frowning.

"I am." She paused. "Ethan? Why do you think this might be your last chance to go to the finals?"

His face darkened. "I never told you that."

"I overheard you mention something to Arnie."

He shrugged. "It's nothing." He glanced at her tablet. "Shouldn't you be moving on this information?"

"Please tell me." She begged with her eyes even though she wouldn't blame him for never trusting her with anything again.

He stared back, then sighed. "You ride long enough your

body's bound to suffer some wear and tear. I've had some trouble with my shoulder. Nothing serious, but I'm going to quit before I blow my future. That's all."

"Really?"

"Really. I'm being sensible. Imagine that."

Sophie smiled. She wanted to kiss him. It would be a stupid move. She'd already proven she couldn't think straight when she was around him. She glanced at the file on her screen just when her phone rang. It was Mandy. Sophie told herself not to get excited yet. "Tell me something good."

"Something good," Mandy said in her usual calm voice.

Sophie's heart lurched. "How good?"

"Mrs. Fullerton turned out to be extremely cooperative once I explained all the possible ramifications of making a false charge against a popular rodeo celebrity. She agreed it would be best to explain she'd misplaced her jewelry and drop the charges. Done deal. I just left the sheriff's office."

Sophie looked at Ethan. "What about the husband?"

"He's out of town again," Mandy said. "But hell, that's her problem. Have you got anything yet?"

"I think I might. Call you in ten?"

"Yep."

The moment they disconnected, Sophie hugged Ethan.

"She found him?" He held her tight, his smile matching hers.

"No, not yet. Wendy dropped the charges. You're in the clear."

He frowned. "I thought you guys were looking for Hawk."

"I am. Ethan. Aren't you excited? No more charges against you. They'll cancel the warrant."

"Well, yeah, of course I am. How?"

"Mandy had a talk with Wendy. She pointed out how

easily a trial could get out of control with other men stepping up to swear Wendy had sex with them and turning
everything into a media circus." Sophie didn't mention that
she'd thought up the tactic during their drive. She'd told
Mandy, who thought it was a brilliant maneuver and volunteered to do the deed. "Of course Wendy didn't know
that you've been trying to keep it out of the media. I told
you. Mandy totally rocks."

Ethan smiled. The relief on his face lifted her spirits.
"Well, now that I've given Brian heart failure," he said,
"I'll call back and tell him to relax. What about Hawk?"

"The prick's real name is Floyd," she said, focusing on
the information on the screen. Sophie had finally realized
what she'd overlooked in his file. Annoyed with herself,
she shook her head. "We got you, you dumb ass."

She grabbed her phone again and while waiting for the
connection, glanced at Ethan.

He was watching her and frowning. "What?" she said.
But then Mandy answered. "He's twenty miles outside
Reno," Sophie told her. "The idiot was too lazy to walk
inside and pay for his gas with *our* money. He used his
credit card."

"Reno's a big place," Mandy said. "Any thoughts on
whether he's passing through or sticking around?"

"I think he'll be hanging around," she said. He'd had
some petty scrapes over gambling with a fake ID when
he was a kid. She should've figured he'd want to go play
big shot in a high-stakes poker game at a casino where
they'd kiss his ass.

"Have you told Lola yet?"

"No, but I bet he's bragged about something or other
that could point us in the right direction. Lola can help
us there."

"Or he's cried over being mistreated," Mandy said. "Either way, I say we meet in Reno."

"I agree." She looked over at Ethan, who of course was still watching her. Why hadn't he gone to call his agent? "Let me know after you book your flight. I'm kind of in the middle of nowhere. Driving might be quicker for me. I'll call Lola."

As soon as she hung up Ethan said, "We can check flights out of Billings and see if it's worth backtracking, but I think you're right. We'd be better off driving."

Hell no, she would not let him tag along. She felt guilty enough for the messes she'd created. Yes, they'd avoided one disaster, but they still needed to nail Floyd before he blew all their money. That was where her focus needed to be. Not on Ethan, who had to get himself mentally psyched for the finals.

Couldn't he see they were reaching the end of the road anyway? The thought hurt. She could barely think about it, so why prolong the agony?

"No. *I'll* be better off driving." She gathered her things. On the way out she'd call Lola. "I'd appreciate a ride to pick up a rental car, though. I'll be fine, Ethan." She wanted to kiss him, but better she stay detached. It was for his own good. And for hers. "You, on the other hand, are driving to Las Vegas."

ETHAN GLANCED AT Sophie's boots scuffing up his once-clean dashboard. "Are you going to sulk all the way to Reno?"

"Probably," she huffed. "Yes, I am. You deserve it. What part of *please drop me at the car rental office* did you not understand?"

Sighing, he nodded to himself. Yep, he knew she was a handful. Stubborn. Irritating. A real pain in the ass when she wanted to be. Sophie was also fiercely loyal. Smart as hell. And she was softhearted, which he could never say to her and expect to live.

She looked so damn tired it made his gut knot. He'd bet anything she was beating herself up over failing Lola. Which really wasn't the case. Not that Sophie would listen.

"It wouldn't hurt for you to get some shut-eye," he said. "Nothing's going to change because you're asleep."

"Why don't I drive for a while?"

"No, thanks."

"You are so damn stubborn."

He snorted. "You would know," he said, turning on the radio. He kept it low and found an easy-listening station.

She surprised him by not complaining. Ten minutes later, just as he'd hoped, she was asleep.

He drove for another hour and then stopped at a motel. Even if they slept for six hours, they had time to get to Reno and meet Mandy. The best flight she could get had two stopovers.

After checking them in and paying for the night, he drove them closer to the room. She slept through it all, even when he carried her inside and laid her on the bed. He thought about undressing her but decided that would be a bad idea. Yeah, they'd both better keep their clothes on or they wouldn't get any rest.

He lightly kissed her parted lips, hid the truck keys, just in case, then set the alarms and crawled in beside her.

THE PALACE CASINO AND HOTEL wasn't the snazziest of the large casinos in downtown Reno, but it looked to be the busiest.

A steady stream of mainly older folks led the way into the hotel, where dings and trills of electronic music mostly covered up the piped-in oldies. The purple carpeting and gold chandeliers had probably been daring in their day.

As they headed toward the front desk, Ethan took her hand, and a shiver ran up her spine. Such a simple touch brought so much pleasure. She'd add this moment to her mental scrapbook.

They had to wait in a short line to reach the front desk. But that was okay, because Mandy was still ten minutes away and Sophie wouldn't proceed without her. So she waited with Ethan, who stood right behind her, draping his arms over her shoulders. Her hands were on top of his where they met on her chest.

She'd meant it when she told him to head to Vegas, but she was still glad he was here. The feel of his body warm and comforting. She was a horrible, selfish person. By tomorrow he would have no more grace period. He'd have to leave first thing to check in for the finals.

"I could eat a whole buffet," he said. "Not including the desserts."

"That's the best part." Dammit, now she wanted chocolate.

It was their turn at the desk, and by the time Sophie explained the importance of speaking to the casino manager himself, Mandy had joined them.

When Sophie made the introductions Ethan thanked Mandy for her help in getting the charges dropped. She looked pleased with the recognition, and not surprised by their clasped hands.

It took a few minutes for the manager to arrive, and he was surprisingly young considering his title. Maybe late thirties? However, the way he sized them up before inviting them into his office said he was going to be a challenge.

His office was small, nothing ornate. Behind him, though, was a door opened just enough for them to see a wall of monitors showing every cash transaction, second by second.

"How can I help you?" Dan Pfizer asked, waving them to the seats in front of his desk.

Mandy took the lead. She showed him her ID, a picture of Floyd, and offered a video of the idiot emptying the company safe.

He stopped her when she brought out the flash drive. "It won't do you any good. Even if I watched him steal from you personally, without a valid warrant there's nothing I can do."

"We're going to call the police," Sophie said. "We already know you have private poker rooms, and that he's in one of them. Probably throwing all our money on the table."

"We saw his Harley close to the valet booth," Mandy added. "So we know he's here."

Pfizer shrugged. "Show me a warrant, and I'll be happy to call the police myself. You have no idea how many times I get asked to do this. Wives wanting their husbands to come home. Vice versa. My hands are tied."

"Actually you might want to reconsider, assuming you want to keep all this quiet. Do you know who this is?" Sophie asked, nodding at Ethan, who didn't even blink at her tactic.

"I'm afraid I don't," Pfizer said. "But I really do have to be—"

"He's the number-two-rated professional bull rider in the world. In fact, I saw a poster out there inviting people to watch the National Finals Rodeo on your HD TVs starting this weekend."

That got his attention. But it wasn't enough.

"Hey, if you can't help us, I understand," Ethan said, shrugging. "Just like you understand why we have to call the police. And since we don't have access to your poker room, I'm pretty sure they'll have no problem meeting us in front of the sports book. That is where people place bets, right?"

Picking up a pen and toying with it, Pfizer frowned.

Sophie could almost hear the wheels turning in his head. "We'll try not to make too big a fuss," she said with a smile.

"By the way," Ethan added, "I saw the odds you have posted out there. I'm the five-to-two favorite. Just out of curiosity, what happens if I get hung up and miss the finals?" His jaw tightened for a split second, and Sophie's heart slid right down to her toes. After that he didn't so much as blink. "Do you guys have to return the money people have already bet?"

And there it was. The look of a man defeated.

"If we could all step outside my office, I'll be with you in a few moments."

They did, and Mr. Pfizer in his neat suit and tie walked hastily toward the poker rooms in the back.

Mandy pulled out her phone and moved a few feet away to give them privacy while she called Lola.

Sophie turned to him. "Why did you say that?"

"Hey, it worked." He looked tired, but he smiled. "Don't tell me you're superstitious."

She didn't buy his act of indifference. He'd been worried about the finals all along. His concern hadn't suddenly disappeared. "No, just a bad-luck charm."

"Come on." He put an arm around her. "Knock it off. What were the chances you'd find Floyd as quickly as you did? That he was still here by the time we showed up? This was a best-case scenario."

No, it wasn't. She and Mandy here taking care of business while Ethan was already in Vegas was a best-case scenario. But she wouldn't argue. He looked so exhausted. Tonight he had to sleep. Tomorrow, if he was still tired, she'd talk him into catching a flight while she took care of his truck.

She dug up a smile from somewhere. "Thank you. Without you here, I don't know— You've been—" She inhaled deeply, hoping it would help keep her eyes dry.

"I would never have deserted you," he said, and squeezed her hand. "I told you I'd help any way I could."

Even if it had cost him the finals? Oh God. She would've just died. But in truth, he wasn't there yet. If she wanted to be a good person, a friend, she'd let him check in to the hotel alone. Sleep as much as he could without her distracting him.

She nodded. "I think it's okay for you to go right after they bring that moron out. If you don't want to stay here, I'm sure you'll find a room in another hotel."

Ethan frowned. "Don't you mean it's okay for *us* to go?"

Mandy, who'd approached and was now on the phone with the Reno cops, turned around again.

"You need sleep," Sophie said. "What you don't need is any more distractions."

"I'm a grown man. I'm pretty sure I know what I do and don't need."

"I didn't mean it like that. It's just— You know I can't go with you now. I have to go back to Wyoming. Once Floyd's arrested, we won't automatically get back what he's stolen. I can't leave everything to Lola." Most of that was true, but she had trouble meeting his eyes.

"Yo," Mandy said.

Walking toward them, right behind the casino manager, Floyd was staring daggers at her. But the two beefy security guards weren't about to let him make a move.

Pfizer stopped in front of Ethan. Behind him, on the

monitor on the wall, Sophie saw a man in a cowboy hat being interviewed. The closed caption said the broadcast was coming from Las Vegas. Her stomach turned over. She literally felt sick. Ethan had claimed he didn't need to be there yet.

"If you'll join us at the security office when you're ready," Pfizer said.

Mandy waited until the guards and Floyd had passed. "The cops will be here in about five minutes. I'll give them what we've got, and then we can head back."

Sophie nodded. "I'll be right there. Ethan has to get his butt to Vegas."

Mandy held out her hand, and Ethan took it. "Good luck. I bet a hundred bucks on you. So get some damn sleep, would you?"

"I'll try," he said, unsmiling.

Mandy shrugged, met Sophie's eyes, then started walking.

"You promised you'd come with me," he said.

"I did, but that was before all this crap happened." She swallowed hard. "I didn't know Floyd was going to rip us off, or that we'd actually find him. But Jesus, Ethan. You told me you didn't have to be in Vegas yet." She motioned to the monitor. "You should be up there being interviewed. Not here mixed up in my mess." She forced a smile. "Look, we had fun, right? But we knew it would end. Like you said, you know what you need to do, and I need to go home. It's as simple as that."

He stared at her as if she'd just ripped his heart out of his chest. "If it's that simple to you, then yeah, I sure did misunderstand."

Despite the pain that squeezed the life out of her, she nodded. He wasn't thinking clearly. She had to be strong for both of them. "I hope you win the title." She stepped back.

"That's it?" He looked stricken.

"I'll call," she said, wondering if she dared. Wanting so much to tell him all the things she couldn't say on the purple carpet of this damn casino. Like how he'd rocked her world. How she used to think she had it bad for him, but now? She'd never recover.

But he didn't need her as baggage or a distraction. He'd never forgive her if he missed the finals, and she'd never forgive herself, either.

Ethan stared, looking confused and angry. But then he turned and walked past the security office, past the police who were headed in to arrest Floyd.

And he just kept walking.

18

SOPHIE SAT IN front of her small TV and shoved another piece of chocolate into her mouth. She wasn't crazy about television. She didn't even have cable or satellite, but she'd watched most of the National Finals Rodeo. Well, she'd kept track of the bull riders, anyway. And now she was watching reruns of Ethan.

Sometimes it had been nearly impossible to watch. Two riders had suffered serious injuries. If Ethan had gotten hurt, she had no idea what she would've done. Except blame herself for having distracted him at the most important time of his entire career.

But she didn't have to worry about that. Ethan had won his second championship title. Last night had been the buckle ceremony.

She'd thought seriously about calling, just to congratulate him. But she couldn't bring herself to pick up her cell. She'd handled the goodbye at the casino so badly. It still stung.

She should've at least offered to drive his truck back to Wyoming. Drop him at the airport first. Sophie had replayed her words and the expression on his face a thousand times in the past two weeks. She'd sounded so cold. How he must hate her.

Seeing the cowboy being interviewed on the monitor had done something to her. Panic had taken over. And she knew if she'd given herself an inch, she would've done the thing she wanted to do instead of doing what was honorable. Intellectually she realized it wasn't completely her fault that he'd driven her to Reno when he should've gone to Las Vegas. She'd begged him to take her to a car rental office. But he'd insisted. And she hadn't fought him hard enough because she'd been thrilled he'd stayed with her.

Someone knocked at the apartment door. She grabbed something to throw at it. Then stared at the bag in her hand. What the hell was she thinking? Not the chocolate. That would make everything worse.

Another knock. It was either Lola or Mandy, most likely Lola. Mandy knew how to buy a clue.

"Go away," Sophie yelled loud enough to be heard by half the residents in the apartment complex.

"Not gonna happen."

"Goddammit, Lola," Sophie muttered, and got off the couch.

She opened the door and growled at her cousin.

Lola walked right in, uninvited, as usual. She surveyed Sophie's mess after three days of hibernation. Every glass she owned was sitting out somewhere.

Finally Lola eyed Sophie's baggy gray sweats and the sock with a hole over the big toe. "You look like shit."

"Should've saved yourself the trip. I could've told you that on the phone." Sophie plopped back down on the couch. Wincing, she lifted her butt and moved the bag of chocolate out of the way. "What do you want?"

"Get up and take a shower, then put on something nice. We're going out."

Sophie snorted a laugh. "Are you high?"

"Come on, Soph." Lola's gaze shifted briefly to the TV. "You can't keep moping."

"Yes, I can. Except I'm not moping."

Lola sighed. "Please get up and get ready. Mandy is meeting us at the—"

"Nice try. Mandy knows better. Yet she's only known me for a fraction of the time you have. Explain that." Sophie stretched her neck back. She'd stayed away from the gym too long. Tomorrow she'd get herself moving.

"The Reno police called. They found the brooch at a pawnshop."

Sophie shook her head. Anyone could tell the piece was an antique and too valuable to sell to a pawnbroker. Anyone but Floyd. "How much did he get for it? Did they tell you?"

"No. I didn't ask. I want this whole thing over with and I never want to hear his name again."

Sophie gave her a sympathetic nod. "I'm glad they recovered the brooch."

"You know what pisses me off, Sophie?"

"I'm coming in to work tomorrow. I'll be my old cheery self. Promise."

"That's not what I'm upset about." She sat at the edge of the couch. "Ethan is a really good man, and you're tossing him away. Do you have any idea what I'd do to find someone like him? What most single women would do? You've never been a quitter. I've always admired that about you."

Sophie had to look away. She wasn't good at hiding her emotions lately. "Not now. Okay, Lola?"

Her cousin sighed. "Please get dressed and come out. Would you do that for me?"

"I can't. I'm sorry."

Shrugging, Lola stood. "You can't say I didn't try."

Sophie watched sideways until Lola opened the door.

She would've felt worse if she thought her cousin really wanted a drinking buddy tonight. Lola was only trying to cheer her up.

Sophie turned her head. Lola had left. Why hadn't she closed the damn door?

Muttering a curse, she pushed to her feet.

Ethan appeared in the doorway. He looked at Sophie, glanced around the apartment and then looked at her again and laughed.

Her mouth wouldn't work. When it finally did, she said, "I'm going to kill her."

"Ah, right. She asked me to remind you that she tried."

"I'm still going to kill her. Stay right there." She skirted the coffee table, thought about taking some glasses and empty bags with her, but what was the point? "Right there," she repeated before disappearing into her bathroom.

She washed her face, brushed her hair and teeth in record time, then splurged with some mascara and scented body cream. She exchanged the sweatpants for jeans. Thank God she'd taken a shower earlier.

When she returned to the living room, plastic trash bag in hand, the door was closed and Ethan was sitting on the couch, staring at the TV. He hadn't pushed her crap to the side. He'd just made himself comfortable.

He looked up at her and smiled.

She pointed at the door. "I told you to stay there."

"You really have to quit being so damn bossy."

"I doubt that's going to stop," she said, sighing, and picked up empty cookie packages, dropping them into the trash bag. She hated feeling this awkward with him.

"I know," he said, his quiet tone making her look up. He nodded at the TV. "You've been watching the finals."

"Oh." She cleared her throat. "Congratulations, by the way." Should she give him a quick kiss or maybe a hug? A kiss wouldn't be out of line. She leaned over and he pulled her onto his lap.

Sophie let out a startled gasp.

"Is this okay?" he asked, uncertainty in his blue eyes.

"Uh-huh."

"I want to explain why I didn't call."

"You don't have to. I never expected you to—"

"Can you please just be quiet for a few minutes?"

She pressed her lips together and jerked a nod.

Ethan gave a short laugh. "At first I was really mad. And then I started thinking about the moment everything had gone sideways with us at the casino. I figured out you weren't trying to get rid of me but get me to Vegas. That was just before the first round.

"I was going to call then. Hash things out. But I knew the moment I heard your voice I'd lose my focus. And I couldn't afford to do that. I owed it to both of us to be on my game."

Sophie blinked. *Us?* A quiver started in her tummy. Like the feeling she'd gotten when she saw him wearing a helmet that first round. He'd worn it until the very end. She'd told herself he was doing it for her and then realized that was the fifteen-year-old inside her who still believed in fairy tales.

"Sophie…" He was watching her, waiting for her to look into his eyes. "Honey, I know you were trying to help get me to finals because you knew how important it was to me. But something had happened that shifted my priorities."

"Okay," she said. "What?"

"You."

"Me? How?"

"By believing in me. When you said my fans would believe me over Wendy, you were probably right. They'd rally around me. But they don't really know me. They just wouldn't want to believe their rodeo idol could be a thief. But you believed in *me*."

"Well, of course…"

"Look, you're a beautiful, capable woman who's built a business and a nice life. And I suspect you got here mainly by yourself. But you don't have to go a hundred miles an hour all the time. You don't have anything to prove. Now, how about believing in yourself, Sophie?"

Her mouth was so dry. Eleven years ago she'd been cowed and humiliated, and she'd been running so fast, so hard ever since to never be in a situation like that again. To be in control at all times. But she hadn't always succeeded. "May I speak now?"

"Go ahead."

"First of all, I'm obviously not all that capable, because I wasn't the one who helped you. It was Mandy. I couldn't even—"

"All right. Stop." He shook his head.

"What? Shouldn't I be able to have my say?"

"You can't expect me to sit here and listen to this crap. Remember, you're talking about someone I love."

The air left her lungs. "You can't love me."

Ethan's eyes blazed. He clearly did not like that response.

"I'm not saying I'm not lovable. I just meant, you don't really know me. You can't. Not after only four days."

He said nothing, just looked at her with a hint of sadness. "Sophie, I know all the things that matter about you. I promise you that. Even if it takes a year, two years, whatever it takes to prove it to you, I'm going to do that. I can be stubborn myself."

She held back a sob and dashed a tear away with impatience. "You're right."

"I am?" He smiled, looking so boyishly delighted, she laughed.

"I think you do know me. Maybe better than I do." She wasn't ready to explain that she had been trying to prove something she hadn't realized until now. She'd needed to feel she deserved the small kindness he'd shown her. Her teenage years had been so damn lonely.

He put his arms around her and pulled her back against him.

That alone made her want to cry as she curled up in his lap. She'd missed his arms so much.

"I owe you a congratulatory kiss." She turned her face, and their lips touched. He kissed her softly, eyes open. She kissed him back and heard the bag of candy scrunch. Now, how could she not love a man who'd seen her mess of an apartment, the mess of her life, and hadn't run in the other direction?

"Dammit, Ethan," she murmured against his lips.

"What?"

"I love you, too."

His smile could've lit the room. "With the finals money, I'm going ahead with the construction of the rodeo camp. And there's plenty of space for you to set up your martial arts studio. If you want to."

She kissed him again, so hard they both nearly fell off the couch. And when she finally caught her breath, she said, "I know the important parts about you, too, Ethan Styles. But it'll be fun to explore the rest."

"I'd like to do a little exploring myself." He stood with her still in his arms. "I'm guessing you have a bedroom somewhere in here."

Sophie grinned. She might not be the best bounty hunter in the world, but she'd set out to get her man and ended up with the man of her dreams. "You can have me anywhere, cowboy."

* * * * *

*Gage Ringer: Powerful, fierce, unforgettable...
and temporarily sidelined from his MMA career
with an injury. Back home, he has one month
to win over the woman he could never forget...*

Read on for **New York Times** *bestselling author
Lori Foster's*

HARD KNOCKS

*The stunning prequel novella for
her ULTIMATE series!*

HARD KNOCKS

Lori Foster

CHAPTER ONE

GAGE RINGER, better known as Savage in the fight world, prowled the interior of the rec center. His stride was long, his thoughts dark, but he kept his expression enigmatic to hide his turmoil from onlookers. He didn't want to be here tonight. He'd rather be home, suffering his bad mood alone instead of covering up his regret, forced to pretend it didn't matter. His disappointment was private, damn it, and he didn't want to advertise it to the world. Shit happened.

It had happened to him. So what?

Life went on. There would be other fights, other opportunities. Only a real wimp would sit around bellyaching about what could have been, but wasn't. Not him. Not publicly anyway.

Tonight the rec center would overflow with bodies of all shapes, sizes and ages—all there for different reasons.

Cannon Coulter owned the rec center. It was a part of Cannon's life, a philanthropic endeavor that, no matter how big Cannon got, how well-known he became in the Supreme Battle Championship fight world, would always be important to him.

Armie Jacobson, another fighter who helped run the rec center whenever Cannon had to travel for his career, had planned a long night of fun. Yay.

Not.

At least, not for Gage.

Earlier they'd had a party for the kids too young to stick

around and watch the pay-per-view event that night on the big screen. One of Cannon's sponsors had contributed the massive wall-mounted TV to the center.

So that they wouldn't feel left out, Armie had organized fun activities for the younger kids that had included food, games and some one-on-one play with the fighters who frequented the rec center, using it as a gym.

With the kiddie party now wrapping up, the more mature crowd would soon arrive, mixing and mingling while watching the fights.

The rec center had originally opened with very little. Cannon and some of his friends had volunteered to work with at-risk youths from the neighborhood to give them an outlet. They started with a speed bag, a heavy bag, some mats and a whole lot of donated time and energy.

But as Cannon's success had grown, so too had the rec center. Not only had Cannon added improvements, but his sponsors loved to donate anything and everything that carried their brand so that now the size of the place had doubled, and they had all the equipment they needed to accommodate not only a training camp for skilled fighters, but also dozens of boys, and a smattering of girls, of all ages.

Gage heard a distinctly female laugh and his gaze automatically went to Harper Gates.

So she had arrived.

Without meaning to, he inhaled more deeply, drawing in a calming breath. Yeah, Harper did that to him.

He watched as Harper assisted Armie in opening up folding chairs around the mats. Together they filled up every available speck of floor space. She stepped around a few of the youths who were still underfoot, racing around, wrestling—basically letting off steam with adult supervision, which beat the hell out of them hanging on street corners, susceptible to the thugs who crawled out of the shadows as the sun went down.

Gage caught one boy as he recklessly raced past. He twirled him into the air, then held him upside down. The kid squealed with laughter, making Gage smile, too.

"You're moving awfully fast," Gage told him.

Bragging, the boy said, "I'm the fastest one here!"

"And humble, too," he teased.

The boy blinked big owl eyes at him while grinning, showing two missing teeth. He was six years old, rambunctious and considered the rec center a second home.

"I need you to take it easy, okay? If you're going to roughhouse, keep it on the mats."

"'Kay, Savage."

Gage glanced at a clock on the wall. The younger crowd would be heading out in a few more minutes. Still holding the boy suspended, he asked, "Who's taking you home?"

"My gram is comin' in her van and takin' all of us."

"Good." Luckily the grandmother was reliable, because the parents sure as hell weren't. And no way did Gage want the boys walking home. The rec center was in a decent enough area, but where the boys lived…

The kid laughed as Gage flipped him around and put him back on his feet.

Like a shot, he took off toward Miles, who was already surrounded by boys as he rounded them up.

Grandma would arrive soon. She'd probably appreciate how the kids had been exercised in the guise of play, schooled on control and manners, and fed. The boys always ate like they were starving. But then, Gage remembered being that age and how he could pack it away.

Briefly, his gaze met Harper's, and damn it, he felt it, that charged connection that had always existed between them. She wore a silly smile that, despite his dark mood, made him want to smile, too.

But as they looked at each other, she deliberately wiped the smile away. Pretending she hadn't seen him at all, she got back to work.

Gage grunted. He had no idea what had gotten into her, but in his current frame of mind, better that he just let it go for now.

Very shortly, the most dedicated fight fans would arrive to catch the prelims. By the time the main card started, drawing a few high school seniors, some interested neighbors and the other fighters, there'd be bodies in all the chairs, sprawled on the mats and leaning up against the concrete walls. Equipment had been either moved out of the way or stored for the night.

This was a big deal. One of their own was competing tonight.

The high school guys were looking forward to a special night where they'd get to mingle more with their favorite fighters.

A dozen or more women were anxious to do some mingling of their own.

Armie, the twisted hedonist, had been judicious in handing out the invites: some very hot babes would be in attendance, women who'd already proven their "devotion" to fighters.

Gage couldn't have cared less. If he hadn't been fucked by karma, he'd be there in Japan, too. He didn't feel like celebrating, damn it. He didn't want to expose anyone to his nasty disposition.

The very last thing he wanted was a female groupie invading his space.

Actually, he'd been so caught up in training, he'd been away from female company for some time now. You'd think he'd be anxious to let off steam in the best way known to man.

But whenever he thought of sex...

Harper laughed again, and Gage set his back teeth even while sneaking a peek to see what she found so funny. Armie said something to her, and she swatted at him while smiling widely.

Gage did a little more teeth grinding.

Like most of the fighters, Armie understood Gage's preoccupation and ignored him. Now if he would just ignore Harper, too, Gage could get back to brooding.

Instead, he was busy thinking of female company—but there was only one woman who crowded his brain.

And for some reason, she seemed irritated with him.

His dark scowl made the stitches above his eye pull and pinch, drawing his thoughts from one problem and back to another.

One stupid mistake, one botched move during practice, and he had an injury that got him kicked out of the competition.

Damn it all, he didn't want to be here tonight, but if he hadn't shown up, he'd have looked sad and pathetic.

"Stop pacing," Harper said from right behind him. "It makes you look sad and pathetic."

Hearing his concern thrown right back at him, Gage's left eye twitched. Leave it to Harper to know his exact thoughts and to use them as provocation. But then, he had to admit, she provoked him so well....

He'd missed the fights. And he'd missed Harper.

The only upside to heading home had been getting to see her. But since his return three days ago, she'd given him his space—space he wanted, damn it, just maybe not from her. At the very least, she could have *wanted* to see him, instead of treating him like one of the guys.

Relishing a new focus, Gage paused, planning what he'd say to her.

She didn't give him a chance to say anything.

With a hard whop to his ass, she walked on by and sashayed down the hall to the back.

Gage stood there, the sting of her swat ramping up his temper...and something else. Staring after her, he suffered the sizzling clench of emotions that always surfaced whenever Harper got close—which, since he'd returned home with his injury, had been rare.

He'd known her for years—grown up with her, in fact—and had always enjoyed her. Her wit. Her conversation. Her knowledge of mixed martial arts competition.

Her cute bod.

They'd recently taken their friendship to the next level, dating, spending more private time together. He'd enjoyed the closeness...

But he'd yet to enjoy her naked.

Time and circumstances had conspired against him on that one. Just when things had been heating up with Harper, just when it seemed she was ready to say "yes" instead of "not yet," he'd been offered the fight on the main card in Japan. He'd fought with the SBC before. He wasn't a newbie.

But always in the prelims, never on the highly publicized, more important main card. Never with such an anticipated event.

In a whirlwind, he'd gone off to a different camp to train with Cannon, getting swept up in the publicity and interviews that went with a main card bout...

Until, just a few lousy days ago—*so fucking close*—he'd miscalculated in practice and sustained a deep cut from his sparring partner's elbow.

A cut very near his eye that required fifteen stitches.

It made him sick to think of how quickly he'd been pronounced medically ineligible. Before he'd even caught his breath the SBC had picked his replacement.

That lucky bastard was now in Japan, ready to compete.

And Gage was left in Ohio. Instead of fighting for recognition, he fought his demons—*and got tweaked by Harper.*

He went after her, calling down the empty hallway, "I am not pathetic."

From inside a storage room, he heard her loud "Ha!" of disagreement.

Needing a target for his turbulent emotions and deciding Harper was perfect—in every way—he strode into the room.

And promptly froze.

Bent at the waist, Harper had her sexy ass in the air while she pulled disposable cups off the bottom shelf.

His heart skipped a beat. Damn, she was so hot. Except for bad timing, he'd be more familiar with that particular, *very perfect* part of her anatomy.

Not sleeping with her was yet another missed opportunity, one that plagued him more now that he didn't have the draining distraction of an upcoming fight. His heart started punching a little too hard. Anger at his circumstances began to morph into red-hot lust as he considered the possibilities.

But then, whenever he thought of Harper, lust was the least confusing of his emotions.

Now that he was home, he'd hoped to pick up where they'd left off. Only Harper had antagonism mixed with her other more welcoming signals, so he had to proceed with caution.

"What are you doing?" he asked, because that sounded better than saying, *"Damn, girl, I love your ass."*

Still in that tantalizing position, she peeked back at him, her brown hair swinging around her face, her enormous blue eyes direct. With her head down that way, blood rushed to her face and made her freckles more noticeable.

There were nights he couldn't sleep for wondering about all the places she might have freckles. Many times he'd imagined stripping those clothes off her, piece by piece, so he could investigate all her more secret places.

Like him, she was a conservative dresser. Despite working at a secondhand boutique clothing store she always looked casual and comfortable. Her jeans and T-shirts gave an overview of sweet curves, but he'd love to get lost in the details if he could ever get her naked.

She straightened with two big boxes in her hands. "Armie had small juice containers out for the kids, but of course adults are going to want something different to drink. Same with the snacks. So I'm changing up the food spread."

Due to her schedule at the boutique, Harper had been unable to attend the party with the youngsters, but she'd sent in snacks ahead of time. She had a knack for creating healthy treats that looked fun and got gobbled up. Some of the options had looked really tasty, but if she wanted to switch them out, he could at least help her.

She glanced at the slim watch on her wrist. "Lots to do before everyone shows up for the prelims."

Since pride kept him at the rec center anyway...

"What can I do to help?"

Her smile came slow and teasing. "All kinds of things, actually. Or—wait—do you mean with the setup?"

"I... What?" Was that a come-on? He couldn't tell for sure—nothing new with Harper. Clearly she'd been pissed at him about something, but now, at her provocative words, his dick perked up with hopes of reconciliation.

Snickering, she walked up to him, gave him a hip bump, then headed out of the room. "Come on, big boy. You can give me a hand with the folding tables."

As confusion warred with disgruntlement, he trailed after her. "All right, fine." Then he thought to remind her, "But I'm not pathetic."

Turning to face him, she walked backward. "Hit home with that one, did I?"

"No." *Yes*.

"I can help you to fake it if you want."

Despite the offhand way she tossed that out, it still sounded suggestive as hell. "Watch where you're going." Gage reached out, caught her arm and kept her from tripping over the edge of a mat.

Now that he had ahold of her, he decided to hang on. Where his fingers wrapped around her arm just above her elbow, she was soft and sleek and he couldn't stop his thumb from playing over the warm silk of her skin.

"Thanks," she said a little breathlessly, facing forward again and treading on.

"So." Though he walked right beside her, Gage couldn't resist leaning back a bit to watch the sway of her behind. "How would we fake it? Not that I need to fake shit, but you've got me curious."

Laughing, she leaned into him, smiled up at him, and damn it, he wanted her. *Bad*.

Always had, probably always would.

He'd had his chance before he left for the new camp. Even with the demands of training, he'd wanted her while he was away. Now he was back and the wanting boiled over.

Her head perfectly reached his shoulder. He stood six-three, nine inches taller than her, and he outweighed her by more than a hundred pounds.

But for a slim woman, she packed one hell of a punch. "Harper," he chided. She was the only person he knew who seemed to take maniacal delight in tormenting him.

Rolling her eyes, she said, "You are such a grouch when you're being pathetic." She stepped away to arrange the cups on a long table placed up against the wall. "Everyone feels terrible for you. And why not? We all know you'd have won. Maybe even with a first-round knockout."

Did she really believe that? Or was she just placating him? "Darvey isn't a slouch." Gage wouldn't want an easy fight. What the hell would that prove?

"No," she agreed, "but you'd have creamed him."

"That was the plan." So many times he'd played it out in his head, the strategy he'd use, how he'd push the fight, how his cardio would carry him through if it went all three rounds. Darvey wasn't known for his gas tank. He liked to use submissions, manipulating an arm or leg joint to get his opponent to tap before something broke. His plan was always to end things fast. But Gage knew how to defend against submissions, how to make it *his* fight, not anyone else's.

"Sucks that you have to sit this one out," Harper continued. "But since you do, I know you'd rather be brimming with confidence, instead of moping around like a sad sack."

Folding his arms over his chest, he glared down at her. "I don't mope."

She eyed his biceps, inhaled slowly, blew the breath out even slower.

"Harper."

Brows raised, she brought those big blue eyes up to focus on his face. "What?"

He dropped his arms and stepped closer, crowding her,

getting near enough to breathe in her unique scent. "How do you figure we'd fake things?"

"Oh, yeah." She glanced to one side, then the other. "People are looking at us."

"Yeah?" Currently the only people in the gym were the guys helping to set it up for the party. Armie, Stack, Denver, a few others. "So?"

"So…" She licked her lips, hesitated only a second, then came up against him. In a slow tease, her hands crawled up and over his chest. Fitted against him, she went on tiptoe, giving him a full-body rub.

Without even thinking about it, Gage caught her waist, keeping her right there. Confusion at this abrupt turnaround of hers stopped him from doing what came naturally.

Didn't bother her, though.

With her gaze locked on his, she curled her hands around his neck, drew him down to meet her halfway and put that soft, lush, taunting mouth against his.

Hell, yeah.

Her lips played over his, teasing, again provoking. They shared breath. Her thighs shifted against his. Her cool fingers moved over his nape and then into his hair. The kiss stayed light, slow and excruciating.

Until he took over.

Tilting his head, he fit his mouth more firmly against her, nudged her lips apart, licked in, deeper, hotter…

"Get a room already."

Gasping at the interruption, Harper pulled away. Embarrassed, she pressed her face against his chest before rearing back and glaring at Armie.

Gage just watched her. He didn't care what his dipshit friends said.

But he'd love to know what Harper was up to.

"Don't give me that look," Armie told her. "We have high school boys coming over tonight."

"The biggest kids are already here!"

"Now, I know you don't mean me," Armie continued, always up for ribbing her. "You're the one having a tantrum."

Gage stood there while they fussed at each other. Harper was like that with all the guys. She helped out, gave as good as she got, and treated them all like pesky brothers that she both adored and endured.

Except for Gage.

From the get-go she'd been different with him. Not shy, because seriously, Harper didn't have a shy bone in her hot little body. But maybe more demonstrative. Or rather, demonstrative in a different way.

He didn't think she'd smack any of the other fighters on the ass.

But he wasn't stupid. Encouraged or not, he knew guys were guys, period. They'd tease her, respect her boundaries, but every damn one of them had probably thought about sleeping with her.

For damn sure, they'd all pictured her naked.

Those vivid visuals were part of a man's basic DNA. Attractive babe equaled fantasies. While Harper hustled around the rec center helping out in a dozen different ways, she'd probably been mentally stripped a million times.

Hell, even while she sniped back and forth with Armie, Gage pictured her buck-ass, wondering how it'd feel to kiss her like that again, but without the barrier of clothes in the way.

"You need a swift kick to your butt," Harper declared.

"From you?" Armie laughed.

Fighting a smile, she said, "Don't think I won't."

"You wanna go?" Armie egged her on, using his fingertips to call her forward. "C'mon then, little girl. Let's see what you've got."

For a second there, Harper looked ready to accept, so Gage interceded. "Children, play nice."

"Armie doesn't like *nice*." She curled her lip in a taunt. "He likes *kinky*."

In reply, Armie took a bow.

True enough, if ever a man liked a little freak thrown into the mix, it was Armie. He'd once been dropped off by a motorcycle-driving chick dressed in leather pants and a low-cut vest, her arms circled with snake tattoos. She'd sported more piercings than Gage could count—a dozen or so in her ears, a few in her eyebrows, lip, nose. The whole day, Armie had limped around as if the woman had ridden him raw. He'd also smiled a lot, proof that whatever had happened, he'd enjoyed himself.

Unlike Gage, Armie saw no reason to skip sex, ever. Not even prior to a fight. The only women he turned down were the ones, as Harper had said, that were too nice.

"Come on." She took Gage's hand and started dragging him toward the back.

"Hey, don't leave my storage closet smelling like sex," Armie called after them. "If you're going to knock boots, take it elsewhere!"

Harper flipped him the bird, but she was grinning. "He is so outrageous."

"That's the pot calling the kettle black." Just where was she leading him?

"Eh, maybe." She winked up at him. "But I just act outrageous. I have a feeling it's a mind-set for Armie."

Ignoring what Armie had said, she dragged him back into the storage closet—and shut the door.

Gage stood there watching her, thinking things he shouldn't and getting hard because of it. Heart beating slow and steady, he asked, "Now what?"

CHAPTER TWO

COULD A MAN look sexier? No. Dumb question. Harper sighed. At twenty-five, she knew what she wanted. Whether or not she could have it, that was the big question.

Or rather, could she have it for the long haul.

"Is that for me?" She nodded at the rise in his jeans.

Without changing expressions, Gage nodded. "Yeah." And then, "After that kiss, you have to ask?"

Sweet. "So you like my plan?"

Looking far too serious, his mellow brown gaze held hers. "If your plan is to turn me on, yeah, I like it."

As part of her plan, she forced a laugh. She had to keep Gage from knowing how badly he'd broken her heart.

Talk about pathetic.

Gage was two years older, which, while they'd been in school, had made him the older, awesome star athlete and popular guy that *every* girl had wanted. Her included.

Back then, she hadn't stood a chance. He'd dated prom queen, cheerleader, class president material, not collect-for-the-homeless Goody Two-shoes material.

So she'd wrapped herself in her pride and whenever they'd crossed paths, she'd treated him like any other jock—meaning she'd been nice but uninterested.

And damn him, he'd been A-OK with that, the big jerk.

They lived in the same small neighborhood. Not like Warfield, Ohio, left a lot of room for anonymity. Everyone knew everyone, especially those who went through school together.

It wasn't until they both started hanging out in the rec center, her to help out, him to train, that he seemed to really tune in to her. Course, she hadn't been real subtle with him, so not noticing her would have required a deliberate snub.

She was comfortable with guys. Actually, she was comfortable with everyone. Her best friend claimed she was one of those nauseatingly happy people who enjoyed life a little too much. But whatever. She believed in making the most of every day.

That is, when big, badass alpha fighters cooperated.

Unfortunately, Gage didn't. Not always.

Not that long ago they'd been dating, getting closer. Getting steamier.

She'd fallen a little more in love with him every day.

She adored his quiet confidence. His motivation and dedication. The gentle way he treated the little kids who hung out at the center, how he coached the older boys who revered him, and the respect he got—and gave—to other fighters.

She especially loved his big, rock-solid body. Just thinking about it made her all twitchy in private places.

Things had seemed to be progressing nicely.

Until the SBC called and put him on the main card for freaking other-side-of-the-world Japan, and boom, just like that, it seemed she'd lost all the ground she'd gained. Three months before the fight, Gage had packed up and moved to Harmony, Kentucky, to join Cannon in a different camp where he could hone his considerable skills with a fresh set of experienced fighters.

He'd kissed her goodbye first, but making any promises about what to expect on his return hadn't been on his mind. Nope. He'd been one big obsessed puppy, his thoughts only on fighting and winning.

Maybe he'd figured that once he won, his life would get too busy for her to fit into it.

And maybe, she reminded herself, she was jumping ahead at Mach speed. They hadn't even slept together yet.

But that was something she could remedy.

Never, not in a million years, would she have wished the injury on him. He'd fought, and won, for the SBC before. But never on the main card. Knowing what that big chance had meant to him, she'd been devastated on his behalf.

Yet she'd also still been hurt that the entire time he was gone, he hadn't called. For all she knew, he hadn't even thought about her. Ignoring him had seemed her best bet—until she realized she couldn't. Loving him made that impossible.

And so she decided not to waste an opportunity.

Gage leaned against the wall. "I give up. How long are you going to stand there staring at me?"

"I like looking at you, that's all." She turned her back on him before she blew the game too soon. "You're terrific eye candy."

He went so silent, she could hear the ticking of the wall clock. "What are you up to, Harper?"

"No good." She grinned back at him. "Definitely, one hundred percent no good." Locating napkins and paper plates on the shelf, she put them into an empty box. Searching more shelves, she asked, "Do you see the coffeemaker anywhere?"

His big hands settled on her waist. "Forget the coffeemaker," he murmured from right behind her. Leaning down, he kissed the side of her neck. "Let's talk about these no-good plans of yours."

Wow, oh, wow. She could feel his erection against her

tush and it was so tantalizing she had to fight not to wiggle. "Okay."

He nuzzled against her, his soft breath in her ear, his hands sliding around to her belly. Such incredibly large hands that covered so much ground. The thumb of his right hand nudged the bottom of her breast. The pinkie on his left hovered just over the fly of her jeans.

Temptation was a terrible thing, eating away at her common sense and obscuring the larger purpose.

He opened his mouth on her throat and she felt his tongue on her skin. When he took a soft, wet love bite, she forgot she had knees. Her legs just sort of went rubbery.

To keep her upright, he hugged her tighter and rested his chin on top of her head. "Tell me what we're doing, honey."

Took her a second to catch her breath. "You don't know?" She twisted to face him, one hand knotted in his shirt to hang on, just in case. "Because, seriously, Gage, you seemed to know exactly what you were doing."

His smile went lazy—and more relaxed than it had been since he'd found out he wouldn't fight. He slipped a hand into her hair, cupping the back of her head, rubbing a little. "I know I was making myself horny. I know you were liking it. I'm just not sure why we're doing this here and now."

"Oh." She dropped against him so she could suck in some air. "Yeah." Unfortunately, every breath filled her head with the hot scent of his powerful body. "Mmm, you are so delicious."

A strained laugh rumbled in his chest. "Harper."

"Right." To give herself some room to think, she stepped back from him. So that he'd know this wasn't just about sex, she admitted, "I care about you. You know that."

Those gorgeous brown eyes narrowed on her face. "Ditto."

That kicked her heart into such a fast rhythm, she almost gasped. *He cared about her.* "And I know you, Gage. Probably better than you think."

His smile softened, and he said all dark and sensuous-like, "Ditto again, honey."

Damn the man, even his murmurs made her hot and bothered. "Yeah, so…" Collecting her thoughts wasn't easy, not with a big hunk of sexiness right there in front of her, within reach, ready and waiting. "I know you're hammered over the lost opportunity."

"The opportunity to have sex with you?"

Her jaw loosened at his misunderstanding. "No, I meant…" Hoping sex was still an option, she cleared her throat. "I meant the fight."

"Yeah." He stared at her mouth. "That, too."

Had he somehow moved closer without her knowing it? Her back now rested against the shelving and Gage stood only an inch from touching her. "So…" she said again. "It's understandable that you'd be stomping around in a bad mood."

He chided her with a shake of his head. "I was not stomping."

"Close enough." Damn it, now she couldn't stop staring at his mouth. "But I know you want to blow it off like you're not that upset."

"I'm not *upset*." He scoffed over her word choice. "I'm disappointed. A little pissed off." His feet touched hers. "I take it you have something in mind?"

She shifted without thinking about it, and suddenly he moved one foot between hers. His hard muscled thigh pressed at the apex of her legs and every thought she had, every bit of her concentration, went to where they touched.

Casual as you please, he braced a hand on the shelf beside her head.

Gage was so good at this, at stalking an opponent, at gaining the advantage before anyone realized his intent.

But she wasn't his opponent. Keeping that in mind, she gathered her thoughts, shored up her backbone and made a proposal. "I think we should fool around." Before he could reply to that one way or the other, she added, "Out there. Where they can all see." *And hopefully you'll like that enough to want to continue in private.*

He lifted one brow, the corner of his mouth quirking. "And you called Armie kinky."

Heat rushed into her face. "No, I don't mean anything really explicit." But that was a lie, so she amended, "Well, I mean, I do. But not with an audience."

Again his eyes narrowed—and his other hand lifted to the shelving. He effectively confined her, not that she wanted freedom. With him so close, she had to tip her head back to look up at him. Her heart tried to punch out of her chest, and the sweetest little ache coiled inside her.

"I'm with you so far," he whispered, and leaned down to kiss the corner of her mouth.

"I figured, you know…" How did he expect her to think while he did that? "We could act all cozy, like you had other things on your mind. Then no one would know how distressed you are over missing the fight."

"First off, I'm not acting." His forehead touched hers. "Second, I am *not* distressed. Stop making me sound so damned weak."

Not acting? What did that mean? She licked her lips— and he noticed. "I know you're not weak." Wasn't that her point? "So…you don't like my plan?"

"I like it fine." His mouth brushed her temple, his tongue touched the inside of her ear—*Wow, that curled her toes!*—then he nibbled his way along her jaw, under her chin. "Playing with you will make for a long night."

"Yes." A long night where she'd have a chance to show him how perfect they were for each other. And if he didn't see things the same as she did, they could still end up sharing a very special evening together. If she didn't have him forever, she'd at least have that memory to carry her through.

But before she settled for only a memory, she hoped to—

A sharp rap on the door made her jump.

Gage just groaned.

Through the closed door, Armie asked, "You two naked?"

Puffing up with resentment at the intrusion, Harper started around Gage.

Before she got far, he caught her. Softly, he said, "Don't encourage him," before walking to the door and opening it. "What do you want, Armie?"

"Refreshments for everyone." Armie peeked around him, ran his gaze over Harper, and frowned. "Damn, fully clothed. And here I was all geared up for a peep show."

Harper threw a roll of paper towels at him.

When Armie ducked, they went right past him and out into the hall.

Stack said, "Hey!"

And they all grinned.

Getting back to business, she finished filling the box with prepackaged cookies, chips and pretzels, then shoved it all into Armie's arms, making him stumble back a foot.

He just laughed at her, the jerk.

"Where did you hide the coffeemaker?" Harper asked, trying to sound normal instead of primed.

"I'll get it." Armie looked at each of them. "Plan to join us anytime soon?"

Unruffled by the interruption, Gage said, "Be right there."

"Not to be a spoilsport, but a group of the high school boys have arrived, so, seriously, you might want to put a lid on the hanky-panky for a bit."

"People are here already?" She'd thought she had an hour yet. "They're early."

Armie shrugged. "Everyone is excited to watch Cannon fight again." He clapped Gage on the shoulder. "Sucks you're not out there, man."

"Next time," Gage said easily with no inflection at all.

Harper couldn't help but glance at him with sympathy.

"If you insist on molesting him," Armie said, "better get on with it real quick."

She reached for him, but he ducked out laughing.

She watched Armie go down the hall.

Gage studied her. "You going to molest me, honey?"

Did he want her to? Because, seriously, she'd be willing. "Let's see how it goes."

His eyes widened a little over that.

She dragged out a case of cola. Gage shook off his surprise and took it from her, and together they headed back out.

A half hour later they had everything set up. The colas were in the cooler under ice, sandwiches had been cut and laid out. A variety of chips filled one entire table. More people arrived. The boys, ranging in ages from fifteen to eighteen, were hyped up, talking loudly and gobbling down the food in record time. The women spent their time sidling up to the guys.

The guys spent their time enjoying it.

"Is there more food in the back room?"

Harper smiled at Stack Hannigan, one of the few fighters who hadn't yet staked out a woman. "Yeah, but I can get it as soon as I finish tidying up here." Every ten minutes she needed to reorganize the food. Once the fights started, things would settle down, but until then it was pure chaos.

Stack tugged on a lock of her hair. "No worries, doll. Be right back." And off he went.

Harper watched him walk away, as always enjoying the show. Long-legged with a rangy stride, Stack looked impressive whether he was coming or going—as all of them did.

In some ways, the guys were all different.

Stack's blond hair was darker and straighter than Armie's. Denver's brown hair was so long he often contained it in a ponytail. Cannon's was pitch-black with a little curl on the ends.

She preferred Gage's trimmed brown hair, and she absolutely loved his golden-brown eyes.

All of the fighters were good-looking. Solid, muscular, capable. But where Stack, Armie and Cannon were light heavyweights, her Gage was a big boy, a shredded heavyweight with fists the size of hams. They were all friends, but with different fighting styles and different levels of expertise.

When Stack returned with another platter of food, he had two high school wrestlers beside him, talking a mile a minute. She loved seeing how the older boys emulated the fighters, learning discipline, self-control and confidence.

With the younger kids, it sometimes broke her heart to see how desperate they were for attention. And then when one or more of the guys made a kid feel special, her heart expanded so much it choked her.

"You're not on your period, are you?" Armie asked from beside her.

Using the back of her hand to quickly dash away a tear, Harper asked him, "What are you talking about?"

"You're all fired up one minute, hot and bothered the next, now standing here glassy-eyed." Leaning down to better see her, he searched her face and scowled. "What the hell, woman? Are you *crying?*"

She slugged him in the shoulder—which meant she hurt her hand more than she hurt him. Softly, because it wasn't a teasing subject, she said, "I was thinking how nice this is for the younger boys."

"Yeah." He tugged at his ear and his smile went crooked. "Makes me weepy sometimes, too."

Harper laughed at that. "You are so full of it."

He grinned with her, then leveled her by saying, "How come you're letting those other gals climb all over Gage?"

She jerked around so fast she threw herself off balance. Trapped by the reception desk, Gage stood there while two women fawned over him. Harper felt mean. More than mean. "What is he doing now?"

"Greeting people, that's all. Not that the ladies aren't giving it the old college try." He leaned closer, his voice low. "I approve of your methods, by the way."

"Meaning what?"

"Guys have to man up and all that. Be tough. But I know he'd rather be in the arena than here with us."

Than here—with her. She sighed.

Armie tweaked her chin. "Don't be like that."

"Like what?"

"All 'poor little me, I'm not a priority.' You're smarter than that, Harper. You know he's worked years for this."

She did know it, and that's why it hurt so much. If it wasn't so important to him, she might stand a chance.

"Oh, gawd," Armie drawled, managing to look both disgusted and mocking. "You're deeper down in the dumps than he is." He tipped up her chin. "You know, it took a hell of a lot of discipline for him to walk away from everyone, including you, so he could train with another camp."

She gave him a droll look rife with skepticism.

Armie wasn't finished. "It's not like he said goodbye to you and then indulged any other women. Nope. It was celibacy all the way."

"That's a myth." She knew because she'd looked it up. "Guys do not have to do without in order to compete."

"Without sex, no. Without distractions, yeah. And you, Harper Gates, are one hell of a distraction."

Was she? She just couldn't tell.

Armie leaned in closer, keeping his voice low. "The thing is, if you were serving it up regular-like, it'd probably be okay."

She shoved him. "Armie!" Her face went hot. Did everyone know her damn business? Had Gage talked? Complained?

Holding up his hands in surrender, Armie said, "It's true. Sex, especially good sex with someone important, works wonders for clearing the mind of turmoil. But when the lady is holding out—"

She locked her jaw. "Just where did you get this info?"

That made him laugh. "No one told me, if that's what you're thinking. Anyone with eyes can see that you two haven't sealed the deal yet."

Curious, eyes narrowed in skepticism, she asked, "How?"

"For one thing, the way Gage looks at you, like he's waiting to unwrap a special present."

More heat surfaced, coloring not only her face, but her throat and chest, too.

"Anyway," Armie said, after taking in her blush with a brow raised in interest, "you want to wait, he cares enough not to push, so he did without. It's admirable, not a reason to drag around like your puppy died or something. Not every guy has that much heart." He held out his arms. "Why do you think I only do local fighting?"

"You have the heart," Harper defended. But she added, "I have no idea what motivates you, I just know it must be something big."

Pleased by her reasoning, he admitted, "You could be right." Before she could jump on that, he continued. "My point is that Gage is a fighter all the way. He'll be a champion one day. That means he has to make certain sacrifices, some at really inconvenient times."

Oddly enough, she felt better about things, and decided to tease him back a little. "So I was a sacrifice?"

"Giving up sex is always a sacrifice." He slung an arm around her shoulders and hauled her into his side. "Especially the sex you haven't had yet."

"Armie!" She enjoyed his insights, but he was so cavalier about it, so bold, she couldn't help but continue blushing.

"Now, Harper, you know..." Suddenly Armie went quiet. "Damn, for such a calm bastard, he has the deadliest stare."

Harper looked up to find Gage scrutinizing them. And he did look rather hot under the collar. Even as the two attractive women did their best to regain his attention, Gage stayed focused on her.

She tried smiling at him. He just transferred his piercing gaze to Armie.

"You could go save him from them," Harper suggested.

"Sorry, honey, not my type."

"What?" she asked as if she didn't already know. "The lack of a Mohawk bothers you?"

He laughed, surprised her with a loud kiss right on her mouth and a firm swat on her butt, then he sauntered away.

CHAPTER THREE

GAGE LOOKED READY to self-combust, so Harper headed over to him. He tracked her progress, and even when she reached him, he still looked far too intent and serious.

"Hey," she said.

"Hey, yourself."

She eyed the other ladies. "See those guys over there?" She pointed to where Denver and Stack loitered by the food, stuffing their faces. "They're shy, but they're really hoping you'll come by to say hi."

It didn't take much more than that for the women to depart.

Gage reached out and tucked her hair behind her ear. "Now why didn't I think of that?"

"Maybe you were enjoying the admiration a little too much."

"No." He touched her cheek, trailed his fingertips down to her chin. "You and Armie had your heads together long enough. Care to share what you two talked about?"

She shrugged. "You."

"Huh." His hand curved around her nape, pulling her in. "That's why he kissed you and played patty-cake with your ass?"

She couldn't be this close to him without touching. Her hands opened on his chest, smoothing over the prominent muscles. What his chest did for a T-shirt should be illegal. "Now, Gage, I know you're not jealous."

His other hand covered hers, flattening her palm over his heart. "Do I have reason to be?"

"Over *Armie?*" She gave a very unladylike snort. "Get real."

He continued to study her.

Sighing, she said, "If you want to know—"

"I do."

Why not tell him? she thought. It'd be interesting to see his reaction. "Actually, it's kind of funny. See, Armie was encouraging me to have sex with you."

Gage's expression went still, first with a hint of surprise, then with the heat of annoyance. "What the hell does it have to do with him?"

No way could she admit that Armie thought they were both sad sacks. "Nothing. You know Armie."

"Yeah." He scowled darker. "I know him."

Laughing, she rolled her eyes. "He's lacking discretion, says whatever he thinks and enjoys butting in." She snuggled in closer to him, leaning on him. Loving him. "He wants you happy."

"I'm happy, damn it."

She didn't bother telling him how *un*happy he sounded just then. "And he wants me happy."

Smoothing a hand down her back, pressing her closer still, he asked, "Sex will make you happy?"

Instead of saying, *I love you so much, sex with you would make me ecstatic,* she quipped, "It'd sure be better than a stinging butt, which is all Armie offered."

"Want me to kiss it and make it better?"

She opened her mouth, but nothing came out.

With a small smile of satisfaction, Gage palmed her cheek, gently caressing. "I'll take that as a yes."

She gave a short nod.

He used his hand on her butt to snug her in closer. "Armie kissed you, too."

Making a face, she told him, "Believe me, the swat was far more memorable."

"Good thing for Armie."

So he *was* jealous?

"Hey," Stack called over to them. "We're ready to get things started. Kill the overhead lights, will you?"

Still looking down at her, Gage slowly nodded. "Sure thing." Taking Harper with him, he went to the front desk and retrieved the barrel key for the locking switches.

The big TV, along with a security lamp in the hallway, would provide all the light they needed. When Gage inserted the key and turned it, the overhead florescent lights clicked off. Given that they stood well away from the others, heavy shadows enveloped them.

Rather than head over to the crowd, Gage aligned her body with his in a tantalizing way. His hand returned to her bottom, ensuring she stayed pressed to him. "Maybe," he whispered, "I can be more memorable."

As he moved his hand lower on her behind—his long fingers seeking inward—she went on tiptoe and squeaked, *"Definitely."*

Smiling, he took her mouth in a consuming kiss. Combined with the way those talented fingers did such incredible things to her, rational thought proved impossible.

Finally, easing up with smaller kisses and teasing nibbles, he whispered, "We can't do this here."

Her fingers curled in against him, barely making a dent in his rock-solid muscles. "I know," she groaned.

He stroked restless hands up and down her back. "Want to grab a seat with me?"

He asked the question almost as if a big *or* hung at the

end. Like… *Or should we just leave? Or should we find an empty room?*

Or would you prefer to go anywhere private so we can both get naked and finish what we started?

She waited, hopeful, but when he said nothing more, she blew out a disappointed breath. "Sure."

And of course she felt like a jerk.

He and Cannon were close friends. Everyone knew he wanted to watch the fights. Despite his own disappointment over medical ineligibility, he was excited for Cannon's competition.

Her eyes were adjusting and she could see Gage better now, the way he searched her face, how he…waited.

For her to understand? Was Armie right? Maybe more than anything she needed to show him that she not only loved him, but she loved his sport, that she supported him and was as excited by his success as he was.

"Yes, let's sit." She took his hand. "Toward the back, though, so we can sneak away later if we decide to." Eyes flaring at that naughty promise, he didn't budge.

"Sneak away to where?"

"The way I feel right now, any empty room might do." Hiding her smile, Harper stretched up to give him a very simple kiss. "That is, between fights. We don't want to miss anything."

His hand tightened on hers, and she couldn't help thinking that maybe Armie's suggestion had merit after all.

GAGE GOT SO caught up in the prefights that he almost— *almost*—forgot about Harper's endless foreplay. Damn, she had him primed. Her closeness, the warmth of her body, the sweet scent of her hair and the warmer scent of her skin, were enough to make him edgy with need. But every so often her hand drifted to his thigh, lingered, stroked. Each time he held his breath, unsure how far she'd go.

How far he wanted her to go.

So far, all he knew was that it wasn't far enough.

Once, she'd run her hand up his back, just sort of feeling him, her fingers spread as she traced muscles, his shoulder blades, down his spine...

If he gave his dick permission, it would stand at attention right now. But he concentrated on keeping control of things—himself and, when possible, Harper, too.

It wasn't easy. Though she appeared to be as into the fights as everyone else, she still had very busy hands.

It wasn't just the sexual teasing that got to him. It was emotional, too. He hated that he wasn't in Japan with Cannon, walking to the cage for his own big battle. He'd had prelim fights; he'd built his name and recognition.

He'd finally gotten that main event—and it pissed him off more than he wanted to admit that he was left sitting behind.

But sitting behind with Harper sure made it easier. Especially when he seemed so attuned to her.

If her mood shifted, he freaking felt it, deep down inside himself. At one point she hugged his arm, her head on his shoulder, and something about the embrace had felt so damn melancholy that he'd wanted to lift her into his lap and hold her close and make some heavy-duty spur-of-the-moment promises.

Holding her wouldn't have been a big deal; Miles had a chick in his lap. Denver, too.

With Harper, though, it'd be different. Everyone knew a hookup when they saw one, and no way did Gage want others to see her that way. Harper was like family at the rec center. She was part of the inner circle. He would never do anything to belittle her importance.

Beyond that, he wanted more than a hookup. He cared about her well beyond getting laid a single time, well beyond any mere friendship.

Still, as soon as possible, he planned to get her alone and, God willing, get her under him.

Or over him.

However she liked it, as long as he got her. Not just for tonight, but for a whole lot more.

Everyone grimaced when the last prelim fight ended with a grappling match—that turned into an arm bar. The dominant fighter trapped the arm, extended it to the breaking point while the other guy tried everything he could to free himself.

Squeezed up close to his side, peeking through her fingers, Harper pleaded, "Tap, tap, tap," all but begging his opponent to admit defeat before he suffered more damage. And when he did, she cheered with everyone else. "Good fight. Wow. That was intense."

It was so cute how involved she got while watching, that Gage had to tip up her chin so he could kiss her.

Her enthusiasm for the fight waned as she melted against him, saying, "Mmm…"

He smiled against her mouth. "You're making me a little nuts."

"Look who's talking." She glanced around with exaggerated drama. "If only we were alone."

Hoping she meant it, he used his thumb to brush her bottom lip. "We can be." His place. Her place. Either worked for him. "It'll be late when the fights end, but—"

"I really have to wait that long?"

Yep, she meant it. Her blue eyes were heavy, her face flushed. She breathed deeper. He glanced down at her breasts and saw her nipples were tight against the material of her T-shirt.

Okay, much more of that and he wouldn't be able to keep it under wraps.

A roar sounded around them and they both looked up to see Cannon on the screen. Gage couldn't help but grin. Yeah, he wanted to be there, too, but at the same time, he was so damn proud of Cannon.

In such a short time, Cannon had become one of the most beloved fighters in the sport. The fans adored him. His peers respected him. And the Powers That Be saw him as a big draw moneymaker. After he won tonight, Gage predicted that Cannon would be fighting for the belt.

He'd win it, too.

They showed footage of Cannon before the fight, his knit hat pulled low on his head, bundled under a big sweat-shirt. Keeping his muscles warm.

He looked as calm and determined as ever while answering questions.

Harper squeezed his hand and when she spoke, Gage realized it was with nervousness.

"He'll do okay."

Touched by her concern, he smiled. "I'd put money on it."

She nodded, but didn't look away from the screen. "He's been something of a phenomenon, hasn't he?"

"With Cannon, making an impact comes naturally."

"After he wins this one," she mused, "they'll start hyping him for a title shot."

Since her thoughts mirrored his own, he hugged her. Her uncanny insight never ceased to amaze him. Then again, she was a regular at the rec center, interacted often with fighters and enjoyed the sport. It made sense that she'd have the same understanding as him.

"Cannon's earned it." Few guys took as many fights as he did, sometimes on really short notice. If a fighter got sick—or suffered an injury, as Gage had—Cannon was there, always ready, always in shape, always kicking ass. They called him the Saint, and no wonder.

Gage glanced around at the young men who, just a few years ago, would have been hanging on the street corner looking for trouble. Now they had some direction in their lives, the attention they craved, decent role models and a good way to expend energy. But the rec center was just a small part of Cannon's goodwill.

Whenever he got back to town, he continued his efforts to protect the neighborhood. Gage had enjoyed joining their group, going on night strolls to police the corruption, to let thugs know that others were looking out for the hardworking owners of local family businesses. Actual physical conflicts were rare; overall, it was enough to show that someone was paying attention.

It didn't hurt that Cannon was friends with a tough-as-nails police lieutenant and two detectives. And then there was his buddy at the local bar, a place where Cannon used to work before he got his big break in the SBC fight organization. The owner of the bar had more contacts than the entire police department. He influenced a lot of the other businesses with his stance for integrity.

Yeah, Cannon had some colorful, capable acquaintances—which included a diverse group of MMA fighters.

Saint suited him—not that Cannon liked the moniker. It wasn't nearly as harsh as Gage's own fight name.

Thinking about that brought his attention back to Harper. She watched the TV so he saw her in profile, her long lashes, her turned up nose, her firm chin.

That soft, sexy mouth.

He liked the freckles on her cheekbones. He liked everything about her—how she looked, who she was, the way she treated others.

He smoothed Harper's hair and said, "Most women like to call me Savage."

She snorted. "It's a stupid nickname."

Pretending great insult, he leaned away. "It's a fight name, not a nickname. And it's badass."

She disagreed. "There's nothing savage about you. You should have been named Methodical or Accurate or something."

Grinning, he shook his head. "Thanks, but no thanks."

"Well," she muttered, "you're not savage. That's all I'm saying."

He'd gotten the name early on when, despite absorbing several severe blows from a more experienced fighter, he'd kept going. In the end, he'd beaten the guy with some heavy ground and pound, mostly because he'd still been fresh when the other man gassed out.

The commentator had shouted, *He's a damn savage*, and the description stuck.

To keep himself from thinking about just how savage Harper made him—with lust—he asked, "Want something to eat?"

She wrinkled her nose. "After those past few fights? Bleh."

Two of the prelim fights were bloody messes, one because of a busted nose, but the other due to a cut similar to what Gage had. Head wounds bled like a mother. During a fight, as long as the fighter wasn't hurt that badly, they wouldn't stop things over a little spilled blood. Luckily for the contender, the cut was off to the side and so the blood didn't run into his eyes.

For Gage, it hadn't mattered. If only the cut hadn't been so deep. If it hadn't needed stitches. If it would have been somewhere other than right over his eye. If—

Harper's hand trailed over his thigh again. "So, *Savage*,"

she teased, and damned if she didn't get close to his fly. "Want to help me bring out more drinks before the main event starts?"

Anything to keep him from ruminating on lost opportunities, which he was pretty sure had been Harper's intent.

"Why not?" He stood and hauled her up with him.

They had to go past Armie who stood with two very edgy women and several teenagers, munching on popcorn and comparing biceps.

Armie winked at Harper.

She smiled at him. "We'll only be a minute."

The idiot clutched his chest. "You've just destroyed all my illusions and damaged Savage's reputation beyond repair."

Gage rolled his eyes, more than willing to ignore Armie's nonsense, but he didn't get far before one of the boys asked him about his cut. Next thing he knew, he was surrounded by wide eyes and ripe curiosity. Because it was a good opportunity to show the boys how to handle disappointment, he lingered, letting them ask one question after another.

Harper didn't complain. If anything, she watched him with something that looked a lot like pride. Not exactly what he wanted from her at this particular moment, but it felt good all the same.

He didn't realize she'd gone about getting the drinks without him until Armie relieved her of two large cartons of soft drinks. Together they began putting the cans in the cooler over ice. They laughed together, and even though it looked innocent enough, it made Gage tense with—

"You two hooking up finally?"

Thoughts disrupted, Gage turned to Denver. Hard to believe he hadn't noticed the approach of a two-hundred-and-twenty-pound man. "What?"

"You and Harper," Denver said, while perusing the food that remained. "Finally going to make it official?"

"Make what official?"

"That you're an item." Denver chose half a cold cut sandwich and devoured the majority of it in one bite.

Gage's gaze sought Harper out again. Whatever Armie said to her got him a shove in return. Armie pulled an exaggerated fighter's stance, fists up, as if he thought he'd have to defend himself.

Harper pretended a low shot, Armie dropped his hands to cover the family jewels, and she smacked him on top of the head.

The way the two of them carried on, almost like siblings, made Gage feel left out.

Were he and Harper an item? He knew how he felt, but Harper could be such a mystery.

Denver shouldered him to the side so he could grab some cake. "Gotta say, man, I hope so. She was so glum while you were away, it depressed the hell out of everyone."

Hard to imagine a woman as vibrant as Harper ever down in the dumps. When he'd left for the camp in Kentucky, she'd understood, wishing him luck, telling him how thrilled she was for him.

But since his return a few days ago, things had been off. He hadn't immediately sought her out, determined to get his head together first. He didn't want pity from anyone, but the way he'd felt had been pretty damned pitiful. He'd waffled between rage at the circumstances and mind-numbing regret. No way did he want others to suffer him like that, most especially Harper.

He knew he'd see her at the rec center and had half expected her to gush over him, to fret over his injury, to sympathize.

She hadn't done any of that. Mostly she'd treated him

the same as she did the rest of the guys, leaving him confused and wallowing in his own misery.

Until tonight.

Tonight she was all about making him insane with the need to get her alone and naked.

"You listening to me, Gage?"

Rarely did another fighter call him by his given name. That Denver did so now almost felt like a reprimand from his mom. "Yeah, *Denver,* I'm listening."

"Good." Denver folded massive arms over his massive chest, puffing up like a turkey. "So what's it to be?"

If Denver expected a challenge, too bad. Gage again sought out Harper with his gaze. "She was really miserable?"

Denver deflated enough to slap him on the back. "Yeah. It was awful. Made me sad as shit, I don't mind telling you."

"What was she miserable about?"

"Dude, are you that fucking obtuse?"

Stack stepped into the conversation. "Hell, yeah, he is." Then changing the subject, Stack asked, "Did Rissy go to Japan with Cannon?"

Denver answered, saying, "Yeah, he took her and her roommate along."

Merissa, better known as Rissy, was Cannon's little sis. A roommate was news to Gage, though. "If you have ideas about his sister, you're an idiot."

Stack drew back. "No. Hell, no. Damn man, don't start rumors."

Everyone knew Cannon as a nice guy. More than nice. But he was crazy-particular when it came to Merissa. For that reason, the guys all looked past her, through her or when forced to it, with nothing more than respect. "Who's the roommate?"

"Sweet Cherry Pie," Denver rumbled low and with feeling.

Stack grinned at him.

Gage totally missed the joke. "What?"

"Cherry Payton," Denver said, and damn if he didn't almost sigh. "Long blond hair, big chocolate-brown eyes, extra fine body…"

"Another one bites the dust," Stack said with a laugh.

"Another one?"

"Obtuse," Denver lamented.

Stack nodded toward Harper. "You being the first, dumb ass."

"We all expect you to make her feel better about things."

Confusion kicked his temper up a notch. "What *things?*"

Slapping a hand over his heart, Stack said, "How you feel."

Striking a similar pose, Denver leaned into Stack. "What you want."

Heads together, they intoned, *"Love."*

"You're both morons." But damn it, he realized that he did love her. Probably had for a long time. How could he not? Priorities could be a bitch and he hated the idea that he'd maybe made Harper unhappy by not understanding his feelings sooner.

He chewed his upper lip while wondering how to correct things.

"Honesty," Stack advised him. "Tell her how the schedule goes, what to expect and leave the rest up to her."

"Harper's smart," Denver agreed. "She'll understand."

It irked Gage big-time to have everyone butting into his personal business. "Don't you guys have something better to do than harass me?"

"I have some*one* better to do," Stack told him, nodding toward one of the women who'd hit on Gage earlier.

"Butting in to your business was just my goodwill gesture of the day." And with that he sauntered off.

Denver leaned back on the table of food. "We all like Harper, you know."

Gage was starting to think they liked her a little too much. "Yeah, I get that."

"So quit dicking around, will you?" He grabbed up another sandwich and he, too, joined a woman.

Gage stewed for half a minute, turned—and almost ran into Harper.

CHAPTER FOUR

GAGE CAUGHT HER ARMS, steadying them both. "Why does everyone keep sneaking up on me?"

She brushed off his hands. "If you hadn't been ogling the single ladies, maybe you'd be more aware."

She absolutely had to know better than to think that, but just in case... "How could I notice any other woman with you around?"

She eyed him. "Do you notice other women when I'm not around?"

Damn, he thought, did she really *not* know how much he cared? Worse, had she been sad while he was away?

The possibility chewed on his conscience. "No, I don't." He drew her up to kiss her sweetly, and then, because this was Harper, not so sweetly.

To give her back a little, he shared his own complaint. "You spend way too much time horsing around with Armie."

Shrugging, she reached for a few chips. "I was trying not to crowd you."

"What does that mean?"

While munching, she gestured around the interior of the rec center. "This is a fight night. You're hanging with your buds. When I see you guys talking, I don't want to horn in."

Whoa. Those were some serious misconceptions. To help clear things up, he cupped her face. "You can't."

"Can't what?"

"Horn in. Ever."

Brows pinching in disgruntlement, she shoved away from him. "I just told you I wouldn't."

He hauled her right back. "I'm not saying you shouldn't, honey, I'm saying you can't because there's never a bad time for you to talk to me. Remember that, okay?"

Astonished, she blinked up at him, and he wanted to declare himself right then. Luckily the first fight on the main card started and everyone went back to their seats, saving him from rushing her.

This time, Gage had a hard time concentrating. He saw the fight, he cheered, but more of his attention veered to Harper, to how quiet she was now.

Thinking about him?

The fight ended in the first round with a knockout.

Instead of reacting with everyone else, Harper turned her face up to his. As if no time had passed at all, she said, "That's not entirely true."

Damn, but it was getting more difficult by the second to keep his hands off her. He contented himself by opening his hand on her waist, stroking up to her ribs then down to her hip. "What's that?"

"There are plenty of times when I can't intrude."

She was still stewing about that? "No."

Like a thundercloud, she darkened. Turning to more fully face him, she said low, *"Yes."* Before he could correct her, she insisted, "But I want you to know that I understand."

Apparently she didn't. "How so?"

Leaning around him, she glanced at one and all to ensure there were no eavesdroppers. As if uncertain, she puckered her brows while trying to find the right words. "I know when you're in training—"

"I'm pretty much always in training."

She looked like she wanted to smack him. "There's training and then there's *training*."

True enough. "You mean when I go away to another camp."

"That, and when you're close to a fight."

Should he tell her how much he'd enjoy coming home to her—every night, not just between fights? Would she ever be willing to travel with him? Or to wait for him when she couldn't?

He had a feeling Harper would fit seamlessly into his life no matter what he had going on.

Being as honest as he could, Gage nodded. "There will be times when my thoughts are distracted, when I have to focus on other stuff. But that doesn't mean I don't care. It sure as hell doesn't mean you have to keep your distance."

The next fight started and though a few muted conversations continued, most in attendance kept their comments limited to the competition. Beside him, Harper fell silent. Gage could almost feel her struggling to sort out everything he'd said.

Again, he found himself studying her profile; not just her face, but her body, too. Her breasts weren't large, but they fit her frame, especially with her small waist and the sexy flare of her hips. She kept her long legs crossed, one foot nervously rocking. She drew in several deep breaths. A pulse tripped in her throat.

By the second the sexual tension between them grew.

The end of the night started to feel like too many hours away. They had at least three more fights on the main card. Cannon's fight would be last. It wasn't a title fight, but it'd still go five rounds.

The current match went all three rounds and came down to a split decision. Gage no longer cared; hell, he'd missed more of the fight than he'd seen.

Around him, voices rose in good-natured debate about how the judges had gotten it right or wrong.

"What do you think?" Gage asked Harper.

She shrugged. "Depends on how the judges scored things. The guy from Brazil really pushed the fight, but the other one landed more blows. Still, he didn't cause that much damage, and the Brazilian got those two takedowns—"

Gage put a finger to her mouth. "I meant about us."

Her wide-eyed gaze swung to his. "Oh." She gulped, considered him, then whispered, "I like it."

"It?"

"There being an 'us.'"

Yeah, he liked it, too, maybe more than he'd realized before now. "I missed you while I was away."

She scoffed. "You were way too busy for that."

"I worked hard, no denying it. But it wasn't 24/7. I found myself alone with my thoughts far too often."

She forced a smile. "I'm sure at those times you were obsessed about the SBC, about the competition, about winning."

"All that—plus you." When it came to priorities, she was at the top. He'd just made too many assumptions for her to realize it.

She looked tortured for a moment before her hand knotted in his shirt and she pulled him closer. With pained accusation, she said, "You didn't call."

Hot with regret, Gage covered her hand with his own. "I was trying to focus." Saying it out loud, he felt like an ass.

But Harper nodded. "That's what I'm saying. There will be times when I need to stay out of your way so I don't mess with that focus."

He hated the idea of her avoiding him.

Almost as much as he hated the thought of ever leaving her again. Yet that was a reality. He was a fighter; he would go to other camps to train, travel around the country, around the world.

He'd go where the SBC sent him.

"You have to know, Gage. I'd never get in your way, not on purpose."

He almost groaned.

"I'm serious! I know how important your career is and I know what a nuisance it can be to—"

Suddenly starved for the taste of her, for the feel of her, Gage took her mouth in a firm kiss.

But that wasn't enough, so he turned his head and nibbled her bottom lip until she opened. When he licked inside her warm, damp mouth, her breath hitched. Mindful of where they were, he nonetheless had a hell of time tempering his lust.

Damn it.

The next fight started. Cannon would be after that.

In a sudden desperate rush, Gage left his chair, pulling her up and along with him as he headed toward the dimly lit hallway. He couldn't wait a second more. But for what he had to say, had to explain, he needed the relative privacy of a back room.

Luckily she'd seated them at the end of the back row. In only a few steps, and without a lot of attention, he had them on their way.

Tripping along with him, Harper whispered, *"Gage."*

"There are high school boys out there," he told her. He glanced in the storage room, but no, that was too close to the main room and the activity of the group.

"I know. So?"

He brought her up and alongside him so he could slip an arm around her. "So they don't need to see me losing my head over you."

She stopped suddenly, which forced him to stop.

Looking far too shy for the ballsy woman he knew her to be, she whispered, "Are you?"

This time he understood her question. "Losing my head over you?" Gently, he said, "No."

Her shoulders bunched as if she might slug him.

Damn, but he adored her. "I lost it a long time ago. I just forgot to tell you."

Suspicious, she narrowed her eyes. "What does that mean exactly?"

Not about to declare himself in a freaking hallway, he took her hands and started backing up toward the office. "Come along with me and I'll explain everything." This particular talk was long overdue.

She didn't resist, but she did say, "The fight you should have been in is next. And Cannon will be fighting soon after that."

"I know." At the moment, seeing the fight he'd missed was the furthest thing from his mind. As to Cannon, well, he'd be in a lot of fights. This wasn't his first, wouldn't be his last. If all went well, Gage would get her commitment to spend the night, and more, before Cannon entered the cage. "The thing is, I need you."

She searched his face. "Need me...how?"

In every way imaginable. "Let me show you."

Her gaze went over his body. "Sounds to me like you're talking about sex."

Did lust taint his brain, or did she sound hopeful? They reached the office door and he tried the handle. Locked, of course. Trying not to think about how the night would end, he said, "Seriously, Harper, much as I love that idea, we're at the rec center."

"So?"

Damn, she knew how to throw him. He sucked in air and forged on. "I thought we'd talk." Digging in his pocket, he found the keys he'd picked up earlier when he shut off the lights.

Sarcasm added a wicked light to her beautiful blue eyes. "Talk? That's what you want to do? Seriously?"

"Yeah. See, I need to explain a few things to you and it's better done in private." The door opened and he drew her in.

Typical of Harper, she took the initiative, shutting and locking the door, then grabbing him. "We're alone." Her mouth brushed his chin, his jaw, his throat. "Say what you need to say."

"I love you."

She went so still, it felt like he held a statue. Ignoring her lack of a response, Gage cupped her face. "I love you, Harper Gates. Have for a while now. I'm sorry I didn't realize it sooner. I'm especially sorry I didn't figure it out before I took off for Kentucky."

Confused, but also defending him, she whispered, "You were excited about the opportunity."

She made him sound like a kid, when at the moment he felt very much like a man. "True." Slowly, he leaned into her, pinning her up against the door, arranging her so that they fit together perfectly. She was so slight, so soft and feminine—when she wasn't giving him or one of the other fighters hell. "I thought it'd be best for me to concentrate only on the upcoming fight, but that was asinine."

"No," she said, again defending him. "It made sense."

"Loving you makes sense." He took her mouth, and never wanted to stop kissing her. Hot and deep. Soft and sweet. With Harper it didn't matter. However she kissed him, it blew his mind and pushed all his buttons.

He brushed damp kisses over to the side of her neck, up to her ear.

On a soft wail, Harper said, "How can you love me? We haven't even had sex yet."

"Believe me, I know." He covered her breast with his hand, gently kneading her, loving the weight of her, how her nipple tightened. He wanted to see her, wanted to take her in his mouth. "We can change that later tonight."

"I'll never last that long." She stretched up along his body, both hands tangled in his hair, anchoring him so she could feast off his mouth.

No way would he argue with her.

Everything went hot and urgent between them.

He coasted a hand down her side, caught her thigh and lifted her leg up alongside his. Nudging in against her, knowing he could take her this way, right here, against the door, pushed him over the edge.

Not what he would have planned for their first time, but with Harper so insistent, he couldn't find the brain cells to offer up an alternative.

"Are you sure?" he asked, while praying that she was.

"Yes. Now, Gage." She moved against him. "Right now."

HARPER GRABBED FOR his T-shirt and shoved it up so she could get her hands on his hot flesh, so she could explore all those amazing muscles. Unlike some of the guys, he didn't shave his chest and she loved—*loved, loved, loved*— his body hair.

God, how could any man be so perfect?

She got the shirt above his pecs and leaned in to brush her nose over his chest hair, to deeply inhale his incredible scent. It filled her head, making her dazed with need.

When she took a soft love bite, he shuddered. "Take it easy."

No, she wouldn't.

"We have to slow down or I'm a goner."

But she couldn't. Never in her life had she known she'd miss someone as much as she'd missed him when he'd left. Now he was back, and whether he really loved her or was just caught up in the moment, she'd worry about it later.

She needed him. All of him.

She cupped him through his jeans and heard him groan. He was thick and hard and throbbing.

He sucked in a breath. "Harper, baby, seriously, we have to slow down." Taking her wrist, he lifted her hand away. "You need to catch up a little."

"I'm there already." She'd been there since first deciding on her course of action for the night.

"Not quite." Gage carried both her hands to his shoulders before kissing her senseless, giving her his tongue, drawing hers into his mouth.

She couldn't get enough air into her starving lungs but didn't care. Against her belly she felt his heavy erection, and she wanted to touch him again, to explore him in more detail.

He caught the hem of her T-shirt, drawing it up and over her head. Barely a heartbeat passed before he flipped open the front closure on her bra and the cups parted.

Taking her mouth again, he groaned as his big hands gently molded over her, his thumbs teasing her nipples until she couldn't stop squirming. She wasn't one of the overly stacked groupies who dogged his heels, but she didn't dislike her body, either.

She'd always considered herself not big, but big enough.

Now, with his enormous hands on her, she felt delicate—even more so when he scooped an arm under her behind and easily lifted her up so he could draw one nipple into his hot mouth.

Harper wrapped her legs around his waist, her arms

around his neck. He took his time, drawing on her for what felt like forever, until she couldn't keep still, couldn't contain the soft cries of desperate need.

From one breast to the other, he tasted, teased, sucked, nibbled.

"Gage…" Even saying his name took an effort. "Please."

"Please what?" he asked, all full of masculine satisfaction and a fighter's control. He licked her, circling, teasing. "Please more?"

"Yes."

Back on her feet, she dropped against the door. He opened her jeans and a second later shoved them, and her panties, down to her knees.

Anticipation kept her still, kept her breath rushing and her heart pounding. But he just stood there, sucking air and waiting for God knew what.

"Gage?" she whispered with uncertainty.

One hand flattened on the wall beside her head, but he kept his arm locked out, his body from touching hers. "I should take you to my place," he rasped, sounding tortured. "I should take you someplace with more time, more privacy, more—"

Panic tried to set in. "Don't you even *think* about stopping now." No way could he leave her like this.

His mouth touched her cheek, the corner of her lips, her jaw, her temple. "No, I won't. I can't."

A loud roar sounded from the main part of the room. Knowing what that meant, that Cannon's fight was about to start, guilt nearly leveled Harper. "I forgot," she admitted miserably.

"Doesn't matter," he assured her.

But of course it did. He was here to watch Cannon compete, to join in with his fight community to celebrate a close friend.

She was here to show him she wouldn't interfere and yet, that's exactly what she'd done. "We could—"

"No, baby." Need made his short laugh gravelly. "Believe me when I say that I *can't*."

"Oh." Her heart started punching again—with excitement. "We'll miss the fight."

"We'll catch the highlights later. Together." He stroked her hair with his free hand, over her shoulder, down the side of her body.

"You're sure?"

Against her mouth, he whispered, "Give or take a bed for convenience, I'm right where I want to be." His kiss scorched her, and he added, "With you."

Aww. Hearing him say it was nice, but knowing he meant it multiplied everything she felt, and suddenly she couldn't wait. She took his hand and guided it across her body.

And between her legs.

They both groaned.

At first he just cupped her, his palm hot, his hand covering so much of her. They breathed together, taut with expectation.

"It seems like I've wanted you forever," he murmured at the same time as his fingers searched over her, touching carefully. His forehead to hers, he added, "Mmm. You're wet."

Speaking wasn't easy, but he deserved the truth. "Because I *have* wanted you forever."

"I'm glad, Harper." His fingers parted her swollen lips, stroked gently over her, delved. "Widen your legs a little more."

That husky, take-charge, turned-on tone nearly put her over the edge. Holding on to his shoulders, her face tucked into his throat, she widened her stance. Using two fingers, he glided over her, once, twice, testing her readiness—and he pressed both fingers deep.

Legs stiffening, Harper braced against the door.

"Stay with me," Gage said before kissing her throat.

She felt his teeth on her skin, his hot breath, those oh-so-talented fingers.

"Damn, you feel good. Tight and wet and perfect." He worked her, using his hand to get her close to climax. "Relax just a little."

"Can't." Her fingernails bit into his shoulders. "Oh, God."

"If we were on a bed," he growled against her throat, "I could get to your nipples. But you're so short—"

"I'm not," she gasped, unsure whether she'd be able to take that much excitement. "You're just so damn big."

"Soon as you come for me," he promised, "I'll show you how big I am."

Such a braggart. Of course, she'd already had a good idea, given she often saw him in nothing more than athletic shorts. And she'd already had her hands on him. Not long enough to do all the exploring she wanted to do, but enough to—

He brought his thumb up to her clitoris, and she clenched all over.

"Nice," he told her. "I can feel you getting closer."

Shut up, Gage. She thought it but didn't say it, because words right now, at this particular moment, would be far too difficult.

He cupped her breast and, in keeping with the accelerated tempo of the fingers between her legs, he tugged at her nipple.

The first shimmer of approaching release took her to her tiptoes. *"Gage."*

"I've got you."

The next wave, stronger, hotter, made her groan in harsh pleasure.

"I love you, Harper."

Luckily, at that propitious moment, something happened in the fight because everyone shouted and cheered—and that helped to drown out the harsh groans of Harper's release.

CHAPTER FIVE

GAGE BADLY WANTED to turn on lights, to strip Harper naked and then shuck out of his own clothes. He wanted to touch her all over, taste her everywhere, count her every freckle while feeling her against him, skin on skin, with no barriers.

Even with her T-shirt shoved up above her breasts and her jeans down around her knees, holding Harper in his arms was nice. Her scent had intensified, her body now a warm, very soft weight limp against him. He kept one hand tangled in her hair, the other cupping her sexy ass.

He let her rest while she caught her breath.

If he'd found a better time and place for this, he could stretch her out on a bed, or the floor or a table—didn't matter as long as he could look at every inch of her, kiss her all over.

Devour her slowly, at his leisure.

But they were in an office, at the rec center, with a small crowd of fighters and fans only a hallway away.

He kissed her temple, hugged her protectively.

His cock throbbed against her belly. He badly wanted to be inside her, driving them both toward joint release.

But this, having Harper sated and cuddling so sweetly... yeah, that was pretty damn special.

"Mmm," she murmured. "I lost my bones somewhere."

"I have one you can borrow."

He felt her grin against his throat, then her full-body

rub as she wiggled against him. "Yes," she teased. "Yes, you do."

"I like hearing you come, Harper." With small pecks, he nudged up her face so he could get to her mouth. "Whatever you do, you do it well."

That made her laugh, so the kiss was a little silly, tickling.

She drew in a deep breath, shored up her muscles, and somewhat stood on her own. "The fight is still going on?"

"Sounds like."

"So all that excitement before—"

"You coming?"

She bit his chest, inciting his lust even more. "No, I meant with everyone screaming."

"Probably a near submission. Cannon is good on the ground, good with submissions." Good with every facet of fighting. "But let's not talk about Cannon right now."

"You really don't mind missing his fight?"

"Jesus, woman, I'm about to bust my jeans. Cannon is the furthest thing from my mind."

Happy with his answer, she said, "Okay, then, let's talk about you." She nibbled her way up to his throat. "There is just so much of you to enjoy."

"You could start here," he said, taking one of her small, soft hands down to press against his fly.

"I think I will." With her forehead to his sternum, she watched her hands as she opened the snap to his jeans, slowly eased down the zipper. "I wish we had more light in here."

Because that mirrored his earlier thought, he nodded. "You can just sort of feel your way around."

"Is that what you did?" Using both hands, she held him, so no way could he reply. She stroked his length, squeezed him. "You are so hard."

"Yup." He couldn't manage anything more detailed than that.

"You have a condom?"

"Wallet."

Still touching him, she clarified, "You have a condom in your wallet?"

"Yup."

She tipped her face up to see him, and he could hear the humor in her voice. "A little turned on?"

"A *lot* turned on." He covered her hand with his own and got her started on a stroking rhythm he loved. *"Damn."*

Harper whispered, "Kiss me."

And he did, taking her mouth hard, twining his tongue with hers, making himself crazy by again exploring her, the silky skin of her bottom, the dampness between her thighs, her firm breasts and stiffened nipples.

Harper released him just long enough to say, "Shirt off, big boy." She tried shoving it up, but Gage took over, reaching over his back for a fistful of cotton and jerking the material away. Anticipating her hands, her mouth, on his hot skin, he dropped the shirt.

She didn't disappoint. Hooking her fingers in the waistband of his jeans, she shoved down the denim and his boxers, too, then started feeling him all over. His shoulders to his hips. His pecs to his abs. She grazed her palms over his nipples, then went back to his now throbbing cock.

"You are so impressive in so many ways."

He tried to think up a witty reply, but with her small, soft hands on him, he could barely breathe, much less banter.

"I've thought about something so many times…" And with no more warning than that, she sank to her knees.

Oh, God. Gage locked his muscles, one hand settling on top of her head.

Holding him tight, Harper skimmed her lips over the sensitive head, licked down the length of his shaft.

Never one for half measures, she drew her tongue back up and slid her mouth over him.

A harsh groan reverberated out of his chest. "Harper."

Her clever tongue swirled over and around him—and she took him deep again.

Too much. Way too much. He clasped her shoulder. "Sorry, honey, but I can't take it."

She continued anyway.

"Harper," he warned.

She reached around him, clasping his ass as if she thought she could control him.

But control of any kind quickly spiraled away. Later, he thought to himself, he'd enjoy doing this again, letting her have her way, giving her all the time she wanted.

Just not now, not when he so desperately wanted to be inside her.

"Sorry, honey." He caught her under the arms and lifted her to her feet, then set her away from him while he gasped for breath. As soon as he could, he dug out his wallet and fumbled for the condom.

Sounding breathless and hot, she whispered, "You taste so good."

He'd never last. "Shh." He rolled on the condom with trembling hands. Stepping up to her in a rush, he stripped away her shirt and bra, shoved her jeans lower. "Hold on to me."

Hooking her right knee with his elbow, he lifted her leg, opening her as much as he could with her jeans still on, his still on. He moved closer still, kissing her until they were both on the ragged edge.

"Now," Harper demanded.

He nudged against her, found his way, and sank deep in one strong thrust.

More cheers sounded in the outer room, but neither of them paid much attention. Already rocking against her, Gage admitted, "I'm not going to last."

She matched the rhythm he set. "I don't need you to... *Gage!*"

Kissing her, he muffled her loud cries as she came, holding him tight, squeezing him tighter, her entire body shimmering in hot release. Seconds later he pinned her to the door, pressed his face into her throat, and let himself go.

For several minutes he was deaf and blind to everything except the feel of Harper in his arms where she belonged.

Little aftershocks continued to tease her intimate muscles, and since he remained joined with her, he felt each one. Their heartbeats danced together.

Gradually he became aware of people talking in the outer room. They sounded happy and satisfied, telling him the fight had ended.

Harper came to the same realization. "Oh, no. We missed everything?"

"Not everything." After a nudge against her to remind what they hadn't missed, he disengaged their bodies. Slowly he eased her leg down, staying close to support her—which was sort of a joke, given how shaky he felt, too.

"Do you think Cannon won?"

"I know he did."

Her fingers moved over his face, up to the corner of his eye near his stitches. "You're sure?"

"Absolutely." He brought her hand to his mouth and kissed her palm. "I was sure even before the fight started."

Letting out a long breath, she dropped her head. "I'm sorry we missed it."

"I don't have any regrets."

She thought about that for a second, then worried aloud, "They'll all know what we were doing."

"Yeah." There was barely enough light to see, but he located paper in the printer, stole a sheet, and used it to wrap up the spent condom. He pitched it into the metal waste can.

"I hope they didn't hear us."

Gage tucked himself away and zipped his jeans. "Even if they did—"

She groaned over the possibility. "No, no, no."

Pulling her back into his arms, he teased, "They won't ask for too many details."

Her fisted hands pressed against his chest. "I swear, if Armie says a single word, I'll—"

Gage kissed her. Then touched her breasts. And her belly.

And lower.

"Gage," she whispered, all broken up. "We can't. Not now."

"Not here," he agreed, while paying homage to her perfect behind. "Come home with me."

"Okay."

He'd told her that he loved her. She hadn't yet said how she felt. But while she was being agreeable... "I'll fight again in two months."

Gasping with accusation, she glared at him. "You knew you'd fight again—"

"Of course I will." He snorted. "I got injured. I didn't quit."

"Yeah, I know. But..." Her confusion washed over him. "I didn't realize things were already set. Why didn't you tell me?"

"Didn't come up." He kissed the end of her nose. "And

honestly, I was too busy raging about the fight I'd miss to talk about the next one."

He felt her stillness. "You're not raging anymore?"

"Mellow as a newborn kitten," he promised. "Thank you for that."

Thinking things through, she ran her hands up his chest to his collarbone. "Where?"

"Canada."

Gage felt her putting her shoulders back, straightening her spine, shoring herself up. "So when you leave again—"

Before she could finish that thought, he took her mouth, stepping her back into the door again, unable to keep his hands off her ass. When he came up for air, he said, "If you can, I'd love it if you came with me."

She was still all soft and sweet from his kiss. "To Canada?"

"To wherever I go, whenever I go. For training. For fighting." He tucked her hair behind her ear, gave her a soft and quick kiss. "For today and tomorrow and the year after that."

Her eyes widened and her lips parted. "Gage?"

"I told you I love you. Did you think I made it up?"

In a heartbeat, excitement stripped away the uncertainty and she threw herself against him, squeezing tight. With her shirt still gone, her jeans still down, it was an awesome embrace.

A knock sounded on the door, and Armie called, "Just about everyone is gone if you two want to wrap it up."

"He loves me," Harper told him.

Armie laughed. "Well, duh, doofus. Everyone could see that plain as day."

Gage cupped her head in his hands, but spoke to Armie. "Any predictions on how she feels about me?"

"Wow." The door jumped, meaning Armie had probably just propped his shoulder against it. "Hasn't told you yet, huh?"

"No."

"Cruel, Harper," he chastised her. "Really cruel. And here I thought you were one of those *nice* girls."

Lips quivering, eyes big and liquid, she stared up at him. "I love you," she whispered.

"Me or Gage?" Armie asked with facetious good humor.

Harper kicked the door hard with her heel, and Armie said, "Ow, damn it. Fine. I'm leaving. But Gage, you have the keys so I can't lock up until—"

"Five minutes."

"And there go my illusions again."

The quiet settled around them. They watched each other. Gage did some touching, too. But what the hell, Harper was mostly naked, looking at him with a wealth of emotion.

"I should get dressed."

"You should tell me again that you love me."

"I do. *So much*," Harper added with feeling. "I have for such a long time."

Nice. "The things you do to me…" He fumbled around along the wall beside the door and finally located the light switch.

She flinched away at first, but Harper wasn't shy. God knew she had no reason to be.

Putting her shoulders back, her chin up, she let him look. And what a sight she made with her jeans down below her knees and her shirt gone. He cupped her right breast and saw a light sprinkling of freckles decorating her fair skin.

"Let's go," he whispered. "I want to take you home and look for more freckles."

That made her snicker. As she pulled up her jeans, she said, "I don't really have that many."

"Don't ruin it for me. I'll find out for myself."

By the time they left the room, only Armie, Stack and Denver were still hanging around.

With his arm around Harper, Gage asked, "You guys didn't hook up?"

"Meeting her in an hour," Stack said.

"She's pulling her car around," Denver told him.

Armie shrugged toward the front door. "Those two are waiting for me."

Two? Everyone glanced at the front door where a couple of women hugged up to each other. One blonde, one raven-haired.

"Why does she have a whip in her belt?" Harper asked.

"I'm not sure," Armie murmured as he, too, watched the women. "But I'm intrigued."

"Are they fondling each other?" Gage asked.

"Could be." Armie drew his gaze back to Harper and Gage, then grinned shamelessly. "But I don't mind being the voyeuristic third wheel."

The guys all grinned with amusement. They were well used to Armie's excesses.

A little shocked, Harper shook her head. "One of these days a nice girl will make an honest man of you. That is, if some crazy woman doesn't do you in first."

"At least I'd die happy." Leaning against the table, arms folded over his chest, Armie studied them both. "So. You curious about how your match went?"

"Wasn't my match," Gage said.

"Should have been. And just so you know, Darvey annihilated your replacement."

"How many rounds?"

"Two. Referee stoppage."

Gage nodded as if it didn't matter all that much. Darvey had gotten off easy because Gage knew he'd have won the match.

Then Armie dropped a bombshell. "Cannon damn near lost."

Because he'd been expecting something very different, Gage blinked. "No way."

Armie blew out a breath. "He was all but gone from a vicious kick to the ribs."

"Ouch." Gage winced just thinking of it. If the kick nearly took Cannon out, it must have been a liver kick, and those hurt like a mother, stole your wind and made breathing—or fighting—impossible.

Stack picked up the story. "But you know Cannon. On his way down he threw one last punch—"

"And knocked Moeller out cold," Denver finished with enthusiasm. "It was truly something to see. Everyone was on their feet, not only here but at the event. The commentators went nuts. It was crazy."

"Everyone waited to see who would get back on his feet first," Stack finished.

And obviously that was Cannon. Gage half smiled. Every fighter knew flukes happened. Given a fluke injury had taken him out of the competition, he knew it better than most. "I'm glad he pulled it off."

"That he did," Armie said. "And if you don't mind locking up, I think I'll go pull off a few submissions of my own."

Harper scowled in disapproval, then flapped her hand, sending him on his way.

A minute later, Denver and Stack took off, too.

Left alone finally, Gage put his arm around Harper. "Ready to go home?"

"My place or yours?"

"Where doesn't matter—as long as you're with me."

She gave him a look that said *"Awww!"* and hugged him tight. Still squeezed up close, she whispered with worry, "I can't believe Cannon almost lost."

Gage smoothed his hand down her back. "Don't worry about it. We fighters know how to turn bad situations to our advantage."

"We?" She leaned back in his arms to see him. "How's that?"

"For Cannon, the near miss will only hype up the crowd for his next fight." He bent to kiss the end of her freckled nose. "As for me, I might have missed a competition, but I got the girl. There'll be other fights, but honest to God, Harper, there's only one *you.* All in all, I'd say I'm the big winner tonight."

"I'd say you're *mine.*" With a trembling, emotional smile, Harper touched his face, then his shoulders, and his chest. As her hand dipped lower, she whispered, "And that means we're both winners. Tonight, tomorrow and always."

* * * * *

REQUEST YOUR FREE BOOKS!
2 FREE NOVELS PLUS 2 FREE GIFTS!

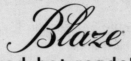

HARLEQUIN®

Blaze

red-hot reads!

YES! Please send me 2 FREE Harlequin® Blaze® novels and my 2 FREE gifts (gifts are worth about $10). After receiving them, if I don't wish to receive any more books, I can return the shipping statement marked "cancel." If I don't cancel, I will receive 4 brand-new novels every month and be billed just $4.74 per book in the U.S. or $5.21 per book in Canada. That's a savings of at least 14% off the cover price. It's quite a bargain. Shipping and handling is just 50¢ per book in the U.S. and 75¢ per book in Canada.* I understand that accepting the 2 free books and gifts places me under no obligation to buy anything. I can always return a shipment and cancel at any time. Even if I never buy another book, the two free books and gifts are mine to keep forever.

150/350 HDN GH2D

Name	(PLEASE PRINT)	
Address		Apt. #
City	State/Prov.	Zip/Postal Code

Signature (if under 18, a parent or guardian must sign)

Mail to the **Reader Service:**
IN U.S.A.: P.O. Box 1867, Buffalo, NY 14240-1867
IN CANADA: P.O. Box 609, Fort Erie, Ontario L2A 5X3

Want to try two free books from another line?
Call 1-800-873-8635 or visit www.ReaderService.com.

* Terms and prices subject to change without notice. Prices do not include applicable taxes. Sales tax applicable in N.Y. Canadian residents will be charged applicable taxes. Offer not valid in Quebec. This offer is limited to one order per household. Not valid for current subscribers to Harlequin Blaze books. All orders subject to credit approval. Credit or debit balances in a customer's account(s) may be offset by any other outstanding balance owed by or to the customer. Please allow 4 to 6 weeks for delivery. Offer available while quantities last.

Your Privacy—The Reader Service is committed to protecting your privacy. Our Privacy Policy is available online at www.ReaderService.com or upon request from the Reader Service.

We make a portion of our mailing list available to reputable third parties that offer products we believe may interest you. If you prefer that we not exchange your name with third parties, or if you wish to clarify or modify your communication preferences, please visit us at www.ReaderService.com/consumerschoice or write to us at Reader Service Preference Service, P.O. Box 9062, Buffalo, NY 14240-9062. Include your complete name and address.

HB15

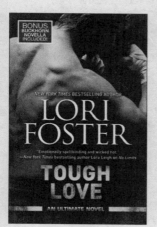

Limited time offer!

$1.⁰⁰ OFF

TOUGH LOVE

New York Times Bestselling Author

LORI FOSTER

She's playing hard to get...to win the
MMA fighter of her ultimate fantasies.

Available August 25, 2015,
wherever books are sold.

HQN™

$1.⁰⁰ OFF

**the purchase price of
TOUGH LOVE by Lori Foster.**

Offer valid from August 25, 2015, to September 30, 2015.
Redeemable at participating retail outlets. Not redeemable at Barnes & Noble.
Limit one coupon per purchase. Valid in the U.S.A. and Canada only.

52612796

5 65373 00076 2   **(8100)0 12073**

® and TM are trademarks owned and used by the trademark owner and/or its licensee.
© 2015 Harlequin Enterprises Limited

PHLF0915COUP

Gray had magic hands. Laney should have gone for sixty or even the full ninety minutes instead of the paltry thirty minutes she'd ponied up for. He was that good.

"You're tight here." He pressed a particularly tense spot on her back, and she stopped caring that she was stretched out, bare-ass naked and vulnerable. God, he was good.

"Trigger point." Not, apparently, that she needed to tell him. The man knew what he was doing.

"Are you a doctor?"

"Trauma surgeon." Was that sultry whisper her voice? Because, if so, Gray was definitely a miracle worker. She felt herself melting under his touch and, wow, how long had it been since she'd done that?

He found and pressed against another knot. "So I should call you Dr. Parker."

He moved around to the front of the massage bed. The bed had one of those circle doughnut things that she'd always thought were awkward. She opened her eyes as Gray's feet moved into view. She'd never had a foot fetish before, but he was barefoot, and his feet were sun-bronzed and strong-looking. Those few inches of bare skin made her want to see more. She'd bet the rest of him was every bit as spectacular.

It was probably bad she found his feet sexy. He was just doing a job.

Really, really well.

He gently pulled her ponytail free before running his hands through her hair, pressing his fingertips against her scalp. Maybe she'd been a cat in a former life, because she'd always loved having her hair played with. For long minutes, Gray rubbed small sensual circles against her scalp. She bit back a moan. *Just lie here. Keep still.* She probably wasn't supposed to arch off the table, screaming *more, more, more.* Although she could. She definitely could.

He moved closer, his thighs brushing against the bed. If she lifted her head, the situation could get awkward fast. Thinking about that made her stiffen up again, but then he cupped the back of her neck, pressing and rotating. And oh, she could feel the tension melting away. The small tugs on her hair sent a prickle of excitement through her entire body.

"Should I call you *Doctor*?" he prompted.

Don't miss
TEASING HER SEAL by Anne Marsh.
Available October 2015 wherever
Harlequin® Blaze® books and ebooks are sold.

www.Harlequin.com

HARLEQUIN™

Blaze®

Red-Hot Reads

A hot shade of lipstick calls for a hot, sexy guy...

Falling into bed with a sexy guy she met on a plane is impulsive even for Chloe. But when Ben's client catches them together, she does something even more impulsive: she pretends to be his wife!

SAVE $1.00

on the purchase of KISS AND MAKEUP by Taryn Leigh Taylor {available Sept. 15, 2015} or any other Harlequin® Blaze® book.

Redeemable at participating outlets in the U.S. and Canada only. Not redeemable at Barnes & Noble stores. Limit one coupon per customer.

Canadian Retailers: Harlequin Enterprises Limited will pay the face value of this coupon plus 10.25¢ if submitted by customer for this product only. Any other use constitutes fraud. Coupon is nonassignable. Void if taxed, prohibited or restricted by law. Consumer must pay any government taxes. Void if copied. Inmar Promotional Services ("IPS") customers submit coupons and proof of sales to Harlequin Enterprises Limited, P.O. Box 3000, Saint John, NB E2L 4L3, Canada. Non-IPS retailer—for reimbursement submit coupons and proof of sales directly to Harlequin Enterprises Limited, Retail Marketing Department, 225 Duncan Mill Rd., Don Mills, Ontario M3B 3K9, Canada.

52612884

U.S. Retailers: Harlequin Enterprises Limited will pay the face value of this coupon plus 8¢ if submitted by customer for this product only. Any other use constitutes fraud. Coupon is nonassignable. Void if taxed, prohibited or restricted by law. Consumer must pay any government taxes. Void if copied. For reimbursement submit coupons and proof of sales directly to Harlequin Enterprises Limited, P.O. Box 880478, El Paso, TX 88588-0478, U.S.A. Cash value 1/100 cents.

5 65373 00076 2   (8100)0 12081

COUPON EXPIRES DEC. 15, 2015

Available wherever books are sold, including most bookstores, supermarkets, drugstores and discount stores.

www.Harlequin.com

® and ™ are trademarks owned and used by the trademark owner and/or its licensee.
© 2015 Harlequin Enterprises Limited

HBCOUP0915

A Sheetcake Named Desire

"A tasty treat for mystery lovers, combining all the right ingredients in a perfectly prepared story that's sure to satisfy."
—B. B. Haywood, national bestselling author
of *Town in a Wild Moose Chase*

"A decadent new series with a Big Easy attitude."
—Paige Shelton, national bestselling author
of *If Fried Chicken Could Fly*

"A mouth-watering new series! Brady's writing is smooth as fondant, rich as buttercream—the pastry shop's delectable confections are just icing on the cake for the appealing characters and intriguing mystery."
—Sheila Connolly, national bestselling
author of *Bitter Harvest*

"A delicious blend of deception, danger . . . and dessert."
—Dorothy St. James, author of
the White House Gardener Mysteries

"Jacklyn Brady whips up a delectable mystery layered with great characters and sprinkled with clever plot twists."
—Hannah Reed, author of the Queen Bee Mysteries

Berkley Prime Crime titles by Jacklyn Brady

Cake on a Hot Tin Roof

Jacklyn Brady

BERKLEY PRIME CRIME, NEW YORK

THE BERKLEY PUBLISHING GROUP
Published by the Penguin Group
Penguin Group (USA) Inc.
375 Hudson Street, New York, New York 10014, USA

Penguin Group (Canada), 90 Eglinton Avenue East, Suite 700, Toronto, Ontario M4P 2Y3, Canada
(a division of Pearson Penguin Canada Inc.)
Penguin Books Ltd., 80 Strand, London WC2R 0RL, England
Penguin Group Ireland, 25 St. Stephen's Green, Dublin 2, Ireland (a division of Penguin Books Ltd.)
Penguin Group (Australia), 250 Camberwell Road, Camberwell, Victoria 3124, Australia
(a division of Pearson Australia Group Pty. Ltd.)
Penguin Books India Pvt. Ltd., 11 Community Centre, Panchsheel Park, New Delhi—110 017, India
Penguin Group (NZ), 67 Apollo Drive, Rosedale, Auckland 0632, New Zealand
(a division of Pearson New Zealand Ltd.)
Penguin Books (South Africa) (Pty.) Ltd., 24 Sturdee Avenue, Rosebank, Johannesburg 2196,
South Africa

Penguin Books Ltd., Registered Offices: 80 Strand, London WC2R 0RL, England

CAKE ON A HOT TIN ROOF

A Berkley Prime Crime Book / published by arrangement with the author

PRINTING HISTORY
Berkley Prime Crime mass-market edition / February 2012

Copyright © 2012 by Penguin Group (USA) Inc.
Cover illustration by Chris Lyons.
Cover design by Diana Kolsky.
Interior text design by Laura K. Corless.

This one's for Valerie Sherry Brown and Vanessa Lee Sthole.

I couldn't do any of it without you.

One

"You'll be here by seven, won't you, sugar? You won't be late?"

My mother-in-law sounded so hopeful, I hated to disappoint her, but how could she ask me to leave work early on a Friday evening during Mardi Gras season? I shifted my cell phone to the other ear and glanced at the chaos surrounding me. Clutter and constant movement filled every corner of Zydeco Cakes, signs of the work overload the staff and I had been experiencing since the first of the year.

Stacks of empty boxes, all decorated in traditional Mardi Gras purple, green, and gold, teetered in every corner of the massive design room. Near the door to the loading dock, boxes filled with King Cakes awaited delivery to businesses and events. More boxes filled the other end of the room, in preparation for the walk-in customers we hoped would be coming in droves to pick them up before the season was over. And that was on top of our regular business: cakes for two weddings, a Valentine's Day party, and a fiftieth birthday party, all scheduled for delivery in the coming week.

I'd only been running Zydeco Cakes for a few months, and this was my first Mardi Gras in New Orleans. I knew the carnival season was a big deal around here, but as a recent transplant to the city, I was still shocked at just *how* big a deal it was. We were already a month into the season, but the sharp increase in business had left me off-balance and scrambling to catch up. I'd been looking forward to the celebration, but I was starting to wonder if I'd be able to find enough free time to enjoy any of it.

But that wasn't Miss Frankie's fault, and I tried not to take out my frustrations on her.

She and I became partners last year, shortly after the death of her only child, Philippe Renier, who'd also happened to be my husband—at least on paper. I was his widow on a flimsy technicality: he'd been killed minutes before he was supposed to sign our divorce agreement, though Miss Frankie liked to imagine that we'd been on the verge of reconciling when he died.

I'm the one with the training and experience as a pastry chef, so I handle the day-to-day work at the bakery. Miss Frankie offers moral support and the occasional cash infusion from the comfort of her living room. Most of the time our arrangement suits me, but today I was frustrated by my partner's lack of hands-on experience.

I'd been working alongside the rest of the staff for days, ignoring the growing heap of paperwork in my office and the even longer to-do list for tonight's Mardi Gras party at Miss Frankie's country club. The same party Miss Frankie was nagging me about at that very moment.

"Rita? Are you even listening to me?"

Her insistent tone pulled me away from my growing frustration and back to the conversation. "I'm listening," I assured her. "But I don't think you realize how crazy it is around here. We're up to our eyeballs in work. Nobody has been able to take a lunch break for two days and things are only getting worse."

"I know y'all are busy," Miss Frankie said, "but tonight's party is important."

And there it was: the crux of our argument.

"It's a *party*," I pointed out.

"A very *important* party," she pointed back. "With very important people. It's not just a social event, Rita. It's the Captain's Court for Musterion. It's crucial to the business that you be here, *and* that you show up on time."

Like I said before, I'm no expert on Mardi Gras, but over the past few months I'd learned a few things. All of the parties, parades, and balls are organized by social clubs known as krewes. There are hundreds of them scattered across the Gulf Coast region. Some krewes take themselves very seriously, others not so much. Musterion (whose membership list topped 2,000) falls somewhere in the middle. The Captain's Court was a sort of last blast for Musterion's movers and shakers, a celebration of all the work they'd done to get ready for Mardi Gras and the prequel to next week's parade and formal ball, which would be open to the entire krewe.

Carnival season may seem heathen on the surface, but it actually has deep roots in Christianity. The whole point of it, after all, is for people to stuff themselves silly on Fat Tuesday before the forty-day austerity of Lent begins on Ash Wednesday. That "last hurrah" starts all the way back at Epiphany on January 6. Which is where the King Cake gets its name—the word *King* refers to the wise men, and the traditional plastic baby figurine baked into every cake represents the baby Jesus. According to tradition, the person lucky (or unlucky) enough to get the slice of cake with the hidden baby in it is obligated to host the party next year.

Philippe, who had been a longtime member of the Krewe of Musterion, got the baby at last year's Captain's Court celebration, which put him on tap to act as this year's host. Thanks to Miss Frankie, I got custody of the baby when he died. This party was, according to Miss Frankie, a *very* big deal, which was why she volunteered me to take over as hostess. I just wish she'd discussed it with me first.

I'm all about doing what's best for the business. I just didn't happen to agree that this party she was so wound up about needed the top spot on my priority list. I'd said so about two million times in the past few weeks, but Miss Frankie wasn't listening.

"I'll get there as soon as the orders for tomorrow morning have been filled," I said, also for the two-millionth time. "That's more important for the business than me standing around with a glass of champagne in my hand." She started to argue, but I went on as if she hadn't spoken. "I don't know any of the people on your guest list. They're not going to miss me if I'm a little late. If you need help entertaining the masses before I get there, I'm sure Bernice will pitch in."

Bernice Dudley is Miss Frankie's neighbor and closest friend. She's a sweet lady with a halo of white hair and a drawl as smooth and Southern as aged Kentucky bourbon.

"Well, of course I can count on Bernice," Miss Frankie said with a tick of her tongue. "That's not the point. A proper party simply cannot begin without its hostess."

That would be me, though not by choice. I was harboring some resentment over the way Miss Frankie had finagled me into the role, which might have been making me slightly more stubborn than usual. I still wasn't convinced that Philippe's predeath party obligations had legally become my responsibilities.

Miss Frankie let out a long-suffering sigh. "Rita. Sugar. Try to understand. This party is important. All the top brass of Musterion will be here, and that includes some very influential—and wealthy—people."

I could have refused, but I was a little concerned about Miss Frankie. Losing her only son had shaken her world to its core. She'd made a valiant effort to keep her spirits up as we stumbled through the holidays together, but by New Year's Eve she'd had enough. The idea of heading into an entire year without Philippe had crumbled her like a stale cookie. She'd spent the whole month of January in a funk, and had only started rallying again in the past week or so. I didn't want anything to jeopardize that.

"These people were friends of Philippe's," she was saying now. "Most of them were clients of Zydeco when he was alive."

"I understand that, but—"

"They'll want to meet you."

I laughed. "I doubt that."

"Why would you? You were Philippe's wife and you're running Zydeco now. Of course they'll want to know more about you. This is your chance to make a good impression. To establish yourself as one of them. Otherwise, they might take their business somewhere else now that Philippe is gone."

But I *wasn't* one of them. I knew it, and they'd figure it out soon enough. Philippe and Miss Frankie had been born into that society. Old money and the genteel Southern breeding might be in their blood, but they weren't in mine.

"I know there are a lot of potential customers on the guest list, but I can't ignore current paying customers just to play nice with people who *might* spend money at Zydeco in the future." It was a lousy excuse. Even I knew that. But the thought of trying to impress two hundred of New Orleans's most influential citizens at once was stressing me out.

"I'm not asking you to ignore anybody," Miss Frankie said. "But you work too hard. I'm asking you to take one evening to have a little fun and make an investment in the bakery's future at the same time. Is that so difficult?"

"Much more difficult than you can imagine," I grumbled, sounding like a moody teenager. Work had always been my comfort zone, and I was resisting leaving it big-time.

Over the phone, I heard the tap-tap of fingernails on a hard surface, a sure sign that Miss Frankie was processing my response and formulating another argument. "What's the matter, sugar? Why does the idea of this party bother you so much?"

She knew me too well. "Besides the fact that I don't know anyone on the guest list?" I rubbed my forehead with the fingertips of one hand as if I could scrub away my nervousness. I had half a dozen solid objections to hosting this party, but Miss Frankie didn't really want to hear any of them. "It's just that it falls at such a bad time. This carnival thing is pretty overwhelming."

Miss Frankie gave a low chuckle. "Relax, sugar. Have fun with it. That's the whole point of carnival."

Relax. Have fun. This wasn't the first time she'd given me that advice. I rotated my head on my neck and tried to work out a few of the stress kinks. "I'll try," I said. But it wasn't that simple. I'd been raised by a master worrier. My uncle Nestor didn't know the meaning of the word *relax*, and he'd taught me everything I knew about stressing out. Part of me wanted to enjoy life more—I just didn't know how.

"Will you?"

"Of course."

Miss Frankie pretended to believe me and changed the subject. "By the way, did I tell you who phoned in an RSVP this morning?"

I stopped rolling my head. "This morning? I thought we turned in the final head count to the caterer two weeks ago."

"We did, but everyone knows that for a party like this, the final head count is just a guideline."

"Not *everyone*," I mumbled. We'd hired a caterer for the buffet, but Zydeco was supplying the King Cakes and I'd been relying on those figures to plan how many we'd need.

"I'm sure we'll have plenty of food," Miss Frankie said. "Nobody expects us to turn away a guest who calls at the last minute. Now, guess who it was."

I wasn't even going to try. "Who?"

"Ivanka Hedge."

The muscles in my neck tightened up again. Ivanka Hedge was one of the wealthiest young women in New Orleans, heir to the Lafitte perfume fortune. Just a week earlier, she'd announced her engagement to Richard Montgomery III, son of an obscenely wealthy businessman with international ties. His grandfather, Richard I, had founded the prestigious Terrebonne Academy, a private school open only to those with the right family background and sufficient money to afford the astronomical tuition. Academic accomplishment factored way below the right genealogy on the list of qualifications.

The city had been buzzing with wedding talk all week, and every business that was remotely tied to the wedding industry had been scrambling to offer their services for flowers, dresses, entertainment, china, silver, and of course, the various cakes they'd need.

At Zydeco, we'd been discussing the possibility of landing

the wedding cake contract—a dream only slightly less ambitious than being hired on by the White House. For the past
four days I'd tried countless times to reach Ivanka personally
or, failing that, to set up an appointment through her assistant.
For all my efforts, I had yet to even speak to a live person.

My heart did a little pitty-pat at the prospect of actually
meeting Ivanka tonight. I nibbled at the carrot cake Miss
Frankie was dangling in front of me. "Are you serious?"

"Would I lie to you?" she asked.

Only if she thought the means justified the end. "How
did you manage to get her to come?"

"I have connections, sugar. The Montgomery men have
belonged to Musterion for six generations. Richard is on the
Parade Committee this year. I knew he and Ivanka were on
the guest list, but I didn't want to say anything until I knew
they were coming. So you see why you have to be here on
time. This really is your chance to make a good impression."

Well. That ought to help me relax. No pressure at all.

I chewed on my bottom lip and argued with myself for a
few seconds. Maybe I *could* leave work a few minutes early.
Someone else on staff could stick around here to make sure
all the orders were filled. My staff was competent and well
trained. They didn't need me to hold their hands to make
sure the work was done. And if leaving early would help me
land the Hedge-Montgomery wedding contract, everyone at
Zydeco would benefit. Win-win.

"Fine, I'll be there by seven," I said, making an executive
decision. "Should I bring anything special with me?"

"Just your sunny personality." I could hear the triumphant
smile in Miss Frankie's voice. "But don't keep the staff
working too late. They're all on the guest list, too, and you
know Philippe wouldn't want them to miss out."

She was right about that. Philippe had loved a good party

more than almost anything else. If he'd still been alive, the whole bakery would have shut down early so the staff could get ready, even if he'd lost business as a result.

I'd always been more practical. It's not that I don't like a good party. I'm fun. I just believe that work should come first, especially in our current circumstances.

Zydeco's reputation had suffered a hit because of Philippe's death. We'd lost enough business to hurt our bottom line, and new orders had been slower to come in since I took over at the bakery's helm. I guess people were waiting to see whether I could maintain the high quality and creative genius Zydeco was known for.

Eventually people would realize that the quality of our work hadn't suffered. But until then, we'd have to rely even more than usual on the income we could make during Mardi Gras. Shutting the whole operation down early and losing walk-in customers wasn't an option I would consider.

I was trying to figure out a tactful way of saying so when Dwight Sonntag looked up from his work table and gave me the stink eye. He jerked his chin toward my own station, where the work was beginning to pile up. "Hey! Rita! A little help?"

I've known Dwight since pastry school in Chicago. He's a talented cake artist with a strict work ethic, but you'd never know that to look at him. He's six-foot-nothing with shaggy hair and an untidy beard, both tucked into sanitary netting when he's working. His clothes hang off his thin frame and he slouches through life looking as if he just rolled out of bed. But there was nothing casual about the frustration glinting in his hazel eyes this morning.

I held up a finger to indicate that I'd be finished in a minute and told Miss Frankie, "I have to go."

"Trouble?"

"Nothing I can't handle."

Since I took over at Zydeco I've tried to protect Miss Frankie from unpleasant reality whenever possible. Partly because losing her only son had left her vulnerable and—let's face it—a little unhinged. But also because my life is a lot easier when Miss Frankie doesn't know about every speed bump Zydeco encounters. If it's earth-shattering, I discuss it with her, but if I ran to her every time one of my eccentric, talented, and emotional staff members got upset, I'd never get anything else done.

A momentary silence fell between Miss Frankie and me, followed by a soft, resigned sigh. "Seven o'clock," she said again. "Don't be late."

Two

❧

Knowing that Miss Frankie would call at least once more before the afternoon was over, I disconnected and stuffed my cell phone into the pocket of my white chef's jacket. As I turned toward the bank of sinks on the far wall, Ox, my second in command, appeared in the doorway leading to the bakery's front offices. He scanned the room looking for someone, and I had a feeling that someone was me.

Ox is a big man, a dead ringer for an African-American Mr. Clean. He's deeply committed to Zydeco and willing to do whatever it takes to make the business succeed. He also has the right breeding to work with our clientele. Known to his mother's highbrow friends as Wyndham Oxford III, he's far more comfortable at society events than I'll ever be. He bucked family tradition to attend pastry school, where Philippe and I met him, and he's in many ways my closest friend. Not that that stops him from trying to prove that he'd be a better choice than me to run Zydeco.

He spotted me and plunged into the chaos, making his way across the room with dogged determination. "Got a minute?" he asked when he reached me.

I shrugged and turned on the water, then squirted soap into my hands. I could feel Dwight glaring at me, but I wasn't in the mood to deal with both of them at the same time, so I avoided eye contact with him. "A minute? Sure," I told Ox. "You have sixty seconds, starting now. What's up?"

He didn't even twitch a lip at my little joke. "Edie tells me you haven't approved the content of the web page I sent you on Wednesday. Is there a problem?"

His question made my smile fade. I couldn't believe he wanted to talk about the website *now*. Couldn't he see how swamped we were?

I rinsed the soap from my hands and used my elbow to turn off the faucet. "No problem," I said, reaching for a paper towel, "unless you count the total lack of time. I'll get to it by the end of the week, I promise."

I'd been saying those last two words far too often lately, and I knew they'd catch up with me soon. In the meantime, I just kept running from crisis to crisis, putting out the biggest fire first and hoping I could get to the smaller ones before the flames got too high.

Wrinkles formed in Ox's usually smooth forehead, and his dark eyes turned stormy. "That web page is supposed to go live today. Or didn't you bother to look at the production schedule I e-mailed you last week?"

"I looked at it," I said.

And I *had*.

Okay. So I'd skimmed it the day he sent it to me and filed

it away in a folder on my computer. The point is, I'd intended to go over it in detail. Later. When I had the time.

Which probably wouldn't be until Mardi Gras was over, Lent was in full swing, and I'd had time to recover from the nervous breakdown I could feel threatening to erupt.

I shot a pointed look at the commotion all around us. "Maybe you haven't noticed, but things are a little busy right now. I'll get to it as soon as I can."

Ox folded his arms across his chest. "The web designer is waiting for it now."

He was making me feel defensive and I *hate* feeling defensive. Last fall, I agreed to hire a couple of guys to create our web presence. They were young, talented, and eager to make their mark. Most important, since they were just starting out, they were relatively inexpensive. I'd left the rest to Ox, hoping that giving him lead on the project would smooth some of the feathers Miss Frankie had ruffled when she'd passed him over and chosen me to take over at Zydeco. So far, all it had done was make him more restless.

"We're paying those guys to wait," I pointed out. "It's their job."

Ox rolled his eyes. "Very professional attitude." He glanced at Dwight's workstation with a scowl. "You wouldn't be so busy if you'd just stuck with our original recipe, you know."

It was my turn to roll my eyes. Against Ox's advice, I'd added two additional varieties of King Cake to our menu this year. He was a purist, convinced that the only good King Cake was one without filling. A large portion of the New Orleans population agreed with him, but there were hundreds of thousands of potential clients who thought a little cream cheese–cinnamon or strawberry filling made the cake better. I happened to agree with them. So far, the new varieties were selling well—a fact that made me happy but stuck in Ox's craw.

"What are you saying?" I asked him. "That the only good changes around here are the ones *you* suggest?"

"Seems to me, you're the one who feels that way."

Like anything else, there are good things and bad about hiring friends. Our friendship means that he can sometimes finish my sentences and guess what I want even before I figure it out. It also means that the lines sometimes blur and Ox occasionally forgets which of us is in charge. We were getting nowhere fast with the finger-pointing, so I pulled us back to the original subject.

"Just explain the situation to the web guys," I said with a brittle smile. "They're from New Orleans. They know all about Mardi Gras. I'm sure they'll understand what we're up against."

Ox's eyebrows beetled over his deep-set eyes. "Approving the content for that page will take you fifteen minutes. Thirty, tops. It doesn't make sense to put it off when you could just do it now."

I dried my hands and returned to my workstation. "I already agreed to the initial launch of the bare-bones site on your timetable," I reminded him. "I need you to be content with that. Upgrading can come later. Right now, we have more important things to think about."

He gave me a look, which I ignored. "Such as?"

"I just found out that Ivanka Hedge and Richard Montgomery will be at the party tonight. I could use some help figuring out the best way to approach them and I'm behind here, as you can see. So instead of arguing with me, why don't you pull up a table and help? The sooner we fill all these orders, the sooner I can get to that page you're so worried about."

The sour look on Ox's face sweetened slightly. He wanted the Hedge-Montgomery wedding business as much as I did. "I have a wedding consult in fifteen minutes," he reminded me. "And I have to deliver the birthday party cake before six. Otherwise, I'd be glad to."

Which kind of proved my point. We were both too busy to be playing around with upgrades to the website. I breathed a silent sigh of relief, thinking that we'd put the website issue on the back burner for now. Allowing two hours with the future bride and groom, I guessed he'd finish the consult just in time to deliver the sculpted football helmet cake to a sports bar across town for a die-hard Saints fan's fiftieth birthday bash. That would put him back at Zydeco just in time to drive to the country club with a van full of King Cakes. That schedule left almost no time to bring up the website issue again until tomorrow.

But Ox wasn't finished yet. "Have you given the other matter any thought?"

My relief died a quick death, and that put a scowl on my face. Rather than snapping at Ox, I channeled my frustrations into rolling out one of the many balls of dough waiting for my attention into a long rope. "If you're asking about the blog, the answer's still no."

"Why am I not surprised? Just tell me one thing: Did you do what I suggested?"

I shook my head. "I haven't had time to read other blogs. Ask me again when Mardi Gras is over. We can revisit the idea then."

"Then will be too late," Ox said, leveling me with a look. "Have you read *any* of the e-mails I've sent you?"

"Of course." It was just a tiny white lie.

He perched on the edge of an unused table. "This is the hot season, Rita. We can only sell King Cakes for a few weeks every year, but we make seventy-five percent of our annual income during those weeks. With business down overall and the economy tanking, we need every advantage we can find."

I couldn't argue with that. "I understand," I began.

Ox went on before I could finish. "A bakery without an online storefront is practically obsolete in today's market. We should have launched the website when Zydeco opened."

I couldn't argue with that either. My almost-ex *had* been notoriously outdated. "That's why I agreed to launch the site to begin with," I pointed out. "I just didn't realize it was going to be so time-consuming. Can't we just push it off another six months? Get the site up and running when we're not so busy so that we're ready for next year?"

Ox shook his head. "That's not a good idea. Nobody looks for businesses in the phone directory anymore. Newspaper advertising is almost obsolete, and we're getting lost on the radio with all the other ads shouting over the top of us. If consumers want to find something these days, they go to the Internet. We need the site up and running now. This year. We can't afford to wait."

"But we *have* a page," I said. "It's working. Orders are coming in. Why can't we wait for the rest?"

His exasperation with me came out on a heavy sigh. "It's not enough to just put a static page on the Internet and hope for the best. We need updated content daily and a presence on the social networks driving traffic to the site. One of us should be tweeting and posting on Facebook every day."

He was passionate about the website, but lack of passion had never been an issue with Ox. Hoping he wasn't going to suggest that I be the one to start tweeting, I glanced toward the boxes stacked near the loading dock. "You really think we need more orders? Between our regular business and the King Cakes for Mardi Gras, we're barely keeping up as it is."

"Yes, I do." He sighed and rubbed his face with one hand. When he spoke again, his tone was a little less severe. "We're in danger of appearing way behind the times, especially since Gateaux just launched their new site. If we aren't competitive, we'll lose more market share than we already have."

He certainly knew which buttons to push. Dmitri Wolff, owner of Gateaux, a rival pastry shop, had been actively trying to put Zydeco out of business since we opened. He'd made a serious effort to buy out Miss Frankie, and he was still our biggest competitor.

I didn't want to make business decisions based on fear, but I could feel my resolve weakening. "Why can't we just make it up after Mardi Gras?" I said with a frown. "The quality of our specialty cakes should speak for itself."

Ox stood again and the corners of his mouth curved into a regretful smile. "I wish it did, but if we lose as much business as I think we will, it could take three or four years to recoup. We're not in a position to take a hit like that."

Logically I knew the drop in business after Philippe's murder wasn't my fault, but that didn't stop me from feeling responsible. My shoulders sagged and I gave in to the inevitable. "Fine," I said with a sigh. "I'll check out the content for the web page before I leave for the day. Will that make you happy?"

"Ecstatic," he said with a grin. "And the blog? You'll write one?"

I'd rather make a thousand buttercream roses using a sandwich bag, but the work was seriously starting to back up and I was the sticking point. "Fine. Okay? Just not *now*."

Triumph flashed in Ox's eyes. "Good."

Yeah. Whatever. He wasn't the one who had to come up with pithy, perky topics to write about several times a week. I made a face at him and shooed him away. "You only say that because you won. Now go. Get back to work. Do something creative and wonderful so I don't regret this moment of weakness."

He grinned. "Your wish is my command," he said as he turned to leave.

If only that were actually true.

Three

I concentrated on rolling and braiding the rounds of dough that kept piling up in front of me. Within minutes, I was caught up in the rhythm of the work and some of my tension began to fade.

Working in the kitchen always helps me relax, and soon I'd destressed enough to enjoy the feel of dough under my fingers and the aromas of yeast and cinnamon that filled the air. After an hour or two, I was even feeling cautiously optimistic about my chances of being able to leave by six.

King Cakes aren't actually difficult to make and they're not especially time-consuming either—unless you're making several hundred at a time. Abe Cobb, Zydeco's baker, works during the wee hours of the morning while the rest of us sleep. He's not really a people person, so he likes it that way. Last night, while the cakes for our regular business orders baked and cooled, he had prepared enough dough to keep the rest of us busy all day. He'd spent hours scalding the milk, activating the yeast, mixing in cinnamon, nutmeg, vanilla, and lemon zest and then kneading and leaving the dough to rise in every available space until the rest of us arrived at daybreak.

Dwight, with his cap and beard mask, takes the next step in the process. When he's not sculpting a cake or working with fondant, he punches down the risen dough and kneads each ball until the dough is smooth and elastic. Then he sets it aside to rise a second time until it's doubled in size, a process that takes about ninety minutes.

And that's where I come in.

Between problem-solving and handling my other obligations, I divide each batch into three balls of equal size, then roll each one into a thin rope. I braid them together, forming each braid into a circle and pinching the ends to create a seal. Once I have a ring of braided dough, I insert the small plastic baby figurine, then place the cakes on baking sheets and slide them to the end of the table, where they rise for a third time, until the cakes are doubled in size. This time the wait is about thirty minutes. Once the cakes have risen, Estelle Jergens breaks away from her gum-paste work to transport each tray to the kitchen for baking. When they come out of the oven, she relays the baked cakes to the cooling racks.

Estelle is short and round, with a riot of red curls that escape every effort she makes to restrain them. At forty-something, she's also the oldest member of the staff. Carting all those cakes around has her moving in and out of the kitchen so quickly, I expect her to lose those forty pounds she's always complaining about by the time Mardi Gras is over.

Her third job is to carry the cooled cakes to Sparkle Starr's corner of the design center—a spot that somehow escapes the sun no matter what time of year it is. The location of Sparkle's workstation is no accident. I'm half convinced she'd turn to dust if the sunlight ever made direct contact. She's the daughter of aging hippie parents who raised their children in a commune long after the lifestyle went out of fashion. I'm still trying to figure out whether Sparkle's dour personality and her love of all things goth is natural or if she's in rebellion against a childhood of flower power and free love. Either way, the name doesn't fit the woman.

When I first met Sparkle, her pale complexion and pitch-black hair gave me the willies. But she was so cool and efficient on the job, not to mention extremely talented, I now hardly notice the piercings in her face or the dragon tattoo that appeared on her wrist two weeks ago.

This week she's spent most of her time creating dozens of carnations out of modeling chocolate for a wedding shower cake. In her spare time she drizzles glaze over each cooled King Cake, creating a decorative pattern unique to Zydeco and avoiding the puddles of glaze created by careless or hurried work. Any cake that doesn't meet her exacting standards is shuffled off for donation to one of the local soup kitchens or homeless shelters.

Once she's finished, Sparkle passes the cakes to Isabeau Pope for the final step in the production process. Isabeau's young, blond, and unfailingly perky. She's also Ox's girlfriend. In spite of predictions that they wouldn't last three months, their relationship is heading into its ninth month and seems to be flourishing. Which is fine with me, so long as it continues not to cause any ripples in the staff pool.

Isabeau has been hard at work making a garden of butterflies from sugar paste, royal icing, and sanding sugar for the tenth anniversary of a popular butterfly garden. Every so often she breaks away to sprinkle purple, green, and gold-colored sugar over each King Cake in carefully measured stripes, then passes the cakes to a couple of the temporary workers I've hired to help out. The cakes are packed into colorfully decorated boxes along with a handful of plastic beads and cheap metal coins bearing the Zydeco logo. When the boxes are sealed, they're routed to stacks designated for shipping, local delivery, or walk-in clients.

It was a good system, established by Philippe when he first opened Zydeco. The work goes smoothly—as long as everyone does their part. Unfortunately, the interruptions that are so much a part of my day as boss often make me the weak link in the chain. I hate being the weak link, especially since I'm also still struggling to prove myself to the staff. Miss Frankie is always pushing me to step back from the actual hands-on work and spend my time supervising everyone else. But that's not why I went to pastry school, so I ignore her.

It was a little after two when Edie Bryce—another old pastry school classmate—came into the design center. Edie wasn't a success in the kitchen, but she's an organizational genius, which is why she's Zydeco's office manager. Her almond-shaped eyes were narrowed and she'd pulled the corner of her mouth between her teeth, two signs that she was worried about something.

But then, Edie worries almost as much as I do.

"Um . . . Rita? Got a minute?"

I pushed a baby into the cake in front of me. "Sure. What's up?"

She glanced over her shoulder toward the door she'd just come through. "I know you're busy, but there's somebody here to see you."

"Now?" I moved the finished cake out of my way and

pulled an empty baking pan toward me. "I didn't see any consults on my calendar this morning," I said. "Did I miss something?" I knew full well I hadn't. Lately Edie's organized and color-coded schedule looked like someone had turned loose a kindergarten class with a year's supply of food coloring, but I checked and double-checked it so often, I knew I hadn't missed an appointment.

Edie shook her head and slid another worried glance at the door to her office. "You didn't miss anything. This isn't a client."

Zydeco isn't a traditional bakery with an open-door policy. Except for the King Cakes at Mardi Gras, our business is by appointment only, and Edie runs a very tight ship. Nobody gets past her, which made her request this afternoon highly unusual. I stopped rolling dough and looked at her. "You want me to talk to a walk-in?"

"Not exactly." She looked almost embarrassed.

Which made me nervous. "What's going on, Edie?"

"You have visitors. They're . . . family."

I made a face at her. "Very funny." Except for Miss Frankie, I have no family in New Orleans. My only blood relatives all live twelve hundred miles away in Albuquerque, New Mexico. Which meant my visitors had to be distant relatives of Miss Frankie's. But this wasn't the time or the place for an impromptu family reunion. "Just take care of whoever it is, okay? Explain that I'm busy."

"I don't think that's a good idea," Edie said, but that's as far as she got. The door behind her opened and a man with a stocky build and hair more salt than pepper stepped through. His skin was tough and wrinkled from years of worry and too much sun, and the corners of his mouth turned down in a scowl.

Uncle Nestor?

His eyes locked on mine and he boomed over the chaos, "What's all this, *mija*? Are you going to keep us waiting out there all day?"

My heart rose at the same time my stomach dropped. I was elated to see him. That went without saying. My uncle Nestor and aunt Yolanda had taken me in and raised me as their own after my parents died. But what was he doing in New Orleans? And why hadn't he told me he was coming?

Four

"Well, *mija*?" Uncle Nestor said again. "Are you going to stand there all day, staring at me?"

Hearing that familiar, gruff, lightly accented voice pulled me out of my stupor. My uncle is moody and opinionated, with a hair-trigger temper. He's also kind and compassionate—in his own stern way. Life with him is never boring, and I'd missed him horribly. It had been only a few months since I'd last seen my aunt and uncle, but it felt like years.

I abandoned my workstation and threw myself into his arms just as my aunt Yolanda appeared in the open doorway. Her chocolate brown hair was cut in a choppy style that made her look younger than ever, and her dark eyes were full of love—the kind I imagine a mother might feel for her daughter.

I'd talked with them at least once a week since I moved to New Orleans, but seeing them again made me realize how worried I'd been that they were angry or disappointed with me for leaving New Mexico last summer and then staying in New Orleans for the Christmas holidays.

"I tried to convince him to wait out front for you," Aunt Yolanda said with a fond scowl in her husband's direction. "But you know how he is."

Did I ever. Uncle Nestor is strong-willed and stubborn and nobody can tell him anything, but at that moment I didn't care. I hugged them both tightly and stepped away to look them over again. "What are you doing here? Why didn't you call?"

"Call?" Uncle Nestor's voice was so gruff, a few of the staff members stopped working to look at us. "What? We can't spend a weekend with our favorite niece without an appointment?"

"Of course you can," I said quickly. But as the first flush of excitement over seeing them faded, the reality of my work schedule began to hit me. "It's not that. It's just . . . well . . . it's nearly Mardi Gras and we're swamped. I don't know how much time I'll be able to spend with you." I owed them both so much, I wouldn't have hurt their feelings for anything in the world. Plus, I could count on one finger the number of times Uncle Nestor had left his restaurant in someone else's hands since he'd opened its doors—the fact that he'd obviously left it to come all this way was significant.

But they weren't staying long. He'd said *the weekend*, right? Surely I could squeeze in some quality time with them over the next couple of days.

"We didn't come here to be a bother," Aunt Yolanda assured me. "Do what you need to do. We'll see you when we can."

That should have made me feel better, but instead it raised the question for me of why they *had* come unannounced. Why this weekend? Why not for Mardi Gras itself?

Uncle Nestor waved a hand over his head to indicate that

he agreed with her, but his attention had been captured by the work going on all around us. "I had no idea your operation was so big, *mija*."

Coming from anyone else, that might have been a compliment. Uncle Nestor managed to make it sound like an accusation. And that left me squirming inside with guilt. I hated feeling as if I needed to defend myself, so I tamped down the urge and said, "It's not usually like this."

Uncle Nestor pursed his lips and clasped his hands behind his back, walking between the tables like a general inspecting his troops. But that only made my irritation flare. He had a habit of taking over whenever he walked into a room, but these were *my* troops. Not his. I was still trying to establish my authority here. I didn't want anything to make me appear weak.

Uncle Nestor stopped at Isabeau's table, raising his eyebrows at the multicolored sugar that had fallen to the floor. After a moment he moved on, this time stopping in front of Dwight and running a look over his wrinkled shirt and threadbare jeans. "What's all this?" he asked, but I wasn't sure whether he was talking about the work or Dwight's appearance.

To my relief, Dwight didn't seem to notice his disapproval. "King Cakes," he said without looking up. "Big tradition in these parts."

"I know what a King Cake is," Uncle Nestor said. "But so many?"

I explained what Ox and I had discussed earlier about the bulk of our business coming from these flaky cakes, which earned a surprised grunt. "Right now we're making around two hundred a day," I explained. "We'll be making at least that many every day for the next week or so."

Aunt Yolanda moved closer and touched my arm. "We've come at a bad time. I knew we should have called first."

I didn't want her to feel guilty, so I grinned, trying for a carefree effect. "It's fine. Really! I'm so glad to see you nothing else matters."

She grimaced. Hard. Which told me I'd gone a little over the top with that last bit.

Uncle Nestor completed his inspection and turned back toward me with his hands on his hips. "So, this is what you left us for."

I shifted a little under the weight of his stare and Aunt Yolanda's scowl and wished they'd chosen to show up on a day when the work proceeded in an orderly and controlled fashion. A day when I looked competent and organized and when dirty dishes weren't piled everywhere waiting for Estelle's nieces to come in after school and load the dishwashers.

"You know why I stayed here," I said. "Miss Frankie needed me." It was a cop-out. I knew it, and so did he. I squared my shoulders and took a more adult approach. "And it was a good chance to strike out on my own. All that money you spent on my education would have been wasted if I'd stayed in Albuquerque."

"Ha!" he said to Aunt Yolanda. "There we have it." Irritation settled like a storm cloud in his dark eyes. "If there was something wrong with working for me, I'd like to know what it was."

"There's nothing wrong with it," I assured him. "Agave is a wonderful restaurant. But if that's what you wanted for me, why did you send me to pastry school?"

"So you could use those skills in *my* kitchen."

"I worked at Agave for two years after Philippe and I separated. I was still doing prep work for other chefs when I left."

He waved off my argument with a flick of his wrist. "Patience, *mija*. Everything doesn't have to happen at once." As if he'd settled that, he put his hands in his pockets, rocked back on his heels, and changed the subject. "Where is Miss Frankie anyway? I'd like to say hello."

"She's at home," I told him, "but I'm sure she'll be thrilled to see you again." Relieved that we'd moved on, I gave him an affectionate nudge with one shoulder. "Come on. Admit it. You're impressed by what you see here."

Uncle Nestor snorted and turned away. "I suppose it's all right." Which in Uncle Nestor–speak is the equivalent of "It's fabulous!" from anyone else. "You're making a mistake to let your people leave so much clutter lying around," he said. "Organization is the key to success."

"Nestor . . ." Aunt Yolanda warned. "You promised."

He growled, but when he spoke again, his voice was a little less brusque. "Your aunt missed you at Christmas. So did the boys."

Meaning my four burly cousins, all of whom were grown and could hardly be considered "boys."

"I missed you, too," I said, hoping he wouldn't rehash the arguments we'd had over my decision to stay in New Orleans with Miss Frankie.

"We could have done with a few more pictures."

"I'll be better about that from now on," I promised. "What are your plans for this evening? Are you free? There's a party I have to go to . . ." I wasn't sure that I wanted Uncle Nestor grumpy-facing it at the Captain's Court, but surely he'd snap out of his mood before then. Besides, not inviting them would be rude, and I liked the idea of having two more people I actually knew among the guests.

Uncle Nestor looked at me as if I'd lost my sense. "We're here to see you, *mija*. We're doing whatever you're doing."

Aunt Yolanda nodded. "We know you're busy. Would you rather give us your key and let us take a cab to get settled in?"

My key?

It took a couple of seconds for her meaning to register. When it did, my stomach rolled over. Omigod, of course they planned to stay at my place. I'd told them all about my beautiful new home (which I'd inherited from Philippe), and had thrown out the invitation for them to come and stay with me anytime—never really imagining they'd take me up on it. At least not without notice.

A mental image of the mound of dirty laundry on my bedroom floor raced through my head, along with the breakfast dishes piled in the sink. And the empty take-out containers from the Thai restaurant next door sitting on the table from last night's dinner. What can I say? Lately I was home just long enough to make a mess, not long enough to clean it up.

And now I had houseguests, one of whom would have a field day pointing out everything I was doing wrong. I spent a few seconds pondering my options. Stay and work like a responsible adult, or scurry home and hide my mess before Uncle Nestor spotted it. There really wasn't any question. I'd rather face half a dozen angry pastry chefs than disappoint my uncle.

As I unbuttoned my chef's jacket, I sensed Dwight tensing with disapproval, but I ignored him and tossed my jacket over an empty chair. I delegated the most pressing jobs and promised to be back as soon as humanly possible, then rushed out the back door to make sure the car was clean before Uncle Nestor got into it.

I almost wondered what else could go wrong today, but I stopped myself just in time. I was afraid I'd get an answer.

Five

As soon as we arrived at the house, I hustled Aunt Yolanda and Uncle Nestor into my second-floor guest room, and while they unpacked their suitcases, I stuffed dishes into the dishwasher and carted trash outside to the bin. I used the Swiffer on the kitchen floor, put fresh towels in the guest bath, and hid dirty clothes in my closet.

The rest of the clutter was almost tolerable, but I still couldn't relax as I showed them through the place. It really is a magnificent house, and I was surprised by how much I wanted them to approve, even as I waited for Uncle Nestor to notice a dust bunny or spot a cobweb. Along with the house, I'd inherited Philippe's substantial bank account and the Mercedes parked on the street. I was slowly getting used to my new lifestyle, but I worried that Uncle Nestor would think it all too ostentatious.

Aunt Yolanda gushed over everything, but Uncle Nestor

grumbled about the stairs he had to climb, the view from the guest bedroom, and the fact that the heater turned on twice while we were there. He'd forgotten batteries for the portable cassette player that lulled him to sleep at night, and apparently New Orleans didn't have a radio station that would satisfy him. His earphones weren't working properly, and the hangers in my closet would leave creases in his pants.

Once I'd left them getting settled and was driving back to Zydeco, I found myself wondering whether time and distance had dulled my memory, or if Uncle Nestor really was grumpier than he used to be. Not that it mattered. Whatever had brought on this foul mood of his was beside the point. I reminded myself that I could tolerate anything for a weekend, and tried to feel optimistic about taking him to the party. Everything would be fine.

Back at Zydeco, I put my family concerns on the back burner and spent the rest of the afternoon trying to work hard enough to make up for my absence. Ox got stuck in traffic trying to reach the birthday venue, so at least I didn't have to take any grief from him. I felt so guilty about abandoning the staff, I changed my mind about closing up early, which went a long way toward gaining me points with them, even if it set us back further on orders. But Dwight was all sharp edges and disapproving looks until the minute we loaded the King Cakes into the van and sent him to the country club, locking the bakery doors behind us.

I was feeling extra prickly myself, trying hard to *laissez les bons temps rouler* but coming up short. It's hard to let the good times roll when you know for certain you'll be paying the price tomorrow for the choices you've made today. I was also nervous about meeting Ivanka Hedge and planning what I'd say when I did. I mentally ran over the outfit I planned to wear, second-guessing the halter neckline, the pleated bodice, and the beaded design at the waist. Were they as flattering as I'd imagined when I bought the dress?

Not that I could do anything about it. I had nothing else even remotely suitable in my closet, and no time to shop. But that didn't stop me from fussing over my choices.

By seven o'clock, as I climbed the sweeping front steps of The Shores with my aunt and uncle, my nerves were stretched taut and ready to snap. I'd been here with Miss Frankie a couple of times, but never for such a large-scale event. Definitely not for an event people might later connect with me and, by extension, Zydeco. I could score in a big way for the bakery if everything went well tonight, but what were the chances of that? I was exhausted, and my new strappy black sandals were already making my feet hurt. I'm not used to wearing heels.

I took a deep breath and let it out slowly to steady my nerves. For months I'd been looking forward to showing off my new life to Uncle Nestor and Aunt Yolanda, but now that they were here, I wondered what they'd think of it. Would they enjoy themselves at the party or would they be miserable all evening? Should I have come earlier to help set up the serving station? And what if Ivanka Hedge didn't show up after all? Would I get another chance to land the all-important contract?

Aunt Yolanda, looking elegant in a pair of black silk pants and a beaded top I'd loaned her, stared at the clubhouse as if she'd never seen anything like it. She probably hadn't. The clubhouse at The Shores is a three-story building that could have been ripped off the set of *Gone with the Wind*. Fronted by a circular drive of crushed oyster shells and backed by acres of lush green lawn, tennis courts, and an Olympic-sized swimming pool with views of the club's world-class golf course, it was way out of our league. The whole area whispers money, history, and long-standing tradition. Though I'm getting more comfortable here, I still sometimes struggle with a sense of inadequacy. I suspected Uncle Nestor was having the same reaction.

While a uniformed valet disappeared with the car, Uncle Nestor climbed the stairs behind us, his hands in his pockets, his shoulders hunched, scowling at everything we passed. The air was cool and dry, lightly perfumed by the flowers blooming on nearby azalea bushes. It was a nearly perfect evening, but Uncle Nestor couldn't even let himself enjoy it.

When I was a girl, we never went a month without worrying how all the utilities and the rent would be paid. Even if we met those basic needs, we were never sure there'd be enough left over for groceries. Uncle Nestor and Aunt Yolanda had worked long hours to make ends meet, leaving my cousins and me alone a lot as we grew older. My aunt and uncle had never once hinted that I was a burden, but I'd secretly suspected that the extra person to feed and clothe—a girl, no less, who couldn't even wear their sons' hand-me-downs—had been the tipping point in their budget.

Aunt Yolanda had taken our circumstances in stride, praising God for blessings she hadn't yet received and urging us to do the same. But Uncle Nestor had gone down a different path. He'd taken those early hardships as a sign of failure, believing that his circumstances were a punishment for some sin he never talked about. Even now, with Agave a success, he walked through life as uncomfortable with his current good fortune as he was in the suit I'd pulled for him from the spare closet where I'd put Philippe's clothes. My poor uncle spent his days just waiting for God to throw the next big roadblock in his path.

I'd fallen somewhere in the middle, unable to rise to Aunt Yolanda's level of faith but not as negative as Uncle Nestor either. I'd found joy in the kitchen as the boys and I scraped together creative meals from the meager contents of our cupboards. Those early days had sparked my love of cooking. Which was actually a little miracle, I guess. It could so easily have gone the other way.

"I didn't realize Miss Frankie was so well off," Aunt Yolanda whispered, pulling me back to the moment.

"She has money," I said, "but it hasn't gone to her head. She's as down-to-earth as they come."

Uncle Nestor eyed the club's broad verandah with suspicion. "Family money?"

"Some of it," I said. "I'm not entirely sure where it all comes from."

He gave me a raised-brow look. "You haven't asked? Or she won't tell?"

"I haven't asked."

He huffed and turned away, and my nerve endings tingled. I wasn't imagining it. He really did seem more caustic than he used to be, but why was that? Was he that angry at me for moving to New Orleans?

There was nothing I could do about it now, so I ignored him and took up the conversation with Aunt Yolanda. "You remember how Miss Frankie was at the wedding, don't you?"

"Utterly charming," Aunt Yolanda agreed.

"And completely genuine," I assured her. "I know you'll like her when you get to know her better."

Aunt Yolanda smiled. "Don't worry so much, Rita. I'm sure we'll like your new friends."

"She's not worried about us liking them," Uncle Nestor groused from behind us. "She's worried they won't like us."

That was so unfair! I turned toward him with a scowl. "That's not true. The people coming tonight aren't exactly friends of mine. Their opinions don't matter." I hesitated on the threshold, taking in the long central corridor lined with glass trophy cases and an impressive library. I could hear the muted sounds of activity coming from somewhere in the back, but the hushed silence that greeted us told me we were one of the first to arrive. That ought to make Miss Frankie happy.

I swallowed my feelings of inadequacy and kept talking to Uncle Nestor as if I weren't battling a giant case of nerves. "Other than the staff at Zydeco, I've probably only met a handful of these people for about thirty seconds at Philippe's funeral. I have no idea what I'll talk about with any of them. I'm a little nervous about that, but there's also a chance that I can make a good impression on some important potential clients tonight. If I'm distracted and edgy, that's why. It has nothing to do with you."

Aunt Yolanda gave me an encouraging hug. "You're an intelligent woman and you have a great sense of humor. You can talk to them about absolutely anything. Don't you dare let anyone make you feel inferior."

I smiled and hugged her back. "Thanks, *Tía*. You always know just what to say. I don't expect you and Uncle Nestor to hang around here all night. If you get tired or bored, just say the word. I'll call a cab so you can go back to my place."

With a soft snort, Uncle Nestor said, "You stay, I stay."

Great. I wasn't worried about Aunt Yolanda. She could hold her own in any social situation, but I wondered if Uncle Nestor would have trouble finding common ground with the other guests in his current mood. He seemed determined to be offended.

I didn't have time to dwell on my concerns, because at that moment Miss Frankie swept into the foyer, greeting us all with her warm, honey-coated smile. She's several inches taller than I am and thin as a rail. Even thinner since

Philippe's death. Her chestnut hair had been teased, styled, and sprayed, and the sequins and beads adorning her outfit gleamed in the glow of the crystal chandeliers overhead.

She hugged me briefly, then tugged me inside. "Thank the good Lord you're here. I was beginning to get worried." Without missing a beat, she turned her smile on Aunt Yolanda and Uncle Nestor. "And how nice to have the two of you here! Isn't this wonderful? I was thrilled when Rita called to let me know you'd be joining us."

That was exactly the reaction I'd been counting on from her.

Miss Frankie snagged Uncle Nestor's arm and led him down the marble-floored corridor toward the staircase that led to the second-floor ballroom. "Rita tells me you surprised her this afternoon. Isn't that fun? I just love surprises, don't you?"

Uncle Nestor has never liked being on the receiving end of a surprise, but he went along without argument and even managed a smile of sorts, which I took as a good sign. Aunt Yolanda and I climbed the stairs behind them and followed them through an archway created by two massive gold-sequined saxophones into the club's ballroom, where dozens of round tables had been covered in crisp white tablecloths and positioned facing the long rectangular table where the krewe's highest-ranking officials would sit. Feathered and sequined carnival masks, strings of beads, and Mardi Gras–themed confetti spilled down the center of each table. Huge vases of cut flowers, each decorated with a different musical instrument, stood between support posts swathed in yards of shimmering white satin and twinkling white lights.

Uncle Nestor gave a little gasp of surprise.

Which Miss Frankie mistook for approval. "Don't you love it? The krewe's theme this year is 'Jazz Hot.' Just wait until the band starts playing. This place will really come to life then."

I was pretty sure Uncle Nestor didn't *love* it, but I was distracted by the mouthwatering aromas that filled the air, reminding me that I'd skipped lunch . . . again. I often get so wrapped up in my work that I forget to eat. My stomach rumbled and I thought about the menu Miss Frankie and I had spent days planning. I could look forward to bacon-wrapped jalapeños stuffed with cheese, crab cakes fried golden brown and served with a creamy lemon-dill sauce, hot and spicy jambalaya, garlic cheese grits, mounds of fresh shrimp accompanied by spicy cocktail and remoulade sauces, loaves of crusty French bread and beignets, and an assortment of desserts, the highlight of which would be the King Cakes that Dwight should have delivered by now.

I made a mental note to check on the cakes after my aunt and uncle were settled. At Ox's urging, I'd delegated the tasks of cutting and serving the cake tonight, and now I was really glad I'd listened to him. Putting Isabeau and Sparkle in charge of the cake service would give me one less thing to think about, especially with Aunt Yolanda and Uncle Nestor here, but I still wanted to make sure the cakes had arrived safely and that someone was on top of the setup.

I was so caught up in my thoughts that I almost plowed into Uncle Nestor's back before I realized that he'd stopped walking. He paused just inside the archway to look around, and the smile on his face faded bit by bit.

"Nice digs," he said when he realized we were all looking at him. "But it's a little out of our league. Wouldn't you say, Yolanda?"

Aunt Yolanda laughed, smoothing over his comments with her customary grace. "It's beautiful. And looks like so much fun. Have you been a member of the club long?"

"All my life," Miss Frankie said. "My mother's people have been part of The Shores for as long as this building has been standing."

"How lovely," Aunt Yolanda said. "Roots are so important. I hope it's all right for us to join you and your friends this evening. Rita assured us we wouldn't be in the way."

"In the way?" Miss Frankie looked astonished at the very idea. "You're family. How could you be in the way?"

Uncle Nestor tugged at the knot in his tie. "Thanks for having us," he said in a flat voice, "but we don't belong here."

"Neither do half the people on the guest list," Miss Frankie said with a laugh. "This is just an informal little get-together for the krewe's board members, the people who've run the committees all year and their spouses. A chance to blow off steam before the work begins in earnest and to honor those who've been so busy behind the scenes. I'm thrilled as can be that you're here, and everyone else will be, too."

Aunt Yolanda ran a glance over the elaborate decorations, the long table laden with dishes for the buffet at the far end of the room, a small four-person jazz band tuning up in one corner, and half a dozen waiters milling about near the kitchen. "This is informal?"

Miss Frankie followed her gaze and laughed again. "We like to do things up big here in the South. It all looks more impressive than it is. Now, why don't the two of you have a seat? I'll have someone bring you some drinks while Rita and I run over a few last-minute details."

"Good idea," I said. "I'd like to talk to you about Ivanka Hedge before she gets here."

"We'll get to that in a minute," Miss Frankie said. She led Aunt Yolanda to a seat near the captain's table and motioned for Uncle Nestor to sit by his wife. He hesitated for a moment before taking a seat, probably looking for the plastic cover to keep stains away.

He finally planted himself on a chair and Miss Frankie motioned for me to follow her as she went in search of a waiter. She has more energy than most women half her age. I had to quick-step to keep up with her, and that wasn't easy in my new sandals. She tossed off instructions as we walked. "I'll try to stick with you as much as possible in the beginning, but don't worry if I slip away. You'll be just fine. Everyone will love you."

"I'm not worried about that," I said, trying not to breathe hard. "I'd like to get your take on the best way to approach Ivanka when she gets here."

Miss Frankie stopped a waiter and sent him to check on Aunt Yolanda and Uncle Nestor before responding to me. "You're just meeting the woman, sugar. You're not cinching a deal. Be personable. Be charming. Be approachable. And don't talk business. With anyone. You promised, remember?"

"I remember," I said, and I *would* try, although I had no intention of forgetting my responsibilities completely. But Miss Frankie didn't need to know that. I'd slip away occasionally to make sure things were running smoothly and she'd be none the wiser.

I must have seemed sincere, because she patted my cheek affectionately and swept an arm to encompass the massive room and all the decorations. "Now, what do you think? How does it look?"

We passed a bank of windows that looked out over the expansive grounds and terraced gardens, where thousands of tiny white lights gave the place an almost magical appearance. "Everything looks great and smells even better. You've done an incredible job."

"Thank you, sugar." Miss Frankie beamed with pride. "That's music to my ears."

"I don't know why you keep insisting that I should pretend to be the hostess tonight. You've done all the work. You should get the credit."

She laughed and started walking again. "That's nonsense. It's your party. I was just happy to help, especially now that your uncle and aunt are here. This will be a great chance for them to see you shine."

I wondered whether Uncle Nestor would appreciate any shining I might do, but before either of us could say more, we heard footsteps and chatter, warning us that new arrivals were heading our way. Miss Frankie clapped her hands with excitement and signaled the band to start the music as she pressed me into duty. "Your guests are arriving, sugar. Shoulders back. Head high. Put a smile on your face. And remember to relax. Tonight's all about having fun. Don't you waste a minute being concerned about your aunt and uncle. I'll make sure they're taken care of."

Relax. Right. I lifted my chin and put a smile on my face, but leaving worry behind was a whole lot easier to say than do.

Six

I spent the next two hours watching for Ivanka Hedge's arrival and experiencing a little dip of disappointment every time someone who wasn't Ivanka came through the sparkling saxophones. I met the guest of honor, Musterion's captain, and his wife, along with the krewe's first and second lieutenants and more of Philippe's friends than I could possibly count. I struggled to connect names and faces with the brief histories Miss Frankie had been sharing with me for the past few weeks, and did my best to remember who'd served on which committee, especially those who'd worked on the Social Committee with Philippe.

I heard countless stories about Philippe's life before we met and more about his life after we separated. Some were charming and amusing. Some made me nostalgic for the early days of our relationship, and some made me wonder how well I'd really known him.

Little by little, most of the staff from Zydeco drifted into the party. Dwight came in first, wearing what passes for formal wear with him—a clean pair of threadbare black pants and a white shirt that looked as if it had been wadded in the bottom of a laundry basket for a month. I saw raised eyebrows as he came through the archway, but he'd knotted a tie—so wide and old-fashioned it must have come from Goodwill—around his neck, and I guess that was enough to put him on the right side of the club's rigid dress code for one night.

He was followed quickly by Sparkle and Estelle. Sparkle wore a dark purple gown with a tight-fitted corset and black ribbon lacing, which she'd paired with lace-up high-heeled boots. Estelle had also cleaned up nicely. In fact, she looked amazing in a silk turquoise sheath and loose-fitting silk jacket. I was pretty sure the outfits had put a hefty dent in both their budgets, which just proved how important Mardi Gras was to the people around here.

Wearing an expression that clearly said, "Don't talk to me," Sparkle settled at a corner table with a glass of champagne, while Estelle drifted from group to group, greeting people she knew. Ox and Isabeau showed up next. After spending the afternoon stuck in traffic, he made a beeline for the alcohol. She headed straight for my aunt and uncle, earning major brownie points and my undying gratitude in the process. Only Abe was missing, but that didn't surprise me. A party like this would have been hell for him.

By nine o'clock, my mind was a blur of details and my feet were killing me—and there was still no sign of Ivanka Hedge. Aunt Yolanda seemed to be making new friends, which didn't surprise me. Slightly more surprising was the realization that after a second (or maybe a third) beer, Uncle Nestor had actually stopped baring his teeth at people. Maybe things were actually looking up.

After the first hour Miss Frankie started drifting away, leaving me on my own for long stretches at a time. When she wasn't at my side, she floated from one group of guests to another, greeting old friends with exuberant hugs and kisses and looking interested in what everyone had to say. I tried to follow her lead—minus the physical displays of affection—but I was so far out of my comfort zone, my head felt as if someone had put it in a vise.

Wishing for some ibuprofen, I snagged a fruity Riesling from a passing waiter and sipped gratefully. The wine danced across my tongue and the burst of flavor I experienced as I swallowed made me want more. I drained the glass quickly and contemplated the wisdom of a second. Many of the guests were showing obvious signs of inebriation, and the noise level created by all that music, conversation, and laughter confined in one room had risen to deafening levels as a result. I didn't want to go overboard with the wine, but a pleasant buzz might ease the ache in my head and even help me relax.

And that *was* the goal, right?

I left my empty glass on a tray and joined the line of guests waiting to place their drink orders. To my relief, the bartenders were fast, and less than ten minutes later I turned back toward the crowd, running a quick glance over the King Cake service station as I did. I hadn't had a chance to thoroughly check out the setup, but with Miss Frankie otherwise occupied and a free moment of my own, this seemed like the perfect opportunity.

Miss Frankie's warning to relax rang in my ears as I wound my way through the crowd toward two long tables draped in white and covered with confetti. The largest King Cake we'd made sat on the table amid the decorations, waiting for Musterion's captain to perform the ritual cake cutting at the stroke of midnight. At the far end of the table, rows of silverware waited beside stacks of napkins that had been arranged in an artistic twist. The rest of the cakes should be in the kitchen, where the kitchen staff would cut and plate them so the waitstaff could deliver them at the appropriate time.

Reassured that everything was in order, I started to turn away. But as my eyes glanced off the stacks of napkins for the second time, I realized that something was wrong. I moved in for a closer look, telling myself the missing Zydeco logo was probably just a trick of the dim lighting. But even when I stood directly over the stack of napkins, I couldn't make that cartoon alligator standing next to the outline of a wedding cake appear.

I didn't know whether to be worried or irritated over the omission. I'd spent a substantial chunk of money on those napkins, figuring they'd work as a subtle form of advertising, and Estelle had assured me that she'd talked with the club's kitchen manager about using them tonight. I knew the box had been in the van with Dwight when he pulled away from Zydeco, so why weren't they on the table?

I glanced around for Estelle or Dwight, hoping one of them could tell me what had gone wrong. I couldn't find either in the crowd, so I decided to check with the kitchen manager myself.

I know, I know. I'd promised Miss Frankie that I wouldn't work, but I couldn't just ignore the problem. And anyway, how long could it take to swap out the napkins? Five minutes? Ten? Even Miss Frankie couldn't complain about that.

After checking to make sure she wasn't watching me, I slipped through the crowd and pushed through the doors I'd seen the waitstaff using all evening. Behind the scenes, the corridors were brightly lit and bustling with the activity that made me feel at home in a way the high-society crowd in the ballroom couldn't.

I followed a line of waiters bearing empty trays along a short corridor and rode the service elevator to the ground floor, drawing up in front of the kitchen just as a heavyset man backed through a set of swinging doors pulling a cart loaded with silver serving trays full of food for the buffet. He was watching his load so intently he almost flattened me in the process.

I jumped back and put out a hand to keep him from plowing right over me. "Hey! Watch out!"

He shot a look over his shoulder that was steely enough to sharpen knives. He looked harried and irritated, and ready to bite my head off. It was an expression I knew well. One I'd seen on Uncle Nestor's face many times when he was working. I'm pretty sure others had seen the same look on my face. When he realized that I wasn't one of his coworkers, he made a visible effort to rein in his temper and even managed a thin smile. "Sorry, ma'am, but you shouldn't be here. This area is for staff only."

I smiled back to show there were no hard feelings. "I understand, and I hate interrupting when you're obviously busy, but there's a problem with the King Cake serving station. Could you tell me where to find the kitchen manager?"

He released his grip on the cart and straightened slowly. "What kind of problem?"

"The napkins are wrong."

He looked confused. "Excuse me?"

"The napkins," I said again. "Someone has put the wrong ones out."

The irritation he'd wiped away just seconds earlier came back with a vengeance, along with a look that said he considered himself several rungs higher up the ladder than me.

"I personally checked that service station earlier. Everything was fine."

I tried not to squirm under the weight of his superior expression. I wasn't that frightened little Hispanic girl from the wrong side of town anymore, and I refused to let him make me feel that I was. "I'm not trying to make more work for you," I said, still determined to play nice. "And I don't want to hold you up when it's obvious you're busy. If you could just tell me where to find the kitchen manager, I'll take care of it myself."

He held out a hand, fingers splayed, as if he was trying to avoid touching something nasty. "I *am* the kitchen manager."

Peachy.

I gripped his cool, limp hand and gave it a firm shake. "Well, then, I guess you're the man I'm looking for. I'm Rita Lucero, the hostess for tonight's party. Could you tell me where to find the box of napkins I had delivered this afternoon? They're embossed with Zydeco's logo."

With a put-upon sigh, the manager started pushing the cart toward the service elevator. "I'm sure they were delivered, but the staff set up that serving station using the club's napkins. That's our usual practice. You understand. It's club policy."

I'm pretty sure my mouth fell open. "Seriously? You have a napkin policy?"

He gave me a tight-lipped smile. "My hands are tied. I'm sure you can use your napkins for some other event."

Maybe, but that wasn't the point. I was 95 percent sure he was lying to me because he didn't want to be bothered, and that just made me angry. Perhaps I should have just let it go, but there was a principle involved. And some pride.

"Obviously there's been a misunderstanding," I said, "but I'm sure you and I can clear it up easily."

The elevator bell dinged softly and the manager gave his cart a nudge, positioning it so I'd have a hard time getting on the elevator. "Not if it means you interfere with the work my staff has done." The doors swished open and he maneuvered the cart inside. "Look, Ms. . . . Whatever. If the napkins you're so worried about were delivered, I'm sure they're here somewhere. I'll make sure they're returned to you when the evening is over. There's no need for you to worry. Just relax and enjoy the party." With that he pulled the cart into the elevator behind him, still blocking the door. An instant later, the doors swished closed, leaving me staring at my very angry reflection in the shiny metal.

Seven

I counted to ten as the elevator carrying the kitchen manager climbed to the upper floors. I didn't want to make waves and put Zydeco in a bad light, but the man's condescending attitude and his refusal to honor our agreement had my blood boiling.

Counting to ten didn't help, but it never had. The time for negotiating was over. I was determined to find those napkins and deliver them to the King Cake station as originally planned. Still seething, I tried every door in that long corridor in case someone had tossed the napkins into a storage room. When that failed to yield results, I stopped a passing waiter and asked directions to the club's service entrance, reasoning that Dwight had probably put the box back in the van when that annoying manager refused delivery.

When the waiter directed me to a narrow hallway on the far side of the kitchen, my irritation jumped a few degrees higher. The club had a policy for napkins, but not for security? I was more convinced than ever that the kitchen manager had lied to me—and I *hate* being lied to.

A few minutes later, I let myself out the back door and headed toward Zydeco's van, parked beneath a solitary streetlamp on the far side of the employee lot. The night was surprisingly chilly, but it felt so good to step away from the craziness inside and breathe the cool, fresh air that I took my time walking toward the van. By the time I reached it, I'd calmed down enough to register that I didn't have my keys.

Terrific.

On the off chance that Dwight had left me a way in, I checked every door on the van, but I was out of luck. Dwight had locked up securely.

A less irritated woman might have given up at that point, but the stubborn streak I'd inherited from my mother kept me going. Cupping my hands around my eyes to block the light, I scoured the inside of the van. Sure enough, the box was there, nestled behind the driver's seat. I swore under my breath and made another circuit, as if I thought one of the doors might have unlocked itself by magic.

All my life I'd struggled with a sense of inadequacy. It had taken years to get it under control, and I hated how quickly it could rise up to haunt me. The kitchen manager's patronizing attitude had infused those napkins with special meaning. Come hell or high water, I was going to get them on the table before midnight.

I hurried back across the parking lot, calculating how much time it would take me to find my keys, retrieve the box, and replace the napkins. Distracted, I tugged on the door I'd come out of a few minutes earlier, but my hand slid off the handle and the door stayed shut. Paying closer attention, I tried again but the door still didn't open. I tried again.

And again. Eventually pulling so hard I broke two fingernails, but the door didn't budge an inch.

"You have *got* to be joking," I muttered to myself, stepping off the pavement into a flowerbed so I could see through
a window. That narrow corridor stretched away toward the
kitchen, but the waiters and kitchen staff who'd been rushing
around a few minutes ago had disappeared completely. Reasoning that they couldn't have gone far, I banged on the door
a couple of times.

Nothing.

I shouted for help.

Nada.

With my mood deteriorating rapidly, I finally conceded
that I wasn't going to get back inside through that door and
set off in search of another way inside.

The grounds were brightly lit on the other side of the
building, the side where members and their guests were
coming and going, but the employees didn't fare so well.
Shrubs and bushes that had appeared lush and green in the
daylight now cast deep shadows across the sidewalk and
lawn, and only a couple of security lamps in the parking lot
helped to chase away the gloom.

The cool air that had seemed so inviting before had grown
uncomfortably cold and I shivered as I walked, cursing the
kitchen manager for the locked door and my lack of a sweater
or jacket. Logical? No. But by that time I was ready to blame
him for just about everything that had gone wrong.

My feet cramped in the strappy little sandals and the hem
of my skirt grew damp from brushing the grass. After what
felt like hours, I hobbled around a curve on the path and
found a small clearing in the trees just large enough for a
lopsided park bench and a trash can.

Almost weeping with relief, I limped over to the bench

and tugged off my sandals, barely resisting the urge to toss them into the trash can at my side.

I could see the members' entrance of the club from there, but it was still at least fifty yards away. A cluster of uniformed valets lounged on the front steps, enjoying their free time until the guests started leaving. Between here and there, the sidewalk I'd been following turned into a pathway that wound in and out of the trees, probably tripling the distance I'd have to walk.

I don't know how long I stayed there, rubbing my sore, tired feet and listening to the sounds of the night. I'd already been gone from the party longer than I'd expected to be and I had no doubt that Miss Frankie had noticed by now that I'd slipped away. I'd have some explaining to do when I got back inside and, frankly, I wasn't in any hurry to have that confrontation.

Bits of conversation and laughter carried on the breeze kept me from feeling isolated, and I closed my eyes for a minute to decompress. That was a mistake. Exhaustion washed over me like a wave at high tide. The next thing I remember was the sound of a door opening and closing somewhere nearby. I sat bolt upright, heart pounding as I tried to shake the cobwebs from my groggy head. I was barely capable of thought, but I was coherent enough to know that if there was a way back into the club that didn't require another fifty-yard hike, I was all over it.

I got to my feet and reached for my shoes, but the sound of voices coming from the bushes stopped me short of actually picking them up.

"There you are," a woman said. "I've been looking everywhere for you. What are you doing out here?"

I heard a soft sound that might have been feet scuffing on pavement followed by a man's voice drawling, "I'm fortifying myself with a drop of liquid courage. Care to join me?"

Apparently, I wasn't the only person who'd bailed on the party. I left my shoes on the bench and followed the walking trail into the bushes, hoping to spot the door they'd used and figure out a way in for myself. I'd only gone a few feet when I rounded a sharp curve and glimpsed a couple standing on a small patch of concrete in front of a door that had been propped open with a piece of cinder block.

I guessed the woman to be in her mid-forties, a striking brunette with a Victoria Beckham haircut. The man was a few years younger. Tall. Handsome. Privileged. His light-colored hair was tousled, as if he'd been running his fingers through it, and he held a silver flask in one hand. But it was the look on his face, a mixture of contempt and pain—obvious even from a distance—that made me pull back into the shadows to avoid being seen.

The woman let out a deep sigh that almost got lost in the sounds of the night and waved a hand toward the flask. "Is that really necessary? There's plenty of alcohol inside."

He studied the flask for a moment before he answered her. "That's true, Mellie dear, but the company out here is infinitely more interesting."

A cold gust of wind blew through the trees and she wrapped her arms around herself for warmth. "That's because nobody else indulges you the way you do yourself."

"Some call it indulgence," the man replied. "I call it survival."

Mellie rolled her eyes. "It's hardly that," she said. "Now please, come back inside. Bradley's going to be looking for you, and you don't want to disappoint him."

The man took a long pull on the flask and carefully

capped it. "Don't you think it's a little late to be worried about that?"

A flicker of conscience told me I shouldn't be listening, but sore feet and curiosity kept me rooted to the spot. I couldn't remember meeting either of them, which only added to my interest. Plus, I didn't want to make a noise and give myself away. They'd think I was spying on them . . . and I was. I knew for certain that both Miss Frankie and Aunt Yolanda would object to that.

Mellie let out an exasperated sigh. "So you'll just hand Susannah a reason to complain about you? I thought you were smarter than that."

The man laughed. "She doesn't need any help from me. That woman makes a career out of complaining. I don't know how my brother puts up with her or . . . or why."

Mellie grinned slyly. "Oh, I think you do."

"Sadly," he agreed. "It's downright pitiful what that brother of mine will do for sex. No offense intended. He made the biggest mistake of his life when he left you, Mellie."

"Water under the bridge," she said. "You need to learn how to put the past aside, Judd."

"Ah, but that's the tricky part about the past," the man countered. "It won't go away. Believe me, I've tried to make it disappear. Repeatedly."

"You're trying the wrong methods. Alcohol won't change anything."

"Perhaps not," he agreed with a lift of an eyebrow, "but it helps me forget those things I cannot change." Ignoring Mellie's disapproving frown, he held up the flask to offer a toast. "I give thanks every day to the good Lord for creating such a useful tool."

Mellie held out a hand as if she thought he might

willingly give up the flask. "Just listen to you," she scolded. "Your mother would roll over in her grave if she could hear the way you talk. Now come back inside and pretend to care about your brother's big night for an hour. After that, I don't care what you do."

The man stared at her outstretched hand for a moment, then shook his head and laughed. "I have a better idea, sister dear. Why don't you run back inside and care about tonight for me? That ought to make him happy."

She smiled sadly and put her hand on the younger man's cheek. "It's not him I'm concerned about, Judd. I thought you knew that."

He patted her hand gently and stepped away. "I know that you've always been decent to me. More decent than any of the others, though God only knows why you should be."

"You're much harder on yourself than anyone else is," Mellie told him. "I wish you could figure that out."

Her words didn't appear to have an impact. Judd just stuffed his hands in his pockets and turned from her. "Go on in," he said as he took a step away from the door. "I'll be in shortly."

A look of weary exasperation crossed her face, but she didn't try to stop him. "I'm going to hold you to that," she warned. He kept walking, and a moment later he disappeared into the trees. With another regretful sigh, Mellie slipped back into the building and I let out the breath I'd been holding.

I stood there just until the sound of his footsteps died away, then hurried back up the path to the bench where I'd left my shoes. Mellie hadn't moved the cinder block when she went back inside, and I was anxious to use the door myself before I lost my chance.

It only took a moment to retrace my steps. I rounded the

curve in the trail and the bench came into view, but my shoes weren't where I'd left them. Slightly winded, I stopped walking and stared at the empty park bench in confusion.

Something at my side rustled and Judd stepped out from the shadow of a huge magnolia tree, my sandals dangling from the fingers of one hand. "Evenin', ma'am. If I'm not mistaken, I believe these belong to you."

He must have known I'd been eavesdropping. I could feel the heat rushing into my face, but I hoped he wouldn't notice in the darkness. "Yes, I—I—" Brilliant. I reached for the shoes. "Thank you."

He moved his hand just out of my reach. "Did I startle you?"

"A little," I admitted. "I wasn't expecting to run into anyone out here. I came out through the service entrance and somehow managed to lock myself out. I've been looking for a way back inside." I realized I was babbling and cut myself off before I could embarrass myself further.

He regarded me for a long moment then dipped his head slightly. "You're in luck, then. I know this place like the proverbial back of my hand. But are you sure you want to go back inside? If you ask me, it's much more pleasant out here."

It was lovely. And quiet. But I shook my head regretfully. "I'm afraid I don't have a choice. I'm needed at the party."

He tipped the flask and took a drink, eyeing me with curiosity as he did. "Duty. She's a tough master, that's for certain." He held the flask in my direction. "Care to imbibe before you go back in? I have in my possession some of the finest scotch my family's money can buy."

I waved away the offer. Whatever he was drinking must have been powerful stuff, though, because I could smell the fumes from where I stood. "Thanks, but I shouldn't. I need to keep my head on straight for the next few hours."

With a shrug, he slipped the flask into his pocket. "If that's the way you want it. So you're looking for a way in, are you? What brings you out here all by yourself in the first place?"

"I needed something from the van," I said. "I'm with Zydeco bakery. We provided the King Cakes for tonight's party."

His lips curved into a sly grin. "Oh, I know who *you* are, sweetheart. You've been the object of much discussion around here. People have been waitin' for tonight with bated breath. They've been speculatin' for months about whether you'd try changin' things."

That didn't surprise me. I'd suspected as much. "And the verdict?"

Judd sketched a mock salute. "Even your detractors have conceded. You've done well . . . for an outsider."

I laughed then shivered a little as a cool breeze blew across the grounds. "I'd ask who my detractors are, but I really don't want to know."

"I couldn't tell you anyway," Judd said in a flat voice. "If I did, they'd have to kill me." He peeled off his jacket and held it out to me.

I accepted it gratefully and slipped it on. "I'm Rita, by the way," I said as I held out a hand. "Lucero."

Instead of shaking, he touched my fingertips and bowed low over my hand. Charming, even if he was pickled. "As I said, I know who you are."

"Ah, but I don't know *you*," I reminded him. "Or did we meet inside and I've forgotten?"

When he lifted his head again, a smile curved his lips. "Fear not, my dear. Your memory hasn't let you down. We haven't met until this moment."

"So then you are . . ."

"A source of never-ending disappointment to my family."

He waved me back toward the sidewalk. "If you'll come with me, I'll show you the quickest way to get inside out of the cold."

He led me a few feet to the right then slipped into a copse of trees where a path had been worn into the grass—which explained how he'd beat me to the clearing.

"You have a secret entryway?" I joked as I stepped around an exposed tree root. "I take it that means you've spent some time here."

He grinned over his shoulder. "I've been coming here since I was a boy. My parents were always busy with something, so I spent a lot of time exploring." He came to a stop in front of the door and held it open for me. "There you go, m'dear. You'll find the stairs to the lobby just beyond the weight room." He handed over my sandals and backed a step away.

"You're not coming?"

He shook his head. "Later, perhaps."

Beneath the gallant smile, there lurked a deep sadness. I wondered what his story was. But I couldn't stand out here talking to him all night. Miss Frankie would have my hide if I did.

"Thank you," I said. "You've saved my life—or at least my feet."

"Then I am a happy man."

I would have bet everything I owned that was the biggest lie I'd heard all night.

Eight

❦

It wasn't until Judd had disappeared through the trees again that I realized I was still wearing his jacket. I thought about going after him, but he'd made it pretty clear he wasn't in the mood for company. Plus, I really needed to get back to the party. And I still hadn't resolved the napkin issue.

And besides, the prospect of meeting up with Judd again later wasn't altogether unappealing.

I forced my feet back into my sandals and climbed the stairs, trying not to wince as I walked through the saxophone arch into the party. The band was playing a slow song that sounded vaguely familiar, and several couples had moved onto the dance floor. I folded Judd's jacket and tucked it under the tables at the King Cake serving station, then looked around to see if Uncle Nestor and Aunt Yolanda had gotten into the spirit. Miss Frankie descended on me before I could spot them.

"Where in the world have you been?" she demanded. Her eyes spit fire, but the smile on her face was faultless.

"Outside," I said, hoping to avoid a long explanation. "I'm sorry. I didn't mean to be gone so long."

"People have been asking where you were."

"Well, I'm back now," I pointed out, then tried to divert her. "Has Ivanka Hedge arrived yet?"

"No, and you're lucky she hasn't. I swear—"

I cut her off as politely as I could. "Can it wait until later? I need to find Estelle. Have you seen her?"

The smile on Miss Frankie's face slipped ever-so-slightly. "Sugar, have you been working?"

"Not exactly." I craned to see over the heads of people standing close by, but that was a waste of effort. The sea of partying humanity had grown in the time I'd been gone. Just as I was ready to give up, I spotted a flash of turquoise near the bandstand. "I'll be back in a minute," I assured my mother-in-law. "I just have to ask her one little question."

Miss Frankie grabbed my hand as if she intended to stop me. I'll never know whether she would have succeeded, because at that precise moment a hush fell over the crowd closest to us and people turned toward the archway wearing expressions filled with such anticipation I wondered if Ivanka had finally arrived and I stopped myself from leaving.

"Who is it?" I asked Miss Frankie.

"I can't tell," she said with a slight scowl. "Let's go see, shall we?"

We made our way through a wall of people who let us through with expressions ranging from impatience to out-right irritation. And all for nothing. Instead of the cool willowy blonde I was hoping to find, a large man with dark hair, close-set eyes, and a broad smile surged into the room.

He wore a ten-gallon cowboy hat and greeted the people around him like a politician on the campaign trail.

I recognized him immediately as Big Daddy Boudreaux, a minor celebrity in New Orleans—owner of half a dozen car dealerships and a string of other small businesses. As far as I could tell, he spent the majority of his time blowing up storage sheds and jumping out of airplanes to prove that his cars were the best and his prices the lowest around—and of course, he did it all on camera for his commercials.

Biting back disappointment that he wasn't Ivanka, I turned away again and glimpsed Miss Frankie's expression. It was gone in a blink, but I knew I hadn't imagined the slight curl of her lip or the coolness in her eyes.

Intrigued by her reaction, I grabbed another glass of wine and moved closer to her. I spoke softly, hoping my voice wouldn't carry. "I take it you're not a fan?"

"Of Bradley's?"

For some reason it struck me as odd that Big Daddy Boudreaux had an actual first name. "Bradley?"

Miss Frankie gave me a smile that was all wide-eyed innocence. "Only a handful of us can get away with calling him that. And why wouldn't I be a fan? He's the life of the party."

"Then why the sour look on your face?"

She shrugged. "Indigestion."

I didn't believe that for a moment, but I didn't get a chance to pursue it.

Big Daddy—with that big-ass hat and look-at-me grin, I couldn't think of him any other way—spotted Miss Frankie and advanced on her with wide-spread arms. "There she is. How are you, darlin'?"

She surrendered to a quick hug, but another pained look

flickered over her face, convincing me that her "indigestion" was a figment of her imagination. "Well, Bradley, I was beginning to think you weren't coming. It's been such a long time since I saw you. I hope you've been well."

He let out a hearty laugh. "Are you kidding? I wouldn't miss the Captain's Court for anything, especially not when I knew it was in your hands."

"How you do go on," Miss Frankie said, smiling at him as if she'd just found a long-lost friend. I knew I hadn't imagined the look on her face, but I also knew that she'd rather die than let an unwelcome guest sense her true feelings. "I'm flattered. I wasn't sure you'd remember who I was."

Her soft-edged response hit its target. He shrugged and glanced at the people around him, playing his audience with a smile that was both haughty and sheepish. He probably practiced it in front of a mirror in his spare time. "I know. I know. I could just kick myself. I meant to call when Philippe passed, but things got the better of me."

Miss Frankie's expression didn't change as she beckoned me closer. "Rita? Come here, sugar. I want you to meet an old family friend. Bradley Boudreaux, this is my daughter-in-law, Rita."

I went eagerly, curious to find out more about their relationship. Big Daddy's smile faltered as I moved closer, and I glimpsed what might have been genuine sorrow in his eyes. "You're Phil's wife?"

Phil? Even I had never called him that.

I told myself not to overreact to the "wife" thing. After seven months in New Orleans, I should be used to hearing myself referred to that way, but it still tweaks my conscience. I've given up trying to explain, though. Our relationship was too complicated at the end, making explanations too convoluted.

I nodded and offered him a hand to shake and a little white lie to swallow. "It's a pleasure to meet you."

Big Daddy bypassed the hand and pulled me in for a hug so enthusiastic it took my breath away—and not in a good way. He smelled of bourbon and cigars, both of which made my gag reflex kick in. "No wonder Phil abandoned us for so long," he said to Miss Frankie over my shoulder. "Just look at her! She's gorgeous."

Double gag. I extricated myself from the hug and smiled, saying the only thing I could think of: "You're an old family friend?"

"Sure am. Phil was my little brother Judd's closest friend when they were kids."

Hearing that name brought my head up sharply. *This* was the brother Judd had talked about with Mellie? I wondered why Philippe had never mentioned his old friend Judd when we were married. I wondered why Miss Frankie had never mentioned the Boudreauxes' absence at the funeral. Or why she'd never once mentioned knowing Big Daddy when we saw one of his obnoxious commercials on TV.

"The two of them used to drive me crazy," Big Daddy said. "Tagging along after me, wanting to do things with me and my friends." He turned the wattage up on his smile and aimed it at Miss Frankie again. "Those were some good times, weren't they?"

Pain flickered in her eyes, so I tried to edge away from those boyhood memories. "I've seen you on TV, but I had no idea you were a friend of Miss Frankie's. I can't imagine why we haven't met before."

Big Daddy's broad smile turned into a deep frown. "It's a damn shame, isn't it? I wasn't at the funeral. It wasn't right, and I hated myself for missing it," he said again. "But the wife and I were on a cruise. I didn't even hear about it until we got back, and by then it was too late."

And he hadn't found a minute to call on Miss Frankie since then? Busy man.

Up close and personal, he was much taller than he looked on TV, and he managed to slip an arm around my shoulders as he talked. My skin crawled, but I didn't completely understand why. I only knew that I didn't like the guy. I made an effort to move away from him, but he tightened his hold, sticking to me like icing on warm cake.

"Judd should have been at the funeral, though. No excuses. But that's my little brother. He's a good kid and he means well, but . . ." His voice trailed off and he shook his head slowly.

I wondered why excuses were okay for Big Daddy but not for his little brother.

"Speaking of Judd," Big Daddy said, craning to see over our heads, "is he here tonight?"

I didn't answer but Miss Frankie nodded. "He came in about an hour ago."

The scents of food, alcohol, and Big Daddy were making my head pound. I rubbed my forehead—at least I tried to. Big Daddy had my arms crushed against my side, giving me very little room to move.

I was getting a little claustrophobic crushed up against him like that, so I finally shrugged him off as politely as I could. That's when I spotted the young woman standing behind him, arms folded across her chest and face pinched in anger. She was probably mid-thirties, close to my own age, with sleek brown hair and a heart-shaped face. She glared at me, her eyes narrowed behind a pair of glasses with rectangular black plastic frames.

I had no idea what her problem was, but I put a little more

distance between the big guy and myself to show her that I meant no harm.

Miss Frankie greeted the woman with her customary warmth. "Violet, dear, it's lovely to see you, too." She turned to me and said, "Rita, you must meet Violet Shepherd. She's Bradley's right arm. I don't know what he'd do without her."

Not his wife, then. Lucky girl. Violet sent me a pained smile and I sent her one back. Luckily I was spared the need to make small talk, because just then a tall man with mocha-colored skin and a deep frown on his face strode up to Big Daddy and jabbed him in the shoulder. "We need to talk, Boudreaux. Outside. Now."

Big Daddy's hot, smelly breath blew over my shoulders and down my back as he turned to face the new arrival, who looked enough like Denzel Washington to make me do a double take.

"Now, Percy, that's no way to act," Big Daddy scolded. "We're at a party, and you're likely to upset the ladies. Whatever it is can wait until tomorrow or the next day."

Percy swept a contrite glance over the three of us. I didn't know about the other two, but I was in no imminent danger of emotional upset.

"I'm sorry, Miss Frankie," Percy said. "But this is important." He looked from one of us to the other and smiled apologetically. "I'm sure y'all understand."

Miss Frankie and I mumbled that we did, but Violet looked at him over the rims of her glasses. "I don't think this is the time or the place—"

Big Daddy gave her a look that stopped her cold, then turned to Percy. "God Almighty," he said half under his breath. "I said *not now*. Talk to me later. Or tomorrow."

Percy held his ground and the frown on his face deepened. "Now," he warned.

Big Daddy gave him a flat-eyed look. "I'm not going to let you stir up a ruckus and ruin the night. Whatever it is that has your boxers in a bunch will keep. Violet, set up an appointment or something. Percy, have yourself a drink and calm down."

Percy looked as if he wanted to argue further, but Violet turned her Vulcan Death Stare on him and ordered, "Call the office on Monday, Mr. Ponter. I'll set up an appointment for you."

"Monday will be too late," Percy said, but he cut a glance at Miss Frankie and me and relented slightly. "My apologies, ladies. I didn't mean to cause a scene." He started to turn away, firing one last shot at Big Daddy before he left. "Don't think this is the end of it, Boudreaux. We'll settle this tonight, one way or another."

Miss Frankie noticed a couple of guests listening to the exchange. Wearing her trademark smile, she took them by the arms and led them away, chatting easily about the music. An uncomfortable silence rang between the rest of us for about two seconds before Big Daddy's plus-one took charge. Turning her death glare into a smile, she tucked one lock of dark hair behind an ear and put a hand on Big Daddy's beefy arm. "Is there anything you want me to do?"

Big Daddy waved her away. "Don't worry so much, Violet. You're my assistant, not my mother. Why don't you go amuse yourself? I'll catch up with you later."

Even though she'd been trying to kill me with her eyes, I felt kind of bad for Violet. Apparently, Big Daddy's on-camera schtick was no act. He really was a jerk.

Violet's face burned, but she pivoted away without another word . . . and plowed straight into a tall young woman with pale blond hair. Ivanka Hedge stumbled backward into her fiancé, Richard Montgomery III, with a cry of alarm. Violet growled something that might have been an apology but probably wasn't, and kept going.

Luckily, Richard, an elegant but plain-faced man of around thirty and slightly balding, kept Ivanka from falling, but the look on her face made it clear that she wasn't happy.

Then again, neither was I. I started toward her, an apology on my lips, but she sailed past me with a little moue of distaste.

My heart sank like a stone. There went my chances of making a good first impression.

If I'd disliked Big Daddy Boudreaux before, I positively loathed him now.

I craned to see where Ivanka had gone, but I'd already lost sight of her.

"You lookin' for the ice princess?" Big Daddy asked in my ear.

I scowled over my shoulder and moved a step away. "If you mean Ivanka Hedge, then yes. Did you see where she went?"

Big Daddy looked out over the crowd and jerked his chin toward a set of doors leading onto the balcony. "Over there with my wife. You want to talk to her?"

"Yes. Thanks. If you'll excuse me—"

He raised one hand over his head and slipped the other around my waist. "Hey, Ivanka! Over here!"

I gaped at him in horror and extricated myself from his grasp. "That's not necessary," I said as nicely as I could. I smoothed my dress, readjusted the parts that had gotten skewed, and looked up to see both Ivanka and a shorter, softly rounded woman with a pale complexion and burgundy hair in a wedge cut, pointedly ignoring Big Daddy's summons. That must be the Susannah I'd overheard Judd and Mellie talking about.

Interesting that neither woman paid attention to him.

"Thanks for nothing," I muttered.

Big Daddy waved that beefy hand through the air, dismissing me, my concerns, and Ivanka all at once. "Listen, darlin', she's not worth getting yourself all worked up over."

Said the man with the bulging bank accounts.

I had a sour taste in my mouth, but I spooned a little more syrup into my smile for Miss Frankie's sake. "I'll keep that in mind."

"I'm serious. She's a friend of my wife's. I know what she's really like. You wouldn't like her."

"Well, hard to say if I never meet her," I said. "Now if you'll excuse me—"

He grabbed my hand and pulled me around to face him. "Listen, darlin', let me give you a word of advice. You can make yourself crazy chasin' after people who don't give two hoots about you. Don't do it. Just be yourself. That's what I do."

That wasn't exactly a selling point. At that moment, Big Daddy Boudreaux was the last person I wanted advice from.

I heard his big booming laugh following me as I walked away, and I made a silent pledge to avoid him for the rest of the night. I had a feeling that Big Daddy was going to be a problem. I just wish I'd known then how much trouble he was going to cause.

Nine

Finally free of Big Daddy, I hurried after Ivanka and Richard, still hoping to wrangle an introduction. I got held up a couple of times, first by Isabeau, who wanted to check on a couple of details related to serving the King Cake at midnight, and next by Estelle, who wanted to show me the pictures Ox had asked her to take for the blog.

By the time I'd asked Estelle to check on the napkins and placated her by slipping her memory card into my evening bag, I'd lost sight of the happy couple again. Luckily, Mrs. Big Daddy hadn't moved, so I decided to take my chances with her.

I made my way through the crowd and stopped in front of her wearing my friendliest smile. "Mrs. Boudreaux?"

She ran a squished-bug glance over me. "Yes?"

"I'm Rita Lucero, I'm the hostess—"

She cut me off before I could finish. "Yes, yes, yes. I saw

you over there with my husband. Is there something you need?"

At least I didn't have to wonder what made the Boudreauxes' marriage tick. They were perfect for each other. "Your husband mentioned that you're a friend of Ivanka Hedge. I'd really love to meet her before the night is over."

She darted a glance at a dark-haired man wearing tortoiseshell glasses who stood a little to one side. Until that moment, I hadn't realized they were together. She shared a little smirk with him and tossed, "Wouldn't everyone?" over her shoulder as they walked away.

Stung by her dismissal, I made two circuits of the ballroom, checked the balcony, scoured the grounds with their twinkling lights, surveyed the tables scattered across the terraced lawn, then made another brief tour inside before acknowledging that Ivanka and Richard must have already left. I'd lost my chance, thanks to Big Daddy.

Big Dud was more like it.

Everywhere I went I heard his booming voice or thunderous laugh. The longer the night went on, the more space he seemed to take up. Like dough left to rise, he seemed to double in size, which may help to explain what happened next.

It was a little after ten and I was locked in conversation with a vague young woman with thin straight hair and winsome eyes. Boredom wrapped itself around my head and squeezed. Visions of my nice, quiet bedroom in my nice, quiet house danced in front of my eyes. While she prattled on about vintage seeds and soil types, I stifled yawn after yawn and looked around for someone—anyone—who might save me.

After several minutes, I saw Uncle Nestor standing near the stairs wearing a look of irritation. An instant later, I saw what had put it there.

Big Daddy had boxed him in beside the staircase, a glass of whiskey in one hand, a cigar in the other. He was talking nonstop, gesturing broadly and leaving a trail of smoke behind with every word.

Uncle Nestor watched him with a caged-tiger look that made me nervous. That was all the excuse I needed to cut my conversation short. I muttered an excuse and started to move away from the young woman, whose name I'd already forgotten.

Apparently, she wasn't listening. "You'd be amazed by the gardens," she said, trailing behind me. I guess she thought I found the subject of chemical fertilizers as fascinating as she did. "So many people think that if a little does a lot of good, a lot will be even better. They couldn't be more wrong."

"I'm sure that's a problem," I said, forcing a smile. "I hope you can find a solution. Now, if you'll excuse me—"

"You have *no* idea. People call me all the time wanting help with some plant they've killed." She droned on, sounding a little like the teacher in the Charlie Brown cartoons. *"Wah wah-wah. Wah wah wah."*

Across the room, Big Daddy threw back his head and laughed at something, and the scowl on Uncle Nestor's face deepened. Even from a distance, I could see color flooding his face.

". . . and of course, aphids can be *such* a problem . . ."

Never again, I promised myself. Never ever again. If Miss Frankie wanted to host a party, she could do it without me.

Uncle Nestor jabbed a finger at Big Daddy and said something I couldn't hear. But I didn't need to hear what he said to know that the situation was deteriorating fast. I glanced around for Aunt Yolanda, hoping she'd noticed what was going on with her husband. I spotted her near the balcony doors, laughing with Miss Frankie and her neighbor, Bernice. I doubted she even knew where Uncle Nestor was.

". . . and you have to dig that into the soil, which can be time-consuming . . ."

Smirking, Big Daddy waved Uncle Nestor's hand away. Cigar smoke billowed between them, but I didn't have to see my uncle's face to know that was going to be a problem. Under normal circumstances, I wouldn't have been as worried, but I was pretty sure Uncle Nestor had been drinking for the past couple of hours, and I still didn't know why he was in such a foul mood to begin with.

I walked away from my gardening friend in the middle of an observation about tree sap just as Big Daddy belted out a rafter-shaking laugh at Uncle Nestor's expense. I slipped past a couple of women and ducked between two men and a waiter carrying a huge tray of hors d'oeuvres. Just a few more feet. Just a handful of people to get past.

But I might as well have been miles away. While I looked on in stunned disbelief, Uncle Nestor blasted Big Daddy with a right hook that would have made George Foreman proud.

Big Daddy rocked under the force of the assault. If I'd been more nimble, I would have vaulted over the furniture to get between them. As it was, I had to skirt tables, chairs, and tipsy guests, and that slowed me down.

I hurried out through the glittering archway as Big Daddy shoved his drink and cigar onto a nearby table and grabbed Uncle Nestor by the lapels of his jacket, slamming him into the wall. A couple of nearby pictures slid off-center from the impact, and I heard the sound of breaking glass just behind me.

It seemed to take forever to push through, but I finally got there and grabbed Big Daddy's arm, trying to pull him off my uncle. "Let go!" I shouted. "I mean it, Big Daddy. Let him go *now*!" He was way too big for me, but I created enough of a distraction for Uncle Nestor to slip out of his grip.

Before I could catch my breath, Big Daddy took his eyes off Uncle Nestor for a split second and my scrappy little uncle launched himself at Big Daddy for the second time. This time he landed a solid blow to Big Daddy's chin, and with it he punched a big fat hole in my bubble of optimism. What was going on? The Uncle Nestor who raised me would never get into a fistfight like this.

I glanced around for help, assuming that everyone had heard the shouting, but the music and laughter must have drowned out the sound. Only a handful of people seemed aware of the scuffle, and I saw Edie trying to distract the few guests who'd noticed.

Thank God for small favors.

Making a mental note to thank her later, I set out to calm both men down before Aunt Yolanda and Miss Frankie got wind of their argument. I waded in a little deeper and tried to get between them, counting on Uncle Nestor to back off rather than hit me. "Stop it!" I ordered. "Both of you. Right now."

Big Daddy wiped a spot of blood from the corner of his mouth and gestured toward Uncle Nestor. "The old man attacked me." He looked around at the small crowd for backup. "You all saw it. Son of a bitch came at me like a crazy man."

Uncle Nestor let fly with some Spanish. I only understood a few words, but every one of them was on the list my cousins and I hadn't been allowed to say when we were younger.

Big Daddy twitched a bit, readjusting his shirt after the tussle. He jerked his head toward Uncle Nestor. "Is this guy for real?"

He had some nerve. Uncle Nestor might be emotional, but even in his current mood I had a hard time accepting that he'd turned into someone who'd start a fight unprovoked. Uncle Nestor didn't start trouble, but he knew how to end it. Big Daddy must have said something to set him off.

But I didn't want to ruin the evening for Miss Frankie by prolonging the confrontation. I forced myself to say, "I'm so sorry," though I had a hard time getting the words out around the big old lump of resentment in my throat.

"Don't you dare apologize for me, *mija*. He's the one who should be sorry." Uncle Nestor shook a finger in Big Daddy's big, ugly face. "You're lucky that's all you got, *pendejo*."

To my immense relief, Big Daddy shrugged him off, but he turned to me with a scowl. "*You're* lucky I'm in a good mood. Otherwise, I might just call the police and tell them to lock the guy up. He's nuts."

That stopped me cold. "He's not crazy. What did you say to him?"

One thick eyebrow rose in surprise. "Excuse me?"

"What did you say to him?" I asked again, deliberately overenunciating.

Big Daddy ignored the question and dug another cigar out of his breast pocket. "This guy's a friend of yours?"

"Yeah. He is."

"Well, then, take my advice and get him some professional help before he hurts somebody." He strode away before I could come up with a good response, which was probably a good thing. I turned away and took a couple of calming breaths before dragging my uncle into a small, unused meeting room.

I locked the door and glared at Uncle Nestor, who was still red-faced and angry. "What was that all about, *Tío*? Why did you hit him?"

Uncle Nestor brushed at his shirt and jacket as if Big Daddy had left traces of something unsavory behind. "Nothing for you to worry about, little girl."

When I was younger, I'd liked it when he called me that. But with my thirty-fifth birthday looming in a couple of months, it had been a long time since I qualified as a child. "I'm not a little girl," I said automatically. "And it sure is something for me to worry about. This is my party, remember? Technically, Big Daddy is my guest."

"Then you ought to be more careful about who you associate with."

"And you ought to be more careful about who you take a swing at," I snapped. "That guy might be a jerk, but he's a local celebrity and a lot of people like him. Your little stunt could give Miss Frankie, Zydeco, and me a big fat black eye in the press."

Uncle Nestor's scowl grew more sullen. "That's all you're worried about? This new life of yours? This new family you've picked out?"

For a moment, I could only gape at him in disbelief. "You have got to be kidding me," I said when I could form words again. "You're jealous?"

He shot a look at me from the corner of his eye. "Don't be absurd."

"What's absurd about it?" I demanded. "You've been taking shots at me, at the bakery, and at Miss Frankie since the minute you arrived."

He shrugged and focused on tucking his shirt into his waistband. "I would never do anything to hurt you, *mija*. You know that."

"You have a funny way of showing it," I said under my breath, but I never could stay mad at him and I didn't want to prolong the drama. I hugged him quickly. "Just steer clear of Big Daddy for the rest of the night, okay? No more trouble."

He gave another shrug. "Of course."

"I mean it," I warned. "And would it kill you to smile?"

He flashed a grin that wasn't entirely genuine, but I'd take what I could get. I stepped away from the door and he walked through it to rejoin the party. After closing my eyes and counting to ten, I did the same.

And I reminded myself that I only had to get through the next couple of hours. After that, I could take Uncle Nestor home. Everything would be better tomorrow. I was sure of it.

Ten

We served the King Cake promptly at midnight.

Estelle had worked her magic, slipping the Zydeco napkins into place when nobody was looking. I told myself not to gloat over this minor victory, but it did reenergize me. And I needed that, since I was anxious about the reception the cakes would receive. Other than the controversial addition of filling in some of the cakes, I'd remained true to Philippe's recipe. I thought they'd turned out well, but these folks were connoisseurs. Most of them had been eating King Cake since they were babies, and the perfectionist in me needed the cakes to score a hit.

I hovered while Musterion's captain made a short speech and introduced the officers for the coming year, a roster that included Big Daddy Boudreaux as captain and Percy Ponter as treasurer, a little detail I found interesting. Several hours had passed since he'd confronted Big Daddy, but Percy didn't look any happier than before. He glared at Big Daddy throughout the ceremony, and several times I thought he was actually going to interrupt. He didn't, though, and Big Daddy seemed oblivious to any negative undercurrents. He beamed and thanked people for their votes and made lavish promises about the upcoming year.

I tuned him out and worried about the King Cakes. Were they still fresh? Would the ceremonial cake hold its shape when the captain made the first cut? Would the guests like the flavor? Would they accept the fillings?

While I hovered, holding my breath in anticipation, I saw Judd lurking at the back of the crowd. So he'd come inside to support his brother after all. I hoped Mellie had seen him and then wondered why it should matter to me. I'd liked him instinctively, and maybe I'd felt some kinship. I'd lived in the shadows of my bigger-than-life ex-husband and cousins, so I had an idea how Judd must have felt having Big Daddy for a brother.

To my relief, the speeches finally ended and the captain pronounced the King Cake excellent. The club's waitstaff surged into the room carrying trays of plated cake, and everything else flew out of my head. Ox and I circulated among the guests, accepting compliments and encouraging anyone who expressed an interest in our cakes to make an appointment with Edie. I lost sight of Judd and didn't think about him again until the party began to break up around 1 a.m.

Miss Frankie and I stood near the glittering saxophones kissing cheeks, accepting hugs, and saying good-bye to the guests in true Southern style. By one-thirty, even my lucky staff had cleared out and what few guests remained had migrated indoors. I could have counted on two hands the number of die-hard guests who were hanging around, and

I hoped they would all leave soon. Miss Frankie would stay until the very end, and she'd expect me to do the same.

After a while, the club's staff began clearing away dishes and glasses, removing the tablecloths, and packing away decorations. I checked to see how many lingerers there were and spotted Mellie across the room deep in conversation with Susannah Boudreaux. Susannah looked upset. Or maybe she was drunk. Or both. It was hard to tell.

I retrieved Judd's jacket from under the serving station and draped it over my arm, then decided against interrupting Mellie and Susannah and instead joined Miss Frankie and Aunt Yolanda, who were sitting on a couple of stray chairs near the head table.

Miss Frankie held a glass of champagne in one hand, but her head was tilted back against the chair and her eyes were closed. Aunt Yolanda sat with her bare feet stretched out in front of her, her shoes abandoned on the floor nearby.

Relieved to have the party behind me, I sank onto a folding chair beside Aunt Yolanda and kicked off the sandals that had all but crippled me. I wriggled my toes, wishing I could curl up and go to sleep right there. If I hurried home, I could maybe catch three hours of sleep before I had to leave for work. I had the feeling it was going to be a very long day.

Miss Frankie opened one eye and smiled at me. "The party was a huge success, sugar. I know it wasn't easy after a full day at the bakery, but all of Philippe's friends were taken with you. You charmed everyone."

Not the important ones. My failure to make contact with the Hedge-Montgomery wedding party was my biggest disappointment. A close second was the amount of time I'd had to spend making sure that Big Daddy's off-color jokes and generally irritating personality didn't offend anyone.

Now that I thought about him, I realized that I hadn't noticed when he'd left. I wouldn't have imagined him leaving without drawing attention to himself but, frankly, I appreciated the silence. I was through with him, that's all that mattered.

I yawned. Stretched. And tried to focus on the positives. "So who got the official baby in the cake this year?"

"Esther McIntosh," Miss Frankie said. "She's the art gallery owner and her husband is an attorney. I introduced you to them, remember?"

I ran through the names and faces I'd tried to mentally catalog in the past few hours. "Tall woman? Thin? Wearing an African-print caftan?"

Miss Frankie nodded. "Her husband looks like he should be coaching the Saints, not teaching tax law."

I was pleased with myself for remembering. "They ought to do a good job with next year's party," I said to be polite. I didn't really care who got the job next year as long as it wasn't me. I stole a glance at my watch and grimaced at how quickly my sleep time was ticking past.

Aunt Yolanda glanced around the ballroom, still littered with plates, glasses, napkins, and silverware. The musicians had packed up their instruments, and the relative silence after a night of rousing jazz numbers made my ears ring.

"I should figure out where Nestor has gone," Aunt Yolanda said. "I haven't seen him in a while."

I hadn't either, I realized with a pang of guilt. After that fight with Big Daddy, I'd vowed to keep an eye on him but I'd been distracted by other things. "Maybe he's slipped away somewhere to get some rest." And by "get some rest" I meant "sleep off all the booze he'd swallowed during the evening." Why else would he have started the fight with Big Daddy? If he was "resting" somewhere, waking him would be like poking a tiger with a sharp stick, but I'd have to risk it. He'd be even angrier if I left him to sleep it off at The Shores.

I stood and realized that I still had Judd's jacket. Yawning, I tried to decide whether to leave it with a member of the staff or give it to Mellie. She obviously knew him well. The one minor problem: She and I hadn't actually met. Which made explaining how I knew to give her Judd's suit coat a little tricky.

Counting on Miss Frankie to help with that, I nodded discreetly toward the two women on the other side of the room. "I don't remember meeting the woman standing with Susannah Boudreaux. Who is she?"

Miss Frankie sat up and took a look. "You didn't meet Mellie? How did I let that happen?"

"It's not your fault," I assured her quickly. "There were so many people here. It would have been impossible to meet each one personally. Is she a friend of yours?"

Miss Frankie nodded. "I've known Mellie since she was a girl. Susannah is relatively new to these parts. Her people come from Charleston, I believe."

That didn't tell me much. "I saw her talking to a guy earlier," I said. "Tall. Blond. Kind of good-looking, I guess." I held up the suit coat. "He loaned this to me, but I never saw him again. She called him Judd. Am I right in assuming he's Big Daddy's brother?"

Miss Frankie brightened. "I'm sure it probably was. He was here earlier."

"So Mellie is his ex-sister-in-law?"

"That's right. Mellie was married to Bradley several years ago. They've been divorced for a while, more's the pity. She was the best thing that ever happened to him." She scowled thoughtfully and lowered her voice a notch. "Susannah is his current wife. The third one. There was one in between, but she didn't last long. Bless her heart, Susannah there tries hard, but she's no match for Bradley."

I glanced again at the two women from the corner of my eye and wondered if the wife/ex-wife thing explained the tension I sensed between them or if there was something else going on. I tried to picture either woman married to Big Daddy. Neither one seemed like his type, but maybe I had a slightly biased idea of what his type was. I'd have bet on platinum blond, dumb as a rock, and 95 percent plastic.

Neither Mellie nor Susannah fit that mold. Neither had Violet, come to think of it, who seemed to be vying for a spot as Wife No. 4. In fact, all three women could have been triplets, separated at birth by a decade or so.

I decided not to interrupt them. I'd hang on to Judd's jacket for a little while longer. Seeing him again to return it would be no hardship. "Why don't we gather our things," I suggested, "and then we can look for Uncle Nestor. Are there any private rooms around here where he might be lying down?"

Miss Frankie got to her feet, but it seemed to take some effort. "Several," she said. "I'll help you look." She smiled at me so fondly, my earlier doubts about the party dimmed. Now that it was over, I could admit that I hadn't really minded playing hostess for the evening. I just didn't want to make a habit of it.

"I have a better idea." Aunt Yolanda reached into the purse at her feet for her cell phone. She pressed a couple of buttons and almost immediately we heard the sound of Uncle Nestor's ringtone coming in through the open doors to the balcony.

"Now, wasn't that easier?" She shut her phone with a snap and crossed the room, calling out as she walked, "Nestor? What are you doing out there? We're ready to go."

He didn't answer, but that didn't surprise me. I still fully expected to find him sleeping it off somewhere. I trailed after her so I could help rouse him if my suspicions proved correct. "Maybe he fell asleep in one of the deck chairs."

"You underestimate your uncle," she said. "He's probably tidying up."

I thought *she* was underestimating the amount he'd had to drink, but I didn't say so aloud. Besides, my uncle isn't the type to "tidy." He cleans the way he does everything else: all out. If he were cleaning up after Miss Frankie's party, he'd be sweeping everything in sight into garbage bags.

Aunt Yolanda waited for me to catch up with her, and put an arm around my shoulders when I did. "You're happy here, aren't you, Rita?"

The question surprised me and so did her timing, but I nodded. "Yes, I am."

"Are you sure? You seem a little . . . jumpy."

"That's because I'm still adjusting. And this"—I gestured toward the party mess—"isn't really my thing. I love Zydeco. I have a great staff and I love the work I'm doing. And you've seen my house. It's incredible. I'm happy with my decision. I'm just not sure that you and Uncle Nestor are happy for me."

"I'm thrilled for you," she said, giving me another squeeze of reassurance. "And Nestor is fine with it, too."

I laughed at her careful phrasing. "Fine with it? I wish I could believe you. He seems hurt. Maybe even a little resentful toward Miss Frankie."

"He's also adjusting, *mija*. If he does feel any resentment, it's only temporary. He's worried about you and he misses you. Just be patient with him. He'll get there."

Guilt tweaked at me again. "You know it was never my intention to hurt either of you. I didn't stay here because I care more about Miss Frankie than the two of you."

"Of course we know that." She turned to face me, resting both hands on my shoulders. "There's *nothing* in the world Nestor and I want more than your happiness. If this is the life you choose, we're in your corner. I hope you know that."

I hugged her tightly, grateful for her steadiness and soft-spoken approval. "Thank you. I don't know what I'd do without you."

She smiled as I stepped away, but I glimpsed something that looked almost melancholy beneath her expression. I had to ask, "Is everything okay with the two of you, *Tía*?"

She pulled back, eyes wide. "With us? Of course. Why?"

"It's just a feeling I get. The two of you showing up here without warning. Uncle Nestor leaving Agave in somebody else's hands. He called three times before we even got here to make sure things were running smoothly. Something's . . . different."

She laughed, but it sounded more brittle than amused. "Such an imagination you have. We're fine. We wanted to see how you're doing, that's all."

Again, I tried to believe her, but I couldn't ignore the anger I'd seen in Uncle Nestor. While I tried to figure out what to say about that, Aunt Yolanda turned away and looked out through the doors, staring into the night, her back stiff, her chin high, but that only made me more convinced that she was hiding something. But we'd been going nonstop since the minute they arrived, so she could have just been tired. I'd ask again tomorrow, when we were both rested.

I held back, thinking I should give her a moment alone, but she called out to me only a heartbeat later.

"*Rita?* Oh my God. Rita! Come here. Quickly!" She sounded frantic. Frightened, even.

"What is it?" I asked, hurrying toward her. "What's wrong?"

With trembling hands—so unlike my unflappable aunt—she pointed at something on the ground below us. "There's someone in the pool. I think he's in trouble." Before I could reach her, she darted across the balcony and started down the steps to the ground level.

"Who is it?" I called after her, but she was already gone.

It seemed to take forever to reach the other end of that long balcony, and by the time I got there, she was racing down the stone steps toward the swimming pool.

It took only one glance to figure out what had upset her. Someone was floating in the pool, facedown and unmoving. With my heart in my throat, I bolted down the steps. Even in the dim lighting from the tiki torches and twinkling white lights, I recognized who it was:

Big Daddy Boudreaux.

"Call nine-one-one!" Aunt Yolanda shouted as she knelt down beside the water. "I think he's dead."

The gentle hum of the pool's filtration system and the soft lap of water against the sides of the pool were deceptively soothing sounds, especially since my pulse was racing frantically as the reality of the situation sank in.

Ignoring the logic that told me that nobody could breathe in that position, I stepped around a small statue that lay near the pool and plunged down the concrete steps into the water. It was only waist deep, but it dragged heavily on me as I made my way toward him.

Big Daddy bobbed gently on the waves I created. He didn't stir, but in spite of a massive, bloody wound on the back of his head, I held on to the frantic hope that he might only be injured. "I need your help," I called to Aunt Yolanda. "We need to turn him over."

She stayed right where she was, shaking her head sadly. "It's too late, *mija*."

"You don't know that." My voice came out high-pitched and sharp-edged. "We need to turn him over and check for a pulse."

"Rita—"

"Please, Aunt Yolanda. We have to at least check."

Reluctantly, she followed me into the water and together we rolled Big Daddy onto his back. But as his swollen and bruised face emerged from the water, I realized that Aunt Yolanda was right.

Just a little while ago he'd been larger than life. Now Big Daddy Boudreaux stared sightlessly up at the sky, his mouth slightly open and his eyes bulging. In horror, I backed a step away, creating a wave that rolled over him and submerged his face again. An angry wound marred his forehead, probably where he hit his head as he fell in. I didn't need to check for a pulse. I could tell just by looking.

He was dead.

Eleven

"Okay, Rita. Let's go over this again. What time did Mr. Boudreaux arrive at the party?"

Two long hours had gone by since I'd placed the 911 call, and I'd told my story in detail at least three times. Half an hour ago, I'd been deposited in one corner of the ballroom and told to wait. Now I was sitting across the table from Detective Liam Sullivan, who apparently wanted me to tell the story again.

Sullivan and I had met last summer, during the investigation into Philippe's murder. He's tall, dark-haired, and yes, handsome. I'd fallen a little bit in love with him when he saved my life, though I'd never confessed that to anyone.

I didn't mind answering his questions, but I wished I could have changed clothes first. My dress was still damp from going into the pool and the wet fabric clung to me like a second skin, chilling me to the bone. I huddled a little deeper into the light blanket Sullivan had asked one of the staff to bring me, and dug around in my fog-filled head for an answer. "I think it was around nine, but I can't swear to it. And no, I don't *know* how he ended up in the pool. He was just there."

I knew I sounded testy, but who wouldn't under the circumstances? There was a dead body in the swimming pool, and my uncle was missing. My aunt and mother-in-law were being interrogated in other parts of the club, as were the handful of guests and the staff who'd still been there when we sounded the alarm. I was worried about how Aunt Yolanda and Miss Frankie were holding up and starting to feel very concerned about Uncle Nestor, who seemed to have disappeared completely.

On top of all that, I'd been running nonstop for almost twenty-four hours and I'd had a few glasses of wine at the party. Exhaustion and alcohol were seriously impairing my ability to cope.

Sullivan glanced at his notes and ran a look over me. "You told Officer Matos that Mr. Boudreaux was drunk."

Usually Sullivan's eyes are a shade of blue so light they're almost disconcerting. Tonight they were dark and gray, like storm clouds rolling in off the Gulf of Mexico. Plus, he was using his stern-cop voice, which, in spite of the charming Southern drawl, was probably sharp enough to cut diamonds.

"I said that I *thought* he was drunk," I clarified. "And that it's possible he stumbled into the pool on his own."

Sullivan lowered his notebook to the table. "And you believed that?"

I shrugged with my face. "It's possible."

"You saw the body," he said. "That explanation might account for one wound, but Mr. Boudreaux has lacerations on his face, bruising on his temple, swelling on his cheeks, and a serious contusion on the back of his head."

Just thinking about that awful head wound threatened to activate my gag reflex. "He could have hit his head when he fell in."

"But he didn't," Sullivan said. "I know that just from looking at him, and I'm guessin' you know it, too."

"I don't know anything," I said stubbornly. I didn't believe Big Daddy's death was an accident any more than Sullivan did, but I resented the implication that I might know more than I was telling him. "You don't know what happened either. Don't you need a coroner's report or something?"

Sullivan fixed me with a hard gray stare. "Yeah. Technically. But it's hard to imagine Mr. Boudreaux going into the pool and hitting both the back of his head and his face on the way down. I'm bettin' he didn't get the wound on the back of his head from bouncing off the side of the pool."

"So what are you saying?"

"I'm saying he had help gettin' that way."

I pulled the blanket a little tighter and let out a resigned sigh. I thought about the statue at the side of the pool and wondered if someone had used it to send Big Daddy to his reward. I sure didn't want the man's death to be deliberate. Neither Miss Frankie nor Zydeco needed to be involved in another murder. Neither did I, and I hated to think of Aunt Yolanda and Uncle Nestor wasting their whole visit talking to the police. "I guess I shouldn't be surprised that somebody killed him," I said. "He wasn't exactly the nicest guy in the world."

One of Sullivan's eyebrows shot up. "What does that mean? Did you have some kind of trouble with him?"

"Me?" I shrugged. "Not really. I only met him for the first time a few hours ago." It was the perfect time to tell him about Uncle Nestor popping Big Daddy a couple of times, but he hadn't asked about anyone else having "trouble" with Big Daddy. Someone was sure to tell Sullivan about the fight, but I just couldn't get the words out. I wasn't ready to throw Uncle Nestor under the bus. I knew it was irrational, but I hoped they'd find the killer so quickly I wouldn't have to rat him out.

Sullivan shifted his weight and propped both arms on the table. "Why don't you define 'not really' for me?"

Another chill shook my body and I huddled deeper into the blanket. "He was loud and obnoxious and grabby. A bit too friendly, if you know what I mean."

"Are you sayin' he made a pass at you?"

"I guess you could call it that. I'm not sure his heart was in it. It seemed almost like a habit. He saw a woman and he made a grab."

"And—"

"And nothing. I handled it. He went away and bothered other people. No big deal."

Sullivan studied my expression for a moment before asking his next question. "Did he bother anyone else in particular?"

I carefully sidestepped the Uncle Nestor factor one more time and stayed focused on the female guests. "Not that I know of. He made the rounds and talked to a lot of people. So you think somebody hit him, and then pushed him into the pool?"

Sullivan didn't so much as blink. "Something like that. I'm told you found the body. Is that right?"

I gave him a thin-lipped nod and linked my hands on the table. "My aunt Yolanda and I found him."

"Tell me about that."

"We were looking for my uncle. The party was over and

we were comparing notes about how we felt it had gone—you know how you do . . ."

He nodded, but didn't say a word. I took that as a cue to keep talking. "Anyway, we realized that neither of us had seen Uncle Nestor for a while, so we decided to look for him."

"You went outside to do that? Why not search the clubhouse?"

If it had just been me, I might've left out the detail about the cell phone—actually, I'd neglected to even mention it to the first cops, it seemed so unimportant. But then I thought about how Aunt Yolanda was a stickler for the truth and realized that she'd probably spilled her guts to the cop interrogating her. After all, she believed that the truth would set her free. And if my story didn't match, we could end up in big trouble.

"We were going to," I explained. "But Aunt Yolanda called his cell phone and heard it ringing outside. She went out onto the balcony and that's when she spotted Big Daddy in the pool."

Sullivan's eyebrow arched high over one slate-colored eye. "I didn't see any of that in the notes Officer Crump gave me."

"That's because I forgot to tell him. I didn't even think about it. And don't give me that look. Nestor's my uncle. He didn't have anything to do with Big Daddy's death."

"Do you have any idea who might have wanted Big Daddy dead?"

"Besides every woman he ever met? Not really."

"I assume you have a guest list," he said, refusing to even crack a smile. "I'll need a copy."

"Miss Frankie has all of that information. Most of the guests were members of the Krewe of Musterion. This was some sort of a bash for the bigwigs. Apparently, Big Daddy was just elected as captain for the coming year." Thinking about all of that made me sit up a little straighter. "You know who you should talk to? This guy named Percy something. Ponter, I think they said. He's one of the officers for next year and he was upset with Big Daddy earlier in the evening."

Sullivan made a note. "Any idea why?"

I shook my head. "Big Daddy told him to make an appointment for next week, that's all I know. Big Daddy's assistant might know, though. She was there. Her name is Violet." I dug around in my memory and came up with the rest. "Shepherd."

Sullivan wrote that down, too. "Anything else?"

I ignored my nagging conscience and shook my head again. "No, that's it." I'd tell Sullivan about the fight once we found Uncle Nestor and I heard his side of the story. Surely he'd be more forthcoming now.

"When you went outside after the party, did you notice anything out of place in the backyard? Anything unusual? Anything that didn't belong?"

The quick change of subject caught me off guard, and exhaustion, worry, and fear made it hard to catch up. Disjointed images flashed through my head. Aunt Yolanda hurrying toward the pool. Me following. The twinkling white lights on the shrubbery and trees. A few tiki torches still burning. A few burned out. Chairs askew. That statue on the cement and glasses scattered about. Most of it telltale signs of a big party, but not especially unusual. Certainly nothing sinister.

"There was a statue," I said after I'd sifted through the details. "On the cement by the pool. Other than that, nothing. I wish I could be more help. It's all too hazy."

One corner of Sullivan's mouth lifted in what passes for

a smile when he's working. "It's all right," he said. "I know it's tough. If you remember anything later, give me a holler."

I nodded to show how agreeable I could be.

He seemed satisfied and moved on again. "Tell me again about finding Mr. Boudreaux in the pool."

"Like I said, Aunt Yolanda saw him first. She called for me."

"Did either of you actually *see* Mr. Boudreaux fall in?"

"No. If we had, we would have helped him."

I got another eyeball, this one directed at my damp clothing. "Looks like maybe you tried to help him anyway."

"I thought maybe he was still alive. He wasn't." I glanced at the clock on the wall, realized how long we'd been sitting here, and felt my empty stomach turn over. "Could you check with your guys to see if anyone has heard from Uncle Nestor? He's been gone a long time."

Sullivan shook his head. "If anyone had heard from him, I'd know it. Let's just get through the rest of the questions and then I'll see what I can find myself." Tough cop faded for a moment and my friend made a brief appearance. "It'll be okay, Rita."

I appreciated the gesture, but we both knew he couldn't make that kind of promise. "And what if it's not? What if something happened to him? What if—" The words got stuck in my throat and tears burned my eyes. I'd been holding it together so far, but the fear of losing Uncle Nestor made it hard to breathe. I tried to remember the last time I'd actually seen him at the party, but those details were lost, too. "He and Aunt Yolanda are all I have, Liam. He *has* to be all right."

Sullivan got up from his seat and came around the table. I wish I could tell you that he gathered me in his arms and comforted all my fears, but he's not that kind of guy. He put a hand on my shoulder and murmured something I couldn't quite make out. Not nearly enough, but I guess better than nothing.

While I sobbed into my hands, Sullivan crossed the room and plucked a couple of Zydeco napkins from the table. He shoved them at me, and I spent a minute or two mopping up so we could move on again.

When I'd dried the tears and blown my nose, I took a couple of deep breaths, trying to get the air all the way to my core, where the panic had taken up residence. It was making images of Uncle Nestor going after Big Daddy flash through my head, and they were images I did not want to remember.

Not that I thought Uncle Nestor was responsible for Big Daddy's untimely demise. But the realization that others might speculate about my uncle made everything inside me hurt.

I wadded the soggy napkins in my hand and glanced at the sequined saxophone archway. "Is it really necessary to drag my aunt off and interrogate her like a common criminal? She doesn't know anything either. And Miss Frankie shouldn't be alone at a time like this."

Sullivan linked his hands together on the table and locked his eyes on mine. "They're fine, Rita. Your aunt is being treated with respect, and Miss Frankie is a lot tougher than you give her credit for. The sooner you answer my questions, the sooner you can check on both of them. I assure you my people aren't roughing them up or shoving bamboo shoots under their fingernails. Now, if you're ready . . ."

I sat back in my chair and made an effort to look calm and collected. "Fine. What else do you want to know?"

"How about telling me when you last saw Mr. Boudreaux alive?"

"Maybe an hour before we found him in the pool," I said.

"Where was he? And what was he doing?"

"He was here, in the ballroom. Near the bandstand, I think. Talking to people."

"Any idea who he was talking to?"

I shook my head. "Like I said before, I didn't pay that much attention to him." At least, I hadn't after the fight. That had been a couple of hours earlier. He'd had time to annoy a dozen other people since then. "He talked to just about everyone in the room and he seemed to know them all, and of course, everyone knew who he was." I rubbed my forehead and looked at him from the corner of my eye. "There's going to be press, isn't there?"

"I'd count on it. Mr. Boudreaux was well known in these parts. And that's going to create pressure from the top to solve this quickly. Why? Are you worried about Zydeco?"

That was as good an explanation as any. I nodded and said, "We don't need any more negative publicity. We're barely climbing out of the ditch we fell into after Philippe died." But the truth was that Zydeco was nowhere near the top of the list of things I worried about. Uncle Nestor, Aunt Yolanda, and Miss Frankie took the top spots.

"We'll try to solve this quickly," Sullivan assured me. "If we can do that, you and Zydeco may not even hit the radar this time around."

I could only hope.

"It's too bad you don't remember who he was talking to," Sullivan said. "In addition to the wound that probably killed him, there's some bruising on Boudreaux's chin and cheek. Looks like maybe he was in a fight recently—like within the last few hours. I don't suppose any of you can shed any light on that?"

I argued with myself for another few seconds, vacillating

between telling the truth and protecting Uncle Nestor. But again, I reasoned that somebody would mention the fight to the police, if not tonight, then soon. So I opted for the truth, even though just the thought of bringing Uncle Nestor into this made my stomach hurt.

Folding my arms across my chest, I said, "It was nothing."

Sullivan's eyes lingered on my defensive posture a moment too long. "What was nothing?"

"The fight. It didn't mean anything. Just a couple of guys who had too much to drink, that's all."

"So you do know."

"It was over in a minute or two. And it happened hours before Big Daddy died."

"Details, Rita. Who are you talking about, and what happened?"

"You have to keep in mind how obnoxious Big Daddy was," I said, trying to smooth out the pavement before I shoved Uncle Nestor under the bus. He already thought I'd betrayed him by staying in New Orleans. He'd never forgive me for ratting him out to the police. "He was loud and abrasive and—"

"I got that part," Sullivan interrupted. "Who are you talking about?"

Hating that I had to choose between truth and loyalty, I ran my tongue across my lips again. I opened my mouth to speak, but the sound of angry shouting cut me off before I could get a word out. Sullivan and I scrambled to our feet and bolted across the ballroom. I had to struggle out of the blanket first, which put him a few steps ahead of me. He paused briefly on the threshold to growl, "Stay here," before pushing the door open and charging out onto the balcony.

Naturally, I ignored him.

I made it outside in time to see him start down the steps toward the pool, where Susannah Boudreaux was leaning heavily on a uniformed officer. She lifted one trembling hand and pointed at something—or someone—hidden from my view by a large flowering shrub. "That's him!" she shouted. "Right there."

Sullivan reached the bottom of the stairs and I craned to see who she was pointing at. I caught a glimpse of Aunt Yolanda and Miss Frankie emerging from separate doors onto the patio and a handful of crime scene techs milling about, all of whom stopped working to see who she was talking about.

"That's him," the woman shrieked again. "That's the man who attacked my husband!"

Everyone in the yard turned to stare—at Uncle Nestor.

Twelve

Silence rang in the night air for roughly two seconds before all hell broke loose. Susannah Boudreaux screeched and pointed and demanded that my uncle be arrested, tried, and executed on the spot. Half a dozen officers drew their weapons and trained them on Uncle Nestor, all shouting at him to get down on the ground and put his hands behind his head.

Uncle Nestor was a child of the 1960s, and his distrust of "the man" was legendary in our family. I didn't know whether to be more frightened that he'd do something stupid, or angry with the police for putting him in a position that might bring out the worst in him.

And I didn't have time to figure it out. With a cry of distress, Aunt Yolanda started down the steps on the other side of the yard, heading straight for her husband. I understood why she wanted to get to him, but running into the middle of all those armed and angry cops seemed like a really bad idea.

I started down the other set of stairs, struggling to keep my balance on the slick stone. "Aunt Yolanda," I shouted. "Wait! Stop!"

She kept going. I wasn't sure if it was because she couldn't hear me over the rest of the shouting, or because she was ignoring me. Panicked, I gathered my still-damp skirt above my knees so I could make better time. "Aunt Yolanda! No!"

She reached the lower terrace and sprinted toward the pool, where Uncle Nestor was, thank God, obeying instructions. Red-faced and angry, he was down on his knees, hands linked behind his head. There'd be hell to pay when we finally got out of here, but at least he was alive to rant about it.

While one scrawny officer patted Uncle Nestor down, two others kept their weapons trained on him. I guess I understood why. He looked capable of almost anything. Relieved that, at least for the moment, he was cooperating, I whipped around to find Aunt Yolanda and spotted her at the far edge of the pool, corralled by a burly officer with a bulldog face.

She didn't look much happier than Uncle Nestor, but I didn't care. They were both safe. That's all that mattered.

I stopped running and paused for a moment to catch my breath. The cool, damp lawn on my bare feet made me wish I'd brought the blanket with me. I shivered and started walking toward Aunt Yolanda, but a uniformed officer with a grim expression and a name tag that read *Kilpatrick* blocked my path.

"Stop right there," he barked. He was tall and thickly muscled, and it was obvious to me that he took his job seriously.

"That's my aunt," I panted. "I just want to make sure she's okay."

"She's fine. I need you to stop right where you are." I might have argued, but Kilpatrick's hand was resting on the butt of his gun and his expression said he had no qualms about shooting me where I stood.

I didn't *think* he would, but I decided not to take unnecessary chances. Nervous energy and impatience made it hard to just stand there, and the sound of Uncle Nestor's voice, gruff and raised in anger, made it even harder. I couldn't make out what he was saying, but the fact that he was saying anything at all made me nervous.

"You're making a mistake," I said to Kilpatrick. "He didn't do anything wrong."

Kilpatrick gave me a heavy-lidded look, but he didn't say a word. He just left me standing there, waiting, watching, and wondering, until Sullivan strode across the lawn toward me.

His eyes had turned ice cold. "You want to tell me about it?"

I wasn't completely sure what he was asking about, so I went with an innocent, "About what?"

"The fight. And don't pretend like you don't know which fight I'm talking about."

I swallowed. Shifted from foot to foot, and then came clean. "Big Daddy and Uncle Nestor?"

"Bingo."

Sullivan wasn't happy. But then, I wasn't either. I could hear someone coming up behind me, but I didn't look to see who it was. "They had a disagreement earlier. I was just about to tell you about it when Uncle Nestor showed up."

The person behind me gasped, and I knew without looking that it was Aunt Yolanda. I couldn't let myself look at her, though. Sullivan was giving me the death glare.

"And you didn't mention it before because . . ."

"Because it had nothing to do with Big Daddy's accident."

"Why didn't you tell *me* about this, *mija*?" Aunt Yolanda demanded.

I slid a guilty glance over my shoulder. "Because it was over in a few minutes, Aunt Yolanda. It was nothing." I tried a reassuring smile, but my lips felt frozen and lifeless. "I didn't want you to worry."

Sullivan gave me a look. "So again, you didn't mention any of this to the police because—"

"Because they're not connected," I said again.

"You mean, you don't *want* them to be connected."

"I mean that I'm *sure* they aren't connected," I said. "Big Daddy said something inappropriate. Uncle Nestor lost his cool. They exchanged a couple of punches and then they went their separate ways."

"It had to have been a minor scuffle," Miss Frankie said helpfully. "I didn't know a thing about it."

"Nestor would never hurt someone else on purpose," Aunt Yolanda agreed. "That woman is blowing the whole thing out of proportion."

"You may be right," Sullivan said gently. "But since neither you nor Miss Frankie actually witnessed the argument, you'll forgive me for keeping an open mind." He turned his attention back to me. "You know for a fact that they went their separate ways?"

Everything inside me wanted to say yes, but I couldn't make myself tell an outright lie. "No. But Uncle Nestor sort of disappeared and I thought maybe he was lying down somewhere. Parties really aren't his thing."

Sullivan let out a heavy sigh. "Okay, tell me now. And tell me everything. No holding back. What did they fight about?"

"I have no idea. I couldn't hear them."

"You didn't ask?"

"Of course I asked. Uncle Nestor wouldn't tell me."

"And you didn't think that was odd?"

I shook my head. "Uncle Nestor keeps to himself when something's wrong. It can be frustrating, but it didn't raise any red flags for me tonight."

"Big Daddy didn't say anything either?"

"He ducked the question," I said. "Frankly, I was glad to steer clear."

"Which was the best thing you could have done," Miss Frankie said. "You know how men are, Detective."

He smiled a little. "I believe I do, ma'am. Anything else you're not telling me, Rita?"

I shook my head. "Not that I can think of."

Sullivan stuffed his notebook into his breast pocket, and then he put a hand on my shoulder and gave it a reassuring squeeze. Which is one of the things I like best about him. "Why don't you take your aunt home? We'll bring your uncle over when we're finished talking to him."

I found the idea that he didn't plan to lock Uncle Nestor up overnight reassuring, but Aunt Yolanda didn't seem to appreciate that subtle distinction. She crossed her arms over her chest and lifted her chin the way I'd seen her do a thousand times when I was growing up. "I'm not going anywhere without my husband."

"It's nearly four in the morning—" Sullivan started to say.

Aunt Yolanda skewered him with a look before he could finish. "I'm not going anywhere without my husband," she repeated.

Sullivan slid a glance at me, but I wasn't about to step in. Aunt Yolanda was already upset with me for not telling her about the argument. I wasn't going to take his side against her and make things worse.

I took Aunt Yolanda's arm and turned toward the clubhouse. "We'll wait inside."

I had no idea how I'd get through another hard day at work tomorrow. Even if we went home right now, I'd barely get any sleep, which probably wouldn't help at all. But those worries fell way below convincing Sullivan that Uncle Nestor wasn't responsible for whacking Big Daddy over the head and then pushing him into the pool to drown.

Thirteen

The seven o'clock alarm jolted me out of a deep sleep long before I was ready. With a groan, I reached for the clock and punched the snooze button. It was barely two hours since I'd closed my eyes. Even though sunlight was already streaming in through my bedroom windows and we had a busy Saturday scheduled at Zydeco, I might have let myself slip back to sleep if reality hadn't punched me in the face with memories of last night's tragedy.

Big Daddy Boudreaux. My devastated aunt. My stubborn uncle, who had flatly refused to answer any of Sullivan's questions. Miss Frankie, who'd been showing definite signs of wear when I drove away. In the end, Sullivan had let us go home around four-thirty in the morning, but only because he had no direct evidence against Uncle Nestor and because I'd crossed my heart and hoped to die if I failed to deliver Uncle Nestor to the police station this morning.

Sullivan's warning echoed in my head as I lay there trying to squash the sick feeling in my stomach. "I need your uncle to tell me what happened between the two of them," he'd said. "Convince him to start talking by morning or my hands will be tied. I'll have to detain him for questioning."

I'd tried all the way home to get Uncle Nestor to confide in me, but all I'd gotten for my trouble was stony silence and a reminder from Aunt Yolanda that the good Lord expects us to honor the people who raised us. Neither of them was speaking to me by the time they climbed the stairs to the guest room.

I didn't for one minute believe that Uncle Nestor had killed Big Daddy Boudreaux, but the circumstantial evidence against him was mounting. Surely Uncle Nestor could understand that, so why wasn't he doing everything he could to clear away suspicion?

Wide awake now, I pulled on my robe and hurried downstairs to the kitchen. Usually Aunt Yolanda got up with the sun, but this morning the house was still quiet. So quiet that if the patent leather pumps she'd worn last night hadn't been lying just inside the front door, I might have wondered if I'd only dreamed their visit.

Determined to start off on the right foot this morning, I pulled a canister of French roast from the pantry and put on a pot. First things first. Aunt Yolanda and Uncle Nestor would need a good breakfast when they got up. Besides, working in the kitchen always helped me think. After breakfast we'd give our statements to the police and then I'd head to Zydeco, where I could at least pretend that it was just another day.

I'd just started the coffee brewing when my cell phone rang, sounding unnaturally cheerful and far too loud in that quiet house. I fumbled with the phone, trying to silence it before it woke up my aunt and uncle.

"Rita? Thank God I caught you," Edie said when I answered. "Where are you?"

"Still at home," I said around a yawn. "I was just about to call you. What's going on? Is something wrong?"

"Wrong?" Edie snorted a laugh. "Besides Big Daddy Boudreaux dying at The Shores, you mean? Isn't that enough?"

My spirits drooped. "You've heard?"

"Um . . . yeah. It's all over the news. I heard it on the radio when I was coming to work this morning, and Good Day New Orleans is all over it. We have the TV on in the back so we can watch the reports. I take it you haven't been watching?"

"I just got up," I admitted. "Didn't get to bed until almost five." I was going to pay for that later. "So what are they saying?"

"Just that Big Daddy Boudreaux is dead under suspicious circumstances. No real details yet except that it happened at the Musterion party."

I was realistic enough to know the news wouldn't stay buried, especially since Big Daddy had been a bigwig in the business community and all, but I'd been hoping for a *little* more time. "So what else are they saying?"

"They're talking a lot about his work, his contributions to the community, and his connections within Musterion. Of course, they're all over the fact that he was elected as captain for next year, and practically naming him a saint for some big-deal charity fund-raiser he was in charge of last fall."

"I'm pretty sure he was no saint," I mumbled. I wondered how Judd was taking the news that his brother had been killed, and what Mellie was feeling.

"So . . . suspicious circumstances. That's code for murder,

right?" Edie asked, cutting into my thoughts. "Do the police have any idea who did it?"

"Not that they're sharing with me. I don't think they have any solid leads yet. It's still too early in the investigation. But I have to take my aunt and uncle down to the station this morning so we can give our official statements. I don't know how long that will take, but I'll get there as soon as I can."

"Of course. Sure. We'll be okay for a while."

"I hope it doesn't take long," I said. "Big Daddy's wife practically accused Uncle Nestor of murder last night. I'm pretty sure it was just the booze talking, but it may take a little while to get that all straightened out."

"The police don't think he did it, do they?"

"Of course not," I said sharply. "My uncle didn't have anything to do with Big Daddy's death."

"I never said he did," Edie said quickly. "But if the police want statements from all of you, you're already connected to the murder in their minds."

"Only because Aunt Yolanda and I found the body. That makes us material witnesses or something."

"That's kind of the point, Rita," she said. After a slight hesitation, she continued, "Don't worry about us. If you need to take a day or two with your aunt and uncle, that's okay."

I blurted a disbelieving laugh. "Considering how much work we have to do? Absolutely not. I'll be in as soon as we're finished at the police station. I'm hoping it won't be later than noon."

Again a beat or two passed before Edie responded. "At least take the day off," she said. "Your aunt and uncle are probably pretty upset. They'll need you around."

Yeah. Maybe. But I was getting a strange vibe from her. "What's going on, Edie? Why do I get the feeling this isn't really about me and my family?"

She sighed heavily, and when she spoke again, her voice was softer, as if she didn't want to be overheard. "It's nothing personal, Rita. It's just that there are already reporters outside. Thanks to the staff at the country club, they've made the connection between last night's party and Zydeco."

The country club staff? My money was on that unpleasant kitchen manager.

"You were the hostess," Edie went on. "So they're going to be looking for a statement from you. Ox and I both think it might be a good idea for you to lay low for a few days—you know, until the police have a real suspect."

She didn't have to say the rest, but I didn't like hearing that she and Ox had been making decisions for the bakery behind my back. I was already tired and cranky, so her argument rubbed me the wrong way. "Listen, Edie, I refuse to cower and hide just because Big Daddy Boudreaux had the misfortune to die at that stupid party. And maybe you should remember that I'm the one in charge at Zydeco, not Ox. He needs to quit trying to take over."

"He's not trying to take over," she snapped back. "He's concerned about the bakery, that's all. If Zydeco goes under, we all lose."

"Zydeco is *not* going under," I insisted. "Instead of anticipating the worst, why don't we do something constructive?"

"Such as?"

I floundered for a moment, trying to come up with something. "Put something on the website maybe. A statement about how sorry we all are over the unfortunate passing of such a beloved public figure."

"We could do that," she said slowly. "Are you going to write it?"

"Ask Ox to do it. If he works fast, he can text it to me for approval and have it uploaded before I even leave the police station. Just please work with me and not against me. My aunt and uncle aren't speaking to me, and I don't need you and Ox throwing up roadblocks and making things worse."

"We're not trying to make things worse," she said. "We're just trying to look out for Zydeco while your attention is splintered." She took a deep breath and let it out slowly, as if I was trying her patience. "Look, Rita, you can't take care of everything all the time, and right now you have your hands full. Nobody's trying to take your job or push you out. Let us help you."

I hesitated, but only for a heartbeat. Accepting help doesn't come easily to me, but she had a point and I'd be foolish not to acknowledge it. Besides, tired as I was, I needed help remembering my own name. I rubbed my temples with my fingertips, as if that might relieve the stress headache I could feel starting. I sat down at the kitchen table. "I wish I knew what Uncle Nestor's argument with Big Daddy was about last night. If I knew that, maybe I could convince him to talk to me about it."

She laughed at that. "Their *argument*? Is that what you're calling it?"

I stopped rubbing and leaned my head against the back of the chair. "Fine. Their fight." A memory of last night wormed its way through the fog of exhaustion and I sat up again quickly. "Hey! You were there. Did you hear what they were talking about before the fight?"

Edie didn't say anything for a few seconds, but I could hear her breathing so I knew we hadn't been disconnected. "I was there," she said after a while, "but I didn't actually hear much. And most of what your uncle said was in Spanish."

"So nothing?"

Another pause. "I don't think it's a good idea for you to get involved, Rita. Just let the police do their job."

"I'm not trying to get involved," I said impatiently. "Sullivan asked me to get Uncle Nestor to talk. I'm just trying to cooperate with the police. If you know anything about that fight, please tell me."

Edie sighed heavily. "All right. But I'm only doing this under protest. I hope you know that."

"Duly noted. What did you hear?"

"Not much, like I said before, but I'm pretty sure your uncle said something about his family's honor. That's it, though. I swear."

Everything inside me turned icy cold. Nothing means more to Uncle Nestor than family. He's not a cold-blooded killer, but if anything was going to push him over the edge, insulting or hurting someone in his family would be what did it. "That must mean Big Daddy said something about Aunt Yolanda," I said, feeling miserable.

"Or you."

"Or me," I agreed reluctantly. Considering what a creep Big Daddy was and the fact that Uncle Nestor doesn't go around punching people indiscriminately, it must have been something completely inappropriate. No wonder he was closed up tighter than a clam. He must know that if he told the police what they fought over, the police would be convinced he had a motive for murder.

Fourteen

Standing in the middle of the kitchen and sipping French roast as if it would save my life, I spent the next few minutes hashing out the day's work schedule with Edie. She tried again to convince me to steer clear, but I still thought she underestimated me. I was perfectly capable of giving the press a brief statement without embarrassing Zydeco. And once the police cleared things up with Uncle Nestor, there would be nothing to worry about on that score.

I made a batch of biscuit dough using ice-cold water and butter straight out of the fridge. When the biscuits were cut out and ready for baking, I pulled an onion, eggs, shredded white cheddar, and bacon from the refrigerator and took out my frustrations and confusion at the cutting board.

Cooking has always been soothing to me, and as I chopped and sautéed, the scents and repetitive motions helped clear my mind and lift my spirits. After a few minutes, I felt good enough to begin my mental to-do list. In addition to the work at the bakery, I needed to call Miss Frankie to make sure she was holding up all right. Even if she and Big Daddy weren't close, they'd clearly known each other for a long time. Finding an old friend dead was bound to have a negative impact on anyone's day. I also wanted to pay a condolence call on Judd Boudreaux. It seemed like the right thing to do, and it would give me a chance to return his suit jacket.

And, of course, I needed to take care of my houseguests.

I crisped bacon and crumbled it, then spread it and the sautéed onions over the biscuits. After whisking together heavy cream and sour cream, I mixed in the cheese and eggs, then poured the whole thing over the onion-and-bacon-covered biscuits. By the time I slid the baking dish into the oven, my mouth was watering in anticipation.

I turned on the TV so I could hear the news for myself. After a few minutes, the sports report gave way to a series of commercials, one of which featured Big Daddy Boudreaux skeet shooting and blasting clay pigeons to smithereens. Each one was painted with a number to represent the price of a used car on his lot, and each one exploded after a blast of his shotgun, showing his adoring public how Big Daddy was slashing prices just for them.

"This van has got to go!" he announced with a cheerful grin. "It's so spotless and the mileage is so low, we could get away with selling it to you for sticker price, but we aren't like that here at Big Daddy's. Come in today and I'll sell it to you. Not for twenty thousand." *Kablam!* "Not for eighteen." *Kaboom!* "Not even for seventeen-five." *Kapowie!* "No siree. Come to Big Daddy's today and you'll walk out the door for seventeen three thirty-nine. That price is so low I ought to check myself in for a psych evaluation."

He brayed a laugh that made my skin crawl. It was eerie watching him preen for the cameras.

While the morning team covered the world news, I sat down with my coffee mug just as Aunt Yolanda shuffled into the kitchen wearing a pink silk nightgown and matching robe. Her dark hair was tousled and her eyes were puffy. From sleep? Or had she been crying?

I watched closely as she poured herself coffee and carried it to the table. I was searching for signs that would help me gauge her mood. She wasn't one to hold grudges, but we were all walking in uncharted territory and I wasn't sure what to expect from her this morning.

Cradling the cup in both hands, she closed her eyes and inhaled deeply. "This coffee smells like heaven," she said when she opened her eyes again. "I really need it this morning."

She sounded normal enough. I smiled with relief. "You and me both. I'm sorry your first night in town was so—"

"Eventful?" She finished the sentence for me and smiled softly. "It certainly wasn't your fault. We'll go see the police first thing and then we can put this whole nightmare behind us."

"It shouldn't take long," I agreed. "What do you and Uncle Nestor have on the agenda after we visit the police station? I wish I could show you around the city, but I have to get to work. Still, that shouldn't keep the two of you from doing some sightseeing."

Aunt Yolanda put her cup on the table and stood. "We haven't talked about that yet. I guess we'll figure it out when we get there. Now, what shall I fix for breakfast?"

"You're not fixing anything," I said. "I've already got a breakfast casserole in the oven, and I was planning to make a tropical fruit salad to go along with it." The salad was a recipe I'd picked up in Chicago. One of my favorites.

Aunt Yolanda sat back down and her shoulders sagged. From this angle I could see shadows under her eyes and lines around her mouth I'd never noticed before. I knew with a certainty I couldn't explain that none of them had appeared overnight. The realization that she was aging made me unspeakably sad. I said the only thing I could force out of my mouth: "If you don't want the fruit salad, I can throw together something else."

"I'm sure it will be delicious." She straightened her shoulders and lifted her chin. As if she willed it, the light shifted and the shadows under her eyes faded. "You don't need to take care of us, *mija*. We'll be fine."

"Are you kidding? You're guests in my home. If I let you fend for yourselves, my aunt would skin me alive. Sit. Enjoy your coffee."

She sank back, looking a little lost. That was another thing I'd never seen before.

I carried my cup back into the kitchen and gathered mango, papaya, pineapple, kiwi, and mandarin oranges. "We'll be down near the French Quarter," I said, trying to keep the tone light. "Maybe you could spend some time there. There's a parade scheduled for later, so it'll be crowded, but you could take one of the walking tours of the Quarter and Jackson Square. Maybe even wander down to the river."

Aunt Yolanda held up a hand to stop me before I could finish. "You're wearing me out already. We didn't come to see the city, Rita. We came to see you. Nestor has been worried about you."

I pulled a fresh mango onto the cutting board. "He doesn't have to be. I just wish we could have a little fun before you leave. Last night's party was work for me, but between now and Mardi Gras there's something going on almost all the time. Is there any chance you could stick around for a few more days?"

She shook her head. "We have tickets on a ten-fifteen flight on Monday morning. We just wanted to see where you've chosen to call home."

I wasn't sure whether I was more disappointed or relieved, but I held out my arms like a game-show model. "Well, here it is. What do you think?"

"It's a lovely home, Rita. Truly beautiful. But that's not what I meant. You know how protective Nestor is of our family, and you have a special place in his heart. You're his only sister's only child. The only girl in our family. He's been worried sick about you here, alone——"

"I was alone in Chicago," I reminded her.

"You were at pastry school, and then you were married. You weren't alone for long."

"So you're here to check up on me." A pebble of bitterness found its way into my heart. I had four strapping cousins, each of whom had disappointed his parents in some creative way—Santos by marrying the wrong woman, Aaron by dropping out of college, Manny by dodging the family business to become a musician, and Julio by fathering a baby out of wedlock. He'd married the mother eventually, but for a while it had filled Aunt Yolanda with a deep and abiding shame. But *I* was the one they'd come to check up on?

Was it just because I was "the girl"? Or because I was my mother's daughter? I knew that my mother had disappointed her older brother with some of her choices. Sometimes it seemed as if he was biding his time, just waiting for me to follow in her footsteps.

I sliced off one side of the mango and made angry gashes

in the pale orange flesh, scoring it with a little too much gusto and slicing through the skin. "I'm doing fine," I said again. "But he doesn't believe that, does he?"

Aunt Yolanda scowled at me over the rim of her coffee mug. "He's concerned. He loves you. Is that so bad?"

I stopped slicing and put the knife aside. "He thinks I made a mistake by staying here."

"He wants to be sure you didn't," Aunt Yolanda said. Her smile was gentle, and I thought about all the times she'd interceded between Uncle Nestor and me when I was younger.

I held out my arms again to encompass the magnificent kitchen in the heart of my magnificent home. "I've managed not to go wild with all of this for months. You'd think he'd realize that I'm not going to lose my head now. And yeah, I'm happy. How could I not be?"

"It takes more than things to make a person happy," Aunt Yolanda chided me.

The grin slid from my face. "I'm talking about more than things, *Tía*. I'm doing what I always wanted to do. The bakery is amazing. The staff is great. And New Orleans is—"

"A long way from home," my aunt said before I could finish. "Your uncle and I miss you."

The look on her face made me uncomfortable. There are few things I hate more than making Aunt Yolanda sad. "I miss you, too," I said. "But don't you want me to make my own way in the world?"

"Yes, of course."

"So here I am. Making my way. I'm not gone, you know. I'm just not underfoot all the time."

Aunt Yolanda scowled at me. "You were never underfoot, Rita. You must know that."

"I do," I assured her, although there was that lingering

doubt. "You and Uncle Nestor saved my life when you took me in. I love you both more than I can say."

"And yet you're happy to live so far away."

I expected guilt trips from Uncle Nestor, but Aunt Yolanda was usually more understanding. Coming from her, this conversation left me tilting on my axis like an off-center cake. "I lived further away than this when Philippe and I were married," I reminded her. "It didn't seem to bother you then."

Aunt Yolanda touched my cheek with her fingertips. "That was different."

"Because I had a husband?" I stared at her in disbelief. "I could almost expect something that archaic to come out of Uncle Nestor's mouth, but not yours."

Aunt Yolanda gave me a look, reached for her mug, and sipped. "That's not what I meant, Rita. Please don't put words in my mouth. Your uncle will talk to you when the time is right."

"When the time is right?" I stared at her, unable to speak for a long moment. "I hope you won't take that attitude when it comes to the police."

"Your uncle knows what's best."

"I'm not so sure," I said. "Look, he's not the king of the castle here. He's one guy on a list of suspects in a murder investigation. He doesn't get to call the shots."

The shadows in her eyes appeared again and her lips formed a thin, disapproving line. "He is not a murder suspect."

"The dead man's wife seems to think he is," I said. "And the police can't clear him if he doesn't tell them what they want to know. I love the fact that you're so supportive of him, *Tía,*" I said, putting my hands over hers, "but throwing up roadblocks to protect him isn't doing him any favors. If you really want to help him, convince him to talk to the police when we get to the station."

Her gaze flashed to my face. "He's not ready."

"He *has* to be ready," I insisted. "It's not up to him."

She shook her head again. "He has a hard head, your uncle. You know that."

I did, but frustration made the headache I'd been fighting all morning spike sharply. "Did he at least tell *you* what happened between him and Big Daddy?"

"Me? No."

"Did you meet Big Daddy last night? Did you hear anything that went on between the two of them?"

Aunt Yolanda nodded. "I met him for a moment. We barely spoke." She turned her hands over and laced her fingers through mine. "Don't worry, *mija*. Your uncle did not kill that man."

"I know he didn't," I said. "Now we just have to make sure the police believe it, too."

Aunt Yolanda smiled softly. "Your uncle will do the right thing," she said firmly. She glanced around, her expression curious. "Where is he anyway?"

I was halfway to my feet, but her question stopped me cold. "What do you mean, where is he? I thought he was in the guest room with you."

"With me? No." A frown furrowed Aunt Yolanda's brow. "He was gone when I woke up. Are you saying you haven't seen him this morning?"

My heart slammed in my chest and all sorts of diabolical possibilities raced through my head as I punched his number into my cell phone. When I heard the phone ringing upstairs, I disconnected and hurried to the front door, cursing myself for not checking earlier. I never should have trusted Uncle Nestor to behave for a couple of hours. Sure enough, the deadbolt had been unlocked and so had the regular door lock.

Sullivan had warned me to keep an eye on Uncle Nestor, but I'd let him stroll right out the front door while I slept.

Epic fail.

Fifteen

❧

Heart thudding, I raced up the stairs to my bedroom. My head shuffled through questions the whole way. Where had Uncle Nestor gone? And why hadn't I heard him leave? Not that I expected answers. I still didn't know where he'd disappeared to last night. Why was he being so secretive? Was he trying to protect Aunt Yolanda or me? If so, what had Big Daddy said that made him think we needed protecting?

I tugged on a pair of jeans and a Phoenix Suns T-shirt so faded I could barely see the logo anymore. Back on the first floor, I stepped into flip-flops just as Aunt Yolanda appeared at the top of the stairs, also fully dressed, and looking worried in spite of her assurances that everything would turn out okay.

"Finding that man's body in the pool has made me jittery, I guess," she said. "Nestor's probably gone for a walk to clear his head. I'm sure he is just fine."

There were two big problems with that theory. First, Uncle Nestor doesn't *take* walks. The idea of him willingly going anywhere on foot was as foreign to me as the idea of putting powdered sugar in an omelet. And second, Uncle Nestor hates mornings. Even if he woke up with a brand-new personality and decided to take a stroll, he wouldn't have done it with the sunrise.

"You're probably right," I said, "but he's not familiar with the area and he doesn't have his phone with him. He can't even call if he gets disoriented." I smiled, trying to hide my own worry and keep hers under control. Somehow, I kept my voice sounding normal when I said, "I'll feel better knowing that he's all right, that's all."

"You don't think something's happened to him, do you?" Her bottom lip trembled slightly. She looked away, trying to hide it from me, but she was too late. It was a little thing, but completely out of character for my aunt. She's a warm and loving person, but she's not a crier. My worry level ramped up another notch.

"Are you sure he didn't say anything to you about going out?"

Aunt Yolanda shook her head and sank into a chair near the window. "No. I didn't even hear him get up."

"That's not surprising," I said, still trying to sound reassuring. "I'm sure you were exhausted after traveling all day and then staying up until almost sunrise. Not to mention all the adrenaline of last night. The surprising thing is that he dragged himself out of bed so early." He must have had a compelling reason.

She glanced out the window, took a deep breath, and closed her eyes as she exhaled. When she opened them again, she treated me to a shaky smile. "You don't have to pretend with me, Rita. It's not becoming."

"I didn't mean to sound condescending," I said. "I just don't want you to worry. But I'm having a hard time imagining Uncle Nestor getting up with the dawn and heading out into a strange city for his morning constitutional. That's just not something he does."

"It is now."

I could only stare at her.

"Times change," she said, but her voice sounded strangely quiet. "People change."

I paused with my hand on the doorknob and looked at her more closely. "I've only been living here for six months."

"Seven."

"Okay. Seven. And in that time Uncle Nestor has started going for walks? On purpose? What's going on? What aren't you telling me?"

"He's not getting any younger, *mija*. Neither of us is. He's been burning the candle at both ends for most of his life. It's time to slow down a little, that's all."

I didn't have time to figure out whether or not I believed that explanation because just then I heard footsteps coming up the front walk and everything else evaporated out of my head. Almost weak with relief, I opened the door.

Lights flashed in my face and a middle-aged man with a hawk nose and graying hair stuck a microphone in my face. I covered my eyes so I could see and registered Uncle Nestor standing beside the reporter, his leathery face creased with irritation.

"Miss Lucero," the reporter said, "could I ask you a few questions about last night's event at The Shores?"

I'd assured Edie that I could handle this, but not here, on my front step, without my hair and makeup done. And not before I'd had a chance to get Uncle Nestor's side of the story. "I'll be happy to talk with you later—" I began.

The reporter cut me off. "You were the hostess for last night's Musterion party, is that right? Were you a friend of Big Daddy's?"

"I met him for the first time last night," I said. "Now if you'll excuse me . . ."

The reporter turned away from me and focused on Uncle Nestor. Not exactly what I had in mind.

"Is it true that you attacked Mr. Boudreaux last night?"

"Where did you hear that?" I demanded before Uncle Nestor could answer.

The reporter gave a little shrug. "I have my sources."

"*What* sources?"

He ignored my question and lobbed another one of his own. "My contacts tell me that the police were very interested in what Susannah Boudreaux had to say when they questioned her. What's your connection to her?"

"There isn't one," I snapped, wondering which big-mouthed police officer had given her my uncle's name. I grabbed Uncle Nestor's arm and jerked him toward the open door. "Get inside," I ordered. "Don't say a word."

He went as stiff as a board and dug in his heels. Which made my anger spike. I needed a little cooperation, not for him to be even more difficult. Putting myself between the camera and Uncle Nestor, I tried hard not to look flustered and nervous. "If you have questions about Mr. Boudreaux's unfortunate death," I said, "please take them to the police."

"I'm told the police haven't ruled out foul play." The reporter made it sound like an accusation. I finally placed him as a reporter with NLTV, a small local station that ranked fairly low in the market share. Behind him, a youthful cameraman in jeans and a T-shirt captured every expression. Viewers of the station would judge our guilt or innocence by what they thought they saw on our faces. I knew they would, because that's what I'd do. It's human nature.

"You'll have to ask the police about that," I suggested sweetly as I gave Uncle Nestor a push toward the door, muttering, "I'm serious, Uncle Nestor. In the house. *Now!*"

He finally started moving, and I trailed behind him. Five feet and one door, and we'd be safe—at least until the next time we opened the door. Four feet. Three . . .

"NLTV has received other tips from concerned citizens about the altercation between the two of you," the reporter said. "I've been told that it happened just a few hours before Big Daddy was found dead. What do you have to say about that?"

"Nothing," I tossed over my shoulder. "No comment." I gave Uncle Nestor one last shove and he was finally inside. I grabbed the door and started to shut it just as Mr. NLTV asked, "What are you trying to hide, Miss Lucero?"

I slammed the door in his face and leaned against it heavily. My heart was thundering like a timpani drum and my breath came in short, raspy gasps. We'd escaped—at least for now—but I had a bone to pick with Sullivan when I saw him.

As my breathing began to even out again, I realized that maybe it wasn't the police who'd connected the dots between the fight and Uncle Nestor for the reporter. Uncle Nestor was a stranger in town, but he'd probably been introduced to more than a hundred people last night. I had no idea how many of them were aware of the fight. I could have sworn that only a few people had known about it. Apparently someone had told Susannah Boudreaux about it, and she'd probably picked up Uncle Nestor's name from the police. If she liked to complain like Judd claimed, she could be venting to anyone who'd listen.

And if Susannah Boudreaux was throwing Uncle Nestor to the wolves, we could be in big trouble.

Not good. Not good at all.

Sixteen

After a few moments, the voice on the other side of the door faded and my heartbeat stopped banging in my ear. As my head cleared, I began to notice details that had escaped me outside, like the fact that Uncle Nestor was wearing jogging shorts and a gray sweatshirt, and that his sweatshirt had several damp patches that hinted at physical exertion.

Aunt Yolanda hurried toward him, her face creased with worry. "What was that?"

"A reporter." He pulled off the sweatshirt and wadded it in his hands. "Asking about last night."

Aunt Yolanda's eyes clouded. "A reporter? Here? Why?"

"He was looking for Uncle Nestor," I said. "Susannah Boudreaux told him about the fight Uncle Nestor had with Big Daddy."

Anger flickered across my aunt's face. "Why would she do such a thing?"

"Apparently, she thinks Uncle Nestor whacked her husband on the head and pushed him into the pool," I said. "Or maybe she just wants the police to think that. She was talking to Big Daddy's ex-wife at the end of the party, and I thought she seemed upset at the time. Maybe she already knew that her husband was dead." It was a stretch, but I was desperate enough to clutch at any straw I could find.

Uncle Nestor grunted. "She's a foolish woman."

"She'd have to be, to marry Big Daddy Boudreaux," I agreed.

As if that had solved all of his problems, Uncle Nestor kissed Aunt Yolanda on the cheek and started walking toward the stairs.

But I wasn't finished with him yet. "Hey! Wait a second," I said. "We need to talk. Where have you been?"

"Out," he said, and kept walking.

Oh no. No, no, no. Outside, he wouldn't move to save my life. Now, he wouldn't stand still for even a second? My frustration level rose a few degrees. I hurried past him and blocked the stairs. "Out where? And don't tell me it's none of my business. You have some explaining to do, *Tío*."

He scowled so hard his neck almost disappeared, and he wiped sweat from his forehead with a sleeve. "I felt like getting some air. Is there a law against that?"

"There ought to be, especially when you're a person of interest in a murder case and there's a reporter camped on the front steps. How did you get past that guy when you left anyway?"

He shrugged and looked at me as if I'd asked a silly question. "I didn't have to get past him. He wasn't there when I left."

That surprised me. "He wasn't? What time did you leave?"

"It was early. I didn't look at the clock."

I didn't believe that for an instant. Uncle Nestor is almost fanatical about the time, and being late for anything makes him edgy. But I realized that he was steering me off-track, so I zeroed back in on what I really wanted to know. "Where did you go?"

Aunt Yolanda put a hand on my shoulder and said, "Let's talk about this later. Nestor only walked through the door a minute ago."

Uncle Nestor waved her off with a flick of his wrist. "It's all right, Yolanda." Turning back to me, he said, "I told you already. I wanted some air. I walked around a block or two, and came back. And now I want a shower."

He started to walk past me, but I held my ground. "Uh-uh. Not yet. I need some answers. I know you both think I'm being pushy, but Detective Sullivan *asked* me to talk with you, and we have to meet him at the station in an hour. Promise me you'll tell him everything."

He looked at me as if I'd said a word he didn't understand. "Everything?"

"Yeah. Everything. What you and Big Daddy fought about last night. Where you were when he died. Why Susannah Boudreaux is trying to make you look guilty. You know . . . the facts."

The frown on Uncle Nestor's face deepened. "How would I know what that crazy woman is thinking?"

"She must have some reason for trying to make you look guilty. Did you even meet her last night? Was she there when you and Big Daddy fought? I don't remember seeing her, but maybe I missed her."

Uncle Nestor's irritation level went from zero to sixty in a heartbeat. "This is ridiculous. You're forgetting who you're talking to, Rita. I don't have to answer to you."

His sudden flash of anger surprised me. "I'm not the one being ridiculous," I said. "I'm not the one who's refusing to explain why I punched a man in the nose who just happened to end up dead a couple of hours later. I'm not the one refusing to say where I was when Big Daddy was being murdered. And I'm not the one sneaking out of the house at daybreak and then acting like it's no big deal. What's going on with you? Why are you acting like this?"

Uncle Nestor's gaze shot briefly to Aunt Yolanda, but whatever he was looking for on her face, I sure didn't see it. She leaned against the wall, arms crossed, eyes narrowed at me as if I'd crossed the line.

Yeah, sure, I was the one being unreasonable. "Come on," I said, pleading with her to help me. "You can't seriously think he's being smart about this. He's in big trouble. Help me convince him of that."

"Everything will be fine," she said. "It's in the Lord's hands."

I plowed my fingers through my hair and growled in frustration. "I'm all for trusting in God," I said, clenching my teeth to keep myself from shouting at her. "But Uncle Nestor can't just sit here, refusing to talk, and expect God to pull his butt out of the fire. It doesn't work that way."

Aunt Yolanda gasped and put her hand over her heart. Uncle Nestor got in my face. "Seems to me, somebody's forgotten the way she was raised. *And* who raised her. Don't you ever speak to your aunt that way again."

"Then talk to me! Give me something I can tell Liam when we get to the station so he can cross you off the list of suspects!"

Something unpleasant flashed through Nestor's dark eyes. "Is this *Liam* a special friend of yours? Is *he* why you turned your back on your family?"

My uncle can be intimidating, and he was working up a heavy head of steam, but we have the same blood flowing through our veins. I felt my temper snap like a toothpick. "Don't you dare try to change the subject."

"Don't you dare try to evade my question. Is that what this is about, Rita? Some man?"

For half a heartbeat I felt about fifteen again. Young. Defenseless. And yes, even a little frightened. But I wasn't a kid anymore. I owned this house. Nobody could send me away because I'd made them unhappy.

I straightened my spine and looked him in the eye. "You're so busy trying to pin the blame for my decision on someone or something," I shouted. "Why can't you just accept the fact that I left New Mexico because I wanted to?"

"Why? Didn't we give you enough? Didn't we do enough for you? You needed this fancy house and that Mercedes?"

I was dimly aware of Aunt Yolanda saying something and trying to wedge herself between us, but I was too angry to stop now. "You gave me plenty," I shouted at the man who'd been like a father to me. "You did everything I could have asked for, and I love you for it. So don't you dare try to make me out to be some ungrateful stray you took in so you can feel better about yourself!"

"That's what you think I'm doing?"

"Isn't it?"

He tossed his wadded sweatshirt onto the stairs and used both hands to punctuate his conversation. "That's the trouble with you, Rita. You've got tunnel vision. All you can see is one thing. You're just like your mother."

I wasn't sure what "one thing" he was talking about, but the last part scored a direct hit. "That's the nicest thing you've said to me in years," I snarled.

"Always chasing the dream," he said. "Always looking for something better." His flying hands came close to my face. I knew he wasn't trying to hit me, but I moved up a step to make sure he didn't accidentally connect.

"So? What's wrong with that? What's wrong with trying to improve my life? And maybe I do have tunnel vision, but that's not a bad thing either. Right now, I seem to be the only one in the family who can see what's going on here."

Aunt Yolanda managed to squeeze in between us. "Stop it, you two! Stop right now."

Uncle Nestor stopped waving his hands and clenched them at his sides instead. "What's wrong with that," he ground out between teeth clenched as tightly as my own, "is that you only see what you want to see. If you had some problem working with me, you should have talked to me."

"I tried, but you wouldn't listen. You were smothering me. You put me in the kitchen and gave me entry-level jobs that were far below my skill level, and you expected me to keep my mouth shut and be happy about it. I'm a trained pastry chef, not a short-order cook."

He shook a finger in my face, but he had to reach over Aunt Yolanda's shoulder to do it. "You're forgetting yourself, little girl."

"I'm not a little girl," I snapped. "That's what you don't seem to remember. If you want to know why I decided to move here, take a look in the mirror."

I wanted to take the words back the instant they left my mouth. Uncle Nestor's expression, filled with a mixture of fury and hurt feelings, made me want to crawl into a hole and hide. He pushed past me again, grabbing his sweatshirt as he pounded up the stairs.

This time I didn't even try to stop him.

Aunt Yolanda started after him, angrier than I'd ever seen her. She stopped halfway up the stairs and turned back to me. "That was a thoughtless thing to say, Rita."

"I know. I'm sorry. He just makes me so mad sometimes."

"Well, obviously, the feeling is mutual. But I won't let you upset him like that again. He's not a well man, so don't say anything you can't take back. He needs rest and quiet, not arguing and accusations."

I heard myself gasp. "What do you mean? What's wrong with him?"

"We'll talk about it later," she said, and headed upstairs to check on Uncle Nestor.

Later. That's all I'd heard since they got here. I had so many questions that needed answers, I could only hope that "later" didn't come too late.

Seventeen

To my relief, the NLTV news truck had disappeared by the time we stepped outside again, but even that didn't ease the tension between the three of us. We made the drive to the police station in stony silence, but not because I wanted it that way. In fact, nothing had really gone my way since yesterday. Big Daddy's murder had thrown my whole life off-kilter, and I wanted it back on track. I wanted to clear Uncle Nestor and find out that he wasn't really sick after all. Not necessarily in that order.

The bright sunlight and clear blue skies overhead mocked the shadows Aunt Yolanda had planted in my heart while we were standing on the staircase. My imagination was working overtime, considering and cataloging every horrible disease it was possible for Uncle Nestor to have contracted. Searching his face in the rearview mirror for clues. Wondering how many possibilities I'd missed.

My mood fluctuated as I drove, alternating between irritation, guilt, and sheer terror at the thought of losing Uncle Nestor. He'd been my rock since my parents died, when I was twelve. I couldn't imagine a world without him in it. What's more, I didn't want to imagine it.

As we drew closer to the French Quarter, traffic slowed to a crawl and people lined the sidewalks, claiming spots for that night's parade. Some were in costume, some in street clothes, but they all seemed in the mood to do what the people in New Orleans do best—they were ready to party.

Under other circumstances, I might have pointed out places of interest on our way, but I wasn't in the mood to play travel guide, and I was pretty sure neither of the grim-faced people riding with me had any interest in the scenery.

We managed to avoid any reporters on our way to the front doors of the station, where Detective Sullivan met us. In spite of my protests, Aunt Yolanda and I were shuffled off with Officer Crump to read and sign our printed statements while Sullivan led Uncle Nestor down a long corridor for more questioning.

I didn't want to leave Uncle Nestor's side. Logically, I knew it was unlikely that Uncle Nestor would keel over while he was with Sullivan, but I wasn't exactly firing on all cylinders. I'd learned at an early age that bad things happened when I let loved ones out of my sight.

But Uncle Nestor strode away as if nothing unusual were happening, and I took my cues from Aunt Yolanda. She appeared calm, so I tried to look the same.

When we were finished, Officer Crump escorted us to a long row of plastic chairs in a hallway lined with doors, and told us to wait there.

It was the first time we'd been alone since Aunt Yolanda

had delivered her bombshell. The first chance we'd had to talk about Uncle Nestor. I waited for her to say something first for as long as I could stand it, which ended up being about five and a half seconds.

"You can't just leave me hanging like that," I said, shifting in my seat so I could look at her. "What's wrong with him?"

Aunt Yolanda slid a glance in my direction. "I'm sorry, *mija*. I should have told you sooner, I know."

"So tell me now."

She sighed softly, but it carried a heavy load of worry and heartache. "It's his heart."

My own heart dropped out of my chest in dismay at the same time it filled with relief that the word *cancer* hadn't come out of her mouth. "What's wrong with it?"

"He had a minor heart attack a few weeks ago, *mija*. He was at work when the pains started. Santos called the paramedics, thank God. Nestor insisted it was just heartburn."

I swear the ground shifted beneath my feet, but I managed to calm myself with the realization that he'd obviously made it to the hospital in time. I made a mental note to thank my cousin for making that call. "Why didn't you tell me?"

"I didn't want to worry you. You're so far away. How would it have helped for you to know? It would only have made you upset. You'd have worked yourself up over things you couldn't help with or change."

Usually I find her unruffled calm soothing. At the moment, it made me want to hit something.

I got to my feet, too agitated to sit still. "I assume the boys all knew about this."

Aunt Yolanda scowled. "Don't go there, Rita."

"I think we're already there, don't you? You told the boys, but you didn't tell me." Whether that was because I wasn't actually one of their children or because of the miles between us, I'd probably never know. It hurt me to think about that, so I tried to focus on the future. "How is he now?"

"Doing better. Well enough to travel, which is a big thing. But his doctor wants him to avoid stress. And you know how he is at the restaurant."

I barked a laugh. So much for avoiding stress on their vacation. Besides, Uncle Nestor thrives on stress. He isn't truly happy unless he's worried about something. "So you came here and left Santos in charge at the restaurant?" Santos has been working at Agave since the day Uncle Nestor opened the restaurant's doors. He's talented and competent, organized and well respected among the staff. He's also one of the big reasons I'd never have risen too far up the ranks if I'd stayed at Agave. He was the oldest son. The heir apparent. "How's Uncle Nestor dealing with that?"

"He's fine with it." Aunt Yolanda slid another glance at me and her lips curved ever so slightly. "For the most part."

I smiled and shook my head. "He hates it, doesn't he?"

"He's struggling," she agreed.

I sobered and thought back over the things I'd seen and heard since they came to town. "So the jogging? That's for real?"

"He's under doctor's orders to get some exercise, to change his diet. To change his life, really."

I sat beside her again, leaning forward so that my arms rested on my thighs. "No wonder he's been in such a foul mood."

She nodded sadly. "It's hard on him, but he's trying. He hates what the doctor has told him to do, but he wants to stay alive for the boys and the grandkids." She touched my arm briefly, "And for you. He loves you like a daughter, Rita. We both do."

Tears welled in my eyes. I brushed them away with the back of my hand, refusing to dwell on the negative and desperate to find something positive to cling to. "So what's the prognosis?"

"If he makes the changes he's supposed to make? It's good. He could live another forty years, get old and crotchety, and make us all miserable."

I laughed and felt a knot of tension loosen between my shoulder blades. "That's the best news I've had in two days. So you didn't come here just so I could see him one last time?"

Aunt Yolanda looked stricken. "No! We came so he could get some peace and quiet."

With a sour grin, I glanced around us. A couple of uniformed officers led a handcuffed young man with dreadlocks into an interrogation room. I could see another cop talking with a businessman in a rumpled suit and two others chatting outside an open doorway over coffee in paper cups. Voices rose and fell. Phones rang and computer keyboards click-clacked, all creating an odd sort of music. "Good choice."

Aunt Yolanda followed my gaze. "Well, of course, neither of us expected to land in the middle of a murder investigation."

I was still worried, but not frantic anymore. Knowing about Uncle Nestor's health problems just made me more determined to clear him of suspicion so he could go home on Monday and get the rest and quiet he needed. Obviously, he wasn't going to get it here.

While I tried to figure out what to do next, a door just down the hall opened and Mellie Boudreaux emerged, followed by one of the officers who'd been at the country club last night. I guessed from the way Aunt Yolanda watched Mellie that she recognized her, too.

Mellie paused just outside the door to shake the officer's hand. "You'll let me know if there's anything else you need from me?"

"Absolutely." He handed over a business card, which she promptly tucked into the Coach bag on her shoulder. "And if you remember anything else, give me a call. Thanks again for coming in, Ms. Boudreaux. You've been a big help."

I caught Aunt Yolanda's gaze and saw curiosity flickering in her eyes. "Is that the ex-wife?" she whispered.

I nodded, pretty sure we were both thinking the same thing. Her being here was no coincidence. She'd obviously just given the police her statement. With Susannah busy pointing the finger at Uncle Nestor, I was desperate to know what Mellie had told the police.

She walked a few feet down the hall and disappeared into the ladies' room. I waited, biding my time, until the police officer went back into the room, then whispered to Aunt Yolanda, "I'll be right back."

"Where are you going?"

"Where else? The ladies' room."

"You're going to talk to her? Do you think that's wise?"

I stood and tried to look shocked by the question. "I'm going to freshen up. There's no law against that, is there?" And then I hurried away before she could give me an answer.

Eighteen

✦

Mellie was already standing at the bank of sinks when I came through the door of the ladies' room. Up close, I could see that she was a beautiful woman, with eyes the deep, rich color of fudge brownies. She gave me a quick noncommittal smile and started to look away, but then her eyes shot back to the mirror. This time she studied me a little closer. "You're Philippe Renier's widow, right? You hosted the party last night?"

I nodded in answer to her first question and gave a little shrug for the second. "It's Rita, please," I said, bypassing the party thing entirely. "I don't think we got a chance to meet last night, but you're Mellie Boudreaux, aren't you?"

She turned away from the mirror, tweaking the collar of a white linen shirt that was unbuttoned far enough to reveal an impressive amount of cleavage. "That's right. I have the dubious honor of being Big Daddy Boudreaux's first ex-wife."

She turned on a smile so open and friendly it was hard not to like her. "I just hope that crazy-ass Boudreaux blood is diluted enough to let our children have normal lives, God bless 'em."

I smiled and moved farther into the tile-covered room. Remembering how hard Philippe's death had hit me despite our separation, I said, "I'm sorry for your loss."

Mellie's expression sobered and she reached for a towel from the dispenser at her side. "Thanks, but I lost Bradley a long time ago. I did my mourning then."

Maybe so, but I was pretty sure I detected some regret in those dark eyes. I didn't want her to know that I'd chased her into the ladies' room, so I moved to the bank of sinks and waved my hands around to get the water started, then pumped soap from the dispenser. "So you're here to give the police your statement?"

She nodded and dug in her bag for lipstick. "Not that it's much of one. I only saw Bradley last night for a few minutes. I guess you're here for the same reason?"

I nodded. "It's such a senseless tragedy. Why would anyone want to kill him?"

Mellie slanted a glance at me. "Oh, honey, if you knew Bradley like I knew Bradley, you wouldn't be asking that. You'd be asking who *didn't* want him dead."

She certainly knew how to get a person's attention. I didn't want to look too eager for information, so I rinsed the soap from my hands and tried for a casual expression. "What makes you say that?"

"Let's just say that it looks like the hens have come home to roost. Bradley hurt a lot of people in his lifetime. Somebody obviously decided to hurt him back."

"Any idea who?"

Mellie shook her head and applied her lipstick—a

fuchsia/wine infusion mix that looked great on her but that I could never pull off. "Like I said, honey, it's a mighty long list. Bradley looked out for himself his whole life. If someone got in his way . . ." She broke off with a shrug, leaving me to fill in the blanks.

"Is that what you told the police?" I asked.

She dabbed at the corners of her mouth with her little finger and leaned back to inspect her reflection. "I have no reason to lie, if that's what you're asking."

"That's not it at all," I assured her. "I'm just trying to figure out what the police are thinking."

Mellie dropped her lipstick back into her purse and zipped it closed. "That's kind of hard to tell, isn't it? They're not sharing much with the rest of us."

"You were there when his body was found, weren't you? I thought I saw you talking to Susannah just a few minutes before that."

She sighed heavily. "You probably did. She's a silly little thing, but I have a soft spot for her. Being married to Bradley Boudreaux isn't easy."

"So you're friendly?"

She laughed again. "Does that surprise you?"

"A little, maybe," I said with a shrug. "You never know how two women who've been married to the same man will get along."

"Well, we get along fine, mostly because I'm so damn happy *she's* the one married to him now." She grinned, but the smile slid from her face after a moment and she turned a sober look on me. "Why do you want to know?"

"She tried to get my uncle arrested last night, and she talked to a television reporter about him this morning. I'm trying to figure out why."

"Susannah's an emotional little thing," Mellie said. "She

thinks with her heart, not with her head. But your uncle *did* attack Bradley, did he not?"

Everything inside urged me to sugarcoat their argument, but what good would that do? "How did you know about that?"

"I was looking for Bradley and happened to overhear some of what went on."

Apparently, more people had been aware of the fight than I'd first thought. "It wasn't a big deal," I said. "My uncle didn't kill Big Daddy."

Mellie plucked at a lock of hair and sent me a pitying smile. "Well, good luck convincing the police of that, honey. I wish I could help, but I may have made things worse for him."

My breath caught. "How?"

"Well, darlin', I have nothin' against your uncle, but I had to tell the police what I saw."

"Are you talking about the fight they had? Because that only lasted for a couple of minutes and it was over hours before the murder."

"Well, yes, I told them about the fight. Bradley really shouldn't have said what he said, but your uncle shouldn't have reacted the way he did. But I also had to tell them about what happened later."

I almost didn't hear the last part of what she said because my attention was riveted on the first part. "You heard what Big Daddy said to Uncle Nestor? What was it?"

Mellie studied me thoughtfully for a moment, probably trying to decide whether to tell me or not. Finally, she let out a resigned sigh and glanced toward the door to make sure we were alone. "I probably shouldn't say anything. The police wouldn't like us talking about the murder."

"We're not talking about the murder," I said. "We're

talking about the fight my uncle had with your ex-husband. All I want to know is what Big Daddy said to Uncle Nestor that set him off like that."

"Why don't you just ask your uncle?"

"I have," I assured her. "More than once. He doesn't want to talk about it. He doesn't want to talk about anything, really. I don't know what's gotten into him." When she still didn't say anything, I tried a different tack. "Please? I'm desperate."

"All right," Mellie said, her voice low, "I guess I really don't think your uncle killed Bradley—though God knows I'd understand it if he did." Her lips quirked slightly. "You see, Bradley had a thing for women and cars. Always did. He traded in his cars every year so he could have the latest model. I found out a little too late that he did the same thing with women."

I mumbled something about being sorry, but I wasn't one bit surprised.

Mellie waved off my apology. "He cheated on me our whole marriage, but it took me a long time to realize what was happening and even longer to put my foot down and tell him it had to stop. Of course, he couldn't stop and that's when he left me for his second wife. She only lasted a couple of years, poor thing. Moved up north to Chicago and remarried, I heard. Anyway, it was like a sickness with him. He was like a moth, and beautiful women were the flame."

"It must have been hard to be married to a man like that."

Mellie nodded. "You don't know the half of it."

I let that settle between us for a few seconds, then followed up. "So what did he say?"

She glanced at the door again and dropped her voice a little more. "He made a couple of comments about what a beautiful woman your aunt is and then told your uncle to let him know if he ever got tired of her."

No wonder Uncle Nestor went ballistic. "And that's why Uncle Nestor hit him?"

"Not exactly." Mellie returned the lipstick to her purse and tucked the bag under her arm. "Your uncle hit him after Bradley said what a treat it would be to get you and your aunt together."

Knowing that Big Daddy had said something so rude, let alone had thought it, made me sick. Imagining Uncle Nestor's reaction made me nervous. I leaned against the cool tile and tried to focus my thoughts again. "Are you sure that's what he said?"

Mellie shrugged. "What can I say? He was a disgusting pig."

I wasn't sure I wanted the answer to the next question, but I had to ask, "So what happened later?"

"Are you sure you want to know?"

"I have to know." I squared my shoulders and lifted my chin, steeling myself. "It's okay. I need the truth."

In spite of my reassurance, Mellie seemed reluctant to go on. "They got into it again an hour or so later," she said after a pause. "I didn't hear what they were saying that time, but I assumed it had something to do with their first brawl."

It seemed like a reasonable assumption, so I nodded for her to go on.

"I was looking for Judd—that's Bradley's younger brother. I don't know if you met him . . ."

I nodded. "We met for a minute."

"I wanted to make sure he was doing all right. Alcohol and Judd do not mix." She flicked a glance at me and said, "Or maybe I should say that alcohol and Judd mix too well. Anyway, I wanted to make sure he was holding up okay. Somebody told me he was out by the pool, so I went down there. Your uncle and Bradley were there, and they were literally at each other's throats."

I thought I'd prepared myself for whatever she had to say, but I hadn't. My knees felt rubbery and my spirits tanked. "They fought again?"

"They sure did."

"What time was that?"

"Around one maybe? I'm not sure. I really wasn't paying attention to the details . . . until I realized what was going on."

"And you didn't hear anything they said?"

"A few words. Not many I could understand. And I think we're about to cross the line here. I probably shouldn't say too much more."

"But you did hear something," I said, nudging her again.

She flicked a lock of hair off her forehead and backed a step toward the door. "I only heard one thing, really," she said, clearly eager to finish the conversation. "I heard your uncle threaten to kill Bradley."

Nineteen

With Mellie Boudreaux's claim echoing through my head, I rejoined Aunt Yolanda on the chairs and made small talk. Maybe I should have told her what Mellie said, but I didn't want to worry her. She had enough on her mind, what with Uncle Nestor's bad heart and all.

Besides, no matter what Mellie might have overheard, I knew my uncle. He might have a short fuse and an explosive temper, but he's not a murderer.

After a while, Sullivan reappeared with a still-sullen and silent Uncle Nestor and told us we were free to go—for now. I wondered if the police were taking Mellie Boudreaux's story seriously, but I didn't want to ask in front of Aunt Yolanda, so I swallowed my questions and promised myself I'd ask Sullivan later.

We dodged reporters on the way back to the car and settled in for the drive home, Uncle Nestor in the front seat with me, Aunt Yolanda in the back. I tried asking Uncle Nestor about his interview with Sullivan, but he still wasn't talking, so we drove back to the house in silence broken only by an occasional observation from Aunt Yolanda about things we passed.

She seemed fascinated by the Mardi Gras decorations and crowds gathering at such an early hour everywhere, but I suspected she was just trying to distract me so I wouldn't upset Uncle Nestor. To a casual observer, I'm sure she looked cool, calm, and collected, but I picked up on subtle clues that revealed how agitated she was. This was tough on everybody.

The minute we got to the house, Uncle Nestor climbed the stairs to the guest room and Aunt Yolanda followed a minute later, saying that she needed to lie down for a while.

Alone for the first time in several hours, I checked my cell phone and noticed that a message had come in since the last time I looked. It was from Miss Frankie, letting me know she was having lunch at The Shores with her neighbor, Bernice, and the police were still gathering evidence from the crime scene. I wondered what she had up her sleeve, but my call to her house phone went through to voice mail and Miss Frankie doesn't carry a cell phone.

I puttered around the house for a few minutes, listening for footsteps coming from upstairs. I needed to get to work. Yeah, I know. Edie had advised me to stay away. But I'm no good at taking advice. Besides, working always helps me think—and I desperately needed to sort through the jumble of questions rolling around in my head.

I waited until I was convinced that Uncle Nestor and Aunt Yolanda were settled in for a while, then changed into a pair of jeans and a T-shirt and scribbled a hasty note explaining that I'd gone to the shop. The bright noon sunlight filtered through the trees as I drove the back streets to the Garden District, and the city began to work its magic on me. Stately antebellum homes surrounded by well-trimmed lawns and ornate gardens filled with flowers stand side-by-side with boutiques and restaurants. It's a trendy, upscale neighborhood with lots of old-world charm. Technically, it was still winter, but it felt like the springs I'd known in New Mexico.

I parked in Zydeco's employee lot and walked inside, where I breathed in the delicious scents of yeast and cinnamon and felt my nerves begin to settle.

"What are you doing here?" Edie snapped when she saw me. "I thought I told you to stay away."

My mood curdled like sour milk. I didn't need attitude on top of everything else.

"I know what you told me," I growled back. "I came anyway."

"So I see." Edie was wearing striped leggings under a lime green tunic and a pair of soft-soled shoes, the toes of which sported intricately embroidered lotus flowers. With her porcelain doll face, the whole outfit made her look young and sweet. Very misleading.

I tried to look calm and in control, completely at ease with my decision to come to work, but I was second-guessing myself like mad. We were standing in the room that had originally served as the home's front parlor and now did duty as the bakery's reception area. It's Edie's domain, and she runs it from behind a wide U-shaped desk lined with stacking trays that are labeled and color-coded. In direct contrast to the organization she prefers, her desk was cluttered with the buildup of paperwork from orders we'd filled since carnival season began. Receipts and invoices teetered in stacks, waiting for her to update Zydeco's books on the computer.

A half-eaten shrimp po'boy sandwich from the corner grocery sat between her computer keyboard and a massive insulated cup, no doubt filled with her favorite, Diet Coke, making me realize that I should have stopped for lunch on my way. I'd never have time to get away for something to eat now.

"How are things going?" I asked, still trying to give the appearance of control. "Are we on schedule?"

Edie slipped behind her desk and dropped into her chair. "Everything is fine. I told you that already. There's no reason for you to be here."

"And yet I am, so it's a moot point," I said and turned toward my office. I unlocked the door and tossed my bag onto the floor beside my desk—also heaped with paperwork and piles of mail. "Where's Ox?"

"Filling in for you in the design room," Edie called back. Her voice was muffled, as if she'd gone back to work on the sandwich. "And he's none too happy about it either. Just so you know."

I ran a quick glance over the heap of work waiting for me, decided that none of it was urgent, and headed for the employee lunchroom. "Is there coffee?" I tossed the question at Edie as I passed her desk.

"I made some an hour ago."

Not fresh, but hopefully not bitter yet. I followed the aroma toward the sunny room that overlooked the street. "Anything to eat in there?"

"Estelle brought bagels and lox from Surrey's this morning. There might be some left." Edie took another bite of her po'boy and got up to follow me. "How did it go at the police station?"

I shrugged. "Aunt Yolanda and I signed our statements. Uncle Nestor spent a while with Sullivan, but don't ask me

what happened. He's still refusing to answer my questions."
I made a beeline for the coffeepot and poured a cup. "I wish
I could figure out what's going on with him. Aunt Yolanda
said he had a mild heart attack a couple of weeks ago.
I'm sure it freaked him out big-time. I don't remember
him ever getting sick when I was a kid, not even a cold. But
even a shock like that doesn't explain why he's refusing to
talk."

Edie shrugged as if to say she had no answer for that and
checked the box from Surrey's on the counter. "You're in
luck. There's one bagel left. The fixings are in the fridge."

Such as they were. A few smears of cream cheese clung
to the edges of the plastic container and two wispy pieces
of lox lay limply on a folded sheet of waxed paper. I scraped
and spread and arranged until the food looked almost appe-
tizing and then tore into it as if I hadn't eaten in days.

Is there a better bite anywhere in the world? A perfectly
boiled bagel, crusty on the outside and chewy on the inside.
The sweetly sour burst of cream cheese mixed with the
smoky taste of the lox almost made me swoon. I wolfed
down half the bagel, pausing only to wag my fingers in
farewell as Edie went back to work, and again in hello as
Estelle came through the door a few seconds later.

She saw me eating the last bagel and frowned in disappointment. "Oh. You're . . ." She waved a hand as if losing
that bagel had flustered her. "That's okay. I had one
earlier."

"It's delicious," I said around the last mouthful. "Thanks
for bringing them this morning."

She gave her spongy red curls a little flip and crossed to
the fridge. "No problem. I thought I should do something.
You know. Because of . . . you know. What happened last
night."

You betcha. A good bagel is the best cure for a murder hangover.

I sipped coffee, added a dash more sugar, and started toward the door as Estelle pulled a Coke from the fridge. "How are you doing, Rita? Are you holding up okay?" she asked.

I nodded, a little surprised by her question. "I'm fine. I'm sorry for Big Daddy's friends and family, but I didn't really know him."

"Yeah, but—" Estelle reached into the cupboard for a glass and filled it with crushed ice from the refrigerator door. "It's just . . ." Her voice trailed away and she chewed her bottom lip for a moment.

I gave her a verbal nudge. "Just what?"

"Well, you know. Edie told us how your uncle is under suspicion." She twisted the cap off her bottle and concentrated on pouring the soda over ice.

"My uncle is innocent," I said firmly.

"Oh, I know! I'm not saying he's not." She glanced at me and away from her task. It only took a second but the Coke foamed over the side. She grabbed a handful of paper towels and started mopping. "I didn't mean to insinuate anything . . . you know . . . bad." She looked so horrified, I almost felt sorry for her, and I reminded myself that I wasn't the only one at Zydeco feeling the effects of Big Daddy's murder. "How's Miss Frankie taking all of this? Poor woman. This must be horrible for her."

"I'm sure it's not easy," I agreed.

She tossed the soggy paper towels and checked her soda to ice ratio, then picked up the glass and sipped. "When you're ready, I have some more pictures for the blog."

"More than what you gave me last night?"

"Ox wanted me to get a variety. I tried."

I nodded and tried to look as if I cared, but if the website and blog had been low on my priority list yesterday, they'd slipped off the list completely today. "Just give the memory card to Edie," I said. "I'll get it from her."

"Oh. Sure." Estelle looked at me over the rim of her glass, her eyes expectant and uncertain, as if she wanted to say more but didn't know if she should.

"Is there something else?"

She put the glass down and moved a couple of steps closer. When she spoke again, her voice was almost a whisper. "For what it's worth, I really don't think your uncle did it."

"He didn't," I said again. "And I appreciate the vote of confidence. I just wish I knew how to convince the police that he's innocent."

Estelle's round face creased in a sympathetic smile. "Seems weird to me that they'd be looking at him anyway. Don't they say that it's usually someone close to the victim?"

After I'd finished the other half of my bagel, I threw the empty box and the cream cheese container into the trash. "That's what they say," I agreed. "I wish I knew more about the Boudreauxes. What did Big Daddy have, a couple of ex-wives? A girlfriend?" I liked Mellie when I met her earlier, but what if she wasn't telling the truth? What if she had a grudge against Big Daddy and resolved it by coshing him over the head?

Estelle shook her head. "Bless his heart. Always searching for love and never finding it."

"Is that your way of saying he slept around a lot?"

Estelle didn't give me a direct answer. "It's my way of saying that the poor man never learned he couldn't run his women the way he ran his business." She slanted a sly glance at me and lowered her voice a little more. "I don't like to speak ill of the dead, but I heard him talking to his wife last night and it was downright shameful. No respectable Southern gentleman would say the things he did."

My ears perked up at that. "What kinds of things?"

Estelle put a hand on her chest and glanced at the door. "I probably shouldn't say."

"You'd better say," I warned her. "And right now. If you know something that could help clear Uncle Nestor, you have to tell me."

Estelle sank into a chair and propped her chin in one hand. She looked miserable, but I didn't let it get to me. I sat across from her and made eye contact—which wasn't easy since she seemed determined not to look at me. "What did he say?"

She sighed heavily. "I'm not sure I can help much. The music was so loud."

I was in familiar territory now. If Miss Frankie had taught me anything since I came to New Orleans, it was the dance of Southern gossip. "Yes, it was," I commiserated. *One, two, cha-cha-cha.*

"And of course I wouldn't think of eavesdropping."

"Of course not."

"But I did hear him say that she had no right to worry about being embarrassed by him. That *she* embarrassed *him* every time she opened her mouth."

It certainly wasn't nice, but considering the other things Big Daddy had said last night, it seemed almost tame. "Poor thing. How did she react to that?" *Three, four, cha-cha-cha.*

"Well, you can understand why she'd be upset, bless her heart."

"Well, of course. Who wouldn't be?" I imagined myself as Fred Astaire and Estelle as Ginger Rogers. I spun her around with a little sympathy and dipped her by musing aloud and looking innocent. "I wonder what she did to embarrass him."

Estelle leaned in closer. We were conspirators now. "I have no idea about that, but I did notice she'd had a few too many. And I heard her tell him that he had to make things right with Percy."

"Percy Ponter? The guy who was just elected as the krewe's treasurer?" The one who'd been so determined to talk to Big Daddy last night?

"I guess. I don't know who he is, but she said he had to do it last night *or else*."

"Or else? She actually said that?"

Estelle nodded, her expression deadly serious. "Or else. But don't ask me what was going to happen if he didn't. Like I said, I wasn't eavesdropping."

I felt a little tingle of anticipation. "Do you remember what time that was?"

"Maybe eleven? It was a while before we served the King Cake. That's all I remember." She delivered the last line with a pointed look that said the dance was over.

I wanted to keep digging, but I knew she wouldn't give me more right now. Getting to my feet, I hugged her quickly. "Thanks, Estelle. At least that gives me a place to start."

"You're welcome." Her cheeks turned pink with pleasure. "Anything I can do to help."

I pondered what I'd just heard as I carried my coffee cup back to my office. I'd had a few questions before, but my conversation with Estelle had brought it up to a full baker's dozen. I tried to sift through them by remembering what I already knew. I thought about Mellie's claim that she'd been looking for Judd by the pool and realized I'd never asked whether she found him. I thought about Big Daddy's connections in Musterion and wondered if someone in the krewe had been responsible for his death. And what about his business empire? After meeting Big Daddy just once, I could easily believe he had a few disgruntled employees in his past, or business deals gone sour, and Mellie had certainly backed up those suspicions.

I knew he had an issue with Percy Ponter, but I had no idea what it was. And now it appeared that the current Mrs. Boudreaux had been unhappy with her husband shortly before he died.

A loud crash sounded from the kitchen, jerking me out of my thoughts. I turned toward it just as someone behind me called my name. "Rita? Thank goodness you're here! Got a minute? We have a problem with the sheeter."

I glanced over my shoulder and saw Isabeau hurrying toward me, her blond ponytail bouncing with every step.

"Sure," I said, trying not to sigh. There were far too many questions and not nearly enough time to find the answers.

Twenty

❧

I called and left a message for my cousin Santos, asking him to get back to me as soon as he had a minute. Then I began sorting through the top layer of paperwork on my desk—all stuff that hadn't been here last time I looked.

I found a few pieces of mail, some important, the rest junk. An updated calendar for the week and an article clipped from the newspaper about the Hedge-Montgomery wedding. Two e-mails from Edie informing me about consults she'd added to my already crowded schedule and a memo from Ox reminding me that I still hadn't approved the content for the web page he was so up in arms about.

The light on my desk phone flashed on and off, alerting me that I also had voice mail.

Groaning aloud, I buried my head in my arms on top of the paperwork. There simply weren't enough hours in the day.

I indulged in my pity party for about three seconds, then lifted my head, vowing to press on. During those three seconds, Ox materialized in the doorway. Dark stubble had sprung up on his usually clean-shaven head, and his chef's jacket was so wrinkled it looked like origami gone wrong.

I gave a little yelp of surprise and sat up quickly. "You startled me," I said. "I didn't hear you there."

"Napping?" he asked with a sardonic quirk of an eyebrow.

"Hardly," I said, doing my best to quirk back. "Wishing for the world to open up and swallow me whole." I motioned him into the office and waved him toward one of the chairs in front of my desk. "What's up?"

"You have to ask?"

"If it's about the web page—" I began.

He cut me off before I could finish. "It's about the murder last night."

I'm pretty sure the fact that I actually felt a ripple of relief says something strange about me. "What about it?"

Ox cocked an ankle on his knee and rested both burly forearms on the chair's arms. "Your connection to it, however coincidental, it's not good for business."

It took a moment for his meaning to sink in. When it did, I laughed in disbelief. "Surely you're not implying that this is somehow my fault."

"No, but your uncle . . ."

I put the cup down carefully so I wouldn't accidentally fling the coffee in his face. "*What* about my uncle?"

"Oh, come on, Rita. He belted the dead guy in the face last night. He's a person of interest in the murder."

My ears began to buzz. "And? Is that it? Come on, Ox. You know better than that. You were in the same position just a few months ago."

Ox held up both hands in surrender. "I never said I thought he was guilty. I'm just saying that I don't think having you front-and-center is the best thing for Zydeco right now."

I scowled so hard my forehead hurt. "I've already had this conversation with Edie. It's not your call."

"It's nothing personal," he assured me. "Frankly, this couldn't come at a worse time. So if you're thinking that I'm trying to nudge you out of the way, stop. That's not it at all."

I stared at him for a long time, surprised to find that I believed him. "I'm thinking about Zydeco, too," I said. "The staff has already been through enough. If I run and hide right now, it's going to make things worse than if I just take it on the chin."

He wagged his head again. "I don't know—"

"Listen," I said, cutting off his argument before he got started. "I'm still trying to establish myself here with the staff. How I deal with this will either make me or break me. They need to see that I'm willing to stand up and fight for this place—and for them if that's ever necessary." *The way I did for you*, I added silently.

I wasn't sure, but I thought I saw a spark of respect in Ox's dark eyes. "And just how do you plan to do that?"

"Show up. Come inside and do the work." I sounded tougher and more together than I felt, but Aunt Yolanda had been telling me for years to fake it until I could feel it and that's exactly what I was going to do now.

Ox regarded me for a long moment and then changed the subject. "How's your uncle holding up?"

Genuine concern tugged at the corners of his mouth and poked big holes in the anger I'd been feeling. I was worried, and the draw of confiding in a friend was impossible to resist.

I told Ox about the heart attack and what I knew about his doctor's orders. "He's supposed to be resting and avoiding stress. Some joke, huh?"

"All the more reason for taking a couple of days off," Ox said. "Stay home. Keep an eye on him. Show both of them the city and party a little. It's your first Mardi Gras, so go enjoy it with your family. It will do you all good."

I laughed. "You don't know my uncle. He's not one for crowds. Really, the best thing for him would be to get him off the police department's radar screen. If I could find a witness who could place him somewhere besides the pool at the time of the murder, I'm sure that would clear him of any suspicion."

Ox shook his head. "To do that, you'd have to interview all two hundred guests and the country club's staff."

"All I need is one reliable witness. What time did *you* leave the party?"

"I don't know. One? Maybe a little after. I don't remember. Why?"

"Were there still guests by the pool? Do you remember? Or had they cleared out by then?"

He gave that some thought before he answered. "There were a lot of people around the pool earlier, but they all started migrating back to the clubhouse around midnight for the captain's speech and the King Cake."

That's how I remembered it, too. "Did you see Uncle Nestor?"

"Not that I recall."

"How about Big Daddy? Do you remember seeing him?"

Ox gave me a look. "Do you really think this is a good idea?"

"What? Asking questions?"

He dipped his head once, a silent affirmation.

"We're talking about my uncle," I reminded him. "The man who raised me. I'm not going to let the police and everyone else treat him like a criminal. So: Did you see Big Daddy before you left the party?"

He gave a reluctant nod. "Yeah."

"Where was he? What was he doing?"

"Upstairs. At the far end of the hall by one of the trophy cases. Big Daddy and his brother were up there together. I got the impression they didn't want anyone to know they were there."

So Big Daddy and Judd had connected during the evening. I wondered how that had gone. "Did they say anything to you?"

Ox shook his head. "No, and I didn't say anything to them. I hit the head and went back to the party. Isabeau and I left about fifteen minutes later." He shifted in his chair, leaning forward to hold my gaze. "Just let the police do their job, okay?"

"Is that what you'd do if *your* uncle was in trouble?"

Ox sighed heavily and looked at me from the corner of his eye. "Yeah. It is."

Sure. And seven-layer double-fudge cake with buttercream icing is low in calories. "I'm not trying to figure out who killed Big Daddy," I argued. "I'm just trying to provide Uncle Nestor with an alibi."

"If he had one, don't you think he'd have told you?"

I shook my head. "He hasn't told anybody anything," I said. "And besides, he doesn't know anyone around here. Even if he was standing somewhere in full view of a dozen guests, he can't exactly name names."

The look in Ox's eyes turned skeptical, which threw cold water on the warm fuzzies of friendship I'd felt only moments before. "He's my uncle," I said again. "I owe him everything. And I'm going to *do* everything I can to clear him."

"I don't like it," Ox said. He stood and crossed to the door, but stopped on the threshold and looked back at me. "Just be careful." His voice was surprisingly gentle.

"Of course." I had no intention of putting myself in danger. I'd just ask a few questions. That's all.

Goes to show how wrong a person can be.

Twenty-one

⚜

I spent the rest of the afternoon working alongside the staff in the production line, trying to prove that I was one of them. As it always does, working with my hands relaxed me, and after a while I felt the knots in my shoulders loosen. Even the headache I'd been blaming on exhaustion began to fade.

I'm sure the staff's mood helped. Their excited chatter about their Mardi Gras plans helped me remember that the world hadn't stopped spinning when Big Daddy left it.

Their enthusiasm was infectious, and soon I was caught up in the planning and laughter. As an outsider, I'd had some preconceived notions about Mardi Gras, but I was quickly learning that it wasn't all alcohol and bared breasts. The people in New Orleans love to party, and since Katrina, they've approached life with a unity that's sometimes surprising. As Estelle had pointed out to me a few weeks earlier, the people of New Orleans party for Jesus, for the devil, for any excuse they can find. The party is the important thing.

When Philippe opened Zydeco two years earlier, he'd decreed the Sunday before Mardi Gras an official bakery holiday. The entire staff and their families attended the Krewe of Musterion parade, followed by the Krewe of Bacchus parade, and everyone went in costume. I'd been warned that they took great pains to keep their costumes secret until the great reveal an hour before the parade started.

I'd been meaning to figure out what I'd wear, but somehow work always got in my way. Now, as I listened to the others talk, I realized it wouldn't be a simple matter of stopping by a costume shop and handing the clerk my credit card. If I'd wanted to do that, I should have come up for air weeks ago.

I could feel tension crawling up my spine again, but I did my best to shake it off. I'd learned at Uncle Nestor's knee, and look how that had turned out for him. I didn't want to worry myself into the hospital.

Putting the murder and my ever-growing to-do list out of my mind for the time being, I concentrated on the music playing on the stereo in the corner and tuned out the conversations around me. I lost myself in the scents and sounds of the world I love best. I could hear the phone ringing almost nonstop in Edie's corner, and I hoped that the calls coming in were orders for cakes, not reporters looking for a story. And then I put that worry out of my head, too.

After a while, Isabeau caught my attention and motioned to something behind me. I turned to find Detective Sullivan lounging against the door frame. He gave me a little chin jerk in greeting and pushed away from the wall with his shoulder.

I had a feeling he wasn't here on a social visit, but I told myself not to assume the worst. Maybe he was here to tell me that Uncle Nestor was in the clear. Maybe they'd arrested someone—someone else. Maybe the nightmare was already over.

I motioned for him to come closer and greeted him with the best smile I could manage, considering the nervous tension skating in my belly and the exhaustion dragging at my mind.

Using the dough scraper, I hacked a large ball of risen dough into three pieces. *Whack! Whack!* "Fancy meeting you here."

He sent back a lopsided grin. I noticed that his eyes were a clear blue today, which gave me hope that things were looking up. "Yeah," he said. "Fancy that. That thing you're wielding looks lethal. Should I be worried?"

I waggled it in front of him. "Plastic. The most damage I could inflict is a serious bruise or a broken finger. What's up, Detective? Are you here on business or looking for the best King Cake in the city?"

"Business, I'm afraid."

"Tell me you're here to announce the arrest of Big Daddy's killer."

"'Fraid not. We've identified the murder weapon, though. Somebody smashed his skull with a small statue we found near the pool."

I shuddered, realizing it must've been the one I'd stepped around on my way to help Big Daddy. "Fingerprints?"

"A couple of partials, but nothing we can use. Actually, I need to speak to a couple of your people. Is this a bad time?"

I was disappointed that the case was still open, but I channeled my frustration into rolling out one of the recently whacked balls of dough. "It's as good as any. Which ones?"

"Sparkle Starr and Dwight Sonntag. Can you spare them for a few minutes?"

"You can take the whole staff if it helps solve the case. Just return them quickly. We're buried."

"Those two will be fine," he said. "Mind if I use the room upstairs to speak with them?"

"If you don't mind sharing it with a few supplies stored there for carnival season. It's usable. We're still having our weekly staff meetings up there, so make yourself at home."

He didn't need me to show him the way or point out the staff, so the fact that he didn't walk off right away made me look up to see what was going on.

"How's your uncle?" he asked.

I shrugged. "Okay the last time I saw him. Did he happen to mention that he had a heart attack a couple of weeks ago and that he's supposed to be avoiding stress?"

Something flickered in Sullivan's eyes, but I couldn't read it. He shook his head. "He didn't mention anything to me. I'll make a note in the file."

Yeah. That would fix everything.

"Has he been any more forthcoming with you?"

I frowned and shook my head. "I wish. He hardly spoke to me on the way home, and I've been here since I dropped him off. I don't suppose you've managed to clear him of suspicion yet."

"Not yet, but I'm working on it. Don't worry."

Easier said than done. "Any suspects yet?" I asked him.

He shrugged. "One or two."

"Any serious suspects?"

He leaned one hip against the table and watched me work. "C'mon, Rita. You know I can't discuss an ongoing investigation with you. Especially not one where you're related to a person of interest."

I really hated that phrase. "There's no law against me sharing information with *you*, though, is there?"

"Absolutely not. It's your civic duty." He dragged a stool closer and made himself comfortable. "What information?"

"I know why Uncle Nestor was so angry with Big Daddy last night."

"He told you?"

I shook my head. "Someone overheard the conversation. I don't know if he told you about this . . ."

"He didn't tell me much of anything."

I filled Sullivan in on what Mellie had told me in the ladies' room, carefully leaving out how I'd come by the information and rushing on before he could ask me about it. "Uncle Nestor's a traditional Latino, very protective of the women in his family. And Big Daddy was a traditional sexist pig. It wasn't a good mix."

"Obviously."

"But Uncle Nestor wasn't the only person who had an issue with Big Daddy. Do you know why he and his wife arrived at the party separately? Could there be something important in that? She was with some guy when I met her."

"With? What were they doing?"

"It wasn't what they did," I said with a scowl. "It's the way they looked when they did it. And why was Big Daddy there with his assistant? I'll bet there was something going on between those two."

Sullivan didn't respond to that, which made me think I was right. "You know, don't you, that Big Daddy was treating his wife pretty shabbily last night? You ought to talk to Estelle about what she heard before you leave here."

"Estelle just happened to tell you about this?"

"No"—I gave him a *duh!* look—"I asked her." I hesitated over how much to tell him about Judd. Sure, I'd liked him when I met him, but my loyalty belonged to Uncle Nestor. "Also, I met Judd Boudreaux when I went outside. I got the impression that he had a few issues with Big Daddy, and he didn't seem to like Susannah much. Ox says that Big Daddy and Judd were having a secretive conversation upstairs right before the party ended. And have you talked with Percy Ponter yet? Like I told you that night, he seemed pretty upset with Big Daddy."

Sullivan folded his arms and stared me down. "I've got it under control. Anything else?"

"Not yet," I said, "but I'll keep you posted."

"Rita—"

I interrupted before he could get started. "If this is the part where you warn me to stay out of the investigation, save it. I won't get in your way and I won't interfere, but if I can find someone who can place Uncle Nestor away from the pool at the time of the murder, I'm going to do it."

"Why don't you let me take care of it?"

I planted my hands on the tabletop and met his gaze. "But will you? Or are you focused on finding witnesses who can place him at the scene of the crime? Because those aren't the same thing at all."

"I'm just tryin' to get at the truth," he assured me.

"Yeah. Well. You keep doing that, and if I find out anything that will help, I'll let you know."

He stood, sighing as if he carried the weight of the world on his shoulders. "Right. Guess I'll get on with my interviews if that's all right with you."

"Knock yourself out," I said, adding a thin smile to show that we were still friends.

He smoothed the legs of his jeans so that the hems fell over his boots. "Just in case your uncle didn't mention it, I've asked him not to leave town."

The smile slipped off my face and landed on the floor somewhere near my heart. "You did what?"

"Just for a few days. Until we can clear up his involvement in the case."

"There *is* no involvement," I insisted. Not that my opinion counted for anything.

"As soon as we can prove that, he's free to leave."

"But—"

He arched a brow, waiting for me to offer some protest, but words failed me. Uncle Nestor stuck in New Orleans until the police cleared him? He'd go crazy. *I'd* go crazy.

"Is there a problem?" Sullivan asked.

I shook my head quickly. "No. It'll be fine."

"You're sure?"

My smile had turned brittle, but I flashed it again. "If I said no, would you let him leave town?"

Sullivan shook his head. "'Fraid not."

"Then I'm sure."

Sullivan looked at me through eyes narrowed with concern, but he kept his distance. My uncle was on the list of suspects in a homicide case, which I guess made all the friendly sort of stuff that usually fell between us off-limits. He ran those piercing blue eyes over my face and then twitched the corner of his mouth. "Chin up. It's gonna get worse before it gets better."

And on that cheery note, he left to interview my employees.

Twenty-two

❧

Okay, I'll admit it. I was going crazy wondering why Sullivan had wanted to talk with Sparkle and Dwight. They'd come back to work without a word of explanation to me, and my mind had been working overtime running through the possibilities. Even a return phone call from my cousin Santos didn't completely distract me.

Santos didn't tell me anything I didn't already know, but he did reassure me that although Uncle Nestor needed to make some lifestyle changes, he wasn't in imminent danger of keeling over dead. Maybe if I heard it often enough I'd really start believing it.

We bantered back and forth for a few minutes, me giving him grief for not letting me know about his dad's heart attack, him telling me I would have known if I'd stayed in Albuquerque. I was having a great time talking to my oldest cousin until partway through the conversation, when it occurred to me that Santos hadn't once asked about the murder or the trouble his father was in.

And that meant that he must not know.

The possibility that Uncle Nestor and Aunt Yolanda hadn't confided in Santos made me feel better in a way. I didn't like the fact that they were keeping secrets, but at least I wasn't the only person they were keeping in the dark.

Of course, that put me in an awkward position. I didn't feel right hiding the truth from Santos, but I wasn't sure how to break the news to him either. Before I could think through the situation, Edie ran into my office to announce another emergency. One of the temporary workers I'd hired had slipped on the wet floor and it looked like the guy had sprained his ankle. Dwight was taking him to the doctor.

Promising to call back as soon as the crisis passed, I hung up on Santos and hurried into the design room to assess the damage. Losing two more people left us seriously short-handed. It also meant that I didn't get a chance to talk to Sparkle or Dwight about Sullivan's visit for the rest of the day.

By the time I dragged myself home, Uncle Nestor and Aunt Yolanda were already asleep. Yes, I checked to make sure.

They'd left a plate for me in the fridge, but I was more tired than hungry. I fell into an exhausted sleep and didn't wake up until Aunt Yolanda knocked on my bedroom door the next morning, bringing me breakfast in bed.

I took that breakfast tray as a positive sign. If Uncle Nestor had been cooking, maybe things were getting back to normal.

I could have lingered for an hour over the coffee, home-made tortillas, fried potatoes, and scrambled eggs seasoned perfectly with onions and peppers and served with Uncle

Nestor's signature salsa. Instead, I wolfed down the meal while Aunt Yolanda told me that Sullivan had stopped by the night before to ask Uncle Nestor more questions—a piece of news that almost took away my appetite.

I peppered Aunt Yolanda with questions about Sullivan's visit, but she couldn't tell me much. He'd shown up at the door. The two men had spoken privately for about an hour, after which Uncle Nestor had gone to bed without a word.

Feeling edgy, I hopped in the shower, dressed, and ran out the door thirty minutes later. Usually, Zydeco is closed on Sundays, but not this month. If the murder and subsequent investigation hadn't been enough to make them regret coming to New Orleans for a visit, I thought, the demands of my schedule certainly would. I needed a day off and a good night's sleep, not necessarily in that order.

Just as the sun crested the horizon, I slung my bag over my shoulder and climbed the steps onto Zydeco's loading dock. It promised to be a beautiful day, and I wanted to be outside enjoying some of the fun.

While coffee brewed, I ran a quick glance over the schedule for the next few days to see if there were any breaks in the lineup that would let me sneak away for an hour or two. I couldn't see any, but I was determined to keep my eyes open for one.

I spent a few minutes prioritizing everything listed on the calendar. A hundred or so King Cakes, a special order for a Valentine's Day party, a meeting later in the week with the website designers to discuss Zydeco's presence on the web, and a three-tier white chocolate cake with white chocolate truffles and henna scrollwork topped by a cluster of white sugar daisies scheduled for a delivery today in the French

Quarter. It was due a good two hours before the Krewe of Barkus parade, but crowds would be thick and the police would have blocked off traffic long before we needed to get through. I checked to make sure Edie had picked up a pass to get us through the police barricades. She had, of course, so at least we wouldn't have to carry the cake through the crush of people on foot.

I could have canceled the meeting about the website, which was far from urgent on my priority list. But it would make Ox happy, and keeping morale high was crucial when we were so busy, so I decided to let it stand.

I worked on the three-tier cake, henna piping until the muscles in my hand were cramped from squeezing the piping bag. Finally finished, I stepped back to admire my handiwork, flexing my hand a few times to stretch the muscles. Isabeau had almost finished the dozens of sugar daisies on wire stems needed to top the cake. All we had to do was place them and it would be ready to roll.

I was focused on my work. Really, I was. But I also stayed alert for an opportunity to talk with Dwight or Sparkle about their interviews with Sullivan the day before. What can I say? I'm a caring boss.

It wasn't so easy to find a spare moment, though. Luckily, the temp agency had sent a replacement worker to cover for the man we'd lost. But that meant Dwight had to train the guy while staying on top of his own work, which took him out of circulation for most of the morning. Which left Sparkle doing double-duty in the King Cake production line, which also put her off-limits.

Shortly after the lunch hour passed (completely unnoticed by everyone but a couple of the temps), Ox started fussing about whether to change the schedule for delivery of the henna cake. Dwight had originally been on tap to drive across town. The cake was large and heavy, but not so heavy he'd have needed a second pair of hands.

I had to agree that pulling him away from his work seemed like a bad idea. He'd established a rapport with the new guy, and if he stepped away now, someone else would have to waste time getting up to speed.

While Ox and I debated the merits of sending this person or that, Sparkle stepped up to the plate with an offer that stunned us both. "I'll take it."

I turned toward her, mouth hanging open in surprise. Sparkle isn't much of a team player. She's a good employee, but like Abe, she's usually happiest on her own, just doing her own thing in her own little corner. So her offer startled me.

Ox looked equally stunned. "You'll—" He got that word out but the rest seemed to get stuck in his throat.

Sparkle curled her black-painted lips and peeled off the cap she'd been wearing over her raven black hair. Her eyes were heavily lined, and her stubby fingernails gleamed under a coat of glossy black polish. "I said I'll take it. It's going to be at least an hour before that last batch of cakes is cooled and ready to glaze."

She was right, but Ox and I didn't jump on the offer right away. I can't vouch for his thought process, but I ran a glance over her outfit and tried to imagine how the conservative middle-aged couple who were going to renew their vows after Sunday service at the Life Fellowship Community Church would react to her black corset with its bright red satin ties, the black leather shorts that revealed a long expanse of bare thigh, and the five-inch wedge boots with industrial-strength metal buckles from ankle to knee. Pulling the whole thing together was an ankle-length punk goth coat with leather cross-straps that looked as if they belonged in a torture chamber.

I didn't want her walking into the renewal ceremony as the sole face of Zydeco, but she so rarely volunteered for anything that I didn't have the heart to tell her no. So I did the only thing I could.

"Thanks, Sparkle," I said. "It's a heavy cake, so I'll go with you. Dwight's a lot stronger than either one of us, but I'm sure the two of us can handle it together." Which was true, and would also give me a chance to talk with her about Sullivan's visit the day before. Win-win.

Ox looked at me as if I'd lost my mind. "You want to go on this delivery?"

"Sure. Why not?" I countered with a friendly smile. I felt a little rush of excitement at the prospect of spending some time in the middle of the celebrations, even if I wouldn't get to stay for the parade.

"Right." Ox still looked skeptical.

I turned away before he could come up with an argument and caught Sparkle's eye. "Ready?"

She shrugged a listless shoulder and held out the keys to me. "Whatever. You want to drive?"

I shook my head as a show of faith and kept walking. "You drive. I'll ride along." It would be easier to focus on the questions I wanted to ask her that way. The two of us maneuvered the heavy cake across the design area and out the loading dock, securing it in the back of the van as if we'd done it a hundred times. While Sparkle started the van and cranked the AC to keep the cake cool, I poked my head back through the bakery door and asked, "Anybody need anything while we're out?"

"Food!" Estelle shouted from her corner of the design room. "I'm starving!"

I sketched a mock salute to show that I'd heard the request and hurried back to the van. I scrambled into my seat and we both buckled up for the ride. Sparkle drove in silence, but I'd expected that. She isn't much of a chatterbox.

I gave her a few minutes and then tossed a casual conversation starter into the space between us. "Nice," I said, nodding toward the bondage-worthy belt on the front of her coat. "Where did you get it?"

Sparkle slid a glance at me. "Why? You want one?"

"Maybe."

Her eyes smiled, which was more than I'd hoped for. "There's a store online," she said after a minute. "I can give you the website later."

"Perfect." I was dying to ask her about Sullivan's visit, but I didn't want to push. Sparkle doesn't trust easily, and if I came across as too eager, I could lose my chance. So I pretended to watch the city go by for a few seconds.

We paused at a stop sign near a parking lot filled with food stalls and craft vendors where hundreds of happy-looking people milled about. Some were in costume, some in street clothes, but all were laughing, singing, dancing, and clamoring to spend their money on trinkets. I thought about Ox's suggestion that I take time away to share this with Uncle Nestor and Aunt Yolanda and felt a pang of longing. Uncle Nestor would hate the crowds and the noise, but Aunt Yolanda would revel in the chance to experience something new.

As I so often did, I fell somewhere in between them. But as I looked at the bright colors and felt the beat of the music work its way into my bloodstream, I realized how much I was missing. I needed to learn how to relax and enjoy more. Otherwise, life was going to pass me by.

"What?" Sparkle's droll voice pulled my head around.

"What, what?"

"You want something. What is it?"

I grinned sheepishly. "I'm that obvious?"

"Duh. Whatever it is, just ask."

I turned toward her as far as the seat belt would let me so I could watch her reactions and make sure I wasn't crossing the line. "I'm just curious about why Detective Sullivan came to see you yesterday."

"He wanted to ask me some questions."

"I kind of figured that."

She took her eyes off the road for a second. "He just wanted to follow up on something I told the other cops I saw."

"Oh?" I tried not to look overly interested even though every one of my nerve endings was buzzing with curiosity.

Sparkle turned her attention back to traffic and we drove in silence for another block or two. "You want to know what it was?"

Yes! Casual shrug. "If you want to tell me."

She processed that for what felt like a very long time. It was all I could do not to unbuckle my seat belt and shake it out of her.

She turned a couple of corners and took us past a rundown strip mall. "That guy who died. Big Daddy? I saw him arguing with that woman he was with."

The buzz turned into a low hum. "Are you talking about his assistant? Violet?"

Sparkle shrugged. "I guess. Dark hair. Glasses."

"Sounds like Violet to me. Did you happen to hear what they were arguing about?"

Sparkle flicked a glance at me as she braked for a red

light. Traffic moving the other way crawled through the intersection at a snail's pace. "I did overhear a few things," she said. "Do you want to know what they were?"

"I would love to know."

Cars stopped moving entirely as a crowd of revelers on foot stepped off the curb and into the street. Sparkle didn't even seem to notice the confusion. "It sounded to me like that girl Violet had just figured out that Big Daddy wasn't going to leave his wife for her after all. She wasn't happy about it."

So I'd been right. They were having an affair. "What did she say?" I held my breath, hoping for something like, *I'll kill you*, or *Stand still so I can hit you over the head*.

The light turned green, but with the intersection full of cars and people, we weren't going anywhere. Sparkle put the van in park, prepared to wait. "She said they were through. And she said that she wasn't going to cover for him anymore."

The hum of anticipation turned to a low-pitched drone that seemed to pulsate in my blood. Or maybe that was the music blaring from some nearby loudspeakers. It was hard to tell. "Cover how? For what? Did she say?"

Sparkle shook her head. "I didn't hear that, but I got the feeling it had something to do with Musterion."

"Why? What gave you that impression?"

Another shrug as the light turned yellow again. A woman dressed as a gigantic purple-and-blue dragonfly floated past the van, followed by another wearing a flower arrangement on her head and then a hairy man in a mermaid costume. "You haven't seen anything yet," Sparkle said with what, for her, passes as a grin.

I must have looked confused, because she nodded toward a couple of harp-playing angels with gossamer wings and said again, "You haven't seen anything yet. We're just getting started."

I laughed and tried to take in the sights, sounds, and smells that bombarded me from every angle. "It's like a gigantic Halloween party, isn't it?"

Sparkle snorted. "Without the ghosts and goblins, I guess, and only about a million times better." We caught a break in traffic and we were moving again—if you can call a slow crawl through the crowded streets "moving." Spectators lined the parade route, waiting for the fun to begin. Music spilled into the air from loudspeakers and street musicians, and we moved from one song to another as we crept along the street.

We made it through the police barrier, but being one of the few vehicles allowed inside the Quarter didn't make it any easier to maneuver. In addition to the costumed crowds, dozens of street entertainers dotted the sidewalks, artists working in every medium I could have imagined—dancers, singers, jazz musicians, all adding to the experience.

"Is that all you wanted to know?"

Sparkle's question broke through my thoughts, but it took me a few seconds to remember what we'd been talking about. Oh yeah. The murder.

"You said that you thought Violet and Big Daddy were talking about Musterion. What gave you that impression?"

"I can't remember exactly," Sparkle said. "She mentioned a couple of names, but I don't remember what they were. Parry maybe? And Scott?"

I forced myself to look away from the spectacle on the street. "Could it have been Percy?"

Sparkle's black-rimmed eyes widened a bit. "Yeah. I think so. Why? You know him?"

"I know who he is, and I know that he was upset with

Big Daddy earlier in the evening. Do you remember what Violet said about him?"

Sparkle inched the van around one last corner and pulled into the parking lot of the church. She put the van into park and shut off the engine. "She said that she was going to back Percy's story, but I don't know what she meant by that."

Neither did I, but I meant to find out. "What about my uncle?" I asked. "Did you see him anywhere?"

She cut a glance at me. "Yeah, I did."

"Where was he?"

"Out by the pool."

My heart stopped beating for an instant, but I told myself not to panic. I already knew Uncle Nestor had been out by the pool, and so did the police. "What was he doing?"

"I'm pretty sure he was talking to Dwight," Sparkle said, and somewhere in the depths of her dark eyes I saw hope flickering. "I know that probably doesn't help."

"It doesn't hurt either," I assured her as I opened my door. "How did Sullivan react to hearing all of that?"

"He didn't. He just wrote it all down and thanked me for my time."

We closed our doors and met at the back of the van. I had one more question for her before we got back to work. "What time did you hear Big Daddy and Violet arguing? Do you remember?"

Sparkle opened the van's back doors and nodded. "Around midnight. It was just a few minutes after we served the King Cake."

The back door of the church opened and our contact came outside to greet us, and the time for thinking about the murder was past. I had to focus on getting the cake inside without smearing the icing or the piping, or knocking off any of the tiny daisies on the top tier.

I didn't know whether Sparkle's story helped Uncle Nestor or not. The argument she'd overhead seemed more like a motive for Big Daddy to get rid of Violet than the other way around. But it did prove that something was askew in Big Daddy's world—and for now that was enough.

Twenty-three

Sparkle and I maneuvered the henna cake through a narrow gate, across a small children's playground, and into the back door of the church's fellowship hall. In spite of the cool weather, I was red-faced and glistening enthusiastically by the time we finished. Sparkle, on the other hand, looked as cool and pale as ever.

On our way back, we stopped at The Joint for a mess of fall-off-the-bone ribs and tubs of creamy coleslaw and slow-cooked baked beans. It was a little out of our way, but we both agreed it was worth the effort. We loaded a couple gallons of sweet tea into the van with the food and headed back to Zydeco to feed the masses.

Traffic was heavier than ever when we finally pulled out of the French Quarter, but this time we were driving away from the parade zone, so we made better time. We still saw people in costume heading toward the festivities, but the carnival atmosphere faded a little more with every block.

Just as Sparkle stopped for a traffic light, a tall black man stepped off the sidewalk and strode across the street right in front of us. He was surrounded by a dozen other people, but I recognized him immediately. Tall. Dark. Denzelesque.

Percy Ponter.

Since we were stopped already, I made a split-second decision. Unbuckling my belt and grabbing my bag in one continuous motion, I waited until he'd reached the other side of the street and opened the van's door.

"Hey!" Sparkle cried as I hopped out into the middle of traffic. "What are you doing?"

"I just saw someone I need to talk to." The light turned and my sense of urgency spiked. "Ten minutes," I promised. "It's really important."

I could still hear music playing along the parade route, but we were far enough away that I could also hear snatches of conversation as people passed me. The air was rich with scents that should have clashed, but instead worked together in a weird way. Hot grease and the yeasty smell of beignets, spicy polish sausage with onions and peppers, shrimp on a stick, and popcorn, all being sold by street vendors. I thought I caught a whiff of cinnamon and curry powder as well, and it all mixed with the mustiness of old buildings.

"I'll call you on your cell in a few minutes," I yelled to Sparkle.

"What in the hell—" The rest of her question got lost when I shut the door between us.

I darted between cars, earning a couple of shouts, one raised middle finger, and three horn blasts. But I made it to the sidewalk in one piece, and that's what mattered. I slipped behind a chalk artist's easel and around the crowd of people watching him work. I had to walk quickly to keep up with Percy's long stride, but following him was easier than I'd expected. Even if he hadn't topped out at a head taller than almost everyone else on the street that day, his tailored and obviously expensive suit stood out in the mostly jeans-and-a-T-shirt crowd.

I tried to remember if Miss Frankie had told me anything about Percy in the weeks before the party, but the details of two hundred lives were all crammed together in my head. I pulled out my cell phone and dialed Miss Frankie's number. The phone rang a few times and the call went to voice mail. There was no answer at Bernice's house either, which probably meant that the two of them were out somewhere together. I just hoped they were staying out of trouble.

Two blocks later, Percy crossed the street and I got caught by the light. I bounced onto my toes so I could keep him in sight. He disappeared into a narrow building midway up the next block and my spirits sank. I shouldn't have hesitated. Now I might have lost my chance to approach him.

Sighing with frustration, I glanced to my left to check the flow of traffic and realized that Sparkle was sitting at the intersection in the Zydeco van. She was watching me with a strange look on her face.

When she saw that I'd spotted her, she rolled down the window. "What are you doing?"

I glanced back up the street to make sure Percy wasn't on his way back and stepped off the curb between two parked cars so I wouldn't have to shout. "I told you. I need to talk to someone. Please, just go around the block and park. I'll call you in a few minutes."

She chewed her bottom lip, considering. "Are you doing something dangerous?"

"No," I said quickly, even though I wasn't entirely sure I was telling the truth.

Her eyes narrowed suspiciously. The light turned green but she didn't move, even when a driver two cars back laid on his horn. "Let me park this thing and I'll come with you."

I shook my head and stepped back onto the curb. "I'll be fine," I assured her. "Now go!"

She didn't look convinced, but at last she put the van into gear and slowly turned the corner. I hurried across the intersection and began the task of trying to figure out which door Percy had gone through.

I'd passed five or six stores without seeing any sign of him when he suddenly appeared on the sidewalk right in front of me. I let out a nervous yelp and sidestepped quickly to avoid running into him.

He tossed an apologetic smile in my direction and prepared to step around me. While I tried to figure out what to say, I saw recognition dawn in his eyes, followed by a minibattle over whether to say hello or pretend not to recognize me.

After a few seconds his shoulders sagged with resignation, a result of his Southern breeding, I guessed.

He hid his hesitation behind a smile, as if he was delighted to see me. "Don't I know you?"

"Rita Lucero." I popped out a hand for him to shake and returned his smile, trying to look as if I was surprised to see him standing there. I won't ever win an Academy Award for my acting skills, but I think I fooled him. "We met at the Musterion party. I was the hostess. And you're . . . Percy? Is that right?"

Something wary flashed behind his eyes, but he kept that friendly smile in place as he nodded. "Of course. I knew you looked familiar."

I glanced at the building he'd come out of—a small neighborhood market. Nothing particularly sinister there. When I looked back at him, he was already making noises about leaving, so I jumped in with both feet. "I suppose you've heard about Big Daddy Boudreaux."

His smile faded and the wariness I'd noticed before spread from his eyes to his face. "Of course. It's been all over the news. It's a horrible thing. Just horrible."

"I met him for the first time at the party, but my mother-in-law has known him for years." I squinted into the setting sun, still trying to look casual and chitchatty. "His death must have come as a shock to you," I said. "It's not easy to lose a friend."

Percy put his hands in his pockets and glanced up and down the sidewalk, just looking for an excuse to walk away. "It was a shock, yes. But we weren't really friends. We were just both members of Musterion."

"Oh? Why did I think you were?"

"I couldn't say." He checked his watch and tried to look regretful. "It's been nice seeing you again. The party was great. You outdid yourself."

I wasn't finished with him yet, so I just kept talking, counting on his being too well bred to leave midsentence. "I guess this creates quite a problem for Musterion, doesn't it? Next year's captain is dead. What happens now?"

Percy reluctantly looked up from his watch. "It's unfortunate, of course, and the timing is delicate, but there are procedures in place to fill a vacancy. The board will take the appropriate steps after Big Daddy has been laid to rest."

I hadn't even thought about the need for a funeral, but now that Percy had mentioned one, I was pretty sure Miss Frankie would be going and she'd expect me to be there. I hate funerals, but it might be interesting to see how Big Daddy's family and friends handled saying their final good-byes.

I tried to look sad, not curious. "Of course. When will that be?"

"I think Susannah has decided on Wednesday afternoon. It will be in the obituary, of course, and we'll post the details on the krewe's website."

I wondered how many hoops they'd have to jump through to secure a venue large enough for Big Daddy's funeral less than a week before Mardi Gras, but didn't ask. I just made a mental note to talk to Miss Frankie about going together and got back to business. "It's all so sad. And for you especially."

"I'm afraid I don't understand. Why me especially?"

"You had unfinished business with him, didn't you?"

There was no mistaking the way Percy's spine stiffened at that or the cautious way he eyed me while he framed his answer. "That was all a misunderstanding. Nothing important."

"Really? It sounded important. You told him that you were going to settle something between you by the end of the night." It was a bold point to make and I was a little nervous making it, but I wasn't about to let him tell me a blatant lie and get away with it.

All pretense of friendliness vanished. "You must have misunderstood. It wasn't like that at all."

I gaped at him. "I was standing right there when you confronted Big Daddy. He'd just arrived at the party. You wanted him to talk to you that night. He tried to put you off until Monday. His assistant told you to call and make an appointment. Are you really going to claim I misunderstood all of that?"

He shifted his weight on his feet and glanced around nervously. "Look, Ms. Lucero, it's not what you think."

"Then what was it? What were you so angry about?"

"I wasn't angry. I was . . . concerned."

"Okay. Fine. What were you concerned about?"

"It wasn't important. Just some krewe business. And it's really none of your business."

Maybe not, but I wasn't going to let him sweep that conversation under the rug. "It was important enough for you to issue an ultimatum. What was it you said? Something about taking care of it one way or another?"

Percy forced a laugh and shifted his weight again so that he was facing me more fully. "Okay. Yeah. I know how that must have sounded, but it really wasn't a big deal. It *wasn't important.*"

"So then you won't mind telling me what he did to upset you."

"That's confidential," he said, his expression cold. "It was a krewe matter. I'm not at liberty to discuss it with you or anyone else." He paused. Shook his head and smiled with wry amusement that almost looked genuine. "Look, you have to know what Big Daddy was like. He was a hard man to pin down. Sometimes you had to get a little in his face to get his attention. But that's all it was, trust me."

Maybe. But not yet. "Did you talk to him again the night of the party?"

Percy shook his head and checked his watch again. "Not that I remember. Now, if you'll excuse me, I have an appointment."

"Just one more question. Please?"

I could tell that he wanted to leave, but he held back and looked at me with exasperation. "What is it?"

I was feeling some frustration of my own. So far nobody

had been able to provide Uncle Nestor with an alibi—or at least nobody was willing to admit they could. Maybe I was barking up the wrong tree. Maybe instead of trying to clear Uncle Nestor, I should be trying to figure out which of these people had the strongest motive to want Big Daddy out of the way.

So I blurted out the question I really wanted him to answer: "If you didn't kill Big Daddy, who did?"

Percy stared at me for a minute before letting out a whooping laugh. "If I—Are you serious? You're standing here in the middle of the street accusing me—Are you *nuts*, girl?"

"I'm just trying to find out who might have had a motive for wanting him out of the way. You knew him. You worked with him at Musterion. If you had to pick a name, whose name would it be?"

Percy put both hands on his hips and turned away so quickly he almost ran into a couple of elderly women coming out of a hair salon. The breeze caught his suit jacket and whipped it out from behind him, making him look like some kind of avenging superhero.

He took a couple of steps away from me, then turned around and came back toward me. "That's a dangerous game you're playing," he said, his voice low.

"It's not a game," I said back. "Who had a reason to want Big Daddy dead? I've heard that he was arguing with both his assistant and his wife that night, and with his brother. And of course, with you. Do you have any idea why he argued with the others?"

Percy barked a sharp laugh. "How would I know that?"

"I just thought you might. Susannah seemed to know about your krewe business. She told Big Daddy that he had to make things right with you that night, or else. And Violet told Big Daddy that she was going to back your story. What did she mean by that?"

Percy's eyes narrowed. "Where did you hear that?" He looked so angry, my heart skipped a beat.

And just in case he was a crazed killer, I wasn't about to give him a name. "From someone who has no reason to lie."

"And you think I do, is that it?" Percy sighed. "Look, Rita, there are a lot of people in this town who aren't exactly losing sleep over Big Daddy's death. But folks in these parts tend to close ranks against outsiders. Take my advice. Quit asking questions."

I didn't know how much of Percy's story to believe. He'd seemed genuinely angry the night of the party, but it was pretty clear he wasn't going to tell me why. He would certainly have the strength to use the statue as a weapon, but was the mysterious krewe business important enough to kill over? Susannah and Violet obviously knew about it, but I wondered who else knew and whether any of them would talk to me about it.

Having delivered his warning, Percy walked away, and I made no effort to stop him. Which turned out to be a smart decision. I set off in the other direction and pulled out my cell phone just as Sparkle came around the corner on foot. Her coattails billowed out behind her as she walked, and her skin looked paler than usual in the bright sunlight.

"Hey," she said when she saw me. "You all right?"

"Yeah. Fine."

"Did you get what you wanted?"

"Not exactly."

Sparkle and I trudged back to the van in silence. I probably should have been thinking about work, or about the murder, or about Uncle Nestor's health, or even trying to devise a new scheme to get an audience with Ivanka Hedge. But for once, all the other voices in my head were quiet, leaving me time and space to think about the way Sparkle had come to check on me.

I was surprised by my reaction to that. Frankly, it gave me the warm fuzzies, but I wasn't going to tell her that. Sparkle isn't the warm fuzzies type, and I wasn't about to repay her kindness with an insult.

Twenty-four

The bakery was in chaos by the time Sparkle and I made it through traffic and back to Zydeco. The new temp had moved all twenty-four chocolate roses for the Valentine's Day cake into a sunny spot near the window, which meant it was all hands on deck to make twenty-four more. Even our baker Abe, who typically kept vampire hours but had recently started coming in earlier to help with the workload, got into the act.

By the time we finished, Dwight was in a thoroughly sour mood, so I decided not to ask him about his interview with Sullivan. Maybe tomorrow.

I had plenty of other things to think about in the meantime. I'd been trading phone calls with Miss Frankie for a couple of days, but I hadn't actually talked to her since the night of the party. We finally made a plan for me to go over that night, once I got off work. Now that Percy had reminded me about it, I needed to talk to her about the funeral. Not to mention, with the date of the Bacchus parade approaching rapidly, I had to get serious about finding a costume, and Miss Frankie was my only hope to find anything remotely appropriate.

As I drove across town, I thought about what Percy had said and pieced it together with what I already knew. Presumably, Violet had been under the impression that Big Daddy was going to leave his wife for her. He hadn't exactly seemed lovey-dovey with her in my opinion, but there's no accounting for some people's choices. It appeared that she'd wanted a big jerk who treated her like dirt, and she was upset to learn that she wasn't going to get him all to herself.

Then again, maybe she hadn't actually been in love with Big Daddy. By all accounts, he had money . . . and lots of it. Maybe that's what Violet objected to losing. At some point during the party, she'd found out she wasn't going to get the future she'd been planning on. Either way, that put her high on my personal list of suspects.

And what about Susannah Boudreaux? If she'd found out that Big Daddy was cheating on her, that could give her a pretty strong motive for murder. I put her in the number two spot on my potential killer list and mentally wrote in Percy's name as number three. He wasn't off the hook. Not by a long shot.

I parked in Miss Frankie's driveway a little after ten that evening. She was waiting for me with a warm smile and a welcoming hug. "Come on back to the kitchen, sugar. I started coffee after you called, and I'm so glad you did. We've been needing to talk. I've warmed some rolls left over from lunch so we can nibble on those."

I was still pleasantly full from the ribs and slaw, but Miss Frankie's homemade rolls are a taste sensation not to be missed. I trailed after, admiring her black silk lounging pajamas with a birds of paradise design that exactly matched the shade of her hair. A pair of black sandals showed off her feet—the recipients of a recent pedicure—with toenails painted the same shade of burnt orange. Which, naturally, matched the shade of polish on her fingernails. At least I knew how she'd been keeping herself busy since the party.

I sat in the kitchen and inhaled the rich aroma of chicory coffee. It's the little things.

Miss Frankie splashed in the condensed milk and filled a mug for me, then put a plate with two steaming dinner rolls and a generous pat of butter on the table in front of me. She gathered some for herself and sat across from me, giving me a look. "So what is it, sugar? What brings you to my door in the middle of the night?"

"It's only ten," I said with a rueful smile. "But if you're ready for bed, I'll come back tomorrow."

"Not on your life. I've been wantin' to see you for a couple of days now. How you holding up?"

"I'm fine," I assured her. "Just a little tired. I'm hoping you can help me with my costume for the Bacchus parade next weekend."

"You don't have one?"

"Not yet," I admitted. "I know, I should have taken care of it weeks ago."

Miss Frankie smiled gently. "Don't you worry. I have plenty of things in the attic. We'll fix you up. Now are you going to tell me why you're here, or are you going to keep me guessing?"

"I left you a message about Big Daddy's funeral. Do you want to go together?"

"You know I do. Shall I pick you up around ten on Wednesday?"

"Perfect." I tore off a piece of roll and smothered it in

butter. "What's on your calendar for the next couple of days? Would you and Bernice have time to show Uncle Nestor and Aunt Yolanda around the city? They're stuck here in town, and I'm not going to have time to spend with them."

"Of course. I'm sure Bernice will be delighted. I'll call her first thing in the morning. Is that all?"

I nodded, then stopped and shook my head. "You could tell me what you know about the current Mrs. Boudreaux."

"Susannah?" Miss Frankie wrapped her hands around her mug and stared at the ceiling for a minute, gathering her thoughts together. "Susannah's an interesting woman," she said after a few minutes. "She was Bradley's third wife, you know."

"So I've heard. How long were they married?"

"Oh, goodness. I don't know. Four years? Maybe five."

"Was it a good marriage?"

"I always assumed it was. Bradley seemed content enough. At least he was as content as he ever got."

"But he was cheating on her," I said. "He was having an affair with his assistant."

Miss Frankie dismissed my comment with a wave of her hand. "Bradley wasn't the kind of man who does well in a committed relationship. He had a tendency to stray, but I'm sure Susannah knew that before she married him. After all, that's how she met him."

My lips curved slightly. "That doesn't necessarily mean she'd be okay with him cheating on her."

"If they'll do it with you," Miss Frankie said, "they'll do it to you."

"That's true," I said with a smile. "What about her? Was she faithful to him?"

Miss Frankie sipped, then put her cup on the table. "I

wouldn't know about that, sugar. She and I don't exactly run in the same social circle."

"Really? I thought you did."

"Gracious no. She's young and energetic and interested in all sorts of things I'm not. The only time I see her is at charitable events or Musterion functions, and then only to say hello. I've always suspected she's the reason Bradley didn't make it to Philippe's funeral."

"He did say they were on a cruise," I pointed out.

"Yes, I know. At times I thought she seemed a little threatened by Bradley's past, as if she felt the need to keep all his attention focused on her."

"So you think she purposely kept Big Daddy away from Philippe's funeral?"

"I'm saying I don't think she'd have rushed home for it, even if they could have."

That made her unlikeable, but not necessarily homicidal. I decided to get right to the point. "Do you think she could have killed her husband?"

Miss Frankie's eyes narrowed thoughtfully. "Of course she *could* have. The question is why would she?"

"Because he was cheating on her," I said. "And because he'd done something she was very unhappy about, and it had something to do with Musterion. Or at least with that guy Percy. Anyway, she gave Big Daddy an ultimatum to make it right, or else."

Miss Frankie's thoughtful expression turned grim. "Are you sure about that, sugar?"

"That's what Estelle overheard. Percy denies it, of course. He claims it was all about some unimportant Musterion business. But you heard what he said to Big Daddy at the party. It sure didn't sound unimportant to me. Did it to you?"

"Percy did seem upset," she admitted. "When did you talk to him about it?" she asked, looking a little worried.

I waved off her concerns. "I ran into him while Sparkle and I were delivering a cake. It was no big deal. The question is, why was Susannah Boudreaux so eager to throw suspicion on my uncle? She had to know Uncle Nestor didn't kill her husband."

Miss Frankie looked skeptical. "How would she know that?"

"Well, because . . . if she saw him do it, why didn't she stop him? Or at least let the rest of us know that something horrible was happening? Why wait until the police were there to make her big, dramatic accusation?"

"That's a good question."

I thought so, too, but neither of us had answers. I finished off one roll and changed my tack. "What can you tell me about Judd Boudreaux? Why would Big Daddy have been upset with him that night?"

Miss Frankie sighed softly. "There's a lot to be upset with when it comes to Judd, I'm afraid."

"He was Philippe's friend?" At her nod, I asked, "Why haven't I heard of him before? Why didn't Philippe ever mention him?"

"Probably because Judd's life is such a sad, sad story. Back when they were boys, Judd was a golden child. Smart. Funny. And so good-looking. He had a way with people and everyone loved him."

I could easily believe that. "He sounds like Philippe," I said, and for the first time I wondered if that's why I'd felt drawn to him when we met.

Miss Frankie nodded again. "They were very much alike, and they bonded almost the minute they met. They went everywhere together, like two peas in a pod. And they both looked up to Bradley."

I made a face. "Please tell me he was different back then."

She laughed a little. "Oh, yes. Both Boudreaux boys were. They got a little older and Judd started playing the guitar and writing music. He was talented, a rising star, and we all thought he'd end up being signed to some big-time record label. Thought we had us our own version of Elvis or something."

I tried to reconcile that dream with the Judd I'd met. If he'd been sober, it would have been easier. "So what happened?"

Her smile faded and deep sadness flooded her eyes. "It was such a terrible tragedy. He was driving a car late one night. He'd been drinking, of course, and he went off the road. The car flipped a few times and he was thrown free. The young woman with him wasn't so lucky."

My breath caught, and the pain I'd sensed in Judd flashed through my mind. Shades of Ted Kennedy, only apparently Judd hadn't bounced back. "She died?"

"Yes." Miss Frankie sighed, reliving a time that obviously still had the power to wound. "It turned out she was younger than she'd claimed to be. Only seventeen. Her parents were devastated. His parents were devastated. And Judd . . . well, that boy has never been the same."

"That's tragic," I said softly.

"You don't know the half of it, sugar. Judd pushed everybody away after that and started drowning his future in a bottle. Their mama took it hard, poor thing. Bradley stood by him, bless his heart. He was just about the only person Judd would let get close. Philippe tried to help, but Judd turned him away time and time again. Bradley never gave up though, even when their daddy threatened to disown Judd if he didn't straighten up, stop drinking, and get his life together."

"Which Judd refused to do?"

"I think he tried a few times, but his heart was never in it. I don't think he's ever forgiven himself for that girl's death. I'm not sure he ever will. For all his faults, Bradley stuck with him. He's bailed him out of trouble more times than I can count."

I tried to reconcile *that* image with the Big Daddy I'd met at the party, but it was even harder to do. One last question hovered on my lips. I didn't want to ask it, but I knew I had to. "Do you think Judd could have killed Big Daddy?"

"I can't imagine why he would," Miss Frankie said. "Big Daddy was just about all Judd had left."

Twenty-five

✣

Monday passed in a blur of work. I was at Zydeco by sunrise and crawled into bed well after midnight. Tuesday flew by as well, and it was Tuesday evening before I found a chance to ask Dwight about his interview with Sullivan and the conversation Sparkle said he'd had with Uncle Nestor. Before I could, though, Edie informed me that I was tardy for the website meeting, and that Ox was already upstairs with our website designers. I rushed into the meeting room, conveniently forgetting that I'd opted not to cancel the meeting and cursing Ox under my breath for scheduling the appointment at all. Frankly, there was no reason for me to be there, and not being all that web savvy, I found that most of what they talked about was over my head. But maybe that's because I was struggling just to keep my eyes open. By the time we all stood up to shake hands and declare our mutual delight to be working together, they'd been discussing meta tags, pixels, and search engines for an hour. That was an hour of my life I'd never get back. But Ox was smiling as he walked them to the front door, so I guess it was worth it.

The sun had gone down and most of the staff had packed it in for the day while Ox and I were otherwise occupied. "Isabeau and I are heading over to the Duke for a drink," he said. "Want to join us?"

I almost said no, but it occurred to me that (1) the Duke served a killer jambalaya, and (2) Dwight was probably there. So I nodded and said, "Sure. Sounds great." You know, for the greater good.

Uncle Nestor and Aunt Yolanda would be waiting for me at home, but I promised myself I'd be quick. Thirty minutes tops.

The Dizzy Duke has been the staff's after-hours hangout since the bakery opened almost three years ago. It's an ancient red-brick building squatting in the midst of a bunch of aging, sagging buildings two blocks east of Zydeco. The whole neighborhood smells faintly of rotting wood. That's not a smell I'm used to, coming from the western half of the country, where dry, not damp, is our cross to bear, but I'm learning to like it.

Ox held the door and I trailed Isabeau inside, pausing for a moment to let my eyes adjust to the low lighting and neon. Here, too, carnival season had left its mark. The whole bar looked as if it had been dusted with Mardi Gras colors. I spotted my favorite bartender, Gabriel Broussard (whom I've mentally dubbed "Hot Cajun"), behind the polished wood bar and waved a greeting. He scooped a lazy hank of dark hair off his forehead and grinned back. The house band was playing a low-key jazz number I didn't recognize— which wasn't saying much. I'm still new to that world, too.

Near the bandstand, someone had pulled a couple of tables together, and most of my staff lounged around them along with a couple of the temps. I was embarrassed to realize I'd forgotten their names. In my defense, I maintain that the brain can only hold so much information at one time. Mine was already chock-full.

I could see Dwight in the center of the group, his usually rumpled clothes looking worse than ever, his face gaunt and pale. We were all burning out fast, and I wasn't sure what to do about it. I made an executive decision and headed for the bar. Maybe I couldn't cut their hours or lessen the workload, but at least I could let them know how much I appreciated what they were doing.

Gabriel spotted me coming, tossed a towel over his shoulder, and leaned on the bar in a sexy sort of way to wait for me. I don't mind admitting that his obvious interest does a little something to my insides, but I was far too tired right then to dwell on it.

I hitched onto a bar stool and offered him a weary smile in response to the slow grin he aimed at me. "Well, well, well," he said as I tried to wrangle my purse onto the bar beside me. He ran a glance over me from head to toe. "Busy day?"

"Little bit," I said. "Why?"

"No reason, except you're a mess."

"Thanks. That means I look better than I feel." I patted the hair I knew had probably frizzed up like a Chia Pet and swiped at a couple of unidentifiable spots on my jeans.

"So what's going on to put that look on your face?"

I shrugged. "Just the normal stuff, times about ten. Surprise out-of-town guests and way too much work."

"You work too hard," Gabriel said. "You need to let your hair down and have a little fun."

"You're not the first person to tell me that," I said, struggling to hold back a yawn. "It's not as easy as it sounds."

"Sure it is. Just let yourself relax."

I propped up my chin in my hand and sighed. "I was raised by a professional worrier. It's in my genes."

"That's a cop-out."

He might have been right, but I was also too tired for self-examination. "Are you going to take my order, or what?"

"Fine. What can I get for you?"

"A virgin margarita," I told him. "And make *sure* it's a virgin. I'm driving." He started to turn away but I called after him. "And jambalaya. Please tell me you have some left."

"Sorry. It's shrimp étouffée tonight." The Duke isn't a restaurant, but the owners throw together a pot of something wonderful almost every night and serve it on a first-come, first-served basis. I miss out far more often than I actually score a meal.

"That's just as good," I assured him. "Make it a small bowl," I said, knowing there was probably a plate of something waiting for me at home. "And send a round of whatever everyone's having over there, on me," I said, jerking my chin toward the staff's tables. "They deserve it."

Gabriel wandered away and returned a few minutes later with a frosty glass on a fragile stem, filled with sweetly sour frozen slush. He knows me pretty well by now, so he doesn't have to ask if I want salt on the rim. If you ask me, drinking tequila without salt is almost sacrilegious; the rule also holds for anything that should have tequila in it, but doesn't.

I sipped cautiously. Not that I don't trust Gabriel to leave the alcohol out . . . but I don't. He's been known to pour with a heavy hand around me, so it's always better to be safe than sorry. When I didn't detect any tequila, I took a healthier swallow and sighed happily. I appreciate a skilled artist, no matter what medium he may work in.

Gabriel filled an order for one of the cocktail waitresses and gravitated toward me again carrying a bowl of étouffée brimming with shrimp, onions, jalapeños, and just enough rice to give it body. I dug in with gusto.

Étouffée-loving foodies have been known to debate certain aspects of the dish. Is it acceptable to use more than one kind of seafood, or does that make it gumbo? Should étouffée be made with a roux (flour and oil whisked together over heat until it's perfectly smooth) or without? Does a proper étouffée contain tomatoes or not? Personally, I loved the Duke's version: single seafood, includes a roux, and excludes tomatoes. It was a well-balanced and flavorful dish with just the right amount of kick to it.

While I shoveled shrimp, peppers, garlic, and rice into my mouth, Gabriel got to work on the order for the staff. "So I hear Big Daddy Boudreaux met his demise at your party," he said.

I stopped eating just long enough to stick out my tongue at him. "It was my party in name only, and I had nothing to do with his untimely demise." I plied a napkin over my mouth to make sure I hadn't left any unsightly bits. "What did people see in him anyway? I don't get it."

"You weren't blown away by Big Daddy's charm and sex appeal?"

I pretended to stick my finger down my throat and made a little gagging noise. "Seriously. I don't get it. What *did* people see in him?"

Gabriel laughed and added 7-Up to the whiskey in Ox's glass. "Money is power, baby. And power is sexy. It's always been that way."

I made a face. "That's a stupid rule."

"It's not a rule," he said. "It's a universal truth. Rules you can break or change. The truth just is. You can't avoid it."

I put down my spoon and took another mouthful of slush. "So you're a philosopher now?"

"I'm a bartender. It's part of the job description."

I licked a little salt from the rim of my glass. "Yeah? Well, I sure hope you're right. Otherwise, my uncle might be paying a very high price for a mighty big lie."

Gabriel pulled a couple of beers from the cooler behind him. "What lie would that be?"

He looked genuinely interested, so I unloaded on him. Bartender, remember? The next best thing to a therapist.

I told him about Big Daddy's behavior at the party and, in the interest of honesty, gave him a brief summary of the fight between Uncle Nestor and Big Daddy. I told him about meeting Judd and overhearing his conversation with Mellie. About finding Big Daddy floating in the pool. About the conversation between Big Daddy and Judd that Ox had witnessed and Mellie's search for Judd later by the pool.

I topped the whole thing off with a second virgin margarita and an account of the Widow Boudreaux making it sound like Uncle Nestor had killed her husband. By the time I'd finished sharing, I felt much better. "She has to know it's not true," I said as I wound down. "Uncle Nestor barely knew the guy. He had no reason to kill Big Daddy."

Gabriel had listened to my whole diatribe without interrupting. Now he cocked his head to one side and asked, "If she knows it's not true, why would she say it?"

"Your guess is as good as mine," I said, yawning again. "Because she's crazy? Because living with Big Daddy drove her nuts? Because she had to be out of her head to get involved with him in the first place?"

Gabriel cashed out a tab for a regular customer I recognized by sight and wiped a spill from the bar, glancing at me from the corner of his eye. "You're not thinking clearly. The woman's not crazy. She might not be the brightest star in the sky, but she's not stupid either. I'm guessing either she believes it's true, or she's lying to divert attention."

I sat up a little straighter and a couple of heavy gray clouds floated out of my head. "You mean, like, from herself?"

"Could be. My understanding is the Boudreauxes weren't getting along all that well."

I started to say something, but sudden realization wiped whatever it was right out of my head. "Wait a minute. Do you know them?"

"Sure. Doesn't everybody?"

"No, I mean, like really *know* them? Not just from the TV? That stuff you said about her not being stupid. How do you know that?"

He dropped a cherry into a tequila sunrise and gave me a half-grin. "I've spent some time with them."

"They're friends of yours?"

"Acquaintances."

"From where? How do you know them?"

He spritzed soda into a glass and reached for a straw. "We're all members of the same krewe."

You could have knocked me off that barstool with a feather. "You're a member of Musterion? Why weren't you at the party?"

"I'm not on the board this year. Not involved in the planning either, thank God. But I'll be there for the ball and for the parade."

"In costume?"

He grinned. "That information's on a need-to-know basis."

I was getting distracted, so I finished my étouffée and licked my spoon—discreetly, of course. With my stomach pleasantly full, I managed to string a few coherent thoughts together. "Does that mean you also know Ivanka Hedge and Richard Montgomery?"

"I do. I was on the parade committee with Rich a couple of years ago."

My exhaustion fell away and I bounced up in my seat. "Are you serious?"

He arched an eyebrow. "Would I lie to you?"

I shook my head quickly. "Not if your life depended on it. Could you introduce me to them?"

"I suppose I could."

"Will you?"

"That depends."

"On what?"

"On what's in it for me."

Everybody has an angle. "How about my undying gratitude?"

He did a little shruggy-thing with his mouth. "That's the best you can do?"

I shrugged back. "I don't know. Maybe." When he didn't relent, I did. "If that's not good enough, what *do* you want?"

"I'll think about it," he said.

"Come on, Gabriel. You have no idea how important this is to me."

He cleared away my bowl, but he didn't say a word.

"This could make or break me," I said. "I really need this."

He turned to a middle-aged man on a barstool a few feet away, pointedly ignoring me.

"Seriously?" I demanded.

He gave the man a beer and turned toward the kitchen. "I'll let you know," he said over his shoulder.

I stood on the rungs of the barstool to make myself taller. "*Seriously?* Oh, come on!" I called to his retreating back. But he just kept walking.

Twenty-six

❧

When Gabriel didn't come back after a few minutes, I picked up my glass and carried it across the room alongside the cocktail waitress who carried the tray laden with drinks for my employees. The group hailed me like some conquering hero and lifted their glasses in salute. I laughed, pleased with myself for doing the right thing. My ex-husband, their former boss, had been fun-loving and gregarious. Picking up the tab for a round of drinks had been second nature to him. I had to work a little harder at making those kinds of friendly gestures, so I always felt a little rush of pleasure when one of them worked out well.

The Duke had a respectable-sized crowd tonight, but it wasn't so busy that I felt claustrophobic. Laughter and chatter rose and fell all around me, but the group clustered around Zydeco's tables was by far the loudest. I positioned my chair close enough to Dwight's to get his attention easily, then waited through two or three songs before I made the effort. "Hey!" I said in the relative silence that fell between songs. "Could I talk to you for a minute?"

Dwight looked puzzled, but he nodded. "Sure. What's up?"

"Not here," I said. "Outside?"

He got to his feet and we wove our way back through the tables while the band's lead singer, an aging man with a graying ponytail and a shaggy Fu Manchu mustache, announced the band's next selection.

Outside, I led Dwight toward a park bench barely illuminated by a nearby streetlight.

He sat next to me, groaning a little from the effort. "I'm getting old," he said with a grin. "I'm starting to sound like my old man."

I scowled at him. "Don't say that. We're the same age."

He laughed and stretched his legs out in front of him. "It's gonna happen to us sooner or later. Might as well accept it."

"Never!"

He laughed again and linked his hands behind his head. "So what do you want to talk about?"

I didn't want to keep him away from the others for long, so I launched right in. "Sparkle told me that she saw you talking to my uncle by the pool the night of the murder. Do you remember what time that was?"

Dwight stretched then linked his hands together behind his head. "A little after midnight, I think. We'd already served the King Cake."

That matched Sparkle's memory and it gave me hope that I was on the right track. We hadn't discovered Big Daddy's body until after two. What were the chances that Uncle Nestor had stayed in the same spot for two hours? "Did you see anyone else out there?"

"Lots of people," Dwight said, cutting a glance at me. "Are you interested in someone in particular?"

"Yeah. Whoever killed Big Daddy."

Dwight grinned and settled more comfortably on the bench. "Wish I could help you, but I wasn't around when he was killed."

"Kinda figured that," I said. "Otherwise, you'd have told Sullivan and there'd have been an arrest by now." A breeze rustled the leaves overhead, a soft, soothing sound. Somewhere nearby a dog barked and music floated out from the Duke as the band began another song. "So what did you and Uncle Nestor talk about?"

"Nothing much. I asked how long they'd be staying, he asked whether you seemed happy."

"How did he seem?"

"You mean was he agitated or did I think he was about to rush off and kill somebody? No. Neither. He seemed normal. Like a guy at a party he didn't particularly want to be at."

"How drunk was he?"

Dwight gave me a funny look. "He wasn't. He might have had a little buzz on, but he wasn't drunk. In fact, when I saw him, he was nursing a ginger ale. Said it was doctor's orders."

That surprised me, but maybe it shouldn't have. I should have known that cutting out alcohol would have been on the same list as "take up jogging." I was just having trouble wrapping my mind around the idea of Uncle Nestor following those orders without argument. But had I actually seen him drinking a lot, or had I just assumed he was drinking because of his behavior? "Did he say anything about the fight he had with Big Daddy?"

Dwight shook his head. "Nope. In fact, he acted as if it never happened."

"I wish it had never happened," I said. "So that was it? That's all you two talked about?"

Again with the funny look on Dwight's face. "Not exactly."

I nudged him in the ribs with my elbow. "Would you just tell me? I'm too tired to pry it out of you."

"He's worried about you, Rita. He's afraid you're . . . how did he say it? Forgetting who you are and where you came from."

"That's ridiculous," I said, but I felt something tugging uncomfortably at my heart. The last thing I wanted to do was hurt Uncle Nestor or Aunt Yolanda, and I hated knowing that he felt that way. "What did you tell him?"

"I told him that you're cool," Dwight said. "That you've got it together and he shouldn't worry so much."

I grinned and slouched down on the bench so that I matched his posture. "Thanks. Did he believe you?"

"I doubt it."

So did I. We sat there for a moment in companionable silence before I asked the other question that had been nagging at me. "So what did Sullivan want to talk to you about?"

"He didn't tell you?"

I snorted a little. "Are you kidding? He hasn't said two words to me about the investigation. So what was it? And please don't tell me it was something that makes my uncle look even guiltier."

Dwight shook his head. "Nope. He wanted to know about an argument I overheard between Big Daddy and Judd Boudreaux."

"What argument? Where? When? Were they upstairs in the clubhouse?"

Dwight shook his head. "They were outside."

So not the secretive conversation Ox had seen them having. That made me sit up a little straighter. "Did you hear what they were arguing about?"

"Not the whole thing, but enough. Big Daddy was furious about something. He grabbed Judd by the shirt and shoved him up against the wall. Looked like he wanted to rip him apart."

The Big Daddy who'd been his brother's protector for all these years? What was that about? "You don't know why?"

Dwight shook his head. "I heard Big Daddy tell Judd that he'd crossed the line big-time this time, but that's about it."

I tried to imagine the soft-spoken Judd under assault from his big brother, and wondered what Judd had done that had made Big Daddy slip from protector to attacker. "What line?"

"I have no idea. Sorry."

"So what did Judd say?"

Dwight lifted one shoulder. "He was pretty sloshed. Kind of hard to understand. He just kept telling Big Daddy that he'd pay him back."

"Pay him back? Like get even?"

Dwight shook his head. "It sounded like they were talking about money to me. Judd said he'd pay Big Daddy back, and Big Daddy told him he'd better get it together by the next day or their asses would both be on the line."

"Judd owed Big Daddy money?"

"That's what it sounded like to me."

For the first time, I gave some serious thought to what the financial situation was in the Boudreaux family. According to Judd, they'd been members of The Shores since he was a boy, so I assumed they were old money. But how was that money split, and who controlled it?

"Then what?"

Dwight shrugged again. "They argued like that for a while and then Big Daddy told Judd he was sending him to rehab. He said this was the final straw."

I couldn't imagine the Judd I'd met getting angry enough to whack his own brother over the head and push him into the pool, but could I have been wrong? "How did Judd react to that?"

"I don't know. Estelle asked me for help with something she did to her camera, and I went back inside. By the time I went back outside, they were gone."

I sat there for a minute, taking that all in and weighing it against what Miss Frankie had said about the relationship between Judd and Big Daddy and what Ox had already told me about the two of them the night of the party. "What about Uncle Nestor?" I asked when I couldn't make all the pieces fit. "Did you see him after that?"

Dwight shook his head. "Sorry."

"How late did you stay?"

"It took me half an hour or so to figure out what Estelle did to the camera. I left right after that." He got to his feet and stood over me for a moment. "Just do me a favor, okay?"

"What's that?"

"Be careful. If you ask me, all the Boudreauxes are crazy as loons. If one of them did kill Big Daddy, they won't hesitate to hurt anyone else who gets in their way."

His warning sent a chill up my spine, but I nodded. "Don't worry about me."

"I'm serious," he said. "The police know everything I just told you. Just let them do their jobs."

"I'm not trying to get involved in their investigation," I assured him. "I'm just trying to clear my uncle."

He walked away a minute later, and I stood there trying

to decide whether to go back inside or head home. I craved some alone time, but Uncle Nestor and Aunt Yolanda had been on their own too much. I was quite possibly the world's worst hostess. It was time to do something about that.

Twenty-seven

❧

I parked three doors away from my house at a little after nine, relieved to see that the lights were still on. I found Uncle Nestor and Aunt Yolanda at the dining room table, talking about something over a pot of decaf. Aunt Yolanda bounced up when I came through the door and spent the next few minutes warming me up a plate, bringing me silverware, and fussing over me in a way I hadn't been fussed over in months. Uncle Nestor didn't say much, but I caught him watching me fondly a couple of times. I hoped that meant that we were okay again.

After I was finally tucked in with a plate of homemade tamales, chili *verde,* and tortillas, all my doubts about their feelings for me faded away. I ate quickly, a little embarrassed that I could put away so much of Uncle Nestor's food after the étouffée at the Duke. In my defense, it had been a small bowl, and the only other thing I'd eaten all day was a blueberry streusel muffin so long ago it seemed like I'd had that in the previous century.

The chili was perfect, flavorful and garlicky, with a bite from the jalapeños that came with a slow after-burn. The tortillas were soft and warm. I tore off one piece after another, using them to scoop up the chili in the time-honored fashion of my childhood. I peeled away the hot corn husk wrapping from the tamales and enjoyed an entirely different taste sensation as the rich flavor of chili *rojo* exploded on my tongue. It was spicy without being hot, and the bland *masa* wrapping acted as the perfect complement.

If ever a meal expressed love, that one did. My stomach was comfortably full as I wiped up the last of the chili with a scrap of tortilla, and so was my heart. I missed my childhood home and the life I'd had in Albuquerque, but I loved living on my own for the first time ever, and my new career was more satisfying than anything I'd ever done. I suppose there are no easy answers to life's hard questions.

They filled me in on their day—a stroll around the neighborhood, a stop at the corner market two blocks down, and phone calls home. I filled them in on mine, minus the stop at the Duke.

The mood was warm and cozy and I hated to disturb it, but there were too many unanswered questions between us. Besides, Uncle Nestor was in a good mood, and I didn't want to let the opportunity to ask a few simple questions slip away. While Aunt Yolanda told me about Santos's oldest son taking a tumble from his bike, I carried my dishes to the sink, rinsed them, and stacked them next to the dishwasher. When she'd finished, I broached the subject uppermost in my mind as gently as I knew how.

"I've been talking to a couple of my employees, Sparkle and Dwight. They had some interesting things to say about the night Big Daddy Boudreaux was killed."

"Sparkle," Uncle Nestor said. "She's the one with the dark hair, am I right?"

"That's right. And Dwight's a friend from pastry school."

"The dirty one," Uncle Nestor said.

I was impressed that he'd made an effort to put names with faces. Resuming my seat, I put my feet up to take some of the pressure off the waistband of my jeans, which had suddenly become too tight. "He's not dirty. He's just . . . cleanliness challenged. And he's very talented."

Aunt Yolanda smiled indulgently. "He seems like a very nice young man."

"He is," I agreed. "But that's not what I want to talk about." I made eye contact with Uncle Nestor and said, "I know why you fought with Big Daddy. You might as well tell the police. If I found out, they will, too."

He looked back at me with an expression of supreme innocence. "What makes you think I haven't already told them?"

"Oh, I don't know. Maybe the fact that Sullivan told me you hadn't."

"And you believe him over me?"

"He has no reason to lie about it," I said without blinking. "So what's up, *Tío*? Why are you still refusing to talk about it?"

Uncle Nestor made a noise like a low growl and turned his attention to my feet on the chair. "Why are your feet on the furniture? Didn't we teach you better than that?"

"My house, my rules." I grinned broadly as I repeated the phrase I'd heard too often as a kid. He was trying to distract me and I wasn't going to let him get away with it. "Now, answer my question."

He scowled up at me and blinked a couple of times. "What question?"

"The one about why you're still refusing to talk about the fight you had with Big Daddy the night he died."

Blink. Blink . . . Blink.

Aunt Yolanda shot me a warning glance. "I don't think we should talk about that just now."

"Well, I do," I said as gently as I could. "Staying silent isn't helping him, *Tía*." I turned back to Uncle Nestor. "If you're trying to protect Aunt Yolanda, she's not as delicate as you might think. She can handle whatever you have to say."

Blink, blink.

I sat up and put my feet on the floor, but only because I was too agitated to sit still. "How about I start then? Big Daddy made some disgusting comments about Aunt Yolanda and about me. You heard them. Maybe he even said them right to you. It made you angry and you blasted him in the face. How am I doing so far?"

Aunt Yolanda looked from Uncle Nestor to me and back again. "What comments?"

Blink.

"You got into that fight because of me?"

Blink, blink.

"Look," I said, hanging on to what little patience I had left, "I understand that you're kind of freaked out after your heart attack—which is another thing we need to talk about, by the way. And I understand that you're worried about me, which you don't have to be. And I can understand losing your temper, especially if you were drinking."

Aunt Yolanda rounded on him, eyes flashing with anger. "You were drinking?"

Uncle Nestor shot me a look, and his wife a smile, clearly intended to placate her. "I wasn't drinking, sweetheart. I promised I wouldn't."

"I just meant that I could almost understand what he did *if* he had been under the influence," I assured her. "But I don't understand starting a fight with one of Miss Frankie's guests if you were stone-cold sober. And not just a fight. You hit him twice while I was standing there, and you went after him again later. *And* somebody heard you threaten to kill him."

His eyes flashed to mine, and for the first time I thought he actually looked worried.

"That's right," I said, pressing my advantage. "Have I got your attention now?"

He sat ramrod straight, his chin held high, his dark eyes narrowed in disapproval. "I was raised to respect women, and that means that there are some subjects a man won't discuss in front of them."

Aunt Yolanda made a noise with her tongue. "What did that stupid man say that you think I can't handle?"

Blink.

He was good, but I wasn't buying it. "If that's the case, why aren't you talking to the police? Sullivan's not a woman. You could tell him what happened."

Uncle Nestor's gaze flicked to mine quickly. "Didn't I teach you to respect your elders?"

"Didn't your mother teach you to tell the truth? Come on, *Tío.* What's really going on?"

He stood, and for a moment I thought he was going to leave the room. To my surprise, he took a couple of steps, then turned back to face us both. "It was that wife of his," he said after a lengthy pause. His haughtiness had evaporated and he looked downright miserable. "I don't know what was going on between the two of them, but she . . ." He slid an unhappy look at Aunt Yolanda. "She kissed me."

My mouth fell open and it was my turn to stare. *Blink, blink, blink.* "She *what*?"

"I didn't know who she was at the time," he said as if that explained everything.

Aunt Yolanda got to her feet, walked across the kitchen, and slapped him across the face. Hard. I was still trying to process what he'd just said, and I waited for her to laugh, to smile, to give some indication that she found the whole thing amusing.

She muttered something under her breath and swept up the stairs before I could wrap my mind around what was happening. When she'd disappeared, I turned my startled gaze back to my uncle and whispered, "What was that?"

Uncle Nestor looked unhappier than I'd ever seen him. "I didn't want her to know. It wasn't anything. It didn't mean anything."

"Well, of course not. Susannah kissed you, not the other way around. Right?"

He nodded, but he didn't exactly look at me, and that gave me a bad feeling inside. "What's going on, *Tío*? What don't I know?"

"It's nothing."

"Are you kidding me?" I jumped out of my chair so fast it rocked back on two legs before slamming onto all four again. "Aunt Yolanda just slapped you. She's royally pissed. It doesn't take a rocket scientist to see that something's wrong here."

"We'll work it out," he said, his voice barely audible.

"Work what out? What's there *to* work out?"

"It's nothing," he said. He turned away, grabbed his jacket

from the back of a chair, and disappeared out the front door, leaving me gaping after him.

I had no idea what was going on between them. I'd never seen them like that, not with each other and not with anyone else. But there was one thing I knew for sure—it most definitely wasn't "nothing."

Twenty-eight

❧

Miss Frankie sailed into Zydeco Wednesday morning wearing a tan linen suit, serviceable pumps, and a wide-brimmed hat that looked as if it belonged at the Kentucky Derby. Her nail color had been changed to match, and her hair had been teased and sprayed, artistically arranged around the hat. She looked sensational.

I looked noticeably less spectacular in a plain navy dress and a pair of low heels, hair pinned up haphazardly, and a whiff of makeup and lip gloss. I hadn't slept well after my conversation with Uncle Nestor and Aunt Yolanda the night before. I was so tired, my eyes felt gritty, and I ached all the way to my bones. I didn't want anyone to ask me why, so I kept a smile on my face and tried to act as if my most pressing concern was how much modeling chocolate we'd need for the next month.

I'm not sure I actually fooled anybody, but at least the

members of my staff pretended not to notice. Miss Frankie went along just until we drove out of the parking lot. "What's wrong, sugar? You look like something the cat dragged home."

I rolled a look of mock annoyance in her direction. "Thanks. Nothing like a sincere compliment to start the day off right."

She waved a hand in the air and weaved between two slower-moving cars. "You know what I mean. You want to talk about it?"

She knew me too well. I hesitated over how much to tell her about Uncle Nestor's encounter with the third Mrs. Big Daddy, but reasoned that the more she knew, the more she could help me. "I found out last night that Susannah Boudreaux kissed Uncle Nestor at the party."

Miss Frankie looked away from traffic for a split second. "I see."

"*She* kissed *him*," I said, wanting to be very clear on that point. "He didn't even know who she was. At least not at the time. He found out later, of course."

"Did he happen to mention why she kissed him?"

I shook my head. "We . . . uh . . . we didn't get that far."

Miss Frankie seemed to understand the rest without being told. It's one of the things I love about her. She took one hand off the wheel and covered one of mine in a comforting gesture. "Well, I'm sure it was nothing."

"Yeah," I said. "Nothing."

"Your uncle is very much in love with your aunt," Miss Frankie said. "It's obvious to everyone."

"Except maybe to her," I mumbled.

She darted in and out of traffic again, taking chances I never would have taken. When she put on her turn signal, I planted my feet to keep my balance as we sailed around the corner. "I take it Yolanda wasn't pleased by the news?"

"That's an understatement. They're not even speaking this morning."

"Well, I know it's hard on you to see them at odds, but I wouldn't worry. They've been together a long time. I'm sure they've weathered storms before, and they'll get through this one, too."

I put on a brave face and offered up a smile, but it felt as fragile as spun sugar. "I'm sure you're right." There was nothing else either of us could say about that, so I changed the subject and told her about my conversation with Dwight the night before. "If Big Daddy was so protective of Judd," I said when I'd finished, "why would he threaten to send him to rehab the night he died? Tough love?"

Miss Frankie let up on the gas a little and shook her head. "That doesn't sound like Bradley. He believed in handling such things privately, and he always thought that Judd would come around if he had the support of his family."

"I think he was a little misguided on that score," I said. "And anyway, I hear he *did* threaten Judd with rehab, and told him that he'd helped for the very last time."

"That's odd," Miss Frankie said, and our speed dropped a little more. We drove in silence while she tried to process the idea of Big Daddy and Judd at each other's throats. "Whatever it was Judd got himself into," she said after a while, "it must have been big. Bradley wouldn't have threatened him that way if it wasn't."

That's exactly what I was thinking. Neither of us said it, but I knew we were both wondering the same thing: Was the trouble Judd got himself into big enough to kill over?

Reporters were camped outside the church, trying to capture the faces of the mourners who'd gathered to say a last farewell to Big Daddy. Luckily, they had no real interest in Miss Frankie and me. We sailed past the cameras and into the cool, dark foyer of the church, where friends were gathered, greeting one another with the appropriate amount of somberness.

Miss Frankie hugged and kissed her way toward the sanctuary, and within minutes, I was following her down the center aisle toward a pew near the front. Flowers filled the room with a scent I'd prefer never to smell again—that odd mix of mums, carnations, and roses that always brings back memories of my parents' funeral. I'd have preferred a seat in the back, but I wasn't going to argue with her.

Bernice Dudley had saved us a seat directly behind the single row that had been reserved for family. We barely had time to agree what a tragedy Big Daddy's death was before the organist began playing and the side doors opened.

We all stood while the pallbearers, none of whom I recognized, carried Big Daddy in for his last public appearance. It seemed that Judd should be one of them, but he shuffled behind the coffin with a black-veiled Susannah on his arm.

The look on his face made my heart twist. I knew how it felt to be alone in the world. It's a feeling I wouldn't wish on anyone.

Mellie came in next with two boys and a young girl, who I assumed were her children from her marriage to Big Daddy. When they were settled, the pastor rose to the pulpit and began the service.

I wish I could say that I figured out who killed Big Daddy while I sat there, but the truth is that it was an entirely unremarkable funeral service. A couple of Musterion members spoke about all the good things Big Daddy had done for the krewe, making it sound as if he'd almost single-handedly planned and executed a fund-raiser last month for the krewe's favorite charity and gushing over how much money he'd raised on their behalf. One longtime employee told us all about Big Daddy's generosity toward the people who worked for him, and another related the story of how Big Daddy had given him a second chance after a brush with the law.

Trying not to be obvious about it, I looked around for the other people on my list of suspects. I spotted Violet a couple of rows back, mostly hidden behind the handkerchief she was using to mop up the tears. I didn't see Percy in the very back row until the service was over and I stood to leave.

The family was ushered out behind Big Daddy, and the rest of us followed slowly. Miss Frankie stopped just outside the doors to speak to an old friend but I slipped away, hoping to find Judd and offer a word of condolence before he left for the cemetery.

I circled around the church toward the side entrance, where the hearse was parked. Apparently, I turned too soon because I found myself in a little garden area between two wings of the E-shaped church. I was trying to decide whether it would be quicker to cut through the inside or go around the outside when I heard voices. One of them belonged to a woman, the other to a man. The choked sobs in the woman's voice made me instinctively slip behind a flowering shrub so I wouldn't intrude on her grief.

"I'm sorry," she said, hiccupping slightly. "It's just that I don't know what I'm going to do now. He was my whole world."

After hearing that, I just *had* to peek around the bush to see who she was. I was a little surprised to see Violet and the dark-haired man in horn-rimmed glasses, whom I recognized from the party with Susannah. I hadn't noticed him inside during the service, but here he was, acting all best-friend-forever-like with Violet.

He gave her a there-there pat on the shoulder, but he seemed almost distracted as he did. "Well, you weren't *his* world. But I guess you finally figured that out."

That was harsh. Even if I did agree with him.

She wiped a fresh batch of tears from her cheeks and sighed. "I know what you thought of him, Tyson. But he wasn't a bad man. He was just . . . busy. Preoccupied. Important."

"In his own mind," Tyson muttered. When she gave him a look of hurt mixed with horror, he relented slightly. "You're going to be okay, Violet. She doesn't hate you. I'll talk to her and make sure she lets you stay on."

She? They had to be talking about Susannah. Interesting.

Violet choked out a disbelieving laugh. "She's not going to want me around, Tyson."

"What I know," he said, "is that you worry too much. Let me take care of it."

Definitely Susannah. I was sure of it. But who was this guy and why did he think he could influence Susannah's decisions? And what was his connection to Violet?

Their voices dropped and the noise of car doors slamming and engines starting drowned out whatever they said next, but eventually Tyson reached for the door handle. "Are you okay now? They're going to be wondering where we are."

"Not *we*," Violet said with a tremulous smile. She let out a sigh that seemed to come from the depths of her soul. "She'd be happy if I fell off the face of the earth."

Tyson clenched his jaw. "Don't be so melodramatic, Violet."

But Violet couldn't help herself. She blew her nose and lifted her chin, but shudders, the residue of her bout with tears, shook her shoulders. "She's got it all now, doesn't she?"

Tyson pulled open the door and waved her inside. "That's the part you never understood, kid. She always did."

The family limousines were gone by the time I got to the parking lot, and Miss Frankie was waiting for me wearing a worried frown. "Gracious, sugar, you gave me a start. One minute you were there with me, and the next you were gone. Wherever did you go?"

"I was hoping to say a few words to Judd," I told her. "I didn't make it."

I told her about the conversation I'd overheard between Tyson and Violet. "Who is he anyway? Do you know him?"

She thought for a minute before shaking her head. "I can't say. Not anyone I know. He's probably an employee at one of Big Daddy's auto dealerships."

That made sense. But no matter who he was, the conversation had convinced me of one thing. Violet might have had a strong motive for killing Big Daddy, but I believed that her motive to keep him alive was even stronger.

Twenty-nine

Uncle Nestor and Aunt Yolanda were asleep when I got home that night and barely speaking when I left for work on Thursday morning. When they did speak to each other, I almost wished they hadn't. The sharpness in their voices reminded me of the way Philippe and I had spoken to each other before we separated. It saddened me.

I tried to hold on to Miss Frankie's assurance that my aunt and uncle had weathered other storms and come out together on the other side, but the knowledge that Philippe and I hadn't made it, as so many couples didn't, frightened me. I'd seen Uncle Nestor and Aunt Yolanda at odds with each other over the years, but I'd never seen them like this.

Thankfully I hit the ground running when I got to Zydeco, leaving me little time to think about family issues or the murder. Since we had only one more weekend until Mardi Gras, everyone gathered in the large room upstairs for our second production meeting of the week. We ran through the schedule, parceling out the work that needed to be done and haggling good-naturedly over who got to do what. I tried to rotate people in and out of the production line, giving everyone an equal chance to work on other orders.

I put Sparkle and Isabeau to work on a butter cake with blueberries and a Bavarian cream filling for a baby shower coming up next week: two tiers, stacked, covered in baby blue fondant and a myriad of white fondant stars. On the top tier they'd attach a molded gum-paste cow jumping over a sculpted cake moon. An adorable design, if I do say so myself. Getting the faces cute enough for a baby shower would have been challenging for most of us, but Sparkle should be able to knock them out easily.

Ox and Estelle would be tackling a tart orange divorce cake with orange custard filling scheduled for delivery on Wednesday. Two tiers again, but this cake wouldn't be stacked. The design called for a flat bottom tier sporting a gum-paste groom with one foot on the top tier, as if he was kicking the bride and her half of the cake to the curb. The little gum-paste bride would be clinging to the side of her tilting tier.

The design was Ox's suggestion, given that the fellow throwing the party was a jilted husband, and I'd approved it wholeheartedly last week. Today, with Aunt Yolanda barely speaking to Uncle Nestor, I didn't find it nearly so amusing.

Dwight and I would work on a four-tier tropical cream cake in a Mardi Gras design. We'd start with sponge cake, lightly dab each layer with coconut syrup, and then spread Bavarian cream, fresh mangoes, and pineapple between the cakes to create each tier. We'd stack the tiers and cover the whole thing with white fondant, then finish the design by applying stripes and harlequin shapes on alternate layers and topping the cake with a gum-paste Mardi Gras mask.

With those details settled, I dismissed the staff so they could get to work and gathered up my notebook and coffee cup, intending to do the same. As I stood, I realized that Ox was still sitting at the end of the table, watching me.

"Have you had a chance to look at the web page?" he asked.

I groaned aloud and shook my head. "Don't start. Please. You have no idea how crazy things have been since my uncle and aunt showed up."

"I'm asking you for fifteen minutes. Thirty tops. Why is that so difficult?"

"Because it is." I shoved a stray lock of hair out of my face and sighed. "Why don't you just approve it yourself? It will save us all time."

"Are you sure you're okay with that?"

"I wouldn't have suggested it if I wasn't." I shoved my chair in the general direction of the table and started toward the door.

"And the blog?"

"Is going to have to wait," I said. He made a noise and I whipped back around to face him. "Seriously, Ox, I can't do it right now. You're just going to have to be patient."

He held up both hands in surrender. "Fine. Whatever. Do I dare ask about the photos from the party?"

It was on the tip of my tongue to say no, but the sudden thought that Estelle might have captured something useful made me cut myself off before I got the word out. Admittedly, it was a long shot, but it was worth a look. "I'll get to them tonight. Will that be soon enough?"

Ox's eyes narrowed as if I'd confused him. "Really? You don't want me to take them? I probably have more time than you do."

"I'll do it," I said as I sailed out the door.

He came after me. "Why so cooperative all of a sudden?"

I grinned at him as I started down the stairs. "You've been complaining because I don't want to help. Now you're complaining because I do?"

He clattered down the stairs behind me, his big feet in their heavy boots making enough noise to raise the dead. "Call me cynical, but I'm highly suspicious of this sudden turnaround."

We reached the bottom of the stairs, so I turned to face him. Edie was away from her desk, leaving us alone in the foyer. "Okay, so it's not entirely about the website. It just occurred to me that Estelle might have gotten some shots of Big Daddy and his killer. I figured I might as well kill two birds with one stone—so to speak."

He frowned so hard wrinkles ran from his eyebrows to what used to be his hairline. "I knew it."

"What's the big deal?" I asked. "I'll look at the pictures. Pick out a few for the website and check for evidence at the same time. You'll get what you want, and hopefully I'll get what I want. We both win."

"Right."

I turned to walk away and another idea hit me squarely in the face. "Hey, Ox?"

He was halfway to the door already, but he wheeled around when I called him. "Yeah?"

"You did such a great job with the design for the divorce cake. How'd you like to throw together something that says, 'Sorry for your loss'?"

The worry wrinkles reappeared on his forehead. "You want a bereavement cake?"

"Yeah. Just something simple. Something appropriate

for a recent widow who may or may not have murdered her husband."

"You're going to take Big Daddy's wife a cake?"

"Why not? Where I come from, taking food to the family after a funeral is the socially accepted way to deal with death. Don't they do that around here?"

Ox gave a grudging nod. "But it's still a bad idea, Rita."

"Maybe. But it's the only one I've got. I need to get a foot in her door somehow."

"No. You don't."

"Yeah. I do. I can't explain why, but I really need to talk to her. Can you have it ready for me by this afternoon?"

Ox took a step toward me, his eyes clouded with concern. "Let the police handle it."

"They can't handle this," I told him. I held up my right hand, as if I were taking an oath. "I swear, it's not about the murder. I need to talk to her about something else."

And it was true. Mostly. I really did want to ask what happened between her and Uncle Nestor. Maybe I could help smooth things over for my miserable *tío*. And if the subject of Big Daddy's murder came up? Well . . . I'd have to talk to her about it, wouldn't I? I wouldn't want to be rude.

Thirty

After work that evening I found Big Daddy's address on the guest list and followed my GPS instructions to a house set back from the road behind a grove of trees. Now that I was here, I started second-guessing my plan.

The cake Ox had pulled together for me in between his regular duties sat on the seat beside me in a box bearing Zydeco's cartoon alligator logo. The cake itself was nothing fancy. He'd found a spare hummingbird sheetcake—a local favorite—in the kitchen and he'd decorated it tastefully with a few pastel peach flowers in one corner. No cheesy hand-piped sentiment. Just cake. It was perfect for what I had in mind.

I turned onto the driveway and wound through forest until the house came into view. A handful of cars were scattered around—two parked in front of the house on a circular drive, two more in front of a garage at the side of the house, and a huge white SUV nosed up next to a serene-looking garden with a lighted fountain surrounded by some exotic-looking broad-leaved shrubbery.

I gathered up the cake and put on a sympathetic expression as I approached the door. A tall, thin man with horn-rimmed glasses and an impatient expression answered my ring and glared down at me from a step above.

Tyson. Well, well, well.

"Yes?"

"I'm here to see Mrs. Boudreaux. Is she in?"

"She's in, but she's not available. Is there something I can help you with?" The look on his face said he'd rather do anything but.

I shook my head, but I didn't back down. Now that I'd run into him, my curiosity was in overdrive. "I really need to see her," I said. "It's important." And when that didn't impress him, I added, "I only need five minutes of her time."

He glanced over his shoulder—the first sign that maybe he didn't actually rule the world and had to take orders from someone else. "I'll see if she's up to seeing you. Your name?"

"Rita Lucero."

Nothing.

"From Zydeco Cakes." I held up the cake box as if that might make a difference.

He still didn't move away from the door.

Desperate times call for desperate measures, so I tried a different strategy. "Her husband passed away at my party," I explained. "I feel so horrible I just won't be able to rest until I offer my condolences."

"The funeral was yesterday," he said.

"That's why I waited until today," I said back.

He still looked hesitant, but he motioned me inside and shut the door behind me. But that's where he drew the line on hospitality. He held up a hand to indicate that I wasn't to come any farther inside and said, "I'll see if she's feeling up to visitors."

I wondered if he'd be so bristly if I told him I'd been in the church garden yesterday. Even if Susannah didn't actually hate Violet, she still might not like learning that her cabana boy was on friendly terms with her husband's mistress.

He kept me cooling my heels for a good fifteen minutes before he came back. His expression was so sour, I expected him to show me out the door again. I could feel aggression pouring off him in waves. Instead, he growled, "Come this way."

I kept my own face expressionless, but inside I did a little skippy dance of joy and followed him through the house and onto a screened porch filled with potted ferns and wicker furniture. Susannah Boudreaux sat on a swinging daybed suspended on chains from the ceiling.

She wore black clam diggers and an open sweater of soft, draped material over a pastel pink tank top. Her legs were tucked under her, and she looked pale and wan, as if sitting was almost too much for her. But her burgundy-colored hair had been carefully teased and sprayed, and her makeup appeared flawless. Which made me think she was stronger than she was letting on.

She offered me a limp hand when I approached, and waved me toward a chair.

I put the cake box on the coffee table and sat. "Thank you for seeing me. I'm so sorry for your loss."

"Thank you." Her voice was soft. Barely above a whisper. A far cry from the fishwife shriek she'd used when she told the world about Uncle Nestor attacking Big Daddy. "You brought me a cake?"

"Just a little something," I said. "It's what I do."

She smiled sadly. "Well. Thanks." She blew her nose and

tucked the tissue into her pocket. "Tyson said you wanted to see me about something important?"

I nodded and glanced toward Tyson, who stood in the doorway, arms crossed and glaring at me from behind his glasses. I took a page out of Miss Frankie's book and dusted my next comment with sugar.

"It must be so comforting to have your family around at a time like this."

Her gaze shot to Tyson and they shared a look. "Tyson's a friend," she said when she looked away. "A family friend."

I wondered whether Big Daddy had been aware of his wife's friendship with Tyson. I'd have bet half of everything I owned that he hadn't. "Friends are good, too," I said, smiling as if I believed her. "The important thing is that you're not alone."

"Yes," she said. "Well. What is it you wanted to see me about?"

I decided it might be best to ease into the subject of that kiss, so I said, "Please understand that I don't mean any disrespect. And I don't want to bring up painful issues, but I'd like to ask you about your brother-in-law. I understand he had a disagreement with your husband the night Big Daddy died."

"He may have," she said. "I don't know anything about that."

"Your husband didn't mention it to you?"

She smoothed one hand down the leg of her pants and I spotted a slight tremor in her hand. Nerves or grief? I couldn't be sure. "No," she said. "And neither did Judd."

"So you don't know anything about the trouble Judd was in?"

She pulled her hand away from her leg and clasped both hands in her lap. "What makes you think he was in trouble?"

"Someone overhead him promising to pay Big Daddy back. In that same conversation, Big Daddy told Judd he was going to put him in rehab. You don't know anything about that?"

She shook her head slowly. "No, but I suppose I shouldn't be surprised. It's no secret that Judd has issues with alcohol. He makes a habit of getting himself into scrapes and my husband was constantly bailing him out." Her voice was hard and flat, and so were her eyes.

"I take it you didn't approve?"

"Approve? Hardly. Judd's behavior is destructive and selfish. But he's family, and my husband was very protective of him."

"And that's why you gave your husband an ultimatum?"

She shot flaming daggers at me with her eyes. "I did no such thing."

"You didn't tell him he had to make things right with Percy—and I quote—or else?"

"I have no idea what you're talking about. My husband was a softhearted and generous man. His brother sometimes took advantage of that."

"His alcoholism?"

"Everyone knows it's a disease," she said. She looked at me through a set of snake eyes. "Big Daddy and I were both very sympathetic toward his brother's illness."

"Until the night he died," I pointed out. "How do you think Judd would have reacted to the threat of being sent to rehab?"

"He would have been angry and upset, but he would have gone. He always did anything Big Daddy asked him to do." She narrowed her eyes and looked to Tyson for direction. He gave an almost imperceptible shake of his head, resuming his position as king of her world.

"I don't understand why you're asking all these questions

about my brother-in-law," she said, shifting position slightly. "What's it to you?"

"I'm just trying to figure out what happened."

"Isn't that a job for the police?" Tyson said from his post at the door.

"Yes, of course. But Mrs. Boudreaux practically accused my uncle of killing her husband." I turned away from Tyson and addressed Susannah again. "I'd like to know what led you to believe that."

She looked stunned and angry. "That man is your uncle?"

"Visiting from out of town," I said with a nod. "He arrived just a few hours before the party. He didn't even know Big Daddy."

"Apparently he knew him well enough," Tyson put in.

Yeah. Thanks, buddy. I stayed focused on Susannah. "Why do you believe my uncle killed your husband?"

"I believe that," she said, "because it's true."

Liar. "You saw him do it?"

She shot another look at Tyson and said, "No. But I'm sure it was him."

"With all due respect, Mrs. Boudreaux, that wasn't my question. I asked why you think that."

Her spine stiffened and the softness around her mouth disappeared. "I think that because he attacked my husband. Twice. And he did it in front of everyone."

"He confronted him because your husband made inappropriate suggestions." At least that's why they'd fought the first time. I still wasn't sure what had caused the second fight, but I assumed it had something to do with the kiss.

She rolled her eyes. "Oh, please. Big Daddy made a little joke. What's the harm in that? That's just the kind of man he was."

I'm not a violent person, but I wanted to get up out of my

chair and show her the harm with the flat of my hand. What can I say? I *am* related to my uncle. I gripped the arms of the chair to keep myself where I was. "It was no joke," I said. "And not everyone found your late husband amusing."

She waved away my comment as if it were a pesky fly. "Clearly, your uncle has anger issues that he's incapable of controlling. I can't help but feel sorry for his wife. To live with that kind of a monster must be horrible."

She really was too much. "If you felt that way," I said, getting to the crux of the issue, "why did you kiss him?"

Tyson's head jerked up as if someone had a string attached to it, but he didn't say a word. Family friend, my ass.

Susannah's eyes glinted, but her hard edges disappeared under a coating of Southern sweet ganache. "Oh, sweetie," she purred. "Someone's been lying to you. I didn't kiss him, he kissed me."

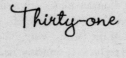

Thirty-one

Tyson showed me to the door, and I held my head high as I walked back to the Mercedes. I drove half a block before anger and frustration forced me to the side of the road. I put the car into park and leaned my forehead against the steering wheel while emotions churned around inside.

Somebody was lying to me. That much was obvious. I just didn't know whether that somebody was Uncle Nestor or Susannah Boudreaux. Gut instinct told me to believe Uncle Nestor, but the way he'd been acting, so secretive, made me begin to wonder.

I don't know how long I sat there before I began to calm down and think rationally again. My family was waiting for me at home. But I wasn't ready to talk to Uncle Nestor just yet. I still needed to process what Susannah had told me.

There was another reason I didn't put the car in gear and head for home. In all the conversations I'd had over the past week, nobody had told me anything that would clear Uncle Nestor for good. But I couldn't just give up. Especially now, with things so rocky between Uncle Nestor and Aunt Yolanda. My uncle might be a lot of things, but he's not a murderer. Somebody out there knew something that would prove that. I just had to keep digging until I found it.

I pulled the guest list out of my bag and flipped through the pages until I found the address I was looking for. I programmed it into the GSP, made a U-turn, and drove to Judd Boudreaux's apartment. He lived in a picturesque complex on Lake Pontchartrain, which consisted of half a dozen three-story buildings scattered across a well-trimmed lawn, all posed in front of the lake and harbor like something that belonged on a postcard.

The road wound around through the buildings, edging off into small parking lots here and there. I followed it until I found the right building and made the rest of the journey on foot.

Unit 203 was on the middle floor, set back from the common staircase to give the illusion of a private entrance. A couple of old newspapers and some dry leaves littered the entryway, and the light over the door flickered on and off as if it was on its last legs.

I rang the bell and the sound of scuffing footsteps reached me a few seconds later. I felt the pricking of nerves and a sudden rush of adrenaline. What was I thinking, coming here alone?

He'd been drinking, and pretty steadily. My clues? The smell, the way he wobbled on his feet and squinted to figure out who I was, and the bottle in his hand. Oh, and the fact that he was still wearing the clothes he'd had on at the funeral yesterday—minus the tie.

He looked tired and sad. Dark circles had formed under

his eyes, and thin spider veins were visible across his nose and cheeks. The charm that had so affected me the first time we met was subdued tonight, diluted by grief and whiskey.

"Well," he said with weak attempt at a grin. "If it isn't the lovely Cinderella. Looking for your shoes again?"

"I have them tonight, thanks. I wonder if you'd mind answering a few questions."

He eyed me curiously. "Questions? What are you, a police officer?"

I shook my head. "Just a friend."

He took a deep drink from the bottle and stepped away from the door, bowing elaborately at the waist. "Well, in that case, come on in."

Inside, the place was a far cry from Big Daddy's home. It was sparsely furnished with a threadbare couch, two lopsided easy chairs, and a coffee table dotted with cigarette burns. Early Goodwill.

He swept a hand toward one easy chair. "Make yourself at home."

I perched on the edge of the seat to avoid a spring I could see coming through the cushion. Judd dropped heavily into a matching chair next to a cluttered TV tray. He bounded to his feet again almost immediately, his once-handsome face clouded. "My mama would have my hide for not offering you something to drink. Can I get you a beer, or would you like something stronger?"

"Nothing," I said with a scant smile. "Thanks."

"You're sure?" He shrugged at my nod and sat. "So what can I do for you?"

"I'd like to ask you about the night your brother died, if you don't mind."

"What do you want to know?"

"First, let me say how sorry I am for your loss. I

understand that you and Big Daddy were close. I know this must be difficult for you."

He didn't say anything, but a muscle in his cheek jumped and I knew he was feeling something.

"I wonder if you could tell me if your brother had any enemies. You know, was there anyone angry with him? Anyone who might have wanted to hurt him?"

Judd let out a deep breath. His cheeks puffed out a little as he exhaled, and he wiped one hand across his eyes. "Bradley had a lot of friends," he said when he finally spoke. "But he also had a lot of enemies. People either loved him or hated him."

"He had a strong personality," I said, trying to put a positive spin on it. "Do you know if he was having any issues at work? Did he ever mention any issues with an employee, or maybe a disgruntled former one?"

Judd shook his head. "Not that I know of. Nothing serious, anyway. I've done some work for him off and on over the years. People came and went. A few people got upset over having to work weekends and late night hours, but that's the nature of the business. Some people stuck around for a while, but some got out of there as fast as they could. With Bradley, it was his way or the highway. You either did what he said, or you walked."

"And people were okay with that?"

Judd shrugged. "It was what it was. He made it clear from the beginning, so nobody could ever say they were surprised."

He seemed to be dodging the question, and I wondered whether he was consciously avoiding the answer or if his brain was just too pickled to form a straight answer. "Did anybody ever try to say they were surprised? Maybe someone he fired?"

Judd shook his head slowly. "Not recently."

I filed that away in case I needed it later. "What about his marriage? What was that like?"

Judd took another drink and capped the bottle slowly. "You ask a lot of questions, Cinderella. Has anyone ever told you that?"

I smiled. "A few people. I do that when I'm trying to help someone."

"That's admirable, but hardly justification for me to spill all of my brother's secrets."

"If those secrets were responsible for his death, I think you'd want to bring them to light."

Judd didn't say anything to that, so I gave him a little more to think about. "I just came from Susannah's house. She accused my uncle of killing your brother. Uncle Nestor didn't do it. I'm trying to help him prove that."

That brought Judd's head up quickly. "Your uncle's the old man? The one who took a couple of swings at Bradley?"

"Yes, but he was only reacting to something Big Daddy said about my aunt."

"That would be the lovely older Latin lady?"

I nodded. "How did you know about Uncle Nestor and your brother?"

"Word gets around quickly. Bradley thought it was kind of a kick, you know. Since nobody actually got hurt and all."

"He didn't seem all that amused at the time."

"Well, that was my brother for you. He could change his mind faster than anyone I ever knew."

"Does that mean that you don't think my uncle killed your brother?"

He flicked something from one pant leg and looked up at me as if the idea of that surprised him. "I guess I don't."

I could have kissed him, and I might have if he hadn't

smelled so bad. "What happened after the fight? Did you see where your brother went or who he talked to?"

Judd cleared a space for his bottle on the TV tray and spent a moment getting it to balance in the small spot. "I didn't see him again after that. I don't know where he went or who he talked to."

Well, that was a big fat lie, but I didn't say so. I had a few more questions to ask before I called him on it. "Why was Susannah upset with your brother that night?"

He scowled. "She was always upset with him. That's not news."

"Are you saying they fought a lot?"

He flicked a glance at me. "It would be hard not to fight with Susannah. She's not exactly easy to get along with."

That was a nice way of putting it. "She gave your brother an ultimatum. Do you know anything about that?"

He yawned, but I had the feeling it was just for show. "Sorry. Can't help you. Ultimatums are her thing. It's how she rolls." He put on a falsetto voice and mimicked Susannah. "Get me that car for Christmas or there'll be no sex for you. Take me to Cancún for our anniversary or I'll spend everything in your bank account."

Interesting, but not surprising. "This ultimatum had something to do with a man named Percy. Do you know anything about that?"

Abruptly, the smile slid from his face. "No, and I'm finished answering your questions." He tried to get up, but he lost his balance and fell back into the chair with a thud.

My heart pounded in my chest at the sudden change in him, but I refused to cut and run. "A friend of mine heard her tell Big Daddy that this was the last straw. That she wasn't going to let him embarrass her. Do you have any idea why she'd say that?"

"I just told you," he snapped. His eyes had taken on a strange focus, and the bleary-eyed drunk turned into something raw and powerful right in front of me. "I don't know anything about what happened between the two of them. I don't care what happened between the two of them." He stood, this time without trouble. "I think you'd better leave now."

He didn't have to tell me twice. I got up and scurried toward the door and freedom. But as I stepped out onto the dimly lit landing, I couldn't leave without asking one more question. "Another friend of mine says he heard you arguing with Big Daddy a little before one in the morning. You promised to pay him back, and he told you he was sending you to rehab. You owed him money. For what?"

"I don't mean to be rude, darlin', but that's none of your damn business." The door slammed between us, and I bolted down the stairs, cursing myself for taking such a stupid chance and grateful that he'd done nothing worse than growl at me.

Judd hadn't exactly been a font of information, but I knew one thing that I hadn't known when I arrived: Susannah wasn't the only Boudreaux lying about what happened the night that Big Daddy died.

Thirty-two

❧

I thought about my conversations with the Boudreauxes all the way home. I was convinced that one of them had killed Big Daddy, but which one? Had Big Daddy found out about Susannah's relationship with Tyson? Maybe he'd confronted her and gotten himself killed in a fit of passion. But if he really was sleeping with Violet, would he have cared that much about Susannah's sexual activities? I might have been wrong, but I doubted Susannah had killed him in a jealous rage.

Their sleeping arrangements must not have been what they'd argued about, I reasoned. Susannah was the one who'd drawn the line in the sand. Whatever upset her, it was something Big Daddy had done, not the other way around.

Judd was clearly lying about his argument with his brother. He'd owed him money, and while he'd promised to pay it back, that hadn't been enough for Big Daddy, who'd threatened to put Judd in rehab. Why? After covering for him all these years, after bailing him out from one trouble situation after another, what had Judd done that had driven Big Daddy to change the way he'd been handling his brother?

I went round and round the questions all the way home, but I wasn't going to find the answers in my own head. I wanted to talk with Violet and find out if she could shed any light on what Big Daddy had going with Percy, but I couldn't do it tonight. It was too late, and I was too tired.

The lights were out on the main floor, so I started upstairs to my bedroom. The door to the guest room was open and I saw Aunt Yolanda on the bed, curled up with a book. Alone. I stopped for a moment to talk with her as I climbed the stairs to my room. We'd done the same thing so many times when I was younger that things felt normal for a moment. If we'd been in Albuquerque, I'd have assumed that Uncle Nestor was at the restaurant. But we weren't, and he wasn't.

Aunt Yolanda might be able to pretend that everything was normal, but I couldn't. I asked her where he was, and she nodded toward the ceiling. "Upstairs on your terrace. He's been up there for hours."

"Is he all right?"

She frowned and gave a little shrug. "I'm sure he is."

That answer was so out of character for her that I moved into the bedroom and sat on the foot of the bed. "How long is this going to go on, *Tía*?"

She kept her eyes on her book. "I'm only going to finish this chapter. It's late, and I'm tired."

"That's not what I'm talking about, and you know it."

She flipped a page, pointedly refusing to look at me. "What I know is that it's never a good idea to get involved in someone else's relationship. I'm sure I've mentioned that to you before."

"Yeah. You have. But this is ridiculous. You know how much Uncle Nestor loves you."

Her gaze finally left the book. She locked eyes with me. "This is between your uncle and me," she said, her voice harder than I'd ever heard it. She marked her place with a bookmark and set the book aside. "I'm tired. I'd like to go to sleep."

Her reaction confused and frightened me, but I stood up and went back to the door. "I'll see you tomorrow," I said.

She mumbled something, but her voice was too low and I couldn't hear it. With my heart aching, I climbed to the third floor, but instead of going into my own bedroom, I kept going to the rooftop garden.

It's a beautiful space filled with large planters holding trees and flowering bushes, a wrought-iron railing allowing a view of the street below, and a stone table with chairs in the center. Twinkling white lights in the trees and along the railing make the whole thing feel like a fairy tale.

Almost losing my life here last summer had turned the fairy tale into a nightmare, but I was slowly learning to relax in this space. New Orleans is never a quiet city, and during carnival season the noise level multiplies. I could hear the revelry all around me. Parties. Music. Laughing. Fireworks in the distance. One of the smaller krewes was having its parade a few blocks away, and the sounds from that hit me softly, as if they'd been wrapped in cotton.

Uncle Nestor sat in a patio chair with his back to the door. He held a glass of water in one hand, but he ignored it and stared up at the sky. I didn't want to startle him, so I cleared my throat as I stepped out onto the rooftop.

He didn't move a muscle. "I wondered when you'd come looking for me. You're home late. Again."

"It's the nature of the business," I said as I walked toward him. "You know what it's like."

He dipped his head a fraction of an inch. "You're very busy. Maybe too busy."

"Only for a few more days," I reminded him. "Once Mardi Gras is over, things will slow down."

He nodded. Sipped. Let out a sigh that came from somewhere near the bottom of his soul.

I worried about how all this stress was affecting his heart. "How are you holding up, *Tío*? Are you feeling okay?"

"Physically?" He darted a glance at me. "I'm fine."

"But . . ."

He turned back to the sky. "Your aunt is angry with me."

"I noticed." I pulled a chair around and sat beside him. "Does she have reason to be?"

He shook his head slowly, leaning forward slightly and resting his arms on his thighs. "For what happened at the party? No."

I didn't like that answer. It was too open-ended. Too full of negative possibilities. The twelve-year-old I'd been when Uncle Nestor took me in after my parents' death wanted to let it go. Since the accident he'd been my rock. My protector. I wanted to protect him now. But my adult self knew I couldn't leave his answer lying in the dark.

"But there's some reason she feels this way." It wasn't a question.

Uncle Nestor let out another of those soul-wrenching sighs. "I suppose so."

"You *suppose* so?"

"It happened a long time ago. It doesn't matter now."

I gaped at him. "Aunt Yolanda is downstairs in bed. Alone. You're up here staring at the stars. Alone. Apparently it matters."

He tried to work up some irritation, but it lacked steam. "It's between your aunt and me."

"Yeah. Right." I let out a sigh of my own and leaned back in my seat. Maybe the stars would have some answers for me. Nobody else seemed willing to give me any. "You know, I'm doing my best to help you, but you sure don't make it easy. I understand you're not big on sharing everything you feel, but would it hurt so much to talk to me?"

He turned his face to the sky again and I figured that was that. Our bonding moment was over. I was just about to give up and go downstairs to bed when he started talking.

"It was a long time ago. Before you came to us."

I didn't breathe for a few seconds. I didn't want to do anything that would make him shut down again. Part of me wanted him to rip the bandage off the wound quickly, but I forced myself to wait.

"It was after Aaron was born," he said. "I made a mistake. A stupid mistake. It meant nothing, but things were rough between Yolanda and me. She was exhausted. Tired from a difficult pregnancy and trying to care for four little boys who had way too much energy. I was exhausted and worried about the money. I had no idea how we'd make it, and every time I turned around, she was telling me about something else we needed to buy."

"So you turned to someone else."

He nodded miserably.

I didn't know what to feel. He'd cheated on his wife. He'd betrayed her, and even though it had happened years ago, I felt as if he'd betrayed me. The idea of him being with someone else made me physically ill. But the pain on his face landed on my heart like a rock. "Did you love her?"

"No!" He dropped his head as if he simply didn't have the strength to hold it up any longer. "It wasn't about love. It was about fear. I hated the way I felt at home. I wasn't making it. I didn't think I *could* make it. Every time I walked through the door and saw Yolanda and the kids looking at me, I felt like a failure."

I put my feet on the cement border in front of me. "That's no excuse, you know."

He laughed without humor. "Not an excuse, just an explanation. It only lasted three months, but I've been paying for it for the past thirty years."

"She hasn't forgiven you?"

The back door of the Thai restaurant next door opened with a loud squeak, followed by the clang of metal as someone tossed trash into the Dumpster. Uncle Nestor waited to speak until the door closed again.

"She's forgiven me as much as it's possible to forgive, I guess. Her God won't let her do any less. But she hasn't forgotten."

"I'm not sure it's possible to forget something like that," I said. "At least, I don't think I could. Not really."

"Well, that's fair," he said with a sad smile. "I haven't forgotten it either. And she's a step ahead of me. I haven't forgiven myself. I'm not sure I ever will."

I put my hand on top of his and we sat in silence for a moment. But we weren't finished. I still had questions to ask. "I went to see Susannah Boudreaux this afternoon."

He looked confused. "Who's that?"

"The woman you kissed at the party."

"I didn't kiss anyone at the party, *mija*. It was the other way around."

I needed to hear him say that, but I couldn't get distracted by sentiment. "That's not what she says."

"Then she's lying."

"Yeah. That's what I thought." I pulled my hand away from his and scooted my chair closer. "Tell me what happened that night. Why did she kiss you?"

"I have no idea. I was standing by the pool, and all of a sudden she was there. We started talking."

"About what?"

"About nothing. About the weather. About the food in the buffet. Small talk. I had no idea who she was. I didn't care."

"Then what? Think about it carefully. What happened right before she kissed you?"

He tilted his head to one side and gave that some thought. I waited, holding my breath until he shook his head. "I just don't remember, *mija*. I wish I could."

I wasn't going to give up so easily. "Think, *Tío*. Did you see anyone else there?"

"There were many people there," he said a little impatiently. "It was a party. But don't ask me who any of them were, because I don't know."

"Did you see her talking to anyone else before she started talking to you?"

He looked up at me from hooded eyes. "She was arguing with Big Daddy. I remember feeling a little sorry for her. And I'll confess that I was amused. He started to walk away in the middle of their argument, and she shouted that she'd show him. I can only guess that's why she did what she did."

"So, was this what your second argument with Big Daddy was about?"

Uncle Nestor rubbed his forehead. He looked tired, and I felt a pang of guilt for pushing him so hard. "Yes. He came back a few minutes later, just as that woman kissed me, and he was very angry. Called me a hypocrite."

"Why?"

"He said I had some nerve blowing up when he made an innocent little comment about my wife, and then trying to . . . you know."

"Hit on his wife?"

He nodded. "It wasn't like that, *mija*. I didn't want anything to do with her."

"I believe you," I said. "But I'm not the one who matters. Aunt Yolanda is really hurt."

"I know."

"What are you going to do about it?" I asked.

He shook his head and got to his feet with a groan. "I don't know. But I'll think of something."

I wanted desperately to believe him. I knew how easily a marriage could unravel, and I needed the two of them to show me that it didn't have to be that way. "It would probably help if you told the police about what happened," I said.

He gave me a thin smile. "I talked with your Detective Sullivan again yesterday. But I don't want anyone else to know. Your cousins don't know about the past, and I don't want them to know."

I could understand that, I suppose. At least he'd told Sullivan the truth, and that made me feel better than I'd felt in days.

"And you're not to worry about this. It's my life, Rita. My problem. I'll deal with it." He crossed the patio and disappeared through the door, no doubt believing that I'd back off.

I'd said the same thing to him more times than I could count while I was growing up, and it had never stopped him from sticking his nose in where I didn't think it belonged. If he saw me in trouble, he was there whether I wanted him there or not.

I loved him enough to repay the favor.

Thirty-three

❧

I couldn't sleep. I just kept thinking about Uncle Nestor and Aunt Yolanda and wondering whether they'd be able to work through their issues. They'd worked through trouble before, I reminded myself several times. But there's a big difference between forgiving someone for a single mistake and forgiving him for appearing to make the same mistake twice. I believed Uncle Nestor's account of what happened with Susannah Boudreaux, but I wasn't the one who mattered. If Aunt Yolanda thought Uncle Nestor's eyes were wandering, he'd have a hard time convincing her otherwise.

After a long time, I got up and booted up my laptop. I found the memory card Estelle had given me at the party and began the arduous task of looking through more than two hundred pictures. I'd left the second memory card in my desk at work, so there were at least this many pictures waiting for me at Zydeco. I figured my odds of finding something useful were relatively high.

Since Ox wanted pictures of the party for the website, I kept that in mind as I scrolled through the images Estelle had captured, but frankly, photos for the website weren't my top priority. I scanned shots of the crowd, looking for any of the major players in Big Daddy's life. I spotted Big Daddy himself in several pictures, laughing with a group of men, flirting with a handful of women. I saw him heaping a plate at the buffet and putting an arm around Miss Frankie.

It was a little creepy looking at those pictures of a man who'd been killed just a few hours after the images were captured. I wondered if he'd had any sense of impending doom, or if he'd been surprised when the attack came.

I paid close attention to the pictures Estelle had taken near the pool, but I didn't see anything that seemed either important or out of place. Frustrated, I downloaded the files to my computer, jotted down the file names of a handful of pictures I thought Ox might like, and tucked the memory card into my wallet so I could return it to Estelle.

By the time I'd finished, I was tired enough to sleep—or at least give it a good try. I tossed and turned all night, waking myself every time I turned over. I was up again with the sun and walked through the door at Zydeco a few minutes after six.

I spent the morning working on the carved Mardi Gras mask for the cake we had to deliver next week, first sculpting the general shape using a serrated knife, then concentrating on the details until I was satisfied with the size and shape. I made a fresh batch of fondant, stirring together corn syrup and shortening, adding salt and vanilla, and finally blending in the confectioner's sugar and stirring until I had stiff dough. I bypassed the electric mixer and kneaded the fondant by hand. It's the best way I know to work through my frustrations.

I spent the rest of the morning cutting out shapes for the Mardi Gras cake, measuring carefully, and storing them in airtight containers so they'd still be pliable when I was ready to use them the next day.

After grabbing a quick lunch from the market down the street, I took my place on the King Cake line, and finally moved into my office around four to check the second memory card. It was slow going and tedious work, but I wouldn't let myself quit until I'd gone through every shot.

I hit pay dirt after only two hundred and fourteen pictures. I'd started zoning out, paying more attention to the headache forming behind my eyes than the images on the screen in front of me. And then, suddenly, there it was.

Estelle had been shooting one of the outdoor tables, but she'd caught Susannah Boudreaux at the edge of the picture. Susannah stood near the swimming pool, her face rigid with anger, her eyes filled with fury. In front of her was Big Daddy's assistant, Violet, who jabbed at Susannah's chest with one finger. Violet's mouth was open wide, giving the impression that she'd been shouting.

I'd fallen into a rhythm as I moved through row after row of photographs, and my finger clicked on the mouse button to move on almost before my brain registered what I'd just seen. I sat up with a jerk and clicked the back button on the browser window so I could study the picture more closely.

I focused on the two women at first, studying their expressions and body language. Clearly, there was no love lost between them. As my focus broadened, I began to notice other details. There, just behind Susannah, the blurry face of Judd Boudreaux. And to her right, Ivanka Hedge.

My heart beat erratically as I sent the image to print and

moved on. I had less than a hundred photographs to go, but my hopes were higher than they'd been in days. If Estelle had captured one argument with her camera, maybe she'd inadvertently caught another one.

Luck was with me just twenty-one pictures later when I found a picture of Big Daddy and Percy standing a little apart from the rest of the crowd. That was interesting enough, considering the fact that Percy denied talking with Big Daddy again before he died. But what I found most interesting was the look on Percy's face.

He looked angry enough to kill.

It wasn't yet five o'clock, so I printed both pictures and tucked them into my purse, then drove across town to the address I found online for Big Daddy's corporate office. It was located in a single-story building that squatted between two of his car dealerships.

Inside, the scent of stale coffee filled the air, and a brunette receptionist who looked all of sixteen sat behind a small desk and tapped slowly on a computer keyboard. She looked at me with bored disinterest, and I told her why I was there.

She made a couple of calls in an effort to track down Violet's whereabouts. After the second one, she pointed me toward a waiting area consisting of a handful of plastic chairs near a coffeepot in the corner and assured me that Violet would be with me in a few minutes.

I thanked her and started away. Big Daddy's operation wasn't what I'd call classy, but it was certainly big. From where I stood, I could see cars in every direction. Chevrolet to the left of me, Nissan to the right, and a large used car lot across the street. These weren't his only enterprises either, and for the first time the sheer scope of his business struck me. I wondered who'd take up the reins now that Big Daddy was gone. Would Judd inherit? Would it all pass on to the next generation of Boudreauxes? Or would Susannah get it all? Getting control of that fortune might have been a motive for murder.

I changed my mind about the stale coffee midstep and turned back toward the receptionist with what I hoped looked like a friendly smile. "I'm sorry about your loss, by the way. It must be difficult to come to work after what happened."

She looked away from the computer screen as if my comment confused her, but she nodded and swept a lock of hair from her shoulder. "I still can't believe it. I mean, who'd want to kill Big Daddy?"

That's what I wanted to know. "So he was a good boss?"

"Yeah. Sure. He was a real nice man."

Yeah. Sure. "I guess his death has made things kind of difficult around here," I said. "Do you have any idea what's going to happen to all of this now that he's gone?"

The girl's expression sobered. "I don't know. We're supposed to have a meeting next week, and I guess they'll tell us then."

I was pretty sure Sullivan would know who inherited Big Daddy's fortune. I just wondered if he'd share that information with me. "Have the police been around asking questions?"

She rolled her eyes as if to say I'd asked a foolish question. "They were here for a couple of days, looking in all our files, checking stuff on the computer. It was awful."

I started to say something sympathetic, but I heard the sharp staccato of rapid footsteps approaching, and an instant later Violet rounded a corner. She looked curious and hesitant until she spotted me. Then her expression turned sour and wary. She nudged her glasses up on her nose and scowled as if I'd just ruined her day. "Can I help you?"

I pretended not to notice the way her mouth puckered up as if she'd tasted something bitter. "I don't know if you remember me," I said. "I'm Rita Lucero. We met at the Musterion party."

She dipped her head slightly. "I remember you. What can I do for you?"

"Is there somewhere we could talk privately? I'd like to ask you a couple of questions if that's okay."

Her mouth puckered a little tighter. "This is a really bad time. If you'll call tomorrow, I'll see if I can arrange a time to meet with you."

I was pretty sure that if I walked out the door, I'd never get this close to her again. "It will only take a minute," I said.

She turned to leave. "Not now. Call to make an appointment."

I wasn't about to let her walk out on me, so I called after her. "Why was Percy Ponter so upset with Big Daddy the night of the murder?"

She stopped walking and turned around wearing an icy expression. "I don't know what you're talking about."

"Would you like me to refresh your memory here, or would you rather talk privately?"

Her nostrils flared slightly. "I can give you five minutes," she snapped. She started walking again, and I had to jog a little to keep up with her.

I trailed her down a narrow corridor to a corner office with windows lining both outside walls. I guessed that it had been Big Daddy's office when he was alive. She sat behind a massive desk that had probably been just right for her former boss, but dwarfed her.

"I don't know what game you're playing—" she began.

I cut her off before she could finish. "It's not a game. Susannah Boudreaux is trying to accuse my uncle of killing Big Daddy, and I'm going to prove her wrong. What do you know about Big Daddy's dealings with Percy Ponter?"

"Nothing."

Nice try. I held her gaze and said, "I don't believe you. I have a feeling you knew just about everything there was to know about Big Daddy's business dealings. How does Percy fit into the picture?"

"Why should I tell you?"

Her attitude was starting to get on my nerves. "Why not tell me? Unless you have something to hide. Why was Percy so upset with Big Daddy the night of the murder?"

"Why don't you ask him?"

"I have. Now I want to hear what you have to say."

She smirked, and I saw some of her tension fall away, as if she'd just dodged a bullet. "It wasn't anything important," she said. "Percy's . . . excitable. He tends to overreact to things."

"What things? Were they in business together?"

"Big Daddy and Percy? No."

"So then why did Susannah tell Big Daddy he had to make things right with Percy before the end of the night?"

Hostility flashed across her face. "How would I know why Susannah did anything?"

I ignored her question and asked another one of my own. "And why did you tell Big Daddy that you'd be backing Percy's story?"

Her face froze, and her eyes took on a deer-in-the-headlights look. She blinked and it disappeared. "That was about an upcoming krewe meeting. Nothing important."

"And Susannah's ultimatum?"

Her lip curled. "I have no idea."

"I take it you don't like her."

"I didn't say that."

"You didn't have to." I pulled the picture of the two of them arguing from my purse and put it on the desk in front of her. "What was going on here?"

She glanced at the picture, then up at me. "Where did you get that?"

I still didn't know if she'd conked Big Daddy over the head with the statue, so I wasn't about to give up Estelle's name. I said only, "That's not important. What were the two of you arguing about?"

Violet's gaze went back and forth between the picture and me a few times before she finally responded. "So we were arguing. So what?"

I bit back the sarcastic retort that rose to my lips and explained what should have been obvious. "I'm trying to piece together what was going on in Big Daddy's life before he died. I'm going out on a limb here, but I think this argument had something to do with him."

Violet rolled her eyes and sat back in her chair. "Yeah? Well, you're right. It did."

"Let me guess," I said. "She found out that you and Big Daddy were sleeping together."

Her cheeks flushed and her gaze faltered. "You make it sound so cheap."

Yeah, well, if it walks like a duck . . . "So you were having an affair."

"Bradley and I were in love. We were going to be together once Mardi Gras was over."

"I'm guessing that Susannah found out about you?"

"That's right. She wasn't too happy about it either."

I didn't know whether to believe that or not. None of these people seemed to truly love each other. But what did

I know? "She certainly looks like she was angry with you. Was she also angry with him?"

Violet nodded and her expression sobered. "She was furious with him. He'd been intending to tell her about us for a few weeks, but every time he got ready to have the talk, she'd come up with some emergency so he wouldn't. First it was something with his brother. Then it was something with one of his kids. They live with their mother, but they used to stay with their father on the weekends. I swear, Susannah knew what was coming and she did everything she could to keep it from happening."

"Even though she was seeing someone else on the side?"

Violet's posture grew rigid. "Who told you that?"

I shrugged. "I don't remember. Did Big Daddy ever say anything about her cheating on him?"

"No," Violet admitted reluctantly. "But I wouldn't be surprised. If you ask me, she probably killed him. She's a real piece of work."

I couldn't disagree with that. "What about Big Daddy's relationship with his brother? What was going on between them?"

"Judd?" Violet seemed surprised by the change of direction.

I nodded. "Big Daddy threatened to send him to rehab the night he died. Do you know why?"

Her gaze flickered away from mine for a moment. "That's not true. He would never have done that."

"But he did," I insisted.

Her gaze locked on mine. "Big Daddy would never have done that," she insisted. "He worried about Judd. He took care of Judd. Big Daddy risked everything for him—" She cut herself off abruptly, eyes wide as if she'd said too much.

I felt a slow flush of excitement. "How so?"

Violet stood, shaking her head angrily.

"What did he risk, Violet?"

She came out from behind the desk and opened the door. "Your five minutes is up. Please leave. I have work to do." I was disappointed but I wasn't going to argue with her. I knew I'd struck a nerve and I was leaving with more than I'd had when I came in. I stood and walked toward the door, thinking back over everything I'd learned in the past week. Susannah had given Big Daddy an ultimatum last Friday evening at the party. She told him he had to make things right with Percy before the end of the night. A few hours later, Big Daddy told Judd that he was through covering for him and threatened to send him to rehab. I didn't think that was a coincidence. "Just one more question," I said. "Who gets all of this now that Big Daddy's gone?"

Fear and anger rippled across her expression, but they were gone in a flash. "As far as I know, Susannah inherits everything as his widow."

Thirty-four

✦

"Susannah did it," I told Gabriel an hour later at the Dizzy Duke. "I know she did. I just can't prove it. Yet."

It was the dinner hour and the bar was nearly empty, which meant that he had time to talk. He leaned on the bar in front of me and listened while I sipped a Diet Coke and laid out my theory. "She found out about his affair with Violet. Big Daddy was going to leave her, but she couldn't let him do that. She'd have lost everything. With him dead, she gets it all. And she accused my uncle to throw suspicion off of herself."

It was nice and tidy, all the loose ends tucked in neatly, and I was proud of myself for piecing it together on my own.

Gabriel didn't look so sure. "So she picked up a statue and whacked him with it?"

"It was what she had. A crime of passion. I don't think she planned it, or she'd have brought her own murder weapon along."

"Why not wait until they got home?"

"Duh! Because then it would have been obvious. She saw an opportunity to pin the murder on a stranger, and she grabbed it."

Gabriel rolled his eyes toward the ceiling for a moment, then looked at me again and shook his head. "I don't know. I don't buy it."

"What's not to buy? It's what happened."

He shook his head again and straightened up, reaching for a couple of dirty glasses someone had left on the bar. "First of all, you're assuming that Violet's telling you the truth. How do you know she is? How do you know Big Daddy really planned on leaving his wife? Do you have anyone else's word to back that up?"

Okay. He had a point there. Big Daddy hadn't seemed all that interested in Violet when I saw them together. Was there any truth at all in her claim?

I'd give Gabriel that one. "No, but if it's true, I'm sure someone will be able to corroborate her story. Why else would Violet and Susannah have argued?"

"I can think of at least half a dozen reasons off the top of my head. One, Violet knew that Susannah was cheating on Big Daddy. You know how protective she was of him. Maybe she got in Susannah's face over that. Or two, maybe Big Daddy told Violet that he *wasn't* going to leave Susannah." He ticked off his ideas on his fingers as he went. "Three, maybe Susannah broke Violet's fingernail or Violet accidentally bumped into Susannah. I've seen people go after each other over less, especially when booze is involved."

I made a face at him. "Funny. Okay, I'll grant you the first two, but this was about more than a fingernail or a misstep." I pushed the picture across the bar toward him, a visual reminder of the incident in question. "Look at their faces."

He glanced. Shrugged. "That doesn't prove anything. You take that idea to the police, they're going to laugh you out of the building. You don't have a single piece of real evidence to prove your theory."

So he had another point. So what? "At least it might convince the police to scratch Uncle Nestor off their list for good so he can go home." They'd been in New Orleans a week already and Uncle Nestor was getting antsy. I hoped that getting back to the restaurant and their own house might help the two of them patch things up.

Gabriel wiped something from the bar and tossed the rag into the sink behind him. "What makes you think they haven't already considered the wife as a suspect? You know what they say. The spouse is always the first person they look at. If the police haven't arrested her, it's probably because they've eliminated her as a suspect."

And just like that, my heart dropped to the floor. I hated to admit it, but he was right. "Fine then," I said grudgingly. "Who do you think did it?"

He shook his head and grinned at me as if we were playing a game. "I have no idea, *chérie*. If you ask me, the best thing you can do is to back off."

"Not while Uncle Nestor is still a suspect." I propped my chin in my hand and ran through my own list of potential killers once again. "How about Judd Boudreaux? In financial trouble and threatened with a stint in rehab. Did he kill his own brother, either because he couldn't pay him back or to avoid being locked up in a detox center for a few weeks?"

Gabriel shook his head. "I don't buy it. I've known Judd for years. He's a mess, but he's not violent."

"You didn't see his face when I was at his house the other night." Gabriel gave me a *didn't I warn you?* look, which I ignored. "Judd stays on the list, at least for now. What about Percy Ponter?"

"As far as I can see," Gabriel said thoughtfully, "he doesn't even have a motive."

"Oh, he does," I insisted. "I just don't know what it is yet. Whatever was going on between him and Big Daddy, nobody's talking about it. And that makes me think it must have been something big."

"Okay, but Susannah's off the list, right?"

"Not even close," I said. "And let's not forget about Tyson. Maybe he wanted Big Daddy out of the way so his girlfriend would inherit all that money. And, of course, Violet," I went on. "She's capable of murder, even if she didn't have a reason to commit one."

Gabriel laughed and walked away to help another customer. When he came back, he put a fresh Diet Coke in front of me and changed the subject. "You still want that introduction to Ivanka Hedge?"

Thoughts of murder melted away like a mouthful of meringue. "Are you kidding me? Of course!"

"All right then. If you'll drop all this murder business, you can go with me to the Musterion Ball. Interested?"

Wow. I had to think about that for a few minutes. It was short notice, but it was also a chance to land a contract for Ivanka's wedding cake and that was huge. But by asking me to stop looking into Big Daddy's death, he was asking me to turn my back on Uncle Nestor.

I chewed my thumbnail for a moment, torn between the biggest opportunity that had come my way professionally and the biggest trouble to hit my family since my cousin Julio told us he'd gotten his girlfriend pregnant.

"Are you in or out?" Gabriel asked. "Make up your mind now or the invitation's gone."

"Hey! That's not fair. Give me a minute."

"Who cares about fair? You asked me for a favor. I'm willing to do it, but you've got to do me a favor in return. Stop poking around in this murder investigation before you get yourself killed."

When he put it that way, what else could I do? I smiled my most agreeable smile and lied through my teeth. "All right," I said. "You win. It's a deal."

He picked me up Saturday evening, just like a real date, and I don't mind admitting that seeing him on my front porch in a tux made me sit up and pay attention. He cleaned up even better than I'd expected him to, and I'd had some pretty high expectations to begin with.

Aunt Yolanda had helped me get ready, which was a good thing, since I'm fashion-challenged. I'd picked up a silk chiffon A-line dress with spaghetti straps and pleating in the front. It was cut so low I felt exposed and vulnerable, but the look in Gabriel's eyes when he saw me made it worth a little discomfort.

Aunt Yolanda and Uncle Nestor greeted him together, which I took as a good sign. They both seemed charmed by his easy smile and laid-back personality, but I wondered if Uncle Nestor would have something snarky to say later.

Gabriel and I made the short trip to the historic Belle Grande Hotel and walked together through the lobby, just like a real couple. Chatter from groups of people in formal evening dress rose and fell all around us, the cacophony of sounds amplified by the hotel's high gilt-edged ceilings. The hotel is a beautiful place, all glitter and opulence—the perfect venue for a formal ball during carnival season.

We walked what felt like two miles through the hotel to

the escalator leading to the brilliantly lit mezzanine, where the party seemed to be in full swing already. I waved to Miss Frankie, who was laughing with Bernice and a few other friends across the room. I'd called to tell her that I'd be coming to the ball with Gabriel, and she'd seemed delighted with the idea . . . but I could tell it was hard for her to think of me moving on with my life. She still held on to the belief that Philippe and I would have gotten back together, had he lived. But I was in no real hurry to get involved, and I knew that she'd come around eventually.

Gabriel seemed to know everyone, and to my surprise, everyone seemed to know him. I wondered how he'd come to be so comfortable in a social class that I'd pretty much automatically assumed was as far over his head as it was mine. My old insecurities rose up to lodge in my throat for a moment, but I shoved them aside. I was going to have a good time tonight.

I still didn't feel like I belonged here, but I had to at least learn to fake it. If I couldn't do that, I'd never make Zydeco a success.

Squaring my shoulders and holding my head high, I walked with Gabriel through the crowd. I smiled at people I recognized and indulged in so much small talk, I thought my head would burst. At last, I spotted Ivanka Hedge and her fiancé, Richard Montgomery, a few feet from where we stood. They weren't alone; it took me a few seconds to realize that the couple with them was Susannah Boudreaux and her brother-in-law, Judd. I felt a flash of disappointment I couldn't entirely explain, and I thought Judd looked a little uncomfortable when our eyes met. Hovering a few feet away and trying to look discreet, Tyson looked on with storm clouds in his eyes.

Gabriel put his hand on the small of my back and steered

me toward them. He greeted the women by kissing their cheeks and spent a few seconds shaking hands and slapping backs with the men. To my surprise, Judd seemed almost sober—or at least not too drunk yet. Susannah seemed unpleasantly surprised to see me there, but she greeted me with a nod before pointedly ignoring me.

My ears were buzzing, but I couldn't tell if it was because I was nervous about meeting Ivanka and Richard, or if some sixth sense was telling me to beware. I decided on the former, if only because I couldn't figure out where Susannah would have hidden a weapon in the slinky black gown she wore.

Gabriel officially introduced me to Ivanka and Richard. She gave me a cool hello and a limp-wristed handshake. Richard greeted me more warmly, and even asked me a few questions about Zydeco. And then it was over. Ivanka turned away from me as if I was of no more interest to her than a gnat, and I wondered for a minute why I'd wanted to make her wedding cake in the first place.

I thought about Big Daddy's advice the night of my party. I could almost hear his big, booming voice when he said, "You can make yourself crazy chasin' after people who don't give two hoots about you. Don't do it. Just relax. Be yourself. That's what I do." And I realized that in spite of all his faults, he might have been right about that.

Gabriel glanced down at me and grinned as if he understood my disappointment. "Got what you wanted?"

"Yeah," I fibbed. "Thanks." And then I turned my attention to more important matters. I nodded toward Susannah and hissed in his ear, "What's she doing here? Shouldn't she be somewhere pretending to mourn or something?"

Gabriel's smile vanished. "Don't start."

"I'm not starting anything," I assured him. "It just seems a little odd, don't you think? Her husband's barely in the ground and she's partying—with his *brother*. What's up with that?"

Gabriel tugged me a few feet away from their cozy little group. "It's Mardi Gras. You're not from around here. You wouldn't understand."

"You're right," I said, making a face. "I don't get it. I'm not sure I want to. What do you think is up with the two of them?"

Gabriel shook his head and propelled me a few more feet away. "You promised. No more with the murder."

"I lied." He rolled his eyes in exasperation, and I said, "Oh, come on, Gabriel. That little nothing introduction was hardly worth the price."

"You," he said, "cannot be trusted." And then he pulled me into his arms and swept me out onto the dance floor.

It was a brilliant move on his part. I didn't think about the murder again for hours.

Thirty-five

❧

I'm not easily impressed, but even I have to admit that the Musterion Ball was a magical event. Gabriel and I danced until we were overheated, then slipped outside and walked together in the moonlit courtyard. He took my hand as if it was the most natural thing in the world, and I surprised myself by not freaking out over it.

Unfortunately, reality has a way of popping even the most dream-filled moments. As we came back into the hotel, I excused myself to answer the call of nature. And that's when the trouble started.

I wandered around for a few minutes looking for a ladies' room that didn't have a line halfway to Biloxi. By the time I found a nearly deserted hallway with a small restroom at the end, the need was truly desperate. I walked past an elderly couple moving slowly toward the lobby and skimmed past a couple of women who were chatting about a new dress shop.

I raced into the ladies' room, took care of business, and was just about to step back into the hallway when I became aware of voices on the other side of the door. I didn't pay them much attention until one of the men said, "Damn it, Percy. This has gotten out of hand."

I froze with the door partway open, just wide enough for me to peek through into the hallway. Percy Ponter and two other men were so deep in their conversation, none of them noticed me. Which I counted as a good thing.

Glancing behind me to make sure I was really alone in the lavatory, I pressed my ear to the opening so I could hear what they were saying. After all, I was stuck here. Even Gabriel couldn't blame me for this.

"I know it's gotten out of hand," Percy mumbled. "I'm telling you, we need to just own up to this."

I recognized Stanton Meyer, Musterion's first lieutenant, a short, round man with ruddy skin and neatly trimmed salt-and-pepper beard. At Percy's words, his ruddy skin turned even redder. He reared back, as shocked as if Percy had suggested they all run naked through the ballroom. "We are *not* going public with this," he barked. "We're going to get the money back from Boudreaux and that will be that."

"How?" Percy demanded. "Judd doesn't have it. He used it to pay off the gambling debt. There's no way he can get the money back now."

Norman Costlow, the krewe's second lieutenant, made a noise of derision. He's a tall, thin man with a shock of red hair and a hook nose. "There's money in Big Daddy's businesses," he said. "Judd can take the money out of there if he has to. I'm sure Susannah would be willing to write a check to shield the family from embarrassment."

I almost choked when I heard that. So that's what Susannah had been talking about when she warned Big Daddy not to embarrass her. That must have been why she'd issued the ultimatum. Protect the family from embarrassment, *or else*. But had *or else* meant murder?

"I've already talked to her," Percy said in a low voice. "If there was money available in one of the businesses, Big Daddy would have skimmed it from there in the first place. There's a reason he pocketed the money from the fund-raiser, gentlemen. I say we just swallow our pride and admit what happened. It will sully Boudreaux's name, but he did embezzle the funds. I don't think we should hide that from the members."

Pieces to the puzzle clicked into place and I had to press my lips together to keep from squeaking with excitement.

Costlow shook his head firmly. "I will not drag his name through the mud now that he's dead. It wouldn't be right."

"I don't give two hoots about Boudreaux's reputation," Meyer snapped. "But I sure as hell care about mine, and I'm not going out there and telling those people that a million dollars of their money disappeared during my watch. Get it back from Boudreaux," he ordered. "I don't care what you have to do."

My heart was pounding so hard I almost missed what he said, and they moved away before I could figure out what to do about what I'd just heard. Big Daddy had stolen money from Musterion to protect his baby brother. That's why his ass was on the line. That's why he was so angry he'd threatened Judd with rehab.

But had Susannah been so determined to protect her own reputation that she'd killed Big Daddy? Had she really thought she could pin the murder on someone else and get away with it?

I had to call Sullivan and let him know what I'd just heard. Trembling with excitement, I fished my cell phone out of my evening bag, but I had no service. Not even a partial bar.

Checking my phone as I walked, I hurried down the hall and out into the crowd. Still nothing.

Gabriel was waiting for me near the escalator, and the smile slid from his face when he saw the look on mine. "You look serious. Is everything okay?"

"I'm fine," I assured him. "But I need to call Detective Sullivan. I just heard something he needs to know about. Any idea where I can get service in this hotel?"

"Not off the top of my head. Shall we go outside? You should be able to get reception there."

I nodded and we moved toward the escalator, but before we could begin our descent, Richard Montgomery stopped us. "I've been looking all over for you," he said to Gabriel. "I need you to settle a bet for me."

Gabriel hesitated, but I waved him off. "This will only take a minute," I promised. "I'll be back before you know it."

He strolled away with Richard, and I rode the escalator to the main floor, then headed toward the lobby, looking for a signal or a side entrance as I walked. The broad corridor was mostly deserted, but there were a few people around. I hadn't gone far when a laughing couple came through a set of glass doors a few feet in front of me.

I veered toward it and checked to make sure I could get back inside—I'd learned my lesson at The Shores—then let the door shut behind me and moved away from the building until a couple of bars showed up on my screen. I punched in Sullivan's number—or at least the first four numbers. That's as far as I got before I spotted Judd and Susannah leaving the hotel by an entrance about thirty feet away.

Judd strolled slowly, hands in his pockets, as if he hadn't a care in the world. Susannah's movements were more furtive. She glanced over her shoulder twice in thirty seconds, and she held one arm in front of her, her evening wrap tossed loosely over her hand.

I had a bad feeling about what I was seeing, so I finished punching in Sullivan's number and waited impatiently for him to answer. "Get over to the Belle Grande Hotel," I said when I heard his voice. "Susannah Boudreaux has a gun. I think she's about to kill her brother-in-law."

Sullivan didn't waste time asking annoying questions, which is one of my favorite things about him. He asked exactly where they were, ordered me to get back inside, and put out a call to dispatch.

I had no desire to get between a crazy woman and her gun, but I couldn't just go back inside and leave Judd on his own. Besides, if I went back into the hotel, I wouldn't be able to call for help if things got worse.

Scarcely breathing, I moved a little closer, keeping to the shadows so they wouldn't see me.

"They know," I heard Susannah say. "They *know*! And they're demanding the money back. They're threatening to destroy Bradley—and me in the process."

Judd sat on the edge of a raised flowerbed. "How can they destroy you, Susannah? You had nothing to do with it."

"Do you think I can hold my head up if this gets out? Do you think anybody in this town will invite me to anything? I'll be a laughingstock. Or worse, they'll feel sorry for me."

Judd smiled sadly. "Now that would be a shame."

"Well, it's not going to happen," she said, her voice growing a little louder. "I'm not going to let it happen. You've embarrassed this family for the last time."

"I sincerely doubt that," Judd said. "Embarrassing the family is the one thing I'm truly gifted at."

Susannah shook her head. I could only see the side of

her face, but I thought she was beginning to look a little wild around the eyes, so I moved closer still. "I don't know how I'm going to manage it, but I'm going to get that money back to the krewe. I'll sell one of the businesses if I have to. But I won't do this again. Big Daddy carried you all these years. He protected you from yourself. He bailed you out, using all of *our* money to do it." She swung her hand and the wrap covering it fell away.

"You're going to leave. Tonight. And you're never coming back. Do you understand me?"

"Why not just let me confess to what really happened the night of the party? They'll lock me up for the rest of my life, and you'll be finished with me for good."

Wait a minute. *What?* My heart stopped beating for an instant and then hammered in my chest so hard I couldn't hear anything else.

Susannah leveled the gun at him. "Never. I'm tired of the pitying looks on my friends' faces when your name comes up. I'm tired of everything always being about you and your *sickness*."

Judd ran a slow glance over her hand and the gun she held. "You'd rather kill me than turn me in?"

"In a heartbeat."

He held out his arms, daring her to take a shot. "Then do it, Susannah. I know I panicked when Bradley died, but this week has been hell and I've realized I can't go through this again." She shifted uncertainly and he pushed harder. "Come on, Susannah. Do you think I care what happens to me now? Life in prison or no life at all, it's all the same to me."

She shook her head and refocused her aim. "I think you're the *only* person you care about, you selfish bastard. I think you used your brother up for his whole life, and you never gave one single thing back to him." Anger twisted her features, making her pretty face almost unrecognizably ugly. "He didn't love you, you know. He took care of you because he *had* to."

Pain seared Judd's face. Her hateful words had found their mark.

"If you cared about him at all, you'd leave," she shouted. "Let me salvage his name. Let me keep this story from getting out. Let me protect his reputation the way you never would."

Judd dropped his head and stared at the ground. When he lifted his head again, he looked different. Resigned. "Why don't you just tell them the truth? Why don't we just get it over with now?"

"Because the truth won't help anything," Susannah shouted. "Do you really think I want to be known as the woman whose husband was murdered by his own brother?"

She'd almost convinced me that she cared about her husband, but that question snapped me back to reality. This wasn't about Big Daddy. It had always been about her.

"I told you, it was an accident," Judd said, but his voice was so low I almost missed it.

"Oh, I know. You didn't *mean* to. You never mean to, Judd. That's the problem, but you still ruin everything for everybody."

I hated knowing that Judd had killed Big Daddy, and I hated Susannah for caring more about herself than she did about either of them. But knowing that she'd tried to throw my uncle to the wolves to protect her reputation made my blood boil.

Sirens split the night, and Judd lifted his head to listen. "Someone knows we're out here," he said. "Looks like I'm not going anywhere."

Panicked, Susannah raised the gun. I didn't have time to

think about what I did next. I'll never know whether she intended to shoot him or not, but I threw myself on her before she had the chance.

I stumbled a little as I grabbed for her hand, and I lost my balance. We fell to the ground together. Pain shot through my knees, and the pavement tore the skin from my arms. My elbow throbbed, but I stayed focused on Susannah's hands and the gun. I just had to keep her from using it until the police arrived.

I expected Judd to run, but he didn't move.

Susannah surged upward, trying to shake me. I jabbed an elbow into her stomach and heard the breath rush from her lungs. Judd still didn't move.

"What's the matter with you?" I shouted at him. "Either get out of here or help me with her. Don't just stand there."

That seemed to rouse him. I could hear the heavy footsteps of New Orleans's finest pounding as help came. I could hear Sullivan shouting my name. But I couldn't tear my eyes from the sight of Judd walking away and leaving me to fight Susannah on my own.

Thirty-six

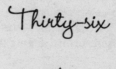

The news of Judd Boudreaux's fatal accident hit the news early Sunday morning and spread like wildfire. He'd been drunk when he drove his car into a tree. The police estimated his speed at around ninety miles an hour.

Everyone said it was inevitable. The way he drank, they'd been expecting something like this for years. I couldn't prove it, and I didn't even want to try, but I suspected it was no accident.

With Big Daddy's murder solved, Sullivan cleared Uncle Nestor and Aunt Yolanda to travel, and they wasted no time booking their flight. My heart was heavy as I drove them to the airport. It had been a hectic week, but it had been great to see them again. And at least they were on speaking terms again.

I pulled into the passenger drop-off and we kept busy unloading their bags from the trunk, avoiding "good-bye" for as long as possible. When we couldn't put it off any longer, I hugged Aunt Yolanda tightly and blinked back tears.

"Are you *sure* you want to leave this morning?" I said, trying to laugh around the lump in my throat. "You should stay until after Mardi Gras."

"You might be able to convince me," she whispered, "but Nestor is anxious to get home again." She pulled back and I could see that her eyes were shimmering, too. "We're going to miss you, *mija*. Come home for a visit soon."

"I will," I promised. I sniffed. Dug in my pocket for a tissue.

And looked up just as Uncle Nestor pulled me into his arms. "I am so proud of you, Rita. Never forget that."

I couldn't see his face. My own tears blinded me. "I love you, *Tío*."

And then they were gone. I watched them walk across the lanes of traffic and into the airport before sliding behind the wheel of the Mercedes and driving away. As painful as saying good-bye was, I still didn't regret the choice I'd made to stay here in New Orleans.

That was good to know.

Memories of the confrontation with Susannah, and Judd's subsequent death, had sparked one of life's clarifying moments for me. I wanted to laugh more and worry less. I wanted to dare more and fear less. I didn't think that was too much to ask. And there was no better time to start relaxing and having a little fun than right then.

I'd spent the past couple of days immersing myself in the Mardi Gras experience with Miss Frankie, Bernice, and the Zydeco crew. Despite Big Daddy's murder and Judd's suicide, Musterion put on a great parade on Sunday. Even the scandal of Big Daddy's embezzlement wasn't enough to dampen Mardi Gras spirits.

I was learning that New Orleans moves to its own unique rhythm, and that's never truer than during Mardi Gras. The music, the crowds, the noise and laughter, the unlikeliest costumes on the unlikeliest people can almost lead to sensory overload. There's nothing subtle or understated about Mardi Gras. The louder, brighter, and more garish the costume or float, the better. It's all about self-indulgence during carnival and self-denial once carnival is over and Lent begins.

I'd had a great time, but I think mostly I enjoyed feeling as if I'd belonged in our little group and being part of a tradition that dates back hundreds of years. I'd spent some time on Bourbon Street, with its beautiful old buildings and iron lacework standing side-by-side with neon signs advertising XXX entertainment. It's an experience, but not my favorite.

I'd been happier at the Uptown parades, where people lined up six or seven deep, and the back rows were made up of people standing on ladders to see over the crowds. I'd loved watching the delight on the kids' faces when someone on a passing float tossed a trinket or stuffed animal their way. And I'd been completely charmed by the people on the West Bank, who'd thrown their arms wide and welcomed me as if I'd always belonged there.

After the intense revelry of Fat Tuesday, I woke up to a quiet, empty house on Ash Wednesday morning. It was the first time I'd been alone in my own home for a long time, and I was enjoying the solitude. For a few hours, nobody needed me and even I couldn't work up anything to worry about. I rolled over and pulled the covers over my head, settling down for another hour of sleep.

The entire staff at Zydeco had been out late the night before, so I'd given everyone the morning off. Which left me free to putter around the house and catch up with some of the chores I'd let slip for weeks. Aunt Yolanda had taken care of the most pressing issues, so I started a load of laundry, whipped up some French toast with cinnamon, and made coffee—strong and black—to kick-start my morning.

Just as I carried my plate and a mug to the kitchen table, the doorbell rang. I cinched my robe around my waist and opened the door to Sullivan. I can't say I was surprised to see him. Along with the rest of the police force, he'd been working double shifts throughout the celebration, but I knew he'd pay me a visit when he could.

He looked good. Strong. Handsome. Steady. After I'd spent the better part of Saturday evening dancing with Gabriel, my reaction to Sullivan confused me. But then, so did my reaction to Gabriel. I'd always been a one-man woman.

I didn't waste time dissecting my feelings. I invited Sullivan in, poured coffee and made him a plate, and then sat across from him. I like my time alone, but I still had unanswered questions, and I hoped Sullivan could clear those up for me. And besides, he's easy on the eyes. "So," I said, "what brings you here?"

He dug into the French toast like a man who hadn't eaten in days. "I thought you'd like to know that Susannah Boudreaux has been charged with two counts of aggravated assault. With your testimony, we should be able to make the charges stick."

"So she'll go to prison? Good. It seems only fair."

He lifted one shoulder and mopped up some syrup with a wedge of toast. "If all goes well. I wouldn't be surprised if her attorney tries an insanity plea, though. She's . . . disturbed."

"Ya think?" I grinned and settled back in my seat, cradling my mug in both hands. "Has she explained how she knew that Judd killed Big Daddy?"

Sullivan nodded. "Apparently, she and Tyson stumbled upon the scene as Judd was running away."

"Who *is* Tyson, anyway?"

"He's the general manager at one of Big Daddy's car dealerships. That's how he met both Susannah and Violet."

"So was he sleeping with both of them?"

Sullivan shook his head. "As far as I know, just Susannah."

"So he and Susannah were together when they found Big Daddy? But they just left him there?"

"That's right. They both say that they didn't actually see Judd hit Big Daddy, but it was pretty obvious what had happened."

"So instead of turning her brother-in-law in, Susannah tried to throw suspicion on Uncle Nestor? The woman really is certifiable, isn't she?"

"I think she was desperate to protect the Boudreaux family, and by extension, her standing in the community. She liked her life, and she saw Big Daddy's name and reputation as her key to keeping it. And I'm pretty sure alcohol was a factor. She'd been at that party for several hours by that time, and the witnesses I've talked to have all said she was drinking heavily. She had a knee-jerk reaction when she found her husband dead. After that, she was afraid to come forward with the truth."

Somehow I thought her decision had been more calculated than that. "Judd said Big Daddy's death was an accident," I said. "Do you think it was?"

Sullivan nodded. "I do, but without Judd's testimony we'll never be able to prove it." And with his past, Judd's memory would probably always be under a cloud of suspicion. I shook off the slight melancholy that settled on my shoulders at that thought and told Liam about Uncle Nestor and Aunt Yolanda and how Susannah Boudreaux had kissed him at the party. "I still don't understand why she did that," I said. "I even asked her about it, but she claimed that my uncle kissed her. I know she's lying."

"She and Big Daddy had a twisted-up relationship," Sullivan said. "They were both sleeping around, and yet they both seemed to genuinely care about each other in an odd way." He held up both hands to ward off the argument he could feel coming and added, "Hey, I don't get it either. I took a statement from Susannah's friend Tyson the other day. He claims that Susannah was trying to show Big Daddy that she meant business. Apparently, she used to threaten to leave him on a regular basis. This time, she wanted him to believe she was serious. So she kissed your uncle right in front of Big Daddy just to prove a point."

"What a crock. Do you believe that?"

"I believe that's what she told Tyson," Sullivan said with a shrug. "But I don't think she had any intention of leaving Big Daddy."

Neither did I. I hated her for involving Uncle Nestor in her mess. He'd had the misfortune of being in the wrong place at the wrong time, and it had come very close to destroying his own marriage, not to mention his life.

"If you ask me," I said, "Big Daddy had already tarnished the name. Other than the way he took care of his brother, he didn't have a lot of redeeming social value."

"He wasn't all bad," Sullivan said.

"He wasn't all good either."

"Who is? If it makes you feel better, I heard from the

Boudreauxes' attorney this morning. Susannah had assumed she was going to inherit Big Daddy's estate, but it turns out he left a will dividing almost all of it between his children. He also left some property a few miles north to Judd. I guess the kids—meaning Mellie, since none of the children is yet of age—have decided to turn that land into a treatment facility: the Judd Boudreaux Memorial Rehabilitation Center."

The melancholy lifted a little further. "I like knowing that," I said.

Sullivan finished his breakfast and sat back with a sigh of satisfaction. "You sure can cook."

I actually felt myself blush. "I'm glad you enjoyed it. Would you like more?"

He patted his stomach and shook his head. "Thanks, but I shouldn't." He glanced around the kitchen. His gaze landed on a pile of sequins and feathers, the costume I'd worn on Bourbon Street. He arched an eyebrow and grinned, leaning over to hold it up in front of him. "New outfit?"

I laughed and nodded. "Yeah, but it was a one-time-only deal. That thing will never again see the light of day with me in it."

He ran another glance over it and looked back at me slowly. "So your aunt and uncle are gone?"

I swallowed. Hard. And tried not to overreact to the way his eyes suddenly turned smoky gray. "They flew out on Sunday. Aunt Yolanda would have liked to stay for Mardi Gras, but Uncle Nestor was ready to get home. He's not really into crowds and noise. They make him nervous."

"I'm sorry their visit was ruined by the investigation," Sullivan said. "I really did try to find someone who could provide him with an alibi."

"Yeah. Me, too." But that was all water under the bridge.

The important thing now was that they were speaking to each other when they left New Orleans. As long as they were talking, I trusted they could work through anything.

Without another word, Sullivan got up and came around the table toward me. He pulled me out of the chair with more gentleness than I would have imagined for a man his size, and put his arms around me tenderly. "I'm glad you called me the other night, but you had me worried sick. Don't do that again, okay?"

I wrapped my arms around his waist and leaned my head on his solid chest.

"Rita? Promise?"

I wanted to oblige, but I don't like making promises I might not be able to keep. "I promise that if I'm ever in trouble, I'll call you."

He pulled back and scowled at me. "That's it? That's all I get?"

"I'm afraid so." I had no idea what the future held for any of us, but I deliberately pushed aside the worry that was so natural for me and let myself enjoy the moment.

I have to admit, it felt pretty good.

He didn't stay. Which was probably a very good thing. If he'd asked, I might have said yes. But I wasn't sure I was ready for that. I had plenty of time to figure out where I was headed. I didn't have to have all the answers today.

After he left, I climbed the stairs to my office and booted up my computer. And then, because Sullivan's visit had left me in such an agreeable mood, I pounded out my first blog entry and e-mailed it to Ox before I could change my mind. Life's too short to quibble about the small stuff, and yeah, it's all small stuff.

Recipes

Rita's Breakfast Casserole

Serves 12

3 cups chopped onion
3 tablespoons margarine or butter
¼ to ½ teaspoon salt
¼ teaspoon pepper
2 (12-ounce) cans refrigerated buttermilk biscuit
6 slices bacon, crisply cooked, crumbled
⅔ cup whipping cream
½ cup dairy sour cream
3 eggs
(½ cup) shredded white cheddar or Monterey Jack cheese
Additional pepper for sprinkling, if desired

Preheat the oven to 375° F.

In a large skillet, cook onions in margarine until tender but not browned. Stir in salt and ¼ teaspoon pepper.

Separate biscuit dough into 20 biscuits and place in an ungreased 15 × 10-inch jelly roll pan. Press over bottom and ½ inch up sides to form crust. Spoon onions over crust, and sprinkle with bacon.

In a medium bowl, combine whipping cream, sour cream, and eggs until well blended. Stir in cheese. Spoon evenly over onions and bacon. Sprinkle with additional pepper.

Bake for 24 to 30 minutes or until crust is deep golden brown.

Serve hot. Store leftovers in refrigerator.

This is a great dish for brunch or when relatives drop in for a weekend visit.

* * *

Dizzy Duke Shrimp Étouffée

Serves 4 to 6

Étouffée is considered one of Louisiana's crown jewels when it comes to cuisine. The word étouffée *basically means "smothered," and it's a common cooking technique here in the South. Shrimp étouffée brings together all the greats of Louisiana cooking: seafood, a flour-and-oil roux, and a mirepoix, otherwise known as the holy trinity: onion, celery, and green pepper. Add some traditional Cajun seasoning and hot sauce, and you can't beat it.*

You can make this dish two ways: either by peeling the shrimp yourself and simmering the stock in your own kitchen, or you can choose the short version, which will cut your prep time to about 20 minutes.

Note that while this recipe calls for shrimp, you can also use crawfish or crab.

OPTIONAL SHRIMP STOCK

> Shells from 2 pounds of shrimp
> ½ large onion, chopped
> Top and bottom from 1 green pepper
> 2 garlic cloves, chopped
> 1 celery stalk, chopped
> 5 bay leaves

ÉTOUFFÉE

> ¼ cup vegetable oil or lard
> Heaping ¼ cup flour
> ½ large onion, chopped
> 1 bell pepper, chopped
> 1 to 2 jalapeño peppers, chopped
> 1 large celery stalk, chopped
> 4 garlic cloves, chopped
> 1 pint shrimp stock (see above), or clam juice or premade
>   fish or shellfish stock
> 1 tablespoon Cajun seasoning
> ½ teaspoon celery seed
> 1 tablespoon sweet paprika
> Salt
> 2 pounds shrimp, shell on (remove shells for use in the
>   shrimp stock; if not making your own stock, you can
>   get shrimp already shelled)
> 3 green onions, chopped
> Hot sauce (Crystal or Tabasco) to taste

FOR SHRIMP STOCK

Pour 2 quarts of water into a pot and add all the remaining stock ingredients. Bring to a boil. Reduce heat and simmer the stock gently for 45 minutes.

Strain stock through a fine-meshed sieve into another pot over low heat. This recipe makes a large amount of stock, which you can use for other recipes. It lasts in the fridge for a week.

FOR ÉTOUFFÉE

Begin by making a roux. Heat the vegetable oil or lard in a heavy pot over medium heat for 1 to 2 minutes. Stir in the flour well, whisking to make sure there are no clumps. Cook for 10 minutes or so, stirring often, until it turns a pretty brown color.

Add the onion, bell pepper, jalapeño, and celery. Mix well and cook over medium heat for approximately 4 minutes, stirring occasionally. Add the garlic and cook another 2 minutes. (Do not overcook the garlic at this stage.)

Slowly add the hot shrimp stock, stirring constantly so it incorporates. The roux will absorb the stock and thicken at first, then it will loosen. Add stock in small amounts until your sauce is about the thickness of syrup. It should be about 1 pint of sauce.

Add Cajun seasoning, celery seed, and paprika, and mix well. Add salt to taste, then mix in the shrimp. Cover the pot, turn the heat to its lowest setting, and cook for 10 minutes.

Add the green onions and hot sauce to taste. Serve over white rice. Great with a cold beer or lemonade.

*   *   *

Zydeco King Cake

Serves 10 to 12

King Cake is a tradition that came to New Orleans with the first French settlers. It's been a part of the culture ever since, though during the early days, the King Cake was part of a family's celebration. It really didn't take on a public role until around 1870.

The sides of the dough should pull away from the sides of the mixing bowl as you knead this dough. If it doesn't, the moisture content in the flour has fluctuated with the humidity, so add a spoonful or two more flour.

CAKE

> 1 cup lukewarm milk (about 110° F)
> ½ cup granulated sugar
> 2 tablespoons dry yeast
> 3 ¾ cups all-purpose flour
> 1 cup melted butter
> 5 egg yolks, beaten
> 1 teaspoon vanilla extract
> 1 teaspoon grated fresh lemon zest
> 3 teaspoons cinnamon
> 1 teaspoon grated fresh nutmeg (more or less to taste)

ICING

> 2 cups powdered sugar
> ¼ cup condensed milk
> 1 teaspoon fresh lemon juice

Purple, green, and gold decorative sugars
1 plastic baby to hide in the cake (can also use a fava
      bean)

FOR CAKE

Pour the warm milk into a large bowl. Whisk in the granulated sugar, yeast, and a heaping tablespoon of the flour, mixing until both the sugar and the yeast have thoroughly dissolved. Once bubbles have developed on the surface of the milk, and the yeast causes it to foam, whisk in the butter, egg yolks, vanilla, and lemon zest. Add remaining flour, cinnamon, and nutmeg, folding the dry ingredients into the wet ingredients. A large rubber spatula works great for this step.

After the dough is mixed well and pulls away from the sides of the bowl, shape it into a large ball. Then knead the dough on a floured surface until it is smooth and elastic, which takes about 15 minutes.

Put the dough back into the bowl, cover with plastic wrap, and set aside in a draft-free place to let it proof, or rise, for 1 ½ hours or until the dough has doubled in volume.

Preheat the oven to 375° F. Once the dough has risen, punch it down and divide the dough into 3 equal pieces. Roll each piece of dough into a long strip, making 3 ropes of equal length. Braid the 3 ropes together and then form the braid into a circle, pinching ends together to form a seal.

Carefully place the braided dough on a nonstick cookie sheet and let it rise again until it doubles in size, about 30 minutes.

Once the cake has doubled in size, place the cookie sheet in the oven and bake until the braid is golden brown, about 30 minutes.

Remove the cake from the oven, place on a wire rack to allow air to circulate, and cool for 30 minutes.

FOR ICING

While the cake is cooling, whisk together the powdered sugar, condensed milk, and lemon juice in a bowl until the icing is smooth and spreadable. If the icing seems too thick, add a bit more condensed milk; if it's a bit too liquid, add a bit more powdered sugar until you have the right consistency.

Spread the icing over the top of the cooled cake and sprinkle with purple, green, and gold sugars while the icing is still wet.

Tuck the plastic baby into underside of the cake and, using a spatula, slide the cake onto a serving platter.

*   *   *

Chile Verde

Serves 6

In all my life, I've never known anyone to make chile verde from a recipe. It's usually made with inexact measurements, and adjusted to taste, so take these approximate measurements and then adjust as you like:

    3 pounds pork roast
    Lard or olive oil to sauté
    3 tablespoons flour
    3 large onions, chopped

3 cloves garlic, minced
1 tablespoon oregano, crumbled (this is entirely
      optional; I usually don't include it)
1 cup green chilies, chopped
1 to 2 jalapeños, deseeded and chopped (optional)
Water
Salt and pepper

Trim away as much fat as possible from the pork roast and cut into cubes. Brown meat in lard or olive oil. Remove from pan and sprinkle meat with the flour. Brown onions and garlic in frying pan until transparent, but not brown. Add meat, oregano, chilies, and jalapeños to the onion mixture and then add water to cover. Simmer 2 to 3 hours. Add salt and pepper during last half hour.

Cool and degrease stew.

Serve with flour tortillas.

*   *   *

Flour Tortillas

Makes approximately 2 dozen

4 cups all-purpose flour
1 teaspoon salt
2 teaspoons baking powder
2 tablespoons lard
1 ½ cups water

Whisk the flour, salt, and baking powder together in a mixing bowl. Mix in the lard with your fingers until the flour
resembles cornmeal. Add the water and mix until the dough
comes together; place on a lightly floured surface and knead
a few minutes until smooth and elastic. Divide the dough
into 24 equal pieces and roll each piece into a ball.

Preheat a large skillet over medium-high heat and add
2 to 3 drops of oil. (Using more oil will make the tortillas
greasy and cause smoking in the kitchen.) Use a well-floured
rolling pin to roll a dough ball into a thin, round tortilla.
Place into the hot skillet, and cook until the exposed surface
begins to bubble. Flip and continue cooking until golden on
the other side.

Place the cooked tortilla in a tortilla warmer or between
the folds of a clean kitchen towel to keep it moist until serving. Continue rolling and cooking the remaining dough.

Someone's out to make a killing . . .

FROM NATIONAL BESTSELLING AUTHOR
PAIGE SHELTON

Crops and Robbers

• **A Farmers' Market Mystery** •

Thanks to her delicious farm-made jams and pre-
serves, Becca Robins's business has been booming.
But when an unhappy customer turns up dead in
Becca's kitchen, she's afraid it will really sour her
reputation . . .

penguin.com
PaigeShelton.com
facebook.com/TheCrimeSceneBooks

M945T0811

"*O*hmigod, that's your guy! The one the psychic told you about!" Jenna whispered excitedly.

I shook my head fast. "No, he's not. It's just coincidence." I sounded breathless. My heart was pounding hard.

"But what are the odds—"

"Look, the psychic probably saw him at some point, and he stayed on her mind and when she was tapping into things, she tapped into her own memory, not my future."

That was the logical explanation, and I liked logical.

"He'd sure stay on my mind," Amber said. "He's totally hot."

ALSO BY RACHEL HAWTHORNE:

RACHEL HAWTHORNE

HARPER TEEN
An Imprint of **HarperCollins***Publishers*

HarperTeen is an imprint of
HarperCollins Publishers.
Labor of Love
Copyright © 2008 by Jan Nowasky

Library of Congress catalog card number: 2007930287
ISBN 978-0-06-136384-9

Typography by Andrea Vandergrift

First Edition

Chapter 1

"*I* see a spectacular sunrise."

An icy shiver skittered up my spine, and the fine hairs on the nape of my neck prickled. I know my reaction seemed a little extreme, but...

When Jenna, Amber, and I walked into the psychic's shop, we didn't tell her our names. So Saraphina had no way of knowing my name is Dawn Delaney.

Sunrise ... dawn? See what I mean? It was just a little too spooky. It didn't help that I thought I saw ghostly apparitions in the smoky spirals coming from the sharply scented incense that was smoldering around us.

Although I certainly didn't mind that the psychic considered me spectacular. If the sunrise she mentioned was really referring to me—and not the sun coming up over the Mississippi River. Her words were vague enough that they could apply to anything or nothing.

I'd never had a psychic reading before, so I wasn't quite sure how it all worked. I was excited about discovering what was going to happen, but also a little nervous. Did I really want to know what was in my future?

My hands rested on top of hers, our palms touching. Her eyes were closed. I figured that she was trying to channel whatever it was that psychics channeled. I'd expected the psychic to be hunched over and old—wrinkled, gray, maybe with warts. But Saraphina didn't look much older than we were. Her bright red hair was barely visible at the edges of her green turban. She wore a flowing green caftan and an assortment of bright, beaded necklaces. Her colorful bracelets jangled as she took a firmer grip on my hands and squeezed gently, almost massaging my fingers.

"I see a very messy place. Broken. Boards and shingles and . . . things hidden," Saraphina said in a soft, dreamy voice that seemed to float around us.

Okay, her words calmed my racing heart a little. We were in New Orleans, after all. I didn't need a psychic to tell me that areas of it were still messy, even a few years after some major hurricanes had left their marks.

"I hear hammering," she continued. "You're trying to rebuild something. But be careful with the tools. You might get distracted and hurt yourself—more than hitting your thumb with a hammer. You could get very badly hurt. And worse, you could hurt others."

Not exactly what I wanted to hear. I wasn't even sure if I truly believed in the ability to see into the future, but I was intrigued by the possibility.

If you knew the future, should you accept it or try to change it?

"Lots of people are around," she said. "It's hot and dirty. There's a guy . . . a red and white baseball cap. The cap has a logo on it. Chiefs. Kansas City Chiefs. I don't get a name, but he has a nice smile."

I released a breath I hadn't realized I was holding.

For Jenna, Saraphina had seen "fire that doesn't burn." The fire part sounded scary, but the not burning was just confusing. And that she saw her at a fair, or something equally mystifying. Jenna's brow was still furrowed, and I knew she was trying to figure it out. She didn't like unsolved mysteries. She couldn't pass a sudoku puzzle without stopping to fill in the empty boxes.

But a nice smile I could live with, as long as that was all he offered, because I was taking a summer sabbatical from guys.

Amber, skeptic that she is about all things supernatural, had tried to mess with Saraphina. She'd been the first one daring enough to ask for a reading. When Saraphina had touched Amber's palm, she'd said she saw color. We'd all been weirded out, amber being a color and all.

Then Amber had asked if she'd find love this summer. Since Saraphina's eyes were closed, Amber had winked at Jenna and me, because she has a boyfriend back home. She's been crazy in love with Chad ever since winter break when they first started going out. He's the first boyfriend she's ever had, and she's been a little obsessive about being with him as much as possible. Quite honestly, I was surprised that she'd come to New Orleans with us, leaving Chad back home in Texas. Glad, but surprised.

Saraphina had said, "Not this summer."

Amber had rolled her eyes and mouthed, "See, I told you. Bullsh—"

"But college . . . one better than you already have," Saraphina finished.

That had been just a little too *woooo-woooo* and had pretty much shut Amber up. Once Saraphina released her hands, Amber started gnawing on her thumbnail. And she was still at it. She had a habit of worrying about things and expecting the worst.

Now, it got really quiet, and Saraphina was so still that it was eerie. How could a person be that still? Was she in a trance?

Sitting on either side of me, Amber and Jenna didn't seem to be breathing. Neither was I. Was Saraphina seeing something horrible? Was she debating whether or not to tell me?

With a huge sigh, as though she'd just finished pushing a heavy boulder up a huge hill,
Saraphina released my hands and opened her
eyes. They'd creeped me out at first, because
one was blue and one was brown. But once I
got used to them, I realized they somehow
belonged together—with her face. With her. It
just seemed like a psychic kind of thing.

"I see nothing else," she said.

Although she didn't look old, she seemed
ancient. I think she had what my grandmother
refers to as "old soul eyes."

"Oh, okay," I said, wiping my damp palms
on my shorts. "Thanks."

"My pleasure."

Maybe she was older than I thought,
because she also sort of sounded like my grandmother.

"If you know something really awful is
going to happen, you'd tell us, right?" Jenna
asked.

Saraphina smiled. "I tell only what I see. I
don't interpret it."

"Yeah, but a fire that doesn't burn. What

does that mean exactly?"

"I don't know."

"But it's the nature of fire to burn, so do you mean it's not actually burning or it's not burning me? See what I mean? It's kinda vague."

Saraphina shrugged, almost as if to say maybe we didn't really want to know anything else. And maybe we didn't.

I touched Jenna's shoulder. "Come on. We should go."

"But I need more—"

Amber and I had to practically drag her out of the shop, before Saraphina told her for the umpteenth time that there wasn't any more.

Once we were outside, the heat pressed down on us. Until that moment, I hadn't realized how cold I was. My fingers were like ice. I shivered again and rubbed my hands up and down my bare arms.

"Well, that was certainly . . . interesting," I said.

"Do you think she means Chad isn't my forever guy?" Amber asked. "Because I was thinking he was *it* for me. You know—my

7

first, my one, my only?"

"Don't get all freaked out," I said. "None of it means anything. Not really."

As we started walking down the street, I slipped on my sunglasses and adjusted my "Life Is Good" cap over my shoulder-length dark hair. The humidity and my hair weren't going to get along, but that was nothing new. After all, I lived near Houston, so humidity was a way of life.

I'd come totally prepared for New Orleans—also known as the Big Easy. I was wearing red shorts, sneakers, a white lacy tank, and lots of suntan lotion. My mom's parents are from Italy—the old country, as my grandma calls it—so I tend to tan easily, but I still take precautions. I'd known we'd be doing a lot of outdoor walking today because we had so much to see and do in the French Quarter.

"Then why'd we do it?" Jenna asked, looking back over her shoulder, as if she thought maybe something was going to jump out at us.

"We thought it would be fun, and we're in New Orleans," I reminded her. "Visiting a psychic is something you should do when you're here."

We'd arrived a few hours earlier, so we had some time to play today. But tomorrow we'd start working. Because, okay, the psychic was right. We were here to help with the rebuilding efforts. So again, she hit the nail on the head — pun intended — with the whole hammering thing. But it was also an easy guess. Lots of students were spending a portion of their summer here, helping with the many rebuilding projects in the city.

"She got our names right," Amber said.

"Color, sunrise, that could mean anything," I pointed out. "For Jenna she was totally off. Come on, a carnival?"

"She didn't say 'carnival,'" Jenna said. "She said 'fair.' Maybe she meant fair as in pale, not dark. My name in Cornish means 'pale, light.'"

"In Cornish?" Amber asked. "You mean, like in serving dishes? That doesn't make any sense."

I laughed, while Jenna rolled her eyes. Amber's comment was just what I needed to shake off the lingering willies. Sometimes she was a little out there.

"Look, y'all, it was something to do for fun. But there's not going to be a fire, Amber isn't going to break up with Chad, and there's definitely not going to be a guy with a red Chiefs cap in my life."

"You never know," Amber said.

"Trust me, I know. I'm taking time away from all things male."

"Why? Because of Drew?" Jenna asked.

"Why else?"

"You really have to get over what happened prom night," Jenna said.

She was right. I knew she was right. But still, it was hard.

Prom night was unforgettable. And that made it a huge problem. Because I totally wanted to forget it.

It was the night I caught my then-boyfriend making out with another girl in the backseat of his car. It had been almost midnight, the dance winding down. I'd gone to the restroom. When I came back to the dance area, I couldn't find him. I was going to text message him, but I realized that I'd left my phone on the front seat of his car.

A few minutes later, it was where I left my broken heart.

Wouldn't those make great lyrics for a country song?

"I'm over it," I said with determination, trying to convince myself as much as my friends. "Totally and completely. But I don't see the point in getting involved with anyone right now."

I'd put my heart on the line with Drew. He was fun to be around. He made me laugh.

He also had what I guessed you called star quality. He was in drama class, and he'd been given the lead in our school's production of *Beauty and the Beast*. He'd made a great beast because he has black hair but startling blue eyes. His performance had made me cry. He'd been so good! I'd been over the moon. My boyfriend had brought the audience to their feet for a standing ovation.

Now I wondered, probably unfairly, how

much of our relationship had been a performance.

The aromas of chocolate and warm sugar
brought me back to the present. They wafted
out of the bakery we were passing.

"Let's stop," Amber said. "Maybe a sugar
rush will wipe out the worries about our future."

"I'm not worried," I stated.

"Yeah, well, I am."

It smelled even better inside—vanilla and
cinnamon added to the aroma.

At one end, the long glass-encased counter
had all sorts of pastries. At the other end were
pralines, fudge, divinity, and an assortment of
chocolates. Several people were in line ahead of
us, so we had plenty of time to make a decision.
And I needed it. I'm totally into sweet stuff.

"I think I'm going for the carrot cake,"
Jenna said. "It's healthy."

"How do you figure that?" Amber asked.

"Carrots."

Amber and I grinned. Jenna is a pseudo-
health nut. Her dad owns a fitness center, her
mother is a nutritionist, and her older brother is

a personal trainer. But Jenna claims she's allergic to exercise. And when she's away from home, she eats every unhealthy thing she can find. Not that you can tell, because she's also on the swim team. She doesn't consider swimming exercise, just fun. Plus she's tall, so she has long arms that give her an advantage in the pool.

But her height gives her a disadvantage when it comes to guys. Jenna is slightly shorter than six feet tall, like an eighth of an inch shorter, which most people would probably just ignore, but she cares about the tiniest fractions because she really doesn't like her height. If someone asks her how tall she is, she'll say, "I'm five feet eleven and seven-eighths inches."

Me, I'd just say six feet.

Or at least I think I would. Having never been that tall, I can't say for sure, and like my dad is always saying, don't judge until you've walked in the other person's shoes. And I could never walk in Jenna's shoes because her feet are a lot bigger than mine.

She's taller than most of the guys at our school. Her mom keeps telling her not to worry about it so much—that boys grow into their height after high school. But get real. She wants a boyfriend now.

Because she spends so much time in the pool—with practice and competition—she keeps her blond hair cropped really short—a wash-and-fluff-dry style.

Amber, on the other hand, wears her dark brown hair in a layered chin-length bob. It never frizzes. She's also the shortest of our group. My dad calls her stocky—which I've never told her because it doesn't sound very flattering. Not that my dad meant to insult her or anything.

Amber's family has a ranch just outside of Houston, and she's used to hard work, which I guess helped her to develop muscles. She's really strong, which will come in handy over the next six weeks as we build a house.

"What can I get you?" the guy behind the counter asked. He was wearing a big smile, and I figured he was a summer employee, still new enough at the job to think it was fun.

My parents own a hamburger franchise,

and I've spent way too much time learning that the customer isn't always right and is usually a royal pain in the butt, but you have to act like you're glad they're buying your burger and not someone else's.

Since I know the truth about waiting on people, I always try to be a good customer.

"Chocolate éclair," I said, smiling.

"To go or to eat here?"

They had a small section nearby with a few tables. Sitting in air-conditioning for a while sounded like a great idea, so I said, "Here."

Jenna ordered her carrot cake, and Amber ordered a pound of pralines. Okay, so maybe working the ranch wasn't the only reason she was stocky.

"A pound?" Jenna asked.

Amber shrugged. "I'll have one here and take the rest back to the dorm, so we can snack later."

Our volunteer group was living in a college dorm, along with other volunteers. Our group is officially H⁴—Helping Hands Helping Humans. Or as its organizer, Ms. Wynder, calls it: H to the Fourth. Ms. Wynder thinks of everything in numbers. She is, after all, our math teacher. And it was her idea to bring several of us to New Orleans.

According to her, voluntourism—"people doing volunteer work while on their vacations"— is becoming increasingly popular. She'd even shown us an article about soap opera actors who'd spent time here, staying in a dorm like normal people and working during the day. Not that the possibility of running into celebrities had influenced my decision to come here— although, yes, I did plan to keep an eye out.

No, my coming here had more to do with putting distance between me and home. Getting away, far away, worked for me. I had no desire to run into my ex-boyfriend. I was hoping that before school started his family would move to Alaska or Siberia. Never seeing him again would totally work for me.

Nudging me, Amber whispered, "He has a really nice smile." She nodded at the guy behind the counter.

Okay, great. Amber, the skeptic, was suddenly a believer. I touched the brim of my white cap. "No hat."

I was a little taller than she was, and I wasn't at all stocky. I wasn't as tall or thin as Jenna, either. If we were in a fairy tale, I'd be the one who was just right—hey, it's my fairy tale.

"Maybe he just doesn't wear it when he's working," Amber said.

Maybe.

"Are you a Kansas City Chiefs fan?" Amber asked the guy as he set our order on the counter.

He scowled, as if he'd been insulted. "Are you kidding? Saints."

"Oh, right." She gave me a look that said, *What's his problem?*

His problem was probably that he was working and we weren't. I knew the feeling.

We ordered sweetened tea, paid for our order, and sat at a nearby table.

"Okay, so he wasn't the one," Amber said.

"There is no 'the one,'" I assured her, before sipping my tea. Nothing is better than sweetened tea on a hot day. I took a bite of my éclair. The filling was a combination of custard and

17

cream, with a wicked amount of chocolate on top. Really good.

"Ohmigod!" Amber exclaimed, after taking her first bite of praline. "This is the best I've ever tasted. It just melted in my mouth."

"I think New Orleans is famous for its pralines," Jenna said.

"Its pralines, its music, its voodoo, its beads. We're going to have so much fun," I said.

"It'll be the best summer ever," Jenna admitted.

"Although I think you're wrong to swear off guys," Amber said. "It's like my dad is always saying: When you fall off the horse, the best thing to do is get back in the saddle."

I started shaking my head. We'd spent hours discussing the unfairness of it all. All I really wanted to do now was escape into summer.

"I think Amber's right," Jenna said. "Look, we're going to be here for six weeks. We're bound to meet guys, guys who are available. Why not hook up with one? Just for fun, just to have someone to do something with? Have a summer fling? Get Drew out of your system, completely and absolutely."

Why not? Because it was scary to think about liking someone new, knowing how much he could hurt me. I didn't know if I could do a casual relationship, if I could keep my heart from getting involved. I'd fallen for Drew really fast. And who could blame me? I mean, how many guys these days bring a girl flowers on their first date? And, okay, it was only three flowers, and I think he'd plucked them from my mom's garden, but still—the thought counted.

"Look, Drew was a jerk," Amber said. "Chad would never hurt me like that. And I don't care what the psychic said. He's the one. I totally love him."

"Because you totally love him, I should hook up with somebody?" Amber is one of my best friends and I love her, but sometimes I can't follow her thought process. Like the comment about the CorningWare.

"No, I'm just pointing out that not all guys are going to do something to hurt us."

"Just don't say absolutely not," Jenna said. "Keep yourself open to the possibility that you could hook up this summer—temporarily anyway."

"But we're not here to hook up. We're here on a mission."

"But I don't see why we can't combine guys and good works. I mean, think about it. Wouldn't it be the sweetest revenge, to post pictures of you with a hottie on my MySpace page? Drew would know you were totally over him."

"I don't care what he knows." Okay, a part of me still did. Yes, he was a jerk; yes, he'd broken my heart. But for a while he'd been everything. He was the one who sat with me in the hospital waiting room when my grandma was sick—even though my parents were there. He was the first one I called when I passed my driver's test. He was the one who got up at five in the morning to be first in line at the electronics store when their weekly shipment came in so he could give me a Wii for my birthday—because I wanted one so badly. Unfortunately I couldn't play it now without thinking of him, so I'd stopped using it. Drew and I did so much together, he was a part of so many things that the memories formed a web, connecting everything and making me feel trapped.

"I'm not hooking up with anyone. That's final," I said.

Jenna shrugged. "Fine. Don't. But I plan to." Having finished her carrot cake, she reached into the box and took out a praline. "I mean, I've never even had a date."

"The guys at school are so stupid," Amber said.

Jenna smiled. "I guess."

"I think you both should get boyfriends while we're here," Amber said.

How many times did I have to say no?

"If we did, you'd be hanging out alone," I felt compelled to point out.

"Don't worry about me," Amber said. "I'll always find someone to hang with. As my dad says, I've never met a stranger."

"I've got a crazy idea." Jenna leaned forward, her blue eyes twinkling. "We should go to a voodoo shop and have a hex put on Drew and get a love potion for me."

"No thanks. I'm still freaked out about the

psychic reading," Amber said. "I'm not sure if I'm ready for voodoo rituals."

The bakery door opened and three guys wearing sunglasses sauntered in. They looked a little older than us. College guys, probably. It looked like they hadn't shaved in a couple of days. Scruffy—but in a sexy kind of way.

They were wearing cargo shorts, Birkenstocks, and wrinkled T-shirts. They grinned at us as they walked by our table. The one in the middle had a really, really nice smile.

He was also wearing a red cap.

A red cap with a Kansas City Chiefs logo on it.

Chapter 2

"Ohmigod, that's your guy!" Jenna whispered excitedly.

It couldn't be. It just couldn't be.

I was trying not to hyperventilate, trying not to lose it. There were probably a hundred guys in the city wearing that hat. Maybe a Kansas City Chiefs' fanatics convention was going on. Or a preseason game. Was it time for preseason games yet?

I shook my head fast. "No, he's not."

Amber leaned across the table and said in a low voice, "Is anyone else totally freaking out here?"

"Don't you think he's her guy?" Jenna asked.

"Well, yeah! Absolutely."

23

"It's just coincidence." I sounded breathless. My heart was pounding hard.

"I'd buy into that if he was wearing a Saints hat. But Kansas City? Why would he be wearing that?" Jenna asked.

"Maybe he's from Kansas City."

"But what are the odds—"

"Look, people visit here from all over. Saraphina probably saw him at some point, and he stayed on her mind and when she was tapping into things, she tapped into her own memory, not my future."

That was the logical explanation, and I liked logical.

"He'd sure stay on my mind," Amber said. "He's totally hot."

Her brown eyes widened. "Oh gosh, don't tell Chad I noticed another guy. He would so not understand."

"You don't think guys with girlfriends notice other girls?" Jenna asked.

"Once you're with someone, that should be your focus," Amber said, but she didn't sound as though she was totally convinced—and she was still eyeing the guys at the counter, with almost as much interest as she had for the pralines.

"My brother says even though he's ordered the entrée, he can still look over the menu," Jenna said.

Her brother—the personal trainer—was five or six years older than she was and living with his girlfriend. If a guy was living with me, I would *not* want him still looking over the menu.

"Yeah, well, sometimes that can make you change your order. Just ask Drew," I said.

"I guess, but still it seems a shame not to be able to look at all," Jenna said. "And I'm crushing on actors all the time. Does that count?"

She'd developed a thing for Nick Simmons. It didn't hurt that he was six feet seven inches tall. She had every episode of *Gene Simmons: Family Jewels* still saved on her TiVo.

"That's just fantasy," I said.

And I didn't want to admit it, but the guys who'd just walked in were sort of fantasy, too. I mean, I couldn't see a college guy really being interested in me, and these three were definitely

25

not in high school. They seemed too confident, cocky almost, but not conceited. Hard to describe.

I looked toward the counter. With one smooth motion, Red Cap removed his sunglasses. Our eyes met. From this distance, I couldn't tell the color, but they looked dark. He smiled. He really did have an inviting smile — a smile that promised fun and maybe . . . more. As though suddenly embarrassed, or maybe he was shy, or not impressed with me, he turned away and said something to one of his friends. The guy he was talking to was amazingly tall.

"How tall do you think that other guy is?" Jenna asked.

"Which one specifically?" I asked.

She glowered, because I was giving her a hard time. It was obvious which one she was referring to.

"Over six feet. Easy," I said. "Maybe close to six six."

I could hear the guys talking in hushed tones, not what they were saying, but I was pretty sure they weren't discussing the pastry options. Maybe I'd picked up some of Saraphina's psychic abilities.

"I think we should probably go," I said.

"Why?" Jenna asked. "We're not on a schedule."

She was making eye contact with the tall guy. He'd removed his sunglasses, and his eyes were definitely a light color, blue or green.

"Stop that," I whispered. "What if they come over?"

"What if they do?"

Okay, this was embarrassing to admit because I had at one time, after all, had a boyfriend, but the truth is, I didn't have a lot of experience flirting. Drew and I got together pretty soon after Mom gave me permission to start dating, and you don't flirt with your boyfriend. I mean, I never flirted with Drew.

I was tutoring him in math after school— part of a program sponsored by the National Honor Society—when he said he was having trouble with a really complicated formula. Then he wrote out Dawn + Drew = x.

He'd looked at me with those gorgeous blue

eyes of his and asked, "Could x equal date?"

And yep, as corny as it was, I'd fallen for it. Totally. That was the middle of my sophomore year, and we'd been together until our junior prom when I'd realized the answer wasn't an absolute constant—that the equation contained hidden variables.

"Look, I'm really not ready to deal with this." I shoved back my chair and stood.

Jenna rolled her eyes and did the same, while Amber closed up her praline box.

"Whoa! You're tall." Tall Guy had walked over and was smiling at Jenna.

Jenna smiled. It was the first time she didn't seem embarrassed by her height. I had a feeling if he asked how tall she was, she'd tell him six feet. No problem.

"So are you," she said.

Tall Guy shot an air ball at an imaginary hoop just over Jenna's head.

"You play basketball?" Jenna asked.

He nodded. "You?"

"Swim team."

He grinned really broadly. Nice smile. Really

nice smile. Maybe all guys had nice smiles, and Saraphina's prediction meant nothing.

"I like those uniforms better," he said. "A whole lot better."

"They're not uniforms. They're swimsuits."

He just winked at her, and I could see her cheeks turning red.

The guy behind the counter, oblivious to the flirting going on, rapped his knuckles on the glass case. "Hey, big guy, you want something or not?"

I sort of expected Tall Guy to point at Jenna and say, "Yeah, I want her."

But he didn't.

All three guys turned their attention to the clerk.

I could tell Jenna was disappointed that the flirting session had so easily and swiftly come to an end. With her cheeks turning even redder, she headed toward the door. Amber and I hurried to catch up.

"See ya!" Tall Guy called out.

Smiling, Jenna looked back over her shoulder and waved. Once we were outside, she said,

"Was he interested or not?"

"I think boys always choose food over girls," Amber said. "It's a caveman mentality of survival."

"Do you even know what you're talking about?" Jenna asked.

"Not really, but it was getting a little intense in there."

"I thought you were okay with Dawn and me hooking up with someone, that you never met a stranger?"

"I am okay with it; I just wasn't ready for it to happen five minutes after we started talking about it."

"So maybe we should have stayed."

"But we were finished eating," I pointed out.

"So? Would it have been a bad thing to be obvious that *I* was interested?"

"Do you want to go back in?" I asked. "Because if you really want to—"

Jenna shook her head. "Nah, no reason to go back in now. It would make us look fickle or something. Maybe desperate. Besides, it'd just be a one-night thing, and we're supposed to be in front of the gate to Jackson Square at eleven tonight so Ms. Wynder can pick us up. Not sure I want to admit I have a curfew to an older guy. But he was certainly tall."

"And cute," Amber said.

"The curfew isn't really a curfew. I mean, Ms. Wynder is providing transportation, because we don't have a car," I said.

"She's responsible for us. Chaperone. Sort of," Amber said.

There were three other volunteers, six of us in all. Because Ms. Wynder had organized our group, she'd promised to look out for us, but it wasn't a school trip and no one had signed any binding contracts, consent forms, or legal documents. She'd driven us here in her minivan and arranged for us to stay in the dorm. She'd provided transportation to the French Quarter with the promise to pick us up later and the warning to not get into any trouble. Although I wasn't exactly sure what she'd do if we did get into trouble. Call our parents, I guessed.

But was she really a chaperone? If she was, wouldn't she have stayed with us, kept an eye on us, instead of cutting us loose to find our own entertainment? Although to be honest, I was glad she hadn't tagged along. I think she's, like, thirty.

"You girls are going to be seniors in the fall. I trust you to be responsible," she'd said when she dropped us off.

Telling us she trusted us was tricky on her part, because it made us feel like we had to behave. Not that we were known for getting into trouble or walking around with fake IDs, but still. Away from home, parents, and anyone who knew us . . .

I think we'd planned to do a little misbehaving.

I thought of the inviting smile in the bakery. I was probably crazy to have walked away. Why was it so scary now to even think about getting together with a guy?

I hated Drew. He made me question everything.

"So what *are* we gonna do tonight?" Jenna asked as we crossed the street after a horse and carriage rattled by.

I almost said that I wanted to ride in a carriage, but it seemed like such a touristy thing to do. Of course, we were tourists, so I supposed it would be okay.

Pointing to a door where a sign proclaimed TAROT CARD READINGS, Amber said, "Maybe we should pop in there. You know, verify what the psychic told us."

"Or maybe we should have our palms read," Jenna suggested. "See if Tall, Dark, and Handsome back there is in my future."

"If he was, don't you think Saraphina would have said something?" I asked.

"I guess there's no way to interpret 'fire that doesn't burn' as applying to him," Jenna said.

"Maybe if he had red hair," Amber suggested.

But his hair had been dark, buzzed short.

"Could 'fire that doesn't burn' mean passion that doesn't happen?" Jenna asked.

I was totally confused.

"What?" Amber asked, obviously confused, too.

"Maybe there would have been passion between us, but I walked away."

Actually, I thought, that sort of made sense.

"If that's the case, then you were supposed to walk away," I said.

"So why predict it? So I live with regret?"

"Who knows? I bet people go insane after a reading, trying to interpret what everything means," I said.

Jenna laughed. "I am obsessing, but you know me and puzzles. I'll stop thinking about it now."

"Sure you don't want to have a tarot reading?" Amber asked.

"I'm sure. Let's just walk around. We've got six weeks to explore things, and I'm not really sure I want the future confirmed. I mean, in theory, it sounds like a good idea, but it's just not nearly as reassuring as I thought it would be."

The French Quarter had been spared most of the devastation that had hit the other areas of New Orleans. There wasn't much traffic, other than foot traffic. I think it was because the streets were so narrow that cars barely missed swiping other passing cars and everyone had to drive so slowly. I wouldn't want to drive here.

Better to park at the outskirts and walk or catch a streetcar.

The buildings revealed interesting architecture, kind of romantic. A lot of brick with wrought-iron balconies decorated with flowers. It reminded me of the Lestat vampire novels. I was a huge Anne Rice fan. Before the summer was over, I wanted to see her house in the Garden District. I could imagine vampires walking these streets. And we hadn't even been here at night yet.

By the time we hit Decatur Street, the sun had dropped behind the buildings and dusk was settling in. We were really hungry, our afternoon snack a couple of hours behind us. Even finishing off Amber's pralines while we'd explored various avenues and shops hadn't ruined our appetite.

"Hey, Bubba Gump Shrimp Company," Amber said, pointing to a restaurant. "I love the Forrest Gump movie. Let's eat there."

"Works for me," I said.

We walked inside. To the right was a bar area and to the left was a gift shop with all sorts of Bubba Gump restaurant and Forrest Gump souvenirs. RUN, FORREST, RUN signs. DVDs of the movie. A suit that Tom Hanks had worn in the movie was on display.

"Three?" the hostess asked.

"Yeah," Jenna said.

"Please come with me."

We followed her through the crowded restaurant to the back and up a set of stairs into a smaller dining area. Booths rested along the wall and tables were in the center. We were the only ones sitting up there.

"Wherever you want," the hostess said.

We took a square table near the window, with Jenna and me sitting on either side of Amber.

"The server will be up in a minute. Enjoy." The hostess walked out of the room.

"Do we stink or something?" Jenna asked as she opened the menu. "That we have to be isolated from the other customers?"

"Well, we have been walking around most of the afternoon," Amber said.

"Still."

"I like being up here," I said. "It's quiet, and

we can hear ourselves talk. It seemed kind of noisy downstairs."

"It was noisy because people were down there. Maybe we'd see something interesting."

"Are you saying we're not interesting?" I teased.

"We're away from home. It just seems like we should meet other people, experience things."

"You're still thinking about that tall guy," I guessed.

"Yeah. Missed opportunity." Jenna sighed. "So, okay, I'm fine now. I've vented. What are y'all gonna order?"

That was the thing about Jenna. She never stayed angry, never held grudges. She probably would have even forgiven her boyfriend if he had ruined her prom night. I was discovering that I held a grudge awhile longer. I wasn't certain if it was an aspect of my personality that I really liked, but at the same time, I thought being too forgiving could be a fault, too.

I just really didn't understand where I went wrong with Drew. We'd always gotten along. We'd never fought. We'd never gotten on each other's nerves. I'd thought he was the one . . . until he wasn't.

"Well, duh?" Amber said. "Shrimp. We have to order shrimp. Boiled shrimp, fried shrimp, sautéed shrimp, shrimp scampi, shrimp cocktail, butterfly shrimp—"

I laughed. "Enough already. We get it."

We heard the footsteps echoing on the stairs.

"I think we're about to have company," Jenna said.

"Unless our server is an alien with multiple legs," I teased.

"Very funny."

"Well, at least putting us up here wasn't personal," Amber said.

The hostess walked into the room, three guys following behind her.

"Hey, we know them!" the tallest guy said.

Amber gasped. I felt my mouth drop open. Jenna's eyes widened.

They were the guys from the bakery.

Chapter 3

What were the odds? That with all the different restaurants in New Orleans, they'd pick the same one as us?

Astronomical.

The hostess told them the same thing she told us, to sit anywhere they wanted, and I halfway expected them to say they wanted to sit with us. They didn't. They took a table at the far end of the room. Once they started talking, we could hear only a low rumble.

"Bummer," Jenna said under her breath. "I thought maybe they'd ask to sit with us. Maybe we should—"

"Are you ready to order?"

The server stood there, and I hadn't even

seen him come in. I'd been paying too much attention to Red Cap and trying not to freak out. Maybe they were stalkers. Maybe they'd been following us all along and we'd been too distracted looking at petunias on balconies to notice.

"Who wants to go first?" the server prodded, obviously in a hurry. He crouched down, put his pad on the table, and started tapping his pencil impatiently against the pad.

We each ordered fried shrimp. When the waiter walked over to the guys' table to get their order, Jenna leaned in. "What do you think it means?" she asked.

"What?" I asked.

She rolled her eyes to the side, toward the guys. "That they're here."

"Either they like seafood or they're huge fans of *Forrest Gump*."

"I think it's a sign," Amber said. "We should have done a tarot reading. Then we'd know for sure."

"You don't even believe in stuff like that," I reminded her.

"Maybe I'm starting to believe. You have to

admit that Saraphina got more things right than she got wrong. I mean, really—did she get anything wrong?"

I wasn't exactly sure how we could judge that. We were assuming a lot of things . . . like this Red Cap was my Red Cap. Maybe he wasn't.

I jumped when I heard a chair scrape across the floor. I'm not usually easily spooked. Nerves of steel, like Superman. But, okay, maybe I was just a little unsettled by how our day was going.

I looked over. The server had left. The guys walked to our table.

"We were wondering," Tall Guy said, looking at Jenna as he spoke, "do you know how much a polar bear weighs?"

Jenna looked at us, looked back at him. "No."

"Enough to break the ice." He grinned, and Jenna grinned back at him.

The other two guys were shaking their heads.

"Seriously," Tall Guy said. "We were talking. We're new to town, don't know anyone, and fate seems to be working here. Three of you, three of us. Running into one another again. What can I say? It seems like destiny."

Did he really say destiny?

"So what say we share a table," he suggested.

"Okay," Jenna said, nodding so rapidly that her head was almost a blur.

The guys moved a chair out of the way, then shoved the closest table against the empty side of ours. Without hesitation, Tall Guy sat next to Jenna. No surprise there. Red Cap and the remaining guy exchanged glances. Finally Red Cap sat next to me, which left Amber sitting across from the third guy.

"I'm Tank," Tall Guy said.

Jenna released a laugh, then slapped her hand over her mouth. "Sorry. It's not a funny name. It's just, were you—are you—in the military or something?"

"Nah, not even close. It's just a nickname, better than Theodore."

Her eyes widened. "Your parents named you Theodore?"

"Yeah, what were they thinking, right? Family tradition. You gotta hate 'em, though."

He pointed to Red Cap. "That's Brady. And Sean."

Jenna introduced our group.

Looking at me, Brady touched the brim of his cap. "Like your hat."

"Like yours, too."

"I thought I noticed you looking at it earlier. You a Chiefs fan?"

I shook my head. "Texans." I wasn't really into football, but I believed in hometown loyalty.

"You from Houston?"

"Yeah. Well, actually, Katy, but most people don't know where—"

"We know where Katy is. We go to Rice."

Okay, so they *were* college guys. Rice University is in Houston, and Katy is about thirty minutes west of Houston.

"Talk about your small world," Brady said, smiling.

"Yeah, really."

He looked past me to Amber. "You know, we should change seats. That way you can talk to Sean."

Amber looked startled, probably because Brady had already stood up.

"Oh, yeah, sure, okay, yeah."

Brady dropped into the chair that Amber vacated. Jenna didn't even seem to notice that she had a different person sitting on the other side of her. She and Tank were talking really quietly, with hushed voices. It was strange seeing Jenna with a guy who seemed totally into her. I mean, I'd never understood guys not giving her attention, but still . . .

"So, you're from Katy," Brady said, drawing my attention back to him.

"Yeah," I said. Did he ever stop smiling? And why did it irritate me? Because I didn't want to like him. This summer wasn't about hooking up with someone. It was about doing good works.

Although I had to admit I was flattered that he was showing interest.

"Where do you go to college?"

I released a self-conscious laugh. "Actually we're high school juniors . . . or we were. We'll be seniors in the fall. I'm never sure what to call myself during the summer. You know? Am I what I was, or what I'm going to be?"

Why was I going on and on about nothing? That wasn't like me. But then, what was these days?

His smile grew. I wanted to reach out and touch the corner of his mouth. Strange, really strange. I'd never wanted to touch Drew's mouth. I'm sure it was only because the psychic had mentioned Brady's smile—correction. She'd mentioned a guy with a nice smile. I didn't know for sure if it was this guy. There were probably hundreds of guys who wore red Chiefs caps over their sandy blond hair.

He removed his cap and combed his fingers through his hair, before tucking his cap in his back pocket. Drew's hair was black, short. Brady's curled a little on the ends, fell forward over his brow. It seemed to irritate him that it did, because he combed it back a couple of more times, then shrugged. "My dad would get after me for wearing a hat indoors," he said. "So, anyway, I'll be a sophomore in the fall."

Even though he was blond, he was really tanned. I figured he liked the outdoors. Drew, even though he was dark, was pretty pale. Not vampire pale or anything, but he much preferred staying indoors.

"At Rice," I reiterated.

"Yep. We're practically neighbors, and here we meet in New Orleans. What are the odds?"

"Five million to one."

His brown eyes widened slightly. The psychic didn't mention that he had really nice eyes. A golden brown, sort of like warm, fresh pralines.

"Really?" he asked.

"No, I was just throwing out numbers. I have no idea."

He laughed. Need I say it? His laugh was nice. Everything about him was nice. And it made me uncomfortable because I didn't want to like him, not even for just one night. Because if we spent time together tonight and I never saw him again, if he didn't ask for my phone number . . . quite honestly, it would hurt. And it would add to all the insecurities that I was already harboring, because I had to have at least one flaw, maybe more. There had to be some reason that Drew abandoned me for someone else. Something had to be lacking in me.

If I'd been brave, I would have asked Drew. Why'd he do it? What was wrong with me? But part of me didn't want to know the truth, wasn't ready to face whatever it was that was wrong with me.

I actually hadn't talked to Drew at all that night after I discovered him cheating on me. I just took my cell phone off the seat, walked away, and called my dad to come pick me up.

"You okay?" Brady asked now, jerking me back to the present—which was a much nicer place to be.

"Oh, yeah. I couldn't remember if I left the iron on." It was something my mom said when she didn't want to talk about whatever it was she'd been thinking about. It made absolutely no sense and was a stupid thing to say. Still, I said it.

"You iron?" he asked incredulously.

"It's obvious you don't."

He looked down at his wrinkled shirt. "Yeah, my duffle bag was pretty stuffed, and we wanted to get in as much sightseeing as we could today."

"So you're just here for the day?"

"Nah, we're here for the summer. Volunteering, building a house, I think. Tank's got the details, I'm just along for the ride."

"That's the reason we're here, too."

There were lots of volunteer and rebuilding efforts in the city. The odds that we were going to be working on the same project could've *really* been five million to one. I was sure it wasn't happening.

So I began to relax a little. What was wrong with having fun—just for tonight?

"Do you believe in love at first sight, or should we walk by again?"

We all groaned at Tank's corny pickup line.

Sometime between the time that the server brought our food and we finished eating, we all seemed to have become friends. Or at least comfortable enough with one another for Jenna to tell Tank that she thought his line about us being their destiny was pretty corny. So the guys had started tossing out their repertoire of worst pickup lines—just to prove that Tank's hadn't been that bad.

"I hope you know CPR, 'cuz you take my breath away," Sean said. He had a really deep baritone voice that sounded like it came up from the soles of his feet.

Jenna and I laughed, but Amber looked at him like maybe she was wondering if he was serious.

He wasn't very tall. But that worked. Because neither was Amber. Not that it needed to work, because she had a boyfriend.

"Do the police have a warrant out for your arrest?" Brady asked. "Because your eyes are killing me."

I laughed.

"No, seriously," he said. "You've got really pretty brown eyes."

"Oh, that wasn't a line?"

"Well, yeah, it's a line, but I do mean it."

"Oh, well, in that case, thanks. I think."

Were we moving into flirting territory?

"You must be tired," he said, "because you've been running through my mind ever since I first saw you."

"Is that a line?" I asked, not certain if I

should laugh again.

"Not really," Tank said before Brady could answer. "We were kicking ourselves for not introducing ourselves to y'all earlier. I'm glad we ran into you again."

I watched as Jenna's cheeks turned pink. "Yeah, we're glad, too," she said.

When the server brought our bill, the guys insisted on paying for everything. Which was so nice and unexpected. I mean, they looked more like starving students than we did.

As we left the restaurant, Tank said, "We're going to hang out on Bourbon Street. Want to come?"

Jenna didn't hesitate. "Absolutely."

Even Amber seemed up for it, which left everyone looking at me. What choice did I have? I shrugged. "Sure."

No way was I going to wander around New Orleans at night alone. And it had gotten dark while we were eating. Besides, I'd heard about Bourbon Street, and I wanted to experience it.

It was obvious Jenna was really interested in Tank. They were even holding hands already.

I'd expected Amber to walk with me, but she was still paired up with Sean, talking to him as we headed over to Bourbon Street. Apparently she wasn't worried about what Chad might think, or maybe she was okay with being with a guy as a friend.

Maybe she was right. What would it hurt if tonight—just tonight—I was a little wild and crazy? If tonight, I had fun with a guy? If tonight, I pretended my heart hadn't been shattered?

Brady took my hand. His was large, warm, and comforting. But still, I jerked a little at the unexpected closeness.

"So we don't get separated," he said, as though he wanted to reassure me that nothing heavy was going on between us. "There's usually a crowd on Bourbon Street."

"I thought you were new to town."

"I am, but I know things."

Chapter 4

Several blocks of Bourbon Street were closed to traffic. The area was a mash of bodies, noises, and smells. I hadn't expected one of those noises to be the *clip clop* of horses' hooves or one of the smells to be manure.

But the police were patrolling on huge horses, and big horses left behind big business.

"Watch out," Brady said, slipping his arm around my waist and hauling me to the side before I stepped in something I absolutely didn't want to. He laughed. "I think my shoes just became disposable." Although we'd missed stepping into a big mess, the street was trashed.

"Mine, too. Definitely."

I smiled up at him, not sure why I suddenly felt very comfortable around him. Maybe it was the revelry surrounding us. Maybe it was everyone shouting and laughing and having a great time. The attitude was contagious, something I wanted to embrace.

I was suddenly very glad to be sharing all this with a guy. Not even Brady particularly, just a guy. Because it seemed like the kind of partying that required holding hands and being part of a couple.

People were acting wild, crazy, totally uninhibited. Dancing, yelling, hugging, kissing, laughing. It wasn't all because of the drinking going on. Sure, some people were drinking freely in the streets, weaving in and out of the crowds. I'm certain a lot of them were drunk on booze, but many were simply drunk on having a good time.

When everyone around you doesn't care what anyone else thinks, why should you?

A guy bumped into us, staggered back, and raised his fist in the air. "Rock on!"

He swerved away, hit a lamppost. "Rock on!"

Brady drew me nearer. "That dude's going to be seriously hung over in the morning if he already can't tell the difference between a post and a person."

"Are you speaking from experience?"

I didn't know why I asked that. It was rude. But I think I was looking for a flaw. He couldn't be this perfect. I wanted him to be not so nice.

He grinned. Obviously he didn't take offense at what I'd said.

"I refuse to answer that question on the grounds that it might incriminate me."

"What are you — a law student?"

"Architecture. We're all architecture majors. It's part of the reason we're here."

"To help rebuild."

"That, and to appreciate what remains."

He made it sound so noble, so . . . un-Drew. The only thing Drew had appreciated was the spotlight, which hadn't bothered me at the time, because it had made him — made us — seem special. I'd never considered him self-centered or selfish, but now I wasn't so sure.

Brady and I walked in tandem, following

Tank and Jenna. Their height made them easy to keep in sight.

The street didn't have a shortage of bars, which you'd probably expect of a street named Bourbon, although the name didn't really refer to booze. At the time New Orleans was founded by the French, the French royal family was the House of Bourbon and *Rue Bourbon* was named to honor them. Yes, I'd spent a lot of time on Wikipedia, looking up facts that were probably only interesting to me. Which is why I didn't share that one with Brady.

We stopped just outside a corner daiquiri bar. The huge doors were wide open. People walked in, got their drinks, and strolled out. Behind the counter were several huge vats of frozen drinks, so it didn't take very long to get served. The tables inside were crammed with people watching a baseball game on the TV hanging on the wall.

"I don't get that," Brady said.

"What?"

"You've got all this stuff happening out here, and people are in there watching TV. I can watch TV at home. Why come here if that's what you're going to do?"

"Maybe New Orleans is their home."

"Maybe."

"Or maybe they're huge baseball fans."

"Still. I believe you gotta experience life, not watch it."

He looked at me like he thought I should agree. I didn't know what to say. Up until this summer, my experiences were pretty limited. I didn't want to get into an experience-listing competition.

"I'm making a run," Tank suddenly said.

He went inside, leaving Jenna on the sidewalk. She had her cell phone out, pointed it at me, took a picture, and winked. For her MySpace page, no doubt. As proof to Drew that I'd totally gotten over him. Moved on.

Who knew pictures could lie?

It was only then that I realized I was still nestled snugly against Brady's side. I didn't want to be obvious about easing away from him, which meant that I stayed beside him because there was no way to move away without being obvious.

So, okay, maybe I was just looking for an excuse to stay close. The weight of his arm around me felt really nice.

"You're not going to get something to drink?" I asked.

He grinned and winked. "I'm not going in to *buy* something, but yeah, I'll have something. Tank's the only one who's twenty-one. I might get carded if I tried to buy it, but I don't usually get carded once I'm holding it."

I wondered if that was part of the reason he kept stubble on his chin, so he'd look older. It was considerably darker than his hair. It gave him a rough, dangerous look. Which gave me a thrill. To be with someone older, someone who looked like he could be trouble, someone who wasn't Drew.

"Sounds like you have a system," I said. There I was again, being snide, trying to find that elusive flaw. What *was* wrong with me?

"I believe in partying hearty. And tonight we're pedestrians, so the only crashing that will take place is when we hit the beds." He gave me his sexy grin. (Did he have any other kind?) "Who am I hurting?"

Tank came out with a frozen red drink.

"Strawberry daiquiri," he said. "They give a free shot of Sex on the Beach, but I couldn't bring it out, so I was forced to drink it myself."

"But you're always willing to make the sacrifice," Brady said.

"You bet! Let's party!"

We started walking up the sidewalk, stepping into the street when the crowds were thick on the sidewalk outside the bars that had entertainment. Music wafted out through the open doors. I wasn't familiar with the tunes but hearing them live made me want to follow their rhythm. I thought I could probably become a fan. Expand my musical horizons.

When we passed through some shadows, Tank passed the drink back. Brady took it and offered it to me. Okay. I wasn't old enough, but I didn't want to seem like a prude, either. I compromised and took a very small sip. It was tasty, so I took another. I was pretty sure all the alcohol was on the bottom and I'd lifted the straw up some, so I was drinking from the middle. The alcohol-free zone. Sounded reasonable to me. Not that a cop would buy into my reasoning.

A vision flashed through my mind of having to call Mom and Dad to bail me out of jail. Wouldn't that be just great? I wondered if that was how things worked for Saraphina. Pictures just flashed through her mind and they could mean nothing, something, everything. How did she know which ones mattered?

Brady didn't bother with a straw. He just gulped down some frozen concoction. We passed another bar, and Tank went inside.

I looked around. "Where's Amber?"

Jenna turned in a slow circle, then shrugged. "I don't know."

"She and Sean ducked into one of the bars we passed back there to listen to the music," Brady said, jerking his thumb over his shoulder.

How had I missed that? I hadn't seen Amber and Sean slip away. I guess maybe I was paying too much attention to Brady. But sitting down and listening to a band sounded like a terrific idea. One way to keep my shoes semiclean anyway. But then, I also wanted to see everything there was to see out here, too.

"We can go back there if you want," Brady said.

He didn't say it with much enthusiasm. I didn't know him well enough to read between the lines, but I had a feeling that he wanted to keep walking. I didn't know how I knew that. I just did.

"No, I'd rather explore."

"Great! Let's at least go to the end of what they've got blocked off. See what other stuff they've got going on. Then we can head back, find the bar they're in."

"Sounds like a plan."

"I'm known for my plans."

"Really?"

"Oh yeah. That's what architects do. Draw up plans."

He gave me a smile that seemed to say I was part of those plans. Or maybe I was just reading things into his expression that I wanted to be there. Maybe he was really talking about blueprints. Although part of me was hoping for the more personal meaning. We were having a good time. And I suddenly wanted to have a good time. A really good time. Show Drew that I was finished moping about him. Have Jenna post a hundred of those pictures for him to see.

Tank came out of the bar with a yellow frozen drink. "Banana," he said, boldly offering it to Jenna.

She took it without hesitating.

We started walking up the street again.

"More?" Brady asked, holding the strawberry daiquiri toward me.

"Uh, no, but thanks."

I felt like a total downer, but my parents had let me come here because they trusted me not to get into trouble. Trust was a heavy burden, a double-edged sword. Too many clichés to name. But I didn't want to do something the first night that would have me back home the second.

Brady finished the daiquiri, crumpled up the plastic cup—why do guys always feel a need to crumple whatever they've been drinking out of? — and tossed it in a nearby trash can.

"We need to get you some beads," he said.

I was pretty sure he wasn't talking about buying me any that were hanging in the windows of the many shops.

Guys stood on balconies, dangling beads, and yelling at girls walking by. Whenever a girl lifted her top, a guy would toss her a strand or two. Unless he was totally wasted, in which case the beads landed on nearby trees or shrubbery. Beads were pretty much all over the place.

"I've decided not to do *everything* the first night," I said. "I want to leave something for later in the summer."

Brady chuckled, leaned near my ear, and whispered, "Chicken."

Okay, maybe I was. I'd never even lifted my shirt for Drew.

"Don't look so serious," Brady said. "I'm just teasing."

"I guess I don't know you well enough—"

"To share what's underneath that tee?"

"To know when you're teasing," I corrected.

"There is that."

He released his hold on me, which I realized felt strange. Not to have him holding me. I almost felt bereft. But that didn't make sense. I'd just met the guy.

He moved so he was standing near a balcony. Waving his arms, he was yelling up at the people leaning over the railing. I'd seen only guys on the balconies, but this one had girls, too. Probably in college. When Brady got their attention, he laughed and pulled his T-shirt up and over his head, then he swung it around like a lasso.

Someone bumped against me. I barely noticed.

Brady was buff. Nothing at all like Drew.

I'd tried to interest Drew in various charity runs. He'd always been willing to sponsor me if I was participating, which I'd thought was nice, but I had a feeling that Brady actually ran. And worked out, and engaged in outdoor activities. Based on the bronzed darkness of his back, I had a feeling he spent most of his time in the sun.

I watched as dozens of beads dropped

through the air. Brady snagged them. He was hamming it up, dancing around, strutting his stuff. The party girls were whistling, dropping more beads, inviting him up.

Brady was being crazy, dancing around, having fun, not caring what anyone thought.

I started laughing. He hadn't struck me as being quite so uninhibited, but it was all in the spirit of New Orleans. I think everyone around him was having as much fun as he was.

I was really, really glad that I was there, involved, part of the madness.

Brady turned toward me, holding up all the strands of beads, smiling like some returning explorer who was delivering gold to his queen or something. He dropped them down over my head.

Then, grinning broadly, he wrapped his fingers around them, pulled me toward him, and kissed me.

Right there in the middle of Bourbon Street, with people pushing past us and music filling the night.

Chapter 5

*B*rady tasted like strawberry daiquiri, and I thought his mouth should be cold from the frozen drink, but it wasn't. It was hot. Very hot.

He brought the beads and his knuckles up beneath my chin. He tilted my head back slightly and started kissing me more thoroughly.

And the thing was — I was kissing him back.

I told myself that the sip of daiquiri had gone to my head. I told myself that it was simply the craziness of Bourbon Street.

But I think part of it was that I wanted to hurt Drew. Like me kissing a guy as though my life depended on it would somehow make us even.

Which was crazy. Because Drew would

never know. And it wasn't fair to Brady. And I knew, I knew, I *knew* that I should stop kissing him. That my reasons for kissing him had nothing at all to do with him, but was some convoluted sense of revenge.

Brady was such a nice guy, with a terrific smile. And he kissed me like Drew never had. Part of me wanted to stay there forever.

But it was wrong.

I drew back.

Brady gave me a broad smile. "Oh yeah."

He leaned back in. I put my hand on his bare chest. His skin was warm and my fingers tingled. I almost moved back toward him. Instead, I said, "I've gotta go."

He looked like I'd just told him that he'd stepped in something gross. "What?"

"I have a curfew."

"A curfew?"

"Yeah, our chaperone is picking us up at the gate to Jackson Square." I looked at my watch, preparing to lie about the pickup time, but it really was almost eleven. How had that happened? Time had completely gotten away from me. "She's picking us up at eleven. I really have to go. Thanks for the beads, for dinner, for . . . everything."

The kiss, I thought, *really, really thank you for the amazing kiss.*

Turning, I hurried back the way we'd come. Or I tried to hurry. It was a little hard when I had to wedge myself between people. "Coming through. Excuse me."

"Wait, you can't just . . . go off by yourself!" I heard Brady call out.

Only I wasn't planning to go off by myself. I was planning to go with Jenna and Amber. I just had to find them.

Brady caught up with me. "Hey, come on. Slow down."

I had my phone out, trying to call Jenna. I didn't know if she'd be able to hear her cell ringing over the saxophones and horns playing their upbeat music and the din of all the people.

"Hey, Dawn, wait up." Brady grabbed my arm.

I spun around. "You're a nice guy, but—"

"It's okay. I didn't realize . . . a curfew.

Wow. Do your friends have one?"

I nodded, wishing I'd used some other excuse. I suddenly felt like such a kid. "It's not really a curfew; it's just that she's picking us up at eleven, so we need to go. Otherwise, she might give us a real curfew."

That sounded worse. Why didn't I just shut up already?

"Okay, I just wish you'd said something sooner."

If I had, he probably wouldn't have brought me to Bourbon Street at all. He probably wouldn't have kissed me.

It took us nearly twenty minutes to find everyone else. Brady didn't say anything the entire time. Didn't hold my hand, although he did keep brushing up against me when the crowds thickened. He'd put his shirt back on — thank goodness. He placed his arm around my shoulders only once and that was when some drunken guy almost stumbled into me — Brady pulled me out of the way, trying to protect me.

I kept thinking I had to be insane for not holding on to this guy with both hands. I probably could have called Ms. Wynder and . . .

what? Our first night here and we couldn't meet up for the rendezvous because we were partying too hard? I was pretty sure that wouldn't go over well.

After we found everyone, we headed for Jackson Square. Tank and Jenna were in the lead again, holding hands. Amber was with Sean, talking. Brady and I trailed behind.

"Look, about that kiss—" Brady began.

"Don't worry about it. It was no big deal."

"Ouch!"

I grimaced. That had really come off sounding bad. I wanted to be cool about it, but I didn't know how. I mean, Drew and I had dated about a month before he ever got up the courage to kiss me. I think it had been his first kiss, too, and it had been, well, awkward. Eventually, we were kissing like pros. I'm not sure pro what. Are there pro kissers?

"I just meant that I know it was the craziness of Bourbon Street that made us kiss," I said.

"You think?"

"Oh yeah. I mean, we just met. It can't be more than that."

"I guess."

"I mean, this wasn't even a date or anything. It was just hanging out."

"Okay. Yeah."

I couldn't tell if he was disappointed or relieved.

When we got near the gate, I saw the other three girls Ms. Wynder had dropped off earlier. They went to my school, too, but I didn't know them very well.

"There's our group," I told Brady.

I turned around, walking backward. "Thanks again."

A familiar minivan pulled up to the curb. Amber, Jenna, and I started running for it.

We were all eerily quiet in the minivan after Ms. Wynder asked how our day was and we all responded "Great." As though a one-word answer would suffice when it most certainly didn't.

It had been one of the most up-and-down days of my life. I'd run through the entire gamut of emotions. I was exhausted. And wondering about the psychic's prediction. Was Brady the guy? Had I seen him for the last time? Was my last memory of him going to be watching him fade into the shadows of the night?

Once we got to our dorm room, we all let out collective sighs and started preparing for bed. Even though it seemed like something needed to be said, none of us was saying anything.

I plugged in the pump and pressed the button to inflate the AeroBed that I'd be sleeping on. Each dorm room had only two beds. I had the choice of an air mattress or a roommate I didn't know—Amber and Jenna had already agreed to bunk together before I realized that I wouldn't be doing a summer tour of Texas water parks with Drew. Yeah, that had been our plan. To be together as much as possible. Slipping and sliding the summer away. It had sure sounded like fun at the time.

Since my life seemed to be a series of adjustments lately, I hadn't wanted to adjust to living with a stranger, so I'd decided to go the air mattress route.

Besides, the summer would be a lot more

fun if we were all together. Every night would be a sleepover.

Amber sat on the edge of her bed. "Okay, guys, I need y'all to promise that you'll never tell Chad what I did tonight."

Crouching on the floor by the mattress, I twisted around. "What did you do?"

"Where were *you*? I hung out with another guy!" Her voice went up a bit; it had an almost-panicked sound to it.

I know after my prom night experience, I probably should have been all over her case, but Amber was innocent. She hadn't done anything wrong, which I felt a need to point out. "Yeah, but you—what? Listened to music?"

She nodded and looked miserable.

"It's not like you were all over him, or sneaking around."

"Still, he's a guy."

"But you can have guy friends."

"Just don't say anything to Chad. Ever."

"We won't tell," Jenna said.

"Of course, we won't," I assured her. "You don't even have to ask."

"Thanks. He just so wouldn't understand."

She looked at Jenna. "What about you?"

"What about me?"

"You and Tank. Are you going to see him again?"

She shrugged. "I gave him my cell phone number, but we were in such a rush at the end, we didn't really say good-bye or make any plans—"

Her cell phone rang. She took it out of her shorts pocket and just stared at it.

"Answer it," I prodded.

"It's Tank. What do I say?"

"Hello?" I suggested.

She took a deep breath, opened her phone, and answered, "Hey."

With a big smile, she said, "Oh yeah. We're fine. I know it was crazy there at the end. I didn't realize it was so late until Dawn found us." She laughed. "No, we don't turn into pumpkins at midnight."

Rolling onto her side, she curled up and started talking really quietly.

"Should we leave the room?" Amber whispered.

"Nah. We can't head out every time one of

us gets a phone call." I turned off the pump and tested the firmness of my bed. It worked.

"What are we going to do if she keeps seeing him?" Amber asked.

"What do you mean?"

"Well, the other two guys will probably be there. I just don't know if it's such a good idea for all of us to hang out together. I mean —"

"Why don't we worry about it if it happens?"

She jerked her thumb toward Jenna. "You don't think his calling means it's going to happen?"

It probably did.

"I'm too tired to solve this right now," I told her. I just wanted to go to sleep. We'd been running around all day.

"I know I'm probably worried about nothing. Gawd, I wish we hadn't decided to visit a psychic." Amber got her stuff together and went into the bathroom.

I fingered the beads dangling around my neck. I didn't know why I'd freaked out when Brady kissed me. Yes, I did. Brady was nice and that scared me. I didn't trust him not to hurt me.

Even for one night. It was a lot easier leaving him than it would be having him leave me.

Jenna had talked about having a summer fling, but I'd never had a casual relationship. Drew had been my first date. I didn't know how to date a guy without caring about him. And why would I want to?

Why spend time with someone I didn't like? And if I liked him, well, the more time I spent with him, it seemed like the more I'd start to like him, and the next thing I'd know . . . I'd be vulnerable again.

The best thing for me to do this summer was to just hang out with Jenna and Amber. And if Jenna was with Tank all the time, then Amber and I would buddy up.

I was probably worrying for nothing.

I'd never see Brady again, anyway. Even if Jenna saw Tank, it didn't mean that Amber and I would hook up with the other guys.

Brady was no doubt going to be just a one night . . . whatever.

Chapter 6

"Okay, I've blogged day one of what I'm calling our Amazing Summer Adventure," Jenna said, leaning away from the desk where she'd set up her laptop.

It was the next morning. Ms. Wynder had knocked on our door shortly after the sun made its appearance. When I'd volunteered for this, I hadn't considered that I'd be sleep deprived the whole summer. Even when I worked for my parents, I didn't go in until just before the lunch crowd hit.

Although I suppose I wouldn't have been dragging so much if I hadn't stared into the darkness for most of the night, thinking about Brady. Reliving the kiss. Wondering if he'd decided that I was a total nut.

What did I care what he thought? I'd probably never see him again. Saraphina's predictions were no doubt all jumbled up. Visions weren't an exact science. Just because she'd mentioned hammering and a red cap didn't mean they were in proximity. Last night was probably it.

Of course, Amber, who was used to getting up with the cows—literally—was her usual perky self. She seemed to be totally over all the doubts she'd had the day before about the psychic encounter.

She and I peered over Jenna's shoulder. Jenna wanted to be a journalist, so she was all about reporting what was happening in our lives—with posting photos and all. And there was the photo of me and Brady.

I looked . . . happy. And he looked . . . sexy. And together we looked . . . cuddly. An item.

And I thought, *Drew, eat your heart out.*

"So Drew is still on your friends list?" I asked, trying not to sound as interested as I was.

"Oh, sure. He's bound to see this."

"Why?"

"Because I write interesting stuff, and he knows it. And he'll be interested. I mean, face it. What we're doing here is way different from what anyone else is doing over the summer. He'll want to know all the delicious details."

She got up from the chair and I sat down. The room didn't have much furniture except the beds, two dressers, a desk, and three chairs — two of which we'd raided from a lounge down the hall.

Amber pressed up against my back as she tried to read what Jenna had written. "You didn't mention Sean, did you?"

"Of course not."

Jenna had written about our visit with the psychic but glossed over her prediction for Amber — no doubt because Chad was on her friends list, too, and he didn't need to know that Amber might find someone better.

Jenna hadn't revealed anything incriminating. Still, it always unsettled me a little to see the intimate details of my life shared with others.

"Oh, by the way," Jenna said as she started getting dressed, "I might see Tank tonight."

I could hear the excitement in her voice.

"Where?" I asked, trying to sound casually interested, instead of anxious to know if that meant that I might see Brady. Did I want to see him? I did. Scary.

Amber moved away to start getting dressed, too. I decided I'd better follow or I'd be left behind. I pulled on the Helping Hands Helping Humans T-shirt that Ms. Wynder had designed for us to wear the first day to identify our group. It had hands all over it. What can I say? She was more into numbers than art.

Jenna shrugged. "I'm supposed to figure out exactly where the dorm is and call him later with directions. He has a car. Said he'd come get me."

"That's awesome!" Amber said at the same time I said, "Aren't things moving a little fast?"

I never would have asked that question before prom night. Sometimes I missed the old me.

"I mean—"

"I know," Jenna said. "You got hurt and now you don't trust boys, and you're worried that I'll get hurt, too."

"I trust boys." I trusted them to hurt me. Drew had really messed me up. I hated that I was giving him that power.

I sat on a chair and started lacing up my

hiking boots. We'd been warned to wear sturdy shoes and jeans because we didn't know what we'd run across in the debris. No exposed legs. No sandals.

"You don't trust boys," Jenna repeated.

What was I supposed to say to that? Do, too? So we could get into exchanging meaningless comebacks like two-year-olds?

"Uh, y'all, do we *have* to wear these T-shirts?" Amber asked.

I looked over at her and saw that the hands on her T-shirt were rudely placed. I dropped my gaze to my own chest. Yep, those little hands were sending a message that I didn't want to send.

Jenna started laughing. "Oh my gosh. I never thought I'd be so glad for a tall body. At least my hands aren't exactly where they shouldn't be."

"Considering the message, I don't think we do need to wear them," I said. "At least I'm not."

I jerked off my T-shirt and scrounged around in my suitcase until I found a faded T-shirt from a vacation my family had taken at Thrill Ride! Amusement Park.

Amber and Jenna changed their shirts, too.

I welcomed the distraction from what might have turned into an argument with Jenna. I was really happy for her, glad she'd met a guy who wasn't bothered by her height. And I really, really hoped . . .

I didn't know what I hoped. That she didn't get hurt, of course, because we were only here for the summer, and he was only here for the summer, and even though he went to college in Houston. . . . I suppose their relationship could last past our time in New Orleans. As a matter of fact, before prom night, I probably would have *believed* in it continuing after we got home. But I used to believe in a lot of good things, like love was forever and boyfriends were neat to have.

Pancakes and sausages were waiting for us in the cafeteria. Several of the volunteers were already eating. Our little group of six, along with Ms. Wynder, gathered at one table. While we ate, Ms. Wynder went over the safety rules again: Watch out for critters, stay alert, don't get in a hurry, haste makes waste, the usual stuff. When we were finished eating, we headed outside, climbed into her minivan, and caravanned with the other volunteers to the site.

We were silent as we drove along, looking out the windows at the devastation. Walking through the French Quarter yesterday, having fun, it was easy to forget how ruined other parts of New Orleans still were. But we could also see the areas that had already been rebuilt. They spoke to the strength and determination of the people of the city.

As my admiration for them was growing, my cell phone rang. I pulled it out of the case attached to my belt. My dad had given me the case because he thought it would make it easier to keep my phone handy and he didn't want me to be without quick access to it. "In case of an emergency."

So maybe he and Mom *were* a little worried about me being away from home—at least, that's what occurred to me when I saw Mom's name pop up in the window.

"Hey," I said, after answering.

"What's going on?" Mom asked curtly.

Her question wasn't at all friendly. Not a *what's happening?* It was more of a *what trouble are you getting into?*

I was sitting on the backseat between Amber and Jenna. They must have heard her through the phone because they both looked at me.

"What do you mean?" I asked.

"Drew e-mailed me a picture of you with some guy—"

"He did what?" That jerk! Why would he do that?

"He sent me—"

"Sorry, Mom," I interrupted again. Mom hated being interrupted, but she was almost four hundred miles away. What could she do, other than growl? "I got you the first time. My question was more of a 'what was he thinking.'"

"So who is this guy?"

"Just someone I met."

She was quiet for a minute. It was never good when Mom was quiet.

"He's a student at Rice," I felt compelled to explain. "He's here for the summer doing the same thing we are."

"Does Ms. Wynder know him?"

Define know, I thought. She'd seen him if she'd been looking out her window last night at the precise moment needed to see him before he disappeared.

"Yes."

I squeezed my eyes shut, hoping she wouldn't ask to speak with Ms. Wynder.

"It's just that I know you're still not over Drew—"

"I am over Drew," I interrupted.

"—and I don't want you doing anything stupid," Mom finished.

"I won't. Don't worry."

Of course, do we ever *plan* to do something stupid? It's not like I wake up in the morning and think, "Today would be a good day to do something stupid."

"It's a mother's job to worry," Mom said. "I just need reassurance there isn't any craziness going on."

"None whatsoever. Please don't worry, Mom. I'm fine. We're in the van now, heading to the site." I thought trying to distract her would be a good move on my part. "We're looking forward to helping to clean things up."

"Yet you don't seem to care about cleaning your room. What's wrong with this picture?"

I could tell that she was teasing and had gotten past whatever had been bothering her. We talked for a little while longer, then said good-bye. I told Jenna and Amber what Drew had done.

"Why would he do that?" Jenna asked.

I shrugged, surprised that he cared what I was doing. I hadn't *really* thought that he'd read Jenna's blog. Why would he? We were so over. Why would he care?

"He's definitely coming off my friends list," Jenna said.

I didn't say anything, but I thought he should have come off sooner.

"Everything all right back there?" Ms. Wynder asked.

"Yes, ma'am. Just my mom missing me."

And my ex-boyfriend trying to stir up trouble.

Chapter 7

Our caravan pulled to a stop in a neighborhood that still reflected the aftermath of the storm. The street had been cleared of debris, but what remained of the houses littered the yards.

No one said anything as we climbed out of the van. I thought I was prepared for this, but I wasn't. It seemed like an impossible task, and yet I was also filled with a sense that we could make a difference. We could get this done.

"Hey!" a guy called out in a welcoming way. "Everyone over here!"

He was standing on a ladder, near the first house on the block, urging us over. He was older, much older. Probably as old as Ms.

Wynder. He wore a black T-shirt with the French fleur-de-lis on the front above the words "Rebuild New Orleans." He had curly red hair that fluffed out beneath his white cap and made him look a little like a clown. All he needed was the red nose—only his was very white, covered in zinc oxide.

Another caravan of vehicles pulled up. I found myself standing on tiptoe, trying to see if I recognized anyone from the dorm or breakfast that morning. Okay, that wasn't exactly true. I was searching for someone I'd seen yesterday, last night to be precise. I was pathetic. I didn't really know what I wanted. To see him again, to never see him again.

I knew he probably wouldn't be at the site, but there was one irritating little spark of hope that wouldn't have been disappointed if he showed up.

And then I saw someone I recognized, the very last person I'd expected to see here.

"Hey, is that—" Amber began.

"The psychic," Jenna finished.

"Hey, Sara! Bring your group over here,"

the guy on the ladder yelled.

Waving at him, she herded her little group over. Wearing jeans and a tank top, with her red hair pulled back in a ponytail, she looked like a normal person. Her group was mostly guys, which was pretty understandable because she was really pretty—gorgeous actually. It took me a minute to realize that, because I was scanning the guys following her.

Okay, I was doing more than scanning. I was seriously searching for the familiar red cap, the nice smile. Which was dumb, because if I wanted to see Brady again, all I had to do was tell Jenna and she'd call Tank and he'd tell Brady and Brady could call me . . . only I didn't know if that's what I wanted.

But I didn't see anyone I recognized.

"Why is she here?" Amber asked. "Is she going to do psychic readings?"

"Based on the way she's dressed, she's probably here for the same reason we are," I said.

"That's weird," Jenna said.

"Not really," I said. "I mean, people who live in New Orleans are working to rebuild it, too."

"Still, a psychic," Jenna said. "Do you think she'll let us know if she gets bad vibes?"

Before I could respond, the guy on the ladder clapped his hands. "All right, people! I need your attention!"

Everyone stopped talking and edged up closer.

The guy clapped his hands again. "I'm John. And this house is our project." He pointed toward the house behind him. "Working together, we're going to gut it, then rebuild it."

Gut it. That sounded so harsh.

"Gutting should take only a couple of days. We're going to move everything out, put it at the edge of the street so we can haul it away. We're going to remove the walls, the windows, the doors. The only thing we'll leave is what remains of the frame."

We'll be able to do all that in a couple of days? I thought. Amazing.

"The woman who lives here is staying with her parents right now. She's already taken all that's salvageable, so anything else — just move it to the curb. Be sure to gear up. We have hard hats, safety goggles, and dust masks over there. Work together and be really careful because you don't know what you're going to find hidden beneath all this stuff."

Hidden? A shiver went through me. Saraphina had said I'd find something hidden.

"Any questions, people?" Without hesitating a beat, he clapped his hands three times. "Then let's go!"

"I had a question," Amber said.

"Did you really?" I asked.

She smiled. "No, but he didn't even give us a chance to ask one if we did."

"Guess he's anxious for us to get started." I caught a glimpse of Jenna off to the side, talking on her phone. I took out the work gloves that I'd stuffed into my jeans pocket earlier. Ms. Wynder had given us tips for how we needed to prepare for this summer of labor. She'd done it last year as well, so she knew what was useful and what to expect. I tugged on the gloves, grateful that I had them. Jenna came back over. She and Amber tugged on their gloves.

Then we walked over to get the rest of

our equipment. A line had already formed. Probably two dozen people were here, many already starting to walk by with their gear in place.

"Does a hard hat leave a hard-hat line around your head when you take it off?" I asked.

"What does it matter?" Jenna asked. "You're not trying to impress anyone."

"Still, with all the gear, we're going to look like we're going into a contaminated zone."

"We probably are—with the mold and stuff," Amber said.

Once we were properly geared up, we grabbed one of the wheelbarrows at the edge of the property and rolled it closer to the house.

"Why don't you girls pick up some of the loose debris that's still around the house?" John asked.

I saluted him. He grinned.

"You okay with us just tossing stuff off the porch and letting you take care of it?" he asked.

"Works for me," I said.

"Good. I love a can-do attitude."

He walked into the house and several people tromped in after him. Amber, Jenna, and I began gathering any broken and rotting pieces of wood that hadn't yet been hauled to the curb. Beneath one board, we found a doll's head, which made us sad thinking of a little girl without her doll.

John came outside and tossed what looked like molding cushions onto the ground.

"Did a little girl live here?" I asked.

He glanced over at me. "Yeah, she's fine. There are two girls, actually. They're with their mom."

"How old are they?" I asked.

"Four and six, I think."

"I guess they have new dolls now."

"Yeah, but little girls can never have too many, right?"

I smiled at him, wondering how he knew what I was thinking. "Right. If I bought something for them, would you be able to get it to them?"

"You could give it to them yourself. When we're finished, we'll welcome them home.

You'll get to meet them then."

"Oh, cool."

I hadn't realized we'd be doing that. I went back to work, picking things up. I was carefully placing the remains of a clay jar in the wheelbarrow when I heard, "Smile!"

I looked up. Jenna snapped a picture and then laughed.

"You look like someone doing something she shouldn't," she said. "Let's try this again."

"Why do you need a picture? I'm all scruffy looking."

"For one—my MySpace page. But I also want to send a pic to your mom so she can see you're hard at work and it'll calm her worries. So smile."

"I'm wearing a mask. You can't even see my mouth."

"So smile, anyway."

Smiling while picking up trash was kind of like those people who smiled in commercials selling exercise machines. It wasn't natural. Still, I pulled down my mask, gave a big fake smile, and a huge thumbs-up.

"That'll do it," Jenna said. "I'm going to see what else I can document."

She walked away. I pulled up my mask and returned to my task. I was reaching down, wrapping my hands around what looked to be a massive table leg attached to a small section of dining table, when I heard a deep voice I recognized say, "Need help with that?"

I jerked up, stepped back. My foot landed on an old board that wobbled. I teetered and would have fallen, except strong hands wrapped around my arms, steadying me.

"Careful," Brady said in a voice that fell between concerned and amused.

"What are you doing here?" I asked.

He was wearing sunglasses so I couldn't read his eyes. Some sort of white powder was sprinkled over his burgundy T-shirt. *Maybe that's his flaw*, I thought. *Maybe he does drugs.*

And how had he even realized it was me, with all my gear on? Had he noticed me when I'd posed for the camera?

"I told you yesterday. I came to volunteer," he said.

"But this site?"

He shrugged. "It's where they sent me."

"So you're into snow?" Wasn't that what they called it? Or was it blow?

"Love snow. Went skiing over spring break."

"I was referring to the powder." I pointed to his chest, trying not to remember how nice it had looked last night without a shirt covering it.

Glancing down, he started dusting off his shirt. "Oh, that. Powdered sugar. We went to Café Du Monde for beignets. Place was packed. It's the reason we're late." He looked up. "You thought it was drugs?"

I felt so silly. Talking to him through the mask. Looking at him through the goggles. Accusing him of dumb stuff.

"I was teasing."

And if you believe that, I have some swampland I could sell you.

He grinned, like he knew I was out of control, but he was willing to tolerate it.

"You eaten there yet?" he asked, taking the conversation back to his breakfast.

"No."

"It's a must-do."

"They feed us breakfast in the dorm."

"Doesn't mean you have to eat there."

Why was I discouraging a hot guy from showing interest in me?

And why was he interested in me?

Why not?

I felt like the before-Drew me and the after-Drew me were on the debate team. And doing a pretty lousy job at substantiating arguments.

"Are you staying at the dorm?" I asked. It would be totally weird if he was, that everything—fate, the dating gods, whatever—was putting him in my path.

"Nah, we've got some cheap rooms in a small hotel in the French Quarter. Tank knew some people who knew some people." He shrugged.

"Is he in charge of your group?"

"We're not official, not really organized. As a matter of fact, very unorganized. Tank asked if I wanted to come to New Orleans for the summer and do some volunteer work, said he'd secured some beds, and since I had nothing better to do—here I am." He made a grand sweeping gesture. "At your service. So let me help you with this."

"But you're not geared up."

"I'll gear up in a minute. Let's get this done."

Squatting, he grabbed the end of the table leg that was still attached to part of the table.

I bent over—

"It's better for your back if you use your legs to lift stuff," he said.

"My toes don't hold things well."

He laughed. "Funny. You grab with your hands, but lift with your legs. See?"

He demonstrated, his legs doing a smooth pumping action, like a piston. He had really nice thighs. Even covered in jeans, they looked firm. Very firm.

"So, you're what? A lifting coach?" I asked.

"Nah. I worked for an overnight package deliverer over winter break. Had to watch safety videos." He shifted the table leg so he was able to carry it by himself and drop it in the wheelbarrow.

It was only then that I noticed Tank and

Jenna working together to remove a screen from a window. How it had managed to remain attached, I couldn't imagine. Most were gone, or hanging lopsided.

"Where's Amber?" I called out to Jenna.

"She went to talk to Sara/Saraphina. I think she wants another psychic reading."

"Now?" I asked.

Jenna shrugged as she walked over to me. "She's still bummed about what Saraphina told her yesterday."

"You had a psychic reading?" Brady asked.

Now it was my turn to shrug. "It's like eating at Café Du Monde. Something you have to do when you're in New Orleans."

"What did she tell you?"

"Nothing that made any sense. Do you believe in that sort of thing?"

"Not really." He reached down, picked up a brick, and dropped it in the wheelbarrow.

Apparently, I had a new partner for the day—whether I wanted him or not.

Chapter 8

"Okay, so her real name is Sara, and Saraphina is, like, her stage name or something. She said it all has to do with marketing," Amber said.

It was a little past noon, and we were all sitting on the curb, eating deli sandwiches called po'boys that one of the local eateries had sent over. Apparently some of the restaurants provided food for the volunteers, which made it really nice on our budgets. It also gave us such a sense of being appreciated—not that we were doing any of this for kudos, but still, it was nice.

"So, did she give you another reading?" I asked.

"No. She doesn't give freebies, and she

doesn't do readings when she's outside the shop. She's just a normal person today—or as normal as she can be with two different colored eyes, but whatever. She said I'm trying too hard to interpret what she saw. I don't know how I can *not* interpret"—she darted a quick glance at Sean, who was attacking his ham sandwich— "what she told me."

I wondered if she thought that since Sean was in college, he had the potential to be the better love.

"It's not like psychic-ism—or whatever you call it—is an exact science," I reassured Amber. "She puts a thought in your mind and then when something similar—"

"Similar? Red Kansas City Chiefs hat is pretty specific," she interrupted.

"What?" Brady asked, taking off his cap and looking at the logo on the front, like he was trying to confirm that it was there.

Before lunch, we'd all taken off our gear and washed up with a water hose. He'd put his cap back on then. I'd put mine on too, because of course I had hard-hat hair.

"Saraphina said Dawn would meet a guy—" Amber began.

"She said she saw a red cap—" I interrupted.

"Close enough."

"What happens with you and the red cap?" Brady asked, settling it back into place.

"Nothing. And look"—I turned my attention back to Amber—"nothing that she saw for Jenna has shown up."

"Maybe it has and we just haven't recognized it."

"You know, I heard a story once about a guy who went to see a fortune-teller," Tank said. "He wanted to know how he was going to die. She told him that cancer would kill him. So he's looking in the mirror one day and sees this strange-colored lump on the end of his nose. He's sure it's cancer and he panics. Jumps in the car, heads to his doctor, and on the way, he's hit by an eighteen-wheeler. Game over."

"So the fortune-teller was wrong," Jenna said.

Tank shrugged. "Maybe, but in a way, cancer *did* kill him."

"That's kinda convoluted," Amber said.

"Exactly," Tank said, "but that's the way all this mumbo jumbo works. You can read anything into it that you want, and practically force what was predicted to happen."

"So you're saying that I'm overreacting," Amber said.

"I'm saying you're letting her mess with your head."

"You don't believe in psychics?"

He grinned. "I didn't say that."

"I just really wish we hadn't gone there at all."

I knew Amber was a worrier, but she'd never believed in stuff like this before. Why was she so troubled now? It made no sense.

I took a long sip of water. I was drinking water like there was no tomorrow.

"I can't believe that y'all were assigned to the same site we were," I said. "What are the odds?"

"Five million to one," Brady said, grinning.

I'd known him less than twenty-four hours and already we had a private joke. I couldn't remember what private joke Drew and I had — or if we'd even had one.

"Are you kidding? The odds were stacked in our favor. Jenna called and told me where y'all were working," Tank said.

I didn't know whether to stare at Jenna or glare at Brady. Jenna was leaning against Tank's shoulder like he was the only thing supporting her, and Brady was studying his sandwich like he was trying to determine what lunch meats they'd stuffed between the French bread.

"You called them?" I said.

"Oh yeah," Jenna said. "They're not with a group like we are. They're like freelancers or something. Just helping where needed, so I called him this morning right after we got here to see if they wanted to help out."

"John was a little freaked that we were here and not on his list. That guy is way too tightly wired," Tank said. "Apparently there are people you're supposed to contact to be an official volunteer, but" — he shrugged — "John decided having our muscles was more important than following the rules."

"It'd be insane to turn away someone wanting to help," Jenna said.

"Exactly the point we made. Who'd have thought we'd even have to argue?"

"John's Sara's brother," Amber announced.

"Really?" I asked.

"According to Sara."

"Guess she wouldn't say it if it wasn't true. Now that you've told me, I can see the resemblance, sort of," I said.

"I asked him if he could see things, but he said no," Amber said. "He said that's Sara's burden."

"I imagine it would be hard to see things, to know things," Jenna said. "It's hard enough just knowing the little bit she told us."

"All right, people!" John yelled. "Five more minutes and we need to get back to work!"

"So much for the Big *Easy*," Sean said.

We all smiled.

"You got that right," Tank said.

Amber smiled at Sean, then dropped her gaze to watch a centipede walking between her feet. Her cheeks turned red, like she was embarrassed to have Sean's attention. Or maybe it was just the heat, which was turning us all red.

The day was only half over and I wanted a shower already. With lots and lots of soap. A bubble shower. I smiled at the thought of filling a shower all the way up with water and swimming in it.

"A dip in a pool would be nice right about now," Brady said.

And I had a vision of him in the water-filled shower with me, and we were cavorting around like seals or something. Way too much imagination.

"Ookay!" I said, standing. "Think I'm ready to get back to work."

I started the exodus from the curb. Everyone crumpled up the sandwich wrappers and tossed them into a nearby trash bin. Then we went back to picking up the debris brought out of the house and putting it into a wheelbarrow. When it was full, the guys hauled it over to the curb and dumped the stuff there.

"I think we've got the absolute best team out here," Jenna said.

She was using the time when the guys went to empty the wheelbarrow to catch her breath. Okay, we all did. But her gaze followed them a little more closely.

"So you really like Tank," I said, although my voice went a little high at the end, and it came off sounding like a question.

"Yeah, I do. And I think Brady might be the one Saraphina was talking about for you. It's obvious that he likes you."

"Or I could just be convenient. You like Tank. He hangs out with Tank. I hang out with you. It's just serendipity."

"Come on. He's here, helping us, just like Saraphina predicted."

"Actually, you sort of orchestrated that, by inviting them. And Sara didn't say anything really happened with me and the guy. She just said she saw him."

"*Whatever*. We could all have so much fun together!"

I know she thought I was being difficult,

stubborn. And maybe I was. But I'd learned the hard way that you can't tell by looking if a guy is destined to hurt you. From the outside, they all look nice.

By about two o'clock, I was hot, sweaty, and ready for another break.

"All right, people," John called out, from atop his ladder. "Can I have your attention?" He made sweeping arm gestures, trying to get us all to come closer.

Jenna, Amber, and I sort of migrated together.

"Wonder what's going on?" Jenna asked.

I shook my head. I didn't have a clue.

"We're making great progress, people," John said. "But we worry that if we work you too hard, you won't come back."

Everyone laughed.

"Soooo . . . you have the rest of the afternoon off."

Applause, a few roars of approval, and some whistles followed that announcement.

John waved us into silence. "For anyone

who's interested, Sara arranged a swamp tour! The bus will be in front of Sara's shop in about"—he made a big production of looking at his watch—"forty-five minutes. Whether you go to the swamp or just hang loose, enjoy your afternoon. Tomorrow morning come back ready to hit it hard again!"

People began to disperse.

"Hmm. Swamp," Jenna murmured. "What do you think? Do we want to go to a swamp?"

"I watched an old movie called *Swamp Thing* with my dad once. That's all I know about them," I said.

"A swamp seems like such an icky thing," Amber said.

"Okay, so what do we want to do?" Jenna asked.

I shrugged. "Maybe we could go down to the French Quarter—"

"Hey, Jenna," Tank called out, walking toward us. "We're going on the tour. Are you?"

"Yeah, we are," Jenna said.

Okay, I guess our plans changed.

"Great! See you at the bus."

She waved at him as he walked away. I watched as he joined up with Brady and Sean, said something to them. Then they headed to his car.

"Hope you don't mind," Jenna said.

"I'm good with it," Amber said. "I mean, we're here to work *and* have fun."

They both looked at me, like they thought I was going to argue with the fun part. I guessed there was no reason why I *had* to go. But I didn't want to spend the rest of the afternoon alone either.

"It'll be interesting," I said enthusiastically. I didn't see how, but I was trying to be a good sport. "But I have an important question here — what *does* one wear to a swamp?"

Ms. Wynder took us back to the dorm so we could clean up — fast. She wasn't going on the tour, but she was willing to drop us off at Sara's.

I changed into shorts. I decided to double layer two tank tops that I had, putting a red one over a pink one that peeked out just a bit. I slipped on my red sandals.

"You know a swamp is probably squishy," Jenna said.

"Yeah, you're right." I changed into sneakers. I didn't want muck getting between my toes.

Quite a crowd was at Sara's when Ms. Wynder dropped us off. The other three girls in our group immediately headed toward three guys who'd shown up at the site with Sara that morning.

"Wow, that didn't take them long," Amber said.

"Looks like a lot of people are pairing off," Jenna said.

"Here we go, everyone!" Sara said as the bus pulled up.

"I guess we can all sit together," Jenna said.

She said it like it was a fate worse than death, obviously worried that Tank wasn't there yet. And then suddenly there he was, grinning broadly, Brady and Sean right behind him.

"Hey," Tank said, taking Jenna's hand. "This is going to be awesome."

Maybe swamps were a guy thing.

Brady and Sean were both standing there with their hands in their back pockets, like they weren't exactly sure what to do. Like maybe they were wondering if we were all going to pair up again like we had last night.

I remembered how worried Amber had been about how things would play out if Jenna was seeing Tank. I hadn't wanted to deal with it then. I still didn't.

We headed onto the luxury bus. Each row had two seats. Sean was leading the way. Amber was following him. I was behind her. Sean dropped down onto a row, reached out, took Amber's hand, and pulled her down beside him. I felt a small spark of panic. Where was I supposed to go now?

I went a couple of rows back and took a seat by the window. Jenna slid onto the seat in front of me, and Tank sat beside her. That was cool. I could sit alone.

But suddenly Brady was there. He eased down beside me.

"I think the bus is going to be packed," Brady said. "Tight fit for everyone, so I figured sitting by someone I knew beat sitting by a stranger."

"These are all people from the site. Don't you know them?"

"Some of 'em, sure, but not like I know you."

What exactly did that mean?

"So should I move?" he asked.

I shook my head. "No, you're fine."

He grinned, wiggled his eyebrows. "Some would say I'm better than fine."

I couldn't help myself. I laughed.

Sara took a head count, and then the bus headed out.

"So . . . Sara predicted I'd walk into your life?" he asked in a low voice.

"Uh, no, she predicted a red baseball hat was in my future. Not exactly the same thing."

"That's weird, though."

"Yeah."

"I mean, how many Chiefs caps could be in the city?" Before I could answer, his grin broadened. "Let me guess. Five million?"

I smiled, shrugged. I didn't want to be

unfriendly. But I didn't want to be too friendly.

"What else did she say?" he asked.

"Not much. That things were a mess. There'd be hammering. Pretty vague."

"And pretty general. That could pretty much apply to anyone."

"That's what I thought. It was interesting, but not something I want to do on a regular basis."

"Well, I'm all about interesting and having fun."

I scowled at him. "But a swamp? Really. How much fun can we have at a swamp?"

"As much as we want."

Chapter 9

*H*oney Island Swamp. I liked the name—the Honey Island part at least sounded sweet—but I still couldn't get past my image of a swamp being, well, a swamp.

It was located almost an hour from New Orleans. I wasn't sure what I'd been expecting. Maybe taking a look at slime covered water from a dock and moving on. Swatting at a few mosquitoes, shooing away flies. Heading back to the Big Easy.

But no, we were getting out *on* the swamp, in a boat. And I soon discovered that the sounds out there were a different kind of music than what we'd heard in the city. Here it was the croak of bullfrogs—some were disgustingly huge and ugly—and the chirp of crickets. There were mysterious knocks and pecks and little trills. Luckily Sara had brought lots of insect repellent for anyone who wanted it. I'd slathered, sprayed, and squirted it on. I was taking no chances. I was not into bugs.

And we were at a very bug-infested place.

We climbed aboard a large, covered boat, like the kind I'd ridden once at a safari ride at a theme park—except this one was real. It didn't run along a rail. It had a motor and a captain, who steered it through the swamp.

Benches lined all four sides of the boat. We all worked our way around the deck. I managed to get a seat near the front of the boat. Brady sat beside me.

I was turned sort of sideways on the bench, so I could see clearly things that approached our side. Brady was twisted around, too, which almost had us spooning.

"You smell really nice," he said in a low voice.

"It's the insect repellent."

"It is?" Out of the corner of my eye, I could

see him sniffing the back of his hand. "Oh God, it is. How sick is that—to like the smell of insect repellent?"

I laughed. "Pretty sick."

"But admit it. You were thinking I smelled good, too."

Okay, I had been, but I wasn't going to admit it. "Maybe."

The motor cranked to life and the boat glided away from the dock. I was surprised that the water looked more like what you'd find in a river than what you might expect to find in a swamp.

Our guide was native to the area, and he shared a lot of the history—especially about pirates and Big Foot sightings—as we journeyed deeper into the swamp. Because so much of the area was protected, he explained, Honey Island Swamp was one of the least-altered river swamps in the country. It probably looked the same more than two hundred years ago when pirates were hiding out there.

"Wow," I whispered. There was an awesome beauty to the place. Huge cypress trees rose from the water.

And I'd expected the marshes to smell . . . well, like stagnant water. There was a little of that, but there was also the scent of wild azaleas. I hadn't expected the sweet fragrance.

"Look," Brady said, pointing.

At first I thought it was a log, resting at the edge of the bank, barely visible through the tall grasses. But it was an alligator. A very large alligator.

"We have more than a million alligators in Louisiana," the guide said.

"Imagine if they ever decided to band together," Brady said. "They could take over the state."

"I think I've seen that in a movie."

"Me, too. I can never get enough of giant alligator movies."

"Really?"

"Oh yeah, the bigger the creature the better. *Night of the Lepus*. A classic."

My dad was a huge creature-feature watcher, so I'd pretty much seen them all.

"Now, see, I didn't get that one. What's

scary about a bunny rabbit?" I asked.

"It's a big, big bunny rabbit."

"Still, not scary."

The guide warned us to keep all our limbs inside the boat. Then he began making a sound I'd never heard before. Alligators—the ones I'd spotted and ones that had been hidden—began slipping into the water and gliding toward the boat.

"Ohmigod!" I couldn't help it. There were so many. I imagined them tipping the boat over. I'd definitely watched too many bad movies with my dad if I really thought that was going to happen.

"It's okay," Brady said, putting his arm around me, squeezing my shoulder.

He was so comforting. But this wasn't a date. It was a group outing, and we were all sitting close together. It was just natural to reassure each other that we weren't about to become alligator dinner.

The guide began tossing something toward the alligators and the *clack* of their mouths snapping shut filled the air.

"Is he tossing marshmallows?" I asked.

"Looks like."

"How did anyone find out that they like marshmallows?"

"Beats me."

Every now and then we'd come in close to the shore, and we'd see other animals: deer, red wolves, raccoons, beavers, turtles . . . and always the alligators.

"I don't think I'd want them for neighbors," I said quietly.

"Me either."

We saw an egret and other birds. It was an untouched paradise. I knew New Orleans had once been swampland, and I wondered if it had looked like this at one time. Hard to imagine.

I looked over my shoulder to see Sara sitting near the captain. I figured we were safe. She wouldn't get on the boat if she saw danger, would she? On the other hand, her visions were so cryptic. Maybe she just saw herself swimming and didn't realize it meant she'd be swimming with the gators.

Amber and Sean were sitting together. He

was pointing stuff out to her. She was smiling. They were just being friendly. Having fun. Like me and Brady. No big deal.

Jenna and Tank were sitting close, his arms around her as they looked out at the swamp. There was no doubt that Tank was really interested in her.

I turned my attention back to the alligators. Sometimes nature was so powerful, you had no defense against it.

It was early evening when we got back to Sara's, and Ms. Wynder was there, waiting for us. Before anyone could say anything, she said, "I've made reservations for eight o'clock. We need to get moving."

Jenna didn't bother to hide her disappointment as she waved good-bye to Tank. I thought Amber looked relieved. I knew I was. It gave me time to think, to try to figure out what, if anything, was happening with Brady and me. We all got along, so I could see our little group hanging out together. But at the same time, did I need to explain to him that more kisses weren't in our future?

On the other hand, did I really want to give that up?

After we were seated at the restaurant and had given our orders to the waitress, Ms. Wynder folded her arms on the table. She looked incredibly serious.

"All right, girls, we need to talk," she said.

I wondered what we'd done wrong. Everyone looked guilty.

"I know some of you are developing . . . friendships." She paused and looked at each of us.

I wanted to raise my hand and say, "Not me!"

But the truth was that maybe I was. A little.

"During the week, curfew is midnight. On Saturday, two o'clock. I already have all your cell phone numbers"—she held up her phone as though to demonstrate—"and I want phones to be kept on at all times."

"What about when we're at a movie?" one of the other girls said.

"Vibrate. I will be making room checks. Or stop by my room and let me know when you get in. Are there any questions?"

It sounded pretty straightforward to me.

She smiled. "All right then. Tell me about the swamp."

The next day, it seemed like the sun had moved a million miles closer to earth. How else could it be so much hotter?

Or maybe it was just that we were working harder. We were actually beginning to see progress. John had given crowbars to some of the guys to start ripping off the outer walls.

Jenna had muttered, "Sexist!"

So Tank had given her his crowbar. Or let her work the crowbar with him. He'd put his arms around her and together they'd ratchet off boards. Boards that Amber and I would pick up after they were tossed to the side, put them in the wheelbarrow, and haul them to the curb.

I caught Brady watching me a time or two. Today he was geared up so much that the only thing that gave him away was when his head was turned in my direction. It felt as if he was studying me, trying to figure me out.

What was there to figure out?

We'd had fun at the swamp yesterday, but it hadn't been anything serious. And it hadn't ended in a kiss like the first night. Actually it hadn't had any type of real ending.

There had just been stepping off the bus and Ms. Wynder ushering us away like a hen going after her chicks. And all of us too surprised to say anything other than "See you tomorrow."

And even though we'd seen each other earlier today, our greeting had been a little cautious. Just a *hey*. Like we were both trying to figure out if yesterday had been more than just hanging out together because of convenience.

Do you like me?

Should I like you?

Where do we go from here?

Should we go from here?

I really wasn't sure. Last night, when I'd asked Amber why she'd hooked up with Sean, she'd said, "Everyone was pairing up. It would have been rude not to."

But if you kept pairing up with the same

person, didn't you eventually become a *couple*? I didn't want to be part of a couple. I didn't want expectations.

Hooking up one night when I didn't expect to see him again was one thing. Hooking up twice was creeping toward dangerous territory.

I thought maybe Amber was feeling the same way, too, because she was staying pretty near me today, helping me haul the debris to the curb.

It kept getting hotter and hotter, and by late afternoon, it was miserable.

John announced that we could quit for the day, but we were so close to being finished with the gutting that everyone protested. We all wanted to stay and get the job done.

Brady, Tank, and Sean walked to their car—a black Honda Civic—pulled their tees off, and tossed them inside. Not that I blamed them. All our shirts were damp from the humidity and our efforts. I thought about how nice it would feel to have the breeze blowing over exposed, damp skin.

They tossed their gear onto a table. I guess

they'd had enough of being safe. They wanted to be not so hot.

Carrying their crowbars, they headed back toward the house. I really tried not to stare at Brady's chest. It had looked nice in the shadows of Bourbon Street, but now there were no shadows. And he was definitely in shape.

Tank walked past us, touching Jenna's shoulder as he went by. "Jenna, help me out over here, will you?"

Only Jenna didn't move. Neither did Amber. Neither did I, for that matter. We were staring at Tank's back. His right shoulder, to be precise.

A shoulder that sported a tattoo of a blue and green flying dragon.

A dragon breathing fiery red and blue flames.

Fire that didn't burn.

Chapter 10

"*I* know you must think I'm insane, but I just can't help it."

Following an afternoon that seemed to have way too many hours—and surprises—in it, we were back at the dorm. Jenna and I were standing in our room, speechless, watching as Amber tossed all her stuff into her suitcase.

"I mean, red Chiefs cap"—she pointed at me—"fire that doesn't burn?" She pointed at Jenna. "I don't care what you say, there is something to that psychic reading. I've got to go home and figure out if things between Chad and me are real or over."

She'd freaked out when she'd seen Tank's tattoo. She'd told Ms. Wynder that her mother called and her grandma had died.

That afternoon, her mother *had* called, to see how things were going, after Amber had left a panicked message on her voice mail saying that she was homesick and wanted to fly home—immediately, that night, the first flight out that she could get.

And her grandmother *had* died—five years ago.

"She didn't say you were going to break up with Chad," I pointed out.

"She said I was going to find something better."

"Well, if there is something better, isn't now the time to find out?" Jenna asked. "You're only in high school—"

"Who are you—my mother? Always thinking that I'm too young to know what I'm doing? I know what I'm doing."

"We've been planning this summer adventure for months!" Jenna exclaimed. "You can't just pack up and leave. We just got here!"

"This is a free country. I can change my mind about what I want to do."

"But we're only going to be here six weeks," I reminded her. "Chad will still be there."

"I'm not going back for Chad. I'm going back for me. You don't understand how I feel about him."

I stepped in front of her, trying to stop yet another mad dash between her dresser and the suitcase on the bed. "I know you're crazy about Chad—"

"Not Chad. Sean. I really, *really* like Sean." She dropped down on the bed, scrunching her clothes between her hands. "That first night when we were listening to the band at that bar, I was leaning into him and he had his arm around me, and I wasn't thinking about Chad at all. I was just thinking about how nice it was to be with Sean. And then yesterday at the swamp—I knew I should have been hanging around with you."

"What could you do? He took your hand—"

"He took my hand because he thinks I really like him. He doesn't even know about Chad."

"He doesn't know you have a boyfriend?"

"How do you tell a guy that?"

"'Oh, by the way, I have a boyfriend?'"

"But what if I shouldn't?"

"What?" Jenna asked, while I said, "Huh?"

I was afraid Amber was about to veer off into one of her strange thoughts that we couldn't follow.

"Look—Chad? He's the only one I've ever wanted to date. I've been crushing on him since I was a freshman. When he finally asked me out over winter break, I thought he was it. Forever. And now, all of a sudden, it's like all I can think about is Sean. And that's so wrong. I know it's wrong. He's like that extra scoop of ice cream that you know you shouldn't have, but you can't resist it. I need to get as far away from the ice cream as possible. I need to go home."

Okay, some of what she was saying was making sense. I wanted to try to convince her that she should stay, but I couldn't anymore. I couldn't without fearing that she'd cheat on Chad—and I'd be encouraging it. She was right. It was better to leave and figure out what was going on.

"I know if we hadn't gone to see the psychic that I wouldn't have all these doubts. Or maybe I would. I just don't know anymore. I mean, what was I thinking to even consider going away for most of the summer? I have a boyfriend and nothing should be more important than him."

Jenna sat on the edge of the bed and drew her long legs up beneath her. "You know, what you're doing is sort of self-fulfilling Sara's prophecy. You're going to make happen exactly what she predicted. Just like Tank was talking about."

"You can't tell me that you weren't a little freaked out when you saw that tattoo."

"I was surprised," Jenna admitted. "But it could be that we're taking her words and seeing things that apply. We're assuming she meant the tattoo because it fits. But it could mean something else."

"Like what?" Amber challenged.

Jenna sighed. "I don't know."

Okay. I thought it was a little difficult to read anything else into that tattoo, but I understood what Jenna was saying — or trying to say. You see what you expect to see, and Saraphina had influenced what we expected to see.

Amber turned to me. "Look at the bright side. You don't have to sleep on the AeroBed anymore. You can have a real bed."

"The bed isn't an issue. I'd rather have you here."

"I can't, guys. I'm sorry, but I just can't stay."

An hour later, Jenna and I hugged Amber good-bye and watched her climb into the minivan. Ms. Wynder, after repeatedly clucking about how sorry she was that Amber's grandmother had died, drove Amber to the airport where she could catch her flight back to Houston.

"Whose idea was it to visit the psychic, anyway?" Jenna asked as we trudged back to our room.

"I think it was Amber's."

"Talk about a fun idea going bad."

"It is a little . . . eerie, though."

"Yeah, but at least I didn't see the tattoo until after I'd fallen for Tank, so my feelings about him are my own. Do you ever worry that what you feel for Brady is because of the reading? I mean, would you have noticed him if you hadn't been looking for a red Chiefs cap?"

"I wasn't looking for a red Chiefs cap."

"Okay, you weren't looking, but when you saw it—I saw your jaw drop, so I know he caught your attention. Would you have noticed him without the reading?"

"Yeah, I think I would have." I sighed. "But I might not have shot up my defenses so fast. Or maybe I would have. I don't know, Jenna. I just really don't want a guy in my life right now."

"At least you're not totally avoiding him and flying back home."

"That would be a bit extreme, especially since I really do want to be *here*."

Jenna smiled at me. I gave her a weary smile back. To say I was exhausted was an understatement. We'd worked harder and longer today than yesterday. On top of that, dealing with Amber's hysterics —

"Dibs on the shower," I muttered.

I wanted the shower first, last, and always. It felt so wonderful to get all the grit and grime off. Amber had hit the shower as soon as we'd gotten back to the room. When she'd come out, she'd gone immediately into frantic I've-got-to-get-out-of-here mode. And Jenna and I had gone into intervention mode. A lot of good that had done.

I guess, being alone with her thoughts, Amber hadn't liked where she and Sean were going.

I was too tired to think of anything except how great the shower felt. And if Jenna wasn't a friend, I probably wouldn't have cared about using up all the hot water.

The bathroom was steamy by the time I was finished; the mirror fogged. Not that I needed a mirror when I only planned to comb the tangles out my hair. When that was done, I massaged my peach-scented body lotion on my legs, arms, and hands. I'd picked up a few scratches on my arms, even though I'd tried to be careful. But nothing serious.

I slipped on cotton boxers and a tank. I was ready to fall into bed and fall asleep.

When I opened the bathroom door, the only light in the room came from the bathroom behind me.

Jenna rolled off her bed and walked toward me, holding her cell phone out. "Here."

"What's that?"

"Phone."

"I know that. I mean, who is it?"

"Brady."

"You were talking to Brady?"

"No, I was talking to Tank, but Brady wanted to talk to you when you finally got out of the bathroom. Did you even leave me any hot water?" She took my hand and wrapped my fingers around her phone. "He doesn't have your phone number. Keep talking until I'm finished with my shower."

She closed the door, leaving me in the dark except for the phone's little bit of indigo glow. I stumbled to the bed, sat down, and stared at the phone for a minute like it was the snake that had slithered out from beneath one of the boards we'd moved that afternoon. Some guy had used a shovel to kill it, and we'd all heard a lecture from Sara about how we should live in harmony with all creatures. The dead snake had upset her. Personally I didn't have a problem with killing anything that slithered and stuck its tongue out at me.

And why did I have to talk to Brady until Jenna got out of the bathroom? It wasn't like she didn't already have Tank's number programmed into her phone, so she could call him back. What about *I really don't want to get involved with anyone this summer* did she not understand?

I moved the phone to my ear. "Hello?"

"Hey."

His voice was as sultry as the Louisiana night. I could almost hear the crickets chirping and the bullfrogs croaking in a bayou. Oh, wait. That could have been them outside the dorm window, since quite a bit of water surrounded the Crescent City.

"You okay?" he asked. "You sound kinda dazed."

"Nah, just totally relaxed after a hot shower."

Which suddenly seemed like a really personal thing to say to him. Maybe he was thinking the same thing, because he didn't say anything. It was definitely a conversation stopper.

"So, uh, Jenna said you wanted to talk to me?"

"Yeah. I, uh . . . this is awkward."

"What?"

"Well, Sean said that Amber's heading home because she has a boyfriend."

"How does he know that?"

"She called him from the airport. Upset. It was strange."

I imagined it was. But Amber was my friend. I wasn't going to call her strange.

"Well, anyway," Brady continued, "I just— it's just that I didn't even think to ask, but do *you* have a boyfriend?"

My heart thudded, because why would he ask unless he was interested? Who was I kidding? He'd kissed me. And we'd hung out a little.

All I had to do was say yes, and he'd move

on. Instead, I heard myself telling him the truth. "No."

"Okay."

What did that mean? I wished we were talking face to face so I could see what he was thinking.

The silence stretched out between us. Finally I couldn't take it anymore.

"Okay?" I repeated. "What do you mean by that?"

"Just okay. Now I know you don't have a boyfriend."

"Do you have a girlfriend?"

"Why do you care?"

"I don't," I responded quickly. I felt like I'd been tricked into revealing something, but I didn't know what. "I mean why would I care? We're just here for the summer, working, having a little fun."

"Okay."

"Okay."

But I felt like something had shifted, and I wasn't sure what.

The door opened. Mist, light, and the scent

of strawberry shower gel wafted out.

"Jenna's ready to take back her phone," I said, hating that I sounded so relieved. Hating even more that I wasn't relieved at all. Should I give him my number? Should I ask for his? Did I even want to continue this conversation?

"See you tomorrow," Brady said.

"Yeah."

I held the phone out to Jenna. "Thanks."

She took the phone, reached back, and turned out the bathroom light. She was whispering quietly as she crawled into bed.

I slipped beneath the sheet and blankets. We'd turned the thermostat on the air conditioner way down and now that I didn't have Brady's voice to keep me warm, I was feeling the chill of the room.

Maybe it was because I was sleeping in the bed that Amber had been sleeping in, but I kept thinking about her telling me that I needed to climb back in the saddle. And I kept thinking of climbing in the saddle with Brady.

Because it was going to be a very long and

lonely summer if I didn't take some action. Now that Amber was gone and Jenna was practically glued to Tank, I was going to be spending a lot of time alone. Unless I wanted to hang out with Ms. Wynder. And I wasn't sure that was even an option because I'd seen her near the porta-potties laughing with John. And no one laughs near porta-potties, so I had a feeling something was going on there.

Suddenly I realized that it was really quiet in the room. That I couldn't hear Jenna whispering anymore. I heard her bed creak as she shifted on it.

"Dawn?" she whispered.

"Yeah."

"You still awake?"

I smiled in the dark. "Nah, I'm talking in my sleep."

She released a small laugh. "You're so funny."

No, not usually.

"Listen," she began, "in the morning I'm going to go have breakfast with Tank at Café Du Monde. Wanna come? It's one of those places you should eat at once in your life."

"Did Tank tell you that?"

"No, actually, my dad told me that he wanted me to eat there. He said Jimmy Buffett mentions it in one of his songs and Dad's a huge Jimmy Buffett fan, so he told me to go eat some beignets on him." She laughed. "Actually everything I eat is on him since he's the one who gave me the money for this trip. So, anyway, do you want to come?"

"Is it going to be just you and Tank?" Not that her answer should really affect my decision but still—

"No, Brady will be there for sure. Maybe Sean. So what do you think?"

I rolled onto my side. I couldn't really see her because of the darkness, but it made it easier to talk to her. "Jenna, if I keep doing stuff with him, he's going to think I'm interested."

"I'm going to keep seeing Tank."

It wasn't like Jenna to be this determined.

"But I want to spend time with you, too," she said. "I'm just talking about you going to get a doughnut with *us*. So what if Brady is there? Big deal."

"I thought it was a beignet."

"Beignet, doughnut—same thing. We wanted to have fun this summer, didn't we?"

Yeah, we did. We'd wanted to do some good, but we'd also wanted some adventure, some laughs, some memories. It was our first summer away from home. Where was my adventuresome spirit?

"Okay," I said. "Yeah, I'm in. Totally."

She didn't take offense that I sounded resigned instead of overjoyed. She just said, "Great."

Yeah, I thought, as I rolled back over and closed my eyes.

Great.

Chapter 11

I'd expected to sleep like a rock, or a log, or something heavy and inanimate. Instead I woke up while it was still dark and couldn't go back to sleep.

I crawled out of bed, grabbed my clothes from the chair where I'd left them the night before, and crept into the bathroom. Once I closed the door, I turned on the light and got dressed as quietly as I could. Today I was going to wear coveralls over a tube top. Coveralls had seemed like a building-house-kinda-thing to wear, but now I was wondering if maybe they'd be too hot. At least my shoulders would be cool.

And bare. Maybe a little sexy.

Oh no, I was thinking about Brady again. I

didn't want to do things to get his attention.

I don't know how long I sat on the edge of the tub and worried about how I could spend time with Jenna, without getting in over my head with Brady. A sudden rap on the door startled me. I nearly fell backward into the tub. Just what I needed—to start the day with a concussion.

"You okay in there?" Jenna asked.

"Oh yeah, I'm fine." I got up and opened the door. "I couldn't sleep and I didn't want to wake you."

She yawned. "Ow. I can barely move this morning. Working with a crowbar was harder work than I thought."

She stumbled into the bathroom as I walked out.

"Call Ms. Wynder and tell her we're going to breakfast with some friends," she said before shutting the door.

"You think she's up?" I called through the door.

"Oh yeah."

I called Ms. Wynder. She was indeed up,

sounding way too bright and cheery for that time of day. She said she was fine with us doing breakfast elsewhere, and she'd see us at the site.

When Jenna came out of the bathroom, we grabbed our backpacks and headed outside.

The dorm was a square, uninteresting brick building, part of a campus that had survived the storm. It was early morning but humidity already hung heavy in the air.

Parked at the front of the drive, in a no-parking zone, was the black Civic. Our two guys were leaning against it—one against the hood, one against the trunk—arms crossed over their chests. Totally sexy pose. Rebels, I thought, and my heart did a little stutter. What was I getting myself into?

"Hey," Tank said as we got nearer.

"Hey, yourself," Jenna said, practically skipping to his side.

He grinned at her. No kiss. No hug. But it seemed to be enough for her as she slid into the front passenger seat, and it probably was. After all, he hadn't tattooed her name on his arm yet. I suddenly wondered if he would someday.

Then I wondered if maybe that was where I'd made my mistake. I always wanted things to happen fast. Drew and I were a steady item after that first date. I'd never questioned where the relationship was going; I'd just followed where it had seemed to lead. Now I was trying to question everything.

Brady just grinned at me, tapped the brim of my "Life Is Good" cap. "You ever not wear that thing?" he asked.

I touched the brim of his. "Same goes."

"Yeah, but I use mine to hide a bald spot. You got a bald spot under there that I need to know about?"

"No. Do you? I mean really? Bald?"

He laughed. "Nah. At least not yet. Someday. If I take after my dad."

"I think bald men are sexy."

I don't know what made me say that.

"Really?" he asked, opening the door to the backseat.

"Really." I climbed inside, scooted across, and he got in.

"Like who?" he asked. "Give me a name."

"Bruce Willis."

"Is he shaved or bald?"

"Is there a difference?"

"Oh yeah. Shaved you have a choice. Bald you don't."

"How bald is your dad?" I asked.

"Pretty bald."

"Bet he's pretty sexy."

"Yeah, and what do you base that assumption on?" His grin was cocky, almost a dare.

And I almost responded with "you." But that would have taken the flirting to a whole new level, and I wasn't even sure that I should be flirting.

Instead I looked out the window as Tank drove along the street. "Looks like it's gonna be another scorcher today."

It was my dad's equivalent of Mom's "I think I left the iron on." A detour in the conversation.

Brady laughed and leaned back in the corner. I could feel him studying me, and I wondered what he was thinking. The easiest way to find out would be to ask. But I didn't.

♥ ♥ ♥

We couldn't find a parking spot near Café Du
Monde, so we parked several streets over and
walked. Although it was early, people were
queued up on the sidewalk. A very small portion of the restaurant was indoor seating. Most
of the seating was outdoors, some beneath a
roof, some beneath a large green-and-white
striped canopy.

As we waited in line, Jenna was nestled
against Tank's side, and they were doing that
quiet talking thing they did. I couldn't figure
out how two such tall people could talk so quietly. And Tank wasn't only tall, he was broad.
He was wearing a tank top today and the muscles of his arms rippled and when they did, so
did the dragon on his shoulder that was peering
out beneath his shirt.

"Like his ink?" Brady asked.

"Oh, gosh, I was staring, wasn't I? That
was rude."

He shrugged. "It's an unusual piece. He
goes to a guy who does original artwork, so
nothing he's ever tattooed on anyone has ever

147

been put on anyone else."

"That's cool. I've never heard of that. I thought you just looked in a catalogue and picked out the one you wanted."

"You can do it that way. But Tank—he never follows the crowd."

"Do you have any tattoos?" Was that question too personal? If he did, they were well hidden because I hadn't noticed any the couple of times I'd seen him without his shirt.

Brady shook his head. "Nah. Been thinking about it, but I don't know if there's anything I'd want forever. I mean, how do I know I won't change my mind? How 'bout you?"

"I did a temporary one once. A peel-on wash-off."

He grinned. "How did that work for you?"

"Not too bad, except I got it out of a machine, like a bubblegum machine, and so I just had to take what it dispensed. It was a skull with a snake coming out of the eye socket. Gross. But I was fourteen, and for a quarter, it was a great deal."

"Where'd you put it?"

"On my wrist."

He looked disappointed, like maybe he'd been fantasizing about it being someplace really personal. And that made me feel very unadventuresome.

"Hey, I had to put it someplace I could reach," I explained.

"Very unimaginative," he said. "Next time you want a tat, I'll help you put it someplace you can't reach."

I narrowed my eyes. "Like where?"

"Your hip, maybe. Someplace so it just peeks out over the waistband of your jeans."

I got warm just *thinking* about him applying the tattoo. I couldn't imagine what would happen if he was actually putting it on. I really wanted—needed—to talk about something else.

"So where's Sean?"

"He hooked up with Sara."

I stared at him. "The psychic?"

Brady grinned. "Yeah. Is that a problem?"

"No, I just"—I shivered—"I don't know if I'd want to be involved with someone who could read my mind."

"Do psychics read minds?" he asked.

"I don't know. They read something. All that paranormal stuff just seems to mesh together. I don't know if there's a line that distinguishes what a person can or can't do."

"She seems nice anyway."

"Oh, well, yeah. I mean, she doesn't seem evil or anything." Then something else occurred to me. I scoffed and muttered, "She didn't have to leave."

"Huh?"

"Amber—she, well, she didn't have to leave. If she'd known Sean was interested in Sara—"

"I don't think he was interested. He was just bummed out because Amber left, so we hit some bars last night." He shrugged. "Sara was at one of them."

"Oh."

So had he turned to Sara because he'd been heartbroken? That made me sad. Why did love—or even just liking someone—have to be so complicated?

We finally got to the front of the line. It was an unorganized type of organization, and

I wasn't at all sure how the staff remembered who had been waited on and who hadn't.

As soon as people got up from a table, people sat down at it—mess and all. Then the server would come clean up the mess, take the order, and head over to another table and do the same thing.

"Over here," Tank said and led us to a just-vacated table.

It was covered in plates, cups, and loads of powdered sugar. We dusted off the chairs before sitting down.

"This is something that just has to be experienced to be believed," Tank said.

The server came over and began clearing the table. "Order?"

"Two orders of beignets and four café au laits," Tank said. Then looked around at us. "Any objections?"

"Sounds good," I said.

Jenna just smiled.

"We're going to be sticky after this, aren't we?" I asked.

"Oh yeah," Tank said. "But it's worth it."

I couldn't believe how crowded it was. And how fast the servers were taking care of people. Apparently Café Du Monde was a tradition for tourists and locals alike.

The waiter brought over our two plates of the little fried squares of dough smothered in confectioners' sugar. He also set down our mugs of café au lait—half coffee, half milk. It all smelled really good.

I picked up a beignet. It was still hot, very hot, just out of the fryer, and the powdered sugar floated around me. There was a jar of more sugar on the table. Not that I could imagine anyone ever needing to add any to the beignets. I bit into the fried dough. Was it ever good!

We made an absolute mess as we ate, leaving powdered sugar all over our faces, our hands, our clothes, but no one seemed to mind.

I kept sneaking peeks at Brady, only to discover him looking at me. It was starting to get awkward. I was afraid I was sending a message I didn't want to send, like that I was obsessed with him or something—when I wasn't. I wasn't going to let myself be.

Even though it seemed like he might be interested in me. Sean had tried to hook up with Amber, and then he'd hooked up with Sara. While Brady, as far as I know, hadn't tried to get together with anyone except me.

So was he interested?

I was pretty sure he was, but he was keeping it cool. Casual. I thought maybe I could handle that.

Maybe.

Chapter 12

"I'm sorry your friend left," Saraphina—oops, she was Sara when she wasn't at the shop—said.

I was in the backyard, sawing off the dead branches of an uprooted tree. The tree itself was dead as well, rotting, and nothing more than an eyesore. But it was also huge. I could imagine the wondrous shade that it had provided for the nearby house. I could certainly use some shade now. It was late morning, and we were waiting for the truck with the lumber and supplies to arrive, filling in the time with odd jobs.

"She just got a little freaked," I explained.

"Sometimes people do that," Sara said, picking up scattered smaller branches and tossing them into the wheelbarrow.

I stopped sawing for a moment and took the red bandanna Brady had given me earlier and wiped my brow. When he'd given it to me, it had been wet and cold and he'd wrapped it around my neck to help cool me down. It had felt so good that I hadn't even been bothered that it was such a boyfriend kind of thing to do. Now all the water had evaporated, and I was using it as a towel to mop my face.

"How long have you been able to see things?" I asked.

"As long as I can remember."

"Do you see your own future?" I thought that would be pretty weird. Would you know what days not to get out of bed?

Hmm. That might be advantageous.

"I see things, but I don't always know who they apply to. Sometimes the visions are stronger when I'm touching someone, but it doesn't necessarily mean it's for that person. It's hard to explain."

"But the things you predicted, they've all sort of happened."

"Sometimes I get them right."

"Do you like being psychic?"

"It has its moments."

"Have you ever helped the police?"

She laughed. "At least you don't think it's a parlor trick. I tried to help them once, but they're as skeptical as your friend was."

I placed the saw on the branch and started moving it back and forth. "I think she's an actual believer now."

"She'll be back here before the end of summer," Sara said quietly.

I stilled the saw and looked over my shoulder at Sara.

She shrugged. "I see her here, but all this looks less messy."

"I didn't think you gave free readings."

"This isn't really a reading. It's just conversation."

But that didn't make it any less spooky.

"Is she just visiting or coming to help?" I asked.

"That I can't say."

"You can't or you won't?"

She smiled. "I don't know why she's here. I only know that she's here. And I see someone else . . . a guy with black hair. I see things getting broken."

Chad had black hair, but how could things get broken if he was here with her? That meant everything was fixed. Didn't it?

"What exactly does that mean?" I asked.

Again, she shook her head.

"I know, I know. You can tell me only what you see, not what it means. You must have been wildly popular at sleepovers."

She laughed. She had a light, lyrical laugh. It seemed to suit her.

Reaching out, she wrapped her hand around mine. "Don't be afraid to rebuild."

I started sawing diligently. "Does this look like I'm afraid?"

"No, Dawn, it doesn't. But looks are often deceiving."

"No offense, but I'd like to have a conversation with you sometime when you didn't tell me the things you were seeing."

"That would be nice. Normal, even," she said, smiling.

"Have you ever seen the endings of movies

that you're watching?" Jenna asked as she walked over and handed each of us a bottle of water. "That would be a total bummer."

She'd missed the rest of our conversation, having gone on another water run. We were trying to drink as much as we could. One girl had fainted yesterday. They called EMTs who had taken her to the hospital. She was going to be fine, but it was a reminder that we needed lots of fluids throughout the day.

"No," Sara said. "And I don't know any winning lottery numbers or who's going to win the Super Bowl. I can't control what I see. It just happens. Anyway, I didn't come over here to discuss my visions. I'm organizing a group to go on a ghost tour Saturday night, and I wanted to see if you were interested in coming."

"That would be fun," I said. I looked at Jenna to gauge her reaction and knew what she was going to say before she said it. Sara's psychic ability was rubbing off on me.

"I'm sort of leaving Saturday night free for now, in case something . . . well, maybe you already know. Am I going to have other plans?"

"No, you won't have other plans."

"Oh." Jenna's face fell. "Then I guess I'll say yes."

"She could be wrong," I told Jenna. "Not everything she sees is an absolute."

"This is," Sara said smugly.

"So you saw her on the ghost tour?"

"No, Tank told me that he and Jenna were coming. So I was just asking you, Dawn, because I figured Jenna's answer was already yes. Are you interested?"

Was I, or did I want to keep Saturday night open? Open for what? A better offer? I wasn't looking for a date. So what could be better than getting up close and personal with ghosts?

"Sounds like fun," I said. "I'm definitely there."

"Good. We'll meet outside my shop at nine." She turned to walk away, then stopped. "And just so you know—I'll be matching people up into pairs. You'll be with Brady."

"He's going to be there?"

She gave me a secretive smile. "I'm pretty sure he is. He asked if you were going, so I just assumed . . ."

Her voice trailed off. I wasn't sure I liked

what she was assuming.

"What if I'd said no?" I asked her.

"I knew you wouldn't."

"How did you know?"

She smiled all-knowingly. "Because I'm a psychic."

She could be really irritating, but I liked her.

She walked away, humming a song that sounded strangely like the theme from *Ghostbusters*. Sometimes I didn't know whether to take her seriously. But how could I not?

"She gives me the creeps," Jenna said, picking up branches and tossing them into the wheelbarrow. "I don't care how nice she is, she gives me the creeps. She just knows too much."

"At least we have something to do Saturday night."

"Are you okay with having a date?"

"It's only a date if he asks, and he didn't," I pointed out.

Jenna held up her hands. "Okay, I guess. It's not a date."

Still, it felt like maybe it was.

And if it was, could I get hurt?

♥ ♥ ♥

"Ow!"

"Hold still," Brady commanded—like a drill sergeant or something—as he studied my palm and the large sliver of wood that had slid under my skin.

"You're not the boss of me," I grumbled.

He looked up and grinned. "That's real mature. I thought only guys were bad patients."

Just before noon, lumber had been delivered on a long-bed truck. We'd been unloading it, carrying it into the yard, and stacking it up. Brady had been there helping me.

We'd been carrying some boards across the yard when I'd tripped and lost my balance. I'd landed hard, and in trying to not drop the wood, I'd ended up with a wickedly long splinter.

I should have been wearing my gloves. But they were hot, making my hands all sweaty, and I was tired of being hot and sweaty. Stupid, I know. But I'd thought I'd be okay. They'd told us we didn't need to wear our hard hats or goggles while unloading the truck.

It didn't make me feel any better that Brady

had wrapped his hand around my arm and hauled me across the front yard. He'd grabbed the first-aid kit from Sara and then led me to a picnic table where the blueprints for the house had been spread out earlier. He'd set the first-aid kit down. Then he'd put his hands on my waist, picked me up, and set me on the table—like I couldn't have gotten up there by myself.

I didn't even know why I had to be sitting down. I wasn't going to faint. I could probably take out the splinter myself.

I knew I shouldn't be irritated, but I was.

"About Saturday night," I said.

He looked up again from studying my hand. I didn't think even a palm reader would look at a hand that much.

"The ghost tour? It's not a date," I told him.

"Okay. I didn't think it was."

"You didn't?"

"Nope."

"But you asked if I was going to be there."

He shrugged—like that was an answer. I suddenly felt bad for being snappish and was worried that I might have hurt his feelings.

"Look, don't take it personally. I'm just not dating this summer."

He studied me for a minute, then said, "Okay."

"I mean, you're nice and all—"

"Nice *and all*? Please. You're going to make me blush with the compliments."

I scowled. "You know what I mean."

"Actually I don't. What's included in 'all'?"

Terrific smile, great shoulders, strong arms—

I shook my head. "You're missing the important part of what I'm trying to say here."

"You're not dating."

"Right."

"But if I get scared on the ghost tour, can I hold your hand?"

I stared at him a minute. Was he teasing? "You're going to get scared?"

"I could. Ghosts. They're frightening." He rolled his amazing shoulders dramatically. "I get goose bumps just thinking about them."

"Do you believe in ghosts?"

"Oh yeah. Especially when they help me get babes."

I smiled. Did he take anything seriously? Other than a splinter in my hand. That he seemed to take way too seriously.

"You don't believe in ghosts," I said.

"Hey, I believed in Santa Claus until I was seventeen."

"Really?"

"My mom told me if I stopped believing, no more presents on Christmas morning. So, yeah. I believed."

"Why stop at seventeen?"

"Got tired of getting toy fire trucks."

I laughed.

He opened the first-aid kit and took out a pair of tweezers. They looked so tiny in his large hand. Had I ever noticed how large his hands were? How tanned? How steady? How strong?

Was I suddenly developing a hand fetish?

"Do you even know what you're doing?" I asked.

He furrowed his brow. Suddenly he seemed

to realize something. He jerked off his sunglasses and hooked them in the front of my coveralls.

"No wonder I couldn't see," he said.

He spread my palm wide, shifted around so he wasn't creating a shadow over my hand.

"It's really in there," he said.

"Let me look."

"I've got it, but this is probably going to hurt."

No surprise there. It did.

But as far as hurts go, it wasn't too bad. And I couldn't help but be relieved. I'd been careless. I'd gotten hurt. Just like Sara had predicted. And that irritated me, too. Even knowing the future, I hadn't been able to change it.

Brady poured alcohol over my palm.

"Ow!" I jerked my hand free and waved it in the air to get the stuff to evaporate.

"Sorry." Then he laughed. "You're such a baby."

"Am not."

"Are to." He moved near, put his hands on my waist, and leaned in. "But that's okay.

Because I have a thing for babes."

I thought he was going to kiss me, but he just lifted me off the table.

"Be careful. I don't like it when you get hurt," he said.

"You think I do?"

I stepped away, thinking I might get hurt again—worse—if I stayed close to him. I handed him his sunglasses. We took the first-aid kit back to Sara.

"You okay?" she asked me.

"Oh yeah, just a little hurt." I smiled. "Which you predicted."

"I predicted a splinter?"

"You predicted I'd be careless and get hurt."

She furrowed her brow and a faraway look came into her eyes.

Oh God, maybe the splinter wasn't the hurt. It probably wasn't. It couldn't be that simple.

"Whatever it is," I said hastily, "I don't want to know. Thanks just the same."

I started walking away, and Brady hurried to catch up.

"Hey, that was kinda rude," he said.

"I really don't want to know what she sees. She says things like they're all innocent, but—" I shook my head. "I just really don't want to know."

That night John arranged for us to have reserved tables at a local restaurant and club— for crawfish étouffée and blues music. The blues originated in the African-American community. To me, it sounded as though the notes themselves were melancholy.

As soon as we walked into the restaurant, he snagged Ms. Wynder and led her over to his table. A table for two away from everyone else.

Jenna waved at someone, and I didn't need to look around her to know who she was waving at. I was slightly disappointed when we got to the table to discover it was a small one, with only four chairs. Tank and Brady were sitting in two of them.

Jenna sat beside Tank, then looked at me as if it was a foregone conclusion I'd sit between her and Brady, so I sat. And then wondered if I should have asked Brady if it was okay.

"John reminds me of a cruise director," Jenna said. "Making sure everyone has something to do."

Tank nodded. "That's one of the great things about volunteering here in New Orleans. You can work during the day, but party at night. The tourist part of voluntourism. And the businesses here need the tourist dollars as much as the people need help getting their homes rebuilt."

Then he leaned toward Jenna and they started that low talking that they did. Drew and I hadn't whispered that much to each other in the entire year and a half that we were together.

Don't compare them to you and Drew, I scolded myself. *Just don't.*

Because they were nothing like us. I didn't want them to be anything like us. But in a way they were. When Jenna was with Tank, he was all that mattered to her.

Just the thought of ever feeling that way again made me nervous.

On John's recommendation, we all ordered

the étouffée, a spicy Cajun stew served over rice. Cajuns were descendents of Acadian exiles—French Canadians. Their influence was strong in the city.

"I think John has a thing for your chaperone," Brady said.

He was leaning near so I could hear him over the music being played. His breath wafted over my ear. It sent a shiver, a very nice shiver, down my back.

I looked at him and smiled. "She's not really our chaperone, she's more like our sponsor, I guess."

"Sponsor? Makes it sound like you're in a rehab program."

"No, I'm in a cleaning-up-New-Orleans program." I tapped the table, trying to decide if I should give him the option of having someone else sit here. Was it fair to him for me to take a seat beside him when I wasn't going to spend the night whispering low?

"Listen—"

"You're not wearing your Life Is Good hat," he said. "Is life suddenly not good?"

"What? Oh." I touched my head, as though I needed to verify that I hadn't worn it. I usually tucked it into a pocket so I could put it on as soon as I took off my hard hat. But tonight I'd clipped my hair back.

"No. Life is great. I don't *always* wear it. You're not wearing your hat."

"True."

And his hair kept falling forward. I wanted to reach out and brush it back.

"So you're sitting here," he said. "Coincidence or intentional?"

That was a hard one.

"It had to be intentional; I mean, I didn't just discover the chair beneath my butt."

He smiled. So maybe I was going to get off easy, without having to actually explain anything about what I was feeling.

"You said you're not dating this summer," he said.

Okay, maybe I was going to have to explain after all. "Right. I'm planning on this being a dateless summer."

"Dateless summer? Wasn't that a movie?"

"You're thinking of *The Endless Summer*."

"A summer without a date would seem pretty endless—or at least it would to me."

I smiled again. And maybe he even had a point. I didn't want to think too much about that.

"The movie was about surfing," I said.

"So we're really talking about the movie here?"

No, we weren't, but it was a more comfortable topic than my whole not-dating thing. Before I could say anything else, he said, "You don't have a boyfriend."

"No."

"So is there someone you're interested in?"

Was he hoping I'd say him? I swallowed hard. This was so hard to say, embarrassing even. "Look, there *was* a boyfriend."

He studied me for a minute and finally asked, "Bad breakup?"

I nodded.

"When?"

"About six weeks ago."

"Okay."

"What do you mean okay?"

"I get it now."

"What's to get?"

"You don't want to date. And I'm okay with that. I don't want to date either."

"Really?" Was I relieved or actually a little hurt? Yes, I think I was—hurt.

"Look, just because you don't want to date, and I don't want to date, that doesn't mean I wouldn't like to hang out," he said. "Or even that we couldn't hang out. I mean, look around. Everyone's pretty much paired up already."

I did take the time to look around then. Yeah, I could see what he meant.

"So, you're saying we're kinda stuck with each other?" I asked.

"Is that such a bad thing? You're fun. I'm fun. We could double our fun."

"You had better pickup lines the other night."

He grinned. "Yeah, but this isn't a pickup." He shook his head. "I'm not sure what this is. Maybe just trying to define what we've got going on here."

What was going on? A casual romance? A summer fling? Summer buddies?

Tonight my thoughts were being influenced by the blues. The thrill definitely wasn't gone. It was fun to have someone to share things with, and Jenna was clearly no longer available.

So I could hang out with Brady. Nothing serious. Nothing permanent. At the end of the six weeks, we'd each go our separate ways. And in the meantime, we'd have fun.

And wasn't that the reason I was here?

I mean, besides helping to rebuild, I wanted to have a great summer.

"I'm not looking for anything serious," I told him.

"Not a problem. I know a thousand knock-knock jokes."

I smiled. "Seriously—"

"Didn't think you wanted serious."

"Look, nothing long-term. Just a New Orleans thing," I said.

"Okay."

I moved closer to him and moved my shoulders in rhythm to the music.

"Then while I'm here in the Big Easy, only while I'm here"—I bobbed my head to the rhythm and blues—"we could hang out together. A friends-with-benefits kind of thing. The benefits being"—I couldn't believe I was being this bold, but if he wanted the relationship defined, I wanted to make sure we were using the same dictionary—"occasional kissing."

That really nice smile of his spread across his face. Reaching out, he wrapped his large hand around my neck and brought me nearer. "I'm good with that. Definitely good."

And then he kissed me.

Yeah, definitely good.

Chapter 13

"So . . . you and Brady," Jenna said quietly later that night as we were lying in the dark.

"Yeah. Me and Brady." I went to sleep smiling.

The next morning I woke up feeling . . . good. Really, really good. Great, in fact, not only in body but in spirit.

Some of the soreness and stiffness had finally worked its way out of my muscles, mostly I think because Brady and I did a lot of dancing the night before. Dancing to the blues. Although it hadn't really been any kind of dancing I'd done before. We'd just moved with the music and had a great time.

I'd always thought the blues meant depressing music, music determined to make you blue, but I'd been happier last night than I'd been in a long time. Being with Brady was a lot of fun. He didn't seem to take anything seriously, and that was what I needed right now. Someone who lived in the moment, someone who was all about fun.

He laughed a lot. He was always smiling. He was nothing at all like Drew. I decided Drew had been a downer. I wasn't certain what I'd ever seen in him.

I thought I actually might be on my way to recovery. And I was loving it.

I'd just pulled on jeans and was working my way into a ratty T-shirt—one I normally wore on laundry day, but decided I should wear for work because who did I want to impress anyway? Brady was already impressed—when my cell phone rang.

I snatched it up, looked at the number, and answered. "Hey, Amber."

Jenna looked up from tying her shoes, a question in her eyes.

"How's it going?" I asked Amber.

"Awesome! I wanted you guys to know that I panicked for no reason. Everything is totally cool between me and Chad. I feel like such a dummy for worrying."

"I'm glad everything's okay."

Jenna rolled her eyes and went back to tying her shoes.

"Things between us are stronger than ever. I just love him so much."

"Great." I didn't see any reason to remind her that the psychic hadn't questioned Amber's current boyfriend. She'd simply said that in college she'd find something better. Of course, that didn't meant she wouldn't find it with Chad. He could be even better as he got older. Or they could break up and another guy would be in Amber's life. Who knew?

"So what's happening with you guys?" Amber asked.

I filled her in on the fact that Jenna was definitely with Tank and I was sort of with Brady.

"Any chance I could borrow your AeroBed if I decide to head on back to New Orleans?" Amber asked.

My knees grew weak and I sat on the edge of the bed. Would Amber freak if I told her that

Saraphina had seen her back here? Yes, she'd definitely freak.

"Absolutely," I said, pushing past my own discomfort with the fact that Sara could, in fact, see into our lives. "Are you going to come back?"

"I'm thinking about it. Next week maybe. Or the week after. I don't know for sure. I was telling Chad about how satisfying it was and how it made me feel good, so he's sort of interested in maybe coming with me. I mean, we haven't worked out all the details. But he has a car, so he'd drive us. I don't know if we'd stay the whole summer, but maybe a couple of weeks. A couple of weeks are better than nothing, right?"

"A couple of weeks would be awesome," I told her. "Every little bit helps."

"Are y'all to the fun stuff yet?"

"What fun stuff? Eating, dancing, shopping?"

"The house. Aren't you going to rebuild it, decorate it?"

"We're rebuilding it. I don't know about

the decorating part."

"If you'll measure the windows, I'll sew some curtains before I come back."

Amber was the only person I knew who could—and loved to—use a sewing machine.

"That'd be great. I'll see if I can get that information for you."

We talked a little more and then I said good-bye.

"What information do you need to get?" Jenna asked, slipping on her backpack.

"Measurements for the windows. She wants to make curtains."

"She's feeling guilty."

"Probably. Although maybe she's just embarrassed that she totally overreacted to the psychic reading."

"Could be. So things are okay with her and Chad?"

"Apparently. The whole breaking up was a false alarm."

"We'll see what happens when she goes off to college," Jenna said. "Although we probably shouldn't point that out to her. She might not apply to any colleges."

"You want to know something freaky? Yesterday Sara told me that Amber would be coming back."

"You're kidding?"

I shook my head.

"Wow."

"Yeah. I didn't tell Amber, though, because her reaction to the other prediction was so out of control."

"Unlike ours. I mean, we took it in stride, right?"

I grabbed my backpack. Had I taken it in stride?

"Well, at least we don't have to worry anymore. All the predictions have been met," I said.

"Have they? Or do we just think they have?"

Goose bumps rose on my skin.

"Is there a statute of limitations on how long after a reading something will happen?" I asked.

"I don't know. Could check with Sara."

"Nah, I'm sure we're in the clear."

And checking with her might result in her having another vision. I'd definitely become a firm believer that seeing the future wasn't all that it was cracked up to be.

It's just a fact that hard-working guys are sexy. Incredibly so. Especially when the afternoon sun beat down unmercifully and they decided it was time to ditch the shirts.

Oh yeah.

It was funny in a way, because when the guys started heading to their cars, the girls stopped hammering. It was like we took a collective breath, and held it, and then released an appreciative sigh. Then we all smiled at each other, a little embarrassed, maybe, and went back to work.

I couldn't believe how fast things were going up. Brady, Tank, Sean, and a couple of other guys were working on the roof. Jenna and I were rebuilding the porch flooring. We'd ripped it up earlier because it had been rotting. I discovered that hammering was an extremely cathartic experience. I just pretended every nail was Drew's tiny, little, stupid head.

Bang, bang, bang.

It was actually fun.

We still wore the hard hats and safety goggles, but we no longer wore the masks.

"Listen," Jenna said.

I stopped hammering, looked around. "For what?"

She rolled her eyes. "To me."

"Okay. What's going on?"

She sighed. "What if Tank stops liking me?"

"He's not going to stop liking you, unless he's an idiot. And if he's an idiot then you want him to stop liking you."

Bang, bang, bang.

I moved up to put the next nail in place.

"Did you just compliment me?" she asked.

"Of course."

"Did you insult him?"

"Only if he stops liking you."

"How do I stop that from happening?"

I pounded Drew's head—I mean, the nail—into the board.

"Jenna, you're worrying for nothing. He's

crazy about you. You've never had a boyfriend. Enjoy it."

"Did you worry when you were dating Drew?"

I gave one more nail a hard pound and sat back on my heels. Had I worried? Good question.

"No, I don't think I did."

"Do you worry about Brady?"

"No. What I have with Brady is perfect. We both agreed it's only while we're in New Orleans. It's finite. No worries."

"What if you decide that's not enough?"

"It's enough, Jenna." I started hammering again. A summer thing with Brady. That's all I wanted. It was nice and safe.

I liked nice and safe.

Chapter 14

"We should have done this days ago," Jenna said.

We were sitting in the hot tub beside the pool at the guys' hotel. It was early Friday evening, and it felt wonderful to have the heated water swirling over my aching muscles.

The hotel was a small one with a very historic feel in the French Quarter. The guys had called that morning and told us to pack bathing suits, so we could stop by before hitting the clubs. Jenna and I had changed in Tank's room while the guys had changed in Brady's room. I thought it was generous of the hotel to give them their own rooms. According to Tank, the owner was married to a cousin of a cousin or something.

I was wearing a bikini and when we'd come out of the room, Brady had wiggled his eyebrows at me and said, "Know what you need?"

"A bubblegum machine tattoo?"

And he'd laughed.

I liked making him laugh, liked watching him smile. Liked watching the way he watched me now as the water swirled around us.

"I've had enough," Jenna said and stood.

"Not me," Brady said, and his eyes held a challenge.

A challenge to me. Was I going to choose him or Jenna?

Tank had also stood up, and I wondered if maybe Jenna wanted to be alone with him.

"I want a few more minutes," I said.

"Okay. Great," Jenna said. "I'll see you in a bit."

She wrapped a towel around her waist, and Tank wrapped his arm around her. I watched as they walked off.

"He's been dying to get some time alone with her," Brady said.

I snapped my attention back to him. "Yeah, it just occurred to me that they haven't really had much of that."

We'd gone to listen to jazz last night, but it had been another group outing. Group outings were safe. I liked them.

Brady glided through the water until he was sitting by me. "But then, neither have we."

I shook my head. Probably a little jerkily. Not being alone with him had seemed like the smart thing to do. And now that I was alone with him . . . I probably shouldn't have been.

"Go out with me tonight," he said.

I stared at him for a minute. "I *am* going out with you tonight."

"No. You're going out with me, Tank, and Jenna. I'm asking you to go out with just me."

"What—you mean like a date? You said you didn't want to date."

"I said *that*?"

"Yeah. The night we had étouffée."

"Are you sure? Maybe I was talking about the fruit, date. I don't eat fruit . . . or vegetables, for that matter."

Why was he giving me a hard time about this? We had an agreement. I shoved on his shoulder. "No, you weren't talking about fruit. You were talking about dating."

"Okay, then, I changed my mind. Is that illegal?"

It could be. When the thought of it made my heart pound so hard that I thought I could die. When we were hanging out with other people, it was easy to find things to talk about—we could always talk about the people around us. If it was just us—

The thought of being with only Brady, with no buffer, no other people, was scary and thrilling. And I suddenly realized that it was something I wanted. I wanted a lot.

I took a deep breath. "Okay."

He grinned at my use of what seemed to be a word that he thought explained everything—when it really explained nothing.

"Just okay?"

I nodded. "Just okay."

We went to House of Blues. Just the two of us. Brady and me. It was in the French Quarter, close enough that we could walk. I never walked as much at home as I walked here—but I was starting to appreciate the fact that we didn't have to get into a car to go everywhere.

Especially when Brady held my hand. He'd changed into jeans and a snug black T-shirt. He looked so hot and smelled so good. And it wasn't insect repellent, this time. The guys had gotten ready in Brady's room, while Jenna and I had showered and changed in Tank's. I was wearing white shorts and a red halter-neck top. I'd left my hair down, brushing my bare shoulders.

"I think it's great that you and Brady are going on a date," Jenna had said, as she ran her fingers through her hair.

"It's not a date."

She'd looked at me, her lips pursed.

"Okay, it's a date."

"We'll meet back here in the lobby at eleven-thirty so Tank can drive us back to the dorm in time for the bed check."

"Sounds like a plan."

She'd hugged me. "Have fun."

"You, too."

"Oh, I will. Definitely."

Now Brady and I were being seated outside in the voodoo garden. My sandals clicked over the bricks as we followed the hostess to a round table covered in a blue tablecloth. A live band was playing—what else?—blues.

Whenever I thought about voodoo, I thought of scenes from shows or movies where voodoo was used for evil. But I'd learned that, like everything, it has two sides, and here was the peaceful, tranquil, bringing-everything-into-harmony side. Lots of lush, green plants surrounded us. It was simply a place that made me glad to be there.

Brady scooted his chair closer to me. "So I can see the band better," he said.

I smiled. "Yeah, right."

"Okay, so I want to be closer to you. Is that a bad thing?"

"No, it's nice, actually."

Very nice.

After dinner, he moved his chair even closer, put his arm around me, and we settled back to enjoy the music—drinking virgin daiquiris so we wouldn't get kicked out for taking space from paying customers.

It felt right. And was no longer scaring me. Or at least not scaring me as much as it had. As long as I kept everything in perspective.

When the band took a break, I said, "This hanging out that we're doing, it's only for the summer."

I needed to be sure that I wasn't expecting more than I was going to get. And that *he* wasn't expecting more than he was going to get.

"Right," Brady said. "That's what we both wanted. Just for the summer, just while we're here."

"I just want to make sure that you understand that it's *only* while we're in the Big Easy, even though we've sorta moved into actual dating territory."

"I get it."

Did he?

"I mean, it's a set period of time. When one of us leaves New Orleans—whoever leaves first—that's it, it's over. No good-bye. Good-bye is understood."

"What? You want me to sign a contract? I

get what you're saying. And it's what I want, too. A hundred percent."

"I just don't want another breakup. I just want an 'it's over' but without either of us saying it's over."

"And you think that'll make it easier?"

"Knowing that it's coming, being prepared? Yeah, I do. We'll be together five weeks, and then that's it. We move on."

"Okay."

I released a long sigh. "Okay."

It would be easier. I was sure it would be.

He absently-mindedly traced his finger across my bare shoulders, back and forth. It felt delicious.

"Where are you going to go to college?" he asked.

"I haven't decided for sure."

"Okay."

"Why do you say that so much? Just 'okay.'"

"So you know I heard you, but don't have anything else to add." He nuzzled my neck. "And sometimes just so you know I understand."

We were in the shadows. No one was paying

any attention to us. He kissed my shoulder, and I thought I might not wear anything that covered my shoulders ever again.

"You understand a lot without me saying much," I said.

"I have three sisters who think I'm Dr. Phil. I've heard about every rotten thing that every guy they've dated has ever done to them. And they always end with, 'If you ever do that to a girl . . .'"

His voice had gone prissy at the end.

"As though I would," he finished in his normal voice.

"What would they do if you did?"

He shrugged. "They never say. But knowing them, it'd be a fate worse than death—forcing me to sit through a marathon of romantic comedies or something."

Brady had a way of always making me smile.

"Still, I bet you make a great Dr. Phil."

He pointed up. "Especially once I get the bald thing going."

I laughed. "You're really bothered about losing your hair."

"Yeah, I think I am. Vain, I guess."

I leaned into him. "You really shouldn't worry about it."

"No?"

"No."

"Okay."

Then he leaned in and kissed me. Being with him without Jenna around wasn't nearly as uncomfortable as I'd expected it to be. Actually, it seemed natural.

He told me funny stories about his sisters. Two were older, one younger, and he finally admitted that he was offended that they'd think he'd ever do any of the jerk stuff guys had pulled on them.

"Why can't relationships be easy?" I finally asked.

He shrugged. "Would they be worth it if they were?"

"I just wonder how you ever know . . . this is the one." I told him about Amber's reading and the reason she'd bugged out on us.

"Sean liked her," he said.

"You want to hear the really weird thing?" I asked.

"There's something weirder than a psychic's

prediction and your friend freaking out because Tank has ink?"

"Well, maybe not weirder, but . . . well, the thing is, Amber has always talked about going to Rice. It's her first choice, and there's Sean . . . at Rice."

"Mmm. So maybe in another year or so . . ."

"Maybe."

"I'll let him know."

"No." I leaned back. "You can't do that. Then you're influencing it and making it happen."

"I've got something else I want to make happen."

And then he was kissing me again. I stopped thinking about Amber and Sean or Jenna and Tank. Or Sara and her predictions.

I was only thinking about how much I liked kissing Brady.

We left the restaurant at ten, which gave us an hour and a half before we had to meet up with Tank and Jenna and head back to the dorm. Neither of us was in the mood for the madness of Bourbon Street, so we just walked along the river. We could see the lights of the riverboats as they traveled along the Mississippi. It was all so romantic.

"You know, I don't even know your last name," I said, when we began walking back to the hotel.

"Miller."

I smiled at him. Brady Miller. I liked it.

"And yours?"

"Delaney," I responded.

"I thought you'd have an Italian-sounding name."

I grinned. "That's my mom's side of the family."

When we got to the lobby, Jenna and Tank were waiting for us. Tank drove us back to the dorm. While he walked Jenna to the door, Brady and I lagged behind.

"So being alone together wasn't so bad," I said.

He chuckled. "You really know how to stroke my ego."

I groaned. "I'm sorry. I just, I don't know, I just feel like I can say what's on my mind when I'm with you. That's a good thing, right?"

"Yeah, I guess."

"Seriously, though, I had a great time," I told him.

"Yeah, me, too."

Then he kissed me good night.

Chapter 15

Saturday we only worked until noon.

Tank drove us back to the dorm with the promise he and Brady would be back to get us in an hour. No way were we going to spend time in the French Quarter without getting cleaned up first. I was going through clothes like crazy. Tomorrow I definitely had to make time for laundry. Or else buy some more clothes.

Hmm. Buying more clothes might be the way to go.

I dressed in a denim miniskirt with cargo pockets on the sides so I could carry money and an ID without having to lug around my backpack. I put on a tank with skinny straps, slipped on sandals, and used a banana clip to get my hair up off my shoulders. I picked one string of red beads to wear. I didn't think I'd be adding to my stash tonight, but I wasn't completely saying no to the possibility.

"Nice," Brady said to me when he and Tank picked us up.

We parked at their hotel, then started making our way through the French Quarter.

"I know just the place for lunch," Tank said. "The home of the original muffuletta."

Central Grocery had been housed in the French Quarter for nearly a century. As we walked inside the red emporium, the tantalizing aromas of salami, cheese, and garlic wafted around us. The worn floor creaked as we made our way around the aisles—displaying various containers of olives, pickles, and spices—to the counter where they took the food orders. The menu was pretty simple. Only one thing was served—the muffuletta. We ordered two to share, because the round sandwich is huge and piled with salami, ham, provolone, olive salad, and other special ingredients.

"Want to split a Barq's root beer?" Brady asked.

"Yeah. Thanks."

"Why don't you grab us some chairs?"

Off to the side was a counter with stools where people could eat. The store was small, the eating area even smaller, but we found four seats together.

"It smells really good in here," Jenna said.

"Yeah, it does."

"I am *so* hungry."

Brady took the stool beside me and unwrapped the sandwich. It was huge, cut into quarters. I had a feeling that one piece was going to be enough for me, and I wondered if we should have just ordered one for the four of us to share.

But Brady and Tank had monstrous appetites, and in no time the sandwiches were gone. They were delicious, and the root beer just topped it off.

I felt incredibly stuffed as we walked out of the store. I didn't think I could have eaten a pecan praline if it was given to me free. Okay, I could have. My theory is that sugar melts, so it doesn't fill you up.

Once we were outside, Jenna pulled me aside.

"Tank and I were thinking of going off and

doing our own thing, but I wanted to make sure you were okay with that, with being alone with Brady."

"That's cool."

"You sure?"

"We've been alone before," I reminded her.

"I know. I just didn't know if you wanted a lot of alone time, because I was thinking we wouldn't hook back up until later tonight."

"I'm fine, Jenna."

"Okay, then, we'll catch up with you at the ghost tour."

She took Tank's hand and led him away.

"What was that about?" Brady asked.

I shrugged. "Just Jenna being silly. They want to do their own thing."

"I'm not surprised. He's got it bad for her." He suddenly looked guilty. "Don't tell her I said that. I mean, it should come from him."

"But it would give me a chance to play psychic," I teased.

"Don't. Please."

I pretended to think it over for a bit. Then finally I said, "Okay."

"You were never going to tell her, were you?"

Smiling, I shook my head.

Holding hands, Brady and I walked to the French Market. It's a covered flea market, so we were at least out of the sun. There were so many vendors.

"This probably isn't the place to be if we're going on a ghost tour tonight," I said, thinking of hauling anything I bought around all day.

"If you find something you want, we can always take it back to my room," Brady said.

"Do you like shopping?"

"Not particularly, but I really like people-watching, and this is a great place for that."

"So you're okay if I stop and look at stuff?" The one time I'd taken Drew shopping with me, he'd moped around and totally spoiled the day. He said guys had a gene that prevented them from having patience at a mall. I didn't buy into it, though, because my dad always went shopping with my mom.

"Look all you want," Brady said. "I've got no appointments to keep."

"Except for the ghost tour," I reminded him.

"Well, yeah, but that's not for a while yet."

We strolled up and down the aisles. A lot

of the vendors were craftsmen, displaying various items they'd made. Some of the vendors had really inexpensive products—knockoffs, trinkets.

Like Brady had said, the most fun was just watching the people, seeing their excitement when they discovered a find, listening to them haggling over prices.

"Hey, I was wondering if you'd do me a favor," Brady said after a while.

I gave him what I hoped was a sultry smile. "Depends what it is."

"I want to find something to take back to my youngest sister. I was hoping you could help me figure out what would be a good thing to get her."

Did he think all girls liked the same things? I didn't have a clue what his sister might like.

"How about a box of pralines?"

He shook his head. "She'd yell at me for screwing up whatever diet she's on when I get home."

"She yells at you?"

"Oh yeah."

"And you want to buy her something?"

He shrugged. "It's what brothers do."

"Not mine."

"You have a brother?"

"Yeah, but he's twelve."

He grinned. "He's probably too young to appreciate you."

"Maybe." I squeezed his hand. "There's so much we still don't know about each other."

It was weird, because we hadn't grown up in the same town or gone to the same school. I didn't know all the details of his life, but I felt like I knew him.

"What's there to know? I have a mom and a dad and three sisters, one who likes to get presents. I go to Rice, majoring in architecture. And I like you. A lot."

He made it all seem so simple, and I knew that he probably wanted me to say back that I liked him . . . a lot. But I couldn't. Even if it was true. So instead I asked, "Why the Kansas City Chiefs?"

"What?"

"Your hat." He wasn't wearing it today. "Why that team?"

"My oldest sister lives in Kansas City now.

I went to visit her, went to a Chiefs game."

"So you're not necessarily a fan?"

"Nope, Houston Texans all the way. So, you and I have something in common."

"Uh, actually we don't. That first night at dinner, I just said that to have something to say. I'm not really into football."

"That's just un-Texan."

I knew what he meant—in Texas, football is king.

I grimaced. "Yeah, I know."

"Might have to do an intervention here. Take you to a Rice game."

It was the first time he'd said something—anything—that hinted at us seeing each other when our time here was finished.

My concern must have shown on my face, because he said, "Sorry. Forgot. We're just summer buddies, right?"

I nodded. "Yeah, just for the summer. That was our agreement."

He studied me for a minute. "Okay. Let's go souvenir shopping."

We stopped at a table of handcrafted jewelry.

He spent about twenty minutes looking over the various selections, asking me my opinion. My favorite piece was a delicate silver chain threaded through a fleur-de-lis charm.

He decided to buy it for his sister.

"I trust your judgment. If you like it, she will, too," he said.

"She might not."

"She will."

"Do I remind you of your sister?"

He scoffed. "No. No way."

"So our tastes might not be the same."

"I can tell you they're not. You have better taste."

He always made me feel good about myself.

"My pockets are a little roomier," I said. "Want me to carry it for you?"

"Sure. Thanks. Good thing I didn't get her a box of pralines, huh?"

I laughed. "Yeah."

We spent some more time walking by the stalls, looking at the various offerings. Then we slipped on our sunglasses and walked back into the sunshine.

It was hot and muggy so we went to the aquarium, to cool off in the air conditioning as much as to view all the exhibits. When we were walking, we'd hold hands. When we were simply standing, looking at something, Brady would slip his arm around me and hold me against his side.

Needless to say, I found an excuse to stand and watch a lot of things.

I loved the way that I fit up against him. My head nestled right into the little curve of his shoulder. His arm would come around me and he'd rest his hand on my stomach or my hip. And sometimes he'd kiss the curve of my neck and shoulder.

It all seemed so natural. So right. I couldn't imagine not being with him.

We rode the streetcar down to the Garden District, famous for its mansions. We got off the streetcar at one end and began walking back up toward the French Quarter. The nice thing about walking through the Garden District was that the area had so many trees we were almost always walking in the shade.

"I think that's Anne Rice's house," Brady said when we got to the corner of First Street and Chestnut.

It was a white two-story house with a balcony on the second floor.

"She lives in California now," I said.

"But doesn't this seem like the perfect place to write about vampires and witches?" Brady asked.

"Yeah, it does."

"Wonder if it'll be on the tour tonight."

I shrugged. "Have you ever been on a ghost tour?"

"Nope. How about you?"

"No. I'd say I was skeptical, except after Sara's reading, I have a feeling that after tonight, I'll believe in ghosts."

Brady chuckled. "Yeah, I know what you mean."

We were walking along, holding hands again.

"I didn't think you believed in psychics," I said.

"I don't . . . or at least I didn't. But yours seemed to be right on and the one I had—"

I stopped walking and pulled him back to face me. "You had a reading? You didn't say anything. When was this?"

"The day I met you."

"Was it with Saraphina?"

"No, someone else."

I grinned broadly. "Come on! Spill it! What did she tell you?"

He removed his sunglasses and held my gaze. He looked so serious that I got a little worried. What could she have told him? Was it bad news?

He cleared his throat, took a deep breath. "She said, 'For you, I see life is good.' Which didn't make any sense at the time, because some stuff was going on in my life that wasn't good, so I figured it was a con, something she probably said to everyone, but then . . ."

His voice trailed off, and I realized where this was going.

"My 'Life Is Good' hat," I whispered, goose bumps erupting along my arms, in spite of the heat of the afternoon.

He grinned. "Yeah."

"Spooky. Way spooky."

"Oh yeah."

I furrowed my brow. "What was bad in your life?"

He shook his head. "Nothing important, nothing that matters anymore, anyway. Now, life *is* good."

And he drew me close and kissed me. No doubt a ploy to stop me from prying into his past.

It worked, because when he kissed me, I could hardly think at all.

Chapter 16

We caught up with Tank and Jenna a little before nine in front of Sara—Saraphina's. It was hard to think of her with her psychic's name now that I knew her as a normal person. Almost normal, anyway.

As long as she didn't give me any secretive, off-the-record readings.

Amber was coming back, just as she'd predicted. But she'd also predicted some hurt when that happened. I didn't like the idea of that. Not at all. Although maybe it would be something simple, something not too painful—like another splinter, or a sunburn. Something small. But then, why bother to mention it?

Palling around with a psychic had its drawbacks. It was one thing for her to give me a reading when I was paying for it, but when she told me something she saw because she felt compelled to tell me—well, quite honestly, it made me worry.

Nearly a dozen people stood around, waiting for our hostess or tour guide or whatever she would be calling herself tonight.

"I don't believe in ghosts," Jenna said—three times—like a mantra.

Which made me think maybe she did believe in them. She sounded nervous. I knew she didn't like scary things.

"I have a feeling Sara will have us convinced before the night is over," Brady said.

"Yeah, well, just don't let go of my hand," I ordered. "And hold me close if I get scared."

"I hope you get scared," he said in a low voice near my ear.

"Me, too." A delicious shiver went through me. "I can practically guarantee it."

He was standing behind me, and he tightened his arms around my waist, pulling me closer. He dropped a kiss onto my bare shoulder.

Oh yeah, I might get scared, but it would be the good kind of scared, where we held each other close and laughed. Or maybe just kissed. I was starting to like him so much—and that scared me most of all.

When she finally arrived, Sara was dressed all in black, a black, hooded cloak swirling around her. It seemed like the fog was trailing in behind her. Her vibrant red hair was the only visible color. She was wearing it down and it flowed past her shoulders.

"Good evening," she said in a very melodramatic, haunting voice. "Does anyone not have a partner?"

Everyone was already paired up.

"Good," she said. "Now, I want you to hold your partner's hand and no matter what happens, don't let go. People have been known to disappear on the streets of New Orleans and never be seen again."

A chill went through me. Yeah, she was going to have us believing in ghosts.

"We are known as the most haunted city in the country," she continued. "And sometimes the spirits get jealous of the living. If you listen closely as we walk through the streets, sometimes you'll hear them crying, sometimes you'll hear them singing, sometimes you'll hear them dying."

I squeezed Brady's hand and rose up on my toes, so only he would hear me. "Are we sure we want to do this?"

"Oh yeah. And if you get so scared you need someone to sleep with you tonight—I'm there."

I didn't think I was going to get that scared, but who knew?

And okay, quite honestly, snuggling up with Brady appealed to me. It was frightening how quickly and how hard I was falling for the guy.

He was nice, he was fun, and he was hot. I just liked the way I felt when we were together. Like we were part of something.

"Follow me as we seek out the lost souls of New Orleans," Sara said in that spooky voice she'd perfected. It sent more chills over my flesh.

Must have sent chills over Brady's, too, because he put his arm around me, like holding hands wasn't enough to keep us from getting lost. We headed up Royal Street.

"New Orleans history is rich with hauntings. Some of the spirits are here because of something left undone. Some feel compelled to remain and re-create the circumstances of their death until justice has been gained. Most spirits are playful, causing mischief. Especially those who died as children. There are rare accounts of spirits causing harm, but rest assured that you'll all be safe tonight. The spirits know me, and they know we mean them no harm. That we mourn their passing, and that we're here to remember."

"That doesn't sound too bad," I whispered, starting to relax.

I felt something brush against my bare calf. I looked down, but there was nothing there. I shivered.

"You okay?" Brady asked.

"I thought I felt something."

"Like what?"

"A cat maybe. A very, very soft cat. It was just a light touch."

"Probably nothing."

"Probably."

But it hadn't felt like nothing.

"Over here we have a mansion that reflects our city's dark history," Sara said.

We stopped in front of a large gray building as Sara told us about Delphine Lalaurie and her physician husband. Wealthy, they were known for their lavish parties until it was discovered that they were monsters, performing surgical experiments on their slaves.

"Within the manor," Sara said, "there have been reported sightings of a man walking about carrying his head."

A shudder went through me.

"Is that what she calls being playful?" I whispered.

Brady chuckled. Did I sound spooked? I thought I sounded spooked.

"And on foggy nights, you can hear the screams of those who were abused within those walls. They are still crying out for justice."

Sara took us down Orleans Street, where on rainy nights the ghost of a priest who'd led a funeral procession to bury the remains of wrongly executed men could be heard singing.

Brady tightened his arms around me and rested his chin on my shoulder. I felt breath whisper across my neck. I told myself it was his. It had to be his.

"Thank goodness it's not raining," he said.

"Really."

"Are you believing this stuff?" He sounded totally stunned.

I twisted my head around. He was grinning.

"Don't you?" I asked.

"No. This is all bogus."

Was it? I didn't know anymore.

At 716 Dauphine Street, Sara told us about the ghost of a sultan who was murdered along with his wives and children and now haunted the four-story house.

"One of my favorite spirits remains here," she said. "I'm fairly certain it's one of the sultan's children. It likes to tickle necks."

I felt a light prickle over my neck. I hunched my shoulders and turned to Brady. "Don't."

"What?"

"I know you're trying to scare me."

"What are you talking about?"

What *was* I talking about? Because he was holding my hand, and no way he could have touched my neck without twisting around — and that I would have noticed.

Maybe it had been a moth or a mosquito. Some little insect of the night.

Every street she walked us along had tales of horrific murders—a man had killed his wife and the ghost of his wife had killed his mistress. What was that she'd said earlier about ghosts not causing harm?

Although the night was warm, I felt chilled. At one point, I thought I saw an apparition—a woman in a white nightgown—but it was gone so fast that I couldn't be sure.

When we'd circled back around to Sara's shop, she seemed really pleased with herself. Maybe because it looked like several people were pale. I probably was, too.

"In two weeks, John and I will take you on a vampire tour. He loves fresh blood! Sleep well," she said, before whipping her cloak around her and walking off. It seemed as if she disappeared from sight sooner than she should have.

"Okay, that was creepy," Jenna said.

"You mean the tour, or John liking fresh blood?" I asked.

"All of it. Sara was a little out there at the end."

"I can't see Ms. Wynder with a vampire," I said.

She laughed. "Me either."

I figured they'd laugh if I told them that I thought I'd felt something. So I kept quiet, but I couldn't stop thinking about it. New Orleans was definitely a city for those who believed in the supernatural. And even those who didn't could have their skepticism challenged.

"Anyone hungry?" Tank asked.

I wasn't, but I welcomed anything to take my mind off the tour.

We went to McDonald's. Not very New Orleans-ish, but it was late and they were open. And the lights were bright—I suddenly had a love of bright lights—so there were no spooky things lurking about.

And actually, once I bit into my burger, I realized that I was hungry. Very hungry. Apparently ghost hunting works up an appetite.

"I don't know if I'm going to do the vampire

tour," Jenna said as she swirled a fry in the ketchup. "I mean, I don't believe in vampires, but then I didn't believe in ghosts either, but that was before tonight. I think I saw one."

"Saw what?" Tank asked.

"A ghost."

He laughed so loudly that several other late-night customers looked over at our table.

"I saw something, too," I said, feeling a need to support Jenna. And okay. I *had* seen something.

"Probably just someone walking by," Tank said.

"If they want to believe in ghosts, I'm down with that," Brady said, scooting closer to me. "As a matter of fact, I'm not certain I want to sleep alone tonight."

"You're scared?" Tank asked.

Brady glared at him, and I laughed.

Then Tank widened his eyes. "Oh. Right. Right. Babe, if you're scared—"

"I might be," Jenna said, "but not if you're going to make fun of me."

They started talking low again, like Brady

and I weren't even there.

"Did you really see something?" Brady asked.

I shrugged, popped a fry into my mouth. "Maybe. I don't know. Could be the power of suggestion. I definitely felt something. On my calf, on the back of my neck."

"Me, too. On the back of my neck."

"Really?"

"No. But if it'll make you not want to sleep alone—"

I shoved playfully on his shoulder. "Get over it. That's so not happening."

We left McDonald's and started walking toward Bourbon Street, as though it was a given that that's where we wanted to end the night.

Since it was Saturday, Ms. Wynder had said she wouldn't do a bed check until two, and I wondered if she'd even bother. What if things got hot and steamy between her and John?

Tank and Jenna were behind us. Brady turned, walking backward. "Hey, we'll catch up with y'all later, at the hotel."

Then he quickened his pace, pulling me along with him. "Come on."

"Where are we going?"

"You'll see."

The guy was nothing but surprises, which I liked. Because every surprise was better than the one that came before.

He brought me around a corner, where a horse and carriage were waiting. The driver wore a top hat, very high society.

"Do you go down to the Garden District?" Brady asked him.

"Yes, sir."

"Hop in," Brady said to me.

Once he paid the driver, and we were settled against the leather seats with Brady's arm around me, I asked, "How did you know I wanted to do this?"

"It's a chick thing. All girls want to do it."

"Your sisters trained you right."

He laughed. "Yeah, but don't tell them that. I'll never hear the end of it."

And I wondered if I'd ever meet his sisters. It didn't seem likely. I mean, why would they come here? And in a few weeks, Brady and I would go our separate ways.

He wound his finger around my beaded

necklace. "So, are you planning to get more of these tonight?"

"I don't think so."

"Yeah. That's what I figured. So I didn't think Bourbon Street would be *that* much fun."

"Watching *you* get beads is fun."

"Yeah, but we should take turns."

That sounded like such a couple thing to say.

"I really had fun today," I said.

"Yeah, me, too."

I nestled my head against his shoulder.

"So tell me about your breakup," he said quietly.

I eased away from him a little and met his gaze. "What does it matter?"

He tucked my hair behind my ear. "I like you, Dawn. I think this guy, whoever he is, is still messing with you."

I looked at the driver. His back was to us. He wasn't paying any attention. And we were talking low. I sighed. "Drew. His name is Drew and he—" I shook my head.

"He what?"

It hurt to think about it, hurt even more to

say it. "He cheated on me."

"Okay."

"Okay? That's all? Aren't you going to tell me that he's a jerk?"

"You already know that."

Yeah, I knew that, but I still found some comfort in hearing it. And while I was usually okay with his single okay, right now I wanted more.

"What you need to understand," he said quietly, "is that I'm not him."

Then, with his hand cradling my cheek and his thumb stroking near the corner of my mouth, he leaned in and kissed me. Something about the kiss seemed different. Like all the others had been for fun, but this one was meant to be more.

It was kind of scary, but at the same time, I realized that it was something that I wanted.

I felt like I had on the ghost tour. Doubting what I was feeling. Wondering if it was real.

Or would it—like an apparition—disappear, and leave me wondering if it had truly ever been there?

Chapter 17

*I*t wasn't until Jenna and I were back in our dorm room—with thirty seconds to spare before the two o'clock curfew—and I was getting ready for bed that I remembered the necklace I'd put in my pocket for safekeeping.

I sat on the edge of the bed and looked at it again. It was really pretty. I wished I'd bought one for myself. Next week, I would. I was sure the vendor would still be there.

"What's that?" Jenna asked.

"Oh, a necklace Brady bought for his sister."

"He buys things for his sister? Wow. My brother doesn't know the first thing about buying me something."

"I helped him pick it out." Saying that

sounded weird. Like maybe we were shopping for something much more important.

"I'm really glad you're hanging out with him," Jenna said.

"Only because it means he's not hanging out with Tank all the time, and you have some time alone."

"Well, there is that. I'm so crazy about Tank, Dawn. It's scary sometimes."

"Tell me about it."

"But it's exciting, too. It's everything." She sat in the middle of her bed and brought her legs up beneath her. "Did you feel that way about Drew?"

Did I? Gosh, it was suddenly hard to remember. All I could remember now was being hurt and angry at him. Like that moment of seeing him with someone else had totally destroyed any good feelings I'd ever had for him. Had I been scared when he asked me out? Nervous? Excited?

"I can't remember, Jenna. That's so weird."

"You know, sometimes I think about what Sara said about you rebuilding. I thought she was talking about New Orleans. But what if she was talking about your heart?"

"She didn't know my heart needed rebuilding."

"She doesn't need to *know* stuff. She just sees things. She said you had to be careful with the tools. I thought she meant hammers and saws. What if she meant Brady?"

I flopped back on the bed. "You're really giving too much thought to all this."

"It's the puzzle solver in me. I can't help it."

I rolled my head to the side and looked at her. "She said I could get hurt. If I wasn't careful. Jenna, I don't think I've been careful. I think I've fallen for him."

"That's a good thing, Dawn. It means you're over Drew."

"No, it means I've set myself up to be hurt again. We agreed this was a Big Easy–only relationship."

"So, change the terms of your agreement."

"What if he doesn't want to?"

She sighed. "Do you have to doubt everything?"

I sat up. "Me? Doubting? You're the one trying to figure everything out, trying to solve the puzzles, wanting all the answers."

She came off the bed. "Well, I've never been in love before, and I don't know if I like it. I thought having a boyfriend would stop all the questions, but there's just more of them."

I smiled. "Yeah, it's a bummer, isn't it?"

"The future is just so"—she threw her hands up—"vague. There are just so many possibilities."

"And going to see a psychic sure doesn't help."

"No, it doesn't." She sat back down on the bed. "So what are we going to do?"

"You think *I* know?"

Laughing, she shook her head. "No, actually, I think you're probably more confused than I am."

"Well, thanks a lot."

Her cell phone rang and we both jumped. Then mine rang.

"Time for good-night calls," she said.

Okay, I guessed tonight we'd moved to a new level. I mean, we'd spoken that one night before I went to bed, but it had been on Jenna's phone, so it didn't really count. Oh, heck, maybe it did.

I answered, "Hey."

"Did I wake you?"

"No." I stretched out, rolled onto my side, and my knee touched the sack the necklace had been in. "I forgot to give you your sister's necklace."

"It's yours."

My brow furrowed. "What? No, I'm not talking about the beads, I'm talking about—"

"The fleur-de-lis."

"Yeah."

"I bought it for you. Why do you think I let you pick it out?"

"But you said it was for her."

"I thought you'd go all weird on me if I bought you something."

"Weird?" I said, offended. "I don't go weird."

"You go weird. You worry about what I really feel or what you really feel or what we're thinking. You're expecting me to hurt you, and I don't know how to make you stop expecting that."

I wrapped my hand around the charm. "I'm a mess. I don't know why you hang out with me."

"I hang out with you because I like you.

You're funny and fun and you believe in ghosts—"

"I don't believe in ghosts. I just had some weird stuff happen tonight."

"Are you sleeping with the light on?"

I hated to admit it, but—

"Yeah, we probably will. Jenna wants to." When in doubt, blame it on your friend. I figured we'd at least keep on the light in the bathroom with the door partially opened.

"About the necklace," I said.

"Yeah?" I heard the impatience in his voice, maybe even a little bit of anger. I couldn't imagine Brady being angry.

"Thank you. I really wanted one for myself, and this one will always be special. Remind me of my time here. My time with you."

"Good."

"But, you were very sneaky having me pick it out."

"I thought it was clever. If I'd known you longer, I might have known what to get, but we're on the short-term plan here. Right?"

"Yeah. Short term."

"End of summer."

"End of New Orleans." And that made me sad.

"Okay, then. See you tomorrow."

"What are we going to do?"

"I figure the least you can do is my laundry."

"What?"

He laughed. "No go, huh? I don't know what we'll do, but it'll be sometime in the afternoon. I do have to get my clothes washed. Maybe we'll just hang out by the pool."

"I like that idea. I could use a day of not doing anything."

"Okay. Then. Tomorrow."

"Yeah. Night."

I closed my phone, set it aside, sat up, and looked at the necklace. I could feel myself smiling. It was the smile of someone who was totally and completely happy. It was the smile of someone who wasn't worried about getting hurt.

I put the necklace on. It felt right. Suddenly everything did. I wasn't even worried about Saraphina's prediction.

But maybe I should have continued to worry about being careful.

Chapter 18

Things were coming along nicely on the house. We were getting to the details. Jenna and I were hammering the trim around the windows that had been replaced.

The four of us had spent last Sunday at a lake near where we were staying, just relaxing. Sometimes we got together after we were finished building for the day. Sometimes it was just Brady and me. It seemed like we could always find something to talk about. And when we weren't talking, we were kissing.

"Hey, catch!" Brady yelled.

I looked over, dropped the hammer, and caught the bottle of water he tossed my way. He'd set his watch to go off every hour and he brought me a bottle when he grabbed one for himself. I sat down on the edge of the porch, removed my safety goggles and hard hat, and set them aside. I twisted the cap and took a long swallow of the cold water. It tasted so good.

Brady leaned against the beam. I watched a droplet trail down his bare chest. A silly thing to be fascinated watching, but fascinated I was. Just about everything about him fascinated me.

"Do you have a sec?" he asked.

I felt my cheeks warm as I lifted my gaze to his, certain my brow was furrowed and a question was in my eyes. We'd been really good about not sneaking off for stolen kisses. I wasn't sure Jenna could say the same. From time to time, she disappeared. Tank was usually AWOL at the same time.

Brady jerked his head to the side. "I want to show you something."

"What?"

He grinned. "If I could tell you, I wouldn't have to show you. Come on."

I got up and walked beside him as he headed toward the street, then sauntered along the line of cars that was parked against the curb. He had a lazy stride—which was odd because I knew he wasn't at all lazy. He was probably one of the hardest workers here. Me, I took a break every fifteen minutes just to catch my breath, dip a towel into ice water, and wrap it around my neck to cool down. I couldn't imagine what it would be like around here come August. Next year, I thought, I'd do this volunteer work over spring break, when it wasn't quite as hot yet.

Yeah, I was already making plans to come back. I really liked New Orleans. It had so much to offer, and we hadn't even explored everything yet.

When we got to Tank's car, Brady stopped, reached into his back pocket, pulled something out, and held it toward me. It looked like white cardboard, folded in half.

"What is it?" I asked.

"Open it."

I set my water bottle on the trunk of the car, took the cardboard, and unfolded it. It was a colorful butterfly. A temporary tattoo. I laughed.

"I saw it at the convenience store where we stopped to get coffee this morning," Brady said. "It reminded me of you."

I squinted up at him. I hadn't put my sunglasses on. The sun was bright, but his smile was brighter.

"I see."

"I could put it on you if you want."

"What? Right now?"

His grin, if at all possible, grew wider. "Yeah. Why not? Lean on the trunk."

He took the towel from around my neck and poured some water from his water bottle on it. I glanced around. It seemed kind of wicked in a way, and sort of silly, too.

"Why not?" I repeated, handed him the tattoo, and leaned against the car. I lifted my T-shirt slightly and pushed the waistband of my jeans down just a tad, near my left hip.

I felt him lay the piece of paper against my skin, felt the damp towel against my back. "That's cold!"

"Bet it feels good, though," he said.

In no time at all he was peeling back the paper. "Perfect."

I moved around him and looked in the side-view mirror, twisting around slightly, so I could see my backside. All I could see was part of the wings peeking out above the waistband of my jeans.

"Sexy," Brady said.

His voice dropped a notch or two, and it sent a shiver along my spine. I'd never had a guy tell me I was sexy before. I liked it. I liked it a lot.

He put his hands on either side of my hips and drew me closer. "I had an ulterior motive in giving you the tattoo. Now I can say something innocent like, 'I'd like to see the bottom half of that tattoo.'" He wiggled his eyebrows. "And it might not be innocent at all."

"Yeah, well, you should have taken a good look at it when you were applying it, because that was probably the last time you'll see the bottom half." I stood on tiptoes and nipped his chin. He had a really nice chin. Strong, sturdy. It matched his strong jaw.

I'd always thought a guy's eyes were his best feature, revealed the most about him. But the truth was, there wasn't anything about Brady that I didn't think was darn near perfect.

"We'll see," he said in a low voice, like a challenge. I knew he was still talking about the tattoo and wanting to see all of it again.

Then he was kissing me, and I thought—
Yeah, we'll see.

A week later, I moved from hammering outside to painting bedroom walls.

I'd called Amber and given her the measurements for the windows and told her that I was going to paint the little girls' rooms pink. Brady had borrowed Tank's car to take me shopping for the paint. I'd bought it myself, because the builder who was donating the supplies had brought only cream-colored paint. And while cream is a nice neutral color, little girls should have something special.

I dipped the roller into the pan, then began rolling it over the walls again. When we'd first started working on the house it smelled of mildew and rot. Now it smelled of paint, of new. It smelled wonderful.

I'd never been involved in something that made me feel this good about myself.

"Hey, guess who just got here?" Jenna asked from the doorway.

I turned around, but before I could answer,

she said, "It's Amber. Come on."

I'd known that, of course. Just as Sara had predicted. Back from her doubts.

I was so ready to see her again. I hurried through the house—in Jenna's wake—and stepped out onto the porch. And there Amber was, running across the yard that when we'd first arrived had been littered. Now the house was almost completed.

I hopped off the porch and rushed to her, reaching her at the same time that Jenna did. We did a three-person hug, laughing. Hopping up and down. Going in a circle. I had so much to tell her. So much to share.

I wanted to hear about everything that had happened at home, too. She'd hardly called, so I knew she'd been wrapped up in Chad. That's the way it is when you have a boyfriend. You spend so much time with him. I wanted to hear it all.

She leaned back, and her smile dimmed. "I didn't come alone."

"I know. Saraphina told me you wouldn't," I said.

She frowned, worried, so typical. "She knew

I was coming back?"

I nodded. "With a guy with black hair."

I looked past her. At the black-haired guy standing a few feet away.

Drew.

The very last person I wanted to see.

I spun on my heel and walked back into the house, back to the bedroom I'd been painting.

Without saying a word to Drew. Without even acknowledging his existence, his presence, his intrusion on my life.

I picked up the roller and started rolling it over the wall in a frenzy—almost insanely. It was a little frightening really. But I thought the problem was that painting wasn't nearly as cathartic as hammering.

I really wanted to feel a hammer in my hand right now.

This place, this city, this house in a demolished neighborhood, had been my paradise. My sanctuary. It had been untainted. No memories of Drew. This was a Drew-less place.

I'd been happy. I'd been really happy.

I'd stopped thinking about Drew before I

went to sleep. I didn't want to see him, didn't want to talk to him, didn't want him to creep back into my life.

I heard footsteps. If it was Drew, I was going to pick up the can of paint and throw its contents on him.

"Dawn?"

It was Amber. I set down the roller, faced her, and crossed my arms over my chest. Jenna was standing beside her. Was she there to support Amber or me? I'd lost my boyfriend. Was I going to lose my friends?

"What were you thinking?" I asked. It was all I could do not to shout.

And knowing Amber, she probably hadn't been thinking.

"Chad and I broke up," she said.

"You're kidding?" Jenna looked dumb-struck.

"Why would she kid about that?" I asked. "And how does that even remotely begin to explain bringing Drew here?"

Ignoring me, Jenna asked, "Why did you and Chad break up?"

"Because I wanted to do something meaningful with my summer, and he wanted to rent DVDs for TV shows he hadn't seen and do season marathons. All the different seasons of *24*. All the different seasons of *Monk* and *Lost* and *Scrubs*. I just wanted more."

"But you told me that he was interested in coming," I reminded her.

"He said he was, but he really wasn't. He was just humoring me. He didn't really care about what I wanted."

"So you broke up with him?" Jenna asked.

Amber nodded. "Plus, I couldn't stop thinking about Sean."

"He's with Sara," I said.

I knew it was mean, but I took some satisfaction in telling her that. I was upset that she'd brought Drew here.

I know sometimes she says things that are out there, but this was beyond out there. This was plain stupid.

"Well, Sean's not *with* her, with her," Amber said. "I mean, I know they've been hanging out together, but they're just friends. She's way older than he is. And he's called me."

I couldn't believe this. Everything was such a mess.

"You broke up with Chad so you could get together with Sean?" Jenna asked.

Jenna still wanted details. I wanted Drew out of there.

"I broke up with Chad because watching TV isn't enough for me. And if Sean isn't the one Sara was referring to—what I'll have better in college—I'm okay with that. I just knew Chad was wrong."

"But you loved him."

Amber nodded. "I know it seems all screwed up, but I know I did the right thing."

"Maybe you did the right thing about Chad," I said, "but Drew? Why bring him?"

"Because I needed a way to get here, and he has a car," Amber explained.

"You could have flown, your parents could have brought you, you could have hitchhiked." Although I knew that was a dangerous option and really didn't want her to risk it—I was upset. Anything was better than seeing Drew again.

"He wanted to help out, though, so it seemed like a perfect solution."

I couldn't believe this. "Amber—"

"I know you're still mad at him, but you should at least talk to him. He's sorry—"

"Oh, he's sorry, all right."

"Prom night was a moment of weakness."

What a crappy excuse. I wasn't buying it. And while she wasn't usually good at figuring things out, she read the expression on my face perfectly.

"Look, he wants to get back together with you," she said.

"Ain't happening."

"But you need closure."

"I hate that word. I had closure. I slammed his car door *closed* and walked away."

"And never talked to him again?"

"There was nothing to say. There still isn't."

"I think you're wrong. I think there's a lot more to say."

No, there wasn't. There was nothing. Absolutely nothing. I didn't care about Drew anymore. I didn't care about him at all.

I headed for the door.

"Where are you going?" Amber asked.

"To take care of something."

I walked into the kitchen where Brady and some other guys were supposed to be working.

And there was Drew.

The guys were standing around talking to him, but I knew that nothing he said was important. Everything was a lie. Especially when he said he loved you.

Brady stepped out of the circle just a little bit when he saw me.

Drew turned around and took a step toward me, his hands out, his smile . . . God, it looked so fake, so stupid. How had I ever trusted it?

"Dawn—"

I walked right by him. Totally ignoring him. I went up to Brady, wrapped my arms around his neck, and kissed him.

Energetically, thoroughly. Maybe even a little desperately.

He pulled back and gave me a funny look. Then he took my hand. "Come on."

He led me past Drew, whose mouth was hanging open.

Good, I thought. *Now you know how it feels.*

♥ ♥ ♥

"What was going on back there?"

Brady was leaning against Tank's car, his sunglasses on, his arms crossed over his chest.

"I was missing you."

"Dawn, I deserve better than that."

I looked down at the grass and could see some shards of broken glass. Would we ever get everything cleaned up?

"He was your boyfriend, wasn't he?"

Nodding, I looked up.

"You were trying to make him jealous."

Well, okay, maybe I was. Maybe I wanted him to see what he gave up.

"Which means you still feel something for him," Brady finished.

"I don't! Not at all. He's such a jerk!" I felt tears burn my eyes. "I hate him."

"Hate's a feeling."

"It's not a good feeling. It's not like I care."

"Why's he here?" Brady asked.

"He gave Amber a lift. He wants to help."

"That's it?"

His voice dripped with skepticism. This was a side of Brady I'd never seen. Impatient.

I shifted from one foot to the other, while I decided whether to confirm what he suspected. "He wants us to get back together."

"Do you?"

I stared at him. "No. No way."

"Are you sure?"

"Yes."

"I'm not."

"You're not what?"

"Not so sure you don't want to get back together with him."

"Are you saying I'm a liar?"

"I think you were using me back there. Maybe I've been using you, too, but you need to figure out how you really feel about him."

Using me? How had he been using me?

"Because if you want to make him jealous," he continued, "it's because you want him back. I've been there, done that, and I'm not doing it again."

"I don't know what you're talking about. What are you saying?"

"I'm saying that we're over."

Chapter 19

*B*rady walked over to Tank, talked to him, then they came back, got in the car, and drove away.

Just like that.

It was just as I suspected: All guys eventually turned into jerks.

It was the opposite of the frog turning into the prince. Eventually, no matter what you did, the prince turned back into a frog.

"Dawn?"

Drew. Behind me.

Even his voice grated on my nerves. Without even looking at him, I started walking toward the house.

"I'm really, really sorry," he said.

I kept walking.

"Won't you even talk to me?" he asked.

Nope.

I just kept walking.

I saw Amber leaning against the new wall of the house, talking to Sean. Smiling. Laughing. He was tucking her hair behind her ear.

At least she'd broken up with Chad, before getting more involved with Sean. I was sure it had been hard to break up with him, and he was probably hurt. But it was easier to get over a breakup than a betrayal.

Or at least I hoped it was.

Right now I was still reeling from Brady's outburst.

What was up with that anyway?

He'd broken our bargain.

Creep.

I felt tears sting my eyes. He wasn't a jerk or a creep. Not by a long shot.

But where had the guy who'd always been "okay" with everything gone?

Jenna came out of the house, hopped off the porch, and came over, stopping me from going wherever it was I was going.

I had no idea.

I was in shock.

"Are you okay?" Jenna asked.

"Brady left. He just left."

"Yeah, I know. Tank called to let me know."

"I don't get it. He's been so understanding—this whole time. And now, when I really need him, he just goes ballistic."

It was a little scary to realize how much I'd come to depend on him being there. That was so not what I'd planned for the summer.

Amber had left Sean and joined us.

"I'm sorry," she said. "I thought you'd be happy to see Drew."

"How could you possibly think that?" I asked.

"I just thought since he wanted to be with you again—"

"But I told you I was with Brady."

"Yeah, but I thought it was just for the summer."

It was. It was. But still.

It was hard to stay mad at Amber. She just didn't think, and I knew she hadn't meant to mess things up for me. But still, she had.

"Brady didn't even give me a chance to

explain," I said. "He just said it was over."

Jenna sighed. "Probably because of Melanie. Don't you think?"

My heart did a little stutter. "Melanie? Who's Melanie?"

Jenna looked surprised. Startled, even. "He didn't tell you about Melanie?"

Shivers went all through me. This was worse than thinking I felt a spirit tickle me on a ghost tour.

"Nooo. What's this about?"

She grimaced. "Oh, I don't know if I should tell you, then."

"Jenna! I need to understand what's going on here."

"Let me call Tank and see if it's okay for me to tell you."

"You need Tank's approval to help your friend?"

"He told me, but I don't know if I can tell you."

"Jenna."

She sighed. "Oh, all right. Melanie was Brady's girlfriend."

"He had a girlfriend?"

She nodded.

Why was I surprised he'd had a girlfriend? Honestly I would have been surprised if he hadn't. I mean, he had way too many smooth moves never to have had one. And he was so cute and nice. Of course he'd had a girlfriend.

"When?" I asked.

"I don't know all the details. Tank just told me about how she broke up with Brady—because it was such a cold way to do it."

"What'd she do?"

"She text-messaged him. He's in class and he gets a text message: 'I'm back with Mike.'"

"Back with?" I repeated.

"Yeah, apparently, she broke up with her boyfriend, then she was dating Brady, then she got back with the other guy."

"Did Brady like her? I mean, a lot?"

She nodded. "Think so."

"This is so weird," Amber whispered. "I don't know if I should have come back."

"You should have come back," I reassured her. "You just shouldn't have brought Drew."

"No, don't you get it? Saraphina said there

would be things hidden. I thought she meant that stupid snake," Amber said.

Another shiver went through me.

Secrets were things hidden. And Brady had one.

Why hadn't he told me?

Then I remembered him saying how he hadn't believed the psychic because life wasn't good. But he hadn't explained why.

I'd finally discovered his flaw.

My old boyfriend showed up and Brady just assumed I'd get back together with Drew.

He was as untrusting of girls as I was of guys.

Weren't we a terrific pair?

I'd never questioned why he'd been so agreeable to the terms of our agreement. Why a New-Orleans-only-no-breakup-predetermined-good-bye had been okay with him. Now I knew.

He was as scared of getting hurt again as I was.

"So what are you going to do?" Jenna asked.

"I don't know. I just . . . I just need to take some time." I looked at Amber. "Go talk to

Sean. That's the reason you came back. And Jenna, go finish painting the bedroom. I'm just going to . . . I don't know."

I walked away, walked across the yard to where we kept the ice chests. I opened one, searched through the icy water until I found a bottle. I closed the chest, twisted off the cap, took a long swallow.

It didn't help. My knees still felt weak. I sat on the chest.

Maybe I'd just go home. Who needed this aggravation?

Drew being here when I didn't want him to be. Brady believing that I'd get back together with Drew—just because he'd shown up.

Only I didn't want to go home. I wanted to be here. I wanted to build a house. I wanted to be with my friends. I wanted to explore the city more.

I'd run away once before because it had hurt too much to stay. But now, no matter how much it hurt to be here, I wasn't willing to leave.

I was vaguely aware of someone opening one of the other ice chests, the pop of a top being twisted off a bottle, the moan of the chest as someone sat on it.

"Sometimes I hate it when the things I see really do happen."

I looked over to find Sara sitting next to me.

"Amber's back," she said quietly. "And the black-haired guy with her? He broke something, didn't he?"

Oh yeah, big time.

Sara looked sad. As sad as I felt.

I nodded. "He used to be my boyfriend. And Brady was just so un-Brady about it. Do you happen to know any voodoo?"

A corner of her mouth quirked up. "Voodoo?"

"Yeah. I was thinking maybe a spell that would send Drew away and bring Brady back."

"You take three hairs from each of their heads, bury them in a backyard"—she jerked her thumb over her shoulder—"like this backyard, and jump up and down on the spot three times."

I looked at her, my eyes wide. "Really?"

She smiled. "No. It's never that simple, Dawn."

"Brady probably wouldn't give me three

strands of his hair anyway. He's kind of protective of his hair. He has this fear of going bald."

She shook her head. "Huh. I don't see him without hair."

I straightened up. "You mean, he's not going to go bald?"

She laughed. "Oh no, I don't *see* him, see him. I just can't imagine him bald."

"Oh. I thought if I gave him some good news . . ."

What did it matter? It didn't.

I sighed. "I don't suppose you see how all this is going to end."

She slowly shook her head. "Sorry."

I nodded. "That's okay. Sometimes it's probably better not to know."

"Yeah, sometimes it is."

And the way she said it made me think she knew more than she was letting on.

"I hate leaving you alone," Jenna said.

We were back in the dorm. I was sitting on the bed.

"I'll be fine."

Amber shifted her weight from one foot to the other. "You sure?"

Tank and Sean were coming to get them for a night of listening to bands. I wondered what Brady was going to be doing. I was a little afraid to ask.

So I didn't ask.

So typical of me. Not wanting to face the truth.

I could see him dancing shirtless on Bourbon Street, gathering beads. I wondered whose neck he'd put them around.

I wondered why he didn't tell me about Melanie.

It was strange, so strange, that all I could think about was him. How much I wanted to be with him.

After Jenna and Amber left, I just looked at the ceiling and thought about him.

When my phone rang, my heart gave a little jump—until I saw who was calling.

Drew.

I almost didn't answer. Mostly because, suddenly, nothing was there. The anger that I'd felt earlier—it was just gone.

"Hey."

"I didn't think you'd answer," he said.

"Then why did you call?"

"Just in case you did. I really want to see you, Dawn."

"Okay."

"Okay? You mean it?"

"Yeah." I gave him the address for the dorm. I changed into jeans and a knit top.

I was waiting outside the dorm when he drove up.

It was kind of funny. There was no excitement. No anticipation. It wasn't at all like waiting for Brady.

I walked over to his car and got in.

"Where do you want to go?" Drew asked.

"McDonald's."

"Seriously?"

"Yep."

I told him there was one near the French Quarter. As he drove, neither of us talked. There seemed to be so much to say and nothing to say.

I showed him where to park.

"Seems like we ought to eat someplace, I don't know, Cajun, I guess," he said as we crossed the street.

"I like this place because the lights are bright. I want to see you."

That seemed to please him. Maybe it sounded like a romantic thing to say, but romance had nothing to do with it. I just wanted to be able to see him clearly when we talked. Wanted him to see me, so there'd be no misunderstanding about what was being said.

Sometimes in the dark, you can misunderstand things.

He ordered a burger and fries. I ordered a soft drink.

"That John guy, he's nice. He found me a place to stay, with some other volunteers," Drew said once we were sitting in a booth.

"Amber said you came here because you wanted to help."

"Yeah. That, and to see you."

I really, really, really wanted nothing more than for him to go back to Katy. But at the same time, I couldn't help but think of him as an extra pair of hands. And New Orleans needed all the helping hands it could get.

So I wasn't here to tell him to leave. I was here to figure out how I could work with him. I didn't think it was going to be as hard as I'd envisioned.

"I thought you wanted to spend the summer doing water parks," I said.

"Yeah, me, too. But I was reading Jenna's blog—"

"Thanks for sending my mom that picture, by the way."

He blushed. "This afternoon, it looked like you were still seeing the guy."

"Yeah, I am." Or I would be, once I figured that part of my life out. I wasn't going to give Brady up nearly as easily as I'd given up Drew. I wasn't going to walk away without talking to him.

"How serious?" Drew asked.

"Serious enough." My arrangement with Brady wasn't any of Drew's business. "I just want you to know that I'm fine with you being here. I'm fine with you helping. I just need you to understand that you and I are over."

I thought about asking what had been wrong with me because I'd always thought it was somehow my fault. But now I knew there was nothing wrong with *me*. There had just been something wrong with *us*.

There wasn't much else to say after that. He drove me back to the dorm.

It may seem cold, but I didn't even bother with good-bye. I just got out.

I heard his door open.

"Dawn?"

I looked back over my shoulder. He just stood there.

"I'm really sorry. About prom night. You have to believe that. I was just getting so much attention from girls after being in the play that I let it go to my head. You were the one."

"Actually, Drew, I wasn't. If I was, you probably wouldn't have kept looking at the menu."

"What?"

I smiled, shook my head. "Just something Jenna said once."

"Are you sure you don't want to give it another shot?"

"You broke my heart, Drew."

"Dawn—"

"You. Broke. My. Heart. We're over. Completely and absolutely."

Now all I had to do was figure out what I was going to do about Brady.

I was lying on the AeroBed reading when Jenna and Amber came back to the room, just before midnight.

"You can have the bed," Amber said.

"Nah. Our original arrangement was that you got the bed, I got the air mattress."

"You don't sound mad at me anymore."

I sat up straighter, folded my legs beneath me. "I'm not. I saw Drew tonight."

They both sat on the floor.

"What happened?" Jenna asked.

I told them about our trip to McDonald's.

"You're not going to get back with him?" Amber asked.

I didn't know how many different ways to say it, so I just said, "No."

She looked confused.

"Are you going to get back together with Chad?" I asked.

"Absolutely not."

"There you are."

"But I left Chad on my terms."

"And tonight I left Drew on mine." Maybe in her spacey sort of way, she'd been right. I had needed some closure where Drew was concerned.

"So you're back with Sean?" I asked.

She nodded. "Yeah. I can't believe how much I missed him. And how much I missed you guys. I even missed the work. I'm thinking about going into construction after I graduate."

"Seriously?"

She nodded.

"But you left before we got to the really hard stuff."

"I know. But just the idea of it, of building. It's something I really want to do. Besides, there are women builders."

"I think that's great," Jenna said. "I'm glad you're back."

"Me, too," Amber replied. She peered at me.

"I am, too." I smiled at her. I knew what it was to worry about what someone thought about you.

"So what are you going to do about Brady now?" Jenna asked.

"Do some rebuilding."

Chapter 20

Much to my surprise, Drew was at the site the next morning. I hadn't really expected him to stay. He was wearing shorts, a T-shirt, and flip-flops. Like maybe he was on his way to a water park. So maybe he wasn't staying.

He walked up to me.

"Hey," he said.

"Hey."

In a way, it was sad that I felt so little for him.

"So what do I do?" he asked.

"What?" Did he still have hopes of us getting back together? Had I not been abundantly clear last night?

He flapped his hand around. "Around here. How do I help?"

"Uh, well, you should probably go talk to

John." *And John is going to tell you to go home and change into jeans and boots*, I thought. Drew really seemed clueless about what was involved in working here.

"Can't I just help you?"

"It doesn't work that way." Usually. Well, okay, if Brady had wanted to help me, I would have welcomed him. "John gives the assignments."

And I'd totally kill him if he assigned Drew to me.

"Okay. I'll see you around, then."

"Yeah."

It was only after Drew walked away that I saw Brady standing a short distance away, watching us.

He turned and went into the house, and I wondered what he thought he'd witnessed.

I went to the bedroom to finish painting. Amber had brought curtains and rods. As soon as we were done with the walls, we were going to hang everything up.

We still had a way to go with the last wall when I decided to take a water break. I went out the front door to the ice chests and grabbed four bottles of water. I walked back into the house, went into the kitchen, and waited while Brady and a couple of other guys finished putting up a cabinet. As soon as he turned around, I said, "Brady, catch."

I tossed him a bottle of water. He caught it, no problem. He had good reflexes—which I already knew.

He studied me, like he was trying to figure out what I was doing.

I just walked out and went back to painting the bedroom.

An hour later, I did the same thing—taking him a bottle of water like he'd always brought one to me.

When we finished painting the bedroom, I went back to the kitchen.

"You guys finished with the ladder?" I asked.

"Sure," one of them said.

I closed it up, tried to carry it—and discovered it was a lot more awkward than it looked.

I heard Brady sigh. Not sure how I recognized his sigh, but I did.

"I'll get it," he said, lifting it. "The legs, remember, it's all in the legs."

He carried it to the bedroom. "Where do you want it?"

"By the window."

Jenna and Amber were in the room, reading the directions for how to hang the curtain rod.

I took one of the brackets, some nails, and a hammer. I climbed up the ladder.

"Do you even know what you're doing?" Brady asked.

Not really, but still I said, "Oh yeah."

How hard could it be to put up a bracket?

I put the bracket against the wall, put the nail in the little hole, brought the hammer back—

"You've got—" Brady began.

And I missed the nail, slamming the hammer against my thumb.

"Ow!"

I jerked back, lost my balance, released a little shriek, fell—

And suddenly found myself in Brady's arms.

"Are you okay?" he asked.

I couldn't help it. Tears started burning my eyes and I shook my head. My reaction had nothing at all to do with the pain in my thumb. It had everything to do with the pain in my heart.

He set my feet on the floor and took my hand. "How bad is it?"

Out of the corner of my eye, I saw Amber and Jenna sneak out of the room, like partners in crime worried about getting caught. If I'd thought it was possible, I'd have thought they arranged all this. But it wasn't possible.

"Doesn't look too bad," Brady said.

I hadn't planned on hitting my thumb. I hadn't planned on ending up in Brady's arms.

"Looks can be deceiving," I said. "I know you saw me talking to Drew."

"You don't have to explain. His being here says it all." He moved away, picked up the hammer that I'd dropped.

"Actually it doesn't say anything," I said. "He's staying to work on the house. Not because of me."

"Yeah, right." He picked up the nail and

bracket. He climbed the ladder and began hammering the bracket into place.

"Are you pretending that's my head?"

He looked down at me. "What?"

"I used to pretend every nail was Drew."

"So you spent the summer thinking about him."

That confession had backfired.

"Only at first. And yes, yesterday, I was mad when I saw him. It was just the shock of it. And yes, I kissed you to try to hurt him. But he doesn't mean anything to me. Not anymore."

"I can't do this." He climbed down the ladder and handed me the hammer. "I just can't do it."

My heart almost stopped. For a minute, I thought he was leaving. Permanently. Going back to Houston.

But I found him in the kitchen, working on the cabinets. Not that he saw me.

I just peered in the open doorway, saw him, and thought, *Okay.*

Then I went to find Sara.

Saturday, Jenna and Amber spent the day shopping with me and walking around the French Quarter.

I told them that they didn't have to. I was okay with them spending the day with their guys. But they didn't want me hanging around the city by myself.

Besides, the three of us hadn't had much time together since that first day.

At least that was their reason. But I knew the truth. They were worried about me.

The past couple of days at the site had been a strain. To say the least. Mostly because I wasn't giving up on Brady.

I took him water every hour. Sometimes I'd just toss the bottle to him. Sometimes I'd stop and talk with him for a minute. Not about anything important. Not about us. Not about Drew.

He'd hold up the water bottle. "You don't have to do this."

"I know. I want to, though." And I'd decided that wanting to do something was enough reason to do it.

And tonight I was going on the vampire tour.

Because I wanted to.

I wanted to because Brady was going on it, too.

Sara had confirmed that for me earlier in the week—after the falling off the ladder incident. I hadn't asked her for a reading. I hadn't wanted her to confirm my future. Or not confirm it. Or give any hints. All I wanted her to do was pair me up with Brady.

And I'd take care of the rest.

Tank and Sean were going to be there as well. Jenna and Amber were going to meet up with them then. And hopefully, if my plan worked out . . . well, I just hoped it would.

So after a day of shopping and talking, we headed to Sara's.

I hadn't expected Drew to be there. I really needed to put a hex on the guy.

He smiled brightly when he saw us. "Hey!"

I just wiggled my fingers.

"This is going to be fun," he said.

"Yeah, it is."

Sara came over—dressed in her black cape

again—and took his arm. "You're going to be with me."

"Really?" he asked.

She winked at me. "Really."

She led him away.

"That was close," Jenna whispered.

Too close. I figured if Brady had seen Drew talking to me—he probably would have walked on by. But the guys weren't there yet.

"They are coming, aren't they?" I asked.

"Absolutely," Jenna said, looking at her phone. "Tank just texted. They're on their way."

I took a deep breath and adjusted the tote bag on my shoulder. "Okay."

Then I saw them crossing the street. They were heading right for us. Brady wasn't trying to avoid me, probably because Tank and Sean were leading the way and he was just following, not really looking the group over. I was standing a little behind Jenna and Amber, so he didn't see me until it was too late.

"Hey," I said.

"Hey."

Sara walked through the group, matching

people up. "Brady, you and Dawn."

She didn't even give him a chance to object.

"Your boyfriend's up there if you want to switch partners," Brady said.

"He's not my boyfriend. He *was*. Past tense. No more."

"You really think you mean that, don't you?"

"I don't *think*. I know." Had I been this obstinate in the beginning about wanting to have a dateless summer? Yeah, I guess I had been.

"Okay, everyone, shh . . . ," Sara said.

John suddenly appeared. It was like one minute he wasn't with us, the next he was.

I don't know how he did that, but I jumped. Brady snickered.

"Are you going to hold my hand if I get scared?" I asked.

He looked at me. He wasn't holding my hand now. I really, really missed him holding my hand.

"I believe in vampires," I said. I'd believe in just about anything if he'd hold my hand again.

"All right, people," John said. He was dressed in a flowing cape. And yes, he had fangs. And he looked pale—bloodless even. "Tonight, I'm going to give you an experience you'll never forget. Follow me."

He started walking down the street, and everyone fell into step behind him.

Everyone except Brady and me.

"Do you really want to do the tour?" I asked.

"Not really. You?"

I shook my head. "I'd rather go sit by the river." I lifted my tote. "I brought a blanket."

"Okay."

We turned and headed toward the Mississippi. He took my hand.

It was a start.

It was late, and night, and dark, and sultry. Even the breeze coming across the water was warm. Sometimes we could hear people laughing or music coming from the decks of the lighted riverboats.

Brady and I were sitting on the blanket.

We'd stopped at one of the many tourist haunts and bought a bottle of water. Just one. For the two of us.

Another step in the right direction.

We'd been sitting there for a while, though, neither of us saying anything. It wasn't uncomfortable. Or at least, I didn't feel that way.

I brought my knees up and wrapped my arms around my legs. "I went to a voodoo shop today."

"A voodoo shop."

I heard the skepticism in his voice. I turned my head, lay my cheek on my knees. "Yeah. Want to see what I got?"

"You bought something?"

"Uh-huh." I reached into my bag and brought out a candle. "If you light this, it keeps the bad mojo away." I set it down near my feet.

Then I brought out another candle: "And this one brings in the good mojo."

"Do you even know what mojo is?" he asked.

"Not really. I think it's like karma. Do you want to light them and see what happens?"

"Sure."

I struck a match, lit one, and then the other.

Brady lifted the first one, studied it. "This smells like peach."

With the flame flickering so close, I could see his face more clearly now.

"Is this really a voodoo candle?" he asked.

I shook my head. "No. But I've learned that sometimes what you believe is more important than what is real. I mean, if I believed that ghosts were really touching me, it didn't matter if it was a moth. And if you believed that I'd get back with Drew, it didn't matter that I wouldn't. You believed it. But you have to understand. I'm not Melanie."

He blew out the flame. "Who told you about Melanie?"

"Tank told Jenna. She told me. Why didn't *you* tell me?"

"What was there to say?"

"I don't know. But you were asking about Drew. So it seems like you should have said something about her."

He sighed. "She doesn't matter."

"Neither does Drew."

And maybe he'd been agreeable to my only-while-we're-here terms because they made him feel as safe as they made me feel. No commitment. No breakup. No heartache.

"We had an agreement," I said quietly. "I'm still in New Orleans. So unless you're planning to leave —"

"I'm not leaving."

"Okay then. I've got you for three more weeks."

"And what's-his-name?"

"I'm not interested in him at all."

He shook his head. "I don't usually over-react to things. But all I could think was that the boyfriend was here and you'd hook back up. I guess I wanted to get out first, on my own terms."

Which I understood completely.

"But our terms are . . . as long as we're in New Orleans," I reminded him.

"And we're still in the Big Easy," he said.

I nodded.

"Okay then."

He leaned in, touched my cheek. "I'm sorry if I was a jerk."

I smiled. "Even Dr. Phil has a bad day now and then. Besides, the reason I was kissing you in the kitchen was wrong. You were right about that."

"I've really missed you," he said.

He leaned in closer and kissed me.

I couldn't have been happier. Not only were we back on speaking terms, we were back on kissing terms.

Chapter 21

I couldn't believe that we'd completed our first house.

The hammers were silent, the rubbish carted away. We'd planted two spindly trees.

The house itself was painted. Inside, it was sparsely furnished. But it did have curtains hanging from the windows to give it a welcoming touch. I had bought some dolls and put them in each of the pink bedrooms.

All the many volunteers stood on the lawn, near the front porch, waiting for the residents to return.

Brady was holding my hand, but then he usually did. He knew that I wasn't going to leave him for Drew. And not only because

Drew was no longer there.

Drew had decided to go back home after only a week in the Big Easy. At least he'd helped for a while.

I couldn't say I particularly liked him, but I did know that I didn't hate him anymore.

The funny thing was — after that first day, having Drew around really didn't bother me. He was not a part of my life any longer.

Brady was.

Things between us were . . . well, developing. We spent most evenings together, going somewhere to listen to a band or a musician.

I was noticing everything about him. I knew he put his sunglasses on two seconds before he stepped into the sun. Always.

I noticed that he looked great in wrinkled T-shirts. And all his T-shirts were wrinkled. Even right after he washed them, because his sorting system was one pile for clean clothes, one pile for dirty clothes.

"Folding, hanging stuff up — not how I want to spend my time," he'd told me.

Yeah, I'd been in his room a couple of times.

To watch pay-on-demand movies. And cuddle without everyone in New Orleans looking on. He never pushed, but he hinted that he was interested in seeing the bottom half of my tattoo—even though it was long gone.

I was thinking about getting another one. A permanent one. One that would be there when I was ready to share it with him.

Now, Jenna and Tank were standing near us. So were Amber and Sean. It was kind of funny that so many couples were around, that so many of us had bonded while building.

A car pulled up in front of the house, and a thrill shot through me. I couldn't believe how excited I was that the family was coming home. That we'd done what we could to ensure that they were able to come home.

John went to greet them. Holding her daughters' hands, the woman walked to the house and stepped up on the porch. She was younger than I'd expected her to be and pretty. She turned to face us, with tears in her eyes.

"Thank you," she said. "Thank you . . . so much."

We clapped and cheered, acknowledging her—that she was home again. That we were all glad.

John opened the door for her, and she walked inside. I could hear the patter of her daughters' feet as they raced through the house.

"Mama! My room is pink!" one of the girls shouted. "I love pink!"

Brady put his arm around me, hugged me. "Good choice," he said.

My throat was tight. All I could do was nod, as tears filled my eyes. I felt a little guilty that I'd originally planned to spend my summer going to water parks. If Drew hadn't been such a jerk, that's what I would have done. And I would have missed out on this sense of accomplishment.

John stepped out on the porch and clapped his hands. "All right, people! Your job is done. Enjoy the rest of the day. We start on the next one in the morning!"

Tank, Jenna, Brady, and I walked to Tank's car. Sean and Amber were catching a ride with Sara. We seldom rode with Ms. Wynder any-more. But, then, she was usually with John.

As we were driving away, I looked out the back window and watched the mother and her daughters waving at us from the front porch. Her daughters were clutching the dolls I'd left in their rooms. I felt . . . happy.

Wiping the tears from my eyes, I leaned my head back on the seat. "One down, and about a thousand to go."

"I think there's more than a thousand," Brady said.

I rolled my head to the side and looked at him. "How many houses do you think there are that need to be rebuilt?"

He shrugged. "A lot."

"Even after all this time?"

"Oh yeah. It takes a long time."

Yeah, I thought, looking at him, rebuilding does take a long time. But it was worth it. It was so worth it.

"I am so glad we decided to spend part of our summer here," Amber said, later that night, as we were holding our own celebration.

She, Jenna, and I were sitting on a park

bench. A jazz band was playing nearby. The guys had decided to take a walk around, do some people-watching.

I think they knew that we wanted some time alone.

"Yeah, me, too," I said, fingering the fleur-de-lis on the necklace that Brady had given me. I wore it all the time.

"This has been the best summer ever," Jenna said.

"And it's not over," I pointed out. "We've still got another week to go."

"Now that we know what we're doing, maybe the next house will go faster."

"Maybe."

"You want to hear something crazy?" Jenna asked.

Amber and I looked at her.

"I've been thinking about asking Sara if Tank and I will get married."

"You want to marry him?" Amber asked.

Jenna lifted her shoulders. "I've thought about it."

"And what if Sara gives you a cryptic answer

like, 'Yes, you'll both get married'?" I asked.

Jenna scowled. "That's the only thing stopping me. I'd worry about whether that meant to each other or to someone else."

"You know, Jenna, it doesn't really matter what she sees. You have to decide what's best for you. Even though she saw things, we were the ones who made them happen," I said. "You were crazy about Tank before you saw the dragon. Amber's reasons for coming back had nothing to do with Sara's predictions. She came back because she wanted to do good things. Have some purpose. And I'm with Brady because I want to be. Not because he has a red hat."

"Are you saying we'd be where we are, even if we hadn't had a reading?" Jenna asked.

"Yeah, I think so. It was fun, but we didn't make any of our decisions because we thought we had to make what Sara saw happen. We determine our destinies."

"That is so corny," Jenna said. "As corny as what Tank said that first night. But I like it. I like it a lot."

I looked up and saw the guys walking toward us.

I grabbed Jenna's and Amber's hands and closed my eyes. "I see a night on Bourbon Street in our future."

They laughed.

"That was an easy prediction," Jenna said. "It's Friday night!"

We got up from the bench.

"We thought we'd head on over to Bourbon Street," Tank said when they got to us. "See what's happening there."

Jenna smiled. "We figured."

I kept myself nestled against Brady's side as we walked along the now-familiar street. We strolled slowly, listening to bands, watching the people, and celebrating the completion of the house.

"You know what you need?" Brady asked.

I laughed, because I knew where this was going. Sara had definitely rubbed off on me.

"Beads," he said.

He grabbed my hand, and I let him drag me farther into the craziness that's Bourbon Street.

Chapter 22

*I*t was our last night in New Orleans. We'd finished gutting another house and were halfway completed with its rebuilding. I wanted to stay and finish it, but we needed to get home, needed to start getting ready for school to begin. Another group of volunteers was going to finish the house. John said he'd let us know when the job was completed, in case we wanted to come back and welcome the family home.

I thought I probably would.

John and Sara had arranged for us to have an all-night party on a riverboat, their way of thanking us for the help we'd given them over the past six weeks. Even though none of us thought thanks were needed, we weren't going to say no to a party.

Brady and I were standing by the railing on the upper deck watching one of the paddle-wheels churn through the water of the Mississippi. There was a romantic element to it, but then, New Orleans is a city of romance. Since I'd been here, I'd come to appreciate what it had to offer: its history, its ghosts, its food, its music . . . its love of life.

Sometimes I think it takes almost losing something to realize how very precious it is.

Like what happened with Brady. I almost lost him. And in the losing, I'd finally discovered what I'd found. During the last few weeks, we'd grown closer, but I felt like I still had so much to tell him, so much he needed to know.

I needed—wanted—to tell him everything tonight, because tomorrow we'd be going our separate ways.

"Feeling better?" Brady asked.

We'd been down below with the other volunteers when I'd started to feel a little seasick. Who knew you could feel seasick on a river? But I guess moving on water is moving on water, regardless of what you call it. So we came up top. I was fine as long as I had plenty of fresh air to breathe. I guessed that was why the swamp hadn't bothered me. We hadn't been enclosed.

"Yeah, I'm okay now."

"Then let's go get something to eat," he said. "I'm starving."

He always was. Still, I nodded. The moment wasn't right for what I wanted to say. Or maybe a small part of me was still afraid— afraid of being hurt again.

But being hurt is part of life. And you learn to rebuild.

New Orleans had taught me that. I figured there would be other storms . . . more rebuilding. The city would shift, reshape, and change, but the heart of it would remain the same.

With Brady holding my hand, we walked past some benches and said hey to the volunteers who were sitting there. Then we went down the stairs that led into the dining room. Jenna, Tank, Amber, and Sean waved at us from a cloth-covered table near a window.

Jenna and Tank—they were tighter than

ever. Definitely in love. They were going to keep seeing each other when we got back to Houston. Jenna was going to apply to Rice, so she could go there next year after she graduated. And if Rice didn't accept her—it had pretty tough academic requirements—well, there was another university in Houston and there were community colleges. They'd find a way to be together. I had a feeling Tank was it for Jenna. The real deal. Forever.

I wasn't quite as sure about Amber and Sean, but then neither was she. She didn't know if he was the college love that Sara had predicted. What she did know was that meeting Sean had shown her that Chad wasn't the right one. And maybe Sean wasn't, either. Time would tell. But I had a feeling there was someone else in Amber's future.

After all, Sara had said Amber wouldn't find love this summer.

Not that I believe in all that mumbo jumbo.

Well, okay, maybe I did a little. It was hard not to after everything that had happened.

Even if I did believe we were in charge of our own destinies.

"Wow. They've got quite a spread," Brady said.

And they did. Red crawfish—piled high on a platter and on Brady's plate. Plus there was gumbo, étouffée, fried alligator, an assortment of shrimp and fish and chicken. I went with the fried shrimp and a bowl of étouffée.

We carried our plates and bowls over to the table where our friends were waiting.

"Sara's over there doing readings," Jenna said once Brady and I were settled. "Twenty dollars a pop. The money goes toward the rebuilding efforts."

I glanced over my shoulder. Sara was in a corner with a large window behind her. The sun was setting and the river visible through the window almost glowed red.

She was also holding Ms. Wynder's hand. I could see Sara talking, but of course she was too far away for me to hear what she was saying.

"Think she's telling her that curly red hair is a permanent part of her future?" Jenna asked.

Watching and grinning, John was sitting

beside Ms. Wynder. They were always together. Ms. Wynder had even stopped doing bed checks. I think maybe it was because she wasn't always back in the dorm on time to make them. Not that I was going to tell my mom that. She might not let me come back next summer if she thought there was "craziness" going on.

But then how could there not be? This was New Orleans.

"Maybe," I said.

"That wouldn't be much of a prediction," Amber said. "Ms. Wynder already told me that she's going to organize a group to come back over winter break."

"I think there is definitely something going on with those two," I said.

"That is just so . . . I don't know what it is." Jenna sighed. "But I just don't think of older people as falling in love."

"She's not that old," I said.

"Still. She's a . . . teacher."

I laughed. "Teachers fall in love. I think it's terrific. I just wish Sara had ended up with someone."

"Do you think she's seen him? Do you think

she knows who he is?" Jenna asked.

We all looked at Sean. He was the one who had spent the most time with her—before Amber had come back.

"What are you looking at?" he asked.

"Did she ever say anything? About her future, about her falling in love?" I asked.

He cracked open a crab claw. "She's married."

I was sure my eyes grew as wide as Amber's and Jenna's. "*What*? But you and she—"

"Friends. That's all. She's fun. Interesting."

"And her husband didn't mind?" Jenna asked.

"He's in the military, overseas." He held up a hand. "But she sees him on their porch, playing with a little boy, and they don't have kids yet, so—" He shrugged.

For the first time, I really, really, *really* hoped there *was* something to what she could see.

"So are we going to ask for another reading before we leave?" I asked.

"No way," Amber said.

"Uh-uh," Jenna emphasized. "From now

on life is a surprise."

"'A box of chocolates,'" Amber quoted. "It's the only way."

On the top deck, a small jazz band—friends of John's—was playing, and the music drifted down to us. It kept everything festive and fun. I was going to miss all this when we left.

I was going to miss Brady most of all.

We danced some, visited with the other volunteers, and said good-bye to the numerous friends we'd made. We all promised to keep in touch, but I didn't know if we would. Maybe at first. But then we'd all get busy. And we'd all just become memories.

That's what was going to happen with Brady.

It was our pact, our understanding, our agreement. We were together only as long as we were in New Orleans. And our time here was ticking away much faster than I wanted it to.

It was getting close to dawn as we stood on the top deck of the riverboat and watched the lights of New Orleans drift past. He'd had his arm around me a good part of the night.

But right now he was leaning forward, his

elbows on the railing, his hands clasped, as the riverboat began heading back to the dock.

"So . . . I guess this is it," he finally said. "The end of our arrangement."

"About that . . ."

He turned his head around and met my gaze . . . and waited.

And waited.

While I tried to figure out if I was willing to risk having my heart broken again. Because I'd fallen for him—hard. And it could break—easily. And this time, it would hurt worse than before. So much worse. Hard to imagine, but I knew it was true.

"I was wondering . . . ," I began.

"Yeah?"

"You were really patient with me in the beginning, when I was so guy shy."

He shrugged.

"Did the psychic see more than life is good?"

"Maybe."

"Tell me."

"What does it matter?"

"It doesn't. I'm just curious."

He sighed. "'I see life is good, but I see hurt. You're trying to rebuild something, but don't build too fast or it'll crumble.' So I decided to go slow."

"But you told me you didn't believe in psychic stuff."

"I don't. But when I met you, I thought, why risk it?"

So he'd gone slow, and been patient, and been understanding. Maybe he'd thought he was rebuilding a house.

But he'd rebuilt my heart.

And maybe I'd helped, just a little, to rebuild his.

"I want to keep seeing you," I blurted. "When we get home."

A slow smile eased across his face. "Okay."

That was all he said, but it was everything.

And then he was kissing me. And that was definitely *everything*. I wrapped my arms around his neck and pressed my body against his. It felt so right. It all felt so incredibly right.

Brady drew back, kissed my nose, my chin,

my forehead. Then he turned me around, put his arms around my waist, and held me close while we watched the sun easing over the horizon in the distance.

Sara had told me that she didn't see how things would end for us. But the truth was that she *had* seen the ending. It was the very first thing she'd seen when she took my hand.

With Brady kissing my neck, I watched as the last of Saraphina's predictions came true. That morning, the sunrise was indeed . . . spectacular.

It always is, when you're in love.

Author's Note

In June 2006, I went to New Orleans to sign books at the Romance Writers of America's exhibition booth at the American Library Association Conference. According to numerous newspaper reports, it was the first conference held in New Orleans following the devastation of Katrina. We were welcomed with open arms.

Friday night, my husband and I ate dinner at Bubba Gump's Shrimp Company. We were seated on the second floor. At another table was a large group of teenagers from out of town. They were laughing, cutting up, having a great time—after a long day of helping with the rebuilding efforts. While I didn't talk to them, after they left, our waiter explained who they were and what they were doing.

They served as the inspiration for this story.

— Rachel Hawthorne

Read on for a sneak peek at

Save the Date

by Tamara Summers

I'm never having a wedding.

When I meet my dream boy—who will not be (a) boring, (b) obnoxiously fit, (c) an enormous role-playing dork, or (d) a Taiwanese model I barely know, like certain other people's husbands I could mention—my plan is to skip the whole inevitable wedding catastrophe. Instead we'll do it the old-fashioned way. I'll club him on the head, drag him off to Vegas, and marry him in a classy Elvis chapel, like our caveman ancestors would have wanted.

None of my five older sisters will have to be bridesmaids. They won't even have to come if they don't want to, except Sofia, who will be my maid of honor. And I won't force her to wear the most hideous dress I can find, because I, unlike most of my sisters, am a kind and thoughtful person with, I might add, a terrific sense of style.

Don't get me wrong; I love my sisters. I'm the baby of the family, so they've always taken care of me and treated me like their favorite toy when we were growing up. In fact, they were always super-nice to me, until they turned into brides. So despite the bridesmaid dresses they have forced me to wear and the weirdos they've married, I do love them.

It's just not safe to get married in this family, at least not if I, Jakarta Finnegan, bring a date to the wedding, which presumably I will to my own wedding. This is because the Finnegan family suffers from a terrible Wedding Curse, or at least I do. I don't know what we did to deserve it.

I didn't figure this out until after Wedding #2. I thought all the insanity at my oldest sister's wedding (#1) was normal behind-the-scenes craziness. When the best man got stuck in a snowstorm in Indiana—in JUNE—I was like,

2

Huh, weird, and then when the organ player at the church came down with the mumps (in this century?), I thought it was strange, and sure, we were all a little freaked out by the flock of seagulls that crashed through the skylight in the reception hall during the cake cutting, but at no point did I think *Oops, my fault* or *Maybe I should uninvite Patrick to the wedding*. Afterwards, when this very first boyfriend I ever had broke up with me and fled in terror, it did cross my mind that maybe fourteen-year-old boys aren't cut out for nuptial ceremonies.

But it wasn't until the next wedding that alarm bells started to go off in my head. For instance, the day I asked my new boyfriend David to be my wedding date, the groom broke his wrist playing tennis and all three hundred invitations arrived back on our doorstep in a giant pile because they were missing two cents of postage. The day before the wedding, on the phone, was the first time I told David I loved him, and at that exact moment I got call waiting. When I switched over, it was one of my uncles hysterically calling to tell us that the hotel where all the guests were supposed to stay had burned down. And *then*, on the way to the wedding, when I kissed David in the limousine, *lightning* struck the car in front of us, causing a massive six-car pile-up in which no one was hurt, but everyone involved in the ceremony was an hour late.

Lightning. Mumps. And *seagulls*. I'm telling you, I'm not crazy. This is a very real curse. And that's not even getting into the emotional wreckage afterwards with David, but I don't like to talk about that.

So you can see why I'm not crazy about the idea of having a wedding myself. Besides, all the good ideas have been taken. There's nothing else I could possibly do that hasn't been done before. That's what happens when you have five older sisters.

My parents are the Ken and Kathy of the Ken and Kathy's Travel Guide series. They travel all the time, always to exotic, fabulous, far-flung locales, and their house is full of wild foreign art and knickknacks. But it's one thing to hang an African mask on your wall or put down a Peruvian llama rug. It's another thing altogether to name your children after the cities you've traveled to, don't you think?

Mine is by far the worst, of course. I mean, it figures; I'm the youngest, with five older sisters, so they had obviously run out of decent names for girls by the time I came along.

My sisters don't have it so bad: Alexandria, Sydney, Victoria, Paris, and Sofia. Those could totally be normal-person names, couldn't they? Not like Jakarta. I mean, seriously.

Alexandria, the oldest, is twenty-eight now. She's a lawyer, and she's tall and thin and blond and perfect-looking all the time. She got married two years ago, to another lawyer, Harvey the Boringest Man on Earth. That was the wedding with the snowstorm and the mumps and the seagulls. The one where Patrick broke up with me.

Then there's Sydney, who's a year and a half younger. She's athletic and short and full of energy, and she's a pediatrician. She married her tennis instructor a year ago. When I say "obnoxiously fit"? You have no idea. Marco makes me tired just looking at him. Even when he's sitting at our kitchen table reading the newspaper, you can tell he's burning major calories. Their wedding was the one where the hotel burned down and lightning hit a car and David was a majorly enormous jerk.

After Sydney came Victoria and Paris, only ten months apart and about as different as two people can be. Victoria, our "romantic" sister, is willowy and pale, wears her hair long and flowing like a nymph in a Pre-Raphaelite painting, and is very sweet and quiet . . . or, at least she was until she became a bride-to-be. Paris, on the other hand, has bright red hair cropped close to her head, a nose ring, and a burning desire to be the world's most famous female glassblower. My mom says she's "an individual."

Paris was enough to keep my parents busy for four years. Personally, if I had a daughter like Paris, I wouldn't ever have sex again, just in case there was another one like her lurking in there. The world couldn't SURVIVE two Parises.

Luckily, what they got instead was Sofia, my twenty-year-old sister who is also my best friend and the biggest genius in the universe. She's graduating from college this year—she triple-majored and still finished in three years.

Then there's me. Recently turned seventeen. I have normal curly brown hair, shoulder-length, and normal gray eyes.

I'm not blond or super-fit or perfect. Not romantic, not "an individual," and definitely not a genius. So what am I? I'll tell you what: a bridesmaid.

It feels like I've been a bridesmaid for three years straight, and we're not even halfway through my sisters yet. Victoria's wedding is this summer and then Paris . . . well, we'll get to that in a minute.

Read on for a sneak peek at

Picture Perfect

by Catherine Clark

"I can't *wait* to see all the guys."

You might have thought that was me talking, as I headed into the town of Kill Devil Hills, North Carolina, my destination for a two-week summer stay on the Outer Banks.

But no. It was my dad, of all people.

And it's not what you might be thinking *now*, either. He was talking about seeing his best friends from college.

We meet up every few years on a big reunion trip with "the guys," their wives, their kids, and other assorted members of their families. I think it's Dad's favorite vacation, because he and his buddies play golf, sit around reminiscing, and stay up late talking every night.

1

Even though that occasionally gets a little boring, I like going on these trips, because I've gotten to be friends with "the guys'" offspring: Heather Olsen, Adam Thompson, and Spencer Flanagan. It had been two years since the last vacation reunion for the four of us, which was *almost*, but not quite, long enough to make me forget what an idiot I'd made of myself the last time, when I was fifteen, Spencer was sixteen, and I'd told him that I thought he was really cool and that we really clicked and that I wished we lived closer because then we could . . . well, you get the gist. *Embarrassing*. With a capital *E*. Maybe three of them, in fact. EEEmbarrassing. Like an extra-wide foot that I'd stuck in my mouth.

But enough about me and my slipup.

We were getting close to the house number we were looking for when Mom shrieked, "Look! There's the house!"

My dad slammed on the brakes, which screeched like the sound of a hundred wailing—and possibly ill—seals. Dad has this awful habit of calling Rent-a-Rustbucket in order to save

2

money. Consequently, we end up driving broken-down automobiles whenever we go on vacation.

Dad backed up and turned into a small parking lot behind the tall, skinny house.

Ten minutes later, after dumping my suitcase in my room, I stood on the giant back deck, overlooking the ocean.

Down by the water, some kids were playing in the sand, building sand castles and moats, while others swam and tried to ride waves on boogie boards.

"I've made a list of top ten Outer Banks destinations. I read eight different guidebooks and compiled my own list," my mom was explaining to Mrs. Thompson when I walked over to them. "We'll need to go food shopping tonight, of course, and make a schedule for who cooks which night."

"Oh, relax, you can do the shopping tomorrow. Things are very casual around here," Mrs. Thompson said to her. She turned to me. "You should go say hi to Adam. He's down there, in the water."

"He is?"

She gestured for me to join her at the edge of the deck. "He's right there. Don't you see him?"

All I could see except for young kids was a man with large shoulders doing the crawl, his arms powerfully slicing through the water. "That?" I coughed. "That person is Adam?"

His stepmom nodded. "Of course."

Wow. Really? I wanted to say. When I focused on him again, as he strode out of the surf, I nearly dropped my camera over the railing and into the sand. "You know what? I think I *will* go say hi." *Hi, and who are you, and what have you done with my formerly semi-wimpy friend?*

I walked down the steps to the beach in disbelief. Last time I'd seen Adam, his voice was squeaking, and he was on the scrawny side—a wrestler at one of the lower weights, like 145. Not anymore. He had muscular arms and shoulders, and he looked about a foot taller than he had two years ago. His curly brown hair was cut short.

You look different, I wanted to say, but that would be dumb. *You look different and I sound like an idiot, so really, nothing's changed.*

4

Why was it that whenever I tried to talk to a guy, I started speaking a completely different language? Stupidese?

"Emily?" he asked.

I nodded, noticing that his voice was slightly deeper than I remembered it. It was sort of like he'd gone into a time machine and come out in the future, whereas I felt exactly the same. "Hi."

He leaned back into the surf to wet his hair. "You look different," he said when he stood up.

"Oh, yeah? I do?" *Different how?* I wanted to ask, but that was potentially embarrassing. Different in the way he did? Like . . . sexy? I waited for him to elaborate, but he didn't. "Well, uh, you do, too," I said.

"Right." He smiled, then picked up his towel and dried his hair. As he had the towel over his head, I took the opportunity to check him out again. Man. What a difference a couple years could make.

Praise for

Michael Robotham

and

THE NIGHT FERRY

"[Robotham] **never fails to entertain**."
—*The Tampa Tribune*

"Popular fiction's **Next Big Thing**."
—*The Times Magazine*, London

"*The Night Ferry* is all about the human heart—**heart-stopping, heart-breaking and heart-wrenching**."
—Val McDermid

"Robotham excels at braiding together **gut-wrenching issues, strong characters and page-turning action**."
—*Mystery Scene*

"**Deeply moving**. . . . Takes us deep into a set of humanitarian concerns by making us care about the characters involved."
—*Sydney Morning Herald*

ALSO BY MICHAEL ROBOTHAM

Suspect

Lost

Michael Robotham

THE NIGHT FERRY

Michael Robotham is the author of *Suspect* and *Lost*. He lives in Sydney, Australia.

www.michaelrobotham.com

THE
NIGHT
FERRY

THE
NIGHT
FERRY

Michael Robotham

VINTAGE CRIME/BLACK LIZARD
Vintage Books
A Division of Random House, Inc.
New York

FIRST VINTAGE CRIME/BLACK LIZARD EDITION, JULY 2008

The Library of Congress has cataloged the
Doubleday edition as follows:
Robotham, Michael, 1960–
The night ferry : a novel / Michael Robotham—1st ed.
p. cm.
1. London (England)—Fiction.
2. Amsterdam (Netherlands)—Fiction.
I. Title.
PR6118.O26 N54 2007
823/.92 22

Vintage ISBN: 978-0-307-27585-1

www.vintagebooks.com

Printed in the United States of America
10 9 8 7 6 5 4 3 2 1

This one is for Alpheus "Two Dogs" Williams,
a mentor and a mate

Acknowledgments

This is a story that could not have been told without Esther Brandt and Jacqueline de Jong, who were invaluable in helping my research. Through them I met Sytze van der Zee, Leo Rietveld and the remarkable Joep de Groot, my guide through Amsterdam's famous red light district.

Elsewhere I am indebted to Ursula Mackenzie and Mark Lucas for their friendship, advice and belief that I have something inside me that is worth writing. For their hospitality I am grateful to Richard, Emma, Mark and Sara. And I'd be lost without my three daughters, Alex, Charlotte and Bella, who make me laugh and forget work.

Yet again, however, it is Vivien who deserves most of the credit. My researcher, plotter, reader, reviewer, lover and wife, she is my love story.

BOOK
ONE

When the first baby laughed for the first time, the laugh broke into a thousand pieces and they all went skipping about, and that was the beginning of fairies.

—SIR JAMES BARRIE,
Peter Pan

1

It was Graham Greene who said a story has no beginning or end. The author simply chooses a moment, an arbitrary point, and looks either forward or back. That moment is now—an October morning—when the clang of a metallic letter flap heralds the first post.

There is an envelope on the mat inside my front door. Inside is a small stiff rectangle of paper that says nothing and everything.

> *Dear Ali,*
>
> *I'm in trouble. I must see you. Please come to the reunion.*
>
> *Love, Cate*

Sixteen words. Long enough to be a suicide note. Short enough to end an affair. I don't know why Cate has written to me now. She hates me. She told me so the last time we spoke, eight years ago. The past. Given long enough I could tell you the month, the day and the hour but these details are unimportant.

All you need to know is the year—1998. It should have been the summer we finished university; the summer we went backpacking across Europe; the summer I lost my virginity to Brian Rusconi and not to Cate's father. Instead it was the summer she went away and the summer I left home—a summer not big enough for everything that happened.

Now she wants to see me again. Sometimes you know when a story begins . . .

2

When the day comes that I am asked to recalibrate the calendar, I am going to lop a week off January and February and add them to October, which deserves to be forty days long, maybe more.

I love this time of year. The tourists have long gone and the kids are back at school. The TV schedules aren't full of reruns and I can sleep under a duvet again. Mostly I love the sparkle in the air, without the pollen from the plane trees so I can open my lungs and run freely.

I run every morning—three circuits of Victoria Park in Bethnal Green, each one of them more than a mile. Right now I'm just passing Durward Street in Whitechapel. Jack the Ripper territory. I once took a Ripper walking tour, a pub crawl with ghost stories. The victim I remember best was his last one, Mary Kelly, who died on the same date as my birthday, November the ninth.

People forget how small an area Jack roamed. Spitalfields, Shoreditch and Whitechapel cover less than a

5

square mile, yet in 1888 more than a million people were crammed into slums, without decent water and sewerage. It is still overcrowded and poor but that's only compared to places like Hampstead or Chiswick or Holland Park. Poverty is a relative state in a rich country where the wealthiest are the first to cry poor.

It is seven years since I last ran competitively, on a September night in Birmingham, under lights. I wanted to get to the Sydney Olympics but only two of us were going to make it. Four-hundredths of a second separated first from fifth; half a meter, a heartbeat, a broken heart.

I don't run to win anymore. I run because I can and because I'm fast. Fast enough to blur at the edges. That's why I'm here now, flirting with the ground while perspiration leaks between my breasts, plastering my T-shirt to my stomach.

When I run my thoughts become clearer, or at least concentrated. Mostly I think about work and imagine that today someone will call and offer me my old job back.

A year ago I helped solve a kidnapping and find a missing girl. One of the kidnappers dropped me onto a wall, crushing my spine. After six operations and nine months of physiotherapy I am fit again, with more steel in my spine than England's back four. Unfortunately, nobody seems to know what to do with me at the Metropolitan Police. I am a wonky wheel on the machine.

As I pass the playground, I notice a man sitting on a bench reading a newspaper. There is no child on the climbing frame behind him and other benches are in sunshine. Why has he chosen the shade?

In his mid-thirties, dressed in a shirt and tie, he doesn't raise his eyes as I pass. He's studying a crossword.

6

What sort of man does a crossword in a park at this hour of the morning? A man who can't sleep. A man who waits.

Up until a year ago I used to watch people for a living. I guarded diplomats and visiting heads of state, ferrying their wives on shopping trips to Harrods and dropping their children at school. It is probably the most boring job in the Metropolitan Police but I was good at it. During five years with the Diplomatic Protection Group I didn't fire a shot in anger or miss one of the wives' hair appointments. I was like one of those soldiers who sit in the missile silos, praying the phone never rings.

On my second circuit of the park he is still there. His suede jacket is lying across his lap. He has freckles and smooth brown hair, cut symmetrically and parted to the left. A leather briefcase is tucked close to his side.

A gust of wind tears the newspaper from his fingers. Three steps and I reach it first. It wraps around my thigh.

For a moment he wants to retreat, as if he's too close to the edge. His freckles make him look younger. His eyes don't meet mine. Instead he bunches his shoulders shyly and says thank you. The front page is still wrapped around my thigh. For a moment I'm tempted to have some fun. I could make a joke about feeling like tomorrow's fish-and-chips.

The breeze feels cool on my neck. "Sorry, I'm rather sweaty."

He touches his nose nervously, nods and touches his nose again.

"Do you run every day?" he asks suddenly.

"I try to."

"How far?"

"Four miles."

It's an American accent. He doesn't know what else to say.

"I have to keep going. I don't want to cool down."

"Okay. Sure. Have a nice day." It doesn't sound so trite coming from an American.

On my third circuit of the park the bench is empty. I look for him along the street but there are no silhouettes. Normal service has been resumed.

Farther along the street, just visible on the corner, a van is parked at the curb. As I draw nearer, I notice a white plastic tent over missing paving stones. A metal cage is propped open around the hole. They've started work early.

I do this sort of thing—take note of people and vehicles. I look for things that are out of the ordinary; people in the wrong place, or the wrong clothes; cars parked illegally; the same face in different locations. I can't change what I am.

Unlacing my trainers, I pull a key from beneath the insole and unlock my front door. My neighbor, Mr. Mordecai, waves from his window. I once asked him his first name and he said it should be Yo'man.

"Why's that?"

"Because that's what my boys call me: 'Yo man, can I have some money?' 'Yo man, can I borrow the car?' "

His laugh sounded like nuts falling on a roof.

In the kitchen I pour myself a large glass of water and drink it greedily. Then I stretch my quads, balancing one leg on the back of a chair.

The mouse living under my fridge chooses that moment to appear. It is a very ambivalent mouse, scarcely bothering to lift its head to acknowledge me. And it doesn't seem to mind that my youngest brother,

Hari, keeps setting mousetraps. Perhaps it knows that I disarm them, taking off the cheese when Hari isn't around.

The mouse finally looks up at me, as though about to complain about the lack of crumbs. Then it sniffs the air and scampers away.

Hari appears in the doorway, bare-chested and bare-footed. Opening the fridge, he takes out a carton of orange juice and unscrews the plastic lid. He looks at me, considers his options, and gets a glass from the cupboard. Sometimes I think he is prettier than I am. He has longer lashes and thicker hair.

"Are you going to the reunion tonight?" I ask.

"Nope."

"Why not?"

"Don't tell me *you're* going! You said you wouldn't be caught dead."

"I changed my mind."

There is a voice from upstairs. "Hey, have you seen my knickers?"

Hari looks at me sheepishly.

"I know I had a pair. They're not on the floor."

Hari whispers, "I thought you'd gone out."

"I went for a run. Who is she?"

"An old friend."

"So you must know her name."

"Cheryl."

"Cheryl Taylor!" (She's a bottle blonde who works behind the bar at the White Horse.) "She's older than I am."

"No, she's not."

"What on earth do you see in her?"

"What difference does that make?"

"I'm interested."

"Well, she has assets."

"Assets?"

"The best."

"You think so?"

"Absolutely."

"What about Phoebe Griggs?"

"Too small."

"Emma Shipley?"

"Saggy."

"Mine?"

"Very funny."

Cheryl is coming down the stairs. I can hear her rummaging in the sitting room. "Found them," she shouts.

She arrives in the kitchen still adjusting the elastic beneath her skirt.

"Oh, hello," she squeaks.

"Cheryl, this is my sister, Alisha."

"Nice to see you again," she says, not meaning it.

The silence seems to stretch out. I might never talk again. Finally I excuse myself and go upstairs for a shower. With any luck Cheryl will be gone by the time I come down.

Hari has been living with me for the past two months because it's closer to university. He is supposed to be safeguarding my virtue and helping pay the mortgage but he's four weeks behind in his rent and using my spare room as a knocking shop.

My legs are tingling. I love the feeling of lactic acid leaking away. I look in the mirror and pull back my hair. Yellow flecks spark in my irises like goldfish in a pond. There are no wrinkles. Black don't crack.

My "assets" aren't so bad. When I was running competitively I was always pleased they were on the small side and could be tightly bound in a sports bra. Now I wouldn't mind being a size bigger so I could have a cleavage.

Hari yells up the stairs. "Hey, sis, I'm taking twenty from your purse."

"Why?"

"Because when I take it from strangers they get angry."

Very droll. "You still owe me rent."

"Tomorrow."

"You said that yesterday." *And the day before.*

The front door closes. The house is quiet.

Downstairs, I pick up Cate's note again, resting it between my fingertips. Then I prop it on the table against the salt and pepper shakers, staring at it for a while.

Cate Elliot. Her name still makes me smile. One of the strange things about friendship is that time together isn't canceled out by time apart. One doesn't erase the other or balance it on some invisible scale. You can spend a few hours with someone and they will change your life, or you can spend a lifetime with a person and remain unchanged.

We were born at the same hospital and raised in Bethnal Green in London's East End although we managed to more or less avoid each other for the first thirteen years. Fate brought us together, if you believe in such things.

We became inseparable. Almost telepathic. We were partners in crime, stealing beer from her father's fridge, window shopping on the Kings Road, eating chips with vinegar on our way home from school, sneaking out to see bands at the Hammersmith Odeon and movie stars on the red carpet at Leicester Square.

In our gap year we went to France. I crashed a moped, got cautioned for having a fake ID and tried hash for the first time. Cate lost the key to our hostel during a midnight swim and we had to climb a trellis at 2:00 a.m.

There is no breakup worse than that of best friends. Broken love affairs are painful. Broken marriages are messy. Broken homes are sometimes an improvement. Our breakup was the worst.

Now, after eight years, she wants to see me. The thrill of compliance spreads across my skin. Then comes a nagging, unshakable dread. She's in trouble.

My car keys are in the sitting room. As I pick them up, I notice marks on the glass-topped coffee table. Looking closer, I can make out two neat buttock prints and what I imagine to be elbow smudges. I could kill my brother!

3

Someone has spilled a Bloody Mary mix on my shoes. I wouldn't mind so much, but they're not mine. I borrowed them, just like I borrowed this top, which is too big for me. At least my underwear is my own. "Never borrow money or underwear," my mother always says, in an addendum to her clean-underwear speech which involves graphic descriptions of road accidents and ambulance officers cutting off my tights. No wonder I have nightmares.

Cate isn't here yet. I've been trying to watch the door and avoid talking to anyone.

There should be a law against school reunions. They should come with warning stickers on the invitations. There is never a right time for them. You're either too young or too old or too fat.

This isn't even a proper school reunion. Somebody burned down the science classrooms at Oaklands. A vandal with a can of petrol rather than a rogue Bunsen burner. Now they're opening a brand-new block, with a junior minister of something-or-other doing the honors.

The new building is functional and sturdy, with none of the charm of the Victorian original. The cathedral ceilings and arched windows have been replaced by fibrous cement panels, strip lighting and aluminum frames.

The school hall has been decorated with streamers and balloons hang from the rafters. A school banner is draped across the front of the stage.

There is a queue for the mirror in the girls' toilets. Lindsay Saunders leans past me over the sink and rubs lipstick from her teeth. Satisfied, she turns and appraises me.

"Will you stop acting like a Punjabi princess and loosen up. Have fun."

"Is that what this is?"

I'm wearing Lindsay's top, the bronze one with shoe-string straps, which I don't have the bust to carry off. A strap falls off my shoulder. I tug it up again.

"I know you're acting like you don't care. You're just nervous about Cate. Where is she?"

"I don't know."

Lindsay reapplies her lipstick and adjusts her dress. She's been looking forward to the reunion for weeks because of Rocco Manspiezer. She fancied him for six years at school but didn't have the courage to tell him.

"What makes you so sure you'll get him this time?"

"Well I didn't spend two hundred quid on this dress and squeeze into these bloody shoes to be ignored by him again."

Unlike Lindsay, I have no desire to hang around with people I have spent twelve years avoiding. I don't want to hear how much money they make or how big their

14

house is or see photographs of their children who have names that sound like brands of shampoo.

That's the thing about school reunions—people only come to measure their life against others and to see the failures. They want to know which of the beauty queens has put on seventy pounds and seen her husband run off with his secretary, and which teacher got caught taking photographs in the changing rooms.

"Come on, aren't you curious?" Lindsay asks.

"Of course, I'm curious. I *hate* the fact I'm curious. I just wish I was invisible."

"Don't be such a spoilsport." She rubs her finger across my eyebrows. "Did you see Annabelle Trunzo? My God that dress! And what about her hair?"

"Rocco doesn't even have any hair."

"Ah, but he's still looking fit."

"Is he married?"

"Hush your mouth."

"Well, I think you should at least find out before you shag him."

She gives me a wicked grin. "I'll ask afterward."

Lindsay acts like a real man-eater, but I know she's not really so predatory. I tell myself that all the time, but I still wouldn't let her date my brothers.

Back in the hall, the lights have been turned down and the music turned up. Spandau Ballet has been replaced by eighties anthems. The women are wearing a mixture of cocktail dresses and saris. Others are pretending not to care, in leather jackets and designer jeans.

There were always tribes at Oaklands. The whites were a minority. Most of the students were Banglas (Bangladeshis) with a few Pakis and Indians thrown into the mix.

I was a "curry," a "yindoo," an "elephant trainer." Brown Indian in case you're wondering. As defining details go, nothing else came close at Oaklands—not my black hair, braces or skinny legs; not having glandular fever at seven, or being able to run like the wind. Everything else paled into insignificance alongside my skin color and Sikh heritage.

It's not true that all Sikhs are called Singh. And we don't all carry curved blades strapped to our chests (although in the East End having this sort of rep isn't such a bad thing).

Even now the Banglas are sticking together. People are sitting next to the same people they sat alongside at school. Despite everything that has happened in the intervening years, the core facets of our personalities are untouched. All our flaws and strengths are the same.

On the far side of the hall I see Cate arriving. She is pale and striking, with a short expensive haircut and cheap sexy shoes. Dressed in a long light khaki skirt and a silk blouse, she looks elegant and, yes, pregnant. Her hands are smoothing her neat, compact bump. It's more than a bump. A beach ball. She hasn't long to go.

I don't want her to see me staring. I turn away.

"Alisha?"

"Sure. Who else?" I turn suddenly and put on a goofy smile.

Cate leans forward and kisses my cheek. I don't close my eyes. Neither does she. We stare at each other. Surprised. She smells of childhood.

There are fine lines at the corners of her eyes. I wasn't there to see them drawn. The small scar on her left temple, just beneath her hairline, I remember that one.

We're the same age, twenty-nine, and the same shape,

except for the bump. I have darker skin and hidden depths (like all brunettes) but I can categorically state that I will never look as good as Cate. She has learned—no, that makes it sound too practiced—she was born with the ability to make men admire her. I don't know the secret. A movement of the eye, a cock of the head, a tone of voice or a touch of the arm, creates a moment, an illusion that all men gay or straight, old or young buy into.

People are watching her now. I doubt if she even realizes.

"How are you?"

"I'm fine," I answer too quickly and start again. "I'm all right."

"Just all right?"

I try to laugh. "But look at you—you're pregnant."

"Yes."

"When are you due?"

"In four weeks."

"Congratulations."

"Thank you."

The questions and answers are too abrupt and matter-of-fact. Conversation has never been this hard—not with Cate. She looks nervously over my shoulder, as if worried we might be overheard.

"Didn't you marry—?"

"Felix Beaumont. He's over there."

I follow her eyes to a tall, heavy-set figure in casual trousers and a loose white shirt. Felix didn't go to Oaklands and his real name is Buczkowski, not "Beaumont." His father was a Polish shopkeeper who ran an electronics shop on Tottenham Court Road.

Now he's deep in conversation with Annabelle Trunzo,

whose dress is a scrap of material held up by her chest. If she exhales it's going to be bunched around her ankles.

"You know what I used to hate most about nights like this?" says Cate. "Having someone who looks immaculate telling me how she spent all day ferrying children to ballet or football or cricket. And then she asks the obvious question: 'Do you have any kids?' And I say, 'Nope, no children.' And she jokes, 'Hey, why don't you have one of mine?' God that pisses me off."

"Well, it won't happen anymore."

"No."

She takes a glass of wine from a passing tray. Again she glances around, looking distracted.

"Why did we fall out? It must have been my fault."

"I'm sure you remember," I say.

"It doesn't matter anymore. By the way, I want you to be a godparent."

"I'm not even a Christian."

"Oh, that doesn't matter."

Cate is avoiding whatever she really wants to talk about.

"Tell me what's wrong."

She hesitates. "I've gone too far this time, Ali. I've risked everything."

Taking her arm, I steer her toward a quiet corner. People are starting to dance. The music is too loud. Cate puts her mouth close to my ear. "You have to help me. Promise me you'll help me . . ."

"Of course."

She holds back a sob, seeming to bite down upon it. "They want to take my baby. They can't. You have to stop them—"

A hand touches her shoulder and she jumps, startled.

"Hello, gorgeous pregnant lady, who have we here?"

Cate backs away a step. "No one. It's just an old friend." Something shifts inside her. She wants to escape.

Felix Beaumont has perfect teeth. My mother has a thing about dental work. It is the first thing she notices about people.

"I remember you," he says. "You were behind me."

"At school?"

"No, at the bar."

He laughs and adopts an expression of amused curiosity.

Cate has backed farther away. My eyes find hers. The faintest shake of her head tells me to let her go. I feel a rush of tenderness toward her. She motions with her empty glass. "I'm just going to get a refill."

"Go easy on that stuff, sweetheart. You're not alone." He brushes her bump.

"Last one."

Felix watches her leave with a mixture of sadness and longing. Finally, he turns back to me.

"So is it Miss or Mrs.?"

"Pardon?"

"Are you married?"

I hear myself say "Ms." which makes me sound like a lesbian. I change it to "Miss" and then blurt, "I'm single," which appears desperate.

"That explains it."

"What?"

"Those with children have photographs. Those without have nicer clothes and fewer lines."

Is that supposed to be a compliment?

The skin around his eyes crinkles into a smile. He moves like a bear, rocking from foot to foot.

"So what do you do?"

I hold out my hand. "My name is Alisha Barba."

He looks astonished. "Well, well, well, you *really* exist. Cate has talked about you a lot but I thought you might be one of those imaginary childhood friends."

"She's talked about me?"

"Absolutely. What do you do, Alisha?"

"I sit at home all day in my slippers watching daytime soaps and old movies on Channel 4."

He doesn't understand.

"I'm on medical leave from the Metropolitan Police."

"What happened?"

"I broke my back. Someone dropped me across a wall."

He flinches. My gaze drifts past him.

"She's coming back," he says, reading my mind. "She never leaves me talking to a pretty woman for too long."

"You must be thrilled—about the baby."

The smooth hollow beneath his Adam's apple rolls like a wave as he swallows. "It's our miracle baby. We've been trying for so long."

Someone has started a conga line on the dance floor, which snakes between the tables. Gopal Dhir grabs at my waist, pivoting my hips from side to side. Someone else pulls Felix into another part of the line and we're moving apart.

Gopal yells into my ear. "Well, well, Alisha Barba. Are you still running?"

"Only for fun."

"I always fancied you but you were far too quick for me." He yells to someone over his shoulder. "Hey, Rao! Look who it is—Alisha Barba. Didn't I always say she was cute?"

Rao has no hope of hearing him over the music, but nods vigorously and kicks out his heels.

I drag myself away.

"Why are you leaving?"

"I refuse to do the conga without a person from Trinidad being present."

Disappointed, he lets me go and rocks his head from side to side. Someone else tries to grab me but I spring away.

The crowd around the bar has thinned out. I can't see Cate. People are sitting on the steps outside and spilling into the quadrangle. Across the playground I can see the famous oak tree, almost silver in the lights. Someone has put chicken wire around the trunk to stop children climbing. One of the Banglas fell off and broke his arm during my last year—a kid called Paakhi, which is Bengali for bird. What's in a name?

The new science block squats on the far side of the quadrangle. Deserted. Crossing the playground, I push open a door and enter a long corridor with classrooms to the left. Taking a few steps, I look inside. Chrome taps and curved spouts pick up faint light from the windows.

As my eyes adjust to the darkness, I see someone moving. A woman with her dress pushed up over her waist is arched over a bench with a man between her legs.

Backing away toward the door, I sense that someone else is watching. The smallest shift of my gaze finds him.

He whispers, "Like to watch do you, yindoo?"

I catch my breath. A half breath. Paul Donavon pushes his face close to mine. The years have thinned his hair and fleshed out his cheeks but he has the same eyes. It's amazing how I can hate him with the same intensity after all this time.

Even in the half-light, I notice the tattooed cross on his neck. He sniffs at my hair. "Where's Cate?"

"You leave her alone," I say too loudly.

There are curses from the darkness. Lindsay and partner pull apart. Rocco is dancing on one leg, trying to hoist his trousers. At the far end of the corridor a door opens and light washes from outside as Donavon disappears.

"Jesus, Ali, you frightened the crap out of me," says Lindsay, tugging down her dress.

"Sorry."

"Who else was here?"

"Nobody. I'm really sorry. Just carry on."

"I think the moment's gone."

Rocco is already heading down the corridor.

"Give my best to your wife," she calls after him.

I have to find Cate now. She should be told that Donavon is here. And I want her to explain what she meant. Who wants to take her baby?

I check the hall and the quadrangle. There is no sign of her. She might have left already. How strange it is to be conscious of losing her when I've only just met her again.

I walk to the school gates. Cars are parked on either side of the road. The pavement is dotted with people. I catch a glimpse of Cate and Felix on the far side. She is talking to someone. Donavon. She has her hand on his arm.

Cate looks up and waves. I'm closing the distance between us, but she signals me to wait. Donavon turns away. Felix and Cate step between parked cars.

From somewhere behind them I hear Donavon cry out. Then comes a tortured high-pitched screech of rubber against tarmac. The wheels of a car are locked and screaming. Heads turn as if released from a catch.

Felix vanishes beneath the wheels, which rise and fall over his head with scarcely a bump. At the same moment Cate bends over the hood and springs back again. She turns her head in midair and the windscreen suddenly snaps it in reverse. She tumbles through the air in slow motion like a trapeze artist ready to be caught. But nobody waits with chalky hands.

The driver brakes and slews. Cate rolls forward, landing on her back with her arm outstretched and one leg twisted beneath her.

Like an explosion in reverse, people are sucked toward the detonation. They scramble from cars and burst from doorways. Donavon reacts quicker than most and reaches Cate first. I drop to my knees beside him.

In a moment of suspended stillness, the three of us are drawn together again. She is lying on the road. Blood seeps from her nose in a deep soft satin blackness. Spittle bubbles and froths from her slightly parted lips. She has the prettiest mouth.

I cradle her head in the crook of my arm. What happened to her shoe? She only has one of them. Suddenly, I'm fixated on a missing shoe, asking people around me. It's important that I find it. Black, with a half heel. Her skirt has ridden up. She's wearing maternity knickers to cover her bump.

A young chap steps forward politely. "I've called 999." His girlfriend looks like she might be sick.

Donavon pulls down Cate's skirt. "Don't move her head. She has to be braced." He turns to the onlookers. "We need blankets and a doctor."

"Is she dead?" someone asks.

"Do you know her?" asks another.

"She's pregnant!" exclaims a third person.

Cate's eyes are open. I can see myself reflected in them. A burly man with a gray ponytail leans over us. He has an Irish accent.

"They just stepped out. I didn't see them. I swear."

Cate's whole body goes rigid and her eyes widen. Even with blood in her mouth she tries to cry out and her head swings from side to side.

Donavon leaps to his feet and grabs the driver's shirt. "You could have stopped, you bastard!"

"I didn't see them."

"LIAR!" His voice is hoarse with hate. "You ran them down."

The driver glances nervously around the crowd. "I don't know what he's talking about. It was an accident, I swear. He's talking crazy—"

"You saw them."

"Not until it was too late . . ."

He pushes Donavon away. Buttons rip and the driver's shirt flaps open. The tattoo on his chest is of Christ and the Crucifixion.

People have piled out of the reunion to see what the commotion is about. Some of them are yelling and trying to clear the street. I can hear the sirens.

A paramedic pushes through the crowd. My fingers are slick and warm. I feel like I'm holding Cate's head together. Two more crews arrive. The paramedics team up. I know the drill: no fire, no fuel leaks and no fallen power lines—they secure their own safety first.

I look for Felix. A dark shape is pinned beneath the rear axle of the car. Unmoving.

A paramedic crawls beneath the wheel arch. "This one's gone," he yells.

Another slides his hands beneath mine, taking hold of Cate's head. Two of them work on her.

"Airways are blocked. Using the Guedels."

He puts a plastic curved tube in her mouth and suctions out blood.

"One seventy systolic over ninety. Right pupil dilated."

"She's hypotensive."

"Put a collar on."

Someone talks into a two-way. "We got serious head trauma and internal bleeding."

"She's pregnant," I hear myself saying. I don't know if they hear me.

"BP is climbing. Low pulse."

"She's bleeding into her skull."

"Let's get her inside."

"She needs volume now."

The spine board is placed beside her and Cate is log-rolled onto her side and lifted onto a stretcher.

"She's pregnant," I say again.

The paramedic turns to me.

"Do you know her?"

"Yes."

"We got room for one. You can ride up front." He is pumping a rubber bag, forcing air into her lungs. "We need her name, DOB, address—is she allergic to any drugs?"

"I don't know."

"When is she due?"

"In four weeks."

The stretcher is in the ambulance. The paramedics

climb inside. A medical technician hustles me into the passenger seat. The door shuts. We're moving. Through the window I see the crowd staring at us. Where did they all come from? Donavon is sitting in the gutter, looking dazed. I want him to look at me. I want to say thank you.

The paramedics continue working on Cate. One of them talks into a two-way using words like bradycardia and intracranial pressure. A heart monitor beeps out a broken message.

"Is she going to be all right?"

Nobody answers.

"What about the baby?"

He unbuttons her blouse. "I'm running two units."

"No, wait. I've lost her pulse."

The monitor flatlines.

"She's asystolic!"

"Starting compressions."

He rips open the final buttons, exposing her bra and torso.

Both paramedics suddenly stop and raise their eyes to each other—a single look, no words, but it conveys everything. Strapped to Cate's midriff is a large piece of upholstery foam, trimmed to fit over her stomach. The prosthetic is pulled away. Cate is "pregnant" no more.

Pushing down hard on her chest, a paramedic counts the compressions, yelling the numbers. The heart monitor is competing with the siren.

"No response."

"We might have to crack her open."

"One amp of adrenaline." He bites off the cap and stabs the contents into her neck.

The next few minutes pass in a blur of flashing lights

and fractured conversations. I know they're losing her. I guess I've known it all along. The dilated pupils, the bleeding inside her head—the classic signs of brain injury. Cate is broken in too many places to fix.

A thin green line on the monitor rises and falls and flattens again. They're counting each inflation with the chest compressions. One squeeze to every five compressions.

"Thommo."

"What?"

"I'm stopping the chest compressions."

"Why?"

"Because they're making her brains come out of her head."

Cate's skull is broken behind her right ear.

"Keep going."

"But—"

"Just keep going."

Half a minute passes. Hard as they try, Cate's heart won't answer.

"What are you going to do?"

"Crack her chest."

A wave of nausea washes into my mouth. I don't remember the rest of the journey or arriving at the hospital. There are no crashing doors or white coats rushing down corridors. Instead, everything appears to slow down. The building swallows Cate whole, less than whole, damaged.

Hospitals, I hate them. The smell, the pall of uncertainty, the whiteness. White walls, white sheets, white clothes. The only things not white are the bodily fluids and the Afro-Caribbean nurses.

I'm still standing near the ambulance. The paramedics return and begin mopping up the blood.

"Are you gonna be OK?" one of them asks. The pillow of upholstery foam hangs from his fist. The dangling straps look like the legs of a strange sea creature.

He hands me a damp paper towel. "You might want to use this."

I have blood on my hands; blood all over my jeans.

"You missed a bit." He motions to my cheek. I wipe the wrong one.

"Here, do you mind?"

He takes the towel and holds my chin in the palm of his hand, wiping my cheek. "There."

"Thank you."

He wants to say something. "Is she a close friend?"

"We went to school together."

He nods. "Why would she—I mean—why did she fake a pregnancy?"

I glance past him, unable to answer. It doesn't serve any purpose and makes even less sense. Cate needed to see me. She said they wanted to take her baby. What baby?

"Is she—will she be OK?"

It's his turn to not answer. The sadness in his eyes is rationed carefully because others will need it later.

A hose spits. Pink water swirls down the drain. The paramedic hands me the prosthetic and I feel something break inside me. Once I thought I had lost Cate forever. Maybe this time I have.

4

Hospital waiting rooms are useless, helpless places, full of whispers and prayers. Nobody wants to look at me. I have tried to clean Lindsay's top in the bathroom, scrubbing it under the tap with hand soap. I only managed to spread the stain around.

Doctors and nurses wander in and out, never able to relax. One patient on a trolley looks like a fly caught in a web of tubes and wires. The skin around his mouth is puckered and dry.

I have never really thought about death. Even when I was lying in hospital with pins holding my spine together, it didn't occur to me. I have faced off suspects, pursued cars, charged through doorways and walked into abandoned buildings but have never thought that I might die. Maybe that's one of the advantages of having little self-value.

A nurse has taken down details of Cate's family. I don't know about Felix. His mother might still be alive. Nobody can tell me anything except that Cate is in surgery. The nurses are relentlessly positive. The doctors are more circumspect. They have the truth to contend with—the reality of what they can and cannot fix.

In the midst of an ordinary evening, on a quiet street, a couple are hit by a car. One is dead. The other has horrific injuries. What happened to Cate's other shoe? What happened to her baby?

A policeman arrives to interview me. He is my age, wearing a uniform with everything polished and pressed. I feel self-conscious about my appearance.

He has a list of questions—what, where, when and why. I try to remember everything that happened. The car came out of nowhere. Donavon yelled.

"So you think it was an accident?"

"I don't know."

In my head I can hear Donavon accusing the driver of running them down. The policeman gives me a card. "If you remember anything more, give me a call."

———

Through the swing doors, I see Cate's family arriving. Her father, her mother in a wheelchair, her older brother, Jarrod.

Barnaby Elliot's voice is raised. "What do you mean there's no baby? My daughter is pregnant."

"What are they saying, Barnaby?" his wife asks, tugging at his sleeve.

"They're saying she wasn't pregnant."

"Then it mustn't be our Cate. They have the wrong person."

The doctor interrupts. "If you'll just wait here, I'll send someone to talk to you."

Mrs. Elliot is growing hysterical. "Does that mean she lost the baby?"

"She was never pregnant. She didn't *have* a baby."

Jarrod tries to intervene. "I'm sorry but there must be some mistake. Cate was due in four weeks."

"I want to see my daughter," demands Barnaby. "I want to see her right this minute."

Jarrod is three years older than Cate. It is strange how little I can recall of him. He kept pigeons and wore braces until he was twenty. I think he went to university in Scotland and later got a job in the city.

In contrast, nothing about Cate is remote or diffuse or gone small. I still remember when I first saw her. She was sitting on a bench outside the school gates at Oaklands wearing white socks, a short gray pleated skirt and Doc Martens. Heavy mascara bruised her eyes, which seemed impossibly large. And her teased hair had all the colors of the rainbow.

Although new to the school, within days Cate knew more kids and had more friends than I did. She was never still—always wrapping her arms around people, tapping her foot or bouncing a crossed leg upon her knee.

Her father was a property developer, she said: a two-word profession, which like a double-barreled surname gave a man gravitas. "Train driver" is also two words but my father's job didn't sound so impressive or have the same social cachet.

Barnaby Elliot wore dark suits, crisp white shirts and ties that were from one club or another. He stood twice for the Tories in Bethnal Green and each time managed to turn a safe Labour seat into an even safer one.

I suspect the only reason he sent Cate to Oaklands

was to make him more electable. He liked to portray himself as a battler from "Struggle Street," with dirt under his fingernails and machine oil in his veins.

In reality, I think the Elliots would have preferred their only daughter to attend a private school, Anglican and all-girls rather than Oaklands. Mrs. Elliot, in particular, regarded it as a foreign country that she had no desire to visit.

Cate and I didn't talk to each other for almost a year. She was the coolest, most desirable girl in the whole school, yet she had a casual, almost unwanted beauty. Girls would hang around her, chatting and laughing, seeking her approval, yet she didn't seem to notice.

She talked like someone in a teen movie, smart-mouthed and sassy. I know teenagers are supposed to talk that way but I never met anyone who did except for Cate. And she was the only person I knew who could distill her emotions into drops of pure love, anger, fear or happiness.

I came from the Isle of Dogs, farther east, and went to Oaklands because my parents wanted me educated "out of the area." Sikhs were a minority, but so were whites, who were the most feared. Some regarded themselves as the true East Enders, as if there was some royal Cockney bloodline to be protected. The worst of them was Paul Donavon, a thug and a bully, who fancied himself as a ladies' man and as a footballer. His best mate, Liam Bradley, was almost as bad. A head taller, with a forehead that blazed with pimples, Bradley looked as if he scrubbed his face with a cheese grater instead of soap.

New kids had to be initiated. Boys copped it the worst, of course, but girls weren't immune, particularly the pretty ones. Donavon and Bradley were seventeen and they were always going to find Cate. Even at four-teen she had "potential" as the older boys would say, with full lips and a J-Lo bottom that looked good in any-thing tight. It was the sort of bottom that men's eyes fol-low instinctively. Men and boys and grandfathers.

Donavon cornered her one day during fifth period. He was standing outside the headmaster's office, await-ing punishment for some new misdemeanor. Cate was on a different errand—delivering a bundle of permission notes to the school secretary.

Donavon saw her arrive in the admin corridor. She had to walk right past him. He followed her onto the stairs.

"You don't want to get lost," he said, in a mocking tone, blocking her path. She stepped to one side. He mir-rored her movements.

"You got a sweet sweet arse. A peach. And beautiful skin. Let me see you walk up them stairs. Go on. I'll just stand here and you go right on ahead. Maybe you could hitch your skirt up a little. Show me that sweet sweet peach."

Cate tried to turn back but Donavon danced around her. He was always light on his feet. On the football field he played up front, ghosting past defenders, pulling them inside and out.

Big heavy fire doors with horizontal bars sealed off the stairwell. Sound echoed off the cold hard concrete but stayed inside. Cate couldn't keep focused on his face without turning.

"There's a word for girls like you," he said. "Girls that wear skirts like that. Girls that shake their arses like peaches on the trees."

Donavon put his arm around her shoulders and

pressed his mouth against her ear. He pinned her arms above her head by the wrists, holding them in his fist. His other hand ran up her leg, under her skirt, pulling her knickers aside. Two fingers found their way inside her, scraping dry skin.

Cate didn't come back to class. Mrs. Pulanski sent me to look for her. I found her in the girls' toilets. Mascara stained her cheeks with black tears and it seemed like her eyes were melting. She wouldn't tell me what happened at first. She took my hand and pressed it into her lap. Her dress was so short my fingers brushed her thigh.

"Are you hurt?"

Her shoulders shook.

"Who hurt you?"

Her knees were squeezed together. Locked tight. I looked at her face. Slowly I parted her knees. A smear of blood stained the whiteness of her cotton knickers.

Something stretched inside me. It kept stretching until it was so thin it vibrated with my heart. My mother says I should never use the word "hate." You should never hate anyone. I know she's right but she lives in a sanitized Sikh-land.

The bell sounded for lunchtime. Screams and laughter filled the playground, bouncing off the bare brick walls and pitted asphalt. Donavon was on the southern edge in the quad, in the shadow of the big oak tree that had been carved with so many initials it should rightly have been dead.

"Well, what have we here," he said, as I marched toward him. "A little yindoo."

"Look at her face," said Bradley. "Looks like she's gonna explode."

"Turkey thermometer just popped out her bum—she's done."

It drew a laugh and Donavon enjoyed his moment. To his credit he must have recognized some danger because he didn't take his eyes off me. By then I had stopped a yard in front of him. My head reached halfway up his chest. I didn't think of his size. I didn't think of my size. I thought of Cate.

"That's the one who runs," said Bradley.

"Well run away little yindoo, you're smelling up the air."

I still couldn't get any words out. Disquiet grew in Donavon's eyes. "Listen, you sick Sikh, get lost."

I rediscovered my voice. "What did you do?"

"I did nothing."

A crowd had started to gather. Donavon could see them coming. He wasn't so sure anymore.

It didn't feel like me who was standing in the playground, confronting Donavon. Instead I was looking down from the branches of the tree, watching from above like a bird. A dark bird.

"Fuck off, you crazy bitch."

Donavon was fast but I was the runner. Later people said I flew. I crossed the final yard in the beat of a butterfly's wing. My fingers found his eye sockets. He roared and tried to throw me off. I clung on in a death grip, attacking the soft tissue.

Snarling my hair in his fists, he wrenched my head backward, trying to pull me away but I wasn't letting go. He pummeled my head with his fists, screaming, "Get her off! Get her off!"

Bradley had been watching, too shocked to react. He

was never sure what to do unless Donavon told him. First he tried to put me in a headlock, forcing my face into the dampness of his armpit, which smelled of wet socks and cheap deodorant.

My legs were wrapped around Donavon's waist. My fingers gouged his eyes. Bradley tried another tack. He grabbed one of my hands and uncurled my fingers, pulling my arm backward. My grip broke. I raked my fingernails across Donavon's face. Although he couldn't see anything from his streaming eyes, he lashed out, kicking me in the head. My mouth filled with blood.

Bradley had hold of my left arm, but my right was still free. In a family of boys you learn how to fight. When you're the only girl you learn how to fight dirty.

Spinning to my feet, I swung my hand at Donavon's face. My index finger and forefinger speared up his nose, hooking him like a fish. My fist closed. No matter what happened next Donavon would follow me. Bradley could break my arm, drag me backward, kick me through the goalposts and Donavon would come with me like a bull with a ring through his nose.

A moan was all I heard escape from his mouth. His arms and legs were jerking.

"Don't touch her. Don't touch her," he pleaded. "Just let her go."

Bradley loosened his grip on my left arm.

Donavon's eyes were swollen and closing. His nasal passages were turned inside out by my fingers. I held him, with his head tilted back and his lower jaw flapping open as he sucked air.

Miss Flower, the music teacher, was on playground duty that day. In truth she was having a cigarette in the staff room when someone came hurtling up the stairs to get her.

Donavon blubbered on about being sorry. I didn't say a word. It felt like none of this had happened to me. I still seemed to be watching from the branches of the tree.

Miss Flower was a fit, youthful, jolly-hockey-sticks type with a fondness for French cigarettes and the sports mistress. She took in the scene with very little fuss and realized that nobody could force me to let Donavon go. So she adopted a conciliatory approach full of comforting words and calming appeals. Donavon had gone quiet. The less he moved, the less it hurt.

I didn't know Miss Flower well but I think she got me, you know. A skinny Indian girl with braces and glasses doesn't take on the school bully without a good reason. She sat with me in the infirmary as I spat blood into a bowl. Two front teeth had been ripped out of the wire braces and were trapped in the twisted metal.

I had a towel around my neck and another across my lap. I don't know where they took Donavon. Miss Flower held an ice pack to my mouth.

"You want to tell me why?"

I shook my head.

"Well, I don't doubt he deserved it but you will have to give a reason."

I didn't answer.

She sighed. "OK, well, it can wait. First you need a clean uniform. There might be one in lost property. Let's clean up before your parents arrive."

"I want to go back to class," I lisped.

"First you need to get those teeth fixed, dear."

Finding an emergency dentist on the NHS normally meant promising your firstborn to the church but I had family connections. My uncle Sandhu has a dental practice in Ealing. (He's not really my uncle, but every older Asian who knew my family was referred to as uncle or aunt.) Uncle Sandhu had fitted my braces "at cost." Bada was so pleased that he would make me smile for visitors, showing off my teeth.

Mama rang my sister-in-law Nazeem and the two of them caught a minicab to the school. Nazeem had the twins and was pregnant again. I was whisked off to Uncle Sandhu who dismantled my braces and took photographs of my teeth. I looked six years old again and had a lisp.

The next morning was fresh and bright and possessed of an innocence so pristine it made a lie of the previous day. Cate didn't come to school. She stayed away for two weeks until we broke for the summer holidays. Miss Flower said she had pleurisy.

Sucking on my glued teeth, I went back to my classes. People treated me differently. Something had happened that day. The scales had fallen from my eyes; the earth had rotated the required number of times and I said goodbye to childhood.

Donavon was expelled from Oaklands. He joined the army, the Parachute Regiment, just in time for Bosnia. Other wars would turn up soon enough. Bradley left during the holidays and became an apprentice boilermaker. I still see him occasionally, pushing his kids on the swings on Bethnal Green.

Nobody ever mentioned what happened to Cate. Only I knew. I don't think she even told her parents—certainly not her father. Digital penetration isn't classified as rape because the law differentiates between a penis and a finger, or fist, or bottle. I don't think it should, but that's an argument for fancy defense lawyers.

People were nicer to me after my fight with Donavon. They acknowledged my existence. I was no longer just "the runner"; I had a name. One of my teeth took root again. The other turned yellow and Uncle Sandhu had to replace it with a false one.

During the holidays I had a phone call from Cate. I don't know how she found my number.

"I thought maybe you might like to catch a movie."

"You mean, you and me?"

"We could see *Pretty Woman*. Unless you've already seen it. I've been three times but I could go again." She kept talking. I had never heard her sound nervous.

"My mother won't let me see *Pretty Woman*," I explained. "She says it's about a whore."

I protested that Julia Roberts is a hooker with a heart, which only got me into trouble. Apparently, it was OK for her to use the term "whore" but I wasn't allowed to say "hooker." In the end we went to see *Ghost* with Patrick Swayze and Demi Moore.

Cate didn't say anything about Donavon. She was still beautiful, still clear-skinned, still wearing a short skirt. Sitting in the darkness, our shoulders touched and her fingers found mine. She squeezed my hand. I squeezed hers.

And that was the start of it. Like Siamese twins, we were. Salt and pepper, Miss Flower called us but I preferred "milk and cookies," which was Mr. Nelson's description. He was American and taught biology and protested when people said it was the easiest of the science electives.

Through school and then university Cate and I were best friends. I loved her. Not in a sexual way, although I don't think I understood the difference at fourteen.

Cate claimed she could predict the future. She would map out our paths, which included careers, boyfriends, weddings, husbands and children. She could even make herself miserable by imagining that our friendship would be over one day.

"I have never had a friend like you and I never shall again. Never ever."

I was embarrassed.

The other thing she said was this: "I am going to have lots of babies because they will love me and never leave me."

I don't know why she talked like this. She treated love and friendship like a small creature trapped in a blizzard, fighting for survival. Maybe she knew something then that I didn't.

5

Another morning. The sun is shining somewhere. I can see blue sky bunched between buildings and a construction crane etched in charcoal against the light. I cannot say how many days have passed since the accident—four or fourteen. Colors are the same—the air, the trees, the buildings—nothing has changed.

I have been to the hospital every day, avoiding the waiting room and Cate's family. I sit in the cafeteria or wander the corridors, trying to draw comfort from the technology and the smiles of the staff.

Cate is in a medically induced coma. Machines are helping her to breathe. According to the hospital bulletin she suffered a perforated lung, a broken back and multiple fractures to both her legs. The back of her skull was pulverized but two operations have stopped the bleeding.

I spoke to the neurosurgeon yesterday. He said the coma was a good thing. Cate's body had shut down and was trying to repair itself.

"What about brain damage?" I asked him.

He toyed with his stethoscope and wouldn't look me in the eye. "The human brain is the most perfectly designed piece of equipment in the known universe," he explained. "Unfortunately, it is not designed to withstand a ton of metal at high speed."

"Which means?"

"We classify severe head injury as a coma score of eight or less. Mrs. Beaumont has a score of four. It is a *very* severe head injury."

At eleven o'clock the ICU posts another bulletin. Cate's condition hasn't changed. I bump into Jarrod in the cafeteria and we drink coffee and talk about everyday incidental things: jobs and families, the price of eggs, the frailty of modern paper bags. The conversation is punctuated by long pauses as though silence has become part of the language.

"The doctors say she was never pregnant," he says. "She didn't *lose* the baby. There was no miscarriage or termination. Mum and Dad are beside themselves. They don't know what to think."

"She must have had a reason."

"Yeah, well, I can't think of one." A trickle of air from the ceiling vents ruffles his hair.

"Do you think Felix knew?"

"I guess. How do you keep a secret like that from your husband?" He glances at his watch. "Have you been to see her?"

"No."

"Come on."

Jarrod leads me upstairs to the intensive care unit, along painfully white corridors that all look the same. Only two visitors per patient are allowed in the ICU.

Masks must be worn and hands must be scrubbed with disinfectant.

Jarrod isn't coming with me. "There's someone already with her," he says, adding as an afterthought, "She won't bite."

My stomach drops. It's too late to back out.

The curtains are open and daylight casts a square on the floor. Mrs. Elliot in her wheelchair is trapped in the light like a hologram, her skin as pale and fine as white china.

Cate lies beside her, hostage to a tangle of tubing, plasma bags and stainless steel. Needles are driven into her veins and her head is swathed in bandages. Monitors and machines blink and buzz, reducing her existence to a digital computer game.

I want her to wake now. I want her eyes to open and for her to pluck away the breathing tube like a strand of hair caught in the corner of her mouth.

Wordlessly, Mrs. Elliot points to a chair beside the bed. "The last time I watched my daughter sleeping she was eight years old. She had come down with pneumonia. I think she caught it at one of those public swimming pools. Every time she coughed it sounded like someone drowning on dry land."

I reach across the marble sheets and take Cate's fingers in mine. I can feel her mother's eyes upon me. A cold scrutiny. She does not want me here.

I remember Mrs. Elliot when she could still walk—a tall, thin woman who always offered Cate her cheek to kiss so as not to smudge her lipstick. She used to be an actress who did mainly TV commercials and was always impeccably made-up, as though perpetually ready for her close-up. Of course, that was before she suffered a stroke that paralyzed her down her right side. Now one eyelid droops and no amount of makeup can hide the nerve damage around her mouth.

In a whisper, she asks, "Why would she lie about the baby?"

"I don't know. She was coming to see me. She said she had done something foolish and that someone wanted to take her baby."

"What baby? She was never pregnant. Never! Now they say her pelvis is so badly shattered that even if she survives she'll never be able to carry a baby."

Something shudders inside me. A déjà vu from another hospital and a different time, when *my* bones were being mended. A price is paid with every surgery.

Mrs. Elliot clutches a cushion to her chest. "Why would she do this? Why would she lie to us?"

There is no warmth in her voice, only accusation. She feels betrayed. Embarrassed. What will she tell the neighbors? I feel like lashing out and defending Cate, who deserves more than this. Instead I close my eyes and listen to the wind washing over the rooftops and the electronic beeping of the machines.

How did she do it—maintain such a lie for weeks and months? It must have haunted her. A part of me is strangely envious. I don't think I've ever wanted something *that* much, not even Olympic medals. When I missed out on the team for the Sydney Games I cried on the edge of the track but they were tears of frustration rather than disappointment. The girl who took my place *wanted* it more.

I know that I shouldn't compare Olympic selection with motherhood. Perhaps my opinions are clouded by the medical reality of a patched pelvis and a reinforced spine that can never withstand the trials of pregnancy and labor. Wanting children is a dangerous ambition for me.

Squeezing Cate's hand, I hope she knows I'm here. For years I wanted her to call, to be friends again, to need me. And just when it finally happened, she's been snatched away like a half-finished question. I have to find out what she wanted. I have to understand why.

Euston Traffic Garage is in Drummond Crescent, tucked between Euston Station and the British Library. The spire of Saint Aloysius Church rises above it like a rocket on a launchpad.

The Collision Investigation Unit is an odd place, a mixture of high-tech gadgetry and old-fashioned garage, with hoists, grease traps and machine tools. This is where they do the vehicular equivalents of autopsies, and the process is much the same. Bodies are opened, dismantled, weighed and measured.

The duty officer, a roly-poly sergeant in overalls, peers up from the twisted front end of a car. "Can I help you?"

I introduce myself, showing him my badge. "There was a traffic accident on Friday night on Old Bethnal Green Road. A couple were knocked down."

"Yeah, I looked at that one." He wipes his hands on a rag and tucks it back into his pocket.

"One of them is a friend of mine."

"She still alive?"

"Yes."

"Lucky."

"How far are you with the investigation?"

"Finished. Just got to write it up."

"What do you think happened?"

"Thought it was pretty obvious. Your friend and her husband tried to tackle a minicab." He doesn't mean to sound callous. It's just his way. "Maybe the driver could've put the brakes on a bit sooner. Sometimes you can be unlucky. Choose the wrong moment to check your mirrors and that fraction of a second comes off your reaction time. Might've made a difference. Might not. We'll never know."

"So you're not going to charge him?"

"What with?"

"Dangerous driving, negligence, there must be something."

"He was licensed, insured, registered and roadworthy—I got nothing on this guy."

"He was traveling too fast."

"He says they stepped out in front of him. He couldn't stop."

"Did you examine the car?"

"At the scene."

"Where is it now?"

He sighs. "Let me explain the facts of life to you, Detective Constable. You see that yard out there?" He motions to an open roller door leading to a walled yard. "There are sixty-eight vehicles—every one of them involved in a serious accident. We have thirteen reports due for the coroner, two dozen submissions for criminal trials and I spend half my time in the witness box and the other half up to me elbows in motor oil and blood. There are no *good* traffic accidents but from my point of view the one on Friday night was better than most because it was simple—sad, but simple. They stepped out from between parked cars. The driver couldn't stop in time. End of story."

The genial curiosity on his face has vanished. "We checked the brakes. We checked his license. We checked his driving record. We checked his blood alcohol. We took a statement at the scene and let the poor guy go home. Sometimes an accident is just an accident. If you have evidence to the contrary, hand it over. Otherwise, I'd appreciate it if you let me get on with my job."

There is a moment when we eyeball each other. He's not so much angry as disappointed.

"I'm sorry. I didn't mean to question your expertise."

"Yes you did." His face softens. "But that's OK. I'm sorry about your friend."

"Would you mind if I took a look at the driver's statement?"

He doesn't see a problem with that. He leads me to an office and motions to a chair. A computer hums on the desk and box files line the shelves like cardboard bricks. The sergeant hands me a file and a video. For a moment he hovers near the door, unwilling to leave me alone.

The driver's name was Earl Blake and his occupation is listed as stevedore. He was moonlighting as a minicab driver to make extra money, he said.

The video is time coded down to the second and begins with wide-angle shots of the street, taken in the shaky camera style of a holiday video. Partygoers are milling outside the gates of Oaklands, some still holding drinks or draped with streamers.

Earl Blake is in the distance, talking to a policeman. He notices the camera and seems to turn away. It might mean nothing.

There are statements from a dozen witnesses. Most heard the screech of brakes and saw the impact. Farther along the road, two cabbies were parked near the corner of Mansford Street. The minicab came past them slowly, as though searching for an address.

I look for any mention of Donavon. His name and address were taken down by investigators but there isn't a statement.

"Yeah, I remember him," says the sergeant. "He had a tattoo." He points to his neck, tracing a cross below his Adam's apple. "He said he didn't see a thing."

"He *saw* it happen."

The sergeant raises an eyebrow. "That ain't what he told me."

I make a note of Donavon's address on a scrap of paper.

"You're not trying to run a private investigation here are you, Detective Constable?"

"No, sir."

"If you have any important information regarding this accident, you are obliged to make it known to me."

"Yes, sir. I have no information. Mr. Donavon tried to save my friend's life. I just want to thank him. Good manners, you see. My mother bred them into me."

6

Earl Blake's address is a small terrace off Pentonville Road in the neglected end of King's Cross. There is nobody home. My legs have gone to sleep I've been sitting here for so long, staring out the windscreen, tapping a rhythm on the wheel.

A drug pusher leans against a low wall outside a pub on the corner, his face half hidden under the brim of a baseball cap. Two teenage girls walk by and he says something, smiling. They toss back their hair and sashay a little faster.

A red hatchback pulls into a parking space ahead of me. A woman in her fifties emerges, dressed in a nurse's uniform. She collects a bag of groceries from the boot and walks to the terrace, cursing as she drops her keys.

"Are you Mrs. Blake?" I ask.

"Who wants to know?" Her blue-gray hair is lacquered into place.

"I'm looking for your husband."

"You trying to be funny?"

She has opened the door and stepped inside.

"Your husband was involved in a car accident last Friday night."

"Not bloody likely."

She is disappearing down the hallway.

"I'm talking about *Earl* Blake."

"That's his name."

"I need to speak to him."

Shouting over her shoulder: "Well, missy, you're six years too late. That's when I buried him."

"He's dead!"

"I sure hope so." She laughs wryly.

The house smells of damp dog and toilet freshener.

"I'm a police officer," I call after her. "I'm sorry if there's been a mistake. Do you have a son called Earl?"

"Nope."

Dumping her shopping on a table in the kitchen, she turns. "Listen, love, either come in or stay out. This place costs a fortune to bloody heat."

I follow her into the house and shut the door. She has taken a seat at the table and kicked off her shoes, rubbing her feet through her support hose.

I look around. There are medications lined up on the windowsill and food coupons stuck under fridge magnets. A picture of a baby in a hollowed-out pumpkin is on the calendar.

"Put the kettle on will you, love."

The tap spits and belches.

"I'm sorry about your husband."

"Nowt for you to be sorry about. He dropped dead right there—face-first into his egg and chips. He was moaning about how I overcooked the eggs and then whump!" Her hand topples onto the table. "I told him

50

not to wear his underwear to breakfast but he never listened. All the neighbors watched him wheeled out of here in his old Y-fronts."

She tosses her shoes in the corner beside the back door. "I know all men leave eventually but not when you've just made 'em egg 'n' chips. Earl was always bloody inconsiderate."

Mrs. Blake pushes herself upward and warms the teapot. "You're not the first, you know."

"What do you mean?"

"Some bloke came here yesterday. He didn't believe me either when I said Earl was dead. He said Earl owed him money. As if! Can't see him gambling from beyond."

"What did this man look like?"

"Had this tattoo on his neck. A cross."

Donavon is searching for Blake.

"I hate tattoos," she continues. "Earl had 'em on his forearms. He was in the merchant navy before I met him. Traveled all over the place and came back with these *souvenirs*. I call 'em skin complaints."

"Did he have one just here?" I point to my chest. "A Crucifixion scene."

"Earl weren't religious. He said religion was for people who believed in hell."

"Do you have a photograph of him?"

"Yeah, a few. He was handsome once."

She leads me to the sitting room, which is full of seventies furniture and faded rugs. Rummaging in a cupboard next to the gas fire, she pulls out a photo album.

"Course it's easier keeping the place clean now. He was a real slob. Dropped clothes like they was crumbs."

She hands me a snapshot. Earl is wearing a jacket with a fur collar and fluorescent strips. He looks nothing like the driver of the minicab, although both are roughly the same age.

"Mrs. Blake, do you ever get mail for your late husband?"

"Yeah, sure, junk stuff. Banks are always sending him applications for credit cards. What's he going to do with a credit card, eh?"

"Did you cancel his driver's license?"

"Didn't bother. I sold his old van. Bought meself the hatchback. Reckon the dealer ripped me off, the Paki bastard. No way that thing had done only four thousand miles."

She realizes her mistake. "No offense, love."

"I'm not Pakistani."

"Right. I don't know much about the difference."

She finds me another photograph.

"Do you ever take in lodgers or have visitors staying?"

"Nah."

"Ever had a break-in?"

"Yeah, a few years back." She looks at me suspiciously.

I try to explain that someone has stolen her husband's identity, which is not as difficult as it sounds. A bank statement and a gas bill is all it takes to get a credit report, which will yield a National Insurance number and a list of previous addresses. The rest falls into place—birth certificates, credit cards, a passport.

"Earl never did anything wrong," says Mrs. Blake. "Never did much right either." She overbalances a little as she stands and her forearms wobble beneath the short sleeves of her uniform.

I don't stay for a cup of tea, which disappoints her. Letting myself out, I stand for a moment on the front steps, raising my face to the misty rain. Three kids are practicing their literacy skills on a wall across the road.

Farther down the street is a triangular garden with benches and a playground surrounded by a semicircle of plane trees and a copper beech. Something catches my eye beneath the lower branches.

When soldiers are trained to hide in the jungle, they are told four main things that will give them away: movement, shape, shine and silhouette. Movement is the most important. That's what I notice. A figure stands from a bench and begins walking away. I recognize his gait.

It is strange how I react. For years, whenever I have conjured up Donavon's face, panic has swelled in the space between my heart and lungs. I'm not frightened of him now. I want answers. Why is he so interested in Cate Beaumont?

He knows I've clocked him. His hands are out of his pockets, swinging freely as he runs. If I let him reach the far side of the park I'll lose him in the side streets.

Rounding the corner, I accelerate along the path, which is flanked by a railing fence and tall shrubs. An old Royal Mail sorting office is on the opposite corner, with tall windows edged in painted stone. Turning left, I follow the perimeter fence. The exit is ahead. Nobody emerges. He should be here by now.

I pause at the gate, listening for hard heels on the pavement. Nothing. A motorcycle rumbles to life on the far side of the park. He doubled back. Clever.

Run, rabbit, run. I know where you live.

———

My hallway smells of bleach and the stale backdraft of a vacuum cleaner. My mother has been cleaning. That's one of the signs that my life isn't all that it should be. No matter how many times I complain that I don't need a cleaner, she insists on catching a bus from the Isle of Dogs just to "straighten a few things up."

"I am defrosting the freezer," she announces from the kitchen.

"It doesn't need defrosting. It's automatic."

She makes a *pffhh* sound. Her blue-and-green sari is tucked up into her support stockings, making her back-side appear enormous. It is an optical illusion just like her eyes behind her glasses, which are as wet and brown as fresh cow dung.

She is waiting for a kiss on the cheek. I have to bend. She is scarcely five feet tall and shaped like a pear, with sticky-out ears that help her hear like a bat and X-ray vision that only mothers possess. She also has an oddly selective sense of smell, which can pick up the scent of perfume from fifty feet, yet allows her to sniff the crotches of my four brothers' underpants to establish if they need washing. I feel like retching at the thought of it.

"Why is there a padlock on my Hari's door?"

"Privacy, perhaps."

"I found it open."

That's strange. Hari is always very careful about locking the door.

Mama holds my face in her hands. "Have you eaten today?"

"Yes."

"You're lying. I can tell. I have brought some dahl and rice."

She uses perfect schoolbook English, the kind they used to teach in the dark ages when she went to school.

I notice a suitcase in the corner. For a moment I fear

she might be planning to stay but one suitcase would never be enough.

"Your father was cleaning out the attic," she explains.

"Why?"

"Because he has nothing else to do." She sounds exasperated.

My father has retired after thirty-five years driving mainline trains and is still making the adjustment. Last week he went through my pantry checking use-by dates and putting them in order.

Mama opens the suitcase. Lying neatly across the top is my old Oaklands school uniform. I feel a stab of recognition and remember Cate. I should phone the hospital for an update on her condition.

"I didn't want to throw things away without asking you," she explains. There are scarves, scrapbooks, photo albums, diaries and running trophies. "I had no idea you had a crush on Mr. Elliot."

"You *read* my diary!"

"It fell open."

Matricide is a possibility.

She changes the subject. "Now you're coming early on Sunday to help us cook. Make sure Hari wears something nice. His ivory shirt."

My father is having his sixty-fifth birthday and the party has been planned for months. It will include at least one eligible Sikh bachelor, no doubt. My parents want me to marry a good Sikh boy, bearded of course; not one of those clean-shaven Indians who thinks he's a Bollywood film star. This ignores the fact that all my brothers cut their hair, apart from Prabakar, the eldest, who is the family's moral guardian.

I know that all parents are considered eccentric by

their children, but mine are particularly embarrassing. My father, for example, is a stickler for conserving energy. He studies the electricity bill every quarter and compares it to previous quarters and previous years.

Mama crosses entire weeks off the calendar in advance so that she "doesn't forget."

"But how will you know what day it is?" I once asked her.

"Everyone knows what day it is," she replied.

You cannot argue with logic like that.

"By the way, your phone is fixed," she announces. "A nice man came this afternoon."

"I didn't report a problem."

"Well, he came to fix it."

A chill travels across my skin as if someone has left a door open. I fire off questions: What did he look like? What was he wearing? Did he have identification? Mama looks concerned and then frightened.

"He had a clipboard and a box of tools."

"But no ID."

"I didn't ask."

"He should have shown it to you. Did you leave him alone?"

"I was cleaning."

My eyes dart from one object to the next, taking an inventory. Moving upstairs, I search my wardrobes and drawers. None of my jewelry is missing. My bank statements, passport and spare set of keys are still in the drawer. Carefully, I count the pages of my checkbook.

"Perhaps Hari reported the fault," she says.

I call him on his mobile. The pub is so noisy he can barely hear me.

"Did you report a problem with the phone?"

"What?"

"Did you call British Telecom?"

"No. Was I supposed to?"

"It doesn't matter."

My mother rocks her head from side to side and makes concerned noises. "Should we call the police?"

The question had already occurred to me. What would I report? There was no break-in. Nothing has been taken as far as I can tell. It is either the perfect crime or no crime at all.

"Don't worry about it, Mama."

"But the man—"

"He was just fixing the telephone."

I don't want her worrying. She spends enough time here already.

Mama looks at her watch. If she doesn't leave now she won't be home for dinner. I offer to drive her and she smiles. It is the widest, most radiant smile ever created. No wonder people do as she says—they want to see her smile.

On the bedside table is a book that I started reading last night. The bookmark is in the wrong place—twenty pages forward. Perhaps I moved it inadvertently. Paranoia is not reality on a finer scale; it is a foolish reaction to unanswered questions.

7

On her very last day of being sixteen Cate found her mother lying unconscious in the kitchen. She had suffered something called a hemorrhagic stroke, which Cate explained as being like a "brain explosion."

Ruth Elliot had two subsequent strokes in hospital, which paralyzed her down her right side. Cate blamed herself. She should have been at home. Instead we'd sneaked out to watch the Beastie Boys at the Brixton Academy. Cate let a guy kiss her that night. He must have been at least twenty-five. Ancient.

"Maybe I'm being punished for lying," she said.

"But your mum is the one *really* being punished," I pointed out.

Cate started going to church after that—for a while at least. I went with her one Sunday, kneeling down and closing my eyes.

"What are you doing?" she whispered.

"Praying for your mum."

"But you're not an Anglican. Won't your god think you're changing teams?"

"I don't think it matters which god fixes her up."

Mrs. Elliot came home in a wheelchair, unable to talk properly. In the beginning she could only say one word: "When," uttered more as a statement than a question.

No matter what you said to her, she answered the same way.

"How are you today, Mrs. Elliot?"

"When, when, when."

"Have you had your tea?"

"When, when, when."

"I'm just going to study with Cate."

"When, when."

I know it sounds horrible but we used to play tricks on her.

"We have a biology test, Mrs. E."

"When, when."

"On Friday."

"When, when, when."

"In the morning."

"When, when."

"About half past nine."

"When, when."

"Nine thirty-four to be precise. Greenwich mean time."

They had a nurse to look after her. A big Jamaican called Yvonne, with pillow breasts and fleshy arms and mottled pink hands. She used to wear electric colors and men's shoes and she blamed her bad complexion on the English weather. Yvonne was strong enough to scoop Mrs. Elliot up in her arms and lift her into the shower and back into her wheelchair. And she talked to her all the time, having long conversations that sounded completely plausible unless you listened closely.

Yvonne's greatest gift, however, was to fill the house with laughter and songs, lifting the gloom. She had children of her own—Caspar and Bethany—who had steel-wool hair and neon smiles. I don't know about her husband—he was never mentioned—but I know Yvonne went to church every Sunday and had Tuesdays off and baked the best lime cheesecake in creation.

On weekends I sometimes slept over at Cate's place. We rented a video and stayed up late. Her dad didn't come home until after nine. Tanned and tireless, he had a deep voice and an endless supply of corny jokes. I thought him unbelievably handsome.

The tragedy of his wife's condition gained a lot of sympathy for Barnaby. Women, in particular, seemed to admire his devotion to his crippled wife and how he went out of his way to make her feel special.

Ruth Elliot, however, didn't seem to share this admiration. She recovered her speech after months of therapy and attacked Barnaby at every opportunity, belittling him in front of Yvonne and his children and his children's friends.

"Did you hear that?" she'd say as the front door opened. "He's *home*. He *always* comes home. Who does he smell like tonight?"

"Now, now, Ruth, please," Barnaby would say, but she wouldn't stop.

"He smells of soap and shampoo. He always smells of soap and shampoo. Why does a man shower *before* he comes home?"

"You know the reason. I've been playing tennis at the club."

"He washes before he comes home. Washes the smell away."

"Ruth, darling," Barnaby tried to say. "Let's talk about this upstairs."

She would fight at his hands and then surrender as he lifted her easily from her chair and carried her up the sixteen stairs. We would hear her screaming and finally crying. He would put her to bed, settle her like a child, and then rejoin us in the kitchen for hot chocolate.

When I first met Cate, Barnaby was already forty, but looked good for his age. And he could get away with things because he was so supremely confident. I saw him do it countless times at restaurants, on school open days and in the middle of the street. He could say the most outrageous things, using double entendres and playful squeezes and women would simply giggle and go weak at the knees.

He called me his "Indian princess" and his "Bollywood beauty" and, one time, when he took us horse riding, I actually felt dizzy when he put his hands around my waist and lifted me down from the saddle.

I would never have confessed it to anyone, but Cate guessed the truth. It wasn't hard. I was always inviting myself back to her place and making excuses to talk to her father. She didn't even know about the times I rode my bicycle past his office, hoping he might see me and wave. Twice I ran into open car doors.

Cate, of course, found my infatuation hilarious beyond measure, thus ensuring I have never admitted to loving any man.

See the sort of stuff I remember! It's all coming back, the good, the bad and the ugly. My mind aches.

———

I've been dreading this moment—seeing Barnaby again. Ever since the accident he has slept at Cate's house, according to Jarrod. He hasn't been to work or answered calls.

The front door has stained-glass panels and a tarnished knocker in the shape of a naked torso. I grab her hips. Nobody answers. I try again.

A lock turns. The door opens a crack. Unshaven and unwashed, Barnaby doesn't want to see me. Self-pity needs his full attention.

"Please, let me in."

He hesitates but the door opens. I move inside, stepping around him as though he's surrounded by a force field. The place is musty and closed up. Windows need opening. Plants need watering.

I follow him to the kitchen and dining area, open plan, looking out into the garden. Cate's touches are everywhere from the French provincial dining table to the art deco posters on the walls. There are photographs on the mantel. One of them, a wedding picture, shows Cate in a twenties flapper dress trimmed with mother-of-pearl.

Folding himself onto a sofa, Barnaby crosses his legs. A trouser cuff slides up to reveal a bald shin. People used to say he was ageless and joke about him having a portrait in his attic. It's not true. His features are too feminine to age well. Instead of growing character lines he has wrinkled and one day, ten years from now, he'll wake up an old man.

I never imagined speaking to him again. It doesn't seem so hard, although grief makes everything more intimate.

"They always say that a father is the last person to know anything," he says. "Cate used to laugh at me. 'Dear old Dad,' she said. 'Always in the dark.' "

Confusion clouds his eyes. Doubt.

"Did Felix know?"

"They weren't sleeping together."

"He told you that."

"Cate wouldn't let him touch her. She said it might harm the baby. They slept in different beds—in different rooms."

"Surely a husband would—"

"Marriage and sex aren't mutually inclusive," he says, perhaps too knowingly. I feel myself growing uncomfortable. "Cate even told Felix he could see a prostitute if he wanted. Said she wouldn't mind. What sort of wife says that? He should have seen something was wrong."

"Why couldn't she conceive?"

"Her womb destroyed his sperm. I don't know the medical name for it. They tried for seven years. IVF, drugs, injections, herbal remedies; they exorcised the house of evil spirits and sprinkled Chinese lemongrass oil on the garden. Cate was a walking bloody textbook on infertility. That's why it came as such a surprise. Cate was over the moon—I've never seen her happier. I remember looking at Felix and he was trying hard to be excited—I guess he was—but it's like he had a question inside him that wouldn't go away."

"He had doubts?"

"For years his wife rejects his sperm and then suddenly she's pregnant? Any man would have doubts."

"But if that's the case—"

"He *wanted* to believe, don't you see? She convinced everyone."

Standing, he motions me to follow. His slippers flap gently against his heels as he climbs the stairs. The nursery door is open. The room is freshly painted and papered. The furniture new. A cot, a changing table, a comfortable chair with a Winnie the Pooh pillow.

Opening a drawer, he takes out a folder. There are receipts for the furniture and instructions for assembling the cot. He up-ends an envelope, shaking it gently. Two sheets of photographs, monochrome images, drop into his hand. Ultrasound pictures.

Each photograph is only a few inches square. The background is black, the images white. For a moment it's like looking at one of those Magic Eye pictures where a 3-D image emerges from within. In this case I see tiny arms and legs. A face, eyes, a nose . . .

"They were taken at twenty-three weeks."

"How?"

"Felix was supposed to be there but Cate messed up the days. She came home with the photographs."

The rest of the file contains testimony of an unborn baby's existence. There are application forms to the hospital, appointment slips, medical reports, correspondence and receipts for the nursery furniture. An NHS pamphlet gives details of how to register the birth. Another lists the benefits of folic acid in early pregnancy.

There are other documents in the drawer, including a bundle of private letters tucked in a corner, bank statements, a passport and health insurance certificates. A separate file contains details of Cate's IVF treatments. There appear to have been five of them. Sohan Banerjee, a fertility specialist in Wimbledon, is mentioned several times.

"Where was she planning to have the baby?"

"Chelsea and Westminster Hospital."

I look at a brochure for prenatal classes. "What I can't understand is how it was supposed to end. What was Cate going to do in four weeks?"

Barnaby shrugs. "She was going to be exposed as a liar."

"No, think about it. That prosthetic was almost a work of art. She must have altered it two or three times over the months. She also had to forge medical letters and appointment slips. Where did she get the ultrasound pictures? She went to all that effort. Surely she had a plan."

"Like what?"

"Maybe she organized a surrogacy or a private adoption."

"Why keep it a secret?"

"Perhaps she couldn't let anyone know. Commercial surrogacy is illegal. Women can't accept money to have a baby. I know it sounds far-fetched but isn't it worth considering?"

He scoffs and smites at the air between us. "So a month from now my daughter was going to nip off somewhere, dump the padding and come back with a baby, custom-made, ready to order from the baby factory. Maybe IKEA does them nowadays."

"I'm just looking for reasons."

"I *know* the reason. She was obsessed. Desperate."

"Enough to explain these?" I point to the ultrasound pictures.

Reaching down, he opens the second drawer and retrieves a different file. This one contains court transcripts, charge sheets and a judgment.

"Eighteen months ago Cate was caught stealing baby clothes from *Mothercare*. She said it was a misunderstanding, but we knew it was a cry for help. The magistrates were very kind. They gave her a suspended sentence.

"She had counseling for about six months, which seemed to help. She was her old self again. There were obvious places she had to avoid like parks and playgrounds, schools. But she couldn't stop torturing herself. She peered into prams and struck up conversations with mothers. She got angry when she saw women with big families, who were pregnant again. It was unfair, she said. They were being greedy.

"She and Felix looked into adopting a baby. They went for the interviews and were screened by social workers. Unfortunately, the shoplifting conviction came back to haunt Cate. The adoption committee deemed her mentally unstable. It was the final straw. She lost it completely. Felix found her sitting on the floor of the nursery, clutching a teddy bear, saying, 'Look! It's a beautiful baby boy.' She was taken to hospital and spent a fortnight in a psych ward. They put her on antidepressants."

"I had no idea."

He shrugs. "So you see, Alisha, you shouldn't make the mistake of putting rational thoughts in my daughter's head. Cate didn't have a plan. Desperation is the mother of bad ideas."

Everything he says makes perfect sense but I can't forget the image of Cate at the reunion, begging me to help her. She said they wanted to take her baby. Who did she mean?

There is nothing as disarming as a heartfelt plea. Barnaby's natural caution wavers.

"What do you want?"

"I need to see telephone records, credit card receipts, check stubs and diaries. Have any large sums of money been withdrawn from Cate or Felix's bank accounts? Did they travel anywhere or meet anyone new? Was she secretive about money or appointments? I also need to see her computer. Perhaps her e-mails can tell me something."

Unable to push his tongue around the word no, he hedges. "What if you find something that embarrasses this family?"

His wretchedness infuriates me. Whatever Cate might have done, she needs him now.

The doorbell rings. He turns toward the sound, surprised. I follow him down the stairs and wait in the hallway as he opens the front door.

Yvonne gives a deep-throated sob and throws her arms around his shoulders, crushing his head to her chest.

"I'm sorry. I'm so sorry," she wails. Her eyes open. "Alisha?"

"Hello, Yvonne."

Manhandling Barnaby out of the way, she smothers me in her cleavage. I remember the feeling. It's like being wrapped in a fluffy towel, fresh from the dryer. Gripping my forearms, she holds me away. "Look at you! You're all grown up."

"Yes."

"You cut your lovely hair."

"Ages ago."

Yvonne hasn't changed. If anything she is a little fatter and her pitted face has fleshed out. Overworked veins stand out on her calves and she's still wearing men's shoes.

Even after Ruth Elliot recovered her speech, Yvonne stayed with the family, cooking meals, washing clothes and ironing Barnaby's shirts. She was like an old-fashioned retainer, growing old with them.

Now she wants me to stay, but I make excuses to leave. As I reach the car, I can still feel Barnaby's stubble on my cheeks where he kissed me goodbye. Glancing back at the house I remember a different tragedy, another goodbye. Voices from the past jostle and merge. The sadness is suffocating.

8

Donavon gave the police an address in Hackney, not far from London Fields. Set back from the road, the crumbling terrace house has a small square front yard of packed dirt and broken concrete. A sun-faded red Escort van is parked in the space, alongside a motorcycle.

A young woman answers the door. She's about twenty-five with a short skirt, a swelling pregnancy and acne scars on her cheeks. Cotton wool is wedged between her toes and she stands with her heels planted and toes raised.

"I'm looking for Donavon."

"Nobody here by that name."

"That's too bad. I owe him some money."

"I can give it to him."

"You said he didn't live here."

"I meant he wasn't here right now," she says curtly. "He might be around later."

"I'd prefer to give it to him personally."

She considers this for a moment, still balancing on her heels. "You from the council?"

"No."

"A welfare officer?"

"No."

She disappears and is replaced by Donavon.

"Well, well, if it isn't yindoo."

"Give it a rest, Donavon."

He runs his tongue along a nick in his front tooth while his eyes roam up and down over me. My skin is crawling.

"Didn't your mother ever tell you it's not polite to stare?"

"My mother told me to beware of strangers who tell lies about owing me money."

"Can I come in?"

"That depends."

"On what?"

"I'm fucking certain I ordered a Thai girl but I guess you'll do."

He hasn't changed. The pregnant girl is standing behind him. "This is my sister, Carla," he says.

She nods, sullenly.

"It's nice to meet you, Carla. I went to school with your brother. Did you go to Oaklands?"

Donavon answers for her. "I sort of shat in that particular nest."

"Why did you run yesterday?"

He shrugs. "You got the wrong guy."

"I know it was you."

He holds up his hands in mock surrender. "Are you gonna arrest me, Officer? I hope you brought your handcuffs. That's always fun."

I follow him along the hallway, past a coatrack and assorted shoes. Carla continues painting her nails at the kitchen table. She is flexible and shortsighted, pulling her foot almost up to her nose as she dabs on the varnish with a thin brush, unconcerned about exposing her knickers.

A dog beneath the table thumps its tail several times but doesn't bother rising.

"You want a drink?"

"No. Thank you."

"I do. Hey, Carla, nip up the road and get us a few cans."

Her top lip curls as she snatches the twenty-quid note from his fist.

"And this time I want the change back."

Donavon gives a chair a gentle shake. "You want to sit down?"

I wait for him to be seated first. I don't feel comfortable with him standing over me. "Is this your place?" I ask.

"My parents'. My dad's dead. Mum lives in Spain."

"You joined the army."

"Yeah, the Paras." His fingers vibrate against the tabletop.

"Why did you leave?"

He motions to his leg. "A medical discharge. I broke my leg in twelve places. We were on a training jump above Andover. One of the newbies wrapped his chute around mine and we came down under the one canopy. Too fast. They wouldn't let me jump after that. They said I'd get a pension but the government changed the rules. I got to work."

I glance around the kitchen, which looks like a craft workshop with boxes of leather strips, crystals, feathers and painted clay beads. On the table I notice a reel of wire and pliers.

"What are you making?"

"I sell stuff at the markets. Trinkets and shit. Don't make much, you know . . ."

The statement trails off. He talks a little more about the Paras, clearly missing army life, until Carla returns with a six-pack of draft and a packet of chocolate biscuits. She retreats to the stairs with the biscuits, eating them while listening to us. I can see her painted toes through a gap in the stair rails.

Donavon opens a can and drinks noisily. He wipes his mouth.

"How is she?"

"She might be brain damaged."

His face tightens. "What about the baby?"

"She wasn't pregnant."

"What?"

"She was faking it."

"What do you mean—faking it? Why would she . . . ? Makes no fucking sense."

The phantom pregnancy seems harder for him to accept than Cate's medical condition.

"Why are you interested in Earl Blake?"

"Same reason as you."

"Yeah, sure. What difference does it make to you?"

"You wouldn't understand."

"Try me."

"Fuck you!"

"You wish!"

"The bastard could have stopped," he says suddenly, his anger bordering on violence.

"Did you see the car speed up? Did it veer toward them?"

A shake of the head.

"Then why are you so sure?"

"He was lying."

"Is that it?"

He raises one shoulder as if trying to scratch his ear. "Just forget it, OK?"

"No, I want to know. You said the driver was lying. Why?"

He goes quiet. "I just know. He lied. He ran them down."

"How can you be sure?"

He turns away, muttering, "Sometimes I just am."

My mother always told me that people with green eyes are related to fairies, like the Irish, and that if I ever met someone with one green eye and one brown one, it meant that person had been taken over by a fairy, but not in a scary way. Donavon is seriously scary. The bones of his shoulders shift beneath his shirt.

"I found out some stuff about Blake," he says, growing calmer. "He signed on with the minicab firm a week ago and only ever worked days. At the end of every shift he handed over eighty quid for the lease of the car but the mileage didn't match the fares. He can't have done more than a few miles. He told another driver that he had regular customers who liked to have him on call. One of them was a film producer but there's no way some hotshot film producer is going around London in a beat-up Vauxhall Cavalier."

He straightens up, into the story now. "So I ask myself, 'Why does a guy need a car all day if it's not going anywhere?' Maybe he's watching someone—or waiting for them."

"That's a big leap."

"Yeah, well, I saw the look Cate gave him. She recognized him."

He noticed it too.

Kicking back his chair, he stands and opens a kitchen drawer.

"I found this. Cate must have dropped it."

He hands me a crumpled envelope. My name is on the front of it. The swirls and dips of the handwriting belong to Cate. Lifting the flap, I pull out a photograph. A teenage girl gazes absently at the camera. She has fine limbs and ragged dark hair, trimmed by the wind. Her wide lips curl down at the edges making her look melancholy rather than gloomy. She is wearing jeans, sandals and a cotton shirt. Her hands are by her sides, palms open, with a white band on her wrist.

I turn the photograph over. There is a name written on the back. Samira.

"Who is she?" asks Donavon.

"I don't know."

"What about the number?"

In the bottom right-hand corner there are ten digits. A phone number, perhaps.

I study the image again as a dozen different questions chase one another. Cate faked her pregnancy. Does this girl have anything to do with it? She looks too young to be a mother.

I take out my mobile and punch in the number. A recorded voice announces it is unavailable. The area code doesn't belong in the U.K. It could be international.

The fight seems to have gone out of Donavon. Maybe alcohol mellows him.

"What are you gonna do?" he asks.

"I don't know yet."

On my feet, I turn to leave. He calls after me, "I want to help."

"Why?"

He's still not going to tell me.

Carla intercepts me before I reach the front door.

"He's losing it," she whispers. "He used to have it together but something happened in Afghanistan or wherever the hell they sent him. He's not the same. He doesn't sleep. He gets obsessed about stuff. I hear him at night, walking about."

"You think he needs help?"

"He needs something."

9

Chief Superintendent Lachlan North has an office on the eleventh floor of New Scotland Yard overlooking Victoria Street and Westminster Abbey. He is standing by the window, beside a telescope, peering into the eyepiece at the traffic below.

"If that moron thinks he can turn there . . ."

He picks up a two-way radio and communicates a call-sign to traffic operations.

A tired voice answers. "Yes, sir."

"Some idiot just did a U-turn in Victoria Street. Did you see it?"

"Yes, sir, we're onto him."

The Chief Superintendent is talking while still peering through the telescope. "I can get his number plate."

"It's under control, sir."

"Good work. Over and out."

Reluctantly, he turns away from the telescope and sits down. "There are some dangerous bloody morons loose on our roads, Detective Constable Barba."

"Yes, sir."

"In my experience, the morons are more dangerous than the criminals."

"There are more of them, sir."

"Yes. Absolutely."

He dips his head into a drawer and retrieves a dark green folder. Shuffling through the contents, he clears his throat and smiles, attempting to appear warmer and fuzzier. A nagging doubt hooks me in the chest.

"The results of your medical have been reviewed, DC Barba, along with your psychological evaluation. I must say you have made a remarkable recovery from your injuries. Your request to return to active duty with the Diplomatic Protection Group has also been noted. Courageous is the word that comes to mind." He tugs at his cuffs. Here it comes. "But under the circumstances, having reviewed the matter thoroughly, it has been decided to transfer you out of the DPG. You might be a little gun-shy, you see, which is hardly a good thing when protecting diplomats and foreign heads of state. Could be embarrassing."

"I'm not gun-shy, sir. Nobody fired a gun at me."

He raises his hand to stop me. "Be that as it may, we have a responsibility to look after our foreign guests and while I have every confidence in you, there is no way of testing your fitness when push comes to shove and Abdul the terrorist takes a potshot at the Israeli ambassador." He taps the folder several times with his finger to stress the point.

"The most important part of my job is shuffling people and priorities. It is a thankless task but I don't ask for medals or commendations. I am simply a humble servant of the public." His chest swells. "We don't want to lose you, DC Barba. We need more women like you in the Met, which is why I am pleased to offer you a position as a recruitment officer. We need to encourage more young women into the Met, particularly from minority communities. You can be a role model."

A mist seems to cloud my vision. He stands now, moving back to the window where he bends to peer through his telescope again.

"Unbelievable! Moron!" he screams, shaking his head.

He turns back to me, settling his haunch on the corner of the desk. A print behind his head is a famous depiction of the Bow Street Runners, London's renowned early police force.

"Great things are expected of you, DC Barba."

"With all due respect, sir, I am not gun-shy. I am fitter than ever. I can run a mile in four and a half minutes. I'm a better shot than anyone at the DPG. My high-speed defensive driving skills are excellent. I am the same officer as before—"

"Yes, yes, you're very capable I'm sure, but the decision has been made. It's out of my hands. You'll report to the Police Recruitment Center at Hendon on Monday morning."

He opens his office door and waits for me to leave. "You're still a very important member of the team, Alisha. We're glad to have you back."

Words have dried up. I know I should argue with him or slam my fist on his desk and demand a review. Instead, I meekly walk out the door. It closes behind me.

Outside, I wander along Victoria Street. I wonder if the Chief Superintendent is watching me. I'm tempted to look up toward his window and flip him the bird. Isn't that what the Americans call it?

Of course, I don't. I'm too polite, you see. That's my problem. I don't intimidate. I don't bully. I don't talk in sporting clichés or slap backs or have a wobbly bit between my legs. Unfortunately, it's not as though I have outstanding feminine wiles to fall back on such as a killer cleavage or a backside like J-Lo. The only qualities I bring to the table are my gender and ethnic credibility. The Metropolitan Police want nothing else from me.

I am twenty-nine years old and I still think I'm capable of something remarkable in my life. I am different, unique, beyond compare. I don't have Cate's luminous beauty or infinite sadness, or her musical laugh or the ability to make all men feel like warriors. I have wisdom, determination and steel.

At sixteen I wanted to win Olympic gold. Now I want to make a difference. Maybe falling in love will be my remarkable deed. I will explore the heart of another human being. Surely that is challenge enough. Cate always thought so.

When I need to think I run. When I need to forget I run. It can clear my thoughts completely or focus them like a magnifying glass that dwarfs the world outside the lens. When I run the way I know I can, it all happens in the air, the pure air, floating above the ground, levitating the way great runners imagine themselves in their dreams.

The doctors said I might never walk again. I confounded predictions. I like that idea. I don't like doing things that are predictable. I don't want to do what people expect.

I began with baby steps. Crawl before you can walk,

Simon my physiotherapist said. Walk before you can run. He and I conducted an ongoing skirmish. He cajoled me and I cursed him. He twisted my body and I threatened to break his arm. He said I was a crybaby and I called him a bully.

"Rise up on your toes."

"I'm trying."

"Hold on to my arm. Close your eyes. Can you feel the stretch in your calf?"

"I can feel it in my eyeballs."

After months in traction and more time in a wheelchair, I had trouble telling where my legs stopped and the ground began. I bumped into walls and stumbled on pavements. Every set of stairs was another Everest. My living room was an obstacle course.

I gave myself little challenges, forcing myself out on the street every morning. Five minutes became ten minutes, became twenty minutes. After every operation it was the same. I pushed myself through winter and spring and a long hot summer when the air was clogged with exhaust fumes and heat rose from every brick and slab.

I have explored every corner of the East End, which is like a huge, deafening factory with a million moving parts. I have lived in other places in London and never even made eye contact with neighbors. Now I have Mr. Mordecai next door, who mows my postage-stamp-size lawn, and Mrs. Goldie across the road picks up my dry cleaning.

There is a jangling, squabbling urgency to life in the East End. Everyone is on the make—haggling, complaining, gesticulating and slapping their foreheads. These are the "people of the abyss" according to Jack London. That was a century ago. Much has changed. The rest remains the same.

For nearly an hour I keep running, following the Thames past Westminster, Vauxhall and the old Battersea Power Station. I recognize where I am—the back streets of Fulham. My old boss lives near here, in Rainville Road: Detective Inspector Vincent Ruiz, retired. We talk on the phone every day or so. He asks me the same two questions: are you okay, and do you need anything. My answers are always: yes, I'm okay; and no, I don't need anything.

Even from a distance I recognize him. He is sitting in a folding chair by the river, with a fishing rod in one hand and a book on his lap.

"What are you doing, sir?"

"I'm fishing."

"You can't really expect to catch anything."

"No."

"So why bother?"

He sighs and puts on his ah-grasshopper-you-have-much-to-learn voice.

"Fishing isn't always about catching fish, Alisha. It isn't even about the expectation of catching fish. It is about endurance, patience and most importantly"—he raises a can of draft—"it is about drinking beer."

Sir has put on weight since he retired—too many pastries over coffee and the *Times* crossword—and his hair has grown longer. It's strange to think he's no longer a detective, just an ordinary citizen.

Reeling in his line, he folds up his chair.

"You look like you've just run a marathon."

"Not quite that far."

I help him carry his gear across the road and into a large terrace house, with lead-light windows above empty flower boxes. He fills the kettle and moves a bundle of typed pages from the kitchen table.

"So what have you been doing with yourself, sir?"

"I wish you wouldn't call me sir."

"What should I call you?"

"Vincent."

"How about DI?"

"I'm not a detective inspector anymore."

"It could be like a nickname."

He shrugs. "You're getting cold. I'll get you a sweater."

I hear him rummaging upstairs and he comes down with a cardigan that smells of lavender and mothballs. "My mother's," he says apologetically.

I have met Mrs. Ruiz just the once. She was like something out of a European fairy tale—an old woman with missing teeth, wearing a shawl, rings and chunky jewelry.

"How is she?"

"Mad as a meat ax. She keeps accusing the staff at the hostel of giving her enemas. Now *there's* one of life's lousy jobs. You got to feel sorry for that poor bastard."

Ruiz laughs out loud, which is a nice sound. He's normally one of the most taciturn of men, with a permanent scowl and a generally low opinion of the human race, but that has never put me off. Beneath his gruff exterior I know there *isn't* a heart of gold. It's more precious than that.

I spy an old-fashioned typewriter in the corner.

"Are you writing, DI?"

"No." He answers too abruptly.

"You're writing a book."

"Don't be daft."

I try not to smile but I know my lips are turning up. He's going to get cross now. He hates people laughing at him. He takes the manuscript and tries to stuff it into an old briefcase. Then he sits back at the table, nursing his cup of tea.

I let a decent interval go by. "So what's it about?"

"What?"

"Your book."

"It's not a book. It's just some notes."

"Like a journal."

"No. Like *notes*." That settles the issue.

I haven't eaten since breakfast. Ruiz offers to make me something. Pasta puttanesca. It is perfect—far too subtle for me to describe and far better than anything I could have cooked. He puts shavings of Parmesan on slices of sourdough and toasts them under the griller.

"This is very good, DI."

"You sound surprised."

"I *am* surprised."

"Not all men are useless in the kitchen."

"And not all women are domestic goddesses." I talk to my local Indian takeout more often than I do my mother. It's called the tandoori diet.

Ruiz was there the day my spine was crushed. We have never really spoken about what happened. It's like an undeclared pact. I know he feels responsible but it wasn't his fault. He didn't force me to be there and he can't make the Met give me my old job back.

The dishes are washed and packed away.

"I am going to tell you a story," I tell him. "It's the sort of story you like because it has a puzzle at the center. I don't want you to interrupt and I won't tell you if it's real or invented. Just sit quietly. I need to put all the details in order to see how it sounds. When I'm finished I will ask you a question and you can tell me if I'm totally mistaken. Then I will let you ask me one question."

"Just one?"

"Yes. I don't want you to tear apart my logic or pick holes in my story. Not now. Tomorrow maybe. Is it a deal?"

He nods.

Carefully, I set out the details, telling him about Cate, Donavon and Earl Blake. Like a tangle in a fishing line, if I pull too tightly the story knots together and it becomes harder to separate fact from supposition.

"What if Cate arranged a surrogacy and something went wrong? Could there be a baby out there some-where—Cate's baby?"

"Commercial surrogacy is illegal," he says.

"It still happens. Women volunteer. They get their expenses paid, which is allowed, but they cannot profit from the birth."

"Usually they're related in some way—a sister or a cousin."

I show him the photograph of Samira. He searches her face for a long time as though she might tell him something. Turning it over he notices the numbers.

"The first four digits could be a mobile phone prefix but not in the U.K.," he says. "You need the exact country code or you won't be able to call it."

It's my turn to be surprised again.

"I'm not a complete technophobe," he protests.

"You're typing your *notes* on an ink ribbon."

He glances at the old typewriter. "Yeah, well, it has sentimental value."

The clouds have parted just long enough to give us a

sunset. The last golden rays settle on the river. In a few minutes they'll be gone, leaving behind a raw, damp cold.

"You promised me a question," he says.

"One."

"Do you want a lift home?"

"Is that it?"

"I thought maybe we could swing by Oaklands and you could show me where it happened."

The DI drives an old Mercedes with white leather seats and soft suspension. It must guzzle petrol and makes him look like a lawn bowler, but Ruiz has never been one to worry about the environment or what people think of him.

I feel strange sitting in the passenger seat instead of behind the wheel. For years it was the other way around. I don't know why he chose me to be his driver, but I heard the gossip about the DI liking pretty faces. He's really not like that.

When I first moved out of uniform into the Serious Crime Group, the DI showed me respect and gave me a chance to prove myself. He didn't treat me any differently because of my color or my age or my being a woman.

I told him I wanted to become a detective. He said I had to be better, faster and cleverer than any man who wanted the same position. Yes, it was unfair. He wasn't defending the system—he was teaching me the facts of life.

Ruiz was already a legend when I did my training. The

instructors at Hendon used to tell stories about him. In 1963, as a probationary constable, he arrested one of the Great Train Robbers, Roger Cordrey, and recovered £141,000 of the stolen money. Later, as a detective, he helped capture the Kilburn rapist, who had terrorized North London for eight months.

I know he's not the sort to reminisce or talk about the good old days but I sense he misses a time when it was easier to tell the villains from the constabulary and the general public respected those who tried to keep them safe.

He parks the car in Mansford Street and we walk toward the school. The Victorian buildings are tall and dark against the ambient light. Fairy lights still drip from the windows of the hall. In my imagination I can see the dark stain on the tarmac where Cate fell. Someone has pinned a posy to the nearest lamppost.

"It's a straight line of sight," he says. "They can't have looked."

"Cate turned her head."

"Well she can't have seen the minicab. Either that or he pulled out suddenly."

"Two cabdrivers say they saw the minicab farther along the street, barely moving. They thought he was looking for an address."

I think back, mentally replaying events. "There's something else. I think Cate recognized the driver."

"She knew him?"

"He might have picked her up earlier as a fare."

"Or followed her."

"She was frightened of him. I could see it in her eyes."

I mention the driver's tattoo. The Crucifixion. It covered his entire chest.

"A tattoo like that might be traceable," says the DI. "We need a friend on the inside."

I know where he's going with this.

"How is 'New Boy' Dave?" he asks. "You two still bumping uglies?"

"That would be none of your business."

Sikh girls blush on the inside.

———————

Dave King is a detective with the Serious Crime Group (Western Division), Ruiz's old squad. He's in his early thirties with a tangle of gingery hair that he cuts short so it doesn't escape. He earned the nickname "New Boy" when he was the newest member of the SCG, but that was five years ago. He's now a detective sergeant.

Dave lives in a flat in West Acton, just off the Uxbridge Road, where gas towers dominate the skyline and trains on the Paddington line rattle him awake every morning.

It is a typical bachelor pad in progress, with a king-size bed, a wide-screen TV, a sofa, and precious little else. The walls are half stripped and the carpet has been ripped up but not replaced.

"Like what you've done to the place," observes Ruiz sardonically.

"Yeah, well, I been sort of busy," says Dave. He looks at me as if to say, *What's going on?*

Pecking him on the cheek, I slip my hand under his T-shirt and run my fingers down his spine. He's been playing rugby and his hair smells of mown grass.

Dave and I have been sleeping together, on and off, for nearly two years. Ruiz would smirk over the "on and off" part. It's the longest relationship of my life—even discounting the time I spent convalescing in hospital.

Dave thinks he wants to marry me but he hasn't met my family. You don't marry a Sikh girl. You marry her mother, her grandmother, her aunties, her brothers . . . I know all families have baggage but mine belongs in one of those battered suitcases, held together with string, that you see circling endlessly on a luggage carousel.

Dave tries to outdo me by telling stories about his family, particularly his mother who collects roadkill and keeps it in her freezer. She is on a mission to save badgers, which includes lobbying local councils to build tunnels beneath busy roads.

"I don't have anything to drink," he says apologetically.

"Shame on you," says Ruiz, who is pulling faces at the photographs on the fridge. "Who's this?"

"My mother," says Dave.

"You take after your father then."

Dave clears the table and pulls up chairs. I go through the story again. Ruiz then adds his thoughts, giving the presentation added gravitas. Meanwhile, Dave folds and unfolds a blank piece of paper. He wants to find a reason not to help us.

"Maybe you should wait for the official investigation," he suggests.

"You know things get missed."

"I don't want to tread on any toes."

"You're too good a dancer for that, 'New Boy,' " says Ruiz, cajoling him.

I can be shameless. I can bat my big brown eyelashes with the best of them. Forgive me, sisters. Taking the piece of paper from Dave's hand, I let my fingers linger on his. He chases them, not wanting to lose touch.

"He had an Irish accent but the most interesting thing is the tattoo." I describe it to him.

Dave has a laptop in the bedroom on a makeshift desk made from a missing bathroom door and saw horses. Shielding the screen from me, he types in a username and a password.

The Police National Computer is a vast database that contains the names, nicknames, aliases, scars, tattoos, accents, shoe size, height, age, hair color, eye color, offense history, associates and modus operandi of every known offender and person of interest in the U.K. Even partial details can sometimes be enough to link cases or throw up names of possible suspects.

In the good old days almost every police officer could access the PNC via the Internet. Unfortunately, one or two officers decided to make money selling the information. Now every request—even a licence check—has to be justified.

Dave types in the age range, accent and details of the tattoo. It takes less than fifteen seconds for eight possible matches. He highlights the first name and the screen refreshes. Two photographs appear—a front view and a profile of the same face. The date of birth, antecedents and last known address are printed across the bottom. He is too young; too smooth-skinned.

"That's not him."

Candidate number two is older with horn-rimmed glasses and bushy eyebrows. He looks like a librarian caught in a pedophile sweep. Why do all mug shots look so unflattering? It isn't just the harsh lighting or plain white background with its black vertical ruler measuring the height. Everybody looks gaunt, depressed, worst of all, guilty.

A new photograph appears. A man in his late forties with a shaved head. Something about his eyes makes me pause. He looks arrogant; as if he knows he is cleverer than the vast majority of his fellow human beings and this inclines him to be cruel.

I reach toward the computer screen and cup my hand over the top of the image, trying to imagine him with a long gray ponytail.

"That's him."

"Are you sure?"

"Absolutely."

His name is Brendan Dominic Pearl—born in 1958 in Rathcoole, a Loyalist district of north Belfast.

"IRA," whispers Dave.

"How do you know?"

"It's the classic background." He scrolls down the screen to the biography. Pearl's father was a boilermaker on the Belfast docks. His elder brother, Tony, died in an explosion in 1972 when a bomb accidentally detonated in a warehouse being used as a bomb-making factory by the IRA.

A year later, aged fifteen, Brendan Pearl was convicted of assault and firearms offenses. He was sentenced to eighteen months of juvenile detention. In 1977 he launched a mortar attack on a Belfast police station that wounded four people. He was sentenced to twelve years.

At the Maze Prison in 1981 he joined a hunger strike with two dozen Republican prisoners. They were protesting about being treated as common criminals instead of prisoners of war. The most celebrated of them, Bobby Sands, died after sixty-six days. Pearl slipped into a coma in the hospital wing but survived.

Two years later, in July 1983, he and fellow inmate

Frank Farmer climbed out of their compound onto the prison roof and gained access to the Loyalist compound. They murdered a paramilitary leader, Patrick McNeill, and maimed two others. Pearl's sentence was increased to life.

Ruiz joins us. I point to the computer screen. "That's him—the driver."

His shoulders suddenly shift and his eyes search mine. "Are you sure?"

"Yes. Why? What's wrong?"

"I know him."

It's my turn to be surprised.

Ruiz studies the picture again as if the knowledge has to be summoned up or traded for information he doesn't need.

"There are gangs in every prison. Pearl was one of the IRA's enforcers. His favorite weapon was a metal pole with a curved hook something like a marlin spike. That's why they called him the Shankhill Fisherman. You don't find many fish in the Maze but he found another use for the weapon. He used to thread it through the bars while prisoners were sleeping and open their throats with a flick of the wrist, taking out their vocal chords in the process so they couldn't scream for help."

Cotton wool fills my esophagus. Ruiz pauses, his head bent, motionless.

"When the Good Friday peace agreement was signed more than four hundred prisoners were released from both sides—Republicans and Loyalists. The British government drew up a list of exemptions—people they wanted kept inside. Pearl was among them. Oddly enough, the IRA agreed. They didn't want Pearl any more than we did."

"So why isn't he still in prison?" asks Dave.

Ruiz smiles wryly. "That's a very good question, 'New Boy.' For forty years the British government told people it wasn't fighting a war in Northern Ireland—it was a 'police operation.' Then they signed the Good Friday Agreement and declared, 'The war is over.'

"Pearl got himself a good lawyer and that's exactly what he argued. He said he was a prisoner of war. There should be *no* exemptions. Bombers, snipers and murderers had been set free. Why was *he* being treated differently? A judge agreed. He and Frank Farmer were released on the same day."

A palm glides over his chin, rasping like sandpaper. "Some soldiers can't survive the peace. They need chaos. Pearl is like that."

"How do you know so much about him?" I ask.

There is sadness in his eyes. "I helped draw up the list."

10

"New Boy" Dave shifts beside me, draping his arm over my breasts. I lift it away and tuck it under his pillow. He sleeps so soundly I can rearrange his body like a stop-motion puppet.

A digital clock glows on the bedside table. I lift my head. It's after ten on Sunday morning. Where are the trains? They didn't wake me. I have less than an hour and a half to shower, dress and get ready for my father's birthday.

Rolling out of bed, I look for my clothes. Dave's clothes. My running gear is still damp from yesterday.

He reaches for me, running his thumbs beneath the underside of my breast, tracing a pattern that only men can find.

"You trying to sneak away?"

"I'm late. I have to go."

"I wanted to make you breakfast."

"You can drive me home. Then you have to find Brendan Pearl."

"But it's Sunday. You never said—"

"That's the thing about women. We don't *say* exactly what we want but we reserve the right to be mighty pissed off when we don't get it. Scary isn't it?"

Dave makes coffee while I use the shower. I keep pondering how Brendan Pearl and Cate Beaumont could possibly know each other. They come from different worlds, yet Cate recognized him. It doesn't *feel* like an accident. It never did.

On the drive to the East End, Dave chats about work and his new boss. He says something about being unhappy but I'm not really listening.

"You could come over later," he says, trying not to sound needy. "We could get a pizza and watch a movie."

"That would be great. I'll let you know."

Poor Dave. I know he wants something more. One of these days he's going to take my advice and find another girlfriend. Then I'll have lost something I never tried to hold.

Things I like about him: He's sweet. He changes the sheets. He tolerates me. I feel safe with him. He makes me feel beautiful. And he lets me win at darts.

Things I don't like about him: His laugh is too loud. He eats junk food. He listens to Mariah Carey CDs. And he has hair growing on his shoulders. (*Gorillas* have hair on their shoulders.) Christ I can be pedantic!

His rugby mates have nicknames like Bronco and Sluggo and they talk in this strange jargon that nobody else can understand unless they follow rugby and appreciate the finer points of mauling, rucking and lifting. Dave took me to watch a game one day. Afterward we all went to the pub—wives and girlfriends. It was OK. They were all really nice and I felt comfortable. Dave didn't leave my side and kept sneaking glances at me and smiling.

I was only drinking mineral water but I shouted a round. As I waited at the bar I could see the corner tables reflected in the mirror.

"So what are we doing after?" asked Bronco. "I fancy a curry."

Sluggo grinned. "Dave's already had one."

They laughed and a couple of the guys winked at each other. "I bet she's a tikka masala."

"No, definitely a vindaloo."

I didn't mind. It was funny. I didn't even care that Dave laughed too. But I knew then, if not before, that my initial instincts were right. We could share a bath, a bed, a weekend, but we could never share a life.

We pull up in Hanbury Street and straightaway I realize that something is missing.

"I'll kill him!"

"What's wrong?"

"My car. My brother has taken it."

I'm already calling Hari's mobile. Wind snatches at his words. He's driving with the window open.

"Hello?"

"Bring back my car."

"Sis?"

"Where are you?"

"Brighton."

"You're joking! It's Dad's birthday."

"Is that *today*?" He starts fumbling for excuses. "Tell him I'm on a field trip for university."

"I'm not going to lie for you."

"Oh, come on."

"No."

"All right, I'll be there."

I look at my watch. I'm already late. "I hate you, Hari."

He laughs. "Well, it's a good thing I love you."

Upstairs I throw open wardrobes and scatter my shoes. I have to wear a sari to keep my father happy. Saris and salvation are mixed up in his mind—as though one is going to bring me the other, or at least get me a husband.

"New Boy" Dave is downstairs.

"Can you call me a cab, please?"

"I'll take you."

"No, really."

"It won't take more than a few minutes—then I'll go to work."

Back in my room, I wrap the sari fabric around my body, right to left, tucking the first wrap into my petticoat, making sure the bottom edge is brushing my ankles. Then I create seven pleats down the center, making sure they fall with the grain of the fabric. Holding the pleats in place, I take the remaining length of sari behind my back, across my body and drape it over my left shoulder.

This one is made of Varanasi silk, elaborately brocaded in red and green, with delicate figures of animals sewn with metallic silver thread along the border.

Pinning up my hair with a golden comb, I put on makeup and jewelry. Indian women are expected to wear lots of jewelry. It is a sign of wealth and social standing.

Sitting on the stairs, I buckle my sandals. Dave is staring at me.

"Is something wrong?"

"No."

"Well, what are you gawping at?"

"You look beautiful."

"Yeah, right." *I look like a Ratner's display window.*

I bat his hands away as he reaches out for me. "No touching the merchandise! And for God's sake, don't have an accident. I don't want to die in these clothes."

My parents live in the same house where I grew up. My mother doesn't like change. In her perfect world, children would never leave home or discover how to cook or clean for themselves. Since this is impossible, she has preserved our childhoods in bric-a-brac and become the full-time curator at the Barba family museum.

As soon as I turn into the cul-de-sac I feel a familiar heat in my cheeks. "Just drop me off here."

"Where's the house?"

"Don't worry. This will be fine."

We pull up outside a small parade of shops. Fifty yards away my niece and nephew play in the front garden. They go tearing inside to announce my arrival.

"Quick, quick, turn round!"

"I can't turn round."

It's too late! My mother appears, waddling down the road. My worst nightmare is coming true.

She kisses me three times, squeezing me so hard that my breasts hurt.

"Where is Hari?"

"I reminded him. I even ironed his shirt."

"That boy will be the death of me." She points to her temple. "See my gray hairs."

Her gaze falls on "New Boy" Dave. She waits for an introduction.

"This is a friend from work. He has to go."

Mama makes a *pffffhh* sound. "Does he have a name?"

"Yes, of course. Detective Sergeant Dave King. This is my mother."

"It's nice to meet you, Mrs. Barba. Ali has told me so much about you."

My mother laughs. "Will you stay for lunch, Detective Sergeant?"

"No, he has to go."

"Nonsense. It's Sunday."

"Police have to work weekends."

"Detectives are allowed to have lunch breaks. Isn't that right?"

Then my mother smiles and I know I've lost. Nobody can ever say no to that smile.

Small feet patter down the hallway ahead of us. Harveen and Daj are fighting over who's going to break the news that Auntie Ali has brought someone with her. Harveen comes back and takes my hand, dragging me into the kitchen. There are frown lines on her forehead at the age of seven. Daj is two years older and, like every male member of my family, is improbably handsome (and spoiled).

"Have you brought anything for us?" he asks.

"Only a kiss."

"What about a present?"

"Only for Bada."

Benches are covered with food and the air is heavy with steam and spices. My two aunts and my sisters-in-law are talking over one another amid the clatter and bang of energetic cooking. There are hugs and kisses.

Glasses graze my cheekbones and fingers tug at my sari or straighten my hair, without my relatives ever taking their eyes from "New Boy" Dave.

My aunties, Meena and Kala, couldn't be less alike as sisters. Meena is quite masculine and striking, with a strong jaw and thick eyebrows. Kala, by contrast, is unexceptional in almost every way, which might explain why she wears such decorative spectacles, to give her face more character.

Meena is still fussing with my hair. "Such a pretty thing to be unmarried; such lovely bones."

A baby is thrust into my arms—the newest addition to the family. Ravi is six weeks old, with coffee-bean-colored eyes and rolls of fat on his arms that you could lose a sixpence inside.

Cows might be sacred to Hindus, but babies are sacred to Sikhs, boys more so than girls. Ravi latches on to my finger and squeezes it until his eyes fold shut.

"She's so good with children," says Mama, beaming. Dave should be squirming but he's actually enjoying this. Sadist!

The men are outside in the garden. I can see my father's blue turban above them all. His beard is swept back from his cheeks and crawls down his neck like a silver trickle of water.

I count heads. There are extras. My heart sinks. They've invited someone for me to meet.

My mother ushers Dave outside. He glances over his shoulder at me, hesitating before obeying her instructions. Down the side steps, along the mildewed path, past the door to the laundry, he reaches the rear garden. Every face turns toward him and the conversation stops.

It's like the parting of the Red Sea, as people step

back and "New Boy" Dave faces my father. It's eyeball to eyeball but Dave doesn't flinch, which is to his credit.

I can't hear what they're saying. My father glances up toward the kitchen window. He sees me. Then he smiles and thrusts out his hand. Dave takes it and suddenly conversation begins again.

My mother is at the sink, peeling and slicing mangoes. She slides the knife blade easily beneath the pale yellow flesh. "We didn't know you were going to bring a friend."

"I didn't bring him."

"Well, your father has invited someone. You must meet his guest. It's only polite. He is a doctor."

"A very fine one," echoes Auntie Kala. "Very successful."

I scan the gathering and pick him out. He is standing with his back to me, dressed in a Punjabi suit that has been laundered and starched to attention.

"He's fat."

"A sign of success," says Kala.

"It takes a big hammer to hammer a big nail," adds Meena, cackling like a schoolgirl. Kala disapproves.

"Oh, don't give me that look, sister. A wife has to learn how to keep her husband happy in the boudoir." The two of them continue arguing while I go back to the window.

The stranger in the garden turns and glances up at me. He holds up his glass, as if offering me a toast. Then he shakes it from side to side, indicating its emptiness.

"Quickly, girl, take him another drink," says Meena, handing me a jug.

Taking a deep breath, I walk down the side steps into the garden. My brothers whistle. They know how much I hate wearing a sari. All the men turn toward me. I keep my eyes focused on my sandals.

My father is still talking to Dave and my uncle Rashid, a notorious butt-squeezer. My mother claims it is an obsessive-compulsive disorder but I think he's just a lech. They are talking about cricket. The men in my family are obsessed with the game even when the summer is over.

Most Indian men are small and elegant with delicate hands but my brothers are strapping, rugged types, except for Hari, who would make a beautiful woman.

Bada kisses my cheek. I bow to him slightly. He ushers his guest closer and makes the formal introductions.

"Alisha, this is Dr. Sohan Banerjee."

I nod, still not raising my eyes.

The name is familiar. Where have I heard it before?

Poor Dave doesn't understand what's going on. He's not a Sikh, which is probably a good thing. If I'd brought a Sikh home my parents would have killed a goat.

Dr. Banerjee stands very straight and bows his head. My father is still talking. "Sohan contacted me personally and asked if he could meet you, Alisha. Family to family—that is how it should be done."

I'm not meant to comment.

"He has more than one medical degree," he adds.

He has more than one chin.

I don't know how much worse this day could get. People are watching me. Dave is on the far side of the garden talking to my eldest brother, Prabakar, the most religious member of the family, who won't approve.

The doctor is talking to me. I have to concentrate on his words. "I believe you are a police officer."

"Yes."

"And you live separately from your parents. Very few single Indian girls have property. So why aren't you married?"

The bluntness of the question surprises me. He doesn't wait for an answer. "Are you a virgin?"

"Excuse me?"

"I'm assuming your mother explained the facts of life to you."

"It's none of your business."

"No comment means yes."

"No, it doesn't."

"In my experience it does. Do you drink?"

"No."

"See? You don't have to be so defensive. My parents think I should marry a girl from India because village girls are hard workers and good mothers. This may be so but I don't want a peasant girl who can't eat with a knife and fork."

Anger rises in my throat and I have to swallow hard to keep it down. I give him my politest smile. "So tell me, Dr. Banerjee—"

"Call me Sohan."

"Sohan, do you ever masturbate?"

His mouth opens and closes like a ventriloquist's dummy. "I hardly think—"

"No comment means yes."

The flash of anger in his eyes is like a bloodred veil. He grinds his teeth into a smile. "Touché."

"What kind of doctor are you?"

"An obstetrician."

Suddenly I remember where I've read his name. It was in the file that Barnaby Elliot showed me. Sohan Banerjee is a fertility specialist. He performed Cate's IVF procedures.

There are 100,000 Sikhs in London and what—

maybe 400 obstetricians? What are the chances of Cate's doctor showing up here?

"We have a mutual acquaintance," I announce. "Cate Beaumont. Did you hear about the accident?"

He shifts his gaze to the mottled green roof of my father's shed. "Her mother telephoned me. A terrible thing."

"Did she tell you that Cate faked her pregnancy?"

"Yes."

"What else did she say?"

"It would be highly unethical to reveal the details of our conversation." He pauses and adds, "Even to a police officer."

My eyes search his or perhaps it's the other way round. "Are you deliberately trying to withhold information from a police investigation?"

He smiles warily. "Forgive me. I thought this was a birthday party."

"When did you last see Cate?"

"A year ago."

"Why couldn't she conceive?"

"No reason at all," he says blithely. "She had a laparoscopy, blood tests, ultrasounds and a hysteroscopy. There were no abnormalities, adhesions or fibroids. She *should* have been able to conceive. Unfortunately, she and her husband were incompatible. Felix had a low sperm count, but married to someone else he may well have fathered a child without too much difficulty. However, in this case, his sperm were treated like cancerous cells and were destroyed by his wife's immune system. Pregnancy was theoretically possible but realistically unlikely."

"Did you ever suggest surrogacy as an option?"

"Yes, but there aren't many women willing to have a child for another couple. There was also another issue . . ."

"What issue?"

"Have you heard of achondrogenesis?"

"No."

"It is a very rare genetic disorder, a form of lethal dwarfism."

"What does that have to do with Cate?"

"Her only known pregnancy resulted in a miscarriage at six months. An autopsy revealed severe deformities in the fetus. By some twisted chance of fate, a reverse lottery, she and Felix each carried a recessive gene. Even, if by some miracle, she could conceive, there was a 25 percent chance it would happen again."

"But they kept trying."

He raises his hand to stop me. "Excuse me, Alisha, but am I to understand from your questions that you are investigating this matter in some official capacity?"

"I'm just looking for answers."

"I see." He ponders this. "If I were you, I would be very careful. People can sometimes misconstrue good intentions."

I'm unsure if this is advice or a warning but he holds my gaze until I feel uncomfortable. There is an arrogance about Banerjee that is typical of his generation of educated Sikhs, who are more pukka than any Englishman you will ever meet.

Finally, he relaxes. "I will tell you this much, Alisha. Mrs. Beaumont underwent five IVF implants over a period of two years. This is very complex science. It is not something you do at home with a glass jar and a syringe. It is the last resort, when all else fails."

"What happened in Cate's case?"

"She miscarried each time. Less than a third of IVF procedures result in a birth. My success rate is at the high end of the scale, but I am a doctor not a miracle worker."

For once the statement doesn't sound conceited. He seems genuinely disappointed.

Aunt Meena calls everyone inside for lunch. The tables have been set up with my father at the head. I am seated among the women. The men sit opposite. "New Boy" Dave and Dr. Banerjee are side by side.

Hari arrives in time for pudding and is treated like a prodigal son by my aunts, who run their fingers through his long hair. Leaning down, he whispers into my ear, "Two at once, sis. And I had you down as an old maid."

My family are noisy when we eat. Plates are passed around. People talk over one another. Laughter is like a spice. There is no ceremony but there are rituals (which are not the same thing). Speeches are made, the cooks must be thanked, nobody talks over my father and all disagreements are saved for afterward.

I don't let Dave stay that long. He has work to do. Sohan Banerjee also prepares to leave. I still don't understand why he's here. It can't be just a coincidence.

"Would you accede to seeing me again, Alisha?" he asks.

"No, I'm sorry."

"It would make your parents very happy."

"They will survive."

He rocks his head from side to side and up and down. "Very well. I don't know what to say."

"Goodbye is traditional."

He flinches. "Yes. Goodbye. I wish your friend Mrs. Beaumont a speedy recovery."

Closing the front door, I feel a mixture of anxiety and relief. My life has enough riddles without this one.

Hari meets me in the hallway. His dark eyes catch the light and he puts his arms around me. My mobile is open in his fingers.

"Your friend Cate died at one o'clock this afternoon."

11

There are cars parked in the driveway and in the street outside the Elliots' house. Family. A wake. I should leave them alone. Even as I debate what to do I find myself standing at the front door ringing the bell.

It opens. Barnaby is there. He has showered, shaved and tidied himself up but his eyes are watery and unfocused.

"Who is it, dear?" asks a voice from inside.

He stiffens and steps back. Wheels squeak on the parquetry floor and Cate's mother rolls into view. She is dressed in black, making her face appear even more spectral.

"You must come in," she says, her lips peeled back into a pained smile.

"I'm so sorry about Cate. If there's anything I can do."

She doesn't answer. Wheels roll her away. I follow them inside to the sitting room, which is full of sad-eyed friends and family. A few of them I recognize. Judy and Richard Sutton, a brother and sister. Richard was

Barnaby's campaign manager in two elections and Judy works for Chase Manhattan. Cate's aunt Paula is talking to Jarrod and in the corner I spy Reverend Lunn, an Anglican minister.

Yvonne is crumpled on a chair, talking and sobbing at the same time. Her clothes, normally so bright and vibrant, now mirror her mood, black. Her two children are with her, both grown up, more English than Jamaican. The girl is beautiful. The boy could name a thousand places he'd prefer to be.

Yvonne cries a little harder when she sees me, groaning as she raises her arms to embrace me.

Before I can speak, Barnaby grips my forearm, pulling me away.

"How did you know about the money?" he hisses. I can smell the alcohol on his breath.

"What are you talking about?"

The words catch in his throat. "Somebody withdrew £80,000 from Cate's account."

"Where did she get that sort of money?"

He lowers his voice even further. "From her late grandmother. I checked her bank account. Half the money was withdrawn last December and the other half in February."

"A bank check?"

"Cash. The bank won't tell me any more."

"And you have no idea why?"

He shakes his head and stumbles forward a pace. I steer him toward the kitchen where "get well soon" cards lie open on the table amid torn envelopes. They seem pointless now; forlorn gestures swamped by a greater grief.

Filling a glass from the tap, I hand it to him.

"The other day you mentioned a doctor, a fertility specialist."

"What about him?"

"Did you ever meet him?"

"No."

"Do you know if he ever suggested alternatives to IVF like adoption or surrogacy?"

"Not that I heard. He didn't overstate Cate's chances, I know that much. And he wouldn't implant more than two embryos each time. He had another policy—three strikes and you're out. Cate begged him to let her try again so he gave her five chances."

"Five?"

"They harvested eighteen eggs but only twelve were viable. Two embryos were implanted each time."

"But that only accounts for ten—what about the remaining two eggs?"

He shrugs. "Dr. Banerjee wouldn't go again. He saw how fragile Cate had become, emotionally. She was falling apart."

"She could have gone to another clinic."

"Felix wouldn't let her. The hormones, the tests, the tears—he wouldn't put her through it again."

None of this explains the money. Eighty thousand pounds isn't just given away. Cate was trying to buy a baby but something went wrong. That's why she contacted me.

I go over the story again, laying out the evidence. Some of the details and half-truths have taken on the solidity of facts. I can see what Barnaby's thinking. He's worried about his political ambitions. This sort of scandal would kill his chances stone dead.

"That's why I need to see Cate's computer," I say.

"She doesn't have one."

"Have you looked?"

"Yes."

The glass clinks against his teeth. He's lying to me.

"The files you showed me—and Cate's letters—can I borrow them?"

"No."

My frustration is turning to anger. "Why are you doing this? How can I make you understand?"

His hand touches my knee. "You could be nicer to me."

Ruth Elliot materializes in the kitchen, her wheels silent this time. She looks at me as though she's spat out a frog.

"People are beginning to leave, Barnaby. You should come and say goodbye."

He follows her to the front door. I grab my coat and slip past them.

"Thank you for coming, dear," she says mechanically, reaching up from her wheelchair. Her lips are as dry as paper on my forehead.

Barnaby puts his arms around me and I move my weight so our thighs lose contact. His lips brush my left earlobe.

"Why do women always do this to *me*?"

Driving away, I can still feel the warmth of his breath. Why do men always think it is about *them*?

I'm sure I could find an excuse or make an argument for what I'm about to do, but whatever way you dress it up, it's still breaking the law. A half brick. An overcoat. The pane of glass shatters and falls inward. So far it's vandalism or criminal damage. I reach inside and unlock the door. Now it's illegal entry. If I find the laptop it's going be theft. Is this what they mean by the slippery slope of crime?

It's after midnight. I'm wearing black jeans, leather gloves and a royal-blue turtleneck sweater Auntie Meena knitted me. I have brought with me a large roll of black plastic, some duct tape, a torch and a USB drive for downloading computer files.

I close my eyes. The layout of the ground floor rises up in front of me. I remember it from three days ago. Glass crunches under my sneakers. A red light blinks on the answering machine.

It shouldn't have come to this. Barnaby lied to me. It's not that I suspect him of anything serious. Good people protect those they love. But sometimes they don't recognize how good intentions and blind loyalty can twist their reasoning.

He's frightened of what I might find. *I'm* frightened. He's worried that he didn't really know his daughter. *I'm* worried too.

I climb the stairs. In the nursery I take the roll of black plastic and cover the window, sealing the edges with duct tape. Now it's safe to turn on the torch.

Precautions like this might be unnecessary but I can't afford to have the neighbors investigating or someone calling the police. My career (what career?) already hangs on a thread. I open the dresser drawer. The files have gone, along with the bundle of letters.

Moving from room to room I repeat the process, searching wardrobes and drawers beneath beds.

Next to the main bedroom there is a study with a

desk and filing cabinet. The lone window is partially open. I glance outside to a moonlit garden, blanketed by shadows and fallen leaves.

Unfurling another sheet of black plastic, I seal the window before turning on my torch. Beneath the desk, just above the skirting board, I notice a phone outlet. The top drawer contains software and instructions for an ADSL connection. I was right about the computer. Right about Barnaby.

Opening the remaining drawers, I find the usual office supplies—marker pens, a stapler, paper clips, a ball of rubber bands, Post-it notes, a cigarette lighter . . .

Next I search the filing cabinet, leafing through the hanging files. There are no labels or dates. I have to search each one. Plastic sheaths contain the domestic bills. Each telephone account has a list of outgoing calls to mobiles and long-distance numbers. I can possibly trace them but it will take days.

Among the invoices there is one from an Internet company. People sometimes leave copies of their e-mails on their server but I need Cate's password and username.

Having finished in the study I move on to the main bedroom, which is paper-free except for the book-shelves. Barnaby said Felix was sleeping in the guest room. His side of the wardrobe is empty. Cate slept on the right side of the bed. Her bedside drawer has night cream, moisturizer, emery boards and a picture frame lying facedown. I turn it over.

Two teenage girls are laughing at the camera; arms draped over each other's shoulders; seawater dripping from their hair. I can almost taste the salt on their skin and hear the waves shushing the shingles.

Every August the Elliot family used to rent a cottage

in Cornwall and spend their time sailing and swimming. Cate invited me one year. I was fifteen and it was my first proper beach holiday.

We swam, rode bikes, collected shells and watched the boys surfing at Widemouth Bay. A couple of them offered to teach Cate and me how to surf but Barnaby said that surfers were deadbeats and potheads. Instead he taught us how to sail in a solo dinghy on Padstow Harbour and the Camel Estuary. He could only take one of us out at a time.

I was embarrassed by my lime-green gingham seersucker one-piece, which my mother had chosen. Cate let me borrow one of her bikinis. As we sat side by side, Barnaby's leg would sometimes touch mine. And to balance the boat we had to lean out over the water and he put his arm around my waist. I liked the way he smelled of salt and suntan lotion.

Of an evening we played games like charades and Trivial Pursuit. I tried to sit next to him because he would nudge me in the ribs when he told one of his jokes or lean against me until we toppled over.

"You were flirting with him," said Cate after we'd gone to bed. We were sharing the loft. Mr. and Mrs. Elliot had the largest bedroom on the floor below and Jarrod had a room to himself at the back of the house.

"No, I wasn't."

"You *were*."

"Don't be ridiculous."

"It's disgusting. He's old enough to be—"

"Your father?"

We laughed. She was right, of course. I did flirt with Barnaby and he flirted back because he knew no other way to behave with women or girls.

Cate and I were lying on top of the bedclothes, unable to sleep because it was so hot. The loft had no insulation and seemed to trap the heat from the day.

"Do you know your problem?" she said. "You've never actually kissed a boy."

"Yes, I have."

"I'm not talking about your brothers. I mean a proper French kiss—with tongues."

I grew embarrassed.

"You should practice."

"Pardon?"

"Here, do this." She pressed her thumb and forefinger together. "Pretend this is a boy's lips and kiss them."

She held my hand and kissed it, snaking her tongue between my thumb and forefinger until they were wet with saliva.

"Now you try it." She held out her hand. It tasted of toothpaste and soap. "No, too much tongue. Yeuch!"

"*You* used a lot of tongue."

"Not that much." She wiped her hand on the sheets and looked at me with impatient affection. "Now you have to remember positioning."

"What do you mean?"

"You have to tilt your head to the right or left so you don't bang noses. We're not Eskimos."

She tossed her ponytail over her shoulder and pulled me close. Cupping my face, she pressed her lips against mine. I could feel her heart beating and the blood pulsing beneath her skin. Her tongue brushed along my lips and danced over my teeth. We were breathing the same air. My eyes stayed closed. It was the most amazing feeling.

"Wow, you're a fast learner," she said.

"You're a good teacher."

My heart was racing.

"Maybe we shouldn't do that again."

"It did feel a bit weird."

"Yeah. Weird."

I rubbed my palms down the front of my nightdress.

"Yeah, well, now you know how to do it," said Cate, picking up a magazine.

She had kissed a lot of boys, even at fifteen, but she didn't brag about it. Many more followed—pearls and pebbles strung around her neck—and as each one came and went there was scarcely a shrug of resignation or sadness.

I brush my fingers over the photograph and contemplate whether to take it with me. Who would know? At the same moment an answer occurs to me. Retracing my steps to the study, I open the desk drawer and spy the cigarette lighter. When we were kids and I stayed the night with Cate, she would sneak cigarettes upstairs and lean out the window so her parents didn't smell the smoke.

Tearing the plastic sheet from the sash window, I slide the lower pane upward and brace my hands on the sill as I lean outside, sixteen feet above the garden.

In the darkness I follow the line of a rainwater pipe that is fixed to the bricks with metal brackets. I need more light. Risking the torch, I direct the beam onto the pipe. I can just make out the knotted end of a thin cord, looped over the nearest bracket, beyond reach.

What did she use?

I look around the study. At the back of the desk, hard against the wall, is a wire coat hanger stretched to create a diamond shape with a hook on one end. Back at the window, I lean out and snag the loop of cord on the hook, pulling it toward me. The cord runs across the wall and over a small nail before dropping vertically. As I pull it a paint can emerges from the foliage of the garden. It rises toward me until I can lean out and grab it.

Pulling it inside, I use a coin to lever open the lid. Inside is half a packet of cigarettes and a larger package wrapped in plastic and held together with rubber bands. Retrieving it, I close the lid of the paint can and let the nylon cord slip through my fingers as I lower it back into the shrubs.

Returning to the main bedroom, I slip off the rubber bands from the package and unfold what turns out to be a plastic bag with documents pressed into the bottom corner. I spread the contents on the duvet: two airline boarding passes, a tourist map of Amsterdam and a brochure.

The boarding passes are for a British Midlands flight from Heathrow to Schiphol Airport in the Netherlands on the ninth of February, returning on the eleventh.

The tourist map has a picture of the Rijksmuseum on the front cover and is worn along the folds. It seems to cover the heart of Amsterdam where the canals and streets follow a concentric horseshoe pattern. The back of the map has bus, tram and train routes, flanked by a list of hotels. One of them is circled: the Red Tulip Hotel.

I pick up the brochure. It appears to promote a charity—the New Life Adoption Center, which has a phone number and a post box address in Hayward's Heath, West Sussex. There are pictures of babies and happy couples, along with a quote: "Isn't it nice to know when you're not ready to be a mother, somebody else is?"

Unfolding the brochure there are more photographs and testimonials.

"HOPING TO ADOPT? If you are looking for a safe, successful adoption we can help! Since 1995 we have helped hundreds of couples adopt babies. Our select group of caring professionals can make your dream of a family come true."

On the opposite page is a headline: ARE YOU PREGNANT AND CONSIDERING WHAT TO DO?

"We can help you! We offer assistance and encouragement during and after your pregnancy and can provide birthparent scholarships. Open adoption means YOU make the choices."

Underneath is a photograph of a child's hand clinging to the finger of an adult.

Someone called Julie writes: "Thank you for turning my unexpected pregnancy into a gift from God to all involved."

On the opposite page are further testimonials, this time from couples.

"Choosing adoption brought us a beautiful daughter and made our lives complete."

A loose page slips from the center of the brochure.

"'This child could be yours," it reads. "Born this month: a boy, white, with an unknown father. The mother, 18, is a prostitute and former drug user, now clean. This baby could be yours for a facilitation fee and medical expenses."

Returning the documents to the plastic bag, I snap the rubber bands in place.

The phone number on the back of Samira's photograph needed a foreign prefix. Cate visited the Netherlands in February. She announced she was twelve weeks pregnant in May.

I pick up the telephone next to the bed and call international inquiries. It feels wrong to call from the scene of the crime, as though I'm confessing. An operator gives me the country code for the Netherlands. Adding "31" this time, I call the number.

It connects. The ring tone is long and dull.

Someone picks up. Silence.

"Hello?"

Nothing.

"Hello, can you hear me?"

Someone is breathing.

"I'm trying to reach Samira. Is she there?"

A guttural voice, bubbling with phlegm, answers me. "Who is calling?"

The accent might be Dutch. It sounds more East European.

"A friend."

"Your name?"

"Actually, I'm a friend of a friend."

"Your name and your friend's name?"

Distrust sweeps over me like a cold shadow. I don't like this voice. I can feel it searching for me, reaching inside my chest, feeling blindly for my soft center, my soul.

"Is Samira there?"

"There is nobody here."

I try to sound calm. "I am calling on behalf of Cate Beaumont. I have the rest of the money."

I am extrapolating on the known facts, which is just a fancy way of saying that I'm winging it. *How much further can I go?*

The phone goes dead.

Not far enough.

Putting the receiver back on its cradle, I smooth the bed and pick up my things. As I turn toward the door I hear a tinkling sound. I know what it is. I made just such a sound when I smashed a pane of glass in the French doors.

Someone is in the house. What are the chances of two intruders on the same night? Slim. None. Tucking the package into the waistband of my jeans, I peer over the banister. There are muffled voices in the hall. At least two. A torch beam passes the bottom of the stairs. I pull back.

What to do? I shouldn't be here. Neither should they. Ahead of me are the stairs to the loft. Climbing them quickly, I reach a door that opens on stiff hinges.

From downstairs: "Did you hear something?"

"What?"

"I thought I heard something."

"Nah."

"I'll check upstairs."

One of them sounds Irish. It could be Brendan Pearl.

"Hey!"

"What?"

"You notice that?"

"What?"

"The windows are covered in plastic. Why would they do that?"

"Fucked if I know. Just get on with it."

The loft seems to be full of odd angles and narrow corners. My eyes are getting used to the dark. I can make out a single bed, a cabinet, a fan on a stand and cardboard boxes of clutter and bric-a-brac.

Squeezing into a space formed by the cabinet and the sloping roof, I pull boxes in front of me. I need a weapon. The iron bed has heavy brass balls on the bedposts. I unscrew one of them quietly and peel off a sock, slipping the ball inside. It slips down to the toe and I weigh it in my hands. It could break bones.

Returning to my hiding place, I listen for footsteps on the stairs and watch the door. I have to call the police. If I flip open my phone the screen will light up like a neon sign saying, "Here I am! Come and get me!"

Shielding it in both hands, I dial 999. An operator answers.

"Officer in trouble. Intruders on premises."

I whisper the address and my badge number. I can't stay on the line. The phone closes and the screen goes dark. Only my breathing now and the footsteps . . .

The door opens. A torch beam flashes and swings across the room. I can't see the figure behind it. He can't see me. He stumbles over a box and sends Christmas baubles spilling across the floor. The light finds one of them close to my feet.

He puts the torch on the bed, facing toward him. It reflects off his forehead. Brendan Pearl. All my weight is on the balls of my feet, ready to fight. What's he doing?

There is something in his fist. A boxlike can. He presses it and a stream of liquid arcs from the nozzle, shining silver in the torch beam. He presses again, soaking the boxes and drawing patterns on the walls. Fluid splashes across my forehead, leaking into my eyes.

Red hot wires stab into my brain and the smell catches in the back of my throat. Lighter fluid. Fire!

The pain is unimaginable, but I mustn't move. He's going to set fire to the house. I have to get out. I can't see.

Vibrations on the stairs. He's gone. Crawling from my hiding place, I reach the door and press my ear against it.

My eyes are useless. I need water to flush them out. There's a bathroom on the first floor as well as an en suite in the main bedroom. I can find them but only if Pearl has gone. I can't afford to wait.

Something breaks with a crack and topples over downstairs. My vision is blurred but I see a light. Not light. Fire!

The ground floor is ablaze and the smoke is rising. Clinging to the handrail, I make it down to the landing. Feeling my way along the wall, I reach the en suite and splash water into my eyes. I can see only blurred outlines, shadows instead of sharp detail.

The smoke is getting thicker. On my hands and knees, I feel my way across the bedroom, smelling the lighter fluid on the carpet. When the fire reaches this floor it will accelerate. The study window is still open. I crawl across the landing, bumping my head against a wall. My fingers find the skirting board. I can feel the heat.

Finding the window, I lean outside and take deep breaths between spluttering coughs. There is a whooshing sound behind me. Flames sweep past the open door. Hungry. Feeding on the accelerant.

Climbing onto the window ledge I look down. I can just make out the garden, sixteen feet below. A jump like that will break both my legs. I turn my head toward the downpipe bolted to the wall. My eyes are useless. How far was it? Four feet. Maybe a little more.

I can feel the heat of the fire on the backs of my legs. A window blows out beneath me. I hear glass scattering through the shrubbery.

I have to back myself to do this. I have to trust my

memory and my instincts. Toppling sideways, I reach out, falling.

My left hand brushes past the pipe. My right hand hooks around it. Momentum will either pull me loose or rip my shoulder out. Two hands have it now. My hip crashes against the bricks and I hang on.

Hand below hand, I shimmy toward the ground. Sirens are coming. My feet touch soft earth and I wheel about, stumbling a dozen paces before tripping over a flower bed and sprawling on my face.

Every window at the rear of the house is lit up. Through my watery eyes it sounds and looks like a university party. The ultimate housewarming.

12

Two detectives have turned up. One of them I remember from training college, Eric Softell. The name sounds like a brand of toilet paper, which is why they nicknamed him "Arsewipe" at training college. Not me, of course. Sikh girls don't risk calling people names.

"I heard you were off the force," he says.

"No."

"Still running?"

"Yes."

"Not fast enough from what I hear." He grins at his partner, Billy Marsh, a detective constable.

Stories about the camaraderie of police officers are often sadly overstated. I don't find many of my colleagues particularly lovable or supportive, but at least most of them are honest and some of them are keepers like DI Ruiz.

A paramedic has flushed out my eyes with distilled water. I'm sitting on the back ramp of the ambulance, head tilted, while he tapes cotton wool over my left eye.

"You should see an eye specialist," he says. "It can sometimes take a week before the full damage is clear."

"Permanent damage?"

"See the specialist."

Behind him fire hoses snake across the gleaming road and firemen in reflective vests are mopping up. Structurally, there is still a house on the block, but the insides are gutted and smoking. The loft collapsed under the weight of water.

I called Hari to come and get me. Now he's watching the firemen with a mixture of awe and envy. What boy doesn't want to play with a hose?

Sensing the animosity between Softell and me, he tries to step in and play the protective brother, which doesn't really suit him.

"Listen, punka-wallah, why don't you run along and fetch us a cup of tea?" says Softell.

Hari doesn't understand the insult but he recognizes the tone.

I should be angry but I'm used to remarks like this from people like Softell. During probationer training a group of us were given riot shields and sent to the parade ground. Another band of recruits were told to attack us verbally and physically. There were no rules, but we weren't able to retaliate. Softell spat in my face and called me a "Paki whore." I practically thanked him.

My left thigh is slightly corked; my knuckles are scraped and raw. There are questions. Answers. The name Brendan Pearl means nothing to them.

"Explain to me again what you were doing in the house."

"I was driving by. I saw a burglary in process. I called it in."

"From inside the house?"

"Yes, sir."

"So you followed them inside?"

"Yes."

Softell shakes his head. "You just happened to be driving past a friend's house and you saw the same man who was driving the car that ran her down. What do you think, Billy?"

"Sounds like bullshit to me." Marsh is the one taking notes.

"How did you get lighter fluid in your eyes?"

"He was spraying it around."

"Yeah, yeah, while you were *hiding* in the corner."

Arsehole!

Casually, he props his foot on the tray of the ambulance. "If you were just gonna hide in there, why bother going in at all?"

"I thought there was only one of them."

I'm digging myself into a hole.

"Why didn't you phone for backup *before* you went in?"

Deeper and deeper.

"I don't know, sir."

Drops of water have beaded on the polished toe of his shoe.

"You see how it looks, don't you?" Softell says.

"How does it look?"

"A house burns down. A witness comes forward who is covered in lighter fluid. Rule number one when dealing with arson—nine times out of ten, the person who yells 'fire' is the person who starts the fire."

"You can't be serious. Why would I do that?"

His shoulders lift and drop. "Who knows? Maybe you just like burning shit."

The whole street has been woken. Neighbors are standing on the pavement in dressing gowns and overcoats. Children are jumping on a hose and dancing away from a leak that sprays silver under the streetlight.

A black cab pulls up outside the ring of fire engines. Ruiz emerges. He steps through the ring of rubberneckers, ignoring the constable who is trying to keep them back.

After pausing to appraise the house, he continues along the road until he reaches me. The white eye patch makes me look like a reverse pirate.

"Do you ever have a *normal* day?" he asks.

"Once. It was a Wednesday."

He looks me up and down. I'm putting most of my weight on one leg because of my thigh. Surprisingly, he leans forward and kisses my cheek, an absolute first.

"I thought you retired," says Billy Marsh.

"That's right, son."

"Well, what are you doing here?"

"I asked him to come," I explain.

Ruiz is sizing up the detectives. "Mind if I listen in?"

It sounds like a question only it isn't. The DI manages to do that sometimes—turn questions into statements.

"Just don't get in the bloody way," mumbles Softell.

Marsh is on the phone calling for a Scene of Crime team to sweep the house and garden for clues. The fire brigade will launch its own investigation. I hobble away from the ambulance, which has another call. Ruiz takes my arm.

Hari is still here. "You can go home now," I tell him.

"What about you?"

"I could be a while."

"You want me to stay?"

"That's OK."

He glances at Softell and whispers, "Do you know that prick?"

"He's OK."

"No wonder people dislike coppers."

"Hey!"

He grins. "Not you, sis."

There are more questions to answer. Softell becomes less interested in what I was doing in the house and more interested in Brendan Pearl.

"So you think this arson attack is linked to the deaths of the Beaumonts?"

"Yes."

"Why would Pearl burn down their house?"

"Perhaps he wanted to destroy evidence—letters, e-mails, phone records—anything that might point to him."

I explain about Cate's fake pregnancy and the money missing from Cate's account. "I think she arranged to buy a baby, but something went wrong."

Marsh speaks: "People adopt foreign kids all the time—Chinese orphans, Romanians, Koreans. Why would you buy a child?"

"She tried to adopt and couldn't."

"How do you buy one?"

I don't have the answers. Softell glances at Billy Marsh. There is a beat of silence and something invisible passes between them.

"Why didn't you report any of this earlier?"

"I couldn't be sure."

"So you went looking for evidence. You broke into the house."

"No."

"Then you tried to cover your tracks with a can of lighter fluid and a cock-'n'-bull story."

"Not true."

Ruiz is nearby, clenching and unclenching his fists. For the first time I notice how old he looks in a shapeless overcoat, worn smooth at the elbows.

"Hey, Detective Sergeant, I know what you're thinking," he says. "You want some kitchen-sink, bog-standard example of foul play you can solve by nine o'clock and still make your ballet lesson. This is one of your colleagues, one of your own. Your job is to believe her."

Softell puffs up, too stupid to keep his mouth shut. "And who do you think you are?"

"Godzilla."

"Who?"

Ruiz rolls his eyes. "I'm the monster that's going to stomp all over your fucking career if you don't pay this lady some respect."

Softell looks like he's been bitch-slapped. He takes out his mobile and punches in a number. I overhear him talking to his superintendent. I don't know what he's told. Ruiz still has a lot of friends in the Met, people who respect what he's done.

When the call finishes Softell is a chastened man. A task force investigation has been authorized and a warrant issued for the arrest of Brendan Pearl.

"I want you at the station by midday to make a statement," he says.

"I can go?"

"Yeah."

Ruiz won't let me drive. He takes me home in my car. Squeezed behind the wheel of my hatchback, he looks like a geriatric Noddy.

"Was it Pearl?"

"Yes."

"Did you see him?"

"Yes."

Taking one hand off the wheel, he scratches his chin. His ring finger is severed below the first knuckle, courtesy of a high-velocity bullet. He likes to tell people his third wife attacked him with a meat cleaver.

I tell Ruiz about the boarding passes and the brochure for the New Life Adoption Center. We both know stories about stolen and trafficked babies. Most stray into the realm of urban myth—baby farms in Guatemala and runaways snatched from the streets of São Paulo for organ harvesting.

"Let's just say you're right and Cate Beaumont organized some sort of private adoption or to buy a baby. Why go through the pretense of pregnancy?"

"Perhaps she wanted to convince Felix the baby was his."

"That's a pretty ambitious goal. What if the kid looks nothing like him?"

"A lot of husbands are happy to *believe* they've fathered a child. History is littered with mistakes."

Ruiz raises an eyebrow. "You mean lies."

I rise to the bait. "Yes, women can be devious. Sometimes we have to be. We're the ones who get left changing nappies when some bloke decides he's not ready to commit or to get rid of his Harley or his porn collection."

Silence.

"Did that sound like a rant?" I ask.

"A little."

"Sorry."

Ruiz begins thinking out loud, trawling through his

memory. That's the thing about the DI—nothing is ever forgotten. Other people grimace and curse, trying to summon up the simplest details but Ruiz does it effortlessly, recalling facts, figures, quotes and names.

"Three years ago the Italian police smashed a ring of Ukrainian human traffickers who were trying to sell an unborn baby. They ran a kind of auction looking for the highest bidder. Someone offered to pay £250,000."

"Cate traveled to Amsterdam in February. She could have arranged a deal."

"Alone?"

"I don't know."

"How did they communicate with her?"

I think back to the fire. "We might never know."

He drops me home and arranges to meet me in the morning.

"You should see an eye specialist."

"First I have to make a statement."

Upstairs, I pull the phone jack from the wall and turn off my mobile. I have talked to enough people today. I want a shower and a warm bed. I want to cry into a pillow and fall asleep. A girl should be allowed.

13

Wembley Police Station is a brand-new building decked in blue and white on the Harrow Road. The new national stadium is almost a mile away with soaring light towers visible above the rooftops.

Softell keeps me waiting before taking my statement. His attitude has changed since last night. He has looked up Pearl on the computer and the interest sparks in his eyes like a gas ring igniting. Softell is the sort of detective who goes through an entire career with his head under his armpit, not understanding people's motives or making any headline arrests. Now he can sense an opportunity.

The deaths of Cate and Felix Beaumont are a side issue. A distraction. I can see what he's going to do: he'll dismiss Cate as a desperate woman with a history of psychiatric problems and a criminal record. Pearl is the man he wants.

"You have no evidence a baby ever existed," he says.

"What about the missing money?"

"Someone probably ripped her off."

"And then killed her."

"Not according to the vehicle accident report."

Softell hands me a typed statement. I have to sign each page and initial any changes. I look at my words. I have lied about why I was at the house and what happened before the fire. Does my signature make it worse?

Taking back the statement, he straightens the pages and punches the stapler. "Very fucking professional," he sneers. "You know it never stops—the lying. Once you start it just keeps getting worse."

"Yeah, well, you'd know," I say, wishing I could think of a put-down that wasn't so lame. Mostly, I wish I could tear up the statement and start again.

Ruiz is waiting for me in the foyer.

"How's the eye?"

"The specialist said I should wear an eye patch for a week."

"So where is it?"

"In my pocket."

Stepping on a black rubber square, the doors open automatically.

"Your boyfriend has called six times in the last hour. Ever thought of getting a dog instead?"

"What did you tell him?"

"Nothing. That's why he's here."

I look up and see Dave leaning on Ruiz's car. He wraps me in a bear hug with his face in my hair. Ruiz turns away as though embarrassed.

"Are you smelling me, Dave?"

"Yup."

"That's a bit creepy."

"Not to me. I'm just glad you're in one piece."

132

"Only bruises."

"I could kiss them better."

"Perhaps later."

Dressed in a dark blue suit, white shirt and maroon tie, Dave has tidied up since his promotion, but I notice a brown sauce stain on the tie that he hasn't managed to sponge away. My mother would recognize a detail like that. Scary.

My stomach is empty. I haven't eaten since yesterday.

We find a café near Wembley Central with a smudged blackboard menu and enough grease in the air to flatten Dave's hair. It's an old-fashioned "caff" with Formica tables, paper napkins, and a nervy waitress with a nose stud.

I order tea and toast. Ruiz and Dave choose the all-day breakfast—otherwise known as the 999 because it's a heart attack on a plate. Nobody says anything until the food is consumed and tea poured. The DI has milk and sugar.

"There is a guy I used to play rugby with," he says. "He never talked about his job, but I know he works for MI5. I called him this morning. He told me an interesting thing about Brendan Pearl."

"What's that?"

Ruiz takes out a tattered notebook held together with a rubber band. Loose pages tumble through his fingers. A lot of detectives don't believe in keeping notes. They want their memories to be "flexible" should they ever get in the witness box. Ruiz has a memory like the proverbial steel trap, yet he still backs it up on paper.

"According to my friend, Pearl was last known to be working as a security consultant for a construction company in Afghanistan. Three foreign contractors were killed in mid-September 2004 in a convoy traveling on the highway leading from the main airport to central

Kabul when a suicide bomber drove into them. Pearl was among the wounded. He spent three weeks in a German hospital and then signed himself out. Nobody has heard from him since then."

"So what's he doing here?" asks Dave.

"And how did Cate meet him?" I add.

Ruiz gathers the pages and slips the rubber band around them. "Maybe we should check out this New Life Adoption Center."

Dave disagrees. "It's not *our* investigation."

"Not *officially*," concedes the DI.

"Not even unofficially."

"It's an *independent* investigation."

"Unauthorized."

"*Unconstrained*."

Interrupting them, I suggest, "You could come with us, Dave."

He hesitates.

Ruiz spies an opening. "That's what I like about you, Dave. You're a freethinker. Some people think the modern British detective has become timid and punctilious, but not you. You're a credit to the Met. You're not frightened to have an opinion or act on a hunch."

It's like watching a fisherman casting a fly. It curls through the air, settles on the water and drifts downstream, drifting, drifting . . .

"I suppose it wouldn't hurt to check it out," says Dave.

———

There are no signs pointing out the New Life Adoption Center, either in the nearest village or at the gates, which are flanked by sandstone pillars. A loose gravel driveway curves through fields and crosses a single-lane stone bridge. Friesians dot the pasture and scarcely stir as we pass.

Eventually, we pull up in front of a large Adam's-style house, in the noise shadow of Gatwick Airport. I take Dave's arm.

"OK, we've been married for six years. It was a big Sikh wedding. I looked beautiful of course. We've been trying for a baby for five years but your sperm count is too low."

"Does it have to be *my* sperm count?"

"Oh, don't be so soft! Give me your ring."

He slides a white gold band from his pinkie and I place it on my ring finger.

Ruiz has stayed behind in the village pub, chatting with the locals. So far we've established that the adoption center is a privately run charity operating out of a former stately home, Followdale House. The founder, Julian Shawcroft, is a former executive director of the Infertility and Planned Parenthood Clinic in Manchester.

A young woman, barely out of her teens, answers the doorbell. She's wearing woolly socks and a powder-blue dressing gown that struggles to hide her pregnancy.

"I can't really help you," she confides immediately. "I'm just minding the front desk while Stella has a tinkle."

"Stella?"

"She's in charge. Well, not really in charge. Mr. Shawcroft is *really* in charge but he's often away. He's here today, which is unusual. He's the chairman or the managing director. I can never work out the difference. I mean, what does an MD do and what does a chairman do? I'm talking too much, aren't I? I do that sometimes. My name is Meredith. Do you think Hugh is a nice boy's name? Hugh Jackman is very cute. I can't think of any other Hughs."

"Hugh Grant," I suggest.

"Cool."

"Hugh Hefner," says Dave.

"Who's he?" she asks.

"It doesn't matter," I tell her, glaring at Dave.

Meredith's hair is just long enough to pull into a ponytail and her nail polish is chipped where she has picked it off.

The lobby of the house has two faded Chesterfields on either side of a fireplace. The staircase, with its ornate banister, is sealed off by a blue tasseled rope hung from brass posts.

She leads us to an office in a side room. Several desks have computers, and a photocopier spits out pages as a light slides back and forth beneath the glass.

There are posters on the wall. One of them shows a couple swinging an infant between their outstretched hands, except the child is cut out like a missing piece of a jigsaw puzzle. Underneath the caption reads: IS THERE A CHILD-SIZE HOLE IN YOUR LIFE?

Through French doors I can see a rose garden and what might once have been a croquet lawn.

"When are you due?" I ask.

"Two weeks."

"Why are you here?"

She giggles. "This is an adoption center, silly."

"Yes, but people come to adopt a baby, not to have one."

"I haven't decided yet," she says in a matter-of-fact way.

A woman appears—Stella—apologizing for the delay. She looks very businesslike in a dark polo-neck, black trousers and imitation snakeskin shoes with pointed toes and kitten heels.

Her eyes survey me up and down, as though taking an inventory. "Nope, the womb is vacant," I feel like saying. She glances at her diary.

"We don't have an appointment," I explain. "It was rather a spur-of-the-moment decision to come."

"Adoption should never be spur-of-the-moment."

"Oh, I don't mean *that* decision. We've been talking about it for months. We were in the neighborhood."

Dave chips in. "I have an aunt who lives close."

"I see."

"We want to adopt a baby," I add. "It's all we think about."

Stella takes down our names. I call myself Mrs. King, which doesn't sound as weird as it probably should.

"We've been married six years and trying to have a baby for five."

"So you're looking to adopt because you can't have your own baby?"

It's a loaded question. "I come from a big family. I wanted the same. But even though we want our own children, we always talked about adopting."

"Are you prepared to take an older child?"

"We'd like a baby."

"Yes, well, that may be so, but there are very few new-born babies put up for adoption in this country. The waiting list is very long."

"How long?"

"Upward of five years."

Dave blows air through his cheeks. He's better at this

than I expected. "Surely it can be fast-tracked in some way," he says. "I mean, even the slowest of wheels can be *oiled*."

Stella seems to resent the suggestion. "Mr. King, we are a nonprofit charity governed by the same rules and regulations as local authority adoption services. The interests of the child come *first* and *last*. *Oil* doesn't enter into it."

"Of course not. I didn't mean to suggest—"

"My husband works in management," I explain contritely. "He believes that almost any problem can be solved by throwing more people or money at it."

Stella nods sympathetically and for the first time seems to consider my skin color. "We do facilitate inter-country adoptions, but there are no children made available from the subcontinent. Most people are choosing to adopt from Eastern Europe."

"We're not fussy," adds Dave. I kick him under the desk. "We're not fazed, I mean. It's not a race thing."

Stella is eyeing him cautiously. "There are many *bad* reasons to adopt. Some people try to save their marriage, or replace a child who has died, or they want a fashion accessory because all their friends have one."

"That's not us," I say.

"Good. Well even with intercountry adoptions, the assessment and approval process is exactly the same as for adopting a child in this country. This includes full medicals, home visits, criminal record checks and inter-views with social workers and psychologists."

She stands and opens a filing cabinet. The form is thirty pages long.

"I was wondering if Mr. Shawcroft was here today."

"Do you know him?"

"Only by reputation. That's how I heard about the center—through a friend."

"And what's your friend's name?"

"Cate Beaumont."

I get no sense of whether she's heard the name before.

"Mr. Shawcroft is normally very busy fund-raising but fortunately he's here today. He might be able to spare you a few minutes."

She excuses herself and I can hear her walking upstairs.

"What do you think?" whispers Dave.

"Watch the door." Skirting the desk, I open the drawer of the filing cabinet.

"That's an illegal search."

"Just *watch* the door."

My fingers are moving over the files. Each adoptive family appears to have one but there is no "Beaumont" or "Elliot." Some folders are marked by colored stickers. There are names typed on the labels. At first glance I think they might be children, but the ages are all wrong. These are young women.

One name jumps out at me. Carla Donavon. Donavon's younger sister. His *pregnant* sister. A coincidence? Hardly.

"Those files are confidential." The disembodied voice startles me.

I look to Dave. He shakes his head. There is an intercom on the desk. I scan the ceiling and spy a small security camera in the corner. I should have seen it earlier.

"If you want to know something, Mrs. King, you should ask," says the voice. "I assume that's your real name or perhaps you have lied about that as well."

"Do you always eavesdrop on people?" I say.

"Do you always illegally search someone's office and look at highly confidential files? Who exactly are you?"

Dave answers, "Police officers. I'm Detective Sergeant Dave King. This is Detective Constable Alisha Barba. We are making inquiries about a woman we believe may have been one of your clients."

The faint buzzing of the intercom goes silent. A side door opens. A man enters, in his mid-fifties, with a sturdy frame and a broad face that creases momentarily as he smiles disarmingly. His hair, once blond, now gray, has tight curls like wood shavings from a lathe.

"I'm sure there must be a law against police officers misrepresenting who they are and conducting unauthorized searches."

"The drawer was open. I was simply closing it."

This triggers a smile. He has every right to be angry and suspicious. Instead he finds it amusing. He makes a point of locking the filing cabinet before addressing us again.

"Now that we know exactly who we are, perhaps I could give you a guided tour and you could tell me what you're doing here."

He leads us into the lobby and through the French doors onto the terrace. The young woman we saw earlier is sitting on a swing in the garden. Her dressing gown billows as she rocks back and forth, getting higher and higher.

"Be careful, Meredith," he calls. And then to us. "She's a clumsy young thing."

"Why is she here?"

"Meredith hasn't decided what she wants to do. Giving up a baby is a difficult and courageous decision. We help young women like her to decide."

"You try to convince her."

"On the contrary. We offer love and support. We teach parenting skills so she'll be ready. And if she decides to give up her baby, we have scholarships that can help her find a flat and get a job. We operate open adoptions."

"Open?"

"The birth mothers and adoptive parents get to know one another and often stay in touch afterward."

Shawcroft chooses an unraked gravel path around the southern end of the house. Large bay windows reveal a lounge. Several young women are playing cards in front of a fire.

"We offer prenatal classes, massage therapy and have quite a good gymnasium," he explains.

"Why?"

"Why not?"

"I don't understand why it's necessary."

Shawcroft has an eye for an opening. It gives him the opportunity to explain his philosophy and he does so passionately, haranguing the historical attitudes that saw young unmarried mothers demonized or treated like outcasts.

"Single motherhood has become more acceptable but it is still a challenging choice," he explains. "That's why I established this center. There are far too many orphans and unwanted children in our society and overseas, with too few options available to improve their lives.

"Have you any idea how slow, bureaucratic and unfair our adoption system is? We leave it in the hands of people who are underfunded, understaffed and inexperienced—people who play God with the lives of children."

Dave has dropped back.

"I began out of a small office in Mayfair. There was just me. I charged £50 for a two-hour consultancy session. Two years later I had a full-time staff of eight and had completed more than a hundred adoptions. Now we're here." He gestures to Followdale House.

"How can you afford this place?"

"People have been very generous—new parents and grandparents. Some leave us money as bequests or make donations. We have a staff of fourteen, including social workers, counselors, career advisers, health visitors and a psychologist."

In one corner of the garden I notice a golf bag propped beneath an umbrella and a bucket of balls waiting to be hit. There are calluses on his fingers.

"My one indulgence," he explains, gazing over the fence into the pasture. "The cows are rather ball-shy. I have developed an incurable slice since my operation."

"Operation?"

"My hip. Old age catching up on me."

He picks up a club and swings it gently at a rosebush. A flower dissolves in a flurry of petals. Examining his fingers, he opens and closes his fist.

"It's always harder to hold a club in the winter. Some people wear gloves. I like being able to *feel* the grip."

He pauses and turns to face me. "Now, Detective Constable, let's dispense with the pretense. Why are you here?"

"Do you know someone called Cate Beaumont?"

"No." The answer is abrupt.

"You don't need to check your client files?"

"I remember all of them."

"Even those who don't succeed?"

"*Especially* those who don't succeed."

Dave has joined us. He picks a metal-headed driver and eyes a Friesian in the distance before thinking better of it.

"My friend faked her pregnancy and emptied her bank account. I think she arranged to buy a baby."

"Which is illegal."

"She had one of your brochures."

"Which is *not* illegal." Shawcroft doesn't take offense or become defensive. "Where is your friend now?"

"She's dead. Murdered."

He repeats the word with renewed respect. His hands are unfailingly steady.

"The brochure contained an advertisement for a baby boy whose mother was a prostitute and a former drug addict. It mentioned a facilitation fee and medical expenses."

Shawcroft lets his palm glide over his cheek, giving himself time. For a moment something struggles inside him. I want a denial. There isn't one.

"The facilitation fee is to cover paperwork such as visas and birth certificates."

"Selling children is illegal."

"The baby was not for sale. Every applicant is properly vetted. We require referees and assessment reports. There are group workshops and familiarization. Finally, there is an adoption panel that must approve the adopter before a child can be matched to them."

"If these adoptions are aboveboard, why are they advertised using post box numbers?"

He gazes straight ahead as if plotting the distance of his next shot.

"Do you know how many children die in the world every year, Alisha? Five million. War, poverty, disease, famine, neglect, land mines and predators. I have seen children so malnourished they don't have the energy to swat flies away and starving women holding babies to their withered breasts, desperate to feed them. I have seen them throw their babies over the fences of rich people's houses or, worse still, into the River Ganges because they can't afford to look after them. I have seen AIDS orphans, crack babies and children sold into slavery for as little as £15. And what do we do in this country? We make it *harder* for people to adopt. We tell them they're too old, or the wrong color, or the wrong religion."

Shawcroft makes no attempt to hide the bitterness in his voice. "It takes courage for a country to admit it can't take care of its smallest and weakest. Many countries who are not so brave would prefer to see abandoned children starve than to leave for a better life.

"The system is unfair. So, yes, I sometimes cut corners. In some countries contracts can be signed with birth mothers. Hollywood movie stars do it. Government ministers do it. Children can be rescued. Infertile couples can have families."

"By *buying* babies."

"By *saving* them."

For all his avuncular charm and geniality, there is steel in this man's nature and something vaguely dangerous. A mixture of sentimentality and spiritual zeal that fortifies the hearts of tyrants.

"You think that what I'm doing is immoral. Let me tell you what's more immoral. Doing *nothing*. Sitting back in your comfortable chair in your comfortable home thinking that just because you sponsor a child in Zambia you're doing enough."

"It shouldn't mean breaking the law."

"Every family that adopts here is vetted and approved by a panel of experts."

"You're profiting from their desperation."

"All payments go back into the charity."

He begins listing the number of foreign adoptions the center has overseen and the diplomatic hurdles he has had to overcome. His arguments are marshalled so skillfully that I have no line of reasoning to counter them. My objections sound mean-spirited and hostile. I should apologize.

"Your friend's death is very unfortunate, DC Barba, but I would strongly counsel you against making any rash or unfounded claims about what we do here. Police knocking on doors, asking questions, upsetting families, that would be very unfortunate."

He has made his first mistake. I can accept his passionate beliefs and his rationale for them, but I don't appreciate emotional blackmail.

Stella appears on the terrace and calls to Shawcroft, miming a phone call with her hand.

"I have to go," he says, smiling tiredly. "The baby you referred to was born in Washington four weeks ago. A boy. A young couple from Oxford are adopting him."

I watch him return along the path, gravel rasping beneath his soft-soled shoes. Meredith is still in the garden. He motions for her to come inside. It is getting cold.

"New Boy" Dave falls into step beside me and we follow the path in the opposite direction toward the car park, passing a statue of a young girl holding an urn and another of a Cupid with a missing penis.

"So what do you think?" he asks.

"What sort of adoption center has surveillance cameras?"

14

"Finding Donavon" sounds like the title of an Irish art-house movie directed by Neil Jordan. "Deconstructing Donavon" is another good title and that's exactly what I plan to do when I find him.

Maybe it's a coincidence, maybe it's not a coincidence, but I don't like the way that his name keeps popping up whenever I trace Cate's movements. Donavon claims to know when someone is lying. That's because he's an expert on the subject—a born deceiver.

On the drive back to London we go over the details of our meeting with Shawcroft. Ruiz doesn't see a problem with adoption having a financial element if couples are vetted properly. Too much control allows black markets to flourish. Perhaps he's right, but a zealot like Shawcroft can turn compassion into a dangerous crusade.

"New Boy" Dave has work to do. We drop him at the Harrow Road police station and I make him promise to run a check on Shawcroft. He kisses my cheek and whispers, "Leave this alone."

I can't. I won't. He adds something else. "I *did* like being married to you."

Timewise it was even shorter than Britney Spears's first wedding, but I don't tell him that.

Nobody answers the door at Donavon's house. The curtains are drawn and his motorbike isn't parked outside. A neighbor suggests we try the markets in Whitechapel Road. Donavon has a weekend stall there.

Parking behind the Royal London Hospital, we follow the insurrection of noise, color and movement. Dozens of stalls spill out from the pavement. Everything is for sale—Belgian chocolates from Poland, Greek feta from Yorkshire, Gucci handbags from China and Rolex watches draped inside trench coats.

Traders yell over one another.

"Fresh carnations. Two-fifty a bunch!"

"Live mussels!"

"Garden tomatoes as red as your cheeks!"

I can't see Donavon but I recognize his stall. Draped from the metal framework there are dozens of intricate necklaces or perhaps they're wind chimes. They twirl in the light breeze, fragmenting the remains of the sunlight. Beneath them, haphazardly displayed, are novelty radios, digital clocks and curling tongs from Korea.

Carla looks cold and bored. She's wearing red woolen tights and a short denim skirt stretched over her growing bump.

I close the gap between us and slide my hand under her sweater, across her abdomen until I feel the warmth of her skin.

"Hey!"

I pull my hand away as if scalded. "I just wanted to be sure."

"Sure about what?"

"It doesn't matter."

Carla looks at me suspiciously and then at Ruiz. A faint, fast vibration is coming off her, as though something terrible and soundless is spinning inside.

"Have you seen him?" she asks anxiously.

"Who?"

"Paul. He hasn't been home in two days."

"When did you last see him?"

"On Saturday. He had a phone call and went out."

"Did he say where?"

"No. He never leaves it this long. He always calls me."

Female intuition is often a myth. Some women just *think* they're more intuitive. I know I'm letting the sisters down by saying that, but gender isn't a factor. It's blood. Families can tell when something is wrong. Carla's eyes dart across the crowd as though assembling a human jigsaw puzzle.

"When are you due?" I ask.

"Christmas."

"What can you tell me about the New Life Adoption Center?"

Her mouth seems to frame something she's too embarrassed to admit. I wait for her.

"I don't know what sort of mother I'm gonna make. Paul says I'll be fine. He says I learned from one of the *worst* so I won't make the same mistakes our mum did." Her hands are trembling. "I didn't want an abortion. It's not because of any religious thing. It's just how I feel, you know. That's why I thought about adoption."

"You went to see Julian Shawcroft."

"He offered to help me. He said there were scholarships, you know. I always wanted to be a makeup artist or a beautician. He said he could arrange it."

"If you gave up the baby?"

"Yeah, well, you can't do both, eh? Not look after a baby and work full-time—not without help."

"So what did you decide?" asks the DI.

Her shoulders grow rounder. "I keep changing me mind. Paul wants me to keep it. He says he'll look after us all." She gnaws at a reddened fingernail.

A crew-cutted teenager stops and picks up a transistor radio shaped like a Pepsi can.

"Don't waste your money—this stuff is shite," says Carla. The youth looks hard done by rather than grateful.

"How did you hear about the New Life Adoption Center?"

"A friend told Paul about it."

"Who?"

Carla shrugs.

Her mauve-tinted eyelids tremble. She doesn't have the wherewithal to lie to me. She can't see a reason. Glancing above her head, I notice the feathers and beads.

I have seen one of these ornaments before—at Cate's house, in the nursery. It was hanging above the new cot.

"What are they?" I ask.

Carla unhooks one from the metal frame above her and hangs it from her finger, watching me through a wooden circle crisscrossed with colored thread and hung with feathers and beads.

"This is a dream catcher," she explains. "American Indians believe the night air is filled with dreams, some good and some bad. They hang a dream catcher over a child's bed so it can catch dreams as they flow by. The good dreams know how to slip through the holes and slide down the soft feathers where they land gently on the child's head. But the bad dreams get tangled in the web and perish when the sun comes up."

Blowing gently, she makes the feathers bob and swirl.

Donavon didn't go to the reunion to "make his peace" with Cate. He had seen her before. He gave her a dream catcher or she bought one from him.

"How well did your brother know Cate Beaumont?"

Carla shrugs. "They were friends, I guess."

"That's not possible."

She bridles. "I'm not lying. When Paul was in the Paras, she wrote to him. I seen the letters."

"Letters?"

"He brought them home from Afghanistan. He kept her letters."

I hear myself quizzing her, wanting to know the where, when and why, but she can't answer for her brother. Trying to pin her down to specific dates and times makes her even more confused.

Ruiz intervenes and I feel a twinge of guilt at having browbeaten a pregnant woman who's worried about her brother.

The afternoon sun is sliding below rooftops, leaving behind shadows. Stallholders are shutting up, loading wares into boxes, bags and metal trunks. Buckets of ice are tipped into the gutter. Plastic awnings are rolled and tied.

After helping Carla load up the red Escort van, we follow her home. The house is still empty. There are no messages waiting for her on the answer phone. I should be angry with Donavon, yet I feel a nagging emptiness.

This doesn't make any sense. Why would Cate write letters to someone who sexually assaulted her? She was talking to him the night of the reunion. What were they saying?

Ruiz drops me home. Turning off the engine, we stare at the streetscape as if expecting it to suddenly change after more than a century of looking almost the same.

"You want to come in?"

"I should go."

"I could cook."

He looks at me.

"Or we could get takeaway."

"Got any alcohol?"

"There's an off-licence on the corner."

I can hear him whistling his way up the street as I open the front door and check my answering machine. All the messages are for Hari. His girlfriends. I should double his rent to pay the phone bill.

The doorbell rings. It should be Ruiz—only it's not. A younger man has come to the door, dressed in a pepper-gray suit. Clean-shaven with broad shoulders and Nordic features, his rectangular glasses seem too small for his face. Behind him are two more men, who are standing beside cars that are double-parked and blocking the street. They look official, but not like police officers.

"DC Barba, we need you to accompany us." He makes a clicking sound with his tongue that might be a signal or a sign of nerves.

"Why? Who are you?"

He produces a badge. SOCA. The Serious Organized

Crime Agency. The organization is less than a year old and the media have labeled it Britain's answer to the FBI, with its own Act of Parliament, budget and extraordinary powers. What do they want with me?

"I'm a police officer," I stammer.

"I know who you are."

"Am I under arrest?"

"Important people wish to speak to you."

I look for Ruiz. He's hurrying down the pavement with a half bottle of Scotch tucked in his coat pocket. One of the men beside the cars tries to step in front of him. The DI feints left and drops his shoulder, propelling him over a low brick wall into a muddy puddle. This could get ugly.

"It's all right, sir."

"Who are they?"

"SOCA."

The look on his face says it all. Fear and loathing.

"You might want to pack a few things for the journey," says the senior officer. He and Ruiz are sizing each other up like roosters in a henhouse.

I pack a sports bag with a pair of jeans, knickers and a lightweight sweater. My gun is wrapped in a cloth on top of a kitchen cabinet. I contemplate whether I should take it with me, but dismiss the idea as being too hostile. I have no idea what these people want, but I can't risk antagonizing them.

Ruiz follows me to the car. A hand is placed on the back of my head as I slide into the rear seat. The brake is released suddenly and I'm thrown back against the new-smelling leather.

"I hope we haven't spoiled your plans for the evening, DC Barba," says the gray-suited man.

"You know my name, can I have yours?"

"Robert Forbes."

"You work for SOCA?"

"I work for the government."

"Which *part* of the government?"

"The part people don't often talk about." He makes the clicking sound again.

The car has reached the end of Hanbury Street. Beneath a streetlight, a solitary spectator, clad in black leather, leans against a motorcycle. A helmet dangles from his right hand. A fag end burns in his fist. It's Donavon.

Traffic meanders at an agonizingly slow pace, shuffling and pausing. I can only see the back of the driver's head. He has a soldier's haircut and wraparound sunglasses like Bono, who also looks ridiculous wearing sunglasses at night.

I'm trying to remember what I've read about SOCA. It's an amalgam of the old National Crime Squad and National Criminal Intelligence Service, along with elements of Customs and Excise and the Immigration Service. Five thousand officers were specially chosen with the aim of targeting criminal gangs, drug smugglers and people traffickers. The boss of the new agency is a former head of MI5.

"Where are you taking me?"

"To a crime scene," says Forbes.

"What crime? There must be some mistake."

"You are Alisha Kaur Barba. You are twenty-nine years of age. You work for the London Metropolitan Police, most recently for the Diplomatic Protection Group. You have four brothers. Your father is a retired train driver. Your mother takes in sewing. You went to Falcon Street Primary School and to Oaklands Secondary. You graduated from London University with a degree in sociology and topped your class at Hendon Police Training College. You are an expert markswoman and former champion athlete. A year ago you were injured trying to apprehend a suspect who almost snapped your spine. You accepted a bravery medal but refused a disability pension. You seem to have recovered quite well."

"I set off metal detectors at airports."

I don't know if his knowledge is supposed to impress or intimidate me. Nothing else is said. Forbes is not going to answer my questions until he's ready. Silence is part of the softening-up process. Ruiz taught me that.

We take the A12 through Brentwood and out of London. I don't like the countryside at night. Even in moonlight it looks bruised and sullen like a week-old fall down the stairs.

Forbes takes several phone calls, answering yes or no but offering nothing more apart from the clicking sound in his throat. He is married. The gold band on his wedding finger is thick and heavy. Someone at home irons his shirts and polishes his shoes. He is right-handed. He's not carrying a gun. He knows so much about me that I want to even the scales.

We continue through Chelmsford in Essex before bypassing Colchester and turning east toward Harwich along the A120. Convoys of prime movers and semitrailers begin to build up ahead of us. I can smell the salt in the air.

A large sign above the road welcomes us to Harwich

International Port. Following the New Port Entrance Road through two roundabouts we come to the freight entrance. Dozens of trucks are queuing at the gates. A customs officer with a light wand and a fluorescent vest waves us through.

In the distance I see the Port of Felixstowe. Massive gantry cranes tower above the ships, lifting and lowering containers. It looks like a scene from *War of the Worlds* where alien machines have landed and are creating hatchlings for the next generation. Row after row of containers are stacked on top of one another, stretching for hundreds of yards in every direction.

Now Forbes decides to speak to me again.

"Have you ever been here before, DC Barba?"

"No."

"Harwich is a freight and passenger port. It handles cruise ships, ferries, bulk carriers and roll-on, roll-off vessels. Thousands of vehicles pass through here every day from Denmark, Sweden, Belgium, Germany and the Hook of Holland."

"Why am I here?"

He motions ahead of us. The car slows. In the middle of the customs area a Scene of Crime tent has been erected. Police cars are circled like wagons around it.

Arc lights inside the tent throw shadows against the fabric walls, revealing the outline of a truck and people moving inside, silhouetted like puppets in a Kabuki theater.

Forbes is out of the car, walking across the tarmac. The ticking of the cooling engine sounds like a clock. At that moment a side flap of the tent is pushed open. A SOCA emerges wearing overalls and white rubber gloves that peel off his hands like a second skin.

I recognize him. George Noonan, a forensic patholo-gist. They call him "the Albino" because of his pale skin and snow-white hair. Dressed in white overalls, white gloves and a white hat, he looks like a fancy-dress sper-matozoon.

He spends a few minutes talking to Forbes. I'm too far away to hear what they say.

Forbes turns toward me, summoning me forward. His face is set hard like the wedge of an ax.

The tent flap opens. Plastic sheets cover the ground, weighed down with silver boxes of forensic equipment and cameras. A truck is parked at the center, with its twin rear doors open. Inside there are wooden pallets holding boxes of oranges. Some of these have been shifted to one side to form a narrow aisle just wide enough for a person to squeeze through to the far end of the truck.

A camera flash illuminates a cavity within the pallets. At first I think there might be mannequins inside it, bro-ken models or clay figurines. Then the truth reaches me. Bodies, I count five of them, are piled beneath a closed air vent. There are three men, a woman and a child. Their mouths are open. Breathless. Lifeless.

They appear to be Eastern European dressed in cheap mismatched clothes. An arm reaches up as if suspended by a wire. The lone woman has her hair pulled back. A tortoiseshell hair clip has come loose and dangles on her cheek from a strand of hair. The child in her arms is wearing a Mickey Mouse sweatshirt and clutching a doll.

The flashgun pops again. I see the faces frozen in place, trapped in that moment when their oxygen ran out and their dreams turned to dust on dry tongues. It is a scene to haunt me, a scene that changes everything. And although I can't picture the world they came from, which seems impossibly strange and remote, their deaths are somehow unbearably close.

"They died in the past twelve hours," says Noonan.

Automatically, I transfer this into personal time. What was I doing? Traveling to West Sussex. Talking to Julian Shawcroft at the adoption center.

Noonan is holding several bloody fingernails collected in a plastic bag. I feel my stomach lurch.

"If you're going to puke, Detective Constable, you can get the hell away from *my* crime scene," he says.

"Yes, sir."

Forbes looks at Noonan. "Tell her how they died."

"They suffocated," he replies wearily.

"Explain it to us."

The request is for my benefit. Forbes wants me to hear this and to smell the sweet stench of oranges and feces. Noonan obliges.

"It begins with a rising panic as one fights for each breath, sucking it in, wanting more. The next stage is quiescence. Resignation. And then unconsciousness. The convulsions and incontinence are involuntary, the death throes. Nobody knows what comes first—oxygen deprivation or carbon dioxide poisoning."

Taking hold of my elbow, Forbes leads me out of the truck. A makeshift morgue has been set up to take the bodies. One of them is already on a gurney, lying faceup, covered in a white sheet. Forbes runs his fingers over the cloth.

"Someone inside the truck had a mobile," he explains. "When they began to suffocate they tried to call someone and reached an emergency number. The operator thought it was a hoax because the caller couldn't give a location."

I look toward the massive roll-on, roll-off ferry with its open stern doors.

"Why am I here?"

He flicks his wrist and the sheet curls back. A teenage boy with fleshy limbs and dark hair lies on the slab. His head is almost perfectly round and pink except for the blueness around his lips and the overlapping folds of flesh beneath his chin.

Forbes hasn't moved. He's watching me from behind his rectangular glasses.

I drag my eyes away. With a birdlike quickness he grips my arm. "This is all he was wearing—a pair of trousers and a shirt. No labels. Normally, clothes like this tell us nothing. They're cheap and mass produced." His fingers are digging into me. "These clothes are different. There was something sewn into the lining. A name and address. Do you know whose name? Whose address?"

I shake my head.

"Yours."

I try not to react but that in itself is a reaction.

"Can you explain that?" he asks.

"No."

"Not even a vague notion."

My mind is racing through the possibilities. My mother used to put labels on my clothes because she didn't want me losing things. My name, not my address.

"You see how it looks," he says, clicking his tongue again. "You have been implicated in a people-trafficking investigation and potentially a murder investigation. We think his name is Hassan Khan. Does that mean anything to you?"

"No."

"The lorry is Dutch registered. The driver is listed on the passenger manifest as Arjan Molenaar."

Again I shake my head.

Numbness rather than shock seeps through me. It feels like someone has walked up and hit me in the back of the head with a metal tray and the noise is still ringing in my ears.

"Why weren't they found sooner?"

"Do you know how many lorries pass through Harwich every day? More than ten thousand. If Customs searched every one of them there'd be ships queued back to Rotterdam."

Noonan joins us, leaning over the body and talking as though the teenager were a patient and not a corpse.

"All right young fellow, *please* try to be candid. If you open up to the process in good faith we'll find out more about you. Now let's take a look."

He peers closer, almost putting his lips on the boy's cheek. "There is evidence of petechial hemorrhages, pinpoint, less than one millimeter on the eyelids, lips, ears, face and neck, consistent with lack of oxygen to the tissue . . ."

He holds up an arm, examining the skin.

"The scarring indicates an old thermal injury to the left forearm and hand. Something very intense, perhaps a blast."

I notice dozens of smaller scars on his chest. Noonan takes an interest, using a ruler to measure them.

"Very unusual."

"What are they?"

"Knife wounds."

"He was stabbed?"

"Someone sliced him up." He flicks an imaginary knife through the air. "None of the wounds is particularly deep. The blade threatened no organs or major blood vessels. Excellent control."

The pathologist sounds impressed—like one surgeon admiring the work of another.

He sees something else. Lifting the boy's right arm, he turns it outward, displaying the wrist. A small tattooed butterfly hovers halfway between the palm and elbow. Noonan takes a measurement and speaks into a digital recorder.

Forbes has shown me enough.

"I wish to go home now," I say.

"I still have questions."

"Do I need a lawyer?"

The question disappoints him. "I can provide you with someone if you wish."

I know I should be more concerned but the desire for knowledge overrides my natural caution. It's not about being invincible or believing my innocence will protect me. I've seen too many miscarriages of justice to be so optimistic.

The terminal has a café for freight drivers. Forbes takes a table and orders coffee and a bottle of water.

For the next hour he dissects my personal life, my friends and associates. Over and over I make the same point. I have no idea how my name and address were sewn into the clothes of Hassan Khan.

"Is it my color?" I ask him eventually.

His countenance falls. "Why do people *always* do that? Play the race card. Whenever someone from a minority background is questioned I can guarantee it's coming. This has nothing to do with your color or your religion or where you were born. *Your* name and address were sewn into a dead kid's clothes. An illegal. That's what makes you a person of interest."

I wish I could take the question back.

He takes out a half packet of cigarettes and counts them, rationing himself. "Have you any idea how big it is—people trafficking?" He puts the packet away, clicking his tongue as though admonishing himself.

"More than 400,000 people were trafficked into Western Europe last year. The Italian Mafia, the Russians, the Albanians, the Japanese Yakuza, the Chinese Snakeheads—they're all involved. And beneath the big syndicates are thousands of smaller freelance gangs that operate with nothing more than a couple of mobile phones, a speed boat and a transit van. They corrupt border guards, politicians, police and customs officers. They are bottom-feeding scum who prey on human misery. I hate them. I really do."

His eyes are locked on mine. His tongue is making that sound again. I suddenly realize what he reminds me of: the Road Runner. Wile E. Coyote was always trying to catch that arrogant, beeping bird, coming up with ridiculous booby traps and snares. Just *once* I wanted the coyote to win. I wanted the hundred-pound barbell or the bundle of dynamite or the slingshot to work, so he could ring that scrawny bird's neck.

As if on cue there is a *beep beep* from Forbes's pager. He makes a phone call on the far side of the cafeteria. Something must have been said during the call because his demeanor changes.

"I'm sorry for keeping you so long, DC Barba."

"So I can leave?"

"Yes, of course, but it's very late. Accommodation has

161

been arranged in town. The pub looks quite nice. I can have you driven back to London in the morning."

He tugs nervously at the cuffs of his jacket, as though worried the sleeves might be shrinking. I wonder who called. Sikh girls don't have friends in high places.

The pub is quaint and rustic, although I've never been exactly sure what "rustic" means. The restaurant annex has low ceilings with fishing nets strung from the beams and a harpoon bolted above the bar.

Forbes invites me to dinner. "I'm a detective inspector but you don't have to consider it an order," he says, trying to be charming.

I can smell the kitchen. My stomach rumbles. Perhaps I can find out more about Hassan Khan.

Shrugging off his gray jacket, Forbes stretches his legs beneath the table and makes a fuss over ordering and tasting the wine.

"This is very good," he comments, holding his glass up to the light. "Are you sure you won't have some?" Without waiting for me to answer he pours himself another glass.

I have been calling him Mr. Forbes or sir. He says I should call him Robert. I don't give him permission but he calls me Alisha anyway. He asks if I'm married.

"You know that already."

"Yes, of course."

He has pale Nordic eyes and his bottom teeth are crooked but he has a pleasant smile and an easy laugh. The clicking sound seems to go away when he relaxes. Perhaps it's a nervous thing, like a stutter.

"So what about your family?" he asks. "When did they come to Britain?"

I tell him about my grandfather who was born in a small village in Gujarat and joined the British Army at fourteen where he became a kitchen hand and then a chef. After the war a major in the Royal Artillery brought him back to England to cook for his family. My grandfather traveled on a steamer that took three weeks to get from Bombay to England. He came alone. That was in 1947.

He earned three pounds a week, but still managed to save enough for my grandmother to join him. They were the first Indians in Hertfordshire but they later moved to London.

My only memory of my grandparents is a story they told me about their first winter in England. They had never seen snow and said it looked like a scene from a Russian fairy tale.

I don't always understand irony, but my grandfather spent his entire life trying to become white only to be crushed by an overturned coal truck on Richmond Hill that painted him as black as soot.

Forbes has finished a second bottle of wine and grown melancholy.

"I have to use the bathroom," he says.

I watch him weave between tables, leading with his left shoulder and then his right. On his way back he orders a brandy. He talks about growing up in Milton Keynes, a planned town that didn't exist before the 1960s. Now he lives in London. He doesn't mention a wife but I know there's one at home.

I want to talk to him about the illegals before he gets too drunk. "Have you managed to trace the truck?" I ask.

"Shipping containers have codes. They can be tracked anywhere in the world."

"Where did it come from?"

"The truck left a factory on the outskirts of Amsterdam early yesterday. The locks are supposed to be tamperproof."

"How did you know Hassan Khan's name?"

"He had papers. We found a cloth bag tied around his waist. According to the Dutch police, he arrived in Holland nineteen months ago from Afghanistan. He and a group of asylum seekers were living above a Chinese restaurant in Amsterdam."

"What else was in the bag?"

Forbes lowers his eyes. "Drawings and photographs. I could show them to you . . ." He pauses. "We could go to my room."

"Alternatively, you could bring the bag downstairs," I suggest.

He runs his socked foot up my calf and gives me his bad little boy smile.

I want to say something disagreeable but can't find the words. I'm never good at put-downs. Instead I smile politely and tell him to quit while he's ahead.

He frowns. He doesn't understand.

For the love of God, you're not even attractive. Call your wife and wish her good night.

Forbes stumbles as he climbs the stairs. "I guess we hit the old vino pretty hard, eh?"

"One of us did."

He fumbles in his pocket for his key and makes several unsuccessful attempts to find the keyhole. I take it from him. He collapses on the bed and rolls over, spread-eagled like a sacrifice to the demon god of drink.

I take off his shoes and hang his jacket over the chair. The calico bag is on the bedside table. As I leave I slide the security bar across the door frame so that the door doesn't close completely.

Back in my room I call Ruiz and "New Boy" Dave. Dave wants to come and get me. I tell him to stay put. I'll call him in the morning.

Fifteen minutes later I go back to Forbes's room. The door is still ajar and he's snoring. I cross the floor, listening for a change in his breathing. My fingers close around the calico bag. He doesn't stir.

Suddenly, there's another sound. A singsong ring tone.

I drop to the floor and crouch between the radiator and the curtain.

If Forbes turns on the lamp he'll see me or he'll notice that the bag is missing.

Rolling half out of bed, he reaches for his jacket, fumbling with his mobile.

"Yeah. I'm sorry, babe, I should have called. I got in late and I didn't want to wake you or the kids . . . No, I'm fine, not drunk. Just a few glasses . . . No, I didn't see the news tonight . . . That's really great . . . Yeah . . . OK . . . I'll call you in the morning . . . Go to sleep now . . . Love you too."

He tosses the phone aside and stares at the ceiling. For a moment I think he's falling back to sleep until he groans and rolls out of bed. The bathroom light blinks on. Behind him, my hiding place is neatly framed by the radiance. He drops his boxers and urinates.

Sliding out of the light, I cross the floor and ease the door shut behind me. Dizzy and trembling, I have broken one of Ruiz's fundamental rules: when under stress always remember to breathe.

Back in my room, I tip the contents of the calico bag onto the bed. There is a pocketknife with one broken blade and the other intact, a small mirror, a medicine bottle full of sand, a charcoal drawing of two children and a battered circular biscuit tin.

Every object is significant. Why else would he carry them? These are the wordly possessions of a sixteen-year-old boy. They can't possibly breathe life into his lungs or tell me his fears and desires. They aren't enough. He deserves more.

The biscuit tin contains a tarnished military medal and a black-and-white photograph folded in half. It appears to show a group of workers standing in front of a factory with a corrugated-iron roof and wooden shutters on the windows. Packing crates are stacked against the wall, along with drums and pallets.

There are two lines of workers. Those in the front row are sitting on stools. At the center is a patriarch or the factory owner in a high-backed chair. Ramrod straight, he has a stern countenance and a far-off stare. One hand is on his knee. The other is missing and the sleeve of his coat is tied off at the elbow.

Beside him is another man, physically similar, perhaps his brother. He is wearing a small fez and has a neatly trimmed beard. He also is missing a hand and his left eye appears to be an empty socket. I glance along the two rows of workers, many of whom are maimed or crippled or incomplete. There are people on crutches, others with skin like melted plastic. A boy in the front row is kneeling on a skateboard. No, not kneeling. What I first imagine are his knees, poking out from beneath short trousers, are the amputated stumps of his thighs.

None of the workers is smiling. They are olive-skinned men with blurred features and no amount of magnifying will make the image any clearer or the men appear any less stiff and glowering.

I put the photograph back in the tin and examine the rest of the curios and ornaments. The charcoal drawing is creased at the corners. The two children, a boy and a girl, are about six and eight. Her arm is around his shoulders. She has a high forehead and a straight part in her hair. He looks bored or restless, with a spark of light in his eyes from an open window. He wants to be outside.

The paper is soft in my fingers. A fixative has been sprayed on the charcoal to stop it smudging. In the bottom left-hand corner there is a signature. No, it's a name. Two names. The drawing is of Hassan as a young boy and his sister, Samira.

Lying back, I stare at the ceiling and listen to the deep night. It is so quiet I can hear myself breathing. What a beautiful sound.

This is a story of parts. A chronicle of fictions. Cate faked her pregnancy. Brendan Pearl ran her and Felix down. Her doctor lied. Donavon lied. An adoption agency lied. People are being trafficked. Babies are being bought and sold.

I once read that people caught in avalanches can't always tell which way is up or down and don't know which direction to dig. Experienced skiers and climbers have a trick. They dribble. Gravity shows them the way.

I need a trick like that. I am submerged in something

dark and dangerous and I don't know if I'm escaping or burying myself deeper. I'm an accidental casualty. Collateral damage.

My dreams are real. As real as dreams can be. I hear babies crying and mothers singing to them. I am being chased by people. It is the same dream as always but I never know who they are. And I wake at the same moment, as I'm falling.

I call Ruiz again. He picks up on the second ring. The man never sleeps.

"Can you come and fetch me?"

He doesn't ask why. He puts down the phone and I imagine him getting dressed and getting in his car and driving through the countryside.

He is thirty years older than me. He has been married three times and has a private life with more ordnance than a live firing range but I know and trust him more than anyone else.

I know what I'm going to do. Up until now I have been trying to imagine Cate's situation—the places she went to, what she tried to hide—but there is no point in calling the same phone numbers or mentally piecing together her movements. I have to follow her footsteps, to catch up.

I am going to Amsterdam to find Samira. I look at the clock. Not tomorrow. Today.

Two hours later I open the door to Ruiz. Sometimes I wonder if he knows my thoughts or if he's the one who puts them in my mind in the first place and then reads them like counting cards in a poker game.

"We should go to Amsterdam," he says.

"Yes."

BOOK
TWO

The bitterest tears shed over graves are for words left unsaid and deeds left undone.

—HARRIET BEECHER STOWE

BOOK
TWO

1

In our second year at university in London Cate missed a period and thought she was pregnant. We were synchronized—same time, same place, same moods. I can't remember which of her bad boyfriends had breached her defenses, but I remember her reaction clearly enough. Panic.

We did a home pregnancy test and then another. I went with her to the family planning clinic, a horrible green building in Greenwich not far from the observatory. Where time began, life ended.

The nurse asked Cate some questions and told her to go home and wait another seven days. Apparently, the most common reason for a false negative is testing too early.

Her period arrived.

"I might have been pregnant and miscarried," she said afterward. "Perhaps if I had wanted it more."

Later, apropos of nothing, she asked, "What do they do with them?"

"With what?"

"With the aborted babies."

"They don't call them babies. And I guess they get rid of them."

"Get rid of them?"

"I don't know, OK?"

I wonder if a scare such as this, a near miss, came back to haunt her during the years of trying to fall pregnant. Did she tell Felix? Did she wonder if God was punishing her for not loving the first one enough?

I *remember* the name of the bad boyfriend. We called him Handsome Barry. He was a Canadian ski instructor with a year-round suntan and incredibly white teeth. What is it about male ski instructors? They take on this God-like aura in the mountains as if the rarefied air makes them look more handsome or (more likely) women less discerning.

We were working during the Christmas break at a ski lodge in the French Alps in the shadow of Mont Blanc (which didn't ever throw a shadow since the clouds never lifted).

"Have you ever seen a Sikh ski?" I asked Cate.

"You can be the first," she insisted.

We shared a room in Cell Block H, the nickname for the staff quarters. I worked as a chambermaid five days a week, from six in the morning until mid-afternoon. I rarely saw Cate who worked nights at a bar. She practiced her Russian accent by pretending to be Natalia Radzinsky, the daughter of a countess.

"Where on earth did you sleep with Barry?" I asked.

"I borrowed your house key. We used one of the guest suites."

"You did what?"

"Oh, don't worry. I put down a towel."

She seemed more interested in my love life. "When are you going to lose your virginity?"

"When I'm ready."

"Who are you waiting for?"

I told her "Mr. Right," when really I meant "Mr. Considerate" or "Mr. Worthy" or any "mister" who *wanted* me enough.

Maybe I was my mother's daughter after all. She was already trying to find me a husband—my cousin Anwar, who was reading philosophy at Bristol University. Tall and thin with large brown eyes and little wire spectacles, Anwar had great taste in clothes and liked Judy Garland records. He ran off with a boy from the university bookshop, although my mother still won't accept that he's gay.

———

Ruiz has scarcely said a word since our flight left Heathrow. His silences can be so eloquent.

I told him that he didn't have to come. "You're retired."

"True, but I'm not dead," he replied. The faintest of smiles wrinkled the corners of his eyes.

It's amazing how little I know about him after six years. He has children—twins—but doesn't talk about them. His mother is in a retirement home. His stepfather is dead. I don't know about his real father, who's never come up in conversation.

I have never met anyone as self-sufficient as Ruiz. He doesn't appear to hunger for human contact or *need* anyone. You take those survivor shows on TV where people are separated into competing tribes and try to win "immunity." Ruiz would be a tribe of one—all on his own. And the grumpy old bugger would come out on top every time.

Amsterdam. It makes me think of soft drugs, sanctioned prostitution and wooden shoes. This will be my first visit. Ruiz is also a "Dutch virgin" (his term, not mine). He has already given me his thumbnail appraisal of the Dutch. "Excellent lager, a few half-decent footballers and the cheese with the red wax."

"The Dutch are very polite," I offered.

"They're probably the nicest people in the world," he agreed. "They're so amenable that they legalized prostitution and marijuana rather than say no to anyone."

For all his Gypsy blood Ruiz has never been a wanderer. His only foreign holiday was to Italy. He is a creature of habit—warm beer, stodgy food and rugby—and his xenophobia is always worse the farther he gets from home.

We managed to get bulkhead seats which means I can take off my shoes and prop my feet against the wall, showing off my pink-and-white-striped socks. The seat between us is empty. I've claimed it with my book, my bottle of water and my headphones. Possession is nine-tenths of the law.

Outside the window the Dutch landscape is like an old snooker table, patched with different squares of felt. There are cute farmhouses, cute windmills and occasional villages. This whole below-sea-level thing is quite strange. Even the bridges would be underwater if the dikes ever failed. But the Dutch are so good at reclaiming land that they'll probably fill in the North Sea one day and the M11 will stretch all the way to Moscow.

On the journey from the airport our taxi driver seems to get lost and drives us in circles, crossing the same canals and the same bridges. The only clue we have to Cate's movements is the tourist map of central Amsterdam and a circle drawn around the Red Tulip Hotel.

The desk clerk greets us with a wide smile. She is in her mid-twenties, big boned and a pound or two away from being overweight. Behind her is a notice board with brochures advertising canal boat cruises, bicycle tours, and day trips to a tulip farm.

I slide a photograph of Cate across the check-in counter. "Have you seen her?"

She looks hard. Cate is worth a long look. The woman doesn't recognize her.

"You could ask some of the other staff," she says.

A porter is loading our cases onto a trolley. In his fifties, he's wearing a red waistcoat stretched tight over a white shirt and a paunch, putting the buttons under pressure.

I show him the photograph. His eyes narrow as he concentrates. I wonder what he remembers about guests—their faces, their cases, the tips they leave?

"Room 12," he announces, nodding vigorously. His English is poor.

Ruiz turns back to the desk clerk. "You must have a record. She might have stayed here during the second week of February."

She glances over her shoulder, worried about the manager, and then taps at the keyboard. The screen refreshes and I glance down the list. Cate isn't there. Wait! There's another name I recognize: "Natalia Radzinsky."

The porter claps his hands together. "Yes, the countess.

She had one blue bag." He measures the dimensions in the air. "And a smaller one. Very heavy. Made of metal."

"Was she with anyone?"

He shakes his head.

"You have a very good memory."

He beams.

I look at the computer screen again. I feel as though Cate has left me a clue that nobody else could recognize. It's a silly notion, of course, to imagine the dead leaving messages for the living. The arrogance of archaeologists.

The Red Tulip Hotel has sixteen rooms, half of them overlooking the canal. Mine is on the first floor and Ruiz's room is above me. Sunlight bounces off the curved windows of a canal boat as it passes, taking tourists around the city. Bells jangle and bike riders weave between pedestrians.

Ruiz knocks on my door and we make a plan. He will talk to the Immigration and Naturalization Service (IND), which deals with asylum seekers in the Netherlands. I will visit Hassan Khan's last known address.

I take a taxi to Gerard Doustraat in a quarter known as de Pijp, or "the Pipe" as my driver explains. He calls it the "real Amsterdam." Ten years ago it had a seedy reputation but is now full of restaurants, cafés and bakeries.

The Flaming Wok is a Chinese restaurant with bamboo blinds and fake bonsai trees. The place is empty. Two waiters are hovering near the kitchen door. Asian. Neat, wearing black trousers and white shirts.

From the front door I can see right through to the kitchen where pots and steamers hang from the ceiling. An older man, dressed in white, is preparing food. A knife stutters in his hand.

The waiters speak menu English. They keep directing me to a table. I ask to see the owner.

Mr. Weng leaves his kitchen, wiping his hands on a towel. He bows to me.

"I want to know about the people who were living upstairs."

"They gone now."

"Yes."

"You want to rent frat? One bedroom. Very crean."

"No."

He shrugs ambivalently and points to a table, motioning me to sit, before he orders tea. The waiters, his sons, compete to carry out the instructions.

"About the tenants," I say.

"They come, they go," he replies. "Sometimes full. Sometimes empty." His hands flutter as he talks and he clasps them occasionally, as if fearful they might fly away.

"Your last tenants, where were they from?"

"Everywhere. Estonia, Russia, Uzbekistan . . ."

"What about this boy?" I show him the charcoal drawing of Hassan. "He's older now. Sixteen."

He nods energetically. "This one okay. He wash the dishes for food. Others take food from bins."

The green tea has arrived. Mr. Weng pours. Tea leaves circle in the small white cups.

"Who paid the rent?"

"Pay money up front. Six months."

"But you must have had a lease."

Mr. Weng doesn't understand.

"A contract?"

"No contract."

"What about the electricity, the telephone?"

He nods and smiles. He's too polite to tell me that he doesn't have an answer.

I point to the girl in the drawing and take out the photograph of Samira. "What about this girl?"

"Many girls in and out." He makes a circle with his left forefinger and thumb and thrusts a finger through the hole. "Prostitutes," he says apologetically, as though sorry for the state of the world.

I ask to see the flat. One of his sons will show me. He takes me through a fire door that opens into an alley and leads me up a rear staircase to where he unlocks a door.

I have been in depressing flats before, but few have disheartened me as quickly as this one. It has one bedroom, a lounge, a kitchen and a bathroom. The only furniture is a low chest of drawers with a mirror on top and a sofa with cigarette burns.

"The mattresses were thrown away," Mr. Weng's son explains.

"How many lived here?"

"Ten."

I get the impression he knew the occupants better than his father.

"Do you remember this girl?" I show him the photograph.

"Maybe."

"Did she stay here?"

"She visited."

"Do you know where she lives?"

"No."

The tenants left nothing behind except a few cans of food, some old pillows and a couple of used international phone cards. There are no clues here.

Afterward, I catch a taxi and meet Ruiz at a bar in

Nieumarkt, a paved open square not far from the Oude Kerk. Most of the outside tables are empty. It is getting too late in the year for backpackers and American tourists.

"I didn't think you were going to buy one of those, sir," I say, pointing to his guidebook.

"Yeah, well, I hate asking directions," he grumbles. "I'm sure someone is going to say, "You want to go *where?*" That's when I'll discover I'm in the wrong bloody country."

A couple at the next table are locals. They could be having an argument or agreeing completely. I can't tell.

"The Dutch can squeeze more vowels into a sentence than anyone else in the world," says Ruiz, too loudly. "And that Dutch 'j' is a deliberate bloody provocation."

He goes back to his guidebook. We're sitting on the western flank of the red light district, in an area known as de Walletjes (the Little Walls).

"That building with all the turrets is the Waag," he explains. "It used to be a gatehouse to the old city."

A young waitress has come to take our order. Ruiz wants another beer, "with less froth and more Heineken." She smiles at me sympathetically.

Opening his marbled notebook, Ruiz relates how Hassan and Samira Khan were smuggled across the German border into the Netherlands in the luggage compartment of a tourist coach in April 2005. They were taken to an application center at Ter Apel and were interviewed by the Immigration and Naturalization Service. Hassan claimed to be fifteen and Samira seventeen. They told the authorities they were born in Kabul and had spent three years living in a refugee camp in Pakistan. After their mother died of dysentery, their father, Hamid Khan, took the children back to Kabul where he was shot dead in 1999. Hassan and Samira were sent to an orphanage.

"That's the story they told in every interview, together and independently. Never wavered."

"How did they get here?"

"Traffickers, but they both refused to name names." Ruiz consults his notebook again. "After they were screened, they were housed at a center for underage asylum seekers operated by the Valentine Foundation. Three months later they were moved to the campus at Deelen where 180 children are housed. In December last year both their visas were revoked."

"Why?"

"I don't know. They were given twenty-eight days to leave the Netherlands. An appeal was lodged but they disappeared."

"Disappeared?"

"Not many of these people hang around to get deported."

"What do you mean 'these people'?"

Ruiz looks at me awkwardly. "Slip of the tongue." He pauses to sip his beer. "I have the name of a lawyer who represented them. Lena Caspar. She has an office here in Amsterdam."

White froth clings to his top lip. "There's something else. The boy made an earlier North Sea crossing. He was picked up and sent back to the Netherlands within twenty-four hours."

"Guess he tried again."

"Second time unlucky."

2

The lawyer's office is on Prinsengracht in a four-story building that deviates from the vertical by a degree or two, leaning out over the brick-paved street. A high arched doorway leads to a narrow courtyard where an old woman is swabbing flagstones with a mop and bucket. She points to the stairs.

On the first floor we enter a waiting room full of North Africans, many with children. A young man looks up from a desk, pushing his Harry Potter glasses higher up his nose. We don't have an appointment. He flicks through the pages of a daily schedule.

At that moment a door opens behind him and a Nigerian woman appears, dressed in a voluminous floral dress. A young girl clings to her hand and a baby is asleep on her shoulder.

For a moment I don't see anyone else. Then a small woman emerges, as if appearing from the folds of the Nigerian's dress.

"I'll send you a copy of the papers once I've lodged

the appeal," she says. "You must let me know if you change your address."

Dressed in a long-sleeved cotton blouse, black cardigan and gray trousers, she looks very lawyerly and businesslike, despite her diminutive stature. Smiling absently at me as though we might have met, she glances at Ruiz and shudders.

"Mrs. Caspar, excuse this interruption. Could we have a word?"

She laughs. "How very English that sounds. Just the one word? I'm almost tempted to say yes just to hear which one you might choose." The skin around her eyes wrinkles like peach stones. "I'm very busy today. You'll have to wait until—"

She stops in mid-sentence. I am holding up a photograph of Samira. "Her brother is dead. We have to find her."

Mrs. Caspar holds her office door open until we follow her inside. The room is almost square, with highly polished wood floors. The house has belonged to her family for generations, she explains. The law practice was her grandfather's and then her father's.

Despite volunteering this information, Mrs. Caspar has a lawyer's natural caution.

"You don't look like a police officer," she says to me. "I thought you might require my services." She turns her attention to Ruiz. "*You*, however, look exactly like a policeman."

"Not anymore."

"Tell me about Hassan," she says, turning back to me. "What happened to him?"

"When did you last see him?"

"Eleven months ago."

I describe the discovery of his body in the truck and how my name and address were sewn into his clothes. Turning her face to the window, Mrs. Caspar might be close to tears, but I doubt if such a woman would let strangers see her emotions.

"Why would he have your name?"

"I don't know. I was hoping you could tell me."

She shakes her head.

"I am trying to find Samira."

"Why?"

How do I answer this? I plunge straight in. "I think a friend of mine who couldn't have children tried to buy a baby in Amsterdam. I think she met Samira."

"Samira doesn't have a baby."

"No, but she has a womb."

Mrs. Caspar looks at me incredulously. "A Muslim girl doesn't rent her womb. You must be mistaken."

The statement has the bluntness and certainty of fact or dogma. She crosses the office and opens a filing cabinet, taking out a folder. Sitting at her desk, she scans the contents.

"My government does not welcome asylum seekers. They have made it more and more difficult for them. We even have a minister of immigration who claims that only 20 percent of applicants are 'real refugees'—the rest are liars and frauds.

"Unfortunately, legitimate asylum seekers are being demonized. They are treated like economic refugees, roaming between countries looking for someone to take them in."

The bitterness in her voice vibrates her tiny frame.

"Samira and Hassan had no papers when they arrived. The IND claimed they destroyed them on purpose. They didn't believe Samira was a minor. She looked closer to twelve than twenty, but they sent her for tests."

"Tests?"

"An age evaluation test. They x-rayed her collarbone, which is supposed to establish if someone is older or younger than twenty. Hassan had his wrist x-rayed. A report was prepared by Harry van der Pas, a physical anthropologist at Tilburg University.

"It backfired on them. Samira appeared even younger. Poor diet and malnutrition had stunted her growth. They gave them both temporary visas. They could stay, but only until further checks were done."

Mrs. Caspar turns a page in the folder.

"Nowadays the policy is to return underage asylum seekers to their own country. Hassan and Samira *had* no family. Afghanistan can scarcely feed its own people. Kabul is a city of widows and orphans."

She slides a page of notes toward me—a family history. "They were orphans. Both spoke English. Their mother was educated at Delhi University. She worked as a translator for a publishing company until the Taliban took over."

I look at the notes. Samira was born in 1987 during the Soviet occupation of Afghanistan. She was two years old when the Soviets left and ten when the Taliban arrived.

"And their father?"

"A factory owner."

I remember Hassan's photograph.

"They made fireworks," explains Mrs. Caspar. "The Taliban closed the factory down. Fireworks were forbidden. The family fled to Pakistan and lived in a refugee camp. Their mother died of dysentery. Hamid Khan struggled to raise his children. When he grew tired of living like a beggar in a foreign country, he took his family back to Kabul. He was dead within six months."

"What happened?"

"Samira and Hassan witnessed his execution. A teenager with a Kalashnikov made him kneel on the floor of their apartment and shot him in the back of the head. They threw his body from a window into the street and wouldn't let his children collect it for eight days, by which time the dogs had picked it over."

Her voice is thick with sadness. "There is an Afghan proverb. I heard Samira say it: To an ant colony dew is a flood."

It doesn't need any further explanation.

"When did you last see her?"

"Mid-January. She surprised me on my birthday. She made me fireworks. I don't know how she managed to buy the chemicals and powder. I had never seen anything so beautiful."

"What about their application for asylum?"

The lawyer produces another letter. "Eighteen is a very important age for an asylum seeker in this country. Once you reach this age you are treated as an adult. Samira's temporary residency was revoked. She was deemed to be old enough to look after Hassan, so his visa was also canceled. Both were denied asylum and told they had to leave.

"I lodged an appeal, of course, but I couldn't prevent them being forced onto the street. They had to leave the campus at Deelen. Like a lot of young people denied asylum, they chose to run rather than wait to be deported."

"Where?"

She opens her arms, palms upward.

"How can we find Samira?"

"You can't."

"I have to try. Did she have any friends at the campus?"

"She mentioned a Serbian girl. I don't know her name."

"Is she still there?"

"No. She was either deported or she ran away."

Mrs. Caspar looks at Ruiz and back to me. The future is mapped out in the lines on her face. It is a difficult journey.

"I have a friend—a retired policeman like you, Mr. Ruiz. He has spent half his life working in the red light district. He knows everyone—the prostitutes, pimps, dealers and drug addicts. Walls have mice and mice have ears. He can hear what the mice are saying."

She takes down the name of our hotel and promises to leave a message.

"If you find Samira, be careful with her. When she finds out about her brother she will hurt in places where it matters most."

"You think we'll find her?"

She kisses my cheeks. "There is always a way from heart to heart."

———

Back at the Red Tulip I call DI Forbes. Straightaway he demands to know where I am. A quiet inner voice tells me to lie. It's a voice I've been hearing a lot lately.

"Have you interviewed the truck driver?" I ask.

"Are you in Amsterdam?" he counters.

"What did he tell you?"

"You can't just *leave* the fucking country. You're a suspect."

"I wasn't made aware of any restrictions."

"Don't give me that crap! If you're running a parallel investigation I'll have you up on disciplinary charges. You can forget about your career. You can forget about coming home."

I can hear the annoying click in his voice. It must drive his wife mad—like living with a human metronome.

Eventually he calms down when I tell him about Hassan. We swap information. The truck driver has been charged with manslaughter, but there is a complication. U.K. immigration officers received a tip-off about a suspect vehicle before the roll-on, roll-off ferry docked in Harwich. They had the license number and were told to look for a group of illegal immigrants.

"Who provided the tip-off?"

"The Port Authority in Rotterdam received an anonymous phone call two hours after the ferry sailed. We think it came from the traffickers."

"Why?"

"They were setting up a decoy."

"I don't understand."

"They were sacrificing a small number of illegals who would tie up resources. Customs and immigration would be so busy that they wouldn't notice a much larger shipment."

"On the same boat?"

"Two articulated lorries haven't been accounted for. The companies listed on the freight manifest are nonexistent. They could have smuggled a hundred people in the back of those trucks."

"Could the air vents have been closed deliberately—to create a more effective decoy?"

"We may never know."

"I don't want a health club, I want a gym," I tell the desk clerk who doesn't appreciate the difference. I shadow box and she backs away. Now she understands.

I know a little about gyms. In our last year at Oaklands, I convinced Cate to take karate classes with me. They were held in a grungy old gym in Penwick Street, mostly used by boxers and old guys in sleeveless vests whose veins would pop out of their heads when they were on the bench press.

The karate instructor was Chinese with a Cockney accent and everyone called him "Peking," which got shortened to "P.K.," which he didn't seem to mind.

There was a boxing ring and a weight-training room with mirrors and a separate annex with mats on the floor for karate. P.K. spent the first few lessons explaining the principles behind karate, which didn't particularly interest Cate. "The mental discipline, physical training and study help build respect toward our fellow man," he said.

"I just want to be able to kick them in the balls," said Cate.

"The two Japanese characters that make up the word 'karate' have the literal meaning of 'empty hands,'" explained P.K. "It is a system of self-defense that has evolved over hundreds of years. Every move is based on a knowledge of the muscles and joints and the relationship between movement and balance."

Cate raised her hand. "When do I learn to hit people?"

"You will be taught the techniques of counterattack."

He then described how the word "karate" came from Mandarin and Cantonese phrases like "chan fa" and "ken fat," which sent Cate into a fit of giggles. The literal meaning is "The Law of the Fist." Attacks to the groin of an opponent are frowned upon by most martial arts. Karate also doesn't approve of targeting the hip joints, knee joints, insteps, shins, upper limbs and face.

"What's the bloody point?" muttered Cate.

"I think he means in competition."

"Forget competition. I want to hurt their balls."

She persevered with learning the theory but every week she pestered him with the same question: "When do we learn the groin kick?"

P.K. finally relented. He gave Cate a private lesson after the gym had closed. The blinds were drawn and he turned off all the lights except for the one over the ring.

She came out looking flushed and smiling, with a mark on her neck that looked suspiciously like a love bite. She didn't go back to self-defense classes again.

I kept going, working my way through the belts. P.K. wanted me to go for black but I was already at the police training college.

Ruiz is on his second beer when I get to the restaurant. He's watching the pizza chef spin a disk of dough in the air, draping it over his knuckles before launching it again.

The waiters are young. Two of them are watching me, commenting to each other. They're trying to fathom my relationship with Ruiz. What is a young Asian woman doing with a man twice her age? I'm either a mail-order bride or his mistress, they think.

The café is nearly empty. Nobody eats this early in Amsterdam. An old man with a dog sits near the front door. He slips his hand beneath the table with morsels of food.

"She could be anywhere," says Ruiz.

"She wouldn't have left Amsterdam."

"What makes you so sure?"

"Hassan was only sixteen. She wouldn't leave him."

"He made *two* North Sea crossings without her."

I have no answer.

So far we have been trying to make inquiries without drawing attention to ourselves. Why not change our tactics? We could print up posters or place an advertisement.

Ruiz doesn't agree. "Cate Beaumont tried to take this public and look what happened. This isn't some seat-of-the-pants operation where someone panicked and killed the Beaumonts. We're dealing with an organized gang—guys like Brendan Pearl."

"They won't expect it."

"They'll know we're looking."

"We'll flush them out."

Ruiz continues to argue, but he understands my point. Chance or fate will not decide what takes place next. We can *make* things happen.

Hotel rooms in strange cities are lonely places where the human spirit touches rock bottom. I lie on the bed but cannot sleep. My head refuses to abandon the image of a child in a Mickey Mouse T-shirt, lying next to his mother, beneath a closed air vent.

I want to rewind the clock back to the night of the reunion and further. I want to sit down with Cate and take turns at talking and crying and saying we're sorry. I want to make up for the last eight years. Most of all, I want to be forgiven.

3

A mobile vibrates gently beneath my pillow.

I hear Ruiz's voice. "Rise and shine."

"What time is it?"

"Just gone seven. There's someone downstairs. Lena Caspar sent him."

Pulling on my jeans, I splash water on my face and brush my hair back in a band.

Nicolaas Hokke is in his mid-sixties with short springy gray hair and a beard. His six-foot frame helps hide the beginnings of a paunch beneath a scuffed leather jacket.

"I understand you need a guide," he says, taking my hand in both of his. He smells of tobacco and talcum powder.

"I'm looking for a girl."

"A girl?"

"An asylum seeker."

"Hmmm. Let's talk over breakfast."

He knows a place. We can walk. The intersections are

a flurry of trams, cars and bicycles. Hokke negotiates them with the confidence of a deity crossing a lake.

Already I am falling for Amsterdam. It is prettier and cleaner than London with its cobbled squares, canals and wedding-cake façades. I feel safer here: the anonymous foreigner.

"Often people want tours of the red light district," Hokke explains. "Writers, sociologists, foreign politicians. I take them twice—once during daylight and again at night. It is like looking at different sides of the same coin, light and dark."

Hokke has an ambling gait with his hands clasped behind his back. Occasionally, he stops to point out a landmark or explain a sign. "Straat" means street and "steeg" means lane.

"This was your beat?" asks Ruiz.

"Of course."

"When did you retire?"

"Two years ago. And you?"

"A year."

They nod to each other as if they share an understanding.

Turning a corner, I get my first glimpse of Amsterdam's famous "windows." Initially, they appear to be simple glass doors with wooden frames and brass numbers. The curtains are drawn across some of them. Others are open for business.

Only when I draw closer do I see what this means. A skinny dark woman in a sequined bra and G-string is sitting on a stool with her legs crossed and boots zipped up to her knees. Under the black lights the bruises on her thighs appear as pale blotches.

The blatancy of her pose and her purpose diminishes

193

a small part of me. She watches me aggressively. She doesn't want me with these men. I will stop them coming to her door.

Negotiating more of the narrow lanes, we pass windows that are so close on either side that it is like being at a tennis match and following the ball back and forth across the net. In contrast, Ruiz looks straight ahead.

A large Dominican woman calls out to Hokke and waves. Dressed in a red tasseled push-up bra that underpins a massive bust, she is perched on a stool with her legs crossed and stomach bulging over her crotch.

Hokke stops and talks to her in Dutch.

"She has four children," he explains. "One of them is at university. Twenty years a prostitute but she's still a woman."

"What do you mean a woman?"

"Some of them turn into whores."

He waves to several more prostitutes, who blow him kisses or tease him by slapping their wrists. Farther down the street an older woman comes out of a shop and throws her arms around him like a long lost son. She presses a bag of cherries into his hand.

"This is Gusta," he explains, introducing us. "She still works the windows."

"Part-time," she reminds him.

"But you must be—"

"Sixty-five," she says proudly. "I have five grandchildren."

Hokke laughs at our surprise. "You're wondering how many customers would sleep with a grandmother."

Gusta puts her hands on her hips and rolls them seductively. Hokke looks for a polite way to answer our question.

"Some of the younger, prettier girls have men queuing up outside their windows. They are not concerned if a man comes back to them. There will be plenty more waiting. But a woman like Gusta cannot rely on a sweet smile and a firm body. So she has to offer quality of service and a certain expertise that comes with experience."

Gusta nods in agreement.

Hokke doesn't seem to resent or disapprove of the prostitutes. The drug addicts and dealers are a different story. A North African man is leaning on the railing of a bridge. He recognizes Hokke and dances toward him. Hokke doesn't stop moving. The African has betel-stained teeth and dilated pupils. Hokke's face is empty, neutral. The African jabbers in Dutch, grinning wildly. Hokke carries on walking.

"An old friend?" I ask.

"I've known him thirty years. He's been a heroin addict for this much time."

"It's remarkable he's still alive."

"Addicts do not die from the drugs, they die from the lifestyle," he says adamantly. "If drugs were less expensive he wouldn't have to steal to afford them."

On the far side of the bridge, we meet another junkie, younger and even less appealing. He points the glowing end of a cigarette at me and talks to Hokke in a wheedling voice. An argument ensues. I don't know what they're saying.

"I asked him if he was clean," Hokke explains.

"What did he say?"

"He said: 'I am always clean.' "

"You argued."

"He wanted to know if you were for sale."

"Is he a pimp?"

"When it suits him."

We reach the café and take a table outside under the bare branches of a large tree that is threaded with fairy lights. Hokke drinks his coffee black and orders a slice of sourdough toast with jam. Afterward, he fills a pipe, so small that it seems almost designed for an apprentice smoker.

"My one vice," he explains.

Ruiz laughs. "So in all those years you were never tempted."

"Tempted?"

"To sleep with some of the women in the windows. There must have been opportunities."

"Yes, opportunities. I have been married forty years, Vincent. I hope I can call you Vincent. I have slept with only my wife. She is enough for me. These women are in business. They should not be expected to give away their bodies for free. What sort of businesswoman would do that?"

His face almost disappears behind a cloud of pipe smoke.

"This girl you want to find, you think she might be a prostitute?"

"She was trafficked out of Afghanistan."

"Afghani prostitutes are rare. The Muslim girls are normally Turkish or Tunisian. If she is illegal she won't be working the windows unless she has false papers."

"Are they difficult to get?"

"The Nigerians and Somalis swap papers because they all look alike but the windows are normally the easiest to police. The streets and private clubs are more difficult. It is like an iceberg—we see only the tip. Beneath the waves there are hundreds of prostitutes, some underage, working from parking lots, toilets and private houses. Customers find them through word of mouth and mobile telephones."

I tell him about Samira disappearing from the care center.

"Who brought her to the Netherlands?" he asks.

"Traffickers."

"How did she pay them?"

"What do you mean?"

"They will want something in return for smuggling her."

"She and her brother are orphans."

He empties his pipe, tapping it against the edge of an ashtray.

"Perhaps they haven't yet paid." Refilling it again he explains how gangs operate within the asylum centers. They pick up girls and turn them into prostitutes, while the boys are used as drug runners or beggars.

"Sometimes they don't even bother kidnapping children from the centers. They collect them for the weekend and bring them back. This is safer for the pimps because the girls don't disappear completely and trigger an investigation. Meanwhile, they are fed, housed and learn a bit of Dutch—paid for by the Dutch government."

"You think that's what happened to Samira?"

"I don't know. If she is young she will be moved between cities or sold to traffickers in other countries. It is like a carousel. Young and new girls are prized as fresh meat. They generate more money. By moving them from place to place, it is harder for the police or their families to find them."

Hokke gets to his feet and stretches. He beckons us to follow him. We turn left and right down the cobbled lanes, moving deeper into the red light district. More windows are open. Women tap on the glass to get Hokke's attention. A Moroccan shakes her breasts at him. Another slaps her rump and sways to a song that only she can hear.

"Do you know them all?" I ask.

He laughs. "Once perhaps, yes. I heard all their stories. Now there is a kind of wall between the police and the prostitutes. In the old days most of them were Dutch. Then the Dominicans and Columbians moved in. Then the Surinamese. Now we have Nigerians and girls from Eastern Europe."

Each of the streets is different, he explains. The Oudekerksteeg is the African quarter. The South Americans are on Boomsteeg; the Asians on Oudekennissteeg and Barndesteeg, while Bloedstraat has the transsexuals. The Eastern European girls are on Molensteeg and along the Achterburgwal.

"It is getting harder to make money. A prostitute needs at least two clients before her rent for the window is paid. Another four clients are needed for the pimp's share. Six men have used her and she still hasn't earned anything for herself.

"In the old days prostitutes would save up to buy a window and then become the landlady, renting to other girls. Now companies own the windows and sometimes use them to launder money by claiming the girls earn more than they do."

Hokke doesn't want to sound melancholy but can't help himself. He yearns for the old days.

"The place is cleaner now. Less dangerous. The problems have gone out farther, but they never disappear."

We are walking alongside a canal, past strip clubs and cinemas. From a distance the sex shops look like souvenir sellers. Only up close do the bright novelty items become dildos and fake vaginas. I am fascinated and disturbed in equal parts; torn between looking away and peering into the window to work out what the various things are for.

Hokke has turned into a lane and knocks on a door. It is opened by a large man with a bulging stomach and sideburns. Behind him is a small room barely big enough for him to turn around. The walls are lined with porn videos and film reels.

"This is Nico, the hardest-working projectionist in Amsterdam."

Nico grins at us, wiping his hands on his shirtfront.

"This place has been here longer than I have," explains Hokke. "Look! It still shows Super-8 films."

"Some of the actresses are grandmothers now," says Nico.

"Like Gusta," adds Hokke. "She was very beautiful once."

Nico nods in agreement.

Hokke asks him if he knows of any Afghani girls working the windows or clubs.

"Afghani? No. I remember an Iraqi. You remember her, Hokke? Basinah. You had a beating heart for her."

"Not me," laughs the former policeman. "She had problems with her landlord and wanted me to help."

"Did you arrest him?"

"No."

"Did you shoot him?"

"No."

"You weren't a very successful policeman, were you,

Hokke? Always whistling. The drug dealers heard you coming from two streets away."

Hokke shakes his head. "When I wanted to catch them I didn't whistle."

I show Nico the photograph of Samira. He doesn't recognize her.

"Most of the traffickers deal with their own. Girls from China are smuggled by the Chinese; Russians smuggle Russians." He opens his hands. "The Afghanis stay at home and grow poppies."

Nico says something to Hokke in Dutch.

"This girl. Why do you want to find her?"

"I think she knows about a baby."

"A baby?"

"I have a friend." I correct myself. "I *had* a friend who faked her pregnancy. I think she arranged to get a baby from someone in Amsterdam. My friend was murdered. She left behind this photograph."

Hokke is filling his pipe again. "You think this baby was being smuggled?"

"Yes."

He stops in mid-movement, the match burning in his fingers. I have surprised him—a man who thought he had seen and heard it all after thirty years in this place.

Ruiz is waiting outside, watching the carnival of need and greed. There are more people now. Most have come to see but not touch the famous red light district. One group of Japanese tourists is shepherded by a woman holding a bright yellow umbrella above her head.

"Samira had a brother," I explain to Hokke and Nico. "He went missing from the care center at the same time. Where would he go?"

"Boys can also become prostitutes," says Hokke, in a

matter-of-fact way. "They also carry drugs or pick pockets or become beggars. Look at Central Station. You'll see dozens of them."

I show them the charcoal drawing of Hassan. "He had a tattoo on the inside of his wrist."

"What sort of tattoo?"

"A butterfly."

Hokke and the projectionist exchange glances.

"It is a property tattoo," says Nico, scratching his armpit. "Somebody owns him."

Hokke stares into the blackened bowl of his pipe. Clearly, it is not good news.

I wait for him to explain. Choosing his words carefully, he reveals that certain criminal gangs control areas of the city and often claim ownership over asylum seekers and illegals.

"She should stay away from de Souza," says Nico.

Hokke holds a finger to his lips. Something passes between them.

"Who is de Souza?" I ask.

"Nobody. Forget his name."

Nico nods. "It is for the best."

There are more windows open. More customers. The men don't raise their eyes as they pass one another.

Prostitution has always confused me. When I was growing up, movies like *Pretty Woman* and *American Gigolo* glamorized and sanitized the subject. My first glimpse of real prostitutes was with Cate. We were in Leeds for an athletics meeting. Near the railway station, where most of the cheap hotels could be found, we saw women on street corners. Some of them appeared washed out and unclean—nothing like Julia Roberts. Others looked so carnivorous that they were more like angler fish than objects of desire.

Maybe I have a naïve view of sex as being beautiful or magical or otherworldly. It *can* be. I have never liked dirty jokes or overtly sexual acts. Cate called me a prude. I can live with that.

"What are you thinking, sir?"

"I'm wondering why they do it," Ruiz replies.

"The women?"

"The men. I don't mind someone warming my toilet seat for me but there's some places I don't want to come second, or third . . ."

"You think prostitution should be illegal?"

"I'm just making an observation."

I tell him about an essay I read at university by Camille Paglia, who claimed that prostitutes weren't the victims of men but their conquerors.

"That must have set the feminists afighting."

"Rape alarms at ten paces."

We walk in silence for a while and then sit down. A swathe of sunshine cuts across the square. Someone has put up a soapbox beneath a tree and is preaching or reciting something in Dutch. It could be *Hamlet*. It could be the telephone directory.

Back at the hotel we start making calls—working through a list of charities, refugee advocates and support groups. Hokke has promised us more names by tomorrow. We spend all afternoon on the phones but nobody has any knowledge of Samira. Perhaps we are going to have to do this the old-fashioned way—knocking on doors.

On Damrak I find a print shop. A technician enlarges the photograph of Samira and uses a color copier to produce a bundle of images. The smell of paper and ink fills my head.

Ruiz will take the photograph to Central Station and show it around. I'll try the women in the windows, who are more likely to talk to me. Ruiz is completely happy with the arrangement.

Before I leave I call Barnaby Elliot to ask about the funerals. The moment he hears my voice he starts accusing me of having burned down Cate and Felix's house.

"The police say you were there. They say you reported the fire."

"I reported a break-in. I didn't start a fire."

"What were you doing there? You wanted her computer and her letters. You were going to steal them."

I don't respond, which infuriates him even more.

"Detectives have been here asking questions. I told them you were making wild allegations about Cate. Because of you they won't release the bodies. We can't arrange the funerals—the church, the readings, the death notices. We can't say goodbye to our daughter."

"I'm sorry about that, Barnaby, but it's not my fault. Cate and Felix were murdered."

"SHUT UP! JUST SHUT UP!"

"Listen to me—"

"No! I don't want to hear any more of your stories. I want you to leave my family alone. Stay away from us."

As soon as he hangs up my mobile chirrups like a fledgling.

"Hello? Alisha? Hello."

"I can hear you, Mama."

"Is everything OK?"

"Yes, fine."

"Did Hari call you?"

"No."

"A Chief Superintendent North has been trying to reach you. He said you didn't turn up for work."

Hendon! My new job as a recruitment officer. I totally forgot.

"He wants you to call him."

"OK."

"Are you sure everything is all right?"

"Yes, Mama."

She starts telling me about my nieces and nephews—which ones are teething, smiling, walking or talking. Then I hear about the dance recitals, soccer games and school concerts. Grandchildren are at the center of her life. I should feel usurped but the emotion is closer to emptiness.

"Come round for lunch on Sunday. Everyone will be here. Except for Hari. He has a study date."

That's a new name for it.

"Bring that nice sergeant." She means "New Boy" Dave.

"I didn't *bring* him last time."

"He was very nice."

"He's not a Sikh, Mama."

"Oh, don't worry about your father. He's all bark and no bite. I thought your friend was very polite."

"Polite."

"Yes. You can't expect to marry a prince. But with a

little patience and hard work, you can *make* one. Look how well I did with your father."

I can't help but love her. She kisses the receiver. Not many people still do that. I kiss her back.

As if on cue I get a call from "New Boy" Dave. Maybe they're working in cahoots.

"Hello, sweet girl."

"Hello, sweet boy." I can hear him breathing as distinctly as if he were standing next to me.

"I miss you."

"A *part* of you misses me."

"No. All of me."

The odd thing is that I miss him too. It's a new feeling.

"Have you found her?"

"No."

"I want you to come home. We need to talk."

"So let's talk."

He has something he wants to say. I can almost hear him rehearsing it in his mind. "I'm quitting the force."

"Good God!"

"There's a little sailing school on the south coast. It's up for sale."

"A sailing school."

"It's a good business. It makes money in the summer and in the winter I'll work on the fishing boats or get a security job."

"Where will you get the money?"

"I'm going to buy it with Simon."

"I thought he was working in San Diego?"

"He is, but he and Jacquie are coming home."

Simon is Dave's brother. He is a sailmaker or a boat designer—I can never remember which one.

"But I thought you *liked* being a detective."

"It's not a good job if I ever have a family."

Fair point. "You'll be closer to your mum and dad." (They live in Poole.)

"Yeah."

"Sailing can be fun." I don't know what else to say.

"Here's the thing, Ali. I want you to come with me. We can be business partners."

"Partners?"

"You know I'm in love with you. I want to get married. I want us to be together." He's talking quickly now. "You don't have to say anything yet. Just think about it. I'll take you down there. I've found a cottage in Milford-on-Sea. It's beautiful. Don't say no. Just say maybe. Let me show you."

I feel something shift inside me and I want to take his large hand in my two small hands and kiss his eyelids. Despite what he says, I know he wants an answer. I can't give him one. Not today, nor tomorrow. The future is an hour-by-hour panorama.

4

Once more I walk past the Oude Kerk and Trompetter-steeg. Hokke was right—the red light district is different at night. I can almost smell the testosterone and used condoms.

As I pass each window, I press a photograph against the glass. Some of the prostitutes shout at me or shake their fingers angrily. Others offer seductive smiles. I don't want to meet their eyes, but I must make sure they look at Samira.

I walk through Goldbergersteeg and Bethlemsteeg, making a mental note of those windows where the curtains are closed so I can return later. Only one woman tries to encourage me indoors. She puts two fingers to her lips and pokes her tongue between them. She says something in Dutch. I shake my head.

In English this time. "You want a woman." She shakes her claret-covered breasts.

"I don't sleep with women."

"But you've thought about it."

"No."

"I can be a man. I have the tools." She is laughing at me now.

I move on, around the corner, along the canal through Boomsteeg to Molensteeg. There are three windows side by side, almost below ground. The curtain is open on the center one. A young woman raises her eyes. Black lights make her blond hair and white panties glow like neon. A tiny triangle barely covers her crotch and two higher on her chest are pulled together to create a cleavage. The only other shadows darken the depression on either side of her pubic bone where the bikini is stretched tightly across her hips.

A balloon hangs from the window. Streamers. Birthday decorations? I hold the photograph against the glass. A flash of recognition. Something in her eyes.

"You know her?"

She shakes her head. She's lying.

"Help me."

There are traces of beauty in her cheekbones and the curve of her jaw. Her hair is parted. The thin scalp line is dark instead of white. She lowers her eyes. She's curious.

The door opens. I step inside. The room is scarcely wide enough for a double bed, a chair and a small sink attached to the wall. Everything is pink, the pillows, sheets and the fresh towel lying on top. One entire wall is a mirror, reflecting the same scene so it looks like we're sharing the room with another window.

The prostitute sips from a can of soft drink. "My name is Eve—just like the first woman." She laughs sarcastically. "Welcome to my Garden of Eden."

Leaning down she picks up a packet of cigarettes beneath her stool. Her breasts sway. She hasn't bothered closing the curtain. Instead she stays by the window. I look at the bed and the chair, wondering where to sit.

Eve points to the bed. "Twenty euros, five minutes."

Her accent is a mixture of Dutch and American. It's another testament to the power of Hollywood which has taught generations of people in distant corners of the world to speak English.

I hand over the money. She palms it like a magician making a playing card disappear.

I hold up the photograph again. "Her name is Samira."

"She's one of the pregnant ones."

I feel myself straighten. Invisible armor. Knowledge.

Eve shrugs. "Then again, I could be wrong."

The thumbprint on her forearm is a bruise. Another on her neck is even darker.

"Where did you see her? When?"

"Sometimes I get asked to help with the new ones. To show them."

"To show them what?"

She laughs and lights a cigarette. "What do *you* think? Sometimes they watch me from the chair or from the bed, depending on what the customer has paid for. Some of them like being watched. Makes it quicker."

I'm about to ask about why she needs a chair, when I notice the strip of carpet on the floor to protect her knees.

"But you said she was pregnant. Why would you need to show her this?"

She rolls her eyes. "I'm giving you the *five*-minute version. That's what you paid for."

I nod.

"I saw her the first time in January. I remember because it was so cold that day." She motions to the sink.

"Cold water only. Like ice. They brought her to watch. Her eyes were bigger than this." The prostitute makes fists with her hands. "I thought she was going to throw up. I told her to use the sink. I knew she was never going to make it as one of us. It's only sex. A physical act. Men come and go. They cannot touch me here or here," she says pointing to her heart and her head. "This girl acted as though she was saving herself. Another fucking virgin!" She flicks the ash from her cigarette.

"What happened?"

"Time's up." She holds out her hand for more money.

"That wasn't five minutes."

She points to the wall behind me. "You see that clock? I lie on my back and watch it for a living. Nobody judges five minutes like I do."

I hand her another twenty euros. "You said she was pregnant."

"That was the next time I saw her." Eve mimes the bump. "She was at a doctor's clinic in Amersfoort. She was in the waiting room with a Serbian girl. Both of them were pregnant. I figured it was a welfare scam or they were trying to stay in the country by having a baby."

"Did you talk to her?"

"No. I remember being surprised because I thought she was going to be the world's last virgin." The cigarette is burning near her knuckles.

"I need the name and address of the clinic."

"Dr. Beyer. You'll find him in the book."

She crushes the cigarette beneath a sling-back shoe. A knock on the glass catches her attention. A man outside points first to me and then to Eve.

"What's your name?" she whispers conspiratorially.

"Alisha."

She reaches for the door. "He wants both of us, Alisha."

"Don't open it!"

"Don't be so shy. He looks clean. I have condoms."

"I'm not a—"

"Not a whore. Not a virgin either. You can make some money. Buy some decent clothes."

There is a small commotion outside. More men are peering through the window. I'm on my feet. I want to leave. She is still trying to convince me. "What have you got to lose?"

I want to say my self-respect.

She opens the door. I have to squeeze past her. Her fingernail runs down my cheek and the tip of her tongue moistens her bottom lip. Men crowd the passageway, where the cobbles are slick and hard. I have to shoulder my way past them, smelling their bodies, brushing against them. My foot strikes a step and I stumble. A hand reaches out to help me but I slap it away irrationally, wanting to scream abuse at him. I was right about Samira. Right about the baby. That's why Cate faked her pregnancy and carried Samira's photograph.

A small patch of gray sky appears above the crush. Suddenly I'm out, in a wider street, drawing deep breaths. The dark water of the canal is slashed with red and lilac. I lean over a railing and vomit, adding to the color.

My mobile vibrates. Ruiz is on the move.

"I might have found someone," he says, puffing slightly. "I was showing Samira's photograph around

Central Station. Most people didn't want to know but this one kid acted real strange when he saw the picture."

"You think he knew her?"

"Maybe. He wouldn't tell the truth if God Almighty asked him for it."

"Where is he now?"

"He took off. I'm fifty yards behind him."

The DI rattles off a description of a teenage boy in a khaki camouflage jacket, jeans and sneakers.

"Damn!"

"What's up?"

"My mobile is running low. Should have charged it last night. Nobody ever bloody calls me."

"I do."

"Yeah, well, that just goes to show you should get a life. I'll try to give you a cross street. There's a canal up ahead."

"Which one?"

"They all look the same."

I hear music in the background and a girl shouting from the windows.

"Hold on. Barndesteeg," he says.

Standing in the ocher glow of a streetlight, I open a tourist map and run my finger down the names until I find the street grid reference. They're not far away.

Movies and TV shows make it look easy to follow someone and not be seen, but the reality is very different. If this were a proper police tail, we'd have two cars, a motorcyclist and two, maybe three officers on foot. Every time the target turned, someone new would be behind him. We don't have that luxury.

Crossing over Sint Jansbrug, I walk quickly along the canal. Ruiz is a block farther east, heading toward me along Stoofsteeg. The teenager is going to walk straight past me.

The pavement is crowded. I have to step left and right, brushing shoulders with passersby. The air is thick with hashish and fried-food smells.

I don't see him until the last moment. He's almost past me. Gaunt-cheeked, hair teased with fingers and gel, he skips from the pavement to the gutter and back again, dodging people. He's carrying a canvas bag over his shoulder. A bottle of soft drink protrudes from the top. He looks over his shoulder. He knows he's being followed but he's not scared.

Ruiz has dropped back. I take over. We reach the canal and cross the bridge, almost retracing my steps. The boy walks nearer the water than the buildings. If he wants to lose a tail, why take the open side of the street?

Then it dawns on me—he's *leading* Ruiz away. Someone at the station must have known Samira. He didn't want Ruiz finding them.

The teenager stops moving and waits. I walk past him. The DI doesn't appear. The kid thinks he's safe but doubles back to make sure.

When he moves again he doesn't look back. I follow him through the narrow lanes until he reaches Warmoesstraat and then Dam Square. He waits near a sculpture until a slender girl appears, dressed in jeans and a pink corduroy jacket. Her hair is short and straight, the color of tea.

He argues and gesticulates, miming with his hands. I call Ruiz on the mobile. "Where are you?"

"Behind you."

"Was there a girl at the station in jeans and a pink jacket? Dark haired. Late teens. Pretty for now."

"Samira?"

"No. Another girl. I think he was trying to lead you away. He didn't want you finding her."

They're still arguing. The girl shakes her head. He tugs at her coat sleeve. She pulls away. He shouts something. She doesn't turn.

"They're splitting up," I whisper into my mobile. "I'll follow the girl."

She has a curious body, a long torso and short legs, with slightly splayed feet when she walks. She takes a blue scarf from her pocket and wraps it over her head, tying it beneath her chin. It is a hijab—a head covering. She could be Muslim.

I stay close behind her, aware of the crowds and the traffic. Trams joust on tracks that divide the wider roads. Cars and bicycles weave around them. She is so small. I keep losing sight of her.

One moment she's in front of me and the next— Where has she gone? I sprint forward, looking vainly in doorways and shop windows. I search the side streets, hoping for a glimpse of her pink jacket or the blue of her hijab.

Standing on a traffic island, I turn full circle and step forward. A bell sounds urgently. My head turns. An unseen hand wrenches me backward as a tram washes past in a blur of noise and rushing air.

The girl in the pink jacket is staring at me, her heart beating faster than mine. The smudges beneath her eyes are signs of the premature or the beaten down. She knew I was following her. She saved me.

"What's your name?"

Her lips don't move. She turns to leave. I have to sprint several yards to get in front of her.

"Wait! Don't leave. Can we talk?"

She doesn't answer. Perhaps she doesn't understand.

"Do you speak English?" I point to myself. "My name is Alisha."

She steps around me.

"Wait, please."

She steps around me again. I have to dodge people as I try to walk backward and talk to her at the same time. I hold my hands together as if praying. "I'm looking for Samira."

She doesn't stop. I can't *make* her talk to me.

Suddenly, she enters a building, pushing through a heavy door. I don't see her use a key or press a buzzer. Inside smells of soup and electric warmth. A second door reveals a large stark room full of tables and scraping chairs. People are sitting and eating. A nun in a black tunic fills bowls of soup from a trolley. A bikie type with a long beard hands out plates and spoons. Someone else distributes bread rolls.

An old man at the nearest table leans low over his food, dipping chunks of bread into the steaming mixture. He crooks his right arm around the bowl as though protecting it. Beside him a tall figure in a woolen cap is trying to sleep with his head on the table. There must be thirty people in the dining room, most with ragtag clothes, body tics and empty stomachs.

"Wou je iets om te eten?"

I turn to the voice.

In English this time: "Would you like something to eat?"

The question belongs to an elderly nun with a narrow face and playful eyes. Her black tunic is trimmed with green and her white hair sweeps back from her brow until it disappears beneath a wimple.

"No, thank you."

"There is plenty. It is good soup. I made it myself."

A work apron, the width of her shoulders, reaches down to her ankles. She is collecting plates from the tables, stacking them along her arm. Meanwhile, the girl has lined up metal tins in front of the soup pot.

"What is this place?"

"We are Augustinians. I am Sister Vogel."

She must be in her eighties. The other nuns are of similar vintage although not quite so shrunken. She is tiny, scarcely five feet tall, with a voice like gravel spinning in a drum.

"Are you sure you won't eat?"

"No. Thank you." I don't take my eyes off the girl.

The nun steps in front of me. "What do you want with her?"

"Just to talk."

"That's not possible."

"Why?"

"She will not hear you."

"No, you don't understand. If I can just speak—"

"She *cannot* hear you." Her voice softens. "She is one of God's special children."

I finally understand. It's not about language or desire. The girl is deaf.

The soup tins have been filled. The girl screws a lid on each tin and places them in a shoulder bag. She raises the strap over her head, adjusting it across her chest. She unfolds a paper napkin and wraps two pieces of bread. A third piece she takes with her, nibbling at the edges.

"Do you know her name?" I ask.

"No. She comes three times a week and collects food."

"Where does she live?"

Sister Vogel isn't going to volunteer the information. There is only one voice she obeys—a higher authority.

"She's done nothing wrong," I reassure her.

"Why do you wish to speak with her?"

"I'm looking for someone. It's very important."

Sister Vogel puts down the soup dishes and wipes her hands on her apron. Rather than walking across the room she appears to float a fraction above the wooden floorboards in her long tunic. I feel leaden-footed alongside her.

She steps in front of the girl and taps the palm of her hand before making shapes with her fingers.

"You can sign!" I say.

"I know some of the letters. What do you wish to ask?"

"Her name."

They sign to each other.

"Zala."

"Where is she from?"

"Afghanistan."

I take the photograph from my pocket. Sister Vogel takes it from me. The reaction is immediate. Zala shakes her head adamantly. Fearfully. She won't look at the image again.

Sister Vogel tries to calm her down. Her voice is soft. Her hands softer. Zala continues to shake her head, without ever lifting her gaze from the floor.

"Ask her if she knows Samira."

Sister Vogel tries to sign but Zala is backing away.

"I need to know where Samira is."

The nun shakes her head, scolding me. "We don't frighten people away from here."

Zala is already at the door. She can't run with the

soup weighing her down. As I move to follow her, Sister Vogel grabs my arm. "Please, leave her alone."

I look at her imploringly. "I can't."

Zala is on the street. She looks back over her shoulder. Her cheeks are shining under the streetlamps. She's crying. Hair has escaped from beneath her hijab. She cannot spare a hand to brush it away from her face.

The DI isn't answering his mobile. His battery must be dead. Dropping back, I stay behind Zala as she leads me away from the convent. The streets and canals are no longer familiar. They are lined with aging, psoriatic houses, subdivided into bedsits, flats and maisonettes. Doorbell pushers form neat lines.

We pass a small row of shops that are shuttered and locked. At the next corner Zala crosses the road and enters a gate. It belongs to a large, rundown apartment block at the heart of a T junction. The shrubs outside are like puffs of green against the darkness of the bricks. There are bars on the downstairs windows and shutters on the upper floors. Lights burn behind them.

I walk past the gate and check there are no other entrances. I wish Ruiz were here. What would he do? Knock on the door? Introduce himself? No, he'd wait and watch. He'd see who was coming and going. Study the rhythm of the place.

I look at my watch. It has just gone eight. Where is he? With luck, he'll get my text message with the address.

The wind has picked up. Leaves dance with scraps of paper at my feet. Hidden in a doorway, I'm protected by the shadows.

I don't have the patience for stakeouts. Ruiz is good at them. He can block everything out and stay focused, without ever daydreaming or getting distracted. When I stare at the same scene for too long it becomes burned into my subconscious, playing over and over on a loop until I don't register the changes. That's why police surveillance teams are rotated every few hours. Fresh eyes.

A car pulls up. Double-parks. A man enters the building. Five minutes later he emerges with three women. Neatly groomed. Dressed to kill. Ruiz would say it smells like sex.

Two different men stop outside to smoke. They sit on the steps with their legs splayed, comfortable. A young boy creeps up behind one of them and covers his eyes playfully. Father and son wrestle happily until the youngster is sent back inside. They look like immigrants. It's the sort of place Samira would go, seeking safety in numbers.

I can't stay here all night. And I can't afford to leave and risk losing my link to her. It's almost nine. Where the hell is Ruiz?

The men on the steps look up as I approach.

"Samira Khan?"

One of them tosses his head, indicating upstairs. I step around them. The door is open. The foyer smells of cooking spices and a thousand extinguished cigarettes.

Three children are playing at the base of the stairs. One of them grabs hold of my leg and tries to hide behind me before dashing off again. I climb to the first landing. Empty gas bottles have collected against the walls beside bags of rubbish. A baby cries. Children argue. Canned laughter escapes through thin walls.

Two teenage girls are sitting outside a flat, heads together, swapping secrets.

"I'm looking for Samira."

One of them points upstairs.

I climb higher, moving from landing to landing, aware of the crumbling plaster and buckling linoleum. Laundry hangs over banisters and somewhere a toilet has overflowed.

I reach the top landing. A bathroom door is open at the far end of the corridor. Zala appears in the space. A bucket of water tilts her shoulders. In the dimness of the corridor I notice another open door. She wants to reach it before I do. The bucket falls. Water spills at her feet.

Against all my training I rush into a strange room. A dark-haired girl sits on a high-backed sofa. She is young. Familiar. Even dressed in a baggy jumper and peasant skirt she is obviously pregnant. Her shoulders pull forward as if embarrassed by her breasts.

Zala pushes past me, putting her body between us. Samira is standing now, resting a hand on the deaf girl's shoulder. Her eyes travel over me, as though putting me in context.

"I don't want to hurt you."

In textbook English: "You must leave here. It is not safe."

"My name is Alisha Barba."

Her eyes bloom. She knows my name.

"Please leave. Go now."

"Tell me how you know me?"

She doesn't answer. Her right hand moves to her distended abdomen. She caresses it gently and sways slightly from side to side as if rocking her passenger to sleep. The motion seems to take the fight out of her.

She signs for Zala to lock the door and pushes her toward the kitchen where speckled linoleum is worn smooth on the floor and a shelf holds jars of spices and a sack of rice. The soup canisters are washed and drying beside the sink.

I glance around the rest of the apartment. The room is large and square. Cracks edge across the high ceiling and leaking water has blistered the plaster. Mattresses are propped against the wall, with blankets neatly folded along the top. A wardrobe has a metal hanger holding the doors shut.

There is a suitcase, a wooden trunk, and on the top a photograph in a frame. It shows a family in a formal pose. The mother is seated holding a baby. The father is standing behind them, a hand on his wife's shoulder. At her feet is a small girl—Samira—holding the hem of her mother's dress.

I turn back to her. "I've been looking for you."

"Please go."

I glance at the swell of her pregnancy. "When are you due?"

"Soon."

"What are you going to do with the baby?"

She holds up two fingers. For a moment I think she's signing something to Zala but this has nothing to do with deafness. The message is for me. Two babies! Twins.

"A boy and a girl," she says, clasping her hands together, beseeching me. "Please go. You cannot be here."

Hair prickles on the nape of my neck. Why is she so terrified?

"Tell me about the babies, Samira. Are you going to keep them?"

She shakes her head.

"Who is the father?"

"Allah the Redeemer."

"I don't understand."

"I am a virgin."

"You're pregnant, Samira. You understand how that happens."

She confronts my skepticism defiantly. "I have never lain down with a man. I *am* a virgin."

What fantasies are these? It's ridiculous. Yet her certainty has the conviction of a convert.

"Who put the babies inside you, Samira?"

"Allah."

"Did you see him?"

"No."

"How did he do it?"

"The doctors helped him. They put the eggs inside me."

She's talking about IVF. The embryos were implanted. That's why she's having twins.

"Whose eggs were put inside you?"

Samira raises her eyes to the question. I know the answer already. Cate had twelve viable embryos. According to Dr. Banerjee there were five IVF procedures using two eggs per treatment. That leaves two eggs unaccounted for. Cate must have carried them to Amsterdam. She arranged a surrogacy.

That's why she had to fake her pregnancy. She was going to give Felix his *own* child—a perfect genetic match that nobody could prove wasn't theirs.

"Please leave," says Samira. Tears are close.

"Why are you so frightened?"

"You don't understand."

"Just tell me why you're doing this."

She pushes back her hair with her thumb and forefinger. Her wide eyes hold mine until the precise moment that it becomes uncomfortable. She is strong-willed. Defiant.

"Did someone pay you money? How much? Did Cate pay you?"

She doesn't answer. Instead she turns her face away, gazing at the window, a dark square against a dark wall.

"Is that how you know my name? Cate gave it to you. She said that if anything happened, if anything went wrong, you had to contact me. Is that right?"

She nods.

"I need to know why you're doing this. What did they offer you?"

"Freedom."

"From what?"

She looks at me as though I'll never understand. "Slavery."

I kneel down, taking her hand, which is surprisingly cool. There is a speck of sleep in the corner of her eye. "I need you to tell me exactly what happened. What were you told? What were you promised?"

There is a noise from the corridor. Zala reappears. Terror paints her face and her head swings from side to side, looking for somewhere to hide.

Samira motions for her to stay in the kitchen and turns to face the door. Waiting. A brittle scratching. A key in the lock. My nerve ends are twitching.

The door opens. A thin man with pink-rimmed eyes and bad teeth seems to spasm at the sight of me. His right hand reaches into a zipped nylon jacket.

"Wie bent u?" he barks.

I think he's asking who I am.

"I'm a nurse," I say.

He looks at Samira. She nods.

"Dr. Beyer asked me to drop by and check on Samira on my way home. I live not far from here."

The thin man makes a sucking sound with his tongue and his eyes dart about the room as though accusing the walls of being part of the deceit. He doesn't believe me, but he's not sure.

Samira turns toward me. "I have been having cramps. They keep me awake at night."

"You are *not* a nurse," he says accusingly. "You don't speak Dutch!"

"I'm afraid you're mistaken. English is the official language of the European Union." I use my best Mary Poppins voice. Officious. Matter-of-fact. I don't know how far I can push him.

"Where do you live?"

"Like I said, it's just around the corner."

"The address?"

I remember a cross street. "If you don't mind I have an examination to conduct."

He screws his mouth into a sneer. Something about his defiance hints at hidden depths of brutality. Whatever his relationship to Samira or Zala, he terrifies them. Samira mentioned slavery. Hassan had a property tattoo on his wrist. I don't have all the answers but I have to get them away from here.

The thin man barks a question in Dutch.

Samira nods her head, lowering her eyes.

"Lieg niet tegen me, kutwijf. Ik vermoord je."

His right hand is still in his jacket. Lithe and sinewy like a marathon runner, he weighs perhaps 180 pounds. With the element of surprise I could possibly take him.

"Please leave the room," I tell him.

"No. I stay here."

Zala is watching from the kitchen. I motion her

toward me and then unfold a blanket, making her hold it like a curtain to give Samira some privacy.

Samira lies back on the couch and lifts her jumper, bunching it beneath her breasts. My hands are damp. Her thighs are smooth and a taut triangle of white cotton lies at the top of them. The skin of her swollen belly is like tracing paper, stretched so tightly I can see the faint blue veins beneath the surface.

The babies move. Her entire torso seems to ripple. An elbow or a knee creates a peak and then slips away. I can feel the outline of tiny bodies beneath her skin, hard little skulls and joints.

She lifts her knees and raises her hips, indicating I should remove her underwear. She has more of an idea of what to do than I have. Her minder is still at the door. Samira fixes him with a defiant glare as if to say: You want to see this?

He can't hold her gaze. Instead he turns away and walks into the kitchen, lighting a cigarette.

"You lie so easily," Samira whispers.

"So do you. Who is he?"

"Yanus. He looks after us."

I look around the room. "He's not doing such a good job."

"He brings food."

Yanus is back at the doorway.

"Well the babies are in good position," I say loudly. "They're moving down. The cramps could be Braxton Hicks, which are like phantom contractions. Your blood pressure is a little higher than it has been."

I don't know where this information is coming from; some of it must be via verbal osmosis, having heard my mother's graphic descriptions of my nieces and nephews arriving in the world. I know far more than I want to about mucus plugs, fundal measurements and crowning. In addition to this, I am a world authority on pain relief—epidurals, pethidine, Entonox, TENS machines and every homeopathic, mind-controlling family remedy in existence.

Yanus turns away again. I hear him punch keys on his mobile phone. He's calling someone. Taking advice. Time is running out.

"You met a friend of mine. Cate Beaumont. Do you remember her?"

Samira nods.

"Do your babies belong to her?"

The same nod.

"Cate died last Sunday. She was run down and killed. Her husband is also dead."

Samira doubles over as though her unborn have understood the news and are grieving already. Her eyes flood with a mixture of disbelief and knowing.

"I can help you," I plead.

"Nobody can help me."

Yanus is in the doorway. He reaches into his jacket again. I can see his shadow lengthening on the floor. I turn to face him. He has a can of beans in his fist. He swings it, a short arc from the hip. I sense it coming but have no time to react. The blow sends me spinning across the room. One side of my head is on fire.

Samira screams. Not so much a scream as a strangled cry.

Yanus is coming for me again. I can taste blood. One side of my face is already beginning to swell. He hits me, using the can like a hammer. A knife flashes in his right hand.

His eyes are fixed on mine with ecstatic intensity. This is his calling—inflicting pain. The blade twirls in front of me doing figure eights. I was supposed to take him by surprise. The opposite happened. I underestimated him.

Another blow connects. Metal on bone. The room begins to blur.

Some things, real things, seem to happen half in the mind and half in the world; trapped in between. The mind sees them first, like now—a boot swings toward me. I glimpse Zala hanging back. She wants to look away but can't drag her gaze from me. The boot connects and I see a blaze of color.

Fishing roughly in my pockets, Yanus takes out my mobile, my passport, a bundle of Euros . . .

"Who are you?"

"I'm a nurse."

"Leugenaar!"

He holds the knife against my neck. The point pricks my skin. A ruby teardrop is caught on the tip of the blade.

Zala moves toward him. I yell at her to stop. She can't hear me. Yanus swats her away, with the can of beans. Zala drops and holds her face. He curses. I hope he broke his fingers.

My left eye is closing and blood drips from my ear, warming my neck. He forces me upright, pulling my arms back and looping plastic cuffs around my wrists. The ratchets pull them tighter, pinching my skin.

He opens my passport. Reads the name.

"Politieagent! How did you find this place?" He spits toward Zala. "*She* led you here."

"If you leave us alone I won't say anything. You can walk out of here."

Yanus finds this amusing. The point of his knife traces across my eyebrow.

"My partner knows I'm here. He's coming. He'll bring others. If you leave now you can get away."

"What are you doing here?"

"Looking for Samira."

He speaks to Samira in Dutch. She begins gathering her things. A few clothes, the photograph of her family . . .

"Wait for me outside," he tells her.

"Zala."

"Outside."

"Zala," she says again, more determined.

He waves the knife in her face. She doesn't flinch. She is like a statue. Immovable. She's not leaving without her friend.

The door suddenly blasts inward as if blown from its hinges. Ruiz fills the frame. Sometimes I forget how big he can make himself.

Yanus barely flinches. He turns, knife first. Here is a fresh challenge. The night holds such promise for him. Ruiz takes in the scene and settles on Yanus, matching his intensity.

But I can see the future. Yanus is going to take Ruiz apart. Kill him slowly. The knife is like an extension of him, a conductor's baton directing an invisible orchestra. Listening to voices.

The DI has something in his hand. A half brick. It's not enough. Yanus braces his legs apart and raises a hand, curling a finger to motion him onward.

Ruiz swings his fist, creating a disturbance in the air.

Yanus feints to the left. The half brick comes down and misses. Yanus grins. "You're too slow, old man."

The blade is alive. I scarcely see it move. A dark stain blossoms on Ruiz's shirtsleeve, but he continues stepping forward, forcing Yanus to retreat.

"Can you walk, Alisha?"

"Yes, sir."

"Get up and get out."

"Not without you, sir."

"Please, for once in your life—"

"I'll kill you both," says Yanus.

My hands are bound behind me. I can't do anything. The acid sting of nausea rises in my throat. Samira goes ahead of me, stepping into the corridor. Zala follows, still holding her cheek. Yanus yells to her in Dutch, threateningly. He lunges at Ruiz who dodges the blade. I turn outside the door and run toward the stairs, waiting for the sound of a body falling.

On every landing I shoulder the locked doors, banging my head against them and yelling for help. I want someone to untie my hands, to call the police, to give me a weapon. Nobody answers. Nobody wants to know.

We reach the ground floor and the street, turning right and heading for the canal. Samira and Zala are ahead of me. What a strange trio we make hustling through the darkness. We reach the corner. I turn to Samira. "I have to help him." She understands. "I want you to go straight to the police."

She shakes her head. "They'll send me back."

I haven't time to argue. "Then go to the nuns. Quickly. Zala knows the way."

I can feel the adrenaline still pumping through my body. Running now, aware of the void in my stomach, I sprint toward the house. There are people milling outside. They're surrounding a figure slumped on the steps. Ruiz. Someone has given him a cigarette. He sucks it greedily, drawing in his cheeks and then exhaling slowly.

Relief flows through me like liquid beneath my skin. I don't know whether to weep or laugh or do both. Blood soaks his shirt. A fist is pressed against his chest.

"I think maybe you should take me to a hospital," he says, struggling to breathe.

Like a crazy woman, I begin yelling at people to call an ambulance. A teenager summons the courage to tell me there's one coming.

"I had to get close," Ruiz explains in a hoarse whisper. His brow and upper lip are dotted with beads of sweat. "I had to let him stab me. If he could reach me I could *reach him*."

"Don't talk. Just be still."

"I hope I killed the bastard."

More people emerge from the flats. They want to come and see the bleeding man. Someone cuts away my cuffs and the plastic curls like orange peel at my feet.

Ruiz gazes at the night sky above the rooftops.

"My ex-wives have been wishing this on me for a long while," he says.

"That's not true. Miranda is still in love with you."

"How do you know?"

"I can see it. She flirts with you all the time."

"She can't help herself. She flirts with everyone. She does it to be nice."

His breathing is labored. Blood gurgles in his lungs.

"Wanna hear a joke?" he says.

"Don't talk. Sit quietly."

"It's an old one. I like the old ones. It's about a bear. I like bears. Bears can be funny."

He's not going to stop.

"There's this family of polar bears living in the Arctic in the middle of winter. The baby polar bear goes to his mother one day and says, 'Mum? Am I really a *polar bear*?'

" 'Of course you are, son,' she says.

"And the cub replies, 'Are you sure I'm not a panda bear or a black bear?'

" 'No, you're definitely not. Now run outside and play in the snow.'

"But he's still confused so the baby polar bear goes looking for his father and finds him fishing at the ice hole. 'Hey, Dad, am I a polar bear?'

" 'Well, of course, son,' he replies gruffly.

" 'Are you sure I don't have any grizzly in me or maybe koala?'

" 'No, son, I can tell you now that you're a hundred percent purebred polar bear, just like me and your mother. Why in the world do you ask?'

" 'Because I'm freezing my butt off out here!' "

The DI laughs and groans at the same time. I put my arms around his chest, trying to keep him warm. A mantra, unspoken, grows louder in my head: "Please don't die. Please don't die. Please don't die."

This is my fault. He shouldn't be here. There's so much blood.

5

Regret is such an odd emotion because it invariably comes a moment too late, when only our imagination can rewrite what has happened. My regrets are like pressed flowers in the pages of a diary. Brittle reminders of summers past; like the last summer before graduation, the one that wasn't big enough to hold its own history.

It was supposed to be the last hurrah before I entered the "real world." The London Metropolitan Police had sent me an acceptance letter. I was part of the next intake for the training college at Hendon. The class of 1998.

When I went to primary school I never imagined getting to secondary school. And at Oaklands I never imagined the freedom of university. Yet there I was, about to graduate, to grow up, to become a full-fledged, paid-up adult with a tax file number and a student loan to repay. "Thank God we'll never be forty," Cate joked.

I was working two jobs—answering phones at my brothers' garage and working weekends on a market stall. The Elliots invited me to Cornwall again. Cate's mother had suffered her stroke by then and was confined to a wheelchair.

Barnaby still had political ambitions but no safe seat had become available. He wasn't made of the right stuff—not old school enough to please the die-hard Conservatives and not female, famous or ethnic enough to satisfy modernizers in the party.

I still thought he was handsome. And he continued to flirt with me, finding reasons to lean against me or punch my arm or call me his "Bollywood beauty" or his "Indian princess."

On Sunday mornings the Elliots went to church in the village, about a ten-minute walk away. I stayed in bed until after they'd gone.

I don't know why Barnaby came back, what excuse he made to the others. I was in the shower. Music videos were turned up loud on the TV. The kettle had boiled. The clock ticked as if nothing had happened.

I didn't hear him on the stairs. He just appeared. I held the towel against me but didn't cry out. He ran his fingers slowly over my shoulder and along my arms. Perfect fingernails. I looked down. I could see his gray trousers and the tips of his polished shoes growing out from under his cuffs.

He kissed my throat. I had to throw my head back to make room for him. I looked up at the ceiling and he moved his lips lower to the space between my breasts. I held his head and pushed against him.

My hair was long back then, plaited in a French braid that reached down to the small of my back. He held it in his fists, wrapping it around his knuckles like a rope. Whispering in my ear, sweet nothings that meant more, he pushed down on my shoulders, wanting me to kneel. Meanwhile, the TV blared and the clock ticked and the water in the kettle cooled.

I didn't hear the door open downstairs or footsteps on the stairs. I don't know why Cate came back. Some details don't matter. She must have heard our voices and the other noises. She must have known but she kept coming closer until she reached the door, drawn by the sounds.

In real estate location is everything. Barnaby was standing naked behind me. I was on all fours with my knees apart. Cate didn't say a word. Having seen enough she stayed there watching more. She didn't see me fighting or struggling. I *didn't* fight or struggle.

This is the way I remember it. The way it happened. All that was left was for Cate to tell me to leave and that she never wanted to see me again. And time enough for her to lie sobbing on her bed. A single bed away, I packed my bag, breathing in her grief and trying to swallow something that I couldn't spit out.

Barnaby drove me to the station in silence. The seagulls were crying, accusing me of betrayal. The rain had arrived, drowning summer.

It was a long journey back to London. I found Mama at her sewing machine, making a dress for my cousin's wedding. For the first time in years I wanted to crawl onto her lap. Instead I sat next to her and put my head on her shoulder. Then I cried.

Later that night I stood in front of the bathroom mirror with Mama's big dressmaking scissors and cut my hair for the first time. The blades carved through my tresses and sent them rocking to the tiles. I trimmed it as short as the scissors allowed, nicking my skin so that blood stained the blades and tufts of hair stood out from my skull like sprouts of wheat germ.

I can't explain why. Somehow the act was palliative. Mama was horrified. (She would have been less shocked if I'd sliced open my wrists.)

I left messages for Cate and wrote her notes. I couldn't visit her house without risking meeting her father—or worse, her mother. What if Ruth Elliot knew? I caught the same buses and trains as Cate. I orchestrated chance meetings and sometimes I simply stalked her, but it made no difference. Being sorry wasn't enough. She didn't want to see me or talk to me.

Eventually I stopped trying. I locked myself away for hours, coming out only to run and to eat. I ran a personal best a month later. I no longer wanted to catch up with the future—I was running away from the past. I threw myself into my police training, studying furiously. Filling notebooks. Blitzing exams.

My hair grew back. Mama calmed down. I used to daydream, in the years that followed, that Cate and I would find each other and somehow redeem the lost years. But a single image haunted me—Cate standing silently in the doorway, watching her father fuck her best friend to the rhythm of a ticking clock and a cooling kettle.

In all the years since, not a day has passed when I haven't wanted to change what happened. Cate did not forgive me. She hated me with a hatred more fatal than indifference because it was the opposite of love.

After enough time had passed, I didn't think about her every hour or every day. I sent her cards on her birthday and at Christmas. I heard about her engagement and saw the wedding photographs in a photographer's window in Bethnal Green Road. She looked happy. Barnaby looked proud. Her bridesmaids (I knew all their names) wore the dresses she always said she wanted. I didn't know Felix. I didn't know where they'd met or how he'd proposed. What did she see in him? Was it love? I could never ask her.

They say time is a great healer and a lousy beautician, but it didn't heal my wounds. It covered them over with layers of regret and awkwardness like pancake makeup. Wounds like mine don't heal. The scars simply grow thicker and more permanent.

———

The curtains sway back and forth, breathing in and then out like lungs drawing restless air. Light spills from around the edges. Another day.

I must have dozed off. I rarely sleep soundly anymore. Not like I did as a child when the world was still a mystery. Now I snatch awake at the slightest noise or movement. The scars on my back are throbbing, telling me to stand and stretch.

Ruiz is lying on a bed in the dimness. Wires, fluids and machines have captured him. A mask delivers oxygen. Three hours ago surgeons inserted a tube in his chest and reinflated his right lung. They stitched his arm, commenting on his many scars.

My ear is wrapped in bandages and an ice pack has melted on my cheek. The swelling has gone down but the bruising will be ugly. At least I can let down my hair to hide the worst of it.

The doctors and nurses have been very kind. They wanted me to leave the DI's room last night. I argued. I begged. Then I seem to remember lying down on the linoleum floor, challenging them to carry me out. They let me stay.

I feel numb. Shell-shocked. This is my fault. I close my eyes to the darkness and listen to him breathing. Someone has delivered a tray with a glass of orange juice under a frilled paper lid. There are biscuits. I'm not hungry.

So this is all about a baby. Two babies. Cate Beaumont tried unsuccessfully to get pregnant through IVF. She then met someone who convinced her that for £80,000 another woman would have a baby for her. Not just any baby. Her own genetic offspring.

She traveled to Amsterdam where two of her fertilized embryos were implanted into the womb of an Afghani teenager who owed money to people smugglers. Both embryos began growing.

Meanwhile, in London Cate announced she was "pregnant." Friends and family celebrated the news. She began an elaborate deception that she had to maintain for nine months. What went wrong? Cate's ultrasound pictures—the fake ones—showed only one baby. She didn't expect twins.

Someone must have arranged the IVF procedure. Doctors were needed. Fertility specialists. Midwives. Minders.

A nurse appears at the door, an angel in off-white. She walks around the bed and whispers in my ear. A detective has come to interview me.

"He won't wake yet," she whispers, glancing at Ruiz. "I'll keep watch."

A local politieagent has been sitting outside the room all night. He looks very smart in dark blue trousers, light blue shirt, tie and jacket. Now he's talking to a more senior colleague. I wait for them to finish.

The senior detective introduces himself as Spijker, making it sound like a punishment. He doesn't give me a first name. Maybe he only has the one. Tall and thin with a narrow face and thinning hair, he looks at me with watery eyes as though he's already having an allergic reaction to what I might say.

A small mole on his top lip dances up and down as he speaks. "Your friend will be all right, I think."

"Yes, sir."

"I shall need to talk to him when he wakes up."

I nod.

We walk to the patient lounge, which is far smarter than anything I've seen in a British hospital. There are eggs and cold meats and slices of cheese on a platter, along with a basket of bread rolls. The detective waits for me to be seated and takes out a fountain pen, resting it on a large white pad. His smallest actions have a function.

Spijker explains that he works for the Youth and Vice Squad. Under normal circumstances, this might sound like an odd combination but not when I look at Samira's age and what she's been through.

As I tell him the story, explaining events, it strikes me how implausible it all sounds. An Englishwoman transports fertilized embryos to Amsterdam inside a small cooler box. The eggs are placed in the womb of an unwilling surrogate. A virgin.

Spijker leans forward, with his hands braced on either side of his chair. For a moment I think he might suffer from piles and want to relieve some of the pressure.

"What makes you think this girl was forced to become pregnant?"

"She told me."

"And you believe her?"

"Yes, sir."

"Perhaps she agreed."

"No. She owed money to traffickers. Either she became a prostitute or she agreed to have a baby."

"Trafficking is a very serious crime indeed. Commercial surrogacy is also illegal."

I tell him about the prostitute on Molensteeg who mentioned seeing a second pregnant girl. A Serb. Samira had a Serbian friend on the campus, according to Lena Caspar.

There could be others. Babies born at a price, ushered into the world with threats and blackmail. I have no idea how big this is, how many people it touches.

Spijker's face gives nothing away. He speaks slowly, as if practicing his English. "And this has been the purpose of your visit to Amsterdam?"

The question has a barbed tip. I have been waiting for this—the issue of jurisdiction. What is a British police officer doing investigating possible crimes in the Netherlands? There are protocols to be followed. Rules to be obeyed.

"I was making private inquiries. It is not an official investigation."

Spijker seems satisfied. His point has been made. I have no authority in the Netherlands.

"Where is this woman—the pregnant one?"

"Safe."

He waits, expecting an address. I explain about

Samira's asylum appeal and the deportation order. She's frightened of being sent back to Afghanistan.

"If this girl is telling the truth and becomes a witness there are laws to protect her."

"She could stay?"

"Until the trial."

I want to trust him—I want Samira to trust him—yet there is something in his demeanor that hints at skepticism. The notepad and fountain pen have not been touched. They are merely props.

"You tell a very interesting story, Detective Constable. A very interesting story, indeed." The mole on his top lip is quivering. "However, I have heard a different version. The man we found unconscious at the scene says he returned home and found you in his apartment. You claimed to be a nurse and that you were trying to examine his fiancée."

"His fiancée!"

"Yes indeed his fiancée. He says that he asked you for some proof of your identity. You refused. Did you conduct a physical examination of Miss Khan?"

"She *knew* I wasn't a nurse. I was trying to help her."

"Mr. Yanus further claims that he was attacked by your colleague as he endeavored to protect his fiancée."

"Yanus had a knife. Look at what he did!"

"In self-defense."

"He's lying."

Spijker nods, but not in agreement. "You see my dilemma, DC Barba. I have two different versions of the same event. Mr. Yanus wants you both charged with assault and abducting his fiancée. He has a good lawyer. A very good lawyer indeed."

"This is ridiculous! Surely you can't believe him."

The detective raises a hand to silence me. "We Dutch are famous for our open minds but do not mistake this openness for ignorance or naïveté. I need evidence. Where is the pregnant girl?"

"I will take you there, but I must talk to her first."

"To get your stories straight, perhaps?"

"No!" I sound too strident. "Her brother died three days ago. She doesn't know."

We drive in silence to my hotel. I am given time to shower and change. Spijker waits in the lobby.

Peeling off my clothes, I slip on a hotel robe and sit cross-legged on the bed, leafing through the messages that were waiting at reception. "New Boy" Dave has phoned four times, my mother twice and Chief Superintendent North has left a terse six-word "please explain." I screw it into a ball and flush it away. Maybe this is what he meant by shuffling people and priorities.

I should call Ruiz's family. Who, exactly? I don't have numbers for his children or any of his ex-wives—not even the most recent, Miranda.

I pick up the phone and punch the numbers. Dave is at the station. I hear other voices in the background.

"Hello, sweet girl, where have you been?"

"My mobile was stolen."

"How?"

"There was an accident."

His mood alters. "An accident!"

"Not really an accident." *I'm not doing this very well.*

"Hang on." I hear him apologizing to someone. He takes me somewhere private.

"What's wrong? Are you all right?"

"The DI is in hospital. Someone stabbed him."

"Shit!"

"I need a favor. Find a number for his ex-wife."

"Which one?"

"Miranda. Tell her that he's in the Academisch Medisch Centrum. It's a hospital in Amsterdam."

"Is he going to be all right?"

"I think so. He's out of surgery."

Dave wants the details. I try to fudge them, making it sound like a wrong-place-at-the-wrong-time scenario. Bad luck. He isn't convinced. I know what's coming now. He's going to get clingy and pathetic and ask me to come home and I'll be reminded of all the reasons I don't want to be married to someone.

Only he doesn't. He is matter-of-fact and direct, taking down the number of the hospital, along with Spijker's name. He's going to find out what the Dutch police are doing.

"I found Samira. She's pregnant."

I can hear Dave's mind juddering through the consequences. He is careful and methodical, like a carpenter who measures twice and cuts once.

"Cate paid for a baby. A surrogate."

"Jesus, Ali."

"It gets worse. She donated the embryos. There are twins."

"Who owns the babies?"

"I don't know."

Dave wants the whole story but I don't have time. I'm about to hang up when he remembers something.

"I know it's probably not the time," he says, "but I had a phone call from your mother."

"When?"

"Yesterday. She invited me to lunch on Sunday."

She threatened to do it and she went and did it!

He's waiting for a response.

"I don't know if I'll be home by then," I say.

"But you *knew* about the invite?"

"Yes, of course," I lie. "I told her to invite you."

He relaxes. "For a moment I thought she might have gone behind your back. How embarrassing would that be—my girlfriend's mother arranging dates for me? Story of my life—mothers liking me and their daughters running a mile."

Now he's blathering.

"It's all right, Dave."

"Brilliant."

He doesn't want to hang up. I do it for him. The shower is running. I step beneath the spray and flinch as the hot water hits my cheek and the cut on my ear. Washed and dried, I open my bag and take out my Dolce & Gabbana pants and a dark blouse. I see less of me in the mirror than I remember. When I ran competitively my best weight was 123 pounds. I got heavier when I joined the Met. Night shifts and canteen food will do that to you.

I have always been rather un-girlie. I don't have manicures or pedicures and I only paint my nails on special occasions (so I can chip it off when I get bored).

The day I cut my hair was almost a rite of passage. When it grew back I got a sensible layered shag cut. My mother cried. She's never been one to ration tears.

Ever since my teens I have lived in fear of saris and skirts. I didn't wear a bra until I was fourteen and my periods started after everyone else's. I imagined them

243

banked up behind a dam wall and when the gates opened it was going to be like a scene from a Tarantino film, without Harvey Keitel to clean up afterward.

In those days I didn't imagine ever feeling like a woman, but slowly it happened. Now I'm almost thirty and self-conscious enough to wear makeup—a little lip gloss and mascara. I pluck my eyebrows and wax my legs. I still don't own a skirt and every item in my wardrobe, apart from my jeans and my saris, is a variant on the color black. That's okay. Small steps.

I make one more phone call. It diverts between numbers and Lena Caspar answers. A public address system echoes in the background. She is on a railway platform. There is a court hearing in Rotterdam, she explains. An asylum seeker has been charged with stealing groceries.

"I found Samira."

"How is she?"

"She needs your help."

The details can wait. I give her Spijker's name and phone number. Samira will need protection and guarantees about her status if they want her to give evidence.

"She doesn't know about Hassan."

"You have to tell her."

"I know."

The lawyer begins thinking out loud. She will find someone to take over the court case in Rotterdam. It might take a few hours.

"I have a question."

My words are drowned out by a platform announcement. She waits. "I'm sorry. What did you say?"

"I have a hypothetical question for you."

"Yes?"

"If a married couple provided a fertilized embryo to a

surrogate mother who later gave birth, who would the baby belong to?"

"The birth mother."

"Even if genetically it had the DNA of the couple?"

"It doesn't matter. The law in the Netherlands is the same as the law in the U.K. The birth mother is the legal mother. Nobody else has a claim."

"What about the father?"

"He can apply for access, but the court will favor the mother. Why do you want to know?"

"Spijker will explain."

I hang up and take another look in the mirror. My hair is still wet. If I wear it down it will hide the swelling on my cheek. I'll have to stop my natural inclination to push it behind my ears.

Downstairs I find the detective and desk clerk in conversation. A notebook is open. They stop talking when they see me. Spijker is checking my details. I would do the same.

It is a short drive to the Augustinian Convent. We turn along Warmoesstraat and pull into a multistory car park. The African parking attendant comes running over. Spijker shows him a badge and tears up the parking stub.

Against his better judgment he has agreed to let me see Samira first. I have twenty minutes. Descending the concrete steps, I push open a heavy fire door. Across the street is the convent. A familiar figure emerges from the large front door. Dressed in her pink jacket and an ankle-length skirt, Zala puts her head down and hustles along the pavement. Her blue hijab hides the bruising on her face. She shouldn't be outside. I fight the urge to follow her.

A large ruddy-faced nun answers the door. Like the

others she is creased and crumbling, trying to outlive the building. I am led down a corridor to Sister Vogel's office, which contains a curious mixture of the old and the new. A cabinet with a glass-front full of books is stained the same dark color as the mahogany desk. In the corner there is a fax machine and a photocopier. A heart-shaped box of candies sits on the mantel, alongside photographs that could be of her nieces and nephews. I wonder if Sister Vogel ever regrets her calling. God can be a barren husband.

She appears beside me. "You didn't tell me you were a police officer."

"Would it have made a difference?"

She doesn't answer. "You sent more people for me to feed."

"They don't eat very much."

She folds her arms. "Is this girl in trouble?"

"Yes."

"Has she been abandoned?"

"Abused."

Sorrow fills every crease and wrinkle of her face. She notices the bruising on my cheek and reaches toward it sympathetically. "Who did this to you?"

"It doesn't matter. I must talk to Samira."

She takes me to a room on the second floor which is stained with the same dark panels. Samira is at the window when the door opens. She's wearing a long dress, buttoned down the middle, with a Peter Pan collar. The light from the window paints an outline of her body inside it. Watching me carefully, she takes a seat on the sofa. Her pregnancy rests on her thighs.

Sister Vogel doesn't stay. As the door closes, I glance around the room. On the wall there is a painting of the

Virgin Mary and the baby Jesus. Both are pictured beside a stream, where fruit hangs from trees and fat naked cherubs dance above the water.

Samira notices me looking at it. "Are you a Christian?"

"A Sikh."

She nods, satisfied.

"Do you dislike Christians?"

"No. My father told me that Christians believe less than we believe. I don't know if that is true. I am not a very good Muslim. I sometimes forget to pray."

"How often are you supposed to pray?"

"Five times a day, but my father always said that three was enough."

"Do you miss him, your father?"

"With every breath."

Her copper-colored eyes are flecked with gold and uncertainty. I can't imagine what they've seen in her short life. When I picture Afghanistan I see women draped in black like covered statues, mountains capped with snow, old caravan trails, unexploded mines, scorching deserts, terra-cotta houses, ancient monuments and one-eyed madmen.

I introduce myself properly this time and tell Samira how I found her. She looks away self-consciously when I mention the prostitute on Molensteeg. At the same time she holds her hand to her chest, pressing down. I see pain on her forehead.

"Are you OK?"

"Heartburn. Zala has gone to get medicine." She glances at the door, already missing her friend.

"Where did you meet her?"

"At the orphanage."

"You didn't leave Afghanistan together."

"No. We had to leave her behind."

"How did she get here?"

"In the back of a truck and then by train."

"By herself?"

Samira's face softens. "Zala can always find a way to make herself understood."

"Has she always been deaf?"

"No."

"What happened?"

"Her father fought with the mujahideen against the Taliban. When the Talibs took over they punished their enemies. Zala and her mother were imprisoned and tortured with acid and melted plastic. Her mother took eight days to die. By then Zala could not hear her screaming."

The statement sucks the oxygen from the room and I feel myself struggling for breath. Samira looks toward the door again, waiting for Zala. Her fingers are splayed on her belly as if reading the bumps and kicks. What must it feel like—to have something growing inside you? A life, an organism that takes what it needs without asking or sharing, stealing sleep, changing hormones, bending bones and squeezing organs. I have heard my friends and sisters-in-law complain of weak nails, molting hair, sore breasts and stretch marks. It is a sacrifice men could not make.

Samira is watching me. She has something she wants to ask.

"You said Mrs. Beaumont is dead."

"Yes."

"What will happen now to her babies?"

"It is your decision."

"Why?"

"They belong to you."

"No!"

"They're your babies."

Her head pivots from side to side. She is adamant.

Standing suddenly, she rocks slightly and reaches out her hand, bracing it on the back of the sofa. Crossing the room, she stares out the window, hoping to see Zala.

I'm still contemplating her denial. Does she love her unborn twins? Does she imagine a future for them? Or is she simply carrying them, counting down the days until the birth, when her job is done?

"When did you meet Mrs. Beaumont?"

"She came to Amsterdam. She bought me clothes. Yanus was there. I had to pretend I didn't speak English but Mrs. Beaumont talked to me anyway. She gave me a piece of paper with your name. She said if I was ever in trouble I had to find you."

"When was this?"

"In February I saw her the first time. She came to see me again in September."

"Did she know you were having twins?"

She shrugs.

"Did she know why?"

"What do you mean?"

"Did she know about the debt? Did she know you were *forced* to get pregnant?"

Her voice softens. "She thanked me. She said I was doing a good thing."

"It is a crime to force someone to have a baby. She did a very *foolish* thing."

Samira shrugs, unwilling to be so harsh. "Sometimes friends do foolish things," she says. "My father told me that true friends are like gold coins. Ships are wrecked by storms and lie for hundreds of years on the ocean floor. Worms destroy the wood. Iron corrodes. Silver turns black but gold doesn't change in seawater. It loses none of its brilliance or color. It comes up the same as it went down. Friendship is the same. It survives shipwrecks and time."

The swelling in my chest suddenly hurts. How can someone so young be so wise?

"You must tell the police what happened."

"They will send me back."

"These people have done very bad things. You owe them nothing."

"Yanus will find me. He will never let me go."

"The police can protect you."

"I do not trust them."

"Trust me."

She shakes her head. She has no reason to believe me. Promises don't fill stomachs or bring back dead brothers. She still doesn't know about Hassan. I can't bring myself to tell her.

"Why did you leave Kabul?"

"Brother."

"Your brother?"

"No. An Englishman. We called him Brother."

"Who is he?"

"A saint."

Using her forefinger she traces the outline of a cross on her neck. I think of Donavon's tattoo. Is it possible?

"This Englishman, was he a soldier?"

"He said he was on a mission from God."

She describes how he visited the orphanage, bringing food and blankets. There were sixty children aged between two and sixteen, who slept in dormitories,

250

huddling together in winter, surviving on scraps and charity.

When the Taliban were in control they took boys from the orphanage to fill their guns with bullets and the girls were taken as wives. The orphans cheered when the Northern Alliance and the Americans liberated Kabul, but the new order proved to be little different. Soldiers came to the orphanage looking for girls. The first time Samira hid under blankets. The second time she crawled into the latrine. Another girl threw herself off the roof rather than be taken.

I'm amazed at how ambivalent she sounds. Fateful decisions, issues of life and death, are related with the matter-of-factness of a shopping list. I can't tell if she's inured to shock or overcome by it.

"Brother" paid off the soldiers with medicine and money. He told Samira that she should leave Afghanistan because it wasn't safe. He said he would find her a job in London.

"What about Hassan?"

"Brother said he had to stay behind. I said I would not go without him."

They were introduced to a trafficker called Mahmoud, who arranged their passage. Zala had to stay behind because no country would accept a deaf girl, Mahmoud told them.

Hassan and Samira were taken overland to Pakistan by bus and smuggled south through Quetta and west into Iran until they reached Tabriz near the Turkish border. In the first week of spring they walked across the Ararat mountain range and almost succumbed to the freezing nights and the wolves.

On the Turkish side of the mountains, sheep farmers

smuggled them between villages and arranged their passage to Istanbul in the back of a truck. For two months brother and sister worked in a sweatshop in the garment districts of Zeytinburnu, sewing sheepskin waistcoats.

The trafficking syndicate demanded more money to get them to England. The price had risen to ten thousand American dollars. Samira wrote a letter to "Brother" but didn't know where to send it. Finally they were moved. A fishing boat took them across the Aegean Sea to Italy where they caught a train to Rome with four other illegals. They were met at the station and taken to a house.

Two days later, they met Yanus. He took them to a bus depot and put them inside the luggage compartment of a tourist coach that traveled through Germany to the Netherlands. "Don't move, don't talk—otherwise you will be found," he told them. When the coach arrived at the Dutch border they were to claim asylum. He would find them.

"We are supposed to be going to England," Samira said.

"England is for another day," he replied.

The rest of the story matches what I've already learned from Lena Caspar.

Sister Vogel knocks softly on the door. She is carrying a tray of tea and biscuits. The delicate cups have chipped handles. I pour the tea through a broken strainer. Samira takes a biscuit and wraps it in a paper napkin, saving it for Zala.

"Have you ever heard the name Paul Donavon?"

She shakes her head.

"Who told you about the IVF clinic?"

"Yanus. He said we had to pay him for our passage from Kabul. He threatened to rape me. Hassan tried to

252

stop him but Yanus cut him over and over. A hundred cuts." She points to her chest. Noonan found evidence of these wounds on Hassan's torso.

"What did Yanus want you to do?"

"To become a whore. He showed me what I would have to do—sleep with many men. Then he gave me a choice. He said a baby would pay off my debt. I could remain a virgin."

She says it almost defiantly. This is a truth that sustains Samira. I wonder if that's why they chose a Muslim girl. She would have done almost anything to protect her virginity.

I still don't know how Cate became involved. Was it her idea or Donavon's?

Spijker is waiting outside. I can't delay this. Opening my satchel I take out the charcoal drawing, smoothing the corners.

Excitement lights Samira's eyes from within. "Hassan! You've seen him!"

She waits. I shake my head. "Hassan is dead."

Her head jerks up as though tied to a cord. The light in her eyes is replaced by anger. Disbelief. I tell her quickly, hoping it might spare her, but there is no painless way to do this. His journey. His crossing. His fight to stay alive.

She puts her hands over her ears.

"I'm sorry, Samira. He didn't make it."

"You're lying! Hassan is in London."

"I'm telling the truth."

She rocks from side to side, her eyes closed and her mouth opening and closing soundlessly. The word she wants to say is no.

"Surely you must be wondering why you haven't

heard from him," I say. "He should have called by now or written to you. You sewed my name into his clothes. That's how I found you." I close the gap between us. "I have no reason to lie to you."

She stiffens and pulls away, fixing me with a gaze of frightening intensity.

Spijker's voice echoes from downstairs. He has grown tired of waiting.

"You must tell the police everything you have told me."

She doesn't answer. I don't know if she understands.

Turning toward the window, she utters Zala's name.

"Sister Vogel will look after her."

She shakes her head stubbornly, her eyes full of imbecile hope.

"I will find her. I'll look after her."

For a moment something struggles inside her. Then her mind empties and she surrenders. Fighting fate is too difficult. She must save herself to fight whatever fate throws up.

———

There is a pharmacy in the heart of de Walletjes, explains Sister Vogel. The pharmacist is a friend of hers. This is where she sent Zala. She was carrying a note.

Turning each corner I expect to see a flash of pink or her blue hijab coming toward me. I pass a greengrocer and catch the scent of oranges, which makes me think of Hassan. What will happen to Samira now? Who will look after her?

I turn into Oudekerksteeg. There is still no sign of Zala. A touch on my arm makes me turn. For a second I don't recognize Hokke, who is wearing a woolen cap.

With his light beard it makes him look like a North Sea fisherman.

"Hello, my friend." He looks at me closely. "What have you done to yourself?" His finger traces the bruising on my cheek.

"I had a fight."

"Did you win?"

"No."

I look over his shoulder, scanning the square for Zala. My sense of urgency makes him turn his own head.

"Are you still looking for your Afghani girl?"

"No, a different one this time."

It makes me sound careless—as though I lose people all the time. Hokke has been sitting in a café. Zala must have passed by him but he doesn't remember her.

"Perhaps I can help you look."

I follow him, scanning the pedestrians, until we reach the pharmacy. The small shop has narrow aisles and neatly stacked shelves. A man in a striped shirt and white coat is serving customers at a counter. When he recognizes Hokke he opens his arms and they embrace. Old friends.

"A deaf girl—I'd remember her," he announces, breaking into English.

"She had a note from Sister Vogel."

The pharmacist yells to his assistant. A head pops out from behind a stand of postcards. More Dutch. A shrug. Nobody has seen her.

Hokke follows me back onto the street. I walk a few paces and stop, leaning against a wall. A faint vibration is coming off me; a menacing internal thought spinning out of control. Zala has not run away. She would not leave Samira willingly. Ever.

Police headquarters is on one of the outer canals, west of the city. Fashioned by the imagination of an architect, it looks scrubbed clean and casts a long shadow across the canal. The glass doors open automatically. CCTV cameras scan the foyer.

A message is sent upstairs to Spijker. His reply comes back: I'm to wait in the reception area. None of my urgency has any effect on the receptionist, who has a face like the farmer's daughter in *American Gothic*. This is not my jurisdiction. I have no authority to make demands or throw my weight around.

Hokke offers to keep me company. At no point has he asked how I found Samira or what happened to Ruiz. He is content to accept whatever information is offered rather than seeking it out.

So much has happened in the past week yet I feel as though I haven't moved. It's like the clock on the wall above the reception desk, with its white face and thick black hands that refuse to move any faster.

Samira is somewhere above me. I don't imagine there are many basements in Amsterdam—a city that seems to float on fixed pontoons held together by bridges. Perhaps it is slowly sinking into the ooze like a Venice of the north.

I can't sit still. I should be at the hospital with Ruiz. I should be starting my new job in London or resigning from it.

Across the foyer the double doors of a lift slide open. There are voices, deep, sonorous, laughing. One of them belongs to Yanus. His left eye is swollen and partially closed. Head injuries are becoming a fashion statement. He isn't handcuffed, nor is he being escorted by police.

The man beside him must be his lawyer. Large and careworn, with a broad forehead and broader arse, his rumpled suit has triple vents and permanent creases.

Yanus looks up at me and smiles with his thin lips.

"I am very sorry for this misunderstanding," he says. "No hard feelings."

He offers me his hand. I stare at it blankly. Spijker appears at his left shoulder, standing fractionally behind him.

Yanus is still talking. "I hope Mr. Ruiz is being looked after. I am very sorry I stabbed him."

My eyes haven't left Spijker. "What are you doing?"

"Mr. Yanus is being released. We may need to question him again later."

The fat lawyer is tapping his foot on the floor impatiently. It has the effect of making his face wobble. "Samira Khan has confirmed that Mr. Yanus is her fiancé. She is pregnant by him." His tone is extravagantly pompous, with just a hint of condescension. "She has also given a statement corroborating his account of what happened last night."

"No!"

"Fortunately, for you, Mr. Yanus has agreed not to make a formal complaint against you or your colleague for assault, malicious wounding and abducting his fiancée. In return, the police have decided not to lay charges against him."

"Our investigations are continuing," counters Spijker.

"Mr. Yanus has cooperated fully," retorts the fat lawyer, dismissively.

Lena Caspar is so small that I almost don't see her

behind him. I can sense my gaze flicking from face to face like a child waiting for a grown-up to explain. Yanus has withdrawn his hand. Almost instinctively he slides it inside his jacket, where his knife would normally be.

I imagine that I must look dazed and dumbstruck, but the opposite is true. I can see myself reflected in the dozens of glass panels around the walls and the news hasn't altered my demeanor at all. Internally, the story is different. Of all the possible outcomes, this one couldn't be anticipated.

"Let me talk to Samira."

"That's not possible."

Lena Caspar puts her hand on my arm. "She doesn't want to talk to anyone."

"Where is she?"

"In the care of the Immigration and Naturalization Service."

"Is she going to be deported?"

The fat lawyer answers for her. "My client is applying for a visa that will allow his fiancée to remain in the Netherlands."

"She's *not* his fiancée!" I snap.

The lawyer inflates even further (it barely seems possible). "You are very fortunate, Miss Barba, that my client is so willing to forgive. You would otherwise be facing very serious charges. Mr. Yanus now demands that you leave him alone, along with his fiancée. Any attempt by you to approach either of them will be taken very seriously."

Yanus looks almost embarrassed by his own generosity. His entire persona has softened. The cold, naked, unflinching hatred of last night has gone. It's like watching a smooth ocean after a storm front has passed. He extends his hand again. There is something in it this time—my mobile phone and passport. He hands them to me and turns away. He and the fat lawyer are leaving.

I look at Spijker. "You know he's lying."

"It makes no difference," he replies.

Mrs. Caspar wants me to sit down.

"There must be something," I say, pleading with her.

"You have to understand. Without Samira's testimony there *is* no case to answer, no evidence of forced pregnancies or a black market in embryos and unborn babies. The proof might lie in DNA or paternity tests, but these can't be done without Samira's permission and invasive surgery that could endanger the twins."

"Zala will confirm my story."

"Where is she?"

The entrance doors slide open. The fat lawyer goes first. Yanus pulls a light blue handkerchief from his pocket and wipes his forehead. I recognize the fabric. He rolls it over and over in his fingers. It's not a handkerchief. It's a headscarf. Zala's hijab!

Spijker sees me moving and holds me back. I fight against his arms, yelling accusations out the door. Yanus turns and smiles, showing a few teeth at the sides of his mouth. A shark's smile.

"See in his hand—the scarf," I cry. "That's why she lied."

Mrs. Caspar steps in front of me. "It's too late, Alisha."

Spijker releases my arms slowly and I shake his fingers loose. He's embarrassed at having touched me. There's something else in his demeanor. Understanding. He *believes* me! He had no choice but to release Yanus.

Frustration, disappointment and anger fill me until I feel like screaming. They have Zala. Samira is sure to follow. For all the bruises and bloodshed, I haven't even slowed them down. I'm like Wile E. Coyote, flattened beneath a rock, listening to the Road Runner's infernal, triumphant, infuriating "beep, beep!"

6

Ruiz's skin is a pallid gray and his eyes are bloodshot from the morphine. The years have mugged him in his sleep and he looks every one of his sixty birthdays.

"I knew you were gonna be okay," I say. "Your hide is thicker than a rhino's."

"Are you saying my arse looks big in these pajamas?"

"Not in *those* pajamas."

The curtains are open and the remains of the day are collecting on the far horizon.

It might be the morphine or his ridiculous male pride, but the DI keeps bragging about the number of stitches he needed in his chest and arm. Next we'll be comparing scars. I don't need a comparison—mine are bigger than his.

Why is it always a competition with men? Their egos are so fragile or their hormones so strong that they have to prove themselves. What tossers!

I give him a big wet kiss on his cheek. He's lost for words.

"I brought you something, sir."

He gives me a quick look, unsure whether to trust me. I pull a bottle of Scotch from a paper bag. It's a private joke. When I was lying in hospital with a busted spine Ruiz brought me a bottle. It's still the only time I've ever had alcohol. A one-off drink, sucked through a crazy straw, that made my eyes water and my throat burn. What do people see in alcohol?

I crack the seal and pour him a drink, adding a little water.

"You're not having one?"

"Not this time. You can have mine."

"That's very generous of you."

A nurse walks in. The DI hides the glass. I hide the bottle. She hands him a little plastic cup with two pills inside. The fact that we've stopped talking and look guilty encourages her to pause at the door. She says something in Dutch. It might be "bottoms up," but I doubt it.

"I think I'm going to stay here," says Ruiz. "The food is much better than the NHS muck and the nurses have a certain charm. They remind me of my house mistresses at boarding school."

"That sounds disturbingly like a sexual fantasy."

He half grins. "Not completely."

He takes another sip. "Have you ever thought about what you'd like to happen when you die? The arrangements."

"I've made a will."

"Yeah, but did you stipulate anything for the funeral? Cremation or burial or having your ashes sprinkled off the end of Margate Pier?"

"Not specifically." This is getting rather morbid.

"I want my ashes put into a rocket."

"Sure, I'll put in a call to NASA."

"In a *firework* rocket. I want to be blasted into a thousand falling stars. They can do that now—put ashes in fireworks. I read about it somewhere."

"Go out with a bang."

"A blaze of glory."

He smiles and holds out his glass for more. "Not yet, of course."

"Of course."

The truth is, *I have* thought about it. Dying. During the autumn and winter of my discontent—the months of surgery and physiotherapy, when I couldn't wash, feed or care for myself—a small, secret, childlike part of me feared that I would never walk again. And an unspoken, guilt-ridden, adult part of me decided I would rather die if that happened.

Everyone thinks I'm so strong. They expect me to face autumns and winters like that and bitch-slap them down, make them heel. I'm not so strong. I only pretend.

"I had a phone call from Miranda today," the DI announces. "I still don't know how she got the number or knew I was in hospital. As far as I can tell I was unconscious for most of yesterday." His eyes narrow. "Try not to look so sheepish, my little lambkin."

"I told you she still cares about you."

"But can't *live* with me."

"That's because you're grumpy."

"And you're an expert in these things, I suppose."

"Well 'New Boy' Dave has asked me to marry him." The statement blurts from me, unplanned, spontaneous.

Ruiz ponders it. "I didn't think he had the courage."

"You think he's afraid of me?"

"Any man with any sense should be a little bit afraid of you."

"Why?"

"I mean that in the nicest possible way." His eyes are dancing.

"You said I was too sharp for him."

"And you said that any man who could *fit* into your pants couldn't *get* into your pants."

"He loves me."

"That's a good start. How about you?"

I can't answer. I don't know.

It's strange talking about love. I used to hate the word. Hate is too strong. I was sick of reading about it in books, hearing it in songs, watching it in films. It seemed such a huge burden to place on another person—to love them; to give them something so unbelievably fragile and expect them not to break it or lose it or leave it behind on the No. 96 bus.

I thought I had a choice. Fall in love. Don't fall in love. He loves me. He loves me not. See, I'm not so smart!

My mind drifts back to Samira. I don't know what to do. I'm out of ideas. Up until now I've been convinced that I would find Cate's babies and then—what then? What did I imagine would happen? Cate broke the law. She rented a womb. Perhaps she didn't realize that Samira would be forced to cooperate. I can give her the benefit of *that* doubt.

Cate always walked close to the edge. Closer to death, closer to life. She had a crazy streak. Not all the time, just occasionally. It's like when the wind changes suddenly before a storm and kids go wild, running around in circles like swirling scraps of paper caught in the updraft.

Cate would get that same gleam in her eye and drift onto the wrong side of crazy.

She is more memory than reality. She belongs to a time of teenage crushes, first kisses, crowded lecture halls and smoky pubs. Even if she had lived, we might have had nothing in common except the past.

I should let it go. When Ruiz is well enough, I'll take him home. I'll swallow my pride and take whatever job I'm offered or I'll marry Dave and we'll live in Milford-on-Sea. I shouldn't have come to Amsterdam. Why did I ever imagine I could make a difference? I can't bring Cate back. Yet for all this, I still can't shake one fundamental question: What will happen to the babies?

Yanus and his cronies will sell them to the highest bidder. Either that or they'll be born in the Netherlands and put up for adoption. Worse still, they'll be sent back to Kabul along with Samira, who will be ostracized and treated as an outcast. In some parts of Afghanistan they still stone women for having children out of wedlock.

Cate lied and deceived. She broke the law. I still don't know why Brendan Pearl killed her, although I suspect it was to stop her from talking. She came to me. I guess that makes me partially responsible.

Am I guilty of anything else? Is there something else I should have done? Perhaps I should tell Felix's family that their son would have become a father in a few weeks. Barnaby and Ruth Elliot are pseudo-grandparents to surrogate twins.

I didn't imagine ever feeling sorry for Barnaby—not after what happened. I thought I saw his true nature on the day he dropped me at the railway station in Cornwall. He couldn't even look at me or say the word goodbye.

I still don't know if he told his wife. I doubt it. Barnaby is the type to deny, deny and deny, until faced with incontrovertible proof. Then he will shrug, apologize and play the tragic hero, brought down by loving too much rather than too little.

When I first saw him at the hospital, when Cate was in a coma, it struck me how he was still campaigning, still trying to win votes. He caught glimpses of his reflection in the glass doors, making sure he was doing it right, the grieving. Maybe that's unfair—kicking a man when he's down.

Ruiz is asleep. I take the glass from his hand and rinse it in the sink. Than I tuck the bottle into my bag.

I'm still no closer to knowing what to do. It's like running a race where I cannot tell how many laps there are to go or who's winning or who's been lapped. How do I know when to kick on the final bend and start sprinting for home?

A taxi drops me at the hotel. The driver is listening to a football game being broadcast on the radio. The commentator has a tenor voice that surges with the ebb and flow of the action. I have no idea who is playing but I like the thunderous sound of the crowd. It makes me feel less melancholy.

There is a white envelope poking out of my pigeonhole at the reception desk. I open it immediately.

Three words: "Hello, sweet girl."

The desk clerk moves her eyes. I turn. "New Boy" Dave is standing behind me.

His arms wrap around me and I bury my face in his shirt. I stay there. Holding him tightly. I don't want him to see my tears.

7

One second I'm sleeping and the next I'm awake. I look at the clock. Four a.m. Dave is lying next to me on his side with his cheek pressed flat against the sheet and his mouth vibrating gently.

Last night we didn't talk. Exhaustion and a hot shower and the touch of his hands put me to sleep. I'll make it up to him when he wakes. I'm sure it doesn't do much for the male ego, having a woman fall asleep on them.

Propped on one elbow, I study him. His hair is soft and rumpled like a tabby cat with tiny flecks of blond amid the ginger. He has a big head. Does that mean he would have big babies, with big heads? Involuntarily I squeeze my thighs together.

Dave scratches his ear. He has nice ears. The one I can see has the faintest hint that at one time it might have been pierced. His hand is stretched toward me on the sheet. The nails are wide and flat, trimmed straight across. I touch his fingers with mine, awkward at being so happy.

Yesterday was perhaps the worst day of my life, and I held him last night like a shipwrecked sailor clinging to the debris. He made me feel safe. He wrapped his arms around me and the pain leaked away.

Maybe that's why I feel this way, lying so still—not wanting this moment to end.

I have no experience of love. Ever since adolescence I have avoided it, renounced it, longed for it. (Such a dichotomy is one of the symptoms.) I have been an agony aunt for all my girlfriends, listening to their sob stories about arranged marriages, unfaithful husbands, men who won't call or commit, missed periods, sexual neuroses, wedding plans, postnatal depression and failed diets. I know all about other people's love affairs but I am a complete novice when it comes to my own. That's why I'm scared. I'm sure to mess it up.

Dave touches my bruised cheek. I flinch. "Who did that?" he asks.

"His name is Yanus."

I can almost see him storing this information away for future reference. He and Ruiz are similar in that way. There is nothing half-cocked or hotheaded about them. They can wait for their shot at revenge.

"You were lucky he didn't break your cheekbone."

"He could have done a lot worse."

I step closer and kiss him on the lips, quickly, impulsively. Then I turn and go to shower. Spinning back to say something, I catch him punching the air in victory.

He blushes.

"It wasn't *that* good a kiss."

"It was to me."

Later, he sits on the bed and watches me dress, which makes me feel self-conscious. I keep my back to him. He reaches across and cups my breasts before my bra embraces them.

"I volunteer for this job," he says.

"That's very noble, but you're not holding my breasts all day."

I gently push his hands away and continue dressing.

"You really like me, don't you?" he says. His big goofy grin is reflected in the wardrobe mirror.

"Don't push it," I warn him.

"But you do. You *really* like me."

"That *could* change."

His laugh isn't entirely convincing.

We breakfast at a café on Paleisstraat near Dam Square. Blue-and-white trams clatter and fizz past the window beneath humming wires. A weak sun is barely breaking through the clouds and a wind tugs at the clothes of pedestrians and cyclists.

The café has a zinc-topped counter running the length of one side. Arranged above it is a blackboard menu and barrels of wine or port. The place smells of coffee and grilled cheese. My appetite is coming back. We order sliced meats, bread and cheese; coffee with frothed milk.

I take Dave through everything that's happened. Occasionally he interrupts with a question, but mostly he eats and listens. This whole affair is laced with half-truths and concocted fictions. The uncertainties and ambiguities seem to outweigh the facts and they nag at me, making me fretful and uncomfortable.

I borrow his notebook and write down names.

> Brendan Pearl
> Yanus
> Paul Donavon
> Julian Shawcroft

On the opposite side of the page I write another list: the victims.

> Cate and Felix Beaumont
> Hassan Khan
> Samira Khan

There are likely to be others. Where do I list those who fall in between, people like Barnaby Elliot? I still think he lied to me about Cate's computer. And Dr. Banerjee, her fertility specialist. It was more than a coincidence that he turned up at my father's birthday party.

I'm not sure what I hope to achieve by writing things down. Perhaps it will give me a fresh slant on events or throw up a new link. I have been searching for a central figure behind events but maybe that's too simplistic a notion. People could all be linked like spokes of a wheel that only touch in the center.

There is another issue. Where was the baby—or the babies—going to be handed over? Perhaps Cate planned to take a holiday or a weekend break to the Netherlands. She would go into "labor"; tell everyone she had given birth and then bring her newborn home to live happily ever after.

Even a baby needs travel documents. A passport. Which means a birth certificate, statutory declarations and signed photographs. I should call the British consulate in The Hague and ask how British nationals register a foreign birth.

In a case like this it would be much easier if the baby were born in the same country as the prospective parents. It could be a home birth or in a private house, without involving a hospital or even a midwife.

Once the genetic parents took possession of the baby nobody could ever prove it didn't belong to them. Blood samples, DNA and paternity tests would all confirm their ownership.

Samira said Hassan was going to the U.K. ahead of her. She expected to follow him. What if that's where they plan to take her? It would also explain why Cate gave Samira my name in case something went wrong.

"Last night you said you were giving up and going home," says Dave.

"I know. I just thought—"

"You said yourself that these babies belong to Samira. They always have."

"Someone killed my friend."

"You can't bring her back."

"They torched her house."

"It's not your case."

I feel a surge of anger. Does he really expect me to leave this to Softell and his imbecile mates? And Spijker doesn't fill me with confidence after letting Yanus go.

"Last night you were crying your eyes out. You said it was over."

"That was last night." I can't hide the anger in my voice.

"What's changed?"

"My mind. It's a woman's prerogative."

I want to say, *Don't be a fucking jerk, Dave, and stop quoting me back to myself.*

What is it about men? Just when you think they're rational members of the human race they go all Neanderthal and protective. Next he'll be asking me how many partners I've had and if the sex was any good.

We're drawing stares from other patrons. "I don't think we should talk about it here," he whispers.

"We're not going to talk about it at all." I get up to leave.

"Where are you going?"

I want to tell him it's none of his damn business. Instead I say that I have an appointment with Samira's lawyer, which isn't entirely true.

"I'll come with you."

"No. You go and see Ruiz. He'll appreciate that." My voice softens. "We'll meet up later."

Dave looks miserable but doesn't argue. Give him his due—he's a quick learner.

———

Lena Caspar's waiting room is being vacuumed and tidied. Magazines sit neatly stacked on a table and the toys have been collected in a polished wooden crate. Her desk is similarly neat and empty except for a box of tissues and a jug of water on a tray. Even the wastepaper basket is clean.

The lawyer is dressed in a knee-length skirt and a matching jacket. Like many women of a certain age, her makeup is applied perfectly.

"I cannot tell you where Samira is," she announces.

"I know. But you can tell me what happened yesterday."

She points to a chair. "What do you want to know?"

"Everything."

The lawyer places her palms flat on the desk. "I knew something was wrong when I saw the interpreter. Samira's English is perfect, yet she pretended not to understand what I said to her. Everything had to be translated back and forth. Samira volunteered no information without being prompted."

"Did Yanus spend any time alone with her?"

"Of course not."

"Did she see him?"

"Yanus took part in a lineup. She picked him out through a two-way mirror."

"He couldn't see Samira?"

"No."

"Did Yanus have anything in his hands?"

She sighs, irritated at my pedantry.

I press her. "Did he have something in his hands?"

She is about to say no but remembers something. "He had a blue handkerchief. He was pushing it into his fist like a magician preparing a conjuring trick."

How did he find Zala? Nobody knew she was at the convent except the nuns. Sister Vogel wouldn't have given her up. De Walletjes is a small place. What did the lawyer once say to me? The walls have mice and the mice have ears.

Mrs. Caspar listens patiently while I explain what I think happened. Zala is not her concern. She has four hundred asylum seekers on her books.

"What will happen to Samira now?" I ask.

"She will be sent back to Afghanistan, which is I think a better option than marrying Yanus."

"He is not going to marry her."

"No."

"He is going to find her and take her babies."

She shrugs. How can she blithely accept such an outcome? Leaning on the windowsill, she looks down at the courtyard where pigeons peck at the base of a lone tree.

"Some people are born to suffer," she says pensively. "It never stops for them, not for a second. Look at the Palestinians. The same is true of Afghanis and Sudanese, Ethiopians and Bangladeshis. War, famine, droughts, flood, the suffering never stops. They are made for it— sustained by it.

"We in the West like to think it can be different; that we can change these countries and these people because it makes us feel better when we tuck our own children into their warm beds with full stomachs and then pour ourselves a glass of wine and watch someone else's tragedy unfold on CNN." She stares down at her hands as if she despises them. "Unless we truly understand what it's like to walk in their shoes, we should not judge people like Samira. She is only trying to save what she has left."

Something else trembles in her voice. Resignation. Acceptance. Why is she so ready to give up? In that split second I realize there is something that she's not telling me. Either she can't bring herself to do it or Spijker has warned her off. With her innate sense of honesty and justice, she will not lie to me directly.

"What happened to Samira?"

"She went missing last night from the migrant center at Schiphol Airport."

8

There is a scientific theory called the uncertainty principle that states it is impossible to truly observe something without altering it. I have done more than observe. By finding Samira I have changed the course of events.

During the taxi journey to police headquarters my fists are clenched and my fingernails dig into the soft flesh. I want to scream. I warned Spijker this would happen. I said Samira would run or Yanus would find her.

I don't expect him to see me. He will hide behind his workload or make excuses that I've wasted enough of his time already. Again I wait in the foyer. This time the summons comes. Perhaps he has a conscience after all.

The corridors are lined in light gray carpet and dotted with palms. It feels more like a merchant bank than a police station.

Spijker is jacketless. His sleeves are rolled up. The hair on his forearms is the color of his freckles. The door closes. His jacket swings from a hanger behind it.

"How long are you intending to remain in Amsterdam?" he asks.

"Why, sir?"

"You have already stayed longer than is usual. Most visitors are here for a day or two."

"Are you advising me to leave?"

"I have no authority to do that." He spins on his chair, gazing out the window. His office looks east across the theater district to the neo-Gothic spires of the Rijksmuseum. Lined on the windowsill are tiny cacti in painted clay pots. This is his garden—fleshy, bulbous and spiky.

I had a speech prepared during my taxi ride, when I vented my spleen and caused the taxi driver a few anxious moments, peering into the rear mirror. Now all my best lines seem pointless and wasted. I wait for the detective to speak.

"I know what you think, DC Barba. You think I have dropped the ball on this. That is a rugby term, yes? A British game not a Dutch one. In the Netherlands we do not *pick up* the ball. Only a goalkeeper can do this."

"You should have protected her."

"She *chose* to escape."

"She's eight months pregnant and eighteen years old. You couldn't hold her for twenty-four hours."

"Did you want me to handcuff her?"

"You could have stopped her."

"I am trying to keep this investigation low key. I don't want it reaching the media. Black market babies make dramatic headlines."

"So it was a political decision?"

"There is no politics in the Dutch police."

"No?"

"No one has talked politics to me."

Despite his down-turned mouth and sad eyes, Spijker comes across as an optimist, a man who has faith in the human condition.

"I have twenty years' service. I know how to make a case. I am like the little pig that builds his house out of bricks. You are like the little pig who builds her house from straw. Do you remember what happens to such a house?" He puffs out his cheeks and blows. A flake of cigarette ash swirls from his desk into my lap.

Sporting metaphors and fairy-tale metaphors, what next? He opens the top drawer of his desk, withdrawing a file.

"There is a fertility clinic in Amersfoort. It has a very good reputation and has helped thousands of couples to begin a family. Occasionally, when IVF has been unsuccessful, the clinic has agreed to implant embryos into the uterus of a surrogate mother. This is called gestational surrogacy. In 2002 there were only four such procedures out of 1,500 normal IVF implantations. In 2003 and 2004 there were two in total." He glances at the file. "In the past year there have been twenty-two."

"Twenty-two! That's an increase of more than tenfold."

"Gestational surrogacy is legal in the Netherlands. Commercial surrogacy is not. Nor is blackmail or bonded slavery.

"Directors of the clinic and staff insist they are unaware of any wrongdoing. They also insist the surrogate mothers were properly screened. They were examined physically, financially and psychologically.

"On January 26 this year Samira Khan underwent

this examination. She was asked questions about her menstrual cycle and was given pills and injections—estrogen and progesterone—to prepare her uterus for the implantation.

"On February 10 she returned to the clinic. The embryo transfer took less than fifteen minutes. A soft tube was inserted through her vagina to a predetermined position. A small inner catheter was then loaded with two embryos and these were injected into the uterus. Samira Khan was told to lie still for thirty minutes and then discharged. She was taken to the car park in a wheelchair and driven away by Yanus. Her pregnancy was confirmed two weeks later. Twins."

Spijker finally looks up at me. "But you know this already."

There are other papers in his file.

"Do you have the names of the intended parents?"

"Legal contracts are required between couples and the surrogate mothers. The clinic does not draw up these contracts, but requires a written statement from a lawyer confirming they exist."

"Have you seen the contracts?"

"Yes."

For a moment I think he's going to wait for me to ask, but he is not a cruel man.

"Each copy of the contract was signed by Samira Khan and countersigned by Cate Beaumont. Is this what you wish to know?"

"Yes."

He returns the folder to the drawer and rises from his seat, surveying the view from his window with a mixture of pride and protectiveness.

"Of the twenty-two procedures I mentioned, eighteen resulted in pregnancies. One of the failures involved a woman named Zala Haseeb. Doctors discovered she was unable to fall pregnant because of earlier damage to her reproductive organs caused by blunt force trauma."

"She was tortured by the Taliban."

He doesn't turn from the window but I know he hears me.

"Twelve of the surrogate mothers are past term but we have no confirmation of the births. Normally the clinic monitors every stage of the pregnancy and keeps a record of each outcome for statistical purposes. In this case, however, it lost track of the women."

"Lost track of them!"

"We are in the process of finding them. The clinic has provided us with their names but the addresses appear to be fictitious."

"I don't think you'll find any trace of the births in the Netherlands," I say. "I think the mothers were smuggled across borders or overseas to where the intended parents live. This meant the babies could be handed over immediately after they were born and registered without any questions."

Spijker sees the logic of this. "We are tracking the intended parents through financial transactions. There are receipts and statutory declarations."

"Who drew up the contracts?"

"A legal firm here in Amsterdam."

"Are they being investigated?"

Spijker pauses for a brief moment. "You met the senior partner yesterday. He represents Mr. Yanus."

His gaze builds into a stare. For the first time I realize what a burden he carries. I have been chasing the truth about a single woman. He now has a case that touches dozens, perhaps hundreds of people's lives.

Spijker turns away from the window. After a long silence he speaks. "Do you have children?"

"No, sir."

"I have four of them."

"Four!"

"Too many, not enough—I can't decide." A smile flirts with his lips. "I understand what it means to people; how they can want a child so badly that they will do almost anything." He leans slightly forward, inclining his head to one side. "Do you know the legend of Pandora's box, DC Barba?"

"I've heard the term."

"The box didn't belong to Pandora; it was built by the Greek god Zeus and it was crammed full of all the diseases, sufferings, vices and crimes that could possibly afflict humanity. I cannot imagine such a malignant brew. The god Zeus also created Pandora—a beautiful woman, inquisitive by nature. He knew that she wouldn't be able to resist peeking inside the mysterious box. She heard pitiful whispers coming from inside. So she raised the lid just a little. And all the ills of the world flew out, fastening upon the carefree and innocent, turning their cries of joy into wails of despair."

His fingers open, showing me his palms. Empty. This is what he fears. An investigation like this risks tearing apart entire families. How many of these babies are in loving homes? Consider how lucky they are when so many children are abused and unwanted. The argument triggers a feeling of déjà vu. Julian Shawcroft had made a similar case when I visited him at the adoption center.

I understand the concerns, but my best friend was murdered. Nothing anyone says to me will justify her death and their ominous warnings sound hollow when I picture Cate lying broken on the road.

The briefing is over. Spijker stands rather formally and escorts me downstairs.

"I spoke to a Chief Superintendent North of Scotland Yard last evening. He informed me that you are absent without leave from the London Metropolitan Police. You are facing disciplinary proceedings for neglect of duty."

There is nothing I can say.

"I also spoke to a Detective Inspector Forbes who is investigating the deaths of illegals on a ferry at Harwich. You are helping him with this investigation. There was also, I think, a Detective Sergeant Softell, who wishes to speak to you about a suspicious fire."

Spijker could have used the term "suspect" but is far too polite.

"These men have asked me to put you on the first available flight back to London, but as I explained to them, I have no authority for this." He pinches the bridge of his nose between his thumb and forefinger. "I also assume you do not wish to leave Amsterdam without your friend Mr. Ruiz. I spoke to him this morning. He is recovering well."

"Yes, sir."

"He has great affection for you."

"We have known each other a long time."

"He believes that you will make a very fine investigator. He used a term I am not familiar with. He said you were 'sharper than a pointy stick.' "

That sounds like the DI.

"I understand why you are here and why you will stay a little longer, but now it is time for you to leave this investigation to me."

"What about Samira?"

"I will find her."

9

I don't normally notice people when I run. I shut out the world, floating over the ground like a vague impression. Today is different. I can hear people talking, arguing and laughing. There are muffled footsteps and car doors closing, the hum of traffic and machines.

"New Boy" Dave is at the hospital with Ruiz. That's where I'm heading, although the strangeness of the city makes it difficult to get my bearings. There are twin church steeples ahead of me. I turn again, running past flat-fronted shops with barred windows or metal shutters. Some of the alleys and lanes are only wide enough for bicycles or pedestrians.

By the time I find the hospital it is almost dark. The corridors are quiet and rain streaks the windows. "New Boy" Dave puts his jacket around my shoulders to stop me from getting cold. Ruiz is asleep.

"How is he?"

"Bored shitless. Today he tried to organize a mass escape from the hospital to the nearest pub. He convinced two guys to join him—both amputees. He said they were legless already so it shouldn't matter."

"How far did they get?"

"As far as the hospital gift shop. One of the nurses uncovered the escape plot and called security."

"What did the DI say?"

"He said the Resistance would spring him tomorrow."

Dave has been talking to the doctors. Ruiz should be able to leave hospital in a few days but he won't be able to fly for a month.

"We can take the ferry," I suggest.

Dave is toying with my fingers, running his thumb across the palm. "I was sort of hoping you might fly home with me tomorrow. I have an Old Bailey trial on Monday."

"I can't leave the DI. We started this together."

He understands. "What are you going to do about the job?"

"I haven't decided."

"You're supposed to have started."

"I know."

There's something else he wants to ask. His forehead creases, wrestling with the question.

"Have you thought about the other thing?" he asks. He's referring to the sailing school and the cottage by the sea. Marriage. The future. I'm still amazed that he plucked up the courage to ask me. The sense of expectation and dread must be killing him. Sometimes life is like the movies, with the audience barracking, "Just ask her. Just ask her."

"I thought you always wanted to be a detective," I say.

"I wanted to be a fireman when I was six. I got over it."

"I fell in love with Mr. Sayer, my piano teacher, and wanted to be a concert pianist."

"I didn't know you played."

"It's still open to debate."

He's waiting for my answer.

"So what happened, Dave? What made you decide to quit?"

He shrugs.

"Something must have triggered it."

"You remember Jack Lonsdale?"

"I heard he got wounded."

Dave silences his hands by putting them in his pockets. "We were following up a tip-off about a bail jumper on the White City Estate. A drug dealer. It's a god-awful place at the best of times but this was Saturday night in mid-July. Hot. We found the place okay and knocked on the door. It was supposed to be a simple pickup. I was putting handcuffs on the dealer when his fifteen-year-old kid came out of the kitchen and stuck a knife in Jack's chest. Right there." He points to the spot. "The kid was hanging off the blade trying to scramble his guts, but I managed to pry him loose. His eyes were like saucers. He was higher than a 747. I tried to get Jack out to the car but there were two hundred people outside the flat, most of them West Indian, screaming abuse and throwing shit. I thought we were gonna die."

"Why didn't you tell me?"

"You had your own shit to deal with."

"How's Jack now?"

"They had to take out part of his bowel and he's taken early retirement. The dealer finished up in Brixton. His kid went to a foster home. His mother was dead, I think."

Dave lowers his eyes, unwilling to look at me. "I know it makes me sound like a coward but I keep thinking how it could have been me spilling blood on that filthy floor—or worse, it could have been you."

"It doesn't make you a coward. It makes you human."

"Yeah, well, that's when I got to thinking about doing something else."

"Maybe you just need a sea change."

"Maybe."

"Maybe you don't really want to marry me."

"Yes I do."

"Would you still want to marry me if we didn't have children?"

"What do you mean?"

"I'm asking."

"But you *want* children, right?"

"What if I couldn't have children?"

Dave straightens up. He doesn't understand.

I try to explain. "Sometimes children just don't arrive. Look at Cate. She couldn't get pregnant and it twisted her up inside until she did something foolish. Don't you think if two people love each other that should be enough?"

"Yeah, I guess."

He still doesn't get my point. There is nowhere else for me to go except the truth. Words tumble out and I'm surprised at how organized they sound. Almost perfect sentences.

A woman's pelvis is meant to expand and tilt forward as a baby grows inside her. Mine can't do this. I have metal plates and rods holding my spine together. My pelvis cannot bend or twist. Pregnancy would put enormous strain on the disks and joints of my lower back. I risk being paralyzed and nursing a baby from a wheel-chair.

He looks stunned. Desolate. It doesn't matter what he says now because I have glimpsed his soul. He wants to raise a child. And for the first time in my life, I realize that I want one too. I *want* to be a mother.

In the hours that follow all possibilities are considered. On the taxi ride to the hotel, over dinner, afterward in bed, Dave talks of second opinions, alternatives and operations. We use up so much air in the room that I can scarcely breathe. He hasn't answered my original question. The most important one. He hasn't said if it matters.

While on the subject of true confessions, I tell him about sleeping with Barnaby Elliot and falling out with Cate. There are moments when I see him flinch but he needs to hear this. I am not the person he imagines.

My mother says the truth is unimportant when it comes to love. An arranged marriage is all about the fictions that one family tells another. Perhaps she's right. Perhaps falling in love is about inventing a story and accepting the truth of it.

10

I wake in the early hours, with his heart against my back and his arm around me. A part of me wants to stay like this, not moving, scarcely breathing. Another part wants to run down the hotel corridor, the stairs, along the street, out of the city, away!

Slipping out of bed and into the bathroom, I dress in jeans and a blouse and fill the pockets of my jacket with cash and my mobile. I bend to lace my boots, accepting the dull ache in my spine for what it is, a part of me now.

Daylight is leaking over the rooftops and the streets are beginning to stir. A machine with spinning brushes seems to be polishing the cobblestones with overnight rain. Most of the windows are closed in de Walletjes, with curtains drawn. Only the desperate and the lonely are on the streets at this hour.

I wonder if this is what it feels like to be a refugee—to be a stranger in a place, despairing and hopeful all at once. Waiting for what will come next. I have never lived like this.

Hokke is waiting for me at the café. He knows about Samira. "A bird told me," he says, raising his eyes. As if signaled, a pigeon flutters onto a branch above us.

The air inside the café is noisy with whistling steam and banging pots. Counter staff and waitresses acknowledge Hokke with waves, shouts and handshakes. He leaves me for a moment, threading his way between tables. The kitchen door is open. Bending low over sinks, scrubbing pans, are three young men who greet Hokke with respect. He ruffles their hair and shares a joke.

I glance around the café, which is almost empty except for a table of hippies who seem to be communicating in a code of clicks and clacks from their beaded hair. On her own, a young teenage girl nurses a hot drink. Waiflike and hollow-eyed, she is just the sort pimps prey upon with warm meals and promises.

Hokke has returned. He, too, notices the girl. Summoning a waitress, he quietly orders breakfast for the girl, thick toast, jam, cheese and ham. She accepts it warily, expecting there to be strings attached, and eats greedily.

His attention turns to me.

"I have to find Samira," I tell him.

"Again."

"Refugees have networks. You said so. You mentioned a name: de Souza. Could he help me?"

Hokke puts a finger to his lips. He leans closer, speaking out of the corner of his mouth like a prisoner under the eye of a warder. "Please be very careful when you speak such a name."

"Who is he?"

Hokke doesn't answer immediately. He pours coffee from a pot, tapping metal against glass. "Despite what you have read, the Netherlands is defined more by what it forbids than by what it permits. We do not have slums. Graffiti is cleaned away quickly. Broken windows are repaired. Abandoned vehicles are towed. We expect our trains and trams to run on time. We queue. It doesn't change the people, of course, just the aesthetics."

He gestures with a slight nod toward the kitchen. "There are half a million illegal workers in the Netherlands—Iranians, Sudanese, Afghanis, Bosnians, Kosovars, Iraqis. They work in restaurants, hotels, laundries and factories. Newspapers wouldn't be delivered without them, hotel sheets wouldn't be laundered, houses wouldn't be cleaned. People complain, but we cannot do without them."

A pipe appears in his hand. He packs it slowly, pressing tobacco into the bowl with his thumb. A match flares and flickers as he sucks in a breath.

"Imagine a person who could control a workforce such as this. He would be more powerful than any trade union leader or politician."

"Is there such a person?"

His voice drops to a whisper. "His name is Eduardo de Souza. Nobody has more real power in this city than he does. He has an army of couriers, cleaners, drivers and spies. He can get you anything: a pistol, a fake passport, a kilo of the finest Afghani heroin. Drugs and prostitution are only a small part of it. He knows which politicians are sleeping with which girls and which illegals are looking after their children or cleaning their houses or tending their gardens. That is *real* power. Destiny making."

He sits back, his soft blue eyes blinking through the smoke.

"You admire him."

"He is a very interesting man."

His answer strikes me as peculiar. It carries a hint that there are things he hasn't told me.

"How long have you known him?"

"Many years."

"Is he a friend?"

"Friendship is something I find harder to understand as I get older."

"Will he help me find Samira?"

"He could be behind it all."

"Why do you say that?"

"Yanus once worked for him."

He places his hands on the table and wearily pushes himself to his feet.

"I will get a message to him."

His pipe slips into his jacket pocket. He won't let me pay for breakfast. The bill has been covered, he says, nodding toward the owner.

Outside it is raining again. The puddles are shiny and black as oil. Hokke offers me an umbrella. "I will call you in a few hours. Give my regards to DI Ruiz. Tell him that old policemen never die. They just miss a beat."

———

Barnaby answers his cell phone quickly as if he's been expecting a call. It must also be raining in London. I hear car tires swishing on a wet road and raindrops on his umbrella. I ask about the funerals. There is a long pause. I swap the phone between hands.

"Saturday at the West London Crematorium. They won't release the bodies until Wednesday."

There is another silence. The knowledge of Samira and the twins expands in my chest. Lawyers and medical ethicists can debate all they want about who "owns" the twins, but it doesn't change the fact that Cate provided the embryos. Barnaby should know.

"There's something I have to tell you."

He grunts a response.

"I know why Cate faked her pregnancy. She arranged a surrogate. Her embryos were implanted in someone else's womb."

Something shifts deep in his chest. A groan. "I told you to leave my daughter's affairs alone."

I don't expect this reaction. Surely he must be curious. Doesn't he want to know the outcome? Then it dawns on me that none of this is new. He knows already.

He lied about finding Cate's computer, which means he must have read her e-mails. If he knows, why hasn't he gone to the police?

"What are you doing, Barnaby?"

"I'm getting my grandchildren."

He has no idea what he's dealing with. "Listen to me, Barnaby. This isn't what you think. Cate broke the law."

"What's done is done."

"These men are killers. You can't negotiate with them. Look what happened to Cate."

He isn't listening. Instead he charges ahead, trying to attach logic and fairness to what should happen next.

"Stop, Barnaby. This is crazy."

"It's what Cate would have wanted."

"No. You'll get yourself killed. Just tell me where you are. Let's sit down and talk."

"Stay out of this. Don't interfere."

The line goes dead. He won't answer again.

Before I can dial Spijker there is another call. DI Forbes's voice is hoarse with a cold and the clicking sound in his throat is muffled by phlegm. I can imagine one of his children bringing the infection home from school and spreading it through the house like a domestic plague.

"Having a nice holiday?"

"It's not a holiday."

"You know the difference between you and me? I don't run away when things get tough. I'm a professional. I stick with the job. I got a wife and kids, responsibilities . . ."

And wandering hands.

He sneezes and blows his nose. "I'm still waiting for your fucking statement."

"I'm coming home."

"When?"

"By Friday."

"Well you can expect a warm welcome. A Chief Superintendent North has been on the phone. Says you didn't show up for work. He's not happy."

"It's not important," I say, trying to change the subject. I ask him about the two trucks that couldn't be accounted for on the ferry that carried Hassan and the other illegals. One was stolen from a German freight yard three months ago, he says. It was resprayed and registered in Holland. According to the manifest it was carrying plumbing supplies from a warehouse in Amsterdam, but the pickup address doesn't exist. The second truck was leased from an owner-driver five weeks ago. He thought it was doing a run from Spain to the

Netherlands. The leasing documents and bank accounts are in false names.

This case is populated with people who seem to be ghosts, floating across borders with false papers. People like Brendan Pearl.

"I need a favor."

He finds this amusing. "I shouldn't even be talking to you."

"We're on the same side."

"Cellar-dwellers."

"Running into form."

"What do you want?"

"I need you to check the Customs and Immigration files for the past two years. Among the stowaways and illegals were any of them pregnant?"

"Off the top of my head I can think of two in the past three months. They were hidden in the back of a container."

"What happened to them?"

"I don't know."

"Can you find out?"

"Yeah, sure. Along with a thousand other fucking things on my plate."

I feel the heat in my cheeks.

"There's something else. Hassan Khan has a sister, Samira. She's pregnant. I think traffickers are going to try to move her into the U.K."

"When?"

"I don't know. You might want to give Customs a heads-up."

"I'm not a free agent here."

"It's only a phone call. If you don't want to do it, just say so."

"How are they going to move her?"

"They'll probably stick to what they know."

"We can't search every truck and container."

I can hear him scratching a note on a pad. He asks me about Spijker and I give him the nuts and bolts of the surrogacy scam.

"I've never known anyone who attracts trouble like you do," he says.

"You sound like my mother."

"Do you take any notice of *her*?"

"Not much."

The call ends and I close my eyes for a moment. When I open them again, I see a class of schoolchildren with their teacher. The girls are dressed like Madeline in navy blue raincoats with yellow hats, and they are all holding hands as they wait for the traffic lights to change. Inexplicably, I feel a lump forming in my throat. I'll never have one of those.

A police car is parked outside the hotel. A uniformed officer waits in reception, standing almost to attention.

"New Boy" Dave hovers like a jealous suitor. "Where have you been?"

"I had to see someone."

He grips my hand tightly.

The officer introduces himself and holds out a police radio. I place it against my ear. Spijker's voice comes from far away. I can hear water. Seagulls. "We've found someone."

"Who is it?"

"I'm hoping you can tell me."

Something soft and wet flips over in my stomach.

The officer takes back the radio to receive further instructions.

"I'll come with you," says Dave.

"What about your flight?"

"There's still time."

We sit in silence on the journey. Frustration is etched into his forehead. He wants to say something planned, thought-out, about last night but it's not the right time.

I feel oddly ambivalent. Maybe that means I'm not ready to marry and I'm not really in love. The whole idea was one of those "what if" moments that doesn't survive the hangover or the harsh light of day.

The Dutch officer has a vocabulary of four English words and is unwilling or unable to explain where we're going. Meanwhile, he navigates the narrow streets and bridges, taking us through an industrial area with docks and warehouses. We seem to pass the same gray squares of water several times before pulling up beside a weathered wooden pier. Police cars nose together as though drinking from the same trough.

Spijker is a head taller than the other detectives. He is wearing a dark suit and polished shoes but still seems miscast in life; as though he's playing dress-up in his father's clothes.

There is a wooden ramp that slopes into the water from the dock. Halfway down it is a Zodiac made of heavy rubberized canvas with a wooden bottom. Another is already waiting on the water with four men on board.

Spijker hands me a pair of rubber boots and a waterproof jacket to wear over my sweater. He finds similar clothes for Dave and then pulls on his own rubber boots.

The Zodiac launches in a fluid movement. Spijker holds out his hand and helps me step on board. The throttle engages and we pull away. The sky is like a solid gray sheet with no depth at all. A quarter mile off I see the flat of a paddle, lifting and dipping, as a canoeist follows the shore. Farther out is a ferry, snub-nosed and puffing smudges of black smoke.

I try to orientate myself. Some six miles to the west is the North Sea. We seem to be following a western dock. The air smells sweet—of chocolate. Perhaps there is a factory nearby. Dave is beside me. I feel him when I rock sideways, brushing his left arm with my breast.

Spijker is comfortable steering a boat. Perhaps it rubs off, living below sea level, protected by dikes and flood barriers.

"How much do you know about the sea, DC Barba?"

What is there to know? It's cold, it's wet, it's salty . . .

"My father was a merchant seaman," he explains without waiting for me to answer. "He divorced my mother when I was seven but I used to spend holidays with him. He didn't go to sea anymore and he wasn't the same man on shore. He seemed smaller."

Dave hasn't said much since I introduced them to each other, but now he mentions the sailing school he wants to buy. Soon they're discussing skiffs and sail area. I can actually picture Dave in an Aran sweater, ducking beneath a boom. He seems suited to outdoors, big spaces full of wind and sky and water.

Five hundred yards ahead of us is a container ship. The Port of Amsterdam spent millions thinking they could match Rotterdam as a hub for international trade, explains Spijker. "It is never going to be so."

Passing the ship, we come to a wooden pier rising twenty feet above the waterline supported by pylons and beams. A floating platform is moored on the nearside.

Spijker disengages the throttle and the engine idles. He steadies the Zodiac and throws a rope around a rusting cleat on the platform, drawing us closer. At the same moment a spotlight is switched on and swings into the darker shadows beneath the pier, searching amid the weathered gray wood. A flash of white appears. A figure suspended above the water, gazing down at me. A noose is looped around her neck. Another rope around her waist disappears into the water, obviously weighted down.

The body swings slightly as if moved by an unseen hand and her outstretched toes seem to pirouette on the surface of the water.

"Is it the deaf girl?" asks Spijker.

Zala's eyes are open. Two crimson orbs. Blood vessels have burst in the whites and her pupils seem to have disappeared. She's dressed in the same skirt and pink jacket that I last saw her wearing. Salt in the air has stiffened the fabric.

The Zodiac is rising and sinking on the slight swell. Spijker steadies it and I step onto the platform. A metal ladder, bolted to a pylon, leads up to the pier. Seagulls watch from the navigation buoys and a nearby barge. The other Zodiac has arrived, carrying ropes and a stretcher cage.

Spijker climbs the ladder and I follow him. Dave is behind me. The planks of the pier are old and deeply furrowed, with gaps in between that are wide enough for me to see the top of Zala's head and her shoulders.

The rope around her neck is tied to a metal bollard normally used for mooring ships.

A police officer in climbing gear abseils over the side. He swings in a harness beside her body and we watch in silence as Zala is lashed into a stretcher cage. The rope around her waist is tied to a cinder block. I can see the cement dust on her hands and the front of her jacket.

They made her jump. The certainty is like a vision. She held the cinder block in her arms and they pushed her the final step. She dropped fifteen feet before the rope stopped her. The cement brick tore from her fingers and kept falling until the second rope, tied around her waist, pulled taut. My stomach shares the drop.

"A fisherman found her just before nine thirty," says Spijker. "He reported it to the coast guard." He swivels to a junior officer, seeking confirmation.

"What made you think . . . ?" I can't finish the question.

"She fitted the description."

"How did she get out here?"

Spijker motions along the pier. "It's fenced off. Warning signs. Of course, that only encourages people."

"You're not thinking suicide?"

"Your deaf girl didn't carry that lump of concrete out here by herself."

In the distance there are whitecaps where the water is less sheltered from the wind. A fishing boat is coming in, its windows flashing in a rare shaft of sunlight.

Despite his veteran's cynicism, Spijker needs to show compassion and offer condolences. Somehow I have become his only link to this girl.

"She came from Kabul. She was an orphan," I explain.

"Another one."

"What do you mean?"

"The list of surrogates from the IVF clinic. At least ten of them were orphans. It's making them difficult to find."

Orphans. Illegal immigrants. What a perfect combination of the unwanted and the desperate.

"Samira mentioned a visitor to the orphanage. A westerner who said he could organize a job for her. He had a cross on his neck. I might know who it is." I give him Donavon's name and he promises to check the files.

The dock gates have been unlocked at the far end of the pier. A forensic team arrives in a van. A second car is summoned to take us back to our hotel.

As I walk along the pier I feel that Amsterdam has changed and become darker and more dangerous. I long for the familiar. Home.

Dave falls into step beside me.

"Are you all right?"

"Fine."

"It's not your fault."

"What do you know about it?" I snap. Straightaway, I feel angry with myself. He's done nothing wrong. After a few minutes I try to assuage my guilt. "Thanks for being here. I'm sorry about last night. Forget everything I said."

"I think we should talk about it some more."

"There's nothing to talk about."

"I love you."

"But it's different now, isn't it?"

Dave puts his hand on my forearm to stop me. "I don't care. I want to be with you."

"You say that now, but think about in five years or ten years. I couldn't do that to you."

An abandoned crane is rusting on the shoreline. It looks like wreckage from an ancient war. Zala's body is still spinning in my mind, pirouetting on her toes in the waves.

I have been a fool. My good intentions have set off a

chain of events that have led to this. And I don't know where it ends or who else will be hurt. I am certain of only one thing: I want to spend every waking moment hunting down the people who took Cate from me and who did this to Zala. This is not about an eye for an eye. It's bigger than that. I want to make their misery more poignant and horrific than anything they have inflicted upon others. Never in my life have I felt so capable of killing someone.

———

Dave's hair is combed. His bag is packed. A taxi is booked for the airport. The clock hasn't moved. Not even a second. I swear it. I hate the last hour before someone leaves. Everything has been said and done. Minutes drag out. Statements are repeated. Tickets are checked.

"It's time to leave this alone," says Dave, rinsing his toothbrush. "It's over."

"How did we get to over?"

"Maybe you think," he says, choosing his words with care, "that this is about you and me. It's not. I'd tell you the same thing if I didn't love you."

"But that's why you *should* understand."

He picks up his bag and puts it down again.

"You could come with me."

"I'm not leaving Ruiz."

He puts on his jacket.

"You could stay," I suggest.

"I have to give evidence in court."

"I need you."

"You don't *need* anyone."

It's not meant to wound but I flinch as though struck.

He opens the door slowly. All the while I'm hoping he'll turn back, take me in his arms, force me to look in his eyes, tell me he doesn't care about anything except me, that he understands.

The door closes behind him. My chest is suddenly empty. He's taken my heart.

11

For twenty minutes I stare at the door, wishing it would open, hoping that he'll come back.

When I was lying in hospital with my damaged spine, fearing I would never walk again, I started to say cruel things to people. I criticized nurses and complained about the food. I called one male orderly Fat Albert after the Bill Cosby character.

"New Boy" Dave came to visit me every day. I remember screaming at him and calling him a moron. He didn't deserve it. I felt sorry for myself because everybody else felt sorry for me. And being cruel to people took my mind off myself for a while.

Dave didn't come to see me after that. I wanted to call him. I wanted to say I was sorry for being mad and could he please come back. I didn't. Instead I wrote him a letter. What a gutless wonder! I don't deserve him.

My mobile rattles on the table.

"You didn't come to lunch today."

"I'm still overseas, Mama."

"Your auntie Meena made kulfi. It's your favorite."

It was my favorite at age six.

"All the boys came. Even Hari."

Typical. He doesn't show up unless he can show me up.

"Your friend Detective King phoned to say he couldn't make it."

"I know, Mama."

"But another very eligible gentleman was here. He was disappointed not to see you."

"Whose arm did you twist this time?"

"Dr. Banerjee seems to be very fond of you."

It cannot be a coincidence. "What did he want?"

"He brought you flowers—such a thoughtful man. And his table manners are impeccable."

If we get married I'll have clean tablecloths.

"Where did you tell him I was?"

"I said you were in Amsterdam. You're being very secretive about this. You know I don't like secrets."

She carries on describing the good doctor and a funny story he told her about his baby nephew. I don't hear the punch line. I'm too busy trying to connect him to Samira.

Banerjee collected twelve viable embryos from Cate. Instead of six cycles of IVF, there were only five, which meant two embryos remained, frozen and stored in liquid nitrogen. He gave them to Cate, which means he knew about her surrogacy plan. That's why he arranged an invitation to my father's birthday party. He tried to warn me off.

"I have to go, Mama."

"When will you be home?"

"Soon."

I hang up and call "New Boy" Dave, who is just boarding his flight.

"Does this mean you miss me?"

"It's a given. I need a favor."

He sighs. "Just the one?"

"When you get back to London, run a ruler over Dr. Sohan Banerjee."

"He was at your father's party."

"That's him."

"What do you want to know?"

"Does he have any links with fertility clinics outside of the U.K.? Also check if he has any links with adoption agencies or children's charities."

"I'll see what I can do."

A stewardess is telling him to turn off his phone.

"Safe journey."

"You too."

Forbes's cold is getting worse and he's developed a seal-like cough punctuated by the clicking in his throat. He sounds like a boom box.

"You should have stayed home," I suggest.

"My house is full of sick people."

"So you decided to infect the rest of the population."

"That's me. Patient Zero."

"Did you find them—the pregnant asylum seekers?"

"I should have locked you up when I had the chance." He blows his nose. "They arrived in early July hidden in a shipping container. A Russian, aged eighteen, and an Albanian, twenty-one. Both looked ready to drop any time. They were fingerprinted, issued with identification papers and taken to a reception center in Oxfordshire. Three days later they were taken to a bed-and-breakfast accommodation in Liverpool. They had two weeks to fill out a statement of evidence form and meet with a lawyer but neither of them showed up. They haven't been seen since."

"What about the babies?"

"There's no record of the births at any NHS hospital but that doesn't prove anything. A lot of people have them at home these days—even in the bath. Thank Christ our tub wasn't big enough."

I have a sudden mental image of his wife, whalelike in the family bathtub.

"It still doesn't make much sense," he says. "One of the attractions of the U.K. for asylum seekers is free health care. These women could have had their babies in an NHS hospital. The government also provides a one-off grant of £300 for a newborn baby, as well as extra cash for milk and nappies. This is on top of the normal food vouchers and income support. These women claimed to have no family or friends in the U.K. who could support them, yet they didn't take advantage of the welfare benefits on offer. Makes you wonder how they survived."

"Or if they did."

He doesn't want to go there.

———

Ruiz is waiting for me downstairs at the Academisch Medisch Centrum. He looks like a kid being picked up from summer camp, without the peeling nose or poison ivy stings.

"The staff wished me a long and healthy life," he says. "They also told me never to get sick in the Netherlands again."

"Touching."

"I thought so. I'm a medical bloody miracle." He holds up the stump of his missing finger and begins counting. "I've been shot, almost drowned and now stabbed. What's left?"

"They could blow you up, sir."

"Been tried. Brendan Pearl and his IRA chummies fired a mortar into a Belfast police station. Missed me by that much." He does his Maxwell Smart impersonation.

He pauses at the revolving door. "Have you been crying, grasshopper?"

"No, sir."

"I thought you might have been pining."

"Not pining, sir."

"Women are allowed to be warm and fuzzy."

"You make me sound like a stuffed animal."

"With very sharp teeth."

He's in a good mood. Maybe it's the morphine. It doesn't last long. I tell him about Zala and can see the tension rise to his shoulders and move to his neck. His eyes close. He takes a ragged breath as though the pain has suddenly returned.

"They're going to smuggle Samira into Britain," I say.

"You can't be certain of that."

"It happened to the others. The babies are delivered in the same country as the parents lived."

"The Beaumonts are dead."

"They'll find other buyers."

"Who are *they*?"

"Yanus. Pearl. Others."

"What does Spijker say?"

"He says I should go home."

"A wise man."

"Hokke says there is someone who might help us find Samira."

"Who is he?"

"Eduardo de Souza. Yanus used to work for him."

"This gets better and better."

My mobile is ringing. Hokke is somewhere noisy. The red light district. He spends more time there now than when he was walking the beat.

"I will pick you up at seven from the hotel."

"Where are we going?"

"Answers at seven."

12

An enormous dishwater moon has risen in the east and seems to move across the sky, following our taxi. Even in darkness I recognize some of the roads. Schiphol Airport is not far from here.

This is a different area of Amsterdam. The chocolate-box façades and historic bridges have been replaced by the functional and harsh—cement-gray apartment blocks and shops protected by metal shutters. Only one store is open. A dozen black youths are standing outside.

De Souza doesn't have a fixed address, Hokke explains. He moves from place to place, never staying more than a night in any one bed. He lives with the people he employs. They protect him.

"Be very careful what you say to him. And don't interrupt when he speaks. Keep your eyes down and your hands by your sides."

We have pulled up outside an apartment block. Hokke opens the door for me.

"Aren't you coming with me?"

"You must go alone. We will wait here."

"No," declares Ruiz. "I am going with her."

Hokke responds with equal passion. "She goes alone or there will be nobody waiting to meet her."

Ruiz continues to protest but I push him back into the car where he grimaces as he folds his arms across his bandaged chest.

"Remember what I told you," says the Dutchman, pointing toward a building that is identical to the one next to it and the one next to that. A teenage boy leans against a wall. A second one watches us from an upstairs window. Lookouts. "You must go now. Phone me if there's a problem."

I walk away from the taxi. The boy leaning against the wall has gone. The second teenager is still at the window. I walk through a concrete archway into a quadrangle. Lights shine on water. Chinese lanterns are strung from the branches of a leafless tree growing amid the weeds.

Pushing through a fire door, I climb the stairs, counting off the floors. Turning left at the landing, I find the second door. A bell sounds when I push a small white button.

Another teenager appears at the door. His polished black eyes examine me but turn away when I meet his gaze. Shoes and sandals are lined up in the narrow hallway. The teenager points to my boots. I take them off.

The floor creaks idly as I follow him to a living area. A group of five men in their forties and fifties are seated on cushions arranged at the edges of a woven rug.

Eduardo de Souza is immediately recognizable because of his place at the center. Dressed in white pantaloons and a dark shirt, he looks Turkish or possibly

Kurdish, with a high forehead and carved cheekbones. Unfurling his legs, he rises and touches my hand briefly.

"Welcome, Miss Barba, I am Eduardo de Souza."

His neatly trimmed beard is black and gray—the gray like slivers of ice hanging on dark fur. Nobody speaks or moves, yet there is a perceptible energy in the air, a sharpening of focus. I keep my gaze down as eyes roam over me.

Through the doorway to the kitchen I spy a young Nigerian woman in a flowing dress of bright colors. Three children, two boys and a girl, jostle at the doorway, regarding me with fascination.

De Souza speaks again. "These are friends of mine. This is Sunday. He is our host this evening."

Sunday smiles. He is Nigerian and his teeth are a brilliant white. Each of the men introduces himself in turn. The first is Iranian with a Swiss German accent. His name is Farhad and his eyes are set so deep in his skull that I can scarcely see them. Beside him is Oscar, who looks Moroccan and speaks with a French accent.

Finally, there is Dayel, a smooth-shaven Indian, with an oil burn on his neck.

"One of your countrymen, although not a Sikh," says de Souza. Dayel smiles at the introduction.

How does he know I'm a Sikh?

There is a spare brocade cushion beside him. I am expected to sit. Sunday's wife enters the room carrying a tray of mismatched glasses and begins pouring sweet tea. Her hair is braided into a curtain of long beaded plaits. She smiles shyly at me. Her teeth are perfect and her wide nose flares gently as she breathes.

Dishes arrive. A meal. Holding his hands together,

de Souza studies me above his steepled fingers, weighing up whether or not to help me. His English is perfect, overlaid with an educated British accent that is especially noticeable on the long vowels.

"This area of Amsterdam is called Bijlmermeer," he says, glancing at the window. "In October 1992 a cargo jet took off from Schiphol and lost two engines. It buried itself into an apartment block like this one, full of immigrant families who were sitting down to an evening meal. Fifty apartments were destroyed by the initial impact. Another hundred burned afterward as jet fuel ran through the streets like a river of fire. People threw themselves off balconies and rooftops to escape the flames.

"At first they said the death toll was 250. Later they dropped the estimate to 75 and officially only 43 people died. The truth is, nobody knows the true number. Illegal immigrants have no papers and they hide from the police. They are ghosts."

De Souza hasn't touched the food, but seems particularly satisfied to see the others eating.

"Forgive me, Miss Barba, I talk too much. My friends here are too polite to tell me to be quiet. It is customary for a guest to bring something to the feast or provide some form of entertainment. Do you sing or dance?"

"No."

"Perhaps you are a storyteller."

"I don't really understand."

"You will tell us a story. The best of them seem to me to be about life and death, love and hate, loyalty and betrayal." He waves his hand as if stirring the air. His amber eyes are fixed on mine.

"I am not a very good storyteller."

"Let us be the judge of that."

I tell him the story of two teenage girls who met at school and became best friends. Soul mates. Later, at university, one of them slept with the other's father. He seduced her. She allowed herself to be seduced. The friendship was over.

I don't mention names, but why would I tell them such a personal story?

Seamlessly, I begin talking about a second pair of teenage girls, who met in a city of widows and orphans. People traffickers smuggled them out of Afghanistan as far as Amsterdam. They were told that they owed a debt for their escape. Either they became prostitutes or carried a baby for a childless couple. Virgins were implanted with embryos in a ritualized form of medical rape. They were the perfect incubators. Factories. Couriers.

Even as I tell this story, a sense of alarm dries my throat. Why have I told de Souza such personal stories? For all I know he is involved. He could be the ringleader. I don't have time to consider the implications. I don't know if I care. I have come too far to back out.

There is a moment of silence when I finish. De Souza leans forward and takes a chocolate from a platter, rolling it over his tongue before chewing it slowly.

"It is a good story. Friendship is a difficult thing to define. Oscar here is my oldest friend. How would you define friendship, Oscar?"

Oscar grunts slightly, as though the answer is obvious. "Friendship is about choice and chemistry. It cannot be defined."

"But surely there is something more to it than that."

"It is a willingness to overlook faults and to accept

them. I would let a friend hurt me without striking back," he says, smiling, "but only once."

De Souza laughs. "Bravo, Oscar, I can always rely on you to distill an argument down to its purest form. What do you think, Dayel?"

The Indian rocks his head from side to side, proud that he has been asked to speak next.

"Friendship is different for each person and it changes throughout our lives. At age six it is about holding hands with your best friend. At sixteen it is about the adventure ahead. At sixty it is about reminiscing." He holds up a finger. "You cannot define it with any one word, although honesty is perhaps the closest word—"

"No, not honesty," Farhad interrupts. "On the contrary, we often have to protect our friends from what we truly think. It is like an unspoken agreement. We ignore each other's faults and keep our confidences. Friendship isn't about being honest. The truth is too sharp a weapon to wield around someone we trust and respect. Friendship is about self-awareness. We see ourselves through the eyes of our friends. They are like a mirror that allows us to judge how we are traveling."

De Souza clears his throat now. I wonder if he is aware of the awe he inspires in others. I suspect he is too intelligent and too human to do otherwise.

"Friendship cannot be defined," he says sternly. "The moment we begin to give reasons for being friends with someone we begin to undermine the magic of the relationship. Nobody wants to know that they are loved for their money or their generosity or their beauty or their wit. Choose one motive and it allows a person to say, 'Is that the *only* reason?' "

The others laugh. De Souza joins in with them. This is a performance.

He continues: "Trying to explain why we form particular friendships is like trying to tell someone why we like a certain kind of music or a particular food. We just do."

He focuses on me now. "Your friend's name is Cate Beaumont."

How does he know that?

"Were you ever jealous of her?"

"I don't know what you mean."

"Friends can be jealous of each other. Oscar, here, is envious of my position and my wealth."

"Not at all, my friend," he beseeches.

De Souza smiles knowingly. "Did you envy Cate Beaumont's beauty or her success?"

"Sometimes."

"You wished she had less and you had more."

"Yes."

"That is natural. Friendships can be ambiguous and contradictory."

"She is dead now," I add, although I sense he knows this already.

"She paid money for a baby. A criminal act," he states piously.

"Yes."

"Are you trying to protect her?"

"I'm trying to rescue the surrogate mother and the babies."

"Perhaps you want a baby for yourself?"

My denial is too strident. I make it worse. "I have never . . . I don't . . ."

He reaches into a small pouch tied to the belt of his tunic. "Do you think I am a criminal, Miss Barba?"

"I don't know enough—"

"Give me your opinion."

I pause. The faces in the circle watch with a mixture of amusement and fascination.

"It's not up to me to say," I stammer.

Silence. Perspiration leaks into the hollow of my back, weaving between the bumps of my vertebrae.

De Souza is waiting. He leans close, his face only inches from mine. His bottom teeth are brittle and jagged, yellowing like faded newsprint. It is not such a perfect face after all.

"You can offer me nothing," he says dismissively.

I can feel the situation slipping away from me. He is not going to help me.

The anger fermenting inside me, fueled by hostile thoughts and by images of Zala, suddenly finds an escape valve. Words tumble out. "I think you're a criminal and a misogynist but you're not an evil man. You don't exploit children or sell babies to the highest bidder." I point to Sunday's wife, who has come to collect our plates. "You would not ask this woman, the wife of a friend, to give up one of her children or force her to have another woman's baby. You support asylum seekers and illegal immigrants; you give them jobs and find them homes. They respect and admire you. We can stop this trade. I can stop it. Help me."

Sunday's wife is embarrassed at having been singled out. She continues collecting the plates, eager to get away. The tension in the room is amplified by the stillness. Every man's eyes are upon me. Oscar makes a choking noise. He would slit my throat in a heartbeat.

De Souza stands abruptly. The meeting is finished. Oscar takes a step toward me. De Souza signals for him to stop. Alone, he walks me to the front door and takes my hand. Pressed between his fingers is a small scrap of paper.

The door closes. I do not look at the message. It's too dark to read it. The taxi is waiting. I slide into the backseat and lean against Ruiz as I close the car door. Hokke tells the driver to go.

The note is rolled into a tube, wedged between my thumb and forefinger. My hands are shaking as I unroll it and hold it up to the inside light.

Five words. Handwritten. "She leaves tonight from Rotterdam."

13

Our taxi driver takes an entry ramp onto a motorway.

"How far is it?"

"Seventy-five kilometers."

"What about the port?"

"Longer."

I look at my watch. It's 8:00 p.m.

"The Port of Rotterdam is forty kilometers long," says Hokke. "There are tens of thousands of containers, hundreds of ships. How are you going to find her?"

"We need a ship's name," says Ruiz.

"Or a sailing time," echoes Hokke.

I stare at the slip of paper. It's not enough. We can't phone ahead and alert Customs or the police. What would we tell them?

"Most likely they want to smuggle her into the U.K.," I say. "They've used Harwich before."

"They might choose an alternative port this time."

"Or stick to what they know."

Hokke shakes his head. It is a wild impossible chase.

Rotterdam is the biggest container port in Europe. He has an idea. A friend, a former police officer, works for a private security firm that patrols some of the terminals.

Hokke calls him. They chat to each other gruffly, in stern sentences full of Dutch consonants. Meanwhile, I follow the brightly lit motorway signs, counting down the kilometers and the minutes. In the moonlight I can make out wind turbines like ghostly giants marching across the fields.

Trucks and semis are nose-to-tail in the outside lane. I wonder if Samira could be inside one of them. What must it be like? Deafening. Black. Lonely.

Hokke finishes the call and outlines the possibilities. Security is tight around the terminals and docks with CCTV cameras on the fences and regular dog patrols. Once inside there are Customs checks, heat-seeking scanners and more dogs. More than six and a half million shipping containers pass through the port every year. These have to be specially sealed. Empty containers awaiting transfer are a different story but even if someone breached the security and reached the containers, they wouldn't know which ship it was meant to be loaded on unless they had inside information.

"Which means they're more likely to target a truck *before* it reaches the port," says Ruiz. "One they know is traveling to the U.K."

Hokke nods. "We're probably looking at roll-on, roll-off ferries. There are two major ferry operators doing North Sea crossings. Stena Line has a terminal on the Hook of Holland. P&O operates from a dock fifteen kilometers farther east, closer to the city."

We're still twenty miles away and it's nearly eight thirty.

Hokke makes another call, getting a timetable of departures, calling out the details. A P&O ferry sails for Hull at nine o'clock. The Stena Line night ferry to Harwich leaves at eleven. Both arrive in the U.K. in the early hours of tomorrow morning.

"Are you carrying a passport, grasshopper?"

"Yes, sir."

"You want to take the first ferry or the second?"

"I'll take the second."

Ruiz nods in agreement. "Anyone know the weather forecast?"

Hokke is on the mobile to P&O seeing if they will hold the passenger gates open. They're supposed to close fifteen minutes before departure, which means we won't make it.

We're basing our assumptions on a ratio of about 2 percent detail and 98 percent desire. Even if Samira is on board one of the ferries, she won't be mingling with other passengers. They'll keep her hidden. How are we going to find her?

My mind aches when I think about her. I made promises. I said I would find Zala and keep her safe. What am I going to say to her?

De Souza asked if I wanted the babies for myself. It was a ridiculous suggestion. Why would he say that? I'm doing this for Cate and for Samira. For the twins.

The docks are lit up for miles. Cranes and gantries act as massive lighting towers, painting the hulls of ships and rows of stacked containers. The water is dark and solid in between, and the waves are hardly waves at all, they're wrinkles on a sluggish river.

The taxi pulls up outside the P&O terminal. Ruiz is out the door before we stop moving. A week of maddening pain and morphine won't slow him down.

"Good luck," he yells without turning back. "I'm going to find her first."

"Yeah, right. You'll spend your entire time throwing up."

His hand rises. One finger extends.

The Stena Line terminal is at the western edge of the port where the Hook of Holland reaches out into the North Sea. The taxi drops me and I say goodbye to Hokke.

"I can never repay you."

"But you will," he laughs, pointing to the meter.

I give him all my remaining Euros for he still has to get home.

He kisses me three times—left cheek, right cheek and left cheek again.

"Be careful."

"I will."

I have an hour until the *Stena Britannica* leaves. The ship dominates the skyline, towering over the surrounding structures. It is the length of two football fields and the height of a fifteen-story building, with twin stacks that slope backward and give the impression, although not the conviction, of speed.

Seagulls circle and swoop for insects in the beam of the spotlights. They appear so graceful in flight yet they squabble like fishwives on the ground. And they always sound so desperately sad, wailing in misery like creatures already condemned to hell.

Many trucks and trailers are already on board. I can see them lined up on the open decks, a few feet apart, buttressed hard against the stern railings. More trucks are queuing on the loading ramp. Meanwhile cars and vans are being marshaled in a different parking area, waiting their turn.

A young woman in the ticket office wears a light blue skirt and matching jacket, like a maritime stewardess. "You will need to write down the details of your vehicle," she says.

"I don't have a vehicle."

"I'm sorry but there is no pedestrian footbridge on this service. We cannot board foot passengers."

"But I have to catch this ferry."

"That is not possible." She glances over my shoulder. "Perhaps . . . ?"

An elderly couple has just pulled up in an early-model Range Rover towing an old-fashioned caravan that looks like a Cinderella pumpkin carriage. The driver is bald with a small goatee that could be a shaving oversight. His wife is twice his size, wearing acres of denim across her hips. They look Welsh and sound Welsh.

"What is it, pet?" she asks, as I interrupt their cup of thermos tea.

"They won't let me onto the ferry as a foot passenger. I really need to get back to England. I was wondering if I could ride with you."

Husband and wife look at each other.

"Are you a terrorist?" he asks.

"No."

"Are you carrying drugs?"

"No."

"Do you vote Tory?"

"No."

"Are you a Catholic?"

"No."

He winks at his wife. "Clear on all counts."

"Welcome aboard," she announces, thrusting out her hand. "I'm Bridget Jones. Not the fat one from the movies—the fatter one from Cardiff. This is Bryce, my husband."

The Range Rover is packed to the gunwales with suitcases, shopping bags and duty-free: Dutch cheeses, French sausage, two cases of Stella Artois, a bottle of Baileys Irish Cream and assorted souvenirs.

They are very cute. A twee couple, with matching lumbar cushions and traveling mugs. Mr. Jones is wearing driving gloves with cut-off fingers and she has road maps, color-coded in a pocket on the dashboard.

"We've been to Poland," she announces.

"Really?"

"Nobody we know has ever been to Poland. Not even our friends Hettie and Jack from the caravanning club, who think they've been everywhere."

"And to Estonia," her husband adds. "We've done 3,264 miles since we left home on August 28." He strokes the steering wheel. "She's managed eighteen mile to the gallon, which is pretty bloody good for an old girl, especially after that bad batch of diesel in Gdansk."

"Gdansk was very dodgy," agrees his wife.

"It must be cold to be caravanning."

"Oh, we don't mind," she giggles. "A spouse is better than a hot water bottle."

Mr. Jones nods. "I get pretty good mileage out of this old girl."

I don't know if he's referring to his wife or still talking about the car.

Ahead of us the traffic is moving. Vehicles pull onto the ramp and disappear inside, maneuvered into marked lanes barely wide enough for their axles. Engines are turned off. The caravan is strapped down. Men in fluorescent vests direct us to the air-lock doors, which lead to stairs and lifts.

"Don't dawdle, pet," says Mrs. Jones. "The buffet is included in the price. You want to beat the queue."

Mr. Jones nods. "They do a fine apple crumble and custard."

A key card is included with my ticket. It corresponds to a cabin on one of the accommodation decks. Deck 8 has signs asking passengers to be quiet because truck drivers are sleeping. Some of them must have boarded hours ago. How am I going to find Samira?

I don't bother visiting my cabin. I have no luggage to stow. Instead I study the ship's floor plan, which is bolted to the wall near an emergency exit. There are four vehicle decks which are restricted to authorized personnel during the voyage. Deck 10 is crew only. It must be the bridge.

The corridors between the cabins are just wide enough for two people to pass. I search them, looking for the familiar or the unfamiliar. This used to be my job when I worked for the Diplomatic Protection Group—looking for small changes, trying to sense the presence of someone in a crowd or notice their absence in the instant of looking. It could be a person who doesn't belong or who tries too hard to belong or who draws the eye for some other reason.

The ship's engines have started. I can feel the faint vibrations through my feet and they seem to transfer to my nerve endings.

The buffet is being served in the Globetrotter Restaurant. Most of the passengers seem to be truck drivers, dressed in jeans and T-shirts. Food is piled high on their plates—congealed curries, cottage pie, vegetarian lasagna. Big engines need refueling.

The Dutch drivers are playing cards, while the British drivers smoke and read tabloids. The ferry has slipped its moorings and pulled out into the river. As the shore lights slide past the window, it feels as though the land is moving and not the ferry. England is five hours away.

Hokke was right. This haystack is too big. I could search the ferry for weeks and not find Samira. She could be locked in a truck or in one of the cabins. She might not even be on board. Perhaps de Souza had no intention of letting me find her and was simply getting me out of the Netherlands.

The cavernous vehicle decks are below me. Some are open to the elements while others are enclosed. I have to search them. How? Do I hammer on the side of each truck, calling her name? Will she answer?

If there's any chance at all that she's on board, I have to find her. Running along the gangways and up the stairs, I stop people and show them Samira's photograph. I'm doubling back on myself, lost in a maze. Have I been down this corridor before? Is that the same passenger I asked earlier? Most of them are in their cabins now, lying down to sleep.

I turn another corner and suddenly I feel it. A shiver in the air. It's an uncanny sensation, as if I'm prescient. Along a long corridor, a figure with his back to me pauses to unlock a cabin door. I see a quarter profile and suddenly flatten myself against a wall. My phantoms are following me.

14

The ferry shifts and I brace myself. We must have reached open water, or maybe it's my heart lurching. I am sure it was *him*. Brendan Pearl. He is here because *she* is here.

My first reaction is to retreat. I pull back and take a few deep breaths on the stairwell, while contemplating what to do. Taking out my mobile, I check the signal. Nothing. The ferry has moved out of range. I should talk to the captain. He can radio ahead and get a message to Forbes.

A member of the crew is climbing the stairs. Although dressed in dark trousers and a white shirt with epaulettes, he looks too young to be at sea. He has a name tag on his chest. Raoul Jakobson.

"Do you have keys to all the cabins?" I ask.

"Is there a problem?"

"There is a man on board who is wanted by the British police. He is staying in cabin 8021." I point along the passage. His gaze follows my outstretched hand. "I am a

British police officer. A detective constable. Is there a passenger list?" I show him my badge.

"Yes, of course."

He opens a door marked AUTHORIZED PERSONNEL ONLY and retrieves a clipboard, running his finger down the page until he finds the cabin number.

"That cabin is occupied by a Patrick Norris. He is a British driver."

Pearl has a new identity.

Is it possible to find out what vehicle he drove on board?"

Raoul consults the list again. "V743 LFB. On Deck 5."

"I need to check this vehicle."

"Passengers are not authorized to be on that deck."

"I'm looking for an illegal passenger. She could be locked inside the truck."

"Perhaps you should talk to the captain."

"Yes, of course, but there isn't time right now. *You* go to the captain. I need him to send a message to this man." I scribble a phone number on the clipboard. "His name is Detective Inspector Robert Forbes. Mention my name. Tell him that Brendan Pearl is on this ferry."

"Is that it?"

"He'll understand."

Raoul looks at the phone number and glances down the passage toward Pearl's cabin.

"Is he dangerous, this man?"

"Yes, but nobody is to panic. Let him sleep." I look at my watch. "We'll be in Harwich in four hours." Moving toward the stairwell, I nod goodbye. "Tell the captain. I have to go."

Taking the stairs two at a time, I swing through the landings and reach Deck 5. Hitting the red button, I hear the air hiss out as the seal is broken. The metal door slides open. The noise of the ship's engines is amplified in the cavernous space and transfers through the floor in pulsing vibrations.

Stepping over the lip of the door, I begin walking down the first line of vehicles. The trucks are parked seven abreast and nose-to-tail, so close together there is just enough room to squeeze between them. I wish I had a torch. The strip lighting can barely cut through the gloom and I have difficulty reading the vehicle numbers.

I walk the length of the deck and back again, following the lanes. When the ferry pitches and rolls in the swell, I brace my hand against a wheel arch or trailer. My imagination puts me inside them. I can picture Hassan and the others, trapped, suffocating. I want to hammer on the metal sides and fling open the doors, filling them with air.

I'm in the second lane on the starboard side when I find it. The rig has a maroon Mercedes cab and a white box trailer. Stepping onto the running board, I grip the side mirror and pull myself up to peer into the cab. Take-away coffee cups and food wrappers litter the floor.

Stepping down, I slowly circle the trailer. Pressing my ear against the steel skin I listen for a sneeze or a cough or a whisper, any sound at all. Nothing. The rear doors are sealed with a metal rod and cam lock. The barrel is closed and padlocked.

Someone holding a torch is walking toward me. The beam swings from side to side, blinding me momentarily. I edge away from the trailer. Darkness feathers around me.

"You're not supposed to be down here," says a voice.

At that same moment a hand snakes around my face, cupping my mouth. Smothering all sound away.

I can't breathe. My feet are off the ground. His fingers are digging into my cheek, tearing at my gums. His other forearm wraps around my neck, searching for my windpipe. I brace my hands against it and kick backward, trying to find his instep or his knee. The blow barely touches him.

He lifts me higher. My toes scrabble at the floor, unable to get leverage. I can hear blood pulsing in my ears. I need to breathe.

Karate training taught me about pressure points. There is one in the soft flesh between the thumb and forefinger, above the webbing. I find the spot. He grunts in pain, releasing his grip on my mouth and nose. I still can't breathe. My windpipe is being crushed. I keep driving my thumb into his flesh.

A knee snaps into my kidneys. The pain is like a blast of heat. I don't let go of his right hand but at the same time I can't see his left fist cocking. The punch is like a punctuation mark. Darkness sweeps away the pain and the memories. I am free of the ferry and the incessant noise of the engines. Free of Cate and Samira. Free of the unborn twins. Free at last.

———————

Slowly the world becomes wider. Lighter. I am suspended for a moment a few inches above my body, staring down at a strange scene. My hands are bound with electrical tape behind my back. Another piece of tape covers my mouth, wrapped around my head like a mask, pulling at my split and swollen lip.

There is a weak light from a torch, lying on the floor near my feet. My head is on Samira's lap. She leans forward and whispers something in my ear. She wants me to lie still. Light catches her pupils. Her fingers are like ice.

My head is pressed to her womb. I feel her babies moving. I can hear the sough and gurgle of the fluid, the melody of their heartbeats. Blood slides back and forth beneath her skin, squeezing into smaller and smaller channels, circulating oxygen.

I wonder if twins are aware of each other's existence. Do they hear the other's heartbeat? Do they hold each other or communicate by touch?

Bit by bit the confusion and darkness work their way into some semblance of order. If I stay relaxed, I can breathe through the tape.

Samira's body suddenly spasms and jackknifes from the waist, squeezing my head against her thighs. Regaining control, she leans back and breathes deeply. I try to lift my head. She wants me to lie still.

I can't talk with the gag. She hooks her fingers beneath the plastic tape and lifts it away from my lips just enough for me to speak.

"Where are we?"

"In a truck."

Our whispers are magnified by the hollowness.

"Are you all right?"

She shakes her head. Tears form at the edge of her eyes. Her body convulses again. She's in labor.

"Who brought me here?"

"Yanus."

He and Pearl must be working together.

"You have to untie me."

Her eyes sweep to the closed rear doors and she shakes her head.

330

"Please."

"They will kill you."

They will kill me anyway.

"Help me to sit up."

She lifts my head and shoulders until I'm leaning with my back against a wall. My inner gyroscope is totally messed up. I may have ruptured an eardrum.

The trailer appears to be full of pallets and crates. Through a square narrow opening I see a crawl space with a mattress and three plastic bottles. Someone has built a false wall to create a secret compartment in the trailer. Customs officers wouldn't notice the difference unless they measured the outside and inside of the truck.

"When did the contractions start?"

She looks at me helplessly. She has no way of judging time.

"How far are they apart?"

"A minute."

How long was I unconscious? Raoul will have gone to the ferry's captain by now. They will telephone Forbes and come looking for me. Forbes will tell them to be careful.

"Undo my hands."

Samira shakes her head.

Letting go of the tape, she tugs a blanket around my shoulders. She is more worried about me than herself.

"You should not have come."

I can't reply. Another contraction contorts her face. Her entire body seems to lock up.

The rear doors swing open. I feel the draft and hear the intake of Samira's breath.

"I told you not to touch her," says Yanus, springing into the trailer. He seizes her, smearing his hands over her face as if covering her with filth. Then he peels back her lips, forcing her jaw open, and spits into her mouth. She gags and tries to turn away.

Then he confronts me, ripping off the gag. It feels like half my face is torn off with it.

"Who knows you're here?"

My voice is slurred: "The captain. The crew . . . they're radioing ahead."

"Liar!"

Another figure is standing in the open end of the trailer. Brendan Pearl. He can't have been there for more than a few seconds yet I have the sensation that he's been watching me for a long time.

The light behind him washes out his features, but I can see how he's changed his appearance since I saw him last. His hair is shorter and he's wearing glasses. The walking stick is a nice touch. He's holding it upside down. Why? It's not a walking stick. It has a curved hook like a fishing gaff or a marlin spike. I remember what Ruiz called him—the Shankhill Fisherman.

Yanus kicks me in the stomach. I roll once and he places a shoe on my neck, forcing it down, concentrating his weight on the point where my spine joins my skull. Surely it must snap.

Samira cries out, her body wracked by another contraction. Pearl says something and Yanus lifts his foot. I can breathe. He circles the empty trailer and returns, putting his heel on my neck again.

I force my arms out, pointing toward Samira. She is staring at her hands in horror. Liquid stains her skirt and pools beneath her knees.

Pearl pushes Yanus aside.

"Her water has broken." Desperately, I choke the words out.

"She pissed herself," sneers Yanus.

"No. She's having the babies."

"Make them stop," says Pearl.

"I can't. She needs a doctor."

Another contraction arrives, stronger than before. Her scream echoes from the metal walls. Pearl loops the barbed hook around her neck. "She makes another sound like that and I'll take out her throat."

Samira shakes her head, covering her mouth with her hands.

Pearl pulls me into a sitting position and cuts the electrical tape away from my wrists. He pauses for a moment, chewing at his cheek like a cud.

"She don't look so healthy does she?" he says, in an Irish lilt.

"She needs a doctor."

"Can't have no doctors."

"But she's having twins!"

"I don't care if she's having *puppies*. You'll have to deliver them."

"I don't know how to deliver a baby!"

"Then you better learn quick."

"Don't be stupid—"

The stave of the marlin spike strikes my jaw. When the pain passes, I count teeth with my tongue. "Why should I help you?"

"Because I'll kill you if you don't."

"You're going to kill me anyway."

"Know that, do you?"

Samira's hand shoots out and grips my wrist. Her

knuckles are white and the pain is etched on her face. She wants help. She wants the pain to go away. I glance at Pearl and nod.

"That's grand as grand can be." He stands and stretches, twirling the spike in his fist.

"We can't do it here," I say. "We need to get her to a cabin. I need light. Clean sheets. Water."

"No."

"Look at this place!"

"She stays here."

"Then she dies! And her babies die! And whoever is paying you will get nothing."

I think Pearl is going to hit me again. Instead he weighs the wooden stave in both hands before swinging it down until the metal hook touches the floor and he leans on it like a walking stick. He and Yanus converse in whispers. Decisions have to be made. Their plan is unraveling.

"You have to try to hold on," I tell Samira. "It's going to be OK."

She nods, far calmer than I am.

Why hasn't anyone come looking for me? Surely they will have called Forbes by now. He'll tell them what to do.

Pearl comes back.

"OK, we move her." He raises his shirt to show me a pistol tucked into his belt. "No fuckin' tricks. You escape and Yanus here will cut the babies out of her. He's a frustrated fuckin' surgeon."

The Irishman collects Samira's things—a small cotton bag and a spare blanket. Then he helps her to stand. She cups her hands beneath her pregnancy as though taking the weight. I wrap the blanket around her shoulders. Her damp gray skirt sticks to her thighs.

Yanus has gone ahead to check the stairs. I can picture crew members waiting for him. He'll be overpowered. Pearl will have no choice but to surrender.

He lifts Samira down from the trailer. I follow, stumbling slightly as I land. Pearl pushes me out of the way and closes the rear doors, sliding the barrel lock into place. Something is different about the truck. The color. It's not the same.

My stomach turns over. There are two trucks. Yanus and Pearl must have each driven a vehicle on board. Glancing toward the nearest stairwell, I see the glowing exit sign. We're on a different deck. They don't know where to look for me.

Samira goes first. Her chin is drawn down to her clavicle and she seems to be whispering a prayer. A contraction stops her suddenly and her knees buckle. Pearl puts his arm around her waist. Although in his late forties, he has the upper-body strength of someone who has bulked up in prison weight rooms. You don't work a regular job and have a physique like his.

We move quickly up the stairs and along empty passageways. Yanus has found a cabin on Deck 9, where there are fewer passengers. He takes Samira from Pearl and I glance at them, fleetingly, sidelong. Surely they can't expect to get away with this.

The two-berth cabin is oppressively neat. It has a narrow single bunk about a foot from the floor and another directly above it, hinged and folded flat against the wall. There is a square porthole with rounded corners. The window is dark. Land has ceased to exist and I can only imagine the emptiness of the North Sea. I look at my watch. It's twelve thirty. Harwich is another three and a half hours away. If Samira can stay calm and the

335

contractions are steady, we may reach Harwich in time. In time for what?

Her eyes are wide and her forehead is beaded with perspiration. At the same time she is shivering. I sit on the bed, with my back to the bulkhead, pulling her against me with my arms wrapped around her, trying to keep her warm. Her belly balloons between her knees and her entire body jolts with each contraction.

I am running on instinct. Trying my best not to panic or show fear. The first-aid course I did when I joined the Met was comprehensive but it didn't include childbirth. I remember something my mama said to my sisters-in-law: "Doctors don't deliver babies, women do."

Yanus and Pearl take turns guarding the door. There isn't enough room in the cabin for both of them. One will watch the passageway.

Yanus leans against the narrow cabin counter, watching with listless curiosity. Taking an orange from his pocket, he peels it expertly and separates it into segments that he lines up along the bench. Each piece is finally crushed between his teeth and he sucks the juices down his throat before spitting out the pith and seeds onto the floor.

I have never believed that people could be wholly evil. Psychopaths are made not born. Yanus could be the exception. I try to picture him as a youngster and cling to the hope that there might be some warmth inside him. He must have loved someone, something—a pet, a parent, a friend. I see no trace of it.

One or twice Samira can't stifle her cries. He tosses a roll of masking tape into my lap. "Shut her up!"

"No! She has to tell me when the contractions are coming."

"Then keep her quiet."

Where does he keep his knife? Strapped to his chest on his left side, next to his heart. He seems to read my mind and taps his jacket.

"I can cut them out of her, you know. I've done it before with animals. I start cutting just here." He puts his finger just above his belt buckle and draws it upward over his navel and beyond. "Then I peel back her skin."

Samira shudders.

"Just shut up, will you?"

He gives me his shark's smile.

Night presses against the porthole. There might be five hundred passengers on board the ferry, but right now it feels as though the cabin light is burning in a cold hostile wasteland.

Samira tilts her head back until she can look into my eyes.

"Zala?" she asks.

I wish I could lie to her but she reads the truth on my face. I can almost see her slipping backward into blackness, disappearing. It is the look of someone who knows that fate has abandoned them to a sadness so deep that nothing can touch it.

"I should never have let her go," she whispers.

"It's not your fault."

Her chest rises and falls in a silent sob. She has turned her eyes away. It is a gesture that says everything. I vowed to find Zala and keep her safe. I broke my promise.

The contractions seem to have eased. Her breathing steadies and she sleeps.

Pearl has replaced Yanus.

"How is she?"

"Exhausted."

He braces his back against the door, sliding down until he settles on his haunches, draping his arms over his knees. In such a small space he appears larger, overgrown, with big hands. Yanus has feminine hands, shapely and delicate, fast with a blade. Pearl's are like blunt instruments.

"You'll never get away with this, you know that."

He smiles. "There are many things I know and many more things I don't know."

"Listen to me. You're only making this worse. If she dies or the babies die they'll charge you with murder."

"They won't die."

"She needs a doctor."

"Enough talk."

"The police know I'm here. I saw you earlier. I told the captain to radio ahead. There will be a hundred police officers waiting at Harwich. You can't get away. Let me take Samira. There could be a doctor on board or a nurse. They'll have medical supplies."

Pearl doesn't seem to care. Is that what happens when you spend most of your life in prison or committing acts that should put you there?

My scalp tingles. "Why did you kill my friend Cate and her husband?"

"Who?"

"The Beaumonts."

His eyes, not quite level with each other, give the impression of lopsidedness until he talks and his features suddenly line up. "She was greedy."

"How?"

"She could only pay for one baby but wanted both of them."

"You asked her to *choose*?"

"Not me."

"Someone else did?"

He doesn't have to answer.

"That's obscene."

He shrugs. "Pitter or Patter—seems simple enough. Life is about choices."

That's what Cate meant—at the reunion—when she said they were trying to take her baby. They wanted her to pay double. Her bank account was empty. She had to choose: the boy or the girl. How can a mother make a decision like that and live for the rest of her life gazing into the eyes of one child and seeing a reflection of another that she never knew?

Pearl is still talking. "She threatened to go to the police. We warned her. She ignored it. That's the problem with folks nowadays. Nobody takes responsibility for their actions. Make a mistake and you pay for it. That's life."

"Have you paid for your mistakes?"

"All my life." His eyes are closed. He wants to go back to ignoring me.

A knock. Pearl slides the pistol from his belt and points it toward me while holding a finger to his lips. He opens the door a fraction. I can't see a face. Someone is asking about a missing passenger. They're looking for me.

Pearl yawns. "Is that why you woke me?"

A second voice: "Sorry, sir."

"What does she look like?"

I can't hear the description.

"Well, I ain't seen her. Maybe she went for a swim."

"I hope not, sir."

"Yeah, well, I got to sleep."

"Sorry, sir, you won't be disturbed again."

The door closes. Pearl waits for a moment, pressing his ear to the door. Satisfied, he tucks the pistol back in his belt.

There's another knock on the door. Yanus.

"Where the fuck were you?" demands Pearl.

"Watching," replies Yanus.

"You were supposed to fucking warn me."

"Would have made no difference. They're knocking on every door. They won't come back now."

Samira sits bolt upright screaming. The contraction is brutal and I scissor my legs around her, holding her still. An unseen force possesses her, racking her body in spasms. I find myself drawn to her pain. Caught up in it. Breathing when she breathes.

Another contraction comes almost immediately. Her back arches and her knees rise up.

"I have to push now."

"No!"

"I have to."

This is it. I can't stop her. Sliding out from behind her, I lie her down and take off her underwear.

Pearl is unsure of what to do. "Take deep breaths, that's a good girl. Good deep breaths. You thirsty? I'll get you a drink of water."

He fills a glass in the small bathroom and returns.

"Shouldn't you be checking the cervix?" he asks.

"And I suppose you know all about it."

"I seen movies."

"Take over anytime you want."

His tone softens. "What can I do?"

"Run some hot water in the sink. I need to wash my hands."

Samira unclenches her teeth as the pain eases. Short panting breaths become longer. She focuses on Pearl and begins issuing instructions. She needs things—scissors and string, clips and towels. For a moment I think she's delirious but soon realize that she knows more about childbirth than any of us.

He opens the door and passes on the instructions to Yanus. They argue. Pearl threatens him.

Samira has another instruction. Men cannot be present at the birth. I expect Pearl to say no but I see him wavering.

I tell him: "Look at this place. We can't go anywhere. There's one door and a porthole fifty feet above the water."

He accepts this and glances at his watch. It's after two. "An hour from now she has to be back in the truck." His hand is on the door handle. He turns and addresses me.

"My ma is a good Catholic. Pro-life, you understand? She'd say there were already five people in this room, babies included. When I come back I expect to see the same number. Keep them alive."

He closes the door and Samira relaxes a little. She asks me to fetch a flannel from the bathroom. She folds it several times and wedges it between her teeth when she feels a contraction coming.

"How do you know so much?"

"I have seen babies born," she explains. "Women would sometimes come to the orphanage to give birth. They left the babies with us because they could not take them home."

Her contractions are coming forty seconds apart. Her eyes bulge and she bites down hard on the flannel. The pain passes.

"I need you to see if I'm ready," she whispers.

"How?"

"Put two fingers inside me to measure."

"How do I tell?"

"Look at your fingers," she says. "See how long they are. Measure with them."

Opening her legs, I do as she asks. I have never touched a woman so intimately or been so terrified.

"I think you're ready."

She nods, clenching the flannel between her teeth through the first part of the contraction and then breathing in short bursts, trying to ease the pain. Tears squeeze from her eyes and mingle with her sweat. I smell her exertions.

"I have to get to the floor," she says.

"Are you going to pray?"

"No. I'm going to have a baby."

She squats with her legs apart, bracing her arms between the bunk and the bench table. Gravity is going to help her.

"You must feel for the baby's head," she says.

My hand is inside her, turning and dipping. I feel a baby's head. It's crowning. Should there be blood?

"They will kill you after the babies are born," whispers Samira. "You must get out of here."

"Later."

"You must go now."

"Don't worry about me."

There's a knock on the door. I undo the latch and Pearl hands me scissors, a ball of string and a rusty clip. Yanus hisses from behind him. "Keep the bitch quiet."

"Fuck you! She's having a baby."

Yanus makes a lunge for me. Pearl pushes him back and closes the door.

Samira is pushing now, three times with each contraction. She has long slender lemurlike feet, roughly calloused along the outer edges. Her chin is tucked to her throat and oily coils of her hair fall over her eyes.

"If I pass out, you must make sure you get the babies out. Don't leave them inside me." Teeth pull at her bottom lip. "Do whatever you have to."

"Shhh."

"Promise me."

"I promise."

"Am I bleeding a lot?"

"You're bleeding. I don't know if it's too much. I can see the baby's head."

"It hurts."

"I know."

Existence narrows to just breathing, pain and pushing. I brush hair from her eyes and crouch between her legs. Her face contorts. She screams into the flannel. The baby's head is out. I hold it in my cupped hand, feeling the dips and hollows of the skull. The shoulders are trapped. Gently I put my finger beneath its chin and the tiny body rotates within her. On the next contraction the right shoulder appears, then the left, and the baby slides into my hands.

A boy.

"Rub your finger down his nose," gasps Samira.

It takes only a fingertip to perform the task. There is a soft, shocked sob, a rattle and a breath.

Samira issues more instructions. I am to use the string and tie off the umbilical cord in two places, cutting between the knots. My hands are shaking.

She is crying. Spent. I help her back onto the bunk and she leans against the bulkhead wall. Wrapping the baby in a towel, I hold him close, smelling his warm breath, letting his nose brush against my cheek. Which one are you, I wonder, Pitter or Patter?

I look at my watch and make a mental note of the time: 2:55 a.m. What is the date? October 29. Where will they say he was born? In the Netherlands or Britain? And who will be his true mother? What a mixed-up way to start a life.

The contractions have started again. Samira kneads her stomach, trying to feel the unborn twin.

"What's wrong?"

"She is facing the wrong way. You must turn her."

"I don't know how."

Each new contraction brings a groan of resignation. Samira is almost too exhausted to cry out; too tired to push. I have to hold her up this time. She squats. Her thighs part still further.

Reaching inside her, I try to push the baby back, turning her body, fighting gravity and the contractions. My hands are slick. I'm frightened of hurting her.

"It's coming."

"Push now."

The head arrives with a gush of blood. I glimpse something white with blue streaks wrapped around its neck.

"Stop! Don't push!"

My hand slides along the baby's face until my fingers reach beneath her chin and untangle the umbilical cord.

"Samira, you *really* need to push the next time. It's very important."

The contraction begins. She pushes once, twice . . . nothing.

"Push."

"I can't."

"Yes, you can. One last time, I promise."

She throws back her head and muffles a scream. Her body stiffens and bucks. A baby girl emerges, blue, slick, wrinkled, cupped in both my hands. I rub her nose. Nothing. I hold her on her side, sweeping my index finger round her mouth and throat, trying to clear the dripping goo.

I drape her over my hand, with her arms and legs dangling, and slap her back hard. Why won't she breathe?

Putting her on a towel I begin chest compressions with the tips of my index and middle fingers. At the same time I lower my lips and puff into the baby's mouth and nose.

I know about resuscitation. I have done the training and I have witnessed paramedics do it dozens of times. Now I am breathing into a body that has never taken a breath. Come on, little one. Come on.

Samira is half on the bunk and half on the floor. Her eyes are closed. The first twin is swaddled and lying between her arm and her side.

I continue the compressions and breathing. It is like a mantra, a physical prayer. Almost without noticing, the narrowest of chests rises and eyelids flutter. Blue has become pink. She's alive. Beautiful.

15

A girl and a boy—Pitter and Patter—each with ten fingers and ten toes, squashed-up noses, tiny ears. Rocking back on my heels, I feel like laughing with relief, until I catch my reflection in the mirror. I am smeared with blood and tears yet have a look of complete wonderment on my face.

Samira groans softly.

"You're bleeding."

"It will stop when I feed them."

How does she know so much? She is massaging her belly, which ripples and sways in its emptiness. I swaddle the baby girl and tuck her next to Samira.

"Go now!"

"I can't leave you."

"Please!"

An extraordinary calmness washes through me. I have only two options—to fight or to fall. I take the scissors, weighing them in my hand. Maybe there is a way.

I open the door. Pearl is in the passage.

"Quickly! I need a drinking straw. The girl. Her lungs are full of fluid."

"What if I can't?"

"A ballpoint pen, a tube, anything like that. Hurry!"

I close the door. He will leave Yanus to watch the passage.

Taking the babies from Samira, I lie them side by side on the floor of the bathroom, tucked between the sink and the toilet. Cupping my hands beneath the running water, I wash away the blood and clean my face.

I have been trained to use a firearm. I can shoot a perfect score with a pistol from thirty yards on an indoor range. What good is that now? My hand-to-hand skills are defensive but I know the vital organs. I glance again at the scissors.

It is a plan I can only try once. Lying on the bathroom floor, I face the bedroom, holding the scissors like an ice pick with a reverse grip. My thumb hooks through the handle. If I look toward my toes, I can see the babies.

Taking a deep breath I open my lungs, screaming for help. How long will it take?

Yanus shoulders the door open, shattering the lock. He charges inside, holding the knife ahead of him. In mid-stride he looks down. Beneath his raised foot is the afterbirth, purple slick and glistening. I don't know what he imagines it to be, but the possibilities are too much for him to comprehend. He rears back and I drive the scissors into the soft flesh behind his right knee, aiming for the artery and the tendons that work his leg. The knee buckles and he swings his arm down in an arc trying to stab me but I'm too low and the blade sweeps past my ear.

I grab his arm and lock it straight, spearing the scissors

347

into the inside of his elbow, severing another artery. The knife slips from his fingers.

He tries to spin and grab me, but I am already out of reach. Leaping to my feet, I jump onto his back and send him down. I could kill him if I wanted. I could drive the blade into his kidneys.

Instead, I reach into his pocket and find the masking tape. His right leg is flapping like the wooden limb of a marionette. Pulling his good arm behind his back, I tape it in a reverse sling around his neck. Another piece covers his mouth.

Yanus is groaning. I grab his face. "Listen to me. I have severed the popliteal artery in your leg and the brachial artery in your arm. You know this already because you're a knife man. You also know that you will bleed to death unless you keep pressure on these wounds. You will have to squat on your haunches and keep this arm bent. I will send someone to help you. If you do as I suggest, you might still be alive when they get here."

Samira has been watching all this with a curious detachment. Crawling off the bed, she takes several painful steps toward Yanus before leaning down and spitting in his face.

"We have to go."

"You go. Take the babies."

"Not without you."

I take the smallest twin, the girl, whose eyes are open, watching me. Samira takes the sleeping boy. Cautiously, I peer into the passageway. Pearl will be coming back soon.

Samira has a towel pressed between her thighs. We head toward the stairs moving as quickly as she can. The passage is so narrow that I bounce off the wall as I try to keep hold of Samira's arm. People are asleep. I don't know which cabins are occupied.

There is a service lift. I can't open the door. Samira's legs buckle. I stop her falling. This is Deck 9. The bridge is on Deck 10. She isn't strong enough to climb the stairs. I have to get her away from the cabin and hide her.

There is a linen room with shelves on either side, stacked with folded sheets and towels. I could leave her here and go for help. No, she shouldn't be left alone.

I hear movement. Someone is awake. Hammering on the cabin door, it opens hurriedly. A middle-aged man, wearing pajamas and gray socks, looks irritated. A fuzz of red hair spills from the V of his shirt and makes it seem like his stuffing is coming out.

I push Samira ahead of me. "Help her! I have to find a doctor!"

He says something in German. Then he spies the bloody towel between her thighs. I hand him the baby girl.

"Who are you?"

"Police. There's no time to explain. Help her."

Samira curls up on the bunk, her arms around the other twin.

"Don't open the door. Don't let anyone know she's here."

Before he can protest, I step back into the passage and run toward the stairs. The passenger lounge is deserted apart from two rough-looking men at the bar, hunched over pints. A woman files her nails at a cash register.

I yell for the captain. It isn't the desperation in my voice that affects them most. It's the blood on my clothes. I have come from a nightmare place, another dimension.

People are running. Members of the crew appear, yelling orders and ushering me farther upstairs. Sentences stream out of me, between snorting sobs. They're not listening to me. They have to get Samira and the twins.

The captain is a large man with shaggy eyebrows and a semicircle of hair clinging to the scalp above his ears and neck. His uniform is white and blue, matching his eyes.

He stands in the middle of the bridge, his head thrust forward, listening without any hint of skepticism. The state of my clothes is proof enough. The chief engineer is a medic. He wants to examine me. We don't have time. The captain is on the radio, using emergency frequencies, talking to HM Coast Guard, customs and mainland police. A cutter has been sent from Felixstowe to intercept and a Royal Navy helicopter is being scrambled from Prestwick in Scotland.

Pearl is somewhere on board. Yanus is bleeding to death. This is taking too long.

"You have to get Samira," I hear myself say. My voice sounds shrill and frightened. "She needs medical help."

The captain won't be rushed. He is following the protocols and procedures set down for piracy or violent incidents at sea. He wants to know how many there are. Are they armed? Will they take hostages?

The information is relayed to the coast guard and police. We are twenty minutes from port. Huge glass windows frame the approaching coastline, which is still blanketed in darkness. The bridge is high up, overlooking the bow. Nothing approximates a steering wheel. Instead there are computer screens, buttons and keyboards.

I confront the captain, demanding that he listen to me.

"I understand that you're a British police officer," he says abruptly, "but this is a Dutch vessel and you have no authority here. My responsibility is to my passengers and crew. I will not endanger their safety."

"A woman has just given birth. She's bleeding. She needs medical help."

"We are twenty minutes from docking."

"So you'll do nothing?"

"I am waiting for my instructions."

"What about the passengers downstairs? They're waking up."

"I don't believe they should be panicked. We have contingency plans to evacuate passengers to the Globe-trotter Lounge, where most of them are due to have breakfast."

The chief engineer is a neat little man with a college-boy haircut.

"Will you come with me?" I ask.

He hesitates. I pick up the first-aid box from the bench and turn to leave. The engineer looks at the captain, seeking permission. I don't know what passes between them but he's ready to follow me.

"Are there any weapons on board?"

"No."

God, they make it hard! This time we use a service lift to reach Deck 9. The doors open. The passage is empty. The deck below has the freight drivers who are due to disembark first.

At every corner I expect to see Pearl. He is a natural at this. Even my presence on the ferry didn't fluster him. He simply adjusted his sights and made a new plan. Yanus is the more unpredictable but Pearl is the more dangerous because he can adapt. I can picture him, waylaid for a moment by the loss of Samira and the twins, but still calculating his chances of escape.

Even before I reach the cabin I can see that something is wrong. A handful of passengers crowd the passage, craning to look over one another's heads. Among them is the Welsh couple. Mrs. Jones looks naked without her lipstick and is squeezed into a gray tracksuit that struggles to encompass her buttocks.

"You can't escape them," she says to the others. "Thugs and criminals. And what do the police do? Nothing. Too busy giving out speeding tickets. Even if they do get charged, some judge or magistrate will let them off on account of their drug addiction or deprived childhood. What about the bloody victims, eh? Nobody cares about them."

The cabin door is open, the lock broken. Sitting on his bunk, the German truck driver holds his head back to stop his nose bleeding. There is no sign of Samira or the twins.

"Where are they?" I grab his shoulder. "Where?"

The worst thing is not the anger. It is the murderous desire behind the anger.

My mobile phone is ringing. We must be in range of a signal. I don't recognize the number.

"Hello."

"And hello to you," says Pearl. "Have you ever seen that TV commercial about the Energizer bunny that keeps going and going and going? You're like that fucking bunny. You just don't quit."

His voice has an echo. He's on the vehicle deck. "Where is she?"

"I found her, bunny."

"Yes."

"Do you know how? The blood. You left a trail of it." A baby is crying in the background. "I also found Yanus. You cut him pretty good, but I patched him up."

"He'll bleed to death."

"Don't you worry about that, bunny. I don't leave *my* friends behind."

I'm already on the move, running along the passage to the first cabin. The chief engineer struggles to keep up with me. Yanus has gone. The floor is polished red with blood and dozens of footprints stain the passageway.

People are amazing. They will walk past a scene like this and ignore it because it's beyond their ordinary, mundane, workaday comprehension. Pearl is still on the line. "You'll never get off the ferry," I yell. "Give them back. Please."

"I need to talk to the captain."

"He won't negotiate."

"I don't wanna fuckin' negotiate! We have a mutual interest."

"What's that?"

"We both want me off this ferry."

———

My head is clearer now. Others are making decisions for me. It is three hours before dawn and the Essex coast is somewhere ahead of us in the darkness. I can't hear the engines from the bridge and without any points of reference the ferry doesn't appear to be moving. Two coast guard launches have joined the *Stena Britannica*, escorting us into port. The captain is communicating directly with his superiors in Rotterdam.

I am being kept away, at arm's length, as though I'm a

liability or worse, a hysterical woman. What could I have done differently? Hindsight is a cruel teacher. I should never have left Samira or the twins. I should have stayed with them. Perhaps I could have fought Pearl off.

My mind goes further back. I should never have gone to Amsterdam looking for her. I have made things worse rather than better. That's the story of my life—good intentions. And being a hundredth of a second too slow—close enough to touch victory in a contest where first and last were separated by the width of a chest.

How can they negotiate with Pearl? He can't be trusted. The chief engineer hands me something hot to drink.

"Not long to go now," he says, motioning to the windows. The lights of Harwich appear and disappear as we ride the swell. Massive cranes with four legs and oblong torsos seem to stand guard at the gates of the town. I stay at the window watching it approach.

The captain and navigator stare at screens, using external cameras to maneuver the ferry, edging it against the dock. We are so high up that the stevedores look like Lilliputians trying to tie down a giant.

DI Forbes is first on board, pausing just long enough to look at my clothes with a mixture of awe and disgust. He takes the phone from the captain.

"Don't trust him," I yell across the bridge. It is all I have a chance to say before the DI introduces himself to Pearl. I can only hear one side of their conversation but Forbes repeats each demand as it is made. The clicks in his throat are like punctuation marks.

Pearl wants the main ferry doors opened and vehicles moved to clear a path for his truck. Nobody is to approach. If he sees a police officer on the deck, or if he hears a fire alarm, or if anything is different or untoward, he will kill Samira and the twins.

"You have to give me more time," says Forbes. "I'll need at least an hour . . . That's not long enough. I can't do it in fifteen minutes . . . Let me talk to Samira . . . Yes, that's why I want to talk to her . . . No, I don't want that. Nobody has to get hurt."

In the background one of the babies is crying—perhaps both of them. Do twins sound the same? Do they harmonize when they cry?

There are CCTV cameras on the vehicle decks. One of them is trained on the truck. Yanus can be seen clearly behind the wheel. Samira is in the passenger seat.

The rest of the passengers are being evacuated down gangways to the main terminal building. The port area has been closed and sealed off by armed response teams in black body armor. There are sharpshooters on surrounding rooftops.

The anguish of the past hours has swelled up inside me, making it hard to breathe. I can feel myself sinking into the background.

Forbes has agreed to take a limited number of vehicles off the ferry, clearing a path for the truck. I follow the detective down the footbridge to the dock as he supervises the evacuation. Men in yellow reflective vests wave the first of the rigs down the ramp.

Forbes has put Pearl onto a speakerphone. The Irishman sounds calm. Confident. Perhaps it's bravado. He is talking over the sound of engines, telling Forbes to hurry. Slowly a clear lane emerges on the vehicle deck. The Mercedes truck is at the far end, with its headlights blazing and engine running.

I still can't understand how he hopes to get away.

There are unmarked police cars waiting outside and helicopters in the air. He can't outrun them.

Yanus is bleeding to death. Even with a bandaged leg and forearm his blood pressure will be dropping. How long before he loses consciousness?

"You definitely saw a gun?" asks Forbes, addressing me directly for the first time.

"Yes."

"Could he have other firearms?"

"Yes."

"What is the truck carrying?"

"This one is empty. There's another on Deck 5. I didn't see inside." I give him the vehicle number.

"So it could be a trafficking run. There might be illegals on board."

"It's possible."

The last of the rigs has been moved. Yanus has a clear path to the ramp. Pearl is still issuing instructions. The twins are silent.

In a beat of flushed silence I realize something is wrong. Pearl is too calm, too confident. His plan doesn't make sense. As the notion occurs to me, I'm moving, pushing past Forbes and sprinting up the ramp. A hundred meters is not my favorite distance but I can cover it in less time than it takes most people to tie their shoes.

Forbes is yelling at me to stop. He's too late. Reacting to the new development, he orders his teams to move. Heavy boots thunder up the ramp after me, sweeping between the outer rows of trucks.

Yanus is still behind the wheel, staring out through the windscreen, unperturbed by my approach. His eyes seem to follow me as I swing on the door handle and wrench it open. His hands are taped to the steering wheel. Blood has drained onto the floor at his feet. I press my hand to his neck. He's dead.

Samira's hands are also taped. I lean across Yanus and touch her shoulder. Her eyes open.

"Where are they?"

She shakes her head.

I swing down and run to the rear of the truck. A sledgehammer pulverizes the lock and the doors swing open. Guns sweep from side to side. The trailer is empty.

Forbes reaches us, puffing and wheezing, still clogged with his cold. I snatch the phone from him. The line is dead.

Amid the commotion of the next few minutes I see things at half speed and struggle to find saliva to push around my mouth. Forbes is bellowing orders and kicking angrily at the truck tires. Someone will have to pop him with a tranquilizer gun if he doesn't calm down.

Teams of police have secured the ferry. Nobody is being allowed on or off. Passengers are being screened and interviewed in the terminal. Floodlights on the dock make it appear like a massive stage or film set, ready for the cameras to roll.

Yanus watches and waits, as though expecting his cue. My heart jolts on the reality of having killed him. Yes, he deserved it, but *I did this*. I took his life. His blood still stains my clothes, along with Samira's.

Paramedics are lifting her onto a stretcher. The towel is still wedged between her thighs. The medics gently shunt me to one side when I approach. She can't talk to me now. I want to say I'm sorry, it was my fault. I should never have left her. I should have stayed with them. Perhaps I could have stopped Pearl.

Some time later Forbes comes looking for me.

"Let's walk," he says.

Instinctively, I take his arm. I'm frightened my legs might fail.

"What time is it?" I ask.

"Five thirty."

"My watch says five fifteen."

"It's slow."

"How do you know yours isn't fast?"

"Because the ferry company has those big fucking clocks on the wall that say *your* watch is wrong in four different time zones."

We walk down the ramp, along the dock, away from the ferry. Refinery tanks and shipping containers create silhouettes against the brightening sky. Wind and smoke and scudding clouds are streaming over us.

"You don't think he's on the ferry, do you?" asks Forbes.

"No."

There is another long pause. "We found a life buoy missing from the starboard railing. He could have gone over the side."

"Someone would have seen him."

"We were distracted."

"Even so."

I can still smell the twins and feel the smoothness of their skin. We're both thinking the same thing. What happened to them?

"You should never have put yourself on that ferry," he says.

"I couldn't be sure she was on board."

Taking a packet of cigarettes from his pockets, he counts the contents.

"You shouldn't smoke with a cold."

"I shouldn't smoke at all. My wife thinks men and women can have precisely the same ailment with the same symptoms but it's always the man who is sicker."

"That's because men are hypochondriacs."

"I got a different theory. I think it's because no matter how sick a woman is there's always a small part of her brain thinking about shoes."

"I bet you didn't tell her that."

"I'm sick, not stupid."

His demeanor is different now. Instead of sarcasm and cynicism, I sense anxiety and a hardening resolve.

"Who's behind this?"

"Samira mentioned an Englishman who called himself 'Brother.' She said he had a cross on his neck. There's someone you should look at. His name is Paul Donavon. He went to school with Cate Beaumont—and with me. He was there on the night she was run down."

"You think he's behind this?"

"Samira met 'Brother' at an orphanage in Kabul. Donavon was in Afghanistan with the British Army. The traffickers targeted orphans because it meant fewer complications. There were no families to search for them or ask questions. Some were trafficked for sex. Others were given the option of becoming surrogates."

"The pregnant illegals you asked about. Both claimed to be orphans."

Forbes still hasn't lit his cigarette. It rests between his lips, wagging up and down as he talks. He glances over his shoulder at the ferry.

"About the other night."

"What night?"

"When we had dinner."

"Yeah?"

"Did I conduct myself in a proper fashion? I mean, did I behave?"

"You were a perfect gentleman."

"That's good," he mumbles. "I mean, I thought so." After a pause. "You took something that didn't belong to you."

"I prefer to think that we shared information."

He nods. "You might want to reconsider your career choice, DC Barba. I don't know if you're what I'd call a team player."

He can't stay. There is a debriefing to attend, which is going to be rough. His superiors are going to want to know how he let Pearl get away. And once the media get hold of this story it's going to run and run.

Forbes looks at my clothes. "If he's not on the ferry, how did he get off?"

"He could still be on board."

"You don't believe that."

"No. What about the crew?"

"You think he took a uniform?"

"It's possible."

He turns abruptly and strides back toward the waiting police cars. The CCTV footage will most likely provide the answer. There are cameras on every corner of the dock and every deck of the ship. One of them will have recorded Pearl.

"Eat bananas," I yell after him.

"Pardon?"

"My mother's remedy for a cold."

"You said you never listened to her."

"I said almost never."

There have been too many hospitals lately. Too many long waits on uncomfortable chairs, eating machine snacks and drinking powdered coffee and whitener. This one smells of boiled food and feces and has grim checked tiles in the corridors, worn smooth by the trolleys.

Ruiz called me from Hull, after his ferry docked. He wanted to come and get me but I told him to go home and rest. He's done enough.

"Are they looking after you?"

"I'm fine."

"Samira?"

"She's going to be OK."

I hope I'm right. She's been asleep for ten hours and didn't even wake when they lifted her from the ambulance and wheeled her to a private room. I have been waiting here, dozing in my plastic chair, with my head on the bed near her shoulder.

It is mid-afternoon when she finally wakes. I feel the mattress shift and open my eyes to see her looking at me.

"I need the bathroom," she whispers.

I take her by the elbow and help her to the en suite.

"Where am I?"

"In a hospital."

"What country?"

"England."

There is a nod of acceptance but no hint of a journey completed or sense of achievement.

Samira washes her face, ears, hands and feet, talking softly to herself. I take her arm again, leading her back to bed.

Motioning to the window, she wants to look outside. The North Sea is just visible over the rooftops and between buildings. It is the color of brushed steel.

"As a child I used to wonder what the sea looked like," she says. "I had only ever seen pictures in books and on TV." She gazes at the horizon.

"What do you think now?"

"I think it looks higher than the land. Why doesn't the water rush in and sweep us away?"

"Sometimes it does."

I notice a towel in her hand. She wants to use it as a prayer mat but doesn't know which direction to face toward Mecca. She turns slowly round and round like a cat trying to settle.

There are tears in her eyes and her lips tremble, struggling to form the words.

"They will be hungry soon. Who will feed them?"

BOOK
THREE

Love and pain are not the same. Love is put to the test—pain is not. You do not say of pain, as you do of love, "That was not true pain or it would not have disappeared so quickly."

—WILLIAM BOYD,
The Blue Afternoon

1

In the nights since the twins were born I have drowned countless times, twitching and kicking at the bedclothes. I see tiny bodies floating in fields of kelp or washed up on beaches. My lungs give out before I can reach them, leaving me choking and numb with an obscure anguish. I wonder if there's such a thing as a swollen heart?

Samira is also awake. She walks through the house at 3:00 a.m. moving as though her feet have an agreement with the ground that she will always tread lightly in return for never encountering another path that is too steep.

It has been five days since the twins went missing. Pearl has soaked through the cracks of the world and vanished. We know how he got off the ferry. A CCTV camera on Deck 3 picked up a man in a hard hat and reflective jacket who couldn't be identified as one of the crew. The footage didn't show his face clearly but he was seen carrying a pet traveling cage. The square gray plastic box was supposed to contain two Siamese cats but they were found wandering in a stairwell.

Another camera in the Customs area picked up the clearest images of the unidentified man. In the foreground trucks are being scanned with heat-seeking equipment designed to find illegals. But in the background, at the edge of the frame, a pumpkin-shaped caravan attached to an early-model Range Rover can be seen. Mr. and Mrs. Jones of Cardiff are seen repacking their duty-frees and souvenirs after being searched. As the car and caravan pull away, a square gray pet cage is visible on the tarmac next to where they were parked.

The Welsh couple were pulled over a little after midday Sunday on the M4 just east of Reading. The caravan was empty but Pearl's fingerprints were lifted from the table and the aluminum door. The couple had stopped for petrol at a motorway service center on the M25. A cashier remembered Pearl buying bottles and baby formula. Shortly afterward, at 10:42 a.m., a car was reported stolen from an adjacent parking area. It still hasn't been found.

Forbes is running the investigation, liaising with Spijker in Amsterdam, combining resources, pitting their wills against the problem. They are cross-checking names from the IVF clinic with the U.K. immigration records.

There has been a news blackout about the missing twins. DI Forbes made the decision. Stolen children make dramatic headlines and he wants to avoid creating panic. A year ago a newborn was snatched from a hospital in Harrogate and there were 1,200 alleged sightings in the first two days. Mothers were accosted in the street and treated like kidnappers. Homes were raided needlessly. Innocent families suffered.

The only public statement has been about Pearl, who has a warrant out for his arrest. Another one. I have taken to carrying my gun again. As long as he's out there, I'm going to keep it with me. I am not going to lose Samira again.

She has been staying with me since leaving hospital on Wednesday. Hari has moved out of the spare room and is sleeping downstairs on a sofa bed. He seems quite taken by our lodger. He has started wearing a shirt around the house because he senses that she disapproves.

I am to face a Police Disciplinary Tribunal. Neglect of duty, deliberate falsehood and abuse of authority are just three of the charges. Failing to show up at Hendon is the least of my worries. Barnaby Elliot has accused me of harassment and arson. The investigation is being supervised by the Police Complaints Authority. I am guilty until proven innocent.

A toilet flushes along the hallway. A light switch clicks off. A few minutes later comes the hum of a machine and the rhythmic suction of a breast pump. Samira's milk has come in and she has to express every six hours. The sound of the pump is strangely soporific. I close my eyes again.

She hasn't said anything about the twins. I keep wondering when she is going to crack, fragmented by the loss. Even when she identified Hassan's body at Westminster Mortuary she held it all inside.

"It's OK to cry," I told her.

"That is why Allah gave us tears," she answered.

"You think God played a part in this?"

"He would not give me this suffering if he did not think I could endure it."

How can she be so wise, yet so accepting? Can she really believe this is part of some grand master plan or that Allah would test her so cruelly?

Such faith seems positively medieval, yet she has an appetite for learning. Things that I take for granted she finds fascinating, like central heating, dual flush toilets and my washer/dryer. In Kabul she had to carry water upstairs to their flat and the power failed almost daily. London has lights along every street, burning through the night. Samira asked me if perhaps we British are scared of the dark. She didn't understand why I laughed.

I took her shopping for clothes at Canary Wharf yesterday. "There is not so much glass in all of Afghanistan," she said, pointing to the office towers that shone in the morning sun. I could see her studying the office workers queuing for coffee and "skinny" muffins: the women dressed in narrow skirts, tight tops and jackets, flicking their short hair, chatting on mobile phones.

The clothing boutiques intimidated her. The shop assistants were dressed like mourners and the shops felt like funeral parlors. I told Samira there was a better place to find clothes. We left and went to Commercial Road where garments were crammed on racks and spilling from bins. She chose two skirts, a long-sleeved blouse and a cardigan. It came to less than sixty pounds.

She studied the twenty-pound notes.

"Is this your Queen?"

"Yes."

"She looks like she has been dipped in plaster."

I laughed. "I guess she does."

The Christmas decorations were up. Even the bagel bakery and halal butcher had fairy lights and fake snow.

Samira stopped and peered into a lobster tank in the window of a restaurant.

"I am never going to swim in the sea."

"Why?"

"I don't want to meet one of them."

I think she had visions of lobsters crawling over one another in the same density as in the tank.

"This must be like science fiction to you."

"Science? Fiction?"

"It means like a fantasy. Unreal."

"Yes, unreal."

Seeing London through Samira's eyes has given me a different perspective on the city. Even the most mundane scene takes on a new life. When I took her underground to catch the Tube, she clutched my hand as an approaching train roared through the tunnel, sounding like a "monster in a cave," she said.

The casual wealth on display is embarrassing. There are more vets in the East End than there were doctors in Kabul. And the animals are better fed than the orphans.

The breast pump has stopped. She had turned on Hari's TV and is flicking between channels. Slipping out of bed, I tiptoe along the hall and knock on her door. She's wearing my old dressing gown, the one with an owl sewn onto the pocket.

"Can't you sleep?"

"No."

"I'll make us a sleeping potion."

Her eyes widen.

She follows me down the stairs, along the hall into the kitchen. I close the door and take a bottle of milk from the fridge, pouring it into mugs. Two minutes in the microwave and they're steaming. Breaking up pieces of dark chocolate, I drop them in the liquid, watching them melt. Samira uses a spoon to catch the melting shards, licking it clean.

"Tell me about your family."

"Most of them are dead."

She licks the spoon. I break off more pieces of chocolate and add them to her mug.

"Did you have a big family?"

"Not so big. In Afghanistan people exaggerate what their family has done. Mine is no different. One of my ancestors traveled to China with Marco Polo they say, but I don't believe it. I think he was a smuggler, who brought the black powder from India to Afghanistan. The king heard of the magic and asked to see a demonstration. According to my father, a thousand rockets streamed back and forth across the sky. Bamboo castles dripped with fire. Fireworks became our family business. The formulas were passed down from father to son—and to me."

I remember the photograph among Hassan's possessions showing a factory with workers lined up outside, most of them missing limbs or eyes, or incomplete in other ways. Hassan had burn scars on his arms.

"It must have been dangerous work."

Samira holds up her hands, showing her fingers. "I am one of the lucky ones." She sounds almost disappointed. "My father lost both his thumbs when a shell exploded. Uncle Yousuf lost his right arm and his wife lost her left arm. They helped each other to cook and sew and drive a car. My aunt changed gears and my uncle steered. My father's other brother, Fahad, lost his fingers during a display. He was a very good gambler but he began to lose when he couldn't shuffle the cards.

"I didn't meet my grandfather. He was killed in a factory explosion before I was born. Twelve others died in the same fire, including two of his brothers. My father said it was a sacrifice that only our family could make. One hand is enough to sin, he said. One hand is enough to save."

She glances at the dark square of the window. "It was our calling—to paint the sky. My father believed that one day our family would make a rocket that would light the way to Heaven. In the meantime, we would make rockets that drew the gaze of Allah in the hope that he would bless our family and bring us happiness and good health." She pauses and considers the irony of such a statement. Perfectly still, she is canted forward over the table, firm yet fragile. Her stare seems to originate at the back of her eyes.

"What happened to the factory?"

"The Talibs closed it down. Fireworks were sinful, they said. People celebrated when they arrived. They were going to stop the warlords and end the corruption. Things changed but not in a good way. Girls could not go to school. Windows were painted over so women could not be seen. There was no music or TV or videos, no card games or kites. I was ten years old and they made me wear a burka. I could not buy things from male shopkeepers. I could not talk to men. I could not laugh in public. Women had to be ordinary. Invisible. Ignorant. My mother educated us in secret. Books were hidden each night and homework had to be destroyed.

"Men with beards and black turbans patrolled the streets, listening for music and videos. They beat people with whips soaked in water and with chains. Some were taken away and didn't come back.

"My father took us to Pakistan. We lived in a camp. My mother died there and my father blamed himself. One day he announced that we were going home. He said he would rather starve in Kabul than live like a beggar."

She falls silent, shifting in her chair. The motor of the refrigerator rattles to life and I feel the same shudder pass through me.

"The Americans dropped leaflets from the sky saying they were coming to liberate us but there was nothing left to free us from. Still we cheered because the Talibs were gone, running, like frightened dogs. But the Northern Alliance was not so different. We had learned not to expect too much. In Afghanistan we sleep with the thorns and not the flowers."

The effort of remembering has made her sleepy. I wash the mugs and follow her upstairs. She pauses at my door, wanting to ask me something.

"I am not used to the quiet."

"You think London is quiet?"

She hesitates. "Would it be all right if I slept in your room?"

"Is there something wrong? Is it the bed?"

"No."

"Are you frightened?"

"No."

"What is it then?"

"At the orphanage we slept on the floor in the same room. I am not used to being alone."

My heart twists. "You should have said something earlier. Of course you can sleep with me."

She collects a blanket and spreads it on the floor beside my wardrobe.

"My bed is big enough. We can share."

"No, this is better."

She curls up on the floor and breathes so quietly that I want to make sure she's still there.

"Good night," I whisper. "May you sleep amid the flowers, not the thorns."

———

DI Forbes arrives in the morning, early as usual. Dressed in a charcoal suit and yellow tie, he is ready to front a news conference. The media blackout is being lifted. He needs help to find the twins.

I show him to the kitchen. "Your cold sounds better."

"I can't stomach another bloody banana."

Hari is with Samira in the sitting room. He is showing her his old Xbox and trying to explain what it does.

"You can shoot people."

"Why?"

"For fun."

"Why would you shoot people for *fun*?"

I can almost hear Hari's heart sinking. Poor boy. The two of them have something in common. Hari is studying chemical engineering and Samira knows more about chemical reactions than any of his lecturers, he says.

"She's an odd little thing," says Forbes, whispering.

"How do you mean?"

"She doesn't say much."

"Most people talk too much and have nothing to say."

"What is she going to do?" he asks.

"I don't know."

What would I do in her shoes? I have never been without friends or family or stranded in a foreign country (unless you count Wolverhampton, which is pretty bloody foreign).

Hari walks into the kitchen looking pleased with himself.

"Samira is going teach me to make fireworks," he announces, taking a biscuit from Forbes's plate.

"So you can blow yourself up," I say.

"I'm very careful."

"Oh yes. Like the time you filled that copper pipe with black powder and blew a hole in the wooden siding."

"I was fifteen."

"Old enough to know better."

"Sunday is Guy Fawkes Night. We're going to make a whistling chaser."

"Which is?"

"A rocket that whistles and has white-and-red stars with a salute at the end."

"A salute?"

"A big bang."

Hari has already compiled a list of ingredients: potassium nitrate, sulfur, barium chlorate and copper powder. I have no idea what this stuff does but I can almost see the fireworks exploding in his eyes.

Forbes looks at the list. "Is this stuff legal?"

"We're only making three-inch shells."

It doesn't answer the question but the detective lets it pass.

Although Samira doesn't mention the twins, I know she must think about them, just as I do. Rarely does a minute pass when my mind doesn't drift back to them. I can feel their skin against my lips and see their narrow rib cages moving with each breath. The baby girl had trouble breathing. Perhaps her lungs weren't fully developed. We have to find her.

Forbes has opened the car door and waits for Samira to sit in the rear seat. She is wearing her new clothes—a long woolen skirt and white blouse. She looks so composed. Still. There is a landscape inside her that I will never reach.

"You won't have to answer questions," the DI explains. "I'll help you prepare a statement."

He drives hunched over the wheel, frowning at the road, as if he hates city traffic. At the same time he talks. With the help of Spijker, he has managed to trace five asylum seekers impregnated at the fertility clinic in Amsterdam who subsequently turned up in the U.K.

"All admit to giving birth and claim the babies were taken from them. They were each given £500 and told their debt had been repaid."

"Where did they give birth?"

"A private address. They couldn't give an exact location. They were taken there in the back of a transit van with blacked-out windows. Two of them talked of planes coming in to land."

"It's under a flight path?"

"That's what I figure."

"Births have to be registered. Surely we can find the babies that way."

"It's not as easy as you think. Normally, the hospital or health authority informs the registrar of a birth but not when it happens in a private home or outside of the NHS. Then it's up to the parents. And how's this? Mum and Dad don't even have to turn up at the registry office. They can send along someone else—a witness to the birth or even just the owner of the house."

"Is that it? What about doctor's certificates or medical records?"

"Don't need them. You need more paperwork to register a car than a baby."

We're passing the Royal Chelsea Hospital on the Embankment before turning left over Albert Bridge and circling Battersea Park.

"What about Dr. Banerjee?"

"He admits to providing Cate Beaumont with her surplus embryos but claims to have no knowledge of the surrogacy plan. She told him she was transferring to a different fertility clinic with a higher success rate."

"And you believe him?"

Forbes shrugs. "The embryos belonged to her. She had every right to take them."

This still doesn't explain why Banerjee lied to me. Or why he turned up at my father's birthday party.

"What about Paul Donavon?"

"He did two tours of Afghanistan and six months in Iraq. Won the Queen's Gallantry Medal. The guy is a bona fide fucking hero."

Samira hasn't said a word. Sometimes I feel as if she has turned off or tuned out, or is listening to different voices.

"We are contacting the orphanage in Kabul as well as one in Albania and another in Russia," says Forbes. "Hopefully they can give us more than just a nickname."

The conference room is a stark, windowless place, with vinyl chairs and globe lights full of scorched moths. This used to be the old National Criminal Intelligence Service building, now refitted and rebranded to suit the new crime-fighting agency with new initials. Despite the headlines and high-tech equipment, SOCA still strikes me as being rather more Loch Ness than Eliot Ness—chasing shadowy monsters who live in dark places.

Radio reporters have taken up the front row, taping their station logos to the microphones. Press reporters slouch in the middle rows and their TV counterparts are at the rear with whiter teeth and better clothes.

When I did my detective training at Bramshill they sent us in groups to see an autopsy. I watched a pathologist working on the body of a hiker who had been dead for a fortnight.

Holding up a jar, he said, "This little fellow is a sarcophagid fly, but I like to refer to him as a crime reporter. Notice the red boozer eyes and his gray-checked abdomen, which is perfect for hiding food stains. More important, he's always first to find a corpse . . ."

Forbes looks at his watch. It's eleven o'clock. He straightens his tie and tugs at the sleeves of his suit.

"You ready?"

Samira nods.

Flashguns explode and render me blind as I follow Samira to the conference table. Photographers are fighting for position, holding cameras above their heads in a strange jiggling dance.

Forbes holds a chair for Samira, then reaches across the table to a jug of water and pours her a glass. His slightly pockmarked face is bleached by the brightness of the TV lights.

Clearing his throat he begins. "We are investigating the abduction of two newborn babies, a twin boy and girl, born in the early hours of Sunday morning on board a ferry between the Hook of Holland and Harwich. The *Stena Britannica* docked at 3:36 a.m. GMT and the babies were last seen thirty minutes earlier."

Flashguns fire in his eyes.

Forbes makes no mention of baby broking or illegal surrogacy. Instead he concentrates on the details of the voyage and abduction. An image of Brendan Pearl is projected onto the screen behind him, along with a detailed description.

"DC Barba was returning from a short stay in Amsterdam when she stumbled upon a people-trafficking operation. She helped deliver the twins but was unable to prevent the babies being taken.

"I want to stress that this is not a domestic dispute and Brendan Pearl is not related to the missing infants. Pearl is on parole after being released as a result of the Good Friday Agreement. He is considered dangerous. We are advising people not to approach him under any circumstances and to call the police if they know his whereabouts. Miss Khan will now make a brief statement."

He slides the microphone toward Samira. She looks at it suspiciously and unfolds a piece of paper. The flashguns create a wall of light and she stumbles over the first words. Someone shouts for her to speak up. She begins again.

"I wish to thank everyone who has looked after me these past few days, especially Miss Barba for helping me on the ferry when I was having the babies. I am also grateful to the police for all they have done. I ask the man who took the twins to give them back. They are very small and need medical care. Please take them to a hospital or leave them somewhere safe."

Samira looks up from the page. She's departing from

the script. "I forgive you for this but I do not forgive you for Zala. For this I hope you will suffer eternal agony for every second of every day for the rest of your life."

Forbes cups his hand over the microphone, trying to stop her. Samira stands to leave. Questions are yelled from the floor.

"Who is Zala?"

"Did you know Brendan Pearl?"

"Why did he take your babies?"

The story has more holes than a Florida ballot card. The reporters sense a bigger story. Decorum breaks down.

"Has there been a ransom demand?"

"How did Pearl get off the ferry with the twins?"

"Do you believe they're still alive?"

Samira flinches. She's almost at the door.

"What about names?"

She turns to the questioner, blinking into the flash-guns. "A maiden can leave things nameless; a mother must name her children."

The answer silences the room. People look at one another, wondering what she means. Mothers. Maidens. What does that have to do with anything?

———

Forbes's shoulders are knotted with rage.

"That was a fucking disaster," he mutters as I chase him down the corridor.

"It wasn't so bad."

"God knows what they're going to write tomorrow."

"They're going to write about the twins. That's what we want. We're going to find them."

He suddenly stops and turns. "That's only the beginning."

"What do you mean?"

"I want you to meet someone."

"When?"

"Now."

"The funerals are today."

"It won't take long." He glances ahead of us. Samira is waiting near the lift. "I'll make sure she gets home."

———

Twenty minutes later we pull up outside a Victorian mansion block in Battersea, overlooking the park. Twisting branches of Wisteria, naked and gray, frame the downstairs windows. The main door is open. An empty pram is poised, ready for an excursion. I can hear the mother coming down the stairs. She is attractive, in her early forties. A baby—too old to be one of the twins— rests on her hip.

"Excuse me, Mrs. Piper."

"Yes?"

"I'm Detective Inspector Forbes. This is DC Barba."

The woman's smile fades. Almost imperceptibly she tightens her hold on the child. A boy.

"How old is he?" I ask.

"Eight months."

"Aren't you beautiful." I lean forward. The mother leans away.

"What's his name?"

"Jack."

"He looks like you."

"He's more like his father."

Forbes interrupts. "We were hoping to have a brief word."

"I'm just going out. I have to meet someone."

"It won't take long."

Her gaze flicks from his face to mine. "I think I should call my husband." Pointedly she adds, "He works for the Home Office."

"Where did you have your baby?" Forbes asks.

She stutters nervously. "It was a home birth. I'm going upstairs to ring my husband."

"Why?" asks Forbes. "We haven't even told you why we're here, yet you're anxious about something. Why do you need your husband's permission to talk to us?"

There is a flaw in the moment, a ripple of disquiet.

Forbes continues: "Have you ever been to Amsterdam, Mrs. Piper? Did you visit a fertility clinic there?"

Backing away toward the stairs, she shakes her head, less in denial than in the vain hope that he'll stop asking her questions. She is on the stairs. Forbes moves toward her. He's holding a business card. She won't take it from him. Instead he leaves it in the pram.

"Please ask your husband to phone me."

I can hear myself apologizing for bothering her. At the same time I want to know if she paid for a baby. Who did she pay? Who arranged it? Forbes has hold of my arm, leading me down the steps. I imagine Mrs. Piper upstairs on the phone, the tears and the turmoil.

"Their names came up among the files Spijker sent me," Forbes explains. "They used a surrogate. A girl from Bosnia."

"Then it's *not* their baby."

"How do we prove that? You saw the kid. Paternity tests, DNA tests, blood samples—every one of them will show that young Jack belongs to the Pipers. And there isn't a judge in this country who would give us permission to take samples in the first place."

"We can prove they visited an IVF clinic in the Netherlands. We can prove their embryos were implanted in a surrogate. We can prove that it resulted in a pregnancy and a successful birth. Surely that's enough."

"It doesn't prove that money changed hands. We need one of these couples to give evidence."

He hands me a list of names and addresses:

Robert & Helena Piper
Alan & Jessica Case
Trevor & Toni Jury
Anaan & Lola Singh
Nicholas & Karin Pederson

"I have interviewed the other four couples. In each case they have called a lawyer and stuck to their story. None of them are going to cooperate—not if it means losing their child."

"They broke the law!"

"Maybe you're right, but how many juries are going to convict? If that was your friend back there, holding her baby, would *you* take it away from her?"

2

The funerals are at two o'clock. I am dressed in a black vest, black jacket, black trousers and black shoes. The only splash of color is my lipstick.

Samira uses the bathroom after me. It's hard to believe that she's just given birth. There are stretch marks across her belly but elsewhere her skin is flawless. Occasionally, I notice a tic or twitch of pain when she moves, but nothing else betrays her discomfort.

She is laying out her clothes on the bed, taking care not to crease her blouse.

"You don't have to come," I tell her, but she has already decided. She met Cate only twice. They spoke through Yanus in stilted sentences rather than having a proper conversation. Yet they shared a bond like no other. Unborn twins.

We sit side by side in the cab. She is tense, restless, as if at any moment she might unfurl a set of hidden wings and take flight. In the distance a chimney belches a column of white smoke like a steam train going nowhere.

"The police are going to find the twins," I announce, as if we're deep in conversation.

She doesn't answer.

I try again. "You do *want* to find them?"

"My debt is paid," she whispers, chewing at her lower lip.

"You *owe* these people nothing."

Again she doesn't answer. How can I make her understand? Without warning she offers an answer, placing her words in careful sentences.

"I have tried not to love them. I thought it would be easier to give them up if I did not love them. I have even tried to *blame* them for what happened to Hassan and Zala. This is unfair, yes? What else can I do? My breasts leak for them. I hear them crying in my dreams. I want the sound to stop."

Twin hearses are parked outside the chapel at the West London Crematorium. A carpet of artificial grass leads to a ramp where a small black sign with movable white letters spells out Felix's and Cate's names.

Samira walks with surprising grace along the gravel path—not an easy thing to do. She pauses to look at the marble and stone crypts. Gardeners lean on their shovels and watch her. She seems almost alien. Otherworldly.

Barnaby Elliot is welcoming people and accepting condolences. Ruth Elliot is next to him in her wheelchair, dressed in mourning clothes that make her skin seem bloodless and brittle.

She sees me first. Her mouth twists around my name. Barnaby turns and walks toward me. He kisses me on each cheek and I smell the sharp alcohol scent of his aftershave.

"Who did you see in Amsterdam?" he asks.

"A detective. Why did you lie about Cate's computer?"

He doesn't answer. Instead he raises his eyes to the trees, some of which are clinging to the yellow-and-gold remnants of autumn.

"I feel you should know that I have instructed a lawyer to gain custody of the twins. I want both of them."

I look at him incredulously.

"What about Samira?"

"They're *our* grandchildren. They belong with us."

"Not according to the law."

"The law is an ass."

I glance across at Samira, who is hanging back, perhaps sensing trouble. Barnaby shows no such discretion. "Does she even *want* them?" he says, too loudly.

I have to unclench my jaw to speak. "You stay away from her."

"Listen to me—"

"No! *You* listen! She has been through enough. She has lost *everything*."

Glaring at me with a sudden crazed energy, he lashes out at a hedge with his fist. His coat sleeve snags and he jerks it violently, tearing the fabric, which billows and flaps. Just as quickly he regains his composure. It's like watching a deep-breathing exercise for anger management. Reaching into his pocket, he takes out a business card.

"The trustee of Felix and Cate's will is having a meeting in chambers at Gray's Inn on Monday afternoon at three. He wants you there."

"Why?"

"He didn't say. This is the address."

I take the card and watch Barnaby return to his wife. Reaching for his hand, she cocks her head into his palm, holding it against her cheek. I have never seen them share a moment—not like this. Maybe it takes one tragedy to mend another.

The chapel is softly lit with red lights flickering behind glass. Flowers cover the coffins and spill out down the center aisle almost to Ruth Elliot's wheelchair. Barnaby is beside her, alongside Jarrod. All three of them are holding hands, as if steeling one another.

I recognize other family and friends. The only person missing is Yvonne. Perhaps she didn't think she could cope with a day like this. It must be like losing a daughter.

On the other side of the church are Felix's family, who look far more Polish than Felix ever did. The women are short and square, with veils on their heads and rosary beads in their fingers.

The funeral director is holding his top hat across his folded arm. His son, dressed identically, mimics his pose, although I notice a wad of chewing gum behind his ear.

A hymn strikes up, "Come Let Us Join Our Friends Above," which is not really Cate's cup of tea. Then again, it must be hard to find something appropriate for a person who once pledged her undying love to a photograph of Kurt Cobain.

Reading from the Bible, Reverend Lunn intones something about the Resurrection and how we're all going to rise together on the same day and live as God's children. At the same time, he rubs a finger along the edge of Cate's coffin as if admiring the workmanship.

"Love and pain are not the same," he says, "but sometimes it feels like they should be. Love is put to the test every day. Pain is not. Yet the two of them are inseparable because true love cannot bear separation."

His voice sounds far away. I have been in a state of suspended mourning for Cate for the past eight years. Trivial, sentimental, everyday sounds and smells bring back memories—lost causes, jazz shoes, cola slushies, Simply Red songs, a teenager singing into a hairbrush, purple eye shadow . . . These things make me want to smile or swell painfully in my chest. There it is again—love and pain.

I don't see the coffins disappear. During the final hymn I slip outside, needing fresh air. On the far side of the parking lot, in the shadows of an arch, I see a familiar silhouette, waiting, tranquil. He's wearing an overcoat and red muffler. Donavon.

Samira is walking through the rose garden at the side of the chapel. She is going to see him when she clears the corner.

Instinctively, I close the gap. Any witness would say that my body language borders on violence. I grab Donavon's arm, twisting it behind his back, before shoving him against a wall, pressing his face to the bricks.

"Where are they? What have you done with them?"

"I don't know what you're talking about."

I want him to struggle. I want to hurt him. Samira is behind me, hanging back.

"Do you know this man?"

"No."

"The Englishman you met at the orphanage. You said he had a cross on his neck." I pull aside Donavon's muffler, revealing his tattoo.

She shakes her head. "A gold cross. Here." She traces the outline on her collar.

Donavon laughs. "Wonderful detective work, yindoo."

I want to hit him.

"You were in Afghanistan."

"Serving Queen and country."

"Spare me the patriotic who-dares-wins crap. You lied to me. You saw Cate before the reunion."

"Yes."

"Why?"

"You wouldn't understand."

"Try me."

I let him go and he turns, blinking slowly, his pale eyes a little more bloodshot than I remember. Mourners are leaving the chapel. He glances at the crowd with a mixture of embarrassment and concern. "Not here. Let's talk somewhere else."

I let him lead the way. Leaving the cemetery, we walk east along the Harrow Road, which is choked with traffic and a conga line of buses. Sneaking side-long glances at Donavon, I watch how he regards Samira. He doesn't seem to recognize her. Instead he keeps his eyes lowered in a penitent's demeanor, framing answers to the questions that he knows are coming. More lies.

We choose a café with stools at the window and tables inside. Donavon glances at the menu, buying time. Samira slips off her chair and kneels at the magazine rack, turning the pages quickly, as though expecting someone to stop her.

"The magazines are free to read," I explain. "You're allowed to look at them."

Donavon twists the skin on his wrist, leaving a white weal. Blood rushes back to the slackened skin.

"I met Cate again three years ago," he announces. "It

was just before my first tour of Afghanistan. It took me a while to find her. I didn't know her married name."

"Why?"

"I wanted to see her."

I wait for something more. He changes the subject. "Have you ever been skydiving?"

"No."

"What a rush. There's no feeling like it—standing in the doorway of a plane at 10,000 feet, heart pounding, charged up. Take that last big step and the slipstream sucks you away. Falling—only it doesn't feel like falling at all. It's flying. Air presses hollows in your cheeks and screams past your ears. I've jumped high altitude, low opening, with oxygen from 25,000 feet. I swear I could open my arms and embrace the entire planet."

His eyes are shining. I don't know why he's telling me this but I let him continue.

"The best thing that ever happened to me was getting booted out of school and joining the Paras. Up until then I was drifting. Angry. I didn't have any ambition. It changed my life.

"I got a little girl now. She's three. Her mother doesn't live with me anymore, they're in Scotland, but I send 'em money every month and presents on her birthday and at Christmas. I guess what I'm trying to say is that I'm a different person."

"Why are you telling me this?"

"Because I want you to understand. You think I'm a thug and a bully but I changed. What I did to Cate was unforgivable but *she* forgave me. That's why I went looking for her. I wanted to find out how things turned out for her. I didn't want to think I screwed up her life because of what I did to her."

I don't want to believe him. I want to keep hating him because that's the world according to me. *My* recorded history.

"Why would Cate agree to see you?"

"She was curious I guess."

"Where did you meet?"

"We had a coffee in Soho."

"And?"

"We talked. I said I was sorry. She said it was OK. I wrote her a few letters from Afghanistan. Whenever I was home on leave we used to get together for lunch or a coffee."

"Why didn't you tell me this before?"

"Like I said, you wouldn't understand."

It's not a good enough reason. How could Cate forgive *Donavon* before she forgave me?

"What do you know about the New Life Adoption Center?"

"Cate took me there. She knew Carla couldn't decide what to do about the baby."

"How did Cate know about the adoption center?"

He shrugs. "Her fertility specialist is on the adoption panel."

"Dr. Banerjee. Are you sure?"

"Yeah."

Julian Shawcroft and Dr. Banerjee *know* each other. More lies.

"Did Cate tell you why she went to Amsterdam?"

"She said she was going to have another round of IVF."

I glance toward Samira. "She paid for a surrogate."

"I don't understand."

"There are twins."

390

Donavon looks dumbfounded. Speechless.

"Where?"

"They're missing."

I can see the knowledge register in his mind and match up with other details. News of the twins is already on the radio and in the early editions of the *Evening Standard*. I have shaken him more than I thought possible.

"What Cate did was illegal," I explain. "She was going to blow the whistle. That's why she wanted to talk to me."

Donavon has regained a semblance of composure. "Is that why they killed her?"

"Yes. Cate didn't accidentally find Samira. Someone put them together. I'm looking for a man called "Brother"—an Englishman, who came to Samira's orphanage in Kabul."

"Julian Shawcroft has been to Afghanistan."

"How do you know?"

"It came up in conversation. He was asking where I served."

I flip open my mobile and punch the speed dial. "New Boy" Dave answers on the second ring. I haven't talked to him since Amsterdam. He hasn't called. I haven't called. Inertia. Fear.

"Hello, sweet boy."

He sounds hesitant. I don't have time to ask why.

"When you did the background check on Julian Shawcroft, what did you find?"

"He used to be executive director of a Planned Parenthood clinic in Manchester."

"Before that."

"He studied theology at Oxford and then joined some sort of religious order."

"A religious order?"

"He became a Catholic brother."

There's the link! Cate, Banerjee, Shawcroft and Samira—I can tie them together.

Dave is no longer on the phone. I can't remember saying goodbye.

Donavon has been talking to me, asking questions. I haven't been listening.

"Did they look like Cate?" he asks.

"Who?"

"The twins."

I don't know how to answer. I'm not good at describing newborn babies. They all look like Winston Churchill. Why should he care?

3

A silver-colored Lexus pulls into the driveway of a detached house in Wimbledon, South London. It has a personalized number plate: BABYDOC. Sohan Banerjee collects his things from the backseat and triggers the central locking. Lights flash. If only everything in life could be achieved with the press of a button.

"The penalty for people trafficking is fourteen years," I say.

The doctor wheels around, clutching his briefcase to his stomach like a shield. "I don't know what you're talking about."

"I don't know the penalty for commercial surrogacy but when you add medical rape and kidnapping I'm sure you'll be in prison long enough to make new friends."

"I've done nothing wrong."

"And I almost forgot murder. An automatic life sentence."

"You're trespassing," he blusters.

"Call the police."

He looks toward his house and then at the houses nearby perhaps conscious of what his neighbors might think.

"You *knew* Cate Beaumont was going to Amsterdam. You gave her a liquid nitrogen canister with her remaining embryos. You told her about the Dutch clinic."

"No. No." His chins are wobbling.

"Were you going to deliver the twins?"

"I don't know what you're talking about."

"How well do you know Julian Shawcroft?"

"We have a professional relationship."

"You were at Oxford together. He was studying theology. You were studying medicine. See how much I know, Dr. Banerjee? Not bad for some uppity Sikh girl who can't get a husband."

His briefcase is still resting on the shelf of his stomach. My skin prickles with something more physical than loathing.

"You're on his adoption panel."

"An independent body."

"You told Cate about the New Life Adoption Center. You introduced her to Shawcroft. What did you imagine you were doing? This wasn't some humanitarian crusade to help the childless. You got into bed with sex traffickers and murderers. Young women have been raped and exploited. People have died."

"You've got it all wrong. I had nothing to do with any of that. What motive would I have?"

Motive? I still don't understand why Banerjee would get mixed up in something like this. It can't be the money. Maybe he was trapped or tricked into doing a "favor." It takes only one mistake and the hooks are planted.

He looks toward the house again. There is no wife waiting for him inside. No children at the door.

"It's personal isn't it?"

He doesn't answer.

Forbes showed me a list of names. They were couples who provided embryos to the IVF clinic in Amsterdam. A surname suddenly stands out—Anaan and Lola Singh from Birmingham.

"Do you have family in the U.K., Dr. Banerjee? A sister, perhaps? Any nieces or nephews?"

He wants to deny it but the truth is imprinted on his features like fingerprints in putty. Mama mentioned that he had a nephew. The good doctor was so proud he told stories about him over Sunday lunch. I take a stab at the rest of the story. His sister couldn't get pregnant. And not even her very clever brother—a fertility specialist—could help her.

Julian Shawcroft suggested there might be another way. He organized a surrogate mother in the Netherlands and Banerjee delivered the baby. He thought it was a one-off—a family matter—but Shawcroft wanted him to deliver other babies. He couldn't say no.

"What do you want from me?"

"Give me Julian Shawcroft."

"I can't do that."

"Are you worried about your career, your reputation?"

Banerjee smiles wryly—a defeated gesture. "I have lived in this country for two-thirds of my life, Alisha. I hold master's and doctoral degrees from Oxford and Harvard. I have published papers, lectured and been a visiting fellow at the University of Toronto." He glances again at his house, the drawn curtains and empty rooms beyond. "My reputation is *all* I have."

"You broke the law."

"Is it so very wrong? I thought we were helping the childless and offering a new life to asylum seekers."

"You exploited them."

"We saved them from orphanages."

"And forced some of them into brothels."

His dense eyebrows are knitted together.

"Give me Shawcroft. Make a statement."

"I must protect my sister and her child."

"By protecting *him*?"

"We protect each other."

"I could have you arrested."

"I will deny everything."

"At least tell me where the twins are."

"I don't meet the families. Julian arranges that side of things." His voice changes. "I beg you, leave this alone. Only bad things can come of it."

"For whom?"

"For everyone. My nephew is a beautiful boy. He's nearly one."

"When he grows up are you going to tell him about the medical rape that led to his conception?"

"I'm sorry."

Everyone is sorry. It must be the times.

4

Forbes shuffles a stack of photographs and lays them out on a desk in three rows as if he's playing solitaire. Julian Shawcroft's picture is on the right edge. He looks like a charity boss straight from central casting: warm, smiling, avuncular . . .

"If you recognize someone I want you to point to the photograph," the detective says.

Samira hesitates.

"Don't worry about getting anyone in trouble—just tell me if there is someone here who you've met before."

Her eyes travel over the photographs and suddenly stop. She points to Shawcroft.

"This one."

"Who is he?"

"Brother."

"Do you know his real name?"

She shakes her head.

"How do you know him?"

"He came to the orphanage."

"In Kabul."

She nods.

"What was he doing there?"

"He brought blankets and food."

"Did you talk to him?"

"He couldn't speak Afghani. I translated for him."

"What did you translate?"

"He had meetings with Mr. Jamal, the director. He said he could arrange jobs for some of the orphans. He wanted only girls. I told him I could not leave without Hassan. He said it would cost more money but I could repay him."

"How much?"

"Five thousand American dollars for each of us."

"How were you supposed to repay this money?"

"He said God would find a way for me to pay."

"Did he say anything about having a baby?"

"No."

Forbes takes a sheet of paper from a folder. "This is a list of names. I want you to tell me if you recognize any of them."

Samira's finger dips down the page and stops. "This girl, Allegra, she was at the orphanage."

"Where did she go?"

"She left before me. Brother had a job for her."

The detective smiles tightly. "He certainly did."

Forbes's office is on the second floor, opposite a large open-plan incident room. There is a photograph of his wife on a filing cabinet. She looks like a no-nonsense country girl, who has never quite managed to shed the baby pounds.

He asks Samira to wait outside. There's a drink

machine near the lift. He gives her change. We watch her walk away. She looks so young—a woman in progress.

"We have enough for a warrant," I say. "She identified Shawcroft."

Forbes doesn't answer. What is he waiting for? He stacks the photographs, lining up the edges.

"We can't link him with the surrogacy plot. It's her word against his."

"But the other orphans—"

"Have talked about a saintly man who offered to help them. We can't *prove* Shawcroft arranged for them to be trafficked. And we can't *prove* he blackmailed them into getting pregnant. We need one of the buyers to give evidence, which means incriminating themselves."

"Could we indemnify them from prosecution?"

"Yes, but we can't indemnify them against a civil lawsuit. Once they admit to paying for a surrogate baby, the birth mother could reclaim her child."

I can hear it in his voice—resignation. The task is proving too hard. He won't give up but neither will he go the extra yard, make the extra call, knock on one more door. He thinks I'm clutching at straws, that I haven't thought this through. I have never been more certain.

"Samira should meet him."

"What?"

"She could wear a wire."

Forbes sucks air through his teeth. "You gotta be kidding! Shawcroft would see right through it. He *knows* we have her."

"Yes, but investigations are about building pressure. Right now he thinks we can't touch him. He's comfortable.

We have to shake him up—take him out of his comfort zone."

There are strict rules governing the bugging of phones and properties. The surveillance commissioner has to grant permission. But a wire is different—as long as she stays in a public place.

"What would she say?"

"He promised her a job."

"Is that it?"

"She doesn't *have* to say anything. Let's see what *he* says."

Forbes crunches a throat lozenge between his teeth. His breath smells of lemons.

"Is she up for it?"

"I think so."

5

Any sport can be made to sound ridiculous if you break it down to its basics—stick, ball, hole—but I have never really understood the appeal of golf. The courses are pretty in an artificial sort of way, like Japanese gardens planned down to the last pebble and shrub.

Julian Shawcroft plays every Sunday morning in the same foursome, with a town planner, a car dealer and a local businessman. They tee off just after ten.

Their club is on the border of Sussex and Surrey, somewhere in the greenbelt and the white stockbroker belt. Brown is a color rarely seen out here unless you take a big divot.

Samira has a battery the size of a matchbox taped to the small of her back and a thin red fiber threaded under her right armpit to a button-sized microphone taped between her breasts.

Adjusting her blouse, I lift my eyes to hers and smile reassuringly. "You don't have to go through with this."

She nods.

"Do you know what you're going to say?"

Another nod.

"If you get frightened, walk away. If you feel threatened, walk away. Any sign of trouble, you understand?"

"Yes."

Groups of golfers are milling outside the locker room and on the practice green, waiting for the starter to call their names. Shawcroft has the loudest laugh but not the loudest trousers, which belong to one of his playing partners. He takes a practice swing beside the first tee and looks up to see Samira standing at the top of a set of stone steps with the sun behind her. He shields his eyes.

Without hesitation, she moves toward him, stopping six feet away.

"Can I help you?" asks one of the other golfers.

"I've come to see Brother."

Shawcroft hesitates, looking past her. He is searching for us.

"Nobody called Brother here, lass," says the car dealer.

Samira points. They turn to Shawcroft, who stutters a denial. "I don't know who she is."

Forbes adjusts the volume on the digital recording equipment. We're watching from eighty yards away, parked beneath the branches of a plane tree, opposite the pro shop.

Samira is a foot shorter than any of the men. Her long skirt flares out in the breeze.

"Maybe she can caddy for you, Julian?" one of them jokes.

"You remember me, Brother," says Samira. "You told me to come. You said you had a job for me."

Shawcroft looks at his playing partners apologetically. Suspicion is turning to anger. "Just ignore her. Let's play."

Turning his back, he takes a hurried practice swing and then sprays his opening drive wildly to the right where it disappears into trees. He tosses his club to the ground in disgust.

The others tee off. Shawcroft is already at the wheel of a golf cart. It jerks forward and accelerates away.

"I told you he wouldn't fall for this," says Forbes.

"Wait. Look."

Samira floats down the fairway after them, the hem of her skirt growing dark with dew. The carts have separated. Shawcroft is looking for his wayward drive in the rough. He glances up and sees her coming. I hear him yelling to his partner. "Lost ball. I'll hit another."

"You haven't even looked for this one."

"It doesn't matter."

He drops another ball and hacks it out, looking more like a woodchopper than a golfer. The cart takes off again. Samira doesn't break stride.

I feel a lump in my throat. This girl never ceases to amaze me. She follows them all the way to the green, skirting the bunkers and crossing a small wooden bridge over a brook. Constantly looking over his shoulder, Shawcroft thrashes at the ball and hurries forward.

"She's going to walk out of range," says Forbes. "We have to stop her."

"Wait. Just a little longer."

The foursome are more than 300 yards away but I can see them clearly enough through binoculars. Samira is standing on the edge of the green, watching and waiting.

Shawcroft finally snaps. "Get off this golf course or I'll have you arrested."

Waving his club, he storms toward her. She doesn't flinch.

"Steady on, old boy," someone suggests.

"Who is she, Julian?" asks another.

"Nobody."

"She's a pretty thing. She could be your ball washer."

"Shut up! Just shut up!"

Samira hasn't moved. "I paid my debt, Brother."

"I don't know what you're talking about."

"You said God would find a way for me to pay. I paid it twice. Twins. I paid for Hassan and for me, but he's dead. Zala didn't make it either."

Shawcroft grabs her roughly by the arm and hisses, "I don't know who sent you here. I don't know what you want, but I can't help you."

"What about the job?"

He is walking her away from the group. One of his partners yells, "Where are you off to, Julian?"

"I'm going to have her thrown off the course."

"What about the round?"

"I'll catch up."

The car dealer mutters, "Not again."

Another foursome is already halfway down the fairway. Shawcroft marches past them still holding Samira by the arm. She has to run to keep from falling.

"You're hurting me."

"Shut up, you stupid slut. I don't know what you're playing at but it won't work. Who sent you here?"

"I paid my debt."

"Fuck the debt! There is no job! This is harassment. You come near me again and I'll have you arrested."

Samira doesn't give up. God, she's good.

"Why did Hassan die?"

"It's called life. Stuff happens."

I don't believe it. He's quoting Donald Rumsfeld. Why doesn't stuff happen to people like Shawcroft?

"It took me a long while to find you, Brother. We waited in Amsterdam for you to come or to send word. In the end we couldn't wait any longer. They were going to send us back to Kábul. Hassan came alone. I wanted to go with him but he said I should wait." Her voice is breaking. "He was going to find you. He said you had forgotten your promise. I told him you were honorable and kind. You brought us food and blankets at the orphanage. You wore the cross . . ."

Shawcroft twists her wrist, trying to make her stop.

"I had the babies. I paid my debt."

"Will you shut up!"

"Someone killed Zala—"

"I don't know what you're talking about."

They're nearing the clubhouse. Forbes is out of the car, moving toward them. I hang back. Shawcroft flings Samira into a flower bed. She bangs her knee and cries out.

"That qualifies as assault."

Shawcroft looks up and sees the detective. Then he looks past him and spies me.

"You have no right! My lawyer will hear about this."

Forbes hands him an arrest warrant. "Fine. For your sake I hope he's not playing golf today."

6

Shawcroft regards himself as an intellectual and a text-book lawyer, although he seems to have mixed up the Crimes Act and the Geneva convention as he yells accusations of inhuman treatment from his holding cell.

Intellectuals show off too much and wise people are just plain boring. (My mother is forever telling me to save money, go to bed early and not to lend things.) I prefer clever people who hide their talents and don't take themselves too seriously.

A dozen officers are going through the files and computer records of the New Life Adoption Center. Others are at Shawcroft's house in Hayward's Heath. I don't expect them to find a paper trail leading to the twins. He's too careful for that.

There is, however, a chance that prospective buyers initially came to the center looking to adopt legally. At our first meeting I asked him about the brochure I found at Cate's house, which advertised a baby boy born to a prostitute. Shawcroft was adamant that all adopting parents were properly screened. This should mean interviews, psych reports and criminal background checks. If he was telling me the truth then whoever has the twins could once have been on a waiting list at the adoption center.

It is four hours since we arrested him. Forbes arranged to bring him through the front door, past the public waiting area. He wanted to cause maximum discomfort and embarrassment. Although experienced, I sense that Forbes is not quite in the same league as Ruiz, who knows exactly when to be hard-nosed and when to let someone sweat for another hour in a holding cell, alone with their demons.

Shawcroft is waiting for his lawyer, Eddie Barrett. I could have guessed he would summon the "Bulldog," an old-fashioned ambulance chaser with a reputation for courting the media and getting right up police noses. He and Ruiz are old adversaries, sharing a mutual loathing and grudging respect.

Wolf whistles and howls of laughter erupt in the corridor. Barrett has arrived, dressed in jeans, cowboy boots, a plaid shirt and a ten-gallon hat.

"Look it's Willie Nelson!" someone calls.

"Is that a six-shooter in your pocket, Eddie, or are you just dawg-gone pleased to see me?"

Someone breaks into a hoedown. Eddie tucks his thumbs into his belt and gives them a few boot-scootin' moves. He doesn't seem to mind them taking the mickey out of him. Normally it's the other way round and he makes police look foolish during interviews or in court.

Barrett is a strange-looking man with an upside-down body (short legs and a long torso), and he walks just like George W. Bush with his arms held away from his body, his back unnaturally straight and his chin in the air. Maybe it's a cowboy thing.

One of the uniforms escorts him to an interview room. Shawcroft is brought upstairs. Forbes slips a plastic plug into his ear—a receiver that will allow us to talk to him during the interrogation. He takes a bundle of files and a list of questions. This is about *looking* prepared as much as *being* prepared.

I don't know if the DI is nervous but I can feel the tension. This is about the twins. Unless Shawcroft cracks or cooperates we may never find them.

The charity boss is still wearing his golfing clothes. Barrett sits next to him, placing his cowboy hat on the table. The formalities are dispensed with—names, the location and time of interview. Forbes then places five photographs on the table. Shawcroft doesn't bother looking at them.

"These five asylum seekers allege that you convinced them to leave their homelands and illegally enter the U.K."

"No."

"You deny knowing them?"

"I may have met them. I don't recall."

"Perhaps if you looked at their faces."

Barrett interrupts. "My client has answered your question."

"Where might you have met them?"

"My charities raised more than half a million pounds last year. I visited orphanages in Afghanistan, Iraq, Albania and Kosovo."

"How do you know these women are orphans? I didn't mention that."

Shawcroft stiffens. I can almost see him silently admonish himself for slipping up.

"So you *do* know these women?"

"Perhaps."

"And you know Samira Khan?"

"Yes."

"Where did you meet her?"

"At an orphanage in Kabul."

"Did you talk about her coming to the U.K.?"

"No."

"Did you offer her a job here?"

"No." He smiles his blameless smile.

"You introduced her to a man who smuggled her to the Netherlands and then to Britain."

"No."

"The cost was five thousand U.S. dollars but it rose to ten thousand by the time she reached Turkey. You told her that God would find a way for her to repay this money."

"I meet many orphans on my travels, Detective, and I don't think there has ever been one of them who didn't want to leave. It's what they dream about. They tell one another bedtime stories of escaping to the West where even beggars drive cars and dogs are put on diets because there is so much food."

Forbes places a photograph of Brendan Pearl on the table. "Do you know this man?"

"I can't recall."

"He is a convicted killer."

"I'll pray for him."

"What about his victims—will you pray for them?" Forbes is holding a photograph of Cate. "Do you know this woman?"

"She might have visited the adoption center. I can't be sure."

"She wanted to adopt?"

Shawcroft shrugs.

"You will have to answer verbally for the tape," says Forbes.

"I *can't* recall."

"Take a closer look."

"There's nothing wrong with my eyesight, Detective."

"What about your memory?"

Barrett interrupts. "Listen, Dr. Phil, it's Sunday. I got better things to do than listen to you stroke your pole. How about you tell us what my client is supposed to have done?"

Forbes shows admirable restraint. He places another photograph on the table, this one of Yanus. The questions continue. The answers are the same: "I cannot recall. I do not remember."

Julian Shawcroft is not a pathological liar (why tell a lie when the truth can serve you better?) but he is a natural deceiver and it comes as easily to him as breathing. Whenever Forbes has him under pressure, he carefully unfurls a patchwork of lies, tissue-thin yet carefully wrought, repairing any flaw in the fabric before it becomes a major tear. He doesn't lose his temper or show any anxiety. Instead he projects a disquieting calmness and a firm, fixed gaze.

Among the files at the adoption center are the names of at least twelve couples that also appear on paperwork from the IVF clinic in Amsterdam. I relay the information to Forbes via a transmitter. He touches his ear in acknowledgment.

"Have you ever been to Amsterdam, Mr. Shawcroft?" he asks.

I speak it here, it comes out there—like magic.

410

"Several times."

"Have you visited a fertility clinic in Amersfoort?"

"I don't recall."

"Surely you would remember this clinic." Forbes relates the name and address. "I doubt if you visit so many."

"I am a busy man."

"Which is why I'm sure you keep diaries and appointment calendars."

"Yes."

"Why haven't we found any?"

"I don't keep my schedule more than a few weeks before throwing it out. I deplore clutter."

"Can you explain how couples who were screened by your adoption center also appear in the files of an IVF clinic in Amsterdam?"

"Perhaps they were getting IVF treatment. People who want to adopt often try IVF first."

Barrett is gazing at the ceiling. He's in danger of getting bored.

"These couples didn't have IVF treatment," says Forbes. "They provided embryos that were implanted in the wombs of asylum seekers who were forced to carry pregnancies to term before the babies were taken from them."

Forbes points to the five photographs on the table. "These women, Mr. Shawcroft, the same women you met at different orphanages, the same women you encouraged to leave. They have identified you. They have provided statements to the police. And each one of them remembers you telling them the same thing: 'God will find a way for you to repay your debt.' "

Barrett takes hold of Shawcroft's arm. "My client wishes to exercise his right to silence."

Forbes gives the textbook reply. "I hope your client is aware that negative inferences can be drawn by the courts if he fails to mention facts that he later relies upon in his defense."

"My client is aware of this."

"Your client should also be aware that he has to remain here and listen to my questions, whether he answers them or not."

Barrett's small dark eyes are glittering. "You do what you have to, Detective Inspector. All we've heard so far is a bunch of fanciful stories masquerading as facts. So what if my client talked to these women? You have no evidence that he organized their illegal entry into this country. And no evidence that he was involved in this Goebbels-like fairy tale about forced pregnancies and stolen babies."

Barrett is perfectly motionless, poised. "It seems to me, Detective, that your entire case rests on the testimony of five illegal immigrants who would say anything to stay in this country. You want to make a case based on that—bring it on."

The lawyer gets to his feet, smooths his boot-cut jeans and adjusts his buffalo-skull belt buckle. He glances at Shawcroft. "My advice to you is to remain silent." He opens the door and swaggers down the corridor, hat in hand. There's that walk again.

7

"Penny for the Guy."

A group of boys with spiky haircuts are loitering on the corner. The smallest one has been dressed up as a tramp in oversize clothes. He looks like he's fallen victim to a shrinking ray.

One of the other boys nudges him. "Show 'em yer teef, Lachie."

Lachie opens his mouth sullenly. Two of them are blacked out.

"Penny for the Guy," they chorus again.

"You're not going to throw him on a bonfire I hope."

"No, ma'am."

"Good." I give them a pound.

Samira has been watching. "What are they doing?"

"Collecting money for fireworks."

"By begging?"

"Not exactly."

Hari has explained to her about Guy Fawkes Night. That's why the two of them have spent the past two days in my garden shed, dressed like mad scientists in cotton clothes, stripped of anything that might create static electricity or cause a spark.

"So this Guy Fawkes, he was a terrorist?"

"Yes, I suppose he was. He tried to blow up the Houses of Parliament with barrels of gunpowder."

"To kill the King?"

"Yes."

"Why?"

"He and his coconspirators weren't happy with the way the King was treating Catholics."

"So it was about religion."

"I guess."

She looks at the boys. "And they celebrate this?"

"When the plot failed, people set off fireworks in celebration and burned effigies of Guy Fawkes. They still do." Never let anyone tell you that Protestants don't hold a grudge.

Samira silently contemplates this as we make our way toward Bethnal Green. It's almost six o'clock and the air is already heavy with the smell of smoke and sulfur. Bonfires are dotted across the grass with families clustered around them, rugged up against the cold.

My entire family has come to see the fireworks. Hari is in his element, having emerged from the back shed carrying an old ammunition box containing the fruits of his labor and Samira's expertise. I don't know how he managed to source what she needed: the various chemicals, special salts and metallic powders. The most important ingredient, black powder, came from a hobby shop in Notting Hill, or more specifically from model rocket motors that were carefully disassembled to obtain the solid fuel propellant.

414

Torches dance across the grass and small fireworks are being lit: stick rockets, Roman candles, flying snakes, crackle dragons and bags of gold. Children are drawing in the air with sparklers and every dog in London is barking, keeping every baby awake. I wonder if the twins are among them. Perhaps they are too young to be frightened by the noise.

I hook my arm through Bada's and we watch Samira and Hari plant a heavy plastic tube in the earth. Samira has pulled her skirt between her legs and wrapped it tightly around her thighs. Her headscarf is tucked beneath the collar of her coat.

"Who would give him such knowledge?" says Bada. "He'll blow himself up."

"He'll be fine."

Hari has always been a favorite among equals. As the youngest, he has had my parents to himself for the past six years. I sometimes think he's their last link to middle age.

Shielding a pale tapered candle in the palm of her hand, Samira crouches close to the ground. One or two seconds elapse. A rocket whizzes into the air and disappears. One, two, three seconds pass until it suddenly explodes high above us, dripping stars that melt into the darkness. Compared with the fireworks that have come before, it is higher, brighter and louder. People stop their own displays to watch.

Hari sings out the names—dragon's breath, golden phoenix, glitter palm, exploding apples—while Samira moves without fuss between the launch tubes. Meanwhile, ground shells shoot columns of sparks around her and the explosions of color are mirrored in her eyes.

The finale is Hari's whistling chaser. Samira lets him

light the fuse. It screams upward until little more than a speck of light detonates into a huge circle of white like a dandelion. Just when it seems about to fade, a red ball of light explodes within the first. The final salute is a loud bang that rattles the neighboring windows, setting off car alarms. The crowd applauds. Hari takes a bow. Samira is already cleaning up the scorched cardboard tubes and shredded paper, which she packs into the old ammunition box.

Hari is buzzing. "We should celebrate," he says to Samira. "I'll take you out."

"Out?"

"Yes."

"Where is out?"

"I don't know. We could have a drink or see a band."

"I do not drink."

"You could have a juice or a soft drink."

"I cannot go out with you. It's not good for a girl to be alone with a boy."

"We wouldn't be alone. The pub is always packed."

"She means without a chaperone," I tell him.

"Oh. Right."

I sometimes wonder why Hari is considered the brightest among my brothers. He looks crestfallen.

"It's a religious thing, Hari."

"But I'm not religious."

I give him a clip round the ear.

I still haven't told Samira about what happened at Shawcroft's interview or, more important, what *didn't* happen. The charity boss gave us nothing. Forbes had to let him go.

How do I explain the rules of evidence and the notion

of burden of proof to someone who has never been afforded the luxury of justice or fairness?

On the walk home we drop behind the others, and I hook my arm in Samira's.

"But he did these things," she says, turning to face me. "None of this would have happened without him. Hassan and Zala would still be here. So many people are dead." She lowers her gaze. "Perhaps they are the lucky ones."

"You mustn't think such a thing."

"Why not?"

"Because the twins are going to need a mother."

She cuts me off with a slash of her hand. "I will *never* be their mother!"

Her face has changed. Twisted. I am looking at another face beneath the first, a dangerous one. It lasts only a fraction of a second—long enough to unsettle me. She blinks and it's gone. I have her back again.

We are almost home. A car has slowed about fifty yards behind us, edging forward without closing the gap. Fear crawls down my throat. I reach behind my back and untuck my shirt. The Glock is holstered at the base of my spine.

Hari has already turned into Hanbury Street. Mama and Bada have gone home. Opposite the next streetlight is a footpath between houses. Samira has noticed the car.

"Don't look back," I tell her.

As we pass under the streetlight, I push her toward the footpath, yelling at her to run. She obeys without question. I spin to face the car. The driver is in shadow. I aim the pistol at his head and he raises his hands, palms open like a mime artist pressing against a glass wall.

A rear window lowers. The interior light blinks on. I

swing my gun into the opening. Julian Shawcroft has one hand on the door and the other holding what could be a prayer book.

"I want to show you something," he says.

"Am I going to disappear?"

He looks disappointed. "Trust in God to protect you."

"Will you take me to the twins?"

"I will help you understand."

A gust of wind, a splatter of raindrops, the night is growing blustery and bad-tempered. Across London people are heading home and bonfires are burning down. We cross the river and head south through Bermondsey. The glowing dome of St. Paul's is visible between buildings and above the treetops.

Shawcroft is silent. I can see his face in the passing beams of headlights as I nurse my gun and he nurses his book. I should be frightened. Instead I feel a curious calmness. My only phone call has been to home—checking to make sure that Samira made it safely.

The car pulls off the road into a driveway and stops in a rear courtyard.

I step out and see the driver's face for the first time across the vehicle's glistening roof. It's not Brendan Pearl. I didn't expect it to be. Shawcroft isn't foolish enough to be seen with a known killer.

A woman dressed in a French peasant skirt and oversize sweater appears at Shawcroft's side. Her hair is pinned back so tightly it raises her eyebrows.

"This is Delia," he says. "She runs one of my charities."

I shake a smooth dry hand.

Delia leads us through double doors and up a narrow staircase. There are posters on the walls with confronting images of hunger and neglect. Among them is a photograph of an African child with a distended stomach and begging bowl eyes. In the bottom corner there is a logo, a clock with letters instead of numbers spelling out O.R.P.H.A.N.W.A.T.C.H.!

Reaching behind me, I slide the gun into its holster.

We arrive at an office with desks and filing cabinets. A computer screen, dark and asleep, is silhouetted against the window. Shawcroft turns to Delia: "Is it open?"

She nods.

I follow him into a second room, which is fitted out as a small home theater with a screen and a projector. There are more posters on the walls, along with newspaper clippings, some dog-eared, torn or frayed at the edges. A small girl in a dirty white dress peers at the camera; a young boy with his arms folded eyes me defiantly. There are other images, dozens of them, papering the walls beneath display lights that have turned them into tragic works of art.

"These are the ones we could save," he says, his pale priestly hands clasped before him.

The wall panels are concertinaed. He expands them, revealing yet more photographs.

"Remember the orphans from the Asian tsunami? Nobody knows their true number but some estimates put it at 20,000. Homeless. Destitute. Traumatized. Families were queuing up to adopt them; governments were besieged with offers; but almost every one of them was refused."

His gaze slides over me. "Shall I tell you what happened to the tsunami orphans? In Sri Lanka the Tamil

Tigers recruited them as soldiers, boys as young as seven. In India greedy relatives fought over the children because of the relief money being offered by the government and abandoned them once the money was paid.

"In Indonesia the authorities refused adoption to any couple who weren't Muslim. Troops dragged 300 orphans from a rescue flight because it was organized by a Christian charity. They were left with nowhere to go and nothing to eat. Even countries like Thailand and India that allow foreign adoptions suddenly closed their borders—spooked by unconfirmed stories of orphans being trafficked out of the country by gangs of pedophiles. It was ridiculous. If someone robs a bank you don't shut down the international banking system. You catch the robber. You prosecute them. Unfortunately, each time a child is trafficked they want to shut down the international adoption system, making things worse for millions of orphans.

"People don't understand the sheer scale of this problem. Two million children are forced into prostitution every year—a million of them in Asia. And more children are orphaned every *week* in Africa than were orphaned by the Asian tsunami. There are thirteen million in sub-Saharan Africa alone.

"The so-called experts say children shouldn't be treated as commodities. Why not? Isn't it better to be treated as a commodity than to be treated like a dog? Hungry. Cold. Living in squalor. Sold into slavery. Raped. They say it shouldn't be about money. What else is it going to be about? How else are we going to save them?"

"You think the end justifies the means."

"I think it *should* be a factor."

"You can't treat people like a resource."

"Of course I can. Economists do it all the time. I'm a pragmatist."

"You're a monster."

"At least I give a damn. The world needs people like me. Realists. Men of action. What do you do? Sponsor a child in Burundi or pledge to Comic Relief. You try to save one, while ten thousand others starve."

"And what's the alternative?"

"Sacrifice one and save ten thousand."

"Who chooses?"

"Pardon?"

"Who chooses the one you're going to sacrifice?"

"I choose. I don't ask others to do it for me."

I hate him then. For all his dark charm and elegant intensity, Shawcroft is a bully and a zealot. I prefer Brendan Pearl's motives. At least he doesn't try to justify his killings.

"What happens if the odds change?" I ask. "Would you sacrifice five lives to save five hundred? What about ten lives to save eleven?"

"Let's ask the people, shall we?" he replies sarcastically. "I get eleven votes. You only get ten. I win."

Fleetingly, unnervingly, I understand what he's saying but cannot accept a world that is so brutally black and white. Murder, rape and torture are the apparatus of terrorists, not of civilized societies. If we become like them, what hope do we have?

Shawcroft thinks he's a moral man, a charitable man, a saintly man, but he's not. He's been corrupted. He has become part of the problem instead of the solution—trafficking women, selling babies, exploiting the vulnerable.

"Nothing gives you the right to choose," I tell him.

"I accepted the role."

"You think you're God!"

"Yes. And do you know why? Because someone has to be. Bleeding hearts like you only pay lip service to the poor and destitute. You wear colored bands on your wrists and claim that you want to make poverty history. How?"

"This isn't about me."

"Yes it is."

"Where are the twins?"

"Being loved."

"Where?"

"Where they belong."

The pistol is resting against the small of my back, warm as blood. My fingers close around it. In a single motion I swing it toward him, pressing the muzzle against his forehead.

I expect to see fear. Instead he blinks at me sadly. "This is like a war, Alisha. I know we use that term too readily, but sometimes it is justified and some wars are just. The war on poverty. The war on hunger. Even pacifists cannot be opposed to wars such as these. Innocent people get hurt in conflict. Your friend was a casualty."

"You sacrificed her."

"To protect others."

"Yourself."

My finger tightens on the trigger. Another half pound of pressure and it's over. He is watching me along the barrel—still not frightened. For a brief moment I think he's prepared to die, having said his piece and made his peace.

He doesn't close his eyes. He *knows* I can't do it. Without him I might never find the twins.

422

8

A large portrait above the fireplace shows a patrician man in legal robes with a horsehair wig that looks surprisingly like a shih tzu resting on his forearm. He gazes sternly down at a polished table that is surrounded by high-backed chairs.

Felix's mother is dressed in a tweed jacket and black slacks, clutching her handbag as though someone might steal it. Beside her, another of her sons rattles his fingers on the table, already bored.

Barnaby is at the window, studying the small courtyard outside. I don't notice Jarrod as he crosses the room. He touches my shoulder.

"Is it true? Am I an uncle?"

His hair is brushed back from his temples and beginning to thin.

"I'm not sure what you are, technically."

"My father says there are twins."

"They don't belong to Cate. A girl was forced to have them."

His eyes don't understand. "Biologically they belong to Cate. That makes me an uncle."

"Perhaps. I really don't know."

The solicitor enters the conference room and takes a seat. In his mid-fifties, dressed in a three-piece pinstriped suit, he introduces himself as William Grove and stretches his face into a tight smile. His whole demeanor is one of contained speed. Time is money. Every fifteen minutes is billable.

Chairs scrape backward. People are seated. Mr. Grove glances at his instructions.

"Ladies and gentlemen, a codicil was added to this will six weeks ago and it appears to be predicated on the likelihood that the Beaumonts would become parents."

A frisson disturbs the atmosphere like a sudden change in the air pressure. The solicitor glances up, tugging at his shirt cuffs. "Am I to understand this marriage produced children?"

Silence.

Finally, Barnaby clears his throat. "It does seem likely."

"What do you mean? Please explain."

"We have reason to believe that Cate and Felix arranged a surrogacy. Twins were born eight days ago."

The next minute is one of exclamation and disbelief. Felix's mother makes a choking noise at the back of her throat. Barnaby is looking at his hands, rubbing his fingertips. Jarrod hasn't taken his eyes off me.

Unsure of how to proceed Mr. Grove takes a moment to compose himself. He decides to continue. The estate consists of a heavily mortgaged family home in Willesden Green, North London, which was recently damaged in a fire. Insurance will cover the cost of rebuilding. Felix also had a life insurance policy provided by his employer.

"If there is no objection, I shall read from the wills, which are each ostensibly the same." He takes a sip of water.

"This is the last will and testament of me, Cate Elizabeth Beaumont (née Elliot), made on the 14th day of September 2006. I hereby revoke all wills heretofore made by me and declare this to be my last will and testament. I appoint William Grove of Sadler, Grove and Buffett to be executor and trustee of this, my will. I give, devise and bequeath to my husband, Felix Beaumont (formerly known as Felix Buczkowski), the whole of my estate provided that he survives me by thirty days and, if not, then I give the whole of my estate to my child or children to be shared equally as tenants in common.

"I appoint Alisha Kaur Barba as guardian of my infant children and I direct her to love and care for them and to expend so much as is necessary from the estate of the children to raise, educate and advance their life."

Barnaby is on his feet, his jaw flapping in protest. For a moment I think he might be having a heart attack.

"This is preposterous! I will not have my grandchildren raised by a bloody stranger." He stabs a finger at me. "You knew about this!"

"No."

"You knew all along."

"I didn't."

Mr. Grove tries to calm him down. "I can assure you, sir, that everything has been properly signed and witnessed."

"What sort of idiot do you take me for? This is bullshit! I won't let anyone take my grandchildren away."

The outburst has silenced the room. The only sounds are from the air-conditioning and distant water pipes filling and disgorging. For a moment I think Barnaby might actually strike me. Instead he kicks back his chair and storms out, followed by Jarrod. People turn to look at me. The back of my neck grows warm.

Mr. Grove has a letter for me. As I take it from him, I have to keep my hand steady. Why would Cate do this? Why choose me? Already the sense of responsibility is pressing against my lungs.

The envelope is creased in my fist as I leave the conference room and cross the lobby, pushing through heavy glass doors. I have no idea where I'm going. Is this it? One poxy letter is supposed to explain things? Will it make up for eight years of silence?

Another notion suddenly haunts my confusion. Maybe I'm being given a chance to redeem myself. To account for my neglect, my failures, the things left unsaid, all those sins of omission and commission. I am being asked to safeguard Cate's most precious legacy and to do a better job than I managed with our friendship.

I stop in the doorway of an off-licence and slide my finger beneath the flap of the envelope.

Dear Ali,

It is a weird thing writing a letter that will only be opened and read upon one's death. It's hard to get too sad about it though. And if I am dead, it's a bit late to fret about spilling that particular pint of white.

My only real concern is you. You're my one regret. I have wanted to be friends with you ever since we met at Oaklands and you fought Paul Donavon to defend my honor and lost your front tooth. You were the real thing, Ali, not one of the plastics.

I know you're sorry about what happened with my father.

I know it was more his fault than yours. I forgave you a long time ago. I forgave him because, well, you know how it is with fathers. You weren't the first of his infidelities, by the way, but I guess you worked that out.

The reason I could never tell you this is because of a promise I made to my mother. It was the worst sort of promise. She found out about you and my father. He told her because he thought I would tell her.

My mother made me promise never to see you again; never to talk to you; never to invite you to the house; never to mention your name.

I know I should have ignored her. I should have called. Many times I almost did. I got as far as picking up the phone. Sometimes I even dialed your parents' number but then I wondered what I'd say to you. We had left it too long. How would we ever get around the silence, which was like an elephant sitting in the room?

I have never stopped thinking about you. I followed your career as best I could, picking up stories from other people. Poor old Felix has been bored silly listening to me talk about our exploits and adventures. He's heard so much about you that he probably feels like he's been married to both of us.

Six weeks from now, God willing, I will become a mother after six years of trying. If something happens to me and to Felix—if we die in a flaming plane crash or should suicide bombers ever target Tesco at Willesden Green—we want you to be the guardian of our children.

My mother is going to pass a cow when she learns this but I have kept my promise to her, which didn't include any clause covering posthumous contact with you.

There are no strings attached. I'm not going to write provisos or instructions. If you want the job it's yours. I know you'll love my children as much as I do. And I know you'll teach them to look after each other. You'll say the things I would have said to them and tell them about me and about Felix. The good stuff, naturally.

I don't know what else to tell you. I often think how different my life would have been—how much happier—if you'd been a part of it. One day.

Love, Cate

———

It is just after five o'clock. The streetlights are smudged with my tears. Faces drift past me. Heads turn away. Nobody asks after a crying woman anymore—not in London. I'm just another of the crazies to be avoided.

On the cab ride to West Acton I catch my reflection in the window. I will be thirty years old on Thursday—closer to sixty than I am to birth. I still look young yet exhausted and feverish, like a child who has stayed up too late at an adult party.

There is a FOR SALE sign outside "New Boy" Dave's flat. He's serious about this; he's going to quit the force and start teaching kids how to sail.

I debate whether to go up. I walk to the front door, stare at the bell and walk back to the road. I don't want to explain things. I just want to open a bottle of wine, order a pizza and curl up on the sofa with his legs beneath mine and his hands rubbing my toes, which are freezing.

I haven't seen Dave since Amsterdam. He used to phone me every day, sometimes twice. When I called him after the funerals he sounded hesitant, almost nervous.

The elephant in the room. It can't be talked about. It can't be ignored. My patched-up pelvis is like that. People suddenly want to give me children. Is that ironic? I'm never sure with irony; the term is so misused.

I go back to the door. It takes a long while for anyone to answer. It's a woman's voice on the intercom. Apologetic. She was in the shower.

"Dave's not here."

"It's my fault. I should have phoned."

"He's on his way home. Do you want to come in and wait?"

"No, that's OK."

Who is she? What's she doing here?

"I'll tell him you dropped by."

"OK."

A pause.

"You need to give me your name."

"Of course. Sorry. Don't worry about it. I'll call him."

I walk back to the road, telling myself I don't care.

Shit! Shit! Shit!

———

The house is strangely quiet. The TV in the front room is turned down and lights are on upstairs. I slip along the side path and through the back door. Hari is in the kitchen.

"You have to stop her."

"Who?"

"Samira. She's leaving. She's upstairs packing."

"Why? What did you do to her?"

"Nothing."

"Did you leave *her* alone?"

"For twenty minutes, I swear. That's all. I had to drop off a mate's car."

Samira is in my bedroom. Her clothes are folded on the bed—a few simple skirts, blouses, a frayed jumper . . . Hassan's biscuit tin sits on top of the pile.

"Where are you going?"

She seems to hold her breath. "I am leaving. You do not want me here."

"What makes you say that? Did Hari do something? Did he say something he shouldn't have said?"

She won't look at me, but I see the bruise forming on her cheek, a rough circle beneath her right eye.

"Who did this?"

She whispers, "A man came."

"What man?"

"The man who talked to you at the church."

"Donavon?"

"No, the other man."

She means Barnaby. He came here, spoiling for a fight.

"He was hitting the door—making so much noise. He said you lied to me and you lied to him."

"I have never lied to you."

"He said you wanted the babies for yourself and he would fight you and he would fight me."

"Don't listen to him."

"He said I wasn't welcome in this country. I should go back where I came from—among the terrorists."

"No."

I reach toward her. She pulls away.

"Did he hit you?"

"I tried to shut the door. He pushed it." She touches her cheek.

"He had no right to say those things."

"Is it true? Do *you* want the babies?"

"Cate wrote a will—a legal document. She nominated me as the guardian if she had children."

"What does guardian mean? Do the twins belong to you now?"

"No. You gave birth to them. They might have Cate's eyes and Felix's nose, but they grew inside your body. And no matter what anyone says they belong to you."

"What if I don't want them?"

My mouth opens but I don't answer. Something has lodged in my throat, a choking lump of desire and doubt. No matter what Cate wanted, they're not my babies. My motives are pure.

I put my arm around Samira's shoulders and pull her close to me. Her breath is warm against my neck and her first sob thuds like a spade hitting wet dirt. Something breaks inside her. She has found her tears.

9

The digital numbers of my alarm clock glow in the darkness. It has just gone four. I won't sleep again. Samira is curled up next to me, breathing softly.

I am a collector of elephants. Some are soft toys; others are figurines made from cut glass, porcelain, jade or crystal. My favorite is six inches high and made from heavy glass, inlaid with mirrors. Normally it sits beneath my reading light, throwing colored stars on the walls. It's not there now. I wonder what could have happened to it.

Slipping out of bed quietly, I dress in my running gear and step outside into the darkness of Hanbury Street. There is an edge to the breeze. Seasons changing.

Cate used to help me train after school. She rode her bicycle alongside me, speeding up before we reached the hills because she knew I could outrun her on the climbs. When I ran at the national age championships in Cardiff she begged her parents to let her come. She was the only student from Oaklands to see me win. I ran like the wind that day. Fast enough to blur at the edges.

I couldn't see Cate in the stands but I could pick out my mother who wore a bright crimson sari like a splash of paint against the blue seats and gray spectators.

My father never saw me compete. He didn't approve.

"Running is not ladylike. It makes a woman sweat," he told me.

"Mama sweats all the time in the kitchen."

"It is a different sort of sweat."

"I didn't know there were different kinds of sweat."

"Yes, it is a well-known scientific fact. The sweat of hard work and of food preparation is sweeter than the sweat of vigorous exercise."

I didn't laugh. A good daughter respects her father.

Later I heard my parents arguing.

"How is a boy supposed to catch her if she runs so fast?"

"I don't want boys catching her."

"Have you seen her room? She has weights. My daughter is lifting barbells."

"She's in training."

"Weights are not feminine. And do you see what she wears? Those brief shorts are like underwear. She's running in her underwear."

In darkness I run two circuits of Victoria Park, sticking to the tarmac paths, using the streetlights to navigate.

My mother used to tell me a folktale about a village donkey that was always mocked for being stupid and ugly. One day a guru took pity on the animal. "If you had the roar of a tiger they would not laugh," he thought. So he took a tiger skin and laid it across the donkey's back. The donkey returned to the village and suddenly everything changed. Women and children ran screaming. Men cowered in corners. Soon the donkey was alone in the market and feasted on the lovely apples and carrots.

The villagers were terrified and had to be rid of the dangerous "tiger." A meeting was called and they decided to drive the tiger back to the forest. Drumbeats echoed through the market and the poor bewildered donkey turned this way and that. He ran into the forest but the hunters tracked him down.

"That's no tiger," one of them shouted. "Surely it's only the donkey from the market."

The guru appeared and calmly lifted the tiger skin from the terrified beast. "Remember this animal," he said to the people. "He has the skin of a tiger but the soul of a donkey."

I feel like that now—a donkey not a tiger.

I am just passing Smithfield Market when a realization washes over me. At first it is no more than an inkling. I wonder what prompts such a reaction. Maybe it's a pattern of footsteps or a sound that is out of place or a movement that triggers a thought. It comes to me now. I know how to find the twins!

Forbes has been concentrating on couples who succeeded in obtaining a child by using a genetic surrogate. They cannot give evidence against Shawcroft without incriminating themselves. Why would they? Science supports them. Nobody can prove they're not the birth parents.

But whoever has the twins doesn't have a genetic safety net. DNA tests will expose rather than sustain them. They haven't had time to fake a pregnancy or set up an elaborate deceit. Right now they must be feeling vulnerable.

At this hour of the morning it isn't difficult to find a parking spot in Kennington, close to Forbes's office. Most of the detectives start work at nine, which means the incident room is deserted except for a detective constable who has been working the graveyard shift. He's about my age and quite handsome in a sulky sort of way. Perhaps I woke him up.

"Forbes asked me to come." I lie.

He looks at me doubtfully. "The boss has a meeting at the Home Office this morning. He won't be in the office until later."

"He wants me to follow up a lead."

"What sort of lead?"

"Just an idea, that's all."

He doesn't believe me. I call Forbes to get approval.

"This better be fucking important," he grumbles.

"Good morning, sir."

"Who's this?"

"DC Barba."

"Don't good morning me."

"Sorry, sir."

I can hear Mrs. Forbes in the background telling him to be quiet. Pillow talk.

"I need access to Shawcroft's phone records."

"It's six in the morning."

"Yes, sir."

He's about to say no. He doesn't trust me. I'm bad news or bad luck. Everything I've touched has turned to shit. I sense another reason. A nervousness. Ever since he released Shawcroft, the DI has backtracked and made excuses. He must have copped some heat, but that goes with the territory.

"I want you to go home, DC Barba."

"I have a lead."

"Give it to the night detective. You're not part of this investigation." His voice softens. "Look after Samira."

Why is he being so negative? And why the briefing at the Home Office? It must be about Shawcroft.

"How is your wife, sir?" I ask.

Forbes hesitates. She's lying next to him. What can he say?

There is a long pause. I whisper, "We're on the same side, sir. You didn't screw me that night so don't screw me now."

"Fine. Yes, I can't see a problem," he answers. I hand the phone over to the night detective and listen to their yes-sir, no-sir exchange. The phone is handed back to me. Forbes wants a final word.

"Anything you find, you give to me."

"Yes, sir."

The call ends. The night detective looks at me and we smile in unison. Waking up a senior officer is one of life's small pleasures.

The DC's name is Rod Beckley but everyone calls him Becks. "On account of me being crap at football," he jokes.

After clearing a desk and finding me a chair, he delivers a dozen ring-bound folders. Every incoming and outgoing call from the New Life Adoption Center is listed, including the numbers, the duration of each call, the time and the date they were made. There are six voice lines and two fax lines, as well as a direct-dial number into Shawcroft's office.

Further folders cover his mobile phone and home line. Text messages and e-mails have been printed out and stapled together in chronological order.

Taking a marker pen, I begin to group the calls.

Rather than concentrate on the phone numbers, I look at the times. The ferry arrived in Harwich at 3:36 a.m. on Sunday morning. We know that Pearl walked off the ferry just after four. At 10:25 a.m. he bought nappies and baby formula from a motorway service station on the M25 before stealing a car.

I look down the list of calls to Shawcroft's mobile. There was an incoming call at 10:18 a.m. that lasted less than thirty seconds. I check the number. It appears only once. It could be a wrong number.

DC Beckley is flicking at a keyboard across the office, trying to look busy. I sit on the edge of his desk until he looks up.

"Can we find out who this number belongs to?"

He accesses the Police National Computer and types in the digits. A map of Hertfordshire appears. The details are listed on a separate window. The phone number belongs to a public phone box at Potter's Bar—a motorway service area near junction 24 on the M25. It's the same service area where Brendan Pearl was last sighted. He must have phoned Shawcroft for instructions about where to deliver the twins. It is the closest I've come to linking the two men, although it's not conclusive.

Going back to the folders, I strike a dead end. Shawcroft didn't use his mobile for the next three hours. Surely if his plan was coming apart, he would have called someone.

I try to picture last Sunday morning. Shawcroft was on the golf course. His foursome teed off at 10:05. One of his playing partners said something when Samira interrupted their game and Shawcroft tried to drag her off the course: "Not again."

It had happened before—a week earlier. After the phone call from Pearl, Shawcroft must have abandoned his round. Where did he go? He needed to let the buyer or buyers know that the twins had arrived. He had to bring the pickup forward. It was too risky using his own mobile so he looked for another phone—one that he thought couldn't be traced.

I go back to Becks. "Is it possible to find out if there is a public phone located at a golf club in Surrey?"

"Maybe. You got a name?"

"Yes. Twin Bridges Country Club. It could be in a locker room or lounge. Somewhere quiet. I'm interested in outgoing calls timed between 9:20 a.m. and 10:30 a.m. on Sunday, October 29."

"Is that all?" he asks facetiously.

"No. Then we have to cross-check them with the adoption waiting list at the New Life Adoption Center."

He doesn't understand, but he begins the search anyway. "You think we'll find a match."

"If we're lucky."

10

"New Boy" Dave hears my voice on the intercom and pauses for a moment before pressing the buzzer to unlock the front door. When I reach his flat the door is propped open. He is in the kitchen stirring paint.

"So you're definitely selling."

"Yep."

"Any offers?"

"Not yet."

There are two cups in the drainer and two cold tea bags solidifying in the sink, alongside a paint roller and a couple of brushes. The ceilings are to be a stowe white. I helped him choose the color. The walls are a misty green, cut back by 50 percent and the skirting boards and frames are full strength.

I follow Dave into the living room. His few pieces of furniture have been pushed to the center and covered in old sheets.

"How is Samira?" he asks.

The question is unexpected. Dave has never met her,

but he will have seen the TV bulletins and read the papers.

"I'm worried about her. I'm worried about the twins."

He fills the roller from the tray.

"Will you help me?"

"It's not our case."

"I might have found them. Please help me."

Climbing the ladder he runs the roller across the ceiling creating long ribbons of paint.

"What does it matter, Dave? You've resigned. You're leaving. My career is finished. It doesn't matter what toes we tread on or who we piss off. There's something wrong with this case. People are tiptoeing around it, playing softly softly, while the real culprits are shredding files and covering their tracks."

The roller is gliding across the ceiling. I know he's listening.

"You're acting like these kids belong to *you*."

I have to catch myself before my head snaps up. He looks down at me from the top of the ladder. Why do people keep questioning my motives? Eduardo de Souza, Barnaby, now Dave. Is it me who can't see the truth? No, they're wrong. I don't want the twins for myself.

"I'm doing this because a friend of mine—my best friend—entrusted to me what she loved most, the most precious thing she had. I couldn't save Cate and I couldn't save Zala, but I *can* save the twins."

There is a long silence. Only one of us feels uncomfortable. "New Boy" has always been defined more by what he dislikes than by what he likes. He doesn't like cats, for instance, or hypocrites. He also loathes reality TV shows, Welsh rugby fans and tattooed women who scream at their kids in supermarkets. I can live with a man like that. His silences are another matter. He seems comfortable with them but I want to know what he's thinking. Is he angry that I didn't leave Amsterdam with him? Is he upset at how we left things? We both have questions. I want to know who answered the intercom last night, fresh from his shower.

I turn toward his bedroom. The door is open. I notice a suitcase against the wall and a blouse hanging on the back of the open door. I don't realize I'm staring and I don't notice Dave climb down the ladder and take the roller to the kitchen. He wraps it carefully in cling film, leaving it on the sink. Peeling off his shirt, he tosses it in a corner.

"Give me five minutes. I need to shower." He scratches his unshaven chin. "Better make it ten."

Two addresses: one just across the river in Barnes and the other in Finsbury Park, North London. The first address belongs to a couple whose names also appear on a waiting list at the New Life Adoption Center. The Finsbury Park address doesn't appear on the files.

Sunday week ago—just after ten o'clock—both addresses received a call from a public phone in the locker room of the Twin Bridges Country Club in Surrey. Shawcroft was there when those calls were made.

It's a hunch. It's too many things happening at the same time to be coincidental. It's worth a look.

Dave is dressed in light cords, a shirt and a leather jacket. "What do you want to do?"

"Check them out."

"What about Forbes?"

"He won't make this sort of leap. He might get there in the end by ticking off the boxes, methodically, mechanically, but what if we don't have time for that?"

I picture the smallest twin, struggling to breathe. My own throat closes. She should be in hospital. We should have found her by now.

"OK, so you have two addresses. I still don't know what you expect to do," says Dave.

"Maybe I'm just going to knock on the front door and say, 'Do you have twins that don't belong to you?' I can tell you what I *won't* do. I won't sit back and wait for them to disappear."

Brown leaves swirl from a park onto the pavement and back to the grass, as if unwilling to cross the road. The temperature hasn't strayed above single figures and the wind is driving it lower.

We're parked in a typical street in Barnes: flanked by tall, gabled houses and plane trees that have been so savagely pruned they look almost deformed.

This is a stockbroker suburb, full of affluent middle-class families who move here for the schools and the parks and the proximity to the city. Despite the cold, half a dozen mothers or nannies are in the playground, watching over preschoolers who are dressed in so many clothes they look like junior Michelin Men.

Dave watches the yummy mummies, while I watch the house, No. 85. Robert and Noelene Gallagher drive a Volvo Estate, pay their TV license fee on time and vote

Liberal Democrat. I'm guessing, of course, but it strikes me as that sort of area, that sort of house.

Dave rakes his fingers through his lopsided bramble of hair. "Can I ask you something?"

"Sure."

"Have you ever loved me?"

I didn't see this coming.

"What makes you think I don't love you now?"

"You've never said."

"What do you mean?"

"You might have used the word, but not in a sentence with my name in it. You've never said, 'I love you, Dave.' "

I think back, wanting to deny it, but he seems so sure. The nights we lay together with his arms around me, I felt so safe, so happy. Didn't I ever tell him? I remember my philosophical debates and arguments about the nature of love and how debilitating it can be. Were they all internal? I was trying to talk myself *out* of loving him. I lost, but he had no way of knowing that.

I should tell him now. How? It's going to sound contrived or forced. It's too late. I can try to make excuses; I can blame my inability to have children but the truth is that I'm driving him away. There's another woman living in his flat.

He's doing it again—not saying anything. Waiting.

"You're seeing someone," I blurt out, making it sound like an accusation.

"What makes you say that?"

"I met her."

He turns his whole body in the driver's seat to face me, looking surprised rather than guilty.

"I came to see you yesterday. You weren't home. She answered the intercom."

"Jacquie?"

"I didn't take down her name." *I sound so bloody jealous.*

"My sister."

"You don't have a sister."

"My sister-in-law. My brother's wife, Jacquie."

"They're in San Diego."

"They're staying with me. Simon is my new business partner. I told you."

Could this get any worse? "You must think I'm such an idiot," I say. "I'm sorry. I mean, I'm not the jealous type, not usually. It's just that after what happened in Amsterdam, when you didn't call me and I didn't call you, I just thought—it's so stupid—that you'd found someone else who wasn't so crippled, or troublesome or such hard work. Please don't laugh at me."

"I'm not laughing."

"What are you doing?"

"I'm looking at that car."

I follow his gaze. A Volvo Estate is parked near the front gate of No. 85. There is a sunshade on the nearside rear window and what looks like a baby seat.

Dave is giving me a way out. He's like a chivalrous gentleman spreading his coat over a muddy puddle.

"I should check it out," I say, opening the car door. "You stay here."

Dave watches me leave. He knows I'm dodging the issue yet again. I have underestimated him. He's smarter than I am. Nicer, too.

Crossing the street, I walk along the pavement, pausing at the Volvo and bending as if to tie my shoelaces. The windows are tinted but I can make out small handprints inside the glass and a Garfield sticker on the back window.

I glance across at Dave and make a knocking motion with my fist. He shakes his head. Ignoring the signal, I open the front gate and climb the steps to the house.

I press the buzzer. The front door opens a crack. A girl aged about five regards me very seriously. Her hands are stained with paint and a pink blot has dried on her forehead like a misplaced bindi.

"Hello, what's your name?"

"Molly."

"That's a pretty name."

"I know."

"Is your mummy home?"

"She's upstairs."

I hear a yell from that direction. "If that's the boiler man, the boiler is straight down the hall in the kitchen."

"It's not the boiler man," I call back.

"It's an Indian lady," says Molly.

Mrs. Gallagher appears at the top of the stairs. In her early forties, she's wearing a corduroy skirt with a wide belt slung low on her hips.

"I'm sorry to trouble you. My husband and I are moving into the street and I was hoping to ask about local schools and doctors, that sort of thing."

I can see her mentally deciding what to do. It's more than natural caution.

"What beautiful curls," I say, stroking Molly's hair.

"That's what everyone says," the youngster replies.

Why would someone who already has a child buy a baby?

"I'm rather busy at the moment," says Mrs. Gallagher, brushing back her fringe.

"I understand completely. I'm sorry." I turn to leave.

"Which place are you buying?" she asks, not wanting to be impolite.

"Oh, we're not buying. Not yet. We're renting No. 68." I point down the street in the direction of a TO LET sign. "We've moved from North London. My husband has a new job. We're both working. But we want to start a family soon."

Mrs. Gallagher is at the bottom of the stairs now. It's too cold to leave the front door open. She either invites me inside or tells me to go.

"Now's not the best time," she says. "Perhaps if I had a phone number I could call you later."

"Thank you very much." I fumble for a pen. "Do you have a piece of paper?"

She looks on the radiator shelf. "I'll get you one."

Molly waits in the hallway, still holding the door. "Do you want to see one of my paintings?"

"I'd love to."

"I'll get one." She dashes upstairs. Mrs. Gallagher is in the kitchen. She finds an old envelope and returns, looking for Molly.

"She's gone upstairs to get one of her paintings," I explain. "A budding artist."

"She gets more paint on her clothes than on the paper."

"I have a boyfriend like that."

"I thought you said you were married." She fixes me with a stare. There's steel behind it.

"We're engaged. We've been together so long it feels like we're married."

She doesn't believe me. Molly yells from the top of the stairs.

"Mummy, Jasper is crying."

"Oh, you have another one."

Mrs. Gallagher reaches for the door. My foot is faster. My shoulder follows. I have no right to enter. I need a warrant or I need proper cause.

I'm at the bottom of the stairs. Mrs. Gallagher yells at me to get out. She grabs my arm. I shrug it away. Above the noise, behind it, in spite of it, I hear a baby crying.

Taking the stairs two at a time, I follow the sound. The first door I come to is the main bedroom. The second door is Molly's room. She has set up a painting easel on an old sheet. I try a third door. Brightly colored fish spin slowly above a white cot. Within it, swaddled tightly, a baby is unhappy at creation.

Mrs. Gallagher pushes past me, scooping up the boy. "Get out of my house!"

"Is he yours, Mrs. Gallagher?"

"Yes."

"Did you give birth to him?"

"Get out! Get out! I'll call the police."

"I *am* the police."

Wordlessly, she shakes her head from side to side. The baby has gone quiet. Molly is tugging at her skirt.

Suddenly her shoulders sag and she seems to deflate in front of me, folding from the knees and then the waist. Still cradling the baby, refusing to let go, she lands in my arms and I maneuver her to a chair.

"We adopted him," she whispers. "He's *ours*."

"He was never available for adoption. You know that."

Mrs. Gallagher shakes her head. I look around the room. Where is she? The girl. My heart skips between beats. Slow then fast.

"There was a baby girl. A twin."

She looks toward the cot. "He's the only one."

Worst case scenarios haunt me now. The baby girl was so small. She struggled to breathe. Please God, let her be safe!

Mrs. Gallagher has found a tissue in the sleeve of her cardigan. She blows her nose and sniffles. "We were told he wasn't wanted. I swear I didn't know—not about the missing twins. It wasn't until I saw the TV news. Then I began to wonder . . ."

"Who gave him to you?"

"A man brought him."

"What did he look like?"

"Mid-fifties, short hair—he had an Irish accent."

"When?"

"The Sunday before last." She wipes her eyes. "It came as a shock. We weren't expecting him for another fort-night."

"Who arranged the adoption?"

"Mr. Shawcroft said a teenage girl was pregnant with twins but couldn't afford to look after both of them. She wanted to put one of them up for adoption. We could jump the queue for fifty thousand pounds."

"You knew it was against the law."

"Mr. Shawcroft said that twins couldn't legally be split. We had to do everything in secret."

"You pretended to be pregnant."

"There wasn't time."

I look at Molly who is playing with a box of shells, arranging them in patterns.

"Is Molly . . . ?" I don't finish the question.

"She's mine," she says fiercely. "I couldn't have any more. There were complications. Medical problems. They told us we were too old to adopt. My husband is fifty-five, you see." She wipes her eyes. "I should phone him."

I hear my name being called from downstairs. "New Boy" must have witnessed the doorstep confrontation. He couldn't stay put.

"Up here."

"Are you OK?"

"Yeah."

He appears at the door, taking in the scene. Mrs. Gallagher. Molly. The baby.

"It's one of the twins," I say.

"One?"

"The boy."

He peers into the cot. "Are you sure?"

I follow his gaze. It's amazing how much a newborn can change in under ten days, but I'm sure.

"What about the girl?" he asks.

"She's not here."

Shawcroft made *two* phone calls from the golf club. The second was to the Finsbury Park address of a Mrs. Y. Moncrieffe, which doesn't cross-reference with any of the names from the New Life Adoption Center files.

I can't leave. I have to stay and talk to Forbes (and no doubt peel him off the ceiling).

"Can you check out the other address?"

Dave weighs up the implications and ramifications. He's not worried about himself. I'm the one facing a disciplinary hearing. He kisses my cheek.

"You make it hard sometimes, you know that?"

"I know."

11

DI Forbes storms through the house, his face hardened into a mask of fury and cold hatred. Ordering me into the rear garden, he ignores the muddy lawn and paces back and forth.

"You had no right!" he yells. "It was an illegal search."

"I had reason to believe—"

"What reason?"

"I was following a lead."

"Which you should have told *me* about. This is *my* fucking investigation!"

His rectangular glasses bobble on his nose. I wonder if it annoys him.

"In my professional judgment I made a necessary choice, sir."

"You don't even *know* if it's one of the twins. There are no birth records or adoption papers."

"Mrs. Gallagher has confirmed that she is not the biological mother. The baby was delivered to her by a man matching Brendan Pearl's description."

"You should have waited."

"With all due respect, sir, you were taking too long. Shawcroft is free. He's shredding files, covering his tracks. You don't *want* to prosecute him."

I think he might explode. His voice carries across the neighborhood gardens and mud sucks at his shoes.

"I should have reported you to the PCA when you went to Amsterdam. You have harassed witnesses, abused your authority and disobeyed the orders of a senior officer. You have failed at almost every opportunity to conduct yourself in a professional manner . . ."

His foot lifts and his shoe remains behind. A sock squelches into the mud up to his ankle. We both pretend it hasn't happened.

"You're suspended from duty. Do you understand me? I'm going to personally see that your career is over."

Social Services have been summoned, a big woman with a backside so large that she appears to be wearing a bustle. Mr. and Mrs. Gallagher are talking to her in the sitting room. They look almost relieved that it's over. The past few days must have been unbearable, wondering and waiting for a knock on the door. Being frightened of falling in love with a child that might never truly be theirs.

Molly is in her bedroom showing a policewoman how she paints flowers and rests them on the radiator to dry. The baby is sleeping. They called him Jasper. He has a name now.

Forbes has peeled off his sock and thrown it into the rubbish bin. Sitting on the back step, he uses a screwdriver to scrape mud from his shoes.

"How did you know?" he asks, having calmed down.

I explain about the phone calls from the golf club and

cross-checking the numbers with the adoption files, looking for a match.

"That's how I found the Gallaghers."

"Did he make any other calls?"

"One."

Forbes waits. "Have I got to *arrest* you to get any cooperation?"

Any remaining vestiges of comradeship have gone. We're no longer on the same team.

"I had an interesting conversation with a lawyer this morning," he says. "He was representing Barnaby Elliot and he alleged that you had a conflict of interest concerning this case."

"There's no conflict, sir."

"Mr. Elliot is contesting his late daughter's will."

"He has no legal claim over the twins."

"And neither do you!"

"I know that, sir," I whisper.

"If Samira Khan decides that she doesn't want the babies, they will be taken into care and placed with foster parents."

"I know. I'm not doing this for me."

"Are you sure of that?"

It's an accusation not a question. My motives are under fire again. Perhaps I'm deluding myself. I can't afford to believe that. I won't.

My mobile phone is vibrating in my pocket. I flip it open.

"I might have found her," says Dave. "But there's a problem."

12

The Neonatal Intensive Care Unit (NICU) at Queen Charlotte's Hospital is on the third floor above the delivery suites and maternity ward. Amid low lights, soft footsteps and the hum of machines there are fifteen high-domed incubators.

The unit manager is two paces ahead of me and Dave two paces behind. Our hands are washed with disinfectant and mobile phones have been turned off.

Passing the nearest crib, I look down. It appears to be empty except for a pink blanket and a teddy bear sitting in the corner. Then I notice an arm, no thicker than a fountain pen, emerge from beneath the blanket. Fingers curl and uncurl. Eyes remain shut. Tubes are squashed into a tiny nose, pushing rapid puffs of air into immature lungs.

The manager pauses and waits. Perhaps people do that a lot—stop, stare and pray. It's only then that I notice the faces on the far side of the crib, distorted by the glass.

I look around. There are other parents sitting in the semidarkness, watching and waiting; talking in whispers. I wonder what they say to each other. Do they look at other cribs and wonder if that baby is stronger or sicker or more premature. Not all of the newborns can possibly survive. Do their parents secretly pray, "Save mine! Save mine!"

We have reached the far end of the NICU. Chairs beside the crib are empty. A nurse sits on a high stool at a control screen, monitoring the machines that monitor a child.

At the center of a plain white sheet is a baby girl, wearing just a nappy. She is smaller than I remember, yet compared to some of the premature babies in the NICU she is twice their size. Small pads are stuck to her chest, picking up her heartbeat and her breathing.

"Claudia was brought in last night," explains the ward manager. "She has a serious lung infection. We're giving her antibiotics and feeding her intravenously. The device on her leg is a blood gas monitor. It shines light through her skin to see how much oxygen is in her blood."

"Is she going to be all right?"

She takes a moment to choose her words. The delay is enough to terrify me. "She's stable. The next twenty-four hours are very important."

"You called her Claudia."

"That's the name we were given."

"Who gave it to you?"

"The woman who came in with her in the ambulance."

"I need to see the admission form."

"Of course. If you come to the office I'll print you a copy."

Dave is staring through the glass. I can almost see his lips moving, breathing as the baby breathes. Claudia has captured his attention, even though her eyes are fused shut by sleep.

"Do you mind if I stay for a while?" he asks, directing the question as much to me as to the ward manager. Every other patient in the unit has someone sitting alongside them. Claudia is alone. It doesn't seem right to him.

Retracing our steps, I follow the manager to her office.

"I called Social Services this morning," she says. "I didn't expect the police."

"What made you call?"

"I wasn't happy with some of the answers we were getting. Claudia arrived just after midnight. At first the woman said she was the baby's nanny. She gave the mother's name as Cate Beaumont. Then she changed her story and said that Claudia had been adopted, but she couldn't give me any details of the adoption agency."

She hands me the admission form. Claudia's date of birth is listed as Sunday, October 29. The mother's name is written down as Cate Elizabeth Beaumont. The address is Cate's fire-damaged house.

Why give Cate's name? How did she even know about her?

"Where is this woman now?"

"One of our consultants wanted to talk to her. I guess she panicked."

"She ran?"

"She made a phone call. Then she walked out."

"What time was that?"

"About 6:00 a.m."

"Do you know who she called?"

"No, but she used my phone."

She points to her desk. The phone console is a command unit, with a memory of the most recently dialed numbers. A small LCD screen displays the call register. The ward manager identifies the number and I hit the redial button.

A woman answers.

"Hello?"

"This is Queen Charlotte's Hospital," I say. "Someone called your home from this number early this morning."

She doesn't answer but in the silence I recognize a sound. I've heard it before—the squeak of wheels on parquetry floor.

I don't have Ruiz's photographic memory or his mother's gifts for telling fortunes. I don't even know if I have a particular methodology. I put facts together randomly. Sometimes leaping ahead or trying things out for size. It's not very efficient and it can't be taught but it works for me.

The woman speaks again. Nervously. "You must have the wrong number."

It's an officious voice, precise, not quite public school. I have heard it often enough, albeit a decade ago, berating her husband for coming home late smelling of shampoo and shower gel.

The line has gone dead. Ruth Elliot has hung up. Simultaneously, there is a knock on the door. A nurse smiles apologetically and whispers something to the ward manager, who looks at me.

"You asked about the woman who brought in Claudia. She didn't run away. She's downstairs in the cafeteria."

A pressure pad opens the doors automatically. The cafeteria is small and bright with white-flecked tables to hide the crumbs. Trays are stacked near the doors. Steam rises from the warming pans.

A handful of nurses are picking up sandwiches and cups of tea—healthy options in a menu where everything else comes with chips.

Yvonne is squeezed into a booth, with her head resting on her forearms. For a moment I think she might be asleep, but her head lifts and she blinks at me wetly. A low moan escapes and she lowers her head. The pale brown of her scalp is visible where her gray hair has started to thin.

"What happened?"

"I did a foolish, foolish thing, cookie," she says, talking into the crook of her arm. "I thought I could make her better, but she kept getting sicker and sicker."

A shuddering breath vibrates through her frame. "I should have taken her to a doctor but Mr. and Mrs. Elliot said that nobody could ever know about Cate's baby. They said people wanted to take Claudia away and give her to someone she don't belong to. I don't know why people would do something like that. Mr. and Mrs. Elliot didn't explain it so good, not sufficient for me to understand, you know."

She draws back, hoping I might comprehend. Her eyes are wet and crumbs have stuck to her cheek.

"I knew Cate weren't having no baby," she explains. "She didn't have no baby inside her. I know when a woman is with child. I can see it in her eyes and on her skin. I can smell it. Sometimes I can even tell when a woman's having another man's baby, on account of the skin around her eyes, which is darker 'cos she's frightened her husband might find out.

"I tried to say something to Mrs. Elliot but she called

me crazy and laughed. She must have told young Cate 'cos she avoided me after that. She wouldn't come to the house if I was working."

Details shiver and shift, finding their places. Events are no longer figments or mysteries, no longer part of my imagining. Barnaby *knew* I was in Amsterdam. And even before I mentioned Samira he *knew* she was having twins. He read Cate's e-mails and began covering her tracks.

At first he probably intended to protect his precious reputation. Later he and his wife came up with another plan. They would finish what Cate started. Barnaby contacted Shawcroft with a message: "Cate and Felix are dead but the deal isn't."

Why would Shawcroft agree? He had to. Barnaby had the e-mails. He could go to the police and expose the illegal adoptions and baby broking. Blackmail is an ugly word. So is kidnapping.

At the funeral Barnaby told me he was going to fight for the twins. "I want *both* of them," he said. I didn't realize what he meant. He already had one—Claudia. He wanted the boy. And his tirade at the lawyer's office and the scene at my house weren't just for show. He was frightened that he might be denied, if not by Samira, then by me.

The Elliots swore Yvonne to secrecy. They charged her with looking after Claudia and hopefully her brother if they could unite the twins. If the scandal unraveled and Shawcroft was exposed, they could play the grieving parents, trying to protect their daughter's precious legacy, their grandchildren.

Yvonne accepted the heaviest burden. She couldn't risk taking Claudia to a doctor. She tried her own remedies: running hot taps, filling the bathroom with steam, trying to help her breathe. She dosed her with droplets of paracetamol, rubbed her with warm flannels, lay awake beside her through the night, listening to her lungs fill with fluid.

Barnaby came to see the baby, his thumbs hitched in his belt and his feet splayed. He peered over the cot with a fixed smile, looking vaguely disappointed. Perhaps he wanted the boy—the healthy twin.

Meanwhile, Claudia grew sicker and Yvonne more desperate.

"I couldn't take it anymore," she whispers, lifting her gaze to the ceiling. "She was dying. Every time she coughed her body shook until she didn't have the strength to cough. That's when I called the ambulance."

She blinks at me. "She's going to die, isn't she?"

"We don't know that."

"It's going to be my fault. Arrest me. Lock me up. I deserve it."

I want to stop her talking about death. "Who chose the name?"

"It's Mrs. Elliot's name."

"Her first name is Ruth."

"Her middle name. I know you don't have much time for Mrs. Elliot but she's harder on herself than she is on anyone else."

What I feel most is resentment. Maybe that's part of the process of grieving. Cate doesn't feel as though she's gone. I keep thinking that she's just walked off in the middle of things and will come back presently and sort this mess out.

I have spent weeks delving into her life, investigating her movements and motives and I still don't understand how she could have risked so much and endangered so many. I keep entertaining the hope that I'll stumble upon the answer in some cache of her papers or a dusty bundle of letters. But I know it's not going to happen. One half of the truth is lying upstairs, pinned like an insect to a glass display case. The other half is being looked after by Social Services.

It sounds preposterous but I'm still trying to justify Cate's actions, trying to conjure up a friendship from the afterlife. She was an inept thief, a childless wife and a foolish dreamer. I don't want to think about her anymore. She has spoiled her own memory.

"The police are going to need a statement," I say.

Yvonne nods, wiping her cheeks.

She doesn't stand as I leave. And although her face is turned to the window, I know she's watching me.

"New Boy" Dave is still beside Claudia in the NICU, sitting forward on a chair, peering through the glass. We sit together. He takes my hand. I don't know for how long. The clock on the wall doesn't seem to change. Not even for a second. Perhaps that's what happens in a place like this: time slows down. Every second is made to count.

You are a very lucky little girl, Claudia. Do you know why? You have *two* mothers. One of them you'll never meet but that's OK, I'll tell you about her. She made some mistakes but I'm sure you won't judge her too harshly. Your other mother is also very special. Young. Beautiful. Sad. Sometimes life can turn on the length of an eyelash, even one as small as yours.

The ward manager touches my shoulder. A police officer wants to talk to me on the phone.

Forbes sounds far away. "The Gallaghers have given a statement. I'm on my way to arrest Julian Shawcroft."

"That's good. I found the girl. She's very sick."

He doesn't rant this time. "Who should we be talking to?"

"Barnaby Elliot and his wife, along with their housekeeper, Yvonne Moncrieffe."

Behind me a door opens and I hear the sound of an electronic alarm. Through an observation window I notice curtains being drawn around Claudia's crib.

The phone is no longer in my hand. Like everyone else I seem to be moving. I push through the curtains. Someone pushes me back and I stumble.

"What's wrong? What are they doing?"

A doctor is issuing instructions. A hand covers Claudia's face, holding a mask. A bag is squeezed and squeezed again. The mask is lifted briefly and a tube is slipped into her nose before being slowly fed into her lungs. White tape crosses her cheeks.

Dave has hold of my arm, trying to pull me away.

"What's happening?"

"We have to wait outside."

"They're hurting her."

"Let them do their job."

This is my fault. My mistake. If I had been stronger, fitter, faster, I would have saved Claudia from Pearl. She would have gone straight to hospital instead of being smuggled off the ferry. She would never have gone to Yvonne or caught a lung infection.

Thoughts like this plague me as I count down the minutes—fifteen of them, stretched and deformed by my imagination. The door swings open. A young doctor emerges.

"What happened?"

"The blood gas monitor triggered the alarm. Her

461

oxygen levels had fallen too low. She's too weak to breathe on her own so we've put her on a ventilator. We'll help her breathe for a while and see how strong she is tomorrow."

The sense of relief saps what energy I have left and I feel suddenly dizzy. My eyes are sticky and I can't get rid of the coppery taste in my mouth. I still haven't told Samira and already my heart has been shredded.

13

Sometimes London is a parody of itself. Today is like that. The sky is fat and heavy and the wind is cold, although not cold enough to snow. Ladbrokes is offering 3 to 1 on a white Christmas in London. All it takes is a single snowflake to fall on the rooftop of the Met Office.

The bail hearing is today. I'm wearing my court clothes: a red pencil skirt, cream blouse and a short jacket that is cut well enough to have an expensive label but has no label at all.

Shawcroft has been charged with people trafficking, forced pregnancy and offenses under the Child Protection Act. The penalty for trafficking alone is up to fourteen years. More charges are pending, as well as possible extradition to the Netherlands.

Samira is sitting on the bed watching me apply my makeup. An overcoat lies across her lap. She has been dressed for hours, after waking early and praying. She won't have to give evidence until the trial, which could be a year away, but she wants to come along for today's hearing.

"Shawcroft is still only a suspect," I say. "Under our legal system a suspect is innocent until *proven* guilty."

"But we know he *is* guilty."

"Yes but a jury has to decide that after hearing all the evidence."

"What is bail?"

"A judge will sometimes let a defendant out of prison just until the trial if he or she promises not to run away or approach any of the witnesses. As a way of guaranteeing this, the judge will ask for a large amount of money, which the defendant won't get back if he breaks the law or doesn't show up for the trial."

She looks astonished. "He will pay the judge money?"

"The money is like a security deposit."

"A bribe."

"No, not a bribe."

"So you are saying Brother could pay money and get out of jail."

"Well, yes, but it's not what you think."

The conversation keeps going round in circles. I'm not explaining it very well.

"I'm sure it won't happen," I reassure her. "He won't be able to hurt anyone again."

It has been three weeks since Claudia left hospital. I still worry about her—she seems so small compared to her brother—but the infection has gone and she's putting on weight.

The twins have become tabloid celebrities, Baby X and Baby Y, without first names or surnames. The judge deciding custody has ordered DNA tests on the twins and medical reports from Amsterdam. Samira will have to prove she is their mother and then decide what she wants to do.

Despite being under investigation, Barnaby has maintained his campaign for custody, hiring and sacking lawyers on a weekly basis. During the first custody hearing, Judge Freyne threatened to jail him for contempt for continually interjecting and making accusations of bias.

I have had my own hearing to deal with—a disciplinary tribunal in front of three senior officers. I tendered my resignation on the first day. The chairman refused to accept it.

"I thought I was making it easier for them," I told Ruiz.

"They can't sack you and they don't want to let you go," he explained. "Imagine the headlines."

"So what do they want?"

"To lock you away in an office somewhere—where you can't cause any trouble."

Samira adjusts her breast pads and buttons her blouse. Four times a day she expresses milk for the twins, which is couriered to the foster family. She gets to see them every afternoon for three hours under supervision. I have watched her carefully, looking for some sign that she is drawing closer to them. She feeds, bathes and nurses them, giving the impression that she is far more accomplished and comfortable with motherhood than I could ever imagine myself being. At the same time her movements are almost mechanical, as though she is doing what's expected of her rather than what she wants.

She has developed a strange affectation around the twins. Whether expressing milk, changing nappies or dressing them, she uses only her right hand. When she picks one of them up, she slides the hand between their legs, along their spine and scoops them in a single motion, supporting the head with the palm of her hand. And when she feeds them, she tucks a bottle under her chin or lays the baby along her thighs.

I thought for a while that it might be a Muslim thing, like only eating with the right hand. When I asked her, she raised her eyes dismissively. "One hand is enough to sin. One hand is enough to save."

"What does that mean?"

"What it says."

Hari is downstairs. "Are you sure you don't want me to come with you?"

"I'm sure."

"I could hold up an umbrella."

"It's not raining."

"They do it for the film stars who don't want to be photographed—hold up umbrellas. Their bodyguards do it."

"You're not a bodyguard."

He's a lovesick puppy. University has broken up for Christmas and he's supposed to be helping his brothers at the garage but he keeps finding excuses to spend time with Samira. She'll even be alone with him, but only in the garden shed when they're working on some pyrotechnic project. The fireworks on Guy Fawkes Night were supposed to be a one-off but Hari has kept that particular fuse burning, for obvious reasons.

"New Boy" Dave is waiting outside for us.

"You're not wearing black?"

"Strange, isn't it?"

"You look good in red."

I whisper, "You should see my underwear."

Samira pulls on her overcoat, which has toggles instead of buttons. It used to belong to Hari and the cuffs have to be folded twice because the sleeves are so long. Her hands find the pockets and hibernate there.

The day is growing brighter, climbing toward noon. Dave negotiates the traffic and parks a block away from Southwark Crown Court, ready to run the gauntlet. Ahead of us, on the pavement, TV cameras and photographers are waiting.

The charges against Julian Shawcroft are merely a sideshow to the main event—the custody battle for the twins—which has everything the tabloids crave: sex, a beautiful "virgin" and stolen babies.

Flashguns fire around us. Samira lowers her head and keeps her hands in her pockets. Dave pushes a path through the scrum, not afraid to drop his shoulder into someone who won't move out of the way. These are tactics from the rugby field, not a sailing school.

Southwark Crown Court is a soulless modern precinct with less charm than the Old Bailey. We pass through the metal detectors and make our way upstairs. I recognize some of the people holding meetings in the corridors, discussing last-minute tactics with counsel. Dr. Sohan Banerjee has hired his own Queen's Counsel in expectation of being charged. He and Shawcroft still haven't turned on each other but the finger-pointing is only a matter of time according to Forbes.

Shawcroft's barrister is a woman, five foot ten in two-inch dagger heels, with white-blond hair and drop pearl earrings that swing back and forth as she talks.

The prosecutor, Francis Hague, QC, is older and grayer, with glasses perched on top of his head. He is talking to Forbes, making notes on a long pad. DS Softell has also turned up, perhaps hoping for some clue in the search for Brendan Pearl, who seems to have vanished completely. I wonder how many different identities he's stolen.

Samira is nervous. She knows that people are looking at her, court staff and reporters. I have tried to reassure her that the publicity will stop once the twins are home. Nobody will be allowed to identify them.

We take a seat in the public gallery at the rear of the courtroom with Samira sitting in between us. She shrinks inside her overcoat, keeping her hands in the pockets. I spy Donavon slipping into the row behind us. His eyes scan the courtroom and rest on mine for a moment before moving on.

Soon the press box is full and there are no seats in the public gallery. The court clerk, an Asian woman of indeterminate age, enters and takes a seat, tapping at a keyboard.

Feet shuffle and everyone stands for the judge, who is surprisingly young and quite handsome in a stuffy sort of way. Within minutes, Shawcroft emerges via a stairway leading directly into the dock. Dressed in a neat suit, speckled tie and polished shoes, he turns and smiles at the gallery, soaking up the atmosphere as though this were a performance being laid on for his benefit.

"You wish to make an application for bail?" asks the judge.

Shawcroft's QC, Margaret Curillo, is already on her feet, introducing herself in plummy obsequious tones. Francis Hague, QC, plants his hands on the table and raises his buttocks several inches from his chair, mumbling an introduction. Perhaps he feels that everyone knows him already or at least should.

The door of the court opens quietly and a man enters. Tall and thin, with an effeminate air, he nods distractedly at the bench and barely raises his polished shoes from the carpet as he glides toward the bar table. Bending, he whispers something to Hague, who cocks his head.

Mrs. Curillo has begun her submission, outlining the many "outstanding achievements" of her client in a "lifetime of service to the community."

The prosecutor rises fully to his feet this time.

"Your Honor, I must apologize for interrupting my learned friend but I wish to request a short adjournment."

"We've only just started."

"I need to seek further instructions, Your Honor. Apparently, the director of public prosecutions is reviewing details of the case."

"With what aim?"

"I'm not in a position to say at this point."

"How long do you require?"

"If it pleases, Your Honor, perhaps we could re-list this matter for three o'clock this afternoon."

The judge stands abruptly, causing a chain reaction in the courtroom. Shawcroft is already being led back downstairs. I look at Dave, who shrugs. Samira is watching us, waiting for an explanation. Outside, in the corridor, I look for Forbes, who seems to have disappeared, along with Softell. What on earth is happening?

For the next two hours we wait. Cases are called for different courts. Lawyers have meetings. People come and go. Samira is sitting with her shoulders hunched, still wearing her overcoat.

"Do you believe in Heaven?" she asks.

It is such an unexpected question that I feel my mouth fall open. Consciously, I close it again. "Why do you ask?"

"Do you think Hassan and Zala are in Heaven?"

"I don't know."

"My father believed we should live our lives over and over, getting better each time. Only when we're completely happy should we get into Heaven."

"I don't know whether I'd like to live the same life over and over."

"Why?"

"It would diminish the consequences. I already put things off until another day. Imagine putting them off until another life."

Samira wraps her arms around herself. "Afghanistan is leaving me."

"What do you mean?"

"I am forgetting things. I cannot remember what sort of flowers I planted on my father's grave. I once pressed the same flowers between the pages of his Koran and made him very angry. He said I was dishonoring Allah. I said I was praising Allah with flowers. He laughed at that. My father could never stay angry with me."

We have afternoon tea in the cafeteria, avoiding the reporters whose ranks are starting to thin. Francis Hague and Shawcroft's barrister still haven't surfaced and neither has Forbes. Perhaps they've gone Christmas shopping.

Shortly before three, a Crown Solicitor finds us. Counsel wants to talk to Samira. I should come too.

"I'll wait for you here," says Dave.

We climb a flight of stairs and are shown through a door marked COURT STAFF ONLY. A long corridor is flanked by offices. A lone potted palm sits at one end alongside a rather annoyed-looking woman waiting on a chair. Her black-stockinged legs are like burned matchsticks sticking out from beneath a fur coat.

The solicitor knocks gently on a door. It opens. The first person I see is Spijker, who looks depressingly somber even by his standards. He takes my hand, kissing my cheeks three times, before bowing slightly to Samira.

Shawcroft's barrister is at the far end of the table, sitting opposite Francis Hague. Beside them is another man, who seems pressed for time. It could be his wife waiting outside, expecting to be somewhere else.

"My name is Adam Greenburg, QC," he says, standing and shaking Samira's hand. "I am the deputy director of public prosecutions at the Crown Prosecution Service."

He apologizes for the stuffiness of the room and almost makes a running gag of his Jewishness, dabbing his forehead with a handkerchief.

"Let me explain my job to you, Miss Khan. When someone is arrested for a criminal offense, they don't automatically go to court and then to prison. The police first have to gather evidence and the job of the Crown Prosecution Service is to examine that evidence and to make sure that the right person is prosecuted for the right offense and that all relevant facts are given to the court. Do you understand?"

Samira looks at me and back to Greenburg. An elephant is sitting on my chest.

The only person who hasn't introduced himself is the man who entered the courtroom and interrupted the bail hearing. Standing by the window in a Savile Row suit, he has a raptor's profile and oddly inexpressive eyes, yet something about his attitude suggests he knows a secret about everyone in the room.

Mr. Greenburg continues: "There are two stages in the decision to prosecute. The first stage is the evidential test. Crown prosecutors must be satisfied there is enough evidence to provide a realistic prospect of conviction against each defendant on each charge.

"The second stage is the public-interest test. We must be satisfied there is a public interest to be served in prosecuting. The CPS will only start or continue a prosecution when a case has passed both these tests no matter how important or serious it might be."

Mr. Greenburg is about to cut to the chase. Spijker won't look at me. Everyone's eyes are fixed on the table.

"The CPS has decided not to proceed with the prosecution of Mr. Shawcroft because it does not pass the public-interest test and because he has agreed to cooperate fully with the police and has given certain assurances about his future conduct."

For a moment the shock takes my breath away and I can't respond. I look at Spijker, hoping for support. He stares at his hands.

"A case such as this raises serious moral and ethical issues," explains Greenburg. "Fourteen infants, born as a result of illegal surrogacy, have been identified. These children are now living with their biological parents in stable loving families.

"If we prosecute Mr. Shawcroft these families will be torn apart. Parents will be charged as co-conspirators and their children will be taken into care, perhaps permanently. In prosecuting one individual, we risk destroying the lives of many many more.

"The Dutch authorities face a similar dilemma involving six children from surrogate mothers. The German authorities have identified four births and the French could have as many as thirteen.

"I am as shocked and appalled by this evil trade as

anyone else, but we have to make decisions here today that will decide what legacy remains afterward."

I find my voice. "You don't have to charge the couples."

"If we choose to proceed, Mr. Shawcroft's counsel has indicated that she will subpoena all the couples involved who are legally and ethically raising children who belong to someone else.

"That is the situation we face. And the question we have to answer is this: Do we draw a line beneath this, or do we proceed and upset the lives of innocent children?"

Samira sits passively in her overcoat. She hasn't stirred. Everything is done with such politeness and decorum that there is a sense of unreality about it all.

"He murdered innocent people." My voice sounds hollow.

Mrs. Curillo protests. "My client denies all involvement in any such crimes and has not been charged in relation to any such event."

"What about Cate and Felix Beaumont? What about Hassan Khan and Zala?"

Greenburg raises his hand, wanting me to be silent.

"In return for the dropping of all charges, Mr. Shawcroft has provided police with the whereabouts of Brendan Pearl, an alleged people trafficker and wanted felon, who is still on parole for offenses committed in Northern Ireland. Mr. Shawcroft has given a statement saying that he had no involvement in the deaths of the Beaumonts, alleging that Brendan Pearl acted alone. He also maintains that he played no part in the trafficking operation that led to the unfortunate deaths at Harwich International Port in October. A criminal gang took advantage of his naïveté. He admits to commercial surrogacy, but says that Brendan Pearl and his associates took over the scheme and blackmailed him into participating."

"This is ridiculous! He's the architect! He forced women to get pregnant! He took their babies!" I can't hear myself yelling, but no other voices are raised. Focusing my anger on Greenburg, I use words like "justice" and "fairness" while he counters with terms like "common sense" and "public interest."

My language is disintegrating. I call him gutless and corrupt. Growing tired of my tantrum, he threatens to have me removed.

"Mr. Pearl will be extradited to the Netherlands, where he will face charges related to prostitution, people smuggling and murder," he explains. "In addition, Mr. Shawcroft has agreed to relinquish all involvement in his charities, including the New Life Adoption Center— effective immediately. The center's license to oversee adoptions has been revoked. The Charities Commission is drafting a press release. Early retirement seems to be the agreed terminology. The CPS will also make a statement saying the charges are being dropped due to lack of evidence."

There is a tone of finality to the sentence. Greenburg's job is done. Getting to his feet, he straightens his jacket. "I promised my wife lunch. Now it will have to be dinner. Thank you for your cooperation."

Samira shrugs me away, pushing past people, stumbling toward the lift.

"I'm sorry, Alisha," says Spijker.

I can't answer him. He warned me about this. We were sitting in his office in Amsterdam and he talked about Pandora's box. Some lids are best kept closed, glued, nailed, screwed down and buried under six feet of earth.

"There is a logic to it, you know. There is no point punishing the guilty if we punish the innocent," he says.

"Someone has to pay."

"Someone will."

I gaze across the paved courtyard where pigeons have coated the statues with mouse-gray excrement. The wind has sprung up again, driving needles of sleet against the glass.

I phone Forbes. Gusts of wind snag at his words.

"When did you know?"

"Midday."

"Do you have Pearl?"

"Not my show anymore."

"Are you off the case?"

"I'm not a high-enough grade of public servant to handle this one."

Suddenly I picture the quiet man, standing by the window, tugging at his cuff links. He was MI5. The security services want Pearl. Forbes has been told to take a backseat.

"Where are you now?"

"Armed-response teams have surrounded a boarding house in Southend-on-Sea."

"Is Pearl inside?"

"Standing at the window, watching."

"He's not going to run."

"Too late for that."

Another image comes to me. This one shows Brendan Pearl strolling out of the boarding house with a pistol tucked into the waistband of his trousers, ready to fight or to flee. Either way, he's not going back to prison.

Samira. What am I going to say to her? How can I possibly explain? She heard what Greenburg said. Her silence spoke volumes. It was as if she had known all along it would come to this. Betrayal. Broken promises. Duplicity. She has been here before, visited this place. "Some people are born to suffer," that's what Lena Caspar said. "It never stops for them, not for a second."

I can see Samira now, smudged by the wet glass, standing by the statue, wearing Hari's overcoat. I want to teach her about the future. I want to show her the Christmas lights in Regent Street, tell her about the daffodils in spring, show her real things, true things, happiness.

A dark-colored car has pulled up, waiting at the curb. Photographers and cameramen spill out of the court building walking backward, jostling for space. Julian Shawcroft emerges flanked by his barrister and Eddie Barrett. His silver hair shines in the TV lights.

He laughs with the reporters, relaxed, jovial, a master of the moment.

I spy Samira walking toward him in a zigzag pattern. Her hands are buried deep in the pockets of her coat.

I am moving now, swerving left and right past people in the corridor. I hammer the lift button and choose the stairs instead, swinging through each landing and out the double fire doors on the ground floor.

I'm on the wrong side of the building. Which way? Left.

Some track athletes are good at running bends. They lean into the corner, shifting their center of balance rather than fighting the g-forces that want to fling them off. The trick is not to fight the force, but to work with it by shortening your stride and hugging the inside line.

A Russian coach once told me that I was the best bend runner he had ever seen. He even had a video of me that he used to train his young runners at the academy in Moscow.

Right now I don't have a cambered track and the paving stones are slick with rain, but I run this bend as if my life depends upon it. I tell myself to hold the turn, hold the turn and then explode out. Kick. Kick. Everything is burning, my legs and lungs, but I'm flying.

The 200 meters was my trademark event. I don't have the lungs for middle distance.

The media scrum is ahead of me. Samira stands on the outside, rocking from foot to foot like an anxious child. Finally she burrows inside, pushing between shoulders. A reporter spies her and pulls back. Another follows. More people peel off, sensing a story.

Samira's overcoat is open. There is something in her hand that catches the light—a glass elephant with tiny mirrors. My elephant.

Shawcroft is too busy talking to notice her. She embraces him from behind, wrapping her arms around his waist, pressing her left fist against his heart and her head against the middle of his back. He tries to shake her loose, but she won't let go. A wisp of smoke curls from her fingers.

Someone yells and people dive away. They're saying it's a bomb! How?

The sound of my scream disappears beneath the crack of an explosion that snaps at the air, making it shudder. Shawcroft spins slowly, until he faces me, looking puzzled. The hole in his chest is the size of a dinner plate. I can see right inside.

Samira falls in the opposite direction, with her knees splayed apart. Her face hits the ground first because her left arm can't break her fall. Her eyes are open. A hand reaches out to me. There are no fingers. There is no *hand*.

People are running and yelling, screaming like the damned; their faces peppered with shards of glass.

"She's a terrorist," someone shouts. "Be careful."

"She's not a terrorist," I reply.

"There could be more bombs."

"There are *no* more bombs."

Pieces of mirror and glass are embedded along Samira's arms, but her face and torso escaped the force of the blast, shielded behind Shawcroft.

I should have realized. I should have seen it coming. How long ago did she plan this? Weeks, maybe longer. She took my elephant from my bedside table. Hari unwittingly helped her by buying the model rocket engines full of black powder. The fuse must have been taped down her forearm, which is why she didn't take off her overcoat. The glass and mirrors of the elephant didn't trigger the metal detectors.

The frayed lining of her coat sleeve is still smoldering, but there's surprisingly little blood. The exploding powder seems to have cauterized her flesh around a jagged section of bone.

She turns her head. "Is he dead?"

"Yes."

Satisfied, she closes her eyes. Two paramedics gently take her from me, placing her on a stretcher. I try to stand but fall backward. I want to keep falling.

I thought I knew everything about friendship and family; the happiness, simplicity and joy within them. But there is another side to devotion, which Samira understands. She is her father's daughter after all.

One hand is enough to sin. One hand is enough to save.

Epilogue

I had a dream last night that I got married in a white dress, not a sari. My father came storming up the aisle haranguing me and the congregation burst into spontaneous applause thinking it was some sort of Sikh floor show.

Samira was there, holding up Jasper, who kicked and giggled and waved his arms excitedly. Hari held Claudia above his head to watch. She was far more serious and looked ready to cry. My mother was shedding buckets, of course. She could cry for two countries.

I am having a lot of dreams like this lately. Perfect-life fantasies, full of ideal matches and soap opera endings. See how wet I've become. I used to be a girl who didn't cry at sad endings or get mushy over babies. Nowadays I have to bite my lip to hold back the tears and I want to float through the ceiling I love them so much.

Jasper is always happy and laughs for no apparent reason, while Claudia watches the world with troubled eyes and sometimes, when you least expect it, she produces tears of abject sorrow and I know that she's crying for those who can't.

Their names have stayed. That happens sometimes; something is given a name and it just doesn't seem right to change it. I won't be changing mine when I get married, but other things are already different. It used to be *me*; now it's *we* and *us*.

Rolling over on my side, I run my fingers across the sheet until they touch Dave's chest. The duvet is wrapped around us and it feels safe, cocooned, shielded from the world.

He's letting his hair grow longer now. It suits his new lifestyle. I never thought I'd fall in love with a man who wears Aran sweaters and waterproof trousers. His hand is lying between us. There are calluses forming on his palms from working the sheets and raising sails.

There is a snuffled cry from the next room. After a pause, I hear it again.

"It's your turn," I whisper, tickling Dave's ear.

"You're getting up anyway," he mumbles.

"That makes no difference."

"It's the girl."

"How do you know?"

"She has a whiny cry."

I jab him hard in the ribs. "Girls do *not* whine. And since when has there been any demarcation?"

He rolls out of bed and looks for his boxer shorts.

"You just keep the bed warm."

"Always."

———

Although it was only three weeks ago, the events of those days have become a surreal blur. There was no custody battle. Barnaby Elliot withdrew gracelessly when faced with charges of withholding information from the police and being an accessory after the fact.

Judge Freyne found Samira to be the mother of the twins, however the DNA test threw up another twist to the story. The twins were brother and sister and the eggs came from Cate, as expected, but they had been fertilized by some third party, someone other than Felix. More than a ripple went round the courtroom when that little piece of information became public.

How was it possible? Dr. Banerjee harvested twelve viable embryos and implanted ten of them in IVF procedures. Cate took the remaining pair to Amsterdam.

There could have been a mix-up, of course, and someone else's sperm may have contaminated the process. According to Dr. Banerjee, the primary reason why Felix and Cate couldn't conceive was because her womb treated his sperm like cancerous cells and destroyed them. In another womb, with stronger sperm, who knows? But there was another issue: the recessive gene carried by Cate and Felix that caused a rare genetic disorder, a lethal form of dwarfism. Should she conceive, there was a 25 percent chance that the fetus would be affected.

Cate would never have cheated on Felix in the bedroom or in her heart, but she desperately wanted a child and having waited for so long and taken such risks she couldn't afford to be disappointed again. Perhaps she found someone she trusted, someone Felix would never meet, someone who looked a lot like him, someone who *owed* her.

It is just a theory of course. Nothing but speculation.

It first occurred to me as I watched the twins sleeping and glanced at the dream catcher above their heads, letting my fingers brush the feathers and beads.

I doubt if Donavon had any idea what Cate planned. And even if he is the father, he has kept his promise to her and never revealed the fact. It's better that way.

I slip out of bed, shivering as I pull on my track pants and a fleece-lined top. By the time I step outside the cottage, it is beginning to grow light over the Solent and the Isle of Wight. Taking Sea Road past Smuggler's Inn, I turn left through the car park and arrive at a long shingle spit that reaches out into the Solent almost halfway to the island.

Wading birds lift off from the marshes as I pass and the beam from the lighthouse flashes every few seconds, growing fainter against the brightening sky. The sound of my shoes on the compacted shingle is reassuring as I cover the final mile to Hurst Castle, which guards the western approach to the Solent. Some days when southeasters have whipped the sea into a foaming monster, I don't reach the castle. Great white-tipped rollers arc upward and smash against the seawall, exploding into a mist that blurs the air and turns it solid. I can barely walk against the wind, bent double, blinking away the salt.

The weather is kind today. There are skiffs on the water already and, to my left, a father and son are hunting for cockles in the shallows. The sailing school will reopen in May. The skiffs are ready and I've become a dab hand at repairing sails. (Those years of watching Mama at her sewing machine weren't entirely wasted.)

My life has changed so much in the past three months. The twins don't let me sleep beyond 6:00 a.m. and some nights I bring them into bed, which all the experts say I shouldn't. They have pushed me around, robbed me of sleep, filled me up and made me laugh. I am besotted. Spellbound. My heart has doubled in size to make room for them.

As I near the coastal end of the spit, I notice a figure sitting on an upturned rowboat with his boots planted in the shingle and hands in his pockets. Beside him is a canvas fishing bag and a rod.

"I know you don't sleep, sir, but this is ridiculous."

Ruiz raises his battered cap. "You have to get up early to catch a fish, grasshopper."

"So why aren't you fishing?"

"I've decided to give them a head start."

He slings the bag over his shoulder and climbs the rocky slope, falling into step beside me.

"Have you ever actually caught a fish, sir?"

"You being cheeky?"

"You don't seem to use any bait."

"Well that means we start as equals. I don't believe in having an unfair advantage."

We walk in silence, our breath steaming the air. Almost home, I stop opposite Milford Green and get a newspaper and muffins.

Samira is in the kitchen, wearing pajamas and my old dressing gown with the owl stitched on the pocket. Jasper is nestled in the crook of her left arm, nuzzling her right breast. Claudia is in the bassinet by the stove, frowning slightly as if she disapproves of having to wait her turn.

"Good morning, Mr. Ruiz."

"Good morning." Ruiz takes off his cap and leans over the bassinet. Claudia gives him her most beatific smile.

Samira turns to me. "How were they last night?"

"Angels."

"You always say that. Even when they wake you five times."

"Yes."

She laughs. "Thank you for letting me sleep."

"What time is your exam?"

"Ten."

Ruiz offers to drive her into Southampton where she's studying for her A-levels at the City College. Her exams aren't until June and the big question is whether she'll sit them at Her Majesty's pleasure or in a normal classroom with other students.

Her lawyers seem confident that they can argue a case of diminished responsibility or temporary insanity. Given what she's been through, nobody is very enthusiastic about sending her to prison, not even Mr. Greenburg, who had to choke back his emotions when he told her the CPS was pressing ahead with the murder charge.

"What about the public interest?" I demanded, acidly.

"The public saw it happen on the BBC, prime time. She killed a man. I have to let it go to a jury."

Samira posted bail thanks to Ruiz and my parents. The DI has become like a grandfather to the twins, who seem enthralled by his craggy face and by the low rumble of his voice. Perhaps it's his Gypsy blood but he seems to understand what it's like to enter the world violently, clinging on to life.

My mother is the other one who is besotted. She phones four times a day wanting updates on how they're sleeping and feeding and growing.

I take Jasper from Samira and hold him over my shoulder, gently rubbing his back. She scoops up Claudia with her right hand and offers her a breast, which she nuzzles anxiously until her mouth finds the nipple.

A missing hand doesn't even seem like a disability when you watch her with the twins, loving them completely; doing everyday chores like washing and feeding and changing nappies. She is a bright, pretty teenage mother of baby twins.

Samira doesn't talk about the future. She doesn't talk about the past. Today matters. The twins matter.

I don't know how long we're going to have them or what's going to happen next, but I've come to realize that we can never know something like that. There are no certainties in life or in death. The end of one story is merely the beginning of the next.

Excerpt from

SHATTER

by

Michael Robotham

*Available in hardcover from Doubleday
in March 2009*

There is a moment when all hope disappears, all pride is gone, all expectation, all faith, all desire. I own that moment. It belongs to me. That's when I hear the sound, the sound of a mind breaking.

It's not a loud crack like when bones shatter or a spine fractures or a skull collapses. And it's not something soft and wet like a heart breaking. It's a sound that makes you wonder how much pain a person can endure; a sound that shatters memories and lets the past leak into the present; a sound so high that only the hounds of hell can hear it.

Can you hear it? Someone is curled up in a tiny ball crying softly into an endless night.

University of Bath

It's eleven o'clock in the morning, mid-October, and outside it's raining so hard that cows are floating down rivers and birds are resting on their bloated bodies.

The lecture theater is full. Tiered seats rise at a gentle angle between the stairs on either side of the auditorium, climbing into darkness. Mine is an audience of pale faces, young and earnest, hungover. Fresher's Week is in full swing and many of them have waged a mental battle to be here, weighing up whether to attend any lectures or to go back to bed. A year ago they were watching teen movies and spilling popcorn. Now they're living away from home, getting drunk on subsidized alcohol and waiting to learn something.

I walk to the center of the stage and clamp my hands on the lectern as if frightened of falling over.

"My name is Professor Joseph O'Loughlin. I am a clinical psychologist and I'll be taking you through this introductory course in behavioral psychology."

Pausing a moment, I blink into the lights. I didn't

think I would be nervous lecturing again but now I suddenly doubt if I have any knowledge worth imparting. I can still hear Bruno Kaufman's advice. (Bruno is the head of the psychology department at the university and is blessed with a perfect Teutonic name for the role.) He told me, "Nothing we teach them will be of the slightest possible use to them in the real world, old boy. Our task is to offer them a bullshit meter."

"A what?"

"If they work hard and take a little on board, they will learn to detect when someone is telling them complete bullshit."

Bruno had laughed and I found myself joining him.

"Go easy on them," he added. "They're still clean and perky and well fed. A year from now they'll be calling you by your first name and thinking they know it all."

How do I go easy on them, I want to ask him now. I'm a beginner too. Taking a deep breath, I start again.

"Why does a well-spoken university graduate studying urban preservation fly a passenger plane into a skyscraper, killing thousands of people? Why does a boy, barely into his teens, spray a schoolyard with bullets, or a teenage mother give birth in a toilet and leave the baby in the wastepaper bin?"

Silence.

"How did a hairless primate evolve into a species that manufactures nuclear weapons, watches *Celebrity Big Brother* and asks questions about what it means to be human and how we got here? Why do we cry? Why are some jokes funny? Why are we inclined to believe or disbelieve in God? Why do we get turned on when someone sucks our toes? Why do we have trouble remembering some things, yet can't get that annoying Britney Spears song out of our heads? What causes us to love or hate? Why are we each so different?"

I look at the faces in the front rows. I have captured their attention, for a moment at least.

"We humans have been studying ourselves for thousands of years, producing countless theories and philosophies and astonishing works of art and engineering and original thought, yet in all that time this is how much we've learned." I hold up my thumb and forefinger a fraction of an inch apart.

"You're here to learn about psychology—the science of the mind; the science that deals with knowing, believing, feeling and desiring; the least understood science of them all."

My left arm trembles at my side.

"Did you see that?" I ask, raising the offending arm. "It does that occasionally. Sometimes I think it has a mind of its own but of course that's impossible. One's mind doesn't reside in an arm or a leg.

"Let me ask you all a question. A woman walks into a clinic. She is middle-aged, well educated, articulate and well groomed. Suddenly, her left arm leaps to her throat and her fingers close around her windpipe. Her face reddens. Her eyes bulge. She is being strangled. Her right hand comes to her rescue. It peels back the fingers and wrestles her left hand to her side. What should I do?"

Silence.

A girl in the front row nervously raises her arm. She has short reddish hair separated in feathery wisps down the fluted back of her neck. "Take a detailed history?"

"It's been done. She has no history of mental illness."

Another hand rises. "It is an issue of self-harm."

"Obviously, but she doesn't *choose* to strangle herself. It is unwanted. Disturbing. She wants help."

A girl with heavy mascara brushes hair behind her ear with one hand. "Perhaps she's suicidal."

"Her left hand is. Her right hand obviously doesn't agree. It's like a Monty Python sketch. Sometimes she has to sit on her left hand to keep it under control."

"Is she depressed?" asks a youth with a gypsy earring and gel in his hair.

"No. She's frightened but she can see the funny side of her predicament. It seems ridiculous to her. Yet at her worst moments she contemplates amputation. What if her left hand strangles her in the night, when her right hand is asleep?"

"Brain damage?"

"There are no obvious neurological deficits—no paralysis or exaggerated reflexes."

The silence stretches out, filling the air above their heads, drifting like strands of web in the warm air.

A voice from the darkness fills the vacuum. "She had a stroke."

I recognize the voice. Bruno has come to check up on me on my first day. I can't see his face in the shadows but I know he's smiling.

"Give that man a cigar," I announce.

The keen girl in the front row pouts. "But you said there was no brain damage."

"I said there were no *obvious* neurological deficits. This woman had suffered a small stroke on the right side of her brain in an area that deals with emotions. Normally, the two halves of our brain communicate and come to an agreement but in this case it didn't happen

4

and her brain fought a physical battle using each side of her body.

"This case is fifty years old and is one of the most famous in the study of the brain. It helped a neurologist called Dr. Kurt Goldstein develop one of the first theories of the divided brain."

My left arm trembles again, but this time it is oddly reassuring.

"Forget everything you've been told about psychology. It will not make you a better poker player, nor will it help you pick up girls or understand them any better. I have three at home and they are a complete mystery to me.

"It is *not* about dream interpretation, ESP, multiple personalities, mind reading, Rorschach tests, phobias, recovered memories or repression. And most importantly—it is *not* about getting in touch with yourself. If that's your ambition I suggest you buy a copy of *Big Jugs* magazine and find a quiet corner."

There are snorts of laughter.

"I don't know any of you yet, but I know things about you. Some of you want to stand out from the crowd and others want to blend in. You're possibly looking at the clothes your mother packed you and planning an expedition to H&M tomorrow to purchase something distressed by a machine that will express your individuality by making you look like everyone else on campus.

"Others among you might be wondering if it's possible to get liver damage from one night of drinking and speculating on who set off the fire alarm in Halls at three o'clock this morning. You want to know if I'm a hard marker or if I'll give you extensions on assignments or whether you should have taken politics instead of psychology. Stick around and you'll get some answers—but not today."

I walk back to the center of the stage and stumble slightly.

"I will leave you with one thought. A piece of human brain the size of a grain of sand contains one hundred thousand neurons, two million axons and one billion synapses all talking to one another. The number of permutations and combinations of activity that are theoretically possible in each of our heads exceeds the number of elementary particles in the universe."

I pause and let the numbers wash over them. "Welcome to the great unknown."

"Dazzling, old boy, you put the fear of God into them," says Bruno, as I gather my papers. "Ironic. Passionate. Amusing. You inspired them."

"It was hardly Mr. Chips."

"Don't be so modest. None of these young philistines have ever heard of Mr. Chips. They've grown up reading *Harry Potter and the Stoned Philosopher.*"

"I think it's '*the Philosopher's Stone.*' "

"Whatever. With that little affectation of yours, Joseph, you have everything it takes to be much loved."

"Affectation?"

"Your Parkinson's."

He doesn't bat an eyelid when I stare at him in disbelief. I tuck my battered briefcase under my arm and make my way toward the side door of the lecture hall.

"Well, I'm pleased you think they were listening," I say.

"Oh, they never listen," says Bruno. "It's a matter of osmosis; occasionally something sinks through the alcoholic haze. But you did guarantee they'll come back."

"How so?"

"They won't know how to lie to you."

His eyes fold into wrinkles. Bruno is wearing trousers that have no pockets. For some reason I've never trusted a man who has no use for pockets. What does he do with his hands?

The corridors and walkways are full of students. A girl approaches. I recognize her from the lecture. Clear-skinned, wearing desert boots and black jeans, her heavy mascara makes her look raccoon-eyed with a secret sadness.

"Do you believe in evil, Professor?"

"Excuse me?"

She asks the question again, clutching a notebook to her chest.

"I think the word 'evil' is used too often and has lost value."

"Are people born that way or does society create them?"

"They are created."

"So there are no natural psychopaths?"

"They're too rare to quantify."

"What sort of answer is that?"

"It's the right one."

She wants to ask me something else but struggles to find the courage. "Would you agree to an interview?" she blurts suddenly.

"What for?"

"The student newspaper. Professor Kaufman says you're something of a celebrity."

"I hardly think—"

"He says you were charged with murdering a former patient and beat the rap."

"I was innocent."

The distinction seems lost on her. She's still waiting for an answer.

"I don't give interviews. I'm sorry."

She shrugs and turns, about to leave. Something else occurs to her. "I enjoyed the lecture."

"Thank you."

She disappears down the corridor. Bruno looks at me sheepishly. "Don't know what she's talking about, old boy. Wrong end of the stick."

"What are you telling people?"

"Only good things. Her name is Nancy Ewers. She's a bright young thing. Studying Russian and politics."

"Why is she writing for the newspaper?"

"Knowledge is precious whether or not it serves the slightest human use."

"Who said that?"

"A. E. Housman."

"Wasn't he a Communist?"

"A pillow biter."

It is still raining. Teeming. For weeks it has been like this. Forty days and forty nights must be getting close. An oily wave of mud, debris and sludge is being swept across the West Country, making roads impassable and turning basements into swimming pools. There are radio reports of flooding in the Malago Valley, Hartcliffe Way and Bed-minster. Warnings have been issued for the Avon, which burst its banks at Evesham. Locks and levees are under threat. People are being evacuated. Animals are drowning.

The quadrangle is washed by rain, driven sideways in sheets. Students huddle under coats and umbrellas, making a dash for their next lecture or the library. Others are staying put, mingling in the foyer. Bruno observes the prettier girls without ever making it obvious.

It was he who suggested I lecture—two hours a week and four tutorials of half an hour each. Social psychology. How hard could it be?

"Do you have an umbrella?" he asks.

"Yes."

"We'll share."

My shoes are full of water within seconds. Bruno holds the umbrella and shoulders me as we run. As we near the psychology department, I notice a police car parked in the emergency bay. A young black constable steps from inside wearing a raincoat. Tall, with short-cropped hair, he hunches his shoulders slightly as if beaten down by the rain.

"Dr. Kaufman?"

Bruno acknowledges him with a half nod.

"We have a situation on the Clifton Bridge."

Bruno groans. "No, no, not now."

The constable doesn't expect a refusal. Bruno pushes past him, heading toward the glass doors to the psychology building, still holding my umbrella.

"We tried to phone," yells the officer. "I was told to come and get you."

Bruno stops and turns back, muttering expletives.

"There must be someone else. I don't have the time."

Rain leaks down my neck. I ask Bruno what's wrong.

Suddenly he changes tack. Jumping over a puddle, he returns my umbrella as though passing on the Olympic torch.

"This is the man you *really* want," he says to the officer. "Professor Joseph O'Loughlin, my esteemed colleague, a clinical psychologist of great repute. An old hand. Very experienced at this sort of thing."

"What sort of thing?"

"A jumper."

"Pardon?"

"On the Clifton Suspension Bridge," adds Bruno. "Some half-wit doesn't have enough sense to get out of the rain." The constable opens the car door for me. "Female. Early forties," he says.

I still don't understand.

Bruno adds, "Come on, old boy. It's a public service."

"Why don't *you* do it?"

"Important business. A meeting with the chancellor. Heads of department." He's lying. "False modesty isn't necessary, old boy. What about that young chap you saved in London? Well-deserved plaudits. You're far more qualified than me. Don't worry. She'll most likely jump before you get there."

I wonder if he hears himself sometimes.

"Must dash. Good luck." He pushes through the glass doors and disappears inside the building.

The officer is still holding the car door. "They've blocked off the bridge," he explains. "We really must hurry, sir."

Wipers thrash and a siren wails. From inside the car it sounds strangely muted and I keep looking over my shoulder expecting to see an approaching police car. It takes me a moment to realize that the siren is coming from the roof.

Masonry towers appear on the skyline. It is Brunel's masterpiece, the Clifton Suspension Bridge, an engineering marvel from the age of steam. Taillights blaze. Traffic is stretched back for more than a mile on the approach. Sticking to the apron of the road, we sweep past the stationary cars and pull up at a roadblock where police in fluorescent vests control onlookers and unhappy motorists.

The constable opens the door for me and hands me my umbrella. A sheet of rain drives sideways and almost rips it from his hands. Ahead of me the bridge appears deserted. The masonry towers support massive sweeping interlinking cables that curve gracefully to the vehicle deck and rise again to the opposite side of the river.

One of the attributes of bridges is that they offer the possibility that someone may start to cross but never reach the other side. For that person the bridge is virtual, an open window that they can keep passing or climb through.

The Clifton Suspension Bridge is a landmark, a tourist attraction and a one-drop shop for suicides. Well used, oft chosen, perhaps "popular" isn't the best choice of word. Some people say the bridge is haunted by past suicides; eerie shadows have been seen drifting across the vehicle deck.

There are no shadows today. And the only ghost on the bridge is flesh and blood. A woman, naked, standing outside the safety fence, with her back pressed to the metal lattice and wire strands. The heels of her red shoes are balancing on the edge.

Like a figure from a surrealist painting, her nakedness isn't particularly shocking or even out of place. Standing upright, with a rigid grace, she stares at the water with the demeanor of someone who has detached herself from the world.

The officer in charge introduces himself. He's in uniform: Sergeant Abernathy. I don't catch his first name. A junior officer holds an umbrella over his head. Water streams off the dark plastic dome, falling on my shoes.

"What do you need?" asks Abernathy.

"A name."

"We don't have one. She won't talk to us."

"Has she said anything at all?"

"No."

"She could be in shock. Where are her clothes?"

"We haven't found them."

I glance along the pedestrian walkway, which is enclosed by a fence topped with five strands of wire, making it difficult for anyone to climb over. The rain is so heavy I can barely see the far side of the bridge.

"How long has she been out there?"

"Best part of an hour."

"Have you found a car?"

"We're still looking."

She most likely approached from the eastern side which is heavily wooded. Even if she stripped on the walkway dozens of drivers must have seen her. Why didn't anyone stop her?

A large woman with short-cropped hair, dyed black, interrupts the meeting. Her shoulders are rounded and her hands bunch in the pockets of a rain jacket hanging down to her knees. She's huge. Square. And she's wearing men's shoes.

Abernathy stiffens. "What are you doing here, ma'am?"

"Just trying to get home, Sergeant. And don't call me ma'am. I'm not the bloody Queen."

She glances at the TV crews and press photographers who have gathered on a grassy ridge, setting up tripods and lights. Finally she turns to me.

"What are you shaking for, precious? I'm not that scary."

"I'm sorry. I have Parkinson's disease."

"Tough break. Does that mean you get a sticker?"

"A sticker?"

"Disabled parking. Lets you park almost anywhere. It's almost as good as being a detective only we get to shoot people and drive fast."

She's obviously a more senior police officer than Abernathy.

She looks toward the bridge. "You'll be fine, Doc, don't be nervous."

"I'm a professor, not a doctor."

"Like Doctor Who. Hey! I could be your female side-kick. Tell me something, how do you think the Daleks managed to conquer so much of the universe when they couldn't even climb stairs?"

"I guess it's one of life's great mysteries."

"I got loads of them."

A two-way radio is being threaded beneath my jacket and a reflective harness loops over my shoulders and clips at the front. The woman detective lights a cigarette, shielding the cigarette from the rain, exhaling slowly. She pinches a strand of tobacco from the tip of her tongue.

Although not in charge of the operation, she's so

naturally dominant that the uniformed officers seem more focused and ready to react around her.

"You want me to go with you?" she asks.

"I'll be OK."

"All right, tell Skinny Minnie I'll buy her a low-fat muffin if she steps onto our side of the fence."

"I'll do that."

Temporary barricades have blocked off both approaches to the bridge, which is deserted except for two ambulances and waiting paramedics. Motorists and spectators have gathered beneath umbrellas and coats. Some have scrambled up a grassy bank to get a better vantage point.

Rain bounces off the tarmac, exploding in miniature mushroom clouds before coursing through gutters and pouring off the edges of the bridge in a curtain of water.

Ducking under the barricades, I begin walking toward the bridge. My hands are out of my pockets. My left arm refuses to swing. It does that sometimes—fails to get with the plan.

I can see the woman ahead of me. From a distance her skin had looked flawless, but now I notice that her thighs are crisscrossed with scratches and streaked with mud. Her pubic hair is a dark triangle: darker than her hair, which is woven into a loose plait that falls down the nape of her neck. There is something else—letters written on her stomach. A word. I can see it when she turns toward me.

SLUT.

Why the self-abuse? Why naked? This is public humiliation. Perhaps she had an affair and lost someone she loves. Now she wants to punish herself to prove she's sorry. Or it could be a threat—the ultimate game of brinkmanship—"leave me and I'll kill myself."

No, this is too extreme. Too dangerous. Teenagers sometimes threaten self-harm in failing relationships. It's a sign of emotional immaturity. This woman is in her late thirties or early forties with fleshy thighs and cellulite forming faint depressions on her buttocks and hips. I notice a scar. A cesarean. She's a mother.

I am close to her now. A matter of feet and inches.

Her buttocks and back are pressed hard against the fence. Her left arm is wrapped around an upper strand of wire. The other fist is holding a mobile phone against her ear.

"Hello. My name is Joe. What's yours?"

She doesn't answer. Buffeted by a gust of wind, she seems to lose her balance and rock forward. The wire is cutting into the crook of her arm. She pulls herself back.

Her lips are moving. She's talking to someone on the phone. I need her attention.

"Just tell me your name. That's not so hard. You can call me Joe and I'll call you . . ."

Wind pushes hair over her right eye. Only her left is visible.

A gnawing uncertainty expands in my stomach. Why the high heels? Has she been to a nightclub? Is she drunk? Drugged? Ecstasy can cause psychosis. LSD. Ice perhaps.

I catch snippets of her conversation.

"No. No. Please. No."

"Who's on the phone?" I ask.

"I will. I promise. I've done everything. Please don't ask me . . ."

"Listen to me. You won't want to do this."

I glance down. More than two hundred feet below a fat-bellied boat nudges against the current, held by its engines. The swollen river claws at the gorse and hawthorn on the lower banks. A confetti of rubbish swirls on the surface: books, branches and plastic bottles.

"You must be cold. I have a coat."

Again she doesn't answer. I need her to acknowledge me. A nod of the head or a single word of affirmation is enough. I need to know that she's listening.

"Perhaps I could try to put it around your shoulders— just to keep you warm."

Her head snaps toward me and she sways forward as if ready to let go. I pause in mid-stride, still holding the coat.

"OK, I won't come any closer. I'll stay right here. Just tell me your name."

She stares upward, blinking into the rain. She reminds me of a prisoner standing in a exercise yard, enjoying a brief moment of freedom.

"Whatever's wrong. Whatever has happened to you or has upset you, we can talk about it. I'm not taking the choice away from you. I just want to understand why."

Her toes are dropping and she has to force herself up onto her heels to keep her balance. The lactic acid is building in her muscles. Her calves must be in agony.

"I have seen people jump," I tell her. "You shouldn't think it is a painless way of dying. I'll tell you what happens. It will take less than three seconds to reach the water. By then you will be traveling at about seventy-five miles per hour. Your ribs will break and the jagged edges will puncture your internal organs. Sometimes the heart is compressed by the impact and tears away from the aorta so that your chest will fill with blood."

Her gaze is now fixed on the water. I know she's listening.

"Your arms and legs will survive intact but the cervical disks in your neck or the lumbar disks in your spine will most likely rupture. It will not be pretty. It will not be painless. Someone will have to pick you up. Someone will have to identify your body. Someone will be left behind."

High in the air comes a booming sound. Rolling thunder. The air vibrates and the earth seems to tremble. Something is coming.

Her eyes have turned to mine.

"You don't understand," she whispers to me, lowering the phone. For the briefest of moments it dangles at the end of her fingers, as if trying to cling on to her, and then tumbles away, disappearing into the void.

The air darkens and a half-formed image comes to mind—a gapemouthed melting figure screaming in despair. Her buttocks are no longer pressing against the metal. Her arm is no longer wrapped around the wire.

She doesn't fight gravity. Arms and legs do not flail or clutch at the air. She's gone. Silently, dropping from view.

Everything seems to stop, as if the world has missed a heartbeat or been trapped in between the pulsations. Then everything begins moving again. Paramedics and police officers are dashing past me. People are screaming and crying. I turn away and walk back toward the barricades, wondering if this isn't part of a dream.

They are gazing at where she fell. Asking the same

question, or thinking it. Why didn't I save her? Their eyes diminish me. I can't look at them.

My left leg locks and I fall onto my hands and knees, staring into a black puddle. I pick myself up again and push through the crowd, ducking beneath the barricade.

Stumbling along the side of the road, I splash through a shallow drain, swatting away raindrops. Denuded trees reach across the sky, leaning toward me accusingly. Ditches gurgle and foam. The line of vehicles is an unmoving stream. I hear motorists talking to each other. One of them yells to me.

"Did she jump? What happened? When are they going to open the road?"

I keep walking, my gaze fixed furiously ahead, moving in a kind of dream. My left arm no longer swinging. Blood hums in my ears. Perhaps it was my face that made her do it. The Parkinson's mask, like cooling bronze. Did she see something or *not* see something?

Lurching toward the gutter, I lean over the safety rail and vomit until my stomach is empty.

There's a guy on the bridge on his knees, talking to a puddle like it's listening. Now he's puking his guts out. Breakfast. Lunch. Gone. If something round, brown and hairy comes up, I hope he swallows hard.

People are swarming across the bridge, staring over the side. They watched my angel fall. She was like a puppet whose strings had been cut, tumbling over and over, loose limbs and ligaments, naked as the day she was born.

I gave them a show; a high-wire act; a woman on the edge stepping into the void. Did you hear her mind breaking? Did you see the way the trees blurred behind her like a green waterfall? Time seemed to stop.

I reach into the back pocket of my jeans and draw out a steel comb, raking it through my hair, creating tiny tracks front to back, evenly spaced. I don't take my eyes off the bridge. I press my forehead to the window and watch the swooping cables turned red and blue in the flashing lights.

Droplets are darting down the outside of the glass driven by gusts that rattle the panes. It's getting dark. I wish I could see the water from here. Did she float or go straight to the bottom? How many bones were broken? Did her bowels empty the moment before she died?

The turret room is part of a Georgian house that belongs to an Arab who has gone away for the winter. A rich wanker dipped in oil. It used to be an old boarding-house until he had it tarted up. It's two streets back from Avon Gorge, which I can see over the rooftops from the turret room.

I wonder who he is—the man on the bridge. He came with the tall police constable and he walked with a strange limp, one arm sawing at the air while the other didn't move from his side. A negotiator perhaps. A psychologist. Not a lover of heights.

He tried to talk her down but she wasn't listening. She was listening to me. That's the difference between a professional and a fucking amateur. I know how to open a mind. I can bend it or break it. I can close it down for the winter. I can fuck it in a thousand different ways.

I once worked with a guy called Hopper, a big redneck from Alabama, who used to puke at the sight of blood. He was a former marine and he was always telling us that the deadliest weapon in the world was a marine and his rifle. Unless he's puking, of course.

Hopper had a hard-on for films and was always quoting from *Full Metal Jacket*—the Gunnery Sergeant Hartman character, who bellowed at recruits, calling them maggots and scumbags and pieces of amphibian shit.

Hopper wasn't observant enough to be an interrogator. He was a bully, but that's not enough. You've got to be smart. You've got to know people—what frightens them, how they think, what they cling to when they're in trouble. You've got to watch and listen. People reveal themselves in a thousand different ways. In the clothes they wear, their shoes, their hands, their voices, the pauses and hesitations, the tics and gestures. Listen and see.

My eyes drift above the bridge to the pearl-gray clouds still crying for my angel. She did look beautiful when she fell, like a dove with a broken wing or a plump pigeon shot with an air rifle.

I used to shoot pigeons as a kid. Our neighbor, old Mr. Hewitt who lived across the fence, had a pigeon loft and used to race them. They were proper homing pigeons and he'd take them away on trips and let them go. I'd sit in my bedroom window and wait for them to come home. The silly old bastard couldn't work out why so many of them didn't make it.

I'm going to sleep well tonight. I have silenced one whore and sent a message to the others.

To the one . . .

She'll come back just like a homing pigeon. And I'll be waiting.

ALSO BY MICHAEL ROBOTHAM

> "*Terrific . . . a classic 'wrong man' thriller that puts its hero in hot water, then raises the Fahrenheit to a fever pitch. . . . Robotham not only builds the suspense masterfully but tops it off with a stunning twist.*" —People

SUSPECT

London psychiatrist Joseph O'Loughlin seems to have the perfect life. He has a beautiful wife, an adoring daughter, and a thriving practice to which he brings great skill and compassion. But he's also facing a future dimmed by Parkinson's disease. And when he's called in on a gruesome murder investigation, he discovers that the victim is someone he once knew. Unable to tell the police what he knows, O'Loughlin tells one small lie which turns out to be the biggest mistake of his life. Suddenly, he's caught in a web of his own making.

Crime Fiction/978-0-307-27547-9

*"An exceptional thriller. . . . [With]
deft dialogue, a fast-paced plot, and
richly drawn characters."*
—Tucson Citizen

LOST

Detective Inspector Vincent Ruiz can't
remember how he got to the hospital. He
was found floating in the Thames with a
gunshot wound in his leg and a picture of
missing child Mickey Carlyle in his pocket.
But Mickey's killer is already in jail. Add
to this the blood-stained boat found near
where Ruiz was pulled from the water,
and the pieces just don't add up. Now, he
is accused of faking amnesia and under
investigation, so Ruiz reaches out to psychologist Joseph O'Loughlin to help him
unlock his memory, clear his name, and
solve this ominous puzzle. Marked by vivid
characters and full of unexpected turns,
Lost is a hair-raising journey of vengeance,
grief, and redemption through the dark
London underworld.

Crime Fiction/978-0-307-27548-6

VINTAGE CRIME/BLACK LIZARD
Available at your local bookstore, or visit
www.randomhouse.com